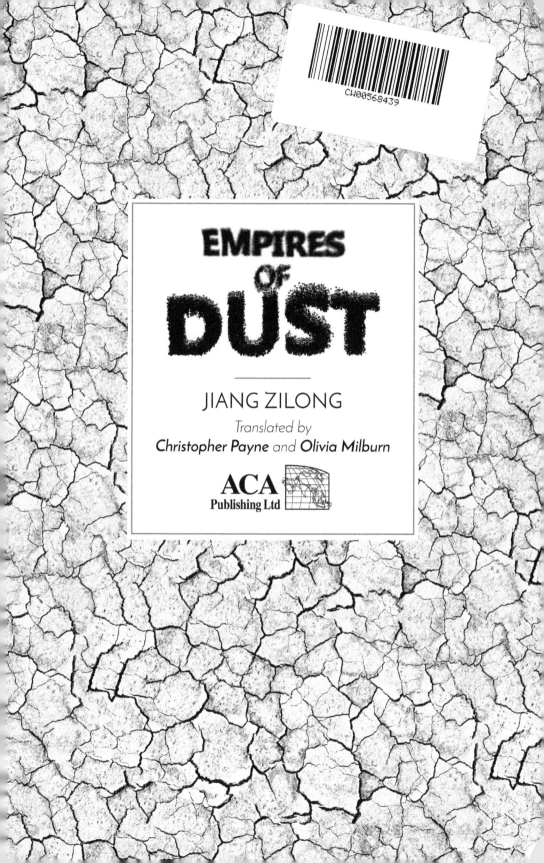

EMPIRES OF DUST

JIANG ZILONG

Translated by
Christopher Payne and **Olivia Milburn**

ACA
Publishing Ltd

EMPIRES OF DUST

JIANG ZILONG

Translated by
CHRISTOPHER PAYNE AND OLIVIA MILBURN

ACA PUBLISHING LTD

Paperback published by
ACA Publishing Ltd.

eBook published by
Sinoist Books (an imprint of ACA Publishing Ltd).

University House
11-13 Lower Grosvenor Place
London SW1W 0EX, UK
Tel: +44 (0)20 7834 7676
Fax: +44 (0)20 7973 0076
E-mail: info@alaincharlesasia.com
Web: www.alaincharlesasia.com

Beijing Office
Tel: +86 (0)10 8472 1250
Fax: +86 (0)10 5885 0639

Author: Jiang Zilong
Translators: Christopher Payne and Olivia Milburn
Editors: Martin Savery and David Lammie
Cover art: Daniel Li

Published by ACA Publishing Ltd in association with the People's Literature Publishing House

Paperback ISBN: 978-1-910760-33-8
eBook ISBN: 978-1-910760-54-3

A catalogue record for *Empires of Dust* is available from the National Bibliographic Service of the British
Library.

CONTENTS

PART ONE

1

THE DRAGON PHOENIX TREES

Guojiadian – despite the name, this wasn't an actual store that bought and sold goods. In fact, it was the name of a country village of roughly two thousand households, nestled in a small sunken corner of north China, in a district by the name of Haijin, not too far away from Shenyang (Mukden). The villagers would say that when it rained, the village would flood; when it didn't, there'd be drought; there wasn't much by way of suitable weather. Life was hard, the people were poor; its only rather dubious claim to fame was its number of single, unmarried men – its so-called bare sticks. Throughout the town's history, there was an unwritten rule known by everyone: whoever wished to use a brick to murder someone wouldn't have to pay with their own lives, nor would what they had done necessarily be considered a crime. After all, any such yarn could only be false, nothing more than exaggerated rumours and hearsay. Why? That was easy: there wasn't a single brick in Guojiadian. The village had risen up from the mud and the sand; all that one could see was the yellow earth stained white in places. When the wind blew, it would whip up the dirt and blind you; when it rained, the houses would collapse having been so shoddily built out of mud. In a village such as this, a place totally bereft of bricks, how could a person kill someone with one?

Residing in Guojiadian was a man by the name of Guo Degui; a docile chap, as pliable as the clay from which the village had been built; a man who worked himself to death building two new rooms for his home. He had married the daughter of a reasonably well-off family from the neighbouring village of Miaojiazhuang, and so, to save face, he endeavoured to work his hardest in all things: two years after their wedding ceremony, she gave birth to twin boys. The village elders, following rural custom, picked two resounding names for the two little boys: Guo Jingtian and Guo Jingshi. They explained to Guo Degui that the heavens had done him a good deed; that his lot in life had changed for the better. In truth, Guo Degui's 'father' was actually his mother's older brother, for he had been given to them to help continue the family line, his uncle having had no children of his own. Now he had had two sons, a sign, perhaps, that his parents' generosity in giving him up had been repaid, that his family would now prosper. On balance, he had fulfilled half the duty of a man's life: he'd had not only one, but two sons. All that remained was for him to build two new rooms so that they could one day have wives of their own.

But in Guojiadian, to realise such good fortune wasn't an easy thing to do. Since ancient times, 'a person' and 'a mouth' went hand in hand, so that village numbers were counted by how many mouths there were to feed. To have a son meant 'adding an extra mouth'; after all, every person has a mouth and every mouth must eat. The Guo family now had two new mouths to feed and, what's more, these mouths couldn't help but be a poor family's 'sacred little treasures' and, at the same time, be as demanding as hell. The whole family seemed to revolve around them. Every morsel of delicious food, rare as it was, inevitably made its way into their perpetually hungry bellies. Before long, their joyful grandfather and contented grandmother, bursting with glee because of these 'sacred little treasures', died one after the other while slaving over the stove.

Contrary to expectations, Jingtian and Jingshi both grew up strong and robust, two hardy lads. Watching them get bigger day by day, Guo Degui's heart should have been overjoyed, but it wasn't. He knew that he had to get started; he had to build rooms for them. As everyone in the village knew, there were three tiresome chores: moulding mud into bricks, weeding fields and shucking wheat. From digging up the earth to form bricks, to pounding the soil for the foundation; to laying the bricks for the walls and raising the roof girders; all the hardest work was carried out by Guo Degui. The two boys weren't yet men so they couldn't help with such an enormous task and, even if they could have, he wouldn't have asked them. This was his lot in life, his task to complete. As he was spreading the reeds to roof the rooms, using leftover wheat husks and mud to seal them, an iron shovel to tap, tap, tap it all down rhythmically like exploding firecrackers. Everything went black, he felt a tickle in his throat and spat up a crimson stream of blood. His eyes opened wide. He thought to use the shovel to fling the reddened earth off the roof but, to his surprise, his arms didn't have the strength to lift it, his mouth filled with a salty taste before it spouted mouthfuls of blood. He thought to close it but couldn't and soon more blood rushed out, fiercely flowing now, whereupon he fell into the mud, convulsing violently. In the twinkling of an eye, this hardy man took his last breath and expired.

The family of Degui's wife wasn't much better off, and so they couldn't help her. Being a poor woman was difficult enough; being a poor widow was harder than death, but it also wasn't something you could have scruples about. There was naught to do but bury her husband and ask the townspeople for help to finish the roofs. Before long, they had frittered away their food and so the widow Guo locked up the family home, lowered her face towards the ground, took the two boys in tow and left the village to beg for alms in the bigger cities. In Tianjin, Beijing, outside the Great Wall to the west of the capital and beyond the Shanhai Pass to the east, for many years she roamed the land begging for food. Some years she would return to Guojiadian for the Lunar New Year festivities and in good years she would return to help plant and harvest crops. She had rules when begging for food: she would smile apologetically, accept people's loathing, bear hardships and endure torments, beseech the grandfathers and talk to the grandmothers, and humbly receive humiliation. All of these things she would bear, but only her. She wouldn't permit her two sons to live a life that wasn't human. In silence, she had accepted her husband's lot in life. She had to preserve the Guo family line and rear the children into adulthood. Every place she went, she would first find lodgings for her children before wandering off to beg; every morsel she obtained would be brought back for them to eat. If she had managed to beg a fair amount, she might have a mouthful for herself, if not she would always let them eat first. Nevertheless, Jingtian and Jingshi grew up fast and strong, so before long it was a wonder how they could bear to see their mother endure such a life. The two brothers had grown up much alike, as if they'd been carved from the same material. Their faces were identical with tall, straight noses, their arms were long and their hands large, and they both had the physique of one day being able to handle heavy work. The older boy, Jingtian, had a somewhat ferocious temperament. He was crafty and astute, and before long there was really nothing that he was afraid of standing up to. During all the years of wandering with his mother, eking out a hard living, he had begun to pick up skills along the way and discovered that he had quite a knack for mending farm tools, cobbling together doors and windows, hammering in horseshoes and repairing pots and pans; indeed, he even learned how to make Buddhist incense sticks, of all things. Guo Jingshi, on the other hand, had an honest and sincere temperament, and was mild and gentle in comparison. He was, in many ways, like a happily wagging tail constantly following his older brother around; he didn't speak much, all he did was listen to his older brother.

In truth, making incense wasn't all that hard, all you had to do was peel off the skin of an elm tree, mulch it into a pulp, add a little scent, mix that with sawdust and that was it. As a result, when the three of them set off on their journeys now, there was a marked change: the two boys would each take turns carrying their loads, one would be their incense and farm tools, the other would be a basket, and sitting inside would be their mother. On their journeys they would now buy and sell their incense and labour. If there was work to be done, they'd do it, if there wasn't, or if they couldn't sell anything, then their mother would resort once again to begging. As the years passed, little by little, things became better and life became easier. In fact, they reached the point when the widow Guo and her younger son, Jingshi, didn't even need to leave the house, only Jingtian would travel and sell incense, or find work to do. Across four townships and eight counties, across many streets and many households, Jingtian could nearly always find a way to sell a little incense, or find some work to do and some money to earn. In fact, finding work wasn't all that difficult. There were always households that needed something doing. In most of these he'd not only be given food to eat, he'd even get a little money and if they didn't have money, they'd at least have food. As a result, the Guo family situation improved and life became much more bearable.

With these easier times, the widow Guo began to make preparations; her boys had to get married after all. But just as she was about to devote herself to finding wives for her boys, autumn floods hit the village, lashing the town for seven days and seven nights, transforming the entire area into a veritable quagmire. She had no idea when the autumn floods might recede and, at that moment, Jingtian wasn't at home. The only thing she could do was to grab her bag and head off with Jingshi into the rain.

There wasn't any other way. With half of her peanut crop already 80 to 90 per cent ripe, if she didn't dig them out now they would only rot, and wouldn't that be a terrible waste of the whole yield! The water had already risen up to her knees so that she couldn't crouch, she couldn't sit, all she could do was bend at her waist, stretch out her hands, and plunge them into the fetid water and mud to dig out whatever she could... mother and son braved the onslaught of rain for an entire day and managed to salvage a great deal of their crop but, in the process, she had torn off all her fingernails. The damage to her hands was horrifying. Her fingertips were bloated and swollen, like bulbous white radishes, fleshy stumps that little resembled actual fingers. People say that the nerves of one's fingers are linked to the heart, but when she was out in the rain driving her hands into the waterlogged dirt, she didn't feel any real pain. She was so anxious to save her crops, she was even willing to sacrifice herself, if need be, throwing caution to the wind to look after what was hers. Jingshi was there too, his hands had been similarly thrust into the mud, and yet he didn't lose a single finger nail.

When the rain stopped, she took the peanuts she had roasted, mixed them with black beans and sautéed them over a fire to make peanut cakes. Then she gathered them together with the little money they had put aside and put it all in a basket for safe keeping. Items such as these would be precious lifesavers in times of disaster. As the waters receded, refugees from the south started appearing in swarms on the roads. The widow Guo used two of her recently made peanut cakes to exchange for a young girl of 17 from Anhui. The girl's family was desperately poor and starving, barely able to trek along the road. Her parents had seen the two peanut cakes and thought that with those, the two of them could last at least half a month — without their daughter of course.

On their wedding day, the widow Guo pulled Jingtian and his new wife into the inner room while she and Jingshi remained outside. Together they laid some sorghum straw on the plank bed, covered it with a blanket and prepared to spend the evening there. Inside the inner room, as Jingtian lay upon the *kang* (heated brick bed), he began to feel increasingly ill at ease. Then, without a word, he jumped down from the bed, stepped outside and pulled both his mother and brother into the inner room and made space for them on the *kang*. His new wife was named Sun Yueqing. At first she was reticent, but after two days of having her belly filled, she began to relax and warm to her new situation, becoming a pretty and delicate flower that couldn't help but stoke feelings of affection. To outsiders, the widow Guo gave off the aura of one immensely satisfied with her lot, but to her family there seemed to be something amiss: she just couldn't understand what the devil a newly married man was doing spending his nights asleep on the same bed with his wife, old mother and younger brother! Deep in her heart she knew she had to think of a way to extend their humble home and then find a wife for Jingshi. Only then would her life's work be complete, only then could she face the spirits of her poor, unfortunate, deceased husband and his ancestors.

Both her sons were strong, strapping lads, easily able to dig up the earth and mould bricks; extending their house shouldn't be all that difficult. Opening a door off the centre room allowed for there to be one bright room with two more on either side, both shaded and suitable for sleeping in. Before work was even completed, the widow

Guo and her youngest son moved in. Nothing breeds success like success, but before long her plan to find a wife for Jingtian encountered problems. She had set out meticulously to find him a wife, she had even arranged meetings and had had numerous opportunities, but none of it came together. As time passed village gossip began to spread with rumours claiming that the two brothers had both married Yueqing and that she was wife to both of them. Some said they took turns, for one month she'd be with Jingtian, the next with Jingshi, others said they swapped between even and odd days. When she later gave birth to a baby boy, Guo Cunxian, there were those who said he resembled his dad, others said he resembled his uncle. Over the next two years, Sun Yueqing would give birth to another boy, Guo Cunzhi, and a daughter Guo Cunzhu. The gossip only increased. The villagers all said that Jingtian and Jingshi truly deserved to be called twins; after all, they both had equal shares in the family: Cunxian looked like the former, Cunzhi like the latter. The only question was, who did the daughter look like? No one could be sure, so perhaps Yueqing had...

Two brothers marrying one woman wasn't actually all that rare in Guojiadian. There were instances where three or four brothers all married the same woman. And in her heart of hearts, the widow Guo wasn't really bothered by such salacious gossip. What widow couldn't endure some bullying? After all, she had two stalwart boys and life wasn't all that bad. Those envious of her situation could say much worse. And it didn't matter whose father was whom, the children were theirs, they were Guos, and that was easy to see; they weren't bought, which was much better than those who hadn't been able to marry, whose family lines had been cut. What really warmed her heart, however, was that Jingshi never once brought up the issue of marriage, of finding his own wife. He liked his sister-in-law, you could even say he loved her more than his brother did. Whenever his brother berated her — and remember, from when they were little, Jingshi had always revered and followed his older brother — he would always take her side and argue her case. Widow Guo was fearful of her eldest boy's temper and of what he might do. There was no way that he hadn't heard the gossip spread round town about them, about their relationship with Yueqing. Was there really nothing he could do about it? She was afraid; afraid that one day he might grab his axe and cleave Jingshi in two!

But that day hadn't come. In fact, it would be Jingtian whose life would end in violence; a bayonet would pierce his heart. It was in the summer of 1943. The 29th Army had scored a great victory over the Japanese imperialists along the Jinpu Line (Tianjin-Pukou Railway), and had then set up camp near Shenyang to make repairs to equipment and allow their men to rest; they thus stationed troops in Guojiadian. Sensing an opportunity to make some money, Guo Jingtian first went to Dadong town to purchase some sticky yellow rice, before setting up a stall near where the garrison was stationed to make and sell sweet, glutinous rice cakes. A sergeant from the platoon had enjoyed the cakes but hadn't paid for them. Unwilling to forgive the transgression, Guo Jingtian immediately informed the garrison commander who flew into a rage. If word of the 29th Army struck fear in the heart of those Japanese bastards, how could it tolerate such a scandal as this? The commander straightaway reproached the sergeant who, on his own life, swore that he hadn't stolen the rice cakes. The commander turned to ask Guo Jingtian whether he was brave enough to accept responsibility for making such an accusation. The commander decided that the only way to resolve the affair was to use his bayonet to tear open the stomach of the sergeant. If the rice cakes spilled out, then his death would be suitable punishment and the commander would pay for the cakes. If, however, no cakes spilled out, Guo Jingtian would have to pay, and not with money, but with his life.

Guo Jingtian couldn't prevaricate. If he did, he'd only prove to the commander that what he had accused the sergeant of was false, so he had to proceed with his claim. Thereupon, with a crowd of people gawking, the commander thrust his bayonet into the sergeant, tearing open his belly. As expected, the rice cakes came spilling out. Guo Jingtian was to be compensated. That evening, a soldier knocked on his family's door to give him the money, saying, as well, that the garrison would be leaving in the morning and that the commander had a request: Guo Jingtian's rice cakes were delicious and he would like very much if Jingtian could make another batch for the troops to take with them. If he could bring them to the two big trees where he had set up his stall earlier in the day, the commander would be most grateful. Throughout the rest of the day and into the night, Guo Jingtian made rice cakes. He didn't even undress when it was time for sleep, instead just grabbing a few winks before the day began to break. Quietly, and without waking anyone, he took the family's small cart, loaded it with rice cakes and made his way to the two trees. In truth, however, the 29th Army had packed up and left late in the night. When day broke, all the villagers could see was Guo Jingtian's corpse slumped against the towering trees, his stomach gorged open and the rice cakes completely untouched. Guo Jingshi stood protectively over the body, his eyes staring blankly, white spittle forming at the corners of his mouth, as though he'd been dumbstruck. While it was difficult to say whether or not Jingshi had, in fact, been scared dumb, what was certain was that from this moment on, he never spoke again.

As for the widow Guo, this strong, resilient woman who had endured so much, the shock of her eldest son's death was too much. She soon fell gravely ill and before a month had passed, she let go of this world and followed Jingtian into the next. For Jingshi, someone who had never led the family, had never really had to, burying his elder brother and then soon after burying his mother, it was all so much, so exhausting. The strain of all this transformed Jingshi into a completely different person. It was hard to judge how long his face had gone without a wash, or how long his hair had gone without a trim; filthy and foul it hung low obscuring half his face, giving him a ghostly look even in broad daylight. Later, when he worked in the fields, he'd haphazardly tie at least some of his hair back but, over time, inevitably all sorts of stuff collected in it. In summer, when they would begin shucking the wheat, the discarded remnants would unavoidably snag in his dishevelled mop of hair. As it happened, a few days after a great rainstorm deluged the village, sprouts of wheat began to peak through Jingshi's hair. Whoever saw him or spoke to him, ridiculed and laughed at him and swore at him, but none of it mattered. He didn't respond. He gave no reaction whatsoever. No one could be sure if he really couldn't hear what others were saying to him, or if he just didn't care. To say he had been scared dumb wasn't really accurate, nor was saying he had gone crazy. When it was time to eat, he'd eat. When it was time to work, he'd do that too. It was just that when he didn't have anything to do, he'd always head to those two trees, plop himself down at their feet, and stare off into space. In the summer, he'd even sleep beneath the trees. Only when his widowed sister-in-law came to collect him would he move; only towards her would he be deferential and obedient. Every so often, Sun Yueqing would get her son to call for the village barber and together they'd heat up a cauldron of water and clean Jingshi from head to toe.

The villagers soon got to saying that Guo Jingshi must've thought that the two trees belonged to his family, one a birch-leaved pear tree, the other an elm. Long ago, there was a small temple shrine dedicated to a local deity just behind the two trees, but in recent years it had endured numerous bombings and the turmoil and chaos of war. While the villagers had been alarmed at the desecration of the temple, no one would dare attempt to repair it; not long after, its walls would completely collapse. And yet, the two trees in front of the temple continued to grow big and flourish, and without anything in between, they soon grew closer and closer together, essentially merging into one, their roots intimately entwined. Soon, the branches tangled together, the leaves grew in pairs, each tree supported the other, and from a distance you'd swear they were one; it wasn't until you drew close that you'd see they were two. The trees soon unfurled to cover nearly half of the village, and from a distance of several dozen *li* (one *li* is equivalent to half a kilometre), you couldn't even see Guojiadian, all you'd see was the trees. Before long, these two massive trees that seemed to beckon to people became symbols for the village itself; they became a place of respite, of peace. When someone died, the deceased's relatives would make their way to the trees to 'inform' them of their family member's passing; and although no one actually said it, in their hearts they all knew: the trees were divine.

When the Eighth Route Army entered the village to enforce the government's land reforms and transform the village into a socialist commune, it caused quite a stir. The villagers, by this time, had grown accustomed to holding town meetings at the base of the two trees. But when the 'Great Leap Forward' was announced, the whole town seemed to change into Guo Jingshi: crazy and only sort of stupid, but only just. Their whole demeanour towards the trees changed. Instead of treating them as divine, the village head rallied everyone together, told them to bring saws and axes, to demonstrate their might and bluster, and to chop down the two towering trees in order to fire the furnaces to make steel. Only Guo Jingshi was unaware of what was happening, still nestled, as he was, at the base of the trees, eyes closed, resting his soul — naturally, his presence prevented the villagers from raising their saws and axes to fell the two giants. But how could this be? How could the villagers of Guojiadian allow a man who feigned insanity to halt the Great Leap Forward?

Among the group that had gathered round the trees, several came forward, wrapped their arms around Guo Jingshi, around his extremities, his head and his waist, and on the count of one, two, three, heaved him away from the trees. After years of silence, the actions of the men around him seemingly stirred Guo Jingshi to respond, mumbling, half to himself, that "a peasant's job was to till the land, forging steel was a worker's job, and people should know their place…" The villagers nearly froze in surprise, all turning their eyes towards Guo Jingshi, staring at him, and yet his mouth didn't move, his eyelids seemed to droop, his eyes themselves directed only towards the ground; he didn't look like a man who could have uttered such words.

There was almost pandemonium among the villagers. Finally, without giving heed to who might've said those words, or even to what words might've been said, two sturdy men with saws slung over their shoulders could wait no longer. They stomped off out of the crowd towards the trees, positioning their saws in front of them and prepared to plunge their metal teeth into the trunk of the birch-leaved pear tree. But as their saws were supposed to be eating into the tree, they heard an ear-piercing wail that couldn't have been human. Saws clanged to the ground and one of the men slumped. His left leg had been torn open and blood gushed everywhere.

Their saws hadn't ripped into the trees; they'd only sliced into their own legs.

How could this have happened? The men had clearly used their saws to tear apart the tree trunks, the bystanders had all seen it so clearly, and yet the trees remained. The villagers could only stand, eyes agape. Adding to their shock was Guo Jingshi, once more sat at the foot of the trees, eyes squinting towards them, calm and collected. The village head flew into a rage, admonishing those around him as though he were scolding a stubborn farm animal, but none would dare step forward and pick up a saw. His verbal insults continued. He railed at them for being superstitious. If saws didn't work, he'd use an axe instead. Eyes red and enflamed, he marched towards the tree, roughly pushed Guo Jingshi out of the way, spat on the palms of his hands, lifted the large axe above his head, and with all his might plunged it into the trunk of the elm tree. Again there was that inhuman wail; lying on the ground in front of the village head was his own forefinger, torn from his left hand at the knuckle.

The villagers only became more infuriated. They shouted out Great Leap Forward slogans and brandished their fists at the sky. If an axe couldn't fell the great trees in whole, then they would enlist strong, able young men to climb into the trees themselves, to use kitchen knives and small axes to prune the trees of their branches. These at least could be used to fire the furnaces, and once the trees were bare, they could slowly chop away at the branchless corpses. By this time, the entire village had come to see the ruckus. The crowd egged on those of stouter hearts to climb into the trees, but before they could even scale the trunks and ascend into the leaves, a viscous substance with a fishy odour fell from the trees onto their heads, drenching their faces in an oozy slime. Looking up, the young men could only stare in horror: both trees were infested with snakes, thousands in number of every colour under the sun, and in all sizes, they wound their way among the branches, their mouths open, dripping saliva onto those below. And in among this writhing mass, a huge snake had wrapped itself around the main trunks; its long glistening forked tongue was reaching out, testing the air for the smell of...

The people gathered round the tree retreated, some so afraid they fell to their knees. And at that moment, a large flock of birds appeared in the sky. Unconcerned by the human ruckus on the ground, nor afraid of the snakes in the trees, they all perched on the treetop and began to caw incessantly. The villagers below fell deathly quiet. No one else would dare take an axe to these trees.

Once the people had collected themselves, they stared at the trees from some distance and soon saw that Guo Jingshi was once again nestled against the tree trunks, his head tilted to one side as though he were asleep. The large snake had slithered down and worked its way to the crown of his head. The villagers began to suspect that Guo Jingshi had brought this poisonous snake there himself to protect the great trees. From this day forward, the great trees oozed a thick black substance from beneath their bark. If it got onto your hands, it was impossible to wash off, and over time it would turn into an ulcerating, festering boil. No one would go near the trees. And while no one really knew why, Guo Jingshi was no longer bullied by the villagers. In fact, people gave him a wide berth, and old and young all referred to him as 'Second Grandfather'.

Of course, it didn't matter what they called him, Guo Jingshi still never responded. At most he would look you over as though he were using his eyes to listen to what you were saying. People soon took to seeking him out when they were ill. While he wouldn't decline such a visit, he wouldn't tell them what ailed them either. His only response would be to reach up and remove a leaf from the birch-leaved pear tree and give it to them. Most minor illnesses were remedied in this manner, with the leaves mulched and drunk as medicine. There were those of some talent in the village who soon gave the trees a most propitious name — the Dragon Phoenix Trees. The name stuck and the story spread. The more it spread, the more fantastic it became, and before long, during New Year festivities, people would take to making offerings to the trees themselves.

2

THE HOE

One winter, there was no snow. The spring that followed on its heels brought drought. Crops were not seeded as the ground would only yield plumes of dust. To make matters worse, the winter crops had died and so the entire village was short of food. This was hard to bear for, as far as the eye could see, the entire area was empty. It seemed as though the only thing remaining were the farmer's beasts of burden, their heads slumped, waists slouching, pulling behind them metal hoes that now seemed to weigh a tonne, tearing through the dry earth, back and forth, back and forth. All around white dust floated through the air, parched and dry, an almost illusory image.

But this illusory scene was real. Following behind his beast of burden was a strong, strapping young man, Guo Jingtian's son, Guo Cunxian. The young man had short, cropped hair that framed his face. He wore a coarse fabric jacket, unlined, with buttons down the front with matching trousers. On his feet he wore a pair of cloth shoes commonly seen in the northeast. From head to toe he exuded a rugged, sturdy image, a certain manhood. His hoe was two feet wide, with two steel bars, much like shiny metal chopsticks, attaching it to the shaft; altogether it weighed around ten kilos. When he thrust it into the earth, it was like one of those old tightly woven fishing nets that unfurled under the water scooping up both big and small fish alike, leaving nothing in its wake. Cunxian's hoe did the same, tearing through the earth, raking up firewood, sticks and branches, farm crops, grass shoots, everything. Only when his hoe had ploughed through the ground and had raked a suitable amount of firewood would he stop, after which he'd pick out the firewood and load it into a clean tree basket that he carried with him.

But Guo Cunxian's hoe wasn't meant to plough up only the new and fresh grasses; it was also meant to plough through last year's dried remains. Only last year, things had not gone to plan. Instead, the townspeople had been organised into a large shovel detail. He had been one of them and they had been instructed to dig deep into the ground, about a metre or more, and to turn the earth over, lifting the moist soil from deep below the surface and burying the sun-parched earth underneath. The plan had been to revitalise the land, allowing fresh new crops to be planted. However, not only had the plan not improved the ground for planting new crops, it had also destroyed the land's weeds, life that had survived and flourished in the earth for thousands of years. In fact, the land had been drained of moisture and transformed into a barren wasteland with little life left in it. And now there was drought, it was difficult for even a centimetre of grass to grow. The land was dry, almost a sparkling white. He felt as though he'd been placed in a bamboo steamer, hoe included, and had been steamed for the better part of a day. And yet, even as day turned to night, all he had collected was half a basket of firewood. To make matters worse, there were more bits of grass than actual firewood, and even that was spongy and damp, more suitable to be mixed up for animal feed than for feeding fires. But he didn't have any animals to feed, they'd all been taken by the commune leaders to look after, so all he could do was use what he'd gathered to light fires. It wouldn't be of much use, though, at most he'd have wood enough to cook a single meal.

In truth, Guo Cunxian wasn't really fussed about how much kindling he'd gathered, he was more concerned about simply having something to do, about putting himself to work, breaking out in a sweat. People had to have something to do. In such hard times this was perhaps the only way forward. Him being out here, almost hiding in this sunken depression, tilling dead soil, was just his way of forcing himself not to be engulfed by the misery all around him. This certainly was a case of joy being turned into sorrow, of the heavens being angry at man's indignation! This time last year, everyone believed they were on the cusp of entering a communist utopia, that soon their bellies would be filled with endless amounts of food, that they'd all have more than enough to clothe themselves and that everything would be in abundance. Who'd have thought that in the blink of an eye they'd be cast out of heaven and thrown into this arid wasteland, and that the key thing they'd be lacking would be food to fill their bellies. Those who were able, the old and the young, had already left the village to beg for food, and it didn't matter where they'd gone or in what direction; leaving was at least a chance to live. Those that remained wasted away their days propped up against walls, crouched in doorways, or hiding behind doors, prostrate on their beds, hoping that another day of motionlessness would help them conserve what little energy they had left. An empty stomach, after all, could endure for at least a short period of time, and empty intestines could actually make one feel a little better. But Guo Cunxian didn't think that such an approach was a long-term plan. It was practically the same as eating whatever one could find and simply waiting for death. Besides, there was no one in his family who could go out and beg for food so he had to think of his own solution.

Just as he was mulling these things over, something flashed across his eyes. In the shade of a dried ditch he spotted a hint of green, a small blooming of seablites no taller than one's palm, thin and narrow, but stubbornly hanging onto the blighted land. His heart skipped a beat. Hurriedly he let go of his hoe and moved toward the seablites. He marvelled at the greenness, at this unexpected life. He spied small swallowtail caterpillars slowly trekking across the greenness, munching as they went. These caterpillars were certainly fortunate, they'd found the only bit of green in this wasted, parched land. These insects were to be marvelled at as well: their main source of food was the fennel plant, but here they were, able to munch away at the much saltier seablites. And yet, there was tragedy here since they couldn't leave the small, palm-sized growth stubbornly clinging to the dried land. Up and down they made their way, over and over again. He quivered; wasn't he much like these caterpillars?

He lifted his foot and viciously kicked at the seablites, spattering the greenness and the little caterpillars that clung to it. Unexpectedly, he then discovered dried willow branches scattered on the slope of the ditch, seemingly placed there deliberately, almost in the shape of a dog's head. Shaped as they were, it was difficult to separate the branches, so much so that even though others had probably seen the pile of kindling with covetous eyes, they'd been unable to pull it apart, and so it had remained here until now. He grabbed an axe from his basket. Grasping its handle, he raised the crescent blade, but he didn't swing it as though he were imitating a master's cut, nor did he take aim. He simply let the blade fall with all its weight, hacking through the bramble of willow branches, shattering it to pieces. His swings came one after the other and soon the smooth, glossy, hard willow stalks were broken into pieces, each piece nearly the same size in length. Guo Cunxian then proceeded to gather the pieces together and load them into his basket before covering the kindling with the grass he'd collected earlier.

The daylight was fading and so he laid down his great hoe in order to attach it to one end of his carrying pole; to the other end he hooked his basket of firewood. Straightening his shoulders and back, he lifted the pole from the ground, took a deep breath and headed towards the village. On the road back to the village, he soon came upon last year's field of sweet potatoes and a solitary figure, a woman, fork in hand, digging in vain at the dirt, trying to find remnants of last year's harvest. Her waist was bowed and her buttocks protruded in hurried fashion. The more she dug the more she came up empty-handed, and so she dug some more, tearing at the earth with her fork as if she'd gone mad. As he drew closer, he could see that it was the young wife of Han Erhu whom the villagers liked to refer to, behind his back of course, as a bit of a dullard. She persisted half-heartedly with her digging, yet not even the hair of a sweet potato did she find. Guo Cunxian slowed his pace and called to her: "Sister, you're still here digging?"

With great reluctance, Erhu's wife raised her head. Her face, her hair, her blue garments, all were covered in dirt. Her expression was one of stubbornness, but there was fear in her eyes: "I didn't believe that the sweet potato field could have been picked clean, but how is it that I can't even find one or two leftover pieces!"

"Don't foolishly waste your strength. I've heard that that field has been picked over at least three hundred and sixty times. Sweet potato? Heh, have a look, not even the leaves of a sweet potato plant are left!"

She plopped herself down into the dirt, flinging her fork away. "Big Brother, to be honest, I'm cursed. I've been married many years, and when things were plentiful I couldn't get pregnant. Now when things are hard and there isn't enough food to go round, this unfortunate child has seen fit to make my womb its home. I want to leave this town to beg for food, but Erhu won't allow it, fearing I will lose the baby. But if I stay home, there isn't anything to eat. If I don't eat, how can this child grow!"

Guo Cunxian laid down his pole and moved towards Erhu's wife, lifting her up.

He then bent down and picked up her fork, putting it back in her hand, urging her to leave the blighted sweet potato field: "Go home. And don't despair, that leads nowhere. If others can make it, so can you. It's foolish to keep returning to this field, digging for sweet potatoes that aren't here, risking your child like this. Tell me, if your child dies out here, would Erhu forgive you?"

Guo Cunxian extended himself and once more lifted his pole onto his shoulder. Together they started back to the village.

The western sky had an azure hue as they came upon the town. Guojiadian was bathed in dusk's meagre light, partly seen and unseen. This was the time of day when the sheep herds were brought home, the chickens returned to their coops and the pigs were fed. It was the time of day when families would be making dinner, and for those who had already prepared their meals, the men and children would enjoy carrying their bowls out into the main street, or they would crouch in their doorways, eating and chatting with their neighbours. Evenings were usually this lively, time for the warm exchange of camaraderie. But as they came upon the town, they didn't see the plumes of smoke issuing from kitchen chimneys, and the main street was virtually empty. Not even the shadows of pigs, sheep, chickens and dogs could be seen, and there were very few people about. The whole village seemed lonely and quiet. A deathly pall hung in the air.

By this time, Guo Cunxian's entire body was drenched with sweat; the great hoe perched upon his shoulder, the basket of firewood hanging from the other side. When the evening wind blew, chills would run through him. But his heart felt even colder. His heart was stuck to the middle of his back and his stomach felt as though a rake were being pulled across it, scratching its way up and down, tearing at his skin. He couldn't help but feel a certain sort of rage. "These people have become so used to being poor; their hunger is eating away at them, shrivelling them up. Even without any food to cook, the kitchen fires should still be lit, there should still be smoke billowing from chimneys, bringing warmth to hearth and home, that's what a village should be like, that's what life should be like!"

Erhu's wife didn't respond. She kept her head low and returned to her own home. Guo Cunxian still had to make his way round the bend before he'd reach home. But as he passed by the communal barn used to house the farm animals, out of the blue he bumped into two young lads standing on the tips of their toes, sorghum branches in hand, vigorously poking at something higher up on the wall. This peaked Guo Cunxian's curiosity, so he stretched his neck to see what it was they were poking at; still he could see nothing. He turned to the boys: "Are you lads trying to drum against the wall?"

The boys stopped what they were doing, but they weren't inclined to tell Guo Cunxian what they were up to. He drew closer to the wall to inspect it more carefully, discovering a black roof tile embedded into the corner of the wall. He asked them once more: "Were you trying to pry this roof tile free?"

Now brazen as could be, one of the boys spoke: "Axe brother, we saw that first, you'd better not try and snatch it from us."

"But what is it?"

"A dried sweet potato."

"What!" Guo Cunxian suddenly realised what it was they'd been poking at. Last year as the villagers thought they were headed towards a communist utopia, many people were inclined to waste things, thinking that the future would be full of plenty. The village children must've taken a piece of cooked sweet potato from the canteen to use as a dart, launching it back and forth between them. And as kids are wont to do, they must've thrown it too high and got it stuck up on the roof tile. There it had been, since last year, and by now it had become hard and congealed, much like a stone. But in hard times such as these, this hard piece of barely edible sweet potato was like treasure. Many had already taken shovels to pry off other pieces to eat. Who'd have thought that up in the corner of this old barn, high up beyond where eyes could easily see, there'd still be a piece of hard sweet potato waiting for these two boys to find? When people were starving, there were few places the eyes couldn't see when looking for something to eat.

Guo Cunxian flung down the pole that he had been carrying over his shoulder and drew it out from the bags hanging over it. Quickly and effortlessly, he reached up and pried loose the dried remnants of sweet potato, dropping it into the hand of one of the children, Dafa. Without considering the caked-on dirt, the child stuffed it in his mouth immediately. The other, Shuichang, howled in exasperation: "I saw it first. We're supposed to share it!"

The sweet potato itself was much too hard and much too small. Sticking half of it out of his mouth, Dafa tried to tear it apart but he couldn't. Shuichang stared coldly at it before moving forward and clamping his teeth down over the extended half. Dafa wouldn't relent. Guo Cunxian moved towards them to try to settle the dispute. He turned to Shuichang: "Is it sweet?"

"Yes."

"The two of you need to treat it like a piece of candy. One of you suck it for a little while, then the other, until it gets soft. Once it does, bite it in two. But make sure neither of you swallows it first, OK?"

Once he had settled the fight, Guo Cunxian picked up his belongings and headed off home. As he entered the door, his mother, Sun Yueqing, must've heard the noise and immediately came out from the inner room. She was not much more than skin and bones, her face dark and sunken, but if someone arrived at the door, proper greetings had to be made. Giving off the image of a certain nimbleness, she said: "Yeah, it's that season again. The land doesn't know that people have been making themselves busy gathering up the dried branches and twigs, over and over again, but how is it that you've managed to collect so much?" The admiration in her voice was clear, either that or she was quite adept at fawning over him.

She turned her head and beckoned to her daughter to come out from the inside room: "Cunzhu, quickly go and get your older brother a bowl of hot water to drink. I've just heated it. That will help to moisten his throat, then we can eat." Hurriedly, Guo Cunzhu went and fetched a bowl of water, returned and placed it in her brother's hands. She then began to unload the basket of firewood before putting both it and her brother's great hoe away... she was only a little more than two years younger than Cunxian, but she seemed much older. Her body was frail and weak but she worked diligently. She showed great deference towards her older brother, or perhaps it was a fearful respect.

Their little home was far too narrow. Beyond the south-facing rampart were the chicken coop, the pigsty and the sheep pen; it seemed rather well planned out, almost hopeful. But, pitifully, everything was deserted except for a pile of firewood on one side and a mound of junk on the other. Facing north stood two darkish rooms straddling a brighter one in the middle. Here they cooked their meals; the side rooms were where they slept. Looking towards the east, Cunzhu and her mother shared a bed; facing west, Cunxian, Cunzhi and their poor Uncle Guo Jingshi were crammed in together. As a result, the western room was the centre of the house, the liveliest room. Here they ate, entertained guests, and discussed important family matters; the western room was customarily used in this fashion.

Cunzhu had previously prepared their small dinner table that was used on top of the heated brick bed. Guo Jingshi, who had already been called in, was squatting down next to it, waiting. Sun Yueqing had given him instructions that, before sitting down to eat, he had to allow his niece to use a moist towel and clean his hands and face. His long white hair was pulled back into a pigtail that hung loosely behind him and his heavy-looking face drooped downwards. His intransigent expression gave him the look of someone burdened with a grave secret; his whole body was shrouded in an odd, almost sinister gloom.

Their so-called dinner was actually a plate of food Sun Yueqing had brought from the production team's canteen. Once she had got it home, she put it in her own pot and re-heated it over the stove, adding water to make a murky, dark gruel. The gruel was a mixture of sorghum flour, seablite seeds, dried cabbage leaves and carrot greens. Sun Yueqing readied a lacquered bowl and first scooped up some gruel for Guo Jingshi. She then took two smaller bowls, ladled in some hot water and added the remaining dark gruel. Stoking the fires, she brought the mixture back to the boil. The watery porridge was for the rest of them to eat.

As she was doing this, she inhaled a whiff of smoke and fell into a fit of coughing. Soon, her face turned crimson red, the cough spreading to her chest, doubling her over. As the children witnessed her plight they couldn't help but suffer it as well. Finally, Guo Cunxian could hold his tongue no longer and said: "Every time it's he who eats and drinks well, and yet all he ever does is sit below that damn tree doing nothing. He can't even be bothered to pluck a few leaves from the Dragon Phoenix Trees to bring home, even though everyone knows that those leaves, once mulched and boiled, can cure illness, break fevers and cleanse the body!"

Guo Cunxian wasn't blaming his younger brother Cunzhi. His anger was clearly directed towards his Uncle, Guo Jingshi. His mother's eyes swept across him before she was able to meekly utter: "How could you say such a thing about your uncle?"

Cunzhu butted in: "I've been thinking about going there in the evening to pick some of the leaves, but there are guards round the Dragon Phoenix Trees that won't allow anyone near them."

Guo Cunxian spun his head around: "What!" Why had Cunzhu blurted out these words? What was she hoping to accomplish? Without saying a word, Guo Cunxian lowered his head and went outside. His mother pounced toward him, grabbing him by his shirt: "What do you plan on doing?" She spoke in a now loud voice.

Guo Cunxian already had one foot in the door: "I'm going to go and see for myself."

"Please eat first and then go and see."

"I'll eat when I come back."

At that moment, in this deathly quiet village of Guojiadian, late into the evening as it was, an ear-piercing, mournful cry came in from outside. Sun Yueqing herself wailed: "Whose house has death visited now?"

"Most likely it's Nan Toucun's mother. Every morsel of food she's got she has given to her child. The only thing she has been eating herself is clay, and all that'll do is swell your stomach. Before long you'll be rolling around on the floor in nothing but pain. People say a good shit will help clean it out, but no matter how hard you try, it just won't come. You'll starve to death and your stomach will be full. Nowadays, living just isn't worth it, people are queuing up to die, just waiting around for it. I've heard there are quite a few who are at death's door."

Cunzhu's words were heard by her mother and elicited an excoriating response: "Stop talking rubbish! It's fine to speak of others when times are good, but don't curse them when death has come!"

Without opening her mouth to respond, Cunzhu took off towards the door to follow her older brother. Sun Yueqing could only yell from the doorway: "Come and eat your dinner. What do you hope to accomplish, eh?" But it didn't matter, brother and sister had already receded into the distance; they didn't reply.

Judging by the crowd of 'mourners' that filled the village street with their grief-stricken wailing, it was most likely an elderly family member that had died. According to Guojiadian custom, upon the death of any villager, the deceased's kin needed to take to the streets immediately in order to lament the loss of their loved one and to announce to the local deities that a villager's soul was on its way; it was like reporting the death to the authorities, in this case the local, spiritual ones. For an entire day, once in the morning, once in the afternoon and then again in the evening, the deceased's family had to 'report' the death. On each occasion, the number of people mourning the passing of their loved one would increase, as would the volume of ferocity of their wailing. It was all meant to show how prosperous and filial the next generation was, and to allow for the deceased to feel gratified that they'd left their kin in such a good state. That said, Guojiadian no longer had a local temple. Instead, all the villagers would make their way to the Dragon Phoenix Trees and at their base they'd burn spirit money, kowtow and make offerings, bringing food to their dead relatives who were, at least temporarily, residing with the tree spirits.

But the people who gathered had empty bellies; they used water in place of wine and chaff in place of food. Surely the deceased's spirit couldn't help but feel wronged. Once the mourners had made their offerings and retreated back to their homes, Guo Cunxian made his way over to the trees. Before he could draw too close, however, he was stopped as expected by the four militia guards stationed to watch over the trees. In a firm voice, the militia leader, everyone's 'favourite young man', a strapping young fellow by the name of Lan Shoukun, bellowed: "What are you doing here?"

Guo Cunxian's stomach rolled over and a sour taste gurgled up into his mouth. How in hell did this boy grow so big? He thought to himself, people were right, we could all be starving, but it would be rare indeed to see a sickly and thin security guard. In this village, all you had to do was take up some official post, to hold even just a little power, then you'd be assured the first bite of whatever came across your plate and be assured that your stomach would never go empty.

Although his own stomach was doing somersaults, Guo Cunxian still managed to respond cheerfully: "I thought I'd come and pick a few leaves from the pear tree. My mother's got this terrible cough and I thought I'd boil up the leaves and give them to her to drink."

Lan Shoukun's mouth contorted, revealing a glimpse of white teeth behind his lips: "Oh, you want to pick some of the leaves to treat your mum's cough. Others have come to snatch the ripe pears from the branches to feed their hunger, still others have come with axes, planning to fell the elm tree to boil its bark and eat that. Everyone in the village has a plan for these trees. How many people do you think come by in a day planning to grab these trees? For some, digging up the roots isn't even enough. That's why the Party has given orders: absolutely no one is allowed near the Dragon Phoenix Trees!"

"But I only wanted to pluck a few leaves!"

"If you pluck some and then the next person does the same, and then the next, the trees would be bare in no time. And without leaves, how long do you think they would live?"

Growing frustrated, Guo Cunxian replied: "But I just want some to help cure an old lady!"

Lan Shoukun's voice grew louder: "Haven't you noticed? There are people dying every day and we can't do anything about it."

"You're just bullying people. It's only a few bloody leaves!" Guo Cunxian was nearly beside himself, shifting back and forth on his feet, itching to spring forward and up into the tree. It was only Cunzhu holding him back desperately that kept him in place. Standing to the side, the other three guards readied their rifles, although one couldn't be sure whether or not they were actually loaded.

Lan Shoukun took a further step forward and spoke to Guo Cunxian rather dismissively: "So what is it, huh? Do you want to cause a ruckus? Stir things up? I know your family, I know the Guo name and what it means, but can't you see where you are? You're standing underneath the Dragon Phoenix Trees. Don't you know that it was these trees that cured your family?"

The three guards chimed in now, adding fuel to the fire: "Really? How can that be, eh? How come we've never heard that? Tell us, eh, tell us, even if it's all just rumour, that doesn't matter."

Lan Shoukun wanted to intentionally ridicule Guo Cunxian now. He had settled an old score and now wished to open a new one. He knew he had already wounded Guo Cunxian and so he struck there again: "I can't help but also say, Guo Cunxian, that perhaps your family background needs to be looked at. Before your father was impaled with that bayonet, your family was fairly well off, wasn't it? You could perhaps even say that they were landowners, right? Or at least petit bourgeois, huh? This is still an unresolved issue, don't you think? Hey, and now you'd like to poke this bear."

Lan Shoukun's words were poisonous, vicious and struck Guo Cunxian to the core. If the village really did decide to re-examine his family's history, if they did decide to label them as petit bourgeoisie, they'd never be able to lift their heads again. Lan Shoukun saw the fear spread across Guo Cunxian's face and he changed his tone, softening it noticeably. In an almost pleasant voice, he advised him to head home. He asked him as well if it would be all right for him to have the guards gather up the pear leaves that had fallen and give them to his uncle, Guo Jingshi, to bring home.

Guo Cunxian could barely contain his desire to throw himself at Lan Shoukun and throttle him, or beat him to death. But he didn't utter a word. He simply turned around and left the Dragon Phoenix Trees. When brother and sister returned home, no one said a word about the leaves, nor did his mother ask him why he hadn't brought any back with him. Sombrely, Guo Cunxian swallowed his watery gruel and then put down his bowl. A dark cloud seemed to hang over him before he suddenly spat out these words: "Tomorrow morning I'm leaving."

His mother was startled: "What the hell for?"

Without lifting his eyes, he replied: "To make coffins. There are so many people starving to death these days, perhaps I'll be able to make a living off it, perhaps even make an extra little bit of money and, if not, then at least I'll be able to earn my keep, enough to get through these days and make ends meet."

Cunzhu couldn't help but throw cold water on his plans: "Brother, I don't think you've thought this through. Just look at our village and at those who've died. Who has been able to handle this properly, to actually bury the dead properly? Most just use their thick mat bedding or their bed sheets to wrap them in and then bury them in shallow graves."

Cunzhi interjected here: "And to be honest, you're not much of a carpenter. In the past you always worked with someone else. Do you think you can handle it all on your own? Perhaps I should go with you."

Guo Cunxian cut off his younger brother before he could say anything else. "No, you can't. If you left, who'd take care of our sister and our mother? Who'd take care of this family?"

Cunzhu nearly blurted out that no one needs to take care of this family, but thought better of it. If one person left that'd mean one less mouth to feed so more food for the rest of them. That'd be the best way to look after this family. Then she glanced towards her uncle, Guo Jingshi, and swallowed her words.

Guo Jingshi was sitting quietly at the head of the *kang*, not looking at anyone; it didn't look like he was listening either.

Guo Cunxian was the head of the family now and what he said went. Even Sun Yueqing could only sigh: "Cunxian, you know that you're not all that young any more, and I've been thinking that in these tough times we ought to take advantage of some poor young maiden passing through, trying to escape this awful famine. If she were suitable, well, then the two of you could marry. But if you leave now, what will become of these plans?"

"You don't need to worry about me." Cunxian straightened up and got down from the heated bed. He walked through to the small south-facing room to rummage around for the old carpenter's bag his father had once used. From inside it, he pulled out an axe, a wood planer, an adze, a chisel, a saw and other carpentry tools. Near the bottom of the bag there was also a whetstone. Gathering everything up, he went into the courtyard. Cunzhu brought him a small bowl half-filled with cold water. He pulled over a small stool and placed it near the door. Squatting down, he took advantage of the little bit of light that shone in and began to sharpen his tools.

As he was sharpening them, his mind wandered to the less than flattering words his younger brother had spoken. He looked at the fine edge he had given his axe and stood up. In the corner of the courtyard were several tree stumps of varying sizes. He pulled one from the pile, the trunk of a jujube tree, and said to Cunzhu: "The wood of the jujube tree is the hardest. This stump here ought to be at least fifty years old or more. You count, I'm going to use twenty swings of my axe to chop it into equal pieces, fit for a coffin. On one side, it won't matter whether it's smooth or not, but for the other sides, I'll slice through them so carefully that they'll be as smooth as though they had been planed."

"Really?" said Cunzhu excitedly as she hollered out to Cunzhi: "Second Brother, come quick! Cunxian is about to show us his skill with an axe!"

Cunzhi leapt up from the inner room and rushed out into the courtyard. There he saw his older brother holding onto the jujube tree stump, sizing it up with his eyes. It was as though he were deep in deliberation, ascertaining the precise angle and strength of the swings he'd have to make.

His deliberations over, he spat into the palm of his right hand, grasped the handle of the axe firmly, and swung. Before his brother and sister could see clearly, Cunxian's axe had already fallen three to four times. His swings were soft and yet heavy, hurried and yet relaxed. From three swings of his axe he'd cut one side of the coffin; with a few more swings into the back of the piece he smoothed it out. By the time Cunzhu reached twenty swings, the once round old jujube tree trunk had been transformed into a perfectly proportioned coffin.

Before the morning grew bright, before anyone else was awake, before his mother and brother could properly say farewell, Guo Cunxian left quietly and without a sound. Over his shoulder he had slung a canvas bag to serve as his carpenter's tool kit. The only things in it were his carpentry tools – his axe, his chisel, his adze and his wood plane – six maize and sorghum pancakes, and an enamelled tea mug. In his hand he grasped a saw – this was for affectation purposes only. After all, he had to make sure that wherever his feet took him he looked the part. People had to know that he was a carpenter and that he was looking for work. He chose to head south. People were leaving the south to escape from famine, heading north to beg for food, going so far as to venture beyond the Great Wall; but for him to make any money at all, he'd have to head south, as far as the south seas if need be.

3

FOOD SUBSTITUTES

In 1958 as the Great Leap Forward reached its apex, scientists at the Chinese Academy of Sciences (CAS) directed their attention towards the following issue: 'increasing food production'. And while you couldn't consider the research into this topic to be complete, near the end of 1959 the central authorities issued new directives, stating that the research project had now changed to the issue of 'managing serious food shortages'. Accordingly, researchers concentrated on the most serious matter: the production of alternative or substitute foods. Since the CAS directed a number of research departments to focus on this issue, and since the CAS itself had been formed on the back of research into biology and biochemistry, the progress made into food substitutes was rather quick so that, to date, they had already achieved a number of experimental successes. These new foodstuffs were not only very nutritious, but they were also free from toxins and the ingredients were abundant. What's more, they were incredibly easy to handle and large-scale production could similarly be extended and popularised according to local needs. Think of acorn kernels: first they needed to be soaked, then mashed up, after which they would be suitable for human consumption. The key was for the authorities to seize the moment and popularise these processes. There were other alternatives, too, such as corn roots, wheat roots and so on. These could all be washed and mashed and made suitable for eating. In addition to these products already available in nature, there were also the substitute foodstuffs created in the CAS laboratories, namely, synthetic meat essence, leaf proteins, chlorella (small balls of algae-based nutrients), platymonas (or green algae), yeast extracted from stalks of celery, wormwood, citron and the Asiatic dayflower (or *commelina communis*). The scientists were also able to extract leaf proteins from more than twenty different domesticated and undomesticated plants and for every fifty kilos of fresh leaves they could produce between one and five kilos of dried protein. Even straw could be used as a foodstuff. According to estimates, the country produced 300 million tonnes of straw per annum. If just ten per cent of that was used for human consumption, that would equal thirty million tonnes of food.

9 NOVEMBER 1960 – A CAS REPORT GIVEN TO THE CENTRAL
AUTHORITIES ENTITLED: *OFFICIAL RECOMMENDATION ON THE
USE OF SUBSTITUTE FOODSTUFFS*

Guo Cunxian had now been heading south for four days, and whether he was far away or not, so long as he could glance and see the railway track, he knew he wasn't lost. He'd passed through more than ten villages by now, and yet he hadn't found any work. The increasing heat was nearly overwhelming him, he had at least two blisters on his parched lips, and what was worse was the fact that the small bit of food he had brought with him was nearly gone. He dared not eat too much. It was only when his legs began to grow weak from the emptiness in his stomach that he'd break off a small piece of his pancakes and stuff it in his mouth. All his hopes were pinned on being able to find a little bit of work to do in order to fill his belly. The days blurred into each other. In the evening he'd often find himself near a well, or perhaps at someone's home where he'd beg for a little cold water to fill his mug, then he'd try to find a pile of firewood somewhere on the outskirts of the village, a quiet place where he could bed down for the night. If he was lucky, he'd find some abandoned building, a more sheltered place where he could rest his weary legs and sip his cool water, which tasted so fragrant and sweet in such circumstances, along with the pancakes his mother had made. In the whole wide world, his mum and her pancakes were the two things he felt closest to. The old saying was right: when you're home, things are good; when you've left, things are hard. But added to his hardship was the fact that he couldn't look back. Never say die, was all he could think. He wouldn't accept that he was trapped on a road leading nowhere.

He had to rely on his youth, on his wits, and not let these things keep him awake; after all, sleep would steal away the things that troubled his mind. When he awoke and opened his eyes, another fierce sun shone overhead, the land stood roasted white underneath, preventing his eyes from looking at the barren expanse that lay in front of him. It was just as Zhu Xi said during the Song dynasty – that during times of war or natural disaster, the land is often made into a "desolate wasteland". Guo Cunxian considered for a moment. These days, at most, he could travel perhaps a few hundred kilometres or so, but that'd be far too few. When would he be able to escape this barren land? Ruminating thus, Guo Cunxian's mind couldn't help but wander to the banal jingles that echoed throughout the Great Leap Forward, doggerels such as: "Why is the earth bathed in such light? Because of the sun shining oh so bright!" This nonsense was too painful. Land bathed with such a fierce light only ended up dry and barren. How were people supposed to live in such a wasteland? It was then that he struck upon a plan: he would cease to wander round this sun-baked earth, frittering away his time and strength. Instead, he'd make his way even further south, looking for any bit of greenery he could find. Only then would he have the means to live. This sun-drenched land only brought starvation; people slumped against walls, waiting for the inevitable. How would he find work in such conditions? It was just as his little sister had observed when he said he was leaving: those at death's door aren't bothered about having coffins.

He decided not to head straight towards the sun, but instead head in a south-westerly direction down a smaller country road. If he didn't come upon any villages, he'd just keep walking. If the road were to meander through a town, well, he'd go and look for work. It'd be easy enough for people to see he's a carpenter, and so if anyone needed work done, they'd call out to him, if not, then at least he'd be able to rest his feet for a spell, beg for a bowl of water, and then continue on his way. And this was how he perhaps whiled away far too many days before suddenly catching a fragmentary glimpse of a small field in the distance. Even though it looked somewhat pitiful, there was still greenness to it, which prompted him to breathe in deeply. A little further on the foliage became even denser, hiding a brook trickling underneath. His entire body was caked in dirt and mud. Glancing around and spying no one about, he stripped off his clothes and threw himself into the gurgling water. Bathing to his heart's content, he then grabbed his clothes and washed them as best he could in the water. Once clean, he wrung them out and put them back on even though they were still cold and damp. The dampness immediately seeped into his bones, making him uncomfortable, but it was worth it. Straightening up, he headed back to the road with a cheerful skip in his step. Even the hot air no longer seemed to scorch his face as it blew around him.

As he continued to walk, a mountain soon came into view in the west. It had a rather steep incline, gradually rising to a precipitous height, but it seemed bare and barren, or perhaps dark and forbidding. It gave the whole area a mysterious quality. His eyes no longer had a panoramic view of the area, drawn as they were to the mountain; he felt excited, or maybe nervous. Suddenly there were signs of movement in front of him. His ears picked up a strange and terrifying sound, a moaning sort of wail. His legs grew taut as he turned towards the sloping land, readying himself for a fierce life-or-death struggle amongst the desolation. Two wild, mangy, almost rabid mutts came into view, battling viciously with a half-grown donkey.

These days are certainly evil; dogs dare to attack donkeys! And this poor thing was already at a disadvantage. Where had its owner gone? The wild dogs were exceptionally ferocious, one mottled white and black, the other a scruffy grey. People these days were all skin and bones, and whatever flesh was left was swollen from malnutrition. Even these crazy dogs were no different. But even during such hardship, turning on each other was madness. This poor beast of burden seemed doomed, its mouth was already bloodstained, which only seemed to provoke the wild dogs even more, increasing their viciousness. The sound of their gnashing teeth carried through the air and then one pounced straight towards the exposed neck of the poor animal. Strangely, though, the donkey didn't try to flee. It kept circling round the same spot, determinedly kicking out its hind legs again and again, trying in vain to fend off the feral attacks. But as it tried to protect its front, its rear was exposed. Its nostrils flared as it endured the attacks, foam issued from its mouth, but still, nothing seemed to be able to make it bellow forth that distinctive donkey yowl. It kept defending itself, huffing and puffing angrily.

Then, suddenly, from below the donkey's extended neck came the blood-curdling screech of a small child. Guo Cunxian was floored and hastily emerged from the slope he had been hiding behind. He could see clearly now. A little boy was cowering beneath the donkey's neck, arms clasped round its front leg. The donkey was trying in vain to position its body between the dogs and the boy. But as the dogs circled, a space became free and the grey dog lunged towards the boy, clamping its jaws onto his buttocks, trying to drag him out from under the beast. Meanwhile the mottled dog circled towards the other side before it too lunged at the donkey, biting at its face, forcing it to turn its head to protect itself, thus diverting its attention away from the boy. Guo Cunxian understood what they were trying to do. They weren't after the donkey at all, but rather wanted to sink their teeth into the soft flesh of the boy. He threw down his saw and rushed towards the melee, brandishing his axe as he came near, swinging it violently in the direction of the grey dog. It yelped loudly as the axe bit into its hindquarters, causing the animal to release the child. It skulked away from Guo Cunxian, dragging its wounded leg behind it. But it didn't flee completely. Once it had got far enough away from the arc of his axe, it stopped, turned, and stared maliciously at Guo Cunxian, biding its time before attacking again. His heart was filled with remorse. If only his axe had been swung a little more ferociously, if only it had torn into the animal's flesh, then its life would have been extinguished and at least one threat ended. But it hadn't, and while he had for the time being saved the child from the maw of the grey dog, the mottled one now turned its attention to Guo Cunxian as well, so that he was facing both of them.

"Ya! You son of a bitch, you really are looking to die!" He didn't try to dodge, but instead waved his axe menacingly toward the animals, inviting them forward so that he could sink his blade into their flesh but his swings were chaotic, random, and failed to strike their target; nor did the dogs succeed in latching their maws onto him. The grey dog stood to one side, barking furiously, almost as though it were egging its partner on. But the barking, filled with rage though it was, served only to lessen the fear in Guo Cunxian's heart. After all, to bark like that meant it was afraid, which allowed Guo Cunxian to pluck up his courage even more. He continued to swing his axe in the direction of the mottled dog at the same time as he hollered towards the dog he had struck, trying to enrage it further, to make it drag its lame backside closer to him so that he could strike another blow. He wasn't trying to scare them off, no, he wanted to kill them, or at least one of them. For so long he'd known nothing but sorrow, it'd serve these two vicious animals right if tonight he ate his fill of roasted dog meat. Perhaps he'd even have dried leftovers, enough for a couple of days at least.

Suddenly, from out of nowhere, a woman's heart-wrenching cry pierced the air: "Fugen! My boy! Oh my boy."

Hearing the approach of more people, the mottled dog ceased its attack, but it also didn't want to concede defeat. It stared at Guo Cunxian, fangs bared as though it would launch itself at him at any moment. There was a ferocious expression across its snout as it barked and howled at him wildly. Guo Cunxian didn't take his eyes off the mottled dog, watching it as it sidled up to the grey beast, the one he thought he had wounded; his work would be easier now. They could bark all they wanted, go crazy, he was almost crazy himself, but there was no way he was letting this dog meat get away.

The woman's cries drew closer and now the boy, hiding underneath the donkey's neck, heard and replied: "Mum, mum!" He dared to cry now and had the energy to do so. A moment passed and then a youngish woman stumbled hurriedly onto the battlefield, grasping a stick in her hand. Hard on her heels, a man holding a stick of his own appeared, although he seemed lame and not all that nimble. The two dogs saw that the tide of battle had turned and thus decided to beat a hasty retreat. But before escaping the battleground, the grey dog, the one Guo Cunxian had struck with his axe, came upon his tool bag and caught the smell of something. Sniffing once, it plunged its maw into the bag, pulled out his last remaining pancakes and then fled. The mottled dog tore off after its partner, snapping at the pancakes it was carrying in its mouth. Guo Cunxian was beside himself, hollering wildly as he chased after them: "You mangy beasts! You sonsabitches!"

While fighting those wretched beasts he had remained silent, but now that they had stolen his last morsel of food, his very lifeblood, he was overcome with anger and rage and couldn't help but holler after them, waving his axe in the air like a madman.

As the animals receded into the distance, the empty pit in his stomach grew worse. He felt overwhelmed. Not only had he not killed the beasts, he'd even let them run away with his last bits of food. What was he going to eat now? Would he have to resort to begging? He hung his head low, picked up his axe and saw, stumbled over to his tool bag, and plopped his behind down onto the ground.

The lame man who had come late to the battle now made his way over to him: "Brother, if it weren't for you today, well… Say, what did those two mangy dogs run away with?"

Without opening his eyes, Guo Cunxian responded: "Dried food."

"Ah, that's no matter, you just ask Sister Liu to make some more for you, any amount, it's no problem."

Guo Cunxian now raised his face to look at the man. He guessed he must be around fifty or so. He had a wide mouth and square cheeks, and a certain strength in his eyes. He'd just called the boy's mother 'Sister Liu', so they weren't family. As he was thinking this, the boy and his mother, with the donkey in tow, came up beside him as well. It was clear then, she only looked about thirty years old. She had a thin, narrow face, drawn tight like the shaft of a straw broom; she was scrawny like a candle that had been nearly burnt down. Bursting with gratitude for what Guo Cunxian had done, she said: "Big Brother, you saved my son Fugen. How can I ever thank you enough?" As she spoke, she made her son kowtow in front of Guo Cunxian, telling the boy to call him uncle.

The boy looked to be about seven or eight years old, a bit rough and tumble, but at the direction of his mother he moved closer and prostrated himself. Seeing this, Guo Cunxian quickly jumped up and grabbed the child: "No, don't, it's not necessary. Quick, let's look and see whether or not the dogs seriously hurt him."

Sister Liu said that the dogs tore his trousers, but luckily their teeth didn't pierce his skin.

"This certainly is a most loyal and courageous old donkey you have. If it weren't for its kicking, encircling the boy and keeping him protected underneath its neck, well, I'd never have made it in time and the boy most surely would have been harmed."

The older, lame man now took the donkey's leash from his sister Liu's hand, patted its back and said: "In truth, this donkey doesn't belong to them any more. Like all the rest, the animals now belong to the collective. But since it was small, this old donkey has always been close to Fugen. The two of them have practically grown up together and share the same heart. Whenever he calls, the beast comes. So when he said he wanted to release it, no one could stop it."

Sister Liu was still upset, still fretting about the ordeal her son had just been subjected to: "My God, people had told me about the wild dogs running around to the north of the village. I knew it was bad, so I asked Old Qiang to come with me, but if it weren't for you being here before us, who knows what might have happened to Fugen?"

"Are there many rabid dogs in the area?" Guo Cunxian asked.

"No, not really," Old Qiang replied. "Since we're all hungry and have little to fill our bellies, most of the dogs have already been killed and eaten. Those that haven't have gone wild, leaving the village to run feral in the woods, attacking anyone who wanders by. There's another reason why these dogs have gone rabid, too. So many of us have died, too many, that we haven't even been able to bury people properly. We've just used grass mats and shallow graves, and these dogs have got into the habit of eating the decaying flesh. Once they do that, madness soon follows, their eyes go red, and there isn't anything that they won't dare to sink their teeth into. They become even more ferocious than wolves."

Sister Liu continued to look Guo Cunxian up and down: "Big Brother, what's your family name?"

Modestly, Guo Cunxian replied: "Guo, my name's Guo Cunxian."

"Come on, let's go Brother Guo, we can speak more at home."

"No, no, no, that's all right. By the way, what's the name of your village?"

"Xinzhuang."

"How far is it from the southern townships?"

"About four kilometres."

"I'm a carpenter, I make a living out of making coffins. If there's work that needs doing in your village, then I'll come and stay a while. If not, then I'd best be moving on to the next village."

Sister Liu and Old Qiang were startled when they heard that Guo Cunxian made his living out of making coffins. As one of the town's menfolk, Old Qiang nodded and spoke in almost reverential tones: "Ah, such a skill to have. In these awful times when there's more dead than living, when there's more going into the ground than what can be harvested, I imagine making coffins would keep you busy indeed."

In a gentle, hesitant voice, Sister Liu interjected: "But there aren't that many families that can afford to have coffins made! When it comes to carpentry, however, I imagine there's a great deal more to do. My own home needs some work, Big Brother. How about coming along to see whether or not you can do anything about it?"

"That sounds about right," Old Qiang added. "I'll let the villagers know as well. I bet you can find work for at least a couple of days or more. The team leader's house, for one, has a lot that needs doing. And besides, those blasted mongrels have already run off with your food. Why not let Sister Liu make you a meal. Surely, after all that's happened, you've nothing better to do today."

Upon hearing that there might be work for him to do, Guo Cunxian's vigour returned. Consenting to their entreaties, he began to gather up his tools. Fugen leapt forward almost immediately and grabbed hold of Guo Cunxian's burnished axe. Raising it over his shoulder, he stepped next to his mother who was still holding on to the donkey's leash and began to head in the direction of the village. Guo Cunxian and Old Qiang brought up the rear. Looking for something to talk about, he asked: "So, Old Qiang, what's your family name?"

"Sun, but everyone calls me Old Qiang. Some years ago when I was working on a local dyke, a stone roller went over my leg, mangling it. Now all I can do about the village is look after the collective's animals. If you'd like, you can spend the night with me in the barn. It's got a very nice heated brick bed."

"Ah, but that'd just put you out, I don't want to trouble you."

"Brother, when everyone is starving like we are, there isn't anything else that can trouble us."

On the road back to the village, Guo Cunxian and Old Qiang passed the time by idly chatting about the town and its people, with Guo learning the odd titbit of information here and there. The village itself wasn't that big, just over a hundred households or so. In the past, there had been three village canteens, but the people round here had been very forward looking, at the vanguard, so to speak, with quite a bit of courage mixed in. Last year, in winter, they dismantled the canteens to construct a single 'model canteen' for the whole village; this was done as a means to satisfy directives from above. When Party cadres visited the village to inspect the initiative, each household sent a single representative to the model canteen and, as was the custom, each brought food with them to contribute to the communal meal; needless to say it was quite the event. Normally, most families would simply eat in their own homes with their own kin. Otherwise, well, who knows, but how else could the village still have half of its population?

The more Guo Cunxian listened to these tales, the more he came to know about the town. And as more of the village came into sight, he began to think that many of its buildings would have fallen into disrepair. But when they finally reached the village gates he understood, it was as though something had been toying with his vision. There was still greenery here, sparse and feeble looking, but green nonetheless, and only the trees that stood in and around the village were bare, their branches naked, even their bark peeled away. He guessed the reason for this, of course, but still his curiosity couldn't help but make him ask: "How did your trees end up as bare as this?"

"The leaves, the bark, all of it, the people stripped it all in order to feed themselves."

Guo Cunxian's body trembled. He thought of his own town, of the guards surrounding the Dragon Phoenix Trees. They were right. He shouldn't continue to bear a grudge against Lan Shoukun. Without thinking he blurted out: "But if the trees are stripped this way, won't they die?"

"In these times when we can't even take care of our own, who's going to care about the trees?"

At the northern gate two trees surrounded and yet didn't obscure the entrance to the town. Because they were bare it was impossible to tell what kind of tree they were. Strangely, the trunks of both trees were layered with a fine yellow mud. Puzzled, Guo Cunxian asked: "What's this for?"

"Ah, that's there to give the impression of tree bark for when the higher ups deign to visit."

"Are they blind then, to not be able to tell the difference?"

"Their eyes mightn't be blind, but that doesn't mean they can see. No doubt some see that the trees have been stripped bare, but they're unwilling to say anything about it. They'd rather not shatter the illusion. After all, they can't think of a reason why they should. Others are happy to go on deceiving the higher-ups, and the higher-ups themselves are happy to remain in the dark, that way it's more convenient for everyone."

Rubbing his forehead, Old Qiang continued as frankly as he had begun: "Don't tell me you still have a pure heart in a world like this. Not too long ago a Party commissioner passed through town. I heard he was once even a member of the Eighth Route Army. People went out into the street to greet him, kneeling in front of him and offering him food. He spent about half a day in the village but, somewhat unexpectedly, he never spoke a word. Then, as he departed the village, he came upon the trees. He patted the trunks and soon realised that what looked like bark was in fact nothing other than yellow mud slathered over the trees. A poor imitation of nature. He then let out a wail that punctured the air, slapped his hands together repeatedly and began to curse himself for his crimes, apologising to his countrymen. Once he finished his verbal tirade he up and left and was not seen again."

Following behind the rear quarters of the donkey, they spoke as they walked and before either realised it, they'd reached Sister Liu's home. Once there, Guo Cunxian's eyes surveyed the humble structure and he couldn't help but be stunned, couldn't help but have second thoughts about coming here. There was no courtyard to speak of, only two rooms facing northwards and a single room to the south. Even more shocking was that there was no door, the north room had but a nail hammered into the doorframe with a grass curtain hanging from it to serve as a feeble barrier across the entryway. The adjacent southern doorway didn't even possess a grass curtain; instead it stood open day and night to the outside world, with no separation between them. Any passersby, or men with certain intentions, could enter as they pleased, even the chickens, pigs and other beasts of burden could come and go at will. How could you call this a home? Was it the custom in this area or was it, in fact, that Sister Liu was just that poor? Guo Cunxian thought that if only he still had his own food, he wouldn't even have considered eating here. How indeed could he swallow anything he might be given?

Without trying to hide or cover anything up, without worrying whether an outsider saw or not, Old Qiang took from his inside pocket a small bundle of something or other and shoved it into the open and welcoming hands of Sister Liu. Guo Cunxian surmised it must be food, and in his heart he wondered what their relationship was. Turning, Old Qiang took the donkey's lead from Fugen and motioned to leave, before instructing the child that after they had eaten he was to bring his Uncle Guo over to the animals' barn. Hearing this, Guo Cunxian thought to curse them all, but he held his tongue. Behind him, Sister Liu spoke: "Old Qiang, why don't you stay and eat with Guo Cunxian and then go together?" Without turning around to decline, Old Qiang only waved his hand and continued on his way, saying: "You don't need to be so courteous to me!"

Accepting of his response, Sister Liu began to collect firewood in order to prepare their meal, leaving Guo Cunxian to find somewhere to sit. Showing great affection for his 'uncle' Guo, Fugen helped with this and also asked if he could make him a wooden sword. Guo Cunxian laughed. Sister Liu hadn't yet given him any work to do, but this small boy had. A smile still on his face, Guo Cunxian was suddenly moved by the fact that he had actually laughed. It had been so long, so many days, so much hardship, but today he could laugh, he could, for a moment at least, forget the torment, forget the worries. This wasn't half bad. His mood improved, he looked upon the boy with a particular fondness and told him that all he needed to find was a piece of wood, and then he could make any sword the boy desired. Taking advantage of the fact that dinner had not yet been fully prepared, Fugen grabbed Guo Cunxian by the hand to begin scouring their house for a piece of wood. First they went into the north-facing room. Like the rest of the house, it too was open to the outside and Guo Cunxian could see the small family stove, a wash basin at the corner of the wall, and a small, short-legged table littered with bits and bobs. The inner room was where they slept; a heated brick bed took up about half of the space. At the foot of the bed stood a wooden bench of about the same width as the bed, flanked by an old, rather shabby wardrobe. The south-facing room also had a *kang* and once looked occupied, but now only kindling for the stove filled its space. Looking at the small branches used for the stove, Guo Cunxian told the boy that with such pieces all he'd be able to carve would be a small sword, a dagger really. Not satisfied with this, Fugen dragged him outside to look for something more suitable. Looking around the house, at the town itself, Guo Cunxian wondered whether he'd be able to work here or not.

Standing in the village, Guo Cunxian couldn't help but be a little surprised. While the town wasn't all that big, there were quite a few old brick buildings, showing the former wealth of the townspeople. Indeed, it must have been a fairly well-off place once. What's more, most of the buildings still had doors, which proved that having none wasn't a local custom but, rather, evidence of Sister Liu's special circumstances, or proof of her extreme poverty.

Lowering his head somewhat, Guo Cunxian asked the boy: "Where's your father gone?" Before he even finished speaking, Fugen blurted out: "He's dead." Not really surprised by the boy's answer, Guo Cunxian let the matter rest. There were quite a few trees in the village too, some locust trees and willows as well, and these even had leaves left on them. Of course, the reason for that was clear: you couldn't eat the bark or the leaves of these trees, or at least only as a last resort. There really were a great number of trees in the village, suggesting that when the calls came out from the authorities for every village to begin smelting as much steel as possible, this village hadn't followed through; perhaps they were a smart bunch. A small river skirted the western half of the village, and while he didn't really understand what good feng shui meant, Guo Cunxian couldn't help but feel that Xinzhuang had it in spades. Near the riverbank he picked up the branch of a jujube tree. Weighing it in his hands, he turned to Fugen and told him that this would do and he'd be able to make any sword he wanted. Overjoyed, Fugen clasped Guo Cunxian's hand and they headed back home.

By the time they reached the house, Sister Liu had finished making dinner. She made the two of them sit first on the heated brick flooring, then placed the short-legged table between them. She then ladled a bowl full of *Gaga* noodle soup for Guo Cunxian and placed it in front of him. It was piping hot and soon the entire room was filled with the familiar aroma of food and of life. The noodles had been made by kneading sweet potato flour and corn flour together, then mixing in dried and crushed Sichuan peppers. The noodles were then boiled with a little salt, some dried vegetables and fried chopped onions, and then served with a sprinkling of cornmeal and makhana (lotus) seeds on top. The soup was both watery and not. It was nice and warm, and very, very comforting to Guo Cunxian. Once he finished his bowl, he made to put down his chopsticks but Sister Liu quickly snatched his bowl away and before he realised what she was doing, she had ladled him up another bowl. Of course, given the emptiness of his stomach, having a second bowl wasn't a problem, but how could he dare do that to this poor widow and her fatherless boy! Defeated, he ate the second bowl she had placed in front of him but this time, once he had finished, he quickly took hold of the bowl and his chopsticks and put them both behind him, thus stopping her from filling it once again. While eating, he'd noticed that Sister Liu's bowl only had three strings of noodles, and now that he'd finished, he saw that there were still two in her bowl.

With his belly full, Guo Cunxian thought it best to state his business and leave for the barn and Old Qiang. If there was work to do tomorrow, then he'd be here, if there wasn't, he'd say his goodbyes now and not pass through her door again. Hmph, there wasn't actually a door to pass through. How did she make it through the day? A poor widow and her only son living in a house without doors! With these thoughts in mind, Guo Cunxian asked her: "Sister Liu, you said that you had work for me?"

Sister Liu let slip a bitter laugh that was filled with a dense, deep heartache. This pitiable, good-natured woman, when thinking of her lot, thought to laugh, but all that escaped from her mouth was bitterness: "Brother Guo, I'm sure you can see, looking at this humble home, that there is more than enough work that needs doing but, when you think about it, I mean really think about it, what difference will it actually make? Why bother?"

What? Hearing this Guo Cunxian couldn't help but feel pained. He wasn't going to be able to find work after all! It became clear that she hadn't really asked him here so that he could actually work, but rather to thank him for saving her son. He got down from the raised heated floor, put on his shoes, offered his gratitude for the meal, and called for Fugen to direct him to the barn. Fugen, however, was unwilling to let him go: "But you said you were going to make a sword for me. When?"

"I'll do it in the barn."

"No, you have to make it here."

Sister Liu paid no attention to her son and instead started clearing away the dinner table. Trapped between staying and leaving, Guo Cunxian looked for a way to change the subject, a way to escape this awkward situation. Turning towards Sister Liu, he blurted out: "I heard that Fugen's father is dead. When did that happen?"

"It must have been over half a year ago by now."

"He couldn't have been very old. What sickness laid him down?"

"He swallowed arsenic."

Oh! Guo Cunxian was startled out of his shoes. He regretted bringing up the subject, but he had, and there was no escaping it now. "In hard times such as these, how did he end up on that road?"

"He wasn't aiming to die." Sister Liu sat on the edge of the raised floor. "Fugen's grandfather was a clerk in the commune and one day he brought home from the central office a bag of arsenic that was to be used to eradicate the mice in the fields. Fearing that if he left the arsenic out in the open in the central office someone might take it and end up poisoning themselves, he decided to bring it home and hide it away, placing it on top of a wardrobe in the south room. At that time, there was an even bigger wardrobe in that room, not just the small one that is there now. We chopped up the big one for a coffin. Just after he put the arsenic away, commune officials called for him and he left, but he forgot to tell Fugen's grandmother not to touch the package on top of the wardrobe. I don't know what she was looking for, but when Fugen's grandfather was out, his grandmother discovered the package. To her, it looked like a bag of flour. And you know, in times like these, she couldn't remember the last time she'd seen so much flour and so she immediately took it down in order to make something out of it, thinking that perhaps her husband had hidden it away for the New Year's celebration. An empty, cavernous stomach can make people act crazy and eat things that will only end up hurting them, no matter what the time of year. Anyway, she took the arsenic, mixed it with some sorghum flour and whipped up some *pak choi* dumplings. As luck would have it, Fugen and I weren't home. My mother was ill and so I had taken Fugen there with me, otherwise all five of us would be dead, a whole household. The commune leaders sent someone to call for me later, to tell me the horrible news. With a house such as this, where was I supposed to get the wood for coffins? So we tore down the doors and the big wardrobe, too, which provided enough wood to make a coffin to put Fugen's grandparents in. As for his father, well, we wrapped his body in grass curtains and buried him next to his parents."

Guo Cunxian exhaled a cold breath of air. Was this a terrible tragedy, or just life? Sitting under the feeble light in the room, Sister Liu looked absolutely miserable, wrapped in an air of futility and misfortune, swallowed up by it. The room was quiet, suffused with despair.

Still somewhat young and sturdy, somewhat enthusiastic about life and its possibilities, even in times like these, standing now in front of this poor widow, seeing her sorrow, her despair, well, any self-respecting man couldn't just up and leave, just abandon her like that. But, at the same time, empty platitudes wouldn't help Sister Liu either; he had to think: "It's good, though, that you have a son, it opens up possibilities for the future. You can keep him close to you or, if someone suitable comes along, you could let them take him. And let me say this now, since you've asked me here to work, I'll be sure to find some way to make you two doors. A home without doors isn't really a home. What's more, it's just you and your son here. What if some no-good bastard were to barge in during the evening, what would you do then?"

"But everyone knows us, there's not much worse that could be done. Besides, I'm already here, in this place, this life, what more could I fear? Heh, even if a dog or a cat were to suddenly burst in I think they'd be the ones scared out of their wits, not us. Do you know, since that fateful dinner, I've never even slept through a full night. When evening comes I feel like going to bed, but sleep doesn't come. It's like I'm out on the street in the middle of the day, wide awake. I've never even thought of making new doors, and besides, I haven't the wood."

"It's such a tragedy what befell your family. Hasn't anyone from the village tried to help?"

"People dying isn't such a big deal these days, so the commune can't really be all that concerned with individual cases. And, to be frank, it was us who ate the commune's arsenic, something that was to be used for the village. Some think it serves us right, that it was deserved."

Hey, did the townspeople really say that? Guo Cunxian mulled it over in his mind. What she told him just didn't seem right. He muttered to himself, smacking his lips in distaste, looked around the room, sizing it up, and slowly an idea came to him. A man's got to piss, it doesn't matter what kind of situation he finds himself in. The crux of the matter was that if a woman were in a difficult spot, a man has to do something. He told Sister Liu not to worry; he wasn't going to make a door so that he could stay inside. He proposed two options: first, when he had been out with Fugen he'd seen a great number of trees, and many of them were already dead, so tomorrow, she was to go to the commune head with Fugen and say she was going to make doors for her home. There aren't many houses that don't have doors, most have them, so she shouldn't encounter any argument. He also said she shouldn't be concerned about whether or not the commune leaders thought she was just borrowing the wood, or if it was some form of emergency relief, so to speak. All he needed was just two coarse old trunks, nothing more, one carried under each arm. And if she didn't wish to embarrass herself by asking the commune for this, if she wished to save what little face she had, then not to worry, in a little while he would go and speak with Old Qiang and get him to ask on her behalf. And if that didn't work, he still had an option two, and that was to take a part of the *kang*, the wardrobe it included as well as the table, and use that to make a door. After all, doors were more important than these things, and besides, he'd be sure to make a new wardrobe for her in the future, that was a promise. He then asked her if she was all right with this.

There was a certain fierceness in Guo Cunxian's voice, a solemn determination to try and do right by them. Both mother and son were dumbfounded and left staring at him, their eyes beginning to moisten and stick together.

Guojiadian was saved. From out of nowhere, the wide river that was so vital to the town began to flow with water. Even if no one knew where it came from, it gurgled and surged, filling at least half of the river trough, bringing life to this most depressed and arid land. There was enough water, in fact, for every production team to irrigate at least forty *mu* of land, and once that was done, sweet potato could be planted. If everything went to plan and the yield was fruitful, each *mu* (one *mu* is equivalent to around 666 square metres) of land should produce at least 1,800 *jin* (one *jin* or catty is equivalent to around 600 grams, just over half a kilo) of sweet potato, certainly enough to save the village.

The village head was, of course, extremely excited at these prospects and took to his loudspeaker over and over again to urge the villagers to act. For their part, the villagers weren't so enthusiastic. In fact, they believed more that he was just talking rubbish. After all, where the hell were they to get sweet potato to plant? And if they really had sweet potato now, would they want to wait until spring arrived to eat it? Of course not. If they had it now, they'd certainly eat it now. But the loudspeaker blared on, slogan after slogan, instructing each work team to gather in the village hall for an urgent meeting to launch the sweet potato planting campaign. In truth, there was enough urgency in the village already, even as the loudspeaker echoed throughout the town, and as each work unit arrived one after the other, the racket grew louder and louder.

"So the plan's to irrigate some of the fields and plant sweet potato, is it? Who the hell is going to be able to implement that plan? Seriously, huh? And why the hell do we need a campaign to do it?"

"That's not for certain," replied Han Jingting, the unit head. "At present the whole village seems to be going crazy from hunger, grabbing whatever they can find and stuffing it into their mouths, the edible and inedible alike. Many have diarrhoea, so much so that they can barely keep their trousers pulled up. Others are so constipated that their stomachs are hard. Even more are bloated and suffering from oedema, listless and hardly able to move. I fear that it's been so long since they've even seen a real sweet potato that to talk of planting some, well, even that will not be enough to get them to move."

At that moment the raucous meeting was pierced by the ferocious sounding voice of the village branch secretary, Chen Baohuai, blaring through the loudspeaker: "All right, has everyone's mind just turned to stone, then? Is that it? Huh? Well let me tell you, it's only when your mind is firm that you have the dogged determination to do something! Right now, all young men between the ages of sixteen and thirty, organise yourselves into a militia. Everyone over thirty, divide yourselves into four work units and start irrigating."

Once the branch secretary had spoken like this, no one dared to appear lazy. Even mad old confused Guo Jingshi could no longer just sit beneath the Dragon Phoenix Trees and snooze, adrift in his own world; instead, he was enlisted into the midnight work unit. At midnight sharp on the first night of this campaign, Guo Jingshi grabbed his iron spade and headed off to the fields, evidently set on digging furrows to irrigate the land. It was on this first night, however, that something strange happened.

When the relief team came in the morning, there was no trace of Guo Jingshi, and so the work unit believed he must have gone home early and was perhaps already asleep by now. By midday however, Guo Jingshi's sister-in-law Sun Yueqing had yet to see him, and so she went looking for him in the fields. When she didn't find him there, she went to the Dragon Phoenix Trees, hoping he was there. When that proved not to be the case, she started to panic as her brother-in-law didn't usually go wandering off, preferring to frequent the places he knew best. With her legs starting to swell, she returned home to enlist her daughter, Cunzhu, to go in search of her uncle, but not before going to get her brother Cunzhi, who was now training to be a member of the people's militia. Together the three of them would go and search for Guo Jingshi. From every door to every household in Guojiadian, from every nook and cranny, whomever they met they asked if they had seen Guo Jingshi, but no one had, nor had anyone heard any news about him either. Sun Yueqing was beside herself with worry. Her brother-in-law wasn't like other people, he wouldn't just talk to strangers on the street, nor would they talk to him as he was too much like a madman, crazy and stupid. If something had happened to him…? You couldn't blame Sun Yueqing for overthinking things, for worrying so. Just yesterday, when the villagers first discovered water trickling through the river trough, some quick-witted fool jumped straight in thinking to catch a fish. Well, if there had been fish that would have been great fortune indeed. Who'd have thought that the first thing he'd grab hold of was a corpse?

With Sun Yueqing nearly at her wits' end, as the morning was passing into afternoon, a county Public Security jeep appeared with Lan Shoukun at the wheel. Cutting a striking figure, he struck only fear in the heart of Sun Yueqing. The jeep soon pulled up to her door and stopped: "Who's Guo Jingshi to you?" came Lan Shoukun's voice.

Sun Yueqing was stunned and her heart stuttered and jumped a beat. Terrible thoughts raced through her mind; she was afraid something awful had happened. Seeing her mother unable to reply, Cunzhu quickly came up alongside her and answered Lan Shoukun's question: "He's my second uncle."

"He's over fifty, his hair and beard about this long?" Lan Shoukun gestured.

"Yes, that's him. What's happened?"

"I really have to ask you, how the hell did he make it to Beijing and what the hell for?"

"He went to Beijing?" Both mother and daughter were dumbstruck. "That's impossible, it can't be him. Last night at midnight he went into the fields as the relief unit to continue digging irrigation drains."

Unable to stifle a laugh, Lan Shoukun replied: "Well then, he dug his irrigation drain all the way to Beijing! Heh. In the morning, as we started our shift, we received a telephone call from the Beijing Municipal PSB [Public Security Bureau]. They told us that some odd, dishevelled country bumpkin had shown up in the city early in the morning. His hands clasping an iron spade, he was seen strolling in the middle of the street, soon attracting quite a crowd. The PSB officers went and got him and brought him to their station. Once there, they asked who he was. That's when they learnt his name and that he was registered here. Guo Jingshi…"

With a pleasant look of surprise on her face, Cunzhu asked: "My uncle spoke?"

"If he hadn't, how would they have known to telephone us? Why, is he mute or something?"

Awoken from her stupor, Sun Yueqing hurriedly explained: "No, when he was younger he spoke like everyone else. It's just now that he's older, well, he doesn't much like talking."

Shaking his head but realising this situation wasn't going to be easily resolved, Lan Shoukun continued: "This really is something serious, it isn't going to be easily fixed. One of you will have to come with me."

Cunzhu wanted to go, but her mother wouldn't allow it, and so in discussion with Lan Shoukun, they decided that Cunzhi would accompany the officers. Just at that moment, the village loudspeaker crackled across the air, momentarily startling them and assaulting their ears. The voice that rang out instructed Lan Shoukun to immediately come to the commune headquarters. Before he left, he turned to Sun Yueqing and her daughter and told them not to worry about Guo Jingshi, and that he'd handle things. He then hopped back into his jeep and sped away, disappearing as quickly as he had come.

The great sweet potato planting campaign had begun. The village was to send people to the commune to collect sweet potato sprouts, and so two ox-drawn carts were dispatched. Accompanying the carts were seven farmers, and four militiamen walking alongside. It all looked rather comical. In truth, this was the work of just two men, or perhaps four at the most. Wasn't sending so many a tad bit of overkill? Perhaps, but if you used your brain you might realise that there was more to it than that: Guojiadian had seven production teams, and so each team had to send one person, that was very clear to everyone in the town. This way, no team would try to take more than their fair share of sweet potato sprouts, nor would any team feel as though they'd been cheated. And to ensure that these seven farmers weren't ambushed on the road, the village sent the four militiamen to watch over them as extra insurance. After all, with so many starving people everywhere, the sight of an unguarded cart carrying a load of sweet potato sprouts would be too tempting, and what should have been a very easy job could have ended up being much more complicated than it needed to be.

However, on the day when they were supposed to actually carry out the work, there was an air of disbelief about the whole enterprise; everyone was suspicious, suspecting the plan itself and everyone involved in it. If they ended up being short even one bushel, well, who's to say that one didn't simply fall off the cart while they were bringing it back, or that the commune officials had accidentally given them one fewer? After all, they were carrying quite a number and it would have been easy enough to make such a mistake; that'd be one possibility. That, or that someone had stolen it to eat. There were eleven men in total, each taking care to watch the others, eyes boring into their comrades. No one would admit to eating it, and no one would say they saw someone else steal it. So what? A ghost ate it? Who'd believe such bullshit! No one. The village branch secretary, Chen Baohuai, pounded viciously on the table. The village head was enraged, and even the villagers themselves suspected the eleven men. No one would give them the benefit of the doubt, no, no, they all firmly believed that the eleven men had stolen the sweet potato, had eaten it themselves and then made a pact to keep it secret, with no one breaking ranks, no one confessing to the crime. And what was this sweet potato to the village? How important was it? Well, it was nothing less than life itself. The great sweet potato campaign had just begun and already such a thing had happened. It seemed as though there'd been no way to stop it, no way to actually plant the damn stuff before someone, some group, had stolen and eaten it. Bastards.

Lan Shoukun soon received orders to gather the militia and take the eleven men into custody. They were then brought to the public square next to the Dragon Phoenix Trees and made to kneel in front of the entire community. Out of the eleven, seven were made to kneel facing north, the remaining four to the south, back to back. There were about four paces between each of them, so that none of them could support each other. The villagers themselves encircled the kneeling men like a pack of frenzied monkeys, hurling accusations and insults at them. What made this spectacle especially pitiful was the fact that the missing sweet potato sprouts wouldn't even have been given to pigs to eat in times of plenty, but now, when so many were starving, such theft could only provoke the gathered people more, thoroughly enraging them! They spat at the kneeling men, cursing them, swearing at them. They'd eaten one extra mouthful, which meant someone else would have one less. So what if they were starving? Who wasn't? Publicly humiliated and reprimanded in this manner, the eleven kneeling men faced the verbal onslaught of the villagers, a public show trial, a way of showing the community's strength and anger over those who would transgress its rules. No one would dare to raise their hand, to try to explain what happened. Whether they admitted to the crime or not, whether they actually stole the sweet potato or not, it didn't matter now. It was all about the public trial.

Kneeling down among the so-called thieves was Guo Cunzhi. Normally, Sun Yueqing wasn't all that interested in seeing such spectacles, but once she heard that Cunzhi was involved, she took off running towards the Dragon Phoenix Trees, worried about her son and his weak disposition, worrying that he might be overwhelmed by humiliation and ridicule. Cunzhu was not far behind, cursing and running at the same time: "These selfish bastards..." But it wasn't really clear just who the bastards were: the men who'd stolen the sweet potato sprouts or the men guarding them? As they reached the hubbub and pushed their way through the throng they saw poor Cunzhi, his head buried in the crotch of his trousers. Sun Yueqing's first inclination was to run towards her son to help him up, or to kneel down beside him and endure the pain together, but just as she was about to do so, one of the militia guards, Ou Guangming, intercepted her: "Auntie, what're you trying to do?"

Sun Yueqing paid little attention to the guard towering in front of her. She was transfixed on her son, yelling out to him: "Cunzhi, weren't you supposed to be off to Beijing to get your uncle? How'd you wind up here in these muddy waters, in this mess?"

Cunzhi let his head droop, not uttering a word.

Beside herself with worry, she continued: "Tell me, why didn't you go to Beijing? How did you end up transporting sweet potato?"

Annoyed with his mother's entreaties, Cunzhi responded: "It was my choice, it's just that kneeling like this is worse than starving."

"What a disgrace. You're killing me! How could you say such a thing?"

Watching the ruckus, a bystander interrupted Sun Yueqing to give her some advice: "OK, OK, you've not been censured by one of the militiamen yet, so don't give them any more ammo to do so. Besides, in days like these, there isn't anything that should make you lose face, hmph. Starving, that's what's disgraceful!"

Letting the man's words sink in, Sun Yueqing's attitude changed. With worry in her voice, she asked Cunzhi: "What about your uncle now?"

Hearing the change in his mother's tone, Guo Cunzhi's voice trembled: "Whether we went to get him or not, he'll return, that's what the others said. If he was able to go to Beijing by himself, he can certainly make his way home."

"That's just what you say, but your uncle is old. How can you think this isn't a problem?" Sun Yueqing's heart was heavy. Her three children no doubt had heard and believed the gossip about their uncle... that's the only reason why they would be so unconcerned about him. Then, from outside the mass of people came a loud voice issuing directives over the air: "First bring Guo Cunzhi forward!" Two militiamen immediately moved through the crowd and grasped Guo Cunzhi tightly, pushing and shoving towards where the authorities would mete out punishment.

Lan Shoukun was in charge of the proceedings. He sat in the centre of the public square on a wooden bench, his eyes staring down, almost closed but not; there was an arrogant gloom surrounding him. It seemed as though anyone could have the chance to play this role now performed by Lan Shoukun. It didn't seem to matter if you'd been to school or not, all you needed was a certain type of intuition, a self-taught knowledge of how things worked. Standing next to Lan Shoukun were several rather excited militiamen. They'd brought forward Guo Cunzhi and acted as though they'd found the weak link among the eleven men, their way in. Looking at the man being brought in, Lan Shoukun could easily see that Cunzhi was not the same kind of man as his brother. No, no, he'd be much more pliable. As they brought him to stand in front, Lan Shoukun gave the militiamen a knowing glance whereupon they swarmed around Cunzhi and boxed his ears. Poor Cunzhi was left dazed and confused, shaking all over.

Once the beating was over, the room grew quiet and Lan Shoukun began to speak. He did not hurry, but nor did he take his time: "You're the one who stole the sweet potato, aren't you?"

"Yes."

"You ate it, didn't you?"

"Yes."

"How much did you eat?"

"Enough to fill half my belly."

"Aiya, still polite, aren't we... why didn't you eat your fill?"

"I heard that if I ate too much I'd be constipated."

None of the militiamen laughed. Lan Shoukun simply struck the wooden bench. In a raised voice he asked: "You knew you'd be constipated and yet you still ate the sweet potato?"

"I just couldn't help myself."

"What a fool! So worried about stuffing your face you never thought about what it would do to your gut. Who put you up to this? Who's the ringleader?"

"What do you mean by ringleader? After we loaded the cart and before we even took stock of how much we had, the hunger was too much, I just grabbed a mouthful. I was scared someone might've seen me, so I looked around at the others, but then I saw all of their mouths munching back and forth, too. Seeing that, well, I think we all must've become a bit more daring and we all started grabbing more. But I didn't care what the others were doing, I just wanted to eat, I really don't know who was the first..."

Getting this off his chest, it didn't matter what else Lan Shoukun asked him, he answered, spilling all the beans. He was honest, frank and held nothing back. And yet they didn't beat him again. With his nose bloody and his face swollen from the first beating he was subjected to, after he finished confessing the militiamen simply grabbed hold of him and returned him to the others, making him kneel once again.

Sun Yueqing's heart ached when she saw him being brought out, his face a bloody pulp, like some rotten, squashed peach. He'd only stolen some sweet potato. Had it really been necessary to beat him so harshly? Before the scene could get worse, Ou

Guangming gave a meaningful look towards Cunzhu, urging her to take her mother home. There was nothing she could do here but make matters worse. Sun Yueqing seemed to realise this as well. She could keep it up but that would only end up in her sharing her son's punishment. It would probably be better if she headed off to the village branch secretary's office to plead with him for leniency. After all, wasn't she making a fuss about nothing? They'd humiliated him publicly, made him kneel before everyone and given him a beating. So what more could they really do? Cunzhi was still a child, there was only so much that they could do. Thinking this, she allowed Cunzhu to bring her back to the village.

The trial continued. Now that he had spoken to Guo Cunzhi, Lan Shoukun understood what had happened, but his heart seemed to be less in it. One by one the next ten men were brought in, those who were forthcoming were beaten less, those who proved to be unyielding were beaten more. The trial continued into the evening until only one man remained, Liu Yupu.

Lan Shoukun laughed, ah hah, the main star of this entire show had come on stage — it had reached a climax!

Calling Liu Yupu the main actor didn't mean that he was the ringleader of this sweet potato fiasco, rather it referred to his special status in the village. He was the only son of Guojiadian's former landowner Liu Chunting. After his father had been struggled against and finally taken down, Liu Yupu's mother soon grew sick and died, leaving Yupu to look after his younger brother and sister. Needless to say, they endured their fair share of discrimination and torment, carrying the burden of a bad class background. Liu Yupu was literate, unlike the rest of the village, but when he saw others in the town he wouldn't give them a friendly smile, nor would he open his mouth, and even if he did speak, it would only be a whisper; he was rather effeminate by all accounts. Behind his back, there were those in the village who liked to use distasteful speech and called him a "sissy". When there were no political movements happening, he'd be brought into the school to teach, but once a new movement began, he'd be unceremoniously told to leave. Ironically, this experience became his political offence. And it didn't matter what movement may start or which way the political wind was blowing, Liu Yupu became the archetypal counter-revolutionary. What type of family would marry their daughter off to the son of a former landowner? He was lumped in with the rest of the village's thirty or forty bare sticks. What made the situation worse for him was his educated background, his generally 'sissyness', as some would say, that made him the target of bullying and ridicule. And today was no different, he took a drubbing like the rest, but the only unexpected thing was that he didn't actually admit to eating the sweet potato sprouts.

Lan Shoukun was surprised and furious. He couldn't believe Liu Yupu could be so pig-headed, so obstinate, that he could withstand the brutality of his interrogation, and if he couldn't get the desired confession, what then? His small face contorted in anger and disgust, he was practically grinding away at his molars: "Everyone else confessed that all eleven of you ate the sweet potato. How can you bloody well say that you didn't eat them?"

Liu Yupu's response was soft, but exact: "If they ate the sweet potato, well, that's their business, not mine. I didn't touch them."

"Do you mean to tell me that you, the son of a stinking landowner, are the only enlightened one, the only one at the vanguard of the revolution?"

"Not bad, not bad at all. You hit the nail on the head. It's precisely because of my background that I dared not touch the sweet potato, but that's not to say I wasn't thinking about it."

"But everyone else said you ate them!"

"Ha, as if they'd know… everyone went wild shortly after the sweet potato was safely onto the cart. They all began stuffing their faces, paying no attention to anyone but themselves. How could anyone see who was eating what and who wasn't?"

"You're spinning quite the yarn, it's better than a good song. But how can you prove it?"

"That's easy, just feel their stomachs and then feel mine and you'll understand. Theirs will all be hard as a rock from eating so many sweet potatoes, especially on empty stomachs. Me, on the other hand, well, I'm as emaciated as I can be. Will that be enough proof?"

"Really now? Alright then, let me feel!" Lan Shoukun drove his fist into Liu Yupu's gut.

Liu Yupu's eyes shut, but he didn't look as though he was in that much pain, or perhaps the punch helped distract him from the pain of his upbringing, his background. Extreme starvation causes a horrible burning sensation in one's stomach, an anxious knot that can't be undone, but now Liu Yupu felt nothing, he only tasted the hot bile that had rushed up into his mouth. It'd been so long since his mouth had tasted anything, even the taste of bile was at least something. Not bad.

Lan Shoukun continued his interrogation: "How about we cut you open to really see if your stomach is empty, huh? I mean, that sunken belly of yours is probably more the result of you swallowing your own courage, you wuss."

"Ya! You're just messing around, trying to distract us, rub your stomach indeed!" Lan Shoukun had suddenly decided to end the interrogation. He stood up: "I'm not going to play your little game any more. You'd like nothing better than for us to kill you, wouldn't you? Fine. String him up boys!"

The militiamen grabbed hold of Liu Yupu and dragged him towards the base of the Dragon Phoenix Trees. There they brought forth a rough hewn rope, slung it over a sturdy lower branch and tied each end to Liu Yupu's hands. They then pulled on the rope, lashing Liu Yupu to the trunk of the tree.

From out of the crowd a piercing voice shouted: "Big Brother!" It was Liu Yupu's younger sister, Liu Yumei. She rushed towards her brother wrapping her arms around his legs, vainly trying to prop him up and take some of the tension away from his arms. Her other brother, Liu Yucheng, then broke through the crowd as well and moved towards his feet, trying to further support him.

Ou Guangming did nothing to prevent them from aiding their brother. Instead, he glared at Lan Shoukun, hurriedly moved over to him and dragged him to one side. In a low voice he said: "What the hell are you doing? If you're not careful, you'll end up killing him!"

"Oh, that's right, isn't it, you're worried about your dear teacher, huh? Well I don't give a damn, we're only doing what he asked for."

"Ai, let me tell you, the branch secretary told you to ask questions, he didn't tell you to kill anyone!"

"Get the fuck out of here, it's not your place to speak to me like this, and if you dare say anything more in support of this bastard I'll string you up with him!"

"Go ahead, I dare you to try!" Ou Guangming steeled himself, his voice suddenly jumping an octave higher. "And what about the townsfolk? They didn't steal any sweet potato, and their class background is no different from yours. Who the hell do you think you are, huh?"

Once he finished, he stamped his foot on the ground and turned to leave.

"Idiot!" Lan Shoukun shouted out after him. "That's right, you leave, go on, but don't think for an instant this rotten prick is going to be any better off."

Lan Shoukun was intent on making an example out of Liu Yupu. The other ten were gutless weaklings. It had taken hardly any effort to get them to spill the beans, but since it had been that easy, how was he going to make an example of Liu Yupu? How could he make them all afraid by only punishing one of them?

The day was quickly turning into night and the dancing shadows of the crowd were beginning to take on an ominous air, but the villagers' curiosity in seeing poor Liu Yupu strung up as he was didn't abate. Perhaps the cruelness of it was taking their minds off food, lessening their hunger, at least somewhat.

Suddenly, a militiaman ran forward with instructions from the branch secretary: since the culprits had admitted their guilt in stealing the sweet potato sprouts, they could be told to return home. The Party would have to carry out further deliberations on subsequent punishment. Upon hearing the instructions, Lan Shoukun announced to the men still kneeling on the ground: "You lot, you've been given permission to leave. Liu Yupu, on the other hand, is to remain where he is, strung up to the Dragon Phoenix Trees until such time as he admits to his crime!"

The assembled crowd slowly began to dissipate and head off towards their homes. The families of those still squatting on the ground rushed forward to help them up and to bring their sorry arses home. Lan Shoukun gestured to the militiamen to leave as well. Soon the square was nearly empty, all except for Liu Yupu and his younger siblings. But they didn't dare to take him down. Yumei simply cried while Yucheng pleaded with his older brother: "Just admit to it, please, there's no need for you to endure such punishment!"

Seeing his younger brother and sister refuse to leave his side brought some strength to Liu Yupu: "Yucheng, I really didn't eat any of it, not even one tiny morsel of sweet potato passed my lips."

With the guards now gone and only the three siblings present, a solitary but brave figure approached the tree: "A wise man knows when to fight and when not to. Admitting to a crime, even if you didn't commit it, shouldn't matter that much."

"But I'm not a wise man, and the pain and humiliation I've felt today pales in comparison to everything the three of us have endured up until this day. But maybe, just maybe I've had enough. I don't think I can take any more, I don't think I can endure it. It has not been easy to come by this opportunity today, to claw back at least some of my dignity." Liu Yupu let out a tortured breath then drew it back in, building up the strength to keep talking: "I haven't been the best of brothers to the two of you. Yucheng, you need to look after Yumei, you need to do right by her, find her a good husband, a good man, and you'd better not use her just to improve your own lot! Things will be better in future, you needn't worry about finding a wife. And if things remain the same as they are now, if you marry and have children, well, they'd be guilty of the same crime we are, they'd still be the son of a landowner, they'd still have the wrong background. Now wouldn't doing something like that be a crime? Wouldn't that add to the bitterness of life?"

"Brother, why are you saying these things?" Clutching desperately at his legs, Yumei's crying increased. Wailing profusely, she continued: "Just hold on a little longer, I'm going to go and talk to Branch Secretary Chen, to beg him…"

Without warning Liu Yupu wrestled against his siblings. Using a tone they'd never heard before, he berated them: "I won't allow it. Even if you weren't my younger brother and sister, I wouldn't allow it. Just go home! Please."

From out of nowhere footsteps were heard, thump, thump, thumping in the darkness as they drew near. Then hands went to work hurriedly untying Liu Yupu, setting him free. It was Ou Guangming. In a raspy voice he spoke: "Go home now, it's alright, this is what Branch Secretary Chen wants."

Then, to the shadows surrounding them he yelled: "Disperse, all of you, it's over, nothing's happening."

In times of famine and crop failure, peasants can do little more than grasp at their empty, hollowed-out stomachs and hope to while away the days, lacking the energy to do anything much else. But in times such as these, that wasn't possible. Early the next day the village loudspeaker shattered the morning calm, barking its directives to the villagers, over and over again, urging them, almost painfully, to get on with the day's work. Yesterday the fields had been irrigated and were now ready. Each production team was to proceed to the next stage of the great sweet potato campaign; one group was to till the land, the other would follow behind, depositing the sweet potato sprouts into the ground.

Liu Yumei was still beside herself because of the previous evening's events. As soon as she'd woken and had pried open her still tearful eyes, still flustered and upset, she raced to her brothers' room. As expected, Liu Yupu wasn't in bed, and by the looks of things, her second brother himself had just woken up. The tone of her voice changed abruptly: "Where's Older Brother?"

"He's gone out I suppose."

"How is it that my heart can still be pitter-pattering?"

"Well, if it wasn't you wouldn't be alive, now would you? It's nothing, don't worry. Last night I waited until Yupu had fallen asleep before I drifted off," said Liu Yucheng, getting down from the bed. "You still don't know his habits, huh? In the middle of the night when there's no one about, Big Brother likes to wander around the village, deep in thought, I suppose. Quickly now, go and get something to eat. You heard the loudspeaker, we've got to get to the fields."

Yumei's heart was still unsettled, but she understood what Yucheng meant. Her eldest brother didn't sleep much after all, and he didn't like meeting people. He'd often go out in the wee hours of the morning to stroll about the area, a willow basket slung over his shoulder, scrounging around for anything edible to bring home.

Afterwards, he'd take what he'd found, dry it in the sun and weigh it into separate piles. Then he'd get the stoneroller and begin to grind the stuff into flour. He had done this more than once before. In fact, he'd done it many times, but the flour never looked like anything more than the dust that hung in the air and got caught in your throat. And even adding water made little difference. All you could do was keep kneading it, over and over again, making a mushy type of dough that didn't really stick together. This is what Liu Yucheng had meant by "getting something to eat". Even though people were starving to death, it was still hard to swallow this stuff. And you couldn't really digest it, at least not much of it; all it did was turn your piss into a clear white colour. Making it wasn't much of a time saver either, so Yumei decided to boil some of the 'flour' and make a thin gruel instead. Besides, it didn't matter what she made, none of it would taste any good; all she could do was make it easier on the eyes and thus maybe a little easier to eat. But before she could even get the water to boil, the loudspeaker sounded again, blaring out its instructions, assaulting her ears: "Liu Yucheng, Liu Yumei, come immediately to the western burial grounds. Something has happened to your older brother!"

Liu Yumei's head spun as though she'd been hit, then she tore off towards the burial grounds. Liu Yucheng yelled after her, but she wouldn't stop. Not wanting their house to burn down, he grabbed some cold water and threw it on the cooking fires, then hurriedly followed.

According to the villagers, the western part of the village was powerful land with good feng shui, and so almost everyone wanted to be buried there. It's hard to say when this first started, but over time the area was transformed into a burial ground. In the centre of the graveyard stood an old, crooked pine tree towering over the burial mounds. Its bark was like steel, the knots of its branches were dark and the branches themselves looked like pythons coiled around it; it was a terrifying tree. Many in the village thought that the tree was the Lord Yama, the King of Hell. In the past, many had hung themselves from the branches of this tree. Today, it had been Liu Yupu's turn. The townspeople who had discovered him early in the morning had already taken him down. The plan was to plant sweet potato in the western fields today, and so more and more people had come.

By the time Yucheng and Yumei arrived, their older brother's corpse had become cold and hard, rigid to the touch. Poor Yumei, this daughter of a landlord who'd been so reserved, so quiet for her twenty years, now exploded. Throwing herself on top of her dead brother's body, she wailed uncontrollably. Through the tears she spoke on and on about how good her brother was. She didn't seem to care any more about who was around her, she let loose all the pent-up pain and torture she had endured over the course of her short life. She lost her father when she was but four years old, her mother a year later, and while in name Yupu was her older brother, in truth he was both her father and mother. He'd loved her the way a parent loves a child and he'd taken care of her. No matter how she might be bullied and tormented in the village, once she came home he'd take her in his arms, spoil and pamper her and let her cry until she felt better. Yupu had also provided clothes for her and her other brother, he'd made them dinner, taught them to read, and he'd even taught her how to sew. When the outside was cold and hard, he'd been her warmth, he'd been her rock to lean on.

Coming up alongside his sister, Liu Yucheng was similarly beside himself.

Grasping his head in his hands, he began pounding it against the pine tree. No one tried to prevent him. Soon, blood began to stream down his face. But he didn't stop. Over and over again he kept hurling his face against the tree, cursing himself: "It's all my fault, Yupu. You just pretended to be asleep, didn't you? How could I let myself fall asleep! I'm such a pig! If I'd watched you, this wouldn't have happened. I'm useless, absolutely worthless."

The bystanders couldn't help but be moved by the scene they were witnessing; their hearts began to ache, too. A villager moved towards them, trying to console them, thinking to pull them away from the horrible scene. Another cursed, voicing the name of the person felt to be responsible for this: "This is all on the shoulders of Lan Shoukun. This is his doing. He hounded Liu Yupu to death."

"I never would've thought that such a bookish man could be so resolute, that he'd give his life to clean his ledger."

"Liu Yupu was a benevolent and righteous character, we can see that now! Look, he used the same rope as that used to bind him to the tree yesterday evening, but he didn't hang himself from the Dragon Phoenix Trees. Instead he just picked up the rope and came all the way here. He didn't want to tarnish or spoil the Dragon Phoenix Trees, didn't want to damage the protective feng shui of the village."

"Those bastard militiamen! Why didn't they take the rope with them when they left, huh? If they had, Liu Yupu wouldn't be lying here on the ground now. He wouldn't have taken this road."

"Heh, it doesn't matter, if someone was intent on killing themselves, well, a belt from their trousers would be enough. Perhaps it's better this way? He'd endured so much suffering, now it's all over, finished."

As the villagers bantered back and forth between them, waxing sentimentality, the team leader Han Jingting ran up. Upon seeing what was happening, he raged at the bystanders: "And you call yourself people? Look at them, distraught, and here you are doing nothing! Quickly, gather the two of them up, get a stretcher and bring Liu Yupu home."

Han Jingting took charge. He looked over the bystanders in front of him, calling forth several names: "You here, for the next two days you're not needed in the fields, instead, you help Yucheng and Yumei prepare their older brother for his last journey."

The rest of the crowd slowly ebbed away. Dispirited and downcast, they made their way to their respective plots of land to begin planting the sweet potato. It was in this most inauspicious and melancholic air that the great sweet potato campaign achieved a success of sorts. That is, the campaign became more about the people than the sweet potato. In fact, you could say that the real objective wasn't actually sweet potato after all, but rather the people who were tasked with planting it in the ground. Since steps had to be taken, of course, to ensure that the sprouts were actually planted instead of being eaten, each production team had guards monitor the work in the fields. There were so many guards, in fact, that they outnumbered the farmers. Those given the assignment were the young people of the village, since they were deemed the most reliable and trustworthy. Those toiling in the fields, on the other hand, were many years older. You could perhaps say that this delegation of work exacerbated an already tense situation, stoking further the hunger pangs of these poor young militiamen as they watched, empty-handed, the villagers planting the sweet potato.

Perhaps because of this building anger in their eyes, or their jealousy, or maybe because of the added seriousness of guarding the sweet potato in order to avoid a repeat of what happened before, whatever it was, it only ended up with both guards and farmers eventually eating their fill. Of course, most of the villagers, and production teams themselves, were all in the fields, and that meant Lan Shoukun was there as well. In a campaign such as this, the Party Security Committee had to be in charge, after all; it was the surest way of monitoring the campaign and of creating the greatest unease among the farmers. Stationed as they were on the edges of the fields, the guards would rove back and forth, supervising relentlessly, shouting out at the villagers when they spotted what they believed to be laziness or sloppy work, constantly issuing new orders, or more often warnings: don't anyone dare think about eating the sweet potato; if you do so, you won't see tomorrow.

In truth, it was all quite absurd and a little terrifying, too. At first, it was almost like a party, but the farmers didn't really have the heart to enjoy themselves. While there were so many people in the fields, it didn't have the same feeling of joviality that it had in the past, there was no easy talk and no laughter. Rather, it was more like a group of prisoners being forced to till the land, a chain gang of sorts, let out to work for the day, but with guards always watching, rifles in hand, waiting to fire on the first signs of disobedience. Nevertheless, and quite unexpectedly, there were still some villagers willing to risk everything in order to eat. And to make sure they didn't get caught, they'd first wait for a moment when no one was really looking at them and then, with great effort, they'd devour a whole sweet potato in one painful gulp. Others got more creative. They'd claim the sprout they were holding had gone bad, turn round to hold it up to the guards watching them, assure them that it was rotten and that it wouldn't grow if planted, and then quick as a whistle they'd swallow it down instead of throwing it away. For the more diligent guards who saw villagers stealing the food, they'd march over to them and give them a swift kick in the rear, or they'd grab hold of their lower backs, pressing them into the ground, not to punish them as such, but rather to make sure that no one else saw what was going on. As it turned out, most of the guards didn't want to cause another fuss or be responsible for another death. It just wasn't worth it, and it just didn't seem right.

This was how the campaign advanced, not with high spirits and elation, but with an oppressive air of furtiveness and suspicion.

It perhaps goes without saying that the productivity of the campaign was less than desired; in fact, it ended up being more about people idling away the time than about anything else. According to the directives, each production team was to plant forty *mu* of sweet potato, but to look around at the fields all you saw were people, and not even ten *mu* of land planted. The authorities were at a loss as to what to do, and so things continued as before and, in any case, they'd be out of sweet potato sooner or later. To make matters worse, the more recently bred sweet potato were much softer and more delicate than the first batches, barely lasting a day before they started to go bad, which only meant that the villagers ate even more, leaving more of the land unplanted, lending credence to the old saying: the poorer you got, the more misery you experienced!

On the third evening of this deathlike campaign, the villagers were startled out of their monotony by an unexpected event, the return of the local madman, Guo Jingshi, who strolled into town, iron spade still slung over his shoulder, as though nothing had happened at all. Immediately, townspeople ran up to him to get a look at him and to pester him with questions. It was quite the ruckus with everyone talking over each other: how'd you come back on your own? Did you walk? Why'd they let you return? You've been to the capital? How? Why? Guo Jingshi looked at them blankly. Hey, was it all confidential?

Despite Guo Jingshi being over fifty, his hair was uncut and tangled and his beard long and messy. He had the look of a man of a very different generation. But upon closer inspection, something stood out: with the exception of the Party cadres, Guo Jingshi's complexion and stature was much better than that of the rest of the village. After all, he'd walked to Beijing and back, that's several hundred *li* at least, which meant that he had a certain vibrancy to him, a certain strength. His clothes, on the other hand, were filthy, making it hard to distinguish white from grey. His pockets on both sides were full and bulging with who knows what. But despite his unkempt appearance, his eyes held a different sort of energy about them. As he scoured through the crowd that had gathered round him, each set of eyes he made contact with couldn't help but be startled. And then he found a familiar set, the eyes of his nephew, Guo Cunzhi. With large strides he bounded over towards him.

Guo Cunzhi no longer had the privilege of being a militiaman, he was no longer trusted to watch over others, nor was he allowed anywhere near the sweet potato. Instead, he had been tasked, punished, as it were, with being responsible for fetching water to keep the land well irrigated. At this moment, however, he was crouched down on the ground, hands covering his stomach, sweat pouring down his face. Guo Jingshi drew close but uttered not a sound. He dropped the spade he'd been carrying, leaned over and lifted his nephew up. With his free hand he felt Cunzhi's stomach, and then moved to lift him onto his back. Realising what his uncle was trying to do, Guo Cunzhi struggled against it, preventing himself from being lifted up onto his uncle's back. In response, Guo Jingshi let his nephew down, instead using his arm to half support, half pull him along. With his other hand he bent over and picked up his spade, making sure not to leave it behind. Together they made their way towards the village. The townspeople could only stare and watch with keen interest as the two of them walked off. Who could imagine that this madman had such strength? Even the production team cadres chose not to interfere. They thought perhaps that Guo Cunzhi had not yet fully healed from the beating he had taken recently, and that the strenuous labour he'd been doing, carrying water back and forth to the fields, had been a little too much for him.

Whatever the case may have been, Guo Jingshi brought his nephew home. While he was away, he had worried about his sister-in-law, Sun Yueqing. And there she was, in the courtyard, hard at work. When she raised her head to see who was approaching she couldn't help but be startled by whom and what she saw, and couldn't help but think that something awful had happened to Cunzhi. But then she wondered, how had the two of them returned together? She just couldn't believe that this madman now standing in front of her had been able to find his own way home. Hearing the ruckus just outside the door, Cunzhu soon appeared, staring at her uncle with great curiosity, looking him up and down, left to right, before launching into a series of questions: did you really go to Beijing, uncle? How'd you get there? And where else did you go besides Beijing? Have you even eaten, you've been away for so many days?

But her mad uncle failed to give a response. He simply threw down the spade he'd been carrying and with both hands dragged Cunzhi into the western room and propped him up on the *kang*, making sure that he could stretch himself out comfortably. He then unfastened his jacket and shirt to expose an enormously swollen belly that looked as though it were about to burst. Sun Yueqing had followed them in and now reached forward to feel her son's stomach. It was ice-cold and rock-hard. For an instant she was stunned because she knew what this meant. These last few days Cunzhi hadn't eaten anything. He'd come back from work and immediately take to bed. She thought this had been because of his punishment, because of the abuse he had endured, and that it had wounded him, not just physically but emotionally as well. She never thought that he might be sick, and with something so serious.

Waving his hands vigorously, Guo Jingshi forced both his sister-in-law and his niece out of the room, before latching the door behind them. Putting the palms of his hands together in front of him and rubbing energetically, he warmed them up. He then placed one hand on top of the other and pressed them against Cunzhi's hardened stomach, massaging it gently at first but gradually increasing the pressure. He massaged one way and then reversed direction, over and over again he repeated this until Cunzhi could bear it no longer and hollered like a stuck pig, crazily calling out. But Guo Jingshi was unmoved, even when his niece yelled from outside, he kept pressing on Cunzhi's stomach, harder and harder; his hands had full control over his nephew.

Cunzhu continued to pound on the door from outside, yelling at her uncle, beseeching him to tell her what he was doing. As she yelled for him to open the door, Sun Yueqing moved towards her and pulled her away. She didn't know why, but for some reason she trusted her brother-in-law. Vainly she tried to console her daughter, assuring her that her uncle was doing his best to help her Cunzhi. Cunzhu, however, refused to believe it. How could her uncle be capable of something like that? If he could, then she'd be able to operate. Gradually, Cunzhi's wailing subsided and turned into quieter, painful sobs. His nose ran and his face oozed sweat that mixed with his tears, making it hard to discern which was which. His crying was filled with a pain unlike anything he'd experienced before, not even when he was being punished and beaten for stealing the sweet potato. It was as though he'd been made to pay twice over for his crime. Once he'd cried enough, once his uncle had massaged away the hardness in his belly and he'd let loose the pent-up wind trapped in his bowels, the pain faded, not just for him but for all of them. His uncle pulled the bedding up over him and told him to rest still, then he exited the room.

As soon as Guo Jingshi stepped outside, Cunzhu grabbed her old mother and rushed to see Cunzhi. The blood had returned to his face and he looked much more comfortable. Sun Yueqing reached out her hand and felt her son's abdomen. It wasn't as cold as before, nor as hard, at least not like the stiff board it had seemed earlier. Now it had slackened a great deal, almost like a soft pimply sort of mound. Cunzhu couldn't help but be surprised. When on earth did her uncle learn how to do this? Sun Yueqing shook her head as well; she was as puzzled as her daughter.

Guo Jingshi was now out in the courtyard at the pile of firewood stacked against the house. He was busily picking and choosing the most suitable pieces to light the stove. In a moment, he planned to heat the pot to make dinner. Pushing aside the lid, he plunged his hands into his overloaded pockets and drew out the squirming mass he had stashed in them. He dumped the whole lot into the boiling pot. Standing just outside the door and stealing a glance inside, Cunzhu couldn't help but gag in disgust. Her uncle had been carrying an assortment of insects in his pocket. There were caterpillars, mung beetles, parasa moth larvae, brown crickets and mole crickets, ants, grasshoppers and earwigs. Some were even still alive as he deposited them into the pot. It was all so revolting. And now, as they were thrown into the boiling water, their chirping and crackling grew louder. In haste, Guo Jingshi covered the pot and waited for the chattering and chirping to fade. He then grabbed a ladle that was next to the stove, lifted the lid and stirred the mixture back and forth. It didn't take long for the aroma of what he was cooking to pervade the entire house, his gruel of dead insects. Once he was done, he reached for a hot bowl mat, placed the scalding pot down on top of it, and then used a rolling pin to mash the hardened insect mixture into pieces; these he dished out into a large waiting bowl.

Leaving that bowl where it was, he bent over to find a small grey fork and proceeded to peel off the baked-on residue from inside the cooking pot. Unconcerned about the heat still emanating from it, he plunged his hand into the pot and gathered up the grey flaky remains, depositing these into a larger bowl nearby. Then, using his fingers, he kneaded the insect flour some more before mixing it with the flaky dregs he'd just scraped out of the pot. Adding a little water, he stirred the broth with a pair of chopsticks and soon walked towards the western room, bringing his 'insect soup' with him. Cunzhu could hold her tongue no longer: "You expected my brother to eat that?"

Guo Jingshi responded as if nothing was amiss and he was a completely normal person: "Foolish girl, of course he's going to eat this, it's treasure. If he doesn't, there's no way he'll get better."

Sun Yueqing helped to prop up her son, who was now much more obedient, or perhaps had no energy left to resist. With the exception of his stomach, his whole body felt like mush, soft and flimsy. After enduring his mad uncle's 'treatment' and feeling much better because of it, he had newfound faith in this man, and so he quickly slurped down the soup Guo Jingshi had brought him. Once finished, Guo Jingshi urged him to lie on his side with his face towards the wall and to try and sleep a little. He assured his nephew that before long he'd be awake again, needing to go to the toilet and that he must pass what was in his stomach before the morning dawned. With his nephew settling down, Guo Jingshi turned towards Cunzhu and told her to go to the kitchen and scrape out whatever was left of the insect mixture and put it somewhere safe. You never know when it might come in handy again. Then to his sister-in-law he gestured towards the bowl holding the insect remains and said that from today onward she didn't need to be concerned about what to eat, just ladle out some of that into a bowl and in half a month's time her dropsy would be much better.

Cunzhu jumped into the conversation, asking him directly if it was really safe to eat the insect mixture, fearing that it might be poisonous. Guo Jingshi's response was confident. That was all he had eaten on his walk to Beijing; he'd relied on them and they hadn't let him down. But still, Sun Yueqing wondered aloud that, if that was all he had eaten these last few days, then surely he must be starving now; she'd go and make him a little something to eat. Guo Jingshi assured her that he wasn't hungry and urged her not to bother with him but just to look after Cunzhu. He was going to go to bed and to watch over Cunzhi. Reluctant to let him go off to bed, Sun Yueqing wanted to ask him how he had managed to go all the way to Beijing and then back again. She wanted to ask him how it was that he couldn't be hungry if he hadn't eaten anything. He simply said that he had followed the river back and forth, and where there was water, there were living things to eat and drink, and quite clean and tasty at that. Hearing him speak like this made Cunzhu gag again. Of course, he was talking about eating those... not waiting for her to speak, to pester him again, Sun Yueqing pulled her daughter away and closed the door behind them.

As soon as Guo Jingshi's head hit the *kang*, he was asleep. When he next opened his eyes it was already the middle of the night; he wasn't sure how many times Guo Cunzhi had gone back and forth from the toilet. He was feeling quite awful, his stomach was churning, but no matter how many times he went to the toilet, he just couldn't release his bowels and so he'd return to bed in more pain than ever. Guo Jingshi thus took to massaging his abdomen again, then suddenly without saying a word he got up and exited the room. A moment later he returned carrying a wicker basket, a length of dried sticks and a coarse iron-wire hook. He told Cunzhi to get off the bed and kneel down beside it, sticking his arse up in the air. He told him to breathe in, to hold his breath and to steel himself for what was about to happen. Guo Jingshi stood next to the bed and his prostrate nephew. With one hand he probed Cunzhi's anus. With the other he inserted the wooden stick, poking and stabbing at the hardened faeces that were obstructing his nephew's bowel movements. They had to be loosened before they could come out. It was fairly dark in the room and he could barely see what he was doing. At times his thrusts missed the mark and instead scraped against his nephew's insides, prompting Cunzhi to let out painful howls. But Guo Jingshi paid no heed and continued to manoeuvre the stick deeper into his nephew's anus, blindly thrusting it in. Half laughing, he told Cunzhi to go ahead, to keep yelling out, to get your sister to come and see him like this.

Slowly the work went, but finally he succeeded in loosening the hardened stool. Guo Jingshi withdrew the stick and grabbed hold of the iron-wire hook, then worked it inside his nephew's arse, probing inward. After a moment he succeeded in hooking the stool and pulling it out. He plopped it into the wicker basket with a thud. The faeces looked a lot like sheep droppings, but it was much, much harder, almost like grey round stones. The fact that he was able to extract these brought some hope to Cunzhi's heart. Guo Jingshi himself let out a long gasp of relief.

Standing outside the door all the while, watching the scene unfold in secret, Sun Yueqing now wiped her eyes, turned around and went to fetch the small lantern in her room. She was determined to help her brother-in-law in his 'work'. If she hadn't seen this with her own eyes, she never would've believed that human faeces could turn into something like that. What Guo Jingshi had scooped out of her son's arse was hard and dark, like stone stakes. No wonder it had sealed him up tight. And this couldn't have happened overnight, no, it must've taken a long time. God, how could people go on living like this? How could soft, and almost mushy, sweet potato sprouts change into something like this and that, once swallowed, they could become as hard as a rock? She couldn't help but blurt out: "Ah my poor boy, how much sweet potato did you stuff into your face to receive such punishment!"

Even though all his energy was going into releasing his bowels, when he heard his mother yell out he couldn't help but whimper a reply: "I really don't know how much I ate. It's about seven *li* from the commune headquarters to here, and I don't think my mouth stopped for an instant."

Sun Yueqing could only sigh in response. She had to be careful. She didn't dare use the iron-wire hook, afraid that she might hurt him seriously and cause real damage, so she used her fingers to pull the hardened turds out. Her legs were still swollen, her back ached, she was old, and before long sweat began to pour down her face. Guo Jingshi stepped in again to relieve her. While almost everyone believed he was mad, deranged, seeing his sister-in-law dirty her hands to save her son, he didn't want to use the hook any more, but his hands were so coarse and rough that they were no better, and so he picked up the hook again. This is how the night passed, each one relieving the other, with Guo Cunzhi prostrate in front of them.

And so they worked. When they could use their fingers, they did, when they couldn't, they'd use the hook to scoop out the faeces; on and on it went. When morning finally started to peak in through the window, the wicker basket on the floor was nearly full. Guo Cunzhi was still constipated to some extent, but certainly not like before, and so Guo Jingshi gave him some broth to drink and instructed him to go outside to the outhouse. He should be able to release the rest of it on his own.

In Xinzhuang, Guo Cunxian felt that he'd done his part.

Over the course of his first days in the village, he had repaired a large number of farm tools, fixed four fences around the animal barns and had even built two coffins for two different households. Not only had he been fed for his work, he'd even made some money, nine yuan and change, as well as four *jin* of sorghum and three *jin* of corn. Of course, he hadn't set these prices. In fact, on his first day working in the village he learned that to make money out of providing the kind of work he did was actually illegal, akin to what the authorities saw and despised as 'speculation and profiteering'. But setting out a mat ostensibly to hawk wares was accepted; that was considered begging, and so the authorities could do little about it. The Chinese always love to ask: What are you doing? Where are you going? If you say you're out begging, well, that doesn't sound all that great. If you say you're out to hawk wares, however, that sounds much better and conjures up a more respectable image. To beg for food in times like these is parasitical. You're like a louse, a good-for-nothing, but who can control that? There just isn't enough food to go around, no matter what the authorities try to do. So if you went out to hawk wares or services, you needed to bring your village ID card and you needed to be identifiable as a poor peasant. If, on the other hand, you were a member of the five black categories – landlords, rich peasants, counter-revolutionaries, bad elements and rightists – well, even hawking wares was against the law.

On this day Old Qiang brought an assortment of farm tools that all needed some work. Guo Cunxian's eyes lit up at the sight of tasks that needed doing, but just as he was about to get to work, the village head came to inspect his documents. He was stunned for a moment. When he had set out on the road, he hadn't thought to go to the commune offices to get the required documents, but he dared not say this now, and so he rummaged through his bags, pretending to look for an ID card that wasn't there, trying to stall for as long as he could in order to think of something to say. Then he shouted suddenly: "Aiya, this isn't good, I think I must've lost my ID documents. I had hidden them safely inside my bag, but that day, you remember it don't you Old Qiang, that day when the dogs attacked, you saw didn't you? I must've lost them."

Standing next to him, Old Qiang began to relate the tale of that day, how Guo Cunxian had arrived and had saved Fugen from a pair of rabid dogs. Without doubt such a heroic deed was worth more than some identity documents, wasn't it? He asked for the village head to be sympathetic. He must've lost the documents, but the goodwill he had earned in the village carrying out odd jobs, and the fact that he'd been doing it for some time now, surely he didn't need such ID any more. But what if he wished to leave Xinzhuang, asked the village head? What then? Old Qiang seized on the opportunity and beseeched the village head to prepare new documents for Guo Cunxian. That was easy enough to do, and so the village head and Old Qiang marched off towards the government offices. In no time at all they had prepared the required letter. On it is stated: "The holder of this letter, Guo Cunxian from Kuanhe County, the town of Guojiadian, is a registered poor peasant. Because he saved the life of a small child from Xinzhuang Village and lost his identity documents, this letter serves as special introduction for the person named above." Stamped in red on the bottom right-hand side of the letter was the village Party seal.

Now that he had this letter, Guo Cunxian showed more confidence in his dealings with customers. When they asked him for a price, his reply would be: "I'm just out hawking my services, whatever you can give me is fine."

If a prospective customer was being stingy, or if he made out that he was poor, insisting that he work for peanuts, or if he just wanted to pay with food instead of money, he'd tell them: "It's hard to find good work these days. If my family weren't so badly off, then I wouldn't need to be out here like this trying to earn whatever I can. I've left four family members at home, and all of them depend on me. If you think you can only afford to pay me with food, then that's all right, I can just bring that back to them. After all, it's just me out here, I can handle it."

Once he made this speech, no one else would order him about, asking him to work for nothing. Especially those who were making preparations for a funeral; they would be particularly nice. And for the others, no one wanted to see him work on an empty stomach so they made sure he always had enough to eat. But for him, the work was the same, he was selling his labour and so he always put maximum effort into it. In most instances, he'd rather not even eat much nor take a rest because he didn't want to hold the work up, particularly when it came to building coffins. This was work that needed to be done punctually. The family preparing the funeral had worked out the most suitable time to bury their loved one, and so he couldn't impede that. His diligence earned him even kinder words from the villagers.

As the days passed and he was kept busy working for the rest of the villagers, he asked Sister Liu to speak to the village head in order to get his consent to exchange the time he had worked repairing various farm tools and old woks, animal troughs, all that sort of stuff, and for these to be brought to the front of her house. Once consent was given, Sister Liu took her son Fugen to scour through the village and the outskirts for dried jujube branches, sticks and willow tree twigs, things of that nature, and those in turn she brought home. The following day Guo Cunxian didn't need to go away to work, rather he just went to Sister Liu's house. First, he took apart the *kang* in the southern room and the wardrobe that had been part of her dowry. With the pieces he made two sturdy doors for her house. The remaining pieces he used to construct a door for the southern room, and although it didn't fit quite right, it would at least prevent the livestock from wandering in. Lastly, he used the branches they had collected to build a fence for their courtyard, even drawing together a rough-hewn gate. While the gate would perhaps guard only against the rich and not the more devious, whatever the case, Sister Liu's house now at least looked like a home.

As Guo Cunxian toiled all day, Sister Liu stood to the side, watching, helping a little when she could, but otherwise simply marvelling at his work. She dared not believe that in a single day, her old, worn-out, dilapidated shambles of a house could be transformed into a solid, clean, proper family home. Up till now her life had been one of suffering and poverty, each day blending into the other. She couldn't figure out why she never thought anything would happen to her. Perhaps it was because she never really thought much about herself and her focus was on her son. If he was doing well, then she could keep on, if not, then it'd be better all round if the end would come. She would never have thought that it was due to her son that Guo Cunxian would come into her life and this warmed her heart. If there was a way she could make him a part of the family, could even make him want to be a part of a family that she herself wouldn't want, if she could just close her eyes for a moment and imagine it all differently... Thoughts like these allowed her cold, dead heart to come alive, to warm again, to grow soft and welcoming; a peacefulness settled over her. It was as though she'd worked too hard, was now exhausted and she could finally rest. These feelings excited her, but also made her nervous, and thereupon a strange feeling swept over her body.

Once finished, Guo Cunxian packed away his tools and cleaned up the courtyard. As the day gradually turned into evening, Old Qiang showed up at Sister Liu's home. Surprised by the transformation, he exclaimed: "Wow, this really looks great! Very well done indeed, Brother Guo. You're amazing, and to do so much so quickly..."

He laughed as he examined the courtyard and the house, then he walked over to Sister Liu and spoke a few words. Turning his head towards Guo Cunxian, he said in a loud voice: "Brother, I'm sorry to say that I haven't got room for you tonight. A few old friends are coming by to talk about some things but, in any case, this southern room here is tidy and clean. I've just spoken to Sister Liu, too. I asked her to let you stay here this evening. You can dump your stuff at my place and when you leave tomorrow you can swing by and get it. That shouldn't delay you."

"Are you sure? I don't want to impose on Sister Liu." Guo Cunxian was being polite, nothing else crossed his mind.

"Of course it's all right," interjected Sister Liu hastily. "Why wouldn't it be? Besides, I need to thank you. It's the least I can do and, in truth, it's not enough." She then turned and went into her own room before bringing out some bedding and a pillow for him to use.

Guo Cunxian saw Old Qiang off and then made sure his own tools were packed safely away in his bag. Afterwards, he grabbed a broom and swept up the remaining pieces of wood and debris, depositing the bits in the bin just outside the courtyard wall. While he finished cleaning up, Sister Liu had gone and boiled some water. She now brought this out to him and told him to go and wash. He took hold of the basin of hot water and went into the south room. There he washed himself from head to toe; it felt wonderful. As he washed, Fugen, wielding his little wooden sword, came up behind him. Playfully, Guo Cunxian flicked some of the hot water at him. While they were playing around, Sister Liu was busy making dinner. First she made noodles out of sorghum flour. This was accompanied by a green sauce that she'd made out of the oil of deep-fried chillies. Fearing that it wasn't quite salty enough, she added a little salt. Then she prepared a small plate of tiny, chopped onions, together with some endives. Once finished, in a clear and loud voice she yelled out to Fugen: "Bring your 'uncle' here, it's time for dinner."

The aroma of the the food – the noodles and the chilli sauce – permeated the entire room. It had been a long time since the room had had such aromas; it had been a long time since she felt so carefree. She recalled how she used to look after her mother-in-law, her child and her husband, and now she was doing the same for Guo Cunxian and Fugen, calling them in for dinner and serving them this splendid food. First she ladled a large helping out for Guo Cunxian, then her son, and then the remaining food she left for herself, serving it into a small bowl. Guo Cunxian didn't dare to gulp the food down, but the aroma of the noodles egged him on and in no time at all he'd cleaned his bowl. He placed the bowl behind him so that she wouldn't try to give him more, and nothing would make him return it to the table. He remembered what had happened before, and appreciated that the amount he had just eaten could have fed both mother and son for three days at least. Nevertheless, Sister Liu was still intent on giving him some more, so all he could do was to grab his bowl and get down from the table. He brought his bowl out to the kitchen and placed it in the basin, turned his head and went straight to the south room with Fugen hot on his heels, wooden sword in hand.

Soon reclining on the *kang*, Guo Cunxian mulled over his current situation. Tomorrow he planned to leave Xinzhuang, but where would he go? Should he head farther south, or perhaps take a more westerly direction? It didn't really matter. Things were now different, not like they were when he first set out. He'd made connections, his heart was rooted, and so it didn't matter what direction he took, he wasn't worried about that any more. The only problem was what to do with the many *jin* of grain he'd been given as payment. Lugging that along with him would be too much, so perhaps he should first bring it back home, or think of a way to send it there, perhaps have his younger brother come and collect it. While he mulled things over, Fugen continued to play at the foot of the bed. Before long however, Fugen became annoyed at seeing his 'uncle' deep in thought instead of playing with him, and so he jumped up onto the bed and snuggled up beside him, shyly asking: "Uncle Guo, are you leaving tomorrow?"

"I suppose so… I have to go in search of work, after all."

"Why don't you stay here and work?"

"But I've done all that I can here, there's nothing left for me to do."

"Can I come with you?"

Patting him warmly on the head, Guo Cunxian responded: "Eh, you must be sleepwalking. Do you think your mother would let you go? Besides, I don't have the means to look after you."

"Aiya, what are we going to do then?"

"Do about what? What are you getting at?"

"I want to learn how to do the same things you do."

"You'll have to wait until you're older, I'm afraid." Wishing to think more about his own situation and what to do, he changed tactics and tried to lull the boy to sleep. After a short while, Fugen's eyes began to grow heavy and soon he was asleep. Picking him up, Guo Cunxian brought him to the north room so he could sleep in his own bed. While the door was closed, it wasn't bolted so he kicked gently at the bottom to push it open. It was dark inside and it felt a little uneasy. Nervously he spoke: "Sister Liu, Fugen's fallen asleep. I've brought him with me."

"Ai, ai….. come in, come in, put him here. That's alright." There was a slightly different tone to Sister Liu's voice. In the dark it sounded as though she were rustling around for her clothes. He soon smelt soap in the air and realised she must've been bathing. He felt a wave of panic and embarrassment wash over him. He quickly put Fugen down gently at the head of the bed near the door, turned around and went straight out. But just as he stepped through the door he collided with Sister Liu. Shocked and unsure of what to do, he blamed his clumsiness on the dark. Inside he felt his face was burning.

Sister Liu on the other hand made no effort to escape. Instead she reached out and grabbed his arm, the smell of soap still wafted from her hair, filling his nose and causing him to feel a mixture of dizziness and ferocity. Soon both her arms were clasped around him, hastily pulling him in towards her. He felt as though he were burning up. His arms, by their own volition, embraced her back. Her skin was moist to the touch, so soft and vulnerable, so gentle, she was so warm to hold onto, it felt so nice. His head pounded, his body tensed, he felt as though he couldn't breathe, while his manhood swelled with a life of its own, hard and fierce. It soon touched up against Sister Liu's body. Nervously he stepped back, his arms released her from his embrace. Sister Liu sensed his worry and spoke to him in a trembling voice: "Brother, you've done so much for me, but I don't have any money to pay you, all I can give you is this body to do with as you wish."

His heart quivered. Flustered, he let go of Sister Liu: "Doing those things for you made me happy. I don't want anything in return. If I took advantage of you now, you, a single mum with a fatherless boy, what kind of man would I be?" Pushing himself away from her, he ran out of the room and straight towards his own. There he quickly gathered up his tool bag and slung it over his shoulder. He was leaving tonight. As he stepped through the courtyard gate, he made sure to close it behind him. Then, after taking a few steps, he stopped and spun around to look at the house once more. In the darkness he could see Sister Liu standing in the doorway to her room, staring at him. Determined, he turned around again and left. He went first to the animal barn. If there was nowhere to sleep, it was a warm night, so it'd be easy enough to find a place to lay his head for the evening.

Guo Cunxian entered the barnyard a little while later and moved towards the inner rooms where Old Qiang slept. Surprisingly, everything was quiet. No one was there, no friends chattering the night away. He pushed open the door and there in the shadows he saw Old Qiang smoking by himself, his face just visible under a small lamp. There wasn't a breeze in the air so the room was filled with cigarette smoke that hung heavily throughout the room, assaulting his nose and causing his eyes to burn. He could barely breathe. Guo Cunxian couldn't help but mumble aloud: "Aiya, just what the hell are you smoking? And what for? If you can smoke it, then surely you can eat it, so why aren't you eating it? I mean, it could fill your belly at least a little. Why roll whatever it is up into a cigarette, only for it to be inhaled and then blown back out again?"

Old Qiang looked up and was surprised to see Guo Cunxian standing in front of him: "Why are you here?"

Placing his tool bag at the foot of the bed, he replied: "I want to ask you something. This is an awfully big bed. Why'd you say there was no room?"

Old Qiang looked him over carefully, staring into his face as though he were searching for something: "I shouldn't be blamed for trying to help you boy, should I? Could it be that Sister Liu didn't want to?"

Guo Cunxian saw the hope in Old Qiang's eyes, saw that he wanted to believe what he said was true, that she hadn't wanted to. Seeing this, Guo Cunxian nodded, then took off his shoes and climbed onto the heated bed. Sitting in front of Old Qiang he asked him: "Do you think I'm blind, that I don't see the connection between you and Sister Liu? They wouldn't be alive if it weren't for you. You're a loyal and upright fellow. These last few days here in Xinzhuang are all because of you. You've made everything possible for me, so much so that I could never repay you. Now tell me, how could I take advantage of someone you care so much about?"

Old Qiang shook his head and waved his hands at Guo Cunxian: "Brother, you only know half the story. I have a family, you know, but it's hard to look after them. At best, and at unexpected moments, I'm able to get away from here, to give her a little attention. But that's not going to work forever. Indeed, many of the barn animals have already died, partly because I've been stealing their food. Oh, that weighs on my conscience! Anyway, on that day I saw you rescue Fugen I got the idea in my head. You seemed like a decent fellow. If mother and son had someone like you in their lives, well, they'd be able to rely on you instead of me. I know, I know, getting you to marry her isn't the best thing for you. I mean, she's older than you and a widow already. But don't forget she's a good, hearty woman, and if you did marry her, you'd also be gaining a son as well, and in a few more years he could prove to be very useful indeed.

"Let's take a step back for a moment. If you don't want to marry her then that's fine. You could just be with her for a few years and see how it goes. You'd at least avoid having to leave in the morning in search of work and, if truth be told, it's not much of a life you've got to look forward to, waiting on handouts in the morning, hoping someone will warm a bowl for you in the evening and relying on your skills, you know, in repairing and building things. Well, I'm afraid to say that I don't think you'll find too much work in the neighbouring villages. So what prospects are there for you, hey? So, what do you think, Brother? Has this old man given you something to mull over?"

Guo Cunxian rubbed his head and sucked on his teeth: "You know, I just wanted to make my way in the world, to find a little work to do, to earn a living. But if I remain here and become the emperor's son-in-law, like Yang Silang,[1] you know, well I'm just not willing to do that. I'm the oldest son with four mouths that depend on me and I can't just discard them."

"Who said you'd have to? Why couldn't you take care of both?"

"Hmph, wouldn't that end up wearing me out? As you said, that wouldn't work forever." Guo Cunxian swallowed hard a few more times, pretending to hesitate still. In truth, after hearing Old Qiang talk like this, listening to what he said, he had had a change of heart. He thought back to the emotions he felt when holding her, when his mind was lost in a lustful stupor. Then he grew interested, very interested in something else Old Qiang had said: "Old Qiang, be honest with me, in a village as small as this, doesn't everyone know you treat her as family?"

"Of course they know, and what does that matter? In any case, I'm just a poor old crippled man taking care of barnyard animals. The Party here, especially the branch secretary, the records-keeping office, they've brushed away far more women, and some of those were young unmarried girls. A household has power, and with power comes food, but to add another mouth, one of the girls that you see today, well, that's of little value. Fifty *jin* of carrots could be exchanged for one virgin girl but most would rather have even just ten *jin* of food to eat. Think about it, if you were to take those bundles of food to a young girl's house, wouldn't she be inclined and happy to wait upon you? We've got an old song in these parts, it goes like this: sand hits the wall but the wall doesn't fall, a dog doesn't bite a newborn babe, stones fill a pit, but not to the tip, a young maiden takes a lover but the wife doesn't get angry."

Guo Cunxian pondered awhile, mulling over the meaning of what Old Qiang had told him. It all came down to this: women weren't as important as food but men still wanted them. Some would even give up their food to get them, even in times like these when food was everything. No wonder there weren't any women around. But what else does a man have? He's not even as useful as a woman. If you were to take all the bare sticks in Guojiadian, you'd be able to line them up in two rows and not find a single woman for them to marry. For the past two years his mother had been looking for a wife for him, but she'd not found anyone suitable. However, the key here was that his family didn't have any food to make such an exchange. It was fortunate that he'd broken free. It had been the right decision and it proved that he could make his way in the world, fend for himself, and that he had the skills to choose a woman for himself, instead of having it arranged for him. He had to thank Sister Liu. She'd given him that kind of self-belief tonight. But that didn't mean he'd be careless and muddleheaded now. No, he couldn't just take on the responsibility of looking after a widowed mother and her son. Ah, his old mother was right. She knew that there was both good and bad to saying difficult things. For a while Old Qiang just looked at him without uttering a sound. He thought that perhaps his words had made some sort of impact. He then reached over, tapped him lightly and spoke in a soft voice: "Go on back. It's alright. She'll blame me in any case for not clearly explaining things earlier."

Guo Cunxian straightened up and spoke resolutely: "No, I can't. I can't go back after I've already left. I can't go and face her like that. Big Brother, please, you go for me. I'm sure she's waiting for me to return. She's a good woman but I can't. I don't want her to be any more embarrassed and humiliated than she already probably is. And tell her this for me: I still have work I need to do. I simply can't look after her and her son, and my family is still waiting for me back at home. They need me to bring food. I owe you enormously for what you've done for me and I appreciate meeting you and Sister Liu. If you can hold on to that, I promise I'll repay both of you in future."

Listening to him speak Old Qiang didn't know if he should be sorely disappointed or inwardly happy. After a heavy moment passed between them, he stepped down from the bed and put on his shoes. Without looking up, without meeting Guo Cunxian's eyes, he spoke: "I'm going to go and talk to her and ask her what she thinks. You look after the barn while I'm gone. I won't be long."

"Don't worry about anything. I'll look after things here. You just go and talk to her."

Once he heard Old Qiang leave the barnyard stables, he got down from the bed. In a corner of the room there was a big burlap bag filled about halfway with sand with a large scoop pushing it down. He unfurled the bag and scooped out three large spoonfuls of sand. These he spread out over the bed in order to make a sufficient place for him to lie down on top of it. He undressed and lay down in the middle of the sand bed, using his inner garments like a blanket.

This sandy bed was to protect against bedbugs. There were two types of bedbugs: 'army' and 'air force' bedbugs, although most were of the former type. At night, from beneath the bed, they'd come out from all directions and seemingly march in formation towards where a person lay sleeping. But when they encountered the sand, they'd become stuck and thus unable to attack. Some of the bedbugs, however, were of the second type. These were much smarter and more daring. They wouldn't try a frontal assault on a sleeping person, no, they'd first climb up to the ceiling and crawl over to just above where the sleeping person lay, and from there they would descend, parachuting onto the prone body waiting below. Once they landed, they'd bite wherever it pleased them – a most happy meal indeed.

In the past, he would fall into a deep sleep almost as soon as he lay down on the sandy bed, well before the first air force bedbug would descend. His body would be left undefended, allowing them to do with it as they wished. They'd bite into his flesh indiscriminately, causing him to itch all over, but he wouldn't wake up; all he would do was squirm and roll about, crushing them by the thousand. But tonight was different. Tonight he lay in bed unable to sleep. When bedbugs bite into human flesh, they don't only cause one to itch, although that is insufferable enough, no, they also make one's flesh burn as though it were being cooked slowly over a low flame. Like a large flatbread burning in a pan, he tossed and turned, his skin on fire but his mind kept working things over. Here he was feeding the bedbugs that had invaded his flesh while Old Qiang and Sister Liu were certainly deep in discussion. He thought he could see her small face turn a scarlet red, brimming with a boundless affection, her eyes filled with an eager longing. He recalled the smell of her freshly washed skin, the softness of her body. Sister Liu had been ready to give herself to him, but he'd sent Old Qiang in his stead.

When the sun sets and the day fades, hunger pangs grow much more intense, as do desires of the flesh; tonight he experienced both. He was, after all, a young man, at a most perilous age indeed, akin to standing on the slippery edge of an abyss. Lying prone on the bed of sand, being attacked by bedbugs, he regretted his actions. He had let go of Sister Liu too easily; now all he could think about was holding her, cradling her in his arms with her arms wrapped around him. Again, he was surprised by the sudden response of his body. His manhood shifted, lifting itself up, stretching the front of his trousers. He felt both the loneliness of his life and the virility of it; his back ached and itched as though there was an oppressive, overwhelming weight pressing down on it. In his heart of hearts he couldn't bear to look at himself. He reproached himself. What kind of man was he? When he'd been given something his body desired, he dared not take it, and now that he couldn't have it, he couldn't stop thinking about it. This was no good. Tomorrow he had to hit the road, head off to somewhere new and find more work. He had to stop letting his mind wander, stop his imagination from running wild. He got up. He remembered that Old Qiang kept a water container in the southeast corner of the barn shack, and that every day he would be sure to fill it to the top. It was for the animals to drink, or to mix up in their feed. He needed the water, a cold shower to put out the flame of these evil urges.

But just as he left the room, he heard a noise coming from the southeast corner of the barn. He'd been here for many days now and had learned to distinguish between animal sounds and human sounds. Could it be that Old Qiang had already returned so fast? Quietly he made his way towards where the sound was coming from and there, by the trough of the village's most noble animal, the old donkey that had saved Fugen, he saw a stranger busily fiddling with something. Were there still people about in times like these who would try and steal barnyard animals? And just what was he doing? Why didn't he just loop a rope around the animal's neck and walk away? In order to get a better look, he tiptoed closer to where the man was, concealing himself behind the animal. Then he saw that the man wasn't interested in the donkey at all, but rather in the animal feed that filled the trough. He was busy driving his arms into the mix, piling it together to scoop up and deposit into a container he had brought with him. The container, already half full of water, was now nearly to the brim and so the man picked it up and gently rocked it back and forth. He then fished out the grassy dregs and placed them back in the trough. Picking up the container again, he drained out some of the water and brought it to his lips, drinking down the remaining sediment. It was only animal feed, leftover grain husks, fit only for donkeys.

Guo Cunxian couldn't help but exclaim in admiration: "Brother, you really have quite a head on your shoulders. Fancy thinking of such a way to get a little to eat!"

The man didn't try to run or hide, he didn't even seem to be all that surprised that he had been discovered: "You're a good man, you are. You already saw what I was up to but you didn't shout out in alarm, didn't yell at me to stop. Instead you waited until I had eaten it. I'm very much obliged to you, Brother!"

"Come now, don't be so polite. You've got gumption, I'll give you that. You knew you were being watched but you kept on doing what you were doing and I guess that what you were doing wasn't a total waste of time because animal feed is still food." Laughing, Guo Cunxian stepped out from behind the animal trough and moved towards the man. He saw then that the man was rather short, a small, compact fellow, with a head the shape of a jujube pit, but all told, it seemed to match. He seemed well proportioned except for his small stature, comical in a way, but not at all unpleasant.

"Well, I'm not worried about what you say. After all, in the predicament we all find ourselves in, well, what else is there to worry about other than going hungry?" He watched as Guo Cunxian moved out from behind the trough, and then reached into his garments and drew out his identity documents. His movements were catlike, as though he were used to sleight-of-hand tricks, and yet the clothes he wore were nondescript. How surprising it was, then, that he had pockets to fill with such useful papers. This man, who'd snuck into the village barn to steal animal feed, still thought he needed to produce his papers, to verify who he was. Guo Cunxian couldn't help but be stunned; he just couldn't get his head around it. And just what would these papers show? That he was a beggar and not a thief, or that he was starving and thus permitted to steal food?

No longer interested in sleep, he decided to argue the point, however pointless that may have been. He ordered the man into the small room and brought the ID papers under the weak light to get a better look at them. He smacked his lips: "Oh ho, you're a Wang from Dingshan County, huh? Wang Shun is it? That's an easy name to remember."

Wang Shun chuckled in reply: "Everyone in my family simply calls me Shunzi, adding the Wang in front of it, well, it just doesn't sound right, makes me a little uncomfortable."

Guo Cunxian returned the identity documents and before thinking further blurted out: "So I suppose you're out hawking your services, too, huh?"

"That's right. I've been away from home for over half a year now, but I've been slowly working my way back. But today's been an especially hard day and I haven't been able to scrounge even a bite to eat. That's how I ended up here, eating animal feed."

"You seem to have a knack for this, yes, quite resourceful. I reckon you've been at this for a while, huh?"

"Well, to tell you the truth, I have certain rules when I'm out begging, the most important being that I don't want to add to the troubles of an already poor household, I mean, they're already hard up, so to ask them for food, well, that's just not right."

"Ya ho, what's there to be righteous about when begging, heh? You're quite a character, aren't you?"

"Whatever you say, but when I come to a new place, I start by heading towards two types of animals. The first is the two-legged kind, the cadres. They're the ones that eat their fill of rice and noodles, even adding a few vegetables on top, and not only do these animals eat well, they even bring some food to their families so that they can eat their fill as well. I've been to more than ten provinces now, and it's always the same thing, so that's where I head first, straight to the Party offices to beg. And if the cadres don't have any family, well, there isn't any need to stand on ceremony. I just barge in and grab what I can, no matter what it is. If I'm unlucky and they catch me, shit, I don't care, all they'll do is throw me in prison, and that'd be all right. At least they feed you in there, and you don't need to do shit."

"What about the other kind?"

"That's the four-legged ones. Well, you've already seen what I do. If I could eat even just a mouthful of that slop per day, at least I wouldn't starve. In times like these you have to do what you have to do. If you can't get into the barnyard, then there're always the communal canteens, the security offices, whatever..."

Guo Cunxian couldn't help but think that this man, Wang Shun, was quite a character. He asked: "So, are you still hungry now?"

"Hungry, shit, how can I not be?" was his frank reply. "I can't remember the last time I haven't felt this empty pit in my stomach!"

As he listened, Guo Cunxian turned towards the chest behind the door. From under one of its legs he pulled out a key and opened it. This is where he'd been storing his several *jin* of grain. He reached his hand into one of the bags and took out a handful of cornmeal. "Eat it."

Wang Shun was overjoyed. He accepted the cornmeal with both hands and then stuffed it in his mouth. He was quite experienced at this and didn't try to swallow it immediately. Instead, he used the saliva in his mouth to moisten it, mixing it as he had done with the animal feed; that was the only way, it'd be too dry otherwise. Once sufficiently moistened, his jaw began to move up and down, vigorously chewing the mixture. The sound of him smacking his lips was clear, fast, as though he were chewing rock candy, something fragrant and sweet, quite satisfying. Seeing him eat so ravenously, Guo Cunxian realised that he hadn't eaten himself. He was curious, too. He hadn't eaten cornmeal like this; he plunged his hand into the bag and followed suit.

And there they sat, at the edge of the bed, face to face, rigorously chewing away. The more they chewed, the tastier it was. It almost felt like they were eating a proper meal. Once they swallowed, their whole bodies felt warm inside, robust even, and if they had a few mouthfuls of cold water, well then, they'd feel very good indeed. Thinking of this, Guo Cunxian reached out for Wang Shun's enamel basin and went outside to the water container to fill it. Bringing it back in, he handed it to Wang Shun who gulped a few mouthfuls and then swished the water all around, making sure to loosen any bits of the cornmeal mixture that had got stuck to his teeth; after all, he didn't want to waste any of it.

Witnessing the scene and seeing how meticulous and how ravenous he had been, Guo Cunxian had to ask: "Are you full now? Or would you like some more?"

Exaggeratedly, he bowed low, both hands in front, and replied: "No, thank you Brother, thank you, thank you. I can tell by your accent that you're not from here, but from the north. You don't seem like a herder. I've been fortunate today to have met such a noble person. I guess the heavens don't want me to die of starvation, at least, not today."

Guo Cunxian couldn't help but be impressed by this man who'd followed the river from down south and had made his way to the north. His ears were especially keen: "I'm from Guojiadian."

Wang Shun slapped his thigh and responded: "You don't say! I've been to your village. It's quite big but quite poor as well. The Guo family name is an important one there, too. How'd you come by such a fortunate name in any case?"

"Fortunate, hah, that's a joke. My name is Guo Cunxian. I make coffins. I've been here in this village for the past little while just doing odd jobs. The cornmeal you ate was payment for these jobs." Guo Cunxian admired the sharpness of his mind. He'd been to so many places and yet he still remembered Guojiadian.

Wang Shun took a moment to look him up and down: "Aiya, Brother, if you've been able to get this as payment in times like these then you must certainly be quite the handyman. And now you've shared some of that with me, I really ought to kowtow."

Guo Cunxian reacted quickly, gripping Wang Shun and pulling him up, stopping him from his performance: "Is a mouthful of grain worth kowtowing for? Huh? Isn't that too much?"

"Aiya, just look around you. A mouthful of grain is worth more than gold these days!" As he spoke, he straightened up: "You didn't turn your back on me, and for that I'm grateful. I can see, too, that you have a righteous heart. From here on I shall act as your faithful servant. I will go before you and find you work, and if there isn't any, then I'll find you a place to rest and go out and beg for food on your behalf, if you'll let me. Without loving parents and being too worthless for wolves and dogs to eat, let us be brothers, hey, poor though we may be."

Guo Cunxian was moved by what he had said. His mouth curled into a smile. If he accepted he wouldn't be lonely, at least, but still he asked: "What about your family?"

"Ah, Brother, my life's been hard. In all the heavens, in all the lands, there's just me. My parents were taken from me last year, and my only sister, well, she's been married off." As he spoke he kneeled, soon almost chanting: "Big Brother on high, please accept me as your younger brother!"

Guo Cunxian pulled him to his feet again: "You really do love a good performance, don't you. OK, OK, I'll take you as my brother, but I must tell you, there's nothing left to do in this town. Tomorrow we set off. Fuck, now I'm making speeches."

"Brother, where do you think we should go?"

"I'm not sure yet. Anywhere, I suppose, will be all right."

"Then why don't we head south? There's a commune not too far from here called Dazhangzhuang. The county government is planning to hold a general food assembly there tomorrow. Perhaps we'll be able to squirrel in there and eat our fill. It's a big village. Who knows? Maybe we'll be able to find work there, too."

"What the devil is a general food assembly, just how do you know this?"

"I overheard the cadres in this village speaking about it. The county government is responsible for organising it, but it's just an assembly in name only. In truth, it's a food competition. All the communes in the surrounding area need to bring their own foodstuffs, and the competition will be about which commune can use the least amount of ingredients to make the largest amount of food. The 'winner', as it were, will then be the subject of the assembly, researching into good methods and all that. I heard that first you have to boil the grains, then boil them again and then place them into a large pot and cook them some more. After the pot comes to the boil, then you boil them some more, then fry, then ferment and, finally, once all that is done, you grind them up. What do you think? Doing this over and over, how much food do you think they'll produce? One *jin* of corn flour, after it's cooked, can make six *jin* of steamed buns. That's surely an increase in production. So let's keep at it, boil up the rice, boil, boil, boil. I'm starving, I'm about to burst."

"I've heard this before, but without dirt, there'd be no walls, and adding water doesn't make more food, nor does it really fill your belly. How the hell can they call for a food-making competition?"

"It's not only this, you know. They also want to see which commune can make food without actually using any of their grain. Talk about a low production target… fruit and veg anyone? Let's mix corn stalks with goosefoot. Adults can eat it and let their legs swell, kids can have some too and only have their brains bulge."

"All right, let's head there in the morning, and even if we can't find work, we can stay and watch the hubbub, and then head south afterwards. Now, let's sleep." Before they did so, however, Guo Cunxian made sure to teach Wang Shun the method for dealing with the bedbugs.

But Wang Shun only laughed, saying he wasn't worried about bedbugs and that they'd better be afraid of him. After all, he hadn't much blood left in him, and his bones had gone hard. If they dared to bite into him, they'd only lose their teeth. He jumped up onto the bed and without even bothering to take off his clothes, he lay down to sleep, remarking: "Wow, this is really comfortable. It's been over half a year since I've slept on a bed!"

Without waiting for Guo Cunxian to carefully lay himself down on the sand-bed, Wang Shun was already fast asleep, murmuring peacefully.

4

CUTTING COFFINS

During these times of extreme hunger, it was said that once even the great Marshal Zhu De was unexpectedly seen out in the gardens of Zhongnanhai, furiously digging up the wild herbs that grew between the lakes and the trees, desperately trying to find something to eat.

And the person who saw him was from Guojiadian, the young wife of Erhu.

As the end of the year approached, the authorities finally sent relief grain, and each person was given one *jin* of black beans. Black beans were great. Not only could they help reduce the oedema that so many suffered from, they were also effective in increasing a person's energy. Think about it, it didn't matter if it was a mule or a horse, if you gave it some black beans before heading to the fields in the morning, it could do an entire day's hard work, no problem at all. But what about people? Erhu's wife collected her two *jin* of black beans from the village, returned home and immediately divided them into three helpings. Why did a household of two mouths need three helpings? Well, because she was still carrying her husband's child, and so that meant she had two mouths to feed. She divided the black beans, placing her husband's portion to one side. Out of the remaining two portions, she took half and placed it in a pan on the stove and began to fry them. Once done, she quickly ate them.

The aroma, well, not much needs to be said about that. It had been more than eighty days since she had last seen grain and it had been even longer since she had felt any movement in her womb. Not moving wasn't all bad, it meant the child could stay inside her a little while longer, and in days like these, wasn't being born earlier a sure-fire way to be blamed that much sooner? In the blink of an eye, she'd finished the beans. She licked her lips loudly, smacking her tongue; she didn't feel full and so she grabbed the second half of her portion and gulped it down. She wondered, then, if times were so hard, what was forbidden and what couldn't be eaten? Then she thought, she'd eaten one *jin* already, why not eat all of it, and so she did, chewing and swallowing down Erhu's black beans. She suddenly felt thirsty and needed some water to wash down the food. Standing next to the water container, she scooped up several ladlefuls of cool water and slurped them down, her throat gurgled repeatedly. It felt wonderful, she felt as though she finally had a full belly.

Rubbing her stomach she went and lay down in bed, feeling as though there was movement inside, like a soft breeze slowly blowing through, but getting stronger and stronger. She felt sated, full, really full, for the first time in a long, long time... and that's how she died.

The villagers, however, saw a silver lining in the foolishness of Erhu's wife, for on the day that she essentially ate herself to death, Guo Cunxian returned, if only for a brief period of time. In fact, he stopped off at home for a moment only before he grabbed his axe and went to help Brother Erhu select the most appropriate wood to make a halfway suitable coffin for his deceased wife. And then on the following day, she was buried. As it happened, over the last few months, Guo Cunxian and Wang Shun had been to a great many different places. They'd walked three to four hundred *li* at least, passing through numerous villages and making well over a hundred coffins. It must be said that social customs are powerful things. The people they encountered might have been living in hard times, suffering starvation and desperately poor, but still they found the will to ensure that their departed ones were properly buried, returned to the yellow earth. For many, that was even more important than having a roof over their heads. Indeed, when death did befall a family, doors would often be torn down, beds broken up – everything would be sacrificed in order to provide a proper burial, a proper coffin. And working all the while, building coffin after coffin, Guo Cunxian made sure to periodically send Wang Shun back to Guojiadian, carrying grain for his family. Each time he went, he'd carry many *jin* of grain with him, always concealed to ensure their safe delivery. It was because of the grain, and the money that he earned building coffins, that his family were able to pass the winter fairly well off, with no more swollen limbs afflicting his poor mother.

Meanwhile, thinking of the approaching spring and being a little better off because of her son's industriousness, Sun Yueqing had started putting some of the grain and money aside, saving it up for when the spring actually arrived. Because once it did, there were sure to be many more refugees on the road trying to escape the famine and perhaps, just perhaps, she could find a suitable wife for her son. But before she had even really thought about discussing this plan with him, Guo Cunxian actually arrived home. He'd been away for nearly a year by then, making his way in the world, and she could see that the experience had changed him; in all respects he now carried himself as the provider for the family. Learning of her plans, he immediately told her, however, not to fuss about it and that she should use the grain and money she'd put aside for them to eat, to live and to ensure that they, that she, didn't suffer from oedema again. Besides, he told her, trying to arrange a marriage for him wouldn't be easy. In fact, it'd be better if he did it himself. Listening to him speak like this, she wondered what must have happened to her son while he was away.

Whatever it may have been, she wasn't about to find out anytime soon as Guo Cunxian didn't stay for long. Worried the village cadres had become envious of him and that they were going to deliberately make things hard for him and not let him leave the village any more, once the weather warmed a little, he slipped away.

Initially he planned to head towards Dingshan County, to where Wang Shun's family lived. He could call upon his old friend again; that would perhaps be the easiest thing to do. He'd be able to find a little bit of work there, earn some money and some grain, too. And Wang Shun was a smooth talker and very good at negotiating. In some cases he was even able to get people to increase the amount they paid him. What's more, if he found some heavier work, say felling trees, he might have a need for a right-hand man. But then again, he thought, there seemed to be a great many more deaths this year than last, and so he'd probably be able to keep himself busy building coffins. Thinking along these lines, he wondered if he could just leave all of that and head straight for Wang Shun's home. Mulling it over, he continued to think that if there were so many more deaths, then if he could get one job making coffins, then that would likely lead to another; that they'd then tell their relatives, and so on. Soon he'd be known as quite the craftsman, a skilful builder of coffins who didn't charge too much. When one job would finish, another would come. Gradually, then, he headed off in a south-westerly direction, walking farther and farther away from Wang Shun's home.

With his tools slung over his shoulder, he eventually wandered to the foot of Lianhua (Lotus) Mountain and came upon a small hamlet by the name of Xiayangpo. As chance would have it, someone just happened to have died and so he was asked to make a coffin. With amazing skill and dexterity, and all with his axe and his two hands, Guo Cunxian cut down the wood and made the smoothest, finest coffin he could. And it didn't matter what kind of wood it was, he was able to use anything, from larger to smaller trees, to discarded cross-beams and wood used for boats, to old doors and wardrobes. All of it would be transformed into the most perfect of vessels to carry the dead. When he had more than enough wood, he'd make a coffin fit for a palace, inscribed with the words of good fortune and longevity. It would stand strong and erect, heavy and sturdy, painted black and polished until it gleamed. And if a family were too destitute and only able to scrape together leftover pieces of wood, it didn't matter, he'd still be able to make a fine coffin. He'd line the inside of it too, filling the bottom half with wood shavings and other bits and pieces. When people looked at it, it would seem heavy and well built, imposing even, bringing good fortune to the deceased and maintaining face for the living. Living was just as hard as dying, and the dead could still see if their loved ones wronged them and didn't give them a proper burial, well... And so Guo Cunxian made sure to work his hardest, allowing the living to pay their respects and fulfil their duty while, at the same time, allowing the dead to show their hidden virtue to the next world.

It goes without saying that, when a villager dies, it's always a major event. Relatives from all over come to help out. This was a way of showing and saving face, not only for the deceased but for the immediate family as well. Each time Guo Cunxian set about building a coffin, there'd always be a swarm of people around him, like a troop of whooping monkeys. The people living at the foot of the mountain hadn't seen anything like this in well over a year, and who could believe that a coffin maker coming to town would be cause for such a show! Guo Cunxian was still young and quite a strapping lad at that. Swinging his axe as he did, he cut an imposing

figure, like someone out of the old tales. Those who watched him work couldn't help
but be awestruck, and Guo Cunxian himself couldn't help but be overly pleased. He
did cut a virile figure, and with each swing of the axe the energy behind them
increased. While they might all be poor, they lived a simple, pure life. It was easy to
find enjoyment, to find happiness even amid such sorrow.

He spent seven or eight days in this village that seemed to be always in the
shadow of the sun, in this town that had misery after misery piled on top of it; it
seemed that death always came one after the other. From what he'd heard, not only
was there little food around, but their water supply had also gone bad, which only
made the starvation worse. And in this shadowy place, the last person who came up to
ask him to build a coffin, a young woman by the name of Zhu Xuezhen, brought
something else with her as well. When he first saw her, he couldn't help but think she
was so delicate, so fragile and distressed. Her face was slender, which served to
accentuate her eyes, but she kept her head low, not daring to look him in the face.

Seeing this poor, beautiful woman so frightened and timid made his heart ache
and he clammed up. She didn't say much either but gestured for him to come with
her. She lived in a small, ramshackle earthen house with just two rooms. A coarse
locust tree stood next to the doorway but its purpose was unclear. The doors to the
rooms were old and battered; a small rotting chest was on the floor inside one of the
rooms, accompanied by a small, short-legged table and a wooden stool with a water
container beside it. Was there enough here to make a coffin? This had become a bad
habit of his over the last little while, a sickness even: as soon as he entered
anyone's house, he would immediately scan its contents to see if there was enough
suitable material to make a coffin, and then he would keep this in mind while he
discussed a price and the type of coffin he could make, its thickness and its style.
But when he looked around Zhu Xuezhen's home and saw the meagre belongings
his heart wept. Her father was slouched on the bed, his head inclined to the side.
Guo Cunxian could easily see that it wouldn't be long now, and his heart wept
some more.

Struggling to look up, it was as though the old man was using the last of his
strength to see the man who'd come into his home, to size him up, as it were. Guo
Cunxian had travelled extensively, but the look in the old man's eyes, the misgivings
he had, the hopelessness, it was something that he would never forget. Here lay this
dying old man, helpless in the face of death, beseeching, willing to risk everything to
hang on a little longer, but knowing that it was impossible. What profound sorrow
was in the eyes of that old man!

Stuttering, gasping for breath, the old man uttered his dying wish. He hadn't told
Xuezhen to go and look for him simply so that he could have a coffin to be buried in.
They didn't have anything to make one with anyway. No, it was something else. He
told Guo Cunxian that Xuezhen's mother had already passed away about six months
ago when the weather was still cold and they had only an old quilt to wrap her up in.
But that didn't matter, they still had one old quilt left, and that would be for him. No,
he wasn't asking for a coffin, all he wanted was for Guo Cunxian to help Xuezhen
bury him, and then for him to take her with him. The old man had heard about Guo
Cunxian, had heard that he was a good man and that he wasn't married yet.

Standing beside her father, tears rolled down Xuezhen's face: her world was crashing around her. Not only was she soon to bury her father but she was about to be sold as well!

With the blood coursing in his veins, without thinking Guo Cunxian knelt down beside the bed. If a dying man makes a last request to you, good or bad, how can one rebuff such a fateful wish? The old man had got to this point in his life, and yet he still had the strength to think about his daughter, to try to make arrangements for her for when he was gone. For most people, life was hard, filled with pain and sorrow. The weight of his request hung in the air. Guo Cunxian, who had startled the old man by kneeling down in front of him, seized the moment to speak: "If Big Sister is willing, let us kowtow to you now so that we can be properly married. Then, after we return to my own home, I can arrange for a proper ceremony and feast. But if Big Sister isn't willing, then I will still consider her family and whenever I eat, I will make sure she has food herself. You might be old and willing to let things go as they are, but I make coffins and I cannot allow you to be wrapped and buried in a tattered old quilt. When the day arrives, I'll have a coffin not only for you, but for your deceased wife as well. I'll make sure the two of you are buried together, so that you can set out on the next journey hand in hand."

Xuezhen fell to her knees next to Guo Cunxian and cried.

Pulling on her arms, motioning her to kowtow together, the two of them bowed and touched their foreheads to the floor three times as was the custom. He then told her to look after her old father and that he was going to go and buy wood, the best he could find to make the most suitable coffin. He was going to make sure he had one ready before the old man breathed his last breath. He wanted him to see what he was to be buried in. After all, a coffin was the vessel in which people left this world and travelled to the next. If you had a good one then that would bode well for where you'd live in the next world. It would allow you to avoid evil winds and cold rain, the lonely spirits and the torment of evil ghosts. Those who died with money had their coffins built well in advance, just waiting for them to take up occupancy when the time came. They were kept in good condition and given a fresh coat of paint each year. Only little kids feared coffins. When they saw them they'd think about death, ghosts and evil things. But for old people, if they could see their coffin before their life left them, then that was not only good fortune, but also evidence that their children were filial and respectful. In some bigger households, once a family member passed fifty years of age, then they'd already make arrangements to have a coffin made, despite some of them living for another thirty or forty years!

Guo Cunxian had worked for some time now in Xiayangpo and so he knew whose house had extra wood. He knew, too, how much wood he needed, that was clear in his mind. With the earnings he had made over the last two months or more, he was quickly able to buy what he required. He then brought this back to Zhu Xuezhen's door and without wasting a moment he got to work. The old man had not yet died, and yet the rigorousness and sincerity Guo Cunxian demonstrated couldn't help but be noticed by the residents of Xiayangpo. Before long a good number of them showed up to see what all the fuss was about. The Zhu family had no heir, and it was desperately poor. It's unlikely that they'd ever seen the respect they were now being shown.

The old man, in a final moment of lucidity, asked Xuezhen to sit him up and move him towards the window. He wanted to see Guo Cunxian at work.

The villagers who'd gathered around spoke continuously among themselves. Quite a few of them now envied old Zhu and his daughter Xuezhen. No one could have expected this: that such a poor family could receive such good fortune. And so they thought of their own houses and whether or not the celestial heavens would send them such a son or son-in-law, a filial man who would look after his aged parents and ensure that they were buried properly when the time came. In times like these, there certainly weren't many men like Guo Cunxian, men with such seemingly innate skill. If the truth be told, there were also a number of other young women in the village who were interested in him. After all, if they were to end up being with him, at least they wouldn't have to worry about having something to eat.

As for Guo Cunxian, he was as honest and upright as they came. If he hadn't been, if he'd been busy scheming, say, then there's no telling how many women he might have had. Ho, but this isn't cause for regret. A man's qualities know no bounds and so there's no need to use them early. In fact, to hold some back meant one would have more in old age. And at this point in his life, Guo Cunxian's mind was set only on earning money and returning home to put his big plans into action. As for finding a wife, for that to happen two conditions had to be met: first, he had to find someone who matched his tastes; second, that person had to have a reliable background, someone able to ensure his family's future.

From the moment he first saw Xuezhen's delicate, small frame, his heart had been touched by a pure, untarnished feeling. The melancholy he saw in her eyes urged him to do his utmost in all things. Later when she cried, her tears were like flames, scorching his heart and melting it completely. Everything about her couldn't help but make any man want to take hold of her immediately, to protect and treasure her, to feel as though there were none stronger and nothing he couldn't do.

By the afternoon of the following day, the coffin he had worked upon so vigorously had been completed. Guo Cunxian asked for some help to lift it up, and then placed it next to the window so that it could be painted. Once finished, he took apart the old rotten window frame that was obstructing the view and went in to pick up his father-in-law. He wanted the old man to inspect the work himself. When his eyes fell upon it, he grabbed hold of Guo Cunxian and looked as though he were about to laugh, but only tears fell down his face instead.

It was as if he had long thought about standing in front of such a magnificent coffin, or perhaps he had long contemplated settling down into the quiet earth, to lie for the last time in such splendid confines, who's to say? But in the arms of his new son-in-law, he then passed away. Those who had come to see the coffin all said that the old man had died most fortunately, that he'd left this world free of sin. The remaining work was straightforward; burials had their procedures and these were especially clear for those to be buried in coffins. Besides, he was now the old man's son-in-law, a respected guest who'd come from afar. He had expended his money and his energy making the finest of coffins, and so now he would wave the spirit banner, carry the crockery, and wail as custom dictated. He was now more than a son. Distant relatives and close neighbours, none would dare challenge his role, no one wished to interrupt the smooth process of sending the old man into the next world, of ensuring that he rested in peace.

Three days later, once the funeral ceremony had ended, Guo Cunxian intended to return to Guojiadian with his new wife.

While Xuezhen intended to sell her father's ramshackle house, Guo Cunxian opposed the idea and figured they wouldn't be able to get very much for it, in any case. She then thought about entrusting the house to the village, asking them to look after it. Again, Guo Cunxian disagreed. He argued that, since the house was in such a state of disrepair, it would probably be impossible to find anyone willing to do it, and if they did, that'd really only be burdening them with a difficult task. After all, what if the roof collapsed, or a wall, what then? Instead he suggested that they board it up, and then who could say whose house it was? But if they didn't board it, how could she claim it to be hers?

Somewhat distressed and annoyed, Xuezhen asked: "But if none of these ideas work, what do you think we should do?"

"This is your home and so we have to hold onto it," Guo Cunxian said reassuringly. "You were born here. On Tomb Sweeping Day we have to return in order to pay our respects to your father and mother. Won't we need a place to stay then? When we have a little money, which shouldn't be long, two to three years at most, I'll return with some men to renovate the whole place. Right now, let's get some mud bricks and fill in the windows, that'll help protect the house and stop animals from coming inside and destroying the place."

Xuezhen burst into tears again; it seemed as though that was all she could do. But she cried as a way to express the mix of emotions she had endured these past few days. It was her way of consoling herself. Guo Cunxian reached out and took her in his arms. Even though there was no one else around, she still hurriedly struggled to free herself. In a soft, delicate voice she spoke: "You're too good to me!"

He laughed to himself and thought what a foolish girl she was being. Men certainly weren't all good. They could be bad enough at times!

Realising that the day was slipping away, Guo Cunxian told Xuezhen to gather up their things. He was going to go into town to find some mud bricks to stop up the windows; it should only cost about five yuan or so. The young men in the village were more than happy to help out, bringing three cartfuls of mud bricks and then working together with Guo Cunxian to tightly seal the windows, even smoothing down the exterior. Once complete, they said their farewells, expressed their gratitude, exchanged platitudes that no one would remember, and then left the village.

On the road leading away from Xiayangpo, when it was just the two of them, Guo Cunxian and Zhu Xuezhen, the realisation of his new life truly dawned on him. The funeral ceremony was over, it was time to change their mood, time to prepare for a much happier event – a wedding feast!

More than two months ago when he left Guojiadian, all he had with him was his axe. Now, however, things were different. While it couldn't really be said that he was returning in silken robes, returning in glory, as the old saying goes, he was returning home with a lovely, beautiful wife, and surely that could be considered a propitious achievement. And while she mightn't necessarily be someone to brag about – she wasn't, after all, some outstanding individual from her village, and yes, she was poor and somewhat weak – she did, however, have a certain distinctive character, a certain air about her. Once they returned to Guojiadian and she was able to eat her fill, well, then we'll see, she might not end up being the best catch, but she'll definitely be the most womanly woman in the village. For now, however, the greatest urgency was getting her to open up. She had to move on from her recent sorrows, losing her father and her mother. Now she had to look to the future, to the happiness of being a newlywed.

He tried to take her hand, but she dodged it, recoiling as though from a scorpion sting. His first attempt failing, he simply reached out and took hold of her arms, feigning as though he were going to grab the bundle she was carrying in her arms, but really he just took her hand and held it under his arm. Using some of his strength, he wouldn't let her pull away. Then, leaning in close, he spoke almost coyly: "What's the matter, hmm? Did I say or do something wrong? You might yet look like a young, unmarried maiden, but in truth you're my dutiful wife. Why then are you so rigid, refusing to lean on me, to save a little energy if nothing else? Why do you keep acting this way, hmm? How long has it been since you ate, since you slept a full night? You're just walking alongside me, but it's like there's a clear dividing line between us, a distinct boundary."

Looking down she smiled faintly, allowing herself to move a little closer.

Guo Cunxian continued: "Hah, so you can smile after all! And you have such a lovely smile, too. So soft, so pure, oh it could steal a man's heart." Disarming her with his compliments, he seized his chance and leaned in and kissed her. "There, now I've marked you as my wife, wherever we go everyone will know we're together."

She put her head down again, shyly smiling once more. But she didn't say a word, only her face turned bright red.

Guo Cunxian continued to tease her: "Today, we're performing the *Fairy Couple*, an opera duet, the two birds in the trees become one. Aren't you going to sing? Your silence will mortally wound me otherwise."

Xuezhen finally responded. Her voice was soft and precise: "But you seem to like speaking so much, please, continue."

He spun in front of her, bringing his face to look directly into hers. The look in his eyes had become more serious: "How can you be so suspicious of what I'm saying, I haven't stolen the words out of your mouth, have I? OK then, I have something serious that I want to ask you, and you'd better answer."

"What?"

"Do you really like me, or did you agree just because it was your father's wish? Do you think you've just sold your body so that you were able to give him a proper funeral?"

She seemed to mumble to herself, but Guo Cunxian wouldn't relent, he pressed her for an answer. Finally she spoke: "I'm yours already, why do you need to ask that?"

"What kind of man do you think I am? It's not like I couldn't find a wife, I didn't just take advantage of your difficult situation. Oh how terrible it would sound if rumours spread that I traded two coffins for a wife! I meant what I said to your father.

You still have your freedom. If you think I'm the right man for you, then we're family and we'll be together for this lifetime. But if you don't fancy me in that way, if you just agreed so that your father could be buried, well, he's in the ground now, and he was given a good send off, we can just call it quits."

Xuezhen stopped in her tracks and blocked his path, looking up into his face she asked: "How about this?"

There was a deepness to her eyes as they teared up.

Trying to deliberately frighten her, Guo Cunxian spoke venomously: "Not two *li* from here there is a long-distance bus station. To the southeast is Guojiadian, to the northwest Jinshan. If you say you don't want to be with me, fine, then I'll take you to Jinshan and sell you there to some old bare stick. I don't care for how much, I just need to make sure that it's the oldest and ugliest bare stick I can find, even better if they're crippled and blind, I'll make you regret for a lifetime that you wouldn't marry me."

The tone in her voice was still gentle, still soft: "Hmph, but you're already old, ugly, crippled and blind, I might as well sell myself to you, huh? I guess that's my lot in life!"

She buried her head in the pit of his stomach. Guo Cunxian took hold of her and tore off running. Huffing and puffing, half running, half stumbling, he ran. On his left shoulder he carried his tool bag, on his right was Xuezhen's bundle with all her possessions in it; in front he was carrying her. He hadn't run far before he was nearly out of breath. With Xuezhen kicking and screaming, he had to stop.

Her face was bursting red, her mood cheerful. She thanked the heavens and the earth for dispersing the dark clouds that had hung over her. She used the arm of her sleeve to wipe his brow. Laughing she spoke: "Foolish boy, that's what you are!"

He interjected: "Just what are you carrying in this bundle of yours? It's so heavy and bangs around so much."

"It's only some clothes and a few books."

"Books?" He watched as she nodded. "On the first day I saw you, I thought you must be Wang Baochuan. Destitute though you were, digging up wild herbs to eat, you still carried yourself with a certain grace. What's the matter, have I said something wrong? Ah, it doesn't matter, even if you are a woman of talent, no family is going to accept you as that. You'll have to get rid of the books."

"You're talking nonsense, those are my favourite books. They're also mementos of when I was younger. My father was the village primary school teacher, and after nine years of marriage they had me. I was his little treasure, his everything, and he made sure that I graduated from middle school!"

"If you were his treasure, then why did he wait until he was on his deathbed to scramble to find you a husband? If it weren't for the good fortune that I happened to come along, then who's to say that the apple of his eye wouldn't have ended up in the deepest of shit!"

A gloom fell over Xuezhen: "You weren't the first, you know. My parents had tried, many times in fact, to find me a husband, but none of them worked out. Thinking there was nothing more to be done, they had no choice but to keep me with them, unmarried. I knew in my heart that one day I would lose them. And they really tried, they had a tacit mutual understanding between them. They wanted to find a man, a son-in-law who would be willing to go against tradition and instead move in with them, but each man that came proved unsuitable, and thus my marriage was delayed, over and over again. Then this disaster struck, and then another when my mother died. What could my father do but grow worried, panicky even?"

"Aiya, good heavens, don't you know what this means? It must have been providence! You must've been waiting for me. That means this was the Will of Heaven and that ours is a match made by the gods!"

Xuezhen dropped her head again, feeling a little awkward: "It wasn't actually my father who chose you. After all, he couldn't get out of bed, so how was he to find out what kind of man you really are? In truth, he entrusted an old colleague from school to learn all he could about you. Later, that man came and told us. He said that by your manner of speech and bearing, you were perhaps a little arrogant. He also said you had somewhat large ears and a broad forehead, that you were tall, with broad shoulders and stout arms."

She continued, still somewhat embarrassed: "He also said you could swing your axe for an entire day without getting tired. Your eyes, he told my father, were clear and piercing. He said you were an imposing figure, opinionated, but reliable. Once we heard all of this, my father then told me to go and take a look and if I was pleased, I was to get you to come home. If I wasn't, then that would have been the end of it. Do you understand? Can you still say then that I don't want you, that you were simply a means for me to give my father a proper burial?"

Guo Cunxian pulled her close, embracing her tightly. Her neck was beautiful and soft and she smelled of the sweetest of fragrances. He drew his mouth close to her ear and spoke softly: "What do they call love at first sight? What love can draw a line between two people over thousands of *li*? That's what we have."

"If you had remained here in this sunken land, whiling away the years, when might our fated love have reached me?"

A woman such as Xuezhen was rare indeed. She didn't speak much but she certainly didn't lack charm or intelligence. After this exchange, their union was assured, but it had a somewhat different flavour to it now. Guo Cunxian picked up her bag and put it over his left shoulder and his tool bag over his right. His right hand he extended towards her lovingly, at times wrapping it around her waist or holding onto her hand. There was a distinct spring in their steps as they walked on.

In those days, not many people travelled by bus. When Guo Cunxian first boarded he immediately looked for a pair of seats so that Xuezhen could sit inside, next to the window. He sat in the aisle seat, protectively shielding her from the other travellers, few though they may be. His tool bag was stuffed under the seat in front of him, and her bag was placed on his lap. He was going to make her a small room once they returned; a place for her belongings. With his right hand, he held on to her left, almost shyly. She leaned against the window. In a soft voice he told her that it was about a three-hour ride to Guojiadian and so she should try to get a little sleep.

She positioned her head as comfortably as she could on the seat rest and, like an obedient child, she closed her eyes to rest. Still, tender teardrops fell down her cheeks. Guo Cunxian held her hand even more firmly, and with his left he gently wiped away the tearstains. He leaned over and spoke to her: "Is leaving home hard, or are you thinking about your parents?" She just nodded her head without replying. Guo Cunxian couldn't help but be a little nervous. If she didn't explain, his heart would remain unsettled.

There was no choice, she moved closer to him and spoke: "A house without an heir cannot help but be mistreated. My home village was big and scattered, we weren't close to our neighbours, and so I was bullied repeatedly as a child. After the first time, when the children bullied me, I returned home and told my parents. But what could they do other than share the pain with me. Afterwards, when the children bullied me, I didn't tell my parents. Those were the times I so wished for a big brother, someone to protect me."

Guo Cunxian understood. She felt a brotherly love from him, a feeling of protectiveness. That was good, after all, wasn't a husband much like a brother, at least a brother of a certain type? She continued: "Many people say that carpentry requires very fine work and meticulous attention to detail. Does that mean then that a carpenter's heart is equally attentive to detail? Since I've known you, I've thought about this. You've helped me so much, doing much more than I could have expected, putting my heart and mind at ease. Are you going to be like this for the rest of our lives? I'm so tired but now I feel I have someone I can count on."

Her voice trailed off into a whisper as she fell asleep. She seemed so peaceful, who knows how long it had been since she had slept so well. Poor, pitiful Xuezhen, be at ease, from this day onwards no one will dare bully you.

These past few days had been very tiresome for Guo Cunxian as well, and a nap seemed like the right thing to do. But his heart was heavy, he had many things on his mind, and he felt it was best to use this free time to try to make sense of them. After they arrived home, he had to organise a wedding feast, but how big should it be? He hadn't planned this to happen, so he hadn't put any money aside for it. Of course, if he borrowed the money, if he could find someone to lend him some, allowing them to earn some face in the process, well, that should be possible. But in truth, if he considered the fact that he and Xuezhen were technically already married, then perhaps they should just save their money and have a simple meal together as a family. Then again, there wouldn't be anyone to invite from Xuezhen's family. He'd always had family next to him, his whole life. Wouldn't a family meal be an inadvertent show of ostentation, an insult to Xuezhen? Certainly it'd be unfair. But he'd made such a show of it in front of her father, said such grand things, if he didn't come through with them, what would Xuezhen think? How would she look at him? He sighed and his thoughts turned to money and how much he would end up spending in the coming months. The house was there, it had been covered up last year. At most it would need only a fresh coat of paint, but still… As he mulled things over he couldn't help but feel he was actually mulling himself over.

When he opened his eyes, the bus had already arrived in the town of Madian. It was late, the hottest time of the day.

His stomach gurgling, he brought Xuezhen into the bus station where there were several food stalls. Using less than one yuan, he was able to buy half a *jin* of sliced vegetables in a braised soup. It was brought out in three large bowls and although it looked very watery, it was quite fragrant and savoury. Xuezhen ate one bowl, refusing quite strongly to eat any more, and so Guo Cunxian finished off the rest which relieved his hunger pangs. Afterwards they went to some small vending stands where he bought Xuezhen some face powder, a small mirror and a comb, the things a newly married woman needed. She cooed then and wouldn't let him waste any more money.

The vending girls crowded together to one side and looked Xuezhen up and down, whispering quietly to each other. He could tell they were talking about his new wife, that she had given him greater stature, more face. Pleased, he spoke in a rather loud voice: "Hey, what day is it today, who's just been married? Money is no object, whatever I spend I can earn again!"

As they drew closer and closer to Guojiadian, as Xuezhen's past receded further and further behind her, as she realised she was embarking on a completely new life, she grew nervous and solemn. Guo Cunxian was the exact opposite. His heart was overflowing, he felt like shouting, like singing, like jumping and laughing. He turned to Xuezhen: "Let's not take the main road, that'll add another three or four *li* to our journey. I know a shortcut. Near the village there's a wide river but it's quite shallow. The water is also sparkling and clear. I'm just dying for a wash and perhaps you could do the same as well. Once we cross the river, it's only about seven or eight *li* to Guojiadian. It's guaranteed that when we reach home you'll set all the married and unmarried girls to talking. You heard what they were saying at the little shop in the bus station, yes? 'Do you see her skin, so fine, so soft, her hands, too, so delicate?'"

Oh how he teased her. Xuezhen could only blush and lower her head, not uttering a sound.

But when they arrived at the river, the water was rushing and gurgling by. It was well over half a *li* wide. The water was exceptionally clear and sparkling, but it only made Xuezhen blanch. She thought to hold her tongue but couldn't, instead, she grabbed hold of Guo Cunxian's arm and for the very first time shouted his name: "Cunxian! How are we to cross such a wide river?"

"Heh, heh, of course it's wide, I said that. If it wasn't, why would anyone say that it was a wide river? But just because it's wide doesn't mean that it's deep. The drought we've had these last two to three years, well, last year it even dried up for a while. Look closely, can't you see some of the river bed showing through in the middle?"

She squeezed his arm tighter: "I can't cross it, I don't dare, let's go around it, find a bridge to cross, please."

"Did I say you had to wade through the water?"

"If I don't, how am I to cross?"

"Well, I'm going to wade across, it's so hot today, isn't it, crossing the river will be a pleasure. You'll see, you'll enjoy it too. I'm going to carry you on my back over the water, and if it gets deeper, well, you can climb onto my shoulders. We've finished singing the *Fairy Couple* ballad, now we'll act out one of Pigsy's scenes from *Journey to the West*, you know, the one when he performs the arduous, and maybe thankless, task of carrying the maiden over the water. Oh, fair maiden, up we go!" Putting his arms around her waist he suddenly picked her straight up and moved to plunge into the water.

Hanging on for dear life, sputtering inconsolably, her face deathly white, Xuezhen wailed at him: "You're mad. Aren't you afraid someone will see us?"

"First, I'd love somebody to see us, all of China even, yes, tell them all to come and see me carry my lovely wife across the river. Second, it's a pity that there's no one here, it'll be a regret I carry with me my whole life. It's a great shame, but there's been no work to do in the village for a long time now. Just look, if you see even the shadow of someone, I'll let you down off my back and carry you in my arms instead!"

Xuezhen didn't turn her head. Instead she relented docilely, muttering playful complaints under her breath: "You're bad, you are, bad."

Letting her down for a moment, Guo Cunxian removed his socks and his shoes and placed them into his tool bag. He then took hold of his bag and hers in his left hand, kneeled down, breathed in a lungful of air and spoke: "All right, I'm ready, climb aboard!"

Xuezhen recoiled a little: "Do you really mean to wade across the river?"

"How else are we going to cross it?"

"If something happens in the middle of the river, are you going to protect your things or your wife?"

He straightened up and looked at her: "Why are you so afraid? We haven't even entered the water and you're already worrying about something happening. If something did happen then, of course, I'm going to look after you. What kind of bastard would be more concerned with their things than with their wife?"

She paid no attention to his jocularity, but instead showed even more concern: "You can really swim, can't you?"

A family of two are a family of two and here he was with a pretty young girl worried about him. What more did he need to make his heart content? He didn't try to frighten her any more. He told her, with great sincerity, that he'd been swimming across this river like a duck takes to water since he was ten years old, and at that time there was much more water and even great waves and surges. He and the other village kids used to swim through the water, climb up into the nearby melon garden, steal some to eat, and then plunge back into the water and swim back.

"All right then, but you take the things across first, and see if the water's deep or not."

That made sense. And although it would be something of a waste of energy, it would help at least to alleviate her fears. Before setting out to cross the river, he asked her to open her bag, take out her most prized possessions and keep them on her, saying: "It's better to be safe than sorry. I don't want some passersby to see our things on the other side and take advantage of us not being there. Or if you'd rather not, I can tie my axe around the top of your bundle. Did you know it can ward off evil? Everyone around here for at least 10 *li* will know that that axe is mine and they won't dare to touch our stuff."

Xuezhen still opened her bag and removed a small, flowery schoolbag. She took the small items Guo Cunxian had just bought her and placed them inside and held it close to her. She then tied up the bundle and handed it to him. "Take it slow, all right, don't overexert yourself. And if the water is too deep, be sure to turn back."

His heart burned over the worry she showed for him, but still he teased her: "My Lord, when'll you be finished worrying? I'll have a beautiful woman waiting for me on this side of the river, and I haven't even really experienced being a husband yet. Lord, even if you asked me to do something risky, I wouldn't."

She leaned over preparing to roll up his trouser legs, but he told her it wasn't necessary. He needed to wash his clothes in any case, and getting them wet now would make them nice and cool, and they'd dry on the rest of the walk home. As he said this he jumped into the water full of excitement and energy and splashed about; it was so fresh and cool. The wide river really was drying out, the deepest part barely reached halfway up his thigh. It didn't take him long to make it across and then back to Xuezhen. He asked her: "You saw what it was like, you shouldn't be worried any more. Come on, up you come!"

She pulled the flowery schoolbag over her right shoulder, and then gently climbed on his back. Embarrassed still, she buried her head in the back of his neck. He straightened up, but didn't immediately wade into the river. Xuezhen had wrapped her bare feet around his torso and he couldn't help but take hold of them for a moment; he had to tickle them, to tease her some more. Without uttering a sound, she squirmed back and forth, nuzzling her face further into the back of his neck. With her two hands she punched playfully at his chest. Smiling contentedly, he jumped into the water and in a loud voice asked her: "I heard that the land and water around your village had gone bad. How is it that your skin is so white and even your feet are so soft!"

She climbed up further onto his back, almost trying to sneak in a laugh, but she didn't answer him.

He continued to tease her, but he was careful not to let her slip. His hands were around her buttocks, rubbing up and down, moving in tandem with the gurgling water underneath. Oh, how beautiful! Wading through the water like this, Xuezhen was afraid to protest too much, only asking: "Can you try and hold your hands a little still at least?"

"How can I? I can't control them. Maybe if you hadn't made me bring the bags over first, well, then my hands would've been wrapped around them, and you'd be a little more settled, I guess. All right, they've stopped now, but I'm not sure if I can keep them from doing something they so heartily enjoyed. And speaking of this, I don't think anything could compare to your pretty little behind, I mean, it's so soft, I almost feel bad for copping such a feel! Oh but a beautiful behind can enrapture an entire household, can take hold of a man's fate, plump, firm, wide, able to bear five boys and two girls. Oh... starting tomorrow you'll have to make sure you feed us well, even when you're stuffed you'll still have to eat!"

"Do you think to turn me into a pig?"

"Oh, if you really wanted to plump up like that, then I'd be fortunate indeed. I mightn't have been to school like you, but the character for house has a pig in it. And in olden times, when a family married off a daughter, they'd call that a 'return', so you haven't really left your home, you're actually returning to it. As they say, if you marry a chicken, follow the chicken, if you marry a dog, follow the dog, you have to be happy with whom you've married no matter his lot, but if you marry Pigsy, on his back, off he'll go! Oh, that reminds me of a story about an old blind man who carried a cripple across the river. I should tell you, if I don't, then you'll never loosen up, your face'll keep turning red, you won't let me pinch your feet, to say nothing about feeling your bum."

"Ah, but you've already pinched my feet quite a bit, and your hands have been all over my bum, in fact, they haven't stopped moving." Xuezhen giggled and blew softly on his neck, moistening it as it tickled him.

"The story goes that an old blind man and a cripple were travelling companions who, while on the road, came upon a river, not too wide, but wide enough, to block their path. Of course, it was up to the blind man to carry the cripple across the river. As they reached the other side, the crippled man saw two young women, naked and bathing in the river. Thinking to test his blind friend, he asked him if the two people he heard bathing were male or female. Needing virtually no time at all, the blind man responded and said they were female. Xuezhen, you guess, if the blind man was really blind, how did he know that it was two women bathing?"

She didn't respond right away, in fact, she didn't move at all. Guo Cunxian arched his neck somewhat and struggled to look round. All he could see was the frustrated, perplexed look in Xuezhen's eyes. But before he could say anything she walloped him over the head: "Eyes in front!"

"Aiya, where's all that book learning gone to, huh? I'll tell you, OK, the cripple saw the two naked women, and whaddya know, the thing between his legs couldn't help but stand up and drive into the back of the old blind man. So, of course, the blind man didn't even need to guess, he knew it must be two young women bathing, heh, heh."

Embarrassed by his story she buried her face, almost driving her chin into the back of his head: "You're just foul-mouthed aren't you? You've only dirty stories to tell me."

In a loud voice, he defended his story: "What I've told you is real, that's life. The whole world is made up of stories about men and women, about one breaking away from the other. Men come from women, from there, and they spend the rest of their lives trying to get back there. I need to tell you another story. Long ago, there was a young man whose family were desperately poor, I mean they had absolutely nothing, but one day they sent a matchmaker into the village to call upon the town's richest moneybag to see about arranging a marriage. They also told the matchmaker to tell the rich man's daughter that their son was well-off. Well, the rich man's daughter believed the matchmaker and agreed to the marriage. Of course, when she went to her new husband's house she discovered that they were penniless, and so she accused them of lying to her and tricking her into marriage. But the young man told her he hadn't lied. Instead, he told her that it wasn't money or wealth that would make a girl happy, but rather his manhood. As he spoke these words, he calmly and unhurriedly undid his pants and, of course, pulled that manhood out. It goes without saying that it was magnificent, tall and long. Immensely pleased with his girth, he told his new wife that this was truly a man's wealth, something she could enjoy for a lifetime without it ever running out. The woman's demeanour changed almost immediately, her furore turned into excitement, and they lived happily ever after."

He heard Xuezhen call him a rude bastard, but only quietly, before she used her fist to tickle him hard in the shoulder.

He pretended then to lose his footing under the water and slip, his body waved back and forth. Frightened, Xuezhen cried out thinking they were going to fall. But with his strong right arm, he held onto her left leg, and then used his other arm to spin her around. She was soon in his arms and no longer on his back. He held her tightly and safely to his chest. Xuezhen put her arms around his neck and held onto him just as tightly, her crimson face directly beneath his nose. They stared into each other's eyes and it was like setting flame to dried wood. Her whole face gave away her modesty, her shyness; she closed her eyes and tried to shift her face away from his. But holding onto her as he was, where could she turn? He lowered his head and without much effort brought his lips to hers.

Oh how he had longed for this. He'd been so thirsty, but now, in the heat of the moment, he grew only thirstier, hungrier. As he drank more, he wanted more, as he kissed her more, he wanted more. The feeling swept over his entire body and his crotch area began to swell; he was so hungry. At first, her body shifted against his and she was afraid of falling into the river but her struggle didn't last. Gradually she became soft, pliable. Instead of struggling against him she fell further into his embrace, entwining herself around him. Their lips grew ever more eager, searching. The water grew shallower and shallower. Carefully he walked up onto the riverbank and placed her gently down in the warm, hot sand, their bodies were aflame, hard, expectant, hungry.

After they finished, Xuezhen laid her head on his chest and cried. Her shoulders throbbed up and down, her hot tears scorching his heart. She looked delicate, lonely and frightened, but she felt no resentment towards him. She had given herself to him, had embraced him just as hard. She'd wanted to feel him inside her. He held onto her with his left arm and with his right he caressed her back. He said all of the things a man would say in such a moment and his hand moved up and down her back. It gradually brought life back into her body but it also made her stiffen.

He loved her deeply and didn't want to hurt her again but his amorous feelings would not abate. Like a tidal wave they rushed in, wave after wave, growing in intensity. His whole body felt it and there was no way to hold it back as his manhood swelled once more. He held her in his arms and she didn't move. Soon he was inside her again, in that familiar place.

5

LEASE HOLDING

Guo Cunxian may have left home to make coffins but he unexpectedly came back with a wife. This was something quite novel, like a scene out of a play or a storybook. The people of Guojiadian were starving and impoverished, there was an oppressive, deathly pall over the village, but Guo Cunxian coming home with a wife was like someone had tossed a live grenade into the village. The whole town seemed to snap to attention and their imaginations soon ran wild. What was this girl like? Was she bald, deaf or handicapped in some way? Had she willingly married him or had he stolen her away? Didn't it seem as though he'd got her as easily as if he'd gone out to collect firewood? Would such a girl even do? Could she be a proper wife? Needless to say, the whole town was abuzz with gossip.

Over the course of the following days, the door to the Guo family house was nearly worked loose. It seemed as though more than half of all the women in town had to come and see Guo Cunxian's new wife, to look her over and size her up. They came one after the other, in groups of twos and threes. They'd climb up onto the *kang* and wouldn't leave until they were poked and prodded, so to speak, to raise their behinds and go. While they were there, they similarly poked and prodded Xuezhen, trying to dig up her life's story, her and her family's background. Their eyes bore into her as though they were trying to peel off the skin of a fruit to get at the pulp underneath; to be blunt, they wanted to know everything. And when they weren't satisfied by what they could see, their mouths worked overtime, asking questions and saying things they normally wouldn't. As custom had it, good manners and etiquette were suspended during this time. The villagers had three days to disrupt the privacy of the bridal chamber. The only problem was that three days had long gone already. And what was even more impudent, they didn't even hold back from crowding overly close to her, clasping her hands, pinching her here and there. Poor Xuezhen, she wanted to run and hide but couldn't. Custom meant she was simply at their mercy.

Her face was flushed. There was nowhere for her to turn. Her head seemed lost among the clouds, engulfed in a warm, misty haze, dizzy and confused. But even though her eyes had become red and her mouth had a sour taste to it, once they'd seen and looked this new wife over, once they'd satisfied their curiosity, their querying persistence became a flood of compliments: for now, she was the talk of the town, the prettiest and loveliest new wife in it. Not only that, but Guo Cunxian received his share of compliments too, the old dog!

The only strange thing about all of this was that while the town's women came in droves, not a single man from the village dropped by. Was this because they were jealous of Guo Cunxian or because they were unable to control their anger that he had been able to find a wife and they hadn't? Was one man's marriage a hindrance to another's? No, not a hindrance per se, but then, not *not* a hindrance. In one small village everyone knew everyone else, everyone watched everyone else and as days blended into each other there seemed to be a clear pecking order. How then, did Guo Cunxian get to the head of the queue? How did he get married before them? In any case, the fact that he had couldn't help but be difficult for the rest of the village's bare sticks to accept. And so it was that, unexpectedly, when the evening of the third night after their return was coming to a close, several of the town's men came clomping up to Guo Cunxian's door seemingly set to relay some important information or other now that the women had all left. Ironically, however, Guo Cunxian wasn't at home.

But what's more, this was no ordinary group of men that had shown up, no, these were all very important players in the village. The ringleader was the village branch secretary, Chen Baohuai, who only had to stamp his feet to make the whole village tremble and shake. You only had to look at his outfit to see his importance. Even in the sweltering heat his blue Mao jacket still hung round his shoulders, an imposing fountain pen protruded from his chest pocket and a bulging black leather notebook stuck out from his trousers. These were all symbols of his power and authority over the village. And it didn't matter what season it was, he was always dressed in this manner. When it got cold, he'd simply cover his shoulders with a heavy overcoat or military jacket. Of course, he was the only one permitted to dress like this in the village. Not even the commune's head cadre was allowed to clothe himself as the branch secretary did and, if he had dared to do so, it would clearly have suggested that he was either about to be named as a branch secretary or that something had befallen Secretary Chen. It was almost like a game. Whenever the branch secretary went to the commune or the county offices, he would always be sure to slip his arms into his jacket and head off, always making sure he looked the part. In situations like these, one only had to scan the assembled crowd to see what they were wearing in order to identify anyone of a higher rank. But there was no other visitor to their house of greater importance than Secretary Chen. Standing behind him was the team leader Han Jingting, as well as a few other men from the Fourth Production Unit. They were all wearing short sleeves or breezy tank tops, clearly less important than Chen. When Xuezhen first saw the men come in, her heart skipped a beat. She immediately wondered if something was wrong. In her old hometown, the village head had never once crossed her doorway.

But it wasn't long before she understood what was happening. They'd come to drink and celebrate. When Guo Cunxian had first returned, he hadn't been back long before starting to make noises about leaving again, and that's how he ended up in

Xiayangpo. And there, well, he had got married, had made vows in front of Xuezhen's old father while he lay on his deathbed, and they'd become husband and wife. For the Guo family, this should've meant that there wasn't a need to have a full wedding ceremony now, no need to invite villagers over and treat them to food and drink. And besides, in times like these, who in the village was really able to do so anyway? Of course, this type of talk only really made sense to one's longstanding neighbours as they'd respect that and not pester you; but it wouldn't work on the party cadres, no, they'd expect a proper meal and a drink. And complicating matters was the fact that Guo Cunxian couldn't really be compared to other men in the village. He'd left, had gone off and earned some money, and had even been paid for work with food. What's more, he brought a wife home with him. Failing to treat them to food and drink just wasn't possible. After all, in their minds, a little bit of food and drink was cheap payment for officially recording Xuezhen's name in his family register, wasn't it? And so, in a great flurry of activity, Sun Yueqing welcomed the men into her home and once more they endured the hypocritical show of friendship and affection. Under normal circumstances, or at least at a less busy time, these would have been the men they would have liked to have invited to their home to celebrate. But they couldn't, not considering their differences in social standing.

After her oldest son had returned, Sun Yueqing gave Cunxian and his new wife the southern room to make their own; she and her two other children would sleep together in the western room. Their uncle, poor Guo Jingshi, would live in the old storage shed in the southern yard, which they had cleaned out and made suitable for bedding down in. It was good that Cunxian had got married and brought a wife home with him. And she quite liked Xuezhen, too, so much so, in fact, that she found it difficult to control her happiness. As she introduced her to such important people from the village, she fluttered about happily, making sure to keep their cups full of water and their cigarettes lit. Then, as soon as her younger son, Cunzhi, came into the room, she immediately instructed him to go and find his older brother. They had important guests and he had to return home quickly. She also pulled out a small wad of money from her pocket and handed it to her daughter, telling her to go to the cooperative to buy some sweet potato wine, and with whatever money was left, she was to buy snacks to go with the alcohol, things like dried tofu, tiger beans and any cheap tins of food if there was enough money. Cunzhu frowned and moved close to her mother, whispering into her ear: "Mother, please, do you really want me to go to the cooperative and bring these things back with me? What on earth for?" She pushed her daughter back a little and told her, more forcefully this time, to go and buy the sweet potato wine.

Having given these instructions to Cunzhu, she returned to the eastern room and her guests. They were in the midst of asking Xuezhen questions, but they lacked proper decorum. The younger cadres were all talking over each other, shamelessly hitting on her. But the two most important men, Secretary Chen and Unit Leader Han Jingting, were sat to one side, seemingly giving her the cold shoulder. Their questions were more direct. Where was she from? How much food was her hometown producing? What did her parents do? Had she been to school? How had she come to know Guo Cunxian? Zhu Xuezhen tried to answer the questions one after the other, keeping her voice calm and clear. She wasn't embarrassed, nor was she timid, but confident and self-assured. Witnessing this, Sun Yueqing's heart warmed to her even more; she was so beautiful and steadfast. She'd watched Xuezhen for several days now, seen her gentleness, her yielding nature, how she had endured the nattering and pestering of the village women and had seemed almost afraid of them. Sun Yueqing hadn't thought that she'd be able to handle herself so well with the village officials, to not be fearful of them, but to answer their questions clearly and unequivocally and so articulately. The Party officials couldn't help but look on wide-eyed; they hadn't expected this at all. Weren't they supposed to be here to tease and torment the newlyweds?

Sun Yueqing then heard the steps of her eldest son. He had returned. Before he actually came into the room, however, his mother, in a barely audible voice, told him to invite the guests to stay for something to eat. In either case, whether they stayed late or left early, it wasn't going to be up to them. Cunxian half mumbled to himself that if these men really wanted to celebrate, then that could be arranged. He just worried that they might inadvertently be letting people with ill intentions into their house, and that was a bad omen indeed. Seeing her son so upset about having these guests here in their home, she thought to ask him why he was so reluctant, but she chose not to push the issue further. Besides, they were going to be sitting down with these men, talking. She'd take advantage of that fact and make dinner. Of course, they had to have noodles as they symbolised a long and happy marriage. As soon as the officials had arrived, she had already been thinking about what to feed them. Sorghum noodles would be the main dish; she'd mix them with sweet potato flour to increase their girth and make them easier to knead into longer strips. She'd add some corn flour too to make them a little whiter so they'd look like proper noodles.

Guo Cunxian lowered his head as he entered the eastern room, but it was clear to everyone there that he wasn't as happy as his new wife had been at seeing the Party officials. In truth, he seemed suspicious of why they had come and he couldn't get that thought out of his head. And so when he actually entered the room, he froze momentarily, unsure of what to do or say. The young cadres who had been relentlessly teasing his young, new wife also froze when they saw Guo Cunxian come into the room. In fact, the whole place seemed to grow silent and still. Even Secretary Chen just stared at Guo Cunxian, unable or unwilling to speak. Perhaps he was thinking that he had never really paid much attention to this boy who was, in truth, a boy no longer. No, he'd gone away and had got married. He was a man now. With his broad forehead, narrow nose and high cheekbones that curved down into his square chin, he was a man, indeed, full of confidence, or maybe it was pride. He hadn't nodded to his guests but rather acted almost as though he were the village head. Han Jingting immediately saw the worry in Guo Cunxian's face, the animosity. This was a quality of all the men in the Guo family; he'd seen it throughout Guo Cunxian's father's life. They were never cowed in front of anyone, not even the old masters of the town. Aware of the tension, Han Jingting spoke: "Cunxian, ah, what have you been doing? You've come back with such a lovely wife and you've hidden her at home, not inviting anyone round, not even for a drink."

"Ah... please, please, I'd like everyone to stay a little longer." It was then that Guo Cunxian suddenly realised that Lan Shoukun was nowhere to be seen, but he didn't know if this made him feel more relaxed, or more annoyed at the whole thing.

Had that prick not come because he felt bad about abusing Cunzhi, or was it because he still felt some hostility towards his family?

With the ice broken, Secretary Chen now spoke as well: "On such a happy occasion, how come you weren't at home when we first came? Where were you? If you hadn't come, we were planning to use the loudspeaker to make sure you came home immediately."

Somewhat embarrassed, Guo Cunxian lowered his head and explained: "I was out looking for some suitable earth to make bricks. Next year I need to extend this room and make two new ones. Since I've brought a wife home with me, I've pushed my uncle out into the storage shed. I just don't feel right about that."

Secretary Chen shook his head somewhat and clicked his tongue: "When all is said and done, you're Guo Jingshi's son. The energy you use on your uncle, no one can say anything about it, but life is about moving forward, taking one step and seeing the next two. Cunxian, ah, these past two years while you've been away working, well, they've enabled you to find a wife and to do all right for yourself. We've discussed it here in the village and we feel that now we have to do right by you and your new wife. Wherever you wish to go, you're free to do so. If you want to earn some money or work for food, that's fine too, we won't interfere. But you're here now with your wife and you should concentrate on the task at hand, enjoy the simple life, but don't forget to carefully consider the more important things. We've come here today for two reasons. The first is to celebrate your marriage. The second is a more serious matter. The unit leader will talk about that now, right, Han Jingting?"

Listening to Secretary Chen speak like this, Guo Cunxian became more serious, more attentive. Sure enough, the village had wanted to stop him from leaving, but they hadn't been able to, he'd left before they could, so what could they do now? He stood, staring at Han Jingting, waiting for him to speak. Just outside the room, Sun Yueqing and her two other children had also heard Secretary Chen's words. It was clear they were going to talk about something serious so they leaned closer to the wall, hoping to surreptitiously eavesdrop on what was about to be said. It seemed that Guo Cunxian had been right: people with ill intentions had indeed come.

Han Jingting was a model farmer. His manner of speaking was mild: "Presumably, this is all very straightforward. Your production team is in rather dire straits and quite disorganised. Take you, for instance. Well, when you felt like it, you just up and left, taking your skills and heading out onto the road to beg for food. If you hadn't… well, it's unlikely that our great sweet potato campaign last year would've turn out as bad as it did, we wouldn't have had to send Liu Yupu along with the cart and he wouldn't have ended up hanging himself. Do you know, over the course of the past two years we've had to change the unit leader three times? No one can do the job properly. Everyone has an opinion about this and no one is completely satisfied about the situation. And so, we've come here tonight to unanimously select you as the new unit leader. We believe that you can right this ship. That's Secretary Chen's opinion as well and the Party offices have already discussed this thoroughly."

Outside eavesdropping, Sun Yueqing couldn't help but pound her hand against her own breast. Her heart had turned to stone and she couldn't breathe. Cunzhi and Cunzhu were all smiles, vainly trying to cover their mouths with their hands. In the history of their family, no one had ever been tasked with such official responsibility, not before the Revolution, nor after. At least their family food rations would increase. After all, Guo Cunzhi was to be a government official now. This was more than Sun Yueqing could have imagined and reminded her of the songs she'd sung when her boys were young: "Oh my boy, grow up quick, grow up to be a leader and no more will your stomach ache!"

But inside the room, Guo Cunxian only laughed, a cold, acerbic, dissatisfied laugh.

Han Jingting was slow, sluggish. He hadn't expected such a reaction. Secretary Chen, on the other hand, was more confused than anything else. Using the authority of his position, he asked bluntly: "Guo Cunxian, just what are you laughing for?"

"Secretary, so many people have left our village over the years, why am I not allowed? Some leave to go and beg, but I went and sold my labour, not an easy thing to do, to try to earn my own way and do a little good. Besides, with me gone, it avoided further conflict and took away the opportunity for those with a grudge against me to come and stir up more trouble for my family. Asking me to be team leader now is nothing more than tethering me so that I can't leave again, anybody can see this. Let's be straight. I'm not saying that I haven't thought about being a team leader. I'm saying that I can't do it. I've enough on my plate taking care of my own family. How could I ever lead an entire unit! There are more than eighty households here and nearly five hundred mouths to feed. Shouldn't I be afraid of taking on the responsibility for all of them? So can I turn the job down, please?"

"Absolutely not!" Chen Baohuai stated emphatically. "If everyone thought the same as you, just what am I supposed to do, huh? Take my advice, don't look for trouble during what should be a joyous time, and don't refuse to say cheers when you'll only have to end up drinking the booze anyway. You don't really have a choice in the matter, there's no room for discussion. Listen to me, the authorities have already given us our orders. We're to mobilise a section of the population and move them to Qinghai in the west. Didn't you say you like to travel? Well then, I'll ensure that you travel pretty damn far. There aren't many people in Qinghai, you know. It'll be a harder life than here, for sure. So what do you think? Should I give your family that order?"

Just at that moment Sun Yueqing burst into the room and began excoriating her son: "Cunxian, don't provoke Secretary Chen any further, don't make him angry. There are many others who'd like to be given the chance you're being given but that'll never happen to them. How is it that you can bring face to our family and then take it away. Quickly, apologise to Secretary Chen!"

His mother jumping into the conversation allowed Guo Cunxian to step off the stage, at least for a moment. In truth, he wasn't dead set against taking on the job, he just wanted to make a good show of it, make it look as though he couldn't care less about the position. He wanted them to think about him, about how they had overlooked him in the past. And now that they wanted him, he would play hard to get. He didn't want to come across as desperate; that would only make him look bad in their eyes. Just what was Chen Baohuai playing at, in any case? Here he was, an important man in the Party. Was he being serious or was he just here to torment him? What was that common phrase? "A guilty team leader is punished by hard labour, an accountant is jabbed by his pen, a guard is burdened with carrying a steelyard weight, a Party secretary is punished by death." Thinking about this, Guo Cunxian realised he'd made a mistake that needed to be rectified as quickly as possible. The shit storm he'd just stirred up had to be cleaned up. Not only did he have to restore his mother's respect, he had to earn some face back for himself. Laughing somewhat bitterly, he pulled away from his mother, and at the same time shot a look towards Xuezhen.

"Mother," he said in a loud voice, "why have you come to think like this? Secretary Chen is not necessarily angry, I know he has arranged this new responsibility for me. All I've done is to exercise my right to voice my own concerns. I was only being honest. I didn't say I wouldn't do it. I just wondered if I was truly able to. Please, go into the kitchen and prepare the meal. I'll apologise to Secretary Chen, OK?"

Zhu Xuezhen took the opportunity to leave the room as well to help her mother-in-law out in the kitchen. With the women gone, Guo Cunxian again reiterated his concerns to Chen Baohuai and Han Jingting: "Although what you said, Secretary Chen, was serious, ominous even, I'm still hesitant. But that said, I certainly don't wish to bring hardship onto my family, and even if Qinghai isn't all that bad, I simply can't leave Guojiadian. I guess there's nothing for it, I'll take the job. But let me be frank, I've no kind of experience whatsoever. With that in mind, Secretary Chen, your advice would be most welcome."

Seeing Guo Cunxian humble himself in this manner allowed the simmering anger in Chen Baohuai to dissipate. He had asserted his authority, especially over Guo Cunxian and his new wife, and now the latter's skills were his so he was quite satisfied. But his face was still stern. In an imposing voice, he said: "I've selected you with the important task of cleaning up this commune, of straightening it out, and implementing a new policy directive issued by the central authorities. If you implement it fully and successfully, then you can be assured of eating well next year, whether you prepare in advance or not. But I warn you, right now, there isn't one man of ability, nor of initiative, in this entire place, so you'll have your work cut out. Don't waste the opportunity, don't end up causing more trouble."

"What policy?"

"Lease holding."

"Lease holding?"

"That's right. After all, isn't the land of the nation owned by the nation? Now, the government is going to take control of land resources and redistribute them via lease holds. And because each lot of land varies in size, the criteria by which the land redistribution will be determined will also vary. The county authorities have determined that every farmer will lend the government three to five *mu* of land, and since our village mediates this land redistribution, we've determined that each person will lend the government four *mu*."

Guo Cunxian thought to himself that if the government had determined the number to be between three and five *mu*, why had Secretary Chen said only four? Why not the full amount? But then he thought some more and realised that he'd just eased Chen's anger and so there was no need to start another row. Instead, he used his words to speak of a related matter: "How long will the land be leased for?"

"That hasn't yet been determined, but according to estimates, at least a year. You also need to ensure that the farmers who work the leasehold prepare a second crop for rotation as well."

"Will those who lend their land be entitled to a share of crops in return?"

"No."

"Can the leaseholders plant whatever they wish?"

"Yes, their lease, their land, so they'll be in control."

"Whether the land is good or fallow, far or near, do the authorities have some rules for how the land is to be redistributed?"

"Each team will determine this according to their own internal decisions and planning. The key is not to spoil something that is good and end up provoking the ire of the population."

"This sounds like an excellent policy, a great initiative indeed!" Guo Cunxian whispered to himself. His mind was already racing, working out ways to implement the policy and devote all his strength to it.

Around the same time as Guo Cunxian returned home with his new wife, the village also welcomed back a member of another household, the younger son of the Jin family. But unlike Guo Cunxian's warm welcome, no one came to greet Jin Laixi. In truth, no one at first really noticed him at all and that's what he was hoping for. He'd rather return unannounced than have the villagers make a fuss. But hopes are just that, hopes, and concealing his homecoming proved to be short-lived, for not long after he returned home with his wife, the whole focus of the town shifted to them and rumours began to swirl. Some said he'd got into trouble, others said he'd broken the law; some said he'd been expelled from the city and some went so far as to say that he'd been escorted home by the police themselves but, whatever the rumours said, the message was clear: trouble was brewing.

As for the other members of the Jin family, Jin Laixi's older brother was in fact an unremarkable man, a well-known, if easily forgotten, bare stick. And if people talked about him, well, he didn't seem to care, and perhaps that's why his ears were so often full. But no matter what the case may be, it didn't seem to make much difference to Jin Laixi's older brother. He seemed to take it all in his stride and, besides, it's not like any of the villagers would try to explain their animosity. And as for Jin Laixi, well, his homecoming had been required by government policy: everyone across the nation had been ordered to return to their place of birth. It's hard to say if this policy was due to the problems faced by those who lived in the cities, or due to the desolation of the land but, whatever the case may have been, for everyone these were simply troublesome times. Ah, but who wants to listen to this and, even if they do, who would trust their own ears? Nah, that would only make things worse.

Since ancient times, there'd always been a city located not too far from the town of Guojiadian. In fact, the city itself was primarily populated by former villagers, those who had headed off to sea, so to speak, to try and make a better life. So it was strange, then, that no one had noticed that one of them had been made to leave. Ah, but saying this is only one part of the problem that was to come. A wealthy peasant would never identify themselves as such. No, when people encountered an unexpected situation, their minds invariably turned to dark thoughts.

As the day began to grow dark, so too did the rooms in the Jin family house, and as the darkness enveloped their home, not a single lamp was lit, or rather, they chose not to. After all, miserable faces seldom want to look upon the same. The only sounds that could be heard in the darkened chambers were the mournful sighs of despair. Reclining at the foot of the bed was Jinlai, the elder, and as yet unmarried, brother. At the other end sat Jin Laixi, the youngest who'd recently been expelled from Tianjin. Nearby was his wife Mi Xiujun. All three sat motionless, struggling to think of something to say, lost in their own individual stupors. As the silence grew nearly unbearable, each began to take turns trying to speak, but whatever they said ended up dying in their throats after only a few words were uttered. All three seemed overwhelmed by their predicament.

Guojiadian, oh, how did this town end up with such a name? Why hadn't anyone ever asked about the origin of this name? Perhaps, when the village was first founded, a family by the name of Guo had had an important and large presence in the area, or maybe the local court official had had the name Guo, and thus he'd named the town? Who's to say, but one thing is for certain – fortunes rise and fall.

When the government land reforms were first enacted, the name Guo couldn't be touched. Attention thus shifted to other families, other targets. There was the landlord name Liu but, due to the recent past, that name couldn't be touched either. No, another, more suitable name had to be found, and so attention was soon directed towards the Jins. For the other residents in Guojiadian, this might be considered good fortune but not for the Jins. And as for the Guos, there was talk about the fact that a certain Guo was serving as the village head, and that he'd shown an expected partiality towards his family name. There was talk, too, of them once being part of the landlord class, or of the rich peasant class, but that such information had been clandestinely removed from the village registers. As for other names, if there were any issues with their papers, their background, then those would be immediately scrutinised. All this resulted in Guojiadian becoming even poorer. That is, if there weren't any landlords, nor even rich peasants, but only the poorest of the poor, then it didn't really sound like a village at all. After all, who'd exploit whom? And if there wasn't any exploitation, then were there really any social classes? Indeed, if there weren't any landlords or rich peasants, how were poor and lower middle classes to be distinguished in the first place?

Jin Laixi's luck couldn't be considered all bad. When he was younger and family histories weren't so strictly monitored and queried, he'd accompanied a relative to the county city where he'd pull a horse-drawn cart. He eventually ended up in Tianjin as an unskilled labourer where he'd carry out all sorts of jobs from disposing of human waste to loading and unloading roof tiles. Later, he was hired by a construction company to make mud roof tiles, joining the proletarian class of urban workers. For many years he worked diligently at his job, and also at finding a fellow worker to marry and start a family with. He finally did and married a girl from Jihe County in Shandong. His older brother, Jin Laiwang, had no skills whatsoever and so had no means of leaving Guojiadian. All he could do was remain in the village and carry on the family legacy of being a rich peasant. Of course, that meant he never found a wife. But you couldn't say that that was necessarily unfair. In the old days only poor men would go through life without getting married, and so there was a certain justice to this now being the curse of the rich. Although there were still both rich and poor who ended up as bare sticks, that's not to say they were the same. Jin Laiwang was a rich peasant bare stick, and that was considerably lower. Now, however, Jin Laixi was in the same boat. He had had to return home and now he too would be a second-class peasant, forced to work under the supervision of the lower middle classes. Or perhaps his position wouldn't be the same as his brother's and he wouldn't be a bare stick, especially an old one. There was still someone to show him sympathy, to play with, to make a little ruckus. Every village has its unwritten rules, and in every household they all had to yield to the bare stick.

Jin Laixi tried to predict his future, but the more he did the more he realised it was short of good prospects. If it weren't for his lack of ambition, then he'd even have considered death! But if he wanted to die, he couldn't do that in Guojiadian. No, if he were to die he had to do it in Tianjin, right in front of the gate to the construction company he had worked for. Nevertheless, he didn't really wish to die; that would truly be an offence, a violation. And, in any case, he'd end up being forced to come back and make amends, or something like that. To be frank, it's not really like that at all, more like being sent to a labour camp to be re-educated. From this day onwards, he had to be especially careful about what he said. Actually, it was better to say as little as possible so as not to give them even more ammunition. The best thing to do was to keep his head down, stay out of sight and give them no reason to take notice of him, then they wouldn't come looking for him. Was this what the authorities had planned? A seeping blood poison?

Jin Laixi grew ever more anxious. He didn't want to end up like his big brother but he couldn't help worrying more than him. For so many years he'd yearned to be the 'big brother', the pride of the Jin family, but now this. And Jin Laiwang didn't even seem all that bothered about being a 'second-class bare stick'. He had, after all, a little brother who was a labourer in the city which had helped protect his heart and harden it; he'd even felt as though he were a little better off than the rest of the village. Especially at New Year and other festivities, Laixi would return for a visit, bringing with him all kinds of things from the city. This all helped Laiwang earn some face in the village. He couldn't help but take his little brother for a walk around the whole town, making sure everyone knew that he worked in the city and had come for a visit. Laiwang had also twice been to Tianjin to see his brother, and when he returned he always brought with him goodies from the city – fruit, fried rice cakes and other sorts of sweets. If there was a family that had something going on, some celebration or other, he'd be sure to send round some fruit. They would, of course, smile at him in response, which pleased him immensely. It must be said that it wasn't all that easy for him to get this kind of friendly, warm reaction from the other villagers, and even then most of the smiles weren't really accompanied with much kindness. Such was his fate. And now, to make matters worse, his brother had been forced to return home and he too would suffer the ignominy of being a second-class peasant. The Jins were ruined!

Jin Laiwang suddenly mumbled: "First, I need to tell you, every day we're only given two to three rations. You'll probably find that quite unbearable, I know. But I should say, too, that it's better not to even eat them all in one day, no, much better to save one or two for later. I mean, you two will have a child soon. How are you to convalesce after childbirth if you don't have anything to eat?"

A moment of deep silence passed between them, but Jin Laixi didn't respond, not seeming to know what to say. Finally, his brother's wife Mi Xiujun spoke, trying to reassure her brother-in-law: "Dear Brother, you don't need to worry about me like that. When the time comes, just ask for my mother to come from Shandong. She'll be able to take care of me."

"I dare say that'd be great..." His voice trailed off. In his mind he wondered, if her family did come, whether that'd only make things harder. How would they feed yet another mouth? There was something else, too, that weighed heavily on the hearts of all three of them, but no one wanted to be the first to break the calm. Right now all three of them were squatting in a two-room house. It had been given to him to use as part of the land reform, and when it was just him, it was all right: he'd sleep in the inner room and cook in the outer one. But now that Jin Laixi had returned, and had brought a wife with him, well, he had no choice, really, he had to give them the inner room and set up a small bedding mat for himself to use in the outer room. Oh, but how was he going to manage that? To make matters worse, he couldn't really say anything to his younger brother and his sister-in-law; that would be too much. But with a bedding mat in the outer room, whenever anyone came in or went out they'd have to walk by it, this poor old mat for an unmarried uncle, a bare stick. And in the summer, when it was hot, he'd only be wearing a flimsy shirt to cover himself, or sometimes nothing at all... oh, can't fate be so cruel? The key, of course, would be how both he and his brother dealt with the cards they'd been given and would they be able to manage it together or would they be better off separate? Perhaps they were all already thinking about splitting up but who would dare bring this up?

"You two rest now, I'll be back in a little bit." Jin Laixi, who had remained silent up to this point, suddenly got up and left.

Dark as it was, how would Laixi be able to see where he was going? And with his younger brother gone, how was he supposed to rest here with his sister-in-law, just the two of them? At a loss, Jin Laiwang got down from the bed and clumsily followed after his younger brother.

Finally the Party members left and Guo Cunxian no longer needed to carry on acting the way he had. He no longer needed to pretend to be neither too happy, nor too morose, neither too toadying, nor too overbearing. In short, he could relax and let the excitement over his new prospects wash over him. He spent the next while simply pacing back and forth, mulling over the opportunity he had been given, his chance to take centre stage, or at least centre stage in the village; after all, he wasn't going to eat like an emperor but he was going to be close to the centre of power in Guojiadian. In the past, a changeover in leadership meant merely thrusting power onto someone and then walking away, so to speak. This time, however, they were going to be watching, observing how he was going to use that power. Take for instance the evening's 'celebration'. He had estimated the weight of the village head's words and had been able to change the way the village authorities looked at his family. No longer were they uninterested in them, in fact, he had become one of them, and from this day onwards if anything happened to any of them, he'd be able to search out the village head directly, and if someone tried to hinder or impede his family, even in private, well, that wouldn't be all that easy any more. Thinking these things over, he couldn't help but feel a little flushed.

In the outer room, Xuezhen was busily washing and cleaning. She hadn't waited to be told, she had simply started tidying up. Once the men had left and Sun Yueqing realised what Xuezhen was doing, she told her to head back to her room. She didn't want her to get tired washing up and she fussed over her saying that Xuezhen didn't need to dirty her hands with cleaning; such was the depth of feeling she had for her new daughter-in-law. As soon as Xuezhen stepped into their room, Guo Cunxian's arms immediately wrapped around her and motioned her to the bed. Gently and affectionately, he lifted Xuezhen onto his lap. Before she had a chance to smile at his warmness, his lips were on hers, kissing her passionately, like a starving man relishes a fresh meal. She didn't dare try to hold back his passion, at least not out loud, embarrassed that her mother-in-law might hear, so she balled up her fist and pushed it gently into the back of his neck, urging him to slow down, to relent. Her actions, however, only spurred him on, and he clenched his arms around her even more tightly. It seemed as though her mouth was not enough to satisfy him; his passion only grew. Slowing giving in, her body became softer, more willing and pliable. Guo Cunxian responded in kind. His manhood swelling, he slid between her legs. With one hand he loosened her trousers and pulled them down, then straightened his back and thrust. Her eyes closed in both pain and pleasure, the heat of his body pressed against her, she soon felt him inside.

When she felt his energy subside, she nibbled at his ear, rebuking him gently: "What's wrong, you've had enough?"

"I've married such a beautiful woman... do you think I could ever have enough? Didn't you see the men around the dinner table tonight, how they looked at you with ravenous eyes?"

"The lights haven't gone out in the other room yet, how about we wait a while?"

"I can't, don't you know I'm mad about you! You're like a treasure to me. Oh my adorable wife, I think you've brought me good fortune. Now that I'm the team leader I can't just go off any time I please to make a little money, but it does mean that I'll be able to spend more time at home with you. I'd just hate to have to leave you here by yourself." As he spoke these soft, tender, sweet words in her ear, his arms moved tightly behind her waist as he thrust himself into her deeper and deeper. Xuezhen soon felt a flood of passion wash over her, wave after wave crashed over her as her body trembled with an indescribable ecstasy.

As she was cleaning the dishes, Sun Yueqing couldn't help but hear the noise emanating from the other room. When she first heard it, she turned to Cunzhi and Cunzhu and told them to go quickly to their room. She remained in the kitchen, silent. Time passed and the sounds grew calmer. Still she waited, silently, listening as Cunxian got up and went to lock the main door, carrying the chamber pot with him. It was then that she finally left the western room. She thought of the family's old bare stick, Guo Jingshi. When they had been eating earlier Cunzhi had not been able to call for him to join them, the reason being plain, his disposition just wouldn't have matched well with the village cadres that had come; they would never have been able to eat at the same table together. People could say he was crazy, that he was a fool, but in Sun Yueqing's heart she understood, there was a certain affability to his madness, a certain carefulness to it. He was afraid that they would resent his shabbiness, dislike him, and this would cause his sister-in-law, his family, to lose face.

Guo Jingshi was unlike many of the other bare sticks in the village. Ever since Sun Yueqing had joined the Guo family, she had never seen him just lounge about like so many other bare sticks. He was always out and about, always off doing something or other. Thinking back on dinner, she realised she should go and look for him. There was still some food left in the pot that she could at least warm up for him. She picked up some firewood and walked off towards the southern room but when she walked into it, she immediately knew that he wasn't there, even without lighting the lamp. She looked around, lit the lamp, and looked some more. The room looked unlived in, even though it had been cleaned up and made ready for him after Guo Cunxian had returned. She cursed herself for the fact that for the past two days she'd been so preoccupied with Cunxian and Xuezhen that she hadn't thought about poor, unmarried Guo Jingshi, her brother-in-law who'd gone his entire life without a wife. Perhaps he'd gone off somewhere to hide, worried that he would have disrupted the festive atmosphere surrounding Cunxian's return if he had stayed? So many people had come by these past two days. Perhaps he hadn't wanted anyone to see him, hadn't wanted them to feel uncomfortable?

The more she thought about it, the more worried she became. She quickly returned to the western room in order to instruct Cunzhi to go out and look for him. The only problem was that when she entered the room, Cunzhi was already fast asleep. She leaned in close to try and wake him, urging him to get up. But before he could open his eyes, Cunxian walked into the room and asked what was the matter.

Plaintively, she replied: "Your uncle hasn't come home for dinner and now it's so late and he's still not back. I was trying to wake up Cunzhi to go and look for him."

"There's no need, I'll go."

His mother opposed him going; he'd been through so much these last few days: "No, no, you rest, Cunzhi can go."

"He won't be able to find him, I should go." Guo Cunxian had already become the head of the family. The tone in his voice exuded a confidence that hadn't been there before. "I also want to talk to my uncle. There are a few things I'd like to discuss with him. If he's unhappy with the sleeping arrangements as they are now, then he can bring his bedding back into the eastern room. Xuezhen likes him. The two of them have really hit it off."

Listening to her oldest son speak like this put her mind at ease. In the past, her children hadn't really shown much care towards their uncle, but over the last half year things had changed. Nevertheless, there was firmness in her voice when she spoke: "I'm sure your uncle won't go for that, he won't stay in the room with you two. Originally, Cunzhu and I were going to stay in the southern room and Cunzhi and your uncle were going to take the western room, but your uncle wouldn't have it. He insisted on moving into the shed. I think you're missing the fact that he wants his own sort of freedom, his own space to do with as he wishes. All right, you go and look for him this time but remember what I've said... start with the tree, that's probably where he is"

"OK, but you go and rest, I'll be sure to bring him back."

Taking hold of his mother's shoulders, he guided her into her room and returned to his own. As he entered it, he saw Xuezhen sitting up. He moved close and cupped her cheeks in his hands, speaking quietly: "You sleep first. I have to go and look for my uncle."

"We'll go together."

"You're not tired? After all that... hard work, it's best to rest, isn't it? I'm sure you'll sleep like a baby."

"Eh, you're just full of yourself now, aren't you." She smiled. "If I'm tired it's your fault, so when I can't walk any more, you'll just have to carry me... you've got the strength for sure." She smiled suggestively.

"Oh, but is that really worth the bother? Me carrying you won't be as nice as lying down here, that's for sure."

"But I've been here now for several days and I haven't left the house. Let's take this opportunity when no one else is about. I can get a little fresh air and you can show me around this town of yours, especially those two big trees."

Guo Cunxian loved listening to her talk like this. She seemed somewhat childlike, as though she were about to throw a tantrum, which only made him love her more. Feeling invigorated by her words, he replied: "OK then, let me take you on my back and let's go and explore Guojiadian."

As they stepped outside, they were greeted by the darkness of the night. The air was heavy with not a star in the sky, to say nothing of the moon. It was pitch black and quiet. The villagers had been starving for years now and they had already eaten almost every animal that would come out in the dark. Guojiadian was thus quiet at night, deathly quiet. In truth, this wasn't too different from when the sun shone overhead. The people had been without food for so very long that there were very few left that had the energy to do anything more than lie about in bed, motionless, day and night. When the moon failed to even shine its light on the village, well, that only made the people even more unwilling to get up off their beds. And so when night fell, doors would be closed and the village would continue to remain silent and still.

Guo Cunxian held on to Xuezhen's hand, bent over and gingerly lifted her onto his back. Comfortably, Xuezhen wrapped her arms around his neck, her chin pressed against his shoulders, and she smiled happily. As they moved at an unhurried pace through the darkness, their eyes grew more accustomed to the dark, so much so that it seemed less and less impenetrable. Soon they were able to make out different shapes in the shadows, to see the rough outlines of the buildings, and so Guo Cunxian began to describe the village to her now that her eyes could at least see it to some degree. As he watched where he placed his feet, he turned to tell her about Guojiadian. Xuezhen had questions of her own, but not necessarily about the town itself.

"You're getting tired, aren't you?"

"I can't say I'm really tired but it wouldn't be true to say that I'm not at least a little tired."

Xuezhen smiled again. She couldn't help but love her husband deeply and so she got down from his back. But Guo Cunxian still held onto her hand tightly to ensure she didn't stumble and trip on the unfamiliar roads. As they walked, he told her the story of the Dragon Phoenix Trees. Enthralled by the tale, she hardly noticed at first that they had arrived at their base. And there in the darkness a shadow seemed to be encircling the trees, strolling around it. Apart from his mad uncle, who in the village would dare come to the trees in the middle of the night? Guo Cunxian called out into the night: "Uncle, is that you?"

The shadow stopped immediately, almost as though it were surprised. Then it hurriedly came towards them. By the way the shadow carried itself he could see that it wasn't his uncle. Xuezhen quickly let go of her husband's hand. When the shadow drew close it extended a right hand and spoke in a rather crisp voice: "It's Cunxian, isn't it? I've just been sent back from Tianjin. It's me, Jin Laixi."

Taken aback by the revelation, almost mechanically Guo Cunxian reached out his own hand and took the one offered. His voice, however, failed him at first as he was unsure of what to say. Then, when he regained a measure of composure, he replied: "I heard about your arrival earlier today. I guess it's true what they say. It doesn't matter how hard you might've worked, if the authorities tell you that you have to return, then that's what you have to do, hey?"

Jin Laixi let out a troubled sigh. This was something he didn't wish to talk about but it seemed as though there was no way around it; everyone he met asked him about it. "Heh, well, what's to be done? We're not worth anything. You know, every villager could become a worker, but it wouldn't matter. We're like old smelly socks. Once we're used up, we're just discarded."

Guo Cunxian was quite furious at his remarks: "Hmph, if city folk are told to return to the land and become farmers, what about us farmers, huh? Are we to be sent to work camps to become criminals? And if not that, then what? Send us to the great northwest as conscripted soldiers? Where's the sense in that!"

That was enough, nothing more needed to be said. Jin Laixi turned in the direction of Xuezhen in an effort to change the topic. In the darkness he couldn't quite make out her face, but he seemed to want to, especially as he could clearly see her figure: "It goes without saying, I suppose, but you must be the young lady that has set the town alight, hmm?"

Guo Cunxian made the introductions: "Xuezhen, forgive my manners, this is Jin Laixi."

Jin fumbled through his pockets before replying in a somewhat embarrassed manner: "I didn't think I'd bump into you two this evening, I haven't brought anything with me. Tomorrow I'll come by your place to properly congratulate you on your wedding."

Guo Cunxian waved his hands deprecatingly. "No, no, that's not necessary. We've already finished our celebrations. We don't need any more."

"Ah, but you've begun something here tonight, you're like the young lovers in the city who go out for evening strolls along the streets."

Even in the darkness Xuezhen couldn't help but feel embarrassed. Guo Cunxian laughed: "That's not bad, heh, but we don't have streets here in the village, just dirt roads. Hey, when you first came here to the Dragon Phoenix Trees, did you see my uncle?"

"Oh, you mean that crazy... um, Uncle Jingshi? When I first walked here I did see someone but I couldn't be sure who. Whoever it was walked off before I arrived, heading towards the north of the village."

"All right then, enjoy your stroll, we'll head north and keep looking for him." Taking hold of his wife's hand once again, they started to walk away. Before they'd taken a couple of steps, Jin Laixi called after them: "Cunxian, would you like me to come with you and help look for your uncle?"

Guo Cunxian responded without even really thinking: "No, that's all right."

Still, Jin Laixi called out after them, this time in an even louder voice: "Cunxian, I can't change the past but I have returned to Guojiadian to stay. I guess there's something to be thankful for in that. In any case, I will have to trouble you before long with some things that need taking care of."

Guo Cunxian stopped and turned round: "If you hadn't said anything, I would've forgotten about it. Well, you've come at a good time, the government has decided to lease out land. Come to the work unit offices tomorrow. I've already got a plan in mind that I want to discuss with everyone."

"Oh..." Jin Laixi didn't think it wise to probe further. The tone of Guo Cunxian's voice had a certain authority to it, as though he were in charge. It was probably best not to say anything more.

As Jin Laixi remained silent, Guo Cunxian thought of something else: "Ah yes, Brother Jin, in the spring I'm planning to build two new rooms. When the time comes I guess I'll have to ask for your help, won't I... given your experience and all."

Jin Laixi's heart jumped. Guo Cunxian's words had inadvertently brought something to mind, had made him see an opportunity in front of him. He couldn't forget that he did have these skills and while Guojiadian certainly wasn't a city, there were people who needed builders: houses had to be made, bricks for beds and stoves laid, pig enclosures, chicken coops... if a household needed such work to be done, then he could surely do it, or at least help out. He could be the architect, the construction worker, available day and night, no job too big, no job too small. He had to make it so that they wouldn't dare not to ask him, and over time, this might be the best way to win the townspeople over, or at least to make himself indispensable, so that they had to ask him for help with these kinds of projects. He knew it couldn't go back to how it was before but could this be a way for him to earn the villagers' respect and make a happy life for himself and his family? If he could start off on the right foot with Guo Cunxian, who obviously held some sway in the village, then perhaps, just perhaps, and with his help, he could open some of the doors blocking his way, or at least make it a little easier to do so.

With these thoughts racing through his mind, Jin Laixi yelled out in response, his voice aping as much sincerity as possible: "Of course, that goes without saying. You're a carpenter, I'm a bricklayer. They both go together to make an excellent team. I guess you could say that we're inseparable, hand in hand we can take on any job."

"You're spot on. So tomorrow morning, make sure you come." Turning round once more, Guo Cunxian and Xuezhen walked off towards the north of the village, but he couldn't help but feel a little apprehensive. To the north it was just open land. Where was he supposed to find his uncle in all of that, especially in the dark? A sense of dread started to come over him. He felt they couldn't just go groping around in the night looking for his uncle. If they did, they'd end up looking until daybreak. As they walked, a light breeze picked up that brought a slight coolness to the air.

It was that time of year when things were sweltering, when there was no rain and even less moisture in the air. But then, as they walked, the silence of the night was split open by the sudden chirping of insects. The heaviness of the evening seemed to break. Guo Cunxian's mind returned to the words Jin Laixi had just spoken... he let go of Xuezhen's hand and, thinking of the young city lovers, he wrapped his arm around her waist. This felt much better, and if he wished, he could steal a kiss on her neck. Even if they didn't find his uncle, the evening walk wasn't bad at all.

The evening walk was also ideal for telling stories, and while they had been out looking for his uncle, he remembered now that he hadn't told Xuezhen the entire tale; only enough, in fact, to stoke Xuezhen's curiosity in her husband's uncle even more. Guo Cunxian asked her why she seemed to care so much for him, to want them to be close. He wondered why she wasn't afraid of his madness and repulsed by his filth, as so many others were. Xuezhen could only respond by saying she didn't know why. All she knew was she didn't fear him, nor was she sickened by him. In fact, she quite liked his eyes; they were so unique, special, and when they looked at her, she could easily see his gentleness. All she wanted was to take his clothes and wash them, to do the same for him, from head to toe.

As they talked, they made sure to look everywhere. But on such a dark night, they could not rely solely on their eyes, they had to use their ears too, and it was Xuezhen who heard it first. Then Guo Cunxian heard it almost immediately – a sound quite unlike the insects that had broken the silence of the evening. They followed the sound forward and as they drew near the sound became clearer. They realised then that it was the sound of a man, curled up on the barren, wild land, snoring ever so loudly. His uncle hadn't run away this time.

Guo Cunxian removed his arm from around Xuezhen's waist and pulled her quickly forward. They had come upon a small stone bridge that spanned the northern swamp. It stood about half a metre high and a third of a metre wide. It was often used as a rest spot for those who had been working all day, or as a place to wait for a friend. Over time and due to some wear and tear, it had gained a certain dignified character. And there upon it lay his mad uncle Jingshi, reclining contentedly with his face towards the sky, his black leather shoes serving as a pillow.

Guo Cunxian felt a weight on his heart. It was difficult seeing his uncle like this, difficult because Xuezhen was there next to him. He didn't know whether to cry or laugh. He leaned over his uncle and gently tried to wake him: "Uncle, get up, please. What would happen if you rolled off the bridge, huh?"

Guo Jingshi, at first dazed at being woken up, finally responded: "Is there any water beneath me? If I fall off, then I'll just climb back up."

Xuezhen was fearful now: "But you might fall and break something... what then?"

His mad uncle looked at her: "If I could fall and hurt myself, where then am I to sleep? But I haven't fallen, have I? Us old gaffers aren't like you young kids, we're not so easy to break, you know."

Guo Cunxian was growing frustrated: "But there's a nice bed for you at home, isn't there? Why do you keep putting yourself in danger?"

"But it's nice and pleasant here, peaceful, comfortable... just breathe in for a second, you'll feel it too... compared with home, well, isn't this much nicer? Hmph, you just don't understand."

"Oh please just come home with us. Mother is worried sick about you, and if you aren't keen on staying in the southern room, that's fine, you take the eastern room and Xuezhen and I will take yours."

"You wretch, don't you dare try to insult me. Looking at me like this how can you even talk about some room or other, sleeping in a bed, huh?"

Xuezhen moved forward and helped support him: "Come on, Uncle, let's go, you haven't even eaten, have you?"

"Eaten, hah, I've eaten better than you... hmph. Do you think if I'd been hungry I wouldn't have returned?" In a wholly relaxed and unhurried manner the old man slowly put on his shoes and stood up, all the while looking longingly at the bridge beneath him, seemingly sad to leave it. "Your mother is something, isn't she? How could she make the two of you come out looking for me?"

"I was afraid Cunzhi wouldn't be able to find you, and even if he did, I didn't think he'd be able to get you to come home." As they spoke, both he and Xuezhen each took an arm to support Guo Jingshi. Together they headed back towards the village. Guo Cunxian then thought to take advantage of this free moment to ask him something, to get his take on a subject that had weighed on his mind: "Uncle, regardless of what others may say, we all know you've quite a keen mind. These past two years I've been away, the family has relied on you. If they hadn't, who's to say something bad wouldn't have happened, like last year when Cunzhi got into trouble."

Mad Uncle Jingshi uttered not a sound, instead allowing himself to be half carried, half pulled along by both of them.

As they walked, Guo Cunxian tried to talk to his uncle again: "Uncle, over these many years, my heart has been burdened with a heavy weight. You were once a well-kept, upright individual, but you changed into what you are now. Of course, we don't know why. But now tonight, when there isn't anyone around except for us, your nephew and his new wife who would so much like to be close to you, well, can you tell us the secret, tell us how you've come to this?"

Guo Cunxian waited patiently in silence for a response, but none was forthcoming.

Changing the topic, he spoke again: "Uncle, I need to ask you something else. Earlier today Secretary Chen and several other important cadres from the commune came to our house and offered me the position of fourth unit team leader. Do you think I should do it?"

Before the words were out of his mouth, his uncle replied: "If I were to say you shouldn't do it, would you really listen and not do it? Ah, if your heart is telling you to do it, then do it, that's what it means to be a team leader."

Guo Cunxian's heart skipped a beat.

Guo Jingshi felt as though he were being carried along by two strangers and he felt increasingly uneasy. He continued to speak, trying to untangle himself from their embrace: "I don't feel like walking along with you at this snail's pace. You go on by yourselves, take your time and watch where you're walking. I'll go ahead on my own." As he finished speaking he slipped away from their hands and before they understood what he was doing, he had disappeared into the night without a trace.

. . .

Since the famine had hit, the commune's fourth unit hadn't had such a well organised and planned meeting. The entire meeting area was filled with people, with the late stragglers being forced to stand just outside the gates. Guo Cunxian was terribly excited; he couldn't help but believe that the hubbub was all due to him being named the unit's new leader.

But in this he was mistaken. The changeover in leaders had occurred more than once, in fact, it had happened over and over again, so much so that the people were quite unconcerned with whomever was newly selected to lead them. They had come today not to witness the change in command, but rather for the redistribution of land. In private many said this was the first instance of small-scale land reform, some called it the second. The first national land reform had been quite the event compared with this: every household had received a plot of land, and then, when collectivisation was enacted, that was quite the event as well, as household after household all returned the plots they had been given. Now they were going to each get land to till for themselves once again. The question was: how much land were they were to be given? How was that going to be decided? And what land were they going to get? Of course, everyone was greatly interested in how all of this was going to play out. People without their own land, well, that's the same as people without a soul; their whole lives would lack certainty. There's an old saying: "The land gives life to a man, and when that man dies, his body returns to feed it."

Because of the great crowd of people, Guo Cunxian thought to move everyone directly into the fields, or to the foot of the Dragon Phoenix Trees in order to have the meeting there. But the more he thought about it, the more he realised that that wouldn't be appropriate either. This was his unit now and he didn't want any other units to know what they were discussing. He wanted to avoid overly nosey people reporting back to the authorities, giving them an excuse to intervene as that would only prevent him from carrying out his own plan. From inside one of the rooms he pulled out a wooden bench and stood on top of it, immediately raising himself above the crowd. He scanned the faces of all the people who had come and felt a shiver of nervousness pass through him. This was the first time he had had to speak in front of such a large crowd and, what's more, from this day forward, whether things were good or bad, whether they had food and drink to fill their bellies or whether they starved, whether they had children or not, all of this would depend upon him. Thinking of this, his mind raced and his heart beat faster, heightening his excitement of standing in front of so many people, causing his face to grow taut and his angular features to become more pronounced. His lips trembled as he began to speak, but the sound of his voice was strange and unfamiliar to him: "Attention, attention everyone, enough milling about."

The courtyard grew silent almost immediately and their faces turned towards him. He saw curiosity and expectation in their eyes. The looks on their faces increased his feelings of excitement, as well as his courage. His voice became much clearer, more fluent, more rehearsed: "We're all aware that the quality of our land isn't all that great. There's too much salt in it, for starters. But I remember the *Earth Song* from when I was young and any decent farmer knows what it means. We're all connected to the yellow earth, our roots go deep into the land. Fertile soil has to be ploughed, for if the weather grows cold, it will only harden and blow away with the wind. But when the sun shines too much and the air is aflame, the land will burn. Only by carefully tending it will it yield its rewards. When it's fat we plant our seeds and care for them like our children. But misuse the land and we bring certain ruin. Our lot is to take care of it, to turn it over and over again, shifting the earth into the earth."

"Oh ho!" came a noise from the crowd, followed by a holler: "Just what kind of meeting is this, huh? Have we come to the theatre? Have we come to watch a show?"

With a notebook in one hand, Guo Cunxian used his free hand to pound upon it. Then, raising his voice, he spoke over the crowd, trying to maintain control of the meeting: "What I've said and what I will say soon cannot be shared beyond our unit. If anyone speaks of it to outsiders, the central authorities themselves will punish you, and I can guarantee you the first thing they'll do is take away your land. Now, why have I said this? Why have I recited the *Earth Song* for you? To be frank, my aim is to ensure the smooth implementation of my plan. I want us to remember the importance of the land, how we need to take care of it, and if we do, it'll take care of us and we won't go hungry again."

The courtyard grew quiet once more and Guo Cunxian continued: "Village rules state that each household is to lease four *mu* of land, but considering what we have is less than ideal, and that most of it is located in the northern swamp and overly salty, I haven't yet been able to come up with the most suitable plan. So, I've been thinking, if we take the fertile land that's closest to the village, it's not really sufficient and there wouldn't really be a way to properly divide it up, would there? Then how about going a little farther afield, that way we could get four or five *mu*. So is that a little fairer?"

In a clear and resonant voice the gathering of people responded: "That's fair, yes, definitely that's fair!"

"That's why Cunxian is to be the team leader!"

"He's got all the makings of a government official. Yes, since he has been given this responsibility, he's a new man. Perhaps there's hope for us after all."

Guo Cunxian wrapped his hand around the notebook again: "Since everyone feels that this is the fairest way to proceed, before we finish the meeting we'll all draw straws. Whichever straw is drawn will determine the land that we use. Now listen carefully, this land is life. Once it comes into your hands you're free to plant whatever you wish. But I need to tell you something first, something unpleasant. From this day forward, from morning until night, rain or shine, you're only to work on your own plot of land when all the other work for the unit has been done. You're not permitted to shirk your duties to the unit in order to plant your own crops. After all, we're all part of the collective, there're no individuals here, but I'm sure you all know and understand this, yes? If anyone decides not to adhere to this, well then that's a crime, of course, the most serious punishment being the confiscation of your land. It's nearly the fifteenth of July, I've heard that planting at this time guarantees a good crop, one that'll be ready to harvest a month later, and that the land is at its best. Now I know you've all seen what the land is like, yes? Uncultivated, dry and desolate. And I know your bellies are empty and that you haven't really got the energy to go and work the fields, but I say never say die, heaven won't block our way. After so many years of hardship, good times will come. Otherwise we'll all end up in the ground and who'll worship heaven then, huh? I'm confident about the year ahead, I have faith things will be better, so let's clench our teeth now and bear it, for when we harvest what we plant we'll have more than enough to fill our bellies and energy to spare, right? Today we divide up the land, tomorrow we all head to the fields to work. Are you with me?"

Their hearts nearly bursting, the crowd shouted out a resounding, "Yes!" It had been so long since they had a clear sense of meaning to their lives. In the past, it didn't seem to matter what was planned, no one really took it to heart to try their best. But this time was different. Guo Cunxian had tapped into hidden reserves, into a power that lay buried under the surface.

Once the meeting was adjourned, Guo Cunxian instructed the villagers to draw lots and, once they were done, they would divide up the land. Regardless of whose land was being given to whom, or if some households ended up with a little more than others, no one would draw attention to it. After all, if there wasn't a household that the extra land could be conveniently given to, they'd have to repeat the whole process of dividing up the land again, something no one wanted to do, and so they left things as they were. In any case, this is how things had always been done. For instance, if you were given some cooking oil, usually the person ladling it out would end up giving you an extra ladleful, or if you were buying seeds you'd end up with a little extra; just like if you went to the market to buy some fabric, you'd nearly always end up with a few more inches than you had asked for. Here now they were dividing up land, and they weren't even selling it, they were 'leasing' it, so a few extra yards shouldn't make any difference.

It didn't matter that Guo Cunxian had exhorted them all to keep this plan confidential to their work unit; that just wouldn't be possible, in any case. Every unit, after all, had to divide up the land they were responsible for and soon the entire village knew how each unit had done this. But no other unit had dared to do it in the manner that Guo Cunxian's unit had done. Certain units only divided up the worst land, and that didn't really even matter, none dared divide up any more than the minimum. Of course, there was discussion and debate in the village over the approach Guo Cunxian had taken; many were especially surprised at the bold initiative he had displayed so soon after being named unit leader. The more astute villagers assumed that Guo Cunxian didn't really care all that much about whether he was the leader or not. After all, were he to be stripped of the position, that wouldn't be all that bad for him. He'd be able to just pick up his tools and begin making coffins again — a good way to earn money in times like these. Besides, he hadn't overstepped his remit, so no one in the village thought it fit to interfere. For their part, the members of the fourth work unit thought they'd grabbed hold of some good fortune and were all quite pleased, very pleased indeed.

But there was something that confused and angered Guo Cunxian. The members of his work unit had been given more than other units had and they were quite happy about that, but the change in mood hadn't affected the way they approached their work, namely, they didn't seem to see the real value of what they had been given, choosing instead not to put their full effort into things, loafing about and only really going through the motions. And so it was quite grating when he was called to see how the work was progressing. At first, as he approached the fields, it looked as though everyone was busy working, tilling the land according to the instructions they had been given. But when he drew close, he saw that this wasn't the case. Instead there were small groups huddled around chatting, some arguing over trivial things, and others just lounging about, doing nothing at all. It was all quite a racket, but all for nothing. The more leisurely they were, the lazier they became, and the lazier they became, the more leisurely they worked, wasting the opportunity they had been given. Guo Cunxian couldn't help but be confused. He had known these villagers for a long time, but now they were like strangers to him, he didn't know them any more, and he felt his anger rise. They were opposing him, toying with him, laughing at the man in the monkey costume. No wonder no one wanted to be the unit leader; power meant nothing if no one obeyed it.

Or, rather, the wielding of power often resulted in unexpected outcomes. While working in the fields, men are able to relieve themselves fairly easily. But what about women who worked in the fields? What did they do? Well, as it happens, they weren't much different from men. When out in the fields, there really wasn't anywhere for them to wander off to, so they would have to do much the same as the men did. In the case of the fourth work unit, well, the women who worked the fields would end up doing very little work before they formed 'pee gangs', walked a little off to one side, squatted down and relieved themselves, laughing and gossiping all the while. In one morning, they'd end up with at least two long pee breaks or more.

And this was how Guo Cunxian encountered the unexpected outcomes of power. One day, when the weather was looking poor, he thought he'd go out before the rain came to get his work done. He never once imagined that the women of the village could have so much urine but as he came up to the field, he saw them off in the distance, milling about and seemingly doing very little work at all. His face dark as he stood well behind them, he thought they would soon finish their business and return to working the fields. But this is not what happened. As he walked into the fields, he was startled by a most unexpected situation. From out of nowhere, he heard Auntie Lin yell out. With her old grey, shrivelled face, he never believed she could be so shameless: "Ladies, look, the unit leader has come to inspect our urine. Attention now, all of you, undo your trousers, squat down, stick out your arses and pee! Can you see clearly unit leader?"

Embarrassed at the shameful situation he had been thrust into, he wanted nothing more than to kick them all in their behinds.

But all he felt was dismay and a degree of obstinacy. He spun round and headed back towards home, but not before calling out to the women saying that he was going to send Xuezhen to deal with them. And if she couldn't, then no one could, he thought. He wondered, too, what else these old ladies might say.

To his great surprise, he never thought that his own mother would yell out after him: "Who would dare send their new wife to the fields? I just can't figure you out. You won't order anyone else about but you would make your wife do it for you, make her save face for you. But Xuezhen is so frail... sending her out into the fields would just end up killing her! In the past, our whole family worked the land to get our work points. Isn't this the same as usual? Aren't we still hungry? No, perhaps not. Thanks to you, we don't need to work for those points, we're not suffering like we did. But how is it that you don't understand? Before you became the unit leader you understood. Why not now?"

It had been many years since his mother had been this annoyed with him; in fact, he couldn't remember when she had ever been so. He was itching to reply but he didn't. Sun Yueqing knew and normally she went along with whatever her son said. She tried to nurture his character, allow him to grow strong, but now she wasn't doing that and he was at a loss as to how to react.

"Oh my son, it's not that you don't have the ability, it's not that you're not a good leader, it's just that we all understand, whether we do the work or not is the same thing. Earning work points... well, they're just useless. You haven't heard what everyone is saying behind your back, have you? Work points are impossible to get, everyone is pissed, so why put full effort into work when one's belly will never be full?"

Guo Cunxian never once thought that he was oblivious to what was happening around him. He always reckoned he was clued in, but now she had scolded him, she'd thrown cold water on his plans. He had lost faith in people and thought that even heaven sought to throw up roadblocks. It was two days before the fifteenth of July, the deadline he had set for his plan. And without warning, the skies opened up and a deluge fell. For three days and three nights it rained. Was heaven playing a joke on them? Or had people caused their own problems? He didn't know, but when the rain stopped Guojiadian was a small, lonely island surrounded by water.

He couldn't even step out of his front door. Looking at all that water, his mouth salivated for a piece of pickled fish, both salty and tart. Or was this how he felt? He thought that it had been fate that he'd been given this position, that he had earned it, but now all he felt was that he'd been played, he'd been cheated. Power was of no use if even the heavens plotted against him.

6

LAND GRAB

Anger is good, and so is despair. Guo Cunxian wasn't young any more but this was an advantage for, when trouble struck, he was able to look on the bright side and that helped boost his morale. He knew the rain wouldn't fall forever and when the nice weather came and the sun returned to the sky, the waters would recede and dry up fairly quickly. And when all is said and done, the land needed the water; it had been too dry for too many years. It's just that it had rained so hard and there was so much water. They needed it to recede quickly. That would allow them to protect at least half of the harvest or more, and that could feed the village or ensure at least that no one starved. He'd only just been named unit leader so he had to make sure that no one went hungry; that was the only way to avoid adversity.

But the heavens weren't part of his family, nor did they care if his life was easy or hard. The deluge stopped for a day, before it began again, day after day, night after night, the skies grew darker and darker and the rain did not cease. The land grew wetter and wetter, the damp soaking into everything. A great dark blanket hung evenly over the village, thick and oppressive. It seemed to stretch everywhere without a discernible depth, without gradations of lightness. The villagers understood why the heavens had shown this kind of face and that it could rain now for months. Guo Cunxian's plan had come to naught and he could think of no new one to deal with this situation. No incantation or spell would magic away the gloom, the darkness that seemed to choke the life out of everything. And so, on the sixth day of the downpour, when he could stand it no longer, he grabbed his conical rice hat and rushed out into the rain.

But what did he hope to accomplish? The heavens weren't going to part the clouds because he'd gone out into the rain. Xuezhen yelled after him, wanting to know where he was planning to go, but he didn't hear her, or he just didn't want to answer. Perhaps he had no answer to give her in any case, perhaps he didn't know where or what he was going to do. In no time he was drenched. His torso was soaked through and his legs were deep in the water. He wasn't walking so much as wading through the swamp his town had become. His mind was as muddled as the water was muddy. Subconsciously his legs dragged him to the commune offices, and it was then finally that he knew what he was doing; he had to talk to the village head about something. He was in the offices of the highest governmental authorities in Guojiadian; they should have a plan. According to regulations, since the rainfall continued to be so heavy, the village head should have already convened meetings with each unit leader to discuss plans to deal with the natural disaster they were facing. How could the village head not think that people would come and look for him, wish to speak with him, wish to figure out how to manage the situation? How could he be so easily annoyed and impatient when they finally did? Perhaps people were better off managing without the village head?

Guo Cunxian couldn't remember the last time he had been in these offices, but he wasn't there to pester the village head to think of some strategy or plan, nor was he there to endure a scolding. No, he went there in the spirit of fraternity, of equality; they were all in the same boat, it wasn't a time for pulling rank. When he came upon the building he saw two soaking-wet transport trucks parked alongside it. Rectangular in shape, the building had five offices in total. One end held the desks and papers of those responsible for the village finances; the other end housed the public security office. The three remaining rooms in the middle were the Party branch offices, and that's where the village head could be found.

Floating out of the offices at this moment, however, was a sound completely different from what Guo Cunxian had expected; the sounds of laughter and giggling, shouting and jocularity seemed to drown out the rain. As he pushed open the door and stepped inside, the sound of rain accompanying him inside, he was greeted by the heavy odour of cigarette smoke that swirled around him, assaulting his nose and throat, forcing him to use all his energy to stifle a cough. People were sat upon the elevated platform, as well as on the floor. Just how many people did it take to manage the affairs of the commune? There were militiamen in the room, as well as several toadies, those who would fawn over the leadership of the commune, shamelessly trying to curry favour. Surprisingly, there were also three or four production unit leaders there as well, some busily playing cards, others engaged in a game of *weiqi*, all of them roaring and laughing. With all the rain, there really wasn't anything else to do. A few of the men in the room had heard him open the door and had looked up, but none uttered a word, instead turning quickly and burying their heads in whatever it was they were doing. Some of the men didn't even bother to look up, they only called out for whoever it was that had entered to close the door to stop the rain from coming in. A few who enjoyed talking acknowledged his entrance and called out to him: "Ah, Cunxian's come... he's an infrequent visitor, isn't he... is there something wrong?"

He didn't respond immediately, but wondered instead how on earth he could talk about anything serious with this lot, the bastards. He scanned the room, seemingly looking for something, or someone, but he didn't see Chen Baohuai or Han Jingting. It was then that several men in the room understood why he had come; they could see his disapproval of them written across his face. He had come looking for the village head, not them. Before he could say anything in response, one of his own militiamen, Ou Guangming, stepped forward. He told Guo Cunxian that Han Jingting had fallen ill because of the damp and was at home with a fever. It had happened when he had called a meeting and had got caught by the rain, unable to return home. Guo Cunxian stared at Ou Guangming, seemingly in a daze. Since he'd come into the room he hadn't opened his mouth. Now all he could do was put his head down and exit the same way he had come in, wondering to himself all the while.

As he stepped back out into the pouring rain, he had no clue, no idea as to where he should go. Should he go to Han Jingting's house? But he was ill. If he were to tromp over there now in the rain, drenched and covered in mud, that would only serve to raise Han Jingting's ire and cause unnecessary animosity. Besides, who would it be for, and was it even worth it? But he wasn't keen on going home either; sullen and downtrodden, he felt like pounding his head against a wall. In any case, he already felt like a downed rat, and so he decided to just keep on walking, wading through the village. He could hear his feet squelching in the mud as he made his way through the swamp that used to be his village, and before he realised it, he turned a corner and found himself in front of the Dragon Phoenix Trees. He didn't think he'd see his mad uncle there but, sure enough, there he was, and as Guo Cunxian came into view he waved to him, beckoning him to come forward. Guo Cunxian's mood improved. At least his uncle was doing well. While everyone else was depressed and filled with worry, he had come and climbed up into the tree to get a better look at the scenery. That said, he still sort of felt like smashing his head against a wall. There was nothing pleasing to look at but then how would it help? Perhaps he'd be better off living like his uncle, being like a small child without a care in the world, without anything weighing on his mind or burdening his heart.

He took off his waterlogged hat and looked up into the tree to where his uncle was sitting, sizing up his climb before taking hold of the branches and shimmying up. Because the trunk of the tree was so coarse and had a girth much too great for him to wrap his arms around, he used all of his energy to drive his fingers into the tree's wet, damp bark and slowly climb up. As he climbed he couldn't help but wonder how his uncle had got himself up into the tree, so difficult was the climb, and so seemingly old and frail was his uncle. But just as he reached the lower hanging branches, his uncle extended a hand, grabbed hold of him, and pulled him the rest of the way up. The wind didn't blow through the branches, so dense had they grown, and his uncle's clothes had already dried. Guo Cunxian couldn't contain his elation: "Uncle, you really know how to pick your places. It's so comfortable, cool and refreshing up here." Guo Jingshi raised his hand and waved in the direction of the village, urging him to look in the same direction. Guo Cunxian wedged himself comfortably between branches and allowed his eyes to follow his uncle's hand but he soon felt his head go numb and a bout of dizziness wash over him. The swamp that lay to the north of Guojiadian had really become a sea. The water seemed to stretch far off to the horizon, gently undulating, boundless and without end. The area around the village seemed vague and indistinct but it was still possible to make out the bits of sorghum and maize bobbing about on the water.

Guo Jingshi spoke: "If the water doesn't stop rising, the village is lost."

Guo Cunxian's mind was racing with thoughts, his eyes staring blankly into the distance. It seemed like half a day or more before he regained his senses. He then looked at his uncle and told him that, when the rain eased a little, he had to head home. Guo Cunxian then slipped down from the tree and ran towards the village.

He returned to the Party offices and without saying a word he grabbed hold of Ou Guangming and then dragged him along as he went from house to house rounding up every strong and able-bodied man in his fourth work unit. Fearing that these poor peasants weren't even enough, he also called on Liu Wangcheng and the Jin brothers. Then, standing on the street in front of them, he issued the lowest level of leadership command in all of Guojiadian. This was an emergency mobilisation: a land grab!

In the pouring rain Guo Cunxian barked out orders: "You mightn't see, but the village is on the verge of drowning in all of this water. At least four-fifths of the sorghum has already turned into mush and the maize has grown soft. Who knows how long it'll need to be dried before we can make even a little bit of corn flour? Some of the beans, too, are nearly ripe. I believe that all of the strongest, sturdiest labourers need to immediately head into the fields to grab the crops, to grab whatever we can, even if only a little."

As sheets of rain continued to fall, Guo Cunxian went on: "We can't just look on our crops helplessly and do nothing. We can't just let them all go to waste in the rain. At least four-fifths of the sorghum has already turned to mush and the corn is growing softer by the day. Even if we were to put some out to dry we wouldn't end up with much. Even the beans are nearly ripe. We need to put all of our energy into this. We must head to the fields immediately and start harvesting what we can, at least bring home a little if nothing else."

Without waiting for Guo Cunxian to finish, Ou Guangming interjected in a loud voice: "Dear leader, have you gone as mad as your old uncle? Even in fine weather, going to the fields is like having to pull the towropes for a boat. It isn't easy. You haven't seen what the weather is like. The water in the fields is surely up to one's waist by now. Even if you were to tie yourself to one of us, that'd be no guarantee they'll go into the fields with you."

"I don't need a rope, I'll brave the rain and head to the fields myself, and one day of work will be counted as three."

"But there's water everywhere. Even if you were to harvest as much as you could, there isn't anywhere dry enough to put it, inside or outside. So what difference would it make?"

"I've already thought about that. Whoever goes out to harvest whatever they can, can bring what they harvest back home with them, and it doesn't matter what you do with it. If you try to store it or throw it all in a pot, it doesn't matter, it's yours to do with as you please. If it's like it has been these past two years, disaster or not, there won't be any rations, so the food is yours, and if by chance the authorities do distribute rations, well, you'll get those, too. So what do you all think?"

Standing in the rain, soaking wet, no one spoke. A quiet rustle could be heard among the crowd. The rain was like a bandit gang that had encircled them, trapping them in a large net. They were all still starving, all suffering, fearful of what there was to eat and of what they might be given in the communal canteen. But now they were being told to take advantage of the rain and to harvest what was available, and even bring home with them as much as they could. At least they'd be able to fill their bellies for a few days; who wouldn't be enticed by this?

Jin Laixi took the initiative and spoke: "I think this is a fine plan. Cunxian, you're a wise leader, and you're not mistaken, allowing us to harvest what we can. You're like a big brother that's looking out for all of us."

One after the other, they all voiced their agreement. Since there was no time to lose, Cunxian set about immediately organising the men into several groups. They were to go door to door and tell everyone in the fourth production team to head to the fields, to harvest and save what they could. But they were only permitted to harvest what belonged to them: first the maize, then the sorghum.

They all consented and then dispersed. Ou Guangming, however, didn't depart. Instead he moved closer to Guo Cunxian, seemingly with something important to tell him: "Brother Cunxian, everyone says that I'm often too rash, that I act without thinking, but I don't think I can be compared to you. You don't seem to waste any time at all agonising over a decision. You know, once we're finished, you'll be finished, too."

Guo Cunxian moved closer to Ou Guangming as well, almost whispering in his ear: "Thanks for the advice. You've been trying to save me from certain tragedy I'm sure, huh? But let me tell you something. Whatever I harvest I'm not taking home, I'm taking it to the Party offices."

In one fluid movement, Guo Cunxian finished speaking and pushed Ou Guangming, sending him on his way to tell his family about the plan.

For his part, Guo Cunxian turned around and headed back to the Party offices to collect a large harvesting basket. He then tied a piece of rope to it as though he were mooring a ship, and pulled himself and the basket towards the field. He knew that those in his unit who had been told of the plan were still standing in their doorways, hesitating, wondering if they really could go into the fields. Bravery wasn't a trait often seen in peasants. They preferred to follow the crowd, especially in matters that seemed to transgress established rules, and so they'd always wait for someone to take the lead and, if no one did, then they'd sit on the fence, waiting and waiting. There was no choice, then; he'd have to start.

And as he trekked on in the direction of the fields, basket in tow, he decided to spin his head round and look. Sure enough, there following behind him in the pouring rain were the farmers of his work unit, all carrying wicker baskets with them, coolie hats on their heads, large sacks slung over their backs. Some were even cleverer; they had brought their wooden animal troughs along with them. Others displayed even more ingenuity by taking the planks of their doors to fashion makeshift rafts. Guo Cunxian smiled to himself. He was pleased. Everyone had followed his orders. Turning his head, he led them all in the direction of the corn.

The rains continued. The village lanes had transformed into small rivulets, orphaning each home, creating little islands in the water, with the villagers trapped within. When there were great deluges like this in the past, the farmers had always been quite happy for the communal holiday from work and, like cats, curled up somewhere warm. They wouldn't get out of bed, wouldn't budge, not except for a fire or something else life-threatening. Before their eyes, it seemed as though the heavens had come crashing down, soaking the land, making even a house fire something rarely to be seen. But there was something that could stir the villages, something even more important than a villager's home going up in flames. But the flood had brought worry and nervousness to the Guo family home; it was as though they knew something awful was going to happen, or that some commotion or other would soon befall them. There was an atmosphere of envy and jealousy about the town, a sense of schadenfreude in the air. As soon as anyone stepped out of their front door, they would be wading in water, but this didn't seem to really stop them. There were still many who would run through the torrential rain picking all that they could. They were waist deep in the water and mud, their torsos and heads similarly drenched. Drowning in the rain, Guo Cunxian watched as his unit set about their work. When they spied him, they called out warm greetings and salutations. The whole mood was carnival-like, as though the town were in the midst of New Year's celebrations. Everyone was entitled to what they worked for, each in their place; what you harvested was yours.

It was disgraceful, like the end of days. Heaven and earth were in disarray, the commune had been disbanded and lawlessness reigned. But it wasn't all bad for them, for while the land allotted to Guo Cunxian's unit was in the northern swamp, who knew they'd take advantage of the chaos and harvest land belonging to neighbouring units? In truth, resolving these suspicions and overcoming such potential jealousy was easy enough to do. All the other units had to do was to go and examine their own plots and they'd easily see that someone had already harvested it, either that or they could simply follow suit and brave the rain as the fourth unit had done and grab what they could. No other unit leaders, however, issued the same orders. They were all too old, too stuck in their ways; they'd experienced and seen too much. There was no way they could follow Guo Cunxian's example and take the initiative; they didn't understand how serious and difficult the situation was. In their minds it was clear: Guo Cunxian was challenging fate and heading for misfortune, and not only for himself. He was going to drag the entire unit down with him. It wouldn't matter who had given the order, the result would be the same for all of them. As soon as the weather turned, the authorities would force them to return all that they had taken. For them, there was no need to be so rushed, no need to be so anxious. This kind of weather was for lounging about, for doing nothing at all, except maybe taking in a show, nothing more.

But for the rest of the many unit members, the common folk, they didn't have the same type of relaxed composure as their leaders had. On the following day, those with a little courage followed suit and headed out into the fields to harvest and grab what they could. On the third day there were more still out in the marshy farmland. Those who had remained indoors, looking on enviously, soon realised that no one was trying to stop them and so they too headed into the fields to dredge up what they could. What a show it was! In fact, before long it was as though whole processions of farmers were in the fields grabbing what they could. Gradually the town was emptied with more than half of the residents of Guojiadian taking advantage of the chaos to get what they could. No one was able to just sit at home and do nothing.

There was something evil about the downpour. For more than half a month there was no change in the sky and it didn't get darker or brighter; everywhere was truly flooded, submerged under the deluge. When the rains finally stopped, it still took over a month before the water fully receded, before they could see the marshy swamp that surrounded Guojiadian. Except for the mud, nothing remained of their crops. And whatever could have been salvaged had already been pulled from the ground and was now in the hands of those who had braved the rain; whatever wasn't grabbed now lay rotting in the soil. In all directions the land seemed empty, barren and crisp, like the shiver one feels when a cool wind blows over one's body. Those households that had harvested what they could in the rain now felt a little downtrodden; those who had remained indoors watching the spectacle unfold outside now felt tired of it all. They weren't looking forward to the prospects of having to beg this winter and into spring, but nor was the thought of trying to get by on eight *jin* a month of dried sweet potato any more appealing. Was there any way they might avoid suffering from oedema again? If they could get by while suffering from it, that would be all right, but there was no guarantee of that. This type of despair and panic was common enough; it virtually enshrouded the entire village, weighing down Guojiadian. Indeed, the weight of this melancholy only increased, becoming heavier and heavier, ultimately mutating into resentment and hatred. They ought to have felt hatred towards heaven, for the lack of care it showed them, but for those who didn't brave the rains and go into the fields, their hatred and resentment was directed solely at those who had, and at their unit leaders who had remained silent throughout and not issued any orders. But once this conflagration of animosity had expired, they all went in search of Guo Cunxian. If he hadn't issued those orders to his work unit, then Guojiadian wouldn't be in the predicament it now found itself. The whole village would be equally miserable, equally suffering the disaster together, everyone hungry and starving. But now, some had bloated bellies while others had liver problems; some ate their fill while others had nothing; some cried profusely while others smiled in private; some cursed other families and not just the living but their ancestors too while others tried to stir up trouble. It was all a great mess.

But Guo Cunxian was no fool, and he couldn't help but feel something. While the village was on tenterhooks, he was surprised one morning when his mad uncle Jingshi, who barely opened his eyes while at home and spoke but a few words, sat staring at him intently across the breakfast table, his hands not touching his chopsticks, nor his bowl, seemingly set on waiting for him to finish his morning porridge. Then, when Guo Cunxian put his bowl back down on the table, his uncle deftly took hold of it and emptied his own bowl into his nephew's before getting down from the *kang* and walking off. He figured his uncle had done this because of the love he felt for him, or perhaps he was trying to console him, or... Guo Jingshi spent his days beneath the Dragon Phoenix Trees, the centre of gossip for the entire town, so for sure he had heard something about what was happening. Pondering this, once he finished his breakfast he didn't head to his own office. Instead he got out his tools intending to work; after all, much of their furniture was showing the effects of the dampness. He pulled out his grinding stone, prepared a little water, and began sharpening his axe.

In the midst of sharpening his precious axe, the expected visitors came. Lan Shoukun with five or six militiamen in tow marched into his yard. When they saw him they laughed irreverently, mockingly: "Oh ho, you're sharpening your axe, huh? Are you preparing to leave again, to head off to make some more coffins and earn some cash? You're quite clever, aren't you, Guo Cunxian! You know you're in trouble. But let me tell you, you're not getting away this time. You're not going anywhere. You're staying here this time."

Guo Cunxian lifted his head and looked at him, but didn't utter a word. He continued to sharpen his axe. Worried, confused and in haste, Sun Yueqing and Zhu Xuezhen rushed out into the yard as soon as they heard the militiamen come. When they saw the scene they couldn't help but grow frightened and worried, and they quickly tried to usher Lan Shoukun into the house to avoid something awful from happening. Lan Shoukun refused. He was there on the authority of Secretary Chen with orders from the Party itself. Guo Cunxian had become too big for his britches. He'd taken advantage of his position and had issued orders he wasn't authorised to do; moreover, he'd instigated a revolt and had destroyed the commune, causing a great crisis for the revolution itself. He was now stripped of his position as unit leader and a request had been made to the central authorities to come and deal with the fallout. While they waited for instructions from the central authorities to arrive, he was forbidden to leave Guojiadian. And finally, all of the food they'd illegally harvested was to be confiscated. But they had a choice: they could willingly return it or the militiamen would enter their home and take it themselves.

With a grunt, Guo Cunxian stood up from the grinding stone and spoke: "Let me tell you something, Lan Shoukun. None of the grain that my brother and I harvested is here. We put it all in the unit offices. Not one grain of sorghum nor one stalk of corn passed through these doors. Everyone in the unit can testify to this. If you don't believe me, fine, go and ask one of your own militiamen, Ou Guangming. He knows. That means you've no right to search my home, so get the hell out of here."

"Oh ho, are you planning to do something with that axe, hmm?"

"The thought hadn't crossed my mind but, you know, I've just been sharpening it. If you want to try something, then I'll happily oblige... your life would be worth it. Me, on the other hand, I'm just a simple worker, my life isn't worth shit."

"Who's here to fight you? I've come to carry out the people's work, since you've said that all of the food you grabbed is in the unit offices, well then, we'll go and make sure that it is. We'll also ask around to see whether what you've said is true or not. If we discover you've lied, then we'll be back."

Taking his men with him, Lan Shoukun departed. The colour still hadn't returned to Zhu Xuezhen's face. Deathly white, she ran to her husband's side. Looking into his eyes she spoke softly: "I was scared to death, you know. If they'd tried to come inside, would you have used your axe?"

The anger in the pit of his stomach had still not subsided. He spat out a venomous reply: "Would that've been polite? They tried to dare me, though, didn't they? I could've cut a few of them down today. I thought of what they'd done to Cunzhi but I guess there's no need to rehash all of that."

Pulling on his arm, Xuezhen replied: "How could you be so rash?"

"When a man needs to fight, then he needs to fight. There's no reason for you to get angry and upset. You just said you were terrified. You know what that means, huh? It means that so were they. If they'd forced their way into our home and made a mess, turning over furniture and stuff while looking for something that wasn't there, then the shit would've hit the fan, I can tell you that. This is our house, our family. I can't let our father lose face."

While the scene had played out, Sun Yueqing had remained by the door without moving. But now, she felt the strength return to her legs. She walked over to her son, put her hands on his arm and lowered the axe: "You don't need to keep sharpening it. You're not going anywhere. Just stay indoors and remain steadfast, that's all you can do. Besides, no one else is going to starve, which means we'll live."

Guo Cunxian relented and watched as his old mother gathered up his tools and carried them back to the storage shed. The whole ordeal seemed like nothing more than a normal day for a carpenter's household. But in his heart, he secretly gave thanks to his axe. He knew that if he hadn't had it there would have been no way to resist Lan Shoukun. He decided then and there that he would make sure to always have it on him.

Once she'd finished packing away his tools, Sun Yueqing returned to her son's side. She looked into his face and comforted him, saying: "I think you'd be better off not being the unit leader. You'll save yourself the grief and hatred that way."

Guo Cunxian averted his eyes from those of his mother and his wife. His head down, he walked away from them and began pacing round the courtyard. His mind seemed trapped within the events of a short time ago. He pinched his fingers together. He'd been the unit leader for only three-and-a-half months. In all of Guojiadian, his tenure had been the shortest. How shameful was that? If he'd known this would happen, he would never have been so rash. Lan Shoukun had also told him that Secretary Chen had requested the higher-ups to deal with him. Had he been trying to scare him or had they really kicked this case up to the central authorities? Even if they had, he thought, what difference would that make? He was just a poor peasant, what more could be done to him? Would they decide to send him to prison or to a labour camp? It had to have been Secretary Chen who had ordered this. Lan Shoukun didn't have that kind of power, that's what was frightening. The more he thought about it the tighter his chest grew as panic seemed to wash over him. Suddenly, he tore off running towards his own room. He had to lie down before he fell over.

Until noon, Xuezhen had been busy helping her mother-in-law prepare the meal. Once finished, Cunzhu was told to lay the table. As they were getting ready, Cunzhi, who'd been out all morning, came home with news of what was happening in the village. In a loud, reproachful voice, he said: "Chaos, just chaos. The whole village has gone to hell!"

Sun Yueqing asked: "Why, what's happened now?"

Guo Cunzhi had left in the morning after he'd eaten breakfast so he was unaware of what had happened, and so he delved straightaway into telling them of the ruckus in town: "The militiamen have been going round, door to door of every member of the fourth work unit, searching for the grain they've harvested. You can guess what the reaction has been! They've been to more than twenty households in the morning alone and you know what? They haven't found a single basket of crops."

Her curiosity peaked, Xuezhen asked him: "Where is all the food that was harvested in the rain?"

"Everyone said that it had all been eaten."

"They were able to eat all of that in a little over a month?"

"That's what they said. I say, they're just like those Japanese bastards, aren't they? I mean, that's a scorched-earth policy if ever I saw one. I learnt about it in year six, in our Chinese class. That said, all the food we put in the unit offices they took, raided it all, everything that we worked so hard to harvest is all gone now. They also told me that Cunxian was sacked from his post. The news has been spreading all over the village."

"They don't need to sack him," Sun Yueqing replied angrily. "He has quit already. Go, now, tell your brother it's time for lunch."

Cunzhi went to get his brother. As soon as he stepped into his room, he saw Guo Cunxian sitting on the edge of the bed, his head against the wall, his left hand holding onto his cheek, and the sound of his laboured breathing echoing through the room. Concerned for his brother, Cunzhi leaned close and said: "Big Brother, are you all right?"

"It's nothing. My teeth hurt. Tell mum I'm not eating."

Upon hearing this nonsense, Sun Yueqing marched straight into his room, walked up to him and grabbed his face to examine his teeth. She felt his cheek as well. It wasn't red or swollen, and she knew that the only problem was the anger in his stomach, the fury in his heart that had made him so anxious. She berated him for being so selfish and told him she would send Cunzhi for the village doctor. He stopped her then: "I won't allow it, and don't let anyone know my teeth hurt. I don't want anyone to laugh at us. I'm not that weak and sickly after all."

At that moment Cunzhu burst into the room saying that she would go, but that she wouldn't say he was in pain, but rather say that it was her own teeth that hurt and that all she needed was a little medicine. She took off back out the door as soon as she had finished talking.

No one thought that the pain in Guo Cunxian's mouth would get any worse, but two days later and he still hadn't been able to eat anything, nor get out of bed. And it was no use trying to have someone come and look at him, to gouge out the offending tooth or to bring him some medicine. Guo Cunxian simply refused. He wouldn't let them call for the doctor, nor would he go and visit one. In the end, there was nothing else for it but for his mad uncle to bring home with him some leaves from the Dragon Phoenix Trees. He told him to chew on them and when one mouthful of leaves were turned into a mulch, he'd give him more. But this didn't seem to work either and so, in the middle of the night when all was quiet, he pulled out some yellow paper (from where no one knew) and proceeded to wrap it three times around Cunxian's head, mumbling, almost chanting, incomprehensibly as he did so. Once he had finished, he left in the direction of the eastern marshes, a pale lantern glowing weakly in his hand. It was as though he had used the yellow paper to wrap up the pain Cunxian was experiencing and taken it with him. The family just didn't know, and Guo Jingshi wouldn't let anyone accompany him. Watching him leave, Xuezhen got up afterwards and closed the door behind him, but without bolting it. Her mother-in-law had also seen Guo Jingshi leave, but Xuezhen told her not to worry and to go back to bed; that she'd wait up for him, and besides, she was too worried to sleep in any case. As they walked back towards the house, from behind them came a loud creaking noise as the gate was pushed open. Xuezhen never expected her uncle to return so quickly. They turned around and then saw that it wasn't Guo Jingshi who had returned but someone else entirely. They both grew nervous and worried.

The man who'd come latched the gate gently behind him and quickly came up to the two of them. In a soft voice he said: "Auntie, it's me, Ou Guangming, I've come to see Brother Cunxian." In his arms he carried a great sack, which he now placed in Sun Yueqing's arms. "This is several *jin* of maize. Hide it somewhere inside."

Startled, Sun Yueqing rebuked him: "Why on earth have you brought this here?"

"Cunxian gave it to me in the first place. He knew that trouble would come, but he also knew that we couldn't be stupid about things and just let them take what we had worked so hard to get. Quickly now, go and hide it."

Sun Yueqing remained obstinate: "Guangming, we can't. Your house is facing the same difficulties we are. Keep it."

"Auntie, whether or not we're facing the same difficulties is another matter entirely. Besides, this is just an armful, there isn't much here anyway, no more than a few mouthfuls, dessert even. Please take it, if for no other reason than that I need my trousers back."

Ou Guangming pushed the sack into her arms, this time more forcefully. She accepted it, reluctantly, and then lugged it inside where it was brighter and she could get a better look at it. Inside she saw that the maize had been packed in a pair of trousers with a string to tie it tight. She stifled a laugh, before her heart was reminded of the pain and bitterness they had been suffering. In a voice no more than a whisper, she asked Ou Guangming: "Your mum's been dead now for a nearly a year, yes?"

"She died last year, just as it got cold."

"Guangming, you need to find a wife, hmm."

"That's easier said than done. What family would marry their daughter off to a man and a family like mine? We're poorer than poor, my father is bedridden, I've an idiot brother, hmph, any woman that'd enter our home would have to take care of three bare sticks. I ask you, what woman nowadays would want to marry into that kind of life?"

"Well, how about letting your auntie take care of things. I'm sure I can find a suitable bride." As she spoke, Sun Yueqing emptied the maize into a large container next to the stove and then shook the trousers vigorously, making sure every grain had been emptied and the trousers were free to be worn again. She then discovered that the backside was nearly worn through, so she called for Xuezhen to take Guangming in to see Cunxian. While they talked she would mend his trousers.

Pretending that he'd just been woken from a deep slumber, Cunxian spat out the leaves his uncle had given him just before Guangming entered the room: "Oh, Guangming, it's you. Why've you come?"

"We've not seen hide nor hair of you for three days. Aren't we allowed to come and visit you? I also need to speak to you about some things."

"I've just thrown away my lousy old cotton-padded jacket, ah... it's difficult these days to even have a couple of days of peace. In any case, if you have something to discuss, shouldn't you do that with the new unit leader and not me?"

"That's what I'm here to talk to you about. The village intends to have Han Dongliang succeed you."

"Brother Erhu?"

"Yes, exactly, but he's as lazy as they come and he doesn't want to do anything. All day today he's been wandering about the village hurling obscenities, shouting that if they wanted him to become the unit leader, then they had to accept the mouth that came with it, no matter how vulgar it might be. He's a real prick."

"So what did they do in the end?"

"They thought to call Guo Cunxiao to do it and everybody agreed. He's your distant relative, a cousin I believe. He has no black marks against him, no skeletons in his closet, and if you were to give your opinion, behind the scenes as it were, then perhaps it'll be all right."

"Guangming, do you think I'm obsessed about being the unit leader? I've been removed, talk to someone else. Eh, why didn't they ask you?"

"In their eyes, I'm still too young and not the brightest. Besides, I don't have the right family circumstances."

As they spoke, Jin Laixi, carrying a small pouch, quietly came up to Guo Cunxian's house. Opening the door and stepping in, he apologised immediately: "Beg your pardon, but I saw that the main door wasn't bolted, nor was the second door closed and there was no one about so I just let myself in." Still speaking, he passed the small pouch to Zhu Xuezhen: "It's just a little bit of maize, quickly, put it away."

Xuezhen, appearing out of sorts and uncomfortable, looked painfully at her husband, who in turn spoke to the two men who'd come: "What's going on here this evening, huh? Just what have you been discussing? Why've you brought me food? Do you think because I've been removed from office I can't manage to fend for my family?"

Jin Laixi responded first: "No one's discussed anything, but the big ruckus of this morning has stretched well into the afternoon. Everyone's saying that, if you're booted out in such a manner, then no one would be willing to take on the post."

Ou Guangming took hold of Xuezhen and ushered her out of the room: "Since we're the ones who have barged in, you needn't be so polite."

Guo Cunxian's heart had warmed a little: "To be honest, these last two days I've felt tormented by everything that's happened. I couldn't help but feel that I've been terribly foolish these last three-and-a-half months, like I've been possessed by an evil spirit or something. I couldn't help but think that none of this is worth it, certainly not worth my life. But listening to you two tonight, perhaps this period hasn't been a total waste after all."

Jin Laixi spoke again: "Brother Cunxian, you're right, you know. Over these last few months you've shown us all something, you've shown us how a team leader is supposed to act. That's what I told everyone else today and sooner or later, I think, you'll be team leader again. But I haven't come here tonight to speak only about this. I also have something else to tell you. We received a letter from my wife's mother in Shandong. They've held a communal meeting and served deep-fried fritters. They've sold steamed bread buns and the people didn't even need food vouchers in order to get something to eat. Can you guess what I'm thinking? Shandong isn't more than a few hundred *li* from here, and if they can do something like this, I think we can, too, and probably even put it together faster than them. All we need is a call to arms, so to speak. What do you think?"

As expected, Jin Laixi's news piqued Guo Cunxian's interest. It excited him enormously. "Really?" he asked. And in his heart he was already making plans. If they were able to organise the same type of gathering, to his mind there wasn't any need to limit it to just Guojiadian. Being a team leader or not was all such bullshit.

Once she had finished mending Ou Guangming's trousers, Sun Yueqing returned and handed them back, interrupting the discussion they were having. "Guangming, when you need sewing done in the future, just bring it to me. It's no trouble."

"Ah... alright then."

Jin Laixi stood up: "We should get going, you all need some rest."

Guo Cunxian got up and showed them to the door. Once outside, however, he dared not speak more about what they had discussed. Both Jin Laixi and Ou Guangming left in opposite directions, and soon not even their shadows could be seen. Guo Cunxian moved to shut the gate, but just as he did the soft voice of his wife startled him. His uncle hadn't yet come home. Quietly, he left the gate slightly ajar, and as he did so he noticed a form making its way towards him. He thought at first that it must be either Jin Laixi or Ou Guangming returning to tell him something more but once the person came into view, he was dumbfounded by who it was: Liu Yucheng had never once crossed his doorway. But now, here he was, and he wasn't empty-handed, either. Slung haphazardly over his shoulder, he carried with him a bag of some weight that he now pulled down to give to Guo Cunxian.

"Cunxian, Big Brother, I've messed up. I didn't take proper care of my corn and now it's gone mouldy. This is the only bit of sorghum I've got. I'm embarrassed and don't mean to put you in a difficult spot but please take it and look after it."

Guo Cunxian wouldn't accept the offered bag, instead grabbing hold of Liu Yucheng's wrist and saying: "Tell me the truth, who issued the orders? Who told you to bring this food here?"

Growing nervous, Liu Yucheng replied: "Big Brother, please don't misunderstand, no one gave me any such order, we all just feel that you've been unjustly wronged. What's more, all the food you gathered has been confiscated, that's something that just doesn't sit well with us."

"Are you really being straight with me? No one's pressured you?"

"No one, really, no one at all!"

"Then why can't I shake the feeling that you all discussed this, planned this?"

"I know I've come on the heels of Jin Laixi, but honestly, we never planned anything. I actually saw him go into your place and so I waited until he was gone and once I saw them leave, well, I plucked up the courage to come forward."

Moved, Guo Cunxian said: "Yucheng, thank you, truly, but I really can't accept it."

"What? Do you think what I've brought isn't any good?"

"What're you talking about? No, it isn't that at all. I know it's just the two of you now, you and your brother, and I know that that can't be easy."

"Big Brother, these last few months when you were team leader you never once looked at me as though I wasn't a person. I know what you're going through now, I know what's happened."

He pushed the bag of grain into Guo Cunxian's hands, turned and left. With one hand holding the bag of sorghum, Guo Cunxian reached out to Yucheng with the other, pulling him back, directing him into the inner rooms and urging him to stay, at least for a little while. Yucheng was adamant, however: "It's too late. Another day, for sure."

Unrelenting, Guo Cunxian spoke: "I'd like to at least ask you something before you do go. Where'd you hide all of the food? How is it that Lan Shoukun and his cronies couldn't find it?"

"It rained so heavily for so long that hiding the food wasn't easy, that's for sure. I mean, whatever hole they dug they'd only end up being able to hide a few hundred *jin* or so now wouldn't they? But hide it well they did. You know Jin Laixi, he's quite a bricklayer. He was able to remove the bricks at the base of everyone's *kang*, store the food underneath and then seal them back up. That was quite clever, and it even kept the food free from the damp. I had a lot so I wasn't able to hide it all. That's how some of it got mouldy and that's what I placed outside for the militiamen to find and confiscate."

Guo Cunxian laughed. The night had become dark, but standing in the meagre light of the lamp, he laughed heartily. And to his surprise, he suddenly realised his teeth no longer hurt.

7

EARTH AND SOIL

There's an old saying: the earth is like a vomiting carcass. Soil is what the earth uses to produce its many creatures. The earth is what adheres to them; it is their essence and therein lies their value. Confucius said: "That which is beneath people, its quality is that of excellent earth! If you plant seeds in it, the five grains will grow there; if you dig into it, sweet springs will emerge. Plants grow there, animals thrive there, living people stand there and the dead lie there. I won't speak of its further abilities: that which is beneath people, its quality is that of excellent earth!" **(The School Sayings of Confucius)**

There's another old saying: the soil brings life, it brings thoughts of plenty. The soil is there to aid us, but it also needs our care. Only when man plants and harvests crops do we call the earth soil. Soil is softened earth. 'The earth is there to be soil, but none of it is for soil', from out of this emerges a careful visage, a harmonious nature.

While autumn had already come, an oppressive heat still remained. But as the peasants knew well, the seasons cannot be ignored and the heat that had arrived with the rains hadn't really been of the proper intensity so now the weather was making up for it. Because of the sweltering conditions, when the local flood control mobilisation team called for a meeting they decided to hold it in the cooler shadows that stretched out from the headquarters gable. That was the plan, at least. But as the people who had gathered there would tell you, the sweat still poured off their brows, and those who had brought straw hats took to using them as fans, for what little good it did.

The main wall of the commune office had been washed in limewater to at first give the building a snow-like hue. Then, from the left-hand corner to the right, from the top to the bottom, eight different bands of colour had been painted, each symbolising a certain rank of attainment. The highest colour band symbolised the rocket. This was followed by the aeroplane, and both bands had been painted in bright red. The third and fourth bands stood for the train and the automobile, both slightly less bright red. The fifth and sixth bands symbolised the horse-drawn buggy and the donkey cart and these were painted grey. The final two bands represented women with bound feet and the abject cuckold. These were, of course, painted black. It's difficult to say when it happened, but black had taken on an inauspicious character and anything associated with it meant something awful indeed. Next to each colour band was an indication of time and the expected progress that was to be made.

Sitting below the wall was a cohort of villagers who served as the secretaries and team leaders of the nineteen communities that constituted the commune, and a few others who had been brought along by those officials with suspect memories. All of their faces looked towards the wall, seemingly entranced by the colour bands painted across it. They nattered and whispered to each other, gesturing at the significance of the colours. At that moment the fifty-year-old director of the commune, Sun Liangjiu, stepped forward. His long face was stiff, rigid and old, and one yellowed eye seemed permanently glued together, but the seriousness of his demeanour, the air of authority he possessed seemed to belie his physical appearance. He issued instructions: the central authorities had ordered that all floodwaters were to be eradicated and in preparation for the inevitable rainy season in the New Year, a sluice-gate was to be constructed that could be no less than 150 metres wide and at least two metres taller than the river banks. If the rains came with the same ferocity and the river was to rise in the future, the excess water would be directed into the sea. The county offices had made their commune responsible for sixty-eight *li*, so each village would be accountable for a *li* and a half.

The courtyard erupted into rancorous bleating with people shouting over each other. There were shouts that this directive was like digging a massive river on their own, that the director must be pulling their legs, having a laugh at their expense. How could such a monumental undertaking be completed in a year? Were they to drop everything else? What about planting crops? And besides, who among them had the strength left to carry out such a task? All they were getting by on was two or three meagre portions of dried sweet potato. Who in the hell would be able to lug the amount of earth that would have to be dredged up for this sluice-gate? Surely someone must be having them on!

A booming voice split through the cacophonous haranguing: "Just what the hell are you all arguing about? And for what, huh?" Sitting in the front row, the commune secretary Liu Dajiang now stood up. He was much younger than Sun Liangjiu, his voice loud and almost threatening, his stature imposing. He grabbed a stick that had been lying near his stool and proceeded to vigorously strike it against the office wall: "You small-minded chickenshits, do you think the nation would set you to work on a worthless task? Those building the sluice-gate will each receive an extra *jin* of rations per day, as well as two *jiao* in cash. What's wrong, you've nothing to say? Fine, then listen to me. Pay attention too, and think about it. When we're done here I'm going to file an official report in which I'll say whether you all intend to be rockets or aeroplanes, or whether you want to be a bunch of women with bound feet, or a worthless cuckold bastard." He ended his curse just short and abruptly sat back down.

But halting his speech as he did, holding back ever so little, had the desired effect. His incisive, penetrating vitriol remained suspended in mid-air, lingering in their hearts, waiting only for the right moment to be called on once again, like a dinner bell waiting to be rung over and over again. At that moment, Sun Liangjiu coughed, somewhat violently, before speaking in a clear, direct voice, issuing specific orders to each village: "In truth, the required pegs are already in the ground. Once we're finished here, you'll all come with me and have a look. The sections each village will be responsible for are all clearly marked."

Once the director had finished speaking he sat down next to the secretary who, seemingly unable to hold his tongue, stood once more and rapped against the wall. He then turned and pointed the stick he held towards the rest of them: "You all understand now, don't you? You've finished thinking, haven't you? So tell me, where do you stand?"

The village branch secretary for Mapodian, Xia Tianyuan, stood up as though he were a primary school student. His eyes were bright, his posture confident, he seemed to be sure of what he wanted to say. He looked the commune secretary straight in the eyes, unflinching, determined. His pose resonated with the others who still sat looking at the wall. Liu Dajiang asked him: "So what will it be, which band do you wish to be in?"

"The horse-drawn buggy."

"The what?" Liu Dajiang gasped in surprise. "Why not the cuckold then, huh? Do you think the rocket and the aeroplane are just for show? Only a painting on a wall?"

Xia Tianyuan wasn't nervous, he wasn't worried, nor was he angry. Calmly he explained: "We're a small village. We don't really have enough young able-bodied men to carry out this job, but being able to sit in a horse-drawn buggy doesn't sound all that bad. It's better to let the bigger villages be rockets and aeroplanes."

"Wangguantun!"

The team leader for Wangguantun, Xu Gaoyang, stood up and lurched forward, his frame akin to a man who'd endured some form of torture or other, crippled and twisted. A heavy silence passed before he spoke: "We'll take the automobile."

Liu Dajiang chose not to ask anything further, instead calling out: "Miaojiazhuang?"

The old team leader of Miaojiazhuang, Miao Jiedi, shuffled forward. There was a certain gentle nature to the way he carried himself, unassuming and friendly. He said softly: "Secretary Liu, do you want an honest answer or do you only want to hear what you want?"

"I want you to be honest!"

"Our village, I think, would perhaps rather choose the donkey cart, if it isn't too much trouble."

"And if it is?"

"It's difficult to say. We'd be willing to take the rocket, that'd make the commune leaders happy for sure, but in case we don't finish the assigned task, then we'd face the consequences, right? And that's a risk we'd rather not take. It's not like we haven't been through something similar to this before. During the Great Leap Forward the authorities spoke in the same grand manner, but if they'd truly listened and done what they said they'd do, if they'd properly stored the people's food, then we wouldn't be in the shit we're in now. Once was enough, there's no need to rehash this drivel."

"Guojiadian!"

Chen Baohuai's voice was piercingly loud: "We'll throw caution to the wind, we'll take the train!"

There was a roar of chattering among them and then someone shouted: "By the sound of his voice you'd think he'd said they'd take the rocket or the aeroplane at least, heh? They'll work themselves dead for half a day at best, then they'll be sitting on the train."

Chen Baohuai responded immediately: "Our village thought to take the aeroplane but didn't know how to buy a ticket and, well, there's nowhere to sit on a rocket. I mean, when have any of you heard about a man on a rocket?" He then changed the subject entirely and spoke directly to Liu Dajiang: "Secretary Liu, when do the authorities plan to exact punishment on Guo Cunxian?"

"Guo Cunxian? Who's that and what did he do?"

"He was a unit leader in Guojiadian. He took advantage of the rain to encourage those under his command to grab what food they could and to hoard it away."

"Oh... yes, that man, that rascal. Let's make his crime serve the people, send him to the river to work."

Just what did that mean? They'd spent half the day arguing over this river project and now work on it was going to be used as punishment for a crime committed against the commune! What was said wasn't what was meant, at least it wasn't intentional on the secretary's part, but to those listening, they heard what they heard. The authorities had envisioned this project as a form of forced labour, of reform through labour. If an urban worker committed a mistake, they'd be sent to the countryside to toil as a farmer. If a farmer were to do likewise, they'd be forced into dredging a river. With this type of approach, how would any of them choose to struggle, choose to work themselves to the bone to take that blasted rocket or to fly an aeroplane? The village cadres turned merciless, wrangling over the meaning of Liu Dajiang's words. But just as they reached a fever pitch, the sound of firecrackers split the air: bang, bang, bang in quick succession, crack... boom!

It was quite an unexpected sound, not heard for the past two years when even New Year's festivities had been quiet. Why had firecrackers been lit now? What was there to celebrate? Sun Liangjiu first conferred in hush tones with Liu Dajiang before he decided they'd all go and see what was happening, then make their way to the river to assign work responsibilities; after all, choosing that now served no real purpose.

Liu Dajiang stared at him questioningly, wondering whether or not he was like some addle-brained drunkard desperately in search of his next fix.

But when the sounds of the firecrackers drifted away, a renewed seriousness came over Liu Dajiang. He turned to announce to the crowd: "The authorities are wise, they'd already considered the possibility of floods, that the food stores had not been properly filled, so they'd made allowances not only for emergency relief, but also for each commune to open a market bazaar. In this manner the population can more readily manage disasters, this current one, and mutually assist each other. We've decided to set up the bazaar in Laodong Township for the fifth and tenth of every month. How about we all walk over to the market now, to browse its wares and see if anyone else has come? Afterwards, we can go directly from there to the river."

The gathered cadres exited the courtyard, turned and went down the main thoroughfare of Laodong Township. The street was the market, the market the street; from south to north it linked the entire town. But on closer inspection it was easy enough to see, more people had come to see the hubbub rather than to buy and sell goods. And even for those who did come to shop, the only items available were the most basic: some woven mats, some wooden logs, a few eggs, a few onions, a couple of aubergines, half a basket of beans… and even though each stall had people milling about, it was difficult to determine whether they were actually interested in purchasing what had become rare items over the last few years, or if they'd come because of the novelty of even going to a market in the first place.

Of course, the market was a welcome sight, but the people had been starving for so many years now and allowing for a market, permitting people to buy and sell things, and even to hawk wares that people could stuff into their mouths, who wouldn't say that this was all very odd? After all, if people had things to eat, why on earth would they sell them and not eat them themselves, in times like these? Surely food was more valuable than a bit of money in their pockets? There could be only one explanation, business was innate to human nature, and it didn't matter what was bought or sold, or how much. Opening a market permitted people to buy and sell things, so it allowed them to live, it gave them back a sense of well-being, however shallow it may actually be. Whether you believed this or not, strolling among the people as they wound their way through the market, there was a certain glimmer in their eyes, even if they ended up buying little or nothing at all. It was just the fact of being there, in the market. What did it bring? Hope, perhaps? A belief, faith that things would work out, perhaps? And weren't the cadres that had come just the same? It really was strange. All you needed was a market to conduct business and, even in difficult times, valuable items could still be sold, and even in times of poverty there were still people who had money to shop.

Sun Liangjiu walked down the middle of the street, taking in the scene. Then suddenly his nose caught a whiff of something and he broke to the right, pushing his way into the crowd, deeper and deeper into the market. As he made his way further into the mass of people, he soon came upon an old man sat behind a stall hawking sweet potato wine, a small bowl adjacent to the bottle. After watching him draw near, the old man spoke: "Director Sun, will you have a bowl?"

It was as though Sun Liangjiu had come on purpose. He reached into his pocket and took out whatever he had. Without even really looking at it, he passed it towards the old man: "I've got just over seven *jiao*, that's a ladleful at least."

The old man opened the bottle and using a small steelyard for measurement, spooned up a little of the alcohol into the bowl. Sun Liangjiu took hold of the offered wine with two hands, enjoying the aroma as he moved his face closer to the lip of the bowl. He knelt down in front of the stall, his back towards the throng of people as though he were afraid someone would try to snatch the bowl away from him. He took one large swig but swallowed it slowly. Raising his face he closed his eyes in exultation, savouring the taste of the wine before letting it slide down his throat. He took another mouthful before opening his eyes again. In the blink of an eye he seemed transformed, now full of energy, his face flushed. The old man who'd sold him the wine pulled a small bundle out of his pocket. Opening it, he took out a small block of salt, proffering it to Sun Liangjiu, who bent forward and touched it with the tip of his tongue. With the salty taste still in his mouth, he took another swig of wine.

A man standing alongside now shouted: "What a show! Director Sun, I think you need to change your name. If that's the way you enjoy your wine, then you ought to be called Old Boozy Sun, that's a much better name for sure!"

Another man shouted: "Don't mock these old-timers. Didn't you know, Sun used to be known as Old Number Nine, that's one, two, three, four, five, six, seven, eight, nine, not Old Boozy."

Sun Liangjiu paid no heed to their jests. He stood and drained the bowl dry, closed his mouth and allowed the warmth of the alcohol to wash over him.

Liu Dajiang finally came up to him and asked: "Another bowl?"

"No, that's all right."

"If you're not drinking any more, then let's go. We'll take your indulgence as a toast to the opening of the market. Everyone now, clap!"

Those who'd gathered round now clapped loudly in unison.

But before they had walked far, they encountered tears. A young, strapping lad appeared before them with a rough, wooden log slung over his shoulder, looking as though he were intent on exchanging the burden he was carrying for half a bag of dried sweet potato. The young man's poor wife came straggling behind, holding on to the end of the log, refusing to let go. She wept pitifully: "How can you take this away to sell? What'll we do when the wind blows and the rain falls? Our house will be without a roof! What then?"

There was no warmth in his response: "What good is a house to people who're starving?"

Watching the sorry confrontation between husband and wife unfold, Liu Dajiang quickly ordered the cadres to hurry along. They couldn't dither any longer, they had to get to work. As they said in olden times, even an honest and upright official would have difficulty resolving a family dispute, to say nothing of today when officials were seemingly impotent to deal with the creeping hunger and starvation that plagued the people; after all, he was only the local commune secretary. In truth, his heart was troubled by other things. Opening this market was quite a nuisance and fraught with potential disruption. Just what would they do if a starving madman were to come and start grabbing at the bits of food available, hmm, what then? For that reason it was rather urgent for him to devote his thoughts to coming up with possible methods to deal with would-be troublemakers.

As the cadres passed through the main street and beyond the market, they soon saw more people making their way into town. Those who'd come first to the market had brought their wares behind them in horse-drawn carts, or they'd pushed the cart themselves, or tied it to one of their farm animals. Others, less fortunate, had come to market carrying loads over their shoulders or baskets in their arms; very few came empty-handed. But the people they saw now had nothing in their arms and that was good, he thought. They'd come simply to browse. But trailing along in the crowd was a solitary figure, a man who looked quite the worse for wear. His steps were uneven and his body tottered back and forth. Then, just as he drew near, he seemed to realise he could move no more and collapsed into the dust underneath. To a man, the cadres all ran towards him, tried to attend to him and to lift him back up but to no avail. The man's body had simply had enough. Looking now at the corpse at their feet, they could see signs of the times across his arms and legs, bloated and festering, his face, too, abnormally enlarged. He was no more than fifty years old or so.

Sun Liangjiu couldn't help but mumble, berating the dead man: "You're suffering from third-stage oedema. Why the hell have you come here, huh? Today is our market day, an auspicious day. Now you've gone and ruined it!"

But there was nothing for it, no way to escape what now lay at their feet. Into the silence Chen Baohuai asked the question: "What'll we do?"

"Does anyone know him?"

A few of the cadres bent low and looked at the man's face, but no one knew him. Liu Dajiang spoke: "We've more important things to manage and, besides, I reckon his family will be along soon. If he's still slumped down here when we return, then we'll just call for someone to come and bury him."

As the sky beyond the window began to brighten, Guo Cunxian awoke. By his estimation, the ground should no longer have been as waterlogged as it was, so he ought to have been able to take his spade and get to work, which in turn would have helped to put his wife more at ease. He'd be able to get out of the house. It was no surprise then that she too had got up with the first rays of sun and had already prepared his clothes for the day. Picking up his spade from alongside the southern wall, he walked towards the courtyard gate, soon noticing that it was slightly ajar. Evidently his mad old uncle had arisen even earlier than him.

Somehow it had just happened. The land around the village became known as private allocations (originally it had been 'lent' to the state as part of the collectivisation initiatives, but some clever higher-up had decided to change all of that and replace the word 'lend' with the word 'retain' instead). This sounded infinitely better and kind of rolled off the tongue, as it were. And it had the effect of making the peasants actually think that the land was truly theirs, or that it had been returned to them. In an instant, then, the authorities had altered the entire perception of the land policies and succeeded in creating little pieces of heaven for each individual farmer which, of course, changed their entire outlook on life. What this all meant for mornings was that the peasants were much more inclined to get up early in order to work the fields. And from far away Guo Cunxian heard them shout: "You're up early today, aren't you?"

"Heh, but aren't you out here earlier than me?"

"Your wife's so pretty. Now that autumn has come you ought to be holding her tight, especially when night comes and one needs to... exert much effort!"

"Ah, but there's nothing for it. Even a pretty wife needs to eat, after all. Where else would one get the energy!"

"Cunxian, what're you planning to sow in your allotment? I think I'll follow suit and plant what you do."

"How's that now, huh? I don't think that'll be allowed. And you know what? I think it's too early yet to sow wheat."

"Heh, you're a smart one you are. You always think of something. That blasted rain, even if it has drained away, has only brought all of the salt to the surface. Just go and look at the farmland. It's practically white and that's all salt. It doesn't matter what we plant, nothing at all will grow."

"You're right about that, it's been on my mind, too."

It was rather odd. The villagers seemed to be speaking to him more than ever now, and there was a certain warmth when they talked, much more polite than ever before. He couldn't figure out why this had happened, no matter how much he tried. It was a truism, one could say, that most farmers lacked courage, preferring not to get involved and to avoid trouble wherever and whenever they could. It was also true that they tended to fawn over their leaders, more than willing to play the role of a toady. Why was it then that now, after he'd been removed from office, that they treated him even better than before? Could it be that they were all really softies at heart and that they knew that his current difficulties were on account of them? Was it because they knew he'd been prevented from leaving town again and that he couldn't go off to make some money making coffins any more? Or was it that they were just resigned to their lot, that they were taking what joy they could in spite of the times. But perhaps it didn't matter. Whatever the reason, he felt much more at ease and much less embarrassed about being sacked from office. As he came upon his own plot of land, he soon saw that Liu Yucheng, who had the field adjacent to his, had already turned over the topsoil and had made the ground ready for planting. Guo Cunxian couldn't hide his surprise: "Yucheng, what did you do? Spend the night here?"

"No, no, I just arrived a little earlier than you, that's all."

There was admiration in his voice when he spoke: "I've been thinking, you know, about getting on here with the work, but I never thought that you'd already be finished."

"I came last night to have a look, but now's the time for putting one's spade to use."

"What're you intending to plant? Aren't you worried about the salt?"

"I'm going to plant some spinach. It's not really affected by the salt. In fact, the more salt there is the more the spinach grows, so much so that a second crop is almost a certainty."

"Why'd you make the ridges between the troughs so wide?"

"Well, that's so the spinach can absorb the salt, to stop it from contaminating the rest of the soil, and then in ten days or so, half a month at most, the land will be ready to plant some wheat crop."

"Aiya, do you think that'll work? If it doesn't, you'll have to find a solution to a very big problem indeed!"

"Try not to worry, Brother Cunxian, we're on it. Hey, did you know I don't really talk all that much? But you didn't bring a fold-away stool with you, nor did I for that matter, so what else am I supposed to do but speak to you a little more."

Guo Cunxian made his way closer so that he could see directly into Liu Yucheng's eyes: "Yucheng, did you know, I'm nine years older than you… a poor peasant as well, just like you. And I'm probably involved in something much shittier, too. But there's something I just don't understand: how is it that you're here planting crops?"

"You've forgotten that my father was a landowner, haven't you? And he wasn't just any old landowner either, no, he was different. Some landowners, they're only in it for the business, they just want to make money, they buy and sell property solely for urban development. But my old man owned the land. For him it was everything. It provided food and made our family wealthy, generation after generation. That meant, of course, that you had to use it, you had to sow crops. In this world, land is the easiest and most difficult thing to understand. I remember my father teaching me this. From a very early age he taught me how to look after the land."

"All right then, you teach me!" Guo Cunxian began to turn over the earth in his plot. Over and over again his spade ate into the ground. Then suddenly he stopped, straightened up and yelled: "Yucheng! I just thought of something. Do you actually have spinach seeds?"

"Of course I do. Do you think I'd be out here working like this if I hadn't any!"

"Where'd you get them? I'd better go and get some myself."

"Do you think there's still time for that? As soon as the floods came I knew what was going to happen. I knew the salt would all be brought up to the surface once the waters receded, so last month I had someone bring me some from Hexi in exchange for some small pittance. I think there's enough for both of us to use."

Guo Cunxian was quite moved: "My dear brother, thank you. If I ever have the opportunity to play a leading role again, I'll be sure to repay you. You'll be my closest adviser."

Liu Yucheng's face turned red and he waved his hands in protest: "No, no, no, I'm only good at sowing seeds and tending to the land. I'm not fit for anything else." From a distance he then spied a figure moving towards them and so he shut his mouth abruptly, not wanting anyone to overhear him. As the figure approached, however, they soon saw that it was Guo Cunxian's mad old uncle. Over his shoulder he was carrying a basket filled to the brim with suaeda (also known as seepweeds or seablites), under his arm he held tight a rake used for night soil and in his hand he was grasping a small sapling a little more than two feet tall. His shoes and trousers were soaking wet. Guo Cunxian gestured him to come closer and helped lighten his load by first taking hold of the night soil rake and then the basket of suaeda hanging over his shoulder. Liu Yucheng took hold of the sapling. "Hey, where did you find this elm sapling? It looks so healthy."

"I found it near the eastern swamp, just alongside the road. If I hadn't moved it then for sure some farm animal or other would've eaten it, or someone would have walked on it." Guo Jingshi then took hold of his nephew's spade. He was going to replant it somewhere suitable near their home. Then he took off his upper garment and in a quaint and somewhat odd fashion he walked away.

Guo Cunxian called out after him but he didn't reply. Teeth bared, he turned towards Liu Yucheng and spoke in hushed tones: "I think your reputation is better than ours. When dealing with my crazy uncle, it's like talking to a wall. We'll ask ten questions and not even get a single response. Damn."

The two men watched the old madman carry his jacket down to the nearby stream and plunge it into the water. Making sure it was soaking wet, he then pulled it out, wrung out the excess water, then walked back up to where they stood and wrapped it around the roots of the tiny sapling. This would keep the roots moist and well-fed, at least until he replanted it.

Watching the scene unfold, Guo Cunxian now removed his own jacket and put it over his uncle's shoulders: "It's still early in the morning and a little chilly. Quickly now, you head home, I'll bring the basket of suaeda when I come."

Guo Jingshi didn't utter a sound. He just bent down, picked up his rake and headed in the direction of the village. Before he got very far, however, he turned round and came back. He picked out a long suaeda stem from the basket, took off the jacket Guo Cunxian had placed over his shoulders and laid it over the top of the basket, then shook out his own soaking wet clothing and put it back on. Liu Yucheng couldn't help but laugh a little: "You're a sturdy one, old-timer... I don't think I've ever seen you fall ill."

Guo Cunxian, in contrast to Yucheng's joking, could only stare blankly at the basket of suaeda. These past few days he'd been so wrapped up in himself and his problems that he'd forgotten about the eastern marshes. The topography of the area was quite low and so the salt emerging from the floodwaters would be even greater than where they were, which meant that the suaeda would have grown even more abundantly, like a weed. But the leaves of the suaeda were edible, and the stems, once dried, could be used for kindling, to say nothing of the fact that the suaeda seeds could be ground up into flour and mixed with other grains to make a gruel that didn't taste that bad. He agreed there and then that both he and Liu Yucheng would head over to the eastern marshes once they had finished tilling their private plots, especially since the suaeda may already be ready for harvesting.

As the sun crept further into the sky, Guo Cunxian's brother, Cunzhi, made an appearance in the fields as well, carrying a spade in his hand. The two were very close, and watching the scene caused a pang of envy to cross Liu Yucheng's heart. His mind drifted back to his dead brother and his heart hurt.

Cunzhi drove the spade into the earth and spoke to his brother at the same time: "I don't think we're digging deep enough into the ground. And if we aren't, what'll we do about all the salt?"

"How deep do you think we should go?"

"Well, Guo Cunxiao was just at our place. He said we all had to form shovel teams, except for those working on the river, of course, and dig at least a metre deep. That'd be the only way to get rid of the salt and make the earth suitable for sowing wheat."

"What're you talking about? What's this about working on the river?"

"That's what he came to our house about. He was looking for you. Apparently, you're supposed to work on the river. I told him I'd go in your place but he said that wasn't permitted and it has to be you because it's your punishment."

Cunxian twisted his head and looked at his younger brother: "That's really what he said?"

"Yup. He also said that these were Secretary Liu's orders, too."

"Fuck. Fuck. Fuck. It's like they're banishing me to some faraway military post! Besides me, who else are they sending?"

"Quite a lot of people, actually. Every household has to send their sturdiest member but you'll get extra grain rations and a little money, one-and-a-half *jiao*."

Guo Cunxian mumbled to himself. Working on the river would be hard, really hard. And what would they get for it? A little extra food and some money. Would that be compensation enough? And they were using this project as punishment, too, reform through labour. Then why wasn't Liu Yucheng coming along too, or was he? In quiet tones Guo Cunxian instructed his brother: "If Liu Yucheng is to be sent to work on the river project as well, then there'd only be his younger sister at home. Our private plots are right next to each other. You'll have to look after both of them, all right, and make sure you don't forget."

While the two of them spoke, Liu Yucheng finished turning the soil over in his plot and decided to lend a helping hand to Guo Cunxian. Before he could start, however, Guo Cunxian interrupted him: "We've got additional orders from the town. Each shovel team is to dig down a metre deep, turn the soil over, then plant wheat seeds. They say that'll take care of the salt. What do you think? Will it work?"

"It won't work," Liu Yucheng responded adamantly, "absolutely not. This village lives on the soil that faces the sun, the soil that's been cooked, you could say. It's this layer that's most fertile. If you dig down more than a metre and turn the soil over from there, shifting the drenched soil underneath, then all you're left with is virgin soil on the top. Planting wheat in that will be a complete waste."

"Well, once you're finished here, why don't the two of you go and see Guo Cunxiao and explain to him what you just told us. He can then let the higher-ups know and convince them not to waste the few wheat seeds we have."

Nervously, Liu Yucheng stepped back: "Brother Cunxian, I can't, I just can't. You know my background. If I were to go, wouldn't it be like deliberately going in search of trouble?"

Guo Cunxian laughed bitterly: "Then I'll go."

Cunzhi immediately blocked his path: "Brother, you can't go either. You're no longer the team leader, why get involved in other people's business? Besides, you know Guo Cunxiao, he's as stubborn as they come and especially hard to deal with. If you mess up and say the wrong thing, that'll just bring more trouble down on top of you, perhaps more than you can handle."

Guo Cunxian thought it over. His brother was right, but still he was unwilling to let it go: "Just because he is a stubborn mule doesn't mean he shouldn't be told the truth and, besides, what more could they do to me, huh? If there's no wheat to harvest next year, well, then that bad luck won't be ours."

Puzzled, Cunzhi and Liu Yucheng both stared at him anxiously. Didn't they already have enough bad luck? If there's no wheat harvest next year, then everyone will suffer, there will be more than enough bad luck to go around, or perhaps that wouldn't be misfortune. If he wanted to take the lead on this, to be the pioneer, then who's to say that any misfortune that did occur would only occur to him? Wasn't the land grab he advocated an example of this? Hadn't everyone but him got off scot free?

Sun Yueqing was overjoyed to see Guo Jingshi come into the courtyard carrying the suaeda. She quickly took hold of it and made her way to the kitchen to wash it, all the while babbling away. She asked him this and that, not really expecting answers; it was just her excitement talking. Strangely, however, mad old uncle Jingshi listened attentively and answered each one.

Where did he find such excellent suaeda?

Near where the frogs nest in the eastern marshes.

There's still water there?

Yes, wherever there were deeper holes, there was water.

But the road was clear; people were able to walk through?

Yes, they could.

Was there much barnyard grass growing?

Yes, there was.

Had it ripened?

By the look of it, yes.

Zhu Xuezhen knelt down by the stove to stoke the fire. Once she saw that the water was nearly boiling, she stood up and went into the western room, ladle in hand, to scoop up some flour. In front of the raised floor was a row of porcelain containers neatly hung on the wall, each in their own place, almost as though they had to be. Inside each jar was stored a little something to eat; not much, mind you, in some only a few spoonfuls but a little just the same. When times had been better, the jars would have been filled with wheat flour, cornmeal or what have you, but now all that was left were the dregs. Perhaps if one were to scrape the bottom hard enough there'd be a little something to make a pancake or two. However, that would only be done as a last resort. It was better to keep a little bit in the jar, for appearance's sake. Unused flour allowed the family to better sustain itself in the face of hunger, at least for another day. To have some flour about the house, well, the importance of that was more symbolic; it wasn't for eating. Besides, the hardships they'd been experiencing had taught them to broaden their horizons, so to speak, and to experiment with myriad things, testing to find out what was edible and what was not. Sometimes this meant that they had more to eat; sometimes it meant they only had too many utensils laid out but their bellies were still empty. Nonetheless, they did expand on their diet.

Speaking only of dried goods, they'd discovered there were many different greens that could be dried and eaten, from radish leaves to purslane (small fleshy-leaved plants that thrive in damp, marshy conditions), endives to sour buds and thistles. Even small, greenish centipedes would make it to their bowls at times. Sweet potato, too, could be divided into different types, from raw to dried, with the latter ground up and used for flour as well. All this meant that each meal ended up being like a herbal remedy or cure for something or other; a matching of this green with that one. But the bonus to this was that each meal was different; breakfast was nothing like lunch and dinner was something else yet again. Meals, too, were dependent on the day's work and the weather. If the men were to be busy, then the meals would be made accordingly. If the day was overcast and cloudy, however, work would end up being rather light and so too would the meals. But the fact that they were able to do this meant that they got on better than most. Before, they had been a little better off because Guo Cunxian had been able to send them food and money. And even if it wasn't enough to truly fill them up, the most important thing was that Sun Yueqing would ration it out, making sure that what they had would last as long as possible. Apart from the two or three portions that the government handed out daily, Sun Yueqing would bump that up with their personal supplies, ensuring that everyone would have at least half a *jin*, with one quarter used for breakfast, two for lunch and the last for dinner. She did the same thing now, and even though Cunzhu was living at school and thus not around, she still had five mouths to feed. Breakfast was always a sticky congee made of cornmeal, sorghum and sweet potato flour. This is what Sun Yueqing was preparing to make, hence she had sent Xuezhen to get the flour. Peering into one of the jars, she scooped up two ladlefuls of cornmeal and placed it on the copper scale that stood on the raised floor. Unfortunately, however, she hadn't brought the required countermeasure and so the scale fell dangerously low on one side, spilling some of the flour.

Making meals in the past had always been Sun Yueqing's responsibility, and things had remained the same, despite Xuezhen's arrival. In fact, her old mother-in-law would only let her help and instead of treating her like her son's wife, another daughter to help with the chores around the house, now more so than ever since Cunzhu had left, she was still treated like a young unmarried maiden. All her mother-in-law tried to do was indulge and spoil her, and while she understood there was no malicious intent, it did seem as though at times she were treated as being too immature, too stupid even, to make a pot of gruel.

In the midst of measuring out the cornmeal, Xuezhen heard a noise coming from the outer room: the water had come to the boil and the cover had begun clinking and clanking as the steam tried to escape. She grew nervous as she couldn't really tell how much cornmeal she had scooped up. Thinking quickly on her feet, she decided she wasn't going to measure out the cornmeal after all; besides, she thought, they were only making it for themselves. What did it really matter? Thinking thus, she slipped her hand into the jar and scooped up two handfuls; she figured that'd be enough. Returning to the kitchen, she was about to dump the cornmeal into the pot when Sun Yueqing came up beside her, a knowing smile on her face from ear to ear. She took the measuring weights from her hand and, with exceptionally deft movements, measured out the specific amount of cornmeal. She then spoke to Xuezhen: "Did you honestly think that I didn't want to bother measuring the cornmeal? For every dead person, for every family with people suffering from oedema, they all rely on their guts to eat, not on these silly measuring weights. When there's food, for sure people want to eat their fill and when there's none, their stomachs rumble. But starving, I mean really starving. That's not just something we've experienced over a couple of days, nor even over a couple of months. It has been years, ever since the Great Leap Forward began two or three years ago. To live through times like these we need to be careful, we need to measure everything, to ration as strictly as we can. What's more, right now this is a test. Cunxian's not only prohibited from leaving town to go in search of work, he also has to work on the river project, which is nothing other than him selling his own labour, or at least being told to do so. Whatever the case, we must make sure that he's always got the energy he needs."

As she spoke, a thought popped into her mind and caused her to shift focus: she was going to change the breakfast menu today. Cunxian and his brother had got up early and had already been out to the fields, shovels in hand, and their uncle, too, had got up early. They all deserved a big meal this morning. She instructed Xuezhen to grab two handfuls of dried vegetables and put them in the pot, along with the two ladlefuls of cornmeal she'd taken out previously without properly measuring it. They'd add some salt and have vegetable pancakes for breakfast.

From the ingredients in front of her, Sun Yueqing nimbly apportioned one *jin* of cornmeal and half a *jin* of sorghum flour and dumped it into a pot. She added some water and stirred the mixture thoroughly, moistening it to make it ready for rolling out, which she did, into one large, round pancake that was to be fried. As her hands busily worked in front of her, she explained her reasoning to Xuezhen for changing the morning meal: "Working men need to start the day right, they can't work properly on an empty stomach... that just wouldn't do, so a proper breakfast was necessary. And if that meant others needed to go without, say the women of the family, then that's how it would be." Then realising something, Sun Yueqing added: "But not you, no, you need to eat too. If you don't, you'll never be able to get pregnant. Do you know, there are over a thousand households in Guojiadian," she continued, "but over the last few years not one has added a new mouth to feed. If that keeps up, soon there won't be a village left at all!"

Listening to her speak, Zhu Xuezhen soon began to understand: the only person who really endured the pangs of starvation in this family was her poor mother-in-law. Thinking of this, her heart ached and burned as though it too were on top of the stove. Still Sun Yueqing worked. She formed six pancakes out of the mixture, wasting not a single morsel, and these she formed into equal-sized balls. Each was placed in the pan, all with the same distance in between. Watching her deftly fry the pancakes, Xuezhen couldn't help but feel a little envious of her skill; it was so graceful.

Once she had finished shaping the pancakes, she covered the pan, moistened a cloth and then wrapped it round the lid, making sure that it was sealed tightly. She then instructed Xuezhen to look after the fire while she got out the cutting board to chop the just washed suaeda. Once diced, she placed the overflowing bowl of suaeda to one side and pealed two heads of garlic; these she mulched with a cutting knife and added to the same bowl. Grabbing a bottle of vinegar, she dripped a little over the vegetables and then added a drop or two of sesame oil. With a pair of chopsticks she mixed it all up, filling the entire kitchen with a pungent aroma. Xuezhen crinkled her nose and asked her mother-in-law what she was making; the smell was certainly enticing. Sun Yueqing looked quite pleased, and responded that not only did it smell enticing, but that it tasted even better. She'd find out soon enough, once they laid the table. She mused, too, that Xuezhen probably hadn't tasted anything like it before, coming from up in the mountains as she did. But here, since they were fairly close to the sea and the salt carried in the air and into the soil, especially during the wet season, farming had become increasingly difficult, but crops like suaeda and barnyard millet flourished. These added a distinctive flavour to the meals they prepared; that was for sure. Once they had finished eating and cleared up, Sun Yueqing promised she'd take Xuezhen to the marshes to gather some themselves and that, if they worked hard, they'd probably be able to pick nineteen or twenty *jin*, which would definitely enhance their meals.

Breakfast was truly delicious, with each man eating two large vegetable pancakes, along with a bowl of lightly salted vegetable gruel. As the men ate the pancakes, Sun Yueqing took one of the additional ones, cut it down the middle and placed a half in front of herself. The other half she forced into Xuezhen's hands, who, out of respect for her mother-in-law, accepted. But she didn't eat it ravenously; instead she took only small bites, slowly savouring the flavour and enjoying the maternal warmth her mother-in-law showed her. Then, as she chewed, she got up and went into the outer room whereupon she took her own pancake and divided it into three pieces, one each for the bowls of gruel prepared for the men. When she returned, however, she noticed that her mother-in-law had not touched her own half of the pancake. She watched and listened to the men as they ate their morning meal, talking about how good it tasted, and before long the bottoms of their bowls began to show. They then expressed the wish that dinner would comprise more of the same fragrant suaeda pancakes. Since both boys needed to tend to the family plot first, once they had finished they lay down their chopsticks and left. Soon, it was just the two of them, Sun Yueqing and her daughter-in-law. They, too, had somewhere to be, so once they had quickly cleaned up and washed their hands and feet, they picked up two cloth bags and sets of chopsticks, locked the doors and headed straightaway to the marshes.

The road to the eastern marshes hadn't totally dried, so they soon found themselves trekking through the mud. Instead of continuing, however, they chose to take a higher path, rightfully surmising that it would be at least a little dryer. The marshland was some distance from the village, and so it was empty of people. Much of the farmland they passed, too, was empty, filled with nothing but a mass of rotting vegetation. The spoiled sprouts from before the rains seemed to hug the ground, suffocating the land underneath; it all looked as though it were some faraway land. The floods had taken away as much of it as they could, so much so that the air that now hung about the area was entirely free of dust. Towards the far end a soft wind blew, and where they stood the sun beat down upon them, allowing for a sense of great comfort to envelope them. But as they were out in the open, Xuezhen kept her head low and her eyes on the road itself. Occasionally she'd lift them to gaze at the landscape, to see if the great waters had really receded. But each time she looked up, all that lay before her was a great expanse of whiteness as far as the eye could see. She spoke then, surprising herself, asking her mother-in-law if that were the sea. Sun Yueqing's mood was good. She answered the question immediately, despite it being rather foolish. Of course, it wasn't the sea but a marshy wetland home to more frog colonies than one could count. Known as Dadongdian, it stretched over some 290km in total!

Near the frog marshes stretched a salty breadth of land nearly overgrown with suaeda, more than half of them taller than a man. Pocketed among the saline soil were small wetlands and in each grew barnyard millet that reached into the sky. The seeds of both were even tastier than the plants, and more nutritious. This was the first thing Sun Yueqing taught her daughter-in-law. They each had a basket, and once they were filled, they dumped the contents into the sacks they had brought with them. Despite their bags being nearly full, it didn't stop them from picking more, especially if the suaeda seemed especially good. Their backs would bend and they would quickly pull the suaeda from the ground and place it in their pockets. They were both quite content, talkative, growing closer and closer, more like family. Xuezhen couldn't help but wonder aloud, if all of this was here, why were they the only ones picking it?

Sun Yueqing replied, saying it might be because of the condition of the road; it was still rather muddy after all. Or perhaps it was that no one knew this was all here.

"Then how did uncle Jingshi know about it?" Xuezhen asked.

Sun Yueqing replied honestly: "He was unique, you know. He didn't think or behave like the rest of them. Their response to disaster was to put their hands up in defeat, acquiesce and give up. And that'd mean they ate less and less and became more and more lethargic, slouching about all day, some not even getting out of bed, resigned to nattering and gossiping about the predicament they were in and doing nothing about it."

The work was deceptive and before the sun reached its apex, they had already filled their two sacks. Sun Yueqing called to Xuezhen, suggesting they should sit down for a rest and after that head home. As they rested, their eyes stared intently at the growing millet and suaeda all around them. Sun Yueqing then let her eyes drop and looked intently at the vegetation underfoot. She discovered that it was, in fact, garlic shoots growing underneath, about half a foot long or more. And that wasn't all, she noticed some grassy sprouts as well and, her eyes flickering, she wondered out loud: "Might these be water chestnuts?"

"Water chestnuts, surely not?" said Xuezhen, even if the question was rhetorical. Regardless, Sun Yueqing answered that soon she would understand, and then she bent over and began collecting the grassy shoots that grew beneath. As expected, they were garlic shoots, despite being comparatively small, more akin to the size of jujubes than garlic bulbs. Nevertheless, her hands worked tirelessly. Still picking, she passed more than one handful to Xuezhen, told her to clean what she'd given her and then use her teeth to peel off the skin. Once the skin was removed they'd be ready to eat. They were quite crunchy and very sweet, with just a hint of chestnut flavour. Xuezhen found them delicious, a hundred times better than the chestnuts that grew in the trees.

Sun Yueqing replied that that was to be expected. After all, who hadn't seen chestnuts growing in trees? Who hadn't tried them? But water chestnuts, no, these were different and even around here in these marshy wetlands they were rare. They'd only grow in the aftermath of heavy rains, after the floodwaters had receded, in the first few days that followed, but this wasn't a sure thing either. Not every flood was the same, so one couldn't be sure if there'd be water chestnuts or not. To be fair, they'd been lucky. Without concern about creating a less than dignified scene, Xuezhen removed her socks and shoes and stomped into the muddy waters, furiously digging with her hands, lifting up mounds of dirt and flinging it up onto the dryer bits of earth. Sun Yueqing would scoop out the water chestnuts and wash the mud off them.

Xuezhen had been part of their family for a while now but Sun Yueqing had never seen her so happy, so full of life, her heart filled with warmth. She thought to herself, just when the heavens seemed intent on destroying their poor old peasant family, it had given them something unexpected. It was just up to them to see it, to take hold of it! She lifted her head and looked towards the sky, then returned to the pile of water chestnuts on the ground in front of her. She yelled out to Xuezhen: "Foolish girl, you're almost as silly as your mad old uncle. It's just the two of us, how do you think we'll manage to carry all of this? Quickly now, wash your feet and put your shoes back on. We need help. Go home and get it. I'll wait here to make sure nothing happens to the food." She made sure, too, to give Xuezhen a few water chestnuts to eat on the road home. Then, just as she was about to set off, she gave her a few more instructions: "You don't need to come back, either. I want you to pick out the ripest suaeda of the bunch, wash and chop them, then put them in a pan with some cornmeal flour. I'll make some more pancakes when I get back."

The men to be sent from Guojiadian to dredge the river first gathered at the foot of the Dragon Phoenix Trees, and while all the other work units had already arrived on time, the fourth work unit was late. The town secretary, Chen Baohuai, waiting to send the men off to work, grew increasingly angry as the time passed and they still hadn't shown up. Exasperated, he finally dispatched a member of another work unit to go in search of them but as the morning faded, even that man had not returned. The team leader, Han Jingting, then took it upon himself to go and find out what was going on; they were surprised when he didn't return either. It was now nearly noon and Guojiadian had not begun their work assignment. The whole town was late. Chen Baohuai thought to himself, how was he going to explain this to the commune authorities? For now, in front of the men who had gathered below the Dragon Phoenix Trees, he decided he'd bluster, make a good show of it, encourage them to work hard, and at the same time refute any malicious gossip. He'd tell them that the work they were about to embark upon was completely different from other initiatives and wouldn't result in the same unfortunate outcomes of previous work projects. But the time for telling the men this had passed so he was left with no choice but to instruct the deputy team leader, Guo Huaishan, to lead those who had come to the river to begin work. He, in turn, would go in search of the fourth work unit.

The courtyard for the fourth work unit was packed with people and chaos reigned, like a mass of chickens and ducks clucking and squawking, everyone trying to talk over everyone else. Chen Baohuai pushed his way into the crowd. In a raised voice he roared at the crowd: "Just what the hell is going on here? Huh?" The courtyard grew silent. He looked them all over, searching their faces for some explanation and spied all the men who were supposed to be at the river but, thankfully, they didn't seem to be striking. That at least, put his mind somewhat at ease and allowed him to regain a semblance of assuredness.

In clear tones, Ou Guangming offered a response: "Secretary Chen, it's good that you've come. Sending me to the river to work is fine but I need some explanation. All of the other units are under the command of deputy team leaders but that's not me. I'm just a common worker. I know my place and I daren't take responsibility for this job. Besides, I also have a sick old father at home who can't even get out of bed. My brother is still too small, and a little dumb, too, it must be said. Everyone knows this. If I go off to work on the river, who's going to take care of them? What if something were to happen, what then? If the work unit could give me some assurances, a letter or something to that effect, then I'd immediately set off to work."

Chen Baohuai played dumb, and then his eyes searched the crowd for Guo Cunxiao, the fourth unit team leader: "That's right, Ou Guangming is in a difficult spot, why was he ordered to work on the river project?" Guo Cunxiao was an honest fellow and his face betrayed him now. He didn't know how to respond. The fact he hadn't wanted to be team leader in the first place only made things worse. Ou Guangming had already asked him this question, too, had asked him too many frigging times, and he'd already answered him. He told him it had been the village's decision, he told him that in front of everyone else, they had assigned him the task of taking the workers to the river; he was to be in charge of them. But when Han Jingting had come, he had told him he didn't know anything about this decision, which only made him look bad in the face of the people, as though he had deliberately put Ou Guangming forward for this difficult task, like working out some grudge or other.

In truth, everyone knew what was going on. And Ou Guangming was no fool either, he knew, too. Guo Cunxiao simply didn't have the balls to make such a decision. The village authorities had manipulated him into doing so. On the surface, it looked as though they were foisting on him the duties of a petty official but in fact they were removing him from the town's militia. All one needed to do was to look at the kind of men they'd earmarked for the river project and those they didn't, and it would be easy to understand what was going on. The first type were those who had suspect class origins or those who needed to be struggled against; they were the ones who couldn't argue with the assignment. The second type were those who were easily controlled, the villagers who were docile and 'well behaved', the ones who didn't dare cause trouble; they wouldn't protest either. Finally, the last type were those the village authorities disliked, the ones given important jobs; they were the ones of some ability, and not a single one of them had been ordered to go to the river. Although the higher-ups had said that dredging the river was a priority, an essential undertaking, a key initiative, as it were, then why weren't the village secretary and the work unit leader also involved? At all levels of the commune leadership structure, only the deputy leaders and work units had been sent, making it plain that the reality of the project didn't match the words used to describe it. And, by coincidence, the fourth unit didn't have a deputy leader, thus complicating things. It wasn't, of course, that no one was on hand. Ou Guangming was certainly capable, after all, but for whatever reason the village leaders just didn't want to make it official, didn't want to give him the title, even if they needed him now to carry out this blasted assignment. What was wrong with them? Why the hesitation about Ou Guangming? Was it because he'd participated in Guo Cunxian's so-called land grab attempt, or that he'd had difficulties with Lan Shoukun even before that over the sweet potato affair? Perhaps they believed he'd been poked and prodded a little too much, had too much pent-up anger inside? Eventually a bellyful of hatred will come bubbling to the surface, and if it isn't released today, well, it will sooner or later drive a person mad!

Chen Baohuai watched as Guo Cunxiao squirmed, whimpered and fretted, struggling and unable to offer an explanation. But at the same time, he didn't want this spineless coward to actually give a reply, so he had no choice but to intervene: "It's like this to me: Guangming's family are in dire straits, so it's all right if he remains home for the time being. We'll reconsider things in the afternoon and make a firmer decision then. As for the rest of you, go, now. This entire project is under the authority of the military and the whole county is involved. Each commune is an integral cog in the machine. Our village, along with the towns of Wangguantun and Mapodian, form links in the chain and that means each work unit in Guojiadian plays a vital role. You were all supposed to be there at the river in the morning for roll call. They had planned a meeting to inaugurate the project. How about this? Let's reinstate Guo Cunxian as unit leader so that you'll have someone in charge. Isn't that perfect?"

The eyes of everyone in the courtyard now turned towards Guo Cunxian, who had been sitting comfortably on his rolled-up mattress and quilt. His head remained low and his eyes closed. He spoke quietly but decisively: "No, that won't work. I was removed from office and so I'll stay removed. My standing in the village has been tarnished. I'm not fit to take the lead on this."

Chen Baohuai had never before been snubbed quite so forcefully and in front of so many people. He was unable to move, unable to step off the stage. Everyone else seemed equally frozen, unwilling to even breathe. The silence lasted for what felt like an eternity before, finally, Han Jingting, who was the unit leader after all, decided to break the awkwardness of the moment. He walked over to Chen Baohuai and whispered some words in his ear as though providing him with a ladder to climb down. Then he turned to the crowd and announced: "Secretary Chen and I have just conferred. We've come to the conclusion that the most suitable person to oversee your unit's contribution to the river project will be your unit leader himself, Guo Cunxiao. This way you can begin work. Later this afternoon, the local Party branch will deliberate and decide upon a suitable deputy leader who will then take charge."

Old Han Jingting was quite clever, after all. The decision they'd just made wasn't going to be re-evaluated, they wouldn't talk about it again. If they'd really wanted to name someone as deputy leader, the time to do that was now, not at some point in the future. Now, that person would be Guo Cunxiao, whether he liked it or not. And he knew it, too. He would be the authorities' scapegoat and, at the same time, he'd have to enumerate the shortcomings of the people. The only loser today was him. What had he done to be so wronged? Of all the individual unit leaders in the village, he was the only unfortunate one that had to go to the river. He couldn't think of a reason to get out of it, either. All he could do was to ask for permission to let his family know, to collect his bedding and then set off to work. Feeling that the issue had been resolved, Chen Baohuai played on the sentiment of the people, especially the honest ones. In a loud voice he exhorted them: "Don't dilly dally, it's already noon, everyone is waiting for you."

Before too much time had passed, Guo Cunxiao returned with his belongings to lead the fourth work unit to the river. Unlike the gathering earlier, there was a carnival atmosphere this time around, with many people coming to see them off. As the men marched off, Han Jingting noticed an axe wrapped up in Guo Cunxian's bedding. He walked over to ask why: "Cunxian, why do you need an axe to dredge a river?"

Thinking he was trying to malign him, Guo Cunxian kept on walking as he answered: "I'm a carpenter. Our rule is that, should we head off anywhere to work, we have to always carry certain household essentials with us. Now, what if these essentials break, huh, won't they need fixing?"

Han Jingting replied: "That's a fine rule, I think. Certainly it's very reasonable."

As they talked, Chen Baohuai stood beside them, but he refused to look at Guo Cunxian. He saluted everyone else but ignored the man who had so publicly snubbed him. Guo Cunxian did the same, minding his own business and exiting the courtyard along with everyone else. He understood, of course, that he had insulted Chen Baohuai and had made him look bad. He knew, too, that Chen still had power, which meant things wouldn't get any better for him, but he was resigned to that fact. Good favour just didn't follow him around. In some ways, he was in the same boat as Guo Cunxiao. After all, hadn't his appointment as team leader for the fourth work unit been similarly inauspicious? If it hadn't been for that flood, none of this would have happened. The key was to control power and not be controlled by it but in Guojiadian, only the secretary had real power. Everyone in the village was stuck in the palm of his hand. Shit, people fooled themselves talking about skills and abilities. Power was all that mattered. That was the skill to have. Power meant others were afraid of you.

Guo Cunxian was listless and distracted the entire way there, his mind plagued by thoughts about his fate. For the past half year he couldn't help but feel like a pancake frying in a pan, lifted up and flipped, over and over, this way and that, one side burning, the other side cold. It was like swinging an axe violently again and again only to have it smash into twisted roots and joints, into knots in the wood, which only tore at the blade, deflecting the thrust of the axe in a different direction. His fate had been twisted like this and shunted onto a different track. For some reason he couldn't fathom, he'd become lumped in with the 'five hated classes'. This whole situation he was in now served to symbolise this. His ill fortune consumed him. Were these the types of obstacles life threw at you?

It was more than five *li* between Guojiadian and the river. The work itself hadn't begun but they were able to see the outline of the new river to be dug. Coloured flags had been placed in the ground to mark where they were to dig, starting in the west and stretching in an easterly direction, the markers fluttered vigorously in the breeze. Next to each flag was a small lean-to with red and green slogans scrawled across them:

"Controlling the water is like treating a disease; managing it is like governing the military!"

"One year to dig a new eastern river will thoroughly transform the entire northeast!"

Since the number four work unit had missed the ceremony to start the project, only now did they understand the monumental task they had been given, the digging of an entirely new river, one that would be called the new eastern waterway. The first thing they did was to locate the other work units from Guojiadian whose lean-tos were all constructed next to each other. Of course, those who'd come early had already been busy. The remaining grassy planks were given to the number four work unit so that they too could construct their own lean-tos. In the winter, this area was known as a wind tunnel, which meant that the other units that arrived earlier in the day had claimed the best locations; the number four work unit was left with less than favourable conditions.

There was a small canteen with men sitting around munching on the dried provisions they had brought with them. In the evening it would properly open, serving food to the entire company of men. The deputy company commander and platoon sergeant sent by Guojiadian, Guo Huaishan, told the number four work unit to quickly have a bite to eat for, in a moment's time, a brass whistle would sound, instructing them all to work. For the newly arrived who weren't up on things, they went off to the communal canteen to get hot water. Some were getting ready to head out to work, and for those who milled about they didn't even have time to finish their snack before the bell rang. The company bugle sounded and the company commander's whistle followed immediately after, both ear-piercingly loud and seemingly growing in intensity. The workers dropped what they were doing and ran out to stand at attention, just like soldiers leading the charge in a film. They all looked very much like a military company, which was a new experience for the farmers, quite exciting. Those who hadn't finished eating stuffed the last bits of food into their mouths and rushed off after the rest of them.

Each company had a technician sent from the county water conservancy bureau who had already assigned sections of the project to individual villages, with pegs placed in the ground to separate each assigned portion from the other. The earliest stages of the work were perhaps the easiest, at least for some, since there was no need to climb up and down the sloping land that was being dug, still shallow as it was. And for those assigned the task of removing the once drought-stricken soil, pushing a wheelbarrow back and forth wasn't all that difficult. Well, not really, at least not at first. Eventually, however, those pushing the wheelbarrows, one after the other, ended up wasting more energy than those who were actually shovelling out the earth. After all, a single wheelbarrow held barely 2,000 *jin* of earth and this had to be pushed for up to 300 metres or more each time. What's more, the constant back and forth was up and down an increasingly steep gradient, which meant the more earth they removed, the more work it took to push the wheelbarrow away. As a result, the work grew increasingly difficult. But for those actually shovelling the earth, well, things were different. That is, between filling the wheelbarrows they could at least take advantage of the lull in work and rest for a while, unlike the men with the wheelbarrows who had to continually keep moving. It was for this reason that everyone believed Guo Cunxiao had deliberately pressed a shovel into the hands of Guo Cunxian. They all knew the mood he was in: annoyed, pissed off, angry. His distant relative was trying to do him a favour, giving him work that was a little easier. A fellow worker standing nearby leaned in close and explained: he was being put in 'charge' of the dirt. Nevertheless, it didn't seem to matter, Guo Cunxian showed no gratitude and expressed no appreciation for the kindness his relative had shown him. Instead, he bent over, grabbed hold of a wheelbarrow and, without uttering a word, headed off towards the section of the river the number four work unit was to be responsible for.

His heart felt heavy, a deep sadness hung over him. His arms ached and sweat poured off his brow. He looked again at the others who had stepped forward of their own volition to push the wheelbarrows. He noticed, then, that they were all tall, strapping fellows, strong, like Jin Laiwang and Liu Yucheng. When the work started, those digging seemed reluctant to fill his wheelbarrow with too much earth, instead only piling it to about halfway, or just about level, and then telling him to go. This didn't really upset him, and it wasn't worth arguing about. After a few times wheeling the dirt back and forth, he grew increasingly adept at pushing the wheelbarrow. The more sweat poured off him, the better he felt; soon a smile came across his face. The anger he felt before left his face. Everyone in the number four work unit was labouring tirelessly. Their bodies were drenched with sweat but their voices had a certain happiness to them, they enjoyed what they were doing and some even began to sing out loud along with the loudspeaker.

Guo Cunxian asked them to add more earth to his wheelbarrow, to pile it higher and higher. The more they added, the more it strained under the weight. It was as though wheeling lesser amounts back and forth wasn't good enough for him, that they were a waste of time and energy. Why should he only shift half a wheelbarrow of dirt at a time? The more he worked the more strength he felt in his legs, pushing the soil back and forth seemed to give him greater energy. Those working alongside him marvelled at his endurance, encouraged him to keep at it, but at the same time they warned him about overdoing it. He didn't want to put his back out, after all. In normal times, they all knew he was a hard worker but he had shifted more than ten wheelbarrows full of earth and that was just beyond expectations and, even though he was panting and breathing hard, he just didn't seem to want to stop. They understood. So did Guo Cunxian. It wasn't that he possessed more energy than them or that he was stronger than them. No, it was all due to their empty stomachs. Over the past two years, Guo Cunxian had never really experienced the same level of starvation as the rest of them, he hadn't felt the same hunger pangs, and even this morning his old mother had made him buckwheat noodles for breakfast, food that stuck to your bones and lasted a long time. Then at noon, she'd brought pancakes made of real flour; pure cornmeal mixed with black bean powder. No wonder his stomach was still so full. Then, the company technician came to take measurements, calculate their progress and weigh how much earth they had removed.

The terrain they were digging in had always been rather low, and with all of the rains they had experienced this year, coupled with the quick pace maintained by the workers from Guojiadian, by the time dusk came they'd already struck water. They were now digging into muddy water, and while that in and of itself wasn't that difficult, it did complicate things for Guo Cunxian and the others who were pushing the wheelbarrows. The technician had experienced this before. He told them that they ought to have prepared a bamboo platform to be placed over the muddy water so that the wheelbarrow could then be pushed over that instead of through the mud, making things much easier. But in practice, it didn't quite work out that way. Not only did the wheelbarrow lurch and groan as it passed over the bamboo raft, it was especially difficult to keep it level; it seemed to bounce as though going over a spring. Consequently, the whole endeavour required quite a lot of arm strength and determination. Fortunately for Guo Cunxian, he'd been swinging his axe since he was young and so his arms already possessed the necessary strength, more than many of the others. As a result, he still managed to derive some enjoyment from even this arduous and somewhat thankless task. He couldn't help but think, however, that this was all a little strange. This job was supposed to be punishment, reform through labour they called it. He never once thought that such exhausting work (and it was exhausting) could bring such enjoyment. The world became simple when all a man had to do was work. Physical exertion had wiped his mind clean and settled the problems plaguing his heart. All the shit he had gone through just seemed all so pointless now.

When the day finally turned to night and the sun had fully set, the bell sounded to end the workday. While it might have been a military horn that signalled the day was over, those who'd been working on the river didn't finish the day in the same manner as soldiers would. Some went to the river to wash their hands, a few others washed their faces as well, but most went straight into the canteen. They were simply too hungry to do anything else. For their part, the canteen seemed to be ready for the men as hot soup and main dishes had already been prepared. There was a large pot of mung bean soup for everyone to share, although it was highly unlikely that anyone would actually scoop up some beans. The canteen cooks seemed to have guessed the men would be desperate for something to eat, and would probably end up causing a ruckus if all they had was mung bean soup. Consequently, along with the strained beans they had prepared *wotou* (a type of cornbread) as well. There were to be two *wotou* for each of the men from Wangguantun and Mapodian, along with half a bowl of stewed radish (well, boiled radish actually) with a little salt sprinkled on it and drizzled with oil. The men from Guojiadian, on the other hand, received only a single *wotou* each along with their half bowl of boiled radish. Looking at the meagre amount on their plates, one wondered whether they would be able to continue work the next day.

Some countries have the tradition of breaking dishes on special occasions but surely that was done after the food on them had been eaten, hmm? Perhaps the best they could do would be to curse their predicament? The three villages ought to have formed a strong link in the chain, and that link should have been made strong by the communal kitchen, but if the kitchen only concerned itself with two out of the three villages, what would happen to the link? Whatever the answer might be, the men from Guojiadian chose to swallow their pride and stamp down the fire that burned in their hearts. They were going to keep it inside, at least until Guo Huaishan arrived and called attention to what was happening. To his mind, the men from Guojiadian had taken the lead in this initiative. They had worked hard, so why the hell hadn't they been treated fairly? Why had they been given so little? One frigging *wotou* is hardly worth the shit it's made from, after all.

Over the years, Guo Huaishan had become known in the village as the 'cow's arse', although no one really knew for sure what that actually meant. Speaking of cows, it was true the hide taken from its rump was the best: smooth and soft to the touch, and equally thick and durable as well. Such a hide welcomed a hard slap as much as it enjoyed a gentle hand being swept back and forth over it. And if a hand wouldn't do, then a stick certainly would. No one would mind, either, when or how many whacks a good rump was given. After all, that's what it was there for. When Guojiadian was established as a production brigade, Guo Huaishan became its deputy commander, a post he had now served in for many, many years, neither being promoted nor demoted. While you could say some people may have looked down at the cow's arse with contempt, you couldn't say that there was no arse to look at at all, which meant the arse played a certain role, even if no one was really sure what that role was. Of course, playing the arse also meant that trouble came from time to time; it was an arse, after all. But when Guo Huaishan finished off his second bowl of mung bean soup, the sole *wotou* and white radish remained there in the bowl. This first invited criticism from the men who were in the canteen but then Guo Huaishan did something wholly unexpected, he dumped the contents of his bowl into the one held by Guo Cunxian and placed into his hand the single *wotou* he had. He spoke loud enough for everyone to hear: "You must be exhausted today, Cunxian. You've worked so hard, you've earned the village some face and I'm not talking about production quotas. You all here are in charge of how much or how little work you do. No, I want you to eat this so that you'll have energy tomorrow to keep up the good work."

Somewhat anxiously, Guo Cunxian stood up: "Uncle, what are you doing? What weight are you trying to put on my shoulders? Haven't you seen that since I've been here in this canteen I haven't uttered a word, that I've just kept my head down and eaten my food? And I'm not the only one, you know. Except for you, we've all worked hard today. I ask you, who here isn't exhausted, huh? Tell us what you mean... hmm... you haven't just given the *wotou* to me, have you? Take it back now, or I'll just throw it away!"

Guo Cunxian's eyes were red with rage. Standing nearby, Guo Cunxiao knew, too, that he wasn't bluffing. Cunxian really would throw everything down onto the ground, and so before things escalated to that point, he reached out a hand and took the bowl and *wotou* away from him, then turned and handed it back to Guo Huaishan. In terms of age, Guo Huaishan was much older than Cunxian; he was from the previous generation. He wasn't a close relative as the family line had split many generations before, so they had little by way of familial interactions, but Guo Cunxian still had to refer to him as uncle and there was still a connection, however weak it may have been. And now, witnessing this response, Guo Huaishan couldn't help but comport himself in the uncle's role. He looked hurt and felt maligned for no good reason. What had he done to deserve such treatment, to be treated no better than the dried shit one accidentally stepped on? His indignation aside, Guo Huaishan wasn't the kind of man to complain, to defend himself vigorously in public. He just smacked his lips, screwed up his face for a moment and then slowly responded as if regurgitating words that had left a sour taste in his mouth: "Cunxian, you don't need to get so worked up. I don't have any ulterior motive. I just thought you could do with a little extra to eat."

It's difficult to say whether or not it was necessary for him to provoke Guo Cunxian as he did, if only inadvertently, but there was a positive outcome as it did bring to an end any and all bickering between the rest of the workers from Guojiadian. As for workers from the other two towns, well, after watching the heated exchange, they could no longer hold their tongues. The three villages altogether formed one company, with the company leader being appointed from Wangguantun, none other than Xu Gaoyang. He stepped forward now and stood in front of the workers from Guojiadian, a small wicker basket in his hand filled with *wotou*.

The Party's political officer, Mapodian's village secretary, Xia Tianyuan, watched from behind him. Remorsefully, he spoke: "My comrades and brothers from Guojiadian, I apologise for what has transpired. The commune authorities ordered our three villages to form one company. They didn't say anything about treating the members of the company differently. Along with the political officer, we've just criticised the canteen cooks and, from tomorrow onwards, we'll all be given the same amount of food. That said, there is something that I need to make clear to all of you, my comrades, my brothers. Initially, the commune had ordered Secretary Chen and Unit Leader Han to take charge of your company. Your village is big with a population to match and so it would've been convenient for them to take command. By coincidence, however, neither of them are in the best of health and so the two of us, Xia Tianyuan and I, have been tasked with this difficult responsibility. Now, the county government gave instructions that each worker here would be given an additional one *jin* of food per day, as well as a small payment of two *jiao* which, in turn, can be used to purchase additional, non-staple foodstuffs, or what have you. In addition, our two villages have committed to providing an extra helping of food to each person, which means everyone here will have more in the morning and in the afternoon. Now, I know this doesn't include non-staple foods at the moment, but plans are in the works to change that soon so that everyone will have even more to eat.

"But you all have to realise something. Mapodian and Wangguantun are both small villages, meaning we haven't sent all that many here to work and so providing additional food is fairly easy. Guojiadian, on the other hand, is much bigger and providing additional food supplies is rather difficult. In fact, the determined amount was to be a little bit less, there was due to be a reduction in the amount of money to be paid out, too, but our two villages thought to make up the difference for you, even if we probably couldn't afford it. This explains why things have turned out the way they have today, I'm sorry to say."

The lean-to was thrown into chaos. The men from Guojiadian refused to work, and the two other villages followed suit. In times like these, the difference over a few mouthfuls of food could drive a wedge between the closest of brothers. Everyone here had come to work, so whose idea had it been to skimp on food? Xu Gaoyang urged all the men to return to their own lean-tos and once they did, he tried to rationalise what had happened to the men from Guojiadian: "Please, everyone, don't get overly upset. Listen to me, please. The county head commissioner and secretary, as well as the secretary from the commune and the director, have all come. Secretary Xia and I have discussed this issue with them and the leadership wish to negotiate with you all to find a quick resolution to this problem. There's still some *wotou* left over, enough for one more each. Let's make do with what you have so that we can start to put this behind us. We can then talk more tomorrow. To be honest, for the amount of work you've done today, I don't think the rations are enough in any case. I think the leadership need to know this also, so that they can think of a better way to equally distribute the food. Don't worry, everyone, we'll fix this."

Guo Huaishan took hold of the *wotou* from the company commander, but no one from Guojiadian extended a hand to take one, nor did they shout, argue or curse. The anger and resentment they felt was simply too intense and no words could do it justice. They just couldn't believe that their own village head could be so unscrupulous. They'd been cheated. This river project would be the death of them and for what? Certainly not for them. Not only had they not been given the extra food promised to them, they'd actually seen their rations reduced... what bollocks! When the project had first been discussed it had sounded so important, so vital to the commune and country that they had been convinced of the need to participate; frightened, even, if they didn't. But it had all been lies. Chen Baohuai showed his true colours here, his maliciousness. Guojiadian had been duped, deceived. They had been used, physically and emotionally. If it hadn't been for them joining up with the other villages, they would have been worked to death for sure without ever really knowing why.

A blaring loudspeaker broke through the tension. Carrying through the air, the county river project propaganda office seemed to be providing the men of Guojiadian with a diversion. The announcement began with almost eloquent words, romanticising the river project: "Worker comrades have rushed forth to take command of the river. The old eastern marshes will soon have a new waterway. Our sixteen hundred kilometre dike will overcome heat. The chanting of our comrades will shake through the land far and wide. Then, following hard on the coattails of the poem was news for the day: the New East River Engineering Project model worker for the first day of the project was none other than Guo Cunxian, from Guojiadian. In half a day, he had removed more seven-and-a-half cubic metres of earth, the equivalent of work carried out by four men, or the work of one man over two days. Such actions make him worthy of the title of wheelbarrow hero. The Party commends Guo Cunxian and urges all workers to learn from his model example!"

A poor farmer could work his entire life without anyone noticing or paying him any attention. But on this day, Guo Cunxian had earned recognition beyond anything he could have expected... it should have given him cause to be happy, but it didn't. No joy welled up inside him. In fact, he felt lonelier than ever, stuck between a rock and a hard place. He grabbed his towel and walked out of the lean-to; washing up and going to sleep was all he could think to do. As he stepped out of the building, he was confronted with a cold evening wind that swept across his sweaty frame and brought on a chill. The moon was perched high in the sky, shining down brilliantly on the eastern marshes, bathing the land in a white radiance. During the day their heads were all kept low, buried, sometimes literally, in work. As a result, he hadn't had the chance to look at the lay of the land and the progress they had made but after only a little more than half a day's work you could start to see the outline of what they were building. Interestingly, because each company worked at different speeds, each section of the project was at different stages, the dyke varying in height, some parts higher than others, all rather uneven, like a winding snake slithering off to the east out of sight. The night sky sparkled across the top of the dyke while the lean-tos stood in the shadows, enveloped in darkness. The loudspeaker continued to blare on, announcing in turn various bits of news related to the project interspersed with patriotic songs.

Not too far from the Guojiadian lean-to was a small watering hole. Guo Cunxian walked over to it and soon spied a man in the darkness holding a kerosene lamp, supposedly looking for crabs in the night. Surprised and intrigued by what he was doing, Guo Cunxian asked: "Brother, are there really crabs about?"

The man, kneeling down by the waterhole, hesitated before answering in an annoyed voice: "Well, there bloody well should be some here in the dark. I mean, because of the rain no one was able to harvest the crops. Shouldn't that also mean they weren't able to fish the fish or dig up the crabs and turtles, huh?"

Engrossed by the scene, Guo Cunxian knelt down beside the man and mumbled some more: "Well, in times such as these I guess there ought to be some, but it seems as though the opposite is more common. After all, if there really were crabs crawling around in the dark, they'd come to the light if they saw it."

The man smacked his lips and Guo Cunxian couldn't be sure if he was betraying his own ravenous greed or if he was simply starving to death. Then he spoke: "You're right, if there really were crabs they'd probably be quite plump too, the oil from their flesh would be..."

By the looks of it, it wasn't only the men from Guojiadian who were going hungry. Perhaps it was better to come out into the dark, to come and scrounge around for anything else to eat. That was infinitely better than sulking in the lean-to, pissed off and hungry. Then, suddenly, from the other side of the watering hole, another man called out: "I've got one, not a crab but a fish."

Someone else appeared and tried to help: "Quickly, fling it up here. How big is it, huh?"

The man who had grabbed it replied somewhat disappointingly: "Not that big, just a small one." Guo Cunxian squatted down and looked at the scene in front of him. He was surprised at it all. He hadn't thought that so many would have come out into the night to try to find something to fill their bellies. As the shadows moved, he guessed there must be at least three or four men actually in the water itself. They were all bent at the waist, their hands deep in the water groping about for whatever they could get their hands on. More men were milling about at the edge, waiting for fish, crabs, anything, to be flung out of the water. Guo Cunxian stood up and thought to move closer, to inspect their harvest, but as he was about to do so, a light shone from the east, casting a reddish glow over half the sky. A strange call then carried through the air; it appeared as though something had happened. Guo Cunxian had never thought there would be such commotion, especially in a place so ill-suited to it. His curiosity piqued, he left the watering hole and made his way towards the growing reddish hue.

As he walked closer, he realised that someone had lit a fire. In the light cast by it, he could make out several men standing round the blaze. They were all especially excited about something, laughing and talking in loud voices. One man chortled loudly, snorted and then shouted: "I can smell it, I tell you, ah the aroma, the smell of roasting meat... I don't know if you believe me or not, but I can smell it, I really can!" Guo Cunxian remained some distance away, listening to the men go on. Gradually, he realised what all the fuss was about. When working this afternoon, he had heard that some of the men had discovered a small ground squirrel burrow. They must have taken advantage of the evening lull to go and catch the rodents. Perhaps they'd collected a container of water and flooded the burrow? That would have been the best way. The squirrels would have had no choice but to flee and run straight into the arms of the waiting men. Guo Cunxian learned later that this was exactly what had happened. And what's more, the men had been fortunate; they'd caught not only one but two ground squirrels. Once they had them, of course, the discussion had shifted to how best to eat them. Would it be better to bring them to the canteen to be stewed, or would roasting them over a fire be better? Before they could decide, however, something else had happened that made the decision for them, at least, that was the way it seemed, for at around the same time another man had caught a hedgehog. With three small animals to enjoy, there was only one way to prepare such a feast: they would cover all three in clay and roast them over a fire. Once the clay had been baked thoroughly, they would remove them from the fire and peel off the hardened clay. As they did so, the fur of the three animals would be torn off as well, leaving succulent meat to enjoy. With a little soy sauce borrowed from the canteen, or some salt, together with a few garlic cloves, well, what an aroma! What a feast!

At the same time as the Party leaders in Laodong Township called for another meeting, the Guo and Liu families were harvesting the spinach they had planted in their private plots, after which they would sow wheat seeds. Since both Guo Cunxian and Liu Yucheng had been conscripted into the river project, the remaining family members had to work the fields. This allowed for a friendship to blossom between the two young women of the houses, Zhu Xuezhen and Liu Yumei; a friendship that would last a lifetime.

Both of them were lonely; it could be seen in their eyes. It was for this reason that they would get along, that they'd be able to talk to each other. When they first met, it was Yumei who spoke first, greeting Xuezhen respectfully in the manner expected between a married woman and one not yet betrothed. For her part, however, Xuezhen did not reply. She only smiled and laughed a little. Yumei thus spoke again: she was happy to have met her here on the way to the fields, especially since it seemed that Xuezhen didn't get out much. To this, Xuezhen only smiled as before and then moved closer to take hold of Yumei's arm; they would go to the fields together and collect the spinach Cunzhi had harvested and then bring it back.

After they had been working for a while, Xuezhen finally broke her silence: "But aren't you the same? I don't think you've stepped beyond your own front door in ages, so it's just as difficult for me to see you, isn't it?"

"Sister, no, it's not like that at all," Yumei sighed. "For me, staying indoors is a way to avoid my family problems. Staying out of sight keeps me from getting angry. But now, well, since most of the men are gone, there's work that needs to be done, and that's better than keeping myself in solitary confinement."

Of course, Xuezhen was fully aware of Yumei's circumstances, so she didn't press the issue further. They continued their work, and just as they had nearly finished harvesting the spinach, Ou Guangming arrived carrying an empty sack over his shoulder. In a loud voice he greeted the two women working in the fields. Yumei was surprised to see him. Why had he come? In a soft voice, Xuezhen told her that her mother-in-law had asked him to come and help. He didn't dawdle, waiting to be invited to get to work, but simply began loading the spinach from Yumei's field into his sack. Cunzhi did the same with the spinach from his own field. Together, they loaded the sacks equally, both to overflowing, but still there was spinach left over on the ground. Cunzhi asked his mother what they should do, considering their bags were already full. Sun Yueqing told them that whatever was left could be theirs to eat. Such wonderful spinach shouldn't go to waste, after all. And if they'd like, they could try to sell some of it as well. She turned to look at Ou Guangming saying that since he was older than her son, Cunzhi was to listen to him once they left, and if the spinach was suitable to be sold, then do so, and if it wasn't, then they were to bring it back. They could at least use it for a meal or two. By the sound of her voice and the warmth in it, she seemed to be treating Yumei as part of the family now.

Ou Guangming heaved the bundle over his shoulder and told Sun Yueqing not to worry; the market the authorities had set up in Laodong Township was not like before, there were quite a few things being sold now, and even more people buying. They were coming from all over, heads bobbing up and down, legs carrying people from stall to stall; jammed in they were, shoulder to shoulder and quite a ruckus it was, with many different accents floating across the air. Ou Guangming told them that planting the spinach had been a good idea. He mused that men's hearts were like grass. All they needed was a small plot of land to dig their roots deep into and they would flourish. Then they needed a market to sell what they grew to make a little money. That was important, after all, for with money men could buy anything they wanted and they wouldn't need to worry about being empty-handed or starving.

Xuezhen understood what her mother-in-law was trying to do. She wasn't only giving Ou Guangming an opportunity to earn some money. No, she was also trying to act as a matchmaker, trying to arrange things between Yumei and Ou Guangming. Thinking about it, he seemed suitable enough. But wasn't there a lot of work to do today? Wouldn't it be easy for something to happen to the two men while bringing the spinach to the market? Her thoughts lingered on this, but she was perhaps more excited by how Ou Guangming had described the market. She and Yumei seemed thrilled by the prospects of going to market. Sun Yueqing saw this in their faces and it made her regret, just a little at least, having asked him to come and help.

Then, as the two young men were about to depart, Sun Yueqing had a change of heart; she didn't want Yumei to go with them. Instead, she gestured towards their mad old uncle who was using the fork often used for the sweet potato to turn over the soil and the spinach roots, indicating that Yumei and Xuezhen should follow after him and collect them. The roots were useful as well. They could bring down a fever, be used in a salad, or even be fried and eaten. They could be dried, too, and ground up into flour and then mixed with other food. As she went on, Xuezhen came up close to her and spoke in a low voice, asking her if she hadn't meant for Yumei to go to the market with the men. Wasn't selling the spinach more important? Sun Yueqing grasped what Xuezhen meant. If Yumei were to go to the market, then she would have to go as well, but she really didn't want them to go. Two young women going off to market would only invite lascivious stares, and with Cunxian not at home, that would just be crazy. What if something were to happen? But she also knew that Xuezhen had essentially been locked up inside for quite a while now, without even someone to talk to, except for her mother-in-law. But could she really talk to her? Xuezhen must certainly have been feeling terribly depressed and she wasn't oblivious of that fact. She raised her head and looked deep into Xuezhen's eyes, probing them for an answer: "Daughter-in-law, are you truly so desperate to go to the market, to see the hubbub?"

In response, Xuezhen spoke in a clear, determined tone: "Collecting the spinach roots could wait until they returned, yes?" She didn't try to conceal her desire. She knew she would never be able to, not with her mother-in-law. Sun Yueqing had to respond; there was nothing else for it. She relented and told the young women they could go to see the market and enjoy its clamour, but that they were not to involve themselves in the men's work. Selling things at the market is not a job for young women. Xuezhen and Yumei smiled at each other. Who imagined Sun Yueqing would hold such an outdated point of view, especially since she herself had actually hawked wares when she was young? She brushed the earth from her clothes, reached into her pocket and took out three yuan. She placed the money in Xuezhen's hand and told her to use it to buy a snack for the two of them; the road back and forth wasn't short and they would be hungry. She also told them to enjoy the market and not to worry about whether the men sold the spinach or how much they got for it. She instructed them to come home early, too, and not to wait for the men. Xuezhen promised to abide by her instructions and obediently took the money, albeit reluctantly. There was no point in protesting. She knew once her mother-in-law had made up her mind that would be it. If she tried to protest, she'd only make her upset.

Standing next to them, Yumei looked at the exchange between them and felt a pang of envy. She couldn't remember her mother, couldn't remember receiving that kind of love and attention. All she could do was wish Sun Yueqing thought of her as a daughter. They hit the road, the two men with the spinach over their shoulders walked in front, with the two women following not far behind. They chatted about a range of topics, none of any interest to the men, partly as a way of getting them to move a little further ahead. Over the last year she hadn't just walked and talked like this. There had always been too much else to worry about. She sighed loudly: "You're so lucky, Sister. You're mother-in-law treats you so well."

Xuezhen nodded her head. Yumei was right. She treated her like a daughter, even though she already had one in Cunzhu.

"Sister, why do you think your mother-in-law had money on her? We were out in the fields. Why didn't she leave the money at home? Was she afraid it would be stolen? Does she always carry the family belongings with her?"

"No, it's just her habit. She believes that, when stepping outside, one needs to have a little bit of cash to hand. It's an old habit, something she's been doing for ages."

"Are you going to use it all?"

"She gave it to me, didn't she? So it's up to me whether I spend it or not. If I don't spend any, it'd seem like I was a stranger to her and she to me. But if I waste it all, well, that would suggest I can't manage money properly. I'll spend a little on us, and also buy a little something for her. That way we'll all be happy."

Yumei's heart was filled with envy but she didn't say anything more. She simply bowed her head and kept on walking. After a few more steps, something popped into Xuezhen's mind and she blurted out without really thinking: "Yumei, if you think my mother-in-law is so nice, then why don't you marry Cunzhi? Then we could be sisters-in-law, wouldn't that be great?" Yumei's face turned bright red. She was both embarrassed and nervous. She told Xuezhen not to mention this again. Not only was she was older than Cunzhi, she also belonged to a bad class, someone their family could never accept. She begged for Xuezhen not to speak of this to anyone. If she did, she'd never be able to show her face again.

Xuezhen realised she had spoken out of turn and tried desperately to explain that it was just a slip of the tongue: "I only wanted us to be real sisters, that's why I said what I did. Please don't take it to heart. I should tell you, too, that our family doesn't care about your background, there's nothing embarrassing about it. Didn't you see how she treated you today? It was as though you were already her daughter, wasn't it?"

Yumei replied that she understood this and she knew Cunxian had always treated her brother really well, too, but that being magnanimous to someone who wasn't family and then having that person become family wasn't the same thing. What's more, she knew there was no easy way for her to bring up the subject of marriage. Her older brother had remained unmarried right up until he was on his deathbed, and as death approached, he was most worried about Yucheng, afraid he'd end up treating me as his wife and not get properly married himself. He instructed him vehemently that that couldn't happen and that he had to let me choose my own happiness, choose my own husband. But you know what? I have a debt of my own, something I need to take care of. I can't let my second brother be like our older sibling. I can't let him live his life out as a bare stick. I can't let our family line end. Just because our father was a landlord, that shouldn't mean our family has to come to an end, does it? That means I wait, I wait until he's twenty-eight and if he hasn't found a wife by then, then I'll marry him!

Xuezhen's eyes turned red. She turned and embraced Yumei tightly. She told her she was such a good sister and that it had been wrong of her to speak out of turn. Yumei replied, urging her to not speak like that. She knew she was only trying to look out for her, to be good to her; there was nothing else to say. They kept walking now, but there was a heaviness to their steps, a melancholy feel in the air. They didn't speak for a long time. Just a moment ago they had seemed like kindred spirits and now there was awkwardness between them.

Yumei thought to herself, Xuezhen had a warm, caring heart. She had to find something to talk about, so she asked if Xuezhen believed in destiny.

Xuezhen knew what she had said had been inappropriate, that it had caused a rift between them, and now she wanted to find something else to talk about, to bring some happiness back into their walk. But talking about fate was much too dangerous. If they weren't careful they might end up discussing something even more serious than before. She had no choice but to decline to respond to her question. Instead she acted as though she were rebuking Yumei and told her not to speak to her with such respect, not to call her 'big sister'. After all, weren't they the same?

Yumei looked at Xuezhen's face. She tried to say she wasn't fussed about such things, but since Cunxian was her senior and she was his wife, what else was she to call her?

Xuezhen bent over and picked up a soft leafy piece of spinach. Cunzhi and Ou Guangming must have dropped it when they rested here a few moments ago, or perhaps they'd seen the tension between Yumei and Xuezhen and had dropped it deliberately as a means to distract them, to change the subject. Xuezhen brushed the leaf clean, blew on it and then placed it behind Yumei's temple. As she did it, her mouth moved close to Yumei's ear and she spoke: her rebuke before had been in jest.

Yumei saw Xuezhen's revived mood and decided to go along with it. Xuezhen, for her part, seemed to enjoy teasing her and began to tell her a tale: there was once a young man who went off in search of a wife, and while on the road he spied a woman out working in the field. She was wearing a round grass hat that covered much of her face, making it difficult for the man to judge her age, and so he just yelled out to her: 'Big Sister-in-law, how much farther to the village?' Upon hearing the man shout out to her, the woman looked up and stared straight back at him. It was clear she was not an older married woman at all, but a young, untouched maiden. Her voice cut into him: 'Are you trying to say that I look old, hmm? That I've already pushed out several children? Is that it?'

Yumei seemed puzzled. Why was being called 'big' sister-in-law enough to make her so upset? And what was the connection to having children?

Xuezhen explained saying the word 'big' gave the impression of age, as in that the person being addressed was much older than the addresser. 'Sister-in-law' also suggested age, the character for it being a combination of 'old man' and 'woman' after all; and if a man and a woman married and grew old together, then wouldn't that mean they also had kids?

Yumei found this explanation quite funny and couldn't help but let out a belly laugh, before quickly covering her mouth with her arm, embarrassed at her response. She didn't normally laugh like that, not out loud in such a raucous manner. But she found the story entertaining and urged Xuezhen to continue. If the young girl had been so upset with being called a 'big sister-in-law', then what happened next?

Xuezhen continued telling her the story. The girl answered the man in a clear and sincere voice; there were still four *mu* until the village. It was now time for the young man to laugh, heh, heh. He asked why they measured distance in *mu* instead of *li*, the former usually being used for the size of a plot of land. This question only irked the girl more and she responded even more fiercely. By rights, she told him, he should address her as 'auntie'! The young fellow was stunned by her manner. He hadn't expected to be berated so vehemently and thought to himself that the women in this place were certainly something indeed! Then his stomach suddenly gurgled. He still hadn't met the proper girl.

Yumei bit her lip. She didn't dare laugh like she had before, although she did ask if there was more to the story.

There was, of course, more to the story. The young man made his way into the town and soon met a matchmaker. Naturally he stayed there for a spell and met several possible wives before he was introduced to the same young woman he had met on his way into town. Now he had the chance to learn about her background. Before long, he was invited to see her family's actual circumstances. This, of course, allowed for both sides to see each other, and once he had met her relatives and friends, he'd asked them to leave so that he could be alone with his prospective wife. But once they were left alone, neither would look at each other, instead keeping their heads low, finding it difficult to think of something to say. In the quiet, the young man thought to himself: it didn't matter what the situation was, since he was a man he should speak first, but she had been so ferocious when he had encountered her in the field that his approach would have to be even more so... he had to frighten her, as it were, to show her that he was the man. Mustering his courage, he asked her if she had ever seen an old tiger, to which she replied she hadn't. She then turned the tables on him and asked if he had. He huffed and puffed for a moment, but then admitted he hadn't see one either. She curled up her lips at his response; she wasn't sure what kind of man he was. Without waiting any longer, she asked him a question instead: would he dare to eat the hottest of hot chillies by itself, with nothing to help mitigate the heat? Bravely and in a clear, loud voice, he answered for sure he would! She remained silent at his response, thinking she had to ask a further question, something that would really stump him. And then she hit upon it. She asked him how far his village was from here. He opened his mouth and answered quickly, eight *mu*. She wondered now why he had used *mu* instead of *li*, and so she asked. But this was what he had been waiting for, and to prove himself he said she should refer to him as 'uncle'! The girl couldn't help but laugh and giggle at his response, remarking that he really was something. When they had met on the road, she hadn't thought very much of him, and now he'd come to her house for what? Reimbursement? Sensing victory, the young man pressed home his attack: he asked her if she would dare to take hold of his hand, to which she put her head down and said no. But she did follow this up with a question of her own: she asked if he'd take hers. His reply came quickly; he would...

Yumei was beside herself with laughter. She grabbed hold of Xuezhen's arm: "Big Sister-in-law..." Xuezhen interrupted her. How could she not remember, she just told her this story all about calling someone 'big' sister-in-law and yet she still started to say it. Yumei replied then and asked just what was she supposed to call her? Call me by my name, or just call me sister. Yumei liked the sound of that, the word 'sister' coming from Xuezhen's mouth sounded like something out of a book. For Xuezhen, since she had arrived in Guojiadian she hadn't once been so brash, so open about her feelings. Her mother in-law was nice, there was no mistaking that, but she wasn't her friend. She hoped, however, that Yumei would be, that she'd be her confidant. Almost inevitably she felt somewhat proud of herself: "Yumei, you're right," she said. "I have had some schooling, and every day we talked about books, but talking about books isn't the same as living them."

After returning from the market, Zhu Xuezhen thought to accompany Liu Yumei back to her house so that the two of them could talk some more, and also because Liu Yumei was terrified of the dark. She had been frightened when she was young and ever since then feared being alone at night. If the lights were extinguished, she wouldn't be able to sleep, and even if the lights were kept on, she was still afraid and unable to close her eyes. She worried that something would come in the night, especially if it were dark. But besides her two brothers, no one knew she suffered from this kind of phobia; that she was able to tell Xuezhen about it really meant the two were sisters, even if there was no blood relation. For a young married woman not to spend the night at her husband's home would be considered quite a big deal, even if her husband were not at home. It was certainly something she would have to clear with her mother-in-law first. Sun Yueqing, however, barely even considered it before saying that it was not allowed. Her reason was clear: the days had already grown cold, and soon the river itself would freeze, meaning the men would be home before long. But Xuezhen persisted and revealed to her Yumei's secret. She would come across as cold and uncaring if she were to refuse again, and she thought, too, that Yumei's situation was quite pitiful, alone in her house as she was, and so she came up with an alternative: Yumei should come here and stay in Xuezhen's room so that was she wouldn't be alone. And since there were quite a few people here, including her uncle Jingshi, then no ghost nor evil spirit would dare try to cross their doorway. Xuezhen replied that she had already suggested this to Yumei, but she said she couldn't, she didn't want to impose, nor did she want Cunxian to return and find her there because it would be too embarrassing and an inconvenience to him. She also worried that, because of her class background, she'd only create trouble for them.

There was perhaps some truth to this, which led Sun Yueqing to regret having a soft heart. Why did she bother herself with other people's business? Xuezhen and Yumei were growing closer too; might not that cause trouble in future with her own daughter-in-law and the daughter of a landlord becoming best of friends? And if that were to happen, then things could indeed go badly for them. But what was she to do? Things had already got to this point and if she tried to obstruct their friendship, well, she just couldn't do it, she had to relent, at least until Cunxian returned, after which Xuezhen certainly couldn't spend the night with Yumei any more. And perhaps Cunzhu would return early as well, in which case she could then spend the night with Yumei instead of Xuezhen. The more she thought about it, the more things became confused. That's what happens when old people's minds wander. There was nothing more she could do. The two of them had already talked it over and over; they'd made plans together, too. Sun Yueqing had no choice but to concede.

The first plan they hatched together was to go to where the river was being dredged so that Xuezhen could see her husband and Yumei her brother. Xuezhen's argument was that the weather had grown cold and she wanted to bring some warmer bedding for Cunxian, as well as a padded jacket and woollen trousers. This made Sun Yueqing quite happy; her daughter-in-law was performing her duty, as it were, and so she thought that maybe, just maybe, she would join them as well. When a suitable afternoon came, when the wind died down a little and the air was less cold, Zhu Xuezhen and Liu Yumei set off towards where the dyke was being built with bundles of clothing tied to their backs. The only problem, however slight it might be, was that the two of them weren't entirely sure which section of the eastern river the men from Guojiadian were responsible for. The only thing to do was to follow the main road and stick to it. Once they reached the river they'd just have to ask around. They talked as they walked and before long the river project came into sight in the distance. There were so many men all busy at work. The whole scene looked like a battlefield with soldiers arrayed in the shape of a snake stretching from the horizon down into the earth, its head somewhere beyond the line of sight. The image made the two women tremble in awe and subconsciously they picked up their pace. But then when they drew close something seemed amiss, forcing them to hold their breath and stop moving closer.

The men working on the river dyke project had seen the two women leisurely walking up and had all stopped working. Their shovels froze in the air, or were left deep in the dirt; wheelbarrows drew to a halt as though they were mired in the mud; all the men's eyes were fixed on the two of them. As the men watched them, some must have felt that simply looking was insufficient and so they took to catcalling and hollering at the women. So there they stood, standing in front of a massive river project with nary a man working. All of them instead were staring at them.

One man shouted: Hey boys, look who's brought extra blankets for some lucky man tonight?

Others joined in the chorus: Oh, it's our pretty wives that've come!

Whose wife?

Mine!

Who?

Then someone asked: What's it like having a wife?

Great!

Horrible, you always have to keep thinking about them!

Stop tormenting them, you'll frighten them to death. You've studied for so long, how about a poem to serenade them?

The loudspeaker rang out every day, broadcasting poems to encourage the men to work;. They all heard it and listened, now one of the men began his own poem. None of them had seen a woman in months, and certainly no one expected any to come here carrying bundles of clothes. It was like the beginning of some theatre show. The braver of them took the initiative: I'll give it a go, listen. 'The blue sky is my blanket, the land my bed, a refreshing cool wind blows. But it has been a long time since I've seen my darling which renders my heart so'.

The men hollered loudly in approval. Who'll try now?

Listen, I will: 'The red flag calls us out to work, but I long to hold my dear one's hand. Digging this river will be the death of us, wine'll warm our hearts more than a blanket will'.

Some shouted their approval, others cursed: "You dirty alcoholic fuckers, I'd trade booze for the warm body of a wife any day. Just look at us, huh? We're all here working on this damn project in summer clothes and now it's winter. What do you think? Our sweat freezes and here comes Lady Meng Jiang[1] in search of her husband, bringing winter clothes. Oh my Lady, don't cry for us, we're not worth it."

Xuezhen and Yumei saw clearly then, the men, all of them, were still clad in summer clothes, some even in sleeveless vests, their arms naked... and here they were carrying winter clothes almost as though they were making fun of the men. Their hearts skipped a beat. They were embarrassed; they'd caused such a fuss and hadn't even seen Guo Cunxian or Liu Yucheng. Were they somewhere else? Mortified, the two young women stared blankly at the men, unable to ask after Cunxian and Yucheng. A silent moment passed. There was nothing they could do. They had to leave, and so they turned and began to walk away, their steps increasing in speed little by little until they were running, fleeing like a scolded child flees from its parents. The men in the background roared with laughter and howled after them: don't run away, you still haven't done what you came for!

The two of them ran until they could no longer hear the men's catcalls echoing behind them. They let the bundles they were carrying fall to the ground and then plopped down beside them. Holding onto the blankets tightly, they tried to catch their breath. Once they'd begun to collect themselves, Xuezhen spoke: "That frightened me to death, those rascals, so rude!"

Yumei also had to catch her breath, and once she had, she replied: "Maybe everyone was right, the only men working on the river project are scoundrels." And then she remembered that her own brother and Xuezhen's husband were there as well. Could they be like the others? She'd never once experienced something like this, had never been ogled and leered at in such a rude manner. She'd only ever been around her second brother, and he was always so well behaved, so docile. Could he be like those men, so coarse and so vulgar, calling after women with such boorish language? The thought deeply disturbed her.

Xuezhen's heart was also pained, traumatised by what had happened. And then she thought that it was fortunate Cunxian hadn't been there. If he had, she would have died of shame for sure.

Still flabbergasted, Yumei looked at Xuezhen and asked her if Cunxian had ever hit her.

Embarrassed by the question, she shook her head in response.

Yumei again looked at her enviously and told her she was just talking nonsense and she didn't mean anything by it. "You're madly in love with him, aren't you? I guess he'd never dare lay a hand on you."

Xuezhen told her, however, that he was terribly jealous and that, not long after they had been married, someone had looked at her the wrong way and he had nearly gone mad with rage.

Yumei replied that that was love.

Strangely, however, the alarming events of just a few moments ago had not completely terrified her, and had certainly not made her want to give up on bringing these blankets and clothes to her husband. In fact, it had only steeled her resolve. She was more intent on it now than ever. Besides, she didn't wish to tell her mother-in-law about what had happened, fearing that she'd only prevent her from going out again. Old people tend to worry so. It would be easier to say that they couldn't find the men, but that they would try again in the evening when Cunzhi could accompany them; after all, he knew the roads better than them. And so they returned home before setting off again later in the day.

But by the time they did, the sun had already fallen and there was no moon to light the evening sky. It was pitch black, as if someone had thrown a dark blanket over the land. The night wind was chilly, too. Liu Yumei's body quivered and shook as she walked, her neck straining in all directions, vainly trying to make out her surroundings. She pulled nervously at her shirt collar, almost beside herself with worry and fear. For her, the night signalled danger; it impaired one's vision and left only a sense of creeping worry in her heart. Xuezhen, on the other hand, was the complete opposite. She thought the night held wonders, was romantic even, that there was nothing to fear about it. Her heart was aflutter, egging Cunzhi on, encouraging him to walk even faster.

Casting aside her inhibitions, Xuezhen walked with greater ease, soon not even feeling the chill in the air. In the distance, they could see the lanterns snaking around the river project like tiny stars sparkling in the night sky, blinking in and out intermittently, but still constant, like a long trailing snake of light. As they walked closer, the lights grew brighter and transformed the evening sky. It was no longer pitch black, not like when they had first left the village. There was robustness to the night and their pace quickened, drawn to the lights shining from around the dyke. Cunzhi led them near to where the lean-to for the men from Guojiadian was located, next to the wood pile used in the canteen. Strips of bamboo cluttered the ground with planks of wood mixed in among them. Wheelbarrows were placed to one side, as well as other tools used by the men. Cunzhi instructed Xuezhen and Yumei to wait just behind a pile of firewood while he went by himself to get his brother and Liu Yucheng. The loudspeaker still blared through the night, airing cultural programmes selected by the workers themselves. There was a moment of silence, and then a heroic song came over the speakers, followed by an insipid poem read in an almost exaggerated tone. As soon as Yumei heard it, she felt a chill run down her back and moved closer to Xuezhen. Xuezhen was reminded of the afternoon and her face flushed red, even in the darkness. A pang of irritation crept into her heart. Mumbling more to herself, she wondered what was taking Cunzhi so long and whether he was having trouble finding them? Had they gone off somewhere else?

She was beginning to have second thoughts when she heard the clatter of approaching footsteps and instinctively held the bundle of clothes a little tighter. Yumei herself nearly froze, seemingly terrified of who it might be. Like a dog's tail she hid behind Xuezhen. But the fear lasted only a minute. Despite the darkness, the rough outline of the approaching man and the sound of his footsteps made it clear to Xuezhen who it was. She knew Guo Cunxian had come. He bounded up to her and grabbed her tightly. How is it that you're here? It's so cold, and pitch-black, too!

In her mind she wondered what he meant: who was cold, huh? He was the one still wearing summer clothes. He should have been even colder than her! But she didn't say anything. She was too happy. The sound of his voice told her that he was overjoyed that she'd come. She didn't want to spoil the moment. They stood facing each other. Guo Cunxian looked at his wife longingly and then spoke to Yumei standing behind her: "From morning until night I think your brother has been freezing to death."

Liu Yucheng stepped into the dim light now too. He greeted Xuezhen: "I must be benefiting from the advantages of having a big sister-in-law to look after me. If it weren't for you, Yumei wouldn't have been able to come here, certainly not at night." Neither of the two young women had a chance to get a word in, both men were so excited to see them. In the dark, Guo Cunxian now laughed and mused that the two of them coming here was like family visiting imprisoned relatives. Xuezhen spoke then, and wondered why they weren't allowed to return home, at least occasionally. And besides, the distance wasn't all that great; they weren't actually in prison, after all. Why was it, she asked, that they were treating them the same as criminals? Guo Cunxian could only reply and say he wished she wouldn't speak of this. If she didn't, then it was easier for him to forget. He then asked both of them a question. A story had made the rounds among the men today, about two young women coming by to bring winter blankets and clothes, but that some brutish fellows with nothing better to do than to wolf-whistle had scared them away. Was that you two?

Yumei couldn't answer. She grabbed her brother and pulled him to one side. Xuezhen asked her husband: "Where's Cunzhi?" Guo Cunxian moved closer and took hold of the bundle of clothes, placing it on the ground next to them. He told her that Cunzhi was in the lean-to, keeping warm. His voice was soft, gentle. He said she must have been out here a long time; her body was trembling. She stretched out her hand to touch his face. He seemed slimmer than before, his face gaunt; she was searching for his warmth, his strength. He submitted willingly to her touch, burying his face in her hand. She started to cry then threw herself into his arms.

Guo Cunxian embraced her tightly, warmly. His grip allowed her to let go. It made her body feel as light as the stalks of grain they took from the fields. Soon she felt the softness of the hay used for firewood against her back. His face was touching hers; his lips kissed away the tears that rolled down her cheeks. She could smell the sour-sweet freshness of the earth on his body and then something strange began to stir inside her. Guo Cunxian's kisses grew more intense as he seemed to be trying to swallow her whole. In tandem with his kisses, her own body grew warmer, her desire washed over her in waves, stronger and stronger they came. His hands moved lower and began to fumble with her belt, soon unfastening it altogether, dropping her trousers to the ground. She had prepared for this, to make things easier for him she had only worn the single pair of trousers. His manhood had already swelled, hard like a stick of firewood, ready to burn. He grabbed hold of her and thrust himself deeply inside; she had been waiting for this. Their bodies were on fire, caught up in the heat of the moment like a violent storm washing over them both, like a lustful wind tearing away at their very souls.

She never would have thought she would experience such a feeling, something she'd never felt, not even on their wedding day, but here, now, in the pitch-dark amid the soft hay used for firewood, she felt for the first time what being a woman could be.

8

BURNING DOWN THE FROG MARSHES

The plans of man mean little to heaven; Laodong Township faced two more years of flooding.

Originally the plan had been to construct the new eastern waterway in one year, but the on-and-off nature of the work meant that it stretched beyond two, and it wasn't until the winter cold front moved in again that the work could be considered complete. The two years brought nothing but pain to Guo Cunxian. His family's small plot helped them make do, but it didn't produce enough to fill their bellies, only enough to keep starvation at bay. But without even a little money, could the whole family really make do? Especially now they had so many expenses with another mouth to feed...

Xuezhen gave him a boy but her own breasts failed to produce enough to feed the baby so they were forced to find suitable supplements. Even if they had some money, buying these things during times like these would have been difficult; without any money... Once his sister reached the appropriate age, she told them of her desire to leave. A former middle school classmate wished to take her as his wife. But they were stuck between a rock and a hard place. They couldn't ask for a proper betrothal but nor could they let her leave in such a shameful manner. That would have upset their poor old mother just too much. Over these past two years her hair had gone almost completely white, such was the worry she was carrying in her heart.

It was Cunzhi who was making her worry most. He was growing increasingly timid and cowardly. He spoke little and did even less, choosing to pass the days away in the small southern room splayed out on the *kang*, his eyes not even looking out through the window but only upwards at the ceiling beams. No one knew what he was thinking about, and if anyone asked, they'd only get silence as a response. It was no wonder that this was worrying their old mother. This form of madness seemed to plague all the young men in the village and there was, of course, a logical explanation: they were all thinking about marriage, about finding a wife. And so it was that this was their job: they had to get him a wife, and quickly. While they were poor, they weren't the poorest family in the village. So no matter what, they couldn't let Cunzhi end up as another bare stick. Nearly every day then, his older brother and mother assumed this responsibility. They were like soldiers fighting a noble cause, all their energies devoted to finding him a suitable wife which, of course, meant asking for help. But as soon as they decided to start their search, a problem arose that none of them could have envisaged. Cunzhi didn't want to marry. For every arranged interview of a prospective wife his mother made, no matter how many times she talked herself blue in the face trying to find him a suitable wife, nothing worked. No matter how much she tried and tried in vain, or how many times she cursed and shouted at him, or tried to force him to at least consider a potential marriage, badgered him with question after question, he wouldn't even give them a response. What woman would want such a man? He wasn't a Party member; he wasn't from the city. In the end, he was nothing but a poor farmer. After entertaining two to three possible wives and their families, it was easy to see nothing was going to come of it.

It was all so very clear to Guo Cunxian. Their mother blamed it on the fact that for the last couple of years Cunzhi had been sharing that room with their uncle and so he must have started taking after him; one old, one young and both bare sticks. Sharing a bed day in and day out couldn't have been good for him, could it? The whole family could see this now. He was always so close to his uncle, they had grown increasingly alike in actions and temperament. But no one could actually say this out loud. They had to wait until Cunzhu was married off, then Jingshi could move back into his own room on the western side of the house. When the time came, whether he was willing or not, well, that wouldn't be ideal, but Guo Cunxian, for his part, traced his younger brother's behaviour back to the punishment he had received for the sweet potato fiasco. To him, that was the root of his brother's illness. From that time onward he had started to change but no one had noticed it until now, so small and gradual had the changes been; not until they had spoken to him of marriage. The village had more than its fair share of bare sticks but that was not for lack of trying. Cunzhi, on the other hand, wanted to be alone, wanted to remain unmarried. Now that would certainly cause an old mother's hair to go white, wouldn't it?

Despite all this, money, too, was a problem. That is, finding a wife would have been easy enough to do if Guo Cunxian actually had some… he'd just buy a wife from somewhere down south. He'd simply bring her into their house and put both of them into a room together, which would serve as their bridal chamber; they'd prepare the proper meal and that would be that. It wouldn't matter if his brother didn't enjoy talking or not, they would simply be husband and wife, until death separated them. Guo Cunxian was determined then, in his callousness, to take advantage of the wintry weather to make some money. In the New Year, they'd first see his sister married and then he'd make changes to their house, building two additional rooms. He would do this himself to make sure the work was done properly, and that should put his poor old mother's heart at ease. The new room could perhaps be used to bring Cunzhi a wife. The only problem was, where to find the money?

There was certainly no point in thinking about using his carpentry skills to earn money in neighbouring towns and villages. The authorities had issued new directives pointing out that farmers who did this would be classified as 'drifters' and punished accordingly. How seriously? Apparently, the punishment would be meted out to the entire family, affecting the most important thing, their food rations. In times like these, any reduction in food rations was tantamount to taking food out of a person's mouth, so wasn't that like a death sentence? If he didn't want to be a 'drifter' at risk of being apprehended, then he needed an official document, a letter from the village that would legitimise his work. With that he could go to the commune offices to get official approval to leave Guojiadian. If he wanted to look for work beyond the county, then he'd have to go to the county offices with letters from both the village and the commune. Shit, there was no way the village government would give him the letter, not now. And even if they did, that wouldn't mean the commune and the county offices would. Besides, in the New Year he'd have to go and repair the reservoir; there was just no way. The only time to think of something would be around the New Year festivities since that was when the whole country shut down and he'd have time to think of some means to get what he needed. But it wasn't like before, he couldn't really just leave. Xuezhen had the baby to look after, his mother wasn't getting any younger, and Cunzhi was... the way he was... is that why people said life sucks the air out of you?

But Guo Cunxian wasn't the kind of man to piss his pants at the first sign of trouble. No, the more difficult things became, the more resolute he was. And so, once he thought through what he was going to do, he sent a letter to Wang Shun to make arrangements. He was going to set his plan in motion on the next market day in Xindian. He also told Ou Guangming, Liu Yucheng and Jin Laixi to each come separately and meet him there. There was a reason for his insistence on meeting in Xindian. Most of the villagers from Guojiadian preferred to shop in the market in Laodong since it was closer and they weren't too keen on walking the more than ten *li* to Xindian. If they were to meet there, they could at least avoid people they knew.

When the day came, they all met in the market and soon found a quiet place to talk things through. Guo Cunxian wanted five wheat pancakes and five bowls of hot water. Jin Laixi, fretting nervously about the whole clandestine meeting, brought these for him. Then, once everyone had calmed themselves, he introduced Wang Shun to his friends from Guojiadian. He told them he was like his younger brother, that they'd once made a living together, years before, when they had all been starving. That was when he had left town in search of work, and all the money he'd earned, well, that had been brought back to his old mother by Wang Shun, every single cent. Nothing was missing. Guo Cunxian then told them that he thought of them in the same way, that they could make a living together, they just had to figure out how... how were they going to make some money? He then told them that, if they were willing, then great, but if they weren't, then he wouldn't hold it against them.

Their intentions were clear, they didn't need any prodding. In fact, they were all quite eager and excited, and urged Guo Cunxian to tell them what he had in mind. How were they going to make some coin?

Guo Cunxian, however, was much more restrained; he didn't show the same impulsiveness as the others. On the contrary, he spoke to them quite seriously: "These last two days I've been wandering around the frog marshes thinking, and do you know what I saw? Reeds as far as the eye can see, growing everywhere. When the New Year rolls around and we have to continue work on the reservoir, all these reeds will go to waste. They will most likely be seen as an obstacle to further excavation and so they'll probably be just set on fire. All these years, the reeds and rushes have just been left to themselves. They grow, they die and they rot. If someone went and cut some to make repairs to their house, or if they were used to burn in the stoves, it wouldn't matter. But if a bunch of us, you know, take the initiative and go and cut them down to sell, then that will be something, let me tell you. Now, you might say it's all a little too much and you'd be right, or you might think this is really nothing, and that'd be right, too, but we're all poor, crazy farmers, right? Shit, if we weren't crazy, then how could we be as poor as we are? Besides, no one owns the reeds. So what if we cut some? That wouldn't make us criminals! Well, what I mean is… it's true, the reeds in the frog marshes don't have any owners, at least not any individual owners but they are owned by the nation, right, which means, I suppose, that we can't cut them all… but that's what I'm planning to do. Wang Shun here has already got the truck we'll need. His responsibility will be driving, as well as finding a buyer. Our job'll be cutting the reeds, wrapping them into bundles and loading them into the truck. Once that's done we'll take the reeds to the buyers and earn our money, and we'll all get equal shares, everyone the same amount. I'd say that one truck load, at least, should get us a couple of hundred yuan. If we load the truck several times then none of us will need to worry about the coming year, that's for sure…" Guo Cunxian stopped suddenly and reached for one of the bowls of water, before taking a bite of one of the pancakes.

No one else spoke. They busied themselves instead with eating their own pancakes and mulling the plan that had been described to them. They were all thinking of the same potential problem: what if they were caught? What would the authorities do? Deliberately, Guo Cunxian gave them time, he didn't want to rush them. He wanted them all to go over the plan in their own minds. He didn't want them to make a hasty decision and then regret it later.

When they'd nearly finished eating their pancakes, Guo Cunxian spoke again, announcing to them all how things were to go down: "No one needs to say anything now. Whether you want to do it or not, you don't need to tell us. If you don't, you still have time to take in the market, I won't say anything. If you want to do it, then be waiting on the northern road near the frog marshes at ten o'clock this evening. Make sure you bring a scythe and make sure it's sharp. That's all you need to bring. The truck'll be parked on the northern road. I know I'll be there, I'm doing it no matter what, even if I have to do it by myself. Oh, one more thing, regardless of what you decide, make sure you don't breathe a word of this to your families. We're the only ones that can know about it, alright?"

When they knew they didn't have to declare their intentions then and there, they all sighed with relief. They still had time to go over things and they could go home and really think it through. They were all thankful to Guo Cunxian and applauded his decision not to force an immediate decision on anyone but to let them mull it over. They'd have no idea what anyone would decide until the evening when they showed up or not. This way no one would influence anyone else and whatever any of them decided, it would clearly be their individual decision, meaning there would be no chance for recriminations later. In their hearts, some of them wanted to just obey Guo Cunxian, to follow along as he showed such conviction about the plan, after all.

Considering the men he'd gathered together, they were all his friends and it didn't matter what their class backgrounds were. If that had not been the case, if their backgrounds had been redder, then perhaps they would have been more shocked by his proposal. But in times like these, the fact he could call his friends together like this, that he could rely on them like this, created a greater sense of security. In truth, for those with a redder class background, their lips would have been sealed even tighter, they would have been even more reliable, for if something happened, then they would be punished as well.

As their meeting came to a close, Guo Cunxian thought to give them some parting words: "Before you all leave, I want to tell you a short tale. It's from Chu Renhuo's novel *Heroes of the Sui and Tang Dynasties*, the part where Shan Xiongxin has been captured by Emperor Taizong of the Tang and is awaiting execution. While in prison, his friend Xu Shiji beseeches the emperor to spare his friend's life, but the emperor refuses. Knowing that his friend is about to die and there was nothing more he could do, he goes to the prison to be with Shan Xiongxin until they take him away. When he sees his friend, he doesn't say a word to him, but rolls up his trouser leg, takes out his knife and swoosh, with one stroke he peels off a piece of his flesh. With two hands he offers this to Shan Xiongxin. Then he tells him: 'Brother, while I cannot save you, I cannot let go of you either. We ought to die together but I still have things to do in this life. Please, take my flesh and swallow it. This way a piece of me will at least die with you, and be buried together. When you're reborn in the next life, we'll be reborn together!'"

The frog marshes were completely pitch-black, the whole area enveloped in darkness. Because of the three years of flooding, the waters were fairly deep, which had enabled the reeds to grow so plentiful and so vibrantly. They swayed in the evening breeze, echoing their soft rustle throughout the night, bringing an eerie feel to the night that made men's hair stand on end. For the four or five men who'd come to cut the reeds, the dark night seemed as bright as day. It was as though they could see everything clearly, the night doing little to interrupt their rhythm or to slow their pace. To be a thief meant to develop the eyes of a thief, or rather to learn how to not need eyes to see, but to feel instead with their hearts, with their courage. The night grew darker and the sounds of the rustling reeds grew more terrifying but their hearts only grew more steadfast and their hands more nimble. Their left hands would clutch hold of the reeds while their right sliced through them, swoosh, swoosh, swoosh. With each swing of their scythes it was as though money was falling into their hands.

They had already carried out four nights of work and fortune had smiled on them, at least for the most part, since the weather had remained dark and foreboding, providing the perfect cover. And while the old northerly wind blew across their faces like a blade slicing through their skin, none of them felt a thing, so engrossed were they in their work, their bodies taut and sweaty, oblivious to everything except for the work in hand. Only the man responsible for wrapping the reeds up into bundles was aware of the night, his hair pulled back, his ears attentive, his whole body vigilant, constantly scanning the area, looking and listening for any signs of movement beyond those in the marshes.

Suddenly, a light from the south appeared and seemed to be rushing towards them. An alarmed voice then broke the silence of their work: "Shit! Cunxian, someone's coming from the village."

Swoosh... the scythes came to a halt. They all looked with concern in the direction of Guojiadian.

Who the hell could it be?

Except for Lan Shoukun, it couldn't be anyone else. These last few days he thought he'd caught wind of something like this; he'd asked around about them privately.

If it's him, then that'll be easy enough to handle.

Easy to handle? You must be joking!

No, shit, there are two or three more torches, it looks like more than a few people are coming.

In a low voice Cunxian instructed them: "Listen, you've all brought your own household utensils, yes? Make sure you don't leave anything behind so that they can prove we were here. We'll make our way round the bend in the marshes and head home that way. There's no way they'll be able to see us if we do that. Once you're home, make sure you hide the money. For now we can't spend a cent of it, and I mean it. Even death doesn't allow for the wind to blow through. Everything else I'll handle.

After a moment of shifting indecision, the men threw their bundles over their shoulders and headed deeper into the reed field, scythes in hand. Worry hung over them, making it difficult to move. And yet the more they walked into the swaying reeds, the greater their worry grew. They needed a cigarette, something to take the edge off their anxiety and steel their courage a little. Seeing the spark of a match being lit, Guo Cunxian turned and snarled: "Who? What the hell? Are you mad?" The man who lit the match froze, then his hand trembled and let it go. The match drifted to the ground and 'whoosh!' – the spark burst into flames.

Guo Cunxian rushed back and grabbed hold of his friend; together they ran. The dryness of the reeds where the match fell coupled with the evening wind soon set them aflame. They crackled and popped like so many firecrackers. The fire was small at first but grew bigger and bigger, higher and higher it reached up the stems, quickly engulfing the reeds. The wind fanned the flames and the flames increased the power of the wind. It howled disturbingly, a strange sound from the depths of who knows where, and then spread, roaring as it consumed the reeds, one after the other until the entire field seemed to glow and burn in the night. Thick smoke billowed up, whirling and rolling through the dark empty sky. The reeds below were being reduced to ashes.

Guo Cunxian and his friends, the men he'd been with these last few nights, turned and watched as the frog marshes were transformed into a sea of fire. There was nothing they could do but flee, or stay and be consumed by the fire itself. As expected, it was Lan Shoukun who arrived at the field first, along with five other militiamen. But it didn't matter how many men he'd brought with him, the reeds were ablaze and all they could do was watch helplessly.

Lan Shoukun kicked at the ground and cursed. Fuck, fuck, fuck... he knew it was that bastard Guo Cunxian, the axe-wielding prick. No one else had the balls!

One of the militiamen mumbled that there was no proof. There was no trace of who had been in the field stealing the reeds. There was nothing left but ashes. Just who the hell was going to be held responsible for this?

But Guo Cunxian and his friends wouldn't be let off lightly, even if they didn't have proof that they were the ones who did it. Lan Shoukun immediately dispatched militiamen to the commune and county offices to file reports, requesting the authorities send men to deal with this as soon as possible. He was going to race back to the village to round up Guo Cunxian and his friends to make sure they didn't try to run away.

The flames burning in the frog marshes lit up half the sky, casting a red glow over everything; it could be seen for miles. The inferno woke up those who'd been sleeping as the night was transformed into day. Who wouldn't be woken by such a ruckus?

By the time Lan Shoukun returned to the village, burning with rage and indignation, there was already a crowd near the northern outskirts of the town watching the conflagration with awe. Some were craning their necks to try to get a better look; others were just milling about and chattering away to no one in particular while others cursed and some shouted their applause. Then, when they saw Lan Shoukun running up, a loose tongue let fly: "What? Lan Shoukun is responsible for the fire, burning such useful reeds... just what the hell were you thinking?"

"That's right, if the nation didn't need them, surely the nation could have let us cut them down. Hmm, that would've been better."

The acid in Lan Shoukun's stomach burned and he roared at them: "Who started the fire, huh? They're mine!"

He pushed his way through the crowd, shining the torch in people's faces, looking for the culprits.

The villagers still cursed and chattered away: the frog marshes had bordered the towns in the area for ages and now with the recent floods they'd flourished, they'd become like one of the family. Once they'd become the responsibility of the commune they took its name, which meant they belonged to everyone and no one. The plan this year had been to transform the reed field into another reservoir so as to join the frog marshes with the other waterway project. The area was to be administered by the county. They would be responsible for it and that would be good but now a great blaze had transformed the field into a massive sky lantern, and for whose benefit?

Unfortunately, Lan Shoukun couldn't find the man he was looking for in the crowd, but that didn't mean he thought he was wrong. The man or men who had stolen the reeds wouldn't have returned to the village, or perhaps they just hadn't had time to make their way back yet. He needed to quickly go to Guo Cunxian's house, and to the houses of his friends, too, and check to see if they were there. If they weren't at home, that would be great, it would prove their guilt. After all, what else could they be up to in the middle of the night? The fact that they weren't at home guaranteed that they were the culprits and he'd have an easy time getting that out of them.

The simplest way to capture a thief was to first catch the lord who hired him. With this in mind, Lan Shoukun went first to Guo Cunxian's house. He rapped on the door for what felt like ages before he finally heard rustling from inside. He then had to wait for that rustling to make its way to the door and open it up. Guo Cunxian opened the door and was nearly blinded by the light from Lan Shoukun's torch. He averted his eyes, seemingly bewildered by Lan Shoukun's arrival at his door. He was only half dressed, standing in the doorway in his underpants, his shoes worn like slippers, his arms bare and a cotton-padded jacket slung over his shoulder. He held his axe in his right hand: "Who the devil...? It's the dead of night, what do you want?"

Lan Shoukun was taken by surprise. With Guo Cunxian standing in front of him, he wasn't sure what to say: "What... what've you been up to?"

"What do you think? I've been in bed. It's the middle of the night. What else would I be doing?"

"The frog marshes are burning, didn't you know?"

"What? Are you here looking for men to fight the fire?"

"I'm here to denounce you! You're the one who has been stealing the reeds. You started the fire to avoid capture."

"What the hell! Screw you and your ancestors! I'll denounce you, huh, you're the one who started the fire. You're trying to cause a ruckus and get the whole town worked up so that you can take advantage of the chaos to look good and hopefully be named village secretary."

"Fuck your ancestors. How dare you provoke me like this! Are you spoiling for a fight?"

Guo Cunxian tightened his grip on his axe: "You're damn right I am. Come on, it might be the dead of night but if you're itching for a fight, I'll give you one!"

Lan Shoukun straightened himself: "But I'm in charge of town law enforcement, are you trying to say you're not going to allow me in, huh?"

"In charge of law enforcement, are you? Hmph, I don't give a fuck. I haven't broken any laws and I haven't done anything wrong. On what grounds do you want to search my home? How about I go and search your home, huh? I've got a mind to." Guo Cunxian was rigid with rage, refusing to move out of the doorway to let Lan Shoukun in.

Nervousness crept over Lan Shoukun. He tried to muster some courage: "So am I permitted to search or not?"

"You're permitted, but I need to make something clear first. If you find a single reed, then I'll freely give myself up for punishment, but if you don't, huh, what then? I'll tell you, I'm going to get men and go to your house and search, and I guarantee you I'll find the supplies you used to start the fire. Do you believe me?"

Backed into a corner, a man will try anything to escape, but at this moment, he was frozen to the spot, unable to move, even if his life depended on it. Guo Cunxian's words had cut to the quick. The two families had known each other for ages; after all, they'd been living in the same village for generations. Lan Shoukun knew full well, too, that Guo Cunxian wasn't the kind of man to provoke too much, but he didn't know where this venom came from, this nasty bile that seemed so easy to stir up, nor did he know how it was that he'd been put in this position.

Lan Shoukun took a step back: "Perhaps I won't carry out the search, at least not right now, but you're not allowed to leave the village. When the commune and county officials arrive, we'll talk about this then."

"Leave? What the hell do you mean, huh? Do you have someone else here with you? You'll have them block my door! Ha!"

Before he finished speaking, Guo Cunxian slammed the door, slipped the lock and stumbled back into his bedroom.

Lan Shoukun had really stirred up a hornet's nest this time, but he was intent on pursuing the matter. He left two militiamen to watch over Guo Cunxian's house, not to shame or humiliate him, no, but to try and frighten him, to make him worry. He was trying to make the other villagers suspect Guo Cunxian, too. By the time morning came, everyone in the town would think that he was the one who'd done it and that the militia had found out.

The first person to rise was his mad old uncle, well, grandpa, really... at least that's what they usually called him. Since he was little, Uncle Jingshi had seemed more like a grandfather to Cunxian, Cunzhi and Cunzhu rather than their uncle. And those feelings of intimacy remained intact today. It didn't matter whether they were at home or out somewhere in the fields or in the village, they all called him grandpa and not uncle.

The first thing Jingshi did in the morning was grab the chamber pot and the night soil fork and head outside. Of course, as he pushed open the door he saw militiamen standing on both sides, their eyes furtively scanning the area, their legs carrying them in straight lines back and forth across the courtyard. The two men had been given orders to prevent any member of the family from stepping beyond the outer gate. They had to ensure that the family didn't try to dispose of their ill-gotten gains, certainly not before the county officials arrived to investigate. Upon seeing Jingshi move towards the outer edges of the courtyard, one of the men shouted, although not all that loudly: "You're not permitted to leave!" Why the low voice? Well, it was clear the militiamen were afraid of waking Guo Cunxian who was nothing if not difficult to deal with. They had witnessed the earlier exchange between Lan Shoukun and Guo Cunxian and they saw how afraid their boss was. Besides, they were just common militiamen; they didn't need the extra hassle. But a madman, and an old one at that, well, that was nothing to be afraid of. It never occurred to them that the old man wouldn't listen to them, wouldn't answer them, or perhaps hadn't even heard them. Whatever the case might be, Guo Jingshi paid them no heed and continued to walk towards the gate. The militiamen grew furious and raised their voices: "Hey, you crazy old bastard, I said you weren't permitted beyond the gate, didn't you hear?"

The old madman continued to take no notice of them, which only enraged the militiamen more. They hadn't wanted to disturb Guo Cunxian but could it be possible that they should have feared the madman? One of the men raised his arms to grab hold of Jingshi but, before he could actually lay his hands on him, he found himself flying backwards through the air before crashing onto the ground, landing squarely on his tailbone and firing a shard of pain straight through his body. The other militiaman was dumbfounded by what was happening in front of him. Just what the hell was going on? He hadn't seen clearly what threw his companion backwards through the air but he now jumped up to act, feeling duty bound to do so. One thing was clear: the old man hadn't stopped walking towards the gate. His feet were moving in a determined rhythm, his arms at his side, the shaft of the night soil fork wedged underneath one of them. Then, suddenly, his body went numb and he felt himself falling forward and his teeth clamped down hard on his lips, breaking the skin.

The old madman didn't even turn his head to see what had happened but kept on walking in the direction of the eastern marshes.

The militiamen picked themselves up off the ground. Their facial expressions had changed. They weren't showing pain but fear instead. If it hadn't happened to them personally, they never would've believed that such a crazy old grandpa was capable of throttling them so easily. One stood rubbing his backside, the other massaging his jaw. They looked at each other with puzzled expressions on their faces. Just what the hell had happened? Then one of them broke the silence: "Do we go after him?" The other knowingly replied: "Madmen have legal protection. Killing him isn't worth it."

"You reckon that's all we can do, kill him... kill a madman?"

"I guess that's our lot. We don't need to hit people, we just need to accept the beating ourselves, hmm. Do you think he's really crazy? I'm not sure, I don't think he has completely lost it. No wonder Guo Cunxian is the way he is, actually their whole family is the same, aren't they? They're all up to the same old tricks."

"Then what're we gonna do?"

"We report to the head, he's the one who ordered us to stay here so he's ultimately responsible. We don't need to bother ourselves with it any more than necessary."

Sun Yueqing had heard the whole ruckus outside. She'd been awake since the knock had come on the door in the middle of the night, unable to go back to sleep. She heard Jingshi get up, collect the chamber pot and night soil fork, open the door and walk out. She heard the commotion as well. How could she remain in bed? She hastened to get up, to see what was actually happening. The courtyard gate was slightly ajar but the road that ran alongside it was quiet and entirely empty. It looked as though the sun was just coming up, bathing the area in the new light of day. Besides their crazy old granddad, who else would be up so early on a winter morning? She then heard someone call out, and wondered if Jingshi was up sleepwalking. Before she could find out more, she heard movement behind her. Xuezhen was up as well. She should have expected this, of course. There was no way Guo Cunxian would still be in bed. Soon he was standing beside her: "Mother, you're up early, huh? Did the nonsense last night keep you up?"

Guo Cunxian looked at his mother. He couldn't help but think her hair had gone white because of his uncle. He never realised the real source of worry was him, because he was so much like his father. Cunzhi, on the other hand, was hardly any trouble at all. Sun Yueqing turned and closed the gate tight, then took hold of Cunxian's arm and pulled him towards the small tree in their courtyard. She stared up into his eyes and asked him a probing question: "What have you been up to? Why did those men come here last night?"

Guo Cunxian laughed in an offhand manner as though he were enjoying the troubles of others: "Last night the frog marshes were set ablaze and the whole northern reed field was completely burnt down. Lan Shoukun was out trying to find out who the culprit was, looking to see if anyone had reeds hidden away at home. If they had, then that would be proof they were the ones responsible for the fire. When he came here to look, well, I had words with him, unpleasant ones, but it did make him leave."

Sun Yueqing was still unsure, still upset: "You really weren't involved, were you?"

Guo Cunxian took hold of his mother by her shoulders and looked deep into her eyes: "Do you think your son's that foolish? If I'd really started it, would I have threatened Lan Shoukun? What would be the point? Besides, the eastern marshes were nothing more than dried reeds, so why burn them? Anyway, have you seen any reeds around here? Whoever it was who caused all the commotion last night, well, people said they were as sly as a fox not to get caught. Others said that the whole marshes were lit up like a flare."

This seemed to put Sun Yueqing a little more at ease and she rebuked him: "That's all nonsense and you know it. Cunxian, my son, you're too much like your father. You act and speak without thinking. You know, we're not all like you. We don't all have the same temperament. You need to consider the rest of us and not just plunge in head first."

In truth, Sun Yueqing had heard movement in the house the last few nights, and on one of them, she was sure she had heard Cunxian head outside, so she got up to follow him only to discover that the door was closed. After she opened it and went outside herself, she saw too that the courtyard gate was similarly closed tight. If Cunxian had gone out first, there would have been no way he could have latched the door from the inside, so she couldn't help but think that perhaps her ears were playing tricks on her, or she had been sleepwalking. Over the last month Xuezhen had been convalescing after childbirth and she hadn't really slept soundly. Whenever the baby cried, she'd wake up to tend to it. She would hear movement, too, in the eastern room. Many years later she finally learnt what it was that she had been hearing at night. She hadn't been sleepwalking or dreaming. Cunxian had really been sneaking out at night.

She had neglected to remember her son was a carpenter. When he had mended the doors to this old house he had also decided to test his skill at wood working, and so he had mounted on the door a small mechanism that allowed people on the outside to latch the inner lock. Later, when one left, there was no need to lock up. Should a thief decide to visit, there'd be no way he could push open the door. Instead, he'd only discover that the door was bolted, and this would lead him to believe that people must be at home. Under such circumstances, no thief would dare try to force it. But after Cunxian had mounted the mechanism he abruptly realised there was a problem: if he told everyone else in the house there was this mechanism built into the door and they in turn accidentally told someone else (a distinct possibility when he thought about his younger brother and sister and their penchant for showing off in front of their classmates), it would result in the townspeople becoming quite curious about the mechanism he'd installed. And once the villagers knew, who wouldn't want to come and check it out? It would be tantamount to their house having no door at all! Consequently, he told no one of the mechanism in the door, and even once thought to remove it altogether. It was only when he discovered its usefulness for him, say, when he didn't want the family to know what he was up to, that he decided to leave it in place.

Once again she heard her grandson crying and Sun Yueqing hurried into the eastern room. As soon as she entered she saw Xuezhen busily trying to get the baby to latch onto her breast. She sat on the edge of the bed and looked at her grandson. His eyes were closed as he sucked at her nipple. The whole scene filled Sun Yueqing with a sense of peace and contentment; being a grandmother was certainly a joyous thing. This moment in time, this place, watching her grandson... it didn't matter if the sky outside were falling, nothing at all could intrude on her happiness, nothing else mattered. She took hold of his little hand and held it tightly. His whole face, his whole body, he was just so lovable. Sun Yueqing asked her daughter-in-law if her breast had produced more milk these last few days as she hadn't heard him cry quite so often. Xuezhen answered in the affirmative but still worried it wasn't enough; perhaps only seventy to eighty per cent of what he needed. In any case, she told her mother-in-law, whenever he cried she simply tried to feed him since a mouth filled with her breast at least muffled his crying. Sun Yueqing tried to console her, telling her not to worry about his crying; that only showed his energy and the strength of his lungs. A crying baby would grow up strong, full of vitality and power. She also told her daughter-in-law that it had now been a month since his birth, that things would get easier from here on and that soon he'll be able to eat soft rice soup. She had even heard that the county seat was selling children's formula, so she'd get Cunxian to go and buy some. Once the winter starts to wane, she'll also tell their granddad to catch some fish, maybe a few prawns, and boil them up in a soup to ensure the little boy grows up big and plump.

The more she spoke about her grandson's future prospects, the more she herself became enraptured in the words. Since today marked the first month, it was now time to give the boy a name. Xuezhen asked her mother-in-law if she had already thought of something suitable. Cunxian had told her, after all, that the naming of the child was, according to tradition, the responsibility of the grandparents. Sun Yueqing had turned it over in her mind more than once, trying to get the right feel for it, and then told her that she had thought of a name and that she'd spoken to their granddad too. Since he was their first grandchild, she told Xuezhen, it needed to be properly auspicious, and what better name could there be but Fuzi, meaning good fortune itself. His life would be far better than theirs. He wouldn't suffer the same poverty they had or the same pain. No, his life would be different... he'd enjoy so much more. For that reason, it made sense to give him the courtesy name Chuanfu, which meant the transmission of good fortune. Not only will he be blessed himself, but he'll bring good fortune to the whole family, passing it on to generation after generation; he'll be our lucky star, happiness and long life will be his. Sun Yueqing revelled in what she was saying, and as she spoke a happy laugh escaped her lips. But with the laugh came worry. A month had passed. What food were they going to prepare for him?

It was Xuezhen's turn to reassure and comfort her. She told her mother-in-law they had had little to eat these last few years but they'd always managed to have something... so they could do it again and handle whatever may happen. But Sun Yueqing's response was direct; she told her daughter-in-law not to be concerned with such matters, then stood up and left the room, mumbling under her breath that that was no way to live, and certainly no way to feed her grandson. It was already bright outside and Cunxian was up, sweeping the courtyard. She spoke to him and asked him where today's market was; she had forgotten. Cunxian stopped his sweeping and looked at his mother. He told her that there was nothing to forget and she wasn't confused; there was no market today, at least not anywhere near Guojiadian. He then asked her what she was thinking of doing. She bit her bottom lip and spoke of her grandson passing one month and how the occasion needed to be celebrated; that they ought to have dumplings at least, even if there was only sorghum flour for the skins and vegetables for the filling. It was a shame they had no meat or fish. Xuezhen also needed to eat something special, she continued, otherwise she wouldn't produce enough milk to feed the child. She then told him that, if he'd already eaten his morning meal, he should head into the county town and see if anything were available.

Guo Cunxian had a little cash on him and had been thinking about going into the county town, but he feared that he wouldn't be able to do so today. He replied to his mother's query slightly hesitantly: "I'll have to wait until things settle down before I can head to town, and if I can't make it today I'll think of something. We have to celebrate no matter what."

Her son's response only stoked the flames of her worry again. She looked him square in the face and asked him directly, probingly: "Is something going on in the village?"

Cunxian avoided giving a clear answer, guessing wildly about the impact the burning of the frog marshes would have on the village, that the authorities would have to be informed, that the people's militia may even be dispatched to monitor the gates in and out of town, and that they would prevent people from coming and going as they pleased. He wondered if she'd like him to talk to the militiamen, if it was worth telling them about his son just passing his first month.

Rubbing her still sleepy eyes, Cunzhu stepped out of her room, complaining to them both: "You've been jawing away the whole morning. The baby is only just over a month old, it's not his birthday." Her mother stared at her and wondered how she could be so flippant. Her grandson might not be a year old but passing his first month in times like these was still a big deal. She told her to start the fire, quickly, and put pots on the stove. In one breath, her mother told her to add water and rice to make the morning porridge and then, once that was done, to bring a bowl of it to her sister-in-law. Once her sister-in-law had been given food, she was to add some more water to the pot and put in the leftover steam cakes from the night before for the rest of them. And in the other pot, she only needed to boil water.

Astonished, her daughter replied and asked her mother if she wanted her to chase down a pig in the yard too... that is if they had one.

Sun Yueqing laughed now herself. Her daughter was to be married next year, she was a grown woman, and yet she had talked to her as though she were still a child. Where did the days go? Boiling a pot of water... you only needed that if you were going to have pork or to shave their old granddad's head, to clean him up, if only a little.

Cunzhu's mouth turned into a smile; catching a pig would be much easier than washing her granddad's head. Of course, she knew that his hair was cut once a year. It was a big family event, a sort of celebration to finish the year and welcome the new one, but there was still plenty of time left before the New Year, she thought, wasn't there?

Sun Yueqing weighed things up in her mind. Hadn't they noticed the change in the days? Soon it would be freezing outside, so cold they wouldn't be able to even step beyond their front door, and certainly too cold to cut their mad old granddad's hair. They should take advantage of the weather now before it got too cold, and what's more it was her grandson's one hundred days; everything ought to be put away and cleaned up. The boiled water could be used for the baby, too, to give him a bath.

Cunzhu couldn't help but still make fun of her mother. Old people really were something. What was she proposing to do? Use the hot water to clean the baby and then use the same water for granddad's head?

Sun Yueqing waved her hand in a mock threat making Cunzhu laugh some more before she ran off to light the fire. Sun Yueqing then turned and walked into the southern room to wake up her other son, Cunzhi. She wanted him to get up and go and search for granddad to get him to come home. There was no way to properly dispose of the night soil in winter and so there was no need for him to wander about, especially in the cold.

Poverty comes with its fair share of difficulties but each new morning presents new opportunities and small comforts. His mother's words had this effect on him now.

As Cunzhu finished preparing the morning porridge, she poured out one hearty bowl to bring to the eastern room. As she walked in, Xuezhen lifted the curtain covering the door and stepped outside, whereupon Cunzhu asked her what she was doing. Hadn't a month passed, she replied. Wasn't it time for her to get up? She told Cunzhu she would take the bowl and return its contents to the pot on the stove. When her mother-in-law saw her walk in, she stood up and asked what was going on, just what was she doing? She told her to return to her room with the porridge, to eat it and then take a warm bath. It was alright for her to get up, her mother-in-law said, for her to do some work even around the house, but she couldn't do any of that on an empty stomach, not just for her sake but for the sake of her child, too.

Cunzhu joined the conversation, agreeing with her mother and telling her sister-in-law that she was, when it came down to it, her baby's canteen, after all! As she spoke she took the bowl of porridge from Xuezhen's hand and brought it into the eastern room, putting it next to her bed. Sun Yueqing followed them in a moment later and took out a small porcelain container from the wardrobe. She spooned out two small ladlefuls of fried noodles and added them to the porridge. This was a tonic for a woman recuperating after childbirth, she told her daughter-in-law.

They added water to the pot and the aroma permeated the whole room. Sun Yueqing sliced some salted vegetables to add to it, and her daughter and daughter-in-law busily finished their own breakfast preparations. As soon as they extinguished the cooking fires, however, they heard a surprised cry coming from outside. Cunxian hollered: "Just what are you doing?"

The two younger women raced out into the courtyard to see what was happening and were just as surprised as Cunxian seemed to be. Their mad old granddad had returned, bare-armed with the night soil basket over his shoulder and the fork in his hand. The sixty-year-old man truly was mad, carrying round a basket of shit in the state he was in.

Cunzhu yelled out, asking no one in particular where her granddad's jacket was.

Cunzhi walked up behind them with his granddad's jacket in his hands. I looked as though he was carrying something quite heavy wrapped up in it. It was winter, freezing outside. Just what could be so valuable that it would make a man take off his jacket and wrap whatever it was up in it? Cunzhi yelled out to them that he needed something to put it in. Cunxian ran over and took the bundle from his brother's hands. He opened the jacket and saw it filled with fine sand.

Sun Yueqing came close and grabbed a handful, rubbing it through her fingers before letting it slip through; it was as fine and soft as flour, and as fluid as water as it slid through her fingers. Smiling, she thought how the sand pouring through her fingers seemed like rays of sunlight. "This is wonderful," she exclaimed. Turning, she went into the kitchen and brought out a container to put the sand in.

Cunzhu was still grumbling about her granddad. It was a new jacket he'd used to carry the sand; she and her mother had just sewn it half a year ago, and now look at it!

Sun Yueqing kept smiling but rebuked her daughter for speaking to her uncle so rudely. She told them the sand was to be treasured. If it were fried a little then it could be woven together with yarn to make a bundle for the baby. When he peed, the sand would absorb it, keeping him dry and clean... warm too. The pee would also be kept away from his skin, so they wouldn't even need to wrap him up tightly in a cloth nappy. Potty training would be that much easier. She told them they had all had the same treatment when they were young. She'd been worried about the child these last few days, with the winter having come but now, after finding this sand, it was a fortunate thing indeed. It also showed how much their granddad loved his grandson!

Guo Jingshi had been busy nearly half the day, his arms tirelessly carrying the night soil container; he hadn't put it down. Cunxian emptied the sand into the container and shook out his uncle's jacket, beating it with his hands to loosen the remaining grains of sand before handing it to Cunzhu to give back to her granddad. He then took hold of the night soil container and placed it on the ground. By the feel of it in his hands he could tell that it hadn't been emptied: "Yah, this hasn't been dumped yet!" He looked in the basket, saw that it was filled with dried grass and thought his granddad had collected it this morning. He didn't think there might still be something else below that. He removed the dried grass and threw it on the pile of firewood near the side of the house, then dumped the remaining contents with the rest of the night soil. But what fell out didn't look like faeces at all, it was much too dark in colour. He turned his head to look at his granddad and asked: "What's this, huh?"

Their mad old granddad had not uttered a word since he walked into the courtyard; it was just as before when he didn't speak at all. Still silent, he walked over to the night soil basket and took hold of it. The dark things that had been dumped out were in fact a roasted rabbit, a now charcoal-feathered bird and several mudfish, charred and hard as a rock. Cunxian understood that his granddad had been to the frog marshes and that these animals had all been baked in the great conflagration from last night, unable to flee. But just where did the mudfish come from? He asked his granddad several times but the only response he could pry out of him was that he'd simply found them in the ashes. The shallow water of the marshes had apparently boiled due to the flames, turning from ice into water in a flash, leaving these poor fish at the mercy of the fire. They had had no way to escape, nowhere to swim to; so there was no way for them to avoid being scorched by the fire. Then, when the land cooled, they froze, although not really like icicles.

Excited by the story, Cunzhu leapt up, laughed and said that her granddad had prepared items for her for the New Year!

Sun Yueqing used her hand to dig out the seared rabbit and saw that it was really only the first layer of flesh that had been burnt; they could still stew it and have some for the New Year festivities that weren't too far off. As for the bird, it was too bad it wasn't a wild goose but what could they do? It was only a much smaller wild duck. Still, that could be used in a soup, something to give to Xuezhen.

This was called 'burning incense sticks to attract spirits'.

Chen Baohuai allowed Lan Shoukun to dispatch two militiamen: one would go to the county offices to report, the other to the commune headquarters. He'd use this event, the conflagration of the frog marshes, to put the fear of god into those nuisance elements in the village. For a long while now he had been unsettled and felt that something was wrong. More and more villagers had stopped listening to his orders and they even dared to look him in the eye, to look past him... well, fuck them all! This fire was just what he needed. It would allow him to reassert his control.

But then something quite unexpected happened. The man he'd sent to the commune headquarters returned without anyone accompanying him. In fact, he hadn't met with anyone in charge at the commune but rather reported that the offices were in complete disarray. Apparently, the old leadership had been overthrown and a new committee had seized power but then, not long after taking control, they themselves were denounced so that no one really knew who was running things. Then, when it was nearly midday, the militiaman sent to the county offices returned as well, and he too had failed to bring the police with him. Instead, there was a group of about a hundred Red Guards following on his tail, all dressed in green military fatigues with red armbands around each and every one of them. Slung over their shoulders were military satchels, and in each hand was a copy of *Quotations from Chairman Mao Zedong*. Some of them looked to be hardly twenty years old but their voices crackled across the electrical speakers they'd brought with them. They were university students from Beijing. Along the way they had rounded up other students as well, those from middle schools between here and the capital, including students from Guojiadian who'd been sent to the county township to study. Among them were students who were known to the village such as Guo Jinghai's younger brother Cunyong, Chen Laoding's boy Erxiong and Lan Shoukun's nephew Lan Xin.

If this were still old China, would there be someone to allow these little brats to act this way? But here they were, marching through the village at the front of a movement that could only be considered most inappropriate. Their faces were contorted and their eyes seemingly possessed with a certain kind of fervour. They looked thoroughly like a bullet that had been fired from a gun and was now hurtling towards its target. Like hailstones pelting down upon the ground before melting in the blink of an eye. They were like countless hailstones falling from the heavens, bringing with them a howling, mad wind, torrential rains and lightning bolts. They were indeed quite amazing, indomitable, sweeping away everything in their path.

Those who resisted would be crushed. Of course, Chen Baohuai knew who and what the Red Guards were but he had mistakenly believed that they were active only on school campuses and only in Beijing and other big cities. He didn't believe their type of calamity would make its way to the countryside; he thought he would've been spared. But now, suddenly, they were standing in front of him, here to root out so-called enemies of the revolution. They seemed even faster and more nimble than the troops that had liberated Guojiadian many years ago.

By now the Red Guards were experts at what they were doing. Their first step once they entered a village would be to take control of the airwaves, and to do that they needed to occupy the highest vantage points in the town. This they would do quickly, and then not long after the loudspeakers would begin to blare, calling the town to attention. Silence would follow as the villagers' eyes would be directed to the tops of the highest buildings, for there on top of each and every one would be Red Guards. Once they had a captive audience, they would bring the loudspeakers back up to their mouths, and if they didn't have a loudspeaker then a rolled-up newspaper would work just as well.

They would begin their exhortations with a broad, general slogan: "Establishing revolutionary networks is the pioneering work of the Red Guards. Chairman Mao supports us in these efforts and encourages us to go out and further the cause of the socialist revolution!"

"Our minds are our weapons. Our task is to spread the words of Chairman Mao to the masses, to every part of the country, to join up with all the rebel factions, to stick together through thick and thin, to be the vanguard and to freeze the sky with piercing cold!"

"Proclaim the great victory of the January Storm!"

"The main aim of the revolution is to wrest control of political power!"

"The Great Proletarian Revolution has begun! Seize power! Seize power! Seize power!"

The slogans carried through the air, rising to a crescendo and slowly engulfing Guojiadian. The political power of the Party in the village had been taken by the Red Guards, and they had taken it effortlessly. There were two symbols of political power in the county, one was the power of the official seal and the Red Guards had taken hold of that quite easily. The second was people, those who actually wielded power. And every last one of them was soon confined to one office including, of course, the core leadership: Chen Baohuai, Han Jingting and Lan Shoukun. Red Guards stood round the building.

There was also another aspect of power in the village, and that was property held by the Party. This was managed by the accountant of the production brigade and the land custodian, who were now called out for interrogation by the Red Guards. Their first question was about their background, for which there were no problems. The interrogation then shifted and it was pointed out that until now they had been walking down the capitalist road of exploitation and their mistake had only worked against the revolution. It was now imperative they act before it was too late. They had to get back on the correct path and be willing to accept the rebel faction as the vanguard of the revolution. The Red Guards also instructed them that it was their responsibility to carry out meritorious deeds in service of the revolution in order to atone for their crimes. The custodian was therefore ordered to arrange dinner for the Red Guards and the production brigade accountant was to organise the people and have them construct a stage to serve as a platform for the impending struggle session. It had to be a bright, open area with enough space for the entire village to gather in front of. The session itself would, before long, entice and excite all of the villagers and in the blink of an eye liberation would be possible and the whole town would be transformed into the vanguard of the revolution.

On this very normal of normal days, something happened in Guojiadian that no one expected nor believed: an opera was performed on stage. There were only a few students performing but they hadn't been instructed to do so by the higher-ups, nor did they have a proper introduction letter from the central authorities. So why had they carelessly roused the entire village? Ordinarily, the village Party cadres were a fearsome lot; they had control over the entire village. But they had instantly submitted and it wasn't the villagers who'd forced them. No, they'd done nothing actually. In fact, it was the Party cadres themselves who had been submissive. They had done what the old-timers would call 'being cowed'. While the Red Guards hadn't been officially dispatched by the higher-ups, they had been sanctioned by Chairman Mao, the supreme leader of the revolution. And it's true they never had the proper paperwork but they did possess the 'supreme directive'. Actually, these were issues the village authorities didn't dare to think about too much and they certainly wouldn't ask the Red Guards about it. Just the sight of them caused men to lose their bearings. If they said 'jump' the men would simply ask 'how high'? No one dared do anything else.

Once the Red Guards were in charge, the messages broadcast over the village loudspeakers changed: "Glad tidings, the rebel faction of Guojiadian and the revolutionary masses as a whole have achieved a great victory. We have assumed power in the village and we've rooted out the capitalist running dogs who have been polluting the village. We've overthrown Chen Baohuai!

"We also have an announcement to make. The burning of the frog marshes was an act perpetrated by the capitalist roaders and class enemies in the service of their counter-revolutionary aims. This afternoon, in the shadow of the Dragon Phoenix Trees, we are calling a struggle session to expose and thoroughly criticise their capitalist conspiracy and crimes. We will resolutely bring down all class enemies!"

This all caused a great ruckus in Guojiadian. Like conjuring up a magic trick it was all so easy and so sudden. The accountant for the production brigade had borrowed the Red Guards' harshness and busied himself with hanging slogans round the necks of class enemies, confiscating whatever he deemed counter-revolutionary, pounding on doors and generally making a big fuss. It was like adding oil to a fire. Guojiadian was thrown into a state of confusion and soon an air of oppression and gloom hung over the entire village, but it would be wrong to say chickens took flight and dogs howled in fear.

And the reason for that was clear: there weren't any chickens or dogs in the village. After all, anything edible had already been eaten by the villagers.

The lack of flying chickens and howling dogs, of course, also meant that the atmosphere in the town didn't seem to be quite as intense as it actually was. The town had already experienced the early land reform initiatives, collectivisation, the

Great Leap Forward and the hard times that followed when starvation stalked them, but it wasn't as though they were going to lose their heads over the Party cadres being stripped of power. So just what kind of poor peasants were they? Most of them were beyond destitute and had been for generations; their blood itself was poor. Before Liberation no one much bothered about the poor but afterwards being poor was no longer considered a personal fault. They could at least claim ownership over their own bones. This all meant nothing much could really scare them, even when they were put into a situation that was truly not a laughing matter; they would invariably look at it as something new and exciting. This was how they approached the day's events. No one would have thought the blaze that had engulfed the frog marshes would turn out as it did. It was a plot twist worthy of the stage. But who caused the fire? And who did it ultimately burn? It was difficult to say.

After lunch, the loudspeakers blared, urging all the villagers to make their way quickly to the Dragon Phoenix Trees where the struggle session stage had been constructed. Soon, wave after wave of music, slogans and the rhythmic clang of gongs and drums emanated from the direction of the trees, making it seem as though an opera indeed was being performed. The so-called 'struggle session' stage was in truth only a theatre stage, about 1.5 metres off the ground, 6.5 metres wide and about 10 metres long. Notwithstanding its dimensions, the platform itself looked rather unfinished, constructed only out of several locust trees and nothing much else. Fortunately, there was no need for people to encircle it completely, otherwise they would have had to go round to each house and borrow mats for the villagers to sit on. The rear of the platform nestled against the Dragon Phoenix Trees, their girth serving to support the struggle session stage, its branches forming the roof. What a pity it was, then, that there were no leaves to shade the proceedings.

And since it looked very much like a theatre stage, who wouldn't wish to come and see the hubbub? Who didn't want to know how the story played out, or who the main characters were? The area in front of the stage filled with more and more people and the gongs rang out ever more stridently. Then the clanging slowed before growing faster again. The rhythm shifted back and forth, from heavy thuds to gentle taps, gradually stoking the onlookers' feelings of suspense. It seemed as though the mallet would soon break, then suddenly it stopped! Everything went quiet and no one dared to even breathe; it was as though their hearts had become lodged in their throats.

Into the silence a tall and rather slim Red Guard stood up and walked towards the microphone. Perched on his nose was a pair of thick glasses that had earned him the nickname 'Four Eyes'. He had a typical Beijing accent but when he opened his mouth he yelled with a certain coarseness that frightened the gathered villagers: "Our supreme leader Chairman Mao has taught us that China has over eight hundred million people and so struggle is unavoidable. Unavoidable! A rooster crows to welcome the day. Seizing power advances the cause of struggle, criticism and reform. There's nothing more to say. When I first saw this village, I asked, just what kind of place is this?"

At first, no one on stage or in the audience dared to speak, as though they'd all been scared stiff and were unsure of what to say. They didn't seem to know what kind of village they lived in. Others mumbled among themselves, wondering why in hell this question was being asked. They were, after all, in Guojiadian!

Four Eyes seemed to have heard what was in their hearts and under their breath and in a loud voice proceeded to denounce them: "Wrong, this place is the Dragon Phoenix Trees! Looking at you people, ah… it's easy to see, many of you are stuck on the feudal, capitalist, revisionist road. Aren't there really two trees behind me? Which one is the dragon and which the phoenix? This is only feudal superstition! If the people of Guojiadian wish to struggle against this trend, then the first thing they need to do is struggle against these two trees here and view them as counter-revolutionaries."

Beside them, a young boy yelled out a slogan: "Down with all feudal, capitalist, revisionist loafers! Down with the Dragon Phoenix Trees!"

The hearts of the townspeople jumped. Fortunately the Red Guards had said "down with" and not "cut down" the two trees.

When the shouting of slogans waned, Four Eyes continued: "From now on, these two trees will be considered as counter-revolutionary! They'll stand as proof of the need for Guojiadian to turn the page on history and to reinvent itself. These two trees, remember them and remember today." Pausing for a moment to let the proclamation sink in, he continued: "Now I want all capitalist roaders, all evil elements in the village to be brought here. I want them detained and put up here on this stage!"

The loudspeaker blared on, a peculiar joviality echoing through the air: "Workers, peasants, soldiers, to battle! The revolutionary line is clear, all political enemies will be purged. Death, death, death to them all!" A squad of Red Guards dragged the day's main actor up onto the stage. Chen Baohuai looked haggard and hunched over, a white paper dunce's hat stuck to his skull with the words 'Guojiadian's key capitalist roader' emblazoned across it. Trailing closely behind him were Han Jingting and Lan Shoukun, each with a dunce's cap perched on their heads, if only a little smaller than the one worn by Chen. They'd been identified as Chen's key lackeys and words to that effect were written across their hats. Coming up behind them were Liu Yucheng, Jin Laiwang and his younger brother, Jin Laixi. They weren't deserving of dunce's hats themselves, so only wooden placards were hung round their necks bestowing on them the moniker of the 'five black categories' of class enemies. Bringing up the rear was a line of company commanders, the second rank of class enemies, the leaders of the production units and men of that ilk. None of them had dunce's hats on, nor were placards draped around their necks, only their hands were bound. Once they had made their way up onto the stage, two columns of Red Guards marched in after them to stand at attention on either side. The three main capitalist roaders took centre stage. There were so many men that the large stage seemed filled to capacity, something no one in the audience had really expected. Then, from amongst the crowd gathered, a large and violent sounding 'DONG' echoed out. No one could have anticipated such a turn of events. It seemed in a world such as theirs, anything at all was possible. Some stood agape, others with a bemused smile across their faces, still others experienced an almost uncontrollable sense of schadenfreude. Needless to say the crowd bustled and murmured like a scene out of some painting.

The loudspeaker pierced the clamour with an intense, sharp clarion call. Then, up on the stage, a single young man and woman walked forward to the microphones.

Their attire made it clear they were important members of the Red Guards that had stormed the town. The slogans that exploded from their mouths confirmed it. Then, when the sloganeering fervour waned, the atmosphere on stage grew tense and quiet. It was as though someone was waiting with baited breath to set the gunpowder alight.

Again Four Eyes roared: "The violent revolutionary wind that has swept through January and that has boosted morale among the people in their targeted attack against capitalist roaders and counter-revolutionaries is reaching another upsurge. It's under these circumstances that the main capitalist flunky in Guojiadian, namely Chen Baohuai, has been struggled against and brought down. It was his plan to set the frog marshes aflame, he'd sent his lackeys to do this, planning to use the conflagration as a diversion, a last-ditch effort to save his own hide. But he has failed! People of Guojiadian, today is your day to rebel, your day to stand up, to denounce these capitalist bastards for what they are and to struggle against their rightist ambitions and machinations. Today is your day to claim back power, to reclaim your revolution!"

A stunned silence spread across the stage and through the audience. Even the Red Guards were quiet, as if they were keen to stoke the sense of suspense on stage, as though they were standing in judgment over the townspeople, gauging the revolutionary fervour of Guojiadian's inhabitants. The silence continued. No one knew what was going to happen next. The silence dragged on. For the men up on the stage, surrounded by Red Guards, the whole atmosphere became unbearable.

Then suddenly a loud voice broke the calm: "I want to rebel!"

The man who'd shouted now pushed his way through the crowd and up onto the stage. Everyone could see clearly then who it was: Guo Chuanbiao, a fat quarrelsome moron from Cunnantou. He stood at the front of the stage and fumbled with his jacket, trying in vain to loosen it. His hands trembled before succeeding in tearing the buttons away, exposing his bare chest. Clutching a badge emblazoned with the face of Chairman Mao in his right hand, he then roared to the audience: "The Red Guards gave me this badge. It demonstrates my loyalty to Chairman Mao and shows my determination to rebel! I want to take this and make it a part of me, part of my flesh. I want it to warm my heart." He pounded his chest: "I want Chairman Mao to always be with me!"

As he spoke he pressed the badge harder and harder into his ample flesh, finally drawing blood that trickled down the front of him.

The Red Guards immediately took their cue and cheered him on: "Learn from the peasants! Pay your respects to them!" The fervour they displayed gave Guo Chuanbiao even more incentive. He walked over and stood in front of Lan Shoukun, raised his hand and walloped him several times across the face with his open hand. The audience were aghast, frozen by his ferocity, by the spectacle they were witnessing unfold.

He then walked over to the microphone and shouted once more: "We must struggle against them. The incorrect path that Chen Baohuai and his cronies have taken us on these past few years has only led to starvation for all of us! You know what, I did actually steal a few of those sweet potato seedlings to try and fill my belly, but that's because Lan Shoukun has been driving us to our deaths. Shit, there are many days on end when I can barely even get out of bed. And what about Liu Yupu, huh? He didn't steal one measly seedling, but Lan Shoukun drove him to hang himself. Oh, wait a minute. Liu Yupu was part of the landlord class, right? Ah, the sonofabitch deserved it anyway!"

He'd lost his train of thought, unsure of what else to say, so perhaps it would be best to stop altogether. But the fat sod had brought up something that stirred the emotions of the audience, rekindled their anger, their sense of having been wronged. They hadn't been sure about how to rebel, thinking it wasn't their turn. They had shown up only to see the spectacle but now they understood today's meeting was about airing grievances, about payback, about getting revenge. It didn't matter where or when, everyone wanted to exact their pound of flesh... after all, who wouldn't? As this new awareness rippled across the audience the energy became palpable. A few of the braver ones, seizing the initiative, jumped up onto the stage. They were going to get their revenge.

Lan Shoukun felt mortified. It was as though his father was Penn Nouth, that Cambodian official who spent his days turning his head back and forth, following whichever way the political wind was blowing, and going through hell all the while. Even his younger sister cursed him for being a selfish child. He'd been brought down and his family along with him. His sister didn't even dare to go outside any more. The growing vitriol and animosity that had bubbled under the surface in the village throughout the hard times had now been released. Every accuser wanted their revenge on both Lan Shoukun and Chen Baohuai; to kick, to pummel and trample them down.

Sensing that his uncle was in more than a little trouble, Lan Shoukun's nephew, Lan Xin, had already spoken to several Red Guards about apprehending the town's crazy old man, namely, Guo Jingshi. Seeing the scene unfold on the stage and realising that his uncle was about to get his comeuppance, he hurriedly reminded the Red Guards of what he had told them and pushed for them to bring Guo Jingshi up onto the stage. As he was dragged forward, the audience fell silent again, with some smiling at what they now saw: where once he was a filthy old man with dishevelled hair constantly whipping about him, here he now stood clean-shaven, his hair cut, his face clean and his clothes washed. Unexpectedly to most, he looked nothing like a man that should be dragged up on stage to face the ferocity of public anger.

Lan Xin made himself scarce. Another Red Guard now marched up to the microphone to bellow out over the audience: "Rebellious comrades, we see the problem here, it's totally clear. Taiwan has its bald leader, old nasty Chiang Kai-shek who still longs to reclaim the mainland. The Soviet Union, too, has its bald master, the vile revisionist Khrushchev. We never thought that Guojiadian would have its own! A man who plays at being crazy! No doubt they're all in league together, one big family of bald counter-revolutionaries! I say down with all of them!"

The audience exploded with laughter.

Guo Cunxian was in the audience, too, chewing his lip, mulling over whether or not he should make his way up onto the stage to rescue his uncle. It was only Ou Guangming that held him back, whispering in his ear: "You can't save him but I can. Let me try."

As he spoke, he reached into his pocket and took out a red armband. In an almost reverential manner, he pulled it up over his left arm. Startled, Guo Cunxian said: "Where did you get that?"

Leaning in close, Ou Guangming replied in a hushed voice: "I exchanged a metre of government-issued stamps for it. Once I saw them take away Liu Yucheng and the Jin brothers, I figured I had to prepare for the worst. But you know what, there's nothing to this rebellious bit. It's quite easy and I thought why should I just let everyone else do it? I might as well do it myself!"

Ou Guangming then turned and marched proudly up onto the stage. Once the villagers saw that it was one of their own who now stood in front of them as a Red Guard they grew quiet. This play was certainly filled with its fair share of twists and turns!

Ou Guangming spoke into the microphone: "I have something to declare. Starting today, I announce the formation of the Guojiadian People's Dictatorship Combat Squadron! It is to be comprised of all of the town's poor peasants and charged with the mission of wiping clean the mistakes of Chen Baohuai and Lan Shoukun, and putting the village back on the correct path. Everyone here is encouraged to sign up."

In a show of support, Guo Cunyong, who was actually a member of the Red Guards, now moved forward to shout out slogans in support of Ou Guangming: "Resolutely support Guojiadian's rebellious faction! Resolutely support the People's Dictatorship Combat Squadron! All cheer for the People's Dictatorship Combat Squadron!"

When the chanting of slogans ebbed, Ou Guangming continued: "Nearly everyone saw clearly and with their own eyes what transpired yesterday evening. When the frog marshes burst into flames, we all saw Lan Shoukun running frantically away from it. Before the fire, we all saw the signal flare, too, but who in the village possesses such a gun? Who has the supposed authority to fire it? Only one person: Lan Shoukun!" Having paid attention to how the Red Guards carried themselves, Ou Guangming now reverted to shouting slogans: "Down with Lan Shoukun! Down with Chen Baohuai!"

His aim was clear, his speech had fanned the flames of anger in the audience even more. Could this have been their ultimate goal? Had they set fire to the frog marshes for this? Lan Xin had lost control of the situation and could do nothing to reign in the fervour of Guo Cunyong, who now pointed in the direction of Guo Jingshi and said: "The class struggle has become confused, our enemies are refusing to accept their failure, our Red Guard comrades have come to Guojiadian, but they haven't immediately grasped the situation. Let me tell you all now, this bald old man is a lower middle class peasant and he's quite mad. Some thirty or more years ago, his brother died at the hands of the Kuomintang. They ripped a whole in his belly and it happened right here at the foot of this tree. That was when he lost his mind. In all of Guojiadian, who doesn't know this story? Huh? Perhaps Lan Shoukun's nephew Lan Xin? He saw his uncle up here, he knew his crimes, but he took advantage of the situation, took advantage of our Red Guard comrades who aren't from the village, who don't know the story of Guo Jingshi. He egged them on, told them to apprehend this old man and force him up here in front of us. His only aim was to destroy our struggle session and to deflect attention away from his uncle and the real enemies of the revolution. Do you dare to deny that this was your intention, Lan Xin?"

The situation exploded. Whether it was what Guo Cunyong had said that had cut to the quick, no one could say, but Guo Jingshi suddenly sprang into action, twisting and contorting his body, and pushing and shoving with both hands. The Red Guards were startled and immediately stumbled backwards, letting go of the crazy old man and nearly falling off the stage altogether. Free of the hands that were restraining him, Guo Jingshi bounded off the stage but not down the steps. Instead, he leapt down into the audience, pushed his way through them and tore off running towards the edge of the town. In the blink of an eye, he was gone.

Guo Cunxian opened his eyes, got out of bed and went straight to his uncle's room to see if he was there. His mother heard him and got up herself, retracing his path step by step to his uncle's room. She asked if there was any sign of him, but she seemed to know the answer to her own question: there wasn't. Unbeknownst to her son, she hadn't slept a wink. Her ears had been trained to every sound that rustled through the night. She had hoped to hear the clang of the main gate but it and the house had remained quiet; there was no sign of Guo Jingshi. Despite fearing the worst, she was still hopeful that somehow he would return. After all, hadn't he done this before? Hadn't he got up to things that no one could have expected?

He had stormed away from the struggle session, and even after it was over, their crazy old uncle hadn't returned home. They had all gone looking for him, continuing their search well into the evening before the darkness finally forced them to give up but there had been no sign of him whatsoever. On his good days, he was really good but on his bad days, well, there was just no way to tell. The whole family was worried and upset but none more so than Sun Yueqing. Their relationship wasn't simply as in-laws, it was something much more. She'd been a young widow with three children to look after and if it hadn't been for Guo Jingshi, it would be hard to say if they would be here today. Now, with more than half their lives over, it seemed as though his madness was growing worse, more severe. Now when he saw her, he'd only mumble incomprehensibly. But he'd never been violent with her. No, their relationship was more like siblings, an older sister and her younger brother, although at times it seemed even like a mother with her son. Then, on other occasions, it was the reverse; she was the younger sister and he the older brother, or even a daughter with her father. She couldn't help but feel terribly upset. Her stomach was doing somersaults and she complained and berated those around her. Why had she heeded their words and cut his hair? If she hadn't, none of this would have happened! What was she to do?

Guo Cunxian was tormented too but not only because of his uncle's disappearance. He saw his mother, he saw her worry, he saw her ageing right in front of him and couldn't help but be pained by this. He tried to console her, told her that his uncle was fine, that he'd disappeared like this before, had been gone for days, and once or twice he'd even been gone for nearly half a month, so now wasn't any different from then. But Sun Yueqing refused to be consoled by her son's words. His uncle had been much younger when he'd gone missing before. Now he was an old man and winter was upon them, to say nothing of the chaos and turmoil spreading across the country. These were evil, wicked times. What was to be done? She lamented, cursing her fate that she wouldn't even be able to die and be with her dead husband or with her own parents! Cunxian tried again to comfort her, telling her that he would look high and low for his uncle, throughout the entire county and province if necessary; throughout the entire country even! He would find him, he vowed. As he professed this vow, however, he kept something back: if he didn't find his uncle, then he would be sure to make that bastard Lan Xin pay. This was his fault and he would have his revenge.

The sun was already well up in the sky and so Guo Cunxian set off for the town offices to request a travel permit, but when he came upon the building he saw that things were in disarray. He was stuck. He couldn't leave the village without a permit as he'd done before, so perhaps at least he could obtain some document or other confirming his class position, some proof that he wasn't a class enemy on the run. The administration of the town had already changed hands and any association he had had with the former town leaders was well and truly buried, he figured, at least to the extent that he wouldn't be prevented from getting some documentation. Practically speaking, however, he had deluded himself. The Red Guards had stormed in like a swarm of locusts. It had all been so fantastic, so chaotic and in a split second they had overturned the established order in earth-shattering fashion. But now... now they'd gone... just as quickly as they'd come, leaving little to mark their passage through the village. No one remained, no one except for two students, who were from the village in any case, positioned as leaders of two factions struggling for supremacy. At the moment, it was Guo Cunyong who seemed to hold greater power. He had sided with Ou Guangming and his People's Dictatorship Combat Squadron. The other faction was commanded by Lan Xin, who despite having had the larger, more imposing flag and expected paraphernalia, controlled far fewer people. If the truth be told, there weren't many in Guojiadian that really gave a damn. For most, power resided in the offices of the Peasant Farmers' Association and the man who headed this was actually a distant relative, a great uncle in fact, a man by the name of Guo Jingfu. Guo Cunxian thought to himself: Surely he wouldn't cause problems for him, would he?

Guo Cunxian walked up to the main building and spied into the offices. They were empty, vacant, except for Guo Jingfu who sat behind the old desk that had just recently belonged to Chen Baohuai. Had he come early this morning to watch over the offices, to guard them against the destruction wrought by the Red Guards instead of remaining nestled in his bed? Shit, this old man had certainly endured enough hardship to last two lifetimes. Ou Guangming and Guo Cunyong were responsible for this. Those two young devils had urged the crowd on and now this old-timer, his distant relative, sat distraught, quite confused about all that had happened. What's more, no one would actually say what they all knew, that he'd been put in this position because he was the poorest of the poor, the oldest, too. He'd spent more than half his life in indentured servitude to the Lü family out near the western river. But all Guo Jingfu ever really enjoyed was whiling away the time crouched down near some wall or other during the day, and then laying about in his meagre bed in the evening. It didn't seem to matter whether it was day or night; his eyes always had a cloudy haze about them, rather lifeless, as it were. Guo Cunxian stepped into the offices and saw the old man, his great uncle, cowering on the small chair, seemingly discomfited about the situation he'd been thrust into. Fearing that he wouldn't hear him, Guo Cunxian walked up close and spoke loudly: "Great Uncle."

This was a title of respect since the old man who sat in front of him was two years his father's senior. His uncle raised his face and stared at Guo Cunxian. His face was wrinkled and deeply pockmarked, like crevasses dug deep into the earth. It was a face that had seen and felt the passage of time most profoundly. His eyes carried a seriousness in them. So deep was it that it startled Guo Cunxian, causing a sense of panic and fear to bubble up inside him. What had he lived through? What had he seen and endured to haunt him like that, to give him those eyes? He stood there with the old man's eyes still boring into him. No sound passed between them, only silence. Had his great uncle not recognised him? Was he as befuddled as most people thought? He could wait no longer: "I'm Guo Cunxian, I'm here to request identity and travel permits."

Guo Jingfu now spoke: "Ah, Cunxian. They always said you had some wits about you. It makes sense they'd ask you to lead the fourth work unit again."

Guo Cunxian was dumbfounded. What the hell was going on? After all that had happened, who would want to appoint him to such a position again? He felt a chill sweep over him. Just what was happening? Who was playing at what? Did this old man really want him to take up such a post? Power was like a drug: for those not suited to wield it, it served only to make them violent, extreme. As if pretending he hadn't heard what his great uncle had said, Guo Cunxian reiterated his request: "My second uncle has gone missing and I've no desire to do anything else. I need the permits so that I can leave the village in search of him."

"Hey!" said Guo Jingfu, raising his voice. "Contrary to what most people think, Jingshi is quite an able fellow. You know, he's two years younger than me, all these years... why did he have it so tough? It's strange that."

The old man seemed oblivious to Guo Cunxian's request, and so he made it yet again: "If someone wishes to depart the village they need a permit and ID papers. Please, give me the papers so that I might go in search of my second uncle!"

"Oh, ho, I heard you, you know. No need to shout, huh!" Guo Jingfu pulled open a drawer and took out some paper and a pen and handed them to Guo Cunxian, saying: "You write it."

He thought for a moment and decided to write two permits, one for himself and one for Cunzhi. The contents of the permits were easy enough to write; they only needed their names and their class backgrounds and the reason for being given permission to travel, namely, that they were looking for their uncle. On his own permit he added a few extra lines: "In order to avoid burdening people, he was also permitted to bring his carpenter's tools to provide service, earn a living and thus enable him to search long and hard for his missing uncle."

Once he'd finished writing the letters, he placed them in front of Guo Jingfu and explained: "I and my brother Cunzhi will have a better chance of finding our uncle if we both head out to look for him, so I've written two permits, one for each of us." Guo Jingfu seemed to be only half listening, or not at all, and in any case, he was illiterate so Guo Cunxian could have written whatever he wanted. His great uncle simply reached into the drawer and withdrew a container of red ink, then fumbled through his jacket before pulling out the Peasant Farmers' Association seal. Attached to the top of the seal was a hemp rope, which Guo Cunxian now saw was tied neatly around the old man's waist.

He nearly laughed: "Aiya! What are you doing with that tied round your waist, huh?"

Guo Jingfu mumbled a reply: "This is the association's seal, what would I do if I lost it? I'm old, too. What if someone tried to take it?"

Amused, Guo Cunxian replied: "You're right, of course. A seal is a seal. Tying it round you is a good idea. You could even keep it close to your heart, you know. That way, if someone were to try and seize power, they might not think to look there."

"That's right, you understand. You get it."

"What about the original village seal?"

"It was tossed into the stove. It's gone."

"Makes sense, but did it actually burn?" It felt to Guo Cunxian that he was playing house with his old, great uncle.

Then, in an almost reverential manner, Guo Jingfu dipped the seal into the red ink and pressed it hard onto the permit letters. Lifting up the seal, he blew gently across the papers to dry the imprint before handing them to Guo Cunxian. He spoke, exhorting Cunxian not to forget: "Once you find Jingshi, bring him to see me. There's something I want to talk to him about. I want to make sure he knows that wandering off like this won't be allowed any more."

This was more an order than anything else. Like a superior instructing his subordinates, like a father reprimanding a child; a clear demonstration of hierarchy, of importance. Guo Cunxian mouthed his compliance, turned and quickly exited the office. If truth be told, he was a little anxious and worried about the whole exchange, and this uneasiness stayed with him now. To his mind, the leadership of Guojiadian had never been all that effective, but what was there to complain about that? Was he feeling uneasy because of Guo Jingfu or was it due to his own predicament? He thought deeply about this and, to be frank, his heart was grieved. He thought of his Uncle Jingfu, about how his eyes had once been hazy and seemingly always half-closed. He recalled how his gait had once been feeble and weak; that of an old, tired man. Now, however, now that he'd been given power, well, his eyes had become bright, his voice loud and forceful, and he commanded respect immediately. But just what the hell did this mean? Was power something everyone craved, an innate desire? Was it the ultimate lure, that which cannot help but entangle and corrupt? And if so, why had he let others pressure him and take it from him? He saw clearly now, he thought, that the future would be all politics, that was certain, and he couldn't help but play his part.

On his way home, he also discovered a red armband on the ground, the same as the one that Ou Guangming had borrowed. He picked it up and hid it in his pocket. He'd take it with him… you never know when something like that could come in handy. Once at home, he shovelled breakfast into his mouth, took out the permit letters and gave one to Cunzhi, issuing orders at the same time: "You look for him in the surrounding villages, each and every one, but regardless of whether you find him or not, before the sun falls I want you back here, understand?"

Sun Yueqing interrupted: "And where will you be?"

"I'll be looking for him farther away. I'll head today to the county city, then follow the railway line northwards. After all, our second uncle once made it all the way to Beijing, didn't he?"

"Absolutely not!" There was steely resolve in his mother's voice. "I don't mind you going far away to look for your uncle but when it gets dark, I want you back here as well. My heart can't handle having both of you gone. I've already lost Jingshi. If you go missing, who'll be left to look for you?"

"Cunzhi is still here, isn't he?"

"But having him isn't enough. I need to see both of you when I get up in the morning. If one of you were gone I daresay I wouldn't be able to eat, let alone sleep. If you're not back here this evening, I won't eat, I won't sleep."

Guo Cunxian promised, before she would need to light the lamp, he'd be back. He then picked up his tools, packed a little food and hurried out onto the road. He didn't take the main road to the county city, however. Instead he headed towards the village. A man out looking for someone was like a man looking for work; the first order of business was to listen to word on the street, to ask if anyone had seen any sign of his uncle, an old bald man, sixty-plus, wearing a dark jacket and trousers. Once he had asked around about his uncle, then he asked if anyone needed some carpentry done, had some work he could do, or if anyone needed a coffin to be made. After he'd passed through two villages his heart calmed and he became much more relaxed, but this wasn't solely due to the fact that he hadn't heard any news about his uncle. It'd been several years since he'd gone off to find work like this, and he'd discovered that things had changed, much more than he could grasp, and as he made his way closer to the county city an odd feeling washed over him. The people he spotted on the road stared at him askew, a deranged, almost mad look in their eyes. When he told them he was in search of work, they would only stare at him even harder as though they were sizing up some strange or never-before-seen curiosity. Finally, he came upon a talkative man who took to listening to him, or rather bombarded him with questions.

He was first asked where he'd come from. How it was that he'd seemingly crawled out of the gutter and onto the road? Didn't he know things were different now? The Red Guards had torn through the area not too long ago and, as a result, the fields lay uncultivated and everything was in disarray. It was unlikely anyone would have need of a carpenter. And while there had certainly been a great number of deaths in the chaos, the authorities had issued orders that cremations were mandatory. They'd even constructed a crematorium. Coffins were… simply put, prohibited, and consequently burials, too. The people had even taken to exhuming their loved ones. The villages that were a little better off allowed for deep burials but others compelled family members to unearth their deceased family members so that they could be cremated and their ashes deposited in urns. These would then be reburied in the same ground, just taking up less space. Guo Cunxian was warned: if he persisted in trying to find work making coffins, he'd end up running into the Red Guards sooner or later, or at least those they had incited to rebel. That would only end up with him being struggled against as well!

Upon listening to the man speak, Guo Cunxian decided to heed his advice and stop searching for work. He'd focus on finding his uncle instead. His heart was troubled, the pace of his steps quickened and before noon he'd already reached the county town. Walking over the bridge that led into the city, he soon found himself thrust into what was once the bustling market street. The noonday sun shone warmly overhead. He thought to himself: if his uncle had made his way here, for sure he'd be on this street scrounging around for something to eat. But things had changed. It was no longer a grand market street but another victim of the recent chaotic past. There were few stalls, few hawkers on the street, and they were greatly outnumbered by those wearing red armbands who towered over everyone. They were inspecting everything that was being sold and confiscating much of it. Some of the street vendors were even taken away with them. Political banners were draped on either side of the road, the most provocative being: 'Violently cut off the tails of the capitalist running dogs!' 'Resolutely crack down on speculative profiteering!'

The meaning of these banners seemed clear: the market had to cease its activities and concentrate on attacking capitalist elements. But Guo Cunxian had come in search of his uncle and so, naturally, his eyes scanned chaotically through the crowd, trying to find gaps in the mass of people. There was no sign of his uncle, however, and no way to find him in this sea of people; it was like fishing with only a single harpoon to hand. Walking through the throngs of bodies wouldn't help either. It was unlikely anyone had seen or heard of his uncle. And no matter how much he scanned the area, there were just too many people, too many disturbed, agitated faces, minds plagued with individual problems, class struggle hanging in the air, and quite a few simply trying to look out for themselves with faces as taut as hardened bricks. Asking anything of these people would be futile, indeed. What would they have to say?

Suddenly he spied a young boy who looked about ten years of age. Dressed in clothes that seemed to bulge with God knows what, both his hands were dug deep into his sleeves while his pupils furtively scanned his surroundings. The boy smirked when their eyes met. Children don't normally lie, Guo Cunxian thought, so he gestured to the boy to come over to him. Bounding through the crowd, in an instant the child was standing next to him, craning his neck upwards to ask: "Big Brother, do you fancy something to eat?" As he spoke he slyly took out two baked sesame-seed buns and tucked them into Guo Cunxian's hands: "Two buns for five mao!"

Before Guo Cunxian had a chance to reply, two youngish men emerged from out of nowhere to stand next to them. One grabbed hold of the boy while the other pulled open his jacket and yanked out five or six baked buns. He stuffed most of them into the satchel he was carrying and then shouted a rebuke at the boy: "You little sonofabitch! You've not done your studies, huh? Instead we find you out here hawking baked buns!"

The child broke out into a wail and struggled with all his might to grab at the satchel the Red Guard had hold of, trying desperately to retrieve the confiscated food: "Give me my baked buns, I need to earn some coin for my sick father!"

The Red Guard berated the boy harshly: "You little shit... you dare to use the same old excuse as everyone else... my father, my mother, my brother... Oh, they're all ill, all sick, hmph. You really want to use that excuse, huh? How about if I go to your house to check your story, hmm, to see if your father really is sick?" The other Red Guard then wrenched the boy's arm tightly and proceeded to drag him away.

The child protested his treatment and struggled against the hold of the men. He howled once more and began to bite and kick to free himself, finally succeeding and then disappearing into the crowd. From not far off, a young girl watched the scene unfold, a basket held tightly in front of her. She turned suddenly and ran towards the river. There had been a lot of rain this year and the river stretched out wide in front of her, the water deep and not yet frozen, even though winter was drawing near. She dug her hands into her basket, pulled out the eggs she'd been carrying and deposited them in the water, using a nearby stone to mark the area. Returning to the riverbank, she took the now empty basket and held it overhead, demonstrating to the Red Guards and everyone else that it was empty.

The young girl waited for the young men to leave, scanned the area in all four directions to make sure no other ones were lurking about, and then hurriedly raced back to the river to retrieve the eggs she'd deposited there. But as she plunged her hands into the water she soon discovered they weren't there. A wave of panic washed over her. She began to frantically search for the eggs with both hands, edging further and further out into the water. Then her feet slipped on the riverbank, she lost balance, and toppled into the water. Guo Cunxian had been watching the scene unfold and now leapt into action. He raced over and plunged into the water, grabbing hold of the young girl and pulling her back to the shore. The girl was drenched from head to toe and Guo Cunxian wondered what he should do and if he was able to give her some dry clothes to change into. Then a young woman ran up shouting out the name Xiao Xiang and soon wrapped her arms around the little girl Guo Cunxian had just saved from the river. It looked as though she was her mother and that she had got the child to sell the eggs while she stood concealed nearby. Guo Cunxian just shook his head, unable to hold back a reprimand: "What kind of mother would endanger her child like this, huh? You made her take all the risk while you hid close by?"

A bystander who'd watched the ruckus now added their two cents: "You misunderstand, Brother. If an adult were out selling goods, well then, that's a serious crime, you know, and they'd surely be arrested and taken away, face censure and criticism, a proper struggle session. They'd also forfeit their food rations. But if it were a child, well, what more could the guards do than to confiscate the goods?"

"Ah, that makes sense, then. I've certainly learnt a lot here today." Guo Cunxian then took advantage of the exchange to ask if they'd seen a mad old man in these parts, or if they had heard any news about such a person. They told him that if he kept on following the main street into the city he'd soon come upon the central square in the southern part of the town. It was there that the Red Guards held their daily struggle sessions and there was always a large crowd gathered to watch the spectacle. If he'd come to the town to find someone, there were certainly worse places to look for him. It seemed everyone ended up in the town square sooner or later.

Guo Cunxian followed their advice and proceeded down the main thoroughfare heading south. As he walked, the atmosphere around him grew ever more tense, electric even, until suddenly, and quite unexpectedly, he came upon what looked to be a street hawker the Red Guards had missed, or perhaps ignored. There were even customers milling about his stand, quite out in the open. Just what the devil was he selling? And then Guo Cunxian saw: he was selling self-criticism notebooks.

His stand was perched on the side of the street, a rather dark and mottled table. The young Red Guard who sat behind it, his red armband prominently displayed, was thin, almost emaciated, looking both erudite and gentle, calm even. Hanging off the table was a wooden placard explaining the purpose of the stand: he was selling self-criticism notebooks, not confessional papers. The sign also stated that absolutely no assistance would be given to class enemies. The self-criticism notebooks were for the peasants and proletariat. Assistance would only be provided to help them better enumerate their own errors; only internal contradictions of the people could be addressed; those from the capitalist, landowner classes were beyond rehabilitation. For example: if a person's struggle session speech lacked a certain force, a certain energy in denouncing their own flaws, or if it contained excuses for not attending struggle sessions, or if it lacked sufficiently vigorous support for the rebellious Red Guard movement, then these were things he could assist with. If a full self-criticism speech were required, he would ghost write it and it would only cost eight *jiao*. If all that was required was, say, ten political slogans or fewer, then that would be only six *jiao*. To write a penetrating, deep self-criticism, that would cost five *jiao*. For just a standard self-criticism speech, the rate was a mere two *jiao*. Finally, a brief biographical letter cost only a single *jiao*.

Guo Cunxian moved towards the table: "How much would a missing person notice cost?"

Without even raising his head, the slight Red Guard answered: "Who are you looking for?"

"My old uncle."

"Two *mao* for an old man, three *mao* for a child."

Guo Cunxian mumbled to himself: "Hmph, looking for someone isn't a crime, why does it cost more than a self-criticism?" As he spoke to himself, a distant rallying cry carried on the wind, growing louder and louder. He moved away from the stand and off to the side. Soon, all eyes were fixated northwards.

Before a moment passed, two large trucks came into view, the first loaded down with more Red Guards than could be counted. They were the ones responsible for the bellowing cacophony of political sloganeering. The truck following close behind held the object of the Red Guards' scorn, those to be struggled against. The enemies of the people all let their heads hang low. Strung about their necks were white placards emblazoned with their crimes, as well as their names, all in thick, black ink. But then, as if to fully demonstrate their guilt, large red "X's" were painted over each and every name.

Their faces betrayed the doom they were soon to experience. One man rapped his head disconsolately against the frame of the truck, wailing as he did so: "I've been wronged, wronged I tell you!" The blood flowed down his face making it indistinguishable, and soon dripped down over the front of him and the placard that weighed down his neck. The sound of his pleas grew increasingly low. The whole scene forced even Guo Cunxian to look away.

The crowd soon lamented over the sight: "Just what kind of punishment is this? He'll be dead soon, won't he? For goodness sake, what's he done?"

"Hey, don't ask. His child doodled over an image of the Great Leader!"

Once the trucks passed, the people who had been milling in the streets all gravitated toward them, following them south in the direction of the central square. Guo Cunxian himself was carried along with the masses. When the mob passed by the county government's offices, he was startled by an ear-piercing laugh that penetrated through the crowd. Guo Cunxian wondered to himself, who had the proper set of balls to laugh at a time like this? Did they have a death wish or something? He stopped walking then and scanned the mass of people. He was bombarded by the overlapping voices of far too many people all gossiping at once. Like multiple flocks of birds chirping and squawking through the forest, the cacophony was nearly overwhelming. Those in the know had a duty to try to explain what was happening but seemed to have lost all control. The Red Guards and those they had easily wound up were ransacking government offices, wantonly flinging objects to struggle against out through the doors and into the streets. It was madness. And there, in the midst of such chaos, stood an old bespectacled man, lenses as thick as bottles. He was the one who had laughed so riotously at the lunacy that was engulfing the town.

Someone then explained the old man had once been a middle-ranking officer in the Kuomintang Army who had switched sides after surrendering and joined the People's Liberation Army. After Liberation in 1949, he had returned to the county and taken up a post as an administrator. During the 'Eliminate the Four Pests' campaign of the Great Leap Forward, he had talked a lot of rubbish, claiming that one of the four pests had to be people; after all, they are the ones that caused food shortages. Because of this, he was trounced out of office and took to spending his days outside the main doors rebuking the authorities. When the Red Guards trundled through they almost immediately declared that he was a 'historical counter-revolutionary'. Today, the Red Guards had given him a conical dunce's hat to wear and had bequeathed on him an additional crime: "A tyrannical leftover bad element of the Kuomintang."

Unexpectedly, the old man refused to wear the hat, arguing that the character for 'tyrannical' had been miswritten. They'd mixed the character up, writing one that meant the 'stem of a plant' instead. Actually, it was the stem of a sorghum plant, one seed of which would grow four or five stalks of grain, which together made up an ear. He argued he was fine with being struggled against but that they couldn't miswrite what it was he was accused of doing; this would cause the whole county to lose face!

In his heart, Guo Cunxian seemed to be poking his thumb at the man; he was in the county city all right, filled with all kinds of people. It seemed as though no one really gave a damn and life or death didn't matter; it was all a big fucking game. He was like a condemned man who somehow hadn't died in front of the firing squad, who had managed to crawl up out of the mound of bodies, only to become the key object of this ridiculous play that was unfolding before them. And what could be done if the Red Guards did seize such a man? Well, they would most likely make him correct the miswritten character that so labelled his fate. Then, just past the government building, a voice cried out passionately; the struggle session was about to begin. The mass of people restarted their forward momentum and swept into the square.

Red flags fluttered in the wind, drums and gongs banged repeatedly. There was a mass of people gathered in the square, all in regimental formation, all rebelling, a genuine sea of revolutionaries singing songs, voicing and shouting slogans, each trying to outdo the other. It was all so surreal. Taking advantage of the few minutes he had before the struggle session formally began, Guo Cunxian worked his way through the crowd, twisting, winding his way through the mass of bodies, searching desperately for any sign of his uncle. But the more he looked, the less confident he was of finding him. His uncle wouldn't be caught dead here, he would avoid it at all costs, and if he hadn't been able to avoid getting swept up into this chaos, what would make him want to be here wandering about this madness?

The Red Guards were still singing their combat songs to the enraptured applause of the crowd. "Open your eyes, people, who would dare to try to stop the Great

Proletarian Cultural Revolution? Smash the headquarters, burn down the county offices, struggle against the five evil classes – the landlords, the rich, the counter-revolutionaries, the bad elements and the rightists – usurp the power of the capitalist running dogs! We're here to realise the revolution. If you're not, then get out of here, out, out, get the fuck out!"

An adjacent formation of Red Guards, who certainly didn't wish to be seen as weak, broke out into song as well, a song of biting sarcasm directed towards those elements of society that longed to protect the emperor and the old ways: "Those on the capitalist road have black hearts but a powerful flame is burning that will soon engulf you, that will incite the masses to rise up. There'll be no escape for you. You wretched fools trying to save the old ways, double-dealing backstabbers, opportunists, you'll all get yours…"

Suddenly, Guo Cunxian's heart skipped a beat, since he hadn't been able to locate his uncle, there shouldn't be any need for him to keep wandering around this place; he'd be better off searching for somewhere to buy a little powdered milk. It didn't matter if he'd be able to find some or not, in truth, it'd just be better if he could return home sooner to avoid making his mother worry any more than she already was. He asked a few bystanders if there was anywhere that sold powdered milk but the only two dried-goods stores they knew of were both filled with nothing but empty shelves. He gave up and decided to simply return home but as he came upon the bridge that led out of town, he spied a somewhat dilapidated dried-goods store and stopped. He might as well pop in and ask and, even if they didn't have what he wanted, he'd be able to get a small bowl of water to moisten his lips at least and eat the buns he'd brought with him.

He never once thought that the store would actually have items to sell. The female shop assistant told him they had two bags remaining and that a single bag cost 1.25 yuan. But she also told him he needed a milk ticket and without such, without any tickets at all, he wouldn't be able to buy anything, let alone a bag of powdered milk. Guo Cunxian realised immediately that there was nothing for him to say. He didn't have a ticket and thus wouldn't be able to purchase what he wanted. He turned and exited the store but before he got very far, he felt something weighing on him, something bothering him. If they actually had milk, shouldn't he try his utmost to get it? There were always ways to get round rules and regulations. His young child was going hungry and that was no way to live. Chuanfu was the family's future and if something were to go wrong, a mishap, anything, then his son's grandma, his old mother, just wouldn't be able to handle it.

He walked back and forth along the riverbank mulling things over. He didn't want to go home empty-handed so he had to think of some way to buy that powdered milk. As he paced, an idea came to him. Since his somewhat docile, submissive behaviour of just a moment ago had yielded no results, perhaps a more hard-ass approach was worth a try. It was good that the store wasn't all that big and that there was only the single shop assistant in it. Everyone else had gone to the central square to watch the ruckus. He fumbled in his pocket and felt for the money needed to buy the milk. Then he took out the red armband he'd 'borrowed', just as Ou Guangming had done, and pulled it up over his left arm. Lastly, he hauled his axe out of his tool bag. Turning around, he walked back into the store, making sure to close the door behind him, before strolling up to the counter.

Astonished, the female shop assistant leapt up from her stool: "What are you doing back in here?"

He gestured, then leaned forward and with one hand grabbed hold of her arm. The other hand, still holding the gleaming axe, now lifted it up and placed it on the counter. The woman's face contorted in fear and she asked: "What, what, what are you doing?"

Guo Cunxian was calm, relaxed, patient in his reply: "Don't be afraid. I just want to talk to you, to reason with you. Us poor peasants are people, you know, and I've a small baby at home. He shouldn't starve, should he? That's not right. What do you think? But we don't have any milk tickets. Today your detachment of Red Guards asked us all to be here to struggle against these capitalist roaders. A whole slew of us have come, too. But you know what? I really need those two bags of powdered milk. Now, you could sell them to me," he dug his hand into his pocket, took out the 2.50 yuan needed for both bags, and placed it on the countertop. "Or I could just take it. You really don't want me to have to use this axe but there's no way that I'm leaving without that milk!"

"I'll give it to you, really, I will." The shop assistant fumbled under the counter with her free hand and produced the two bags of powdered milk, placing them in front of Guo Cunxian. He relaxed his hold on her in turn, picked up the milk and deposited it in his tool bag. With his right hand still holding the axe, he turned to leave. Then, after taking just a single step, he stopped and looked back at her: "Comrade, you'd better keep quiet after I leave, no hollering for help. There's no one out here anyway, everyone's in the town square for the struggle session. No one would get here before me. Don't make a fuss, I'll pay you back, I swear. I'm sorry, too, for frightening you today. I'm a man who keeps his word. If I didn't, well... I wouldn't be human, would I?"

As he spoke, he ran his right ring finger over the blade of his axe, quickly drawing blood.

The shop assistant was shocked by his actions and turned away: "I won't say anything, now please, leave."

Guo Cunxian remained unmoving: "Comrade, what's your name?"

"Ma... Ma Yufen."

"OK then, I won't forget. I'm in your debt. Thank you."

9

THE GREAT DEBATES

From the day it was constructed, the struggle session arena in Guojiadian was never vacant. Whosoever had an itch to be scratched or a tickle in their throat that needed lubrication, all they had to do was to call someone out and they would soon have them dragged up onto the stage to be struggled against. And if they couldn't find a suitable person, then any old capitalist roader or one of the bad classes would serve as their object of scorn. It only took a few words to have someone dragged up here and the people's victory was assured, that was beyond certain. There were times, however, when it was difficult to find a capitalist flunky to struggle against; after all, familial connections throughout the village tended to be rather complicated. While it was expected that arms would be held up in support once a political slogan blared out through the air, in private it would be difficult to say who called out whom. For instance, the big-character posters plastered across town to denounce Chen Baohuai and Lan Shoukun wouldn't last very long before someone would end up tearing them down. There were no ready-made groups as it were, no clear distinctions between 'rebels' and 'bad elements'. The only classes that were easily identifiable were, of course, the landowners and the wealthy. And it was evident who belonged to these classes, none other than Liu Yucheng and his sister, as well as the brothers Jin, Laiwang and Laixi. Who else would the Red Guards name?

It was due to this that in Guojiadian, the 'four freedoms', namely, the freedom to speak out, to air views fully, to write big-character posters and to hold great debates, ended up being about really only the last of these and not much else. And in truth, the great debates were enough. Men share many characteristics with dogs. You only needed to call out to them and a whole bunch of people would come blindly running. The great debates soon became popular as well, despite the rather inarticulate nature of the villagers. But once the whole idea of the great debates, the struggle sessions as they were euphemistically known, were out there, it didn't take long for people to give them their own distinct qualities and make something new. As a case in point, while midday was generally time for lunch, that didn't stop those who supported Lan Xin's faction from grabbing hold of the loudspeakers and abruptly announcing that Liu Yucheng and the Jin brothers were to be brought up on stage to be struggled against!

The rebel factions all understood that blaring something across the loudspeakers would always have the effect of making people drop whatever it was they were doing and rush towards whatever it was that was happening. The Red Guards had three rich landowners kneeling on the platform with a small table positioned in front of them. One of the Red Guards then removed a single egg from his pocket and ordered the kneeling men to make it stand up erect. Naturally, of course, they knew there was no way to succeed and so they hesitated. But they were stuck and they all knew this, too. On the one hand, they were mortified by the prospect of touching and potentially breaking the egg; on the other, they knew what the Red Guards would do to them regardless. Their indecision only riled the Red Guards themselves. And so it would go, the 'enemies' of the people were caught no matter what, waiting patiently for the beating that was sure to come. And this was how virtually every struggle session proceeded.

Finally, the Red Guards, realising the men would not stand, would walk over to the table themselves, pick up the egg and essentially drop it. Of course, the egg would already have been cooked and thus not easily broken; in fact, it would be rather easy to make it stand up. Quite satisfied with their performance, in loud voices they'd chant that familiar refrain: without destruction there can be no construction. The men would then be accused of attempting to thwart and resist directives issued by Chairman Mao himself. The Red Guards would then beat the men mercilessly and for quite a while, too, at least until they were satisfied with their own violence. They'd pummel them with their fists, or slap them, or even use their feet.

During this particular struggle session, this great debate, Guo Cunyong instructed the Red Guards he'd brought with him to drag both Lan Shoukun and Chen Baohuai up onto the stage so they could be properly dealt with. The audience who had gathered to witness the spectacle all possessed a ravenous desire for payback, like hungry, rabid wolves, they were looking to sink their teeth into warm flesh. After all, the Red Guards had behaved much like this and set the example for everyone else to follow. But still, it was a great debate and so it needed a suitable issue to turn over, and so the Red Guards made sure to ask questions that couldn't help but be answered incorrectly.

Guo Cunyong bellowed: "So... tell me you two, how many shitters are there in Guojiadian?"

How were they to answer? Didn't every household, even the poorest of the poor, have one? Wasn't that expected? Not only was it more convenient, it also helped to keep one's fertile waters from flowing into a neighbour's. Some houses had the toilet inside their own courtyard, some alongside the street and others out in the fields, well, anywhere would do. Who the hell would be able to count that? The two capitalist roaders remained silent, not uttering a sound. Guo Cunyong took to ridicule: "You've been in power here in Guojiadian for too long, your minds possessed by capitalist reactionary thoughts. You never once showed true concern for the people. The Chairman has taught us, the Party needs to understand the suffering of the people, to understand and be concerned for their daily lives. But what did you two do, huh? Well, my question is easy enough to answer. I mean, if I'd asked you how many shitters were in the entire county, or the entire country, that would be a near impossible question to answer. But I only asked you about your own village, and still you can't answer. Well, I'll tell you what that means. It means you two've spent your time stuffing your faces, getting fat off the people and not paying any actual attention to them! Let me tell you, Guojiadian has three shitters, one for women, one for men, and one in each household for both of them to use. What do you say to that, huh?"

Before his words were enunciated, of course, the two men were beaten even more violently than before.

Gradually the Red Guards and those who'd come to watch the great debate realised they were just going round in circles, belabouring the slain tiger that lay prostrate in front of them. It ceased to hold any particular meaning, but the phrase calling them to struggle against class enemies nevertheless became quite popular. If a person didn't like the look of someone else, or if they had been looked at the wrong way, it didn't take much to muster people together 'for a great debate'! If there was some disagreement between people, they would just report it to the Red Guards, and the same thing would happen: a 'struggle session'! And if someone wanted to fix someone up, all they needed to do was look for any excuse to blare out 'struggle'! These words weren't dissimilar to the idea of 'rehabilitating' someone; it just meant using language first to curse them, and then finally one's fists and feet to bring the point home.

To increase the momentum of the movement, the local Red Guards would regularly invite the county ones to come and cheer them on, which worked out well since those in the city had already been organised into two main groups or factions. They would burst into anyone's home without so much as a 'by your leave'. In private, the villagers took to saying they weren't really out in search of counter-revolutionaries but rather in search of a meal. And heaven help the household that wasn't prepared, didn't have the stove hot and food seemingly waiting for them. It wouldn't turn out to be just an inconvenience, they would end up being dragged away to be struggled against. The idea behind the movement, a show of great unity among the people, ended up being more about a chance to get payback, real and imagined.

Guojiadian had never experienced anything like this before. The tension in the village was palpable and most ended up being afraid to even speak a few words to fellow townspeople. If they passed people on the streets, they would avoid eye contact just to be safe, just to avoid being possibly brought up on stage to be struggled against. There was, of course, no way to know who might wish to call out whom. Some people dared to strike first, thinking it was to their advantage to go on the offensive instead of just waiting meekly for an attack to come. The village soon lost its sense of togetherness, eyes became suspicious and unwelcoming. A creeping sense of animosity worked its way through the town, vile and disturbing.

And so, like so much of the rest of the country, Guojiadian was plunged into chaos.

It even seemed as though the heavens wanted to get in on the act as well, for the winter was bitterly long and cold, the ground frozen so hard you could almost walk across it and snap it to pieces. It would lie beneath everyone's feet, like cracked shards waiting to be picked up by some hapless fool. It truly seemed as though winter was vehemently intent on maintaining its icy grip over the village. The days were dark and short as if the pent-up rage of the season knew no end. And when the spring thaw should have begun, the town was blanketed with even more snow. White and sparkling, clean and cold, the snow enveloped the sordidness the village had fallen into; heaven and earth seemed bleached and limpid. The snow was almost half a metre deep and spread across the town; some even hoped anxiously that the weather would at least bring some respite from the chaos that had ravaged Guojiadian, if only for a few days.

But the days don't always pass smoothly, and movements, it could be said, are defined by that key quality: they moved and moved continuously. Enemies of the people had to be rooted out, and if they couldn't be found, they would be made up. Those who acted early did more; those who stood at the forefront of the movement naturally possessed the greatest power.

The Red Guards who had accompanied Lan Xin from the county town could be heard bellowing out their slogans about "cleaning up class contradictions", arguing that this movement was equally deserving of a stage like the great debates. Before long, just such an initiative was put into place in Guojiadian with its own catchphrase outlining their ambitions: "Winter serves to clean the land, spring does likewise, now it's time for us to forge ahead and welcome the month of July, just as the Party's founders did!"

But just where to begin? Of course, the five class enemies were the most reprehensible and needed to be dealt with. They were also the lowest-hanging fruit and the easiest to deal with. So attention was then directed towards the landowners, the rich, the counter-revolutionaries, the rightists and the bad elements; to dispose of these class enemies would certainly give the movement impetus and strength. Naturally this meant the usual suspects were targeted, Liu Yucheng and the two Jin brothers, all of whom were soon brought up onto the stage as class enemies. Unlike the previous struggle sessions however, on this occasion even Liu Yucheng's sister was dragged along with them. After all, even a girl or a woman could be a class enemy. Liu Yucheng and both Jins had their clothes stripped off them and stood humiliated and quite naked up on stage. Liu Yumei as well as Jin Laixi's wife and their young two-year-old daughter, on the other hand, were allowed to remain clothed. Together they stood in front on the stage along with other class enemies, abject and wounded. Lan Xin then stepped over towards Han Erhu and clasped his bare arm, writing his crime on it: he was a counter-revolutionary. Having lost his wife, he was barely able to get by on the meagre rations he had been given and so, when the Red Guards had marched into the village, he hadn't been all that welcoming, going so far as to say things he shouldn't have. As a result, he'd got himself into trouble and now found himself up here.

As expected, once this new stage of the movement had begun, it was like gunpowder going off. Soon Guojiadian was aflame again and the Red Guards tore through the streets apprehending people from all over, determined to make examples of them and destroy class enemies. They were going wild, stealing things that didn't belong to them and causing general chaos throughout. All it took was for someone to be reported and the Red Guards would soon be there to drag them away. This was how Guo Cunxian finally found himself up on the struggle session platform, naked and branded a coward, someone who had shirked his duty to the revolution and had tried to run away; a man who had wandered over the entire region getting up to heaven knows what. Surprisingly, or perhaps deliberately on his part, when they came to get him he didn't brandish his axe and violently protest; rather, he was quite docile, submissive even. When they told him to undress, he did so, and when they came to take him away, he went.

For months he spent his days out wandering, searching in vain for his uncle and seemingly forgetting the rest of his family. For more than a few years now the family hadn't really celebrated anything, even the importance of the New Year had seemed to diminish. And not just for Guo Cunxian's family, it was much the same for every other family in Guojiadian. But this was perhaps beside the point; for Guo Cunxian, a deep sorrow and sense of despair hung over him and he couldn't help but feel that he would never find his uncle. But he couldn't say this out loud as it would be torture for his old mother and he had to protect her from that, no matter what. So, every day, he would go out and look yet again. She still clung to the hope that after one more day, just one more, and perhaps, yes, perhaps, Guo Cunxian would bring his uncle home. He had seen the tumult in the village these last few days and it left him uneasy. He thought that on the morrow he would wake early and head out as soon as he could. But when morning came and he had readied himself to go and look for his uncle once more, he opened the front door and was stunned to see a red armband hung near the front gate. Emblazoned across the fabric was the mark of not just the local Red Guards but the Revolutionary Committee of Peasants, Workers and Soldiers of Kuanhe County, the largest and most powerful organisation in the area. A wave of joy washed over him. No one else in the village would have hung up this armband by their door, nor could a similar one be seen anywhere else in Guojiadian. No, the only person who would do such a thing would be his crazy old uncle. The intent was clear, too: this armband would work like a protective shield warding off danger. Once it was hung by one's house, no other Red Guard faction would dare to challenge it, to say nothing of trying to cause trouble. He thought it had been a little strange. Yesterday, it had snowed quite heavily and the Red Guards that had come from far away had been unable to leave and so they had gone and stirred up trouble in a number of houses but none of them had bothered him and his family. He wondered why that was and thought maybe they had been afraid of the reputation of 'Old Man Guo', his crazy uncle, and had been too scared to poke the bear, as it were. The armband outside explained it though. It also meant something else: his uncle was still alive and he couldn't be all that far away, either. Thinking this, he decided to break into a run to see if he could catch sight of him, and if he didn't see him in the village, then he would head towards the county town, running so fast he would barely leave a footprint in the snow. But before that, he had to let his mother know his uncle was still alive. The world is a strange place, however, and just as he lifted the armband from where it had been hooked, a Red Guard appeared out of nowhere, apparently on the orders of Lan Xin: Guo Cunxian was to be arrested. He turned and placed the armband in his mother's hand, speaking in a bittersweet voice: "Last night he came back, this armband is his, he hung it next to the door."

Those who had been made to strip now stood on the platform virtually freezing to death, their lips blue, their whole bodies trembling uncontrollably, thinking that if they could just stay on their feet they might be able to survive the ordeal. Three other class enemies, each from once rich families, however, were already on their knees, arms clasped round their shoulders, trembling side by side in pitiful rhythm. But they weren't being cursed, nor were they being abused, no, time and the cold would do far more damage to them. Who among them would be willing to freeze to death? Did these bastards all really deserve this fate? Had they committed such evils? As he stood on the platform, Guo Cunxian was eighty per cent sure something awful was going to happen to him. Even if nothing happened to anyone else, however, he knew he would only last up to a certain point and then he was bound to lose control and cause a commotion. There was just no way he was going to allow himself to freeze to death; he wouldn't give them the satisfaction! Like a puss-filled sore that had to be squeezed, time was running out. Something else also became clear as he stood on the platform. There was no sign of Guo Cunyong and his faction, they had not deigned to come thus proving he was a man of little courage. Ou Guangming hadn't come either, the useless twat! How could he just let poor Liu Yumei stand up here and freeze? He looked her over now, her face purple from the cold, standing as close as she could to her brother. Mi Xiujun held her daughter tightly to her breast and, in the effort to keep her from freezing, stood leaning on her husband, Jin Laixi. The Red Guards were off at the side, busy with heaven knows what and seemingly unconcerned with the suffering on the stage. Guo Cunxian took the opportunity to step a little forward to stand next to Jin Laiwang, then wrapped his cotton trousers around his arms. This left only two women and the three naked, kneeling men in the centre.

The north wind howled, nipping at them remorselessly, squirrelling into each nook and cranny of their bodies. On the loudspeaker Lai Xin began to explain in a booming voice the importance and meaning of the class movement: "Just what does it mean to enact this purification of class? Well it means to expose and criticise class enemies, then eliminate enemies of the people and mete out punishment. It means to settle accounts once and for all."

He spoke these words with a profound sense of righteous indignation but as he did so, a loud, bustling movement stirred behind him. There was a clatter of footsteps rushing forward as though the river banks had burst and now threatened to inundate the whole area. With growing panic he asked into the loudspeaker: "Just what the hell is going on?" The sound of his voice reverberated across the stage, amplifying his query.

Before he fully understood what was happening, the entire platform was surrounded by the men of the People's Dictatorship Combat Squadron, all of them brandishing clubs quite menacingly. The People's Militia were alongside them as well. Quickly, efficiently, they leapt up onto the stage, grappled with Lan Xin's supporters and soon brought them to heel.

Ou Guangming stood now as the militia commander with much more power than Lan Xin. He declared in a booming voice over the loudspeaker: "Members of the People's Dictatorship Combat Squadron, we mustn't permit any of these sonsabitches to leave. Each and every one of them is a counter-revolutionary. They have already inflicted enormous damage on our town and all must be apprehended."

He turned and spoke in a low voice to the so-called bad elements on the stage: "You're still here? Go, now. Get out of here."

In a somewhat confused rustling of feet they quickly vacated the platform. Family members waited to greet them with blankets as they stepped down from the stage. Those who didn't have family waiting for them ran as fast as they could in the direction of their homes. Soon the platform was empty. Ou Guangming then instructed his subordinates to bring Lan Shoukun and the other members of Lan Xin's faction out in front, forcing each of them to their knees. He said for all to hear: "Remove their clothing, let's give them ten minutes, let them see how it feels. Capitalists might be the more numerous class enemies but this small group right here are the most dangerous, the most destructive!"

He gestured to Guo Cunyong to come forward and handed the loudspeaker to him. Ou Guangming then stepped back.

Holding a notice in his hand, Guo Cunyong proceeded to interrogate Lan Xin: "Ai, look up at me when I'm talking to you. You see this notice here? We've just pulled it down from your headquarters. You're responsible for putting it up, yes?"

Defiantly, Lan Xin answered: "Of course we put it up. You don't understand, you just can't grasp what it's about."

"What does that mean, huh?"

"Ah, perhaps you're all illiterate then? Well, I'll tell you what it says, it's quite good news, too, and you have to know it's only us that can deliver such. What's more, it's absolutely true. So this is it: a very well known and respected doctor in Beijing has just given Chairman Mao a complete check-up and he guarantees the Great Helmsman is in exceptional health and that he'll live to at least a hundred and fifty years old. What great fortune for us, for our country!"

Guo Cunyong walloped Lan Xin across the mouth: "You really are something, aren't you? A reactionary through and through! You even dare to curse Chairman Mao in public. What balls saying he'll only live to a hundred and fifty! Don't you know? The whole country, revolutionaries across the world, we all know Chairman Mao will live for ever. Long live the Great Helmsman. Long live the revolution!"

Lan Xin was left aghast, stunned. His supporters, too, all let their heads droop, stunned by what they had heard.

Guo Cunyong spoke through the loudspeaker even more vigorously: "The malevolent demon longs to wreak havoc but never realises he is more bluster than menace. Mayflies cannot help but dash themselves against the wall, droning helplessly, fitfully, mournfully." He shifted gears and stated: "In the name of the revolution I hereby declare, from this moment onwards, the Red Guard faction led by Lan Xin in Guojiadian is disbanded and prohibited. Lan Xin and his cohort are, from top to bottom, counter-revolutionaries of the worst kind. To resist their machinations we must strive forward to establish our proletarian dictatorship and we must ensure they are never again given the chance to put their evil plans into motion!"

"Down with Lan Xin! Down with the Lan Xin faction!"

Chen Laoding's wife, whose family lived in the southern part of town, came to see Sun Yueqing and when she first arrived, a smile stretched across her face. Soon after seeing Guo Cunxian's mother, however, she couldn't help but stare blankly, the smile quickly turning upside down, creasing her face sharply: "Is there anything wrong? I know fortune has smiled on you and you've been gifted a grandson. I just haven't had the time to come and properly express my best wishes but, seeing you now, what's happened to make your hair go so white?"

Sun Yueqing was surprised at the infrequent visitor but smiled and gestured her in towards the inner room: "But how could my situation be compared to yours, Aunty? No, I'm just worried, that's all."

Despite the invitation to come inside, Chen's wife declined, instead leaning forward to speak softly to Sun Yueqing: "I remember you talking about finding a wife for Cunzhi. Have you settled upon any one yet?"

"No, not yet. Do you have someone in mind?"

"If I didn't, would I have mentioned anything, hmm? Come, I'll make the introductions, and might I suggest you ensure that Cunzhi is around, just in case, you know… after all, you wouldn't want to let a potential daughter-in-law slip through your fingers and it might be good to introduce them sooner rather than later." Chen's wife took hold of her hand and pulled her towards the door.

Sun Yueqing laughed a little and freed her hand. "Even at your age you can still be so giddy. And with what you've been through recently… you still have a mind to introduce me to someone's daughter?"

"They're from Wangguantun, Chen's niece, his wife's sister's daughter. I've heard her uncle isn't doing so well and his posture is suffering. Come and see. I really think she'll be a suitable daughter-in-law. It's too bad, really, that my own daughter is too young, otherwise she'd make an excellent wife for Cunzhi."

Sun Yueqing turned and went to speak to Xuezhen and Cunzhu: "Keep an eye on Cunzhi for me, OK? Make sure he doesn't wander off anywhere. I'll be back soon with a prospective wife."

Cunzhu stared, surprised, at Xuezhen, and said: "Again? It's just like the rebel factions and their constant struggle sessions, over and over again!" Sun Yueqing had no time to reply or chose not to bother. She turned and left in the company of Chen's wife.

As they walked, Chen's wife talked incessantly, relaying the family details of the prospective daughter-in-law, her family background, character and temperament, and how they had fallen on hard times. It went without saying she had already told them everything she could about Cunzhi. That was fortunate, for it saved Sun Yueqing the trouble of doing it herself. It also meant she didn't need to ask any more questions; she only needed to look at the girl and make a decision.

The girl's name was Huang Suzhen. She was of the right age, just a little younger than Cunzhi. She wasn't the prettiest, with a rather high forehead encircled by close-cropped, dense, dark hair. She didn't look that smart or intelligent even. For Sun Yueqing, it was her eyes that determined she was the right choice for her son. They were bright, joyous, possessing a certain sparkle. She looked sturdy enough, as well, giving off an air of strength and freshness. She'd be the perfect match for Cunzhi who was, after all, a little on the weak side. He needed someone who could carry her own weight and help out with the daily chores, not some dainty, shy wallflower.

The two old ladies wasted no time at Chen Laoding's home. After brief greetings, they took Huang Suzhen by the hand and led her back to the Guo family home. As soon as the young woman saw the very neat courtyard and the tidy rooms, her heart was filled with joy; this home certainly had more influence and power than her uncle's. Zhu Xuezhen and Guo Cunzhu welcomed them as they arrived and ushered both her and her aunty into the western room. The room was soon filled with a flurry of questions and chatter; an investigation of sorts before any decision on marriage was made. As the exchanges continued apace, Sun Yueqing slipped out to get her son, Cunzhi. It had been more than two years now that she'd been trying to find him a suitable wife, a fruitless search until now that had caused her no small amount of worry and stress. She feared she'd end up on her deathbed unable to close her eyes for not having found her youngest son a wife. There had been a heaviness weighing her down, anxiety about his fate, and fear; fear that he would spend his life as a bare stick. As she said these words to her son, tears poured down her face. Cunzhi bowed his head hurriedly; he understood her meaning. Cunzhu appeared then and shepherded her brother into the room where Suzhen was waiting. She introduced him and then everyone but the potential couple left the room.

It was quiet. There was little trace of the excited chatter of a few moments ago; only the two young people remained. A certain awkwardness crept into the room. Guo Cunzhi had been through these meetings numerous times already and so you couldn't say he suffered from stage fright but still he didn't dare to make eye contact; in his heart he just wished desperately for the whole ordeal to be over. But his mother approved, she wanted him to marry, so perhaps it was enough that Suzhen wasn't missing a limb and wasn't crippled in some way or other.

For her part, Suzhen had kept her head low, stealing only a glance at the young man who stood in front of her. She noticed that he, too, was keeping his eyes on the floor. She plucked up her courage and figured she might as well get a look at him, size him up. She thought to herself he didn't seem too bad. He was not short at least and had a sort of earnest manner about him. Her heart was already warming to him. All that she needed now was for him to speak, for her to hear his voice to see what kind of man he was. Normally, Cunzhi was rather passive, always waiting for the other person to speak first. They'd question, he'd answer; rarely did he initiate a conversation. Before he'd come into the room, his mother had made her desire clear but she hadn't actually given him any instructions. In these situations, it was for the man to speak first, but...

Huang Suzhen began to worry. Was this prospective husband a mute, or worse, a dim-witted fool? Had her aunty lied to her and talked him up as some kind of gentleman? She could wait no longer: "Has the cat got your tongue?"

Cunzhi kept his head low but he could feel the growing heat of her eyes boring into him. He opened his mouth to reply but had no idea what to say. His voice shook: "Ah... I was... waiting for you to say something first."

His response worried Suzhen. Just what kind of man was he? She had to test him to find out: "So you want me to speak first, hmm? Alright then, what's the reddest thing in this whole world?"

Guo Cunzhi lifted his head then and looked into her eyes. She must be, in her heart at least, a member of the rebel faction! If he were to marry her and bring such a woman into his house, what kind of family life would they have? Every day would be a struggle session against his poor old uncle, that's what! He grinned sharply: "You've never heard of the monkey's flaming arse, have you? Let me tell you, that backside is the reddest of the red!"

Her response was immediate and severe: "Reactionary!"

She spun round and marched out of the room. Seeing the commotion, her aunty hurriedly followed after.

Xuezhen and Cunzhu, both of whom had been listening in, laughed together. Cunzhu looked her brother up and down taking his measure: "I have to tell you, brother, you're quite a talent, yes indeed! You know, I don't think I've heard you speak so much for more than a year now." She laughed again: "What in heaven made you think of a monkey's arse?"

His mother was much less amused: "You, you… what a disappointment! Even I know the answer to that question. Isn't the reddest thing the red star over China?"

Xuezhen tried to comfort her mother-in-law: "Mother, you don't think that Cunzhi doesn't know, do you? His answer was deliberate. In fact, there's no correct way to answer it, so perhaps a monkey's behind isn't such a bad answer after all. I mean, in this whole world there are quite a few things that are really red… red apples, pomegranates, the rosy cheeks of a child. And when Cunzhu is married she'll take red flowers with her. So, you see, it isn't only the Red Star, it's the loyalty of the troops and the blood of the soldiers. But she was cute, wasn't she? Despite this misunderstanding, perhaps there's still room for discussion."

It was in the middle of the day when Lan Shoukun's wife took her eyes off her little four-year-old son for just a minute, when she'd lost him there in the street.

Both husband and wife were beside themselves with worry. Lan Shoukun enlisted the help of his older brother, Lan Shouyi, and together they searched in every nook and cranny for the boy but found not a trace of him. As the time stretched on and there was no sign of the boy, their worry increased, as did their fear. In times like these, when even an adult could easily be stomped on and crushed, what hope was there for a little missing boy?

No one in the village actually deigned to help them search but that didn't stop them from watching the commotion from the sidelines. Peoples' hearts can be fickle things and can change easily, as they had in terms of the sentiment the village held towards Lan Shoukun; the days of them bowing in front of him had passed. There were some who seemed to sympathise with him, who seemed to want to help, but given all that had recently happened… and, well, a child nowadays could be exchanged for at least one peck of grain. Who's to say the little boy wasn't a prime target to be kidnapped, slipped a little something to knock him out and then scooped up… the child like a primer for something else… society seemed to have lost its moral code after all. Or perhaps he had fallen into some ice.

Lan Shoukun was filled with worry. He didn't know if he wanted to believe his son had fallen through the ice, somewhere, even though the alternative seemed to be much worse. Along with his family, they inspected every frozen body of water in Guojiadian and in the surrounding area. They looked in the irrigation canals, in the new Eastern River that had recently been dredged and in the frog marshes but they found nothing suspicious; no potential holes in the frozen waters. Their worry grew even more pronounced and severe, their panic increased, their minds and hearts raced. They seemed to be going mad, racing from one town to the next, following any word they might have heard about a small boy going missing from his family until finally they arrived at that place...

Lan Shouyi was extremely worried, too. His younger brother had lost his son and the implications of this were far-reaching. As for himself, he'd become accustomed to having the shit piled on. When his brother held his position of power, well, he benefitted, but that didn't last. Then when his son, Lan Xin, led his Red Guard faction, things were all right again, sort of. But that didn't last, either. No, all that Lan Shouyi could do was to try and manoeuvre things as best he could, to claw at what small advantages existed and try to avoid as much of the shit as possible. Thinking about what had happened, he knew of course that his brother had persecuted more than a few people but the more he thought about it, he just couldn't get his head round who might want to actually harm his nephew. And as he worked this over in his mind without arriving at a resolution, he became increasingly agitated, scared and on edge. His nephew's disappearance could only mean one thing: someone was out to finish them off, to destroy the family, and yet that someone was still in the shadows, unidentified, or perhaps even worse, the whole damn village might be in on it. Talk about hitting someone when they're down! The thought of this gave him cold shivers and he thought of his own son again. Lan Xin was being held by Guo Cunyong and the others, the People's Combat Dictatorship Squadron. His mind went blank. The fates were cruel indeed. All of this was their retribution... hmph, there were even quite a few of Lan Shoukun's own thugs in this new so-called squadron, opportunists they were, bending whichever way the political wind blew. But that was to be expected, he supposed. Politics and loyalties were ruthless after all. Would his son be safe, he wondered? He knew what could happen, well, anything, really, and this only worried him more.

His mind then returned to his nephew. He wondered, as he mulled it over in his mind, why was it that the supposedly upright and honest citizens of Guojiadian couldn't figure out a way to find a missing boy? This was the reason why he had endured such torment for so many days. He hoped that the Red Guards would return; those who had come from elsewhere, not the local ones. They would be able to save Lan Xin if they came back but they were like rats fleeing a sinking ship, weren't they? The bastards, sonsabitches, they didn't have the balls to come back. These last two days as he brought Lan Xin some food to eat he'd heard titbits of news: the Red Guards who had come and caused such a disturbance had all been forced to write confessions, admitting they'd cursed and gone against the plans set out by Chairman Mao. They were found guilty and had to fully desist from their reactionary organising activities. If they dared to return to Guojiadian, for whatever reason, they would be apprehended immediately and turned over to the county military offices to be punished. They really were something, he thought. They had caused such havoc and all for nothing. Still, what they did required talent, he supposed. His mind then turned to something else he'd heard. The authorities had issued a complaint against someone but who? And how was the complaint to be made? If the truth be told, he wasn't even sure who the authorities were at the moment and if they couldn't find the right person, might that mean his son would take the fall. Whichever way the axe fell, it wouldn't be good for them. No, there was no alternative; he would have to forsake what little reputation he had left in order to curry whatever favour he could from the village leaders.

His mind turned over and over. The venom Guo Cunyong held against Lan Xin was extreme; approaching him on behalf of his son would likely result in nothing. Ou Guangming, on the other hand, was a different matter. He was frank and straightforward like a reliable old mule. It would be much easier to persuade him, to get him to intervene. He then recalled that Ou Guangming's father was still infirm, unable to even get out of bed. If he were to bring them, say, two *jin* of mung beans in a small bag, perhaps that would help, too. Having decided on a course of action, he set off to activate his plan. From some distance away, he waited and watched Ou Guangming's home until the moment he saw him return to prepare dinner. Still watching from a safe distance, he let Ou Guangming open the door and go inside before walking slowly up to the house and knocking. When he saw who it was, Ou Guangming immediately understood why he had come but instead of being riled by Lan Shouyi's audacity, he looked at him with a calm, unemotional face, not the least concerned about why he was there. He let Lan Shouyi plead his case, to ramble on about his son, but his face remained stern. He wasn't about to give in, no matter what Lan Shouyi said.

Lan Shouyi bit the bullet. He was going to lose whatever face he had left but he accepted that. He had given up on his own ambition. Ironically, someone in the position he now found himself in wasn't all that easy to drive away, intent as they were on trying to get their point across. And besides, he still had one thing he hadn't yet tried. If that didn't get a response out of Ou Guangming, well, then there would be nothing else for it. His last resort was, of course, the two *jin* of mung beans. At first, he planned to present the beans straight away but then thought better of it, thinking perhaps he'd be able to convince Ou Guangming without the bribe and thus save the beans for himself. And if he had given the beans right away and then not been able to persuade Ou Guangming, then he'd be out of everything. The only problem with all of this, however, was that Ou Guangming hadn't said a word one way or the other. He reached into his pocket and pulled out the small bag of mung beans.

Placing them on the table he said: "I've heard Uncle isn't doing well and that he has back problems. I've brought these mung beans that are supposed to help relieve inflammation."

Before letting him finish, Ou Guangming picked the bag of beans up and returned them to Lan Shouyi's hands. "Beware the bearer of false gifts, they say. I know what you're trying to do. What a nerve! Do you know what crime I'd be guilty of should I accept these beans, huh? Covering up for a counter-revolutionary, that's what. Tomorrow I'd be arrested for sure and end up just like your son. Put them away, now, otherwise I'll throw you out on your arse, or report you to the authorities. Then you'll have a struggle session all for yourself!"

Lan Shouyi had no choice but to put the beans away. Then his legs buckled, he didn't really know why, and he found himself kneeling in front of Ou Guangming: "Brother Guangming, I know you're a straight-talking fellow, outspoken, but what of your heart? That's where your fire is. Please, I beg you, do what you can to save Lan Xin."

His voice choked and his throat grew dry and he began to sob uncontrollably.

"So you've been reduced to this, huh?" Ou Guangming gripped him under the arms and lifted him back up, putting him on the *kang*. "Why didn't you do something before now, huh? You saw what your son was doing, the trouble he was causing. Why didn't you try to stop him then? He was out of control, ruthless and violent for the sake of violence itself. I mean, come on, making people kneel prostrate in the freezing cold with no clothes on. And he was doing it to his own people, men and women who've lived in this town for generations, just like yours. If they'd died, would your family have taken responsibility? It was immoral, plain and simple!"

Lan Shouyi kept his head low, mumbling in agreement: "You're right, you're right... what kind of son have I raised?!"

It seemed as though Lan Shouyi accepted what had been said but Ou Guangming persisted. There was more he had to say and none of it pleasant: "Do you know what crime your son is guilty of? A few days ago, the county authorities executed a number of people, including those who'd slandered Chairman Mao. They'd said awful things, apparently. A small boy painted what he'd seen and later showed it to his family. They were all horrified at the image. Now consider what your son is charged with. Do you think it's worse than this? When it comes to Cunyong, who's but a young pup himself, well, he seems kind and honest enough, but if he sends Lan Xin off to the military authorities, it probably won't be long before you need to go and collect his corpse, now will it?"

Abruptly and without warning Lan Shouyi began to strike himself, violently: "This is our sin, you know, the Lan family curse. It's my fault for not better educating my own son. Brother Guangming, please, you must do something to save him!"

"There's no point in asking me, I'm not in charge. Guo Cunyong is. What's more, new regulations are soon to be posted that'll end up changing everything yet again." His voice trailing off, Ou Guangming put his arms round Lan Shouyi and half carried, half dragged him out the door.

A new fear overwhelmed Lan Shouyi. He had no idea what these 'new regulations' might be but he needed to comport himself. There might yet be a chance. Although Ou Guangming had said there was nothing he could do, he had helped him nonetheless and Lan Shouyi knew Guangming wasn't the kind of man who would be kind on the surface but hold evil in his heart. He wouldn't do anything to help Lan Xin but nor would he say anything to make matters worse. He needed to go and plead with Guo Cunyong. It was abundantly clear that this was his task. He had to get him to save his son and if that didn't work, he'd kowtow to the entire village and beg them for mercy, beg them to forgive his wayward son, to feel some compassion. Surely they wouldn't want to see his family lose both its youngest sons.

The weather finally started getting warmer and new life and greenery began to show on the trees. The day of Cunzhu's wedding was growing near but all around it didn't seem that way. The expected atmosphere and excitement for a wedding was absent, as were the signs of preparation. If the truth be told, these past few years hadn't really lent themselves well to a wedding. Their family was fairly well off and it was expected they'd send a set of bedding and pillows as part of Cunzhu's dowry for whenever she got married, so these had been prepared by Sun Yueqing some time ago. After all, if she hadn't waited until closer to the actual event, she'd never have had time. Cunzhu had her clothes as well and on her wedding day, it would be easy enough to wrap them up so that she could take them with her.

For families that were harder up, they also hoped to get a little something in return for marrying off their daughter which meant, of course, that she couldn't get married empty-handed. The key to all of this going off smoothly, however, was the family's mood and, unfortunately, no one seemed all that happy about the impending nuptials. Or perhaps it was the opposite. As the day grew close, perhaps they were all suffering cold feet. Whatever the cause was, there was a veritable gloominess that seemed to permeate the air throughout the entire house. For Sun Yueqing, she seemed to be constantly wiping away the tears from her face. Her daughter was soon to be married, and to a man from the county city, no less. She expected the other villagers would look at her with envy for 'successfully' marrying off her daughter, all the while she worried about Cunzhu, about a rural girl in the city and whether or not she'd be accepted by the other wives. Would her daughter be bullied? The county city was so far away, too. She'd find it difficult to visit her daughter, and it wouldn't be easy for Cunzhu to come to her either.

Then, on the day before the ceremony was due to take place, Cunzhu changed her mind. But she didn't tell her mother straightaway. Instead, she waited for her to go out to visit friends, and then Cunzhu raced to her brother's room and beseeched him to run to the county city to let her prospective husband know that she couldn't get married the following day, that she wanted to wait for two years and that, if he wasn't willing, then they should call it quits. Both Cunxian and Xuezhen stared at her in disbelief; was she out of her mind? Tomorrow was to be the wedding. What had just escaped from her lips was impossible. Was she trying to ruin them? Had she been dishonest about her desire to marry all along? When they asked her why, she wasn't even able to give a clear answer, and when they persisted in their questioning, she broke down and cried uncontrollably. Without even really thinking about it, one of them passed her a pillow and she proceeded to bury her face in it, sobbing nonstop.

She looked wounded and in enormous pain. Xuezhen immediately placed her young child on the bed and then put both her arms around her sister-in-law. Unconsciously, her own eyes began to grow moist and soon she was crying along with Cunzhu. Guo Cunxian stood to one side kneading his forehead, unsure of what to do. He didn't understand and couldn't rationalise it. What play was his sister acting out? From the looks of it, it didn't seem that her future husband had done anything wrong. After all, she wanted to ask him to wait, so he must be wholly innocent in this... this... whatever this was. It certainly wasn't the case that he and Xuezhen had caused her to make this decision. If they had, well, she certainly wouldn't have come into their room crying about it. So that meant only their mother and Cunzhi could be responsible, but Cunzhi would never bully her. What about their mother? Had she said something? Done something? She only had Cunzhu, a single daughter she loved deeply. Would she treat her so poorly? It was a hard thing to do, marrying off one's daughter. Cunxian kept rolling it over in his mind. For the moment there was nothing he could do. No, he'd wait until she stopped crying and then they would try and talk some more. In any case, wasn't it common enough for a girl about to be married to get cold feet, to need to cry a little... or a lot? He wondered and then thought some more. But wouldn't they cry together with their mum? Surely not with their brother and his wife, no?

Perhaps these were tears that had been held back for far too long. She'd soaked the pillow nearly all the way through, and then finally lifted her face. She seemed to have cried enough. Guo Cunxian reached for a towel that had been hanging nearby and passed it to her. He also grabbed a dry cloth used for the baby and passed it to his wife: "Here, to dry your face as well. I might not understand why you cried but you did and, well, perhaps you felt the need to join in?"

The two of them smiled at his awkwardness, her caring, and wiped their faces dry. Guo Cunxian looked at his sister; would she be able to explain now, after she'd had a good cry? She looked at him and a few more tears rolled down her cheeks but not the torrent like before. And through a somewhat sobbing voice, she described her worry: "As soon as I'm gone, mum will be by herself in that room, alone. I'm afraid something will happen."

Guo Cunxian replied: "What? Why?"

"For a while now she's not been sleeping at all and she coughs throughout the night, so severely, in fact, that I've been using a blanket to muffle the sound. I didn't want it to wake you. When she does manage to fall asleep, she snores horribly as though she's having trouble breathing. It frightens me half to death and I usually have no choice but to wake her. I don't think there's anywhere she doesn't feel a little pain and with her not sleeping, I'm really worried and afraid there's something very seriously wrong. It's not that I don't want to get married. I just want to delay it. And what's two years, anyway? If something were to happen to mum, then what?"

Xuezhen moved then to put her hand over Cunzhu's mouth. There was no need to talk such nonsense.

Guo Cunxian asked: "So that's the reason why?"

"It's not enough? Marriage can wait, and if he doesn't want to, then another man can be found, but I only have one mother! And she's had such a hard life. She's had to take care of the three of us by herself and wait upon our uncle as well."

"Enough!" Guo Cunxian had heard all he wanted to hear. "Do you think that I don't know what it has been like for her? Do you think Xuezhen doesn't know? She has aged a lot over these past two years. Her back's giving out, she barely eats... her heart's sick with worry. That's the main problem. There're two things tormenting her. If she could get over them, then things would be better... a little better, at least. Now, if you don't get married tomorrow, what do you think'll happen, huh? It'll only add to her worries, won't it? It'll be the proverbial last straw."

"Now who's talking nonsense!"

"I'm talking nonsense? Hmph, you're just looking for excuses, you know that? Tomorrow is your wedding day, you're getting married, to someone from the city no less. Don't you know how happy that'll make her? What family in the village with a daughter to marry wouldn't be envious? I'm even chuffed about it, myself. Look, once the weather warms, you'll be in the county city, so get in touch then with a good hospital and I'll get us a ride and bring mum in to see the doctor. That's better than you acting the foolish, petulant child, isn't it? So enough, put this aside and grow the hell up!"

"You said there were two things tormenting her?"

"Isn't it obvious? One thing is our poor old uncle. We don't know if he's alive or dead. I can't help but feel that he's doing well, that he's fine and that once things are calmer in the village he'll be back. These past few days I've been thinking a lot about him. I think he disappeared in order to help Cunzhi and I, to help all of us. I mean, think about it, for quite a while now we haven't done anything but look for him. We've been everywhere and, as a result, we've been spared involvement in what has been happening in the town. And you know me and my temperament. If I hadn't been so busy looking for him, for sure I'd have been dragged into the commotion the Red Guards started, one way or another, and that would have probably led to something much more serious happening."

Cunzhu and Xuezhen thought it over, and the more they did, the more they believed he might be right. Cunzhu then wondered aloud, thinking that if this was the case, then surely their uncle wasn't crazy at all. No, he was perhaps some Daoist immortal or other? Xuezhen agreed. She thought the same thing. Cunzhu then pressed her brother further: "If that's one thing that's bothering her, what's the other?"

"The other is Cunzhi and his marriage prospects. After recent events, I went to Chen Laoding's place to try to smooth things over. Their daughter isn't a Red Guard, rather… well, apparently she's a bit of a prankster. She likes to tease and torment people but I think our mum quite likes her. When I paid them a visit, I actually brought that ointment your sister-in-law never uses as a gift for her aunty, and when Xuezhen has a little free time, she's going to visit Wangguantun, you know, to apologise to them and, hopefully, if their daughter is still amenable, then tell them that Cunzhi would make a good husband. It would be great if uncle were to return as that would solve both problems but, in any case, I guess we'll wait for that before actually having the ceremony for Cunzhi, he won't mind. So what do you think? There's nothing for you to worry about, right? I mean, I still have quite a few things to do but that's my job, not yours."

Cunzhu was happy. Her brother's words had eased her anxiety and lifted the burden from her heart, but there was a slight pang for her sister-in-law. It seemed she had work to do herself, work that didn't sound all that great.

Xuezhen pushed her a little: "Why are you still leaning against me?"

Guo Cunxian got up and said: "Alright then, if you're fine, I'll go to the village offices to borrow a vehicle, a big one. After all, my little sister needs a proper ride for tomorrow, she's on her way to be married in the city and must make a suitable impression." Cunzhu demurred and told him it wasn't necessary. Her fiancé's family had given her a bicycle as a betrothal gift and they'd planned to use it tomorrow. Qiu Zhantang, her husband to be, was going to ride it with her on the back. Together they'd go into the city. She blushed then, a bright red, and felt a little embarrassed talking about this in front of her older brother and his wife.

Xuezhen clapped her hands enviously. It certainly sounded better than riding in the back of a farmer's cart!

Guo Cunxian wasn't displeased; their plans would make it easier on him, in any case. All he needed to borrow from the village offices would be a small trolley, enough to carry the two bundles their mother had prepared for her. At that moment, Cunzhu wondered if she shouldn't give the bicycle to Cunzhi, to impress his potential bride. Hesitantly, she raised the idea with Cunxian.

His response was quick: absolutely not! He waved his hands rigorously, adamantly. He spoke as the head of the family then, unyielding and strong. Her brother wouldn't want it, nor would their mother agree to it. He told her to stop being silly, to stop worrying about them and to think about her wedding tomorrow. If she had nothing to think about, then she should spend the time with their mum. Having finished what he wanted to say, Guo Cunxian left the room but, as he stepped outside, he spied his mother sitting not too far away. She must have heard everything they had just talked about. He stuttered: "Mum, I thought you'd gone out."

"What, I'm not allowed to come back?"

"No, no, that's not what I meant, um..." He tried to recover his confidence: "You know, Xuezhen and Cunzhu have just had a good cry about tomorrow. Why don't you go in and talk to them, heh? What young girl doesn't cry on the day before her wedding, right?"

Guo Cunxian bent over a little to help his mother up, but she pushed him away, hard, and rebuked him: "So you say... quick, go on, go and take care of your business!"

Shit! There was nothing more to say, and in any case, all his sister's crying and moaning had really messed with his head. There was nothing for it but to leave, and so he took off through the gate like the wind. First, he'd head to the village offices to borrow the pushcart and then take it to the river to wash. It had to be clean and sparkling for tomorrow. Once done, he'd bring it home and leave it in their courtyard to dry. After that, he had to go to the commune store and buy a few sheets of crimson paper and two strings of fireworks, then head to the school to ask for the finest calligrapher to write three rhyming couplets for his sister's wedding, along with the character for double happiness, a dozen or more at least of these, all in varying sizes. Then he'd bring it home and find some way for the rest of them to make the paste in order to stick the double happiness characters all around the house; it didn't matter where, so long as they were prominently displayed.

The rhyming couplets, naturally, had to frame the main doorway on either side, as well those to the southern and northern rooms. The double happiness character would be pasted above the door and on the walls, the top of the wardrobe, the windows, the kitchen, the water cistern, everywhere, even on the wheels of the pushcart he was going to use to bring his sister's dowry on. What a great din! The house was flush with activity as everyone hustled and bustled to get things ready for the happy event. The scene was joyous and soon red was everywhere, creating an auspicious, jubilant atmosphere.

On the following morning, the family ate the traditional meal of noodles together and then waited for Cunzhu's husband-to-be, Qiu Zhantang, to arrive in the village on the bicycle his family had given them as a wedding gift. The children who had come out to see the excitement set off fireworks as he passed by and soon it was as though the entire village of Guojiadian had come out to see the wedding. Everyone knew Guo Cunxian's younger sister was being married off to a man from the county city. Guo Cunxian instructed his brother to bar the door to make sure no uninvited guests made their way in, and then he took charge, acting very much like their father would have done. He escorted the new husband into the house and towards Cunzhu's room, and together they all kowtowed the required three times in front of Sun Yueqing.

Their old mother was moved to tears as she watched them pay the proper respect.

When Cunzhu rose to say she was now going to leave, her mother's tears flowed even more copiously.

Qiu Zhantang accompanied his wife-to-be out to the bicycle, made sure she was seated safely on the back, and then he mounted the bicycle himself. On both sides of the road people had come to watch the celebration, with many having come from the city to greet and receive the new wife into their family. The villagers had never seen such a spectacle before and soon took to whispering, wondering what kind of position the new husband's family held in the city.

Guo Cunxian followed behind with the pushcart. Inside it he was carrying two bundles: one the bedding that was a gift from his mother, the other his sister's clothes. This was her dowry. Cunzhi walked alongside him but his hands were empty. The bicycle with his sister on it soon started to pull ahead; it was moving much faster than he was pushing the cart but he seemed not to mind, or perhaps preferred to fall behind. In any event, the two brothers were soon left in the dust as the bicycle sped away, or so they thought. As they approached the village limits, there, just a little way away, stood their sister and the wedding party.

As they came up alongside them, Cunzhu spoke and told him she'd be better off sitting in the pushcart; perching on the back of the bicycle was hard and uncomfortable, to say nothing of her being afraid she might fall off. Guo Cunxian laughed and said he figured as much, and then told her he would be more than happy to carry his sister into the city. He helped hoist her into what was now the marital carriage and prepared to get underway. The two bundles she picked up to hold in her arms and, as she did so, she discovered a quilted red bridal cushion underneath. Her joy was plain to see and she exclaimed to her brothers: "Oh how thoughtful mum is!"

Still grinning, she sat down and waited for her brother to use his sturdy arms to push her and her dowry the remainder of the way to the city. Needless to say, the pushcart-cum-carriage would be a much better ride. Before they started, Guo Cunxian told his sister to place one bundle behind her, that way she'd be able to rest against it. It would feel as comfortable as her bed, he assured her. She thought of her mother and smiled again; smiled, too, at her brother, and thought that nothing in this world could compare to the affection between a parent and their child!

Guo Cunxian then took hold of the two handles and tied the cotton straps attached to them around his neck. He lifted with both arms, straightened his back, positioned his legs, and started off. Soon there was a rhythm to his movements, the pushcart wheel complementing his strength, the wheel in turn helping with forward momentum. Compared with simply walking, the connection between man and cart, the unity of movement, allowed them to make much quicker progress without completely tiring themselves out. Before too long, it was now Cunxian and his sister who had pulled away from the others, Cunzhi and Qiu Zhantang, both of whom had been walking slightly behind, pushing the bicycle alongside them. Realising how this might look, Qiu Zhantang decided to mount his bicycle again to better follow after them, forcing Cunzhi to run to keep up. It didn't take long for the sweat to start pouring down his face.

Once they caught up with Guo Cunxian and Cunzhu, his brother laughed. Here he was pushing the cart with little trouble at all while his younger brother, empty-handed no less, looked much worse for wear. Feeling sympathetic, Guo Cunxian slowed his pace and decided to make small talk: "Zhantang, I've heard you work in the city. Tell me about it."

Pleased at being asked such a question, Qiu Zhantang replied: "That's right, I work in a factory doing mechanical repairs. My father's a model worker there. He takes care of the place and helped me get the position I have."

"Sounds great. But what about the Red Guards? I mean, they're everywhere. Are there movements taking place in the factory, too?"

"That's over with now. The factory has reinstated its Revolutionary Committee, even the old foreman has returned, and we're in the process of promoting increased production to fully realise the revolution. There's so much work to do that we haven't been able to do it all."

"Is this the way it is for all the units in the city?"

"Just about, the Revolutionary Committee is in charge again now, so it's much like it was before the recent turmoil."

"You don't say? Do you think Cunzhu will have the opportunity to work, then?"

"There're some formalities to take care of first but my mum has already spoken about these. Cunzhu will be given a post in the Commerce Bureau."

"Excellent! I guess much of the trouble has really died down, huh?"

"Yes, exactly. The factories are up and running again, schools have reopened, even the capitalists are returning one by one. As for the rebel factions, well, they've lost their power and influence, they're being disbanded and the key trouble-makers arrested. And we're linking up to form Revolutionary Committees. It's like we have fulfilled our responsibilities and are looking towards the future and getting on with the work that needs to be done."

No one knew for sure what effect Qiu Zhantang's words had on Guo Cunxian but he didn't speak for the remainder of the journey. He just walked, seemingly depressed, his mind deep in thought. He continued pushing the cart, almost mechanically, and his pace picked up again. Soon, Cunzhi and his sister's new husband were left further behind. Seeing his older brother-in-law move ahead, Qiu Zhantang grew cautious and held up a little until he was again walking side by side with Cunzhi. Hearing the conversation end, Cunzhu turned round to look at her brother. She saw the heaviness about him and thought she should say something, quietly, so that the others wouldn't hear. She talked about her soon-to-be parents-in-law, and told him they hadn't been pushing her to get married too quickly as they wanted her to have the opportunity to work but they were afraid about her family status, that to enter the Commerce Bureau meant they would look at her *hukou* (residence permit). Zhantang is their only child, she told him, and they loved him unreservedly. Then she returned to a familiar topic, saying she still wasn't entirely comfortable with getting married before Cunzhi.

Guo Cunxian replied somewhat harshly and told her it was none of her business. Besides, what if Cunzhi never married, he asked? Would that mean she shouldn't as well? He berated her a little more and told her if she were still a child then her worries would make sense but that she had to stop treating him like he was her little brother! He ended his rebuke by telling her that no great aunty should be involved in so much!

Stunned by his choice of words, Cunzhu replied: "What? How did I end up being a great aunty? I'm not even married yet!"

"There's Chuanfu, he calls you aunty. Won't his children call you great aunty!"

"Hey, Chuanfu is still a baby and already you're talking about grandchildren! Even Cunzhi's prospects for getting married are dim." Suddenly, what they'd talked about yesterday popped into her mind; her voice took on an interrogative tone: "Brother, what you said about Cunzhi, about him getting married, about not having a door. Is that true?"

Cunxian replied that not only did Cunzhi have no door but he had no window either. If things in the city were as Zhantang said they were, that things had quietened down, then the same should be the case for Guojiadian. There'd be a good harvest this year, so he'd been thinking about ways to build an extension to their house for Cunzhi. If they had that, he'd be a much better prospective husband, and if Huang Suzhen wasn't keen, there was always Bai Suzhen.

"If you want to build an extension, Zhantang and I will help out with some money at least."

Guo Cunxian's hands slipped on the handles, giving Cunzhu a jolt and frightening her quite a bit. His voice was serious: "Cunzhu, you've just reminded me of something. You know your family, we're just poor farmers. You mustn't let your in-laws look down on you, OK? Don't entertain any more ideas about giving us money or anything. It's not your place. Besides, Cunzhi and I are fine, we're not good-for-nothings, you know. You certainly can't give us money to build an extra room for your brother to get married, absolutely not!"

The vehemence in his voice frightened her, but today wasn't like other days. No, first, she was to be married, it was a happy occasion and he couldn't get really angry. Second, she was leaving her home today, she was entitled to act like a spoiled child, at least to some extent. She pouted and mumbled to herself, complaining that it was him who looked down on women. Didn't he know that, once she was married, that was it, she'd be gone, like spilt milk. But she wasn't married yet so why was he treating her like an outsider already?

"OK, OK," he half apologised, coaxing her to calm down. "Please, we're nearly there, sit."

Cunzhu wouldn't relent. She continued to pout: "I won't, I won't enter my husband's house riding in a second-class cart. I should be in first class, you know. That's how I should enter his home!"

"Alright then, you're still my little sister!" His spirit had returned, and now it was his turn to probingly question her: "You're really not afraid of them looking down on you, not afraid that these city folks will think you're just a dirty peasant bumpkin?"

"No, I'm not. Entering into my husband's house in a pushcart doesn't mean I'm some country redneck, it means I'm a very rare thing indeed and maybe a bit dangerous, too!"

"In that case, let's hold on here for a moment until Zhantang and Cunzhi catch up, then he can ride his bicycle in front to give you a proper entrance. Cunzhi can walk alongside as your bodyguard, and I'll perform the *Yangge* (a popular rural folk dance), that will make it a real send off indeed. We'll take that turn up ahead, march round as much of the town as we can, you know, really show them how a wedding's done! Ah, it's a pity we're missing..."

"Missing what?" Cunzhu laughed.

A proper theatre troupe. If they were marching, singing, dancing and beating a drum on both sides, that would make it even better."

"Heh, heh, that would certainly break the 'four olds' and start our own struggle session, too!"

Brother and sister continued to talk and laugh until the others caught up with them. Cunzhu told Cunzhi and Zhantang what they'd been planning and the four of them all happily agreed to comply with it. There was an ulterior motive as well to Guo Cunxian's plan. He wanted to avoid the dried-goods shop just on the other side of the bridge. He didn't want the same female shop assistant to see him again, not after what he'd done before in brandishing his axe so that she'd sell him the milk.

It was in this ostentatious manner that they arrived at Cunzhu's husband's house, the dormitory adjacent to the mechanical repair factory. The courtyard was large, the neighbours all fellow workers in the factory. On either side, no other family had lit their fires, they were all partaking in the happy event. Altogether there must have been at least fifty or sixty tables decked out. The wedding ceremony itself was quite simple, the most important thing being they bowed towards Chairman Mao. After that, three bows to her husband's family and then the party could begin. Seated at a table with numerous strangers, the two brothers were soon a bit out of sorts. The people sitting around them were chatting and jesting nonstop, so much so that the incessant banter soon weighed on Guo Cunxian's heart, causing him to become increasingly agitated. His ears began to block out the sound and the food soon lost its taste.

The humorous story he'd heard that troubled him had to do with the recent winter and the supposed haunting of the main hospital morgue. Every evening, the story went, people would hear talking, singing, slogans being shouted off the walls... at times, the people suspected the dead must have been finding the steel metal boxes they were enclosed in to be a little too cold and so took to wandering about trying to find a grass sack to at least cover up in. And if they couldn't, they grabbed hospital comforters and used those instead. At least, that was the explanation given for the mess the hospital had been in. Guo Cunxian didn't want to say anything but his heart beat fast. Pretending, however, as though he wasn't all that interested in the story, he asked the man who'd been telling it why there hadn't been someone in the morgue to manage and take control of things. The man answered with a question and a laugh of his own: everyone had been called out to rebel, hadn't they? The hospital, he added, had already fallen into turmoil and if there had been no one to take care of the living, well, who in hell would look after the dead! He laughed again. Now, however, with the recently formed Revolutionary Committee, well, they'd set out to arrest those in charge of the hospital but who would dare to go into the morgue? After all, it was still haunted, wasn't it?

Excusing themselves, Guo Cunxian and his brother bade farewell to their sister, exchanging a few words as was customary, before hurriedly departing. Once they were out on the main road, however, Guo Cunxian stopped, gave the cart to his brother to push and said: "You head home first, tell mum about the wedding, and don't skimp on the details. I've got something I need to take care of. I'll be back a little later this evening. Tell them not to worry."

Cunzhi wasn't a child and wouldn't be fooled so easily. Of course, he asked his brother what it was he had to do.

Guo Cunxian fumbled with an excuse, telling his brother he wanted to search around town to see if he could find some powdered milk to buy.

Cunzhi didn't let it rest there. And, if the truth be told, he seemed a little out of sorts today himself, perhaps because it was his sister's wedding and he had had a few drinks but, whatever the case, he persisted: "I should help. It won't be easy trying to find some milk to buy."

Guo Cunxian's voice was nervous: "Shit, you're talking a lot today. Normally you don't say a word. What the hell's wrong with you? Don't you know mum's at home waiting to hear how things went? You head home now so she won't worry."

His voice was quite loud and seemingly stressed, so Cunzhi dared not push the issue further. It was better if he took the cart and headed home. After his brother had walked a suitable distance and was a fair distance away, Guo Cunxian immediately took to searching for a public bath. Granted, the rebel factions had wrought havoc in the town but surely there would still be a public bath? He searched for quite a while, but finally discovered one; the only one, in fact, in the entire city. He asked how much a single ticket cost: 2.5 *jiao*. He followed up by asking when they closed: every evening at eight o'clock was the answer. He then told them that he and his uncle were in the city working and that they would both be incredibly tired by the time the evening rolled around but they wouldn't finish work until midnight, and by that time all they would want to do is shower and wash up. He wondered if they would be willing to allow them to do that; he'd pay 5 *jiao* for it. As luck would have it, the man at the counter agreed, and even told Guo Cunxian he didn't need to pay at that time, and that he would let the night shift know they'd be coming since he finished at eight. He assured Guo Cunxian it was no problem; peasants, city folk, it didn't matter, according to him they were all one big family.

While he'd sorted things for the evening, his heart was still heavy. He had to find the hospital, he had to go through it, searching; finally, towards the rear of the building, he came upon the morgue. The door was ajar, the lock having long since been torn out. He pushed it open, gently, and a shiver coursed through his body causing his hair to stand on end; goose pimples popped out all over. Even in the middle of the day this place was dark and terrifying. He dared not step further into the room but instead quickly withdrew, pulling the door closed. Once the sun fell, he returned with a brick, found a dark, shaded corner, and then plopped his arse squarely down on the brick he'd brought with him. There he waited, quietly, intently, his eyes firmly fixed on the door to the morgue immediately in front of him. It was pitch black in the corridor, with only the small, flickering shards of light that snuck in from the street lamps outside that split the darkness. The entire hospital was quiet, deathly so, as though the entire building was vacant. Guo Cunxian was nervous and worried but not afraid.

He wasn't sure how long he'd waited, but then, finally, he heard the footsteps he'd been expecting. A dark shadow traversed the flickering light, something wedged under its arm. Its gait was brisk and silent. It moved directly towards the door to the morgue, pushed it open, stepped inside and closed the door behind it. Guo Cunxian stood up nimbly and went towards the door. He bent low and peered in through the hole where once there was a lock. With the aid of the light from outside, Guo Cunxian saw that the figure had placed what he'd been carrying under his arm down on one of the tables, a grass mat, and then opened the metal box that stood in the deepest recesses of the morgue. Carefully and expertly the figure lifted the corpse up out of the box and propped it up next to the wall. He then took the grass mat, placed it inside the box and then climbed in himself, seemingly settling down for the evening.

Guo Cunxian found it difficult to suppress his excitement. He had to open the door, he had to see who was inside. He stepped into the morgue and walked directly over to the metal box, bent down beside it and stared into the sparkling eyes of his uncle. He couldn't contain his emotion and blared out: "Uncle! You certainly made it hard enough for us to find you. You found a good hiding place, indeed, enough to frighten the whole town! Do you know they've been trying to reorganise and rectify operations at this hospital? Do you know how important this place is to the city, the county? It's not a place for you to bed down for the night. If only you knew the troubles that have come to pass in Guojiadian. Lan Xin, that vile bastard, he has been arrested. Mum is worried to death about you, her back's giving out and she hobbles around day in and day out. We've been out looking for you every day, you know. Get up, now, we'll go together to the public bath, clean ourselves up, sleep a little, and when the sun comes up, we'll head for home. How does that sound? And don't run off again. We don't have the energy to keep looking for you."

His mad old uncle refrained from protesting and was entirely acquiescent. He got up out of the metal box. Guo Cunxian helped him remove the grass mat and together they put the corpse back into it. They were neither hurried, nor overly worried. Once the body was safely inside, they left the morgue.

10

UNDERMINED

Spring finally came. And in the fields of Guojiadian something strange had happened. Because the great majority of the production team had already devoured more than half of the grain the authorities had provided, the land had been left mostly fallow. Over the winter season, the snow hadn't totally blanketed the landscape, so once spring had returned it was expected that the land would burst forth with new life; there should have been green everywhere. But that hadn't happened. Instead, with the land uncultivated, the sun was free to scorch what little foliage had grown, leaving the ground mostly barren and bereft of vegetation. All that grew were traces of wild grass near the irrigation troughs. It was a rather offensive sight.

Against this backdrop, however, in one part of the village fields, the wheat had actually grown and was now up to waist height, vibrantly green. Something else that drew the townspeople's attention was the fact that in among the wheat stalks, rapeseed was also thriving. More shocking still was the shape the rapeseed had taken on, for it was clear to see the words 'Long Live Chairman Mao' emblazoned across the field. Indeed, the rapeseed had seemingly grown rapidly, now towering over the wheat. It was thick and lush, with yellow flowers that glistened in the sunlight and dazzled the eyes, making it easily visible from a great distance away. Its fragrance carried on the wind, too. Like a green velvet mat inlaid with gold, the rapeseed seemed to be paying homage to the Great Helmsman himself. And as if standing on guard, several dozen small trees surrounded the area. With their thick trunks and verdant foliage, they seemed to frame the scene most perfectly.

Such a sight couldn't help but create quite a commotion. Once word spread, the inhabitants of Guojiadian came one after the other to the field; they came by the dozen and later in their hundreds. Before long, people from throughout the countryside, some even more than ten *li* away, made their way towards Guojiadian, prompted by their curiosity to witness the scene. As more and more people came, the field took on a more and more spiritual air. Some said that the strange formation had first been seen after a dramatic lightning storm that had cut across the night sky. Others said it must have been the sublime work of aliens. Of course, the more people told stories about it, the more word spread, and soon reached the ears of the authorities. Seizing the opportunity, the commune and county leaders in the Revolutionary Committee issued a statement urging the people of the need to "grasp this sign of the revolution and further advance production". Not long after, official visits to the field were organised for all the surrounding inhabitants. The whole area soon took on the likeness of a bustling street market, which had the effect of angering poor old Jingshi, who soon took to guarding the field, preventing friend and foe alike from approaching 'his' wheat, and the trees he'd diligently planted several years ago and had protected ever since. To better fend off encroachment, he ultimately cordoned off his entire personal plot, ensuring that no one could step foot on it. By this point, it was clear to everyone that the land was Guo Cunxian's allotment and that the wheat along with the rapeseed had both been planted by him and his younger brother.

Guo Cunxian's point of view on all of this was quite uncomplicated, due in large part to the fact that he had been apprehensive about this particular issue for some time. It was as though a sword were perched precariously over his head. He was the one who had rounded up his friends to clandestinely harvest the nearby reeds that had ultimately led to the conflagration of the frog marshes. When the Red Guards ravaged the town, they never followed up on this incident, nor did he try to meddle. After all, he didn't want to drag his family into his problems. But here they were again, once more being given directives to increase production quotas. He could reveal his hand or try to ensure the truth about the frog marshes remained concealed. At the same time, he figured this might be a way to guarantee his uncle stayed. From the moment the rebel faction had renamed the Dragon Phoenix Trees and placed the stage for their struggle sessions at their feet, his uncle had not returned to their base, nor would he idle away his time in their branches. But he had no wife and there was no simple way to keep him tethered to their home. Who's to say he might not just up and leave one day? Guo Cunxian hadn't expected this would all cause such a fracas. His heart was perplexed and troubled, uncertain as to whether this whole affair was something to be welcomed or to be greatly troubled about.

Whatever the case may be, it was an unavoidable situation. Reportedly, he'd just been dispatched from the provincial capital. He went by the name of Feng Hou and held the position of Kuanhe County Revolutionary Committee Production Team Leader. He was accompanied by the Laodong Commune Revolutionary Committee Director Liu Dajiang, who was in charge of the production team and assisted by his Deputy Director Xin Chuan. Naturally they visited the now sacred ground emblazoned with the golden 'Long Live Chairman Mao'. Amazing. They praised the formation in the field to no end and then their eyes expectantly scanned the surrounding area... and just like that their entire mood changed. The excited, charged emotions they had when they initially arrived were now dissipated and replaced with a dreary coldness. There was dismay in their eyes, annoyance at the emptiness of the adjacent fields. They saw numerous people who had come from far away to visit the fabulous natural praise of Chairman Mao but, apart from these people, there was not a single villager from Guojiadian out working in the fields. They should all have been out busily ploughing the fields, tilling the land and planting crops. They might not have carried out this work the previous year but the time was perfect now for seizing the day and replanting what had been lost previously.

What was wrong with the people of Guojiadian? Did they think time had stopped for them? The workers on the much-delayed river project hadn't been dispatched, the fields lay fallow. This town was truly in dire straits, more so than any other village in the county. And yet, it was in this desperate town that someone had planted rapeseed in praise of Chairman Mao, and that had brought attention and fame to this little corner of the county. It was certainly an interesting place, that couldn't be denied.

The village head had, of course, received notification that the commune and county heads were going to pay the town a visit to inspect its productivity. The loudspeaker had been in use since early in the morning, letting everyone know. The head had even sent men round town to inform every household but quite a few homes were padlocked and empty, the visit of higher-ups having coincided with many taking their entire families out to beg for food. Credit for this sorry state of affairs lay squarely with the Red Guards and the total disruption they had caused. As it was, it was due to their free transportation and free movement that had led others to assume and expect the same. In the past, it had been different. Official permission was needed for everything; even going out to beg required papers. But that was no longer the case. Now, if a person or family decided they were going to do something, they simply went off and did it. It was, after all, Chairman Mao who had advocated that the masses rebel and many had taken that as an excuse to do as they pleased. It wasn't all that surprising, then, for the villagers to suppose that what was good for the goose must also be good for the gander. Colloquially, they renamed what it was they were doing; begging for food, at the end of the day, didn't have the greatest ring to it. Borrowing the same grandiose terms used to describe the activities of the Red Guards, going out and begging for food was soon known as making 'serial connections'! These past two years when the villagers from Guojiadian had taken to begging beyond their own town, they had quite enjoyed taking their whole families with them. The result was huge numbers of people criss-crossing the landscape, causing quite a ruckus, just as the Red Guards had done previously. Fortunately, the town officials had been in time to foil a mass exodus. In fact, they had prevented a hundred or more families from marching off; men, women, old and young. They had all been called to the eastern square to wait for the higher-ups to issue their commands.

As he entered the village, Feng Hou's heart was torn. In a village this size, he wasn't expecting to see such a lack of standard housing. Instead of the usual mud-clay walls, the houses here were constructed out of bricks, pale white in colour, the walls somewhat crooked and twisted, with a fair number ringed with fences and small lanterns. He wasn't expecting to see piles of stored foodstuff but even the stockpiles of firewood were rather small, and without wood, well, there'd be few fires lit and fewer things cooked, he assumed. A lack of firewood suggested little was harvested in the previous year. Why cut wood when there was nothing to use it for? Without crops, he continued to think, there'd be little grain to eat. He thought some more and wondered if that hadn't saved them in terms of collecting firewood, but then, if they didn't make many meals, what did they eat? Had they fought over the seeds and ended up begging? They were trapped in a vicious circle. For Feng Hou, it was no wonder Guojiadian seemed cold and cheerless, lacking in the energy and vigour it should have had. Feng Hou pondered the situation. It was not at all surprising to see that poverty, once it reached this extreme level, led inevitably to any number of evil deeds. But as he walked towards the eastern part of the town, he began to hear an unexpected noise.

Feng Hou called to Liu Dajiang and instructed him to bring him immediately to the eastern square. Even from a distance it was easy to see the mass of people that had gathered in the square, even women and children. Feng Hou grew suspicious. What the devil was going on? Had something new now transpired in Guojiadian? As he drew closer, he spoke to a peasant standing on the outskirts of the crowd: "What's this gathering for, huh?"

Guojiadian might be poor and its people fairly destitute but they had seen enough of the world to know how it worked. The man turned towards Feng Hou and knew immediately he was of a certain rank, and a high one at that. His response was delivered in a matter-of-fact manner. The town head had called them all together. They were doing revolutionary work. He told the man to listen. It was a great meeting for them to demonstrate their loyalty; one could say it was a 'great assembly for making serial connections'. The town head had asked them to wait. Once the gathering was finished, food coupons and travel money would be provided.

"And what about your village head?"

"The villager leaders don't leave the town for food. Why would they need to expose themselves to that, huh? No, they all wait in the central offices for the more senior leaders to visit, of course."

The peasants were all talking at once. It was quite a lively atmosphere, so much so that Feng Hou was unable to clearly hear the gist of what was being said. Liu Dajiang, since he was more familiar with the area, was fulfilling the role of '*tuguan*' (a 'local official'), a leadership role that was once hereditary, but even he was unsure of what was being talked about and found it challenging to break things down and explain them to Feng Hou. Today was actually the central market day for Laodong County, and with the rebels no longer causing a commotion, the capitalists, whose tails had never quite been cut off, now allowed the market to be revived. But an outcome of the once more bustling market was a corresponding increase in the numbers of people who would come from far away to solicit food from those who were a little better off. For most of these people, market days were viewed as being quite propitious, lucky days to go begging, for one could often find a way to fill one's belly before noon, and then still have time to scrounge for a little money to find a ride or buy a train ticket heading north. Such tactics would allow them to be a little better off. All they needed to do was to leave Guojiadian and wander around the markets as paupers, passing the year without having to worry about starving to death, at least. Of course, living in such a manner meant a person couldn't totally avoid hardship but, again, that was infinitely better than feeling one's stomach hollow out. Besides, begging for food wasn't quite as difficult as might be imagined. In fact, you got to meet any number of interesting, strange people and to see and hear many interesting, strange stories, to say nothing of seeing how many other people lived very different lives. It was like watching a performance on stage, life as it is lived, so to speak, and there were even times when you could participate yourself. It could really become rather addictive.

Feng Hou sighed with exasperation. Addicted to begging! That was rather outrageous, wasn't it?

Whatever the case may be, whether there was some new trick to begging that was hard to imagine, or whether it had been an activity long practised in the area, it was at least a tradition in Laodong County to go out begging. Of course, over the last few rather difficult years there had been a change in the perception of who was begging from whom and what all that meant. In the past, most people would have considered begging to be a shameful loss of face, and those who regularly took to the streets would find it near on impossible to get married, to say nothing of having a proper family. But things were different now. Begging was no longer seen as being shameful. It was out in the open, aboveboard, a chance to call out to friends; there was even a certain honourable quality and strength to it.

This changed attitude of the peasants was quite possible to comprehend. If you were to say rebel, then they'd rebel; if you were to say you ought to seize power, they'd assist you in doing so; if you were to say they should criticise, they'd do it; if you were to say they should struggle, they'd struggle. Instigating movement after movement among the population, causing disruption after disruption, well, that didn't stop them from being poor. In fact, it had only made matters worse. But at the end of the day, who's willing to do all of that on an empty stomach? They'd be much better off making serial connections, taking the initiative, as it were. So when spring came and the land remained yellow instead of green, the only option for Guojiadian's residents was to beg. You could call it a meal of great misfortune. The past returning once again. Those from Laodong County who decided to roam about the area begging soon obtained quite a reputation. It didn't matter where one went, as soon as they saw people out begging, as soon as they heard them speak, it was easy to tell where they'd come from. Eight or nine out of ten would be from Laodong. Half the north of China knew that Laodong County's production of beggars was flourishing.

Feng Hou cast his eyes on Liu Dajiang and then proceeded to ridicule him: "You've assuredly struck the right path here, hmm. One can rely on begging to make one's reputation. That's fairly unique, to say the least."

These past few years Liu Dajiang had received more than his fair share of torment. He'd been in office, then out, and now in again. No one else in Laodong had gone through quite what he had, and even though he was now back in a position of leadership his belly was still full of resentment and discontent. To make matters worse, now, here in front of his superior, these villagers had given his boss further reason to vent. There was not much he could do but let his face blush with embarrassment and meekly accept the cutting remarks. He had had several dealings with Feng Hou by now and figured he had experienced his fair share, too. Feng Hou never held back. He said what he thought, regardless of his interlocutor's position, whether it was a rebellious youth or part of the old guard, it didn't matter, he showed no fear. Take, for instance, the title of 'group leader'. It could be a highly regarded rank, or not much more than a lowly pencil pusher, a member of a village cooperative or part of the ruling politburo. Who knew just what position Feng Hou held? Whatever the case might be, Liu Dajiang didn't dare to say too much in front of him. The villagers of Guojiadian, on the other hand, didn't seem to pay much attention to this, or they just didn't care. They were like an army of poor beggars, uncooperative and obstructionist. There really wasn't any way to convey to them the gravity of the situation they were in. In fact, as more of the gathered people saw that a higher-up was in their presence, they became even bolder, deliberately raising their voices for him to hear: "It's nearly gone noon already. How is it that you still haven't given us permission to go?"

Some followed suit and echoed the question, while others took it a step further: "Alright, it's fine if we're not permitted to go but somebody sure as hell better sort out our dinner!"

Still others piled it on, playing the fool and asking: "But who's able to do that, huh? Feed the whole village. Well, surely not anyone from Guojiadian."

"That's right, there's a very old, old saying that goes something like this: Guojiadian, ah, its land is more salt than sand, in drought they drink bitter bile, and in floods they beg."

Feng Hou stood silently, but the more he listened the more he grew cold. Poverty was a sickness, a communicable disease. He could hold his tongue no longer. He shifted towards Liu Dajiang and reproached them: "Haven't the central authorities issued emergency rations? The county has repeatedly issued orders to energetically promote self-help to put an end to people wandering far and wide begging for food. How is it that things have become even more severe here? It's like a gang of bandits is in charge of the house!"

Most things aren't easily explained, at least not in a few words. Liu Dajiang could only offer an incomplete explanation: "The emergency rations, well, they've been consumed already. They lasted just through the winter and when the land remained dry and brown into spring, there wasn't anything left to do but go out and beg. As for the self-help initiatives, well, you need to be producing something in the first instance, and right now, that's the problem... nothing's being produced. It's a combination of natural disasters and man-made calamities that have conspired against them. Without seeds to plant, there's not much work to be done, to say nothing of..."

"Well then, if that's the case, who had seeds to plant 'Long Live Chairman Mao'?"

Several mouths clamoured to offer an answer: "Ah, those words were the work of Guo Cunxian and his singular skill. In our opinion, he must have borrowed the seeds to sow the land. It gives him something to harvest this year and saves him and his family from having to beg."

Another voice then interjected with a sigh: "Borrowing seeds is all well and good, but just who has them to lend?"

Feng Hou ignored the lament. If Guo Cunxian was able to do it, then why weren't the others? He spoke once more: "So, is this Guo Cunxian here then?"

"Well, we've already said his family doesn't need to beg, so why the hell would he be out here today sweltering under this sun?"

"Then what about the local cadres?"

A militiaman who'd been put in charge of the square and tasked with preventing the people from leaving, replied: "They're all in the central offices waiting for the authorities to show up." Before he finished speaking, he saw Guo Cunyong come running up and decided it was best for him to stop.

Guo Cunyong was quite young but he knew enough not to slight nor embarrass a senior party leader who'd come to Guojiadian. On the contrary, he greeted Feng Hou with excitement and seemed completely unperturbed with the discordant atmosphere rippling through the eastern square. In a bold and forthright manner he said: "Fellow comrades, welcome, welcome!"

Seeing the age and temperament of the cadre now standing in front of them, Liu Dajiang immediately surmised he must be from the rebel faction and did nothing to hide the distaste in his voice: "Who are you now? You've certainly not skimped on your welcome, huh!"

Guo Cunyong didn't back down, instead he welcomed Liu Dajiang's seeming reproach and replied confidently: "My name's Guo Cunyong. I'm the deputy director for the local committee. The director and the remainder of the cadres are waiting for your instructions in the central offices." Liu Dajiang's stomach churned. He thought to rebuke the boy for his arrogance. He and Feng Hou had arrived much earlier in the day, after all, so what the hell were they still doing sitting around in their offices supposedly waiting for them? Guo Cunyong seemed to guess what Liu Dajiang was thinking and sought to offer an explanation. He smiled, telling them that the director Guo Jingfu had taken ill and found it difficult to breathe. He'd been bedridden for days now, he added, but once he heard that the commune and county leaders were coming to inspect the village, he had dragged himself out of his sickbed and had been waiting patiently for them.

Feng Hou smiled in response but remained silent. With his eyes he tried to curb Liu Dajiang's growing irritation and introduce himself. Then, waving his hands, he directed the boy to lead the way to the central offices. Before departing, however, Guo Cunyong leaned close to one of the militiamen and gave orders, quietly. The villagers were to head home, the director had ordered, and if any of them dared still to leave the town to go and beg, then they'd have a year's worth of rations confiscated.

Some of the gathered people heard the order directly, others guessed what it was, and even if they didn't, they all still knew what it was that Guo Cunyong had whispered to the militia. Immediately a voice blared out over the crowd: "Who dares, huh? Whoever confiscates my rations, well, I'll sure as hell be eating at their house!"

"Damn right! Do bare feet fear wearing shoes? If we've already nothing to lose, then what the hell, hey!"

"Poor old Guo… once a tramp, always a tramp… a model worker, hmph. That may be but he sure as hell didn't have a proper bed on which to lay his head. You know, he sold his own child. He's a beggar through and through. His debts accumulate all year long, despite the fact he spends most of his time sitting on his arse. He's running the village association. Ha, perhaps he thinks his fate's changing and he's a rich old bastard now!"

The people roared with laughter.

Feng Hou leaned toward Guo Cunyong and asked: "Who're they talking about? Who's Old Guo?"

Hoping not to embarrass the senior Party members in front of the crowd, Guo Cunyong pretended the laughter had nothing to do with them and instead smiled and replied: "It's our village committee director, Guo Jingfu. He also heads the Peasant Farmers' Association."

Feng Hou didn't say anything further, nor did he laugh. He was beginning to realise being here in this town was going to be exceptionally troublesome. Their poverty gave them ample justification to rationalise any subsequent behaviour. They'd endured so much hardship that they'd earned a right to a certain obstinacy and the poorer they became, the more obstinate they were. Their resentment far outweighed that of the Red Guards; he thought the whole town was on the verge of falling into anarchy itself.

They accompanied Guo Cunyong to the Party offices. The structure was fairly imposing and had been constructed not long after the great flood. Inside there was a large room that could hold at least twenty or thirty people. The air was thick with smoke, burning the lungs. The current village leaders were all seated in the room, waiting for Guo Cunyong to make the introductions. First, there was Guo Jingfu who served as director. Cunyong, as they knew, was the deputy director, and so too was Ou Guangming, whom they were now introduced to. They'd also recently welcomed back into the fold two more senior cadres, Han Jingting and Guo Huaishan.

Liu Dajiang followed up immediately by making introductions for Feng Hou. His tone of voice was particularly serious: "Team Leader Feng has come to Guojiadian for two reasons. The first has to do with the frog marshes reservoir which is of great concern for the entire county. It's also a provincial project of great importance. The other villages across the area are all buzzing with activity and making excellent progress, but your village has only dispatched a few former landlords and wealthy class individuals to assist in the work. As a result, you've not only slowed down the progress of this commune but, much more seriously, you've slowed down the progress of the county as a whole. The second reason he has come has to do with the spring planting. He has already seen the fields and witnessed that the land is still lying fallow. Are you still farmers or something else? To his endless surprise, he has also learnt that you actually gave most of the seeds provided by the authorities to your people to eat and that, once they had gorged themselves, you permitted them to go out begging for food. It might be more appropriate for you to formally change the name of the village and simply call it Beggars' Town." As he spoke, the fire in Liu Dajiang's voice grew. Feng Hou, on the other hand, uttered not a word but stood watching, observing intently the reactions of the village leaders.

To a man none betrayed their emotions, choosing instead to look cold and detached. In truth, they were much more interested in watching Liu's heated tirade, one and all believing that the problems he raised had nothing to do with any of them. Guo Jingfu sat placidly. His hair hadn't been shaved or trimmed in quite some time; it framed his face as the dry blades of grass framed the dry fields outside. Feng Hou wondered how this poor old peasant had been put in charge of the local cadres. No doubt he'd endured countless hardships over the course of his life. His face was bruised, his posture crooked and hunched over; his breathing was raspy and laboured; age had ravaged him and left him weak; it seemed as though one gust of wind would topple him. And yet, here he was, giving the orders and after all that had happened over these past few years, he was in command. No one knew for sure who was playing what game on whom. The only thing that was certain was that even a man of his advanced age wouldn't let go of the reins now that he'd finally grabbed hold of them. He was calling the shots in Guojiadian and, as protocol would have it, he was required to respond to the criticism to be levelled by the commune leadership. But just as he began to mumble to himself, and before anyone could really hear clearly what it was he was trying to say, the old man broke out into a fit of coughing so severe that his pain and infirmity could be felt by everyone in the room.

Nevertheless, the higher-ups wouldn't relent. They launched their attack, sparing no amount of venom in the words they chose, even if neither Feng Hou nor Liu Dajiang could outline exactly the underlying reasons for their animosity. It, of course, begged the question: who else in the village was willing to take the initiative to accept responsibility and take the blame? The two older, recently rehabilitated, members of the village leadership were wont to withdraw from the heated exchange that had just erupted but were prevented from doing so; instead the troubles of the village were piled upon them as well, and so it was in their best interests to try to first exculpate themselves. Two others whose stomachs weren't all that fortified were absent. They had been in charge of 'advancing the revolution' but had been negligent with respect to sowing the fields and sending workers to the reservoir, despite these two activities being clearly in the realm of 'promoting production'. Feng Hou then turned to Liu Dajiang and asked if he could see the crux of the matter. For the former it was clear that Guojiadian, from top to bottom, was disorganised and suffering from paralysis due to inaction. It wasn't a failure of the chain of command as the directives from the central authorities were delivered. No, the problem was in the village itself, in the fact that no one could carry out the directives or, to put it another way, no one had the gumption to implement central commands.

Abruptly, he turned his attention back to the village cadres: "Who's the team leader?"

No one answered but all eyes shifted to Han Jingting, who finally replied: "Why the hell are you all looking at me? I was team leader before but I was I brought down by the Red Guards, wasn't I? That was several years ago now, too. There is no team leader in Guojiadian." The nervousness in his voice was evident to all.

Feng Hou continued his interrogation: "Who was the Party Secretary then, hmm?"

Liu Dajiang answered this question: "That would have been Chen Baohuai, but I'm not sure what his situation is at the moment nor where he is."

Ou Guangming, in a straightforward manner as usual, added additional details: "He really was brought down by the Red Guards and had lost whatever support he may have had. No one respected him any more nor would they follow his commands. The last I heard, was that he'd suffered a total breakdown."

Feng Hou continued to probe the matter: "So who in the village do the people respect and admire? Is there anyone?"

Ou Guangming smiled and laughed a little. Glancing at the pouting lips of Guo Jingfu, he answered: "Well, that's an issue best answered by the director, I think."

Holding his asthma at bay, the old man spoke: "All I know is it's a job I can't do. I'm too old and I don't have it in me. Shit, who's to say if I'll even be around tomorrow? No, giving me the responsibility would only botch the whole thing."

Feng Hou changed his demeanour and attempted to soothe his concerns: "Well, your appointment wouldn't cause things to go off the rails. They're already off the rails, if I may be so blunt. That said, the blame doesn't lie entirely at your feet and no one is questioning the performance of your farmers' association. I'll go so far as to say the village committee is also performing as expected. It is organised by the people after all, but these organs cannot stand in for the main production brigade nor for the Party branch. The first order of business is to reinstate the production brigade. Let me ask you, who do you think is best suited to assume such duties?"

"Guo Cunxian, I think he's perhaps best suited to manage Guojiadian."

Feng Hou's eyes penetrated deeply into the cadres there in front of him: "And what do you all think?"

As the old saying goes, they'd been painted into a corner. They couldn't put themselves forward for the position, rural decorum wouldn't allow it. They could only wait for someone to express an opinion and then parrot it. Unexpectedly, Ou Guangming broke ranks, as it were, and added his thoughts to the discussion: "Guo Cunxian won't accept the post. We asked him once before and were rebuffed, and that situation is unlikely to have changed now."

This new information suddenly stoked Feng Hou's interest. His look was steady and self-assured. He first instructed Ou Guangming to go and get Guo Cunxian and bring him back. Then he had to find them a private room. Feng Hou intended to speak with him personally. He was convinced he wouldn't be rebuffed. Finally, he ordered Guo Cunyong to inform each and every production team to send their team leaders to this location. He was going to convene a meeting for all of them and if the teams had no leader in place, then they were to send a responsible representative at least.

After dispatching two youths with his instructions, Feng Hou turned to speak to Liu Dajiang, directing him to host a meeting to select the new team leader for Guojiadian. Once the selection was made, however, he was told not to conclude the meeting but rather wait until Feng Hou himself had had the chance to talk to Guo Cunxian. Then, and only then, would Feng Hou come. There was another issue he also wished to discuss with Liu Dajiang, namely, who was to be the Party secretary? For the time being, he suggested Comrade Xin Chuan might be a suitable appointment, then, after the Party branch had been properly reinstated, a more permanent selection could be made.

The two commune leaders nodded their heads repeatedly, convincing themselves of the decisions they were making, learning a new skill themselves.

The loudspeaker blared once more its familiar refrain, dead set on pressuring the people to comply. One by one the production team leaders began appearing while Feng Hou, however, made his way to an adjacent room to wait for Guo Cunxian. Ou Guangming had already reasoned it out. He knew why Feng Hou had come to the village and he had relayed this to Guo Cunxian in advance of his meeting. As a result, when he entered the door Guo Cunxian didn't have the usual chip on his shoulder. On the contrary, he had an awkward, somewhat uncomfortable smile on his face. Up until now, Feng Hou was the most senior Party representative he'd ever met but his demeanour was not what Guo Cunxian expected. He was surprised to see the man stand up and offer his hand to shake. Feng Hou then invited him to sit down. His eyes, Guo Cunxian thought, contained an inner warmness, a friendliness he was surprised to see. The former Party secretary had never been so polite. Guo Cunxian couldn't help but respect the man now seated in front of him. As he looked at the man, Guo Cunxian could see that he wasn't all that much older than him and yet he'd already been appointed to the highest position in the county. His face had the look of an intellectual: clean and unspoiled by manual labour, possessing a certain intensity.

Feng Hou prevaricated. He wanted to shoot the breeze a little before turning to the real reason he'd wanted to meet personally with Guo Cunxian. He wanted him to feel at ease. "Cunxian, it's alright if I call you Cunxian, isn't it? Calling you Old Guo wouldn't feel right. You're much too young for such a form of address."

Guo Cunxian nodded his consent hastily. It was no problem, everyone in the village called him that.

"What made you think to sow those rapeseeds as you did, huh? It's quite something, you know. There's nothing to compare with it for hundreds of kilometres. I haven't investigated it or anything but I'd hazard a guess that there's nothing like it in the entire country. It took real intent, real heart to lay the seeds like you did. Perhaps you've created a new model form for trees, hmm."

Guo Cunxian was a little embarrassed but he didn't dare tell the man the whole truth. Instead, he shifted in his chair and spoke: "I didn't really intend for the crops to grow as they did. I was thinking more about my family. I really just wanted the seeds to grow and flower, to make the best use of our allotment, so that we'd be better able to manage, that's all."

"Good, good, you're being honest with me, not trying to tell tall tales about how it was planned and deliberate. The most frightening thing in this world, you know, is empty talk in disregard of the truth. But I'll tell you something. I think Guojiadian is wasting a valuable resource. It's wasting your skills, dedication and hard work. Tell me, what do you think of the work units in the village, huh?"

"Guo Jingfu isn't a bad fellow. It's not that he doesn't want to do the job, it's just that he can't. Han Jingting himself is old. As for Guo Huaishan, well, he's a crafty old bird. Guo Cunyong is smart enough but in his heart he's not a farmer. Ou Guangming is diligent and hardworking but he's not a leader."

Feng Hou burst out laughing, "I've found the right man. No one else in the village quite fits the bill!"

There was a firm, if somewhat sullen look on Guo Cunxian's face. "Team Leader Feng, I'm sorry, but please don't yank my chain. I was once in charge of Guojiadian, and that didn't turn out so well. I can't be put in the same position once again."

"Why?"

Guo Cunxian began to tell him about the flood, about the orders he'd given and the consequences they led to, and as he did it was easy to see the bile coming up in his throat and an almost murderous look in his eyes: "Ah, everyone's happy to get you to do the work, and they won't let you know how to do it, but as soon as things don't go the way they want them to, they turn on you in a flash and treat you no better than the sheep shit they try to wipe off their shoes. And it doesn't stop there, no... no, they try and fix you, control you. Hmph, why should I sell myself so low, huh?"

Feng Hou tried not to betray the effect the story had on him. He didn't want Guo Cunxian to see how it riled him and made him angry to hear about how he'd been mistreated and wronged. He remained steadfast, staring into Guo Cunxian's eyes as he spoke, nodding in agreement. Finally, he replied: "I've heard about this, you know. At the time, I thought it was good news, indeed. I didn't realise it was you. Excellent! You aren't just a simple peasant, are you? It's a great pity, you know, that there aren't more like you. If there were, if there had been, people wouldn't have starved like they did in the aftermath of that great flood. And I'm not just talking about Guojiadian, I mean across the whole commune and county. The story of this has earned you a great amount of credit. People have been told to remember your actions. I reckon it's the reason why people feel comfortable in giving you responsibility for the village instead of refusing your appointment.

"I'll ask you again, please, step out of the shadows and assume this position. Both the county and commune authorities will testify to your appointment. Then it should just be a formality for you to be selected by the village cadres, after which no one, including the leadership in the commune and county governments, will be able to remove you from office. There'd be no legal recourse, no reasons whatsoever."

On the surface this all seemed so great. Guo Cunxian had never once heard before about a village cadre being chosen by the county leadership. And in his heart of hearts, it wasn't as though he didn't want the position. In truth, he did, but he couldn't let on too quickly. He had to hold back and so he had to ask, had to get an answer to a burning question: "Team Leader, now isn't really the best time. The people are troubled, they have lost faith, those who haven't starved, well, they've only survived to witness internal strife spreading like wildfire. It has only been two years since the market reopened and already capitalists are taking advantage of the people. Very few have the backbone to deal with this. Team Leader, are you able to give me any inside info, a clear picture of just what's going on and what's planned? I don't want to get halfway through the job only to see it all dashed on the rocks again."

Feng Hou laughed suddenly, sharply: "Cunxian, you really are unique, a singular person to be sure. To tell you the truth, I do have some inkling about what's going to happen. What, you may ask? Well, that's difficult to say. But I'll ask you another question: is so-called real inside info necessarily real, in fact? The land needs only to be cultivated for people to have food in their bellies, that's the hard truth. Chairman Mao instructs us to read the original works, to study theory and that Marxism is our actual situation. If you hear what he says, the economy is more fundamental than politics and wealth is a problem related to progress. That much is obvious. You're not the only one who doesn't understand... most don't. Why, if we're already so poor, do we need to be even poorer? The reason, hmm, well, that's the nature of poverty, it self-replicates, over and over, without scruples. It's like that old saying, you know the one, about bare feet not fearing shoes. Because bare feet already have nothing, it's much easier to magnify the hatred, to increase the bile in one's stomach. To repeat this over and over again leads to even greater destitution. Marx himself spoke of this. The barbarian doesn't know and doesn't understand what wealth is. Early humans relied on trade and commerce. That's how civilisation was built and that's how it flourished. Where there's wealth, there's inequality, but that's not to say if we're all poor we'd all be equal. Didn't we already try our hand at egalitarianism, hmm? That resulted in the Cultural Revolution."

When he got to the most interesting part, Feng Hou abruptly stopped. Why had he rambled on this way in front of a simple peasant? He was pathetic. Perhaps the stress had got to him and he needed to vent. He just never thought he would have ended up here in the countryside babbling on to a poor farmer who had no clue what he was talking about. He had to admit, though, that it was probably much safer, even if still inevitably pathetic. He never thought for an instant, however, that his interlocutor would be so attentive, nor that he would encourage him to carry on. Feng Hou stood up: "You stay here for a moment, alright? I'm going next door to see what's happening. If they've selected you to be team leader, you'd better live up to their expectations and not let them down. It'll be up to you to bring Guojiadian and even the whole of Laodong out of poverty. And if they haven't chosen you, well, that'll be fine too. It will give me the chance to find you some suitable position in the commune or county government. You're a character, that's for sure, and we certainly can't let that be overlooked."

Guo Cunxian sat there a little perturbed. He hadn't said whether he was willing to take the post or not, and yet hadn't Feng Hou already arranged for the others to make the selection? And if he were chosen, he still had to say yes or no. But if he wasn't, then wouldn't that mean he'd be ridiculed again? Before he could work things out for himself, Feng Hou returned with a smile across his face: "Cunxian, ah, I knew it, they've all had a change of heart. After all, who wants to go poor and hungry? It was unanimous. They all chose you. Come, I'll accompany you, it's time for you to show your face and say a few words or perhaps outline your plans for the future."

Guo Cunxian stood up but he didn't move: "Team Leader, you can be assured that I'll follow whatever commands you give but I'm afraid I can't distinguish the good from the bad. May I make a request of you?"

"What is it?"

"Call a town meeting and order Han Jingting, on behalf of Chen Baohuai, to publicly apologise to me. They disgraced me when they removed me from office. I need that to be rectified but not only for my own reputation. The whole village needs to know that the Party can make mistakes but, just as it highlights its achievements, it can also acknowledge its mistakes. I want the people to know that."

"Alright then. This afternoon we'll call for a public meeting to announce your appointment. Any other requests?"

"Well, considering that both you and Comrade Liu are here, I'd like to take advantage of this and have you discuss the troubles Guojiadian has faced over the last couple of years. I'd like these issues to be resolved, those that can be, in any case. You know there are still a number of prisoners being detained. I'd like that to be sorted. I want it to be made clear that that has no connection to me. After all, I don't want them influencing the proper work I need to carry out."

"That's as it should be. We'll resolve these issues during the meeting this afternoon. That's two requests, is there a third?"

Somewhat uncomfortable, Guo Cunxian said there was: "There is one other small thing, but you're the only one who can deal with it. Since you're a learned man, I'd like to ask if you could give the two big trees standing at the gates to the village a name. And don't laugh at this request, please. The whole village, young and old, those with problems, those without, everyone, we all liked to rest at the foot of those trees, to while away the time. The whole area is treasured for its feng shui. The trees, too, are our symbol, they stand watch over the town and help determine its fate. Most of us call them the Dragon Phoenix Trees, but the Red Guards told us that that was reactionary, feudal and capitalist to boot. They renamed the trees after themselves but that doesn't sound right, does it? It's wrong. But as a result, everyone avoids the trees now. Before they were believed to be quite auspicious, now they're considered to be the opposite so no one dares to go near them. That's wrong, too." Guo Cunxian continued on with his story, relaying as briefly as possible, the history of the Dragon Phoenix Trees.

Completely engrossed in the story, Feng Hou finally replied: "I'd be only too happy to help. In a moment I shall have to go and see the trees myself, think of a name and then discuss that with you, alright? Aside from these requests, is there anything else?"

Guo Cunxian shook his head.

"Well then, let's go and make the announcement."

There wasn't much in the village that could be concealed for long. Word spread quickly about the afternoon meeting, meaning most people arrived exceptionally early for it. Even more surprising, considering, of course, that the villagers had been told not to leave town to beg, the loudspeaker didn't even need to sound before the place was already packed with people. The stage the Red Guards had used for their struggle sessions had changed, however. Browbeaten capitalists and other bad elements were no longer the central actors. Of course, ghosts and monsters still have qualities that make people want to look, just as men have theatrical techniques and flowers have their allure. These are all means to attract the attention of an audience. Towards the front of the stage a small lectern stood ready. A long table had been placed in the middle of the stage and there in the centre sat the county head. Both sides were taken up with the commune heads but it was who was sitting beyond them that drew people's interest. To one side sat three men of the old guard: Guo Jingfu, Han Jingting and Guo Huaishan. Opposite them sat Guo Cunxian, Ou Guangming and Guo Cunyong, all young men by comparison. Seeing how the stage had been arranged and the power structures it suggested, the audience couldn't help but smile and openly discuss the significance of such an arrangement.

Han Jingting and Guo Huaishan were old hands at this. They'd been up on the stage innumerable times, down on their knees, humiliated and ridiculed. Now, however, they were seated. Apparently, public office was open to all kinds of men, the crooked and the straight.

Whatever the case may be, much of life is about having a little good fortune or none at all.

And of all the men up on the stage, whose life could be considered good and whose bad? Life itself is a performance, which means roles invariably change, one day the spotlight might be on me, the next day on you, back and forth, each of us taking turns to lead. This explains the popularity of the theatre; people are enthralled by the show and how it will all end.

Children live in fear of heaven and earth being plunged into chaos, of evil men going scot-free. An audience that is oblivious of this is the source of great sorrow for those on the stage!

Fuck your mother's stinky arse! The reverse ought to be true, it was the audience after all that had suffered.

Being the youngest, the loudest and full of spit and vinegar, Guo Cunyong was chosen to host the meeting. But even he chose not to be nonchalant about it, not like before when he would stand in front of the microphone and spew out whatever came to mind. No, at this meeting, he was paying attention to the details, he didn't want to speak off the cuff, despite his gift of the gab. In fact, he'd made use of dinnertime to prepare properly, his hands clutching a few sheets of paper with the words he was to speak clearly written out. He stood in front of the microphone and spoke in a tone very different from the past: "Fellow villagers!"

The audience gasped. What had happened to comrades-in-arms? The rebel faction?

It seemed that had gone out of style. After all, didn't everyone see the once denounced capitalists on centre stage. Those on the capitalist road were on it once again, their faction was now back in power, which meant only one thing, of course: that the rebel faction had all been mad.

Guo Cunyong called for attention. He might have looked older now, more mature than he had before, but inside he was the same. He still held onto the fervour of the recent past. This became all too clear as his voice took on the tone of previous inflammatory speeches: "From this day forward, Guojiadian is turning a new page, we're marching towards an ever greater victory and we'll be testing the achievements of the recent battles. We've experienced great struggle, great criticism, great reforms and now we're striding into a new era. The legacy of those great struggles and criticism have given us the power, energy and high spirits to greet even more profoundly this new period of change! Change that means we take down the old and bring forth the new. We can't forget the past. The debts we have to history will have to be paid. So, with that in mind, let us first ask for the president of the Guojiadian Farmers' Association, who also serves as the chair for the Revolutionary Committee, namely Guo Jingfu, to give us a report on the troubles of the past and our bright new future."

Wow, Guo Jingfu can still deliver reports! Well, if a dung beetle were to wander up onto his table, I'm sure he'd figure out a way to make a meal of it.

The items on the meeting agenda had all been mutually decided upon by the county and commune heads. As convention would have it, the first issue was the bitterness of the past and the promise of the future, as well as providing Guo Jingfu with the opportunity to save face. The old fellow wasn't bad. He was about to relinquish power but in a dignified manner. He walked up to the lectern somewhat nervously, surprised he hadn't burst into a coughing fit, then craned his neck as much as possible and navigating his mouth towards the microphone, he said: "Us old-timers know, there are three types of poverty here, poor people, poor land and finally poor village." He coughed a little and continued: "There are five other things too that I wish to talk about, five things we have too much of. The first is begging for food, which we've taken to calling, euphemistically of course, hawking our wares or, more recently, the making of serial connections... ha! The second is the amount of back-breaking work we carry out, the daily slog that never seems to end but never seems to make us any better off. The third is the number of bare sticks in the village, there are certainly too many of them. Fourth are our debt burdens and, lastly, the practice of selling off our children. I fall under the second category without a doubt. I've spent most of my life as an indentured labourer, toiling for the Lü family, and even when we struggled against the landlords and took ownership of the land, even when that land was redistributed, nothing really changed." He coughed again, a little more this time before carrying on: "And at that time, for one year's work, the Lü family gave me eighteen litres of sorghum."

Taking advantage of the pause, an audience member jumped in: "Hey! That's a larger quota than what you've given us today!"

"That's right, with eighteen litres of sorghum we'd have no problem at all taking care of our families"

Guo Jingfu coughed more rigorously now, trying to clear his throat. The echo of what he'd said reverberated through the crowd, encouraging him to continue. He was still in good spirits and willing to talk some more. Somewhat unexpectedly, he even began to show off: "Ordinarily, I could control my appetite and eat what was available. Hell, I'd often only bathe once a year. When my son was due to come home, I went to the station to meet him. Because I used to plough the fields, I'd earned a little cash." He coughed some more then continued: "Lü was able to treat illnesses you know. His family took advantage of the land they possessed, twenty thousand *mu*! That allowed him to have several wives and concubines, who gave him a great number of sons and daughters, a whole gang. And then after liberation, he was given the position of bureau chief, became a pilot and then a general in the military." He trailed off into a coughing fit...

Someone else from the audience shouted out: "Hah, maybe you should be called Guo Laofu, then, a rich man's toady, president of the landlords' association?"

"Are you talking about the bitterness of the past and the promise of the future, or are you recalling the sweetness of yesterday and the unpleasantness of today?"

The audience was congealing into a mass of people talking, shouting, complaining... both Liu Dajiang and Ou Guangming looked at each other nervously. Liu had told the younger man to help Guo Jingfu prepare what he was going to say. It didn't matter if he had a lot to say or not, but he shouldn't have been allowed to say what he has, moaned Liu Dajiang, complaining the old man was making a laughing stock of the whole meeting and riling the audience up! Ou Guangming defended himself, saying that any script he'd prepared would be of no use since Guo Jingfu was illiterate, after all. In private he'd tried to instruct the old man on what to say and how to say it but who knew his mouth wouldn't be able to keep up with his legs and that he'd touch on such a sore spot for everyone, huh? Ou Guangming couldn't contain his laughter. Liu Dajiang cast his eyes in the direction of Feng Hou, who was sitting speechless; he wasn't laughing but nor did he seem to be angry. He sat stiffly as though he was an outside observer watching a play unfold. Liu Dajiang then waved his hand hurriedly to get the attention of Guo Cunyong, gesturing for him to get the old man off the stage and to get on with the agenda.

Guo Cunyong walked up to the lectern with the aim of smoothing things over: "It seems as though our director's chronic condition has reared its head again. You can all see that, hmm, his cough and…"

That's right! His coughing has brought the truth out into the open.

There's nothing much wrong with what he said, it proves he's a decent fellow, at least!

Guo Cunyong grew suddenly agitated and had a mind to unleash a political slogan of the kind he'd used to denounce the tyrannous landlord class not all that long ago. Such a slogan would surely have had the immediate effect of silencing the raucous audience. But such tactics were no longer permissible, especially not when the county head was on the stage behind him.

He moved closer to the microphone and spoke loudly through it: "Fellow villagers, this here's an old labourer. It's clear he has been exploited for most of his life, for so many years that it's impossible for him to forget the person who exploited and took advantage of him for so long. And what does this mean, huh? It means we've still a long struggle ahead of us! Eighteen litres of sorghum a year and a bar of soap. Is that enough to purchase one's soul? We mustn't forget that even the soul needs revolution. We must think of a proper method to conquer it! Following is a prepared speech notifying you all of the outcome of the village committee's research that has been ratified by the Revolutionary Commune Committee: the investigation into Lan Xin's culpability with regard to recent calamities is over. He's to be released immediately. However, he is to be subject to your supervision. He must work hard and undergo reform. Moreover, he's not permitted to leave the village or to try and collude with other disruptive agents from outside the town for the purposes of causing mayhem. If he violates any of these directives, both his past crimes and any future ones will be weighed together according to military justice in order to determine a suitable sentence! Moving on, we now invite the former team leader Han Jingting to the microphone to speak."

Han Jingting had already been through this type of situation, this type of battle. He stood up but instead of walking to the lectern, he stepped around it and to the front of the stage. There he bowed deeply to his fellow villagers before speaking: "In the past, I've committed many, many mistakes. Two, especially, weigh heavily on me, the first being that, in all my many years at the helm of Guojiadian, I never effected real change and never transformed the appearance of the town. On the contrary, our poverty only became worse. My second greatest mistake occurred during the flood when Guo Cunxian encouraged you all to take what food you could get from the fields before it all rotted. It's clear now that that was the correct action. Secretary Chen and I removed him from office for giving that order. That was wrong. In front of you all now, I wish to offer my sincerest apology to Guo Cunxian!"

He turned round and bowed deeply to Guo Cunxian, who hurriedly stood up to acknowledge it. Watching the apology unfold, the audience soon burst into applause.

The remaining agenda items were actually the most important. First, Liu Dajiang announced to everyone the selection that had been made in the morning: "The result of this morning's deliberations, as you should know, was unanimous. The village committee and production team leaders have elected Guo Cunxian as the new team leader for all of Guojiadian. Ou Guangming and Guo Cunyong will serve as deputy team leaders. Do you all approve? Please applaud if you all agree and welcome Guo Cunxian to give us a few words."

Again, Guo Cunxian seemed hurried, but not because he didn't have important things to say. In truth, there was much he wanted to speak about but he wasn't entirely sure this was the best time. The result was a more ad-hoc speech than what he had intended: "Thank you to the Party leadership and to you all for putting your faith in me. I wasn't expecting this in the least. Truly, in my deepest heart of hearts, this is a surprise. The roots, the foundation of our village are weak and we've squandered opportunities for many years but I will do my utmost to change that. I remember the winter when I was up here on this very stage, naked, being struggled against. I suppose, in a manner of speaking, I'm up here again. But, now, I have a request for all of you: you all know the trees guarding the entrance to the village. You know they've grown strong, that they've done nothing to make us turn on each other and that, in the past, none of us dared to call them by name. But then the Red Guards went and changed it, nonetheless. We didn't approve but I think that became a sort of illness that crept through Guojiadian, infecting all of us. Fortunately, today we have with us Comrade Feng. He's a learned, educated fellow. What do you think of us asking him to give the trees a new name?"

The audience roared in agreement: "Yes!"

"And it should be a properly auspicious name, too!"

Feng Hou rose from his seat: "These two trees are the symbol of Guojiadian. Once, they were two separate trees but over the past hundred years they've happily shared the soil and grown strong together. Perhaps it has even been several hundred years. If the opportunity arises, I shall have to get an expert to determine the case, for sure. Together, the two trees support and help each other, and they mutually yield to each other. I have to say, they're certainly an impressive sight! I'll say, too, that there are extraordinary people here, as well. Guo Cunxian's rapeseed homage to Chairman Mao is but one example. Today is a memorable day. We're not criticising anyone nor taking anyone down. No, instead we're announcing the selection of a new leader for Guojiadian. Heaven welcomes this news as do the land, the people and the trees. This is a day of great joy, of great happiness! And with great happiness come great expectations for the future. I think, therefore, that we shall rename the trees 'Lucky'. Formerly they brought boundless joy to Guojiadian, to the extent that whosoever came upon them would immediately see the good fortune they brought... you, me, everyone. So what do you think? Is it a suitable name?"

"Yes, yes indeed! It's an excellent name!"

They roared in unison: "Lucky Trees, Lucky Trees, Lucky Trees!"

Guo Cunyong announced that the meeting was adjourned and the production team leaders were dismissed. Each team, however, was required to select three sturdy, able-bodied labourers to remain behind.

Guo Cunxian gathered the workers together to deliver his first order as team leader for Guojiadian. A curious crowd stood some distance away, keen to hear what mission Guo Cunxian was to give them. Feng Hou had been around long enough and knew what Guo Cunxian was experiencing. He was also curious to see how Guo Cunxian would act now that he had been given such power.

For his part, however, Guo Cunxian seemed not to be overly concerned. His whole attitude had changed. He was firm, almost rough with the men he'd asked to stay behind: "Do you know why I've asked you to remain? I want you to dismantle this stage, immediately!"

None of the men had expected such an order and stood there in front of Guo Cunxian dumbfounded, unmoving.

Guo Cunxian spoke again, his voice betraying his growing agitation: "Tear it down, and if you run into trouble, then dammit I'll do it! What? You're not keen to do it? Well, if we don't tear it down the chaos caused by the rebel faction will never end. We won't be able to move on until it's gone. It needs to be taken down so we can put to rest the ghosts that linger here. To have peace and stability it must be destroyed. This is good land. We get a northerly wind during the winter and the summers are cool and breezy but this stage, well, it's like a dagger plunged deep into the pit of our stomach. But you know what? That's not even the most important reason. No, I need the wood. I'm going to exchange it for seeds. We've still got time to till the fields but to do that, we need something to plant: some maize, sorghum, black beans... If we wait any longer, it'll be too late, and if we're too late, well, I ask you, what will we eat, hmm? Will the whole village have to go and beg? Dismantle the stage and place the wood in the central buildings.

"Guangming, ensure there's someone to watch over it and then find out where there's a market open tomorrow. Wherever it is, we'll load the wood onto a cart and sell it there. Cunyong, you manage the project and the sale of the wood. You're the best talker among us. You'll be able to haggle for a better price. And make sure you take someone with you who'll be able to select the best seeds; someone like Han Jingting, Liu Yucheng or Guo Cunxiao. Any of them would be fine. Just make sure you come back with seeds. If you can't purchase enough, then I'll have to think of some way to borrow some and, if that doesn't work, I'll have to ask the county authorities to pay out the river reservoir allowance to supplement what we can buy ourselves. Do you all understand?"

"Yes sir!"

"Good, then get to it."

Without wasting another moment, the men began to dismantle the stage.

While they worked, Guo Cunxian continued to fill the rest of the production teams in on the details: "Why weren't men dispatched to work on the reservoir? Even the hard-line ones who went returned before too long, apparently because they were only paid work points instead of in cash. But work points are worthless shit, so who can blame them for that? If men aren't compelled to do the work, then they'll never develop their skills. From this moment on, I'm issuing a new directive: whoever heads off to work on the river, I assure them that the fruits of their labour will be delivered into their hands. Whether that's an allowance or food coupons, their households will be their unit, and that goes for work, food and money. The family will be in charge and I guarantee whoever goes to work on the river will be rewarded accordingly. Not only should we send a great number of men to the frog marshes, we want also to make sure they strive to excel at this engineering project. Our purpose is clear. We can't allow the salaries paid to be given to other villages. We've got the men, we've got the strength, we're only missing the money, but there's money to be had if we work for it!

"I've also heard from Comrade Feng that there's another way of making money in the county, too. About thirty or forty *li* to the east, there's an even bigger national engineering project that has started in Dahua, a great iron and steel manufacturing initiative. They need a huge number of workers so I'm going to dispatch men to establish links with it immediately. That's my plan. I'm dividing the work units into three contingents: one will remain in the village to sow the crops, one will work on the reservoir in the frog marshes, and the other one will be sent to Dahua to earn extra income. If you all agree, then start arranging things at once. If you don't agree, then let's discuss things some more right now. And whatever we decide, we'd better make sure to tell those who've got ready to hawk their wares, so to speak, that they need to stay. You've all seen it, haven't you? The authorities have grown increasingly agitated about people going out begging and they don't want it to continue. Tell anyone who still plans to go that they'll be facing prosecution when they return. Tell them, too, that the village head guarantees they'll have food to eat should they stay, whether from work on the reservoir project or from temporary work. Either way they'll be making money."

The year witnessed many new initiatives, which certainly provided no end of enjoyment for those who loved to watch the excitement. Good things were happening in Guojiadian. The commune had assigned five 'Beijing educated youths' to the village. There were two young men and three women, and while the boys went more or less unnoticed, the three girls got people's tongues wagging, especially among those families that hadn't been able to find wives for their sons. If they were able to arrange a marriage, especially to one in particular, a girl by the name of Lin Meitang whom everyone considered to be exceptionally pretty and healthy looking, whose skin seemed to glisten as though she'd just stepped out of the water, well...

It was rumoured the five youths had wound up in Guojiadian for a particular reason and not just by chance. Apparently, when the orders had first been given, there had been talk of sending them to Inner Mongolia or somewhere in the northeast. But because one of them had family connections somewhere, in the commune, with the county government or with some state organ in Beijing (who's to say?), they'd been sent down to Laodong County instead. Laodong, of course, wasn't all that far from Beijing, and if they ever felt homesick, they could fairly easily get a ticket and return, say, once or twice a year, or even every couple of months. The village provided them with lodgings, the boys in one room, the girls in the other, with a shared kitchen between them. For the first year they were provided with food by the central authorities but in the second they were required to more fully participate in the community and the work units they were assigned to. Guo Cunxian was in charge of this, so each of the educated youths was sent to a specific work unit. The youths themselves had no say in the matter, they simply obeyed. If Guojiadian were to receive additional educated youths, then they would summarily be assigned to the work units that hadn't yet received one.

Lin Meitang was assigned to the fourth work unit. This year in Beijing, the 'Up to the Mountains, Down to the Countryside' policy initiative specified that the eldest children would remain in the city and the younger ones would be dispatched to the countryside. Many were to be sent to the northeast while some were given the option to select a place themselves. For Meitang's family, it was her younger brother who was to be sent down but, because he had just begun his first year of high school, Meitang requested that she be sent in his stead. Reluctant at first, her parents eventually relented and her mother set about making arrangements and establishing connections, and ultimately had her daughter sent to the work units in Guojiadian. In any case, a poor peasant was a poor peasant and there wasn't much difference. Wherever she was to be sent she'd receive the same education. But Meitang could never have expected the difference would be so great. Her first year in Guojiadian was certainly a learning experience beyond comparison to anything she'd received up to this point in time.

She never thought the area surrounding Guojiadian could be so vast. She could walk for well over half an hour and still not encounter another village, not even another building. She was literally in the middle of nowhere. If they had to walk that distance every day, she'd be miserable indeed. Her mother had prepared cotton shoes for her but they soon felt as though they had nails in them. When she walked, it felt as though the balls of her feet and her heels had spikes driven into them. They were sore and aching, and waves of pain would work their way straight to her heart. Her pace slowed considerably. Soon she would find herself at the end of the line on a daily basis, trudging along with her hoe in hand, staggering on sore feet, her eyes searching longingly towards the east and west. She was desperate to find a building, bricks, a structure of any kind, but she saw nothing. Her only companion was the nails that continued to pierce her tired feet. She remained aloof from her work unit comrades, partly because of her shoes or, rather, because she refused to admit they hurt her feet and that she was afraid to talk to anyone for fear they might detect her discomfort. After all, she thought, it wasn't proper for a girl to cry out for help. Many of the young farmers wanted to strike up a conversation with her but none of them had the courage to start first. Instead they pretended not to look at her, even though they were. They weren't afraid of her. No, they were more afraid of the other men in the village gossiping about them and the jealousy they would no doubt encounter. So, instead, they talked among themselves, rambunctiously, pretending not to be interested in her. Perhaps this was the reason why there were so many bare sticks in Laodong. The boys were all much too naïve. That and the crushing poverty, of course.

As a result, the work unit would march along and Lin Meitang would fall farther and farther behind. No one would stop, nor would anyone take the initiative and turn around to try to help her. In their minds, the work didn't depend on her; what needed to be done was done. At most, she contributed very little at all, prone as she was to being so far behind them, swaying back and forth as she sang *yangge* melodies. Then one day something happened. A member of the work unit disgraced themselves in a most unspeakable manner that ultimately influenced the entire unit. They had been trudging through a particularly rough area and they were surrounded by great clods of muddy soil. In such terrain, Lin Meitang had no choice but to wear her shoes despite the constant pain they caused. It was at this moment she learnt what it really meant to be away from home, to be far away from family. She began to fathom how life on one's own often had a bitter and sour taste. It was much like in a novel, perhaps, one in which the heavens seemed to be deaf to the protagonist's desperate entreaties and the land unmoved by their cries, when all that was left for the character to do was to cry out mournfully. Of course, it was easy enough to count these moments for Lin Meitang. All she needed to do was to think of crying and her eyes would well up immediately and, before another second passed, her face would be wet. She wailed shamelessly and plaintively. Then something unexpected happened. Someone seemed to have heard her lament and had turned round. Closer and closer they came, making their way towards her.

The man who had turned round to walk towards her was none other than Guo Cunxian. In the past cadres studied and learned one thing at a time, from all directions, from back to front. Guo Cunxian's smarts came from the fact he'd grasped the lesson Chen Baohuai had provided him that one's uniform and rank didn't mean one should ignore the ordinary people under one's command. He never just whiled away the time in the central offices, nor did he just have Ou Guangming carry out his own duties and deal with the daily matters that arose. Ou Guangming was put in charge of public security and administrative duties, which meant he had to keep the peace and ensure no rebellious activities broke out. What, in the town, might disrupt the peace? What, in turn, needed to be guarded against? Well, perhaps not much at all, and if such was the case, Ou Guangming and his subordinates would simply be tasked with various odd jobs; there were always plenty of those.

Guo Cunxian had a great amount of freedom and flexibility in terms of the work he needed to do. In fact, he essentially did whatever he wished. If that meant carrying baskets of kindling, then that's what he did; or if it meant lugging around canvas sacks, then so be it. Today, several work units had been tasked with thinning out seedlings and preparing the land for cultivation. It was also the first day of actual work for the educated youths from Beijing. Guo Cunxian had already made the rounds to each work unit, ensuring that things were prepared for the work ahead. That's who Lin Meitang now saw walking towards her. She raised her head and wiped her eyes, and thought to herself that, even though he was coming towards her, he wouldn't actually do anything right away. No, he'd expect her to take the initiative and ask for help first. She and the other educated youths had been in the village for several days now and they had heard things about Guo Cunxian, about how 'Grandfather Guo' was a frightening fellow, thin and tall in stature with a dark and foreboding face. They had heard, too, how he didn't speak much. People would ask him several questions and get but a single sentence or perhaps only a single word in reply. Even stranger and more disconcerting was the fact he seemed to always have an axe ready to hand. When something needed to be chopped or pounded, the axe would appear. Perhaps the wicker basket he now carried over his shoulder held it, that oh so mysterious axe.

Guo Cunxian walked closer and closer, moving directly towards her. She couldn't remain silent and she couldn't hide, even though she wanted to, and the face she'd just raised to look at him, she now buried in her chest once more. The sun was behind him, allowing his frame to cast a tall, long shadow that seemed intent on swallowing her up entirely. But she didn't dare lift her head; she felt exceptionally lonely and isolated. A creeping sense of dread began to well up inside her. A deep, profound moment passed and then a coarse, hard voice spoke from above her head: "What's the matter? Why are you just sitting here?"

"My shoes have spikes in them. I'm looking for a brick or something to pound them down."

"Have you found one?"

"No."

"There aren't any in Guojiadian, you know."

Lin Meitang raised her face: "How's that? A village without bricks, is that even possible?"

"There's nothing that's impossible in this world. That's called poverty. If someone had said in the past they'd committed murder with a brick in Guojiadian, well then, they wouldn't pay with their life. If a man went to report it to the *yamen* [a government office in feudal China] or the county officials, they'd say the man was lying. That's because the officials knew there wasn't a brick or tile in all of Laodong that could be used to commit such an act."

"Then what's to be done? Is that why you carry an axe with you wherever you go?"

"You know about my axe, do you? Take off your shoes and let me see."

Lin Meitang removed her left shoe and gave it to Guo Cunxian. He held it in his hand, feeling its weight, and then seemed to laugh, curling his lips slightly: "The soles of your shoes are as thick as the hooves of an ass. Are you trying to frighten us poor peasants, hmm? Or did you expect to wear the same pair of shoes for the rest of your life?"

Lin Meitang didn't understand. Was she being criticised, ridiculed, restrained? Or was he showing concern?

Guo Cunxian put down his basket and tossed aside the shoe he'd been holding. He then turned and headed back towards the rest of the work unit that had continued to walk on in front. Lin Meitang craned her neck to look into the basket and there she spied, as she expected, the axe, glistening in the sunlight. She lifted it up, intending to pulverise the spikes in her shoe, but the butt of the axe wouldn't fit into the mouth of her shoe.

Guo Cunxian then returned, this time carrying a hoe in his hands and a small padded sole to place in her shoe. With the butt end of the hoe he attached the new sole and subsequently used his axe to bend down the spikes. It was all quite simple, quick and easy. His hands had moved efficiently, expertly. She would no longer have any trouble with her shoes. Having finished with the left shoe, he now asked for the right one to give it the same treatment. Once he had finished, he returned them to Lin Meitang. Job done.

While he fixed her shoes, Lin Meitang couldn't help but cut an extremely sorry figure. She knew her face was blushing a bright red but she didn't dare say anything nor even look at him. She'd not been down in the country all that long and already she'd caused trouble and not just with anyone but with the village head himself. She'd made him use his axe for her. Had she been fortunate or terribly unlucky? It was almost as though that frightening man had not actually fiddled with her shoes at all but, instead, had touched her own bare feet.

Guo Cunxian seemed not to notice her discomfort. He bent over and picked up his willow basket and the extra hoe he'd brought, and without making a sound he marched off in the direction of the rest of the work unit. When he failed to hear any signs of movement from behind him, he turned his head and saw Lin Meitang, still rooted to the spot, distracted as though she'd had her soul stolen. He shouted to wake her out of her stupor: "Come on, let's go!"

Her mind screeched at her, told her to move her feet, and slowly they did. After all, what was she going to do about it? There was no need for her to be so embarrassed, was there? He'd only repaired her shoes. What was so wrong with that?

11

ATTACKED ON ALL SIDES

G uo Cunyong was surprised to be named a deputy team leader for the village. His selection surprised the villagers as well, most lumping him in with the rest of the Red Guards such as Lan Xin and the other youths who had caused such disruption only a short time ago. Perhaps the authorities had issued some command or other requiring their representation on the new leadership committees, he couldn't be sure. Whatever the case may be, Guo Cunxian had put him in charge of engineering projects for both the commune and the county. The only problem was Guo Cunyong wasn't entirely sure what that meant, nor did he have a clue what projects the village might actually have. Just how in hell was he going to lead on this? He had no choice but to wait until Guo Cunxian was alone so that he could ask him for instructions: "Big Brother, you've given me responsibility over engineering projects but what are these exactly? How am I supposed to administer them?"

Guo Cunyong was about a head shorter than Guo Cunxian. The latter used his index finger to tap his young comrade's forehead and spoke to him in a jocular yet serious tone: "You know, you've grown up, haven't you? I remember when you were young, you once climbed up into one of the date trees to steal some dates but then you couldn't climb down. You started to cry out something fierce and terrifying. That's when I came upon you, solely by chance, too. I remember climbing up into the tree to help you down. You put both arms round my neck and promised to give me the dates you had stolen in your pocket. But as soon as you were safely on the ground, you took off and ran away. You didn't give me a single date."

Guo Cunyong blushed and played dumb: "Big Brother, don't bring that up, please."

Guo Cunxian replied in a more serious tone: "Cunyong, do you know there are three special qualities about you?"

Guo Cunyong shook his head. He wasn't sure where this was going.

Guo Cunxian used his hands to enumerate and explain: "First, you're young and quick-witted, you catch on fast. Second, you're brave, confident and unafraid. Third, you despise us peasants, you loathe the idea of tilling the land and only think about getting the hell out of here. Tell me I'm wrong."

Guo Cunyong felt as though a strip of flesh had been peeled off him. He felt exposed and raw: "If that's your opinion of me, why did you name me a deputy leader?"

Guo Cunxian's jocular demeanour had now disappeared completely. His face was rigid, which served to frighten Guo Cunyong: "I'm just trying to accentuate your stronger qualities and give you the opportunity to avoid more, shall we say, manual, farm-based labour. What's more, if you oversee these projects well, I'm sure you'll soon get the chance to leave Guojiadian. You've asked what these engineering projects are. Well, the work is quite easy. Now, give me your nose and lend me your ears. I want your fullest attention. In the past, such work was reserved for those who were quick-witted and resourceful. You know the type, they're able to size up a situation in a flash, analyse it from many different angles, from top to bottom, and always figure out a way to make some money. There are three specific things you need to do. One, you need to take charge of the water reservoir being constructed in the frog marshes. Two, you need to establish relations with the Dahua iron and steel factory so that we can dispatch a work unit or perhaps even take the lead on one aspect of the initiative. Three is nothing much but I want you to visit the various markets in nearby areas to evaluate them, so to speak. You know, take their pulse, and then I want you to report back to me. Understand?"

Guo Cunyong agreed with Guo Cunxian's assessment of him and aimed to validate the trust placed in him. He promised to himself that he wouldn't dare let him down but instead would act quickly and confidently, especially with regard to the first two tasks. He wanted to please the village head, that much was certain. Guo Cunxian was right about him: he hadn't grown up working the land and getting his hands dirty so where would he get such strength now if he was asked to till the land? And who would argue and say he wasn't one of the brightest bulbs in town? He was clever after all, particularly with regard to using his connections to persuade or intimidate others to get what he wanted. That's what he'd done when the Red Guards marched through the village and now he was going to do the same with Guo Cunxian's plans. Take the first initiative, for instance, the reservoir project. Even those who had been most unwilling to go to the river to work before had changed their tune; they were all clamouring to go now. That's because the village work unit would award them work points that could be exchanged for food rations in the autumn; some would even be able to make a little money. This was, of course, all connected to the authorities and their food distribution subsidies. Had it ever been so good before?

Once the necessary number of men was dispatched to the frog marshes, he'd have to quickly make arrangements and send men to the ironworks. Forty or so strong and strapping lads should be enough, he surmised. He wouldn't need to explain, either, what the work was, that didn't really matter. No, it was more important they had arms like tree trunks. Unfortunately, his plans hit a snag as no one volunteered, which was more than a little embarrassing for Guo Cunyong, especially since he couldn't identify a leader. He'd have to go and talk to Guo Cunxian about it. His response wasn't what he expected. He told him that, since he'd made the contacts with the ironworks, then he would have to lead.

Guo Cunyong was startled. Really, he asked? Was it Guo Cunxian's intention to toughen him up, by any chance? What about the other work he was supposed to do? Was he to give that up?

Guo Cunxian stared at him. Give it up? That's choice, hmph. Everything I've told you to do needs to be done. Telling you to lead isn't the same as telling you you need to be there working with everyone else, unless you'd rather spend your days at the ironworks? It means that every few days you go and check on things. The things that only you can do, well, you have to do them. You will just have to maybe draw them out a little bit. I'll help by assigning you an able-bodied assistant to oversee the daily work at the factory.

Guo Cunyong grinned and exclaimed that it was so far away, that he only had two legs and that it would be the death of him for sure if he had to keep going back and forth!

It was Guo Cunxian's turn to laugh and then something conveniently came to mind. It was true that the work unit had very little money and that Guo Cunxian himself had even less, so he told Guo Cunyong that whatever money he could make for the village, the first bit would be his to use to purchase a bicycle. After all, a bicycle was necessary for the job he'd been given.

Guo Cunyong seemed pleased by that and told his village head how thrilled he was to be working for him. His soon-to-be poor broken legs would feel the same. His concerns addressed, he set about marshalling the troops to head to the factory. Before taking his leave, however, he made sure to express his gratitude to Guo Cunxian. Then, just before departing, Guo Cunxian kept true to his word. He called out to Jin Laixi and asked him to step to one side, adding that the men would be his to take charge of once they were under way.

Jin Laixi was startled by the news and protested that he wouldn't be fit to assume such responsibility, worried that if something were to happen he'd not be able to deal with it!

A sombre look came over Guo Cunxian's face. He thought to himself, when had Jin Laixi ever been given responsibility for anything? Why was he now so reluctant? When he'd been brought up on the stage to be struggled against, Guo Cunxian had been there with him. That was all over with now. Guo Cunxian instructed Cunyong to make a mark next to his name; in practice, he would do what he was instructed to do. It was an opportunity, one that he couldn't let slip through his hands. In the end, with Guo Cunxian in charge of the village, would the heavens still fall?

Jin Laixi's face blanched and then turned crimson; he relented. Guo Cunxian gestured for him to return to the rest of the men but indicated that he should stand at the front. In a loud, clear voice, he said: "Take note, you're not simply temporary or migrant workers, you're the engineering squad for Guojiadian! You all know the plan, everyone gets equal shares, twenty-seven yuan per calendar month. Eighteen of that will be put to one side so you'll each get nine yuan and the one yuan left over will go to the work unit. The other nine yuan will be used to purchase work points and at the end of the year, these points can be exchanged for foodstuffs, one to one. To be honest, I've thought about all of this already. As team leader, besides earning money, what else is there to do? If one doesn't do the job, they'll rightly be cursed and blamed. Alright, alright, there's no point saying any more about this. I just have a question for you all. Do any of you know anything about architecture? Have any of you laid bricks?

"Fellow comrades, I can tell by the look in your eyes you don't understand what I'm getting at, do you? You've spent your whole lives in this village. Are you telling me you're not sure who has done what?" Guo Cunxian paused a moment and then answered his own question: "Do you mean to say none of you have a clue about bricklaying? Then let me make it clear here and now, Guo Cunyong is in charge of the engineering work unit." Again he paused, deliberately, trying to gauge the response of the audience but they reacted with indifference. He continued: "The deputy team leader is Jin Laixi!" The crowd immediately responded with astonishment, confusion and no small measure of discontent. Guo Cunxian, almost shouting over the hubbub he'd caused by his announcement, made it clear that if anyone had an opinion, now was the time to voice it.

The crowd grew silent once more.

Guo Cunxian's voice was stern: "I know what's on your minds, Jin Laixi's a rich peasant. But you need to understand something. His father was of that class, not him. Laixi's a worker like the rest of us, solemn and serious. Now, if someone wants to say they're better suited then speak now and the responsibility will be yours. Alright, I've got some things to say before you go. Once you leave here, you're representatives of Guojiadian, so take care not to stir up trouble with work units from other villages and don't do anything to cause disagreements between yourselves. I don't mean to sound blunt but should anything arise, just return to the village. We deal with our own issues ourselves, we don't air our dirty laundry in front of outsiders. I've given this responsibility to Jin Laixi, so I'm responsible for him. If anyone has anything to say, now's the time. Laixi, you listen too. If you don't want to take on this job, if you're afraid you'll botch it up or cause something bad to happen, well, it doesn't matter, I still want you to do it." He paused for a moment and then finished: "Fine, if no one has anything to say, then it's time for you all to set off. If any of you have a problem, then stay!"

Who would be willing to stay? Who would dare to do it? Guo Cunyong was quite pleased with how everything had turned out and stole a moment to give Guo Cunxian the thumbs up.

Before being completely dismissed, Guo Cunxian urged them all one final time: "Each and every one of you has a job to do, a role to play. Stay on track and, if you need to, think about what I've said."

Guo Cunyong added his own thoughts now: "And relax. Going to work for a big company is nothing like working on the reservoir. The work you'll do is clearly planned, all outlined in detail. You'll arrive today and start work immediately tomorrow."

His words were reassuring, and surprisingly prophetic, for this was exactly how things went. A few days later, Guo Cunyong was back in Guojiadian to report to Guo Cunxian. It was evening when he came up to his superior's door but he didn't go in. Somewhat mysteriously, he asked for Guo Cunxian to step outside instead. There in the courtyard, Guo Cunyong gave his report in a hushed, apprehensive tone.

"Big Brother, I've discovered something strange, but I can't make my mind up about it. I'll leave that to you."

"What is it?"

"I've visited quite a few markets and they all seemed to be selling animal skins, well, sheepskins and cowhides, most going for between seven and eight yuan, but the better ones even bringing in nine. Now guess how much a live sheep was going for in the same market? A fat one'll get you only eight *yuan* at most, the average-sized ones between six and seven, the smaller ones three or four. The meat's going for even less."

Guo Cunxian was puzzled: "That's odd. Shit, why would anyone buy just the sheepskin when buying a live one is cheaper?"

"I don't have an answer for you. It's mad, that's what it is. I reckon those buying the skins must be from a leather factory. I mean, they're all state-run. I suppose there's no way to properly settle an account for a live animal, no way for them to process the meat, and regardless of whether or not they ate it themselves, I mean, they'd still have to sell it, wouldn't they. And that's wrong, isn't it? The same skewed pricing was true for the cowhides, too. An average skin was eighty-five yuan whereas a live cow was eighty. I just don't understand it."

"Could you tell if the people buying the skins came from the county or from the city?"

"Definitely from a prefecture-level city. For sure a place much bigger than Kuanhe."

"If we sent skins as well, would they be willing to buy?"

"Yes, for sure. They were buying whatever they could get their hands on!"

"Where's the market for tomorrow?"

"Zhangzhuang. It's a big one."

"Later on I want you to inform Han Wulin about this. He used to be the village butcher, pigs mostly. He could even neuter them if you wanted. Tell him I want him to bring his tools and to make sure they've been sharpened. Then get what's-his-name. We'll need a cart. Oh, and find five planks. In the morning I'm going with you."

"Are you really going to do it?"

"Why, do you think I'm pretending? The whole village is on the edge, we've got nothing. We have to seize any and all opportunities that come our way and once we have hold of them, we can't let go. I'm going to write a letter to Wang Shun, too. He's an expert at these sorts of things."

"Big Brother, there might be a problem. You need money to get a stall for the market. Didn't you say we were broke?"

Guo Cunxian laughed sheepishly: "Oh, we need money, do we? Well, I guess that's to be expected. You need money to make money after all, right?"

Guo Cunxian sucked on his teeth for a spell, then suddenly stiffened and marched back inside. He returned holding a few sheets of paper and a fountain pen. He sat down at the dinner table, told Guo Cunyong to shine his torch so he could see what he was doing, and then began to write a loan request. Before he had two words on the page, however, he stopped, raised his head and looked at Guo Cunyong: "Who's the head of your family. Your uncle or your auntie?"

"My father of course," replied Guo Cunyong, trembling a little, unsure of what Guo Cunxian had planned. "What are you thinking about doing?"

"I'm thinking about borrowing some money. What else can I do?" It didn't take him long to write his request and when he had finished, he read it out loud, checking to make sure he'd written everything he needed to: "Uncle, our village intends to open an abattoir but lacks the capital to begin the project. I'm therefore requesting you lend us fifty yuan. In three months' time, we'll double your investment and return to you a hundred yuan. If you wait until the end of the year, it'll be three hundred yuan." On the reverse he signed his name: "Village head, Guo Cunxian."

He then gave the loan request to Guo Cunyong, who was troubled by what his superior had written: "Big Brother, may I try something myself? Do I really have to ask my family?"

"You need the money, I need the money. Do you know what they say about that? It's like two grasshoppers bound by one rope: you're not able to run and I'm not able to jump. But if we fight like our lives depended on it, we can only succeed and not lose any money!"

Guo Cunxian instructed Cunyong to look over the loan request he'd written, and then told him to write one of his own but address it to 'Sun Yueqing', Guo Cunxian's mother. He was to copy the request word for word but to sign his own name at the bottom instead. Once they had finished writing both letters, Guo Cunxian dispatched his subordinate to find Ou Guangming so that they could be officially stamped, and then proceeded to wait for his return. After he came back with both letters freshly stamped, he directed Guo Cunyong into his mother's room.

Sun Yueqing had yet to go to sleep, even though she'd been lying down for quite some time already. In fact, she was busy stitching a pair of tiger shoes for her grandchild. She'd been working on them for quite a while but it wasn't as though her grandson was waiting to wear them. It was more a question of her having to keep busy and giving herself something to do. If her hands were idle, she'd start to worry, fret and end up tying herself in knots. It was Guo Cunxian who interrupted her train of thought: "Mother, the work unit has decided to open an abattoir. Cunyong would like to make a request for some money, to help with setting things up: about fifty yuan. It would be returned in three months."

"So much!" was her startled response. "You'll waste that for sure. Just what's this talk about an abattoir?"

Guo Cunxian knew his mother had a keen, quick mind, so he stepped into the conversation now, trying to support their request. Sun Yueqing sighed heavily. She'd worked hard to save up what she had. The idea of lending it for what she thought was a dubious plan didn't sit well with her at all. "You're asking too much of me, you know. This cuts to the quick. The money is supposed to be for Cunzhi's wedding."

Guo Cunyong saw an opening and interjected: "Please, auntie, rest assured if something goes wrong and his wedding's delayed, I'd be willing to forego my own marriage and make sure Second Brother has a wife first."

"Rubbish! Don't talk nonsense. Your future bride is still running round the legs of her mother!"

She cursed and raged some more. Guo Cunxian knew there was nothing for it. He took hold of Cunyong, ushered him towards the door and told him to wait outside.

. . .

The area for the planned reservoir had been transformed into a deep pit. Because of the depth they had dug to, the wind no longer blew through the construction site, meaning the humidity was trapped near the ground. When the sun blazed, the area was oppressive and the workers barely able to breathe. The reservoir base was uneven with dips and rises throughout, and everywhere flag markers poked out of the ground, little wooden posts wedged in every which way painting a white line across the earth. The commune had assigned each village an area to work on, and within each, the village authorities divided the area further, assigning each family work unit a spot to focus on. There was a great deal of work to do but the energy behind much of the workforce was equally great. For some, this resulted in swift progress and some family units had already been able to return home, their work completed. For other units that lacked the same degree of vigour, they still had work to do. Unfortunately for them, their pace only seemed to go in the wrong direction, meaning their work fell farther and farther behind, and became increasingly arduous in the process. The earth also conspired against them as it became ever more damp and heavy, even spurting out running water in some places which, in turn, amplified the work required to remove it.

Of course, in situations like these there were always a few men who seemed entirely unconcerned about the work and the corresponding difficulties, men who could even find joy in it, find the bright spot in a dark sky, as it were. A young lad from Wangguantun spotted and managed to snag a frog, a big one, and yelled in delight as he pinched it between his fingers. The frog croaked incessantly to be free. A few others winked mischievously at another young man, a bare stick by the name of Liu San, before pouncing on him and pulling down his pants. They were going to give him the chance to fuck the frog.

"How was it?" they demanded.

Liu San wasn't the cleverest but he knew if he remained silent they'd never let him go. He answered as honestly as he could: "It felt cold, like clammy noodles." The young men roared with laughter. Some were egged on by his honesty and began to repeat his refrain: cold and clammy like noodles... shit! Liu San just fucked a frog!

During this raucous scene, an older man from Mapodian, Cui Liang, had been in the midst of pushing a barrow full of earth when it had tipped over, pinning his right leg underneath. No one could be sure what had happened. Whether he'd been distracted by the riotous nature of the younger men or if he'd slipped, in either case, he hadn't been able to evade the wheelbarrow and now his leg seemed crushed beneath it. Mapodian had begun their work fairly early and most of the man's fellow villagers had already finished and gone home. The only person working alongside Cui Liang was Liu Yucheng from Guojiadian, who heard the man yell out and raced over. He set to work freeing the man's leg from beneath the wheelbarrow, finally succeeding and pulling him to one side. Cui Liang's eyes were shut, his skin sweaty and cold to the touch, and for a long while he seemed not to be breathing. Finally his eyes opened and he mouthed the words to Liu Yucheng: "Thank you, little brother Liu."

Liu Yucheng moved his arms up and down the man's leg to feel if it was broken.

As his hand touched Cui Liang's knee and calf, the man winced in severe pain, his whole body trembled and his breathing quickened. It was broken, of that Liu Yucheng was certain. Since he was by himself and wouldn't be able to work with such a lame leg, Liu Yucheng asked him if he'd like him to take him home. Of course, they would first have to find the village doctor so he could have a proper look at the man's leg and, if that didn't work, they'd have to go to the county hospital.

There wasn't much choice but still Cui Liang shook his head and breathed in hard: "That's too much, you needn't trouble yourself. Besides, the work will be delayed should you leave and we can't have that."

"Ha, I've heard that more than once before!" Liu Yucheng pushed Cui Liang's wheelbarrow back onto the main path, propped it up against a mound of earth and returned to the older man. Slowly, he helped him up and into the wheelbarrow, made a makeshift splint for his leg and then stepped behind the handles and began to push. Cui Liang, sitting uncomfortably in the wheelbarrow, was also perturbed at what Liu Yucheng had done and felt the younger man had made his leg worse with such a shoddy splint which, in turn, would only delay his recovery. Liu Yucheng himself was concerned about something entirely different. His sister was due any minute now with his lunch. He couldn't recall how many times he'd told her he'd bring his own lunch. The bastards that worked here, shit, they'd see a young woman and lose all control and decorum, spewing forth all kinds of obscenities. He didn't want his sister Yumei to endure that sort of treatment. Such language would scar her. But Yumei wouldn't hear of it. Everyone was working at something and this was her responsibility, she thought… let the men say what they wanted… he just had to ignore it. She'd be here any minute, he thought. Would she be worried when she didn't see him?

It was only about ten *li* or so to Mapodian from the frog marshes, but pushing a man in a wheelbarrow, someone who weighed a couple of hundred *jin* at least, to say nothing of the weight of the wheelbarrow itself, coupled with the uneven terrain, well, it was heavy enough to kill even the strongest man. Despite the difficulties, however, Liu Yucheng persevered and before he felt all that tired, he'd arrived at Mapodian. Strangely, however, once they came upon Cui Liang's fellow villagers to ask after the doctor, Cui Liang played down the fact he'd broken his leg, suggesting that it was only sprained instead.

Puzzled at his demeanour, Liu Yucheng asked: "Uncle Cui, what's your social status?"

His response was equally odd for he ended up asking himself what class he was before confirming, to some degree, that he was a poor peasant.

"That's the best then," Liu Yucheng offered in reply. "So why won't you be honest about how seriously you're hurt?"

"Ai, it's difficult to say. I'll try to explain once we're inside."

Cui Liang's home wasn't much, just a single old room with a small cooking area attached to the side; not a proper kitchen at all. As they rumbled up to the door, the older man's daughter heard the commotion and raced outside. Once she saw her father she panicked, called out his name and attempted unsuccessfully to help him out of the wheelbarrow. Her voice alternated with worry and questions about what had happened. By the looks of her she was in her early twenties or thereabouts, skinny, malnourished and with a voice that inspired pity. Cui Liang tried to console his daughter, telling her it was nothing, that he'd been careless, that the wheelbarrow had toppled over on his leg and that the most unfortunate one was Liu Yucheng who'd been so inconvenienced by his carelessness. He then told her to fetch some warm water for their guest.

Liu Yucheng was silent. He slowly pushed the wheelbarrow and propped it safely against the wall. Wrapping his arms around the older man's waist, he lifted him gently up onto his back and brought him inside. The room contained a raised bed and nothing else but it was exceptionally clean. Liu Yucheng placed Cui Liang on the bed in a sitting position with his back against the wall. This would be better for his injured leg, too. He urged him once more to seek treatment. His leg was seriously hurt and he had to pay attention to it, otherwise it would only get worse and if it became infected somehow, then he'd lose it for sure.

Cui Liang heaved a sigh. The village doctor was a useless crank who couldn't treat even the most minor problems and, for those that were more serious, he just told people to go to the commune to seek help. Cui Liang continued: "And where do I have the money for that, huh? I've got other worries too, you know. If the village authorities learn about my injury and my inability to work, the work I've already done will be a complete waste, I won't get anything for it. If that happens, what will my daughter and I eat?"

A great sense of worry and desperation hung in the room.

His daughter interrupted the silence: "Should I go and find my brother?"

Cui Liang's eyes grew hard: "Don't you dare! Even if I were at death's door I still wouldn't let you go and find that bastard!"

Liu Yucheng, embarrassed by the older man's vitriol towards his son, tried to alleviate the tension by saying there was a wise old man in Guojiadian and that perhaps he'd be able to think of something. He said he could go and get him and bring him back this evening, that is, of course, if the wise man had some way of treating his leg. Liu Yucheng then told him not to worry about the reservoir work, saying there were only eighty to a hundred cordoned-off sections remaining for him to do and Yucheng could do that for him. Just tell anyone who asks, Liu Yucheng insisted, that you have completed the work already. This way he wouldn't lose out when the village sorted out payment for work done. After saying what he had to say, there wasn't time for a proper goodbye, so he turned round quickly and left. Once out on the road, he quickened his pace, running back to the reservoir. There was work to do.

From far off he could see Yumei waiting for him, looking anxiously in all directions. He hurried his pace and by the time he returned, the sweat was pouring off him. Yumei was not a little annoyed. She interrogated him, asked him where he'd been and rebuked him for causing her to fret. In between breaths, Liu Yucheng replied: "Don't ask. Old Cui Liang hurt his leg. I reckon it's broken. I had to take him home."

Yumei passed him a towel to wipe the sweat that still drenched his face before they sat down together to eat what was a very simple, basic lunch. After eating, Liu Yucheng wasted little time before getting back to work. Yumei helped with the work, shovelling what she could, which wasn't all that much, if the truth be told. Every day passed in this manner. They'd work until evening, with Yumei leaving a little before her older brother so that she could prepare his dinner. Liu Yucheng would always remain a bit longer to get a little more work done. When there wasn't a moon, he'd stop at sundown, unable to see the trench he was digging. If the moon shone, however, he'd work until his muscles cried out for him to stop. His stomach would rebel with hunger and his waist would protest at being bent over for so long; then he'd stop. He didn't want to be struggled against like before so working until he could work no more seemed a fair exchange to avoid that.

In the afternoon while they worked, neither talked about where Yucheng had been or what he had done. Then suddenly Cui Liang's daughter appeared with the wheelbarrow. She was certainly a sight, not much taller than the wheelbarrow she was pushing, and by the looks of it, she'd never pushed one before in her life. She struggled mightily with it, tumbling back and forth over the uneven path, her arms and face were mottled green and purple, her hair wet and matted, her greenish trousers and grey upper garment were soaked with sweat as though she'd just been dredged up out of the water. The poor girl had grown up quite emaciated and weak, and this was the main reason Cui Liang had never made her go out and work. All she ever did was fetch the water and the dried foodstuffs when needed. She had no idea that the earth she was walking on and tumbling over was the land her father had been working on. As she approached, she waved in greeting and began to ask them what they were doing. Liu Yucheng gestured at the scene in front of her and then told her they were halfway through digging up a small mountain. Her brow creased and her lips pursed, she seemed to be deep in thought, weighing his words carefully. Even over a lifetime of digging there was just no way they could remove all of the soil. She remained silent, chewing her bottom lip, then, after a moment passed, she picked up the shovel and started digging. She didn't dare load too much earth into the wheelbarrow, afraid she wouldn't be able to push it. So back and forth she went with a half-full barrow in front of her each and every time. She spent as much time digging as on wheeling the cart, over and over again, shifting the soil beneath her.

After watching the spectacle several times, Liu Yumei had had enough and raced over to help her, finally pushing the empty cart back to where she'd been digging. She spoke to break the awkward silence between them: "I'm Liu Yumei, over there, that's my brother. Should I call you Older Sister or Younger?"

"My name's Cui Lan, I'm twenty-three."

"You're older than me, so I guess I call you Older Sister. I'm twenty-two. Is there no other man in your family that could do the work?"

"Just my bastard brother, but that's complicated."

Surprised at what she'd heard, Yumei couldn't help but ask: "Why did you say that?"

"Eh, don't ask. It happened when there was little food to eat and when things were really difficult. Well, he was starving so badly, we all were, but he broke down, unable to endure it any longer and ate a month's worth of food all by himself. Mum hit him then but he hit her back, with the handle of a hoe, right on the side of her head. She'd been starving worse than the rest of us. She didn't even have the chance to swallow a breath of air before she died."

Cui Lan's face was wet with a mixture of sweat and tears. Her story was tragic. And reason enough to sever all contact with her brother. Liu Yumei also felt her heart grow heavy; she was pained by what she had heard. After a little while passed, she spoke: "Working like this won't solve anything, and working yourself to death won't help either. Besides, there's no guarantee you'll be recognised as a model worker or anything. Who knows, you might face censure by your village for not finishing the work and if that happens, well, then the chicken has really flown the coop and not only will you not get what's yours, you might even end up being punished."

Cui Lan hadn't really thought things over like this. She only thought she'd better try to finish the work her father was responsible for, just so that they could get their yearly rations. After listening to Liu Yumei, however, she had no idea what to do.

"Sister Cui Lan, if you won't be offended, I do have an idea I'd like to share."

"Look at me. Do I look like someone who should be offended by anything? It's more that other people find me offensive."

"If we work together, you and I shovelling and my brother wheeling the dirt out of here, then we'll both be finished much more quickly and, more important, we'll be on time. But there's one thing I have to say. Our father was a landlord and if you cooperate with us, it's likely to get peoples' tongues wagging. There could be all kinds of gossip and they're liable to lump you together with us which might even make matters worse."

"That's right. I knew I recognised your family name. But look around you, we're surrounded by poor peasants, aren't we? And they can already see I've supposedly transgressed social boundaries by simply standing here. Tell me, when my dad hurt himself, who helped him? It wasn't any of them, it was your brother. That's who brought him home. There are many poor peasants in Mapodian and when each of them finished their work, did any come to help my father complete his? No, they all went home, that's what they did. From the moment my mum died to my father being hurt here today, I haven't received one nice, comforting word from any of them. Don't talk about your father being a landlord or that you're some kind of bandit. When I needed your help, you gave it and for that I'm incredibly grateful. We women rely on our noses. One sniff and we can tell whether someone's got a good heart or not." The more she spoke, the less she was able to contain her emotions and suddenly she burst out crying.

The entire atmosphere of Guojiadian was transformed. It seemed a strong wind could blow its aroma for miles.

What flavour? Well, during the day, a rank odour of beef and mutton hung over the town. In the east of the town, a row of shacks had been constructed to house the cows, sheep and even some donkeys that had 'come from far away'. What did that mean? Well, these were the animals Wang Shun had purchased and brought with him and he, along with Han Wulin and Old Fatty, were responsible for slaughtering them. While the animals waited for their imminent demise, they had to be fed and provided for, hence the shacks. If any of the beasts took the eye of one of their caretakers, then perhaps they'd be given to that person, a reprieve of sorts from the abattoir's blade. In the evenings, Wang Shun and his crew would get to their bloody work and then the meat would be brought to market in the morning. The skins, however, would be sent to the leather factory in Juedian. Every day was much the same: before Wang Shun and his men returned from the market to slaughter the next batch of animals, the livestock would listlessly wander and lie about in the shacks, some cooing and making other noises, others weeping silently.

Then in a split second, a pungent, thick, rank odour would filter its way through the town. If there was a westerly wind, the villagers would be happy as it would carry the stench off to a neighbouring community. If the wind blew from the east, however, then the smell would linger, the cost of engaging in such business. Evenings had taken on a gory rituality, with rivers of blood flowing daily from the eastern parts of Guojiadian. Their poor old crazy uncle couldn't stand the sight of such a messy endeavour and soon set upon trying to alleviate it as best he could. Every morning he'd get up early and head out to the fields and stroll about for hours, filling a basket full of soft grass each time. This he would bring to the animal shacks and then spread it among the poor beasts of burden; he wanted them to meet their end on a full stomach at least. Later on, he improved the walls of the shacks, packing new dirt along the base so that the blood would no longer stream out and inundate the town. Once he'd fixed the enclosure, he then dug up the stained earth, piling it high in morose fashion and then carting it off. Most of it he buried near the Trees, which ended up benefitting greatly as the soil around their roots became even more fertile. At the same time, he gave the abattoir workers a new layer of fresh, unbloodied soil to tread on. The old man performed this service daily, which made Cunzhi worry greatly that he was working himself to death. Understanding that his mad old uncle would not stop, he brought several carts from the frog marshes reservoir to at least lighten the workload a little.

Afterwards, the aroma wafting through Guojiadian was less pungent and smelled more of a delicious offal stew instead of a blood-soaked abattoir. At the base of the Lucky Trees in the western part of the town, a dozen or so wooden benches had been arranged. Alongside the benches three great pots bubbled and boiled, the fragrant scent of mutton and offal wafting heavily around them. Many of the villagers believed that Wang Shun had brought the seasoning for the offal stew from Damu Hui Autonomous Region, the specialty of some famous old restaurant or other; at least, that was the reason for its distinct and unique flavour. Wang Shun would, however, always leave the last bit of the stew in the pot to ensure the next batch would taste the same and, in any case, the more the offal was stewed, the more fragrant it became. Every day he'd be there stirring the broth and the entrails, and every day people would come from near and far, bowls in hand, eager to slurp it down.

Wang Shun was also skilled at exhorting others to come and try: "Ai! You'd better buy it quickly and try it before it's gone. It's a recipe handed down from olden times using nothing but the freshest meat. There's nothing else like it. If you miss out, you've never really lived."

His excited sales pitch and the offal stew went hand in hand. People would eat the offal, drink the soup and listen to his refrain. It was all quite addictive and well worth it, too! He only had to open his mouth and people would holler in reply: Yes indeed, I'll 'ave another! Over and over again, Wang Shun displayed his gift of the gab, belting out his catchphrases and luring people in to eat. He soon had his own chorus, too. Men standing just outside cheered him on, playing a vital role in attracting more and more people. Before long, he took to tapping the ladle on the pots, ratcheting up the level of his performance: ding, ding, dang.

Ding, ding, dang;
Don't forget your mum once you've found a wife.
All young wives love to eat offal.
Mums love the idea of drinking soup,
Only five cents'll get you a bowl.

You could make the whole family smile and be happy for such a pittance? Yes indeed, it was that cheap. If you talked about a bowl, for outsiders the cost was three cents, for the residents of Guojiadian, it was two and after ten at night. If there was any left, there was a free bowl for whoever wanted one. Had they returned to the communal canteens of the Great Leap Forward? Just about, because selling the animal hides returned all of their investment; the stew was simply surplus and not for making money. Did people from other villages really come to purchase the stew? Not only did they come but the numbers grew greater and greater, such was the power of word of mouth. They all came, young and old, and once they'd had a bowl of offal stew, nice and warm, so much better than a simple steamed bun, well, it was no wonder that Wang Shun's fame spread. It was addictive. Even going a few days without it became difficult; one's tummy craved it. The people of Guojiadian had lived a countless number of poor lifetimes; destitution and decline was just how it was, they'd resigned themselves to that, but eating the mutton stew brought a renewed vigour, a renewed robustness to the whole town!

Gradually, Wang Shun's makeshift kitchen was transformed into the centre of activity for Guojiadian's residents. Even on hot days with pockets hardly overflowing with change, in the evenings they would find themselves there. And if they were broke, well, it didn't really matter, the aroma was free. Besides, it wasn't as though Wang Shun was an insensitive lout. If someone came with nothing but an empty bowl, he wouldn't let them go home empty-handed; after all, he knew what it was like to starve. He'd experienced it himself since nearly the day he was born. Now that he had a little more, if he didn't look after his poor fellow peasants, who would? It was comparable to what it was like in the old days when the wealthy landlord would occasionally arrange a communal meal of porridge for those less well off, except, of course, that Wang Shun was giving them meat and not just gruel, which was much better for a strong constitution, especially a man's!

Others began coining ditties as well, and so did Shopkeeper Wang.

In fact, Wang Shun greatly enjoyed this. He was able to work and prattle on:

Sticky steamed buns and mutton stew,
A full belly and a fragrant aroma for your nose, too.
A bowl for the boss with nothing expected in return,
I say, isn't it heaven beneath our Lucky Trees?

There were shouts of agreement and some tapped their bowls: how about some vegetables!

Always quick with his tongue, Wang Shun replied: "I'm selling a meat stew, who the hell said anything about being vegetarian?"

"Alright then, be vegetarian I suppose, but I can't promise there won't be some hint of offal and mutton in your bowl."

"That's easy to take care of. Now listen, everyone, I'll tell you a story. There's a carob tree in Guojiadian, right? A Chinese scholar tree that shifts in the wind to watch the arrival of officials. Mothers are given to asking their unmarried daughters, 'What are you looking at?' Are they waiting to watch the tree flower? It's a small tree, you know, it flowers something beautiful. A stage is set up just beneath its branches for all the young wives to come to but I ask you, is there someone for me?"

"Are you married, Wang Shun?"

"Nah, not yet."

"But you're a man of certain skills. Why haven't you found a wife?"

"Shit, it's my foul mouth. What family would marry their daughter off to an oaf like me, huh? And what about this stench that clings to me now? Fuck, you can smell me a mile away and people do, then they start running, heh, heh."

His self-deprecation sparked smiles and gentle laughter among his patrons. While many had come for the stew, many others hadn't. No, they'd simply accompanied friends, come to see the show and hear the latest gossip. Others would linger even longer and end up playing Chinese chess under the light of lanterns or sing various verses from local dramas. Some dared to try their hand at Peking opera. Wang Shun's kitchen became the town's restaurant, a place to meet family, make friends, talk business and find a wife. Everyone eventually found their way there.

It was into this relaxed scene that Jin Laixi had purposefully returned from the metalwork factory and, by the looks of him, he had something serious on his mind. After all, he hadn't first gone home but rather went directly to see Guo Cunxian. Despite the seeming urgency, however, Guo Cunxian didn't give him the chance to open his mouth. Instead, he grabbed two flat cakes, turned to his mother to ask for four cents, and then gestured for the younger man to follow him towards the Lucky Trees. There they found a clean and quiet place to sit. Jin Laixi was surprised at the transformation; he'd only been gone for a few months. Where had this entire hubbub come from?

Guo Cunxian put the four cents down on Wang Shun's long table: "Shopkeeper, two bowls of offal stew. In one give us a little less meat and more broth."

"Right away!" Wang Shun hurried over with two bowls of stew and placed one in front of each of them. Then he said in a low voice: "Big Brother, you've got to assign me some help. I'm working myself to death from morning until night. I barely have a chance to even blink I'm so busy."

Guo Cunxian swallowed a mouthful of the soup and sunk his teeth into the flat cake. He chewed eagerly, savouring the flavour, before bursting out laughing: "Hey, it's really quite something. Delicious. Is it really an old secret family recipe, passed down through generations?"

"If I'm lying, I'll give you back your money! Hey, don't slurp it all down so quickly. Did you hear what I just said?"

"Ho ho, you need some help, an extra body to do some work, heh? Let me tell you, the whole village is short-handed but not just short of men. It's best if you find someone yourself. Once you do, just let me know and I can make it official. I've thought of a name for your factory, too. You've said before, right, there's nothing else like it. I think that should be it, that's the name: 'There's nothing else like it.' From tomorrow onwards, when you go to market to sell the meat, you need to have a shop sign with you. On top write 'There's nothing else like it', and on the bottom write 'Guojiadian'. That'll let everyone know where your shop is, and also that there's nowhere else like here!"

"Sure, that's not a bad name, it kind of roles off the tongue, I'll give you that! Hey, brother, you know who I've been thinking about lately?"

"Who?"

"That cripple from Xinzhuang. Old Qiang, wasn't it? He could size up livestock like no one else, even tell its fortune just by looking at it. If he were here to help me, well, it would certainly make my life a hell of a lot easier."

"You know, I've been thinking about him too, lately. Old Qiang must really be getting on now but, you know, he's got family to look after. How could he drop all that and come here? Why don't you write to him and ask? I wonder how old Fugen is now? If he has graduated and has nothing to do, then perhaps he could come. I could give him some work to do."

"OK." Wang Shun couldn't stay any longer and chat, there were too many customers to take care of.

Before leaving, Guo Cunxian added: "Shopkeeper, I think you ought to be a little more generous, huh? Stop charging different prices to outsiders. It should all be the same for everyone, alright? You're a food factory, after all. Can't you be a little more magnanimous?"

Wang Shun deliberately put on airs before responding: "Sure, sure, let's talk about it later."

"So, is something wrong?" Guo Cunxian finally directed his attention towards Jin Laixi, who had been sitting silently watching the exchange between the two men.

"I've come up with a good idea. I want to see what you think of it, if you'd be willing to…" He hesitated, hoping to build suspense, as well as Guo Cunxian's interest.

Staring, Guo Cunxian interrupted the silence: "Speak!"

Perhaps the offal stew had given him greater nerve. His eyes seemed to sparkle and he even undid the top buttons of his jacket. Then, in a low voice dripping with mystery, he finally continued: "The ironworks are in the midst of putting things together. As you know, it's a huge project that's going to transform the country and make us a steel kingdom, I tell you. Well, to build the actual factory they're planning to use bricks and I was thinking, we've been removing so much earth as we dig the frog marsh reservoir, if we were to construct an earth kiln to make bricks and then sell them on to help build the ironworks factory, well, that'd be great for Guojiadian!"

Guo Cunxian's eyes lit up as he listened: "Can it be done? I haven't a clue about firing a kiln to make bricks, to say nothing of the fact that there are probably people in Guojiadian who've never even seen a brick."

"Well, the easiest factory to build is one made of bricks, that's for sure, and I know I could make the kiln. Then all you'd need to do is send Guo Cunyong to find an expert, someone from far away. Ask him to look for someone beyond the county limits. Once he has found someone, they could come back and teach us how to do it."

"What about the cost? How much of an upfront investment would we need?"

"Ah, I've already thought about that. I don't think it's a big problem. We could request the ironworks to pay us a year in advance. I've already mentioned this to them and they seem willing. You just need to come in person to vouch for what we're planning, as the village head, you understand. Afterwards, we could use the same approach you and Guo Cunyong used to set up the abattoir, a high-interest loan, but not from people outside the village. We've got to keep this opportunity for our own people, so we'll ask them to put up the money. The other men from Guojiadian working with me at the ironworks all understand the plan, too. They're happy for their salaries to be deferred if they see that they'll be doubled at the end of the year."

Guo Cunxian tipped the bowl of stew into his mouth and drained it completely. His eyes turned in the direction of Wang Shun and he shook his bowl: "Could you add a little more broth?" Then, in a quieter voice, he spoke to Jin Laixi: "To decide on this, I need to go to the office and get Guangming and Cunyong to come. We'll need to think of a plan."

As they were about to depart, Liu Yucheng raced up towards them and in a reverential tone directed a question at Guo Cunxian: "Team Leader, I need to find your uncle. It's quite urgent. He's not at home nor is he here. Where could he be?"

Liu Yucheng's nervousness upset Guo Cunxian and made him feel ill at ease. There were so many people all round, he couldn't help but think his overly timid behaviour was nothing but a show for the men working. He massaged his head and spoke at the same time: "I'm truly sorry but Wang Shun has created such a hubbub, chaos even, that my poor old uncle can't bear to come here. Have you seen Cunzhi?"

"No, I haven't. If I had, I wouldn't be bothering you."

Something came to Guo Cunxian's mind: "Try the small wooded area to the north. He planted all of it. He might be there."

"Small wooded area? What are you talking about?"

"It's right next to our family allotments. My uncle and I secretly planted trees there right at the edge of the field marking its border. They're saplings now. If you have time, you should plant some yourself, it doesn't matter what kind of tree."

"Ah... I know where you mean." He turned and headed northwards. The moon was shining brightly, bathing the evening in light. It wasn't much darker than in the day. When Liu Yucheng finally came upon the personal allotments, he soon spied Guo Cunxian's uncle there, as expected, nestled at the base of a small tree, fast asleep. Cunzhi's jacket was draped over him as a blanket, with Cunzhi standing bare-chested beside him. Liu Yucheng walked up and spoke in a low voice to the younger man: "I should've known the two of you would be together. I've been looking for him and now I've found both of you."

Cunzhi acknowledged that that was often the case these days; his uncle couldn't be left to his own devices. He then asked if Liu Yucheng minded letting him sleep a little.

"Why doesn't he go home and sleep?"

"Who knows? Perhaps he just can't sleep at home. It looks like something's bothering you, huh?"

"That's true, I do have a something quite urgent I wanted to ask your uncle about, but he seems to be sleeping so peacefully. Shit, how can I disturb him?"

"Well, why don't you bother me with it first?" Suddenly, Cunzhi's crazy old uncle stood up, shook the jacket he'd been given and returned it to his nephew. He ordered them abruptly: "You need to go and get me leaves from the Dragon Phoenix Trees." He never asked why Liu Yucheng had come looking for him. He simply put his head down and marched off towards the village. Liu Yucheng came up beside him and told him how old Cui Liang from Mapodian had hurt himself. Cunzhi's uncle seemed to be only half listening. He didn't say a word in reply. They came upon his house and he went directly into his room to get a cloth bag. On the wall, grass of all kinds had been hung to dry. He pulled a clump down, shook it a little and then deposited it in the bag.

Cunzhi returned shortly thereafter with the leaves his uncle had asked for which were deposited in the bag as well. He then went into his mother's room to say hello, before accompanying Liu Yucheng and his uncle towards Mapodian. Prior to setting off, however, Liu Yucheng, thinking of Cunzhi's uncle and his advanced age, figured they should bring a cart for him and place a cushion and a big pillow in it, too. That way the old man could be comfortable and they wouldn't need to worry about him possibly stumbling and hurting himself. It had, after all, become quite dark. Guo Jingshi didn't protest, nor did he stand on ceremony. He simply climbed into the cart, made himself comfortable and before long was snoring away. Liu Yucheng and Guo Cunzhi talked as they walked, briskly pushing the cart along the road to Mapodian. About halfway to the village, Guo Jingshi abruptly sat up, stirred from his slumber as though by some noise or other. The two younger men halted their steps immediately and pricked up their ears. From the fields all around them came the chirping of insects, soon drowning out all other sounds.

Guo Jingshi leapt out of the cart onto the ground and, before either of the young men could say anything, he darted into the fields. Cunzhi took off after him, but he soon realised he had no idea which way his uncle had gone and so was unable to follow. Then, as quickly as he had disappeared, Guo Jingshi reappeared, clutching something small to his chest. It was tiny and dark, possibly a cat, a dog, or some wild animal. It seemed to be barely alive, or perhaps already dead as it didn't make a sound nor try to wriggle free. Just what in heavens was it? Holding onto whatever it was, Guo Jingshi climbed back into the cart, found his comfortable spot and then proceeded to stick his finger into the animal's mouth.

The three of them continued on their way to Mapodian. Cunzhi was already used to his uncle's odd behaviour and general lack of communication, so it didn't affect his relationship with him. Liu Yucheng, on the other hand, was terribly intrigued by the old man's actions and was quite beside himself with curiosity as to just what Guo Jingshi was doing. He didn't dare ask him, though. Seeing the growing agitation in his walking companion, Cunzhi finally leaned close to try to explain things. The animal was a small dog, abandoned by its mother; it was nearly dead. But it wasn't just any old dog, according to his uncle. Its heritage was unclear. The animal had become so weak with hunger it was barely able to make a sound. The two men hadn't heard anything either; no sounds of movement whatsoever. So how the hell had such an old man heard the animal whimpering? Cunzhi didn't try to explain further that his uncle was unique. Liu Yucheng could only bottle up his thoughts, twisting and turning them over in his mind on the remainder of their journey to Mapodian. Later, as they drew close to Cui Liang, Guo Jingshi straightened himself up and Cunzhi hinted to Liu Yucheng that they should stop pushing the cart. Once they had helped the old man down, he quietly marched off as though he were a sentry around the building, seemingly sizing up the situation as he did so.

Liu Yucheng went and knocked on Cui Liang's door. A brief moment passed and then his daughter, Cui Lan, opened it. As soon as she saw that Liu Yucheng had been true to his word and had brought the supposed old mystic, her eyes filled with hope and with a great flurry she began to usher them inside. But when Guo Jingshi came close, she couldn't help but be a little frightened and surprised. "My heavens," she mumbled under her breath. In the pale moonlight this dark figure had approached her with his hair long and dishevelled, his face as black as the rest of its body and with something equally dark held close to his chest. A mystic or a ghost? Before the situation got away from them, Cunzhi jumped in and spoke: "Do you by chance have anything to eat? It doesn't matter what, anything will be fine. My uncle's holding onto a little dog, it's almost starved to death."

Cui Lan was struck by his question. Had this mystic come to help her father or save some mangy animal? Whatever the answer, she walked out to their little half-kitchen and brought back some steamed buns to give to Cunzhi. Taking the poor dog from his uncle, he gently laid it down beside the wall and placed the food in front of it. Unnoticed by Cui Lan, Guo Jingshi's eyes had actually fixed on her father the moment he'd stepped inside. It was as though he'd shrunk into his bed; his face had no colour at all. He'd managed to briefly open his eyes when he'd heard them arrive but quickly shut them again, having no energy to properly greet the men who had come to his home, nor even the strength to tell them he was quickly losing consciousness.

Liu Yucheng asked the girl if the doctor had dropped by to see her father.

She cried by way of response and then through a tear-soaked voice she told them the doctor's advice: her father's leg was broken and they had no option but to seek treatment at the county hospital.

Cunzhi looked at his uncle and then spoke to Cui Lan: "Don't worry, give us a small handkerchief and then take the contents of my uncle's bag, the dried herbs, and boil them up. Then you wait outside." Once he had finished speaking, he climbed onto the bed along with Liu Yucheng and together they propped up the injured old man. They wedged the handkerchief between his teeth. Cunzhi then positioned himself behind Cui Liang and took hold of the man's torso, grasping it tightly. Liu Yucheng put his arms round the man's remaining good leg and held it down with all the force he could muster. Guo Jingshi clutched the broken limb and worked his hands up and down it for a moment, then, in one sudden thrust, he deftly snapped the bone back in place.

Cui Liang spat out the handkerchief and roared out in pain. Listening the whole while outside, Cui Lan rushed back in. She saw her father's eyes now open. The pain from not too long ago was gone. She turned to Liu Yucheng: "How will I repay you?"

"It was Guo Jingshi who reset his leg, there's nothing to thank me for."

Gesturing in Guo Jingshi's direction, Cui Liang said to his daughter: "Show your respects girl, kowtow to him."

When she raised her head to look for the old mystic, there was already no sign of him. He had already gone outside and was again cradling the little dog. It seemed the steamed buns had restored some of its energy because it was burrowing into his arms and licking him repeatedly, to Guo Jingshi's great amusement. Cunzhi instructed Cui Lan to fetch the herbs she'd been boiling in the kitchen and to bring them here, and then find two bamboo reeds and a short strip of cloth. Cunzhi dipped the handkerchief into the herbal mixture and then washed Cui Liang's injured leg with it. Once complete, he took the two bamboo reeds and tied them tight on either side. He told Cui Liang not to get out of bed for at least a month, and then not to put any pressure on it for at least another two months. In three months' time, he assured him, it should be fully healed.

Liu Yucheng also told Cui Lan that Guojiadian had an abattoir and that he would provide her with bones to boil up into a broth to give to her father to aid his recovery.

Both father and daughter were overwhelmed with gratitude, but they had no idea how to properly express it. As Cui Lan escorted them out, Cunzhi suddenly abruptly asked her a question he'd not really thought through: "Who lives in that big mansion not too far from here?"

Cui Lan's response was brief: "It used to be where the town's branch secretary lived. I think it still is."

Cunzhi leaned close to his uncle: "Do you think something's wrong with them?"

In an almost off-the-cuff answer, Guo Jingshi told them about their brother who used to live there. They were always getting into fights and making a racket, not among themselves, but with others from the area. They had already gone a good number of years without having a hot meal but it didn't seem to matter to them if the steamed buns were only half cooked. Cui Lan opened her mouth to speak but caught her tongue before saying anything. What Guo Jingshi had said was right on the money. When all that stuff was happening, they would often come and ask to borrow their cooking fires.

Holding the dog tenderly, Guo Jingshi climbed back into the cart. Cunzhi picked up the handles and prepared to push once more. He wouldn't let Liu Yucheng assist him this time, arguing that he'd already been put through enough coming to get help for old Cui Liang; he couldn't be expected to give more.

They had not gone far from the village when they heard a voice holler out behind them. Guo Jingshi immediately provided a reply: "No need to see us off!" He then directed his attention towards his nephew: "Afterwards, you tell him, in the courtyard of Cui Liang's house there's a locust tree. Once he's married, he can cut that down to make furniture. Now he should just buy some sprouts from the market to plant, that'd be fine."

Before another moment passed, a young man, gasping for breath ran up to them. He was the one they had heard. He bowed to Guo Jingshi and then spoke: "My name's Xia Tianyuan, from the house next to the one where you just were. I'm here to ask for your help."

Cunzhi, however, was trying to work out what his uncle had just told him. There was no way Xia Tianyuan could have heard what his uncle had said, but still he was a little uneasy. Unconvinced by what his uncle had said, he asked him: "Was it that easy? What if the newly planted trees didn't take root? What then?"

Guo Jingshi opened his eyes wide: "Don't worry. All you need to do is plant the sapling in the soil and it'll be sure to germinate."

Sun Yueqing was an old lady who'd already been through quite a lot but now she seemed to be even busier than ever, at least, that's how she felt. There was really nothing to say about it. As soon as the sun lit up the horizon and she opened her eyes there would be mouths waiting to be fed: the chickens, two pigs, one small the other not so much, and three sheep, and now Guo Jingshi had brought a dog home. Admittedly, the dog was different; all it ever did was follow close behind Jingshi, day and night. To be honest, she really had no idea what it ate, only that it always seemed hungry but, at the same time, it seemed to be getting bigger and bigger by the day. It must have been eating something, otherwise how else could it be growing?

For most peasants, this was how the days went, a constant feeding trough, mundane and yet unique. At least, this was how they went now. In the years immediately before, during the shortages, there had only been human mouths left gaping, certainly no animals. The village had been much cleaner then but also cold and desolate, lifeless. The past two years things had changed enormously, of course. People weren't going hungry any more and there was a corresponding rise in the number of four-legged animals about, and creatures with wings, too. They all seemed to be increasing in number. They had to remember to shut the gates in the evening now. And usually they were woken in the morning by the sounds of life bustling in the courtyard; it was becoming quite the menagerie. The trees Guo Jingshi had planted a few years ago had also grown and would now flower and bear fruit. There was an entirely different atmosphere, a new life, but for Sun Yueqing, her own energy seemed daily to be on the wane.

The clear indication of this was that before she even really got started with the day's work, before she'd really even done anything, she'd already be feeling tired. She was also becoming forgetful. She would think of doing something and then the thought would slip her mind. For instance, when preparing some cornmeal pancakes, she'd get the pans ready and then forget to bring the cornmeal, or she'd have the water boiling and gurgling away, but she'd be wandering back and forth between the rooms not sure what she was supposed to be doing. Today, as she woke up, the first thing she spied hung behind the door was the bundle of clothing she had received from Ou Guangming three days ago. She had meant to give it to Liu Yumei to wash but she'd forgotten that, too. She couldn't help but violently berate herself; she'd just simply forgotten them and had no excuse.

A few days before, she'd heard Ou Guangming's father had taken a further turn for the worse. They had been neighbours for ages so she had to pay him a visit but, at the same time, she was struck by what she had seen. The Ou family home was in such a filthy state. The bed was no longer a bed, the comforters no longer comforters, no, it was all just a large bundle of fabric in dire need of a wash. The whole house was the same. She thought, then, that this would be a good opportunity to try to arrange a match between Guangming and Yumei. She had promised as much to Guangming, after all. She'd told him that getting Yumei to help out with the washing and cleaning was a good way to start the discussion. Why in heaven had she left it there behind the door, out of sight and out of mind? People get old, she thought, there was just no way round it. Nowadays, she'd wake up and feel just as tired as though she'd spent the previous day out husking wheat. But she'd started to come round to the realisation she was getting old. Even though she knew there was so much to do, she'd begun to lie in as opposed to getting up early. She'd wait until her son and his wife were awake and then bring her little grandson into her room. If he was still asleep, she'd cradle him a little while but if he was awake, she'd play with him instead. Her heart would be strengthened by this, enough to get up to welcome the new day.

But on this morning, afraid she would again forget the clothes bundle behind the door, she called out to Xuezhen to remind her that after breakfast she had to give the clothes to Yumei to wash. Xuezhen replied to say she would do it; it wasn't worth it for her to strain herself. Grateful to her daughter-in-law for her willingness to help, Sun Yueqing was still a little worried. It wasn't just about the clothes. Xuezhen didn't understand this. It was something much bigger, something she had to do herself. Xuezhen smiled but didn't argue the point. She knew what her mother-in-law had on her mind and that it wasn't just about dirty bedding and clothes. She also thought she might be better able to learn Yumei's true feelings about the matter, more at least than her mother-in-law might learn. But she left these thoughts unsaid.

For Sun Yueqing, it was simply something that had to be taken care of, regardless of what her daughter-in-law might think. Arranging a wedding was as essential and as important as taking care of the animals that chirped and squawked each and every morning. What had to be fed needed to be fed, just like one had to clean up the kitchen after cooking or sweep up the courtyard after feeding. Pondering this for a moment, Sun Yueqing changed tack and asked Xuezhen what she wanted for breakfast. After receiving a reply, she made quick work of getting the food ready. The men would soon be coming to the table one after the other. Guo Jingshi and Cunzhi brought the fresh grass and vegetables. As they walked into the kitchen area, the little black dog trailed close behind, a bone stuck in its maw. Their uncle hadn't given the beast a name and so they'd initially just grunted and whistled at it. Guo Jingshi, however, in his own unique way, had established an intimate connection between himself and the dog. They often only needed to exchange glances and the creature would know immediately what he wanted. If it were napping, a quick "hey" by the old man would rouse it and get its attention. In a certain way, it was like Guo Jingshi's child, albeit covered in dark fur. Before long, someone coined the name Blackie and it stuck. Before the grass could be given to the sheep, the vegetables had to be chopped up and eaten. Once finished, the leftover water was used with the husks of the grain and all boiled into a slop that would be given to the pigs to eat. Everything was carried out methodically. After the morning work was complete, Xuezhen collected her child from her mother-in-law with one hand while carrying a bundle of clothes in the other. She'd help her mother-in-law carry it, at least, but she wouldn't go into the Liu family home. She'd just wait outside until Sun Yueqing had had the chance to speak to Yumei. They could then return together.

Sun Yueqing, however, did not appreciate her daughter-in-law's assistance and instead roughly pulled the bundle out of her hand. Scolding Xuezhen, she said there was no need, that she wasn't a three-year-old child and was quite capable of carrying the bloody bag herself. Xuezhen didn't protest; it wasn't her place. Rather, she waited for Sun Yueqing to depart and then, child in hand, she followed on behind, right up until her mother-in-law arrived at Liu Yumei's house. Since Sun Yueqing was convinced of the magnitude of these discussions, they had to be handled in an appropriate manner. Her expression, once she stepped inside the house with the filthy clothes and bedding, was therefore solemn and serious. Yumei had no idea what was on Sun Yueqing's mind. She simply received the bundle and hastily deposited it into water. After that, Sun Yueqing explained why she had come, at least superficially, making sure not to forget to give herself a plausible reason. After all, she was terribly busy with so many things to take care of that it was difficult to find the time to wash someone else's dirty laundry. But that didn't stop her, of course, from feeling sympathy for what Ou Guangming and his family were going through, what with his father bedridden. She was just too old, she added, to properly wash clothes any more. She didn't have the strength in her arms. Xuezhen, too, was so busy with her own child and with making meals that she'd forgotten to wash them herself, even though they'd promised Guangming. If it wasn't too much trouble, she asked, might Yumei help them out?

Yumei was, by nature, gentle and kind-hearted but she was also quite introverted and often felt detached from the people around her. In many instances, she would almost intentionally guard against getting too close to anyone. It perhaps goes without saying that this was primarily the result of torment she'd endured while growing up the child of a landlord father but, whatever the case, listening to Sun Yueqing talk set her heart racing. Regardless of whether or not she would end up being a good match for Ou Guangming, she couldn't help but feel an enormous amount of gratitude to the old lady. The tone of her reply was filled with joy. She said she'd be sure to wash all of the clothes today and then return them directly to Guangming's home. There was no need, after all, for Sun Yueqing to trouble herself running back and forth.

Sun Yueqing clasped Yumei's hand and told her she couldn't just bring the clothes back herself. It wasn't Sun Yueqing's intention for her to have to do that. No, she'd get Guangming to come and pick the bundle up but maybe not today as that would be a little too rushed; tomorrow would be better. That way he'd be able to express a proper thank you as well. As for Guangming himself, Sun Yueqing added, she could certainly do much worse. Guangming had a good heart, he wouldn't raise his voice towards her, nor would he make an issue of her family background. Sun Yueqing mused that he could be considered a proper man. If he wasn't, then surely Yumei's brother would have faced much more serious accusations. Besides, it wasn't as though his family didn't also have skeletons in their closet. His father might not be long for this world but he also had an idiot for a younger brother who he no doubt would have to look out for in the future. Therefore, becoming his wife wouldn't be without difficulties. She paused before continuing and spoke plainly, admitting she wasn't entirely sure of the match, worried she was getting too involved, afraid she might be doing wrong by her and that Yumei might end up holding a grudge against her.

Listening to Sun Yueqing voice her reservations and worries suddenly weighed heavily on Liu Yumei. So this is what it was like to grow old. Were they trying to help or trying to undermine her? Sun Yueqing used to be so sure of herself. When she set her mind to something, she would do it, quickly, confidently and audaciously, even. But now she was old and dithering, nagging, turning things over and over in her mind, unable to reach a decision. She tried hastily to console her: "Auntie, I've nothing but gratitude towards you and your family. That won't change. You've been so kind to me and my brother. He wouldn't be where he is now if not for Guo Cunxian. How could I ever bear any resentment towards you? I know Ou Guangming's a good man. Please, please don't worry."

There was no point in saying any more. And besides, at the present time she couldn't decide whether to go through with it or not even if she had wanted to. Things with her brother still weren't sorted so there was no way she could promise herself to Ou Guangming. And, come to think of it, there was no way to be sure her brother would agree in the first place. Perhaps he wouldn't want her to marry. Perhaps she'd end up having to be his wife, in any case. Ou Guangming might do right by her but she didn't really fancy him. He could be loud and uncouth, character traits that didn't always go over well. He was always bustling with energy, causing a fuss and a racket. It was true he had a good class background but did she really want to marry him? Is that what he wanted? After all, everyone in the village knew she was the daughter of a landlord. If she listened to her heart, it would be better to marry someone from far away, a complete stranger who knew absolutely nothing of her family background. As Yumei grew distracted by her own problems, Sun Yueqing was left to plop down on a nearby seat, seemingly incapable of standing any longer, to say nothing of speaking further on the subject. Instead, her thoughts shifted to her grandson, to her own family's situation. Even if she couldn't be sure exactly what her family had to face. She reproached herself. She hated growing old and hated the waffling back and forth that it entailed. When she wanted to stay at home, she thought about going out. Then when she was out, she immediately thought about coming back.

After Sun Yueqing had been sitting for a while, she slowly felt the energy return to her legs. With her strength somewhat recouped, she stood up to take her leave. Yumei reached forward to help steady her. Together they walked to the door and stepped outside. In the distance she could see Zhu Xuezhen waiting, trying to look as though she'd only just arrived. She walked up to her mother-in-law to escort her home. Yumei turned and went back inside, immediately lighting a fire to boil the water to wash the clothes. Once it started to bubble, she dropped the lot of them in and waited. After a spell, she removed the clothes, put them out to dry in the air and then started to prepare a meal. Once the the food was ready, she wrapped it up and headed off towards the construction site. She worked with her brother and Cui Lan in the afternoon digging the water reservoir. When evening came, she'd come back. The clothes should be dry by then, so she could collect them and fold them all up, wrapping them safely once more into a bundle. She'd then put it to one side and wait for Ou Guangming to fetch it. Two days passed, however, and there was still no sign of Ou Guangming. She thought to herself, she hadn't been all that wrong about him. He didn't always follow through with things, just as many had said. She wondered what kind of man he really was. The idea had been for her to do his family's laundry and for him to collect it, and have a look at her. Now he'd demonstrated a lack of concern about it, would he really be all that good for her?

By the evening of the third day, Yumei was beginning to give up on the possibility of seeing Guangming come for his clothes and bedding. It was already getting late. Her brother had returned from another day of exhausting work and had gone straight to bed. Liu Yumei herself was tired and figured she'd get some rest as well. Then, suddenly, there was a knock at the door, hurried and nervous. A knock at their door at this hour always seemed to bring bad tidings, so much so that Yumei was frightened, unable to get out of bed to see who it was. Liu Yucheng, however, stirred immediately. It had become a habit of his; whenever he heard a noise outside their door, he'd wake up at once, quickly get up and holler that he was coming to open the door. At the same time he'd instruct his sister not to move, not to make a sound. Yucheng pulled his jacket on, slipped his feet into his shoes and moved quickly to see who had come. Two people were waiting outside, Guo Cunxian and Zhu Xuezhen. He was startled by the sight of them, his voice betraying his surprise: "Brother Cunxian, what's wrong? What has happened?"

Guo Cunxian sighed and started to speak. From the adjacent room, Liu Yumei could hear who it was and so she decided to get up and join them in her brother's room. Their expressions were anxious as they looked at Guo Cunxian and his wife, waiting for them to speak. Seriousness hung in the air but at the same time they tried to ease their anxiety, told them not to worry and indicated what they had to say wasn't earth-shattering. They began from the beginning: late that evening Ou Guangming's father had started to hyperventilate, almost uncontrollably, so much so that he could barely breathe and couldn't say a word. They all thought this was the end. No one, however, could figure out why this had happened so suddenly. They didn't know what was bothering him, weighing on him. After some more fretful moments, his breathing finally eased a little but his expression became morose, heavy, especially when he looked at his two boys. Then, one of their aunties, their father's younger brother's wife, figured out what was wrong. The old man was worried to death about whether his boys would find wives or not, whether their family would continue or whether they'd end up being bare sticks. The auntie then spoke to Guangming in low tones, suggesting they figure out a way to make it look like he'd got married, even if he hadn't. Guo Cunxian then told the siblings that was when Yumei's name was mentioned. If she were to go to Guangming's house and address the old man as father, then he'd be able to close his eyes in peace and set off on his final journey, steadfast in the belief that at least one of his boys had found a wife.

Neither brother nor sister could have guessed that this was what had brought Guo Cunxian and his wife to their house so late at night. Yucheng wouldn't force the issue and was unwilling to pressure his sister, so he stood, silent, unsure of what to do. Xuezhen walked towards the younger woman and clasped her arm.

Guo Cunxian could feel the tension in the room and longed to leave but he couldn't, there was still more to explain: "They were worried that if someone else had come, you wouldn't even consider it. That's why they asked us to do it. I even talked to them about it before coming to find you. Trying to put an old man's mind at ease before the end comes is important, it's a family's duty. So when they asked for my help, there was no way I could decline. But I can't compel you to do it. It has to be your choice. Using an old man's dying wish is no excuse to force a marriage onto someone who isn't willing to agree to it. So don't feel like I'm giving you no say in the matter, Yumei. You decide for yourself. You don't need to do it and, even if you decide to go, that doesn't mean you'll marry Ou Guangming either, I guarantee you. That's why I've come here with Xuezhen. I went home first and got her instead of coming straight from Guangming's. If you want to go, she'll accompany you. If you don't, she'll go instead. After all, Guangming's father has never seen Xuezhen. We're not trying to fool or deceive him but we're all from the same village so we have a duty to go and see them. I mean, it's not such a big deal to just go and call someone father, is it? Besides, whatever's really in the old man's heart, he'll take to his grave."

Guo Cunxian seemed to have finished what he had wanted to say, so Yumei broke her silence: "Brother Cunxian, I hear what you're saying and you've said it in front of my brother, too, so I know what I have to do. Give me a moment and then we'll all go. After all, Ou Guangming also once helped my brothers. I need to do this. But I have three conditions. One, I won't leave this house until my brother finds a wife. Two, if that happens quickly and without a hitch, well, I'll wed Ou Guangming, if he still wants me. Three, if things don't work out, whoever can help me find a sister-in-law, well, then I'll marry whomsoever."

Liu Yucheng could hold his tongue no longer: "Yumei, is all of this worth the trouble? Have you forgotten what our older brother said to us before he died?"

Guo Cunxian nudged Yucheng and interrupted him: "It's not your decision. Yumei has given us her point of view and I agree to her three conditions. I'll go first, alright?"

Liu Yucheng found his voice again: "Shouldn't I go with you?"

Guo Cunxian waved his hand: "You're not needed tonight. It's better if you wait at home. I'll get Xuezhen to bring Yumei over a little later. When they hold the funeral the day after tomorrow, then we'll need you to come. You'll need to help."

Yumei was sure not to forget the bundle of clothes. When they reached Ou Guangming's home, there were people milling all about. The Ou family was actually the smallest clan in town. Ou Guangming didn't have a lot of uncles and cousins like most other men but when things were bad for them, there was no shortage of people eager to help. It also demonstrated something else: Guojiadian had healed. After the years of pain and starvation, there was again a sense of camaraderie among the villagers. A few short years ago, a dying villager was worth less than a dying dog. A dog's carcass, after all, could provide food for a few people, at least. When the people gathered round the Ou family home saw that Yumei had really come, they seemed to part immediately and someone yelled towards the inside: "Quickly, make way for Yumei."

The people inside did the same when Yumei came up to the door. They stepped to either side, allowing Guo Cunxian to clear a path for Xuezhen to bring Yumei forward. The two women saw the poor old man prostrate on the bed. His hair had been cut and his face shaved. Someone had helped him into burial clothes and he looked as though he already had two feet in the grave, except for his eyes, which were wide and clear, possessed with a penetrating stare. His mouth was wide open as well. He seemed to be about to say something but the words wouldn't come out. He lifted his arm towards them. Liu Yumei felt no fear. She moved close to the old man, clutched his hand and called him father. Her eyes then welled up with tears.

Ou Guangming's father tried to utter a response. His lips moved and for a brief moment a smile crossed his face. There was a look of contentment before his eyes finally closed. The room exploded into mournful weeping.

All of Guojiadian was witness to it. Tang Hao, a youth sent down from Beijing, was at first healthy and active, a stout young lad with thick arms and legs. But after two years of labour in the countryside, his right leg had become lame. No one knew why or how it had happened, and Tang Hao was giving nothing away. Some suspected he was playacting as a way to avoid doing more work or for an excuse to request that he be allowed to return to the capital. The treatment for his leg saw him go back and forth between Beijing and Guojiadian quite a few times, actually, but from beginning to end, the leg showed no signs of improvement. In fact, the opposite was the case. It got worse and worse, and much more serious. Any little bit of exertion was so excruciatingly painful that it made him grimace in severe discomfort. It was then that the villagers finally accepted the truth: his leg really had been hurt somehow and he really was lame. Of course, this started the rumour mill as the reason for the injury remained a mystery. How could a strapping young man become lame for apparently no reason at all?

On that day, another youth sent down to the countryside, a boy by the name of Ye Yuan, accompanied Tang Hao in search of the local Party branch secretary, Han Jingting.

When exactly had Han Jingting been named branch secretary, one may ask? Well, it ought to be remembered that when Guo Cunxian was first selected to be team leader, the county leadership declared at the same time that the deputy director of the commune, Xin Chuan, was to double up on his duties and be the Party branch secretary for Guojiadian as well, due in large part to the fact the Party's presence had been so disrupted in the area during the first few chaotic years of the Cultural Revolution. Once the Party apparatuses had been sufficiently restored and various people put back in the necessary positions, it was decided that Han Jingting was the most suitable person for the role of branch secretary, even though he'd now be in a more senior position than Team Leader Guo Cunxian.

The reason for his promotion was due in large part to the fact that Guo Cunxian himself wasn't an actual Party member and so was ineligible for such a post. For Han Jingting, he'd spent the better part of his life in some leadership role or other and felt a degree of familiarity in this new role. He also believed the most important thing for the future development of the village was to ensure that Guo Cunxian gained his Party membership. That would eventually enable him to be promoted to the role of deputy Party secretary and to make the greatest contribution to the town so long as he remained in the more junior role. Ironically, however, and despite his position of seniority over Guo Cunxian, Han Jingting was rarely called upon by the villagers to make decisions or deal with troublesome issues. It seemed most were inclined to talk things over with their team leader, almost ignoring the branch secretary altogether. As far as the senior Party leadership was concerned, Han Jingting was the central man in charge in Guojiadian, which was the reason he was always called to attend the senior Party meetings. It didn't seem to matter that he was more the messenger than anything else, for each time he returned he'd simply relay the directives to Guo

Cunxian and then accept that he wouldn't be the one who actually implemented them. This was both good and bad, of course. If Guo Cunxian was amenable and happily listened to the orders, fine, but if he disagreed with what the central authorities planned, then the plans simply wouldn't be implemented. In these latter instances, it was Han Jingting who received criticism from the senior Party leadership and more than a few times over the last year he'd been caught up in more than his fair share of squabbles between both sides. That was why it was so unexpected to have two youths that had been sent down to the countryside come suddenly running up to his house in search of his counsel. He couldn't help but listen intently to the explanation as to why they'd come.

Tang Hao was incredibly polite, showing great deference to Han Jingting. He talked about the policies implemented by the central government and of how there were special instances when youths that had been sent down to the countryside could return to the cities. He made the case for how he'd come down to the countryside full of energy and vigour but had ended up a cripple through no fault of his own. There wasn't much he could do now and so he thought it would be best for him to return to Beijing to seek proper treatment, at least while he was still young. He was here to request permission to do so. As he listened, Han Jingting was moved by the young man's earnestness and quickly gave his consent: "Yes, you should return to the capital. The village will provide you with whatever paperwork you need."

Ye Yuan now chimed in, stating that it wasn't simply a matter of getting the proper paperwork. No, Tang Hao had been injured while working for the village, he argued, yet he was still young. What about the rest of his life? Surely, he suggested, Guojiadian should be responsible in some form or other? Surely they had to look after him.

Han Jingting quickly understood what was being implied. They were resorting to extortion, trying to put Guojiadian on the hook for Tang Hao's injury. He'd had an inkling of something being amiss as soon as the youths came to find him. He tested them: "Hmm, you might be right but tell me what you have in mind."

Ye Yuan continued to speak for his friend: "There are two options. One, the village could provide him with a lump sum for the cost of medical treatment up front. That way this unfortunate incident can be quickly put behind us and, should something arise in future, well, the town wouldn't be held responsible. The second option is that the village and my friend here could sign an agreement stipulating that, regardless of how much money is spent on his treatment, he would have the right to seek full reimbursement from the village."

Han Jingting had a further question: "If we take option one, how much do you think you'll need?"

Ye Yuan replied confidently, thinking he had the upper hand: "I think that's best left to the hospital in Beijing to determine. They could provide us with an evaluation to get an idea of the cost. If I were to make an estimate, considering it is his thigh area, I can't see it being any less than eighteen thousand yuan."

Han Jingting sucked in a cool breath of air before replying: "Phew, I'm just an old peasant and not very worldly, you know. I've never seen such a sum of money before. I can't even say I know how much that really is." He took another breath: "Young Tang, what were you doing when you injured yourself, especially so seriously?"

Tang Hao's answer was vague: "I'd worked so hard during the day, when I fell asleep, I caught a draught."

"It's winter and you didn't use a quilt?"

Ye Yuan interjected: "You've never had to use the toilet in the night? It was just at that moment of exertion as he got up to relieve himself that he caught the draught."

Han Jingting thought things over for a moment before continuing with his penetrating questions: "Was there no chamber pot in the room?"

Ye Yuan was quick-witted and seemingly skilled at prevarication: "No, there wasn't. He'd left it outside in the morning and it had frozen and cracked. Who'd have guessed it could be so cold here!"

As though agreeing, Han Jingting nodded his head and then spoke almost more to himself than to the young men standing in front of him: "So perhaps what the villagers had been saying was true?"

Tang Hao seemed a little nervous: "Secretary Han, please, tell us, what gossip have you heard?"

Han Jingting rubbed his forehead a moment and then said: "It's not gossip, you confirmed it after all. One wintry night you were awoken by your overflowing bladder but you didn't want to actually go to the outhouse, you had no chamber pot, and so to save yourself the trouble you stood in the doorway to relieve yourself there. Because you weren't properly dressed, you caught a draught and when you woke in the morning your leg had gone lame. It's a good thing you're young. Shit, if you'd been a little older and caught the same draught you'd probably be paralysed right now."

Tang Hao blushed with embarrassment. He hadn't wanted the old man to know all of the details, to look at him and know his shame. He regretted coming here and speaking to the old secretary. His gaze turned towards Ye Yuan, beseeching him with his eyes to save him from this humiliation. Han Jingting saw the intent and grew suspicious. It was probably Ye Yuan who'd encouraged him to come and pressured him into this course of action.

Han Jingting, feeling sympathy for the boy, tried to smooth things over: "Young Tang, if you'd spoken the truth earlier, you could have avoided the embarrassment and received treatment sooner, at the very least your leg wouldn't be as bad as it is now. But in any case, what's happened has happened here in Guojiadian, we're not wholly free of responsibility. Nevertheless, it's something that needs to be decided by the work unit. You need to go and speak to Guo Cunxian, the team leader."

Ye Yuan protested at this, arguing that Han Jingting was the Party branch secretary and in all villages what the branch secretary says goes!

"Heh, I don't know about that. I mean, it's true that in essentially all of the other villages in the region the Party secretaries are the village heads but that's not the way it is here in Guojiadian. Here the team leader's in charge. He's young and quite capable. I, on the other hand, am an old man. Surely that's plain to you two."

Ye Yuan, this young whippersnapper, could feel his temper boiling. Naturally, the secretary didn't want to be considered as some old local deity or wise man but surely Guo Cunxian should be under his command and not the other way round!

Han Jingting laughed at his reaction. Had he learned that in Guojiadian? Doubtful. He was in the wrong place for those ideas. It's true, he agreed, he could be considered the old wise man of the area, the old farmer. He wasn't trying not to be, but no one else looked upon him like that, not in Guojiadian. The townspeople knew, Han Jingting told them, why the two young men had come to see him. They thought it would be easier for them to get what they wanted by talking to an old, confused man, and that they didn't have the courage to go and talk to Guo Cunxian. Wasn't that right?

Tang Hao offered an explanation: "No, that's not true. It's just that Guo Cunxian isn't the easiest person to talk to, nor does he talk all that much. He just looks at you with those eyes of his. It's so unnerving. And in any case, you are his superior so hopefully you can say something to him on our behalf. I need to seek treatment, after all, so that means I need to return to Beijing."

Han Jingting tried to reassure them: "Don't worry, I will speak to him."

Seeing the two youths off, Han Jingting made a firm decision: the title of Party branch secretary was important and it shouldn't be further tarnished. He might be old but it wasn't as though he was inexperienced. Didn't the title come with some authority? Didn't he have the right to take the lead on things? And if he didn't take the initiative now, by the time the harvest came round, if any other problems emerged, it would be too late for him to make any attempt to deal with them and his position would be meaningless. He wasn't just talking about the situation with Tang Hao and his medical expenses, either. That's not what the old man had in mind. No, he was thinking of the serious and important directives the central authorities had given him, the tasks he was responsible for, namely the 'Learn from Dazhai in agriculture' initiative. They had to move mountains to make farmland, move heaven and earth, and work bitterly, diligently and with extra energy to transform the country. This was a national movement, after all, a solemn duty and a great project for the entire nation. But Guo Cunxian had set his mind wholly on the factory. He wasn't listening to him or paying him any attention at all. How had he let things turn out this way?

On the following day, he claimed he'd taken a tumble and had broken his leg, but because he didn't have a son, only three daughters, he had no choice but to call on a distant relative, Han Erhu, to take him to the commune offices in a small pushcart. There was something he had to discuss with the commune leadership. Once there, Han Erhu helped him into the building where he spoke to them about his age and about how he'd been fortunate not to seriously injure himself even more than he may have done already. He also talked to them about his duties and about how he didn't want his current infirmity to adversely affect the projects that needed to be carried out. He therefore requested that Guo Cunxian serve in his place as Party branch secretary. Not only did his performance allow him to keep his dignity but it also excused him from the responsibility of implementing central policy. Nominally speaking, you could say he had killed two birds with one stone.

In truth, there wasn't a soul in the commune offices who didn't know that Han Jingting had been given the position of branch secretary as punishment for past infractions. But, that said, they didn't much like Guo Cunxian either. They loathed his presumptuousness, his brazenness and that certain look he'd often get in his eyes. Unfortunately for them, Guo Cunxian was being protected by members of the county government and there was really nothing they could do. Han Jingting served as their intermediary. He could smooth things over between the commune and the village when necessary and save them the trouble of having to deal directly with Guo Cunxian. Now that the old man had come to them with this, what were they to do? Things hadn't been easy for him these last couple of years. Perhaps their only option was to accede to his wishes and let him save this little bit of face.

As soon as Han Jingting returned to the village, he called a Party meeting. He relayed to them what had happened and how he'd hurt himself. He also spoke of his visit to the commune government and the decision they had arrived at. He was systematic in the details he gave them. The handover of authority would be clean and neat and, from this point onwards, Guo Cunxian would be the Party branch secretary.

Stunned by this revelation, it was clear to everyone Guo Cunxian had been wholly unprepared for the announcement. His voice betrayed his surprise and his degree of regret, making it clear that he wasn't entirely happy at the prospects of this new responsibility: "Uncle Jingting, I've always considered you an honest and sincere man. Surely you're just toying with me. I envisaged your role as dealing with the central authorities for me and keeping them off my back so that I could actually get things done and improve things for all the residents of Guojiadian. And things seemed to be working. But thrusting me into the pole position is just a recipe for disaster."

The morning sky was still dark when the motorcade set off from the factory. The lead truck of the convoy was adorned with flags with deep blue backgrounds with oxen and white sheep embroidered on either side and in the middle large, red characters were stitched bearing the words: 'Nothing else like it'. The vehicles were carrying 500 *jin* of beef and 300 *jin* of lamb as well as 200 *jin* of marinated beef and another 100 *jin* of pickled donkey meat. The truck following behind the first had its flatbed divided into six sections, three of which contained pork. This was a relatively new product but then what food factory wouldn't produce pork? The higher-ups had stipulated there needed to be three long tables for the sale of meat. In each truck sat three men, all looking quite excited.

Alongside the convoy was Wang Shun, riding the newest Red Flag bicycle. Seated on the shafts of the second vehicle's cart as though he were a warrior from some story, was Han Wulin, whose heart was a little uneasy. As Wang Shun rode abreast of him, he anxiously asked: "Do you think we've brought too much meat? Will we be able to sell it?"

Seemingly well prepared for such a query, Wang Shun's reply was quick: "Brother Wulin, you asked will we be able to sell it all? Well, I say change that question into a statement: we will sell it all. I'm more worried about whether we have brought enough or not. I've spread the word, you know, to every market across the whole region within a radius of more than fifty *li*. I've been holding my breath for so long waiting for this day. To use our leader's words, today the village encircles the city. Today Kuanhe County will be ours! Just you wait and see. It won't be long, either, before he comes to the city himself to oversee things, you watch."

"Cunxian's coming?"

"That's right. He has been waiting for this for a long time, too. What makes it even better is that we couldn't have picked a better day for it. There are tens of thousands of people in the city. I'm not tempting fate but, if we can get them to try my meat, shit, if we can get them to even just smell it, they'll know there's no other place like Guojiadian!"

"Why do you say that? What's happening in Kuanhe today?"

"People have three days off to celebrate National Day, that's what. Shit, they've all been so down in the dumps these last few years with nothing to celebrate, well, everything's different now. Lin Biao is dead, Jiang Qing has been apprehended, the Cultural Revolution is over, new policies are on the horizon and, best of all, well, is that we're leading this motorcade. I tell you, to get rich is to make revolution!"

Laughter echoed throughout the convoy. Old Fatty chimed in: "Boss, eh... no, sorry, factory director, I mean. You seem to know quite a bit. Have you been to Kuanhe before?"

"Been to the city before? Let me tell ya, I once occupied this here city. You could say I helped clean it up, you know, root out the enemy. Shit, it must have taken a month. And I'm not blowing my own horn, either, it's the damn truth, I tell ya. I wouldn't lie."

Ah, really? Most seemed to think he was shooting his mouth off. What regiment? Could he have been part of the Eighth Route Army?

Wang Shun laughed loudly: "Ha! Did I say that? Eighth Route Army? Shit, I was certainly more formidable than they were. I know, I know, whenever they liberated a town they'd be sure to take from the villagers as little as possible. Well, I did the same. And you know what? I did even more. Do you know how many streets there are in Kuanhe? How many *hutongs* [lanes]? I carried a plate down each and every one of them."

Two younger members of the convoy didn't quite understand: "What are you talking about? What did you do exactly? What year was that?"

Wang Shun felt annoyed and begrudged the fact he had to explain: "Hawking wares, that's what! You mean to tell me you don't know what I'm talking about? I mean begging, that's what I mean. Down every single street, knocking on every single door."

Everyone roared with laughter. A sweet scent wafted on the morning air. Their enjoyment was palpable. Wang Shun was from a different town, not from Guojiadian. He'd been put in charge of the factory because of his relationship with Guo Cunxian; quite a responsibility. In the beginning, no one in the village dared say anything but there was resentment among the people. As time passed, however, he'd gained a lot of friends. He wasn't some dirty moneygrubber. He was kind, honest and generous. He was always good for a laugh, too. He didn't seem bothered by what anyone said, serious or otherwise. His pet phrase was always something along the lines of him being a bare stick with no family, no property but always with food in his belly. Shit, he even had enough extra to feed a dog. He had come to Guojiadian to share in the work. What use had he for money?

Under the leadership of this clown they entered Kuanhe and found the busiest, liveliest street they could find to set up shop. There they sold both their raw and prepared meat, right in front of the county's own commerce bureau stall. It was tantamount to thrusting the people into making a choice between their own leaders and the upstarts from Guojiadian.

Business was outstanding! The stalls drew a great deal of attention. The meat, which had been freshly slaughtered, looked exceptionally fresh, suggesting a deliciousness not seen for some time. But what really put them over the top was the fact that their prices were much lower than what the state officials were selling theirs for. To make matters worse for the officials, the government was at the same time emphasising the need for everyone across the country to spend their money as wisely as possible, to make it go as far as possible, which was certainly a plus for the people from Guojiadian!

Wang Shun wasn't in the least bit worried about selling the three types of meat they'd brought but that didn't mean he wouldn't give it his all to bring people to their stall. With great verve and energy, he pummelled the meat displayed on the long table, then held his hands high in the air for everyone to see. At the top of his lungs he bellowed towards the people in the market: "You can all see, right? This is the meat we've brought. No matter how you might handle it, your hands are still clean, not sticky at all. That proves our product is fresh, free of contaminants and additives, and that it all comes from healthy animals with just the right amount of fat and juicy meat to sink your teeth into. If you don't believe me, then come on over and see for yourself. You'll know I'm telling the truth."

It didn't take long for a queue to form. The people at the market knew when to snap up a bargain and when not to. They'd lived through difficult times. Besides, they weren't really given to questioning what they were told and the meat was cheap. There was really no reason to wait.

With the stage set for brisk sales of the uncured meat, Wang Shun now wiped his hand and moved behind the tables displaying the marinated products. For him, these were the most important, the meat he just had to sell. It perhaps goes without saying but it was doubtful anyone in Kuanhe had ever purchased this kind of thing before but the marinated meats would bring in greater profits, so the focus had to be on them. From beside the table he pulled out a finely sharpened blade that glimmered in the sun. His cutting board was immaculately clean, putting the onlookers' minds at ease that the meat wouldn't be soiled. He took hold of a piece of sinew and sliced into it with his knife, separating it into several delicious looking morsels. A crowd stood round him, watching the expert at work. With a look of great sincerity in his eyes, he handed out samples of the meat to those closest to the table, for them to try. Again, he spoke loudly over the market hubbub: "Hey everyone, come and take a look. This here is marinated beef. There's donkey which is our specialty, an old recipe of mine. Come and have a taste. If you like it, then buy some... or don't. To be frank, I'm not worried about selling this here meat. There's nothing else like it, if I do say so myself. If you don't want it, well, that's just your loss, not mine!"

Soon smacking lips and satisfied sighs were heard among those who'd tried the meat. Heads nodding up and down, enjoying it thoroughly, another queue quickly formed. Wang Shun's approach to business was straightforward. A customer could buy as much as they wanted. If they had more money, then he'd sell them more; if less, well, you get the idea. Sales were rapid and customers were happy, all praising the taste and texture of the meat. Wang Shun's spirits grew more and more, setting his tongue wagging: "I tell you, there's nothing else like it, no other taste that compares. If you don't believe me, try for yourself. I guarantee, even just a small bite is unforgettable. Then you'll know what I mean when I say there's nothing else like it. Come on and try it, don't miss out!"

Since Liberation, had anyone in Kuanhe seen anything like this? The commerce bureau employees, the supply and marketing cooperatives, the state-run butchers, all of them came running to see the ruckus. Those that tried the marinated meat quickly bought some, while others couldn't hide their annoyance. Wasn't he underselling state-produced goods in favour of his own? All forms of commerce were supposed to be state-run, weren't they! It didn't take long for someone to put the question to them: where were they from and did they have the proper papers and certificates to sell meat products?

A rather obsequious, deferential smile came across Wang Shun's face: "I didn't realise national approval was needed for honest commerce? We're from Guojiadian, an industrial cooperative. Do you know where that is? In Laodong, part of Kuanhe County, when the Twenty-Ninth Battalion of the People's Army were fighting those Japanese bastards, the village did all it could to provide support and now it's using all of its resources, human and natural, to aid and support the development of the country into a modern industrial nation. This isn't a private stall, you know. It belongs to the village. It's our industrial cooperative. Please have a look at the sign above. It bears the emblems of the town, the commune and the county. That's all three levels of government... I assure you!"

The men who'd asked the questions raised their heads and, as expected, saw all the certification Wang Shun had just spoken of. The bystanders watching the exchange now chimed in as well. They couldn't help but praise Wang Shun, admiring his savvy in dealing with the officials, before requesting he continue with his performance.

Seemingly carefree and unworried, Wang Shun continued hawking his meat, collecting money, calculating sums in his mind, and all the while gabbing nonstop: "Shit, I'm here selling all this meat for such a pittance while my stomach goes empty. Aren't I mad for selling the lot?"

"Ha ha, how about another?"

"One more? Alright, listen. In Guojiadian my old man's married to a ripe old bird with a dodgy eye and a crooked mouth. Well, let's just say she's not much to get excited about! Heh, heh. But let me tell you, one word about someone selling marinated meat, well, quick as a flash and bare-assed to boot, he'll be there with money to shoot!"

The crowd roared with laughter. The men who had come to check his credentials were left impotent, unable to pursue the issue further. If this had been during the so-called Cultural Revolution, well, they'd immediately have dragged his arse off to a struggle session. But things were different now. The government was promoting the revitalisation of the country. What could they do with such brazenness? Those more interested in purchasing meat began to push forward now, pressuring the men who'd challenged Wang Shun to step out of the way.

Unbeknownst to Wang Shun and the others, Guo Cunxian had already arrived at the market and had been watching things from the side. Everything looked to be in order. It was barely noon and already the tables were nearly empty. He'd thought it best if he didn't get in the way then, suddenly, he decided to step forward and call out to Wang Shun. He asked him to cut two pieces of marinated meat and wrap them up in separate packages. He then walked over to the table selling pork and asked for two more pieces to be cut and wrapped up. With the meat in hand, he got back on his bicycle and left.

He, too, was riding a new Red Flag bicycle. When he purchased it, Guo Cunyong had thought about buying a Phoenix bike or a Flying Pigeon that were well-known brands, after all. But Guo Cunxian was adamant, he wanted a Red Flag model. That was the name he was after. He asked the younger man to think about what came to mind when he imagined Guo Cunxian riding such a bicycle? The senior leadership of the country were all driven around in Red Flag limousines and he wanted to do the same, if only a two-wheeled one, so the town bought five Red Flag bicycles.

Guo Cunxian lacked experience, however, in riding a bike. He'd also loaded the rear basket area with far too much stuff. Coupled with the number of people all milling about the city roads, he was afraid he'd end up crashing into someone and making a fool of himself. That's why he wasn't actually riding the bicycle at this moment but instead pushing it out of town and across the bridge. As he did so, he spied once more the dried-goods shops. Employees at state-owned businesses always finish the day early, and so it was at that moment that the shop attendant, Ma Yüfen, removed her dark uniform, put on her own clothes and walked out the door just in front of Guo Cunxian. It seemed clear she was on her way home to eat lunch and would return fairly quickly. Like clockwork her actions appeared to be well rehearsed. Guo Cunxian continued to push his bicycle some way behind her. They passed two *hutongs* before she came to a stop and entered a small house facing the street. The city folk lived in less than ideal homes. They were old, small and crowded, too. A family of four or five could apparently squeeze into each one. Guo Cunxian walked up to the door she had entered, positioned his bicycle safely against the wall, removed a *jin* of marinated beef and one of pork from the basket and then called out to 'Comrade Ma'.

Ma Yüfen turned round and stared suspiciously at the man who'd called out to her: "You're looking for me?" From behind her, three or four other faces appeared and immediately tried to get the measure of this man who had suddenly shown up on their doorstep, particularly with regard to what he had in his hands.

Guo Cunxian moved a little closer and placed the package he'd been carrying in Ma Yüfen's hands: "It's some marinated beef made in my village. Try it and let me know what you think." He then moved further into the house and placed the pork belly on a countertop before withdrawing and stepping back outside.

Ma Yüfen had remained by the door, stupefied and surprised at this unexpected visit: "You've brought so much. Are you sure you've got the right place? Do we know each other?"

Guo Cunxian smiled in reply: "No, you don't know me, but I can't forget the good turn you did me. Do you remember, heavens, it was some years ago now, I once came into your store brandishing an axe and forced you into selling me two bags of dried milk powder?"

"Oh." Ma Yüfen smiled herself, now. "So you really do have a heart. Huh, you remember that? It was nothing, you know. Please come in and have a seat."

"No, no, I'm just here as we've set up a meat stall. The day's coming to a close and I'd better get back and make sure they're packing everything up."

Ma Yüfen started: "You mean to tell me that it's your village that's caused such a ruckus in the market?"

Guo Cunxian smiled disarmingly: "My apologies if we've affected your business today."

Ma Yüfen laughed loudly now: "Hah, whatever the country buys or sells, well, none of it belongs to any one individual, so what's there to worry about. If you're able to come daily, well, it won't take long before we all get used to you."

Guo Cunxian thought for a moment before speaking: "Well, to be honest, our plan is to open a shop here in the city or perhaps even a factory outlet. But we've only just started and don't quite have the expertise yet, at least, not with regard to running accounts and keeping track of money. If it's not too much trouble and not too embarrassing on your part, I'd like to maybe ask you from time to time for advice and guidance. In return, if ever you're in need, well, you won't need to stand on ceremony, you can just ask me and I'll help out in any way I can." As he spoke these words he shifted his body, put his hands on the bicycle and began to walk away slowly, leaving Ma Yüfen standing at the door with the package of meat in her hands, unsure of how to respond to what he had said.

Without stopping, Guo Cunxian pedalled to his sister's house but neither Cunzhu nor her husband were at home, as her father-in-law informed him. Evidently, they'd heard of the commotion Guojiadian had made when they came to the city market and so they had both run off to see it at first hand. Guo Cunxian smiled at the older man and handed him the remaining packages of meat he had with him. They exchanged a few pleasantries before Guo Cunxian took his leave and rode straight back to the market. As he pulled up near the village stands, he soon saw the long tables had been cleared of meat. Apparently they had sold everything. He was confused, however, by the number of people still milling about and began to worry that something had happened. Moving closer to get a better look and to hear what was being said, he soon realised it was only Wang Shun, spinning yet another yarn, another scam.

He was standing there beneath the sign 'Nothing Else Like It', holding a strip of cured donkey meat that looked rather like the skinny arm of a child, purplish due to the soy sauce, gleaming and shiny. With his finger he gestured to the audience and explained in a booming voice: "You all see it, don't you? This is the most expensive product I've brought here today and let me tell ya, heavens, there are some who even consider it sacred! It's better known as Donkey Money. That's true, honest. Eating this is not only good for your kidneys and your...," he said, shaking his waist, "it also enriches the blood, giving you more energy and vitality. Normally, a strip like this would cost between thirty and fifty yuan, so even if many of you still have some money in your pockets, I'm afraid to say you won't be able to buy it. That's because it's already spoken for. I mean, we've had discussions with a certain well known fellow in Beijing and we have an agreement with him. He wants however much we produce. You all know this is our first day here in Kuanhe selling our meat, so you ought to know we couldn't actually come without bringing our finest product. That said, we didn't bring all that much and so some of you here, my friends, well, you haven't been able to buy anything and I'm really sorry about that. It really pains me, you know. So I tell you what: I don't feel much like putting this back in the truck to take back with us," he remarked, again holding up the meat for everyone to see. "How about we play a little game?"

Once he got to this point in his story, he abruptly stopped, holding back on revealing the climax. Instead, he pulled a gaudy roll of paper out of his pocket, held it up high so everyone could see it and then explained what kind of game he had in mind: "This paper here will serve as lottery tickets. There's a hundred here, I think. It'll be two *mao* [20 cents] for one ticket. Once they're all sold, then we'll choose the winner. There's a number on each ticket, so don't worry, I know what I'm doing. One of those numbers is the correct weight of that oh so special donkey meat. Whoever buys the right ticket, well, you're the winner. Come on, who's up for it, huh? It's only two *mao*. Who wants to try their luck?"

As though the place were set on fire, a forest of hands stretched up into the air, clutching whatever change they had left. Everyone wanted a ticket.

Just at that moment, however, a man leading two sheep appeared, seemingly intent on causing trouble for Wang Shun, or at least some measure of inconvenience. In a loud voice he bellowed above the crowd: "Hey shopkeeper, do you take goats here, too?

Wang Shun handed the lottery tickets to Han Wulin and replied: "We certainly do. Cattle, donkeys, we take pretty much everything. On one condition, however. They have to be of good quality. As you can see, we've pretty quickly established a name for ourselves. I can't accept just any old animal now, can I?"

His one condition made plain, Wang Shun proceeded to inspect the two mountain goats the man had brought with him. He ran his hands over them from front to back and from top to bottom, and then nodded his head: "They're not bad. I think they'll do."

"How much per *jin*?"

"How much does the county cooperative give you?"

"Four *mao*."

"I'll give you four point two *mao*."

"Sound, I agree."

Finally Guo Cunxian found his sister and her husband, Qiu Zhantang, in the mass of people. He pulled them over to one side and told them he'd been to their place not too long ago and delivered some meat to them, and that he only wished he'd known they'd be coming here as it would have saved him the trip.

Cunzhu could barely contain her happiness at seeing her brother but she felt a little bad about having wasted his time. She then remarked on the skill Wang Shun had for working a crowd. He was quite a performer.

Satisfied, he welcomed the praise: "He is rather good, isn't he?"

"That's for sure!" Cunzhu noticed her brother was alone and said: "I'd like to come with you when you return home. I miss mum. How's she doing?"

"She's fine, good." Then, directing his attention to his brother-in-law, he said: "Zhantang, you should come, too. There's actually something I'd like to discuss with you."

Qiu Zhantang was somewhat surprised: "What's on your mind?"

"I'm planning to open a factory in the village and I'd like to hear your opinions, both of you. After all, you're city folk, you've also worked in a factory and you know the ins and outs of it, where the opportunities are, right? I've come to a decision I don't want to be a simple farmer. I want to be well off. I just can't imagine any more going back to that life, planting crops and tilling the land. It's just no longer for me."

There was a burst of commotion and then riotous laughter. Someone had won the donkey meat! Some became green with envy while others turned to Wang Shun to ask when he'd have more. He hadn't actually discussed that with Guo Cunxian, so he didn't dare give a definite answer. He mentioned only that it wouldn't be too long. As he dealt with the remaining customers, he also began to pack up. The day's trading was finished.

Once things were packed up and ready to go, Guo Cunxian invited his sister and her husband to join the rest of them for a meal before they headed home. He turned to Wang Shun: "I know a place that does braised pancakes. They're not bad. You remember that place we ate at when we met your brother's wife? You know, the first time they came to Kuanhe. We can go there, buy some of those pancakes and braise a bit of that donkey meat. I think that'd be fantastic!"

Wang Shun's expression, however, was not what he expected. Directing his attention towards Han Wulin, Guo Cunxian pursued the matter: "Ah, do you mean to tell me you didn't even save a little of the marinated meat for us?"

Wang Shun looked pained: "I'd planned to, honest, but there were just so many customers, it didn't feel right to hold back. I mean, in business you have to look after your customer, don't you? What they think matters, so I ended up selling the whole lot."

"Ah, you great joker, you. You've got money on the brain. You've had a taste of it now and that's all you can see!"

12

A TIME FOR WEDDINGS

When it came to considering a family's prosperity and well-being, things were far from straightforward. In fact, they could be downright strange. No more so than for a once rich landlord family who'd suffered a great deal and who'd been persecuted and struggled against for quite some time. Yet despite these troubles, it seemed to do little to tamp down the desire for more children. Jin Laixi, for instance, already had a young daughter but that didn't stop him from wanting a son and so when his wife gave birth to a boy not long after his daughter was born, you could say his heart was quite content and the young babe incredibly cherished. When the boy reached five months old, however, that joy was turned on its head. No one really understood how or what the boy may have contracted but night and day he would cry incessantly. He stopped eating, eventually prompting the family to start forcing even just a little milk down his throat. Unfortunately, most of it would be vomited back up. Jin Laixi's wife, Mi Xiujun, had little recourse but to bundle the boy up and go in search of the village doctor and, although it was probably of little help, she also called on the boy's uncle, Jin Laiwang, to accompany her. The local clinic, such as it was, ended up being a waste of time and she had no option but to head to the main county hospital to seek help for her boy. At the same time, she dispatched someone to the ironworks to collect her husband. Once Jin Laixi returned and saw the state of his boy, he was even more worried than his wife. His son was the family's future, its lifeline, and he hoped beyond hope for things not to become more serious than they already seemed. Directing his attention to his wife, he begged for details of what the doctors had said. Her reply did little to allay his fear, however, for the doctors seemed to have no idea what was afflicting their son, nor any idea of how to treat him. To compound matters even further, an old lady who'd come to see the doctor herself said the child looked as though it was frightened, scared out of its wits as it were.

Upon hearing the old women speak, Jin Laixi could do little to control his rage:

"How is fear a bloody illness, huh? What in hell are you saying? Is there even such a sickness?"

"That's right, the doctor had asked the same thing, before saying that that was just superstition," said Mi Xiujun but before she could finish speaking, Jin Laixi seemed to be suddenly stricken by his own sense of fear and clutching his son tightly in his arms, he took off running. At first startled by her husband's abrupt actions, Mi Xiujun soon collected herself and tore off after him, yelling as she ran: "Just what are you doing? Slow down before you scare the child even more!"

Jin Laixi didn't answer her entreaties, nor did he let up but continued running until he reached the gate that led into Guo Cunxian's house. Pulling it open he stepped inside and finally stopped to catch his breath. Guo Cunxian's son was now old enough to run about the courtyard and to speak, too. Jin Laixi could see him busily chasing a few scraggy chickens under the watchful eye of his granny Sun Yueqing who was sitting near the house. Upon seeing the torment in Jin Laixi's face, the worry in his enflamed eyes and the screeching child clutched in his arms, she sprang from the bench in suitable fright: "Laixi, what's wrong? Why are you scaring your child like this? What has possessed you?"

Before he could utter a reply, his wife came running up behind him and, without pause, launched into cursing him for his rashness. Jin Laixi paid no attention to her and instead directed his attention toward Sun Yueqing, beseeching her: "Auntie, is uncle in? Please let him be here?"

Pointing in the direction of the old man's room, she answered him: "He's in there, incubating eggs!"

Incubating eggs? Jin Laixi suspected his ears had betrayed him.

Sensing his confusion, Sun Yueqing gestured towards the chicks scurrying about the courtyard: "These are his. He bred all of them and not even one has died. Can you imagine? A dozen altogether and he's still got five more in a makeshift coop. Anyway, why've you come looking for him?"

Jin Laixi's eyes turned towards the child he still held tightly in his arms. The baby looked terrified.

Her grandson, Chuanfu, who'd been in earshot, now ran towards Guo Jingshi's room and hollered after him: "Poppy, someone has come looking for you and he's brought a small baby with him. The baby's really crying, too. I think he's afraid of something."

From inside a reply could be heard: "Oh, I'll be there in a minute. Just ask him to hold on."

A long moment passed before the door finally opened and the crazy old man stepped out. The day was sweltering, and yet here he appeared fully clothed in heavy trousers and overcoat. He hadn't shaved for what seemed like ages, nor had he had his hair cut. But surprisingly, there were no beads of sweat to be seen, only a slightly flushed look amid the long hair. It was hard to determine his age. He looked very much like he had now many years ago. In contrast to the heavy clothes he wore, his feet were bare and as he walked over the bits and pieces of firewood scattered about the courtyard there was a terrible cracking and snapping sound. He walked up to Jin Laixi, extended a hand and felt the forehead of the baby in his arms. The child stopped crying almost immediately, its two dark onyx eyes stared at the old man who now stood in front of them.

Jin Laixi and his wife were dumbstruck.

Sun Yueqing chimed in: "Quickly now, let Guo Jingshi hold the baby, our little Chuanfu has never been ill, never been hurt and never endured any unpleasantness at all."

With little hesitation, Jin Laixi passed his son into Guo Jingshi's arms. The small child reached out its arms, seemingly wanting to grab hold of the old man's beard. Jin Laixi seized the moment's respite to poke his head into Guo Jingshi's room. His reaction was honest. Shit, it was hot in there and populated with chickens, ducks, a dark-furred dog and sheep. A veritable menagerie was wedged into his room every which way. On his bed, squawking and fluttering about, some munching away on whatever it was he was feeding them, other animals were sleeping, each and every one of them seemingly living together in one harmonious mess. The heat in the room seemed to weigh heavily but there was no malice in the air. Instead there was an earthy, natural pleasantness to it. Jin Laixi couldn't help but be a little startled however and felt the hairs on the back of his neck stand up. Slowly and carefully he pulled his head out of the room, turned around and bowed deeply to Guo Jingshi: "Uncle, you're really something, you are!" There was more he wanted to say but the words died in his mouth. If Guo Cunxian ended up in hot water again, surely his crazy old uncle would be able to utter some blessing or other to get him out of it!

Guo Jingshi returned the child to his mother's arms and no sooner was it safely against her breast, the baby's mouth searched almost ravenously for his mother's nipple. Mi Xiujun opened her blouse and once the baby latched on, it began to suck vigorously as though it had long been denied. Chuanfu then seized the opportunity to grab hold of his granddad's leg before being lifted up and brought into the room with him; with his free hand, the old man closed the door behind them. Jin Laixi and his wife were extremely grateful and with Guo Jingshi having already left, they expressed their gratitude to Sun Yueqing before getting ready to depart. But just as they were about to leave, Guo Cunxian arrived home. Jin Laixi looked at the town leader and said: "What a coincidence, huh?"

"Coincidence? Nah, I heard you were back. I actually came looking for you and now here you are. How's your boy?"

Jin Laixi raised his thumb to show all was well: "Your uncle's a mystic for sure!" He turned to his wife and told her to head home, then looked at Guo Cunxian: "What's wrong, what do you need me for?"

"Oh, it's only a small thing." Guo Cunxian, however, didn't invite the man inside. Instead, he directed him towards the main gate and together they stepped outside. Some distance from his home but still in view of it, Guo Cunxian found a place to sit and gestured for Jin Laixi to crouch down with him. Once seated, Guo Cunxian spoke: "I've a builder's question for you. Do you think it's possible to add another room to my house?"

"More than enough space, for sure," confirmed Jin Laixi, scanning the house and courtyard. "With the structure the way it is now with the courtyard attached to it, well, you could keep the main gate where it is and build adjacent to it, or you could shift the gate and cut a new one. Either is doable. When are you thinking of?"

"The sooner the better, to be honest." Guo Cunxian sucked on his teeth: "Right now wouldn't work, there's too much going on. I haven't even decided on a site. Let's discuss it some more but don't talk to anyone else about this. Cunzhi isn't getting any younger. It's just that he doesn't seem to want to marry. He spends his days with our uncle, learning god knows what kind of medicine and talking about philosophy. Either that or he's growing his green thumb and taking care of the zoo he has brought into their room. But he won't dare say anything about not getting married as he's worried he'll upset our mother or provoke her ire. He's just hoping it will quietly go away, that no one will notice. But it has been brought up more than once, you know, and quite recently, actually, things got kind of serious too, by the sound of things. But, well, it just didn't work out and now we're worried if we don't hurry up and arrange something, we simply won't be able to do anything at all. The girl... let's just say she had a... a way about her. Our mum thought she'd be a good match but also that she seemed a little rough around the edges. She was blunt, too blunt, said Cunzhi was spineless, that her family was looking for someone who could take care of things, you know, manage a household, and that that just wasn't Cunzhi. Mum has been ever so upset about it. She hasn't been sleeping and she has been nagging me about it repeatedly. Well, let's say this has all steeled my resolve and convinced me that I need to extend our house by adding another room. That should be enough to make him take things more seriously so that he'll see the light and realise he'd better get married and soon!"

"Sounds like a plan. I can round up some lads from the factory to help. I can mark out the lines and get them to raise the walls. It should only take three to five days. Set the date and we'll make things happen. Just bear in mind the New Year festivities as no one will be available then."

"Do you think there's time to get it done before the New Year? I haven't even made the earthen bricks. That takes time."

"What're you talking about? You're thinking about earthen bricks? What's wrong with you? Our engineering team has access to a proper kiln to fire the clay into proper bricks. Take a look at the building Wang Shun has for his food factory. That's redbrick from ground to roof. Why would we use simple earth to build your extension? Shit, who'd want to waste their energy on trying to make those any more? Besides, you'd only end up seeing it fall apart in a couple of years and having to rebuild again from scratch."

"But you're talking about structures that belong to the community, to all of us. Aren't I just talking about extending my own individual home?"

"Are you separate from the collective? Shit, if it wasn't for you, would Guojiadian be in the position of strength it now is? To my mind, the collective ought to build you a grand structure, two storeys at least. You're our standard-bearer, if we wouldn't dare to even build something like that for you, then how have we been able to strike out as we have and improve things for all of us, huh? How have we been able to work so hard, hmm? We've lived forever in mudbrick houses but now we're not worried about where our next meal comes from or about whether or not we'll have even enough to drink. Shit, we've got time enough to stand around and shoot the breeze, argue about this and that, and have a little bit of fun."

Guo Cunxian lifted himself up from the ground: "You know, what you've said, it has affected me. How do you think we've made things better for Guojiadian? I mean, to be frank, it's just about getting rich. If I hadn't taken the lead and grabbed the bull by the horns, as it were, we might be poor but we'd have our honour. Isn't there a certain reason to poverty, a desire and need to strive to overcome it? Fine, I hear what you're saying. Build the extension for Cunzhi as you see fit."

"You're right and, what's more, let's let the whole neighbourhood see, huh? Never before has anyone lived in a brick house, not even the richest landlord, but that's what I'll build for you. Give it to me and don't you concern yourself with it at all. You just make the proper requests and then inspect the work once it's done."

Guo Cunxian was still a little uneasy and urged Jin Laixi once more: "For the sake of the collective, I won't use a cent of its money. Tell the accountant to keep a record."

"Of course, that's as it should be. Are you still worried about me taking charge? I'll make sure everything is accounted for and properly recorded, and that none of the collective's funds are used. Tell me, over the past two years, who hasn't got at least a little bit of money, hmm? Don't just speak of adding a third room, if you'd prefer a small three storey building, well, we can make that happen. You know, it would be our pleasure."

"I want the cost of the building works taken out of my year-end salary. Once it's finished, I want the costs clearly marked and shown on the wall. That way, if anyone else in Guojiadian would like a similar extension, then they'll know how much it takes."

"Don't worry, it'll be a piece of cake!"

The autumn was dry and parched. So, too, were feelings in the town.

And at the reservoir, Liu Yucheng and Cui Lan had become virtually inseparable, much like a young married couple. This was clear to Yumei, at least, and she soon found herself spending less and less time in their company. When Cui Lan had first starting coming to the reservoir to work, Yumei had told her she needn't bother to bring her own food and that she instead would prepare enough for the three of them to share. This arrangement, however, didn't last all that long and soon Cui Lan ended up bringing her own meals, not because she wasn't grateful to Yumei, but rather due to her father and the worry that would grow within him if he continually saw her head off each and every day without anything to eat. By bringing her own food, at least, the appearance would be that she was taking care of things by herself. This is not to say they ceased to enjoy their meals collectively. In fact, the opposite was true; there was just more food to go around. Before Cui Lan had joined them at the reservoir, Yumei had generally brought lunch and then stayed on for part of the afternoon to lend a hand. It wouldn't be until much later in the afternoon that she would head home to make dinner for her older brother. Now, however, she no longer did this. Once lunch was finished, she simply went straight home, leaving Yucheng in the company of Cui Lan. Alone together, the two would toil the day away, loading the earth into the wheelbarrows before pushing them away. Cui Lan couldn't be considered strong but the more she worked side by side with Yucheng, the more their bodies began to move in unison together, the more strength and vigour she seemed to possess. And as this intimacy grew stronger day by day, actual physical contact between them increased. Soon, it became quite frequent for Cui Lan's breasts to brush up against his arms, for her body to draw ever closer. The effects of this closeness became plain. Yucheng would break out in a sweat and have difficulty containing the lustful fires growing within him. There was often nothing for him to do but to turn away and to try to tamp down the urges swelling up inside. This, however, only seemed to egg her on. She would, almost fervently, chase his gaze, or take out her own handkerchief to wipe his brow, to feel his skin beneath her hand, a seductive if not wholly intentional look in her eye.

Labouring, sweating, toiling as the men were, the whole situation couldn't help but be ripe for frayed emotions and potential havoc. Whenever they had a free moment, they would immediately launch into all manner of raucous storytelling in language that would make the most brazen blush. If a woman happened to be passing by the reservoir at these moments, they'd be unable to contain themselves and the catcalling would commence, their eyes immediately undressing the passerby. It would make one wonder how they could tolerate the son of a landlord like Liu Yucheng among them, to say nothing of how he was now seemingly consorting with a poor farmer's daughter, daily playing at being a 'good married couple'! They roared with laughter at the scene, shouted slogans and foul curses, too. But nothing could make them think that this young woman, who seemed so gentle and agreeable, and with a good background, too, would be stirred on further by their salacious gossip. It was as though she had steeled her heart to stay close to this landlord's son, to be swallowed up together and destroyed by the humiliations they hurled at him!

The more disreputable, unsavoury of the men working at the reservoir often wondered just what in hell he was doing here, especially considering his class background. And when they saw Ou Guangming arrive one day with militiamen in tow, they simply assumed they had come for him. They never once suspected they'd come to assist him. Of course, Ou Guangming couldn't help but be a little amused by their reaction and so, in a loud and quite clear voice, he spoke to Liu Yucheng: "Cunxian has asked me to come and see how you're getting on and to see if you need any help making sustained progress. After all, he's got plans for you, even more important work he wants you to do. So he's hoping you'll be able to finish sooner rather than later."

Nearly everyone working on the reservoir project heard the few sentences Ou Guangming had uttered and then saw him instruct the men he'd come with to begin working themselves. Without hesitation they immersed themselves in the task, spending the better part of a day assisting Liu Yucheng and Cui Lan with their assignment. Many couldn't help but wonder at what kind of horseshoe this bastard old son of a landlord had up his arse. From then on, each time Ou Guangming would visit Liu Yucheng, he'd bring men with him to help with the work, all the while talking in a relaxed and amicable fashion with both Yucheng and Cui Lan, often joking about when they'd formally tie the knot. The other workers could only marvel at such a prospect. Could there be a bigger mismatch? No one saw, however, that Ou Guangming helping Liu Yucheng was like helping himself. After all, if Yucheng were to marry Cui Lan, Yumei could be his. It wasn't surprising, then, that Ou Guangming's frequent and lively visits ended up causing quite a bit of consternation among Guojiadian's bare sticks. But if the locals from the town weren't up in arms, then those from elsewhere certainly couldn't cause a ruckus themselves.

Before much more time passed, the work Liu Yucheng had been assigned, along with the work he'd undertaken for Cui Lan, reached its final stage. All that remained was a couple of days' work at best, which could be completed at a much more relaxed pace if they so wished. Liu Yucheng, however, recalled what Ou Guangming had told him, namely, that Guo Cunxian had a more important task for him to carry out, and so the two of them put all their effort into one last burst of energy to complete everything as quickly as possible, ensuring that they'd be able to save a couple of days and actually leave earlier than planned. Taking a moment to review the task they'd completed and seeing how uniformly they'd dug and how precise everything was, both Yucheng and Cui Lan let go a sigh of contentment. They had really done a fine job, something to be proud of; or at least, they should have been happy but before the satisfaction could sink in, it was replaced by a sense of loneliness and despair. Neither of them could speak. Instead they only regretted the fact they'd finished so quickly. With the work finished, it was time for each of them to return home, and who's to say when they'd get the chance to see each other again? Perhaps if they had thought about that first, they wouldn't have been so keen to finish with such a flourish of speed. But neither of them was willing to say this. They didn't want to shatter the perceived reverie of having completed the work so efficiently.

Standing there together, in a night filled with more stars than one could possibly count, Liu Yucheng could see a sparkling radiance in Cui Lan's eyes. The sight itself melted him and he felt a hot urge bubbling up within him as though his blood were boiling, and the sound was echoing in his ears. The rising tide was becoming too much and he struggled to hold it back. He was starved, famished and desolate. In a quiet voice he broke the silence: "Come on, let's go."

Cui Lan slowly lifted her face towards him. Softly she responded: "Yucheng, it's so late. I'm afraid. Can you walk with me and escort me home?"

He hesitated a moment: "Sure, yes, erm, that's for the best." They tidied up the site, packing away the tools, the water container and the odds and ends, and placing all of it in the push cart. Liu Yucheng then took hold of the handle while Cui Lan sat astride the wheelbarrow. Together they headed off towards Mapodian. Unspoken words hung in the air between them but neither dared to open their mouth. At the end of the day, Cui Lan was still but a young woman. She believed wholeheartedly that Liu Yucheng was aware of her feelings; she'd made that plain enough while they worked together. As a man, she believed it was his responsibility to speak first, to make the first move, to pull open the window to let their feelings through. But would he have the gumption to do so? Since he was a boy, he'd only ever faced persecution as the son of a despicable landlord. Of course, doing a good turn for someone invoked feelings of warmth but could those feelings be reason enough to broach such a subject? Could she, could anyone get past the fact of his background? Could he ever take off the hat of a landlord's son? In matters of the heart, could he risk it? She was fond of him, he could tell, but did he want to disrupt what they already had? He certainly didn't want to cause her any more trouble than she already had. He was afraid to, but he had to let the feelings go.

The two of them sauntered down the road quiet and uncommunicative, and before long they arrived in Mapodian where Liu Yucheng halted the wheelbarrow. He'd rather not bring her directly to her doorstep for if he did, her father would certainly invite him in and he'd find it difficult and impolite to refuse. Clutching the handles tightly, he waited for Cui Lan to step down. She, however, didn't move an inch, seemingly glued to the spot. Then, in a quiet voice, she said: "Yucheng, my legs are so tired, I can't move them. They won't budge. Lift me out, please."

For a spell he was stupefied, unsure of what to do. The only sound he could hear was the pounding of his own heart. Without answering, he positioned the wheelbarrow securely then reached over the side of the cart and put his arms gently around Cui Lan. In one smooth, effortless motion he began to lift her up but as he did so, her scent crossed his face and he was paralysed with confusion. Another moment passed, and fear and worry topped his confusion. It was as though one sensed the presence of some spirit or ghost creeping up from behind. For her part, Cui Lan wrapped her arms around Yucheng's neck, drawing him in even closer, then her soft, supple and moist lips met his own dry, parched mouth.

Abruptly, from out of the darkness of the evening, a stern voice shattered the moment of intimacy: "In public, hell, just what're you two up to, huh?!"

Cui Liang stepped out of the shadows, a rough stick in hand, and rushed towards the two figures he saw in the dark with his stick flailing about wildly. Liu Yucheng shielded Cui Lan from the blows, twisting his frame so that the blows fell on his back. The old man's arms continued to pump up and down like pistons and, at the same time, he kept up his rebukes: "Liu Yucheng, you dirty bastard, I knew you were up to no good!"

Liu Yucheng remained where he was and let Cui Liang continue to wail at him. Shifting her frame, Cui Lan removed herself from Yucheng's embrace and reached out to take hold of the stick her father was swinging. Tears streaming down her face she shouted at her father: "Dad, have you gone mad? Have you lost your mind? Have you no conscience?"

Cui Liang shouted in reply: "I am crazy but it isn't me who has no conscience. Heh, I wonder what his motives were when he saved me and my poor leg, huh? What was it? A leg for a daughter perchance? Well, not on my watch, that's for damn sure. I'll give this bloody leg right back to him!" He stopped pummelling Yucheng and directed his ire towards his own still lame leg, pummelling it mercilessly.

Cui Lan was on the verge of hyperventilating but his anger was unrelenting. She snatched the stick away from her father and flung it into the darkness: "I'll tell you who to strike. Hmm, you remember when my brother left, right? He left because of you. So, what is it? Will you beat me until I run away, too? If that's the case, who'll be left to look after you, huh? Let me tell you something. My heart already belongs to Liu Yucheng. I love him. If you give us your blessing, we'll be here to take care of you. If you don't, I'm leaving with him, right now, this very night. You do what you please!"

During this whole exchange, Liu Yucheng stood quietly alongside them, not uttering a word. But upon hearing Cui Lan's declaration he was both surprised and elated. Surprised because she'd made such a public declaration in front of her father to save him, and elated because she felt the same way he did and she wanted to be with him.

Cui Liang was powerless to resist. He looked at his daughter forlornly, responding to the resoluteness she'd shown: "My sweet little Lan, he comes from the landlord class. If you marry him your life will be ruined, and not only this one. Your children, if you end up having them, will face the same shame, generation after generation. Oh!"

"I know there'll be hardships and that we'll be bullied and persecuted. I accept that. But I know he's a good man. Over the past three months, he's been nothing but kind and decent to me, never once trying to take advantage of things, never asking for any kind of repayment for helping you. It's only the darkness in your own heart that's seeing this. What's more, he's not a landlord. His father might have been but not Yucheng. So tell me, what's there to hold me back? What better prospects are there? I've got you to look after." Cui Lan stopped talking abruptly, turned and walked beside Liu Yucheng. She proceeded to rub his back where her father had struck him. In a low voice she said: "You're alright, aren't you? Nothing broken?"

Liu Yucheng shook his head: "I'm fine and I know what you're trying to say. Don't provoke your father any more. If there's more that needs saying, we can talk about it later."

Cui Lan turned him round so that she could look into his face. Gently she caressed it. Her eyes were soft but there was a brilliance to them as well. She could see the warmth in his heart and his forgiving nature. But at the same time her voice was firm, unyielding: "There's nothing more to say. I think we've said everything tonight and caused quite a stir. We might as well say it's done. In three days I'll be here, waiting for your bridal party to arrive. Let's set the date, there's nothing more I could ever want. And if I can't wait that long, then I'll come to you. Yucheng, don't you dare throw me aside now. My life is in your hands."

Once she had finished speaking, she put her arms around him and he soon felt her tears roll down his neck.

Guo Cunxian could feel the sullen mood that hung over the town, so he immediately set about organising a grand meeting to discuss things. And he really did want it to be 'grand', meaning that all forty heads of the production brigades were to attend, as well as their deputies. Wang Shun, as factory director, had to attend, as did the engineering teams, both team leaders and their deputies. Guo Cunxian even went as far as to require those in charge of running the kilns to come and the builders. He really meant it to be a 'grand' meeting, regardless of whether the attendees were all Party members or not. What made the summons even more extraordinary was that Guo Cunxian even had former 'class enemies' attend the discussion, namely, Liu Yucheng, the former landlord's son, and the once rich peasant Jin Laixi. But despite their shock at seeing who was in attendance, no one among the rank and file dared to say a word. All they could do was wonder: just what was this meeting all about?

The people were packed in but Guo Cunxian hadn't yet announced the start of the meeting. Instead he sat solemnly on a bench in front of them, slowly inhaling on a cigarette. After a few drags he coughed, threw the cigarette butt onto the ground, waited for his coughing to subside and then lit another. He repeated the process, methodically, one after the other. It was the first time anyone in the village had actually seen him smoke. Once he'd smoked a few more, he no longer coughed but his complexion had changed, transformed into something hideous as he swayed unsteadily on his chair. Wang Shun interrupted the scene, shouting that the cigarettes must be poisoned! He abruptly stood up, grabbed a mug of boiling hot tea, added a little cold water to it and then tried to get Guo Cunxian to raise his head and swallow a few mouthfuls. With some difficulty he managed to drink a number of mouthfuls and slowly the colour returned to his face. Wang Shun deftly squirrelled the pack of cigarettes out of Guo Cunxian's sight, depositing them in his own pocket, before turning to his friend to berate him almost good-humouredly: "Just what're you playing at, huh, wasting my fags!"

Guo Cunxian didn't reply and a heavy silence fell once more over the gathering. Then, as though he were mumbling to himself, Guo Cunxian spoke: "Things have gone wrong, let me tell you. The higher-ups aren't pleased, some below are opposing, our village hasn't learned from Dazhai [held up as a model village for agriculture in the late 1960s], we've not terraced our fields and the day before yesterday I was severely reprimanded for just this failure! But it's not that we haven't learned from Dazhai. You know, when that initiative was first announced, well, I asked some experienced farmers, people who know about the land, and they all said that terracing our fields was a waste of manpower and time. Useless, that's what they told me. Dazhai sits abreast a mountain, so it makes sense to terrace their fields, there's really no other way. I mean, you can't separate the fields from the slope of the land so it makes sense terracing their fields. All you need is some water and you can easily preserve the moisture of the soil.

"But Guojiadian is flat, the whole blooming area. If we set about deliberately building burial mounds across the whole area, shit, we'll just end up with stagnant and motionless water, and with the soil nutrients unable to circulate; then how in the hell would we grow anything? Later on, hmm, you'll see what'll happen to our neighbouring villages, won't you? Their whole fucking fields will be barren like some old man's bald head with a few roots and that will be all. Who'll they blame then? Hmm... but will the higher-ups be pleased? You betcha, and no criticisms will be forthcoming, even though they won't meet their production quota. No, I'll be the one they criticise because I didn't follow the directive!

"There's more too. To help find a wife for my younger brother Cunzhi, who's nearly thirty, I've been trying to add an extension to our family home to provide a room for him, you know. But this has led to nothing but a deluge of rumours and gossip spreading throughout the town which is really drowning me, that's what it's doing. I see their faces, green with envy, covetous of what others have, you know? I wouldn't have thought it possible of our town. Shit, didn't I post the details? Aren't they there for all to see? Hell, if you're that envious, then build the same damn thing! Right here, right now I swear this to all of you, once I'm finished building an extra room for my brother, I'll start one big building here, alright? It'll be fancy, too, and if it's not, well, you won't be blamed for tearing it down! You know, when Cunzhi was a boy he was quite clever but then he endured that beating from Lan Shoukun and that changed everything. If not for that beating, well, I doubt he'd be this old and still unmarried.

"Oh, and speaking of which, there's something else I want to say. I heard that for the past few years, Lan Shoukun has been looking for his child, that he finally found him in Qinghai and that he has decided to settle there but I wish he'd come back and see Guojiadian right now. We're not going through that terrible class struggle that he once led. Guojiadian has changed, hasn't it!"

The assembled people began to whisper among themselves, surprised at Guo Cunxian's candour. They hadn't expected the meeting to be a chance for Cunxian to vent his feelings.

Guo Cunxian pulled himself up from the bench he'd been sitting on. His eyes bored into the crowd but no one had the gumption to meet his stare head-on. He spoke again in even harsher tones: "You know, today isn't supposed to be about me whinging about this and that. After all, there's little chance it'll change anything, so I guess there's really no point to it." He paused before continuing: "No, maybe it does have a purpose. We can't complain to the higher-ups but we can to those below and we shouldn't berate ourselves. When you all first came here, you felt something was amiss and that there was a strange atmosphere. You wondered just what kind of meeting this was going to be and why so many of you had been called here, right? Let me tell you, this isn't a Party meeting. That's why I've called everyone from the village, from all walks of life. Well, it's Guojiadian's own Zunyi Conference, just like the one they had during the Long March. I want us to decide together the future direction of this village, its destiny. And because of this, everyone here will have to give their own point of view and, once we've all done that, then we'll announce our decision to the rest of the town, explaining, too, that whatever decision we arrive at isn't solely mine but has been made by all of us together. We'll all put forward ideas and thus we'll all be responsible."

He gestured to Guo Cunyong to record the meeting agenda he had just set out, making sure that each and every word was duly noted. The entire factory was silent, the attendees eyeing each other. To a man, they all realised the seriousness of what Guo Cunxian was proposing.

The quiet was broken again by Guo Cunxian who began to lay out the formalities: "The first order of business is the assigning of work units in Guojiadian and whether or not we should follow suit. You may have heard that certain other towns have recently set off fireworks, shall we say. They've divided their villagers up into various work units and most have responded quite happily to this. Of course, we're not talking about how things worked during the land reform efforts. I mean, that was about assigning a plot of land to each and every household and giving each family a small piece of land that was theirs to till. Dividing up into teams is about dissolving the production brigades, which would mean each home undertaking the job of cultivating their own piece of land. So I guess it's similar to how things worked before. In any case, other villages have already put this into practice. They've decided to divvy things up and they've done so, partly because they don't have a factory to be thinking about. I mean, their only concern is the farmland, day in, day out.

"But Guojiadian is different. At present there's quite a lot of interest in what we're doing. Hundreds are coming round to the idea that they don't want to just till the fields any more. No, they want to come and work in a factory. We've got the taste for industry now and it's sweet indeed. Last year, we produced about a million tonnes. I estimate that this year we'll reach at least three million tonnes or more and some are content with that. But if you ask me, well, I don't think that's up to par yet. You know what? I think we're still pretty small-scale. To be frank, I think we're still on the first step at best and that there's still so much more to accomplish. Think about it, we're talking about a food processing factory. Shouldn't we also want our own chicken farm, our own piggery and dairy farm? Shouldn't we want to grow our industry, to have our products distributed throughout Kuanhe County and even all the way to Beijing? Don't we want people in Tianjin to be drinking our milk and eating our meat? Should we even be thinking about boundaries? There's also the iron and steel works to think about, and the possibility of manufacturing electrical products and chemicals. I'm quite hopeful, you know, about a possible chemical factory. We're close to the sea and have abundant resources. Things like PVC and sodium hydroxide, well, they're things to be treasured and there's demand for them. However much you can make, there's sure to be someone who wants it and we could, essentially, set our own price.

"These past few years we've been busy setting off down this road of industry and I've come to know a few things, to realise something, that even the name of our town, Guojiadian [literally, Guo Family Shop], well, it has the word 'shop' in it. I mean, that's what '*dian*' is. After all, if we want to profit and do well for ourselves, we need to visualise what's in front of us, to seize that opportunity, and the means to do that is by opening up shop. That's what a factory is all about. All we need to do is eliminate our poor-peasant mentality. That's the only way to become prosperous. And that's where the problem lies. If we divvy up the land like other towns have done and give each household their own plot, where in hell will we build a factory? Let's think about it. If we do divide up the fields, well, some of us might do alright, some might get rich and they might even have a better piece of land, who's to say? But in the long run, won't we only be paving the way to the end of Guojiadian, the destruction of our town? You know, I've been tormented by this, thinking about what to do. My head's pounding, so that's why I'm here asking for your point of view. If someone has something they'd like to say, then go ahead."

The whole building broke into a cacophony of voices, bubbling over like a pot on the stove. People in the back were straining to get their views heard while those in front did the same. Everyone was talking over everyone else, some in loud voices, some more quietly. But the more discussion there was, the more they all seemed to coalesce around a particular focus. Guo Cunyong, who'd been tasked with recording everything, now chimed in to try and sum things up: "From the discussions I've recorded, it seems a unanimous decision is clear. You all oppose dividing Guojiadian into work units and you support being more entrepreneurial and more industrialised in the pursuit of enriching the lives of everyone in the town together. However, since national policy is geared towards divvying up villages and land, if Guojiadian does not follow this directive, you're all concerned about what may happen, yes? If we understand correctly what has been said, allocating plots of land to people ultimately means that the collective will have no business with regard to what happens to the individual plots and, when year-end calculations are made, any collective material and social benefits would exclude that individual. He would go about his daily life and the collective would do the same, to each his own. This point is clear. Finally, then, by all estimates, no one is in favour of this policy."

Guo Cunxian stood up once more. A smile had at last come to his previously dark visage: "All right then, we now have to discuss the second item, which is our plan for Guojiadian's future. The land round our village, well, you all know what it's like. The eastern marshes are quite large but that's also the worst soil, where the salt is closest to the surface, especially in the area nearest the frog marshes. It's much the same for the southern marshes. The salt content of the soil there is high, too, which all means there's not much by way of fertile land that we can rely on, no matter how hard we might try to till the land and make it productive. True, our ancestors tilled these lands and weren't seemingly ready to accept defeat. For many generations they planted crops and made a go of it, and it wasn't as though the more they tried, the poorer they got. That's because of the western and northern marshes. They might not be as broad as the other areas but the soil's alright, good enough to support the village, which is the reason why we've built this here factory on the eastern marshes. This is also the reason why we should continue to build here, in the eastern parts of town. We'll make this area our industrial sector and when we've exhausted this space, we'll have the southern marshes at our disposal. Are you all agreed on that?"

"Yes, of course. That makes sense, indeed. What other choice is there? There's no grounds to oppose it."

Hearing their response, Guo Cunxian continued: "There's more we need to consider, namely, the fact that Guojiadian is a farming town. It doesn't matter how much we develop our industrial capacity, each household will still need its own plot of land. I mean, we can't be left in a position of not having anything to eat. Yes, industry will allow us to be better off and it can make us rich but our roots are still in the soil, in tilling the land. So, we're not going to divide things up further but, to be honest, we also need to do away with the work units themselves. Before, we had forty of them and the land was distributed equally among them, regardless of the quality of the soil. But now, it's all a mess. Some team leaders have gone off to work in the factory, Wulin set up the abattoir and now runs that and Cunxiao's in charge of the mill. Oh hey, Cunxiao, let me tell you something: you don't need to mill all of the wheat by hand, we've some communal funds left over from the end of the year. Take some of that to buy a proper machine to do it. That way, we'll be able to mill not only rice but other grains as well, corn, sorghum, you name it, we can industrialise that sector as well as a subsidiary of Wang Shun's operation, producing a range of high-quality flour. You understand what I'm saying, yes? Good.

"Umm, to return to what I was saying, we've got to decide what to do with the more productive soil to the west and north of the town, right? What I've got in mind is this. I'd like to industrialise the whole agricultural process, to professionalise the use of the land. Of course, it has to be tilled properly. Compared with what our neighbouring villages are doing, well, we'll have to see who better manages the land, who gets the most out of it. Am I right? I've heard in the United States, one farmer produces enough to feed fifty people. I reckon fifty of our farmers could produce enough for an entire city. After all, one bad master ought not to have five hundred farmers looking after him, now, should he! That said, I think there's something we need to see from this American example. Shit, it's hard for me to admit this. Do you know why? Because I've got hold of a little money, that's why. Next year, we need three machines we need: a tractor, a harvester and a water pump. This is what we need to discuss. We need someone to take the lead on this, someone who's happy and willing to do it, and someone who'll do a proper job and make sure the land is cultivated as best we can. We need someone in charge. It doesn't matter what they did before or what their class background is, or whether or not they're a Party member. The only requirement is that they can work, and work hard, and that they're capable, right? I mean, we're not searching for someone to lead the Red Guards. You understand?"

"Yes!" the crowd replied together excitedly. They all seemed to know whom Guo Cunxian was referring to, and at the same time understood why Liu Yucheng had been summoned to attend the meeting as well. There was no way anyone could protest. Guo Cunxian had manoeuvred things so adroitly. There was nothing to say about Liu Yucheng's ability to till the land for he was the logical choice, perhaps the only choice to take up the reins of such an agricultural initiative. He'd already made a name for himself in managing the industrial efforts already launched. While it was almost inconceivable that such wonderful opportunities seemed to land at his feet, there really was no other choice.

Ou Guangming, sensing the moment, jumped into the conversation to give his two cents' worth: "I've a name to put forward. I think Liu Yucheng is ideally suited for the role. After all, the whole town knows that whatever he touches turns to gold!"

In chorus, the attendees replied: "Yes, Liu Yucheng is an excellent choice!"

Guo Cunxian turned towards his friend: "Yucheng, do you have anything to say?"

Hurriedly, Liu Yucheng stood up, stooped and then bowed respectfully, reverentially: "Thank you, thank you all for your faith in me. I'll try to devote all my energies to making it a success."

Guo Cunxian extended the palm of his hand, gesturing for Liu Yucheng to raise his head: "Hey, lift your head up, I want to see you standing up straight. We've chosen you to lead this project. It's not a struggle session!"

Guo Cunxian's teasing nature inspired the audience to cheer and laugh. The earlier seriousness had dissipated, giving way to a more relaxed atmosphere.

Guo Cunxian continued: "Afterwards, I'll send men to work under you. You'll need several dozen. You'll be in charge, their leader. Now, you won't want them to see you with your head down and think you're inferior. How will you ever be a leader if that's what they think, hmm? They chose you," he said, gesturing to the crowd. "If someone opposes, well, they can come and talk to me about it. Today, now, I'll give you your first name. Guo Cunzhi is willing to tend the fields and later on he can be one of your guards. Alright then, that's settled. Does anyone have anything to say?"

A "no" came from the crowd.

"Let's turn our attention to the final matter, namely our intention to enrich the lives of everyone in the village, to see everyone prosper. For that to happen, two main factors need to be considered. One, we need capable men who know about wealth. Two, we need information and contacts. That's how we'll know we're on the right path. And since this is what we need, I want to mobilise the entire village. Whoever has the most helpful information, ideas, knows the right direction to take, or can introduce us to the most capable men and whoever can put the town on the most beneficial path, well, let me say you'll be well rewarded. How does that sound?"

"Yes, great, excellent, wonderful idea, that's the way it should be."

. . .

The autumn harvest was nearing its end and all that remained in the fields surrounding Guojiadian were a few hauls of beans, mostly black ones, with a number of mung and soybeans mixed in as well. The bean pods had already begun to turn yellow, indicating their ripeness. Most burst open as the thresher was pushed through the field, the beans falling quickly to the ground. The pod carcasses were then raked up and piled into a heap to one side, the remnants of a successful harvest.

Out of the group of five youths sent down to the countryside who'd been living and 'learning' among the farmers of Guojiadian, only Lin Meitang accompanied the other ladies of the town in collecting the beans. The other female in the group, Hong Fang, was more fortunate. Wang Shun had noticed her some time back and had ordered her to report to the food processing factory to do the books. Her days were thus spent there, amid the wafting, pungent aroma of Wang Shun's distinct recipes. Of the other youths, Shen Liangbao had become sick, weak and utterly useless in terms of farm work, so he'd been sent back to Beijing. The remaining two young men were similarly useless: Tang Hao and his lame leg had also returned to the capital; Ye Yuan had told the town authorities he was working on some project for the village and had essentially disappeared from sight.

For his part, Guo Cunxian looked upon the youths with a certain amount of respect for their supposed city education, and consequently was disinclined to burden them with much work, choosing instead to let them manage their own affairs, more or less. After all, their numbers didn't make much of a difference and the town had got on alright without them in the past. They certainly wouldn't be discouraged from working in the fields but nor were they forbidden from leaving, if that was what they wished. In fact, Lin Meitang didn't need to be in the fields, they could have used her number skills in the mill, getting her to take care of the accounts. Given that the mill director was actually in charge of her work unit, all it would have taken would have been one good word and she'd have been off. But she never once broached the topic. Perhaps she felt that doing so would have been akin to enacting the abuse a daughter-in-law so often faced in the old society? There was another reason, however. Guo Cunyong wouldn't allow her because he had something much more appropriate for her to do. He just wouldn't tell her what it was, at least not yet.

On this day, while she toiled in the fields, Guo Cunyong suddenly rode up on his Red Flag bicycle, the one the commune had purchased. He looked imposing, well groomed, with a crisp white shirt neatly tucked into his blue trousers. His face was held high, the look of a young man apparently content in his place and in what he'd accomplished (whatever that may have been). The townspeople, those well experienced in matters between young men and women, always considered Guo Cunyong to be good-looking, if not handsome in his way. His features were broad, his complexion fair. And there always seemed to be an air of good fortune about him as well, although it would be difficult to say exactly what this stemmed from. Once he'd manoeuvred his bicycle up to where the women were working, Guo Cunyong brought it to a halt and in a loud and confident voice, he hollered out to them: "Meitang... Meitang, come here."

Guo Cunyong enjoyed making a show of his closeness to Lin Meitang, especially in front of everyone else, and they, too, knew of his intentions and the circumstances he was in. It probably went without saying that word spread like wildfire through the village, throughout the whole commune, really. But was setting his sights upon one particular girl reason enough for him to act like this? It was difficult to say. In any case, things weren't all that straightforward, especially since Lin Meitang hadn't taken the plunge and resigned herself to spending the rest of her life in the countryside. No, she worried about accepting his amorous advances and whether or not that'd mean she'd be able to return to Beijing or remain in Guojiadian. According to the farm girls, Guo Cunyong was considered a fairly good catch but from her side, she hesitated. She wasn't about to throw caution to the wind and embark on a life with him, not when she had other things to think about. This was why she didn't come bounding up to him when he first arrived. Instead, she simply straightened her waist, looked towards him with the rake still in her hand and replied clearly and emotionlessly: "Comrade Guo, is something wrong?"

Guo Cunyong gestured towards her, urging her to come close. His voice still rang out above the other women working: "Yes, you need to come with me."

She hesitated and betrayed a slight peevishness at his impetuousness: "But I'm right in the middle of work here."

The women standing round her now egged her on: "Come on dear, it must be something important if he has come all the way here like this. Go. Quick."

Still she didn't budge, worried he was simply putting on a show for the other women: "If it's so important, why don't you tell me what it is?"

Her obstinacy seemed to cut him to the quick, and at the same time it increased his resolve. If she wouldn't come, then he'd go to her. With the bicycle in hand, he navigated his way through the working women and came up alongside Lin Meitang. Her heart became more vexed every time she encountered Guo Cunyong. No matter where or when, his hands always took liberties, touching her here, brushing up against her there, enough to raise her ire. And even now, in the midst of so many onlookers, he was the same, overly affectionate, one hand tugging at her collar, the other picking out the blades of grass stuck in her hair. She blushed crimson and tried to turn away. In a purposefully soft voice he told her he was heading to the ironworks where there was a large department store and asked was there anything she wanted? If so, he could fetch it and bring it back in the afternoon.

Lin Meitang took a step back to put some distance between herself and Guo Cunyong, saying as she did so: "I'm fine, there's nothing I need, thanks!"

Perhaps surprisingly, Guo Cunyong didn't push the issue. Instead, he shifted tactics: "Would you like me to take care of it, then? Oh, and don't work yourself too hard, you don't want to overdo things. I'd better get going myself. There are people waiting for me. I'll come and see you when I'm finished."

Lin Meitang didn't dare respond herself, but that only seemed to encourage the ladies behind her to chime in, creating quite a ruckus. Someone yelled for Comrade Guo to bring her back something nice and that she'd wait for him patiently. Another hollered for Cunyong to buy her a gold ring, before things became raunchy and there was talk of breasts. Guo Cunyong ignored them all, and perhaps this was the kind of outcome he had been hoping for in the first place. He wanted everyone in the town to know that this pretty Beijinger, Lin Meitang, was his. It seemed to be a question of when they'd get married, not if.

Humming a tune, he set off directly towards the ironworks. Although the workshops were all bustling with activity, there was still quite a bit left to do in order to fully implement the civil engineering plan, so as soon as he arrived, he went in search of Jin Laixi. Together, they inspected the work being done on the essential infrastructure, ensuring everything was in order and that the cooperative project for next year was on track. Once the inspection was over, Jin Laixi and Guo Cunyong, along with the men tasked with building the infrastructure, took the afternoon off and enjoyed a happy lunch and drink to celebrate their progress. When they had finished the meal, Guo Cunyong made sure not to forget his planned visit to the department store. He intended to purchase a small radio for Lin Meitang. Once he'd found a suitable one, he returned to his bicycle and swung his leg over the crossbar, gingerly setting off on the Red Flag, with a tune soon on his lips again. As he came upon Guojiadian, he soon spied a short distance in front of him a young woman crouched down near the side of the road clutching her ankle and moaning in pain. She wore a short, flowery tunic that exposed the soft white skin of her arms. Her trousers were black and figure-hugging, accentuating the curve of her legs that sloped gently upwards to her rather plump buttocks; a sight to behold, for sure. Guo Cunyong's heart skipped a beat, his stomach churned and a certain urge began to well up inside him. He halted his bicycle awkwardly: "Is something wrong? Are you alright?"

She raised her head, and to Guo Cunyong's surprise, she was a local named Ou Huaying who was once his classmate in middle school. At first her brow was furrowed but once she recognised who it was, she soon thought a gallant white knight had chanced upon her and her eyes took on a distinct sparkle, seemingly bursting with life and vigour: "Cunyong! It's you. Bless my luck. I've just come from my auntie's place and I've twisted and sprained my ankle. You must help me, please."

Guo Cunyong stepped down from his bicycle, thinking first to take hold of her but sensing the situation, he moved closer and knelt down next to her, extending his hand to take hold of her swollen ankle. As soon as his hand touched her, she squealed in pain, her arms suddenly clasping hold of his. Her whole body felt warm to the touch and he soon found himself pulling her close with an unconscious urgency to his actions. His hands moved across her body. The fabric of her clothes was thin and soft, as he imagined her skin underneath must be. Ou Huaying's mouth quivered and she let herself fall into his embrace. His movements were effortless, strong. All she needed to do was straighten her one good leg before he deftly manoeuvred her onto the rear seat of his Red Flag. He pushed the bicycle a few steps then swung his leg over the crossbar and began to pedal. But the country roads weren't the best and the bicycle wobbled to and fro, threatening to throw both of them to the ground.

Ou Huaying spoke from behind: "Please take it easy and pedal a little more slowly. I'm frightened. May I put my arms round your waist so I can hold on a little tighter?"

This was exactly what Guo Cunyong had been hoping for: "Sure, of course. Hold on tight and don't let go."

Ou Huaying didn't hesitate. She wrapped her arms round his torso, clasping her hands together over his stomach, and laid her head against the small of his back. The warmth of her body so close to his set his blood rushing but also gifted him with a great sense of comfort. Her voice, soft and bashful, interrupted his reverie: "Oh, you've been drinking. I can smell it. Oh, but a man with a little alcohol in him smells much more like a man should. I remember you were such a cute boy in school and now you've become such a... such a man. Do you know most of the town thinks you're responsible for the turn in its fortunes, at least for eighty per cent or more."

"Really, do they really say that?" Guo Cunyong was clearly elated. He let go of one of the handlebars, reached behind him and squeezed her arm. Her skin was smooth and supple. The longer his hand lingered on her skin, the more ravenous it became and the more his manhood beckoned. Ou Huaying pushed her chin into his waist and twisted teasingly, coquettishly: "Mind what you're doing, you're going to make me fall."

The bicycle wobbled dangerously, forcing Guo Cunyong to put his hand back on the handlebars to steady it. Ou Huaying shifted and pulled herself closer towards him, giggling in a clear, light-hearted manner as she did so. As she laughed, she also reminisced about things that happened when they were school kids: "Cunyong, you remember, right? When we were in primary school, the games we used to play, the extracurricular stuff we got up to, and how you'd try and find any excuse to hold my hand, hold it tight and not let it go? How when we started middle school your hands wandered to places where they shouldn't have, not at that age anyway... copping a feel... oh, you were just sooo bad."

"What was I supposed to do huh? Your mum had given you such beautiful clothes, it was just too tempting. I bet you've forgotten what our classmates used to call you. Hmm, you were such a tease."

"Fuck you, huh, you know they're sensitive, don't you? Squeezing like you did was really painful. But, I didn't blame you, did I? Afterwards, when you went to high school, you didn't come looking for me, even though I waited. And after that, well, the only time I got to see you was when you were up on stage. Change, that's what it is, we've all changed so much."

Guo Cunyong released one handle grip again and swung his arm backwards to pat her behind: "Change for the better or for the worse, hmm?"

"Better, I think, well, at least they do think, makes them remember. No, no, forget that, for the worse, definitely change for the worse!" Her finger poked at the little paunch he now carried, tickling the extra flab he'd not had when they were kids. Her toying with him, however, moved something inside him and he felt his manhood harden once more.

By the time they arrived in the village, it was already late in the day and the town was mostly quiet and free of people milling about. Before he knew it, he was at her door. The gate to her house was closed and bolted, causing his mind to race: "No one at home?"

"They're all at my auntie's." She gestured then for him to help her step down from the bicycle, unbolted the gate and opened it. She then told him to bring the bike inside the courtyard and lock the gate behind him. As he did as he was told, she waited. After all, he had to carry her indoors, given the fact her ankle was sprained. Her room was clean but decorated somewhat garishly. A smell hung in the air; that certain, distinct smell of young womanhood. A pink mattress lay across the raised bed, embroidered with two lightly coloured mandarin ducks. The bed itself was unmade, a red quilt bunched up and left to one side. Inside such a room, Guo Cunyong seemed to lose focus and concentration, seemingly overcome with the fragrance that wafted through the air, slowly enveloping him.

Ou Huaying instructed him to sit on the edge of the bed and not move. She'd invited him in here so she expected and wanted him to listen. Before beginning to say what she wanted to say, she turned and grabbed a small, personal towel, then poured out some warm water from the thermos flask in her room. Dipping the towel in the water, she let it warm thoroughly, pulled it out, wrung it dry of excess water and presented it to Guo Cunyong: "You're tired and very sweaty, here…" He reached out to take hold of it but, as he did so, she brushed his hand aside and then, with one hand caressing his face, she used the warmed towel to wipe his brow and his cheeks. Her voice came soft, gentle and as warm as the towel: "I want to really thank you, and not just for today but for everything, our noble minister who has performed so outstandingly. Your clothes are soaked through with sweat. Quickly, undo the buttons and I'll wipe your chest."

Ou Huaying moistened the towel again and continued to bathe him, her hands working across his torso and then, suddenly, they brushed up against the swelling in the crotch of his trousers. Startled, she cried out: "Oh my, I… what's this?" Before she could say more, she was wrapped in his embrace, paralysed and unable to move. Her pampering had unleashed an uncontrollable desire in Guo Cunyong. Frantically, his arms pulled her close, then they twisted and she was beneath him. His hands moved to undo his own trousers first, then hers, before sliding between her legs. His fingers felt her moistness as their bodies entangled, both overcome with lust and the physical pleasures of the flesh, they twisted and contorted in a rhythmic dance. His blood boiled and he longed to be inside her, to ravage her like a beast overwhelmed by desire. He thrust ferociously while she yelled and bit down hard, animal-like, on his shoulder, her voice drowning out his own feverish noises, egging him on, encouraging him more, hardening his manhood, driving him mad with lust. He swelled more and more and then, abruptly, he burst. His orgasm tore him from his body, his spirit sailed and then his body slumped, sated and fulfilled.

The New Year had yet to arrive but Guojiadian was already crackling madly with the sound of firecrackers. Those who had endured the famine, the bare sticks who had experienced the difficulties of the Cultural Revolution, they were all now celebrating a happy occasion together. How could the atmosphere be anything but lively? Onlookers would, of course, be envious.

Seated at the front table were the central figures, Guo Cunzhi and Liu Yucheng. Both had selected the same auspicious day. What's more, and due to her having fulfilled her familial obligations to her brother, Liu Yumei was now upholding her promise to Ou Guangming and giving her hand to him in marriage. She wondered to herself at this moment, too, whether or not her brother might one day experience such a happy occasion? After all, Guo Cunxian had seemingly demonstrated a degree of flexibility with regard to personal backgrounds. That said, Guo Cunxian's 'flexibility', also resulted in raising the ire of other bare sticks, especially those with comparatively clean backgrounds. They perhaps couldn't help but be bitter about how former landlord families were being treated. Others were envious of Guo Cunzhi. If the town hadn't experienced such a din, such commotion, well, to use the way outsiders would describe it, a little bit of money seemed simply to go straight to one's head. The Guo family were the first in Laodong County to have a redbrick extension added to their home, and all Guo Cunzhi could think of, what he was fearful of, was that he was on the same road as his poor old uncle.

It goes without saying, really, that Cunzhi's mother had been working on finding a wife for him for years but now that the day had finally arrived she couldn't help but turn her mind to obsessing over other worries and problems. Of course, this usually meant worrying about her brother-in-law, poor old Guo Jingshi. Indeed, it wasn't until the bridal party had left that Guo Cunxian was able to get Xuezhen to bring him a bowl of warm water so that he could make his uncle at least a little more presentable. Taking care of him, especially keeping his mess of hair in order, had always been Guo Cunxian's responsibility since he had the steadiest hand and the greatest skill with a blade. But the demands on his time as village head hadn't allowed him to keep on top of his more immediate familial chores. And so, there the old man sat in a dishevelled, filthy state, seemingly oblivious to it all. A reed of dry grass was stuck between his teeth, slowly being mulched by the rhythmic movement of his jaw. Blackie, his mangy mongrel dog, who had grown quite big, was curled up by his feet. And there, not too far behind, two old mountain goats meandered, apparently caught in the old man's orbit. Sun Yueqing sat beside her brother-in-law, holding her grandson tightly in her arms. As she watched Guo Cunxian wield the blade through his uncle's matted hair, she took the opportunity to voice what was troubling her.

"Jingshi, you know I've long been oh so worried about Cunzhi's prospects for marriage, or lack thereof, but now that it seems to be happening, my heart's still troubled. I've been thinking about what to do with the two of us, you know, oh, Jingshi, what do you think? Should I move in with them in the new extension or should you? I mean, we're doing alright now, there's no need for you to remain in that little old room. It'd be better used for storage. And, you know, it's not like it was before when we were all more concerned about where our next meal was coming from, when we didn't have anything… we do now… and it doesn't look good leaving what we do have all piled up outside in the courtyard. Oh, it just looks so awful. But I'm worried about Cunzhi. His wife's family is a bit rough around the edges, I think. Ah, but Xuezhen, well, I've been around her too long now and, to be honest, I've grown accustomed to having her next to me. I'm willing to move in with her and with my grandson, naturally, he's my treasure after all… I can't sleep at night without him near me you know. And, well, thinking of you, I think you'd be better off moving in with Cunzhi. You've had such a hard life, it seems only right you should have some enjoyment and live a little better in your golden years, don't you think? Your brother never had that, bless him."

The mention of her long-dead husband brought tears to her eyes and gave Cunxian the opportunity to interject: "Again with this, hmm? On such a happy day there's no need to bring this up."

"But since it's a happy day it's so easy for the mind to wander to such things. If your father had been alive to see this day, oh, it would have been so good!"

It was the dead of winter, the twelfth month of the lunar calendar, and their crazy old uncle was wearing a cotton-padded jacket, a hand towel wrapped round his neck, and behind him Guo Cunxian continued to move the blade through his hair. Somewhat unexpectedly, the old man had fallen asleep. The scene caused Chuanfu to giggle, amazed at how his grandfather could have dozed off while his hair was being trimmed. His nanna assured him that, even though his granddad may be asleep, he could still hear every word that was being spoken. In fact, she told the little boy his granddad was praising his father and his skill with a razor. The way he was able to move it so deftly across his granddad's scalp, allowing him to sleep while doing it, was indeed quite a feat.

Cunxian joined the conversation once more: "Ma, you need to move into the new extension, that's really the only option, and Chuanfu, well... he'll be fine... I mean, Cunzhi has only just got married, it's all new and unfamiliar, but it's because of that we don't want to give anyone any reason to start their tongues wagging. We don't want to cause unnecessary problems and destroy what happiness we've got. Besides, aren't you already concerned about Cunzhi's character? If you have Uncle move in with him, it'll only mean he's next to him day and night, and mightn't that make things worse? And it isn't just Uncle, you know, that mangy dog follows him everywhere, to say nothing of the sheep, the chickens, shit, even the ducks are never too far away. I mean, we've grown accustomed to it, sure, but will his new wife be able to handle living in a zoo? At least let's make do as we are for the first few months until things settle down and Cunzhi gets used to being a married man. And for his wife, too, the first months can be the most difficult so we don't want to make them any more tumultuous and, who's to say, perhaps someone from her own family will come, then you can use that excuse to move out. In any case, Uncle can stay with me and Xuezhen, alright? Please."

Looking at her eldest, Sun Yueqing beamed. Being of a certain age meant it was difficult to admit that things might not work out but still she understood what he meant. It was just that, to her, this was so important, such a big deal, that she'd turned it over and over in her mind but hadn't been able to arrive at a solution. Her son's words made sense; she'd have to follow them. She pulled her grandson even closer to her breast, swayed a little to make the child smile, and then told him tonight they were moving into a new room.

Suddenly, Guo Jingshi opened his eyes and told them in no uncertain terms that he was going nowhere and they should leave his room alone. Cunxian placed his hands on his uncle's scalp and massaged it a little, pleased at how well he'd shaved it while, at the same time, conceding defeat. Fine, fine, he told his uncle. He understood what the room meant to him, that he had his own prized possessions in it and that he'd grown used to being there. They'd talk about it more in the New Year but, for now, everything would be left as is.

Of the tidal wave of marriages that swept through Guojiadian, the most unexpected was that between Guo Cunyong and Ou Huaying. Everyone in the village knew the object of Guo Cunyong's affections was Lin Meitang, so how he'd ended up marrying someone else was just beyond the realm of understanding. There was gossip, naturally, and some with a keen eye suggested a plausible reason for Ou Huaying to marry Guo Cunyong. After all, wasn't it clear she was putting on weight, at least around her belly? If she were indeed pregnant and unmarried, well... Besides, Lin Meitang had never once openly promised to marry Guo Cunyong, despite what most villagers thought. She'd always been very noncommittal, if the truth be told. There were some who said they'd just been fooling around, that she was just a fling for him, that he'd had his fun and then simply tossed her aside, that, unfortunately for her, she hadn't got pregnant and so there was no way for her to hold onto him. It was as though, before at least, everyone thought she was just the same as him, just out for fun and nothing more, but now, whatever the case, she just couldn't... refused to admit that she'd been used, toyed with, and that things were that straightforward. Or perhaps thinking like this only made matters worse. Regardless of what may have been the case, now when she came face to face with other villagers, they always looked at her sideways, doing double takes to try to figure out what she knew or didn't know. It was quite pitiful, really, for she could see the sneers and sense they were looking down on her.

What was most irritating about this whole situation, however, was Guo Cunyong himself, for he went so far as to call upon her to explain things, to profess his love for her, to tell her he'd been drunk that fateful night, that he'd not planned to get Ou Huaying pregnant, but that now that he had, marriage was the only option. He tried to convince her that this was temporary, a stopgap measure and that after a year or two, he'd divorce Huaying and then they could get married. They would still be young and what was a couple of years after all? Hearing his words served only to make Lin Meitang shiver and tremble with growing rage. She'd never cursed someone before, choosing instead to be reserved, but now she had no choice. She swore at Guo Cunyong, calling him a bastard, a hooligan and many other names as well, before asking him when she'd ever promised to marry him, in any case. Besides, what was it to her that he'd got married? And now he was here talking to her about divorce. What kind of man was he? Was he even a man or an animal?

Regardless of what she said, it all seemed to roll off him like water off a duck's back. That's because he wasn't angry, nor did he feel guilty about anything. All he'd told her was the truth about his deepest feelings being all for her. Was that so wrong? She hated him, but that wasn't all. Fear too accompanied her growing hatred. In spite of everything, the fact he was married yet he still wanted, dared to be with her, and had the gall to ask her if she was angry, to reach out to her, to try to embrace her, to tell her a kiss and a hug would make things better... He tried to tell her he understood, accepted that she was getting angrier by the second, jealous, but then didn't that prove she loved him after all?

Lin Meitang couldn't help but feel as though she had now come face to face with a real scoundrel. There was nothing more to say, no words to describe it, the sight of him repulsed her, made her sick, and she had to flee, to get away from him. But it was cold outside. Where could she run to? She thought first of returning to Beijing but she had no money to speak of and the end-of-year salary had yet to be paid. What about going in search of Guo Cunxian, of asking him, begging him, to tell the commune accountant to hurry up with the distribution of year-end salaries? She could perhaps then find someone with a bicycle who could take her to the county town and then she could take the night train to the capital. As she pondered frantically what to do, her two legs had unconsciously taken her directly to Guo Cunxian's home. She looked up, prepared to knock on the main gate, but just before she did so, the excited and rabid barking of a dog echoed out, followed almost immediately by a forceful reprimand. It could only be Guo Jingshi, Guo Cunxian's mad uncle who had hollered out, as the dog ceased barking straightaway.

Another moment passed and Lin Meitang extended her arm to rap on the gate. There was no more barking. Clearly the beast knew to obey its master. Then, from inside the house, a woman emerged to see who it was who'd come and to let her in. Seeing that the person who'd come to open the gate was Guo Cunxian's wife, Lin Meitang deferred at once, showing her the respect due to her position. She was curious, at the same time, for according to the villagers, Xuezhen was the town's first lady but this woman who'd come to open the door didn't fit the profile of someone like that. She didn't seem to have the arrogant swagger that many other wives of prominent men had. In truth, Xuezhen wasn't seen much around town. She was still fearful of strangers and when she did come upon them, she rarely smiled, rarely spoke and, if she did, her voice would be quiet and low, and carry with it the accent of an outsider, even though she'd been in Guojiadian for many years. Now, coming to open the gate, seeing who it was standing beyond it, never once thinking that such a person would be there knocking on their door, thinking, too, that so many people came in search of her husband, although she wasn't sure if this girl had come before or not, Xuezhen spoke no word of greeting, unsure what to call her, in any case, and simply released the latch, gestured for her to come in, and then closed it behind her.

Lin Meitang was curious about Guo Cunxian's house as a whole, not just his wife. With the aid of the stars in the sky, as well as the light that shone through a window in the room to the north, she scanned the courtyard. It was filled with the smells of a farmer's house. Against the southern wall was a pile of firewood and next to that a mound of drying grass and something else she couldn't identify. Beneath the light of the window, she saw sweet potato, ears of corn and other grains, and produce that hadn't yet been husked, cleaned or prepared for dinner. There were a few trees in the northern quarter of the courtyard and beneath them lay bundles of wool. When she'd walked over here, she was in a vile, vicious mood, but that now changed and a smile came across her face. This was quite a courtyard with so much going on, demonstrating beyond a doubt that the family that lived here was fortunate indeed. With Zhu Xuezhen leading her, Lin Meitang was brought into the part of the house that was lit. Thereupon she saw three solitary, vacant rooms.

She turned to her host and asked: "Has Secretary Guo not returned yet?" Zhu Xuezhen informed her he wouldn't return this evening. He'd gone to the city to speak to his sister and her husband, something to do with the electrical factory. She said he might even have to travel to Tianjin, she wasn't sure, but he could be gone for several days. Lin Meitang then replied with another question: "What about your son?" He was with his grandmother, she was told. They'd just moved rooms and were with her husband's uncle, Guo Jingshi. Actually, the whole family had just been having dinner together, which explained why these rooms were empty and cold. Then, sensing Lin Meitang's discomfort, Xuezhen hastened to add she'd just put several logs in the stove so the bed was beginning to heat up, at least. Directing the young woman to remove her shoes, she invited Lin Meitang to sit on it to warm herself up. Zhu Xuezhen's demeanour and friendliness was genuine and natural, Lin Meitang thought, not forced. She wasn't trying to be polite for politeness' sake. Lin Meitang understood there would be no return to Beijing tonight, as Guo Cunxian wasn't there to help her. At the same time, however, she didn't want to return to her dorm nor risk seeing that vile man again. There was little else she could do but to remove her shoes and lift herself onto the bed. The heat, weak though it was, immediately warmed her buttocks and sent a wave of comfort through her body. Gradually, she felt more at ease.

Zhu Xuezhen joined her on the bed. Seating herself opposite Lin Meitang, she smiled and asked: "It's at least a little warm, isn't it?"

"Oh, it's quite warm."

"So, may I ask why you've come looking for Cunxian? Is something wrong?"

"It's… it's nothing major. Have the production teams all been disbanded? I was thinking of returning home, so I wanted to ask the secretary for a leave of absence."

"Eh? You need to ask for permission to return home? Go on home tomorrow morning, alright? Hasn't he got enough on his plate already to worry about? You needn't trouble him with this. Besides, it's nearly the New Year, your family must be worried about you."

Zhu Xuezhen's interest and feelings were sincere, Lin Meitang could tell, but she didn't want to talk any more about herself and didn't want to answer any more questions. Instead, she directed the conversation towards her host: "Sister, do you still have family back in your hometown?"

Xuezhen sighed and told her there was no one, no one at all. But that didn't stop her from thinking of home. She often wished to return to see the house she once lived in, the village, too, and to burn some joss paper for her dead parents. Cunxian at least took some time out each year to go and make the expected offerings and later, when her responsibilities allowed for it, she too would travel and see them. Xuezhen's thoughts then returned to Lin Meitang. If she wanted to return to the little town she came from, nestled as it was at the foot of a mountain, destitute and poor, then surely someone who was born and raised in Beijing, such a marvellous and no doubt exciting city, would have to be thinking of it, especially at this time of year.

Lin Meitang sighed herself now, but not over her predicament. Listening to Xuezhen talk about her husband, about how Secretary Guo took time out each year to travel to his in-laws' graves, she was thinking what a dutiful, filial man he was. Lin Meitang then asked her how they had met, especially considering the distance between Guojiadian and her hometown. Had someone played matchmaker?

Perhaps it was the time of year, a cold, dark winter's night, she couldn't be sure, but Xuezhen felt a pang of loneliness. At the same time, however, she also felt a bond with Lin Meitang as they'd both come from so far away. She couldn't help but feel some sympathy for the young woman, to keep her tone soft and welcoming, and to talk more with a stranger than she normally would. She told her the story of how she'd met Guo Cunxian, starting with his work as a carpenter and builder of coffins. It was a curious coincidence, to say the least, that he had ended up in her town. Her family circumstances at the time were hard and in came Guo Cunxian like some brave knight-errant with a heart of gold. With great mastery he handled all of the arrangements for her father's passing and then, on that fateful day, her father entrusted her to Guo Cunxian. She didn't really have any other option, even though it was a little like selling herself into slavery. Zhu Xuezhen couldn't recall the last time she'd talked about her own story with someone else, it had been so many years, but talking about it now, retelling the story of how she'd met her husband, it had a different flavour to it. Time had really flown by, and it made her think of what had just recently happened, just yesterday, in fact. In the blink of an eye, her own son had grown so much. When good fortune finally called upon the Guo family, it wasn't because her mother-in-law's family hadn't been bullied, hadn't been through tough times, no, even when they were in the most dire straits, when they were facing their greatest difficulties, Cunxian never felt embarrassed, nor did his mother, his uncle or his sister. None of them ever treated her as an outsider.

Lin Meitang asked after Guo Cunxian's uncle, wondering if he was still around and whether or not he really was mad?

Zhu Xuezhen nodded her head and responded that he wasn't all that strange and that, in fact, he was affable and upright. What's more, she told Lin Meitang, his presence in the house, and only his presence, truly set her heart at ease.

Lin Meitang was floored by what she had said, astonished and surprised at the affection shown a supposedly crazy old man. She told Xuezhen they were to be envied, that they weren't what she had expected when she had first knocked at the gate. They'd experienced so much. There was a story here, romance and an exceptional life, indeed.

Zhu Xuezhen smiled at these words and told her there's no point in thinking about such things, that the past and the future were all so far off, and that the only thing that matters is now and how one lives one's life presently. Her mother-in-law was old, meaning she had to stay put, but otherwise she fancied doing something for the village, serving as a substitute teacher, for instance. She really thought that would be ideal, that she'd be able to help out the teacher already there and the village, too.

Listening to Xuezhen's words, Lin Meitang's stomach churned. Not because of what she was hearing but, most likely, because of Guo Cunyong. She couldn't shake the feeling that ever since she had arrived here she'd done absolutely nothing but spend her days carrying out miscellaneous tasks with the other middle-aged, uncultured women. But here was Zhu Xuezhen, a woman like her, someone from a cultured family, someone learned. They had spent the evening talking and Guo Cunyong's name had not come up once, nor had any of the other gossip she'd so often heard among the other women whose lips were constantly flapping. And most important of all, she had not felt any embarrassment whatsoever about her predicament. Finding someone else in Guojiadian who could understand her, who could touch her heart and mind as Xuezhen had, well, that was downright impossible, she felt. But it was getting late and she had to depart, she couldn't keep her up any longer. It's just that she didn't want to, her body wouldn't obey her mind. Zhu Xuezhen broke through the awkwardness and asked her if she'd lit the fire in her small room.

Lin Meitang laughed somewhat bitterly at Xuezhen's question. She was the only one left in the room they'd been given. What would be the point of lighting the fire? And besides, it never worked properly in the first place.

"Oh my," was Xuezhen's initial response. "Why didn't you say something before? When the weather was warmer, you should have asked for it to be repaired. It's probably too late now. Stay here tonight. I'll get you some bedding and you can head back tomorrow."

Lin Meitang hesitated. In her heart she wanted to stay, or rather not to return, but she didn't want to impose. It was asking too much, wasn't it?

Xuezhen wouldn't hear of it; it was no imposition at all. Besides, Guo Cunxian wasn't at home, which meant she had a clean set of bedding in the wardrobe that could easily be used. "At least it'll be warmer here than in your own room," Xuezhen assured her.

"But what if Secretary Guo returned in the middle of the night, what then?"

Xuezhen replied confidently: "Ah, no problem, I'll just put him in the adjacent room. After all, it's empty too and there's plenty of extra bedding."

Lin Meitang relented, accepting the hospitality of Secretary Guo's wife. "Sorry to bother you more, but may I ask where the toilet is?"

"I'll go with you," was Xuezhen's reply. "It's in the courtyard, but it's only for us ladies." Zhu Xuezhen picked up an electric torch and the two of them went outside. First they went to the main gate and made sure it was properly bolted. The toilet was nestled in the southern corner of the courtyard wall. Xuezhen illuminated their path with the torch and, once inside, Lin Meitang could see how clean it was, further emphasising, to her at least, the hardworking nature of this family. Returning inside the main house, Zhu Xuezhen opened the trunk that held the blankets and quilts, removed what would be necessary and laid them out on the heated bed. At the same time, she pulled out some small towels, then went into the kitchen and poured out a basin of cool water before adding the hot water to it to make it bearable to the touch.

"Here, this is to wash your face," she said to Lin Meitang. Once the young woman had washed her face, Xuezhen passed her her own cold cream, urging her to use some; the wintry weather would dry her face something awful otherwise. Once Lin Meitang was finished, Xuezhen proceeded to wash her own face in the water used by the other woman. Seeing this, Lin Meitang was moved and a little embarrassed. Once she had finished, Xuezhen poured the water into a larger receptacle and then added boiling water to it to warm it back up. Once it reached a suitable temperature, she turned to Lin Meitang and told her to soak her feet for a little while, and that it would help her sleep.

Lin Meitang was further embarrassed: "Sister, you're too kind! Too attentive!"

Zhu Xuezhen laughed gently and assured her it was no trouble at all: "It's nothing, really. All through the winter I do the same for Cunxian every evening."

Placing her feet into the water, Lin Meitang couldn't help but feel a strange feeling wash over her. The basin was theirs, for husband and wife to use together. She wasn't guilty or anything, but... Once her feet were washed, Zhu Xuezhen lifted the basin and moved towards the door, then poured the water out into the gutter that ran alongside the building. Leaving it just outside, she picked up the chamber pot and put it near the bed, then turned and latched the door. "If you need to, use this," she said, pointing towards the chamber pot. "There's no need to go outside in the middle of the night."

Hastily, Lin Meitang explained she wouldn't need to since she rarely woke up during the night. Zhu Xuezhen told her they were the same, and ever since their son began spending his nights with his grandmother, they hadn't had much use for the chamber pot, but it was still nice to know it was there should the need arise. Together they climbed under the covers and continued their conversation for a brief period before Xuezhen drifted off to sleep. Lying next to her, Lin Meitang listened to the other woman's rhythmic breathing, in and out, in and out, steady and strong. She felt her own eyelids grow heavy. Her whole body could feel the warmth of the bed; the quilts were dry and clean. She was so comfortable. It felt as though she were home, back in Beijing and that Zhu Xuezhen was like an older sister she never knew existed but that she'd missed for so long. Her eyes closed and she fell into a deep, sound sleep.

While dreaming peacefully, Lin Meitang felt as though someone had joined them under the covers, and soon there were arms around her, holding her in a tight embrace. In her heart she welcomed the closeness, perhaps Xuezhen disliked the cold; two bodies wrapped in each other's arms would be that much warmer. Whoever it was, their hands began to move, caressing her body up and down. The person shifted and she felt the weight on top of her. Her arms were then pinned and a tongue pushed its way into her mouth. She felt a sharp pain below. Lin Meitang cried out and woke up, startled and a little disturbed.

The person who was on top of her rolled off and in a low voice spoke: "Who're you?"

Startled by the noise, Zhu Xuezhen woke as well and hurriedly lit the lamp. Realising what was going on, in one seamless action she flung her own blanket over her husband's naked form and in a mortified voice asked: "Cunxian! What're you doing here? I wasn't expecting you!"

The room lit up by the lamp, Guo Cunxian could see poor Lin Meitang, seemingly frightened out of her wits, cowering beneath his own bedding. "Just what the devil is going on, huh? Isn't this my place? Am I not allowed to return?"

Zhu Xuezhen stepped down from the bed and seemingly moved to protect Lin Meitang. Her face betrayed her growing anger: "I asked you what you're doing back, and more important, how you got in, since I know I bolted the door."

Without raising his voice, Guo Cunxian explained: "I made these gates, these doors, you know that. It doesn't matter if they're all bolted and locked up tight, I can still get in."

"I don't believe you. Get out and I'll lock the door behind you, then you can show me if you can get back in. I want to see this for myself." Zhu Xuezhen was furious at her husband, but not at poor Lin Meitang. As a matter of fact, wasn't this the least they could do to appease the poor young woman they appeared to have traumatised?

Guo Cunxian gestured to the chair where he had haphazardly thrown his clothes before climbing into bed. Zhu Xuezhen picked them up and threw them at her husband. Putting them on hastily, he exited the room after which he heard his wife fumbling to lock the door behind him. She then yelled out: "Alright, come in, see if you can!" Before she had finished speaking, Guo Cunxian had noiselessly released the bolt barring the door and pushed it open.

Zhu Xuezhen was dumbstruck: "That's the work of a ghost. Who else knows about this, huh?"

Guo Cunxian shook his head: "Only me."

Zhu Xuezhen was flustered. She had never yelled at her husband as she did now:

"Why in hell did you toy with the doors like this? I don't like this at all and it makes me worry, you know, what was your plan, huh? To make it easier for you to get up to no good?"

It dawned on Guo Cunxian that this wasn't something she was going to get over quickly. Nor had he ever replied to anyone in such a servile, meek manner: "No, no, when I made these doors you weren't even here. I was young then and I was just showing off, you know, marvelling at my own carpentry skills. I added a mechanism to each door throughout the house, you know, to allow us to lock them from the outside, but that meant they could be unlocked too, and then, well, afterwards I realised this was a problem and that if anyone else knew, well, there soon wouldn't be any doors in the house at all. So I had no choice but to keep it secret. Later, when I found some free time, I was going to remove the mechanism, honestly. I mean, who knew you'd have someone else sleep over? You never told me."

Zhu Xuezhen told him to leave, to go and sleep in the adjacent room. Guo Cunxian hesitated for a moment, mulling over whether to protest or not, but decided to keep his mouth shut, then turned and walked away. Zhu Xuezhen returned to the bed and put her arms round Lin Meitang. In the softest, gentlest voice she could muster she apologised to the young woman: "I'm so sorry, truly I am. You're not too frightened, are you?"

Lin Meitang was inconsolable. She pulled the covers up over her head and burst into tears. She wanted to cry, she had to, she had to let it out, but not because she was just overwhelmingly depressed. She was hurt, in pain and her body ached. And there amidst the pain, was a certain sense of surprise and astonishment. She'd dreamed so much about love, had fantasies about being with someone, and considered sex to be something spiritual. Making love was something noble, she thought. But these dreams had been shattered: sex was just that, sex. Her womanhood, her virginity, something she was supposed to hold onto until she met the right man, could it so easily be lost? A case of mistaken identity and that was it? Seeing Lin Meitang crying her eyes out, Zhu Xuezhen grew more upset. She realised that for her to be so beside herself, something more than just her husband getting into the bed next to her must have happened. She removed her arms from Lin Meitang and felt the bedding beneath her. It was damp and her heart felt a sharp pain. She grabbed the lamp and pointed it over the bed. The bloodstain was clear. Terror and anger welled up inside Zhu Xuezhen. A moment passed and then the barrier broke. Xuezhen let loose a tirade of vitriol, cursing her husband, calling him a no-good bastard and worse; like some ravenous, starving wolf unable to control his urges. Oh, what was to be done?

Her cursing continued as she got down from the bed and marched into his room, prepared to have it out with him. It wasn't really an argument, more her swearing at him and Guo Cunxian quietly enduring the barrage. But whatever she said, this was a problem between a husband and wife that no amount of arguing was going to resolve. This was a pain that cut too deep to be relieved by shouting. The verbal bombardment continued for some time, a conflagration not unlike that which tore through the frog marshes. Finally, she had said what she had to say and she regained her composure. Zhu Xuezhen returned to her room, reached for a warm towel to wipe the tears from her face and then tried to soothe Lin Meitang: "Little Sister, don't cry any more, what's happened has happened. Crying won't change anything. To be honest, I'm the one who should be crying. I really like you, I do, and I enjoyed our talk. We really connected, I thought, but who could imagine such a thing might happen? We, my husband and I, we didn't plan this. It wasn't deliberate, some scheme we hatched to trick you."

Lin Meitang interrupted her: "Sister, please, don't say any more. I know you're a good person. Who could imagine heaven could be so cruel, could see fit to put a woman in such a position to cause such trouble for a husband? I'm crying because my life has brought nothing but pain and bitterness. Whatever could go wrong has gone wrong and ill fortune stalks me like a predator stalks its prey."

Zhu Xuezhen reiterated that it is what it is and that they would do whatever they had to do. In any case, the responsibility lay with her. She held no grudge against Lin Meitang, nor would Cunxian. Besides, according to the law, causing harm to a youth sent down to the countryside was a serious offence. The only thing she hoped for was that when it came time to testify, Lin Meitang would simply tell the truth about what happened.

At that moment, Guo Cunxian pushed the door open and stepped into the room. There was a look of resolve in his eyes. He had thought of a way to deal with the situation. There was confidence in his voice. The stern demeanour he had become known for was present. He spoke to both of them: "Since you've both been talking about involving the legal authorities and criminal punishment, I too have something to say, something I want the two of you to hear. There's most likely a legal provision for dealing with cases like these and, for sure, the rape of a youth sent down to the countryside entails severe punishment. But you need to remember something. What happened, well, it happened in my home, in my bed. So is it correct to say I raped a youth sent down to the countryside in my own bed? With my own wife lying next to us? In cases such as these, the most important evidence is what the medical examiner can determine after examining the victim, I mean, traces that the man has really done what he's accused of doing, but I'm sure there's no trace of that. As soon as you opened your mouth I knew the sound of your voice was wrong, that you weren't my wife, and I got up immediately. Now, can that truly be called rape? If the man supposedly perpetrating the rape really wanted to do you harm, if he were really an evil man, there'd be no way for him to stop like that, not at that moment. To be frank, ever since our son began sleeping with his grandma, it has just been the two of us here in this bed, and now this has happened, whether it's a cause of some deep shame between the three of us or not, whether we can speak about it or not, well, it doesn't change the fact that under these blankets it has just been me and my wife and if I don't put my arms around her each and every night, sleep just doesn't come to me. I'd planned to go to Tianjin today but my sister and her husband told me there was no point because it's nearly the New Year and whatever I had hoped to achieve would be impossible. So, even though it was late, I rushed back home. I wanted to give out the year-end bonuses to everyone. I've been running round all day and it has been hard and I'm tired. The only thing on my mind was to get home, crawl into bed and feel my wife in my arms. As soon as I smelled Xuezhen, well, I'm intoxicated by her, I can't help myself."

At this point, Xuezhen could no longer contain her own growing anger. She launched into him once more: "You, just look at you, do you think your wife's the only person to use cold cream on their face, huh? Really?"

Guo Cunxian looked at his wife: "Don't interrupt, I'm only telling you what happened. You're the one who invited young Lin here into our bed and let her sleep where you usually do. It's not like I climbed into the wrong bed, is it? That's the truth. Trying to punish me for what has happened... at most, I owe you both an apology, some compensation. And I've apologised. To keep on saying I'm sorry would only cause even greater shame for the victim and blow things even more out of proportion, and that would only make things worse for you, wouldn't it?

"As to the issue of compensation, what would suffice? How does one provide reparation for the loss of one's virginity? Well, I've thought of something, I'm in debt to you for the rest of your life and mine. From now on, I consider you part of my family. You're my little sister, which means I'll look after you for a lifetime. If you wish to return to Beijing, then I'll regularly go and visit you. What's mine is yours and if, in future, you get married, it won't change a thing. You'll still be my sister. For now, I'd like you to stay. Don't return to the capital before you find a suitable husband. I want you to stay here under this roof. This room is yours. You needn't return to that dorm you were living in. It's nearly the New Year. If you'd like to head home to see your family, then I'll take you myself. Our village is doing alright, it's got money, things, you can introduce me to your relatives and not be ashamed about it. We three are the only ones who know what happened here tonight, right here, in this room. But let's settle it here, too. I think my proposal is the best option for all of us. Anything else will just cause us even more pain and torment. Think about it, both of you. I'm not worried, worrying doesn't help with anything. When something happens one must meet it head-on. I guarantee you won't be able to think of a better way to deal with what has happened."

Once he had finished speaking, Guo Cunxian turned and exited the room.

It's difficult to say if it was a case of counting their chickens before they hatched, or whether it was the fatigue that often followed the New Year festivities, but by the fifteenth of the first lunar month, Sun Yueqing took to her bed and could not get up.

The year that had just passed had had its fair share of joy. First there was Cunzhi's wedding, which had eased the nagging worry in her heart. Then there was the addition of Lin Meitang to the family, another daughter, although she was unsure of the reason why. Surprisingly, her 'new' daughter had remained with them over the holiday instead of returning to Beijing. Unbeknownst to Sun Yueqing, Lin Meitang didn't dare to return to the capital, fearful her 'secret' might be exposed and cause nothing but further torment. Sun Yueqing was confused about her presence, unable to fathom why she was there, unable to understand her desire not to return to see her family in Beijing. The only thing she was sure of was that Guo Cunyong had harmed the girl, but was that reason enough to stay with them? Was Cunxian taking sides against Cunyong, or was there something else going on, something else that had happened? She didn't know. Nor did she have much time to think about it since the most surprising turn of events was heaven giving her another grandson due early in the year. Liu Fugen showed up in search of Guo Cunyong. He'd grown in the years since Cunxian had first met him during the time he'd spent roaming the countryside making coffins. Now a middle school graduate, the boy had been unable to find work, but after receiving a letter from Wang Shun, he'd decided to seek shelter, and hopefully a job, with his 'adoptive' father. He referred to Sun Yueqing as his granny, and contrary to expectations, the two became quite close.

To say she was tired was one thing. But in truth, it was her heart that was worn out. To make matters worse, everyone was at a loss as to what to do. What could get her out of bed? She'd spent most of her life tormented by the world around her and had grown accustomed to worrying. Every little thing seemed to find its way into her heart and mind. Finally, when the day of the Lantern Festival arrived, she mustered what strength she could to enjoy the customary sticky rice dumplings, but shortly after eating a few, she was overcome, her stomach weighed down by the festive food, unable to pass even a morsel. As soon as her daughter and son-in-law heard the news, they made arrangements to have her immediately brought to the main county hospital.

The only problem, however, was that she wouldn't go. She said to Cunxian: "You're the head of the family, yes, but before I die, you still need to heed my words, yes?"

At the tone of his mother's voice, Guo Cunxian fell to his knees next to her bed: "Mother... mum... whatever the case may be, you need to go to the hospital and you need to see a doctor. You must understand what I'm saying, don't you? Nothing else matters."

Sun Yueqing smiled: "It's all of you that don't understand, I know what's what. Your uncle knows, too. If he didn't, he'd already be in here dragging me off this bed and out to do my chores. Let me tell you, I'm not sick, I'm just old. Do you mean to tell me death's not allowed? We all die. Do you mean to say the town can't bear it? That the world will lose its lustre after I'm gone? I've lived a worthy life but it's enough, it's time for me to go. Now please leave, all of you, and when my grandson calls out, then that's who I'll want to come in."

She let her head fall once more, but still held on tight to her dear grandson, her precious Chuanfu. The small boy understood what was happening. After all, he spent his days and nights with his granny, and like the good filial child of lore, he soon hollered out to the person Sun Yueqing wished to speak to. Zhu Xuezhen was startled to hear her name; she hadn't expected it would be her. She thought her mother-in-law would wish to see her eldest son first, not his wife. Perhaps she had something she wished to entrust to her? Whatever it might be, Xuezhen followed her husband's action and, upon entering the room, she knelt down by the bed as well, leaning her face in close to her mother-in-law. Using what little remained of her strength Sun Yueqing extended her free hand. The smile that had often graced her face was absent, replaced by a deep-seated worry and affection for someone she considered her blood: "Has Cunxian done something to hurt you?"

Taken aback by the question, Xuezhen attempted to explain: "No, no, not at all, he's never done anything to hurt me."

"Xuezhen, I'm worried about you. You're too kind-hearted, too easily taken advantage of. If, in future, Cunxian does wrong by you, then leave him, take your son and go. I have faith Chuanfu will have a bright future. And after I'm gone, if Cunzhi wishes to move out, don't try to stop him. I think the departure of him and his new wife would be best, for you especially. Xuezhen, my daughter, you and I are kindred spirits. I feel closer to you than to my own flesh and blood, Cunzhu is…"

"Mother!" Xuezhen could control her emotions no longer. She moved towards her mother-in-law, tears streaming down her face. Startled and frightened by the sounds coming from within, the rest of the family that had been waiting outside now burst into the room thinking that the worst had happened.

Sun Yueqing spoke to Chuanfu: "Tell them to leave, and then tell your uncle to come in." Obeying her instructions once more, he ushered them out of the room again and then asked after his uncle Guo Jingshi. It was rare to see him waiting so obediently, like a well behaved child. He entered the room, sat down on the edge of the bed and took hold of the hand his sister-in-law had extended.

Even though much of her energy had dissipated and her voice was barely audible, Guo Jingshi was able to clearly hear what she was saying: "Jingshi, I know life's dealt you a bad hand and that you've had more than your fair share of pain, some of that caused by me. I know you love me dearly but I also know you feared that love, feared the awkwardness it would cause for both of us and that you so didn't want to bring more pain to the family. I know that's the reason you played at being crazy and pretended to be a mad old fool. It was your way of dealing with things and also of ensuring that no one else would try to find you a wife. It allowed you to be here and to help me raise three children. When I leave this world and enter the next, I'll be sure to tell your brother, tell him what a good man you are. My time's nearly up. I need to tell you this. You were, rather you are, a good brother and you did right by him. Thank you for that. I need to tell you that. Thank you."

"Sister, I think you've got it wrong, hmm? You're my sister-in-law, more like my mum. It's you who took care of me. I've been heartless, lived a carefree life, much too easy, I reckon. My brother was fortunate to have met you, we all were, are. It's you who've put up with so much pain and sorrow. It makes me happy to see that you understand what living means and you know that death is part of that, in fact, the most important part. You've lived a perfect life, perfect! Close your eyes now, rest, I'll be here… right up until the moment you see my brother, your husband."

Guo Jingshi's voice was gentle and soft, and he had a smile on his face. He reached, too, for Chuanfu's hand and removed it from hers. Then he saw Sun Yueqing smile as well: a serene, peaceful look in her eyes. Guo Jingshi picked up the boy and walked out of the room.

Anxiously, nervously, Sun Yueqing's children pressed their uncle: "Uncle, our mother, she's alright, yes?"

"Yes, everything's fine. She's gone."

Three days after she was buried, the family piled earth around her grave to make the customary burial mound. Not long after, Guo Jingshi and his constant companion, Blackie, disappeared. Guo Cunxian and the rest of the family, as well as village friends, searched frantically everywhere but there was no sign of him. Guo Cunxian couldn't bring himself to tell them not to bother. Those words couldn't pass his lips. But in his heart of hearts he knew they'd seen the last of their uncle. This time he would not return.

13

WOMEN'S FATE

When Guo Cunxian announced to the rest of the village that Lin Meitang was to be part of his family, he chose his words well. He didn't use the word sister but, rather, said first that his mother, before passing, had decided to adopt Lin Meitang as her daughter. Thereafter he called her sister. As surprising as the announcement ought to have been, it didn't really faze the villagers. Guojiadian was flourishing and so it was bound to attract more and more people looking for work. But if those people truly wanted to make a go of it in the town, they'd need to have some kind of connection with a local. After all, that would be the only means by which the villagers themselves would welcome those who had come. For instance, if the person hadn't come to the town as someone's new wife or new husband, they'd need some other reason for coming, wouldn't they? They'd need a connection. Like Wang Shun, for example, who ran the food processing factory. When Guo Cunxian was roaming the countryside looking for work, the two of them met and helped each other out, becoming firm friends in the process, closer even than brothers, and a deep bond now existed between them, clarifying Wang Shun's connection to Guojiadian.

Besides, when Guo Cunxian made the announcement, the villagers were all still so compliant with his directives and trusted him implicitly, ascribing the decision to make Lin Meitang part of his family to his boldness. After all, he'd decided to welcome into his home a young girl other work units had flippantly shunned; to protect a girl who had endured and was still facing an enormous amount of hardship. No one would dare to bully her from here on out, that was for certain. There were quite a few villagers who offered their congratulations, and at the same time chuckled gently at the situation he was in, remarking on the good fortune that had come in twos, for not only had his old mother adopted a daughter, he also welcomed an adopted son.

It was because of these developments that Guo Cunyong felt that his relationship with his boss had changed. It had become awkward and somewhat delicate. And although he couldn't say Guo Cunxian had begun to treat him any differently, that didn't stop him from feeling a tad guilty about his previously wanton and at times fame-seeking demeanour. In fact, his entire behaviour changed. He grew more cautious, more circumspect when handling official and unofficial duties alike, fearful that Guo Cunxian would seize upon any wrong step to come down hard on him.

If things in Guo Cunyong's case had changed for the worse, the opposite was true for Lin Meitang. For starters, she'd been given an office job and no longer needed to perform the manual tasks she had in the past. She was soon responsible for the flow of information, her position of note-taker leading to broadcasting and ultimately the dissemination of official propaganda. Following close on the heels of these developments, she was soon admitted into the Party and then not long after given the formal role of propaganda officer. Together with Ou Guangming, the two became diehard Party members for the Guojiadian branch. One man, one woman, a perfect match. The more the villagers saw of the relationship between Guo Cunxian and Lin Meitang, the more they could see that it was a bond that seemed to come straight out of the folk songs of old, a connection that went deep, beyond the ties of blood to something much more spiritual.

It goes without saying, too, that the nature of their relationship had changed as well. What began through misunderstanding and awkwardness had now become a relationship of mutual affection. A first time is followed by a second and a third. Guo Cunxian had been assured of his convictions and felt that the fault was not entirely his own but he'd also imposed his will somewhat tyrannically: "You're my woman, you gave yourself first to me. In the old society things would be handled easily, you'd simply become my second wife, which would have simplified matters to say the least. Now, in New China, dealing with situations like these in that manner is no longer permitted. But until you're married, you're my woman." Together, they resided in both the eastern and western rooms, which was convenient for the time being. Once Guo Cunxian's mother died, Zhu Xuezhen took up a position as a substitute teacher at the village school, which meant she rarely saw her husband any more and the distance between them grew. In the evenings, Lin Meitang would listen for the sounds of Xuezhen drifting off to sleep, real or otherwise, and then she would steal into Guo Cunxian's room. Of course, Zhu Xuezhen realised early on what their relationship was, or what it had become, and she began to suspect that this had been their plan all along, and that Cunxian hadn't mistakenly bungled his way into making Lin Meitang a part of the family. Why else had his mother, on her deathbed no less, asked her whether or not Cunxian had wronged her, mistreated her?

The only question was why someone as young as Lin Meitang possessed such intense and lustful desire? Being honest with herself, Zhu Xuezhen couldn't help but be a little fearful of it. Lin Meitang just seemed to thirst for any chance to climb into her husband's bed. It was as though she could only feel safe and protected by being with him, and only by being with him could she believe that he needed her, that he loved her. There were even times when she could barely contain her affection and attachment to Guo Cunxian. At times, you could see her finishing off the water he'd leave in his glass, or if he appeared to want a cigarette, she'd take one out, put it to her mouth to light it, and then pass it to him. To the villagers, it was all a bit tawdry, to say the least!

Lin Meitang also felt fearful. Her relationship and feelings towards Guo Cunxian were far from normal, and she also worried about the lasting effect it would have on Zhu Xuezhen, someone who had been so good and kind to her. Nor did she wish to provoke the ire of the villagers. In all honesty, however, it was difficult to say what these two women meant to each other, nor was it clear who really hurt whom. Finally, when news came that the central authorities were releasing the youths sent down to the countryside from their duties, Lin Meitang decided to leave Guojiadian and return to the capital.

She had been sixteen when she'd been sent to Guojiadian, and spent the better part of seven years in the village. One might say she gave the prime years of her youth to the town. And while it wouldn't be accurate to say that she had deep feelings for it, it was at least true that she'd grown accustomed to the lifestyle and its people. When she first heard the news, she felt as though a great weight had been lifted off her shoulders, but when she had actually returned to Beijing, things didn't go as planned. At first, she was unable to find work and ended up as a street vendor selling ice lollies.

Her younger brother had already married and their mother was living with him. There was, therefore, no room for anyone else in the tiny home he had, and so she was forced into seeking lodgings elsewhere in the city. The result was an itinerant lifestyle. She would bed for a while in one place, then move to another for a couple of months, then somewhere else thereafter. She was no longer young, either, at least not according to most. Nor was she simply a girl. No, she was a woman, had experienced what that meant, and now truly realised the difficulties and embarrassment that often came with it, especially when there was no husband in the picture. Ultimately, she ended up boarding in the factory where they produced the ice lollies. In the day she'd sell them on the streets and in the evenings she'd bed down alongside the machines and guard them. Her day would start at three in the morning, after all, the other street pedlars would come to fetch their day's worth of lollies before the sun rose over the horizon.

Then, one day, she suddenly realised the nature of her predicament. She'd returned from the countryside as a former youth sent down to the rural areas, and now she was back in the city and in exactly the same position she was in seven years ago when she first arrived in Guojiadian. It was all so frustrating. She had never once thought she'd have to face days like these. Could she even consider herself a Beijing local any more? Was being in the capital any better than being in Guojiadian? Mulling this over in her mind, that's what she realised: she was no longer a Beijinger and the city hadn't welcomed her back. She'd been away too long and all that she was now to her family in Beijing was a nuisance and a disruptive influence on their lives. The city just didn't need her and she meant nothing to it. In truth, she felt, society as a whole had no use for her, she was superfluous to it, an object of sympathy to those who gave her a little something to eat, the lowest of the low. Her whole life had been a series of mistakes; that was all clear to her now. The only option left to her was to quickly find someone to marry but that would be easier said than done. After all, she wasn't exactly a lucky catch, at least, not any more. No, she was more like someone to avoid and ignore. Few would be willing to give her a chance as she just wouldn't do, she was not suitable. Gradually, this realisation only hardened her heart.

In the eyes of those around her, she was a youth who had been sent down to the countryside, nothing more. It was this that hurt for when she'd first been ordered to head to the countryside, to learn from the peasants, her heart had been filled with joy and excitement, but back in the city, what was there for her to do? There was no path for her to take in the city, which only sent her mind frequently back to her experiences in Guojiadian. At least she wouldn't be looked down upon in the village and wouldn't be discriminated against. Was there really all that much difference between the city and the countryside any more in this day and age? The food was certainly fresher in Guojiadian and perhaps there was more variety, too. And it wasn't only the food, either. If she thought of having her own home, well, that would be much easier to come by in Guojiadian. There was one, she thought, waiting for her. She could return to Guo Cunxian's home without much difficulty, couldn't she? Turning this over in her mind, she first resolved to return; she wouldn't get anything better in Beijing. But then worries crept into her train of thought. Would Guo Cunxian welcome her back? Should she take that chance, keep her plans concealed from her real mother and return to Guojiadian? It was as though fate, destiny, whatever one wished to call it, had bound her to the countryside, to that village. However reluctantly, she had to admit, a Beijing *hukou* meant very little. She was better off without it.

There were some who said this was the debt history owed to the youths sent down to the countryside. But who would step in and settle these historical accounts?

The tight spot she found herself in served as cause, at least on the surface, for her to think of returning to Guojiadian. But there was another reason as well, one that she chose not to speak aloud. She couldn't escape the feeling she'd not learned to be a proper, upright woman, not learned the behaviour society expected. No, she had this nagging feeling that she was nothing but a lascivious, vile woman, a jezebel. It was already impossible for her to leave Guo Cunxian; he was a devil. It was because of him she had learnt what it meant to be a woman before she was ready, but he was her first, she couldn't leave him, didn't really want to. Being next to him allowed her to forget what he'd done, his devilish impulses were compartmentalised and resigned to the recesses of her memory. For all intents and purposes, she was his. He made her see herself, know herself. He made her a woman, but what kind? Then, thinking like this, she tricked herself, allowing herself to believe that she was special, that not all women were as fortunate as her, and that not all of them had known the pleasures she had come to know. This was a woman's foolishness. For most, being a woman meant getting married and having children; that was what was expected of them. But she knew that having all of that and conforming to society's expectations was no guarantee of being a real woman.

She had hated him and cursed him but not because he'd destroyed her life. No, sometimes he could be so callous, rude and unreasonable, too focused on his own power and prestige, wholly uninterested in her and what she was doing. It was then that she hated him. But that hatred never went as deep as her love; she was too willing to throw everything else away, all for that man. Yes, she'd had her fits, there had been times she'd grown so pissed at his insensitivity that she'd fled back to Beijing. There, she would do her utmost to defame and speak ill of him. He was, after all, nothing but an old, uncouth, uncultured country bumpkin, wasn't he? He was so uncaring, so harsh and cold, rarely reciprocating the feelings she felt for him, so what was so good about him? Was he worth loving? These questions would plague her mind for a few days but after simmering for a time, her hatred would dissipate and she'd wonder how she could ever think and say those evil, nasty things about him and see no good in him whatsoever. And then she would long for him once more. She'd rather throw everything else away just to be with him. Whatever self-respect, pride or inner fire she might have had, as soon as she saw him, all of it would disappear. She'd go as giddy as a school girl on seeing him, willing to give him everything. She lacked the will to resist and couldn't help but go weak at the knees when she saw him and submit to whatever he wanted. She couldn't leave him, could she? Without him she was nothing, nothing but a little girl of no importance to anyone.

The more she thought about her situation, the more she felt that a woman's fate was irrevocably tied to one thing: loving a man. And with that love, however misguided, she'd do her utmost to idealise him, no matter what. But the pressures of society and family were too much. When she first returned to the capital, she thought she could make a clean break with Guo Cunxian, find someone else, someone better, but no one could compare to him, at least in her eyes. There was no one as manly as him. Guo Cunxian had made her, moulded her. She couldn't help but feel that he was the one for her and that no other man would do. Her lot had been thrown in with the devil. The only problem was that the devil didn't seem to want her.

This riled her and hurt her pride. No, she wouldn't return to Guojiadian, despite the implications of this decision. She'd live her life alone, solitary and impoverished, no better than a street urchin, sometimes with a full belly, sometimes not. She'd never have a place to call home, never feel that kind of security, nor would she dare think or plan for the future. No, she couldn't even ask herself that question: did she have a future? What would happen to her when she was old? It wasn't as though she lacked qualifications. She had skills and experience. She could handle all sorts of things. But far too often, even when she was alone or with Guo Cunxian, she had no control over herself and her emotions. She'd cry or get upset for little or no reason, fuss over the smallest of things, and then, once whatever commotion had died down, her heart would return to him, to Guo Cunxian.

There was another Beijing girl still in Guojiadian but her fate was entirely different, it seemed. Hong Fang had come with Lin Meitang. She, too, was a youth sent down to the countryside. But Wang Shun had taken a liking to her almost immediately. He asked if she'd been to high school, to which she had answered yes, at least the first year of it. How was the homework? Fine. What rank was she in the class? She'd never once placed lower than the top three. Then, suddenly, like the loveable scoundrel he often was, he laughed suggestively and gave her the thumbs up. On the following day, Guo Cunxian informed her she was to head to the food processing factory and report to Wang Shun as he had need of an accountant.

Hong Fang wasn't all that pretty. She carried more weight than she should on her smallish frame. Her face, too, was plump and her eyes were narrow. A little mouth completed her face but when she smiled and showed her teeth, she looked so happy and joyful that those around her couldn't help but feel a certain fondness for this youth sent down to the countryside. On that first day at the food processing factory, when Wang Shun arrived in the afternoon, he carried with him an old worn canvas sack filled nearly to the brim with cash. He was happy, of course, and called for all of the workers to gather round. That's when he introduced Hong Fang.

"From this day, our factory is on the correct path and we now have our own 'minister of finance'," he said, gesturing towards Hong Fang. "I've invited a professional accountant to join our ranks. She's an exceptionally talented student from Beijing, never ranking outside the top three in all her tests in class, which certainly can't be said about us. In primary school I was always in the bottom three! In the past, it was often said those with the longest and sharpest teeth ate the best. Now look here at our accountant, Miss Hong. She's got the cutest little teeth, especially the little pointy one on the left. Oh my, when she smiles she's so pretty. Now, what do we say about someone like this, hmm? I'll tell you, yeah, a smile like that means they're quite good at managing household affairs, that's what! You just watch, our factory will soon be rolling in it and so will we. You see her face, hmm, its plumpness. Well, in the past, that's exactly the kind of face the emperor looked for in his empress. She'd be the one living in the eastern palace while the western palace would be filled with concubines, you know, those used for... Hey! Stop laughing. Huh, when I was a beggar, you know, before I came to Guojiadian, I saw all kinds of people. I even spent a few months with an old fortune teller. I learned a few things, too. Certain wives with certain faces, faces like our dear Miss Hong here, well, they were sure to bring good fortune and wealth. A man who finds such a wife is destined to do well. Eh, stop it now. Huh, you're putting indecent thoughts into my mind. I may be a toad but I'm not thinking of eating the swan! Miss Hong here is our goddess of wealth, alright, so you'd all better treat her with respect, eh? You dirty bastards you, hmm... behave."

Foul mouths find it hard to utter nice words. Wasn't this supposed to be a model factory? Whatever the case, poor Hong Fang couldn't help but blush; there was little she could do. Wang Shun was trying to be serious and upright. He wanted to say something nice. But his mouth betrayed him, his words lacked the seriousness intended. Once he had finished his garrulous and colourful banter, he dug his hand into one pocket and pulled out a key. Stepping over to a nearby table, he inserted the key into the drawer and pulled out several notebooks, the kind students used to practice their sums. He handed them to Hong Fang: "These are the informal ledgers for the factory. I've been scribbling things down, you know. This one here is for livestock to record the heads of cattle, sheep, donkeys and pigs. This other one records our sales of uncooked meat and this one our sales of cooked... From today, these are all your responsibility. I'll buy you a new notebook, too, so you can keep making records."

Wang Shun then turned and opened another drawer, pulling out a formal Accountancy Manual, before telling her he was going to have a sturdy, thick wooden cupboard built to place next to the table to be used for holding the factory's profits. She was to be responsible for all of the money coming in and out; everything would go through her hands. He then passed her the canvas sack he had brought: "It's not gonna be easy, let me tell you, you've got quite a job on your hands. First, according to the rules, you need to produce formal accounts, it all has to add up. Hopefully you won't have to do it all on your own for too long. I'll try and find you an assistant, then one of you could take charge of the money while the other does the books, but for now, it's just you."

After Hong Fang had worked through the notebooks for the factory and had sorted out the finances, her opinion of Wang Shun changed. She no longer dared to look down on him, even if he was a fast-talking scoundrel. He might have recorded the cash flows of the factory in a rather haphazard way, but there wasn't a number out of place. Afterwards, Wang Shun left things completely to her. He trusted her judgement and followed her word. It was as though, after handing the ledgers and responsibility for doing the numbers to her, he'd unburdened himself of a heavy load and could again spend his time in a much more carefree manner, whiling away the days with idle and sometimes wild chatter about numbers and... But at the end of every month, and then every year, when financial and profit reports were due, the numbers he reported varied little from those she had recorded. Each time he did this she couldn't help but be amazed. Here he was, a coarse, flippant kind of country bumpkin with a loose tongue, not the kind of person you'd expect to be all that bright, demonstrating greater insight into numbers and finances than even the most proficient accountant... and all without the aid of a ledger! She soon thought there must be some other reason for the job he had given her.

When that day came, when the order was received allowing the youths sent down to the countryside to return to the cities, when even the more well-known and somewhat 'influential' Lin Meitang had departed, most still assumed she would stay behind. But once the official formalities were taken care of and the paperwork releasing them from their duties in the countryside was prepared, Hong Fang, too, decided to leave. But it was a difficult decision as she really didn't want to leave the factory, nor leave Wang Shun. Feelings are strange things, however, and her desire to return to Beijing ultimately won out. Her mind made up, she thought to go in search of Wang Shun to give him the news but when she came upon him, he was deep in deliberations with a group of men about setting up a dairy farm.

He might have been uncouth and much too flippant in his manner of speaking but no one at the factory dared to call him anything but boss. He might have been coarser than all of them but they would never treat him as such. The only person to disregard this unwritten rule was Hong Fang. She would call him by name and he'd answer very naturally. No one really knew when this had started and it didn't seem to matter. Hong Fang had always been open with him, saying what was on her mind regardless of who else was around, and this wasn't going to change: "Wang Shun, I've made the preparations, I'm returning to Beijing tomorrow. That means you should treat me to dinner tonight, to see me off, shouldn't you?"

Everyone was startled. Wang Shun raised his head, looked at Hong Fang and spoke frankly: "OK, tonight we'll go out." He turned his attention back to the men gathered round and continued their discussion. But it was clear their minds were no longer on the dairy farm. Hong Fang hadn't expected this kind of a reaction from Wang Shun. He didn't seem to be surprised by her announcement, she thought. The bastard. Nor did he show any desire to hold on to her, to try to get her to stay. It was as though he had already assumed she was going to leave and knew that whatever he said would be a waste of words, or perhaps he just didn't care. One would think that a farewell party for someone who'd done the job she did would have involved everyone

that worked there; a proper, lively party. In truth, Wang Shun generally spent his
nights enjoying the company of friends, colleagues and villagers. To do otherwise just
wouldn't do for a man like him; a quiet meal would be out of order, to say the least.
But tonight, something strange happened. As the work day ended, everyone departed,
quickly and neatly. Everything was tidied up and put away. Had Wang Shun decided
not to call anyone else to come, she wondered? Had everyone else just assumed they
would have a party, a proper send-off for someone who had done so much for the
factory, and that they were going to meet somewhere? She didn't know, for the only
person she saw was Wang Shun. Had something changed?

Wang Shun was carrying some of their own product, a package of marinated
meat, as well as some small cooked snacks. In his other hand, he had two bottles of
alcohol. He'd come to the room they'd made especially for her. As he stepped inside,
he saw that Hong Fang was busy packing up her belongings. He blurted out: "Aiya! I
think I've been too good to you, hmm." He scanned her room and continued: "I've
given you so much and now you're planning to leave, and so quickly too! Your
heart's all set on it, hmm?, I'll help you pack all this stuff tomorrow, OK? There'll be
plenty of time for that. I can't send you off properly and watch you packing at the
same time, it'll only make me cry like a baby and that'll only do my head in. Oh, I'm
miserable, I tell you. My heart's breaking!"

Hong Fang listened and was once more surprised by the man. His previous
attitude had been only defensive. Now he had gone on the attack. Fine, she decided
she wanted to see him weep. If he didn't, then he certainly wasn't the man she'd
thought he was!

Wang Shun put down the things he'd brought with him and with both hands
pounded the table. His head flailed back and forth as if he were crying out to heaven
and cursing the earth at the same time. His eyes still dry, he wailed: "Heavens, ah!
Ah! How can she be so cold and ruthless? She cares nothing for me... ah... ah... ah.
It's killing me and my factory too. Oh I just don't want to live any more. No one
touch me... oh...oh. Just let me die here."

His lament echoed around the room and finally Hong Fang had heard enough. She
feared the villagers would hear him and wonder what was going on. No matter
whether his grief was real or not, her heart was pained by his actions. She moved
closer towards him, removed some of the marinated meat he'd brought and put it in
his mouth: "Wang Shun, oh Wang Shun, have you no shame?"

Wang Shun pulled the piece of meat out of his mouth and said: "I'm doing
nothing shameful, I'm not playing games. Even a louse can cry and bemoan its lot
in life."

Hong Fang soon felt it hard to control her own emotions but she didn't know if
she wanted to cry or laugh at what he was doing. Not sure what to do, she
straightened up the table and laid out the food. She poured out some of the wine and
the two of them raised their glasses. But with their glasses in the air, what were they
to drink to? To her leaving, to wishing her the best once she returned home? Wang
Shun didn't want to say anything at first, but with their hands aloft, he changed his
tune and said: "Thank you, Miss Hong, your contributions to our factory will not be
forgotten. You've not helped it flourish but you've given me a lot of face, you've
always respected me and helped us to truly succeed!"

"Hey, why are you being so polite? Are you being honest? Do you mean it? Do you really want me to leave or not?"

"You still need to ask that? Of course I want you to stay, who'd be willing to give up their soul, hmm?"

"Lose your soul? Is it really as serious as that? Do you mean the factory or yourself?"

"Both!"

"Then why haven't you made more of an effort to try to get me to stay?"

"Do you mean you'd consider it?"

Wang Shun went silent. Could he really do that, just get her to stay? She asked herself, too, but no answer was forthcoming. Her heart and mind were in turmoil. All she could do was drink the wine she held in her hand and look for something to postpone where the conversation had been heading: "I'm like Cao Cao sipping chicken soup and being misunderstood. Who's Yang Xiu?[1] What should I do? It'd be a pity to just throw it away as it does have some flavour, after all. But if I keep it, well, the soup only contains ribs and not much meat at all."

Wang Shun's head swayed: "That's not right. It's not just bones, there's a lot meat on them, enough to satisfy any hunger and keep the mind working well. And in times of plenty, well, you'd think the meat is too greasy and too much would cause you to get fat. You can't throw it away. If you do, you'll regret it for sure."

"Don't use your smooth talking on me, OK?" There was a strained look on Hong Fang's face. "I want to leave but I want to be honest with you, I'm not reluctant about leaving Guojiadian, I'm reluctant about leaving you. There's just something about you, I don't know what it is, but whenever I'm with you, I'm happy and relaxed. But that isn't enough, not for a lifetime, is it? I've been going over it in my mind, maybe I'm not feeling reluctant about things, after all, maybe it's just my mind playing tricks. Maybe I should go. That would be best, I think."

"Do you really have no feelings, or are you afraid to let love in?"

"Why are you asking me that? Were we talking about me staying or not? But when I first told you I was leaving, you didn't seem to care. How am I to know if I should stay or not?

Alright, I want to ask you something. I'm going. What do you think about that? Is there love in your heart? You're a man. Do you even dare to love?"

"No, I don't," he admitted frankly and changed the tone of his voice, "because I'm a saint and a sage. I mean, I've been a rascal and a rogue all my life but with you, I'm not. You know what other people think. Well, you need to think that too. If we were living in the past, or if you weren't a Beijing girl, I would have popped the question already, long ago even. We'd already have kids by now, a life together and all the hassles that come with it. I wasn't always like this but with the life I've lived, how in hell can I be a saint? You already said, didn't you, that there's nothing honourable about me. But let me say this. I've never grabbed you or torn at your clothes. Isn't that honourable? Is there something more I should've done? Sure, I don't always grasp what's going on but I could give you a good life, I'd treat you as my lady, I'd provide for you, make you laugh and pamper you too. I'd be your toad and you'd be my swan, I know I could make you happy. I'd give you everything I could but there's one thing I know I can't give you, and that's the city! If we married, who's to say you wouldn't one day think of Beijing, or you'd wake up unhappy and regret staying here. What then?"

Hong Fang's heart was burning and she feared it was melting, too, feared that she was losing control and would end up staying. She had to change the topic: "Let's not talk about it any more, it's too much, too overwhelming. We'll both end up drunk if we carry on like this. Let's talk about something else. Tell me about when you were young, that should be easy enough for you. You always seem to tell such great tales. I bet you've always had this natural talent, haven't you?"

"Natural talent, ha, more like bullshit! And I can do it like the best of them because I have practised ever since I was little. I was fond of singing when I was young and whenever anyone got married, they'd always come and ask me to sing a jolly song or two. I'd dress up, too, the gaudier the better, with one of those pointy hats on. I'd sing along with the loudspeaker," he said, breaking off to hum. "And after I sang, I'd always get some morsel of food, sometimes even money. There were times when I'd be given something that wasn't fit to eat, or they'd only give me a little bit of money, so I'd sing to curse them, you know, sing about how they liked to talk big but were as cheap as hell, how they had a child with no arsehole, stuff like that. I used to even sing at funerals. I'd get all dressed up in black and lead the funeral procession. When the drums began to beat behind me, I'd inhale deeply then wail 'Ooooohhhh' all the way to the burial site. I'd sing in rhythm with the bells, too. If it was a well-off family, you know, one with a wide courtyard, when they ought to have had two of us, well, when I was there they didn't need it. When one long, deep breath was finished, I would immediately start another."

As she listened, she felt the happiness well up inside her: "No wonder then that tongue of yours has been in training since you were but a boy. But I've found something else out, too. There's one person whom you don't speak to in the same garrulous manner."

"Guo Cunxian."

"But his family name is Guo and yours is Wang. How come he's your senior?"

"When I first met him, well, I had to kowtow. I was starving, on my last legs, to be honest. I'd been begging, like so many others, but even that wasn't getting me anything to eat any more. I was all skin and bones, I tell you. Later on that night, I spied a village that still had some livestock so I knew they must be feeding them something, you know, some coarse grains or whatever. I waited until it was dark and then crept in to steal some. Using a bit of water, I mulched up some bits of grain, whatever I could find, and then gulped it down. That evening, Guo Cunxian was helping out the old caretaker, so he was standing guard over the animals, but when he discovered me he didn't raise the alarm. No, he did something I never would have expected. He shared his own food with me, the cornmeal he'd earned by making coffins, and even gave me a bowl of cool water, too. I tell you, after I ate that, well, I felt the life come back into my body, honestly.

"We stuck together after that night and learned how to get by on whatever grain we could get our hands on. He had the skills with his hands, you know, carpentry, you've seen their extension, and, well, I have the gift of the gab, right? I helped find him work. When I was in school, I remember our teacher telling us about the Red Army and the Long March, and how they'd eat leather because they had nothing else.

I reckon that was a helluva lot harder to swallow than what we had but, shit, there was once, about five or six days I reckon, when we couldn't find any work to do, nor beg for any food. Even washing down barns and all that animal filth wouldn't get us a mouthful of anything. Well, I remember taking an old donkey's harness, cleaning it and then boiling it up to make soup. It wasn't half bad. We were able to fill our bellies, and once the broth was gone, well, we chewed on the soft leftover leather but, hell, there was no chewing that into pieces, let me tell you. That's when it dawned on me, what if we roasted it over a fire? You know, grill it until it was black and then eat it. Hey, what flavour! That got us through the following two or three days. Not bad I'd say. That's when I understood, too, how the Red Army won. If they'd been able to make do on roasted leather, well, they could take on anything."

Hong Fang laughed and then playfully rapped her chopsticks on his head: "You're incorrigible. You dare to speak sarcastically of such things. You've drunk too much, haven't you? Sing me a drinking ditty, hmm, I need a good laugh."

As though he was on stage and his audience had spoken, he got into character, rapped his skull and thought of a tune: "We're having a drink but I swear I haven't touched a drop yet I feel it, ho! It's bubbly we've drunk and our legs are the first to go, followed by our tongues and then we say stuff we shouldn't. Ah hey, to hell with it all anyway!"

"You scoundrel, you're calling me the devil?"

He opened his eyes wide in mock surprise and stared at Hong Fang. There was a smile on his face. His brow was furrowed in good humour. The more he looked at her the more his feelings welled up inside. Finally he spoke: "The tune's about a man."

"And what if it was about a woman?"

"Heh, heh, well sweet words often have the opposite effect but the more I look at you the prettier you get!"

Her face went crimson red. Then, in a gentle voice she asked: "Is this just more sweet talk or do you really mean it? Do you think I'm pretty?"

"There are countless pretty women about but you're something special. Some kinds of beauty are dangerous and do only harm. Yours warms the heart."

"You're just trying to flatter me," said Hong Fang, training her eyes on him. They felt as hot as the sun. She continued: "Everyone says you've got talent, especially when it comes to dirty limericks... I don't really know what they mean. Let me hear one."

With the booze coursing through his veins, he looked at her with bloodshot eyes and decided why not? He'd let his inner demon out: "Burning incense in the Buddhist Temple, I come across a young monk. He loves that I'm young, I love his smooth head. We cuddle up together under a red damask quilt, lying across an ivory-framed bed. Wrapped in each other's embrace I urge him to take it slow, I don't wish to wake my dear mother."

Hong Fang's face flushed ever more crimson: "Those are words from a play, aren't they?"

"Of course they are, do you think I could write that myself."

"If we're together, could you write one of your own?"

"When it's something I'm doing at first hand, the words come naturally. Here, what about this? 'Virtuous sister, sister of virtue, please don't resent a brother's lowly background. Together we can be happy, I love your sweet heart. Let's have children, a whole big brood. Our intimacy will last more than a hundred years'."

"You want me to be some kind of sow? You're already raising some pigs but that's not enough for you? You want me to be one too, popping out piglet after piglet?"

"But pigs are great. They eat and sleep without a care in the world, without thinking too much. People born in the year of the pig are said to be honest, true and blessed with good fortune. A face that is round like a pig's is said to reveal an open and bright mind!"

Hong Fang didn't smile. She looked at his face. There were so many stories there it drew you in and promised thrills and excitement but, at the same time, she felt shy and embarrassed by the desire he'd awoken in her. She moved her face closer to his and in a barely audible voice she dared to speak what was in her heart: "I want you to take me in your arms."

"Oh, what a wild little piglet you are. I can certainly do that but it won't be easy to make me let go." Wang Shun's mouth might have been boorish but his embrace was soft and tender, his hands careful and delicate. Gently he began to caress her, his fingers were warm to the touch as though they were aflame. The more he moved his hands the more excited she became until finally his hands reached the place she'd been longing for them to reach. His whole body came alive then and they were soon entangled with each other. His foul, dirty mouth didn't stop either: Oh my dirty little piglet, my treasure, I'm yours. I long for you, you eat me up. I've been waiting for this for so long. My wild little piglet, I've wanted to kiss those little piggy teeth of yours forever. Oh, they're just so... I can't help but love them.

Wang Shun stayed the night and Hong Fang never mentioned returning to the capital again. In the few years that followed, they had three children together and each one was like a tiny piglet, sturdy and always full of energy.

14

A WINTRY SPRING

A yellowish hue descended on the afternoon sky as desert sand was carried on the wind.

It tore through the town, pushing vehicles as it went, forcing their tyres to spin faster and faster. And as it blew, it gathered more and more dust, twirling and swirling like ferocious little tornadoes. A moment to open the bus door was all the wind needed to blanket everything and everyone in a layer of yellow sand. Guo Cunxian stood at the open door, about to speak but his voice was immediately swallowed up by the dirt flying through the air and forced down his throat by the wind.

"Hurry up, come on!" The ticket seller roared. Everyone was shouting the same words, those trying to get off the bus and those trying to get on.

Guo Cunxian was gasping and struggling to breathe, his throat raw because of the sand. At his feet lay a package of mechanical components, jamming the path towards the door.

"Eh, old-timer, yes, you, come on and hurry up!"

"He's carrying such a big bag with him, he ought to be penalised. I'd say he should have to buy another ticket."

A bus was never short of those wishing to share their opinions, and at this moment they formed a veritable mob, all roaring together to bully poor old Guo Cunxian. Perhaps the passengers didn't know he was a man who couldn't easily control his temper, or perhaps they were simply seizing an opportunity to vent some of their long pent-up frustrations. Of course, Guo Cunxian was no ordinary peasant. He'd received his fair share of animosity before, ranging from outright hostility to smaller annoyances, from trivial matters to much more serious ones. It goes without saying he'd been between a rock and a hard place once or twice in his lifetime but this almost feral anger the passengers were directing at him now, just where was this coming from? Unfortunately, he couldn't stop to mull it over; his only option was to swallow it as he swallowed the sand.

As he made his way to the exit, he kept his anger to himself, instead using all of his energy to push towards the front with his bag behind him. Motherfuckers, he thought. He'd just turned forty and here they were calling him an old-timer! To his mind he was still young, or perhaps he was wrong, perhaps he'd never really been young to begin with... he'd only thought that seizing the opportunity to become village leader had been what a young man would have done and now that seemed to be in doubt. Or maybe it was a case of the position itself exacting a far greater toll than he'd have thought, the worries and problems it came with prematurely ageing him, like rust forming at the ends of a metal plate. He thought some more. If he were being honest, he supposed, he had noticed how his cheeks had begun to sink, how lines had deepened across his brow. The sweat and the dirt of life in the countryside had become ingrained into his face, cutting lines across it, splitting it and cracking it open.

There was a growing urgency on the bus, those getting on began to kick and trample over each other while he could only use his strength to push against the shifting weight of humanity. Finally he stepped down from the vehicle, his bag flung down unceremoniously after him.

Then, as the bus set off again, he was enveloped in a cloud of dust and smoke. There was nowhere to flee, no fan to clear the air, and no way to cover his mouth. The smoke swirled up around him, forcing him to breathe it in. There was no escape from the earth, from the soil. It's in our bones, it provides us with food and when we die, we return to it, we're buried in it, or we're burnt to ashes and then spread across it. People are fearful of dust and feel it has no purpose, no reason, but there really is no point in being afraid of it; it's part of us. He squinted to watch how the sand carried on the wind, how it surrounded him, clung to his frame like strands of silk, sticky, irritating and coarse. He felt it on his tongue. It was rough, salty and almost tasted like the sea. Sand and dust loved causing havoc with the wind, loved being picked up and flung through the air to ultimately settle on everything and everyone, finding its way into the smallest nook and cranny. And then, as violently as the wind had been blowing, it stopped and all was silent.

Guo Cunxian had to straighten himself up. There was still quite a way for him to go before he reached Guojiadian. He wasn't sure, either, whether or not he'd be able to make it home before dark dragging this heavy bag with him. He stuck to the side of the paved road and started to walk, finally turning off at the dirt road that led to Guojiadian. The bag rattled and clanged as he walked. Fear grew inside him. He was worried he'd end up breaking the instruments he'd brought with him. Finally, he decided to hoist it over his shoulder and keep on walking. The weight bent him over at nearly ninety degrees. The metal and iron on top, flesh and bones underneath. His back hardened and soon lost all feeling. The more he walked, the heavier the bag became. His breathing became increasingly laboured and the sweat rolled down his face. Dizziness then began to take hold. His chest grew tighter and tighter as though it was waiting to explode. His back worsened and grew harder. Unfortunately, this also brought searing waves of pain. The sun dropped further and further in the sky, darkening his path. He hunched even more but his feet kept trudging along.

What bastard would dare call me old, huh?

I'm old? Ha! What youngster even could carry this load?

Didn't this road usually feel flat? How was it now so pitted with holes and ridges? When the village is wealthier than it is now, the first thing we'll do is repair this road and then build new ones linking Guojiadian to the city, to the provincial capital. We'll have roads stretching in all directions. After all, without proper roads, who'd be able to come to the town? And without people, how will it prosper and get rich? His face inched closer and closer to the ground. It was getting harder and harder, more and more painful to even lift his legs. It felt as though his waist was about to snap but still he lumbered on.

Constructing a chemical factory was his idea and so he was responsible for it, no one else. And if he didn't try his hardest, who else would? It was his burden to carry and his alone. Everyone in the village knew he was a capable man and that once he'd thrown his hat into the ring, then surely he would succeed. It was even clearer to him. He knew he could handle it. He'd endured hardship all his life, faced official censure and punishment, and he wasn't afraid to open his mouth to get the help he needed. That's why he'd gone to the northeast, to replace the components for a high-pressure pump they needed. He hadn't brought much money with him, certainly not enough to buy a new piece outright, nor had he brought the broken component. After all, admitting to the fact they'd damaged the original component would be exposing too much of their operations and would have made it obvious they'd installed the component incorrectly so that when they had test-driven the machine it had broken. What would be the point in telling them this? It certainly wouldn't help them get a replacement, would it?

Without a factory, there'd be no way to make the village rich, but farmers weren't all that familiar with heavy machinery. You could say it was as though the machinery had an all too easy time bullying farmers. But what farmer couldn't put up with a little bit of bullshit, hmm? Everyone thought they were easy targets, so sometimes the best response was to go along with it and tell the truth, half-truths or blatant lies when the need arose, anything really, to make the city folk take them at their word. And this was exactly what Guo Cunxian had done. He'd been frank, told them that his workers had installed things incorrectly, that there'd been some problem or other and that now they needed some spare parts. That was all they needed and they'd be sure to make a go of it. Besides, the parts only cost a fraction of the total and nobody would miss a small pittance out of 170,000 yuan for the project as a whole, right? Still, asking for favours wasn't always the easiest thing to do, especially when it was some old country bumpkin asking favours from a city man; that made things much more complicated.

Of course, Guo Cunxian had already experienced his fair share of shame and humiliation, like when he'd gone down on his knees and prostrated himself in front of the entire village; that had been hard to bear. But from that experience, he had a grasp of what he was able to do and what he could achieve or take, like offering empty talk while those below him did the heavy lifting. But there was something he didn't quite grasp, at least not fully. In those instances when he had to bow humbly and low, when he had to brownnose, play the subservient fool and willingly shame himself, he had to do these things all by himself without anyone under his command knowing about it. That way, he could return to the village triumphantly, his dignity intact, his power and prestige undamaged. He'd endured so much beyond the town limits, had accepted so many injustices, but these things all had to be kept to himself. For seven days and seven nights, he hadn't enjoyed a proper meal, hadn't slept, not comfortably in any case, nor had he thought that when he got off the bus there'd be no one around. Could this be the reason why he now had to carry everything back to Guojiadian by himself?

Something was wrong. Why was the road so empty today, so cold and cheerless? Spring had already come and there should have been people out in the field, tilling the soil, gathering fertiliser, visiting relatives. There should have been someone about. And what about the factories they had already set up? This road was usually filled with people day and night. Guo Cunxian dawdled a little, his waist hadn't broken, his legs were still underneath him, but now his stomach started to churn and tie itself in knots. A cold wind rose and nearly overwhelmed him, sending frigid air down his throat. He felt exhausted. His feet were frozen to the ground, unable to take another step forward. Carefully, gingerly, he lifted the weight off his back and placed it on the ground. He was still bent over like a bow, powerless to straighten his back. All he could do was collapse alongside the road and rest his tired frame against the bag he had been carrying. He reached for a cigarette, only to find the pack empty. His hand then shifted and he pulled out a dried pancake. Bringing it close to his mouth, he bit off a small piece and chewed it slowly. His hunger only became intensified as though a stake had been been driven into his abdomen. He felt the bile rise up in his throat and before he could do anything else, he vomited the undigested pancake. The contents of his stomach were bright red. Then another wave of nausea welled up and burst out.

Guo Cunxian was afraid, his head swam and his heart pounded in his chest. He threw down the pancake and used his hand to root out any remaining bits. He closed his mouth as tightly as he could and then used both his hands to massage his stomach. He was trying as hard as he could to manoeuvre the remaining blood towards his intestines and out of his body. But if his body wanted to vomit blood, could he really keep his mouth shut? He kept kneading his belly, vainly trying to force the bile back down. Once his stomach settled and he no longer felt the urge to vomit, Guo Cunxian picked up a stick and poked it into the mess he'd made on the ground, wondering what was in it. Just what the hell was going on with him? Was he just exhausted or had he swallowed something?

A cold shiver ran up his spine as another freezing blast of air swept through. Guo Cunxian turned the collar of his old jacket up and pulled the garment more tightly around him. His mind was busy disproving possible hypotheses for what was ailing him. Impossible, he thought. He knew his stomach. He'd probably just picked up a bug, nothing serious. His belly was nearly empty, after all. He had stuffed too much in too quickly and this was the result. He remembered when he was small and his crazy old uncle had made a bet with another man about pulling an ox cart. He had worked so hard he vomited blood but the old man had lived beyond sixty. He'd just been hunched over so much, too, that it had made him nauseous but there was nothing in his belly but blood to spit up.

Guo Cunxian continued to console himself, to calm his nerves. Another moment passed and he picked up the pancake once more, intent on eating it. But his bites were small and tentative. He had to get something into him. He couldn't leave his stomach empty and, as he did so, he began to feel a little better, or at least not like he had before. But as he took his third bite, something felt off: the sesame seeds were moving. When he inspected it more closely, he was stunned to see the sesame seeds weren't seeds at all but ants. Disgusted, he threw the pancake down again and once more took to massaging his stomach.

At the same time as Guo Cunxian was left powerless to walk any closer to Guojiadian, an investigation team was waiting with a trap prepared, ready to ensnare him. Over the past few days, the tranquillity of Guojiadian had taken on an evil air. On the occasions when a dog's bark would echo out, or when a pig would squeal, the entire village would leap in fear. A palpable sense of fear seemed to stalk the town.

And whatever was causing it, it was only a matter of time before all would be revealed.

Over the past few years, the offspring of most Chinese families had come to understand that organisations such as 'investigation teams' and 'work units' all possessed certain implications, even if those implications weren't always clear. Most political initiatives, for example, the 'Four Cleanup Movements' that took place between 1963 and 1966 (a movement to rid or 'cleanse' the political, economic, organisational and ideological fields of reactionary elements), or the Cultural Revolution that followed, started with investigation teams or work units. Those who hadn't experienced events such as these really had no inkling as to the myriad implications and potential for upheaval such wording held.

The arrival of an investigation team spelled only trouble; that much was certain. For anyone who was to be investigated, well, they became a pariah almost immediately. Once the investigation team arrived, every factory was ordered to cease production and await investigation. It was as though a cold frost had settled on the farmland, destroying crops and forcing farmers into a resigned listlessness. With little or no work to do, fewer and fewer people could be seen walking about the town. Many took to spending their days slumped against some wall or other, basking in the early spring sun. A cold, cheerless atmosphere hung over everything and everyone. And the longer this mood gripped Guojiadian, the more restless and anxious the villagers became. The greater their anxiety, the more they began to ask discreet questions and keep their ears close to the ground for any and all titbits of news. Their eyes were constantly shifting, inspecting friend and foe alike.

If the day was the domain of the sun and the night belonged to the moon, then sleep was how man endured the passage of the netherworld. The morning brought freshness and new hope. The impending noise and excitement that Guojiadian was about to endure began first in the eastern part of the town. When the villagers opened their eyes and made their way to the communal well to fetch the day's water, they spied the signs of what was to come. Upon seeing it, they immediately called to their neighbours and news spread like wildfire, meaning further announcements were irrelevant. The early risers, the most diligent and earnest ones, asked the first questions: "What's happening today, hmm? What movement are we about to start?" In the immediate past, whenever a new movement was to begin, everyone, all the production teams and work units, would be called to the town well to listen for instructions. Every Tom, Dick and Harry, every minority group, would put aside what they had planned to do and make their way to the communal well.

One night, as a villager slept soundly, peacefully, two feet trod close. Two water pails, one at the foot of the bed, one at the head, swayed rhythmically and a folk tune carried on their lips. Then a clear, resounding, sharp voice shattered the calm scene: "Old man, just what the hell were you up to yesterday, huh? Why's your leg bowed as though you'd been riding a horse all day? Did you forget to dismount?"

"Hey there old-timer, what's wrong with your eyes? You can't seem to open them, huh. Did your wife make you sleep on the floor last night?"

Every household has endured their fair share of pain and delight. Each family has gone through its ups and downs. And they all have their own temperaments. But in the morning, standing next to their bed, you can pretty much tell what kind of family they are.

This day was fortuitous, for everyone woke up with a smile on their faces, their teeth shining white in the morning sun, with some even nodding their heads. There was no music in the air and no folk songs sung as people were afraid to raise suspicions. Even raised voices might be considered an offence. The only sound that could be heard was the gentle lapping of water in the pails alongside the beds.

An oppressive sense of dread hung in the air. Everyone was waiting for whatever was about to happen.

At the same time, something else never before seen in Guojiadian happened: a man, with seemingly nothing better to do, was running. Early mornings are precious, especially for a farming village, so it was natural that the man running was not from Guojiadian but, rather, the head investigator Qian Xishou. City folk didn't much like the village, its lifestyle and people, but they certainly enjoyed the country air. Especially the early mornings when it was already mild but at the same time cool and crisp. Such weather had the effect of awakening the senses to the world all around them. One gulp of that kind of air penetrated deep into the lungs and purged them clean. Qian Xishou took care of himself. After getting out of bed, he wouldn't wash and gargle as most do, but instead headed straight outdoors to jog for at least forty minutes. He'd wear a sleeveless, tan-coloured cotton top, blue sports shorts and white trainers. He looked the picture of health, clean and nimble, and cut quite a figure around the town. But the sound of his rhythmic footsteps would shatter the general calm and tranquillity of the early morning.

To the villagers, he seemed to be running laps around the town as a show of force. It was as though suddenly and abruptly an aura of death had invaded Guojiadian, imposing its domineering will over the fragrant, gentle freshness of the early dawn. He ran at a leisurely pace, his head held high so that his eyes could scan the environs closely and methodically. Those he encountered on his run received no polite greeting, not even a simple bow. His face looked serene but for an odd smirk that never seemed to leave it. His eyes were cold and indifferent. His smile almost immediately made the villagers think of Guo Cunxian's weeping but no one could really explain just what the connection was. The only thing they were certain of was that Qian Xishou had come to Guojiadian for a purpose, and that meant someone was going to die. He hadn't come to share laughter with them; his smile brought with it death instead. You could say his smile indicated his own satisfaction with his position and all the severity it entailed. As a result, those villagers who saw him out running would immediately retreat from his sight if they could, and if they couldn't, they'd keep their heads low, doing their utmost to avoid making eye contact. Some would even go so far as to pretend they hadn't seen him. Those less fortunate endured his stare as though they had been stapled to the spot where they stood, dreading the potential outcome.

As for Qian Xishou, he cared little about what the villagers thought of him. His pace was unhurried, his gait light. All that mattered was how he felt about himself, and in that regard, he was thoroughly pleased. He knew the townspeople would regard him as some sort of oddity and laugh at him and curse him behind his back. That was all very natural. And the reason for their demeanour towards him was plain: he had come to Guojiadian as leader of an investigation team, which meant the villagers' responses would vary. Some would welcome his arrival while others would oppose it, at least when among their own friends. Some would feel utter hatred for him and his team, while the rest would simply fear them. So it didn't really matter what kind of attitude he displayed. To a man, everyone in the village was keenly aware of what his arrival signified. The fate of Guojiadian was in his hands, which meant they all had to be deferential towards him, regardless of their own inner sentiments. Of course, this resulted in quite a few townsfolk openly trying to curry favour with him, some egging him on to come down hard on the village, others hoping he might be more lenient.

What made the inhabitants of Guojiadian most anxious, however, was precisely why he had been dispatched in the first place. To his mind, there was trouble in this town; that much he was certain about. After all, his team had been sent because those in power believed there was still time to actually do something about it. So for Qian, he hoped his investigations would clearly identify what was wrong. At the same time, he also hoped that, as they looked into things, they would uncover more and more issues, and that each one would be more serious than the last. Such a turn of events would naturally draw more attention to him and what he had been able to achieve.

There were six members in his team, including even a cook, as it was expected they would prepare their own meals. This 'battle deployment', as Qian likened it to, was different from the past when they would have shared their meals with the village work units. Their task was to ferret out undesirable elements, which meant they had to remain separate from the townspeople at all costs. Maintaining this type of clear boundary, they wouldn't accept a single morsel of food, not one ladle of soup. That would allow them to carry out their investigation in a cold and detached manner. It was to be entirely businesslike, impersonal and emotionless. In fact, the only imposition they made on the village was with regard to their lodgings; they couldn't, in the end, stay in tents, could they?

After the team arrived in Guojiadian, they were immediately divided into smaller units and assigned specific tasks, each responsible for a part of the whole investigation. Interviews were held, questions asked and evidence gathered. The local public security bureau and prosecutor's office were involved as well. Those in uniform kept watch over the town, carefully doing their rounds and striking a rather imposing image as they did so. If the villagers entertained thoughts that things would work out in the end, they were soon dispelled. This investigation team, it seemed, was hell-bent on making arrests.

It only took a single person to guess what was going on, and within half a day the story would be on the lips of everyone in town. A thousand mouths telling the same story. Well, then, before the day ended, everyone for miles around, in all the eight counties, would be sharing the same tale, believing for sure that more than a few people from Guojiadian had been taken into custody. The first such arrest would be Guo Cunxian, of that there could be no doubt. For most, they couldn't be sure if Guo Cunxian's life was blessed or cursed, but ever since his return with a wife so many years ago he had experienced his fair share of crises. Today he'd be arrested and investigated by the authorities; tomorrow he'd be rehabilitated. Over and over again the cycle seemed to be repeated.

The day before in Wangguantun market, which was only about thirteen *li* away, people were telling their stories, each purporting to be relaying the most accurate version, of how Guo Cunxian had been hauled away in shackles and how his wife had trailed behind him, crying out uncontrollably.

In Guojiadian, rumours were flying about, worming their way into every nook and cranny, hot on everyone's lips. Conjecture swirled and questions abounded:

Did you say Guo Cunxian had returned?

I heard he'd run off with the mechanical components he'd gone off to buy!

Hey! How the hell would you know, huh? Besides, somebody's already seen him being hauled off.

The villagers could barely contain their excitement. Their curiosity and speculation about what was happening knew no bounds. As for the actual truth, the real impact this would have on their lives, that wasn't really important. No, their attention was on the gossip and the hours of conversation this would give them. It didn't matter if someone as important as Guo Cunxian was getting some supposed comeuppance or other, or if he was finished as town leader; they didn't fear things like this. Life was complicated and being at centre stage only meant that one would eventually have to step down, whether by force or not. The events they were witnessing now simply formed part of the scenery, startling though they may be.

Of course, such malicious gossip did raise the ire of those who supported Guo Cunxian, those who hoped he wasn't done for.

Ultimately, Qian Xishou had no recourse but to intervene, to clarify what was happening. If there was anything that worried Qian Xishou, it was that his investigation team would turn up nothing. Arriving in town was one thing, that was simple; departing was an entirely different matter altogether. The more things got out of hand, the harder it was to rein things in.

But the nature of his worry and the anxiety shown by Guo Cunxian were of a different order of magnitude entirely. Wanting to carry out an investigation was one thing but had they come to the right place? Were they looking into the right people? This wasn't the first time he'd been the hunter.

It was as though a seed of grass was growing in the pit of her stomach. Lin Meitang had come to make discreet inquiries about Guo Cunxian, or to at least find someone to talk to, to get some things off her chest. But as she walked through the village a deep-seated worry and fear grew. Who could have known that at this moment they'd be talking about her and Guo Cunxian? Was it perhaps just bad timing on her part? What would... what could she say if she barged in now? What kind of eyes would they look at her with? Might her appearance now cause only further misunderstanding and provoke only more malicious gossip? That certainly wouldn't be worth it, she thought. Regardless of what she thought herself, however, she was known in the village. Stories had persisted, even though she had left. Most people considered her to be like one of those prized consorts from the past who had wormed their way into the heart of the emperor. But if something had really happened, who could she talk to, besides Guo Cunxian? There wasn't anyone else. So she kept walking, aimlessly, without anywhere to go. Then, before she knew it, she was in front of Ou Guangyu's home. A sudden and urgent thought occurred to her. Ou Guangyu's young wife was pregnant with their second child and she had to discuss something with her, had to set a time to abort the child growing in her belly. She was, after all, director of the Women's Federation in Guojiadian and responsible for family planning policy. This was in the nation's interest, regardless of the joy or pain it brought to the Ou family, and she had to deal with it sooner or later, despite the headache it gave her.

She knocked on the courtyard gate and a pair of eyes belonging to Ou Guangyu's old mother peeked out through the window at her. The eyes disappeared as quickly as they had appeared before Lin Meitang heard a flurry of activity from inside. The old woman had taken down a lock from on top of the wardrobe and made her way to open the door. As she stepped outside, however, she pretended not to see anyone straightaway, instead turning quickly and bolting the door tightly behind her. Her actions were swift and fluid, practised. Once the door was safely shut, she turned leisurely around once more and acted as though she was surprised and flustered upon seeing Lin Meitang: "Oh, it's you, Director Lin. Um, my son and his wife have gone to her parents' home and I'm on my way out, too. Sorry I can't let you in at the moment."

Lin Meitang didn't believe her. She had seen this kind of act many times before. But today she wasn't in the mood and didn't feel like wasting her breath. She simply turned her head and began to walk away. As she did so, she gave instructions: "Make sure you tell me when they return. Time is of the essence here and things need to be handled sooner rather than later."

"Eh," the old lady promised in reply and then waited for Lin Meitang to leave before cursing her: "You barren, cold-hearted woman. Like a hen that hasn't laid any eggs, all you do is chirp and squawk at those that have, trying to prevent them from having more. Not everyone has to be like you, loveless and with no one to care for, last in the family line!"

Lin Meitang came to a halt. What's this old lady been eating today to give her such fire, such impudence? She hadn't said anything. What cause had she given the old woman to curse her so viciously? She should straighten this old hag out. If she didn't, she'd probably end up inciting others, wouldn't she? Today there would be curses thrown at her back, tomorrow those hurling them would become even bolder. Before long, she'd have all kinds of shit heaped on her and be bullied and browbeaten by everyone. How would she deal with that? But anger begets anger and hatred stirs only more hatred. Lin Meitang chose not to turn round. If this were the past, the old lady would never have had the nerve to say these things about Lin Meitang, but things were different now. She'd found the nerve to say what was on her mind. The investigation team that was looking into how the town was being run gave the old woman the gumption she needed. If she did turn round, Lin Meitang thought to herself, what could she do? Curse the old woman? Drag her off to the Party offices in town for re-education? The family planning policies weren't all that bad, Lin Meitang pondered, but considering what was happening, having fewer things on one's plate was better than having too much. Guo Cunxian was already in a big enough jam; she didn't want to add to it. She pretended she hadn't heard anything and forced her legs to move. She had to leave. The only problem was that she wasn't sure where she ought to go. Perhaps there was nothing else to do but return to her own little room and wait… for what, she wasn't sure.

As she passed by the agricultural depot, she saw the old hands inside, idle, squatting around telling each other dirty jokes. When they spied her, they immediately exploded into laughter and began catcalling, howling and hooting like rabid dogs. The village women knew there was only one way to handle such a situation: whenever they met or bumped into a crowd of men like this, the only thing they could do was close or avert their eyes and run. Lin Meitang put her head down and stepped up her pace.

Still, the foul language and obscene words pelted down on her:

"Hey y'all, do you see who has come? The director of the Women's Fed!"

"I reckon us bare sticks are bare because of her. She ought to take responsibility for that herself, huh, especially the difficulties we have in the evenings, whaddya say?"

"You're right on the money there! Go on, ask her, why are there wives for some men but none for us, huh?"

"Who? If you've got the balls to, then why don't you go ahead and ask her?"

While they bantered on, Lin Meitang slipped away and returned home, her face wet with tears. Had everyone in the village gone mad today? Was it the end of the world or something? Was there no tomorrow? They might not be afraid of her but did that mean they were no longer afraid of Guo Cunxian hearing about how she was treated? Just whose end was it? Surely they didn't think it was their own; could it really be Guo Cunxian's? Was that why they'd been so brazen and so crude? But for the moment at least, Guo Cunxian wasn't finished, perhaps they were just tempting fate. Whatever the case may be, the way the townspeople were acting certainly showed the underbelly of resentment they felt towards him. Ordinarily, Guo Cunxian accorded himself a particular level of prestige. He came across as strong and formidable, as ferocious and even a little difficult to deal with, and that was all due to the real power he wielded. But for them to treat her like that, sure, the rascals did it to most women, leering was their main pastime, but this was something more, it was as though they no longer cared a wit about Guo Cunxian either, no longer feared him.

A cold, sharp pain gripped her heart. If Guo Cunxian was going to be removed, then she feared the worst. She wouldn't be able to stay in the town. If he was brought down, there'd be no one in the village to give her the time of day, so what would be the point of staying? She'd be better off returning to the city to try and find a man, someone to marry her. Either that or remain a spinster living out the rest of her days with her old mum. Would she still have done what she'd done had she known this would be the outcome? She'd been mistaken about everything but she couldn't figure out why. Had she sacrificed everything for love? Was that really what love was? And even if she thought it was, did Guo Cunxian feel the same way? She tormented herself with these thoughts, allowing them to spin over and over again in her mind. But she didn't once utter the word 'love'. The villagers didn't talk about such things and didn't even believe in them. All they would do was let loose their dirty mouths when it came time to actually climbing into bed.

It was all clear to her now. When the villagers looked upon her relationship with Guo Cunxian they had two opinions of her. One, she was nothing but a pair of old, worn-out shoes, useless and of poor quality to begin with. The other was that she was the victim, she'd been trapped, taken advantage of and deserved to be pitied. Would her future hold promise? Her fate had been decided. Her love for Guo Cunxian, from the very beginning, had been entangled with misfortune. Time and again this proved to be true that disaster and trouble came hand in hand with her feelings, uninterrupted. She'd already felt this. She knew in her heart of hearts they wouldn't be together forever and that sooner or later their relationship would end. But had it come already? What were the chances that, when the investigation team burst into town, Guo Cunxian would be gone? Had the authorities planned this and seized on this moment to topple him, to bring him down, just when he wasn't there? When he'd left, there was no inkling of these developments on the horizon, there had been no whispers on the wind; she couldn't believe that such a thing could even happen. It had been ages since he'd come to see her. He hadn't even exchanged many official words with her for some time. She'd waited knowing full well he wouldn't come. Feelings of the heart are hard to contain. She hoped she had the stamina to wait for him, for even the slightest hint of his shared feelings for her, just a glance, a small gesture, anything… but it never came. Her despair grew day by day as the thought of a pleasant surprise diminished more and more; even chance seemed to have abandoned her.

Lin Meitang was distraught and her heart was in turmoil. She sat in her room staring blankly out the window as the day slowly turned into night. Finally she got down off the *kang* to make some dinner. She didn't feel like eating, didn't really feel like making anything to begin with, but she forced herself to put something together. Living alone was hard, something as simple, natural and necessary as preparing a meal was, at times, a struggle. If she thought for a moment she couldn't be bothered, then she wouldn't and her stomach would go empty; those types of days were the hardest. Why was it so hard at times to drum up enthusiasm for life? Why in hell had she returned to Guojiadian?

Sitting there, going over these things in her mind, she resolved to make herself live like everyone else, three meals a day, not one less. She had to eat, sometimes more, sometimes less, that was fine so long as she ate and even when she really didn't feel like eating, she still had to make something. When it came to cooking, she had to ensure the fire was lit and the chimney flute was open. She had to make sure the room was warmed; it wouldn't do to sit down and sleep on a frozen bed. She lifted the lid of the water jar to get some water for the pot but the ladle only scraped against the bottom of the jar; there wasn't a drop of water in it. It seems as though whatever could go wrong today had done. It was late now. Did she really want to go to the well? What if she were to slip and fall on the way there? But if she didn't go to fetch any water, what then? She took hold of her flask. There was drinking water at least, she didn't have to worry about that but was there enough for her evening wash?

Before she'd met Guo Cunxian, before he'd made her his, all the daily little things that one had to do in life had been taken care of by him, and on the occasions when he couldn't do it himself, he'd send someone else to handle it. She was his heir, but he couldn't show outward concern for her. No, it wasn't that he couldn't, it was more as though he were a thief with a guilty conscience, and that he had to act in a manner that didn't arouse suspicion. She had requested he act like this because she knew he enjoyed the public image he cut and the power he possessed; he was a man, after all. To everyone else he was bold, brazen and afraid of no one, of nothing, but that wasn't the whole story. She knew what worried him, she knew what made him weak and cowardly. Like a wife knows her husband, she knew what caused him distress, what would make him suffer.

But Guo Cunxian did nothing, so somebody else did. It didn't matter how many people might be talking behind her back, spreading rumours and lies. For some, it was just what they did, an uncontrollable need to blather away, to gossip about other people. Some, they just wanted to join in the fun and offer their own two pennies' worth. In truth, he had always liked her and had sought ways to worm his way in closer to her. He had been willing to give her work to do. There were always men like this and Guo Cunyong was most certainly this type of man. As a woman, Lin Meitang knew what he wanted, she was clear about that. The desire, the lust he had had for her hadn't totally dissipated; the embers still burned. But he was ashamed of these feelings, he didn't want to cause further trouble for Guo Cunxian, nor did he dare to fully stoke the small fire he still had for her. He just had to keep it smouldering so he couldn't get too close nor too far away. The distance and energy it took to maintain it had to be just right. That was the only way to make it work, to satisfy his need to be connected to her and at the same time protect his relationship with Guo Cunxian. One thing was clear: he wanted her to be happy, to be able to walk down the street and freely greet whomever she encountered. He wanted her life to be free from problems.

But she wasn't happy.

In a village like this, Lin Meitang thought, when the time came to cook a meal, women of her age would first go and fetch water and, for the most part, that was the life of a widow. No, she thought, she wasn't like a widow. A widow would carry herself with a certain strength and uprightness, and they would also receive other people's sympathy, respect and care. But her? She was no better than a grass widow! Who would look after a woman like her? Who would treat her with respect? To make matters worse, in truth, she didn't even possess the status of a grass widow. She steeled herself. She would rather eat nothing, drink nothing, nor even fetch water. She didn't care about the rule she made for herself; rules were made for breaking, after all. She threw the ladle down onto the counter and went back inside. She walked outside again a minute later. She had to find something to do. She couldn't just shut herself in her room with her thoughts; she couldn't torment herself like that. Just as she was mulling things over, the sound of footsteps echoed from beyond the courtyard. They were coming closer. She hoped that whoever it was was coming to see her, would relay some news or anything, really, and it didn't matter who it was. She would invite them in regardless and ask them to sit for a while. Even some mangy dog or a stray pig would do, just someone or something to keep her company.

"Meitang," said the voice. And just like that, the man she'd been thinking of appeared, for it was none other than Guo Cunyong.

She answered him and opened the door. There he stood, two pails of water slung over his shoulders: "It has been a frantic couple of days. I'm not sure if you've got water in your jar or not but I'm off for a few days and wanted to see you before I went, to bring you some water, too, just in case."

His earnestness warmed her heart and she felt her eyes moisten. But she remained silent. Polite language wasn't appropriate under the circumstances. It would have been like treating him as a stranger, an outsider. Guo Cunyong stepped in through the door and put the pails of water down on the floor, then opened the lid to her water jar: "Hey, it's dry!" He emptied the pails into it and then stood to take them back outside.

Lin Meitang had despised him once but in a flash that feeling had disappeared. She wanted him to stay: "Come in and have a rest. You can leave later."

"First let me fill your water jar."

"That's alright, there's no need. You've brought enough for me to last a day at least."

"But you need water to wash, too. Someone like you loves being clean." He had one foot out the door when he suddenly stopped and remembered he had something to give her. From his inside pocket he took out a letter and handed it to her: "It's from Beijing. Perhaps your mum is missing you."

He left to get more water. Lin Meitang stood at the door and tore open the envelope. As expected, it was from her family. The handwriting was her younger brother's but the words were her mother's. Her mum had been putting aside money for some time now, all with one objective in mind. He was forty-three years old, a factory worker; his wife had run off and left him to care for their son, a young teenager. Most important, however, he didn't care that she had a rural *hukou*. Her brother had underlined this sentence, although she wasn't sure why. Had their mother told him to do it? It seemed to stress how difficult it had been for her mother to find a city man willing to take her as a wife and that she shouldn't be picky. The letter ended with her mum beseeching her to return to the capital... and quickly. She wanted to make introductions.

Lin Meitang's heart was wounded. Was she really that miserable, that wretched? A factory worker, a man about the same age as Guo Cunxian, a man abandoned by his wife... but he was what? Someone of high moral integrity who was unexpectedly willing to overlook her *hukou* and prepared to stoop to her level? Did her mother think she was not even good enough for a man like this? He was supposedly willing to do her a favour. Lin Meitang pondered the letter. If her mum's proposition had been even just a little bit better, who knows, she might have considered it, might have returned to the capital to at least meet the man.

Guo Cunyong returned with enough water to fill the jar. The remainder he poured into the pot on the stove. Lin Meitang let him inside, prepared a cup of hot tea and some cigarettes to go with it, as well as some sweets. She still had the manners of a city girl, especially when guests were present. She had to make a good impression, to feel as though she wasn't the same as everyone else in this village. Guo Cunyong unwrapped a sweet and popped it into his mouth.

"You're not smoking?" Lin Meitang had thought to light a cigarette for him but he declined it. And as he did so, her hands were soon in his, although he wasn't sure how it had happened. It was like an electric current had drawn them together but then had frozen them to the spot. Lin Meitang's face was flushed and hot. There was a bashful look in her eyes as well as a glimmer of fear. A lonesome, monotonous life was quite easily given over to passion. She didn't know if Guo Cunyong wanted something to happen between them or not, but if he did, would she be able to refuse? She didn't even know what she wanted. Was she afraid to give in to her desire? Her hands trembled slightly. They were soft but cold.

Guo Cunyong wanted to embrace her. He'd longed to hold her for so many years but now his courage deserted him. Who knew how many eyes were outside peeking in? He couldn't give in and allow himself to be led round like a donkey on a string. He finally let his hand go limp. He smiled: "Your room's immaculate, you know, and it smells nice, too. You ought to put up a 'no smoking' sign. You don't need that stink in here."

Her gaze was deep and clear. She felt a pang of disappointment, as well as appreciation: "Cunyong, you're a good man."

"But good men go unnoticed."

"True, but you do good deeds outside the home. Be happy about that."

"Don't you do more good? I mean, if we're talking about your intentions, about how you carry yourself, can any other woman compare? Isn't that worth talking about? You've probably gone over this problem in your mind a hundred times or more."

Lin Meitang lowered her head. Teardrops escaped from the corner of her eyes. This type of resentful melancholy drove men mad; they couldn't stand it. The stories of heroism, those magnificent feats to rescue the damsel in distress, they all began here, with that look, that show of emotion. And Guo Cunyong was a man. What's more, you could say he was famous throughout the village for leading with his heart. Seeing Lin Meitang like this, his chest began to pound. He was soon overcome by what he could only call a heroic desire to pull her into his arms. But was this the right time? He'd just brought several pails of water into her home, there had been people who must have seen him. Their eyes would have followed him and who's to say Ou Huaying wasn't about to burst in on them or that someone would soon holler at them from the window?

But at this crucial moment, he wanted to be her hero, to be worthy of stories and songs. He only needed Guo Cunxian's consent and gratitude, and if he really gave it, then Lin Meitang would show her appreciation, too. She could rely on him and perhaps even become his... That said, what did it matter if this caused more problems for Guo Cunxian? Lin Meitang was the victim here, after all. If he could take care of her forever, then she'd never have to worry again. But then again, of all the women in the world, Lin Meitang was the one who couldn't, at least not now, go down this road with him.

Guo Cunyong might have been ruled by his emotions but he was no fool. He shifted his body, encouraging her, this poor, pitiable, beautiful woman he held close to his heart, to look him in the eyes: "Meitang, can you see yourself continuing like this? You need to think about the future, about what comes next. I'm telling you, you need to move on. So let me also say that before you do go, I'll come to see you, and if you have this thing on your mind, then beyond this town maybe I could be that man for you, or, even better, I'll help you find someone not unlike the two of us... someone who'll take you to the city and settle down there with you and give you the life you deserve, better than what you have in Guojiadian. My only advice is this: if this is what's on your mind, then act on it quickly. You're still young and beautiful. The sooner you decide, the better. That's how you'll save yourself and Cunxian."

All the times he'd been in her company before, he had never once uttered Guo Cunxian's name. But tonight, he did. They'd arrived at this point and there was no need to hide from the truth any longer. Lin Meitang looked at him but instead of answering his question, she responded with one of her own: "And at this moment, where will you go?"

"I'm not lying to you. It's because of the situation you're in that I'm saying this. The situation I'm in... hell, what have I got to keep me here? Wouldn't it be torture for me to stay! I need to take advantage of the fact that the investigation team has given me orders to stay. I need to get out, too, and soon. The timing is right as well. The chemical factory has product to sell and I need to find a market for it. It's a chance for both of us. As the saying goes, the sky imposes no limits on the birds that take to the wind, nor does the sea forbid fish from swimming far and wide. I just need to hear what you think. Beyond this village, I can be your knight-errant. If you're willing, then leave and come and find me."

Lin Meitang mumbled under her breath. She wanted to speak but felt dejected and dismayed at the same time. But the bitterness she held inside welled up: "Cunyong, I know your intentions are sincere, I know that we once shared feelings that ultimately went bad and that I blamed you for that. That now... you're willing to do this for me... I can't explain fully how happy that makes me. As you said, if you think of the situation I'm in, on the surface things look fine and I'd be considered a catch, but as soon as they learned the smaller details, who would want me then? And how could I involve you in that? If Cunxian ever found out, if he knew that you made the introductions, wouldn't your relationship be ruined? I know you once felt you'd been wronged by me."

He cut her off: "I'm not afraid. If Guo Cunxian really does love you, then he'll thank me." Guo Cunyong rarely showed such intensity, despite his reputation. It was as though he had to demonstrate to her the profound sincerity of his feelings and open up the depths of his heart to tell her how he felt: "Meitang, I'm truly not trying to come between you two, but if you really want to marry, Cunxian needs to let you go. His whole family, the village, everyone that's been good to you both, they need to release you. I think he knows this but he doesn't have the courage to tell you. He's afraid you'll only curse him for being cruel and heartless. But let me tell you, I'm sick and tired of seeing you beholden to him. You're young and pure, it's just too much. We've all had trouble at some point in our lives but you've been trampled on, taken advantage of, used and discarded! I know he values loyalty but there's no way he can blame you, nor can any one in his family. I think they need to thank you. If you really wanted to hurt him and cause him pain, one word to the investigation team would see him in chains immediately, don't you think? If your aim is to leave Guojiadian, you need to put an end to your relationship with him, once and for all. That's the only way you'll find happiness."

The affection in his voice and the warmth and sincerity of his words forced her to relent: "OK, OK, Cunyong, I hear what you're saying."

"And if the investigation team wants to make an issue of any of this, there'll be those in town who can speak for you and plead for leniency for Cunxian. You probably aren't aware of this but the investigators have restricted documents with them. They list seven charges against Cunxian, the most serious is that he used his position of power to take advantage, over a long period of time, of a youth sent down to the countryside."

Lin Meitang's heart skipped a beat: "What did you say?"

"They're restricted documents with black characters printed very clearly on white paper. Quite official. It's like a memorandum once presented to the emperor accusing someone who'd transgressed heaven. It has been presented to the central authorities. On the top, it states that the situation is dire and lists his various transgressions. The document is tantamount to him being sentenced to death. You know what he's like. He has lobbed criticisms at more than a few political movements and flaunted official instructions. All that is in there."

"Are the authorities going to act on all the charges in the dossier?"

"I don't know the answer to that."

"Do you know who wrote it?" Lin Meitang was becoming increasingly flustered.

"How would I know? The investigation has an official note-taker, a woman who records absolutely everything, that's for damn well sure, although she'll never be accused of any wrongdoing."

He stared intently at Lin Meitang, drawing her in. She couldn't help but become entranced whenever she looked into a man's eyes, or they looked into hers. He noticed her reaction and took the opportunity to speak even more candidly to her, showing his deep concern and his willingness to take care of her. His confident demeanour, the certainty in his eyes, swallowed her whole. Guo Cunyong became equally captivated by her reaction but still knew he couldn't move closer. He had to maintain the moral high ground and look after her from a distance. Theirs was an intimate connection, yes, but words were unnecessary. That is how he would obtain a sense of satisfaction, of joy. "Meitang, it's already late, I don't think you need to bother preparing a meal. Come home with me and we'll eat together."

Lin Meitang raised her head and smiled reluctantly: "I'm human like everyone else. Can't I go a day without making food? I can't bother you any more. I don't want to give anyone else reason to gossip."

"Hey, I bet you don't know this but if I put my mind to something, if I really want to do it, well then, Ou Huaying doesn't dare to challenge me. Do you know, back when... well, she wormed her way into my life, that's the only reason I'm with her. I wouldn't have pursued her otherwise. I have to tell you, I'm not afraid of being put in a bad spot every now and then, and I certainly don't care an iota about what others say. Don't forget, I've seen a lot of what this world has to offer. But to be frank, aside from Cunxian, no one else would dare spread rumours about me. Yes I've come here tonight but only to invite you to dinner, to give you some work to do. Everything's above board and my intentions are nothing but honourable. Not a few people saw me this evening, and to a man they all asked who I was bringing water for. I said they were all blind not to see, of course, I was bringing it for you. Ou Huaying knows this as well, so now tell me, what more is there to say? The whole village knows that I'm a selfless model citizen just like Lei Feng. I'm just standing in for Cunxian and looking after you, making sure you've got things to do. If he's not concerned about anything, then there's no reason any one else should be either. I'm certainly not bothered, so there, what do you say? It's not easy for a young woman to make it in this world and that's the truth."

Guo Cunyong certainly had a silver tongue this day, thoroughly playing the part of hero.

"OK, OK, it's clear to me now. Let's go. I'll take you up on your offer, so, quick, we shouldn't make them wait for us too long."

It goes without saying that this was an unusual turn of events, as normally Lin Meitang would never have found herself heading off to Guo Cunyong's home for dinner. This was the difference between him and Guo Cunxian: he was able to put on airs, to deceive when he had to. But the mention he'd made of that restricted document weighed on her mind and troubled her heart. If it weren't for this, she wouldn't have played hard to get and essentially tricked Guo Cunyong into inviting her to his home. She just didn't want to be alone tonight; she needed some company. Why was she so different from other women? Why couldn't she allow herself to be happy? It wasn't as though she loathed men. Why couldn't she just have a good time and enjoy a nice meal together?

Guo Cunyong urged her to get ready to go and, as they stepped outside, he scanned the area to see if anyone was about. Seeing that they were alone, he embraced her tightly and proceeded to smother her in passionate kisses.

At home, village women have no cause to gossip. That's because they're always calling on their neighbours; they wouldn't be able to live if they didn't. And calling on neighbours is simply a means to set tongues wagging. Most rural towns would be divided up into a countless number of female domains, social circles, groups and coteries. This was their means of social interaction. In each individual circle, all types of news and titbits of information would be shared and exchanged. A wind blowing from the south, rain falling in the north sea, news emerging from the east, a scandal in the west; true, false, vulgar, mundane, chaotic and some downright evil. The more the women chatted, the greater the enjoyment, more so than they ever could from the man they shared a house with and shared a bed with. In many instances, the source of their stories came from their husbands. The idle chatter the men shared with their wives became fully developed stories among the women's circles. These stories would then be brought back into the home, constructing the social community as a whole.

As the central most important figure in Guojiadian, Guo Cunxian seemed to be well aware of the town's destiny. He was involved in everything, even when such involvement wasn't all that welcome. He was a celebrity, which naturally meant that he was the focus of most gossip. That gossip increased tenfold after the investigation team arrived, so much so that his poor wife, Zhu Xuezhen, could no longer sit idly by.

She needed more information, someone to talk to, so she set off to visit Guo Cunyong's wife Ou Huaying. She felt they were both in similar predicaments, one married to the Party secretary and the other to his assistant, in charge of the town's business interests. They seemed to be tied together, bound to the same fate. If something happened to one, it would happen to the other; the reverse was true as well. As the saying goes, misery loves company, after all. Ou Huaying might have been young, but she had already experienced a great deal and there was much going on in her mind. A lot revolved around ways to deal with the investigation that was currently being carried out in the town, so perhaps listening to someone grumble about their plight would be a suitable diversion.

Upon seeing the look on Zhu Xuezhen's face, she put on a show of shared anxiety, although her heart experienced a wave of delight. Ou Huaying believed her husband was the most able man in the entire village and that his current position as an assistant in charge of industry was due to Guo Cunxian standing in the way, refusing to share even a smidgen of power with him. The secretary had to have his hands in everything, it seemed. Her husband was dispatched to do all sorts of menial tasks, acting the fool when necessary and expending all his energy for Guo Cunxian. She'd sulked and squabbled with him more than once, accusing him of being servile and cowardly, of being afraid of Guo Cunxian, and lacking the courage to challenge him and do what had to be done. She had also voiced her opinions on what he should do, quite a few times, but each time he left the house, he'd never follow through. So when the investigation team arrived, she didn't feel worried, there seemed to be no need to panic. In fact, she felt more joy than anything else, a sense of delight at others' misfortune. If Guo Cunxian was really brought down, his position might fall to her husband, she thought, and then he'd have the power over the town that he deserved.

Life could be so bitter, so hard. Zhu Xuezhen thought of Ou Huaying as a sister, despite them having no familial connections. There was no one else to turn to, no one left in her mum's family to pour her heart out to. The only person she had was Ou Huaying. It wasn't as though Ou Huaying felt no sympathy for Zhu Xuezhen. When Guo Cunxian had returned with her so many years ago, the other young ladies in the town felt they couldn't compare to her. She had the face and the body that men desired. She could work, too, enduring hardships like so few others, and she did it all with a silent, calm disposition, never once uttering a complaint. The other men in the town all gave her the thumbs up and looked enviously on Guo Cunxian's good fortune. Envy was useless, however; Guo Cunxian simply had a certain quality that most other men lacked. But didn't a man have to anticipate what might come, and if so, what then?

Zhu Xuezhen had aged a great deal. The youthful exuberance her face once had had disappeared, replaced by deep lines and creases. This was the one good thing about finding a prominent man! To Ou Huaying's mind, there were four types of men: prominent and powerful men; good men; small, cowardly men; and, finally, fake men. Finding the first was a woman's good blessing but it was easy for things to go south since such men tended to attract too much attention to themselves, and such attention was usually difficult to deal with, and even harder to talk about. But the most unfortunate of women married small cowardly men, or men who weren't really men at all. The safest choice, naturally, was finding a good man, someone who could work and make money, handle the obstacles that life threw at them and also share their company. This type of man didn't easily attract the opposite sex, so a wife rarely needed to worry about philandery. Guo Cunyong was of the first type; otherwise Ou Huaying would never have married him. It was just a freak combination of factors that had placed Guo Cunxian above him, that had forced him to feign ignorance and play at being a good man. It had also resulted in her life being fairly comfortable. When Zhu Xuezhen had first come to the village, everyone had been envious and covetous of her position but should that position now come to her, Ou Huaying wasn't sure if that would necessarily be desirable, at least, not any more.

She no longer pretended to be worried but stood up and poured some warm water for Zhu Xuezhen. Turning to prepare some food, she spoke: "Hey, the radish has a purple core, that's a good omen. It means I'll get what my heart desires!" A smile stretched across her face and a feeling of contentment and confidence for the future washed over her.

No smile spread across Zhu Xuezhen's face. All she could do was force a grin: "You can say that for yourself, but I wonder if I'll ever be given the same. Cunxian's not at home, again. I don't even know if the investigation team has turned something up. I'm just completely in the dark."

"Well, I know what all the women are talking about, and from what I can see, I think everything goes back to that sly, sneaky witch!"

"But if that's true, what's to be done?"

Zhu Xuezhen seemed to be lost in thought. Standing in front of her, Ou Huaying felt empowered and that good fortune was smiling on her. She felt a responsibility, too, a need to hatch a scheme for the town's first lady: "Think about it: Cunxian hasn't been found guilty of corruption or of trying to take the credit for someone else's work. He hasn't been found guilty of stealing or trying to appropriate things he shouldn't; nor has he been caught out for murder or arson. So, tell me, could there really be anything that could bring him down? And what about a wanton little whore getting her teeth into him? I mean, if we're talking about crimes, I suppose the less serious offence would be him forcing himself on a young woman, with the more serious one being bigamy, having two wives at the same time. But if this means he loses his position as Party secretary, well then, I guess you could say the shit has really hit the fan and there's not much more that can happen, is there?"

Zhu Xuezhen couldn't help but be frightened, but she only mustered a muted response: "Then what's to be done?"

The more Ou Huaying spoke, the more her plan came into focus. At this moment, she was both Zhu Xuezhen's master and saviour: "The best thing you can do is find her a husband. The longer she remains unmarried, the more harm and damage she'll do to you."

"That would be best, for sure, but who could really make it happen? And if she doesn't leave, well, what then?"

"True, but I suppose even if she were to disappear for a few months and return to Beijing, well, that would be alright too."

"But who can explain this to her?"

"True, but before all we thought of doing was to hate, curse and ignore her. Now, tell me, was that really punishing her? I don't think so. No, we ought to have her dragged before the investigation team. That would be a far better way to punish her."

Before Ou Huaying had finished detailing her plan, several women showed up rather unexpectedly, all looking to play some poker. They all talked together but opinions varied and soon the discussion grew tense. Zhu Xuezhen knew the women were being evasive, afraid she might report on them to her husband, worried she was just seeking company for some feigned illness and that later she'd be fine. The women all had small children in tow, each one quiet and seemingly used to such gatherings; the women had come to chat, laugh and joke about. In gatherings like these, however, Zhu Xuezhen was like a fish out of water, uninterested and aloof from the exchange of easy banter between the other women. Feeling very much the outsider, she soon got up and left. As she stepped outside, an echo of laughter followed her and she wondered what could be making the other women laugh so heartily. Naturally, they were talking about Guo Cunxian and Lin Meitang. Good people put others first as much as possible, thought Zhu Xuezhen, especially when it came to pleasant things, but she'd come to know that for most people this was all an act. The more she thought about it, the more perturbed and flustered she became.

It wasn't yet dinnertime, so if she went home now she'd end up wallowing in more pity, her mind wandering off to who knows what kind of dark thoughts. She didn't think she was unaware of the world around her and she was experienced enough in life, but ever since she had arrived in Guojiadian as Cunxian's wife, she'd gradually changed. In rural communities, it was common for a new wife who'd come from far away to be bullied, especially one with no maternal family to call on, but Guo Cunxian's position had protected her from all of that. No one really dared to treat her in such a manner, at least, not overtly. Of course, this only meant her sense of isolation was even more acute, more unavoidable. It also meant, however, that the gossip was unrelenting, if always under the surface, like waves billowing across the sea despite the stillness of the air. She nearly always felt eyes following her around and whispers tickling her ears. As if this wasn't bad enough, Guo Cunxian made things worse. It was as though he loved to cause a stir, to rile people up. Life with him had certainly not been what she'd expected nor dreamed of. She had to take greater care but it was hard. For so many years she'd carried a sense of fear with her. Zhu Xuezhen was never one for talking much but she talked even less now. She just couldn't help but feel that those around her had become even more foolish than ever before.

Finally she decided to call upon Liu Yumei, her one true friend. She'd be able to really talk to her, to get things off her chest, but before she got halfway there, she changed her mind. Yumei's brother-in-law, Ou Guanghe, was a fool and she hated being round him. He had an eye for women, especially married ones, and whenever his sister-in-law had friends over he'd always stick around and try to involve himself in whatever the conversation. Perhaps she could pay a visit to Jin Laixi's home? His wife, Mi Xiujun, was an outsider like her. She might be a bit older but they had similar temperaments. Neither one liked to talk too much and they'd actually spent time simply seated together, face to face but essentially quiet, exchanging only a few sentences every now and then. Despite this lack of verbal communication, she felt rather close to Mi Xiujun and, considering the circumstances with the slanderous stories that abounded throughout the town and the stress this was piling on top of her, perhaps just sitting together with someone quietly would be just what she needed. But she was mistaken, for when she reached Jin Laixi's home, she soon heard the voices of another coterie of women busy chewing the fat. Nothing seemed to be making any sense in the town these days. She made her way closer to the door, thinking to knock, but as she did so, she could hear they were talking about Guo Cunxian, about his manly prowess, how he was so unlike other men in the village, especially when it came to being a man. They sniggered, their words laced with heavy sarcasm. Zhu Xuezhen was at breaking point. Again she heard the name Lin Meitang, this young woman, a vixen, fully twenty years her junior. She chose to confront the giggling head on.

Zhu Xuezhen pulled across the curtain that hung in the doorway and burst into the room. She seemed intent on asking them if they'd really seen Guo Cunxian's manhood and if they'd shared his bed, too. The women went deathly quiet. Their eyes bore into her. They seemed to be staring at her from a distance with a malicious look hidden behind their cool demeanour, and then, as though they'd held their tongues for too long, the room erupted in unbridled laughter. Zhu Xuezhen had never earned a prize for anything. All she could do in response was to lower her head and beat a hasty retreat; from head to toe her entire body trembled uncontrollably. Mi Xiujun got up immediately and followed her out. Catching hold of her, she pulled Zhu Xuezhen close and began to sob. She spoke to her in a low voice: "Xuezhen, oh, don't be angry with me. The other women knew you'd come looking for me. They wanted you to hear what they were saying. It was all deliberate on their part; they wanted to hurt you. You know my family background, it's problematic. Cunxian isn't here and the investigation team has dragged another man off. I had no way to stop them. Please don't blame me."

Zhu Xuezhen tore herself away from Mi Xiujun's embrace as though she were keen to flee Jin's home. Things felt like they did before, at the height of all the political movements. Again she'd been shunted to the outside, ostracised from the other women of the village. It hadn't been like this before the investigation team had come. Previously the women had tried to curry favour with her, and now they treated her like a stranger. A gulf existed between them, and the other women seemed intent on stabbing her in the back. They spat on her now. She'd spent so much of her life in Guojiadian. How had it changed so rapidly, soured so quickly? She had always been careful about what she said, never bad-mouthed anyone, and certainly never harmed a soul, but again, her husband was the target of attack. Did she really deserve to be treated like this? She walked home, her mind plagued with dark thoughts. Stepping inside, she flung herself down on the bed, letting her anger seethe. Time passed, although she had no idea how much. Then she heard footsteps outside; someone had come. There was a sense of urgency about their arrival but they were silent, quietly opening the door and coming inside. It wasn't her son, she was sure. Who could it be? Who'd dare to pay her a visit at a time like this?

Sure enough it wasn't a total stranger but not a family member either. As soon as Lin Meitang spied Zhu Xuezhen on the bed her face blanched, a look of terror in her eyes, worried that Zhu Xuezhen had fallen ill. She hurried over to where she was lying: "Sister, what's wrong?"

Zhu Xuezhen stared in astonishment. Lin Meitang was the last person she expected to darken her door. She violently pushed the other woman's hand away, not wanting to feel the touch of the woman who'd caused her so much pain: "Just what the hell are you doing here?"

"I came to see if the secretary had returned. Has he sent no letter to tell you what is going on?"

Unable to control her rage, Zhu Xuezhen spat at the woman: "Unbelievable! Do you honestly think that's reason enough to come here? What is it? Haven't you caused us enough trouble already?"

Lin Meitang was stunned by her ferocity and froze, unable to respond. But she didn't retreat. She stretched out her hands and took hold of Zhu Xuezhen's.

Zhu Xuezhen's mood changed abruptly. Why was Lin Meitang here? No words were immediately exchanged. She stared into Lin Meitang's eyes, looking them over and over, trying to find some explanation. Lin Meitang persisted, but fear crept across her face. They were close enough to feel each other's breath. They were sizing each other up as if they were strangers. Looking into this younger woman's face, what was she feeling? Hatred? Jealousy? Or curiosity? Was she wondering why such a face, no longer as young as it once was, was still so white, still so pretty and seemingly free of shame?

Lin Meitang stared at the older woman's face and felt fear. She'd once found Zhu Xuezhen's face so familiar and had for a long time enjoyed looking at it, and even envied the warmth it projected. Now, however, it was a stranger's face; everything about it had changed. It had become cold, bereft of feeling, seemingly detached from the filth of the world around her. For a long time Lin Meitang had felt a sense of guilt whenever she looked at Zhu Xuezhen. Most of the other women in the village surmised that she was desperately waiting for Zhu Xuezhen to go mad and die but, in truth, she felt an enormous degree of sympathy and pity towards her. She longed very much for them to talk, to share their pain, to have a good, long cry about everything.

With these thoughts running through her mind, Lin Meitang couldn't help but start to cry. She pulled Zhu Xuezhen close to her: "Sister, Xuezhen, why are you looking at me like this? Am I really a stranger to you? It's me, Meitang! I know you're a good person, I know you feel wronged and that you hate me. I don't blame you for that. You're still my sister. In fact, I envy you, more than you can know. You have a husband, a family, a son... what do I have?"

Zhu Xuezhen didn't try to evade the question, nor did she respond. Her face took on a peculiar look. There was a sharpness in her eyes.

15

A WOMAN AND HER PIGTAIL

No one really knew when the day took on three different shades of colour. The west brought to mind the yellow earth, the east a charcoal, industrial feel. The centre, meanwhile, had a pallid hue and there stood Guo Cunxian. It was a deep, textured paleness that blanketed the centre with sinisterness. Nearby was a pale yellow cemetery that blended into the bare yellow terrain around it. The poplar trees that stood guard on both sides of the road were similarly ashen in appearance, neglecting to sprout the green buds they ought to have had at this time of year. The sky, too, was dark. A wind blew, growing more forcefully with each gust, and colder, too. A wind that began in the evening would blow through the night. Could he really stay here, despite the growing hostility of the weather? But even if he left what he was carrying and returned home, he'd still be worried. After all, what if someone were to happen by and walk off with the mechanical components he'd brought from the city? Wouldn't that be a complete waste of all of his energy?

He wrapped his arms more tightly around the bundle, at a loss as to what to do. It wasn't that he didn't want to move, he just didn't have any power left in his body. This was his responsibility, his domain. He just needed a path forward, some way to let the village know he was here and for them to send someone to help. As the western part of the sky grew darker, he then really heard the sound of footsteps drawing close. Raising his head to look in the direction of Guojiadian, his eyes met those of the approaching woman who quickened her pace and called out to him at the same time: "Cunxian, Cunxian!"

Guo Cunxian grunted and stood up, straightened his waist and released what he was carrying. She was the last person he had expected to see but her arrival helped to warm him, if only a little. For a city woman of such exquisite beauty to treat a man like him so well, he couldn't count how many lifetimes he'd need to see such good fortune visited on him again. It was Lin Meitang. She'd been to his house and discovered he wasn't there, so she decided to head towards the city to meet him and welcome him home. The evening sky was grey and dim but the scarlet winter jacket she wore as director of the Women's Federation served to keep the cold night at bay. Her body moved in rhythm with her feet, the front of her jacket glittered and her hair flowed loose and free behind her. She looked as graceful as a bird fluttering its wings to land gently in front of him.

She was gasping as she came up alongside him and he could feel the hotness of her breath on his face, fragrant and intoxicating. Her skin was still white and soft. She'd spent more than a decade in Guojiadian, amid the yellow earth and the dirt of country life but the sun hadn't darkened her complexion nor hardened her skin. She was fond of rural life but she'd not become a villager. Because she'd run up to him just now, her cheeks were flushed and had a reddish hue. Perspiration glistened on her brow and increased her allure. Her very presence seemed to transform the blighted landscape into a beautiful scene out of some book or other, pure and untouched. Guo Cunxian didn't know when it began but every time he saw her, he couldn't help but feel this sense of freshness, newness and fragility. He felt a familiar urge well up inside, threatening to overwhelm him. The more he looked at her, the greater his thirst grew. He wanted to take hold of her immediately, to swallow her whole.

She moved close to him, seemingly startled and concerned by his appearance. His face was gaunt and angular, creased and wan. It was like newly ploughed earth, with deep crevasses and troughs marking a bumpy and ravaged terrain. His lips, too, were blistered and parched. It had been only a few days, but he was thinner than before and his whole frame seemed different.

"What's wrong? What's happened?"

"Nothing, nothing at all."

"If it's nothing, then why do you look like you do?" Anger flashed across her eyes. "You went to the city on official business. Why didn't you take someone with you? It would have made the journey that much easier. You need to take better care of yourself." She had hoped that one day he'd take her with him, but she didn't dare say this to him now. She knew he'd not answer, in any case.

Guo Cunxian was a man, all man. He didn't delegate but took care of everything himself and managed everything. That was his rule; he didn't trust anyone else. There were times she was afraid of him, afraid of the underlying despotism he wielded, and then other times when she found this irresistible. He grabbed her hand. It was soft, warm and moist. Enveloped in his coarse hands, she felt a wave of contentment wash over her.

"Where are you off to?"

"I've been waiting for you."

"How did you know I'd return today?"

"I guessed you would, and if you didn't come today, I'd be back here tomorrow and the day after that."

He took her into his arms and pulled her to his chest. His blistered lips met her tender, soft and moist mouth, and then worked its way over her cheeks, eyes, neck and ears. His longing roared and extended out; his passion was aflame, rigid and hard. The excitement he felt came as somewhat of a surprise, considering the circumstances. But he was overjoyed. His bulging manhood proved that his body was fine, that he'd not contracted a serious illness and that the blood he'd spat up was just due to what he'd eaten. He moved his mouth closer to her ear and whispered hungrily: "I've been thinking of you, really, deeply. You're all that's on my mind."

He pulled her over towards the cemetery, the larger of the mounds would provide respite from the wind. The ground was fairly flat as well, with even some dried grass to serve as bedding. He was seemingly young again and full of virility. But then he stopped abruptly, turned and embraced Lin Meitang once again, tightly, forcefully. On each burial mound a living head rose up, each with their own emotions, each yelling out to him. He couldn't hear them clearly, but he didn't dare take another step. The hair on the back of his neck stood up straight, rigid. His legs grew stiff and unmovable.

Lin Meitang felt the rapid change in his body, from searing heat to cold clamminess. She didn't know what was going on but followed his eyes to gaze in front of them. There was nothing there. Guo Cunxian analysed her reaction but, seeing no inkling of fear or terror in her face, he knew that she had not seen what he had. This put him at ease, at least a little. To be truthful, he didn't really believe his own eyes, that he'd seen severed heads sprouting out of the burial mounds, that they'd called out to him. No, it must have been just a trick of the mind, an illusion and nothing more. But when he lifted his head again, the hairs on his neck prickled once more and the heads without bodies wailed to him even more urgently than before. He was Guo Cunxian, village head but what was going on? Slowly he tried to calm himself and in a low voice he spoke to Lin Meitang: "You told me you were here waiting for me. Has something happened?"

"Yes, sort of... but please don't blame me."

Guo Cunxian's heart skipped a beat. Something had happened, something bad, and not like before. He kept these misgivings to himself: "There are enough things every day to make a man angry but if I really wanted to be, I already would be."

"The authorities have sent an investigation team. It includes the police and the prosecutor's office responsible for Party discipline. The reason they have come must be quite serious. According to the stories flying round town, the person heading up the investigation is a man by the name of Qian Xishou. It seems as though he's got a hidden agenda."

Guo Cunxian's mind spun as though all the blood from his body had rushed to his head. It didn't matter any more if he was really sick, if he had gut rot or anything similar, or even more serious. None of that mattered now. The town was being investigated. He'd heard how that process worked and knew what it meant, and that it didn't really matter why they'd come. He knew they had come for him. He was, after all, in charge of Guojiadian. From the smallest detail to the largest project, his hands were all over everything. His face grew yellower and darker but a grin spread across it as well. Lin Meitang soon realised he didn't care. He looked at her again: "So this is the bad news you've brought?"

"I was afraid you wouldn't be prepared, that you'd return without suspecting anything was wrong and be apprehended immediately. I wanted to let you know they were in the village and to give you advance warning so that you can think of how best to deal with this."

"Have they stripped me of my title?"

"No."

This was essential, he thought. If he still held the position of Party secretary for Guojiadian, it meant the village was still his. That would make things easier.

"Have they said what they are looking for?"

"No, it's as though they're investigating everything but especially the village factory. It's as if they suspect we're pulling resources away from agriculture and putting them all towards industry. Wang Shun is perhaps in the most trouble, They suspect him of misappropriating profits for illicit gambling, which is a crime against the nation. They've begun to examine all official accounting records but Wang Shun seems to be bearing up under it all. The electronics and chemical factories haven't ceased production but the brick factory and electric mill have." Her eyes welled up with tears prompted by the anxiety and worry that strained her heart. She stared at Guo Cunxian's face.

He stared back and the look in his eyes gave her encouragement and helped strengthen her resolve to persevere: "Meitang, let me tell you, I'm not worried about any investigation. I've done nothing wrong, nor has the town. I'm not afraid of being thrown into a deep fryer, that's for sure!"

They both knew and understood what they had to be afraid of; words weren't necessary. Their relationship had to remain secret, there was nothing else to fear. Of course, they knew, too, that there probably wasn't a soul in the whole town who didn't already know they were intimate with each other but it was clear that no one had dared to say anything about it because it was too embarrassing to do so. That was the only explanation for them not having been arrested already. If the investigation team really did uncover the truth, then the dam would break and they'd be drowned for sure. It was quite easy for something like this to be blown out of proportion, for people to sully their names and cause his downfall. But there was something that weighed on his heart, questions that remained unanswered: the authorities had to have a reason for launching the investigation, which meant someone had skeletons in their closet. Otherwise they wouldn't have attracted notice, would they? Or had the authorities simply caught wind of something? Was some new movement on the horizon? What was their objective?

He couldn't voice these questions aloud, however. He didn't want to overburden Lin Meitang. If he thought she knew, then certainly he'd have asked but if she didn't, which was most likely, then pestering her with questions would only saddle her with more stress than she already had. His mind then drifted to other things. Why had it been Lin Meitang who'd come to find him? What about the other work units in Guojiadian? What about his wife or his child? None of them had come. Had they not thought about it? Were they afraid? But she had come, at some personal risk, to warn him. A man had only one life but if they were fortunate enough to meet a woman like her, then it didn't matter what the future might bring, it was all worth it!

The most important thing was to make sure she was safe: "Did anyone see you leaving the village?" But as soon as he spoke those words, he regretted them. What if someone had seen her? Why was he trying to frighten himself?

"No one, I'm sure. I was out and about, pretending to call on different families."

"Then head home, quickly, and find a few people you can trust, I mean really believe, and ask them to come and collect these components," he said as his voice trailed off. Who could be trusted in times like these? His son was too small... his wife... his young brother... he was the most reliable... no, Xuezhen wouldn't be able to lift the bundle, if she'd even come... nor could Cunzhi, for that matter. At this point in time there was little hope of relying on them. No, Lin Meitang was the clear choice. He had to rely on her to make arrangements. Still, thinking things over, another name came to mind: his adopted son Liu Fugen. He gave instructions to Lin Meitang: "Go and get Fugen to bring the bicycle here."

"You return first," was Lin Meitang's response. "I'll stay here and watch over the bundle."

"No, no. Remember, I can't cause you any more trouble." Guo Cunxian still felt the need to demonstrate his heroic nature, his willingness to die rather than bring more harm to someone he loved.

Lin Meitang wrapped her arms round him: "Don't worry... it doesn't matter what might happen, the only thing I can be sure of is that I won't cause you any more problems."

"You've never caused me any problems, believe me, it's more the other way round."

"I'm not afraid. I'm just worried about you."

Lin Meitang cried and her tears ran down his neck, moistening the collar of his jacket. His heart pounded but nothing stirred below. He was impotent, like a neutered animal, worth less than the air it breathed. He pushed her away gently and with the cuffs of his coat, he wiped away the teardrops staining her face: "I don't have a handkerchief but if you don't wipe them away, your face will be dried and chapped once you return."

He demonstrated remarkable tenderness towards her, a sincere and deep affection. She didn't want to leave. Women could certainly cause one to fret. You only needed to show them a little kindness and they wouldn't want to let you go. But at this moment, Guo Cunxian had no more room in his heart; he couldn't worry about her and deal with what was to come.

He urged her once more: "There's nothing to worry about. I've been in their sights before. The higher-ups have sent people to Guojiadian before but nothing has ever stuck. I'm a peasant, so long as I don't break the law, then there's nothing anyone can do to me. And besides, past or future, restricted or not, what happens between a man and a woman will always happen. There's no society that can prevent that, not yesterday, not today and certainly not tomorrow. Especially in the countryside, for every couple caught in the act of adultery, there's always a pair, and a wife calling the husband out is like the pot calling the kettle black. That's just the way it goes. Besides, isn't it all a kind of planting... tilling the soil? Now tell me, what kind of society wouldn't let a farmer sow his own seeds?"

He pushed her softly again, encouraging her to leave. Her red jacket disappeared slowly into the darkness. His heart felt empty. No, that wasn't true. Her departure left him with a sense of dread and foreboding. He ought to be clear-minded, he had to think rationally about how to handle the investigation she'd warned him of, but his thoughts were chaotic, jumbled, and he couldn't concentrate. The sun had faded fully by now and the night had engulfed him. In all directions, blackness stared back at him. The westerly wind seemed to take its cue and increased in strength, soon howling like some ghostly banshee. The hairs on his arms and the back of his neck stood on end. He kept his eyes away from the direction of the graves, not daring to look. Had he really seen a ghost? Or was it a premonition? Was disaster lurking nearby?

Those heading up the investigation were confident they had the backing of the authorities, so they assumed once Guo Cunxian returned he would immediately report to them as he was the man responsible for the village, the first citizen, as it were, so he wouldn't just ignore them and pretend to be unconcerned about their arrival in town. After all, if the police were to knock down your door, you'd have to be a little nervous; you'd have to treat them with respect, wouldn't you? At the very least you'd offer them some tea, a cigarette and ask in polite tones what you could do for them. Otherwise, well, in the case of Guo Cunxian, if he didn't show the proper attitude towards the investigators, they'd think he was all beside himself, unable to eat, tossing and turning throughout the night; very much an ant in the frying pan.

But as it happened, Guo Cunxian didn't match their expectations. In fact, he waited for them to come and find him instead of the other way round. He had his reasons, too. In his mind, as long as he hadn't been removed from power, as long as he was still Party secretary for Guojiadian, then it didn't really matter why an investigation team had come, it was their duty to report to him first. Without his permission to actually begin their enquiry, then how could they start questioning people without cause, and causing a general fuss throughout the town?

Guo Cunxian had his own motives, that much was certain. And to those in the know, it was clear what he was trying to do. He wanted to see just how much power the investigation team had been given and if they could really remove him from office. In short, it was a pissing contest. He knew, of course, that the road forward for the village was linked to what happened to him, and that what happened to him was in the hands of the investigation team, the bastards, but what caused him to hesitate a little wasn't the investigators themselves. No, it was the power behind them that caused him to worry, for he could never be sure who was actually wielding it or where it truly emanated from. All he could be sure of was this: great power was merciless, ruthless and exact. If that power had decided to use a lowly sheep as its symbol, then that sheep would immediately be transformed into a ravenous wolf, a ferocious tiger, regardless of outward appearances.

Besides, it was usual for initiatives like these to take on the aura of a fierce tiger, a voracious wolf. If they didn't, how would they properly demonstrate the power behind them? The ability to dominate others, to strike fear into their hearts was something he understood; it was something he didn't really need to be worried about either. Ultimately, it was how things should be, he accepted that, contented even! But he suspected the fates were conspiring against him, that he'd been given a black mark when he was born. He was over forty now and had endured poverty, hardship and being the target of official attacks. There wasn't really much else to say about these things but the whole experience of the latter was wearing on him, he had to admit. In this instance, it was clear to him that the investigation was launched by the most senior officials, that it was a major policy to query what was happening in Guojiadian but that they'd directed their attention to private matters first, to affairs of the heart.

This brought things much closer to home, it brought his family into the firing line, and it almost seemed as though that was their firm intention. What was he to do? He couldn't show weakness, nor would he allow himself to be a pushover. He wouldn't give them the upper hand. Besides, there was much going on in the village, other issues they could focus on. He had to shift their attention to these things and get the townspeople to go along with it as well; anything to deflect attention away from his own personal affairs. With this in mind, the morning after his return to Guojiadian, Guo Cunxian sought to demonstrate his own stature in the town. Shortly after the sun came up, he walked out into the early day and strode through the village as though he were surveying the battlements. He wanted to make it plain to everyone in the village. He wanted the investigation team to see things clearly: I, Guo Cunxian, have returned!

If the crops had grown, then his morning ritual would be to get up, take a piss and move his bowels, somewhere near the fields was always best. Yes, shitting in the grass was a farmer's joy. Heaven-made latrines, that's what the fields were. Farmers couldn't help but enjoy that. And for a farmer, it was all about the mornings. If they started poorly, then the rest of the day would be shit, quite literally. Now, however, the fields lay barren so there were no crops to fertilise. He spied Wang Shun's dairy farm, the chicken coop and the pig pen. There was nowhere he could squat down and relieve himself. So he walked on and finally found a public toilet, clean and uncontaminated. If nothing else, this would allow him to inspect his own faeces. He could see what colour it was and whether or not there was any blood.

He hadn't moved his bowels for two or three days, and what he did now relieve himself of was dark and swarthy like sheep's droppings. Somewhat surprisingly, there was no reddish tint to any of it, neither bright nor dark. It proved, he thought, that his stomach was no longer bleeding very much and that whatever ailed him before was relatively minor. This was a good sign; he could stop worrying about it. And in any case, the greater concern had to be what was happening in the village, something that had nothing to do with his own body, something that plagued his mind, not his gut.

Suitably relieved, he set off for the chemical factory. He was highly concerned about it. Most of his interest lay there and it was also the perfect stage for him to demonstrate his return to the town, the perfect stage for him to dance with the investigation team. For someone to be brought low, to be toppled out of office, didn't solely depend on the strength of one's opposition. Of course, their intention was to attack, so it would be incorrect to think they weren't trying to inflict a mortal wound which meant, naturally, they would try to target your most sensitive spot. But the key to this is that first they need to see whether or not you have the means to defend yourself, to endure their first volley. The food processing factory, the brick-making kiln and the motorised mill all fell under the scope of agriculture and so the wretched investigation team wouldn't dare target these industries. Their target would be the chemical and electronics factories. The latter was run by his sister and her husband, so he had to make sure to keep these dirty waters away from that. Which left the chemical factory; this was his key to defending against their attack. Since they had established it, the money had been flowing in, allowing the villagers to see and experience for the first time what having money could mean. It also convinced them that his plans had been right, which meant that should this be attacked, he'd have the whole village on his side.

As he was about to walk inside, he heard the bustling sounds of industry. They were sounds that used to make him so excited and reminded him of the trials and tribulations he'd gone through to set up the factory. For a brief moment, his heart felt a measure of respite. He recalled, too, the early discussions of where to establish the plant, and the need for there to be some distance between it and Wang Shun's food processing factory. Ultimately, he'd settled on the southern marshes. He decided, too, to use own his kiln to make the bricks, and with those he had constructed two bright and spacious workshops. As he stepped inside, he was welcomed by a somewhat unexpected sight. Wedged up against the walls were wooden stakes and each stake had a mesh-bag hanging from it. In each bag were myriad things: some had *mantou* (a Chinese steamed bun), others salted vegetables. There were cornmeal pancakes, leeks, large flatbreads, salted eggs, steamed pastries and even stinky tofu. Guo Cunxian stared at the food in a daze. He was aware of the circumstances of nearly every household in the village but whose rations could these be?

It had never occurred to him that the first opportunity to make some money by means of modern industry would result in those working in it to spend their cash on a dazzling display of earthly bounty.

The sight brought a carefree easiness to Guo Cunxian's mind. As he paused to ponder the scene, a sturdy young lad came rushing up. His forehead was broad and his eyes were large, as was his mouth. His face, hands and clothes were covered in grease and grime. For the young people in the village, being covered in grease and grime was something to be proud of. It meant they had escape from toiling in the fields and was a symbol of them having joined the industrial age. There were even some who wouldn't wash the grime off after a hard day's work, such was the value they placed on what it symbolised. The lad who had come to greet Guo Cunxian was Chen Laoding's oldest, Chen Erxiong. He'd never expected Guo Cunxian to visit them this early in the morning but, in a loud voice, he announced his arrival: "Greetings, Secretary."

Good. They were still quick to greet him and call him Secretary; this would be helpful. He pointed in the direction of the bags hanging against the wall: "It's quite a lot of rations you have there, isn't it?"

Erxiong grinned: "Us lads all agree, if we don't produce the plastics we need, then we don't go home."

This titbit of news was music to his ears. It proved to him his position was still secure, that he still commanded respect and obedience. There was a noticeable rise in the pitch of his voice: "But won't the food go dry if it's left hanging like that?"

"It might go off a little but that's no worry, the wind won't make it go bad." Chen Erxiong stopped for a minute, fearing the secretary might misunderstand what he was saying, before continuing: "Once the machines are turned on, we can't stop them, so there's really no time to go home and eat."

Contentment welled up inside Guo Cunxian, as well as a feeling of warmth. He gestured to the young man to usher him in and show the machines at work, and was welcomed by a blast of hot steam. Pipes snaked in every direction, the machinery sparkled, and every man operating the instruments was a young strapping lad. He leaned closer to Erxiong: "And Cunyong? Shouldn't he be here busy working with the rest of you?"

Chen Erxiong informed him that two days ago Guo Cunyong had left the town, presumably he'd taken off towards the city to find a market for their wares. He had to find a buyer so that when they were ready, they could immediately sell what they had produced. Later, when they had the money in their hands, then they'd be happy for sure. Chen Erxiong seemed sturdy and strong but shrewd, too. As he told Guo Cunxian of Cunyong's plans, he smiled.

Guo Cunxian couldn't help but let out a little cheer. This was excellent news, better than he could have hoped for, and certainly much better than the young Chen Erxiong could understand. To himself, he acknowledged Guo Cunyong's intelligence. Not only had he removed himself from the line of sight of the investigation team, he'd also escaped Guo Cunxian's presence as well. Of course, Guo Cunyong hadn't committed any offence, nor had he meddled in things he shouldn't have. At the end of the day, whatever happened in the village was his responsibility, not that of his underlings. He wouldn't be cut down by the daily squabbles of village life, no, if he were to be brought down, it would be on account of something serious, and it was good that Guo Cunyong had escaped the possibility of being tarnished by it. In fact, if Cunyong were still here it would make things more complicated than they needed to be; he might even be forced into cooperating with the investigation and causing even more harm. And what if he were put in the position of superseding Guo Cunxian? Then causing his downfall would be in his own best interests, wouldn't it? And what then? This was what worried Guo Cunxian most, the emergence of a traitor from within the village itself. The investigation team was comprised of outsiders, so it made sense they would have little compunction about bringing him down. But a traitor? That would be a demonstration of cold-hearted ambition. Was there someone in the village who planned this and, if so, would he be able to work out who? Whatever the case may be, he was more relaxed than resentful that Guo Cunyong had left.

Fine. He was ready. He could meet the investigation head-on. The chemical factory would be his ace in the hole. It was the town's barrier against poverty, Guojiadian's bank that they wouldn't jeopardise for anything. And with that being the case, what could the investigation team do?

He turned to Chen Erxiong and instructed him to tell everyone to come to the chemical factory. He was calling a town meeting. A Party cadre had to call a meeting. It demonstrated their prestige, power and authority; it was also a declaration of war. He made clear that this meeting was not to delay production at the factory but that they were to attend the meeting as well; everyone had to be there.

It wasn't long before the village loudspeaker echoed through Guojiadian: "This is an urgent notice for the entire town. All members of the village committees must immediately report to the chemical factory." Good. This was exactly the result Guo Cunxian was hoping for. Before long, they started showing up. Each and every one of the village work units began to file into the factory, most probably unaware that Guo Cunxian had actually returned. As soon as they saw him, the very image of a leader, their backbones straightened and their courage grew.

To his surprise, his sister's husband also made an appearance. Qiu Zhantang now moved close to Guo Cunxian: "When you've time, I'd like you to come and see the progress your sister and I have made. We've got everything set up. We just need you to come, to lend us your strength and give the order, then we'll start production."

"Once we're done here, I'll pay you a visit. Now, is Cunzhu here?"

"No, she couldn't come. She's still in the city looking after Chuanfu. Do you know? He reads like a real trooper and he has finished his exams, too, coming top in his class. He's going to be something else, I tell you. He has a great future ahead of him. You ought to tell Xuezhen to come to the city to see him. It would be better if they're together and, besides, the village isn't exactly the best place to be at the moment."

Guo Cunxian nodded: "It's because of what's happening that your sister-in-law can go."

"Big Brother," Wang Shun now called out to him. "Have you managed to get a little rest? You must've been shattered after yesterday, weren't you?"

Guo Cunxian smiled broadly and nodded.

"I reckon you slept well last night. After I went back and got a little something to eat and a bottle of wine, well, I thought we'd enjoy it together, you know, and each have a few swigs but when I went to fetch you, you were already in bed, fast asleep and snoring like a baby."

"Heh, heh… I'll have that drink with you tonight, alright? I'll come to your place. I'd like to see your three little treasures, too!" There was an easy joviality to their exchange, like something out of a comedy sketch. But Guo Cunxian didn't once use his name, referring to him instead as Shopkeeper or Boss Wang. "Do you know, when I was in Tianjin changing buses, I thought about buying some of your wares, your marinated jerky would certainly have filled my belly, but there was such a queue, I had no time. But let me tell you, even though my stomach went empty, my heart was warmed. You've definitely made a name for Guojiadian. Throughout the whole northeast, they all know about us. I even heard that orders have been made as far away as Beijing, is that right?"

Wang Shun was quite pleased: "Big Brother, that's inspiring news alright, but there's more I haven't had time to tell you about. Our Beijing buyers have put in an order for our marinated donkey jerky, as much as we can give them. They want the most high-end jerky, too, and it's not for resale. They want to keep it all themselves. I had men that went to the Laodong market today and not one of them dared to bring the prized donkey jerky."

Quite a few people in attendance were surprised at the scene. The whole village knew the investigation team had uncovered evidence of his gambling but, in spite of that, he was still willing to jest with Guo Cunxian? Some had difficulty believing it: "Boss Wang, you've still got the balls to go to market?"

"Of course I have. If I don't, who the hell else am I going to sell it to?"

"OK then, Boss Wang, how about you tell us a tale. It's been ages since we heard one. Give us a good laugh, huh." The whole gathering seemed to be bustling with positive, kinetic energy.

Wang Shun understood well the mood of his audience and knew he couldn't just sweep it away, but he couldn't tell one of his usual ditties: "OK, OK, I have one, I think. It came to me the other day. I was out walking past the northern marshes and saw Director Liu Yucheng hard at work tilling the soil. I tell ya, boy oh boy, does he have some skill or what! Anyway, I gave him a song. So then, would you all like to hear it? Untilled earth is as flat as a mirror, while turned-over soil is like a face. Those strips of high ground always run straight. One link in a chain is connected to another, and through all those links the key issue can be grasped. And the key issue is where we are now!"

There were pockets of laughter: "That's pretty good... you even included reference to the commune secretary!"

"Heh... I don't know about that. All I know is I'm exhausted. A half day's work, that sounds about right for a commune secretary, but I was thinking I did the secretarial job for the whole damn county at least!"

Laughter erupted among the crowd. On such a morning as this, the villagers encircled Guo Cunxian as though they were performing some welcoming ceremony straight out of some story or other. The townspeople had been under enormous pressure recently. The light-hearted mood of this gathering gave them the chance to let off some steam and to enjoy themselves. As they did so, Ou Guangming seized the opportunity to speak closely with Guo Cunxian: "Cunxian, the county head commissioner has asked me to tell you that you need to go and see him."

"Which county commissioner?"

"Have you forgotten? Director Feng who headed the reservoir project. He's deputy commissioner now, in charge of daily operations for the entire county, and perhaps even deputy director for this investigation?"

"Him? I was the one who put him forward, and now he has come to take me down?"

Ou Guangming cut Guo Cunxian off with a wave of his hand: "Hold on, hold on... I think he knows he made a mistake when he selected that city boy to lead the investigation," said Ou Guangming, making a gesture of two bulls locking horns. "He told me as much. The original remit of the investigation was to carry out research. It wasn't supposed to be like the 'Four Cleanups' or the Land Reform efforts. Those were political movements targeting specific things. This was supposed to be different."

Guo Cunxian's heart dipped a little. He lowered his head, drawing his mouth closer to Ou Guangming's ear: "If they take me down, I want you to replace me, and don't be polite about it. I know you haven't been involved in what we've been trying to do with industrialising the town. You don't want the conflict that comes with it but, let me tell you, you can't let the town fall into someone else's hands, no matter what. That'd destroy everything we've tried to accomplish these last few years."

Ou Guangming's mouth twitched and he extended his index finger towards Guo Cunxian: "It'd be a great pity to let your efforts go to waste and, besides, where will you go? You need to see things through. The whole village might see me as your closet friend and ally but have you forgotten? My wife comes from the landlord class! Do you know what the townspeople say about that, hmm? They say I just wanted to find a wife and it didn't matter who... that I only wanted a son, that's it."

Guo Cunxian smiled a little at his response.

He lifted his eyes to scan the audience. He could see the looks on their faces, the swirl of emotions they had felt while he was away. The investigation team had fired the first volley but these were his people, his diehard supporters, his village. And a plan without supporters was no plan at all. On this stage, Guojiadian was the solid base he stood on; they supported him and lifted him up. Of course, there were some eyes among the group that avoided his; there were always cowards. Things were clear to him now: as long as the investigation was prevented from bringing him down, these people would never betray him. But if he were removed from office, then these very same people would be powerless to protect him, except for the few comrades-in-arms, his brothers, that would stay by his side no matter what.

The confidence in his face, the way he stood there in front of them, the aura he was portraying, it couldn't help but encourage the villagers and bring smiles to their faces. They had had enough of the heavy mood that had been hanging over the town. But at times like these, extra care had to be taken about what was being said. Nonsense or overly flowery words would serve no use. Guo Cunxian looked at the audience some more and then in a resounding voice declared the meeting would begin: "We find ourselves in very special circumstances. Hence I've called this meeting." He paused and shifted his piercing gaze towards Chen Erxiong: "Has the equipment been properly installed?"

"Yes, everything's in order."

"Any problems?"

"No, it's all top-notch." The young men nodded their heads enthusiastically. His path forward was clear. His destiny was mortgaged to the chemical factory and not to the yellow earth, not to farming. This was what Guo Cunxian needed, his fate linked to these young men.

The sun had reached its zenith and warmed the faces of the gathered crowd, burning off the dread that had filled their hearts. Guo Cunxian raised his voice noticeably: "It's clear to everyone, I think, that our number five factory, the Four Seas Chemical Plant, is all set for production. Yes, today, this morning, it's clear, we've got two names on our lips. The seas provide the raw materials for our plant and we're right next to it. Chairman Mao once said: 'The four seas are rising, clouds and waters raging, the five continents are rocking, wind and thunder roaring.' That's where we take our names from. Our chemical plant is the Four Seas and Zhantang's electronics factory is the Five Continents. Now tell me, doesn't that sound great?"

"Yes, great indeed!"

"You're really something else, Cunxian, to think of such things at a time like this!"

Guo Cunxian took advantage of the remark and continued: "There's really nothing to it, I'm just heeding the call for reform and opening up, I'm... we're on the road to becoming rich, which is glorious indeed. I'd like to also take the opportunity now to appoint Chen Erxiong as factory director. Does anyone object?"

"No! Excellent choice!" Their voices rang out in unison, loud enough to shake the mountains.

Who could protest? The investigation hadn't turned up anything that could remove him from his position, he was simply exercising his power as he was wont to do, handing out appointments and commenting on successes to ensure the villagers' loyalty and allegiance. He wasn't bribing anyone. No, he was trying to inspire them. With consensus from everyone there, Guo Cunxian turned once more to Chen

Erxiong: "I'm giving you the position of factory director. Do you think you're up to it?"

Chen Erxiong was unusually calm, as though he'd expected this all along: "If you're willing to put your faith in me, then I'll be sure not to let you down."

"I believe in you, true, but at the moment we also have to think about the investigation. Do you have the resolve to deal with this?" He turned his head in the direction of the other factory workers to solicit their opinion. "If I were to let you select your own factory director, who would it be?"

They spoke in unison: "Erxiong."

He looked back at Chen Erxiong and stared into the other man's eyes, forcing the younger man to meet his gaze: "Erxiong, you've had time to think about it. You ought to know they're investigating our decision to shift from agriculture to industry and the impact this decision has had on our farm yields. No doubt they're also querying our failure to redistribute land, and probably other decisions we've made, too. Accepting the post of factory director means accepting responsibility for it. It won't be easy, and there'll be some degree of risk involved. What do you say to that?"

"Secretary, you telling me that only makes me want to take on the role even more. To be honest, us workers here, well, we aren't interested in politics. For us, the town's decision to welcome industry, to fully support it, is great. It means we don't have to leave to find a way of making a living. And hey, won't it mean school wasn't a total waste?"

Chen Erxiong's words caused a ripple of uneasiness to spread through the crowd but Guo Cunxian needed men like him, and if he was a little rash, well, that would have its uses. Besides, those more interested in politics tended to be more concerned about observing which way the political wind was blowing, but things hadn't got to that point yet. There wasn't any need to maintain a certain distance from what was happening, at least, not for the moment. For now, he'd make use of the men around him, and that meant stirring and stoking their resolve, and their mood about what was happening in Guojiadian. He had to bind everyone to his plans: "Alright then, we've settled that. We have our own industrial association! If we want our village to shake off poverty and realise a great future, well then, we need industry. Without it, we can never succeed. How will we do it? Well, that's where all of you come in."

It seemed as though Chen Erxiong knew in advance that the chemical plant would need a director and that sooner or later it would be him. At Guo Cunxian's words, he spoke up straightaway with a plan seemingly in mind: "This year, our output will only be a hundred tonnes, or thereabouts, and we ought to be able to clear about four or five million yuan."

"What about longer term? We need to think about that. Tell me, when do you think you'll be able to manufacture polypropylene? If the circumstances call for it, we can always expand production capacity by building an extension to the factory. To my mind, I think the manufacturing of even more plastics is the way to go. It's much easier to earn a profit that way and a helluva lot quicker. We don't want to restrict ourselves. No, we ought to pursue whatever might benefit us. There's a broad range of fields we can involve ourselves in as chemical manufacture is incredibly diverse. I'm talking about the production of dyes, medicines and fertilisers, all of which involve chemical industry."

On the surface, it appeared as though Guo Cunxian was issuing instructions to the young men working in the factory but, as a matter of fact, his words were aimed directly at boosting the morale of the already weakened village committee and demonstrating the backing they had. He had used the prospects the chemical factory gave them, as well as the youth and enthusiasm of Chen Erxiong and the young men working there, as a palliative to put at ease the flustered, rattled hearts and minds of the village work units. And at the very least, the meeting helped to calm his own nerves. With that in mind, he urged the young men on a little more: "Now remember lads, regardless of whether it's an individual or the whole group, the most difficult thing is choosing a path forward. Once the way forward has been chosen, then you have to get on with realising it, the sooner the better. The places that've already started down the road to prosperity, well, they all made that decision quickly and got to work even faster. Whoever can grab hold of the reins of change, whoever can seize the opportunities change presents them with, they're the ones who'll be rewarded in the end. I'm not sure if everyone understands this but I know all of you certainly do."

Guo Cunxian could see in Chen Erxiong's face a newfound self-respect engendered by the role he'd just been given. He must have heard, Guo Cunxian thought, what the other villagers had said about him, namely, that he was the most capable man in Guojiadian. And in truth, that's really where his ability lay; he just needed to see it himself. For most villagers, a man's ability was tied to how well he kept his word. This was how he'd been able to hold onto the secretary's position for as long as he had. But if he had learned anything else from this morning's meeting, it was that he could also play the long game and he had the courage to meet things head on. Courage and a little bit of luck; without it, well, one's ability wouldn't really matter all that much, that was obvious. Guo Cunxian had provided the spark for Chen Erxiong to develop the self-confidence he needed for what was to come: "Don't worry, Secretary Guo, I know what to do. Give me a few days and I'll be sure to formulate a plan going forward."

Guo Cunxian searched the faces in front of him and, in fact, had already spotted Guo Cunxiao trying to hide behind the others, but that didn't stop him. He spoke loudly and clearly over the crowd: "Is Cunxiao here?"

Guo Cunxiao was caught and he knew it. He stood up straight and answered: "Yes."

"Cunxiao, has the investigation team spoken to you already?"

"Yes, they have."

"Have they told you to shut things down?"

"No, they haven't, not in so many words, but I'm worried nonetheless."

It was rare to see Guo Cunxian exercise such control over his temper, as he was usually so willing to let things get out of hand, and to rage and curse like a sailor. But he remained calm and continued to speak to Cunxiao and the rest of the men in an even tone: "Now tell me, how long do you think we should have to continue eating rations, hmm? Surely the investigation team dispatched by the central authorities can't stop us from eating, can they? It's true that establishing a chemical plant, as well as an electrical factory, I suppose, is evidence of our intentions to industrialise the village, but surely a mill belongs to the agricultural sector. Tell me, was there any household in the past that didn't have a mill? Ha! Every village in the whole area mills grain. Taking that away from us is the same as sentencing us to death. It would make more sense to just line us up and shoot us. What then? Hey, Cunxiao, you know I'm not trying to make things difficult but you can't shutter the doors to the mill. You need to keep it operating, or should I send someone else to do it?"

"No, there's no need, and you don't need to worry, Cunxian. I'll reopen it, right now, I promise!"

Guo Cunxian arched his head again as though he were searching the crowd for someone else. Jin Laixi, standing at the back of the mass of people, surrendered to the inevitable and raised his hands: "Cunxian, my apologies, I accept my punishment, too, and to help quell your dissatisfaction, I shall give myself a thrashing!"

He immediately proceeded to strike his own face, although not with a great deal of force. The men surrounding him burst out laughing. Even Guo Cunxian could not contain himself: "How did you know I was looking for you?"

Jin Laixi snorted bitterly: "Am I not guilty? I'm in charge of the brick-making kiln and I shuttered its door. But yesterday evening, when I heard you'd returned, I relit the fires. Cunxian, please forgive me. I know I'm not worth it, and I know I'm not very good at taking responsibility for things, but I'm afraid there's something I must tell you, something that will likely make your own fires burn hot. There are serious criminal charges awaiting you, ones that will bring ruin. There's more, too, I'm afraid to say, but I think I've saved a little only to lose a lot and I've destroyed all my plans. I accepted work in Tianjin for a rather large project but the city, well, it has gone mad. It's like they're launching new construction projects as though their lives depended on it but while there are so many opportunities, I think I've bitten off more than I can chew. The only way forward, I think, is to establish a proper construction firm, something large enough to handle what I've committed to do. I've been waiting for you to return to get your point of view."

Guo Cunxian mulled things over for a minute. He knew there had been poor people and, at the same time, wealthier people in the past, and in most cases, a family's situation was due in large part to how quick-witted its members were. He wouldn't let this get to him. In fact, his face still conveyed a happiness that was surprising, even to him: "This morning I toured the eastern section of town and saw the smoke billowing out from the kiln, so I knew the fires had been relit. You say you wish to establish a proper construction firm. Do you have a plan for that? You'd have to manage it and select someone to be your secretary. You wouldn't want to install someone in that kind of position that you didn't trust, would you? Let's talk about it some more once you've had the chance to think about it, and let's march together into Tianjin!"

Jin Laixi breathed silently to himself.

Guo Cunxian returned his attention to the men as a whole and scanned their faces: "Does anyone else have something to say?" The crowd was quiet. Wishing to end on a high note, Guo Cunxian thought he'd take advantage of the emotions he'd stirred and call the meeting to a close, pre-empting any further distractions. He'd accomplished his goals, and he didn't want to keep people from their lunch. He raised his voice and addressed everyone: "I know we're facing special circumstances at the moment but there are maybe some ugly words that I have to get out into the open, right now. You're all individuals concerned with your own little stalls, each working for their own interests, each blowing their own horn. I need to change this. Now, I'm not saying we can't be individuals, but it should go without saying that if we want to achieve something great here, we all need to be playing the same tune, otherwise the town is doomed and I'd rather that didn't happen. I'm telling you this because, whatever happens, I'll assume responsibility. The old folks used to say, those in high positions must have broad shoulders, and those with broad shoulders ought to take on more responsibilities. A village official is still an official. If you're not all willing to march to the tune I'm singing, then I'm afraid to say you'll have to take responsibility for whatever happens. Deal?"

Once more they agreed unanimously. Guo Cunxian had sold them on what he'd said. With hearts confident and carefree, the meeting came to a close and the men departed.

In the hustle and bustle of people departing the meeting, Guo Cunxian had failed to spot Liu Fugen. When everyone had finally left, he asked after the boy, and Erxiong gestured to the pressurised valves in the back: "He's probably still asleep."

He felt a pang of anger and walked purposefully towards the rear of the building. As expected, Fugen's bedding was there behind the pressure valves, with the young man curled up on a straw mat. He was sleeping comfortably, wrapped in a cotton-padded jacket Guo Cunxian had never seen before. For a moment he was disappointed and then annoyed; it was already quite late in the day. But surprisingly, his disappointment and annoyance soon dissipated. These were special circumstances he found himself in. While everyone else seemed to be engaged in a life and death struggle, his adopted son remained fast asleep. He wondered how they could all stand so fast and be so determined while Fugen seemingly couldn't? Did he lack spirit or motivation? He wasn't sure but, at the same time, standing here in front of Chen Erxiong and the rest of the young men, he didn't want Fugen to completely lose face. He gave the boy a kick: "Go home, now. Tell your adoptive mother to cook some noodles and then bring the soup here."

Chen Erxiong hurried to intervene: "Secretary, that's not necessary. Fugen doesn't need to go."

Still half asleep, Liu Fugen was bewildered by the scene. Guo Cunxian couldn't help but raise his voice: "You're still here!"

Liu Fugen's indolence had darkened his spirits somewhat, and once he left the chemical plant, he no longer felt like returning home. Instead, he decided to follow the sun and head east towards the Lucky Trees. He wasn't sure why, but he felt an urge to see the two entwined trees, like a man who longs to see his family after he's been away. If he went even a few days without seeing them, he just didn't feel right.

The Lucky Trees were just beginning to bud. A greenish hue enveloped the branches and glimmered brilliantly in the sunshine, bathing the whole area in a sparkling glow as though the ground was festooned with gold and silver. The trees stood there magnificently, a perfect spot to welcome the first rays of sun each and every day. From a distance, its aura spoke of history, of grandeur and majesty, and a seeming awareness of the unpredictability of fate, as though one could see all of this if one were to stare into its soul. But upon coming up close to it, that feeling of majesty changed. One could see the vicissitudes of history, the torment it had laid upon the trees and the endurance it had to remain. It didn't matter who stood in its shadow, they couldn't help but feel small and insignificant, and that their passage through this world paled in comparison to that of the trees. For a man, life was short indeed.

Guo Cunxian raised his head to look at the trees. Transfixed by its power, he barely noticed the burnt offering paper under his feet, still smouldering away, as the fires had yet to completely consume them. Then he came to his senses. It wasn't the holiday season and there were no ancestors here to pay respect to, so who had come the previous evening to make such an offering? The trees often served as the village temple, he knew this, but which family had felt the need to make offerings to it? What hardship or worry were they facing? Or had there been a wedding, a funeral wake, or had some honourable and upright person come to pay their respects and seek good fortune from the trees? Whatever the case, why had they stolen through the night to perform such a ceremony? Were they afraid of the investigation team or worried that such a ceremony would be seen as being in opposition to the official inquiry? Had they come to ask the trees to look after and protect Guojiadian? He wondered and became intrigued at the same time.

He sat down on a root that had curved up into the air with his back resting gently against the trunk and his face staring towards the sky and the sun. It was warm and he felt the sun's radiance all over. Each and every time he returned to the village after being away, he had to spend a little time here, just like he was doing now. He felt an unusual and extraordinary closeness to the trees, an intimacy that spread through his entire body and washed over him in an inexplicable feeling of safety as though all the problems he faced were gone, at least for the time being. Women, power, prestige, position, wealth, all of it... was it really so important? Was being a simple peasant, a man who just worked the fields, really so bad? That kind of life had fewer worries and fewer problems. He'd be able to eat his fill at the end of each day and then sit here beneath the Lucky Trees watching the sun go down without a care in the world. Wasn't that kind of life better than the one he had right now?

He breathed deeply with his eyes closed and, for a minute or so, his mind was free of worry. But it lasted only a minute before his problems came rushing back. He couldn't simply give in and surrender. This might be his only chance. If he did nothing, his life might very well be at an end. He wasn't willing to let things go and sacrifice everything he'd worked for.

At the time, it never occurred to Lin Meitang that Guo Cunxian's fate would be thrust into her hands. But sure enough, teams of investigators came one after the other to talk to her. The goal was clear; they wanted to use her to get to him.

The first to visit her was a man named Gao Wenpin. His face was smooth and unblemished, and his eyes were shifty. He assured her he was there to speak privately, and that she could "divulge secrets" without anyone else knowing that she had, but his cloak of uprightness was just that, a cloak covering his true feelings. She was little more than a whore in his opinion. She let herself get angry with him and proceeded to prevaricate, giving him nothing of use. The next person to visit her was named Wu

Lie. He wore a police uniform and carried himself in an arrogant, bullish manner. He spoke in tones expected of the police when dealing with young people, both soothing and threatening at the same time, offering to save them before they headed too far down the wrong path. He tried to persuade her that she was the victim and that she needed to free herself from his clutches, to disassociate herself from him and the serious offences he was guilty of, and that if she didn't, she would be charged along with him. Her response was clear. She asked how she'd been harmed and whether Guo Cunxian done something wrong to her? Wu Lie's initial plan had been to use suggestive language to tease out Guo Cunxian's crimes by implication only, but after being led on a merry dance, he changed tactics and decided he might as well be direct and put all his cards on the table: someone had made an official accusation claiming Guo Cunxian had used his position of power and influence to take advantage of her.

This was not the first time she'd heard of this terrible-sounding accusation but instead of responding with anger, resentment and shame, as Wu Lie expected, she was the very image of composure, displaying a degree of complete indifference towards the accusation that surprised him. Her answer was confident. She told him in no uncertain words that no man could take advantage of her, especially not over such a long period of time. She then asked him if he knew what year it was because stories like this were reminiscent of the past, not the present. Hadn't New China been established based on a socialist system? Yes, she had been a youth sent down to the countryside, but once the order had been rescinded she returned to the capital. Unfortunately, it had been rather difficult to find suitable work in the city and so she decided to return to Guojiadian to resume her former position as director of the Women's Federation, a role she was most suited for. And if things hadn't worked out in the long run, she would have left. After all, she had the freedom and independence to do so, which proved her point: how in the name of heaven had she let herself be taken advantage of, especially by a man? Lin Meitang continued her rebuttal, arguing that whoever wrote that letter in the first place was trying to vilify the village, slander the good work they'd been doing, as well as defame modern women as a whole. He was a police officer, too, she pointed out, so didn't such testimony need scrutiny? Shouldn't he double-check the circumstances of whoever made the report and verify it? And if she needed to, she'd certainly confront the accuser. If they hadn't yet checked, if they'd simply gone on the basis of a rumour, on the word of someone who maybe had an axe to grind, well then, she was within her right to file her own lawsuit against them for libel.

Surprised by her words, Wu Lie was left dumbfounded. He had underestimated Lin Meitang. Or perhaps he'd underestimated women in general, especially those willing to throw caution to the wind and endure whatever shame, humiliation and catastrophe life threw at them. These were the kind of women ordinary men had no way of imagining, to say nothing of how to handle them. His failure was due entirely to his own misconceptions about Lin Meitang. In his mind, to his wishful way of thinking, it didn't make sense for her to remain in Guojiadian. For him, it didn't seem worth it. He believed that, by using gentle language to frighten her, sprinkled with a few kind words, she would have gone all soft, regretted her decision to stay, and may even have cried, kind of lost her wits and, ultimately, divulged the information he wanted. Who would have guessed she'd do the opposite, that she'd feel some sense of duty not to betray him, and that she'd fight back? To make matters worse, all he had was an anonymous letter, which was hardly sufficient proof. In short, she'd shot him down, exploded his plans and sunk his ship. He was at a loss as to what to do. He could speculate or engage in more conversation, but he knew that wouldn't work. They were deadlocked, so there really wasn't much point in continuing. Desperate to find the most dignified way to leave, Wu Lie fell back on his official position and the uniform he was wearing, cleared his throat, straightened his clothes and left.

Stepping outside, Wu Lie felt stupid and cowardly. He was embarrassed with himself. He'd been a police officer in the city for years and now he was stuck in this village. And to make matters worse, he'd failed and let himself be beaten by some loose woman. There was really only one explanation that made sense. He'd felt sympathy for her before beginning his questioning. He'd believed she was the victim and that she'd been taken advantage of and used; if not that, then perhaps he'd let his own curiosity in this woman get in the way. He'd planned to be cordial, to try and help her. Who knew she would provoke his anger, wouldn't trust him in the least and wouldn't be deserving of his kind intentions? Considering his position, for a woman like her, a whore, to treat him so disrespectfully and to turn her nose up at him, he couldn't help but feel insulted. He just had to make sure no one else ever found out.

Since Wu Lie had been unable to extract anything useful from Lin Meitang either, the only female investigator in the whole team, Ms An Jinghui, volunteered to see if she would have better luck. And on one rather dull and gloomy afternoon, she paid Lin Meitang a visit.

Lin Meitang thought to herself that the investigation was coming in waves, determined to breach her walls. Volley after volley they fired as they attacked relentlessly. It was as though they believed that one word from her would be enough for them to apprehend Guo Cunxian and bring him to his knees. They wanted to strip him of his position, but did they have to arrest him first in order to do that? She had become the key to taking him down, whether she wanted to or not. For her to be in this position whereby Guojiadian's singular man of ability relied on her for protection... she didn't know if she should be happy or sad. If she had been of questionable character, she could have taken advantage of the situation to destroy him, but what then? She knew she couldn't do that and that she wouldn't give him up, no matter what. But it was interesting to speculate about what if she did? What would Guo Cunxian do? How would he treat her then? Would he wish her dead? Would he try to make that happen with his own hands? While his heart might turn in that direction, he'd never really be able to do it. He didn't have that kind of strength.

If she did betray him, she knew she'd lose him forever; that would be the cost. But she still wondered if catastrophe truly befell him, how would he respond? Would he remain so inflexible and hard? Would he still show such strength? Men in power made the same mistake: they thought the world was theirs. She loved seeing him angry. To her mind that was when he was most manly, when he would set her heart racing, when her admiration for him would grow. He had a way about him, a demeanour that could be overwhelming. You could see it in his face: a sternness and businesslike manner that showed through when he was handling official matters. His words were always chosen carefully and for maximum effect. Most people felt a sense of dread when dealing with him but she didn't fear him. She loved it when he gave in to these character defects, when he let himself fly into a rage. It was at times like these, she felt, that you could really see his true power. To the other villagers, he was an imposing figure dazzled by his presence. For the inhabitants of Guojiadian, and for those who arrived from outside, Guo Cunxian was a man you couldn't help but like and respect. But Lin Meitang thought that his faults were only fully apparent to her and that she was the only person who could truly say she knew him. And so she thought perhaps she would test herself and bring Guo Cunxian down to the level of a common peasant, maybe even to the level of a criminal, just to see if she would stay with him. Did she really love him? No one else seemed to believe she did; perhaps she didn't really understand it herself. People in rural communities never used the word 'love' between a man and a woman as it was considered to be unimportant. It was more about whether a husband and wife got on and whether they made do, not about whether they were intimate or whether they loved each other. That was just regarded as fooling around.

The other villagers might curse her behind her back but they never went too far, at least, not to her face. And the more aloof she seemed from the rest of the townspeople, the more polite they were towards her, waving and nodding their heads in deference to her and her position in Guojiadian. There were also those who often tried to ingratiate themselves or to curry favour with her; there were quite a few of them, to be honest, and she knew, too, that most of this was due to her connection to Guo Cunxian. If she had repaid his kindness, or the fear he'd felt way back when they'd set off down the road they'd travelled, then perhaps his power would have been all his own, but one year after returning to the city, she'd come running back to Guojiadian and had decided to settle here, so it didn't really matter what reasons she may have had, it was impossible to say there was no connection to Guo Cunxian. How many women were like her, willing to risk so much? If her actions weren't a sign of love, then they were at least the starting point, and even if it was just fooling around, she was putting her all into it, just like in those television dramas, so didn't that make it worthwhile at least? Who wouldn't be convinced by her actions? After all, they certainly seemed to attract attention, didn't they? If she did test herself, would he lose respect for her, to some degree? In the whole town, was there anyone who would dare be flippant with her? Was there anyone who possessed even the right qualifications to try? And if some of the women in the village hated her, then fine; if they were jealous of her, good. In their hearts, she believed they knew they had to obey her, defer to her and even envy her, at least a bit.

But calling someone jealous or envious was all too easy; trying to get someone to understand was much more challenging. The investigators could see it as soon as they entered the village. The popular feeling of the population was a mess and because of that, it was unpredictable. The villagers' mood could change on a dime, as could their willingness to implicate others to save their own skin and their willingness to use her as a scapegoat. Lin Meitang had no relatives or friends in the town. She was an outsider and she hadn't even married anyone in the village so it was all too easy for them to plot and scheme against her, to destroy her, or to at least drive her out of the town altogether. In the past, Guo Cunxian had protected her, perhaps because she'd so readily given herself to him. But now, not only could he no longer protect her, it was his association with her that was a problem. And to make things worse, he actually needed her support. The world could play cruel tricks on people and things could go topsy-turvy all too quickly. A strong powerful man who found himself in trouble would likely turn towards his supposedly weak woman as though she were his nurturing, caring mother. But was she really the love of his life? She knew at least she wasn't the only one. Did she still have the strength to see this through? And in affairs of the heart, things were always much more complicated. It was true, people were less inclined to give you the third degree to your face, but behind your back there'd be no end to the speculation and gossip, with people playing wilfully with words and adding all kinds of embellishment and often sordid details. For a man, these kinds of situations weren't necessarily bad, they might even provide the opportunity for them to impose themselves on women, but for a woman all of that distasteful talk stuck with her, sat in her belly and gnawed at her. You could say that a woman in such a predicament could feel only loneliness and, to add to the troubles of the last few days, her heart felt like it was tied in knots, twisted and tight. It was all becoming so unbearable for her.

While Lin Meitang was busy pouring over these details in her mind, An Jinghui seemed to appear out of nowhere to knock at her door. She wore a smile that stretched across her face and seemed to betray a flighty disposition.

She was wearing sunglasses and her hair was cut short and sharp, making her look handsome like a tomboy. Dressed in a bright, fashionable buttoned jacket, she looked intelligent and quite capable, as well as a tad overbearing and imperious. She entered Lin Meitang's room and immediately looked her up and down. There was no overt malice in her eyes, but rather a desire to take the measure of her, to size her up and suss out the connection to Guo Cunxian. Before long, an awkward atmosphere permeated the room which they could both feel. It was as though an impassable gulf stretched between them. The only way to cut through the tension was to speak but what pleasantries could either woman share? And what if words only made things worse and instead of putting each other at ease, they further strained the situation? Fortunately, An Jinghui had been in similar circumstances before and knew how to use her words to alleviate the awkwardness. In a soft, gentle voice, she set to work: "Well, you do live up to your reputation, I must say. A truly outstanding member of the community. I had assumed you'd have, to be frank, a somewhat provincial deportment, that you'd be unwilling to attract too much attention to yourself, but the clothes you're wearing, this round-collared shirt and the rather snug trousers, certainly show off your figure. Quite catching I must say. I imagine you get all kinds of envious looks in the village. You're really quite fetching. Hey, you know it's hard to believe, but I've been in the village a few days now and I haven't yet had the opportunity to look you over carefully. So I just don't understand, the wind blows like mad and the sun seems to burn everything it touches, but every unmarried girl, and even the young wives, too, all have such lovely skin, such wonderful complexions. Much better than what you'd see in the city. I mean, you're not tanned by the sun at all, and it doesn't look like any of you would need to wear blusher. You look all so natural, really quite pretty. And your manners, well, there's nothing wrong with them."

She seemed to be a little overexcited, carried away by her own words. Then suddenly, in the midst of talking, she broke out into a rather odd fit of laughter, so much so that even tears began to well up in her eyes and roll down her cheeks. Her breasts, which seemed much too large for her figure, heaved as the fit of laughter continued, like two large melons jostling with each other behind her buttoned coat. She seemed to be losing all control, before she seized the opportunity to pull Lin Meitang close and wrap her arms round her.

They were strangers, and yet here she was rashly showering her with compliments, praising her skin and her figure. Lin Meitang was left in a daze. It all felt so artificial and she knew she had to be on her guard. No airy-fairy words would sway her into mistaking the reason why this woman had come and yet, despite knowing all this, her animosity towards An Jinghui ebbed. She was a woman after all and kind words were something every woman loved to hear, especially if they came from the lips of another woman. Most women seemed to look at others as competition, which meant they often chose to mock and ridicule them, to belittle them and point out their shortcomings. Either that, or they'd feel jealous of other women, in the belief that they had something more, were more beautiful, or what have you. Had An Jinghui's words of admiration been evidence of that, a sign of her jealousy? Lin Meitang wasn't sure. But when a man said words like these, a woman had to be careful and she had to read between the lines because, far too often, men with silver tongues harboured evil intentions, and they usually had only one thing on their minds that had little to do with love. But when such words were spoken by another woman, they were much easier to accept, much easier to believe. An Jinghui's words had caught Lin Meitang off guard and had left her a little bewildered. She wasn't sure how to respond.

As the laughter died down, the room began to go silent again. But An Jinghui hated those awkward silences; they were just something she couldn't bear. In situations like these, she often gave in to her own discomfort and began to ramble on. There were even times when she would cut others off and interject her own opinions just to deal with the awkwardness. This is what she did now. "Meitang, oh my, Meitang. Do you know why I was laughing so hard? Something just came to me, you know the saying, a beautiful flower blooms in a stinking pile of manure! They grow tall and straight but certainly no lovely flower ever chose to grow in such a place. I just can't believe that. But you've been rumbled, haven't you? You've such a charming face but your guilt by association, well, even the Yellow River can't wash you clean. You're beautiful and pretty, and you're on the minds of just about everyone in the town. The men... we know what they want. They'd eat you up given the chance. And as for the women, they'd rather see you dead, or worse. But here you are playing at being a chaste woman from old China, fighting for what? Honour and loyalty to your man? To the townspeople, you're nothing but a floozy. If I lived in the village, if I were from Guojiadian, I think I'd want the worst for you, too. You're fortunate, then, that I'm not a local. I'd rather give you a kiss than sink my teeth into you."

Her mind turned to her own family before she nudged Lin Meitang, who was still a little at a loss for words, over towards the bed. She sat down next to her and continued to ramble on: "Meitang, look at my face. I have what you farmers might call a pale, flat, rather dry face. Certainly not what you'd call pretty. But it's not ugly either, not an offence to the eyes, as some would say. It's a safe face, though. Men feel comfortable around me and find me easy to talk to, even in central government buildings like the city hall. I'll give men like the mayor a hug and it doesn't matter whose office it is, if I want to push the door open and step in, I'll do it, and if I want to do something, well, it's easy. This world might belong to men but I have them in the palm of my hand. You just wait, I'm preparing this world for us, that's my plan. And if things get complicated, you know, if I take a more senior man to bed, well, there won't be one whiff of scandal. And do you wanna know why? It's because I'm not all that pretty, that's why. No one would believe that some leader or other would take me to bed. But when all is said and done, I am a woman. It doesn't matter if my face isn't the prettiest, my skin is fine and soft to touch. Go ahead, feel it. The texture of it is really quite nice, quite sensual, if I do say so myself. Apart from a pretty, round face, there're two other important parts to a woman's body. One is our breasts, now look at mine, hmm, men just absolutely love them. The other is our bum. Now check out mine, its shape. Why, it rounds out so well you could place a wine goblet right on it. With this kind of ass, let me tell you, the world can be ours, especially during times like these, when things seem so crazy and out of hand. Men just love an ass like mine, they'd give their life for it!

"Think about it. For a woman to fully please a man, to not cause him any trouble, well then, wouldn't they have to treat you like the empress you are? To be honest, I've already had one of these flings with someone high up in the provincial offices; it was really quite torrid. Right now, two of my lovers are younger than me but we're discreet. We have an understanding, too, that whoever I feel like being with, or if one of them feels like being with me, it just takes a phone call and they'll come, or I'll go to them. It's as simple as that and enjoyable, too. I'm their safe, cosy harbour, a romantic port when they need it, or a place just to unload, discretion assured. Heh, heh, heh. Oh my. Hey, do you have anything to eat or drink? I'm dying of thirst."

Now it was Lin Meitang's turn to laugh. She'd listened to An Jinghui tell of her romantic, somewhat sordid, escapades and felt there was really no other response but to laugh. It was a raucous type of laughter, rude even, and it continued while she went and grabbed some snacks as well as some water for tea. Her display of mirth helped conceal her embarrassment. She hadn't expected this type of person to be among the investigation team. From the point of view of the villagers, An Jinghui was a brazen, seemingly carefree sort of jezebel. She was now holding the cup of tea Lin Meitang had poured for her, staring intently at the tea leaves floating inside it, before she pursed her lips and began to make a fuss about seemingly nothing at all: "Oh, you have such wonderful tea!"

And off she went again, beginning another tale that echoed throughout Lin Meitang's room: "Your room is really immaculate and well organised. Tidy and comfortable, too, I might as well come and stay with you, hmm. Don't be sensitive about it, I won't impose. I really don't have any interest in village gossip and I'm not formally part of the investigation team. I've just come along for the fun of it. Besides, I'm too tired. I just helped run down a bigwig, it was all over the news, and to be honest, I'm still feeling knackered. It was coincidence, you know, that I was in the municipal offices when I heard about the investigation to be launched in Guojiadian and I thought I'd tag along. You know, it was a chance to get away, breathe some fresh air and see the scenery. I didn't think I'd spend most of my days in meetings. It has been terribly boring... depressing, too. Hey, I heard tomorrow is market day in Laodong. How about you taking me along to it, to do a little shopping together?"

Lin Meitang felt she was in the company of a child. The investigation had thrown the town into a state of chaos and yet this tomboyish woman had come for a bit of fun and some fresh air. It didn't matter if what she had said was true or not, for her to even speak like this showed her true colours. She didn't seem to let anything get to her and she was willing to say whatever was on her mind. When she first arrived, Lin Meitang had wondered why she'd come to see her, that much was true. But she hadn't expected the other woman to answer so immediately, to disclose so much, not to even suggest she move in with her. Unconsciously, she breathed a sigh of relief. Besides, she thought, she didn't have any reason to be afraid and having one of the investigation team stay with her might actually make her position even more secure. It would at least demonstrate the trust they still had in her. Having such a dope like her move in would provide sufficient diversion, to say nothing else, an excellent cure for boredom, and she'd have the inside track on the investigation, too.

An Jinghui cracked some sunflower seeds between her teeth and then suddenly the content of her verbal gymnastics switched to the topic of food. She asked Lin Meitang if there were any good restaurants in the area since Guojiadian was, after all, quite far from the city. The food the investigation team was eating was terrible, according to An Jinghui. She wondered if Lin Meitang could borrow two bicycles so that they might go and find somewhere nice to eat together. Lin Meitang's reply was to ask if she minded staying in, to which An Jinghui demurred and said that she didn't want to impose, that she hadn't come for that reason and that, besides, it would be much too much of an inconvenience; another day would be best.

"Today's the first day we've formally met and, I must say, I like you quite a lot. I'd like to think we could be sisters. So, please, why don't we take advantage of the day and the good mood we're both in, and go out and do something, eat somewhere, or whatever. We'll eat until we can't eat any more. Oh, look at my hair. It's a mess, more like a bird's nest, wouldn't you say? How about we find a hair salon and get a perm, if they can do it." As she prattled on she got down from the bed, pulling Lin Meitang along with her. She was light and graceful on her feet with a purposeful gait. With her head held high, she urged Lin Meitang to quickly close the door and bolt it, and then the two of them would find bicycles to borrow.

It was easy enough to find two bicycles, every family had them, but Lin Meitang didn't think it would be wise to bring An Jinghui along with her to knock on some villager's door. Instead, they walked to the chemical plant to borrow the bicycles the workers used, which would be newer ones, at least. Bicycles in hand, they rode off together. As they left Guojiadian, a cool wind buffeted their faces and howled through the trees that lined the road. The land opened up and spread colourfully in front of them. An Jinghui marvelled at the sight before turning towards Lin Meitang and remarking: "It's so beautiful, oh my... oh!"

Her mood rubbed off on Lin Meitang and the worry, stress, nerves and anxiety of the last few days dissipated. She felt a pang of envy towards this woman riding next to her, the way she comported herself with seemingly not a care in the world and how she would laugh riotously without cause or need, with little provocation at all. It couldn't help but make some people jealous, but she lived her life in the moment, untroubled by the vagaries of the world around her. She seemed to be genuinely at ease with herself, a rare sight indeed.

As she rode her bicycle, An Jinghui continued to speak, although she was shouting rather than talking: "I love this breeze. These past few days I've been bored out of my mind. This is much better. Meitang, I know your secret, the secret all the women in town share. You're all so fit and toned because of this, this beautiful scenery, this fresh, moist air. It's all so wonderful! I swear, if I could find the right circumstances to build a little place for myself here, you know, to come and stay for a couple of months each year, then this would be peach blossom land, my utopia. And if I could bring one of my lovers, too, we could live, at least a few months, without a care in the world, like some Daoist immortal out of those old stories!"

"Ms An, you really have a way with words but haven't you seen how the investigation has impacted the village? Everyone is so worked up, worried and frightened, and yet you still think this place could be a utopia? Is there any such place in all of China?"

"Why are you being so formal? We're not strangers any more so why are you being so awkward round me? Call me Jinghui, OK? Or Sister An, if that's easier. Meitang, let's not think about what other people see or what they say. You and I are kindred spirits. As soon as I saw you I knew I'd like you. Let me tell you, the world's filled with nobodies, people of no character and of even less interest. They're everywhere, the common crowd, stiff and inflexible, the masses. If there's someone who stands out from the crowd, then they can't help gossiping but let me tell you, such people are special, despite what others may say. I can say what I feel with you, I can be straightforward and not hold anything back. We're friends now and that means I'm thinking about you, and your problems are mine. I know the situation you find yourself in, of course I've heard, but I'll do what I can to protect you, and whoever tries to cause you harm, well, they'll have me to deal with, I guarantee you that!"

She was being candid, intimate. She was even trying to lighten the mood and laugh. Unwittingly, Lin Meitang felt herself being drawn to her. She felt a certain kind of peace and tranquillity envelop her and fill her with happiness. It was easy for a woman to feel this way towards someone who was so different from her but, at the same time, she knew she couldn't let her guard down completely.

"To be honest Meitang, I'm really quite curious about you, you know. I have to admit, the great majority of people would rather live in the city. I mean, can you show me a young rural boy or girl who doesn't want to move to the city? You're from the city, too. You're a Beijinger, really. But what kind of place is it? It's the centre of government, of the economy and culture too. And what does that mean? Well, it means people of ability all want to move to the capital and they want to become officials. Once posted to Beijing, they want to be part of the central government, that's what. Scholars and professionals share the same dream. They want to live in Beijing, too. They think that's how they'll be considered the most talented. And it doesn't matter who or where they come from, they all think the capital will give them a better life. But you, you gave up on Beijing, left the capital and came here, to this dirt-poor rural village. Can you explain that to me? I mean, can you make a woman like me understand your reason?"

This was a question An Jinghui had to ask, but it didn't have the bite one might have expected. In fact, it wasn't a sensitive issue, at least not to Lin Meitang. That said, it was a question she couldn't answer, for if she did she'd be telling An Jinghui everything. But it was An Jinghui who'd been forthcoming to begin with and had talked about the details of her life, things she'd probably not want anyone else to know, and she'd really gone into the ins and outs of her affairs, and had almost literally shone a bring light on them, allowing Lin Meitang to learn about her most private secrets. She'd felt hostile towards the investigation and disgusted with their methods and intentions, but she was beginning to understand something, at least about An Jinghui, and that couldn't help but change her mind. She could see herself becoming friends with this woman. In fact, Lin Meitang had been prepared, and had expected An Jinghui would pay her a visit, and she seemed to sense, too, that such a visit wasn't about ridiculing her or about trying to catch her out but that's not to say she expected the visit to turn out the way it had.

She gripped the handlebars of the bicycle and manoeuvred it closer to the other woman: "I think everyone I know has asked me that question, and no matter how sincere I've been with my answers, no one has really ever fully believed me. They think I must be holding something back. It has been a long time now and the annoyance I once felt about this question has waned, but I don't think there's more I can give by way of explanation. So no matter what I do, there'll always be people who just don't understand, but I can't be concerned about that, it's their prerogative. Of course, I do have my reasons, that goes without saying."

Lin Meitang, twisted her neck and looked at An Jinghui. She'd expected her to interrupt as she'd been so talkative already but An Jinghui was instead listening intently, aware that if she did try to interject, she'd end up changing the topic and not learning anything more. Her best recourse was to remain silent and wait for Lin Meitang to continue. When she was ready, she'd pick up where she left off, at least, that's what An Jinghui was hoping for. Sure enough, once Lin Meitang calmed down a little, she began again, relating the difficult circumstances she found herself in when she first went back to Beijing and how she finally decided to return to Guojiadian. As she spoke, An Jinghui could see her eyes growing increasingly red.

An Jinghui stopped her bicycle and got down, laying it on the ground beside the road. She waited for Lin Meitang to do the same, then took her by the shoulders and hugged her tight. They sat down together. Lin Meitang pulled out a handkerchief and wiped the tears from her eyes. As she did so, An Jinghui spoke: "So, what about getting married? Someone like you... do you think you can find someone suitable in a rural village like Guojiadian?"

"That will be up to fate, and if it's my fate to be here, then I'm sure I'll find someone suitable and, if it's not, whatever happens, I know my fate is not in Beijing, which means there's nothing for me to return to there."

"OK, fine, I can admire you for that. You're willing to accept life as it's given to you. You have your faith and you're sticking to it. But since we only have this life, shouldn't we follow our heart? Sure, there's no logic to love and some women find themselves bound to tired, tedious men for their whole lives when they'd be better off following their hearts and actually living. That way they'd have their freedom at least. You're not married but you seem to be waiting for that most beautiful of weddings. And you know what? A wedding like that serves only as the prelude to divorce. Most people would prefer not having to think. They'd rather exchange anything for a so-called happy life but, in my experience, a woman that longs daily for that kind of life will only end up sacrificing everything." It was as though these last words had been directed inwards, or as if they were words that some memory or other had brought to the fore. In any case, An Jinghui stopped what she was saying, absorbed in the emotions her words had stirred.

Lin Meitang was deep in thought, too. She knew what question was coming, knew An Jinghui would ask her about her relationship with Guo Cunxian.

But An Jinghui was well versed in matters of the heart and knew that the crucial moment had yet to arrive. Yes, they ha established a level of mutual trust but she knew that the time wasn't quite ripe. She'd get the answer she was looking for, sooner or later, but it would take a little more time yet. She'd have to let the trust she'd established with Lin Meitang take root first. She shifted her frame and then pulled Lin Meitang up alongside her: "This is all a little too heavy, I think. Let's stop now before we ruin our plans for the evening. We'll not want to eat anything if our minds are preoccupied with affairs of the heart. Look, the day is already getting on. Let's go, quickly, and find somewhere to eat. We can eat and talk at the same time, in any case."

They picked up their bicycles and set off once more, chatting away about nothing in particular. Before long, they arrived at the gates of the county city. Since they were both essentially strangers, they asked for directions to the finest restaurant in town. As they entered, their eyes scanned the scene before them. The floor was dark and covered in filth, the remnants of fruit juice, fish bones and chicken carcasses. The tables were covered in grease, as were the shelves leaning against the walls. Even the waitress, leaning similarly against the shelves, was bedecked in oil-stained clothes, busily cracking open sunflower seeds... crunch, crack, crunch. She was quite practiced, deftly cracking the shells, eating the seeds and spitting the leftovers onto the floor. She looked at the two women who'd come in with a degree of curiosity they'd never seen before, but she didn't open her mouth to welcome them. An Jinghui returned her stare for a moment, then turned and pulled Lin Meitang along with her. Smacking her lips in disgust, she muttered under her breath: "How could it get so grimy? Would anyone dare eat there?"

Lin Meitang smiled but didn't answer. She feared they wouldn't be able to find a suitably high-end restaurant that An Jinghui supposedly wished to eat at.

Fortunately there was only one main thoroughfare in Kuanhe, a road that split the city horizontally. They pushed their bicycles as they strolled along trying to identify somewhere decent to eat. They did come across two places, one better looking than the other, but despite the rather fancy look of the restaurant, An Jinghui's unforgiving mouth conveyed only sorrow: "Is this really a county town?"

Lin Meitang answered with a question: "So what do you think a county town should be like? For the inhabitants of the area, Kuanhe is considered fairly large, and in most cases, it's not so easy for them to find reasons or time to visit."

"That's a shame. Peoples' minds are so often directed elsewhere. For a capital city, even a provincial one, to be so poor and bereft of amenities, what's the point of wasting time here?"

Lin Meitang thought to interject her opinion that it wasn't that the people in this area were wasting time but rather it was far too often the case that higher-ups kept tormenting them. The investigation team, for instance, had been dispatched to Guojiadian, they had not been invited. The words hung on the tip of her tongue. She was unconcerned about An Jinghui's penchant for speaking harshly without really meaning what she said, and about how she could accuse someone without explicitly doing so, but she was still part of the investigation and Lin Meitang had to be careful not to openly offend her. As she turned this over and over in her mind, something else occurred to her: "Oh, I've heard there's a committee guest house in Kuanhe where all the officials stay when they visit. It should be clean at least, shouldn't it?"

They immediately asked around, quickly discovering the location of the guest house but learning as well that they were currently hosting an official conference and thus not open for outside business. An Jinghui promptly flashed her credentials; she was, after all, an official reporter for the municipal committee. In a manner that suggested credentials were much more important than words, the two of them were ushered into a small room. After being seated they requested a menu, to which the server replied they did not have one. Before they could respond from their shock, the server went on to tell them a menu wasn't necessary, and that in a moment or so, plates of hot food would be delivered. The food arrived, enough for a meeting of ten or more people. There were eight plates in total, each piled high with food. Crispy-fried chicken, spring onions and scrambled eggs, cabbage and tofu, mung bean vermicelli and stewed meat. There was also a large bowl of radishes and mutton soup, followed by rice and steamed *mantou*.

The two women were both astonished by the elaborate display: "So much!"

"This is standard regulations," the server responded, "eight dishes and one soup."

"What if we can't finish it all?"

"Eat what you can, you can leave the rest."

True enough, there was no way they could force down all of the food now laid out in from of them. An Jinghui accepted the situation they were in, the more the better. Guests shouldn't decline what was offered, after all. She turned towards the waiter and asked for a bottle of wine.

The server replied that they didn't have wine, only beer and *baijiu* (white wine or liquor made from grain).

"What's the best *baijiu* you have, then?"

"Sichuan Lang liquor."

An Jinghui slapped the table: "Excellent, that's just what we've been missing today. Go, quickly, and fetch it. We'll take on that challenge and drink until we can drink no more!"

The two women seemed to be participating in a martial arts competition, each taking turns to toast the other, gulping down cup after cup of the liquor at the same time as their chopsticks stabbed at the meat in front of them, mouthful after mouthful. An Jinghui seemed to be able to hold her drink, or she was good at pretending she could. For her part, Lin Meitang had spent many a night alone in the company of cigarettes and booze, so she wasn't afraid of *baijiu*. She simply wanted to drink as much as she could, drink herself into a stupor. And if she really could lose herself in drink, wouldn't that solve all of her problems?

After polishing off half a bottle, the two women were feeling quite tipsy, relaxed and at ease; a true sense of contentment had washed over them. Lin Meitang's face had a peachy hue, even her eyes were red. An Jinghui's face was blanched, and the more she drank the whiter it became. Sweat was beading on her forehead and her eyes were hazy as she stared at Lin Meitang. Abruptly she reached out her hand and slapped Lin Meitang's shoulder: "Meitang, you really are gorgeous, you know, really alluring, like a cherry-apple dangling from a tree. I can see how men just want to grab hold of you. I tell you, I wish I were a man right now... whoo-hoo! I'd really like to have my way with you!"

"Sister, you ought to have a little drink every day, the more you do the whiter and softer your face becomes. It gives you a certain... quality."

"What quality... hmm? Humiliation, that's what! Sure, a woman's essence is her beauty but, let me tell you, it doesn't last. That's what makes us vulnerable and weak, the fact that our beauty is short-lived. Ah, but in truth, what does it matter? Modern love... more and more it's just a fucking game, there's no real emotion involved. And because it's a game it doesn't matter whether you're beautiful or not, you can still play, or not... ah who cares?"

"But you're an important, well respected reporter, I'm sure you're a player. My thoughts are different, you know, I think... I believe love is the most terrifying, heaviest type of feeling there is and that it's the most dangerous, most painful bait imaginable!"

"You feel that way because you've been duped, you've been hurt. But in truth, there's nothing to be done about that now. No matter where you are or what you do, you're going to run into all kinds of men, and you'll have some torrid affairs and adventures. Who's content with their lot in life, hmm? We've all got different tastes."

"Sister, what kind of man do you like then?"

"I'm a feminist, I've got smarts and I'm not lured by pretty looks. I like helping men resolve serious problems. That way I get to control them and get them to obey me. Before they know it, they'll be kneeling at my feet and I'll be the centre of their world. What about you? What's your type?"

"I like a powerful man, someone I can depend on."

"You stupid cunt. Are there really men like that? Have you ever come across one?"

"I thought I had..."

"You mean Guo Cunxian?"

Lin Meitang dodged the question but it evoked fond memories of the past. Before she realised, she was relaying to An Jingshi her first encounter with Guo Cunxian and how he'd come to her rescue and repaired her shoe. An Jingshi pursed her lips: "Wow, quite a story. He's truly a man with vision, huh? He took advantage of the tight spot you were in and fixed your shoe, capturing your heart in the process. It's like something out of an opera... and then what?"

"What do you mean, then what? You already know the rest." She was back in that dream again but deep inside she knew it was dead. She went silent, raised her head and poured another glass of *baijiu*. Her heart ached as though a great weight was pushing down on it.

An Jinghui reached over and squeezed her shoulder, then drew closer and pecked her cheek: "Sweet Meitang, it doesn't matter, OK? You're not the only one who's gone through something like this. We've all got our flaws, you know. We have to find what joy we can in sorrow."

Lin Meitang remained silent with a forlorn look on her face as she raised glass after glass up to her lips. The sense of ease the alcohol had first brought was gone, replaced by a deep-seated melancholy. How could she have let it happen? How had her life become so entwined with that man?

Once the bottle was finished, An Jinghui wanted another but she couldn't find the waiter. In fact, the restaurant was empty, the staff had already left for the day and theirs was the only room with the light still on. "Shit, they left without giving us the bill. What now?" She helped Lin Meitang get to her feet, thinking they ought to get some air, but their first step felt as though they were walking on soft cotton padding. Unsteady, they crumpled into a heap almost as soon as they had stood up.

An Jinghui put her arms round Lin Meitang's neck and spoke softly to her: "I don't think we'll make it home tonight. I think we should get a room here. I want to let you in on a little secret. I know how a single woman can manage that deep craving that sometimes gushes up inside."

It doesn't matter what kind of organisation it is, all it takes is for someone to put it together and it will develop its own characteristics and resist becoming a monolithic block. The investigation team was no exception to this rule. Qian Xishou was a certain type of individual and Feng Hou was quite another. He didn't go for runs in the morning, only strolls. He was like a man with nowhere special to be and not a lot to do. He especially enjoyed wandering round the central town well, watching the residents of Guojiadian come and fetch their water for the day. He'd listen to their banter, the petty bickering, enjoying the convivial atmosphere it conveyed. At times, he'd even interject himself into the verbal jousting he was often witness to, adding his own titbits of idle gossip. As a result, the village cadres were inclined to welcome him. They appreciated his demeanour and would wave politely in greeting whenever they saw him. They'd also use the respectful title of head county commissioner, despite the fact his position was only deputy chief investigator.

And so his presence each morning began to be taken for granted. Once, after seeing Liu Yucheng, evidently the only agricultural team leader in the whole area, walk up to the watering hole carrying two steel buckets for the umpteenth time, he couldn't help but call out, commenting on the other man's clockwork-like routine: "I say, every morning I see you come to fetch water. An excellent display of diligence, I must say. Either that or you're obsessive about keeping your house clean. You certainly use quite a lot of water."

Liu Yucheng smiled somewhat darkly, an honest look on his face. He was reluctant to address the hidden implication behind what Feng Hou had said: "It's just my lot I suppose."

A keen listener, Feng Hou picked up on the other man's response and decided to be more overt: "I say, Guo Cunxian's been back for two or three days now, hasn't he? How is it I've never seen him come to get water? Does someone else fetch it for him?"

Liu Yucheng caught on too late to the shift in Feng Hou's tone and replied with the truth: "His son, Liu Fugen, fetches the water, but he doesn't follow a set routine. He just shows up when they need it, two or more times a day in some cases."

"Eh? How is it that his son has the family name Liu?"

Liu Yucheng quickly realised he'd said something he shouldn't have but there was little point in trying to cover it up: "Ah, there's a story there. He first met the boy years ago now, when he was roaming the countryside building coffins… for about two years, if I remember correctly. The boy, well, by that time he was a young man, well, he just showed up on his doorstep. I suppose he had nowhere else to turn to."

"Ah. I see. Changing topics, I have something I'd like you to do. When you return home, check in on Guo Cunxian for me to see if he's awake, OK? Afterwards, I want both of you to come and see me. There's something I'd like to discuss."

"Here?"

Feng Hou nodded: "Yes, here."

He was being asked to go and fetch Guo Cunxian? Feng Hou wanted to speak to the two of them together here. For a moment, a brief shiver of fear ran up his spine. It was early, the sun hadn't long been in the sky, but already the deputy chief investigator had thought to engage with his supposed foe Guo Cunxian. And on top of that, he'd been called into the fight, too, the son of a landlord. No doubt the villagers would come in droves to see the spectacle. The ears of those who'd been milling about near the watering hole would help spread the news of the impending battle like wildfire. Liu Yucheng wondered what on earth he wanted to discuss. As he thought more about it, he figured there was about an eighty per cent chance that battle would soon be joined. He just wondered why in hell he'd been dragged into it. Standing still, he wasn't sure what to do.

Feng Hou looked at him strangely, breaking his brief moment of stupor: "Well, hurry up then. I'm waiting."

Of the bystanders who'd dawdled to watch the exchange, many of them now placed their buckets on the ground and took out their cigarettes, eager to see what was going to happen next. The others quickened their pace; they had to take their water home as soon as possible so that they could return just as swiftly. What was clear to everyone was that it seemed they were all keen to see Feng Hou and Guo Cunxian come together and have it out. While he waited, Feng Hou once more began to chat freely with the remaining villagers, asking questions about the watering hole, the water that was in it, and other random bits of conversation.

Before long, Liu Yucheng returned with Guo Cunxian. Neither knew what to expect and so they couldn't help but feel nervous. They walked up to Feng Hou but did not open their mouths. Instead, they chose to watch closely the man who'd summoned them. To Guo Cunxian, Feng Hou seemed chubbier than he had been before, his face fuller and rounder. He looked peaceful and serene, betraying nothing of why he wanted to talk to them. Time passed and all the three men did was stare at each other. There was complete silence for what seemed like ages. Finally Feng Hou broke the calm and asked a question, one Guo Cunxian would never have expected to hear: "By the look on your face, I'd say you've got intestinal problems. Am I right?"

Guo Cunxian was at a loss for words. He had no idea how the investigation team might have learned that he'd vomited up blood and that his stomach had been doing somersaults. As a cloud of suspicion grew in his mind, he shook his head and chose to admit to nothing. If there was anything wrong with him, it must only be the anxiety and stress someone in his position ought to feel. There was certainly nothing wrong with his stomach. Of course, Guo Cunxian didn't want anyone to know his true condition. He also knew that this was just Feng Hou's opening salvo, the prologue to the play they were about to perform. Feng Hou hadn't asked him here to speak about his stomach, of that he was sure.

"When I was younger, I studied medicine. Maybe you didn't know that. These past few days I've been watching the residents of Guojiadian, taking the pulse of the town, as it were. Drinking from this watering hole every day, well, there are bound to be quite a few cases of stomach complaints, I'd say. The fact that there aren't any other more serious illnesses in the village is remarkable. At any rate, I've had to watch from the sidelines. I don't expect many of you would be open to coming for a real examination." There was a penetrating sharpness in Feng Hou's eyes as he stared at the two men. They had a certain presence in the town but now they were left utterly confused and unsure of what was happening. Had the investigation been launched to inspect the foodstuffs, the water and the health of Guojiadian's residents?

A moment of silence passed before Feng Hou lobbed what Guo Cunxian thought to be another volley: "Do you know, I'd previously instructed Ou Guangming to deliver a summons to you demanding that you come to see me. Since you didn't, may I ask where you've been hiding?"

Guo Cunxian gesticulated but was unable to think of an appropriate answer.

Noticing his indecision, Feng Hou volunteered an explanation: "I understand, you had to ready yourself. It is an official investigation after all. You have to admit you're an influential figure in the town, so I'm sure you would approve of not coming to see me immediately but others might not. We've been sent by the central authorities, that's true, and we'll have to submit an official report but we're not here to launch some movement or other, nor are we here to remove you from office. Do you understand? We're here to investigate something much more serious. So, as I've already asked you, tell me, when has this watering hole ever gone dry?"

The deputy chief investigator seemed to be a man intent on wielding two blades. As the saying goes, a man with a hammer in one hand and a wooden club in the other is unable to concentrate solely on one thing. But in any case, his words served only to confound Guo Cunxian. Liu Yucheng noticed this, too, and subsequently sought to come to Guo Cunxian's rescue: "What are you talking about? This water hole's never gone dry? It's been here for four thousand years, probably longer than that, and it has always been in use. I'm not exaggerating when I say it's the lifeblood of the town. So, once again, how can you say it has never been dry? Shit, the old-timers even say there's tortoise essence at the bottom of it and you know what that means: the water ensures long life, just like those reptiles that live forever."

Guo Cunxian stepped in now to correct Liu Yucheng: "No, that's not true. By my reckoning, it has gone dry twice since liberation."

"And when it did, what did the town do for water?"

"They dug deeper."

"Well, let me tell you, there's a good chance this watering hole will go dry again, most likely this year." There was a certainty to Feng Hou's voice, as though he were sure it was going to happen. He then directed the two farmers' gaze towards the long piece of wood wedged into the ground a few feet from the water's edge. "We placed that there the day after we came to serve as a marker. Have a look. I'd say the water has dropped by two fingers at least, what do you reckon? Now, as the days get warmer, you're all using more and more water. Some of you are even using it to water your vegetable gardens and it's because of such usage that, well, I'd say it'll be dry by June at the latest. I've consulted the national meteorological office and I've read their weather reports, too. They say there'll be drought this year for sure. Rainfall is expected to be about thirty per cent less than normal. Now, if you don't think of a means to deal with this, well, not even your tortoise essence will survive."

The bystanders guffawed. They'd been loafing around hoping for an exciting show, crouching and standing nearby, they'd not dared to venture too close. But once they realised the men were simply talking about the watering hole and not something more sensitive or more secret, they quickly lost their sense of reserve and became rather impudent instead. Some even dropped what they were holding and walked deliberately over to the men, intent on giving their own two pennies' worth.

Guo Cunxian's head had been swirling with thoughts of political struggle, of crackdowns and entrapment. He was confused. He had had a great deal of respect and appreciation for the former county commissioner but, owing to his current position as deputy head of the investigation team, he had had no choice but to exercise caution. And he was Guo Cunxian, after all. His feelings of enmity weren't all that easy to tamp down. Besides, could he really believe his own eyes and ears? Had the investigation team really come to town to talk about watering holes, and about theirs in particular? The onlookers, those who'd stayed in the hope of seeing fireworks, all seemed to understand, or were at least primed to keep talking over one another. But he couldn't. The more he listened, the more befuddled he became.

Feng Hou seemed nonplussed by the fuss. He simply raised his voice, gestured for the bystanders to stop their ranting, and then, in an orderly manner, he relayed to them his own thoughts on the matter: "My point is this. There aren't many villages left that rely on watering holes any more. That's a fact. Watering holes are just unreliable. I mean, you can go for days without food but not without water. That's a fact, too. But even more important, it's impossible to ensure that watering holes remain safe and clean enough to drink from. Look, your own livestock, the chickens, ducks, pigs and sheep, are all here drinking from it. That confirms it isn't the cleanest, and it's still water, too, you know. There's no current, and that means its quality can't be that high. If water is left for a hundred days, it turns poisonous, did you know that? It becomes bog water. People are the same. If we are idle and motionless for the same amount of time, well, we get sick too. So let me ask you, why do you insist on using this watering hole? Why not use well water instead?"

This time, Liu Yucheng seemed to have his wits about him: "We've dug more than a few wells but the water is always salty and bitter."

There was urgency to Feng Hou's reply: "Then dig deeper!"

The men standing round the watering hole had never once considered this problem. For generations they'd made use of this watering hole. They liked it and believed it to be sweet and quite good for them. Dig a well? No one was willing to do that. They preferred drinking from the watering hole. Well water wasn't sweet, after all. Liu Yucheng voiced these thoughts: "Is water from a deeper well that much better?"

Feng Hou's eyes bore into Liu Yucheng: "Now listen, I want you to hear this, especially you, since you're in charge of agricultural production. I know the quality of the soil here, it has a high alkaline content. Some years ago a reservoir was built with the aim of addressing the soil quality, of fixing it, but no one expected the more the land was irrigated the saltier it would become. Have you seen the frog marshes and what the land there has become like? Well, I won't go into details right now, I've got data back in our office. A little later we'll go and look at it together. But let me say this, our scientists have devised a new method for dealing with the alkali in soil, and it's simple too: irrigate it with well water. That will not only keep the soil moist, it will also solve problems associated with where it comes from. What's more, it will hold back the increasing salification of the land, too. And to top it off, the water's clean, and since it will be coming up from deep in the ground, there's every likelihood that it will be loaded with all kinds of minerals the body needs."

Liu Yucheng's eyes sparkled, his excitement palpable. But at the same time, he didn't want to blather on. Fortunately, the man standing beside him stood in: "But won't digging a deep well cost an enormous amount of money?"

Feng Hou now stared at Guo Cunxian: "That's why I've asked you to come. I want to discuss this very issue. To provide the village with a suitable well, I shall come up with a plan to fund the project. As to the water your agricultural sector uses, it should be easy enough to find a bank to loan us the money necessary to dig a well. This year our main objective is to prepare for the impending drought. If the idea is to promote industry, well, that requires its own supply of running water, and a lot too. All this means to say that water is the key issue. If Guojiadian insists on continuing to use this watering hole to drink from, well, let me tell you, all your plans will come to nought and nothing you say will make any difference. Of course, the water in the frog marshes reservoir is there to be used but have you tried it yet? I wonder, considering all the work you've done these last few years, how has it all become so salty?"

Liu Yucheng's face was creased with laughter lines and in an excited voice he bellowed: "I say, it sounds good to me!"

The other farmers round the watering hole joined in chorus, some laughing, some shouting their agreement. The investigation hadn't been a waste of time.

Guo Cunxian seemed to finally grasp what was happening but not because Feng Hou had assured the villagers that he'd help construct a well. No, he'd teased something out. The investigation was being pulled in different directions and what the director wanted wasn't the same as what the deputy director wanted. It was clear to him now: Feng Hou was on his side, here to support him and the other farmers in Guojiadian. Of course, this meant he was putting his neck on the line. It was tantamount to open resistance towards his own superior. But that realisation imbued Guo Cunxian with renewed courage and vigour. The morose and abject feelings of the past few days waned, as did the sense of fear and helplessness. He wouldn't smile obsequiously as those around him were doing. No, he would address Feng Hou with the respect he deserved: "Commissioner Feng, I appreciate you've come here as part of an official investigation, but let me say, it's much like you did in the past, when you came as a leading cadre to learn from firsthand experience what it was like in the countryside. You looked for problems then, too, and found solutions, put forth ideas and plans, and advanced the work in the village, and you did it all for us."

"Stop, there's no need for you to speak like this. I just want to say one thing. You can't let rumours get to you. People have grudges, sure, and they say things. They praise you on one hand and criticise you on the other but you can't let that weigh on your mind. You've been village head now for a while, not just for a few days, and this village is yours, it belongs to all of you, and if you do right by it, you'll all benefit but if you don't, if you let niggling problems stand in your away, then Guojiadian is doomed. Right now, your top priority is to begin construction of a well as soon as possible, so that means you need to select a site quickly. Once you do, I'll be able to dispatch a team to actually begin the digging, say in about three to five days."

There was a certain severity and graveness to Feng Hou's voice, an implication that hard work lay ahead. He paused for a moment, straightened himself up and used his hand to point in the direction of the western part of the town. He then continued: "I like that spot there, just south of the Lucky Trees. There's open, unused space there that would be ideal for a well and I guarantee the water quality will be top-notch. If it wasn't, well, the trees wouldn't have grown so large and so sturdy. The western marshes are the best spot around the village, am I right?"

Liu Yucheng chimed in, amazed at Feng Hou's insight: "You're right, yes, definitely. It's the best place. Commissioner, I don't suppose you understand feng shui, do you?"

"Feng shui? Don't be silly, all it takes is a little bit of common sense for anyone to see that's the best spot."

16

CURSES

There are many forums and arenas in this world. You have football stadiums, boxing rings, lecture halls, stages, cinemas, amphitheatres and theatres but everyone likes best the places where they can really hurl abuse at someone else. Take a football stadium. That is an excellent place to scream insults at other people. Who would feel uncomfortable shouting abuse in a place like that? Alternatively, you can write anonymous letters or hurl abuse at other people right to their faces. You can make snide remarks or you can scream like a fishwife. You can curse while laughing or you can be absolutely furious. You can genuinely mean every word you say or you can simply be pretending. You can shout your insults on your own or as part of a crowd. One sarcastic remark can change the whole situation where a cartload of abuse would be completely pointless. You can also curse X when you mean Y, curse because you might as well, curse and then discover that nobody is paying the blindest bit of attention and even though you know there is no point, you still carry on. You can use the insults hurled at the football to complain about how useless your boss is, about problems at the factory, about the fact that you haven't had a raise or a promotion, about the fact that society is rotten to the core, that life is pointless and that your fate is terrible. You can curse your colleagues, passing strangers, your own family, and then move on to abuse the poor, the rich, pimps and whores, this, that and the other!

When you are trapped in the queue waiting for a train or a bus, or you are in the departure lounge of an airport surrounded by hordes of travellers because the plane is late, or when you walk along the main drag or go to the shops, or even better when you find yourself part of the crowd in one of the markets, you may suddenly discover that you are in the perfect place for hurling abuse at other people. There are all kinds of things that go wrong in life and sometimes it can seem as though everyone you meet has a million complaints to make and as if they simply cannot open their mouths without a torrent of abuse coming out.

You should not imagine even for a moment that hurling abuse at other people is something that only 'vulgar' people do, or that this is restricted to the poor and disadvantaged. There are also plenty of sophisticated people, 'high society' types who are really good at saying horrible things. Some of them will swear in the most appalling way while others will curse the government in the most virulent terms. It is a fact that there are some well known and very stylish women, people that you will have heard of, who only seem to use crude or filthy words when they open their mouths in public. And these curses just roll off their tongues, completely naturally and yet really startling at the same time. This is where you begin to understand the attraction of traditional Chinese swear words. They can highlight the modern style of a trendy young woman. It can almost bring you round to the view that the elite ought to use swear words all the time since vulgarity and sophistication are two sides of the same coin, and filth from the very gutter can be the height of fashion.

According to the newspapers, in some developing countries cursing people has become a new kind of career, with great prospects. Say there is someone who you really hate and you don't want to kill him because that would have legal consequences, then you can employ someone good at hurling abuse to humiliate them in public. After all the Chinese character for 'to curse' has two mouth radicals on top of it, representing two sets of teeth and two tongues ready to release a tidal wave of insults, so it will not surprise you that a good number of fine cursers are women. Women have great intuition when it comes to picking the most wounding things to say. They can really make their insults count and they can make the person they have been paid to abuse feel that they have been stripped naked in public as they feel the world turn dark before their eyes. Indeed, sometimes they end up thinking that it would be best if they could just die right then and there.

In China, the popularity of abusing your fellow man has resulted in various products being placed on the market, including the 'Cursing Doll'. You can take it with you wherever you go, and if you come across someone you don't like, you just pinch the doll's leg, and it starts swearing and using the most filthy language. The best thing is that it never gets tired. It won't stop until you feel you've had enough and turn it off.

Why has swearing become so fashionable? Sociologists give us many answers: people now are permanently stressed, competition is so severe, everyone is under terrible pressure, and then there are also social inequalities and injustices. The latest medical research now tells us that shouting abuse can calm us down and that it is beneficial to our health. But that doesn't explain what happens to the person who is being abused! Are we to believe that humiliation is a necessary part of growing up? Can it possibly be true that being sworn at makes you live longer?

It was the turn of An Jinghui to cook for the investigation team but she was lazy and didn't want to get up early to make porridge, so she restricted herself to boiling a pot of water. She used this to reheat the buns left over from the day before and then she poured everyone a cup of the coffee she had brought with her while the rest of the hot water went to fill the thermos flasks. After that, she chopped up a dish of pickled vegetables and then considered breakfast ready. Clucking softly to herself somewhat in the manner of a hen that has just laid an egg, she waddled out of the room to call everyone in to eat. The first person to come was Qian Xishou, and he came rushing in so quickly that he almost bowled her over. An Jinghui couldn't care less about this, but Qian Xishou gave an almighty jump as he came to a dead stop, and then overbalanced.

An Jinghui very kindly went over to help him to his feet but he was determined to brush her off. However, in his hurry to wave her away, he managed to bang his head against the doorframe. An Jinghui burst out laughing, her whole face alight with amusement. Meeting a woman this early in the morning and, given that she was not his wife, then to have her laugh so heartily, so vulgarly, so confidently, and with such lack of respect for his position, Qian Xishou was now feeling even more uncomfortable. He was chilled and numb, and he could feel the goosebumps on his skin. He was quite sure that people were watching him from every window and door in Guojiadian, hidden in every nook and cranny. This bloody woman, this lunatic. Really, she was impossible!

An Jinghui looked from side to side. Sure enough, various passers-by had been stopped by her bellow of laughter and come over to see what was going on, and now they were standing around watching, while those who had been working had also stopped. However, she decided that she had had enough of teasing him and whispered in Qian Xishou's ear, a stage whisper that could be heard halfway across the town: "You do look gorgeous with your face done like that, Mr Qian!"

A cloud of cheap and nasty perfume enveloped Qian Xishou, like a gas attack. He flinched and tottered back a few steps. It wasn't clear whether he was trying to get away from An Jinghui's perfume, or whether he was trying to avoid having to listen to her speak.

"You went off for your run without even pausing to wash off those red marks," remarked An Jinghui, trying not to laugh as she whipped out a handkerchief from her pocket and began to wipe down Qian Xishou's face. Qian Xishou was horrified and humiliated. The reason all of those peasants had been giggling at him wasn't because they were surprised to see someone out for a morning jog but because they had seen the paint on his face. He felt that he had really embarrassed himself and, although that in itself wasn't important, the whole investigation team had been brought into disrepute in the estimation of the locals. Where they should have been respected and feared, these people now thought they were all a group of clowns!

Qian Xishou was a careful man who made demands on his own behaviour. You might imagine that he was the last person to get into trouble but, since the investigation team was having problems finding anything out in Guojiadian, he had to make a show of solidarity and encourage his people to make more efforts together. In this way the investigation might reach a conclusion more rapidly. That is why he did not refuse when An Jinghui invited him to a poker party the night before but the problem was that the woman suggested that anyone who lost a game should have a red circle of lipstick drawn on his or her face by the winner. Several people had immediately applauded this suggestion and, since he didn't want to annoy everyone, he felt obliged to agree. Maybe they had agreed earlier that this would be a great opportunity to make fun of him.

An Jinghui was by far the most enthusiastic member of the party. She was a bubbly personality at the best of times, and she liked men. The night before she had been the first to climb into Qian Xishou's lap and grab him round the neck while, with the other hand, she marked his face with her lipstick. At that moment, the serious and dull atmosphere that pervaded the investigation team was completely destroyed, and even Qian Xishou found that he couldn't but laugh. However, it was an awkward moment, and he was clearly embarrassed. An Jinghui's face was right in front of his, her lips were level with his lips, her eyes level with his eyes, and he found that he had to just shut his eyes and let her get on with it, which his team members found absolutely hilarious. After that, winners still didn't feel comfortable smearing their lipstick over Qian Xishou's face, so they would ask An Jinghui to do it for them. An Jinghui was by far the most extrovert of any of them: she was happy to show off her flirtatious and frivolous side, and the enjoyment she got from it all ensured that everyone else found it hysterically funny as well.

When she lost, she found herself being hugged by other team members as they daubed her lipstick on her face. She was a thin woman with prominent cheekbones but her lips were full, which made her extremely sexy. She was dangerously attractive.

After that, someone brought out a bottle of spirits, and now anyone who lost had to drink a cup, but Qian Xishou and An Jinghui were always asked to drink a loving cup. Normally Qian Xishou never drank alcohol but everyone at the party seemed to have gone berserk and they didn't show the slightest respect for his position. There seemed to be no way for him to regain control of the situation. Whatever he said they simply ignored, or rather, the more he said he couldn't possibly drink, the more determined they were to make him do so. When a group of people get together like this at a party to torment one of their number, their wretched victim is going to find himself in serious trouble.

With Qian Xishou's personality, even though he was forced to drink a few glasses, he was perfectly able to cope. Furthermore, he could well remember having had this kind of thing happen before, so he was not completely unprepared. If he ever went to a party or attended an event with colleagues, somehow or other he always ended up being the person that everyone else wanted to make fun of, though he had no idea what it was that made complete strangers want to gang up to torment him. It was perfectly true that he did not have much of a sense of humour and was not the kind of person to enjoy a good laugh. In fact, there was nothing he disliked so much and he was terrible at any kind of light socialising with people he didn't know well. He was much better in situations that required rules and good order, where he could exert his authority and show his impartiality. Of course, he was quite sure that last night things had not gone too far. The moment he realised that he was in danger of losing control, he had walked out. He could always manage to do that. If he was really determined, his subordinates would have to give up harassing him. He had a simple rule concerning his own behaviour: at all times he had to maintain the ability to assess the situation clearly. So why had he gone back to his room and gone to sleep without washing his face? Of course, it was the best night's sleep he had had since coming to Guojiadian. So when he woke up early, he was relaxed enough to feel like an early morning run, and he completely forgot about the marks on his face.

Perhaps it was because of what happened last night and he had simply forgotten?

What was yesterday? Ah yes, a water day. That would explain it. He hadn't used soap to wash his face and that is why the lipstick hadn't come off. Some years earlier, Qian Xishou had happened to read a report in the newspaper that washing with soap every day was bad for the skin and, since he liked to take care of himself now he was over fifty years of age and his skin was getting delicate, he felt that he ought to do his best to look after it. As a result he only washed with soap on Tuesdays and Fridays. On all other days he washed with water alone, just quickly rinsing his skin.

In actual fact, the night before, Qian Xishou really became the focus of the party only after he left. Everyone sat around playing cards and discussing his personality which they all found deeply mysterious. They got so absorbed in their discussion that they put down their cards to really concentrate on their analysis of the situation. Of course, it all began with An Jinghui: "Do you know why I let Mr Qian go? He was getting paler and paler until it was really scary. He looked just like an old woman. I simply couldn't bear to go on with our joke. Making fun of someone like that you have to be careful not to go too far because people with physical problems aren't going to be psychologically normal, so you don't want to put them in a position where they feel cornered. If you want to know the truth, I thought this would be an excellent opportunity to find out if he is interested in women or terrified of them."

"What was your conclusion?" one of the others asked. "Do you think he fancies you, or is he scared of you?"

"Both," said An Jinghui. "He fancies me but he is terrified of the fact. I've already noticed that sometimes he likes to chat with women and he seems to want to get close to them but if a woman really seems to respond to him, he gets frightened and stressed, and then runs away. Tell me, what should we think of someone like that? Is he some kind of eunuch or is he bisexual? Wu Lie, you're in the police, you must know something about it, so tell us."

Wu Lie shook his head: "Good God, woman, we don't care about things like that in the police. The local people call that kind of person 'a waste of a ball', where a man doesn't have his full equipment or where his balls don't work... what doctors call testicles. I've heard that in the past eunuchs were just like castrated pigs today. It wasn't that their sticks were snipped but they cut a hole so that their balls could be popped out. People round here called men like that *eryizi*."

"Easy?"

Wu Lie hesitated: "Not easy, but the *yi* meaning suspicious, dubious or weird, so '*eryizi*' means that they were confused about their sexuality and didn't know whether they were male or female, yin or yang. Actually, I don't know which character it should be, so I am just guessing here."

Feng Hou, who hadn't said anything so far, but had just been sitting to one side and giggling, suddenly broke in to explain authoritatively: "Actually it should be *erweizi* with the *wei* that means 'tail', not the *yi* that means 'dubious'. Creatures in the animal kingdom have various different types of tails and people are animals too, so *erweizi* (someone with two tails) means that the person concerned has the characteristics of both sexes and could be considered male or female. So they are hermaphrodites, both yin and yang, if you see what I mean. These people are what are called *nikei* ('dimorphs' or, more literally, 'two shapes' or 'forms') or *hangetsu* (literally 'half month' or 'half moon') in Japanese. Right now, according to An

Jinghui, Mr Qian may have a physical problem of some kind but it doesn't mean that he isn't interested in women. As you all know, he was married for a few hours when he was a young man but on the wedding night, the bride ran away. According to my information, he hasn't looked at a woman since but that doesn't prove he doesn't have normal desires, does it? Why would he have got married if he wasn't interested in women? If you ask me, a better comparison would be a eunuch back in olden times."

Here, An Jinghui found that she had things she wanted to know. "Eunuchs were castrated, so what's up with Mr Qian?"

Feng Hou stood up and said with the utmost seriousness: "In the Bible, in the Book of Matthew, there is a line where it says that there are eunuchs who were born that way, and some who have been made eunuchs by others. We Chinese have the Buddhist sutras that say that there are five kinds of non-male and five kinds of non-female that are subject to evil desires. The five kinds of non-male are the *sheng*, the *jie*, the *du*, the *bian* and the *ban*. *Sheng* means that the man is born with a shrivelled-up penis, and he cannot experience an erection. *Jie* means that the person is born gender neutral and that their sexual orientation will depend on the gender of their partner. People in the past explained that, if such a person met a man, they would become female, and if they met a woman, they would become male."

Gao Wenpin squawked at that: "Wa-hey! That sounds great. You can swing both ways, just think how much fun that would be!"

An Jinghui immediately shushed him: "Look at you, you're just sex-mad! Can I remind you that you're tiny. You couldn't possibly cope with having sex with both men and women! And can you all stop interrupting so that Mr Feng can carry on with his explanation."

Feng Hou laughed in a leisurely way and carried on: "*Du* means that the sex organs are missing. *Bian* is when a person is half-male and half-female, or where they are male for half the month and female for the other half. *Ban* is where the sex organs don't appear to have any abnormality at all but the man is infertile. That is the reason why people in the past called men like that *ren'a* which literally means 'human waste'."

By this time, everyone was interrupting. Hey, are there really that many different kinds of men? Couldn't you provide a few more details? An Jinghui shouted louder than everyone else: "Can you all shut up! Let us hear what Mr Feng has to say."

Her suggestion was immediately adopted: OK, OK, nobody is allowed to interrupt. If anyone has a question can they please wait until Mr Feng has finished speaking before they say anything.

Feng Hou laughed and carried on showing off his knowledge of the past which he had never before had an opportunity to display like this: "In the past, legend has it that men who were castrated as small children could sometimes grow back their penis as adults with the help of the right medication. It seems that some eunuchs did indeed get married and have children. On the other hand, it was a particularly horrible kind of medicine that they used, since it was composed from the brains and bone marrow of little children. However, if you are talking about Mr Qian, a born eunuch, his penis will be naturally shrivelled up, and there is nothing that modern medicine can do to help. Just look at his appearance or listen to his voice and you will know. And since we are talking about Mr Qian, when he was young his skin was just beautiful and white, just like a woman's. Now he is over fifty and has so many wrinkles, which twist across his face in a fine network, not to mention the fact that his flesh is all kind of soft and flabby, so he looks more like a middle-aged housewife than anything else. The older that kind of person gets, the thinner they become, and ultimately he's going to be positively skeletal as the mouth sags and the chin is really sharp and pointed. It's all to do with endocrine.

"In imperial times, there weren't too many eunuchs that got fat. And then there is the ultimate sign, that high-pitched voice. In the past, countries in Europe all had opera troupes where castrated men sang soprano roles, and as theatrical traditions developed, there were many castrated men that sang women's parts. To their way of thinking at the time, this was a gift from God, with biblical sanction. You see? Mr Qian, when he speaks, deliberately slows right down, because he is trying to make his voice strong and deep, but the moment he is anxious and speaks quickly, the tone goes way up, all sharp and shrill, so that it assaults your eardrums and is really horrible to listen to. Given that his personality is very difficult for other people to get along with at the best of times, I am sure that everyone understands that since he is neither yin nor yang, it is not surprising that he has some psychological problems. Throughout history, people like him are noted for their abnormal characters. They are moody and vengeful, and they are inclined to make a huge fuss about things that normal people would regard as trivial. Since society as a whole or, indeed, you could say since life has proved unjust to them, as social animals they end up being perverted, and so they have a strong anti-social streak. That is why, throughout history, there have been very few eunuchs who proved capable of greatness, such as Cai Lun, who discovered how to make paper, or Zheng Zhong who ended a civil war and saved the dynasty in the Eastern Han dynasty, or the famous eunuch Zheng He who sailed across the sea. All the other eunuchs we have ever heard about are notorious for their abuse of power and the chaos that they brought to the government, or the murders they committed within the palace. An Jinghui was absolutely correct in the way that she behaved because Mr Qian did very well last night and you got to tease him pretty much to your heart's content but when the time came to stop, you did, before things went too far."

Maybe because she found herself entranced by Feng Hou's disquisition on eunuchs, or because she was overcome by his showmanship, An Jinghui clapped her hands excitedly. "Goodness, Magistrate Feng, you have kept all of this very quiet. Normally you don't say anything at all, so we thought that you had had the stuffing knocked out of you by all these years of supervising agricultural labour. We had no idea you were so very well educated!"

"I wouldn't say that I am well educated or that supervising agricultural labour is soul-destroying work, but I will admit that I like to read."

By now everyone was talking about the stories they had heard concerning Qian Xishou. They all agreed that he had changed work units loads of times but that wherever he went, nobody really got on with him.

Some people had heard that he was always punishing his subordinates and that he was really strict: probably this was his eunuch nature coming out. Since he was angry about not being able to enjoy a relationship with a woman himself, he was jealous of normal men who could. Of course, you could also turn that around and say that women didn't like him and men found him objectionable, so nobody was prepared to befriend him, and they all said horrible things about him. Since people tended to dislike him on sight, naturally they would want to get rid of him at the earliest possible opportunity.

But they had also heard that, after he joined the municipal party committee, he calmed right down. Clearly he was exactly the right kind of person to become a politician and he enjoyed himself immensely in this era of class struggle with one campaign coming hot on the heels of the last. Abstinence and birth control, fighting selfishness and denouncing revisionism; clearly he would be happy if every man in the country was prevented from having sex. This kind of situation was terrible for everyone else but he liked it. He could be on his own, he had no ties, he didn't care about anyone else, and so he could fix his eyes on the goal. As the saying goes, a man with nothing is afraid of nobody, and right now, that was his trump card.

Think of the investigation team: everyone lived and ate together, and they spent all their time with one another, so even if they didn't want to get to know one another, they didn't have any choice in the matter. So they knew every last little thing about each other, and they would chat about their families, good things and bad, the people they liked and didn't like, who they missed and who they remembered, who they were going to write to and who they were going to phone, all without the slightest hesitation. But nobody had ever heard Qian Xishou mention his family and, equally, they had never seen him write a letter or make a private phone call. Maybe he had been hatched from an egg and didn't have any family or friends, quite apart from the failure of his marriage. They all felt that a formal term of address was the best way to talk about someone like that.

No wonder that, when the city decided they had to send an investigation team to Guojiadian, the higher-ups thought of him. Once he turned up, he immediately got onto the relationship between Guo Cunxian and Lin Meitang. It was just really bad luck that there was a 'sexual problem' involving the two of them, and it was Qian Xishou who was in charge of the investigation. If he were put in charge of the anti-pornography bureau he would really have gone to town. All Party institutions would have been turned into monasteries and the Women's Federation into a nunnery!

Feng Hou sighed. "In the past, Chinese people used to use the term of respect 'an official or eunuch family'. Why put officials and eunuchs together? The fact is that people used to call eunuchs, 'eunuch-officials,' which tells you that eunuchs were also government officials, and that it was hard to distinguish between the two. If you couldn't be an official, you could become a eunuch, and if you were ruthless enough, you could get quite as rich and powerful as any official. Perhaps you could say that eunuchs were ideally suited to become government officials."

The moment he mentioned eunuchs, An Jinghui had another question: "Just now, you mentioned five kinds of non-female. What does that mean?"

"The non-females are what are vulgarly called 'stone virgins'. There are five kinds as well: the *luo*, the *jin*, the *gu*, the *jiao* and the *xian*, and in each case, the women concerned cannot give birth. Actually, this is what doctors today call 'infertility', and in most cases now you can have an operation to fix the problem."

"You said that eunuchs used to get married. Does that mean they were really having sex, or were they husband and wife in name only?"

"That is kind of complicated, and there are three possibilities. You have the fake eunuchs, like the famous Lao Ai at the court of Qin. He was supposed to be a eunuch but he was having an affair with the mother of the First Emperor for years and they ended up having two children together. And then, in the time of the Chenghua Emperor in the Ming dynasty, there was Achou who had an affair with Consort Wan. According to the secret histories of the reign, normally there was no difference between Achou and any other eunuch, but every month when the moon was full, the second penis hidden in his belly would pop out and his erections were then much longer-lasting and more powerful than any normal man's. At the same time, his eyes would turn red and if any woman looked into his eyes, she would lose all control, her face would become flushed, her heart would be pumping, her thoughts running wild, and she would let him do whatever he wanted with her. There is also An Dehai who had an affair with Empress Dowager Cixi and later on there was Zhang Yongfu, who was also called Little Dezhang, who had a relationship with Empress Dowager Longyu and various other palace women simultaneously. There are lots of examples of this kind of thing.

"The second kind is the sort who plays a female role in order to get imperial favour. In the past, it used to be said that women needed five qualities: *pan*, *lu*, *deng*, *xiao* and *xian*. The third character, *deng*, refers to the eunuch Deng Tong, who was the favourite of Emperor Wen of the Han dynasty, who is supposed to have been the richest man in history. This means that a woman needs hard currency. What the *History of the Han Dynasty* says is that Emperor Wen loved Deng Tong so much that he gave him all the copper in Mount Yandao in Sichuan, and let him mint his own money, to the point where Deng coins were accepted across the empire. If you can mint your own coins, you can make as much as you like, that's why he was the richest person ever! I'm sure that you have all heard the story of how the emperor cut his sleeve. That is about Emperor Ai of the Han dynasty and his favourite, Dong Xian. Emperor Ai wanted to get out of bed and go to court, only one of his sleeves was caught under Dong Xian's body, and the emperor didn't want to wake up his homosexual lover, so he used a knife to cut the sleeve off.

"As for the third kind, they would openly get married. In the Tang dynasty, eunuchs like Gao Lishi and Li Fuguo had massive wedding ceremonies, and they were given special permission by the emperor to hold them. In the Ming dynasty, in the reign of the Jingtai and Tianshun Emperors, it seems that it was perfectly normal for eunuchs to get married and have concubines. Pretty much all of the palace women had their own partner. There was a courtship, discussion about getting married, and then after the engagement there would be a swearing of oaths, and the whole thing was not really any different from a marriage ceremony outside the palace. At that time, there was a special name for eunuchs and palace women who had got together. They were called *caihu* (literally, a 'vegetable household'). If an emperor wanted to tease a palace woman, he would ask her, who is your *caihu*? There were more than ten thousand eunuchs in the palace in those days, so it is not surprising that sometimes there were abuses, or people managed to smuggle themselves in or perhaps that there really were cases of them growing their penises back. Way back in the Eastern Han dynasty, there was a eunuch called Luan Ba, who is supposed to have been the first recorded instance of a eunuch regrowing his penis. With the situation that existed in those days, there were some women who divorced their husbands in order to marry eunuchs. According to what it says in history books, there were some women who were thinking about how much money the eunuchs had, and then eunuchs had to do other things in bed to satisfy the desires of their lovers. Of course, there are also many instances of eunuchs who were really evil people, where their disability resulted in perversion or they were seeking psychological compensation, and there were situations where they would use dildos to torment the women that they married."

At this point someone whispered: "Who knew that eunuchs had so much fun!"

"What, you want to give castration a try?"

"It is kind of tempting. If one of you would give it a go, then Mr Qian could have a partner."

And so the conversation turned back to Qian Xishou.

When interfering types got busy with their calculations, they worked out that there were seventy-three bachelors in Guojiadian over the age of thirty. If they dropped the age two years, and counted those over the age of twenty-eight, then there were more than 108 bachelors in Guojiadian. These unmarried men were a force in the village, and their power was a problem, because it was internecine, it broke out in strange places, and you never knew quite how or why they would be moved to violence.

The one thing these unmarried young men had in common was their physical strength, but what they lacked was a suitable place to show it off. For them, the strongest forces in their lives were hunger and the desire for sex. Unfortunately, they were far too poor to be able to do anything about this, so they had to improvise. Since none of them had the slightest chance of getting married, they would get depressed and then they would hurl abuse at other people, or they would gossip with one another, playing chess or poker, smoking, sunning themselves or taking a nap.

Everybody else, which here means married couples, called the place where these men regularly congregated 'Bachelors' Hall'. At New Year's, they had gone so far as to put up a red paper notice on either side of the door to Bachelors' Hall, saying: "If you want to be happy, you should know your place."

The various bored and restless unmarried men of the village had no idea what this notice was supposed to mean. Was it a sarcastic reference to their problems or was it praise? So they put up another notice themselves above the door, reading: "Unmarried and unemployed!"

Bachelors' Hall had been the communal dining room back during the Great Leap Forward, and later on it had been rejigged to act as a shed for the animals belonging to the commune. There were two old bachelors employed to look after the animals, and this naturally led other unmarried men to congregate there, and it ended up with the place being the centre of activity for all the bachelors in the village. The girls and young married women in Guojiadian all avoided the road in front of Bachelors' Hall, because anyone foolish enough to walk that way would find themselves the main topic of discussion for the men for the rest of the day.

When the investigation team came to the village, Bachelors' Hall was even more busy than normal. People came in and out all day, and not just the bachelors, but married men as well. They talked about the investigation team, of course, but they were also worried about what would happen to Guo Cunxian and the whole village of Guojiadian, and then gradually they started to discuss the people in the investigation team about whom all kinds of things were said. Sometimes the entire hall was rocking with the bachelors' laughter. During the last couple of days, the bachelors' interests had become focused on the only woman in the team: An Jinghui. These unmarried men were naturally interested in discussing women and she offered them a fantastic opportunity. They could really exercise their imaginations, and the more they talked, the better it sounded and then, somehow or other, An Jinghui ended up becoming linked with a thirty-two-year-old bachelor named Ou Guanghe.

I've heard that she isn't married, not because nobody has ever asked her but because she wants to try them all, but that now she's had enough of city boys and has come out to the countryside for a change of pace. Everybody knows that our village has the largest number of bachelors for miles around, all virgins. But in this here Bachelors' Hall, I reckon only Ou Guanghe is good enough for her. He's about the right age, and they would look good together. If you look at that woman's face, her skin is so fine and pale, you just want to reach out your hand and stroke her, and then maybe pat her a bit, and then get closer so that you can kiss her... aahh! Just think how great that would be!

She isn't particularly pretty, but that mouth is gorgeous. Big lips are great for kissing!

Have you seen her when she is smoking? She really is super-sexy! Her cigarette never leaves her hand, and do you know what that means? She is definitely up for it!

If you ask me, it is that tiny waist that makes her so attractive. You could span her waist with your hands, and then take it from there.

You are all quite wrong, the best thing about her is those massive tits. You don't need anything else if you can be giving those a good suck.

This village couldn't turn out any man good enough for such a gorgeous woman. Well, except for Guanghe. He's got those big old eyes and thick eyebrows, and beefy shoulders. Guanghe is clearly really strong, so he could make a woman like that submit.

When all of this kicked off, 'Big Head' Ou Guanghe wasn't too bothered. He just leaned his head against his hand, but soon he was grinning, and then laughing, his face alight with happiness at the fantasies the other bachelors were spinning for him.

Now all of the unmarried men crammed into the room picked up the joke: you know, I've heard that she's really interested in our Guanghe, she's been asking lots of people about him, and yesterday she went off specially to talk to Ou Guangming, to see what he had to say. Hey, Guanghe, if you don't believe me, you can go home and ask your brother about it.

Now one of the others immediately chimed in: that may be true, but I've heard that one of the other people on the investigation team is interested in her, and you know what they say about distant water being no help to present thirst? If you want my advice, we ought to be giving Guanghe here a few pointers, so he can seduce her as soon as possible.

That won't be difficult. After all, she has chosen to come to our village so she's asking for it. She's always off talking to Lin Meitang, and Lin Meitang is the head of the Women's Federation in our village, so she's responsible for finding wives for our bachelors. If Guanghe lies in ambush near Lin Meitang's house, he can wait until she comes out and force himself on her. Once he's had her, she'll have to marry Guanghe.

That's the dumbest idea I've ever heard of; that's what is called rape. If he rapes a member of the investigation team, do you think Guanghe is going to be walking around as a free agent afterwards? Let me tell you, Guanghe, the team is out every day talking to people in this village, right? So if you go and chat to her every day, and you just talk to her, not to anyone else, you might be able light a spark in her that means she's happy to take things further.

Or maybe you can do something amazing, make yourself a hero for the whole of Guojiadian, and then she'll seek you out herself.

Everybody was laughing heartily as they gave their own suggestions, and nobody noticed that the main protagonist of today's joke, Ou Guanghe, was starting to change colour, and that his face was becoming more and more flushed. Who knows whether he was planning to follow someone's advice, or whether he had a better idea himself, or whether he was getting angry, or whether he was tempted? Suddenly he got up and went out without a word, slamming the door behind him.

Bachelors' Hall just rocked with laughter.

Quite a different situation pertained in the investigation team. Having had such fun the night before, they were all really formal the next day, and even when they were eating, they were not as friendly and chatty as normal. They didn't even dare to crack a joke together, let alone behave with the freedom that they had shown at the party. This was because Qian Xishou was behaving in an unusually stiff manner. He told everyone that there was going to be a meeting after lunch and then didn't say another word. His staff kept their eyes on their own plates and teacups. With the atmosphere so heavy and unnatural, they didn't dare even to glance at each other.

When the meeting began, everyone resumed their normal ability to look each other in the eye, since when you are talking, you can't fail to have eye contact. It was Qian Xishou's turn to report on progress, and he enjoyed presiding over meetings, so he became even more serious than normal. Since the team members could now look at him directly, they were studying Qian Xishou in the light of Feng Hou's analysis of the night before. That cadaverous face covered in a network of fine wrinkles did indeed look rather like that of a eunuch with those protruding cheekbones, those pendulous cheeks and that sharp chin without a single hair on it. The more they thought about it, the more they felt that he looked like a feeble old lady. His voice was also just as Feng Hou had said, he was speaking really slowly and rasping his throat to keep the tone low.

"Everybody knows the situation that brought us here. Village people have confused thinking, violations of the law are rampant, and the leaders of the municipality are greatly concerned about the results of our investigation. They are waiting for us to bring them evidence so that they can research this problem. If it turns out there is some important guiding principle at work, it may have a much wider application. The masses are watching us and asking what this team is going to do. We have a heavy burden on our shoulders, and there is a lot of pressure on us. We have been here in Guojiadian for quite a few days now, and the people in this village clearly do not have a stable way of thinking, and there has been an awful lot of gossip. Therefore we need to sort out the facts and establish some preliminary conclusions, and then discuss what we are going to do next."

Wu Lie was a young man and couldn't help but grumble: "That Guo Cunxian hasn't shown his face since he got back. Clearly he doesn't have any respect for us at all."

Gao Wenping immediately put his oar in: "I think it goes beyond not having any respect for us. It is more like he has locked horns with us to see who is stronger. He's a right piece of shit. But when it comes down to it, what can he do?"

"That is hard to say," said Luo Denggao in a shy voice, "because right now it seems to me that he has the upper hand. I am not sure he couldn't make things very difficult for us."

Gao Wenping didn't agree at all. "What? When our investigation concludes, we are going to be relying on you in the Prosecutor's Office for support. You can't just give up on us!"

Qian Xishou now moved quickly to turn the conversation towards a more fruitful topic: "Comrade Wu Lie, someone denounced Guojiadian for having cheated the state out of tens of thousands of yuan with false reports of water conservancy projects. Did you find any evidence for this?"

"No. The people in charge of the earthworks have all moved on, and I can't find any of the people who performed the inspections, so it was impossible to get any evidence about what really happened."

Qian Xishou now turned to Luo Denggao: "How about the bribes offered by Guojiadian to facilitate the implementation of large-scale business projects? Do we have any evidence of the law being broken there?"

Luo Denggao was about thirty years of age, with a noble air and a calm way of speaking. "Dealing with a case of this kind has changed a great deal in recent years. Outside investigations are now really difficult because everyone lies. If anyone were to say that Guojiadian offered bribes, it is like admitting that they took them, and the punishments for taking a bribe are much worse than for giving them. Do you think they are all stupid? They've formed a network where they all trust each other, and they cover one another's backs. Anyone who were to betray their connections would be cutting the pipeline that funnels a lot of money into their own pocket, and then when other people find out that you aren't trustworthy, they would take steps to defend themselves. You'd be out in the cold, or at the very least you would find that you didn't have too many friends any more. If you don't have connections, how do you make any money? The economic bubble has made people desperate to get rich, and their respect for the law has decreased. As a result, even though we went to lots of different work units, we didn't find any real evidence of wrongdoing."

Luo Denggao had handled many important cases for the Prosecutor's Office, but when he said this, Qian Xishou, who hadn't been in a good mood to start with, now got really cross. "What that means is that we haven't done enough, or we haven't found the right approach to take. There are problems here in Guojiadian, otherwise the municipality wouldn't have sent us out here."

Luo Denggao was a very calm person and he didn't show the slightest sign of impatience: "The situation now is quite different from what it was even just a few years ago. We simply don't have the authority that we used to, and the law is no deterrent. Either people won't talk to us or they lie, and there is nothing that we can do about it. We cannot be in too much of a hurry, because if we wait until we have some real evidence, we can begin the legal process properly, and then it will be much easier to make them tell us the truth."

The expert auditor, Gao Wenping, now shouted: "Can't we just arrest him?"

"Arrest who?" Luo Denggao asked.

"Arrest Guo Cunxian!"

"Why?"

"Because nothing happens at Guojiadian without him being involved."

"When you audited his accounts, did you find any evidence of wrongdoing?"

"Don't talk to me about those accounts, they are in a complete mess. There were loads of problems. Of course, if we are going to arrest Guo Cunxian it might be best to do so on the basis of his personal behaviour. He treated those girls who were educated youth sent to the countryside as his own personal harem and didn't allow them to go back to the city. We have plenty of complaints about that. We also have eye-witness accounts from pretty much the entire village. I'm sure people would like him to be punished for the way he behaved."

Of the various members of the investigation team, Gao Wenping was one of the sillier ones, and what he said was rarely worth listening to, though his words often conveyed a sense of superiority that on closer examination turned out to be entirely superficial. Whatever everyone else was talking about, he would quickly turn the conversation to the subject of women, and he simply could not conceal the importance this topic had for him. His self-righteous attitude in these matters happened to make Qian Xishou feel really uncomfortable, and the feeling that he normally had that he was in charge, that he was the master of other people's destiny, completely disappeared. He had the impression that the masses had changed, that they had regressed to being the way they were several decades ago, and that nobody could escape unscathed when such terrible moral delinquency was revealed. Way back when, the moment the investigation team appeared, the people in the village would be telling them all about things, and a large part of their work was calming people down, then making sure that government decisions were carried out. It was all so much easier than today, when you were faced with people who wouldn't tell you anything. He had participated in or led so many investigations, and there wasn't a single one that had failed to be successful. It was unthinkable that you wouldn't get brilliant results! But now? Even the investigation team was quite different from the groups that had carried out mass movements in the past. The people that had participated in investigations of this kind in the past had a sense of pride in what they were doing, they felt they were on a mission, they obeyed orders, they struck while the iron was hot, they got results! Now it was all so much more difficult, and it was all because they couldn't agree, everybody had their own ideas, everyone wanted to prove their theory was right, they were all waiting patiently for events to prove them correct, and there was simply no cohesion within the team.

It seemed as though he had to face up to the fact that the era of task forces and investigation teams was over.

Qian Xishou would have been happy if everyone on the investigation team had been like Gao Wenping. Although he was a silly man, and arrogant, he was the kind of person who stirred things up, and having arrived in Guojiadian, he was prepared to make a fuss and not shut up. People like that are easy to motivate and easy to control. If everyone on the team was as energetic and ready to deal with the problems that arose, he would be able to relax. But there were also people like Luo Denggao, who was rather a headache, but also not really too hard to keep under control. Luo Denggao had his own opinions about things, and he had had ideas about the investigation team right from the moment it was set up. Whatever he said or did, he first considered his own theories. He never once thought about how this would affect the investigation as a whole. He acted in the light of his own experience and ideas, and he was determined to show that he was better than anyone else. His every word and action smacked of a kind of professional arrogance. If he liked to look down on the inhabitants of Guojiadian, nobody was going to mind, but he clearly thought himself a cut above the rest of the investigation team, and that annoyed other people.

However, by far the most difficult person for Qian Xishou to deal with was his deputy, Feng Hou, and his slave, Cui Daben. He was the head of the community in which Guojiadian was to be found, and he did whatever Feng Hou seemed to want. The pair of them were supposed to be in the team to help everyone else understand the situation in the countryside, but nobody was quite sure whether they were helping the investigation or hindering it. Feng Hou had actually publicly discussed the problem of getting drinking water to the village with Guo Cunxian, sitting by the side of the pond, and he had agreed to bring well-builders from the county seat out to Guojiadian. But just when the investigation team was going at it hammer and tongs, hadn't he put the brakes on and prevented them from making any further progress? That got Guo Cunxian off the hook and made it clear to everyone that there was dissension within the team. Qian Xishou had already decided that he was going to kick this problem over to the municipality as soon as possible. He was going to ask that either they got rid of Feng Hou, or they gave him some more people.

Feng Hou had good connections with the local government and his intelligence had at no stage been used to help the investigation. Instead, he had used his position as the deputy leader to shackle the team... and then there was his slave, Cui Daben. For all that Qian Xishou was head of the investigation team, who was prepared to genuinely help him? He felt more and more isolated and when he started to think about it, he was stunned: exactly how had Feng Hou come to be appointed as his deputy? The only explanation was that not everyone in the municipality was interested in seeing this investigation succeed, and bringing Feng Hou in was perhaps the result of some kind of compromise. Qian Xishou could feel a cold shiver running down his spine as he realised that the strong institutional support that he had imagined stood behind him quite possibly wasn't there.

The success or failure of this investigation was very important to him. He had spent a long time in the Political Science Research Division and if he carried on working there, this is where he would end his career. Furthermore this was a staff department, so when the party bosses want you for something, you have an opportunity to speak out, but when they don't want to listen to you, then you have to keep silent. You don't have any real power, and fewer and fewer people were prepared to pay any attention to you. There was a reason why the senior officials in the municipality had sent him out with this team. If past practice was anything to go by, this was part of the process of promotion. Next year at the municipal elections, he might well become head of the local division of the Party, or secretary of Political and Legal Affairs, or Party secretary for the municipality as these three posts were all up for grabs, and then he would automatically become a member of the standing committee. He wasn't a very ambitious man and he didn't expect promotion much beyond that. He was just hoping that the success that had eluded him in other areas of his life could be attained in the field of public service.

Gao Wenping had no idea that Qian Xishou was quietly stressing out next to him. Once he started talking about women he simply couldn't stop. "When you think about it, it is quite clear. If you look at Lin Meitang's arse, her waist or her tits, does she look like she's still a virgin? She's shaking them about, and they've obviously been handled by men. Plus, she's nearly thirty, yet she isn't married and doesn't have a boyfriend. What is she waiting for? Who is she waiting for? There has got to be something going on! Don't think that Guo Cunxian is too ugly for that. He's got form for this kind of thing. After all, he didn't show much mercy to that girl from Beijing that he fiddled with."

An Jinghui was not pleased. "That's a disgusting thing to say."

Just at that moment, a torrent of abuse began to be hurled just outside the window, and the longer it went on, the more foul the language became. "Fuck your bitch of a mother and your grandmother. You come over here and I'll kill you, and I'll enjoy it!"

"Bastards! I hope every member of your family dies!"

The investigation team now couldn't possibly carry on with their meeting. Who was screaming abuse like that out in the middle of the road? And who were they swearing at?

If you go and shout underneath the windows of the investigation team, who can you be swearing at? Wu Lie and Luo Denggao were the quickest on their feet and got out first, everyone else following in their wake. They left Qian Xishou sitting all by himself. The meeting hadn't finished and they hadn't waited for him to give permission, but the moment someone said something outside the window they all rushed off. Qian Xishou was silent for a moment and then he decided it would be awkward if he just remained seated on his own, so he went out as well.

A filthy sow was making grunting noises as it moved its head back and forth across the ground. Behind it, there was a young man in his twenties with the long hair fashionable among young men in the big cities, wearing a Western-style blue jacket, black trousers and a pair of beat-up brown leather shoes. His appearance wasn't too outlandish but he didn't look like anyone else in the village and that made him seem out of place. It looked as though he was trying to imitate the way city people dressed but hadn't quite worked out how to do so, like he was trying to keep up with the latest trends but was too stupid to get it right. Everywhere you looked there was something that just wasn't right, and then he just stood there with his mouth hanging open and his eyes practically popping out of his head, which made him appear both violent and unpleasant.

There was a whole bunch of idle busybodies trailing along behind him, and when he got tired of shouting abuse and stopped, they would put in a word or two to make him start up again. Each time, he came back stronger than ever: "Fucking bitch, fucking whore, why don't you stay in your own hovel. Is this the place for you to be licking and biting and grubbing up everything you see? Aren't you afraid of getting into trouble?"

The people standing around enjoying the fun and excitement were applauding loudly: "Wow... Guanghe really has a lot to say, doesn't he?"

Gao Wenpin had no appreciation of the fact this might be something he'd be better off avoiding, so he rushed forward to ask: "Who are you shouting at like that?"

"Are you blind?"

"What do you mean?"

"What do you think I mean? Can't you see?"

"You were there shouting outside the window, but we had no idea what you were on about."

"What a pig-ignorant piece of shit you are!"

Gao Wenpin was normally pretty quick to reply, but he was now so furious that his face had turned bright red and he couldn't think of a thing to say.

Ou Guanghe could see that his opponent was at a loss for words, so he pressed on with his attack. Raising his voice so that it was even louder, he shouted: "That pig is mine and if I want to swear at it I can. Get out of my way, bastard, before I kick you out of the way!"

Gao Wenpin realised that he had been publicly humiliated by one of the local pigmen, and he was not about to let it go at that. He now also raised his voice and asked: "What's your name?"

Ou Guanghe was eyeing him and hadn't yet had time to reply when one of the other people standing around chipped in: "We all call him Dickhead."

"Dickhead, you are just using this pig as an excuse..."

"Who's a dickhead? You're the dickhead! Your older brother is a son of a bitch, you're the dickhead and your younger brother is a ponce."

"You're nothing but a foul-mouthed hooligan! And if you're not a dickhead, what are you?"

"I'm your old man!"

"You...!"

"What about me?" Ou Guanghe was now really starting to enjoy himself, and there was a huge number of people now standing around to enjoy the whole spectacle. His red face seemed to take on an extra flush, his neck stuck out at an even more prominent angle, and his eyes were popping. Clearly he wasn't planning to back down for anyone.

Wu Lie was going to intervene at this point, but Luo Denggao stopped him. "Keep calm," he whispered. "Let's see what the boss wants us to do."

The local peasantry standing around watching this could see that the situation was now getting out of hand, and instead of enjoying Ou Guanghe's apparently inexhaustible supply of swearwords, they began to take more of an interest in the attitude displayed by the investigation team. How were they going to respond? How were they going to put a stop to this? The head of the team, Qian Xishou, was right there, and if he picked up the gauntlet there was going to be trouble, but if he ignored it, it would look bad. Since he had to deal with this situation, what would be the right way to go about it? If he couldn't bring it under control immediately, what would that look like? He would be letting this bastard get away with humiliating them all. If the investigation team ended up looking weak, if they were so feeble that they didn't dare answer back when someone swore at them, how would they be able to stay in Guojiadian? On the other hand, if he was going to take a hard line, how was that supposed to work? If the team started shouting back and hurling abuse themselves, and they couldn't make him eat his words, it would look even worse and his position would be completely untenable. He was hoping that some suitable person would come forward right at that moment to get them out of this predicament. Had all the cadres in Guojiadian just gone and died? Or were they behind this in some way?

Just as Qian Xishou was finding his position as the head of the investigation team more and more untenable, and he was getting increasingly anxious about what on earth he was going to do, Feng Hou marched out in front of Ou Guanghe with a grim expression on his face. Glaring at him, he spoke to Cui Daben: "Mr Cui, you're in charge here. Go and find Guo Cunxian and bring him here immediately!"

A cold smile hovered at the corners of his mouth, and his gaze was fixed sharply upon Ou Guanghe, who pretty quickly started to show signs of fear where before he had been entirely confident. Slowly, he opened his mouth to begin: "Well, well, Guojiadian has produced a real hero, you are really good at shouting at pigs, aren't you? And the pig played its role well, didn't it? And then there were so many people in the audience encouraging you on, you've done really well, haven't you? I'm telling you right now, if you want to shout at your pig, you can go and do it in the pigpens. If you don't like that, you can scream at people in your own home. This is Guojiadian's main road, and this is for people. Your pig here is an animal, and it doesn't understand. You don't have that excuse. If you've got the guts, why don't you pick another window in the village to shout abuse at, and see what happens to you? What? You think a Communist Party investigation team, Communist Party cadres are a suitable target for your foul language? The way I see it is that the pig running away is just an excuse, you are here to try and cause trouble. Right, off you go! Why don't you swear a bit more? I'm listening."

Feng Hou was pointing his finger at Ou Guanghe's head, but now he inadvertently turned his head to look at Wu Lie.

Wu Lie, who was there dressed in his police uniform, suddenly stuck his right hand deep into his pocket. He was still glaring at Ou Guanghe, and looked as if he were ready to attack him at any point. The people standing around were starting to get nervous now, and not one of them dared to say a word. In the same cold tone as he had employed before, Feng Hou looked at those present and demanded in a loud voice: "Isn't there a single village cadre here?" The people in the crowd looked at each other, but nobody said a word. "Really, not a single one? Of course, you people have views about your village cadres, and in particular, you have views about Guo Cunxian. However, you don't dare to say a word about this, and you don't even dare answer the questions put to you by the investigation team, because you are afraid that Guo Cunxian will take revenge. So you thought of doing this instead. You get this young idiot to cause a rumpus. OK, so you want to complain about Guo Cunxian, but what you've done is cause trouble for Guojiadian. You've really embarrassed yourselves. You might as well just have answered the investigation team's questions.

Well done! Right now, I want you to come with me into the office, and you can tell us all that you know."

As he said this, the crowd simply melted away. The only people left out on the street were a handful of children and Ou Guanghe.

Ou Guanghe, who only moments before had been at the height of his powers, now suddenly seemed to have deflated. He would have liked to grab his pig and get away, but he was stopped by Feng Hou. "You can't go anywhere, you are responsible for all of this. You have been shouting at the top of your voice all this time and must be exhausted, so why don't you come in and have a drink of water?"

Ou Guanghe was now really worried. "Mr Feng, you aren't really going to arrest me, are you? It's all because I am so poor, you know, I couldn't afford to buy animal feed so I let the pigs out to forage, and since I was miserable, I thought I would swear a bit. You aren't going to say that I am guilty of class struggle, are you?"

Feng Hou looked him up and down. "Oh, since you are poor, you are allowed to get away with this kind of thing. And it's not just that you can't afford to buy feed, looking at you I guess that you aren't married either. You don't look as if you have someone to take care of you. No wonder that you came running to cause trouble. That is what all the unmarried men do round here. You don't like your life, you don't get on with anyone else, you quarrel with other people, and every day there are half a dozen fights underway. That's how you take out your problems on everyone else. Today you have been quarrelling with the people in the investigation team. I suppose that tomorrow you'll be off to Beijing to argue with people there. You think that, just because class struggle is over, the Communist Party doesn't have any rules? That they can't punish you for your hooliganism? Tell me, did Guo Cunxian put you up to this?"

Now Ou Guanghe began to panic: "No, no, absolutely not. I haven't seen him for a couple of weeks. This was all my idea. Mr Feng, I wasn't doing this to get at you."

"So who were you trying to get at?"

"I… I was getting at myself, having nothing better to do, I guess I was trying to cause problems for myself. I'm a bastard, OK?"

Having found Guo Cunxian, Cui Daben now came back and reported to Feng Hou: "Guo Cunxian is on his way."

Now Feng Hou could deal with the situation: "Fine, you are head of this village and Party secretary here, so you can deal with this tiresome pigman. Guo Cunxian and the Guojiadian Party branch had better sort this out so that the investigation team is happy. Was someone behind all of this? What was he trying to achieve?" Now, Feng Hou turned his gaze towards Qian Xishou. "Mr Qian, what do you think?"

Qian Xishou was looking furious but he had to take advantage of this opportunity to get out of this ridiculous situation: "Fine, let them deal with it, we will carry on with our meeting." Having said that he turned round and went back into the room. He wasn't going to be standing in the doorway when Guo Cunxian arrived, as if the whole investigation team had been sworn at and were now just waiting for him to arrive and deal with the situation. If he, Qian Xishou, had to meet Guo Cunxian, then one of two things would happen. Either Guo Cunxian would take the opportunity to explain his position, or he would have to give an order to make Guo Cunxian speak, in which case he could equally start making a fuss about his own view of the problem.

Everyone else wanted to wait and see how Guo Cunxian dealt with the situation. Whether he was behind it all or not, this would only become clear when he was face-to-face with the pigman. Would he apologise to the investigation team in the name of the secretary of the local Party branch? However, Qian Xishou and Feng Hou had already gone inside, so everyone else just had to follow along behind them.

Gao Wenpin had just been cursed in front of such a large crowd of people that it was going to take him a while to recover from his humiliation, and he complained loudly: "What do we do now? If this carries on we aren't going to be safe here. A few days ago, the people in this village didn't behave like this at all, but since Guo Cunxian came back, the whole situation has become totally chaotic!"

An Jinghui tried to cheer him up: "You can stop that right now, because didn't Mr Feng deal with him for you? Mr Feng is hot stuff. At the crucial moment he was really able to get the situation under control. And it wasn't at all difficult. Once he had mentioned Guo Cunxian, the villagers all ran away because they were frightened and didn't want to get involved. When the crowd had disappeared, that hooligan was easy to deal with." An Jinghui realised that Qian Xishou was looking cross and glaring at them, so she shut her mouth as quickly as she could.

Spring in the north comes with gales and it leaves with gales. The winds that had been blowing for a couple of days on end stopped, and everyone immediately realised that summer was beginning: the soil had become moist, the grass had turned green, the air was warmer, and there was a kind of sweet smell coming from the ground. Everywhere was buzzing with life, as if every living creature wanted to stretch its arms and legs.

The sun now had some heat in it, and people found themselves getting warmed through, so they didn't need to wear their padded jackets any more.

Guo Cunxian wore a dark Mao suit with brand new cloth shoes on his feet and his chin clean-shaven. Earlier in the year he hadn't dressed up like this, since when you get into trouble, it is best not to draw further attention to yourself. The more people are trying to get at you, the more you need your wits about you. He was heading for the mill, and just as he passed the northern fields, he saw a bunch of kids were having fun playing at being beggars. They were bent over and hanging their heads, a stick in their hands, and when they got to a haystack or a pile of firewood, they would pretend they had reached a door, and were begging for food.

Some of them said: "Sir, madam, I am desperate for something to eat."

Some of them said: "Ladies and gentlemen, boys and girls, do your good deed for the day."

Some of them said: "Giving alms means that you'll enjoy luck in the years ahead."

Some of them were singing:

"Generosity will bring luck to your door,
such has ever been the law.
You will find yourself a wonderful wife,
and your children will care for you for the rest of your life. "

Every haystack or pile of firewood had another child standing in front of it, and when the beggars sounded appealing, and the child liked the sound of what they were saying, it would stretch out its hand and pretend to be giving them a bun or a bowl of water.

There was one annoying little boy who said:

"I'm a beggar who does as he pleases,
who wants to be as rich as sneezes?
Your sons are all a bunch of thieves,
when they get going, it's nothing they leave.
They cry, they scream, they threaten to die,
with a splitting headache in your bed you lie."

This joker naturally didn't get given any food. The rest of the children simply fell on him and pushed him to the ground while they yanked his clothing off, and then they made him kneel down right there. Village children wear very simple clothes, and on this occasion some of them were just wearing a little jacket which was easy to take on and off, with nothing on their lower halves.

Guo Cunxian stood there in a daze, watching the children, and it was a while before he could pull himself together. The children were all perfectly well aware of who he was, and seeing him there staring at them and not moving, they decided to stop their play and run away. The little pest who had been stripped naked was equally quick to get up and put his clothes back on.

Guo Cunxian called out to them, and said to the tallest of the children: "You're the one they call Stumpy, right? I don't want you to run away, I am going to get some people together to watch you play, and if you do it just like you were, I am going to give everybody five coppers at the end of it all. You don't need to hand the money over to your parents, you can keep it and buy yourselves some sweets, or maybe a bowl of mutton stew or soy milk. What do you think?"

Of course, they were happy to oblige. They all ran back to one of the haystacks to discuss who was going to play the role of the joker who got stripped naked. Guo Cunxian turned round and shouted at someone to stop, and then told him to go as quickly as possible to tell all of the Party cadres, the Party members, and the members of the Youth League in the village, as well as the team leaders and the managers of the various factories that they should immediately come here for a meeting.

It didn't matter that the investigation team was right there on the ground. If Guo Cunxian gave an order, nobody dared to disobey. Plus, besides which, it had been a long time since there had been any big get-together in Guojiadian, and it was going to be outdoors, at the northern fields where there weren't any nice trees to sit under. That made everybody even more curious. The Party cadres came, and the people who weren't Party members also came. Guo Cunxian was squatting there, and he very quickly heard the sound of footsteps and people chatting with each other. However, when they walked past him, they didn't say a word.

There were now more and more people in the northern fields, but nobody knew what this meeting was supposed to be about, and nobody dared to ask. They were all sitting there in silence, guessing. The people in front saw that Guo Cunxian was squatting there, and they then squatted down behind him in good order. The Deputy Branch Secretary and Chief of Security Ou Guanghe then leaned forward and whispered in Guo Cunxian's ear that pretty much everyone had arrived.

Guo Cunxian stood up and turned round to look at his cadres. Oh, it wasn't just cadres that had come, half the village was here and there were still more people coming running. His cold gaze seemed to be as sharp as a knife, piercing other people's entrails. Those present, the most important people in Guojiadian, who would normally be happy to be laying down the law, were now squatting down and watching him. He was standing tall, like a thunderbolt wrapped in dark clouds, and nobody had a clue where the bolt would fall, or how bad it would be when it hit.

He now began to speak: "You see this, you see what game the children here in Guojiadian are playing? They are pretending to be beggars! If you don't get given food, you have all of your clothes ripped off you and you are punished by being made to kneel to the others. I played that game as a child myself, and I am sure that everyone else here did too, and who knows for how many generations our ancestors played this game too. Why have our parents and grandparents in Guojiadian for umpteen generations done this? One word: poverty. Right from birth we have had to learn how to beg, how to be happy when we have nothing, so that we can enjoy our begging. I'm asking you, is this what we want for our children and grandchildren? Are we going to carry on playing this game forever?"

Ah, so it was a meeting to discuss poverty. However, it couldn't be that simple. Guo Cunxian must be up to something.

The northern fields were silent. Everybody was looking straight ahead. A few of the children had become alarmed at having so many people watching them, and so the begging game finished with them running away. The only thing that could be heard was the sound of Guo Cunxian's loud and coarse voice: "Your families have been farming here for generations, and you've had to go out as beggars the whole time. Why don't you realise that you can't just rely on the land you have here to eat? Even if you don't care about anything else, just think about how many bachelors we have. Seventy something, isn't it? What's going to happen to them? Are we all just going to sit around and wait until these kids here grow up and add another thirty or forty to their number? Other places can sort themselves out. There are some villages to the south that have been really successful with opening businesses. Even the newspapers say there can be no political stability without the development of agricultural production, we cannot stimulate interchange without trade, and we cannot become prosperous without industry. Right now, we need to be seizing this opportunity, because this is not going to work if we delay. After all, the chemical works is already in business, and the manager, Chen Erxiong, says that at the end of the year he is going to be paying the village at least four or five million yuan."

The silence that had fallen over the northern fields was no more. People were now murmuring to one another, and Guo Cunxian stopped speaking.

He had deliberately tossed this bombshell, and now it was time for everyone to feel the effects. At the same time he had laid his lure, and it was time to see whether they took the bait and bit down on the hook. Was there ever a peasant who didn't want to earn a bit more money? It took a good long time before the northern fields were silent again.

When everyone had their eyes fixed on him again, Guo Cunxian continued: "The last few days I had to go away for a while because of some business related to the chemical works, and wherever I looked there were people building houses, and because they were building houses they needed materials, they needed steel. When these houses are finished they aren't going to be sitting empty, they'll need furniture. I have been in touch with various people about how this year our village could be opening a furniture factory and a plant for producing building materials. In addition to that there various other irons in the fire, ideas that need more research and planning. We are going to be bringing in a few Gods of Wealth from outside, of course, but we will still have our own God of Wealth, namely, the land. Everything was going well, everything was under control, and Guojiadian was on the verge of achieving something really big. And then out of the blue here comes trouble. Someone is determined to bring us down, and they write anonymous letters saying that I have embezzled a few hundred thousand yuan of funds set aside to buy equipment and legged it. You lot really have underestimated me! Do you genuinely think that I care about a few hundred thousand yuan? In a few years, Guojiadian is going to have some work units that are earning billions of yuan. There will be food processing plants, chemical works, electronics factories and who knows what else besides. There have also been other kinds of allegations made to the higher-ups that are currently under investigation. They say that we have interfered with land distribution to individual households, that we aren't carrying out the policies established by the central government, or saying that the businesses we have started are illegal, and that it is having a bad impact on agricultural production. I've been accused of all sorts of crimes. Now tell me, last year, was the harvest less than normal? Did we pay less in taxes? Were the tractors and pipes for irrigation and drainage not available for everyone to use? The towns and villages around here are all gossiping about how I am supposed to have been arrested I don't know how many times, and yesterday when I was on the bus coming back, there was someone who asked me if it was true that Guo Cunxian had committed suicide in a sleeping car on the railway. I said that I am Guo Cunxian. Are you telling me that I'm a liar?"

Some people laughed. Others found they couldn't laugh. The atmosphere was now becoming even more tense.

Guo Cunxian looked far from amused. His eyes were bloodshot but still as cold as could be. It seemed as though he was deeply indignant, but what he was actually doing was very cleverly turning the attention of the crowd in a different direction. He wanted to use the motive the investigation team had in coming to the village in the first place, to turn the attention of the people listening to him towards the bigger picture. He was determined to run the risk of mentioning government policy and economics.

"Here in China," he said, "everyone is busy with their gossip and lies, and then the Party leaders find themselves at their wits' end. The gossip has to be investigated, and then they have to punish people. Some have told me not to bother, what do I get out of it? If I were doing this for my own benefit, I would have been driven mad years ago! But no, I am doing this for us peasants. We are poor because we haven't had the opportunities, we are poor because we haven't been ambitious! We can't allow our children to carry on playing at being beggars. I, Guo Cunxian, am not the kind of person that takes being insulted lying down, and you can't bully me just because you feel like it. However, I can see as well as the next person that government policy has changed, but this doesn't scare me. If you get scared every time the wind blows in a different direction, you are going to get into trouble. When it comes to reform and opening up, you cannot be changing your mind every five minutes according to what the Politburo says, you need to think about what is best for the people. In the past, every mistake came about because they didn't care about what was best for the people: collectivisation, the Great Leap Forward, the Cultural Revolution, when everything was given over to agricultural production we were grindingly poor, and when everything was given over to class struggle, we were terrified.

"We've been treating Party leaders as if they were our own parents, and the moment they make an announcement we set about carrying it out. The result is that we've made every possible mistake, we've been the ones to get punished, and the leaders are still leaders, and their directives still change every year. Dealing with natural disasters, dealing with poverty, encouraging wealth creation, all of these things are easy. It is dealing with the stupid that is difficult. Dealing with stupid leaders is basically impossible. What are you supposed to do if the person you thought of as a loving mother starts treating you like a stepmother? Since we can't stop the leadership from doing dumb stuff any time soon, we have to deal with stupidity in our midst first, and we need a plan. My plan is that it would be best for all of us if we stopped being peasants. A village that doesn't look like one is the very best kind of village!"

Guo Cunxian knew how to get people worked up and how to create momentum, and he was prepared to show that he didn't agree with higher-ups and he could curse his subordinates in the cruelest possible terms. Of course, he was good at swearing at people, because in doing so you can kill them without having to pay the smallest price yourself. What boss fails to curse other people, when power is so often obtained by cruel words? However, it is true that not all bosses have been able to establish their authority solely on their ability to say horrible things to others. Guo Cunxian had decided to make a display of power and prestige on this occasion, because he believed that after today, he could put a stop to pretty much all the rumours about him and Guojiadian, as well as suppressing evil elements within the village, at the same time as giving his own supporters a bit of encouragement. He wanted everyone, whether they came from this village or not, to understand that he was still in charge of Guojiadian, just as he always had been. He was not going to let anyone get away with not understanding, or not admitting, that point.

Loads of folk had come to listen. Some of them were interested in what was going to happen to the village, but there were others who saw that something was occurring in the northern fields and had no idea what it was, so they came over to find out and then didn't leave again. Some people were squatting down, some were sitting, some were standing. Guo Cunxian wasn't worried that they'd be able to hear what he said, in fact, he was hoping that as many people as possible would hear him. The wrinkles on his face didn't hide the force of his personality, his ability to move the crowd. Now he turned the topic to praising Wang Shun, Chen Erxiong, Liu Yucheng, Qiu Zhantang and Jin Laixi, and having acclaimed each of his diehard supporters in turn, he announced that even at this moment, they were busy helping him plan for new developments, and that they had gone out of their way to bring business and investment into the village. He encouraged everyone in Guojiadian to take advantage of these opportunities. Anyone who set up a project would be responsible for carrying it out, whereby they could take advantage of the preferential policies for the entire village.

Finally, he deliberately chose to say a few words about Lin Meitang: "If your family is in trouble, is there anyone here who wouldn't turn to her? The head of the Women's Federation has to be friendly and kind, doesn't she? But she also has to be prepared to annoy people, she has to be able to cope with people getting angry and cursing her in public. After all, the worst job right now in the countryside is anything to do with family planning, and there, Lin Meitang has done her best, even if it hasn't always been successful." Guo Cunxian also explained that she had been really active in trying to help the villagers make money, and that she had written to family and friends in the city to encourage them to invest and set up factories in Guojiadian.

That was the kind of person Guo Cunxian was: the things that he wanted to hide, he would drag out and discuss with the largest possible number of people. Lin Meitang was sitting with the others, with a handkerchief spread out across the ground under her bottom. She found Guo Cunxian almost unbearably attractive at that moment, since she had always found him most sexy when he was angry or shouting at someone. Wave after wave of excitement broke over her, and she felt a burning desire.

Every member of the investigation team was present, except for Qian Xishou and the various people carrying out external enquiries. Everyone wanted to know what Guo Cunxian was going to say, and what he was up to. Guo Cunxian was perfectly well aware that by summoning everyone to this meeting he would be going into open conflict with the investigation team. However, it was not a choice, since if he didn't fight back, he was going to be in big trouble. He decided that he would have to try and come out in opposition. Perhaps there might turn out to be a way out for him. Of course, he could oppose them in various different ways: he could offer violent or gentle opposition, or both in turn. His good sense warned him that whatever he did he should not go for violent opposition, since that would be like throwing eggs at a rock. There had been so many mass movements in recent years in China, which had killed so many people, and it wasn't as though they didn't have evidence of his shortcomings. However, he had to encourage his subordinates and build up his own courage for the attack, because once it had begun, there would be no turning back. If they were determined to bring him down, then it was still not clear who was going to be the egg and who was going to be the rock. Besides which, it might turn out that the egg was unexpectedly hard, or that the rock had a very soft centre.

He noticed the arrival of the members of the investigation team, but even if none of them had turned up, he knew that what he said would quickly have been reported back to them. However, Guo Cunxian was not a stupid man, and when it came down to it, he was prepared to leave some room for manoeuvre.

"Today, there is someone I want to criticise in the strongest possible terms, and that's Ou Guanghe. He let his pig go, and then used that as an excuse to stand outside the window of the investigation team and hurl abuse. Are you completely stupid? Are you so obsessed by your problems with getting married that you've gone insane?

You've embarrassed everyone in Guojiadian, and you've caused me a lot of problems. Just think about it, how can I have someone as useless as you helping me out, carrying out my orders? It has ended up in a situation where it looks like I really could be pulling the strings behind the scenes, having made such a mess of things, who can say? Right here and now I am formally apologising to the investigation team on behalf of the Guojiadian branch of the Party and the village committee. I've also heard that, for the last couple of days, everyone has been hiding from the team. That's just not right. Since they have come to our village, we should be offering them a warm welcome and looking after them. If they are investigating us, they are helping us. When they finish their investigation and it turns out there aren't any problems, that will put a stop to all this gossip and it will show that we here in Guojiadian are innocent of any wrongdoing. Shouldn't we be grateful to them? I am hoping that Party members and cadres will lead the way, and that they will set an example to the masses in taking the initiative to help the investigation team with their enquiries, so that they can understand what has been going on here."

Given what he had been saying earlier, no one was expecting him to finish on such a note. He was being polite and showing off the intelligence and leadership ability underpinning his right to be in charge of this village. He was using the game played by the children as a mechanism for removing the bad feeling and sense of impending disaster that had been hanging over them. He was talking about the bigger picture and using national policy to dent the investigation team's arrogance. It sounded good, and it was very difficult to criticise him for it. The inhabitants of Guojiadian looked at one another, and some of them laughed bitterly. They seemed to have inferred something quite different from what Guo Cunxian had to say.

The investigation team had picked a really hard nut to crack this time.

Some of those present were carefully keeping an eye on Feng Hou, who was sitting on a stack of firewood towards the back. His square face was deliberately neutral: he looked as calm and peaceful as ever, with not the slightest sign of anger; the classic expression of a senior Party cadre. Occasionally he muttered something to Cui Daben in a low voice, and at other times he seemed detached. An Jinghui, on the other hand, was looking excited when at the end of the meeting she rushed up to Guo Cunxian: "Can I talk to you for a moment?"

Guo Cunxian stiffened. "What do you want to talk about?" he asked cautiously.

"We could talk about anything. We could talk about you! I find you really fascinating."

Guo Cunxian couldn't decide whether she was being sarcastic or whether this was a genuine compliment. However, it seemed impossible that a member of the investigation team would be complimenting the target of the investigation in public. He knew that he couldn't show the slightest weakness in front of his own villagers. "I don't think there is any point. Maybe you are used to investigating people and just don't care any more, and so when you see the people you are punishing suffer, or the place that you are punishing reduced to ruins, you find it amusing."

The inhabitants of Guojiadian standing around them burst out laughing at this.

An Jinghui gave a start. Did he really not appreciate that she was trying to be polite? Just now, she had been trying to get him to talk, and she had said every nice thing that she could think of, so why was he now having a go at her? She had rarely encountered a man who dared to speak to her like that, and she was now beginning to get cross: "Who's punishing you? If you haven't done anything wrong, you aren't scared when people bang on your door in the early hours!"

"I certainly haven't done anything wrong, but I don't like people banging on my door in the early hours, because it stops me sleeping."

Yet again the peasants burst out laughing.

An Jinghui was stopped dead in her tracks. She was totally unprepared for this country bumpkin being able to gain the upper hand, and she suddenly realised that she wasn't going to be capable of outsmarting him. She had thought that Guo Cunxian would be flattered by her making the first move to talk to him, and that he'd be grateful for this. Clearly she had underestimated his level of hostility. She was now silently cursing him: bastard, mother-fucker, how dare you speak to me like that. At the same time, she had to admit that she had brought this on herself by sticking her nose in where it wasn't wanted.

Guo Cunxian couldn't care less what she was thinking, he had already forgotten all about her. He walked away, talking with a couple of locals about something completely different. There were still a couple of peasants standing around watching An Jinghui, and they looked to be smiling, but they weren't necessarily feeling sympathetic towards her. To begin with, she was feeling humiliated, but the awkwardness was quickly replaced by a kind of terror. She could see in these people's eyes what they really thought of the investigation team. If someone had raped her or tried to murder her right at that moment, there probably wasn't a single person in Guojiadian who would have tried to rescue her.

She was looking for Lin Meitang but there wasn't a single woman among the people laughing. Instead she saw Ou Guanghe walking towards her with his gaze fixed upon her.

17

UPROARS

People like causing an uproar. On a large scale, there are revolutions and uprisings. You can have an enjoyable uproar at a wedding, or the Lantern Festival, or New Year's, or at any kind of party, really. And then there are the unpleasant occasions, like quarrelling with your spouse or with your family and friends. If you do it well, you create a friendly, lively atmosphere that everyone enjoys; if you don't do it well, then you are a trouble-maker, causing problems for everyone else, making a mountain out of a molehill. Even more seriously, you can cause a disaster, or you can make yourself sick over it.

The child known as Dog's Bollocks had run so fast that his little face was bright red. He had been all over the west side of the village, and the east, when he finally tracked down his father, Ou Guangming, out at the mill. Without a thought for all those standing around, the moment he came through the door, he started shouting at the top of his voice: "Uncle is in a foul temper again and he has broken our water tank. Mum's locked inside the house and doesn't dare come out, so she can't do any cooking. She wants you back home as soon as possible!"

Ou Guangming turned quite white, then turning around, he started running in the direction of his home. No matter what kind of facade he put on in front of others, when there was this kind of problem at home, it was going to look bad. But as he ran, he started to slow down, because he was becoming more and more frightened. Even if he ran all the way home, what would that achieve? Was he really going to kill his own brother? God knows he wanted to, but he simply didn't dare, besides which, if he got into a fight with his brother, it might well be him that got killed. No matter how much he might hate his brother, it was nothing compared to how much his brother hated him. How about shouting at Guanghe? Guanghe had a much louder voice than he did, and a much worse temper, and when he got to hurling abuse, he didn't care what he said or who was listening, he caused such an uproar that the whole village would come running to watch and enjoy the fun.

The problem was that Guanghe had never had the slightest sense of shame; he didn't get embarrassed, but he was bloody good at embarrassing other people! OK, so I can't kill him, and I can't hit him, and I can't shout at him. In fact, I can't do anything at all, not even tell him that he has behaved badly. It was all because Guanghe was quite convinced that everyone else in the family had done him wrong. He has made it obvious that he thought working for his older brother all these years was completely pointless, he hadn't bettered himself, and he hadn't even been able to get himself a wife. He was sure that, if he'd been on his own, everything would have worked out, and maybe he'd even have been able to save up enough money to get married.

Ou Guangming felt more and more discouraged, more and more confused. In the end, when he got back, the only thing he could do was try to cheer his wife up. In this family, his position was about the worst. In front of other people he could seem to be successful, it looked like he was in charge of things, and that no matter what happened he'd be able to cope: he could deal with whatever the hell it was that had happened. No matter how angry he got, he could control himself, and all the while he would be driving other people up the wall. Ou Guangming was well known as a pretty tough customer in Guojiadian, someone who could throw his weight about. The one thing that he couldn't do was to control his younger brother.

His younger brother was Ou Guanghe. If you are prepared to curse other people right outside the window of the investigation committee, is there anyone you'd be scared to hurl abuse at?

If Ou Guanghe had been stupid or insane, it would all have been so much easier. No villager or family member was going to complain or make fun of an insane person, so Ou Guangming could have taken charge, punishing him if he misbehaved. Even if he hit him or shouted at him, there wouldn't have been any gossip about it. Unfortunately, Ou Guanghe wasn't in the least bit insane, and he also wasn't stupid. The real problem was that he didn't have a wife. All of the men in the village who couldn't find a wife ended up being a bit weird sooner or later, and the most obvious sign of this was the way they became more and more ill-tempered, to the point where they would quarrel over nothing, and they didn't care who they annoyed. It had been the same for countless generations already. This was the reason why anyone who was having trouble with their disobedient sons would try to get them married off. Even real bastards could be controlled a bit better once they had a wife.

Men need women to make them tractable, but the bachelors in this village who couldn't get married for whatever reason, would regularly go back to their homes and have a quarrel, smashing pots and bowls, shouting and screaming. This was considered perfectly normal. The parents of such a man believed that they owed him something and so did his married brothers and sisters. As long as you were unmarried, you were in the right whatever you did, and you wouldn't be blamed no matter how much trouble you caused. The principle that bachelors were in the right had been handed down from one generation to the next, and they understood themselves that they could do what they liked, with the result that there were huge upheavals quite regularly, while less serious quarrels took place every day. Even if they had jobs, they didn't bother working at them, they spent their time building up fantasies, and when they set out to cause trouble, it quickly got quite out of control because, from their point of view, there wasn't any point in not making it all as unpleasant for everyone else as possible.

Ou Guangming's home was a three-room adobe house that he had inherited from his parents. He and his wife and child lived in the east room, Guanghe had the west room, and the middle one was the kitchen which was also Guanghe's favourite battleground every time he decided to cause a major family row. The floor of this room was sopping wet, and water was still collecting in some of the depressions, and the hopper of grain standing in front of the stove was also completely soaked. In the corner where the water tank normally stood there were now just the various smashed pieces of ceramic. Just opposite it was a rickety black table, which was leaning over at an angle suggesting that it would fall apart if anyone so much as touched it.

Ou Guangming was furious. With the water tank, this house really felt like a home, but now it was broken. Hey, Guanghe, if you've got the balls, why don't you go right ahead and smash all our cooking pots too? That would be a real energy-saving measure, because then we wouldn't be able to get anything to eat or drink, and we might as well just kill ourselves. Because Ou Guanghe was a cadre in the village, it wasn't possible for him to get a factory job, so that is why he didn't earn much. In addition, he had his own ideas about where his savings were going to go, so he didn't waste money on trying to make the house anything other than a hovel. He'd managed to make sure there was pretty much nothing that his brother could break in one of his rages. When it came right down to it, all of their problems stemmed from poverty. If he had enough money to buy Guanghe a wife, then the two of them could divide the property; he, for one, could think of nothing he desired more. He had it all planned out. It was going to take a while to save up, but that bloody Guanghe couldn't wait!

Ou Guangming felt a kind of ringing in his head and he was so furious that he was getting a headache. He wanted to find something to vent his anger on, so that he would feel a bit better. However, though his younger brother could just go and smash something, as the responsible older brother what could he do? Besides which, if he did anything of the kind it wouldn't work out well for him. He might as well hit his brother and shout at him openly so that everybody knew how much they couldn't stand each other! Since he hated him, why should he be afraid of him? At the very least, Ou Guanghe wasn't afraid; why should he be when he had absolutely nothing to lose? Ou Guangming might say that he wasn't afraid, but he knew perfectly well that this was just something he told himself: he had a wife and a son, he had responsibilities, and no matter how furious he was, he'd have to make sure that they were fed and cared for.

He shouted at Dog's Bollocks to carry the hopper out and then swept up the pieces of ceramic tank, righted the rickety old table, and put a few shovelfuls of earth into the dips in the floor where the water had collected. When the kitchen had been tidied up, he wanted to go to their room to tell his wife that it was safe to come out, so that she could restart the fire and cook some food. However, just as he got to the door of the east room, he stopped. No, that wasn't a good idea. He couldn't go to his own room first. It wasn't like this was the first time that this kind of thing had happened, where his wife had quarrelled with his younger brother. If he went first to his wife to sort things out, when he got back then Guanghe would say that he was showing favouritism to her, that he was nothing but a hen-pecked husband, and that the two of them were ganging up on him. He felt he had no choice but to go first to his brother's room, but he knew that this would really annoy his wife.

The room was in pitch darkness, but he could just about see where the huge mud-brick *kang* stuck out, occupying half of the room. Ou Guanghe was lying on top of the *kang* with his eyes shut, pretending to be asleep. Ou Guangming swallowed his anger and walked forward, ready to try and cheer him up: "What's up, Guanghe?"

Guanghe didn't lift his head or open his eyes. He spat out a single word: "Nothing."

"If nothing's happened, why did you smash the water tank?"

Ou Guanghe sat straight up, but his eyes slid away from his brother. "Who cares if I did smash it? Other people sneer at me, they look down on me, and then when I come home, I get sneered at as well. Is there anyone who cares about me at all? I wanted to say a few words to your wife, and she didn't pay any attention to me. Then I was going to help her with the firewood, and she got cross and refused to cook. In fact, she ran into her room and locked the door, refusing to come out. So I'm asking you, what do I count for in this family? You treat me like I'm some kind of idiot, and you're always trying to find a reason to get rid of me, so you can have the house to yourself. If you're determined to get rid of me, fine! Let's stop this farce of trying to live together and divide the property."

With his younger brother being so stubborn, Ou Guangming decided that his only option was to try to be as gentle as possible. "I know you're cross, but this just won't do. When dad was dying, he told us that we shouldn't divide the property until after you were married. It wouldn't be doing right by you otherwise."

"Great! You're trying to kill me!"

"What are you talking about, Guanghe?"

"You need me to explain? If it weren't for having to live with you lot, do you think I'd be like this today?"

With the conversation having taken this turn, Ou Guangming simply couldn't hold his temper any more. He could feel his pulse throbbing, and he was becoming light-headed: "OK, you're the one that wants this, so we'll divide it up. How do you want the property shared out?"

"There's nothing to divide other than this three-room house. You move out, and everything will be fine."

"You want the house?"

"Didn't you just say that you were going to do right by me? How am I supposed to get married if I don't have a house?" Ou Guanghe was quite confident of his rights in this matter.

"So where are we supposed to live?"

"Wherever you go and live, you are still a family. You can't ask me, a bachelor, to move out! If I leave then I'll be homeless, and everyone in the village will say that you forced me out. How do you think you are going to look then?"

Ou Guanghe was just trying it on, but he had hit Guangming's Achilles heel. This wasn't a division of property. He was trying to force his brother and sister-in-law out. However, bachelors are in a strong position when it comes to this kind of thing. If he spoke in a loud enough voice, he'd be able to leave his older brother with no way to fight back. Having already quarrelled so badly in the past, the two brothers had no affection for each other to fall back on, so he might as well carry on and push it through. Ou Guanghe laid his cards on the table: "If I'd been able to get married like you, I would have moved out ages ago. It's the old rule, whoever gets married has to move out. Why should you have the house so that I have to stay as a bachelor until the end of my days?"

With the quarrel having gone this far, it didn't matter any more if his brother was saying this in a fit of anger, or whether there was somebody else provoking him, Ou Guangming didn't want to say another word. There are three important things that happen in the lives of peasants: building a house, marrying a wife and having children. If his brother couldn't get married, then that branch of the family would die out, and that was a responsibility that he had no wish to shoulder. Ou Guangming wasn't angry any more, or rather, he was feeling sorry for himself and he was furious with himself. He was furious because he hadn't been able to do anything, he simply didn't have the money, and at over thirty years of age, he couldn't even make sure that his wife and son had a place to rest their heads. "OK," he said, resentfully. "Within the next three months, I'll hand the house over to you."

When Ou Guangming went into the other room, his wife, Liu Yumei was sitting on the *kang* sewing. She was a good tailor, so there were plenty of people who wanted her to make clothes for them. As usual, she didn't look at her husband, nor did she speak to him, because she was waiting for him to complain. She might listen to his complaints, but then if she didn't want to, she had plenty say about how annoying his brother was, in which case, having cried and shouted a bit, it would be his turn to comfort her. She was busy with her own work, since she was trying out a new style, so there she was spreading out the fabric, turning it over and then marking it out. Pretty soon a spring coat for a village girl was all cut out and ready to sew, and her husband still hadn't said a word. She was starting to find this kind of odd. "What's wrong? I thought you were going to talk to your brother?"

Ou Guangming sat down on a stool next to the *kang* and put his head in his hands. "I haven't talked to him. Even if I did, he'd do the same thing tomorrow. When will there be an end to it?"

Since her husband wasn't complaining, she was beginning to feel a bit concerned: "What do you have in mind?"

"Dividing the property!"

"Dividing the property?" Liu Yumei wasn't entirely displeased at this idea. She had often thought how nice it would be to live quietly with her husband, if only they could get rid of his horrible brother and all of the problems that he caused. When she got angry, she had thought a lot about this, but no matter what, no matter how much she wanted this, she knew that these words could not come out of either her mouth or that of her husband. She had to turn round and try and encourage her husband to make peace with his brother. "How on earth is someone as lazy and foul-tempered as Guanghe going to survive if you divide the property? He's going to get himself into trouble and then people will say that it is all your fault, or mine because I was too narrow-minded to cope with a bachelor brother-in-law."

"The thing is that, even if we don't want to divide the property, we are not going to have a choice, since it was his idea. And it is not him who is being forced out, it is him forcing us out!"

Liu Yumei didn't understand what he was talking about.

Ou Guangming didn't dare look his wife in the eye. This kind of division was nothing but bare-faced robbery, and even the most gentle of women wasn't going to agree to it. However, he had to tell her the truth. "He wants this house and I've agreed. If Dad was still alive, we'd have had to move out anyway. Think of it as though he were still with us."

Liu Yumei could never have imagined that this would be the outcome of their quarrel. Although her husband had not said a word of complaint, she now began to complain about herself: "This is all my fault, all my fault. He was just shooting off his mouth, it wasn't like he was really going to do anything to me. I shouldn't have shouted at him like that, I shouldn't have annoyed him."

Ou Guangming was sitting right by the *kang*. He stretched out one hand and patted his wife's shoulder: "What did he do?"

Liu Yumei sighed. Then she began to explain what had brought all of this about. This afternoon when he left the house he was in a really good mood, and he said that Guo Chuanwu and Ou Guangyu were going to introduce him to a possible wife: they were going to meet this afternoon. Then a little bit later, Dog's Bollocks came back to tell me that the two bastards had decided to 'introduce' Guanghe to a sheep, and they told him that in other countries that kind of thing is perfectly OK, so they were going to hold the marriage ceremony and put them in bed together right then and there. When Guanghe came back he seemed a bit strange. There was a nasty look in his eyes and he kept staring at me. He was also talking rubbish. He said that in lots of poor parts of the country, where men can't get married, two brothers share the same wife. On odd-numbered days she sleeps with the older brother and on even-numbered days with the younger brother, or else it's half the month with one and half the month with the other. He said that's what married men with serious health problems used to do all over the Northeast, and they still got to sleep on the *kang* with their wives. Then he asked how come he couldn't even match up to a sick man? He used fetching firewood for me as an excuse to grab my leg, and then he was feeling up my arm, and the whole time he was saying the most disgusting things. I got goosebumps all over just listening to him. I wanted to get away from him, but he was determined to stop me. Whichever way I moved he was right there with me, and I got so cross that I ran into my room and locked the door. He was right outside trying to beat down the door. I was really scared and didn't dare move. Then a little while later he smashed the tank.

Ou Guangming was looking black with fury. This time he really was going to kill him! "Fine! I'm glad we're leaving, because otherwise one of these days I'd have to kill him, before he really gets us into trouble."

Liu Yumei didn't dare say another word. After all, she understood her husband's temper, not to mention that of her brother-in-law. She decided to change the topic of conversation: "When we move out, where are we going to live?"

"Yumei, you really made a terrible mistake when you married me." Ou Guangming would have been happy if he could have found a crack to hide in. He couldn't even look at his wife as he outlined his plans for their future. "It's easy to find somewhere to live right now. After all, we don't have to go and beg Guo Cunxian and Wang Shun to get permission to build ourselves a house. However, we can't do that, because then the people in the village would imagine we were hiding from my brother. Guanghe has been a right little pest ever since he was born. Everybody in the village knows that he is quite stupid and impossible to deal with, and those in the know would quite understand that it is him throwing us out, but those who don't know the full story would say that we are trying to get away from him. You've been a wonderful wife to me, and I don't want other people to think they can say a word against you. So, we are going to have to suffer for a few months, living in a hut in the fields outside the village, to make sure that absolutely everyone here knows the truth. Then, come the autumn, I promise you that I will build us a new brick house to move into."

Liu Yumei thought that her husband's idea sounded perfectly sensible, and she did actually have some savings of her own, which at one time had been set aside with a view to helping Guanghe buy himself a wife. She wasn't quite sure, however, that she wanted to spend it on building a house. "We'll do as you say," she said, "and you don't need to worry about me. It's not as though I haven't been through bad times before. He's your own brother, whether you divide the property or not, and you don't want to lose face over this. Could you go and get me two buckets of water and I'll cook some food. Once it's ready you can call Guanghe to come and eat. Until the property is divided, you are in charge of this household. Once we move out, if he wants to come round to our place to eat, he's going to have to go down on his knees and beg. He may be a right bastard, but at least we know how to behave!"

This was the busiest time since the investigation team had arrived at Guojiadian. Ever since Guo Cunxian had held that meeting of his out at the northern fields, it seemed like all the inhabitants of Guojiadian had agreed that they needed to form a long line outside the office to report their problems to the team. They announced that they had come to help the investigation, and there were plenty of them who refused to speak to anyone other than the team leader. From the moment Qian Xishou opened his eyes in the morning there was a long queue of villagers waiting to see him outside, and he was so tired that he couldn't summon up the energy to go for one of his usual early morning runs. In fact, on some days he didn't even have time to eat. If he got painfully hungry, he would make some excuse to go back to his room and hide there while he ate a little, while the peasants waiting to report problems to him squatted down outside the door. The investigation team would throw open the doors early in the morning, and it would not be until late into the night that they could close them again.

Each of the peasants had their own idiosyncrasies. Some were very mysterious. They would lean forward and whisper in your ear, as if the problem they were reporting was a matter of national security. Some of them shouted, and they would be there inflating their lungs for a good bellow the moment they got through the door: "I'm here to report a problem. Guo Cunxian, the secretary of the Party branch in this village, has been involved in feudal superstition and building a personality cult." It sounded serious, like the kind of thing they should be looking into, so the investigation team were quite pleased. "Last year, Jin Laosi built a new house right here in the village and then he got married. Then at New Year's he didn't hold a ceremony for the Stove God, but he put up Guo Cunxian's photograph instead. He said that praying to Guo Cunxian was working out much better for him than praying to the Stove God. Does that count as a problem?"

"Did Guo Cunxian ask Jin Laosi to do this?" Qian Xishou asked.

"I'll bring Jin Laosi along and you can ask him yourself."

Jin Laosi had a loud voice, and they could hear him shouting long before he arrived: "Why can't I do that if I want? Are you telling me that it is illegal to have a photograph of Guo Cunxian up in my house? As far as I'm concerned, I have a lot of time for anyone who makes my life easier, and if someone gives me the opportunity to earn a bit of money, I'm happy to honour them like I would the Stove God. The year before last I suggested that the village start a mill, and Secretary Guo took up my recommendation and put me in charge of it. The mill has earned a bit of money, which means I've been able to build a new house and get married, but what's that to do with you? Are you jealous? Are you angry? If you find it annoying that I'm doing so well, you are just going to have to suck it up."

"Why should I be angry? I'm talking about the principle of the thing."

When the pair of them started quarrelling, Qian Xishou had to calm the two of them down, and afterwards he was able to ask Jin Laosi: "Did Guo Cunxian know that you were worshipping him in this way? Or did someone encourage you to do this?"

Jin Laosi hastened to reassure him: "Guo Cunxian knew nothing about it at all, and I hope that the investigation team won't say a word about what happened today. If he knew that I had his photograph up like that, there'd be all kinds of trouble!"

Qian Xishou didn't understand this. "Why?"

Jin Laosi lowered his voice: "It could result in him dying younger than necessary. After all the Stove God is a god, and it is only after you die that you can become a god, right?"

At this point, someone right at the back started to shout: "Haven't you people finished yet? Why are you monopolising the investigation team like this? Isn't it time to let someone else get a word in?" The peasants who had just arrived wanted to tell Qian Xishou about something quite different, which seemed to be significantly more serious than putting up a photograph of Guo Cunxian for worship.

Peasants are exceptionally concerned about lineage. If you don't have children then your family line gets cut off, which was called 'the end of the lineage'. Traditionally, it was said that your ancestors must have done something dreadful and that is why your generation didn't have any children. Although it wasn't considered suitable at this time to mention this traditional understanding of the situation, every family was still deeply concerned about manpower. Whether any individual household did well or not was basically dependent on manpower, and because they all understood this to be the case, everybody wanted sons. If the first baby was a girl, then all hopes were fixed upon a second baby, and there were plenty of women who got pregnant in secret. How do you think Guo Cunxian punished them? He would convene a meeting for the entire village and then complain about how couples with a daughter wanted a few sons, but those with sons thought about having a daughter, and then they would want to have both, until you have families with five sons and two daughters. Where was this all going to end? But the national family planning programme wasn't set by me: there are rules for the city and rules for villages, and if any village has even one baby beyond its quota, then the branch secretary gets fired, so if you insist on having a second baby then I am going to lose my job. If you have a problem with me being the Party secretary here then just say so, you don't have to go about it in this underhand fashion! Who could do anything to him when he was busy attributing motives like that? So any woman who got pregnant a second time was forced to have an abortion. Guo Cunxian really is a right bastard! Who cares whether he stays as Party secretary or not, and how could that compare in importance with whether a family gets a son?

"I want to report another problem. The Party in our village is still engaged in 'extreme left-wing' activities. Think of what is happening elsewhere in the country, but in Guojiadian we are still attacking the rich, while there are fears about making any kind of investment. People here are still being encouraged to be proud of their poverty. The more left-wing you are, the better. If you pretend to go along with this you can get away with anything, that's how you get power round here."

They were excited and impassioned, but Qian Xishou found himself feeling more and more uncomfortable. This was not because he was reading too much into the situation; just think about the kind of problems that the peasants were reporting! Who exactly were they complaining about? Were they reporting problems about Guo Cunxian, or were they actually trying to get at the investigation team? Qian Xishou was not a man given to introspection. He liked to come down on his suspects like a ton of bricks, but this time he kept wondering to himself if there wasn't something wrong with his own attitudes. Why was it that every time people wanted to talk about some sign of 'extreme left-wing' activities, they would insist on discussing it with him? Could it be that in their minds, the investigation team was 'glorifying poverty', that they thought 'the more left-wing the better', and that they were just a bunch of overly suspicious hypocrites?

No matter how much he kept himself on a tight rein, Qian Xishou was finding it very difficult to cope with this situation. It seemed as though someone, or to give him a name, Guo Cunxian, was pulling the strings from behind the scenes, and he was using a rotating cast of peasants first to confuse him and then to lay siege to the entire investigation team. To begin with, he did not have the experience to deal effectively with the sudden enthusiasm displayed by the inhabitants of Guojiadian. When they finished making their complaints, he had been asking them further questions, and encouraging them to explain in further detail, questioning them on specific points. The people who were so helpful were actually busy with their red herrings. They weren't going to tell him anything in the least bit useful, but they did take up every moment of his time.

The other investigation team members weren't idle either. In order to ensure that everyone who came to make an accusation was treated with the appropriate warmth, they were kept busy right through the day until late into the night. They didn't have any time to rest, they couldn't leave to gather evidence or make further investigations, they couldn't talk to the people that they needed to talk to, and the office was packed with people endlessly coming and going. The investigation team headquarters felt like a truck stop, with the team members reduced to the level of waiters and waitresses.

They couldn't stop for a moment to exchange information. Of course, they weren't bothered about being busy nor about being tired: what where they here for, after all? The crucial thing was whether they were going to get anything of value out of this exercise and was it going to be worth it? After a few days of this kind of thing, the members of the team knew perfectly well that they were being bamboozled. The peasants were using the opportunity offered to them to 'complain' about Guo Cunxian's activities, but this was actually being used to get him off the hook. First Peasant A would come in to tell you all about something completely pointless, and when he'd gone, you'd have Peasant B on the same subject, and when he'd finished, it would be Peasant C's turn. The team had heard the same thing over and over again, and if you tried to cut them short and say that you already knew about this, then they'd glare at you and say something about how you didn't want to listen to peasants reporting serious problems. Since saying anything was a waste of time and would only get you into trouble, you kept your mouth shut and let them get on with it. Who would have thought that this was what being part of an investigation team entailed? You had to listen to something that you didn't want to hear, that you'd already heard half a dozen or more times before, and you were perfectly well aware that they were doing it on purpose but you still had to appear to be sincerely interested... it really was a form of torture, and it was ruining the morale of the entire investigation team.

Once they had got the last round of complainants out of the place in the evening, the investigation team didn't want to say another word, and they couldn't keep their eyes open for another minute. They just lay down on the *kang*, without even bothering to wash their faces or brush their teeth. Their heads were spinning to the point where it was impossible to sleep. Wu Lie cursed without even opening his eyes: "Fuck! What kind of investigation is this?"

Luo Denggao also had his eyes shut. Maybe he was trying to provoke him, or maybe he simply didn't have the energy to try to calm him down: "Well, it's a kind of investigation. We've found out what the people here want, and we know how little we can do, and quite how powerful Guo Cunxian is, and we've got another round coming tomorrow so we need to get to sleep as soon as possible."

This was all great fun for the residents of Guojiadian. Where in the past, the investigation team had been watching the uproar in the village, it was now the turn of the village to enjoy the problems of the investigation team. Everywhere you turned there were peasants pointing and laughing, whispering in each other's ears, giggling away, telling each other all kinds of gossip and rumours about Qian Xishou.

Qian Xishou was able to grab Feng Hou and take him off on his own to a quiet corner, to discuss the situation. "Right now we need to be on the attack. The villagers have had their minds disturbed, there is a lot of gossip flying around, and so we ought to immediately convene a meeting for everyone to attend, at which we announce that Guo Cunxian is being stripped of his position as branch secretary of the Party because he has been instigating people to cause trouble for the investigation team, and interfering with our work. He is a nasty piece of work, and if we don't bring him down, it will be impossible for the investigation team to carry on here in Guojiadian."

Feng Hou could see that Qian Xishou had made his decision, and to give himself time to think, he spoke more slowly than usual: "Mr Qian, coming here to make an investigation is one thing, but it is quite another if you are really going to punish one of the cadres. This is something that ought to only take place after the final results of the investigation have come in, and it should wait until you have received permission from the Municipal Party Committee and the County Party Committee. I am afraid that the investigation team doesn't have the right to do this. Besides which, the investigation is still ongoing, and you need to think very carefully about stripping the office of the branch secretary of such a big village as Guojiadian. As the old saying goes, this is a place with ten problems and ten difficulties. I don't remember all of them, but I think it was problematic thinking, problematic personal connections, problematic geography, as well as housing problems, and then there were difficulties with getting enough to eat, difficulties with getting warm clothing, difficulties with getting drinking water, difficulties with growing enough food, difficulties with getting married, difficulties with getting any decent cadres in.

"In the past, the village head used to change every five minutes, and whoever we put in didn't last long, and then we got Guo Cunxian who has managed to hold the place together for a few years, and now there are signs of good things happening in this village, and people are beginning to sit up and pay attention. If you want to strip him of office, that's easily done, but who is going to take over? I am told that you don't actually have evidence of any wrongdoing in spite of all the complaints, including what you were just talking about, the gossip flying around and the people disrupting the work of the investigation team. Are you sure that you can prove that Guo Cunxian is behind all of this? If you are going to hold a general meeting and dismiss him, how are you going to explain this to the masses?"

Qian Xishou didn't agree with this at all: "I can get permission from the Municipal Committee, and as for evidence, there are eyewitnesses, since a couple of days ago he held a big meeting at which he openly encouraged villagers to assist the work of the investigation team. The peasants here are 'helping' in the way that he told them to! If someone wasn't doing this deliberately, if he wasn't there supporting them, do you think that the peasants would have suddenly come to take over our investigation headquarters the way that they have? Would they dare to scream and shout like this over nothing? There are a number of people who have been telling us exactly the same thing, so it is clear that someone has been providing them with a script. Guo Cunxian has nothing to fear, he's in charge here, and he has already become the single biggest obstacle to our investigation work. If we don't get rid of him, those who would like to report real problems won't dare to come, and people who have a problem with Guo Cunxian himself are even less likely to report them to us."

Qian Xishou was speaking in a very determined tone, but Feng Hou was equally strong in defence of his own convictions: "We've come to Guojiadian to make a proper investigation, not to listen to gossip, and in particular we should not be tricked into imagining that every time someone says something bad about Guo Cunxian they are telling the truth, and if they say something good about him they are lying."

This was a very clever thrust on the part of Feng Hou, and Qian Xishou knew that it would be impossible to bring his deputy round to his own way of thinking, so that the investigation team presented a united front. However, this gave him just the excuse he needed for his report back to the Municipal Committee. If they were going to investigate Guojiadian, they would have to first investigate problematic thinking on the part of team members. Furthermore, it wasn't just that the team was having problems working well together, somewhere within the organisation there was a person deliberately messing up the investigation from the inside. As far as Qian Xishou was concerned, this was the most aggravating thing, but he couldn't tell anyone about it. He knew that right now people in Guojiadian were having a whale of a time gossiping about him and laughing at him for his physiological secrets, and that was something that could only have begun from within his own team.

If you want to investigate other people, you first have to consider whether there are any aspects of your own life that you would be afraid to have brought to light. The real difficulties and defeats in official life come from when someone has discovered your secrets. Secrets are weak points, and in any kind of struggle, they are likely to come to public attention. The more of other people's secrets that you know, the more proactive you can be. If someone else knows the things that you need to keep secret, your life is in their hands. This principle is one that everyone understands, and everyone tries to keep their own secrets safe. Is there anyone in this world who doesn't have secrets? Qian Xishou was really the kind of person who didn't have any secrets at all, and as a political animal, he ought not to have had secrets. So how could it be that he was in this kind of situation now? He couldn't have explained it himself, and the only thing he could say was that, if you have a secret, you cannot expect to keep it forever.

Of course, by the same token, if you are all set to reveal someone else's secrets, they are going to fight to the death to stop you.

Qian Xishou sighed. He had made his decision. "Mr Feng, clearly even the two of us cannot agree on how to proceed. Tomorrow I will have to report back to the Municipal Committee and see what they say. They should get back to us within a couple of days, or a week at the longest."

"It isn't urgent," Feng Hou said cheerfully, "and you've been working so hard lately. You ought to go home and have a good rest."

Qian Xishou was now feeling really annoyed. Feng Hou hadn't seemed in the least surprised when he suddenly came out with his decision to report this back to the Municipal Committee, and he'd been grinning away when he suggested that he go home and rest. Could it be that he simply didn't care, and that he wasn't at all concerned that he might complain to the Municipal Committee about him? Maybe Feng Hou had foreseen this move ages ago, and would like to see him leave and never come back. He didn't know whether Feng Hou was an inveterate schemer or simply completely brass-faced? He was sure he was up to something, but he just didn't know what.

Qian Xishou took refuge in conventionalities: "You'll have to take charge of the work of the investigation team, and punishing Guo Cunxian will have to wait until after I get back." He added this last sentence in order to make it clear to Feng Hou that he was still determined that Guo Cunxian should be dealt with severely, and to let him know that things weren't over yet!

As to whether things were over or not, only time would tell, but the situation right now was one that allowed Feng Hou to relax a bit.

With Qian Xishou going like this, clearly he had decided not to fight with the odds against him.

With Qian Xishou gone, all of a sudden the entire village decided to leave the investigation team alone. In fact, they didn't see a soul from one day to the next. Guojiadian was a peculiar place, and undoubtedly there were more people behind this than just Guo Cunxian. One shouldn't imagine that just because Qian Xishou said that he was going to call a general meeting of the entire village and put all the blame for messing up the investigation on Guo Cunxian that he thought this to be true. The fact is that, even in the investigation team, there were plenty of people who didn't believe that this was all Guo Cunxian's work; he couldn't possibly be that stupid! It was quite possible that there was someone quietly fanning the flames because they didn't get on with Guo Cunxian, and the objective was to get rid of him, and that by annoying and attacking the investigation team they were hoping that Guo Cunxian would take the blame, and that he would get into such serious trouble that he would never be able to prove his innocence.

Who could this person be? They couldn't think, and until they knew that, what happened at Guojiadian would remain unsolved.

After Qian Xishou's departure, the other members of the investigation team didn't show their faces much, and it wasn't quite clear if some of them had taken advantage of this opportunity to slope off home, or whether they were holed up inside their rooms looking through the accounts, or perhaps chatting and playing cards. There weren't any quarrels between the inhabitants of Guojiadian and the investigation team during this time, since they seemed to be leaving each other alone. However, although it appeared that everyone was relaxed, it was quite clear that there was more going on beneath the surface, and that neither side was clear what the other was up to or what they were going to do next. When people don't know what is going on they are inclined to think the worst: Qian Xishou must have had some evil plan in mind and that is why he had gone back to the city. He was testing the waters, going to get warrants, and when he came back, Guo Cunxian would definitely be for the chop.

But would Guo Cunxian just sit there and do nothing when someone else was out to get him?

That night it was pitch black.

By contrast, the stars seemed unusually bright, scattered across the sky, shining together and yet alone, keeping forever a set distance from each other. Liu Yumei felt herself to be in the same position, and yet she was even more isolated than a star, hiding as she did in the darkness. She had never experienced a night this black before, and the darkness spread out in all directions, deep and terrifying, surrounding the little house in which she lived with impenetrable blackness. The hut itself was also black, and it was only when she stood outside that she could see a few twinkling lights coming from the village. It was warm there, there were other people around, but it was far away, as distant as the stars. During the day she didn't mind it, but once it got dark she felt that she had been thrown out of Guojiadian, that other people had given up on her.

The darker it got, the more frightened she was about lighting a lamp. Spring was coming and the weather was warming up, so she was afraid that lamplight might attract foxes, weasels, bugs or centipedes. The very thought made her skin prickle with tension. Once dusk began to fall, Dog's Bollocks would grab hold of a corner of her skirt and simply refused to let go, hanging on her like a dead weight. The kid was terrified, afraid of the dark and unaware of what dangers might be lurking out there. Peasant children are brought up on ghost stories from birth, and living here out in the fields you were far from the village and close to the cemetery, or to put it another way, you were far from people and right next to the ghosts. This was just the sort of place that was likely to be haunted.

After they moved out of the village, Ou Guangming did his very best to be there at night with his wife and child so that they wouldn't be frightened to live there. He brought out the hunting gun that he had kept from his time in the local militia and propped it up against the mud wall of the hut. It didn't matter whether the gun was actually useable or not, it was there to scare people off and make his family feel a bit better about being out there. In a crisis, at the very least it could be used like a club in self-defence. What he hadn't anticipated was that when he brought out the wretched gun and showed it to his wife and son, not only were they not cheered up by the sight, they were now utterly convinced that he was terrified of living there too. If a grown man, the head of the family, felt the need for an unloaded gun to bolster his morale, then how could women and children not be scared? Liu Yumei now wasn't just worried that a lamp shining all by itself out in the darkness was going to attract poisonous insects and wild animals, she was terrified lest it bring them to the attention of two-legged criminals.

At the back of the little hut there was a large road heading to Dongxiang, which ran through the western fields, and this was where the Dahua Iron and Steel Company was based. People from other parts of the country were often to be found on this highway, quite apart from the fact that Dahua Steel trucks roared past day and night, shaking the little hut from top to bottom and covering everything in a cloud of dust. Who knew whether one of these days someone would decide to break into this little hut? And then there were the thugs from the village. If they knew that Ou Guangming was away, what was Liu Yumei supposed to do if they came out here to rape her? The door was made from a few planks of rotten wood, and would open with a single kick! Even if she screamed herself hoarse, there wasn't anyone to hear. She could shout for help until kingdom come. For as long as she could remember Liu Yumei had been bullied and abused, so it was natural for her to think the worst whatever happened, and she kind of enjoyed scaring herself in this way. The more she scared herself the more terrified she became, and the more terrified she became, the more her imagination ran wild.

During the last couple of days Ou Guangming had been busy working on his own plans and so, once he had eaten supper, he would tell his wife to clear everything away and get their son to bed, since he would creep out as soon as the two of them were asleep. However, as soon as they moved into this little dark hut, Dog's Bollocks had developed a tiresome new habit: he wouldn't go to bed unless his parents went to bed too, and if someone wasn't cuddling him, he wouldn't go to sleep. Really, he was too old for this kind of thing, but it seemed like the older he got, the more tiresome he became. Ou Guangming was so cross he really felt like giving the kid two hard slaps.

Liu Yumei could see what her husband was thinking, and she wasn't the kind of woman not to be considerate of others, but she didn't say anything about how he should just go. The fact is that when it got dark she really didn't like to be alone to look after her son in that horrible dark little hut. At the same time, she was quite well aware that whatever Ou Guangming was up to wasn't right. The busier he got, the more chances there were that he would get himself into serious trouble. Ou Guangming was now the security officer, and although he couldn't control his own brother, he interfered in absolutely everything else going on in the village. In the past, when they had all been engaged in class struggle, he'd done fine, he could say whatever he liked to people and they didn't dare not listen; they were terrified of him. But who cared now about what a security officer said? The previous security officer hadn't been able to protect his own son, who'd ended up being thrown out of Guojiadian. Right now everyone was complaining about the way Party cadres interfered and pried into other people's business. They were busy with pickpockets but left thieves and muggers alone. They were happy to tackle a few hooligans but gangsters got away with murder, and while they were content to make life miserable for the little guy they wouldn't say a word against their superiors no matter what they did. Once Ou Guangming had crossed almost every single person in the village, what was going to happen to him then? There were plenty of people complaining about him already, saying that he was nothing but one of Guo Cunxian's running dogs. Was this a good way to proceed? Everybody hated him. If you have a good life with enough to eat, even if you don't get much time off, you can still relax. But now he had been forced to live outside the village by his own brother, who had bothered to ask after you, or was worried about you? Who stood up for you and took your side? For all you know, they are all hiding from you and laughing about what has happened.

Liu Yumei had been thinking along these lines for quite a few days now, but she wasn't actually going to put these thoughts into words. She didn't want to harm her husband's sense of self-respect and, even more than that, she didn't want her husband to yell at her and say that she was ungrateful. Way back when, it had been because Ou Guangming came from a good background and was a member of the village militia, that he'd been able to protect her older brother and her. One had to admit that in those years, Ou Guangming had helped the Liu family a lot and it had seemed like they were destined to be together. He didn't mind her family background, and she didn't care about the fact that his family was poor. They really were made for each other. But was she really happy like this? She had never known what happiness was. Did she regret their marriage? Not really. She'd given birth to a son, and the life that she lived wasn't that much worse than any of their neighbours, and Ou Guangming was important in the village, he had status. Liu Yumei wasn't in any way a harridan, she couldn't shout and scream at anyone, so in order to make sure that Ou Guangming stayed at home, she just came up with a string of murmurings, where she mentioned one problem after another, because until he had fixed them he couldn't possibly leave.

"Right now it's fine having the three of us crammed into this little hut, but once the weather starts to warm up, aren't we going to fry?"

"What do you think happens when three people stay here in the ordinary way of things? I've never heard of any of them ending up fried."

"In the summer, it's going to get really hot out here, and we're going to be eaten alive by the mosquitos."

"We can kill them if they come into the hut, and outside we can have smudge pots. But who is bothered by mosquitos at this time of year?"

"But what about the winter? Without a *kang* aren't we going to be frozen into icicles?"

"What is it with you today, Yumei? I've already told you that we'll be moving into a new brick house in the autumn. It is cold out here. How about we move into the hut and carry on this conversation lying down on the mat? Look at Dog's Bollocks, he can hardly keep his eyes open."

Dog's Bollocks suddenly opened his eyes: "I'm not tired. The moment I go to sleep you're going to leave. Do you think I don't know that?"

"So what if you know that? You're a man, and your mother is relying on you, so how can you let her down?"

Dog's Bollocks had dreams of becoming a hero, but when he looked out at the all-encompassing darkness, he got scared again and decided to prevaricate: "I'm only little, so what happens if a ghost appears? Or if someone comes and attacks us?"

Ou Guangming was a bit irritated by this: "There's no such thing as a ghost. Have you ever seen one?"

Liu Yumei also tried to cheer up her little boy: "There aren't any ghosts here, and nobody is going to come and attack us. I just wanted to step outside and look at the stars because it was stuffy in the hut, and I couldn't breathe properly. Look at how pretty the stars are today. You can see loads more than usual and they are really bright."

Ou Guangming sighed heavily: "I promise you, come the autumn we are going to be moving into a new house."

"That's just a castle in the air. How are you going to get us a whole new house?"

Ou Guangming was feeling a bit irritable and tense now: "I knew you wouldn't believe me, so I wasn't going to say anything until it was all fixed up." He now explained his plan: for the last couple of days Guo Cunxian had been discussing setting up a construction company at Guojiadian with Jin Laixi, and they'd already contracted for a big project in Tianjin. But Jin Laixi doesn't have a good family background, so he needs a Party cadre to go in with him, and I would like to go. While I'm gone, you are going to have to go back to your mother's. If there isn't any more serious trouble in the village, and if Guo Cunxian gets out of this, everything is going to be fine. If I'm a manager at the construction company, then I won't have to do very much, and when the workforce comes back, we'll spend a bit of money on buying the materials, and they can build a three-room house for us in the twinkling of an eye.

Yumei could see that he was serious about this, and she was happy, but at the same time worried. The happiness was in discovering that he had understood that he was going to have to do some work, but she was worried because Ou Guangming had never had anything to do with house building. Building a house isn't something you should undertake lightly, because if something goes wrong people could get killed. "But you don't know anything about architecture, and you've never worked with bricks and mortar."

"Not again! We haven't even begun and you're finding things to worry about. It never seems to end. The architectural design is going to be done by them, we just need to see to the construction. If we have the plans and the money, we can get the experts that we need, not to mention the skilled workforce. This evening I've got to go and discuss things with Jin Laixi and Guo Cunxian, because time and tide wait for no man. Spring is when construction work has to begin."

"Well, you had better be off then." Liu Yumei took her son by the hand and went into the hut.

The child wasn't feeling very happy about this and shouted: "Dad! Come home as soon as you can!"

"I will." Ou Guangming was already on his way out as he said this. He was in a great hurry to get there because it was going to be this evening that he found out if this construction company was going to get off the ground. For many days now he'd been trying to push this good thing along, hoping to strike while the iron was hot, and praying that Jin Laixi wouldn't mess it up for him. Ou Guangming was sure that if this project was going to work out, Jin Laixi would have to be involved, at least at the outset. But he'd been to talk to him loads of times, and somehow Jin Laixi had not been willing to say the necessary words.

He was a slippery customer. Although he might look all meek and mild, deep down he was ready to take any opportunity to wriggle out of whatever it was. He was pretty sure that he had worked out what Jin Laixi was actually up to, and he didn't really want Ou Guangming to come with him as some kind of figurehead. He was thinking of going to Tianjin on his own and taking charge of everything himself. Then if things went wrong, he'd ask Ou Guangming to deal with it, but that wasn't going to happen. Ou Guangming had quite another idea of how this was going to work. He was planning to use this opportunity of going to Tianjin with the construction team to finally stop having to do all of these exhausting and pointless tasks around the village. He was confident in his own ability to deal with Jin Laixi. With someone like that, Guo Cunxian could cope, but if you tried it he wouldn't take you seriously. Sometimes with people like that you have to be pretty tough, and that was something he'd learned during struggle sessions. It was the only way to deal with people of his kind.

The reason why things get so complicated in this world all comes down to human relationships. Ou Guangming and Jin Laixi were both Guo Cunxian's strongest supporters, but because they were so much on his side, they couldn't stand each other. Maybe they were just natural enemies. Ou Guangming had got to his position through class struggle, while Jin Laixi had always been someone he'd struggled against, so even though Ou Guangming had actually protected Jin Laixi from the worst of it, he still had an intense antipathy towards anyone who had worked for the Party in those days. In addition to that, the two men had completely different personalities. Ou Guangming liked to shout at the top of his voice and glare, as if he were just about to come out with a stream of abuse at the least little thing. That kind of behaviour might scare other people, but Jin Laixi was getting to be somebody now, and he wasn't going to let Ou Guangming get away with putting one over on him with sheer bluster. Even more important, taking Ou Guangming to Tianjin with him was going to be a problem. The original contract had been negotiated by Jin Laixi, and there were plenty of aspects of the deal that neither side would be too happy to explain to a third party, so what would it look like if he now turned up with Ou Guangming glued to his side? Jin Laixi was going to be taking people back to Tianjin as the head of his own construction company, and he wanted to let the people who'd prevented him from going home see that he'd done well for himself without them. In fact, he might be able to grab a few good people from his old work unit. But when it came to the company, he had to have complete control.

However, as the situation stood right now, without Ou Guangming as a figurehead this construction company was never going to get off the ground, and there was an investigation team in the village getting up to God knows what. Who knew what would happen in Guojiadian in future? Ou Guangming might be a very useful card to play. He would just have to grasp the nettle. The fact that he didn't personally care for Ou Guangming was one thing, but to say so openly was quite another. Right now, Jin Laixi couldn't afford to annoy someone like that. Given that it seemed he was going to be lumbered with Ou Guangming whatever he did, Jin Laixi could only mutter to himself: what happens if he gets angry and kicks me in the teeth? Then he said to himself Ou Guangming wouldn't do that; he's a simple soul, really. He would realise that Jin Laixi had got hold of him, but he wasn't the kind of person to understand that he'd been baited and hooked. Running around like that after him, Ou Guangming had shown him plenty of respect, and Jin Laixi had now made up his mind that he'd have to hang his head and keep his eyes averted as he announced: "Guangming, as a senior member of the Party, I trust you, but with the situation being what it is, with the investigation team here, if Cunxian doesn't give the word, and if the local branch of the Party doesn't agree, I can't promise you anything."

This was actually an insult to Ou Guangming, but there was nothing he could do about it because Jin Laixi had hit the nail right on the head. He wanted everyone in the village to know that it was Guo Cunxian, and the local branch of the Party, that had decided to set up this construction company, and that they had appointed him as the manager. What did Ou Guangming have to offer in comparison? A private individual cannot expect the same treatment as a government official. On the other hand Ou Guangming now felt his worries roll away. He'd asked Guo Cunxian for permission to do this ages ago; otherwise he wouldn't have dared approach Jin Laixi. "That's what I was expecting you to say," he said, "so let's get going. Cunxian and the others are expecting us."

Ou Guangming dragged Jin Laixi round to Guo Cunxian's house, only to discover a thick cloud of cigarette smoke obscuring the entire place, and a host of people packed in there, some on the *kang* and some sitting on the floor. Ever since the investigation team had arrived in Guojiadian, Guo Cunxian had been operating out of his own home, deciding all aspects of life in the village from a corner of his own *kang*. When he spotted Jin Laixi coming through the door, Guo Cunxian immediately got up from his place on the *kang* and said cheerfully: "Laixi's here. Come and sit down."

Jin Laixi sat down on one edge of the *kang*. He'd arrived in the middle of a discussion, and the people sitting around were all much bigger wheels than him, so he couldn't get a word in edgeways. He just had to keep his head down and hear them out. Guo Cunxian quickly made the necessary decisions in response to the questions posed by these men, and then he allowed them to leave. The room emptied out. Now Guo Cunxian turned to face him: "Laixi, the local Party branch has already decided that we can establish a construction team here at Guojiadian, and I've already thought of a name for you. We'll call it the Guojiadian International Construction Company. We have big ambitions for it, and we are going to be building a new world. What do you think, Guangming?"

Ou Guangming was thrilled: "International sounds pretty grand to me!"

Jin Laixi agreed to this. Then Guo Cunxian continued: "I want Guangming to join you. From the professional point of view, you're in charge, but Guangming can help you out by keeping an eye on the workforce. Guangming's got his own problems. Since his brother threw him out of the house he doesn't have anywhere to live, and he's too proud to borrow a place from anyone else. I'm putting you in charge, Laixi, and this year you're going to have to build him a three-room house."

Jin Laixi was only too happy to agree. "If that's what you want, Cunxian, no problem. I can deal with it."

Guo Cunxian carried on speaking: "The two of you are also going to be in charge of the brick kiln. There will be some profit for you in selling bricks, and it will be beneficial for our whole project. The central government says we have a lot of work to do, and that the things that have gone wrong are going to need to be rebuilt. Rebuilding is construction, right? I think the construction industry has a great future in this country, and if we can really develop this, we can turn our brick kiln into a whole factory for producing building materials."

Jin Laixi now knew where he was, but he pretended to look uncomfortable. "You know my background, Cunxian. Is it going to cause you trouble to put me in charge, what with the investigation team still being here on the ground and all?"

"Well, Laixi, it seems to me that the village is going to be in much greater trouble if we can't employ anyone in Guojiadian who knows how to earn a bit of money. Do you think my position is necessarily any better than yours? Right now they're busy investigating me, and you might imagine from the way that some people are carrying on that I'm the worst villain ever to have come out of Guojiadian." Guo Cunxian was clearly very confident about what was going to happen, and as he spoke, he became quite as decisive as before. "From the perspective of class struggle, you're a rich peasant and a class enemy. From the perspective of people during the Cultural Revolution, you are a bad element who has been sent back to the countryside. But when we think about you from the modern commercial perspective, you are a very capable man with vital specialist knowledge, and you can benefit the economy of the whole of Guojiadian. I'm telling you, we need to move beyond the perspectives of class struggle and the Cultural Revolution when we think about other people. In this day and age we need to think about economics, and we should be looking at you from that point of view."

Jin Laixi was perfectly well aware of what kind of day and age this was himself, but he wanted the most important man in Guojiadian to say this to his face, to Ou Guangming's face, and with all the other senior cadres in the place in attendance. That would make his position in the construction team secure. However, he still felt that he had to hang his head, keep his eyes down, and let his feet hang off the edge of the *kang*. "Thank you, Mr Guo. Construction is a very important industry, and we can't afford to make any mistakes. I'm worried that I won't have the status to be able to give orders to my team and that they won't listen to me. If something goes wrong, what happens then? If I'm supposed to take responsibility, I'm afraid that I can't."

Jin Laixi had a point, but above and beyond that, he wanted to have some authority from Guo Cunxian to deal with Ou Guangming if he caused any trouble for him in future. If he couldn't command the obedience of his workforce, and Ou Guangming didn't know the first thing about construction work, and his only idea was to shout at people when he felt like it, how was he supposed to cope? They might not like to hear this, but he was going to put it to them straight. As it happened, Guo Cunxian had also already considered this point. "We've discussed this, and you are going to be the general manager. You'll be responsible for the company, and you'll be in charge of the project and the technical side of things. If you need to take control, you can. You are in complete charge. If something goes wrong, that's your fault. If you give orders and other people disobey them, then you can punish them according to the rules. Guangming, in his capacity as a Party cadre, is going to help you deal with political and ideological work, but he's got things to do back here in the village too, so he won't be able to spend much time in Tianjin. To put it bluntly, he's only going to join you as and when people are out to cause trouble for you."

Jin Laixi was very pleased. He hadn't expected Guo Cunxian to put things quite so frankly, and this made him feel confident in his position. He didn't need to say any more. If he had said another word, it would have been rude to Guo Cunxian and just made things more difficult for himself in future.

Having finally got rid of all of the visitors, Zhu Xuezhen passed Guo Cunxian a hot towel to wipe his face with, and then they put out the lights and went to bed. A good while later, while Guo Cunxian was still hovering on the edge of sleep, he thought that he could hear someone knocking on the door, which startled him into sitting straight up. Xuezhen wanted to get up herself and answer the door, but he pushed her back down. He pulled on his clothes, jumped down from the *kang* and went to open the door with an axe in his hand.

Standing in the door was Guo Cunyong. He'd been gone from the village for ages. Why had he suddenly come crawling back now? Some distance behind him, a small car was parked in the shadows, with the headlights blazing. A figure was standing in the light, which dazzled him. What the hell? He'd managed to get himself a car to drive him back here. He was just showing off!

Guo Cunyong thrust a bag into Guo Cunxian's hand, and then turned round to talk to the person standing in front of the car. How about you spend the night on the *kang* here, and then set off first thing tomorrow morning? The man wasn't happy with that, since he said that he had to be in Shandong the following day. Since you've got to where you wanted to go, I need to be on my way. Guo Cunyong said something about how, if that was the case, you should be off then, my home is just a few steps away. I'll go there once I've had a few words with Mr Guo here.

So Guo Cunyong had come to talk to him even before going to his own house! At this time Guo Cunxian wasn't going to think positively about anything that happened to him, so he immediately started jumping to the very worst conclusions. Guo

Cunyong had arrived in a car in the middle of the night and wasn't going straight back to see his family. Had something bad happened? Or had he perhaps heard something important? The questions were tumbling over each other in his mind as he led Guo Cunyong into the house. By that time Zhu Xuezhen had also dressed and was putting all the lights on.

After they got indoors, Guo Cunyong took out a fashionable open-collared sweater from his bag and said that this was a present for Zhu Xuezhen. There was also a beige scarf to go with it. Xuezhen felt embarrassed and tried to refuse the gifts, saying that she couldn't possibly wear something so lovely, and suggested that he keep them for his own wife. Guo Cunyong said that he'd buy his wife something nice some other time; I just can't stand the way that she goes gabbing on about things. If she has anything new she has to show off about it until the whole village gets to know. He then pulled out a pile of expensive foodstuffs, which he'd bought for Guo Cunxian, and then he sat down to ask about what was going on in the village. The fact is that he knew perfectly well what was happening in Guojiadian, since he was kept up to date by family and friends, but he had decided to take advantage of Qian Xishou's absence to find out whether the investigation team was likely to cause a lot of trouble, to weigh up the chances of some major change.

The two men lit their cigarettes. Guo Cunxian looked curiously at Guo Cunyong as he puffed a few times, and then said: "You've picked just the right time to come back. Before he left, Qian Xishou was making it quite clear that he was determined to arrest me, though he didn't succeed because Mr Feng stopped him. I imagine he has gone back to the Municipal Committee to get some kind of extra powers. The investigation team was sent out here by the Municipal Committee, so they won't want to stop halfway. When he comes back, I'm sure to be arrested, in which case either you or Guangming will be selected as a temporary replacement."

With a thud, Guo Cunyong jumped down from the *kang* and started shouting: "Stop that! You've got the whole thing absolutely wrong. Nobody's going to arrest you. The last couple of days, quite apart from being busy with my own work, I've been trying to find out what is going on in the big city, and the whole atmosphere is quite different when you think about the kind of rock-hard teams that they used to send out. There wasn't agreement in the city to begin with, and I've heard that, right at this minute, the people supporting economic development in the countryside are in the ascendant again. Besides which, the Municipal Committee answers to the Provincial Committee, and even if the municipality wants to get at you, if they don't agree at the provincial level, do you think they'd dare to touch you?"

In actual fact, he wasn't too sure of the truth of any of what he was saying, since he was working on various bits of gossip and rumours he'd heard around and about, together with a few educated guesses about what was going on, but he wanted to convince Guo Cunxian. Realising that Guo Cunxian was listening to him attentively, he spoke with even greater confidence: "Everybody else is busy earning as much money as they possibly can, so what is going on here that there are investigations and people being punished? Who has time for that kind of thing nowadays? If you've got the money, you're lord and master. I'm telling you, supposing that you do lose your position here, you'd be in luck. The two of us could go in together and I am promising you, in less than three years, you'd have a nice new Western-style house to live in, you'd be driving your own car, and you'd have a couple of hundred thousand yuan in the bank. If you want me to take over from you, think again! One, I couldn't possibly do your job and two, I don't want it. Right now my only interest is in earning money. Let me explain."

He took a couple of contracts out of his pocket and put them down in front of Guo Cunxian. "You see, these are worth real money. These are contracts I've signed for the village. If you're in charge here, we're working for the village. If you lose your job, then we work for ourselves. This here is the contract for building a new dormitory for Guofeng Middle School, and this is the Urban Construction Bureau contract agreement. We've worked on projects for them for a couple of years now. This is a foreign trade agreement. They want as much PVC as our chemical plant can produce. You see the list, we've got caustic soda, soda ash, steel... The things on this list are just the most pressing commodities right now, and there are a couple of them that we could do. And then there are the city banks. I've already been to talk to them, and if we put forward a project, they will do the financing for us, and we can have as much money as we want. This is the country's money and if we don't take it, someone else will. We can borrow the money now and then pay it back slowly. The reason that I came back this time was because I wanted to discuss setting up a retail business. I could sell products produced in this village across the country. I want you to pick out a name and the sooner the better, because then I can register it immediately as our trade name."

Guo Cunyong was putting all of his efforts into making it sound good and covering every angle. As he spoke, his lips were covered in spittle, and the more grandiose his plans, the more entrancing Guo Cunxian seemed to find them. He was bewitched and bewildered. In future, even if this biggest of all wheels in Guojiadian managed to keep his position, he'd have to listen to him and obey his orders. If Guo Cunxian lost his job, then Ou Guangming would be easy to keep under his thumb. This was the happiest Guo Cunxian had been for ages, but he was trying to conceal his joy. He bent his head and studied each of the contracts in turn in the lamplight.

Guo Cunyong was determined to strike while the iron was hot, so he suggested another idea: "We can't just sit here and wait for them to come and get us. Since I'm here, how about we invite Mr Feng and Mr Cui to dinner. Right now it might be awkward to do this in your name, so I'll be the host. Ou Huaying can put a little banquet together, and you can be in attendance. When the villagers see you sitting there, won't they all understand what end is up? It would have quite the same effect as if you were the host, and if the pair of them come, it'll prove that they're on your side. We can show our appreciation, and we can get some idea of what is going on. One of these days Mr Feng might well find himself promoted to the municipal level, in which case that would be a great connection for us to make. Afterwards I'll go back to the city and get busy, and there's nothing that money can't do in this line. If we can get enough people on board, it would to be possible to stop Qian Xishou from ever coming back to Guojiadian, and then the investigation team will have to be recalled sooner or later. What do you think?"

Guo Cunxian perked up: "Do you really think you can pull the necessary strings?"

Guo Cunyong giggled. "To tell you the truth, I've made a few friends in the city in recent days."

"How much money do you need?"

"Oh good God, we have the money, it's not about that at all. We can get what we need from the food factory and the chemical works. I'll deal with that, don't worry about it."

Guo Cunxian had believed every word that Guo Cunyong said, and he was deeply grateful: "We'll do as you suggest. It's late and you ought to get home as soon as you can. Discuss the situation with Huaying, and then tomorrow we can get busy."

When Guo Cunyong got home, he wasn't in any kind of hurry to talk to his wife. He needed to think about something that Guo Cunxian had said first. How much of it was true? Could Guo Cunxian possibly get away with it? That really didn't seem very likely. However, even if he did lose his position, he might well still have a big say in who took over from him as village secretary. So why didn't he just hand everything over to Ou Guangming, who'd been such a loyal supporter. Why even mention my name? It couldn't possibly be his own idea, he'd never trust me to that extent. It must have come from a higher-up person, like for example Mr Feng, someone like that must have suggested it to him. Maybe he was being completely impartial. Maybe he'd decided that the only one who could possibly deal with this mission was Guo Cunyong; he could handle the investigation team and put Guojiadian on the right path. If that was the case, then he should take the job. Who in Guojiadian could possibly be considered more important than himself? The crucial thing was to make sure that the higher-ups were on board, and that is why he had suggested inviting them to dinner.

Guo Cunyong was a clever man, and he was sure that he was the only person in the whole of Guojiadian who stood a chance against Guo Cunxian in any battle of wits. However, whether intentional or not, that one word from Guo Cunxian had caught his attention more than anything else. He was excited and worried but also suspicious. He was breathing hard, the pitch of his voice rose, and all of a sudden he found that he was using more swear words in every sentence. It had been quite a while since his last return home, and the moment he came through the door he was in a temper. When his wife asked him a question he didn't reply, but he was uncomfortable because he couldn't say anything about what was really bothering him. Until he'd made up his own mind about what to do, he couldn't say a word. Ou Huaying was a notorious gossip. As far as she was concerned, molehills were there to be turned not into mountains but into the Himalayas, and she could twist a couple of incautious words into a scandal that engulfed half the village. But in this instance anything mentioned out of turn would ruin the whole thing.

The problem was that, supposing he couldn't talk to his wife, then he couldn't talk to anyone. It wasn't comfortable to keep such a big piece of news to himself, and he really didn't know whether to laugh or cry. Should he be throwing his weight around in the village or should he be keeping his distance? Should he be parading his close relationship with Guo Cunxian or should he avoid the man? Should he be thanking the investigation team or yelling at them? All of these questions filled his mind and he simply could not decide what to do for the best. Power is somewhat like a woman: if you can't see it or feel it, then you can maintain your detachment. The moment you can see it, the moment you can feel it in your hands, you'd be lying to say that you weren't attracted. No matter what kind of person you are, whether tricky and nasty or loyal and upright, even the dumbest of people can't escape the temptation, not to mention a clever and active man like Guo Cunyong. However, when it came right down to it, Ou Huaying wasn't stupid. The moment Guo Cunyong came through the door, she knew that something was up. To begin with she thought that he was overtired and that was why he was cross, and indeed right then all the important people in the village had good reason to be irritated. However, she quickly realised that there was more to it than that. For some time Guo Cunyong just sat there in a daze, and his conversation was completely disjointed, with each sentence seemingly unrelated to the previous one. Clearly he was worried about something, he was busy thinking over something important. He was deliberately holding back, he was being vague and slippery, and that was not fun for her to deal with. If a husband is really worried about something and he doesn't tell his wife about it, he has to be up to something that she wouldn't like! She asked and he didn't reply. She asked again and he still didn't reply, and so she didn't ask a third time. She was absolutely furious. She lay down on the *kang* with a long face, like a cat that has missed its mouse.

When Guo Cunyong was in a good mood, he liked to say that he'd been very lucky, and this luck consisted of marrying a wife who could hold her own in conversation. When he was angry, she could cheer him up; when he was stressed, she could give good advice. The feeling that he had a comfortable home, somewhere he was happy to come back to, that was all thanks to his wife. And indeed whether his home was comfortable, and whether he was happy there, all depended on whether his wife was in a good mood or not. The moment Ou Huaying started to look cross, Guo Cunyong also began to feel that his house wasn't really very welcoming. He hadn't been back for such a long time, and his wife had already gone to bed. She'd wrapped the bedclothes tight round her body to make it absolutely clear that she was going to bed and she didn't want him anywhere near her.

"What's up with you?" Guo Cunyong asked irritably. "I've come back home after a long trip, I'm absolutely exhausted, and you can't even be bothered to heat up a bowl of water to let me wash my feet?"

Ou Huaying snorted and sat up. "Who are you talking to?"

"What is wrong with you? I'm talking to you! Who else is there in the house?"

"Oh, so you've noticed that I'm here? Am I running a hotel or a spa? You go off to God knows where and get up to God knows what, then you come running back, and then this isn't right and you don't like that... Who asked you to come back? Why don't you just leave me alone?"

"Don't be cross. I've got something important that I want to talk to you about, but first get me some hot water so I can have a wash."

Ou Huaying now saw that he was really angry, so she didn't keep on at him. Turning over, she got down from the *kang*, went to heat up a bowl of water and then put it by his feet. Then she wrung out a hot towel for him to wipe his face with and she dipped the towel in hot water again to scrub his back and chest. Seeing that his wife had suddenly cheered up and was looking quite happy, Guo Cunyong suddenly felt much more comfortable. The blood was pumping through his veins and his feet were quite cozy in their basin of hot water. With a tug he pulled his wife onto his lap.

Wait a bit, wait a bit. Ou Huaying put one arm round her husband's neck, while her other hand grabbed hold of Guo Cunyong's crotch. "Look at you! You've been out poking your dipstick into every pot you can and then you come home with this measly little worm!"

Guo Cunyong realised that he wasn't out of the woods quite yet. "What are you talking about? You've got hold of it, so you tell me whether it's a measly little worm or not? You want me to show you what a worm can do?"

Ou Huaying didn't let go, but she started to laugh: "That's all for show, that is. One thrust and it's all over. That might be OK for some little hooker that you found on a street corner, but you can't fool me! I know just what you're like! OK, tell me, what have you been up to?"

"What do you mean, what have I been up to?" As he spoke, his erection really did start to soften.

"If you'd been up to something good, there'd be no reason to keep it a secret. If you're keeping it a secret, it's because you've been doing something that you shouldn't. Right, have you been following in Guo Cunxian's footsteps and found yourself a mistress on the side?"

"What the hell? What on earth are you talking about? Just now, Guo Cunxian told me that he reckoned he was for the chop sooner or later, and that he wouldn't be able to keep his position as Party secretary in this village. When Qian Xishou comes back, there's about a ninety per cent chance that he's going to be gone, so he was thinking that I might take over. He wants me to invite the people from the investigation team to dinner here, to make a few connections. Do you think that would work?"

"Really? He should have thought of that ages ago. If you ask me, he's going to be lucky if the worst that happens is that he loses his job!" Ou Huaying had never dreamed that one day she might become the wife of the village Party secretary. That would make her the most important woman in Guojiadian. She got off her husband's lap as quickly as she could, and helped him to dry his wet feet. Then she allowed him to get into his nice warm bed on top of the *kang*, while she herself went outside to pour the water away from the basin in which he had washed his feet. Having bolted the door properly, she grabbed the chamber pot and brought it back with her, going first to the bedroom on the western side to look at her son, and tucking him up in the quilt that he'd kicked aside. Then she went back to her own room and got onto the *kang*. Before she'd even begun to take her clothes off she was prodding Guo Cunyong in the arm and asking: "Do you think Guo Cunxian was serious? What did you say when he put it to you?"

"I didn't have a clue whether he was serious or not, so I thought it best to refuse absolutely in the first instance. Remember, it doesn't matter whether this works out for us or not, we are not going to say anything to anybody. Whatever happens, you must not tell anybody."

"I don't understand why you're so scared of him. Things have been bad in the past, it's true, but now is your time to shine. It's a fact that all of these years Guo Cunxian has just been talking, but when it comes to action, isn't that always your job?"

"Oh, I'm not scared of him, and I don't care that much about whether I get to be secretary or not. What bothers me is the thought of a whole lot of trouble over nothing. It seems that right now it is often very difficult to get a handle on what people are up to, and Guo Cunxian may have been brought down a bit, but he is still far from out. Even if I really wanted to be secretary, I'd have to pretend that I didn't want the job. In fact, it would be best if it looked like he was forcing me to take it. And I haven't told you yet, the last few days I have been dealing with a couple of projects, and it looks like I could be earning big money on them. If I get to be secretary, then we'll handle them one way. If I don't get to be secretary, then we'll handle them another way, but whatever happens we'll be doing OK out of it."

Ou Huaying had already thought of another point: "If you ask me, this is a great opportunity. If you get to be the Party secretary here, then everyone in Guojiadian will have to do what you say. If you don't get to be secretary, then our future will depend on whether whoever it is feels like giving us permission to go ahead."

"You have a point there. You are good at thinking of these things. However, taking over from Guo Cunxian is not going to be easy."

Having been praised by her husband, Ou Huaying was busy thinking even more. "What do you mean about it not being easy? If you have no power, nothing is easy. If you have power, you can do what you like! Guo Cunxian got where he is because of the way he can talk. But when you come right down to it, there is a limit to what you can do with just yap, and the way he speaks to other people means that he has annoyed everyone. The villagers don't like him, so they've reported him to the authorities, and now the higher-ups want to punish him. Do you think he's going to get out of this in one piece? You're an educated man, you know stuff and you're competent. Everyone in the village knows that. You get on with people in a way that he just can't, and I reckon that you could do a much better job here than Guo Cunxian does."

Guo Cunyong was enjoying everything that his wife said. "OK, we'll do as you say. Tomorrow I'll invite Mr Feng and Mr Cui here to our house, and we'll see what they have to say."

Ou Huaying's eyes were glittering. Having taken off her clothes she slipped between the covers and, sliding over towards him, she started wrapping herself around him. "Darling, you're so lucky. You're going to be in charge here!"

"Ha! Just a moment ago you were saying that I'd been going to hookers!" Guo Cunyong was beginning to feel he could throw his weight around, even though he didn't have an official position yet. However, he didn't push his wife away but hugged her closer.

"What are you talking about? That was just a joke! I've missed you so much! Let me have a good feel of you. Have you missed me? Oh, my God, that's a massive erection! Don't be in such a hurry, I've got other ideas..." She looked like a fish that has swallowed a hook. Since her soft little mouth had taken the bait she had to follow in the direction of the person holding the line. But it wasn't her that had been hooked, it was Guo Cunyong. He wasn't fishing for her, she was fishing for him. Guo Cunyong found his whole mind unable to take any other direction. He was plunging deeper and deeper, until he felt that his spirit and soul were being hooked out of his body. She was in charge, she was directing him, and he was just floating along, all in a daze. His voice could still be heard though, sometimes moaning softly, sometimes muttering words of love.

She kept going until Guo Cunyong felt that he was going to explode at any moment, and then he hoisted himself up and pressed his wife down underneath him.

. . .

The following day, Guo Cunyong found that Feng Hou was determined to refuse his invitation, so only Cui Daben would be coming to dinner. This didn't matter, because it was all about getting the necessary information, and it might well be that Cui Daben was more inclined to talk if Feng Hou wasn't there. In actual fact, he was restricted in his movements because he was a member of the investigation team, otherwise what would have been the point of inviting this Cui Daben? Otherwise, half of Guojiadian would have had him to dinner by now.

The moment he came in through the door, Cui Daben felt his authority return. He was given the seat of honour on the *kang*. Compared with the other local leaders who'd come to Guojiadian in the past, Cui Daben seemed a bit rougher, and thus more friendly. Guo Cunyong and Guo Cunxian sat to one side, in subordinate positions. Ou Huaying had done her very best to put on a spread. When he arrived there were five dishes set out on the table and three eating bowls. There was shredded pork with laver, celery cooked with nuts, tofu with vermicelli and a leek-flower omelette. None of these dishes contained any expensive ingredients, but they gave a good appearance. There were also two bowls of potatoes, a plate of chopped pickles and a plate of chopped braised meat, in addition to salted duck eggs, pickled garlic, onions and dipping sauce. For anyone who was still hungry there was flatbread to fill up on, as well as noodle soup. There were hot and cold dishes, meat and vegetarian dishes, and things in sauces and things served dry. All in all, this was the finest kind of banquet that Guojiadian could provide.

It was obvious that Ou Huaying had pulled out all the stops. She wanted to make her husband look good and understood how this was to be done. She served the food, but did not sit down at table, nor did she try to interfere in the conversation. When she wasn't required, she went into the other room and sat by the table where she could hear the three men talking.

Having eaten and drunk their fill, the men began to talk. Their voices were now raised, and they put more emphasis on what they were saying. When men are drinking, they need to start talking with the first round of food, because if they don't, even the most delicious dishes lose their savour. Good food and good wine is there to encourage people to speak, and to say something useful when they do. Today, Guo Cunyong was the host, so he had to rack his brains for topics of conversation, while hoping to work them round to something he'd like to know while, at the same time, leaving Guo Cunxian with the impression that he was just being polite. The moment the slightest silence fell, there he was encouraging the others to eat and drink some more.

Of the three men in the room, Guo Cunxian found himself in the most awkward position. He had to stop himself from monopolising the conversation, ensure that he didn't come across too strong and find ways to make Cui Daben talk. The more alcohol Cui Daben poured down his throat, the more relaxed he became. He'd been depressed and feeling put-upon lately. Normally he was the head of the entire community, with seventy or eighty thousand people at his beck and call, but the moment the investigation team arrived he'd become the most insignificant of mortals: who cared what someone like him thought about anything? He wasn't even as important as that crawler, Gao Wenping! Even that whore, An Jinghui, got to boss him about! The moment he got away from the investigation team, however, he was the most senior person in the place. Just like now, other people had to flatter and fawn on him, and as he felt things return to normal, he became happier and happier, and had more and more to say.

"If the people in the investigation team knew that I was sitting here eating with you, I'm sure I don't know what they'd say!"

Guo Cunyong immediately took up the burden: "Are the people of China allowed to eat in peace or are they not? Sometimes it seems like even eating a meal can be treated like a crime! Anyone would think it would be possible to destroy the Party and ruin the principles on which we are governed by eating! Way back when, if the Communist Party and the Eighth Route Army hadn't been eating the food given to them by the people, if they hadn't been sleeping on *kangs* belonging to the people, how could they have defeated the enemy, eliminated traitors, killed the landlords and redistributed the land? They wouldn't have been able to do anything at all."

"Yes indeed. People now have forgotten the old days. Everybody thinks they can throw their weight around and bully people." The irritation Cui Daben had been feeling lately seemed to have been brought to the surface by all the alcohol he'd drunk. "Cunxian, you must not think this is all aimed at you. You are being treated in this way as a warning to others. If anything happens in Guojiadian, then we in the community also have some responsibility. I'm going to have to pick up some of the pieces after you."

This really did stick in Guo Cunxian's craw. He didn't want to hear this. Who was picking up the pieces after whom? I didn't ask the investigation team to come here, and you, Mr Cui, are my superior. What do you mean that you are having to pick up the pieces after me? It would be more accurate to say that my problems are all your fault!

Guo Cunxian could have been emboldened by wine into showing quite how angry he was, but he didn't dare do anything that would endanger his position. The words trembled on the tip of his tongue, but he managed to say something completely different: "Mr Cui, there's nothing for you to worry about, nothing is going to happen to me. And supposing that I do get into trouble, it's all my own fault. It has nothing to do with you, or with Cunyong and the others. If the investigation team want to have me dismissed, then they can go ahead. I've had enough of this job, and I don't want to do it any more. However, I asked you to come here today so that I could put one point to you. When it comes to selecting a new branch secretary for Guojiadian, you cannot let the investigation team have it all their own way. If you get someone or other who only knows how to lick the arses of the team, Guojiadian is going to be in serious trouble. It's got to be your choice who gets to be the new branch secretary. You know the situation here, and you can pick someone young who knows what they are doing. I know I shouldn't be saying this in front of Cunyong, but he'd be the best choice. Unfortunately he's refusing. I wish I could force him to do this, but I simply don't have the authority."

"Things haven't got to that point yet, so you'd better keep quiet for now." Cui Daben was speaking in a very loud voice. He was determined to cut Guo Cunxian's conversation off short. He understood that this banquet was about protecting Guo

Cunxian, and that was the reason why he was ignoring his host, Guo Cunyong. His aim was to try to cheer Guo Cunxian up. "Even if things have got a bit out of control here, you aren't unique in that. There are plenty of villages and counties in exactly the same position. Why don't they go and investigate them? Why haven't all their officials lost their jobs?"

This remark was quite justified and it was exactly what Guo Cunxian wanted to hear. It was now time for him to stop speaking up for Guo Cunyong and to take this opportunity to put in a word for himself: "Whose fault is it that things have got out of control? Is it the peasants here, or is it the government? There are people right now going around saying that peasants are so desperate to make money that they'll do anything and so they are ruining the whole society. Since when have peasants been able to do something like that? If the government goes wrong, why are the little people expected to put it straight? Everyone bends with the wind, so why should we peasants be expected to stand up to the blast? We are just doing what everyone else does, so why should we be the subject of an investigation team? If we'd stood up to the blast, I doubt any of us would be here today to join you in a cup of wine!"

From her position outside, Ou Huaying could hear that the conversation had taken a dangerous turn, so she quickly pushed aside the curtain covering the door and bustled in. "Is the wine still warm enough? Drink up everyone and I'll go and open another bottle for you." She took advantage of the opportunity offered by handing over the bottle to pinch her husband's hand, and he immediately picked up his cup. "Mr Cui, Cunxian, drink up and then we can have another round of warm wine."

"Bottoms up!" Cui Daben downed his cup in a single draft. Ou Huaying poured him another cup, filling it to the brim. He praised the food that she'd cooked and suggested that she join them. Ou Huaying waved this off with a laugh, saying that she had no tolerance for alcohol, and she went back to the other room. Guo Cunxian raised his cup a second time. He had calculated that Cui Daben must now be feeling a bit light-headed from the alcohol but that he was still far from being drunk. While everyone was still able to pay attention, there were things that he needed to say: "Mr Cui, to protect your own village cadres, you've gone up against that Qian Xishou. Let me drink this toast to you!" As he spoke, he drained his cup again.

Cui Daben's face had turned a little bit red, and he was obviously angry: "Who the hell does he think he is? I reckon that if you want to stand up to him, you can. Let's not talk any more about that. Drink up! Drink up! Let's talk about something more cheerful. Cunyong, I know that you've been off finding opportunities for Guojiadian to earn some money. Of all of the young cadres in these villages, you've shown the most initiative. Let me drink this toast to you and your family. You are very lucky to have such a wonderful wife. No wonder you look so well. Clearly she feeds you up with half a dozen dishes every day!" Cui Daben's red face showed that he was now quite drunk. There wasn't any point in encouraging him to continue drink, the problem was going to be how to stop him from having any more.

And what was worse, he was starting to talk rubbish, meaning that there was no hope of getting anything out of him now.

Guo Cunxian decided to bring the evening to a close. He started praising Ou Huaying's flatbread and noodle soup to Cui Daben, saying that if these weren't the best in the county, they were certainly the best in the village. After that he was able to call in Ou Huaying and tell her not to serve any more wine, and that they wanted the bread and noodles served to fill up any gaps. Cui Daben was not too drunk to think. He was afraid that if he went rolling back it wouldn't look good to the investigation team. He didn't want someone making a formal complaint to Qian Xishou or the city, and he had managed to get something out of this little escapade as it was.

It had taken them a long time to eat, and afterwards they had spent some time talking together. Cui Daben could feel his eyelids drooping, so he stood up and said goodbye. It was completely dark outside, and Guo Cunyong was afraid that he wouldn't make it back safely, so he said he'd escort him to where he was staying. Guo Cunxian wanted to go too, but Ou Huaying stopped him, suggesting that he wait where he was until Guo Cunyong came back. Guo Cunxian thought that this must mean that the pair of them still had something they wanted to discuss with him, so he felt that he had to sit back down. Ou Huaying told him to put his feet up on the *kang*, and that if he was tired it would be perfectly fine if he lay down and went to sleep. She would go and sleep with her boy in the other room. As was usual in the village, it was very awkward and uncomfortable when a senior man had to talk to the wife of one of his juniors; everything had to be very polite and formal. No matter how important the subject of the conversation, it had to be discussed as quickly as possible so that they could go their separate ways. If there was nothing to say, they weren't supposed to meet at all. The relationship between a senior man and the wives of his juniors was considered to be the most sensitive, the most difficult; one conversation too many, one touch out of place, and everyone would be suspicious. Or perhaps it would be more accurate to say that, ever since the dawn of time, if a senior man wanted to seduce someone, the wife of one of his juniors would be the easiest person to pick, so people tended to view this kind of interaction with a great deal of concern.

Ou Huaying wasn't interested in this kind of thing, or at least she didn't behave in her own house as if she were interested. She didn't use a formal term of address for Guo Cunxian, and she didn't tell her son to call him 'Uncle'. Instead, she always used his own name when she talked to him: "Cunxian, I'm going to make you a bowl of jujube tea. I'm told it's good for people who have had too much to drink."

Guo Cunxian tried to stop her. "Don't worry about that, I haven't had that much to drink."

"You've all been drinking as much as each other, and Mr Cui has already had his face turn the colour of pig's liver. How can you not have had too much to drink?"

All this wine was having a depressing effect on Guo Cunxian, and he had a lot to think about. He wasn't happy to talk it over with the wife of one of his subordinates, so he sat there smoking. Ou Huaying stood in front of him and said seriously: "Cunxian, in future, I don't want you to say any more about Cunyong taking over from you. You don't understand him, he's been really worried and upset ever since he came back last night. I've had to repeat over and over I don't know how many times that if you're involved he should help you, and if you're not involved, then he should get out. If the worst comes to the worst you can go in together and open a little factory, and just be self-employed."

Guo Cunxian looked up at Ou Huaying. He didn't say a word, and he wasn't smiling. In fact, it was quite impossible to say what he was thinking.

Standing right next to Guo Cunxian, Ou Huaying was more and more aware of his... what you could only call might. It had nothing to do with his physical appearance; he wasn't anything like as strong as Guo Cunyong, but Guo Cunyong simply did not have his air of authority. Guo Cunxian's might seemed to come from his very bones. It made her feel nervous and self-constrained, but at the same time, she also felt excited, and as though something new and strange was happening. She was worried that he didn't believe what she'd just said. What is more, that entire evening, there hadn't been a single sign that Guo Cunxian was on the way out and her husband was going to be promoted in his stead. Cui Daben didn't seem to be thinking that way at all. Guo Cunxian didn't seem to be considering seriously about what he would do after he lost his job either. That whole meal had gone by without any one putting their cards on the table. However, she didn't in the least regret hosting this banquet, for all that it had proved pointless, because thanks to this evening, she now had another idea.

Ou Huaying realised that she was sweating. Normally she just hung her head in Guo Cunxian's presence, and she had no idea that she was quite so scared of him. She got up and went to the other room, where she found a handful of jujubes. These she put on the fire to roast, immediately filling the whole place with the smell of hot jujubes. Then she put them in with the tea leaves, and topped up the mug with hot water, after which she handed it to Guo Cunxian. This gave her an opportunity to calm down and get her breathing back to normal. The smile on her face was perfectly natural and lit up the whole room. However, whatever she did, she couldn't attract Guo Cunxian's attention even though the two of them were alone together.

He was too arrogant. He'd been through all kinds of experiences and met all kinds of people. How could someone like him care what the wife of one of his distant relatives thought? He was used to being the biggest fish in the pond: everyone was frightened of him, everyone was trying to get on his good side and trying to say ingratiate themselves with him. Ou Huaying suddenly felt her heart leap. She wanted to say something to him that nobody else would dare to even mention, to provoke him and see what happened.

Without the slightest thought for the possible consequences, she burst out: "Cunxian, there are a lot of people here who would be happy to see you lose your position tomorrow and would like it even better if you were arrested and dragged off to prison. You are talking all the time about how you are going to be dismissed, and that's really tough on those who've worked for you. Whatever happens, you really must not go and visit Lin Meitang again. The investigation team has people watching you, and you know exactly who I mean. She has been round at Lin Meitang's place every five minutes. She has even been introducing her to possible marriage partners! What she's actually trying to do is get evidence against you. If you ask me, you should just let this one go, let Lin Meitang get married, and then it'll all be over. She may well still care about you, but once she's married she can do as she likes, things will be easier and she'll have more freedom, and nobody will dare to gossip about you. Otherwise you are going to end up being responsible for her for the rest of her life. How can you take that upon yourself? You have no idea when this might not blow up in your face."

She suddenly found that she couldn't say another word.

Guo Cunxian hadn't shouted at her or moved aggressively; equally, he hadn't done anything to cut her short. He had no intention of arguing. He just sat there in stony silence listening to what she had to say, with a tired and gloomy expression in his eyes. A man like that can seem very impressive and very attractive. Ou Huaying drank a couple of mouthfuls of the jujube tea that she'd made for Guo Cunxian, and then used the back of her hand to wipe her mouth and clear the sweat from her forehead. Her eyes were like two deep pools of water as she turned to look at Guo Cunxian. "Really, look at me! I'm saying all of these unpleasant things to you!"

"Why not? If you have something to say, then go ahead."

"You're not cross?"

Guo Cunxian got down from the *kang* and pulled on his shoes. "I should go."

Ou Huaying had no idea what he was thinking, and she was getting a bit anxious. "I meant it for the best, Cunxian!"

As he walked off, Guo Cunxian said: "I know that. You meant well, and you're not stupid. It might be that there is a job for you in future."

Ou Huaying stood stock still thinking about what Guo Cunxian might have meant by that, and by the time that she'd pulled herself together and gone out the door, he'd already walked away. Anyway, she'd given Guo Cunxian a good talking-to tonight, and that made her feel very excited and proud. There wasn't another woman in Guojiadian who'd have dared to do that. With a man like Guo Cunxian, women could rely on him without thinking about it. He was someone you could trust unconditionally. Men would be better off making friends with him since he would be a bad enemy. Ou Huaying understood that her husband had to be very careful in handling the hot potato of whether he was going to lose his position or not.

Guo Cunxian's legs were wobbling, and he felt a little bit as though he were floating. As he made his way home, he kept feeling that he wasn't walking quite right. However, he was still perfectly capable of thinking clearly, and he knew that he'd done well. He had a strong sense of his own self-control. In fact, although he'd matched Cui Daben cup for cup, he could have drunk twice as much without showing any sign of it. In the old days, he'd gone out to cut timber for use in coffins every winter, and a lot of time had been spent drilling the boards while squatting down in a corner, so he'd had to drink alcohol to warm himself up; he'd never been bothered by the thought of having to drink. This time he hadn't been careful enough, though. The wine was much more bitter than he was used to, and he was furious. It is a bad idea to drink when you are angry, and the more bitter the wine, the more stressed it makes you, and the more you drink the more irate you become, and the worst of it is when you have to drink while asking a favour from someone else, and you have to be there smiling and cracking jokes. Wine under those conditions makes you dead drunk. He could feel that his stomach was undergoing unusual strain, it was churning and he was becoming frightened. He didn't want to throw up. What might not come out that way? If he threw up all over the street, first thing tomorrow morning people would see it and try and make something of the occurrence. If they found out that it was him who'd been throwing up, there would definitely be a story about it. And if the worst really did come to the worst, there were endless possibilities for scandal! He wasn't going to provide any opportunity to those who wanted to get at him.

On leaving Guo Cunyong's house, he'd still been feeling fine, but once he got out in the wind he suddenly came over all funny. Maybe that was because he'd been putting on a show for his wife, trying to look in charge of everything. Besides which, Ou Huaying was a woman who liked to interfere with other people, and was always convinced that she was in the right. How dare she speak to him like that? How dare she point her finger at him? Although he knew perfectly well that she was trying to get into his good books, he found her an immensely tiresome woman. She was far too sharp. What kind of man can cope with a woman who is always throwing her weight around, always self-righteous, and always trying to control every least little thing? It might have seemed as though Guo Cunxian was like an enormous millstone that Ou Huaying was neither brave enough nor strong enough to move and that, by trying to do so, she'd only shown how feeble and hypocritical she really was. However, his own sense of self-esteem was very weak and very easily wounded.

As Guo Cunxian was weaving his way home, Zhu Xuezhen was waiting for him to go to bed, the blankets spread out on the *kang* and the chamber pot ready. The moment she saw him and smelled the stale alcohol about his person, she was shocked. "Oh my God, how much have you had to drink to get in this state?"

Guo Cunxian smiled. It was a sincere and loveable smile, such as he had not produced for who knows how long. "Hey, we've been married for ages. Since when have you seen me drunk?"

It was a fact that they had been married for many years, and Zhu Xuezhen had never seen him like this before. She rushed out to get him some hot water because she wanted him to wash his face. By the time she came back with the basin, Guo Cunxian was lying in bed with all his clothes on.

"How can you say that you're not drunk? Are you going to go to sleep like that?"

Guo Cunxian sat back up again. "Who said that I was going to sleep? I was just lying down for a bit."

Zhu Xuezhen laughed. "You're impossible to talk to when you're drunk."

Having wrung out a hot towel she wanted to help him wash his face. He didn't want her assistance and scrubbed himself down as normal, then he took off his clothes. It seemed as if his mind was quite clear as he said: "Has Chuanfu gone to bed?"

"He went off to find his old school friends. He doesn't come back often, and they miss him, so he's been visiting them and chatting."

"What do you mean? He's gone to the county town to study. It's not like he's gone abroad. Can't he come home whenever he likes?"

This made Zhu Xuezhen feel so much better. Normally he never even mentioned things like that, and even if he cared about how his son was getting on, he wouldn't actually say anything. It was very rare for the two of them to have this kind of conversation. Having washed and taken his clothes off, Guo Cunxian now crawled under the bed covers. If he was upright, he felt sick, but lying down he couldn't sleep. Some people go straight off to sleep when they're drunk, but he was one of the ones that can't.

Having put everything away, Zhu Xuezhen turned out the lights and lay down next to him. Guo Cunxian found himself overwhelmed by an unexpected feeling of guilt towards his wife, so he stretched out his arm and took hold of her hand. "You really are wonderful," he whispered across the pillow. "There are plenty of people in Guojiadian criticising me, but there isn't a single person who doesn't love you. Look at Cunyong's wife, always causing trouble, always going around gossiping right and left. I daresay Cunyong can cope with it, but anyone else would have broken her neck or cut her tongue out years ago!"

"That's a horrible thing to say. She invited you all to dinner and you can't say a single nice thing about her." Zhu Xuezhen was touched by how affectionate her husband had become as a result of the wine, and she was really regretting not having realised years ago that it had this effect on him. If she'd known, she could have been getting him drunk every evening. They had the money now, and they could buy whatever kind of wine he wanted. She put out her other hand and began to stroke his chest: "Are you feeling any better?"

"Oh, I'm feeling fine. Who would drink if they felt bad? Everybody drinks because they enjoy the feeling it gives them, and I'm feeling fine right now. I'm remembering all kinds of things that happened way back when. I remember your father wanted me to promise him, when he was dying, that I'd make sure you were OK. If I lose my job, we'll go ahead and open a factory, so we'll be earning good money. I reckon that, after a few years, we'd be rich."

"I'm not asking for you to get rich. As long as you're fine, as long as our whole family is safe and sound, I'm going to be perfectly happy."

"Xuezhen, everyone else seems to be totally mercenary. How come you never seem to think like that?" Guo Cunxian hugged his wife to his chest. "Do you remember how I brought you to Guojiadian to get married? I carried you on my back when we had to ford rivers, and your arms were clasped tight around my neck and your sweet little face next to my ear. Your breasts were pressed against my back so that every time I moved, they bounced against me. You bit my earlobe, and as you did so your breath tickled my ear, so right at that moment I wished the river was twice as wide. In fact, I would have liked it to have been many miles across. Then, when we got up the bank on the other side, I refused to go another step, but it was not because I was tired, but because I couldn't stand it any longer. The riverbank was flat and smooth and clean, so I put you down there, and took off my coat. That was our wedding night, as it were. Your blood stained the bottom half of my coat, and I told you to keep it safe. I don't know if you did or not?"

"When Chuanfu was born, I cut it up for nappies."

"Just then, the sun was shining high in the sky, and the river was burbling along at our feet, and we had the earth and the sky as witnesses for our wedding and the riverbank as our bed. It was the very finest wedding that anyone could possibly have. Afterwards you couldn't walk, so I had to carry you as we followed the bank. You were there on my back, chirruping away. First you bit my earlobe, then you licked my neck, and as we went on, I couldn't stand it one minute longer all over again."

Guo Cunxian found that he was being excited by these memories, that he now desired Zhu Xuezhen's body again. He couldn't remember when it had begun, but he had gradually lost all interest of that kind in his wife. It was a long time since the two of them had last had sex. He hadn't done right by her, since it was the responsibility of every husband to make sure that his wife was satisfied. If she was sexually satisfied then she'd trust him, she'd calm down, and everything would be fine.

Xuezhen was very relaxed and slippery inside, and he stuffed himself in. For the first couple of thrusts, he was feeling pretty good about things, but afterwards whatever he did, he simply couldn't get to the right level of wonderful engorgement. Because of this, he couldn't give Xuezhen an orgasm. She was doing her best to facilitate things, she was waiting for him, but he couldn't help it, he had lost faith in himself, and now he was becoming more and more tense. He kept reminding himself, encouraging himself: don't give up halfway. If he couldn't do this, what on earth was he going to say to his wife? Since he was so tense, so incapable of thinking about anything else, his penis simply wasn't doing the job. Instead of getting harder, it was becoming more and more soft. He was on top of his wife's body, he was trying to have sex with her, but he wasn't enjoying the experience in the slightest. All that was left was a sense of responsibility. It was his duty, it was a matter of face. He was forcing himself to thrust, to go faster, in the hope that he might be excited by the passion of the moment. Who could have imagined that there would prove to be such a big gap between fact and fantasy? His useless penis, instead of responding to the excitement of the situation, took this opportunity to retreat yet further into its shell. In the end, it was just no use. No matter what he did, it was pointless.

He would have liked to hide himself in one of the cracks in the *kang*. This was the most tragic kind of failure any man can experience, and all that was left was the shell. Since he wasn't a real man any more, what would be the next step? He was worried that Xuezhen wouldn't believe that he was genuinely impotent. She might well imagine that this was the result of some affair on the side. He rolled off Xuezhen's body and buried his head between her breasts. This was the first time he'd have to ask his wife for forgiveness and understanding.

"I can't do it, Xuezhen. I just can't do it any more. I can't bear it, but I'm already useless and I'm not even fifty years of age! I haven't been having an affair, there isn't any other woman in my life. You've had me under your eye for the last couple of months, and you have seen what I've been doing every minute of every day. I'm so, so sorry. I had no idea this would ever happen to me." As he spoke he began to cry, and his warm tears soaked Zhu Xuezhen's breasts.

Zhu Xuezhen held his head pressed against her breasts. Sometimes he seemed like such a tyrant, throwing his weight around and determined to win at all costs, but right now he seemed more like a child. She cuddled him just like she would have cuddled her son, and a powerful feeling of warmth bubbled up inside her, so she hugged him even tighter. She could feel how much he relied on her, how much he needed her trust, her bosom, her embraces and the sense of security that she provided. She was becoming more and more important to him. It was a good feeling. She wanted him and actually couldn't care less whether he was impotent or not. If anything, if he couldn't have sex any more their lives would be a lot simpler, he wouldn't be off with one whore after another, and other women wouldn't be endlessly trying to seduce him. His family would be more important to him after this. She would have him to herself. However, she felt sorry for him, and stroked him softly on the back as if he were a child that she was trying to cheer up.

The worst part was now over, and Guo Cunxian was feeling thirsty, but he couldn't bear to ask Xuezhen to get up and pour him a glass of water. He got up, pulled on his trousers and then got off the *kang*. First he found a towel to wipe his face and then he reached for the thermos to pour himself some water. Having just got up from his warm bed, and rushed about like that half-naked, his stomach decided that enough was enough. Bile launched itself against his throat, and he bent down quickly to throw up into the chamber pot. Once the first mouthful had gone down, it was impossible to prevent the rest from following it, and he retched and gagged until everything had been vomited out.

The room was filled with the sharp, sour stench of alcohol.

Zhu Xuezhen hastily got out of bed and into some clothes. Without noticing, at some point in the proceedings their son, Chuanfu, had come home, and hearing them up and about in the other room, he came in. One of them patted him on the back, while the other poured a cup of warm water for him to rinse his mouth.

Since he was now in middle school, their son now spoke more like an adult: "You shouldn't drink when you're upset, it just makes you feel worse."

Having thrown up everything he had in his stomach, Guo Cunxian was now sitting crouched on the floor, unwilling to get up. His head was in the way of the chamber pot, so his wife and son couldn't see what it was that he'd vomited, but he couldn't stay sitting there forever. Xuezhen told him to rinse his mouth, and having done so, he thought that he could go and tip the pot out. This was not normal, so his son grabbed it out of his hands. When he saw what was in the chamber pot he just stood there, with a furrowed brow, frowning. He almost lost his grip on the pot: "What have you been throwing up? Why is it all red?"

"That's the pork with laver." Now that he had vomited all that food and drink, Guo Cunxian was feeling a lot better, and the fumes of alcohol had completely cleared from his mind. "Go and throw it away, it smells terrible!"

"Pork with laver wouldn't be that red. You've been vomiting blood!" He was still a child, after all. If it had been Zhu Xuezhen, she wouldn't have been making such a fuss about it.

Zhu Xuezhen was horrified when she heard that he'd been vomiting blood. She looked at the chamber pot, then at Cunxian, and the whole time she was muttering: "What are we to do? What on earth are we going to do?"

Guo Cunxian was deeply worried, and he said in a rough voice: "Throw it away and then we can talk."

Chuanfu emptied the pot into the refuse heap outside the door, and then cleaned it with fresh water before bringing it back into the house.

By then, Guo Cunxian had got back onto the *kang* and was sitting with the window behind him. Zhu Xuezhen was sitting by his feet, looking at him. From time to time she would close her eyes and shake her head. Then she would rub her eyes, but her expression was strange. She seemed shocked and frightened, uncertain of what to believe. Chuanfu was worried that his mother might get sick again after such a scare, so he looked at his father. Guo Cunxian's expression told him that they were both worried about the same thing.

Guo Cunxian already had himself well under control: "Xuezhen, just now I threw up, and there was a bit of blood towards the end. It's not serious. I guess I must have been overtired and overly irritated the last couple of days, and then I ended up drinking too much today. Don't worry about it. I know my own health situation."

Chuanfu was very worried. His mother was in such a state and if anything happened to Dad, well, the whole family would be ruined. "Dad, how about I go with you tomorrow to the city for a checkup?"

"No. You have to understand, you cannot let anyone else know about this. In a few days, once I've lost my job, I'll go for a checkup. And if I don't lose my job, I'll still go."

"Dad, whether you lose your job or not really isn't that important. It's your health that matters. If there really is some problem with your stomach, the longer you wait, the more dangerous it gets."

"What do you mean? At the worst I've got an ulcer, or maybe stomach cancer, but it seems to me that the problems with my job are much more serious."

Zhu Xuezhen cut short their argument: "Chuanfu, your father isn't growing a tumour or anything like that, he's just got a sensitive patch on his stomach and can't tolerate alcohol any more." This was just to calm him down. If you are vomiting large quantities of blood, you must have some internal bleeding somewhere. However, once Zhu Xuezhen started minimising the danger, neither her husband nor her son wanted to quarrel with her, so they had to go along with what she said.

"How do you know that?" Chuanfu asked.

"I saw it."

"You saw it?" The more she said, the weirder she sounded, and Guo Cunxian was by now quite prepared for her to have another of her turns.

"You're bleeding from an old injury. That day when I got sick, you'd just come back from shopping, and I could see at a glance that you had internal bleeding. However, at the time I didn't say anything, because I was feeling so ill I was about to pass out at any moment."

Now it was Guo Cunxian's turn to look sharply at her, with a shocked and surprised expression. He said nothing.

Zhu Xuezhen shut her eyes. She looked like a witch, and she was mumbling something inaudible.

Guo Cunxian could feel his hairs prickling. However, Chuanfu rushed over and put his arms round his mother's neck. Jokingly, he said: "Isn't that great! Mum is just like Uncle and can communicate with the spirits!"

Guo Cunxian's face changed colour. "Chuanfu, you must not say anything about your mother," he instructed his son.

He agreed. The things that had happened this evening were more than strange. Having thrown up all the alcohol he had drunk, Guo Cunxian was now feeling more clear-headed than ever. He knew that he wouldn't be able to get to sleep any time soon, so he made the excuse of having suddenly remembered a problem which meant that he had to go to the chemical works. So he got dressed and leapt down from the *kang*. He told his wife and son to go to sleep and not to wait up for him.

In actual fact, he was going in the middle of the night to pray at the Lucky Trees, to sit by himself and think things out.

18

DEATH

Lin Meitang had cooked her supper early, and even though she didn't have any appetite, she forced herself to eat it. When it was time to go to bed she went gone to lie down, but she simply could not calm herself down enough to be able to go to sleep. She had drunk all the wine that she'd bought to cheer herself up when she was feeling low, and she had smoked one cigarette after the other until she had a bitter and numb feeling in her mouth. However she was feeling more and more restless. That afternoon An Jinghui had come round and stayed for ages, and in their conversation she had inadvertently told her something of what the investigation team was up to. Did Guo Cunxian know? Did he have any other news?

Experience told her that she was unlikely to get much sleep tonight. She'd be tossing and turning until the early hours and then drift off into confused dreams. Unfortunately this kind of thing was happening to her more and more, and it was all because Guo Cunxian wasn't visiting her any more. Nothing had happened to him yet, but he'd already dumped her. That was all that she could see. If anything ever happened in Guojiadian or to Guo Cunxian, she'd be the first victim. Having realised that, it was impossible to avoid getting angry and upset. She was feeling sorry for herself and furious with herself as well. Why was she putting herself through this? Who was to blame for all of this other than herself? When would there be an end to it all?

Of course, it was now too late to complain, it would be pointless. Instead of lying there on her *kang* like a pudding, she decided it would be better to get up and walk about outside. Since she couldn't sleep whatever she did, what did it matter whether she was lying down or standing up? There is one good thing about living on your own, nobody is going to interfere with you, and you can sleep or stay awake just as you please.

She got dressed, got down from the *kang* and then, grabbing a torch, she headed out of the door.

The moon was very full and seemed to be grinning, which amused the stars scattered across the sky so that they winked and twinkled in their turn. The whole scene seemed so bright that the village of Guojiadian was thrown into clear relief. Only the mountains behind, with their peaks and ravines, threw shadows into dark corners, hazy and obscure. The breeze was warm, like a silk scarf brushing against her face, but that warmth did not touch her heart. She was beyond being moved by the beauty of the night landscape. This night-time vista was nothing to do with her, it made her feel more helpless and melancholy. Other people couldn't understand what was hidden beneath this soft and peaceful light, nor did they know the terrible things that had happened there. One year earlier, on just such a lovely moonlit night, she had been lying on a haystack near the foot of the embankment, looking at the moon, counting the stars, happy and carefree. Then Guo Cunxian had gone to cover her with his coat. He stood there before her, unmoving, like a dark cloud covering the moon. After that, he didn't actually cover her with his coat at all; instead he had moved on top of her. That was the first time she had really experienced true pleasure in sex; she screamed and cried like crazy. At the time, she had believed that he brought a whole new joy into her life. Afterwards he had dried her tears and promised her everything he could think of, but she hadn't demanded anything of him. Even then, there were things that she wanted from him. He made a lot of promises, but they all stopped short of suggesting that he might marry her, and at the time, she wasn't at all sure that she'd ever want to marry him. The moonlight was the only witness to the fact that she'd really given everything to him. In the past there were stories in which a goddess would mate with a human, with only a tree or a stone as witness. That night, she'd had the moonlight as witness to her love, and all she wanted in future was for him to come to her every time the moon was full and make love to her again.

Suddenly she gave a start, and she stopped dead in her tracks. Without realising what she was doing, she'd walked to Guo Cunxian's front door. If anyone saw her and it got out, they would say that she had gone in the middle of the night to see him. What would that have looked like? She hastily hid in the shadow of the wall, and then got away from his door as quickly as she could. No matter how angry she might be, no matter how furious, the person she really wanted to see right now was Guo Cunxian. But whatever happened, she couldn't possibly go to his house. She was afraid of bumping into Zhu Xuezhen. Supposing that Zhu Xuezhen got sick because she'd burst in on her, she would be in really serious trouble. Even if other people didn't say the worst, she wouldn't be able to forgive herself.

Without any clear direction in mind, she started walking towards the light: that meant the chemical works. The lights were blazing there, it was one of the sights of Guojiadian. As Guo Cunxian had planned right from the beginning, this first step in his programme to enrich the entire village had been a great success. It was not yet clear, however, whether he was going to be allowed to get away with it or not. Lin Meitang would have liked to go in and talk to the people working nights there. Maybe there was something that she could do for one of them. The problem was that, with the situation she was now in, if people knew that she couldn't sleep, the entire village would be gossiping about it. Who knows what they might think or say? She walked quickly down one side of the factory building and then turned to head out of the village, walking lightly, but with a sad heart.

Knowing that she could not see the man she loved so much, she wanted to see him even more. It so happened that on this night the moonlight was unusually bright, as though it were flooding her veins with warmth, as if to deliberately make her feel worse. And then there was that warm breeze, blowing against her face until it flared, bringing with it a rich aroma of fresh greenery. It was such a beautiful scene and such a delicious scent, but it made her feel even more alone, and she found herself feeling even more uncomfortable and tense. On a night like this it seemed a shame to carry on as normal. She was desperate for something to happen. She wanted to talk, drink, get drunk and cause a scene, and she wanted to hug someone while she screamed and shouted.

Suddenly she felt surprised at herself for having such an idea in her head and quickened her pace as she walked to the north of the village, and then she turned to head west, in the hope that she might enjoy the moonlight and the sky full of stars, and the peace that had fallen over Guojiadian. She was in no hurry to go back to her own little house. She was going to spend a bit of time outdoors, and if she wanted to take a turn round in the moonlight, who was going to say that she couldn't? If she managed to wear herself out, to make herself really exhausted, then she could return home and go straight to sleep. Wouldn't that be lovely?

The landscape beyond the village looked absolutely lovely, and here there was no need to worry that anyone might be watching her, trying to guess what she was up to and gossiping about it. This allowed her gradually to relax and feel more at peace. Far in the distance, the vista was blurred by a few wisps of fog, shining like silver, covering the fields and the trees in a soft haze.

She now saw that the Lucky Trees to the west of the village were bathed in dazzling light. The branches looked like they had been forged from silver, stretching high into the night sky, holding up the bright moon, while at the same time throwing a vast, dark, mushroom-shaped shadow across the ground. Lin Meitang found herself drawn to the light thrown by the Lucky Trees, and she walked over almost involuntarily. When she got close, she could see something even darker standing in the shadows. She stopped still, but it didn't occur to her to be frightened. The things that terrified her always happened during the day. She'd not once had anything horrible happen to her overnight. Things that occurred at night were good things, things that made you unforgettably happy. All of the trysts she'd had with Guo Cunxian had taken place at night, in various places outside the village. She was afraid of what people would say, so places that were deserted were safe for her. She felt free when she was out in the middle of nowhere in the dark. If something scary happened now, such as a ghost turning up, that would be dreadful.

She could hear the sound of a voice coming from the shadows of the Lucky Trees. Lin Meitang was brought up short, the hair prickling on her scalp, her whole body trembling. She nearly ran away. But in the blink of an eye, her terror turned to delight, because she realised that the person speaking was Guo Cunxian, the very person she was so desperate to see.

"There's nothing to be scared of, Meitang. It's only me," Guo Cunxian said.

Guo Cunxian was kneeling down, facing the Lucky Trees.

"Cunxian, is that you?"

Lin Meitang rushed over and threw her arms round Guo Cunxian's neck, hugging him tightly as if she was afraid that he might run away. "Are you OK?" she said.

"I'm fine."

"If you are fine, why are you kneeling here?"

"I felt like it. I feel better after kneeling for a while."

"You believe in the spirits?"

"Yes and no. It would be more correct to say I believe in these two Lucky Trees. There would always be some special sign from the trees every time something big happened in Guojiadian. Just now when I arrived I could see them shining."

"Really? I think I saw that too." Lin Meitang raised her head to look up at the trees, mysterious and awe-inspiring, which formed a dark canopy overhead like a roof. "It was a kind of white light, wasn't it? You know, I always liked the old name for these trees. One was called Dragon and the other one was Phoenix."

Guo Cunxian didn't understand why Lin Meitang had come out from the village so late at night and all on her own. Maybe she had heard some bad news, or someone had been tormenting her beyond what she could bear. Maybe the very thing that he had been most worried about had finally happened? "Why aren't you asleep?" he asked. "What are you doing here?"

"Did you really think I'd be tucked up in bed and fast asleep? I came out to find you."

"How did you know I'd be here?"

"The trees told me... Actually, I have no idea why I walked in this direction."

"Has something happened?"

"Something really important." Lin Meitang wasn't planning to start complaining the moment she saw him. Many people had recently brought him bad news, and she wasn't going to add to their number. She knew Guo Cunxian's temper only too well. He was very sensitive to what others thought about him. If he was suffering, he would treat that as a kind of Achilles' heel, and simply refuse to allow anyone else to even mention it. Even those closest to him had to pretend that everything was just fine.

"What on earth is the matter?"

"I miss you, I really miss you so much! Is there anything that could be worse than that?"

Guo Cunxian sighed with relief but he still wasn't entirely convinced.

In the circumstances, she couldn't simply take account of his feelings, she'd been under such strain for so long. Now something had finally gone her way, and the emotions that she could not bear to bottle up any longer threatened to spill over into the moonlit night. She turned his face so that he was looking at her, eye to eye, and the sparks in her eyes matched those in his. She found herself more and more entranced by the look on his face, and she began to shower kisses on him. She had lost all sense of whether she was ever going to stop, she put her hands all over his face and body, now stroking, now grabbing hold, not thinking about what she was doing. All the time she was murmuring: "I miss you, I miss you, I have really missed you so much. I'm sure you have no idea! Why didn't you come to see me? You really are a bastard. Look at the moon! Have you forgotten that this time every month is when we meet? You are completely selfish and only ever think of what it is that you want. I hate you, I love you, I wish I could eat you up." Now her murmurings had gradually become moans. She began to bite him on the lips, the nose, the earlobes. Her whole body seemed to have come to life, and her desires threatened to overwhelm her.

Guo Cunxian was starting to get a bit nervous. He simply had no faith in his own body any more, and the shadow left in his mind by his failure with his wife was still casting a dark spell. He no longer had control over his emotional state. Think of what had happened to him lately! But the greater the danger, the more intense the excitement. Lin Meitang was writhing in his lap, and the passionate words she was murmuring to him were getting him into a state. Danger makes people tense but that tension can result in great explosions. He could feel his erection growing, as if beyond his control, and the more determined he was not to become excited, the more stiff he could feel it become. It was the only thing he could think about, and it was in control, it was going to do what it wanted to do. Quick as a trice, he'd pulled Lin Meitang's trousers down and pushed himself between her legs. A sudden wild excitement brought the two of them together, driven by an intense desire. One pair of lips sought the other, one tongue sought the other, the knife plunged into the wound and the finger placed itself on the trigger, as their hips thrust in unison. She wanted her body to become one with his as they mated like a pair of wild animals.

The leaves of the tree above their heads rustled, and the insects chirped away as the moon slid slowly to the west. Guo Cunxian was more happy than he could say. His self-respect had been restored. He was still the man he'd always been, the Guo Cunxian who could have any woman he wanted. He wasn't tense or nervous. The burden that had been weighing so heavily on his spirits had been removed. He wasn't thinking about anything any more, as he lost himself in the pleasures of the flesh, enjoying their mutual arousal. He could feel that Lin Meitang was moving more and more gently against him, that she was stretching her limbs, that her breathing was becoming more rasping, and her moans and murmurs softer. He was feeling very pleased with himself, and as always he enjoyed the way that Lin Meitang expressed her pursuit of pleasure. She wasn't like the peasant women who were so restrained, who couldn't let themselves go. He wanted her to orgasm, so he clasped Lin Meitang's firm waist between his hands as like a battering ram he thrust against her, first vigorously and then more gently, as he proceeded with the most basic and animal of connections. He said all the things that are only ever said at moments like this.

Having been engulfed by passion, they now lay on the ground in each other's arms.

The Lucky Trees protected them from the falling dew, and the night scene around them was very peaceful and still. Lin Meitang really wished that she could lie there forever, locked in her lover's arms.

Her body had offered Guo Cunxian exactly what he needed. He was feeling content, his worries had vanished, and he found that he wasn't scared of anything any more. He felt as if he'd turned into a different person, and been renewed from inside out. It was really odd. He'd been quite sure that he was impotent but then, all of a sudden, it had worked out with Lin Meitang. The best things in life are the things that you really need but they aren't necessarily either right or legal.

Lin Meitang was quite shameless. She was lying on the ground not feeling like moving, and she had her arms round his neck and was refusing to let go. He hugged her in his arms and then started to help her get dressed again: "Lying on the ground, you'll get cold. Your warm body is pressed against the cold earth and it's easy to get sick that way."

"You're worried I might get sick? I was just thinking it would be best if I died like this!"

She didn't want to leave him. After sex, she found it amusing to quarrel a bit.

Guo Cunxian didn't care. If you have a young woman as a girlfriend, sometimes you have to be patient and cajole her as you would with a small child: "It wouldn't matter if I died, I've had a good life. But you cannot die yet."

"Why not?"

"You haven't begun to bloom."

"What do you mean 'bloom'? I'm withering on the vine! And it's all your fault!"

"It's not all my fault. I've been tending you, to make sure that the prettiest flower in all of Guojiadian blooms even more beautifully. Otherwise how would you be getting so many offers of marriage? Haven't Guo Cunyong and An Jinghui both been trying to introduce you to suitable men?"

"How do you know that?"

"Is there anything in Guojiadian that I don't know about?"

"Are you jealous?" Lin Meitang was pleased at this idea. She put her two arms back round Guo Cunxian's neck. "You know how much you mean to me. What kind of man would be good enough for me now? If the man is young and handsome, he seems silly and useless. If he is gentle and refined, and tries to please me, then I find that he isn't manly enough for me. What am I to do?"

Guo Cunxian didn't even smile. "You're the kind of person to attract attention, and so you get a lot of people wanting to help out, and a lot wanting to give you advice. In my opinion, there are two things to consider here. First, you cannot go home right now, because the moment you leave here, everyone will say that you are running away, and they will be quite sure there is something in it, that you've done something wrong. Besides which, going back to the city won't take you far enough away. You might hide from the first round of questioning but they'll find you sooner or later. Second, while I think that it would be a good idea for you to get married, you can't do anything about it right now. Trying to cover things up would only make it worse. We can't underestimate these people, and you can't just pull a suitable fiancé out of your hat. If you can't find someone suitable straight away, it's going to be a while before you can get married anyway. Then everyone will say that you are trying to pull some kind of trick and distract attention from the main issue. Everything is going to have to wait a little while."

Guo Cunxian always seemed to think more deeply about things than those around him, and he often came up with an unexpected opinion. That was his style. Seeing the dark and unhappy expression in his eyes, Lin Meitang felt uneasy. "Are you cross?"

"No."

"I'm not going anywhere, I'm not marrying anyone else. I'm going to stay here in Guojiadian with you. If anyone thinks they are going to punish you over this, then I'll tell them that I seduced you. I will take all the blame for breaking up your family."

"Are you completely stupid? That would mean admitting everything! If they don't have your confession it's going to be really difficult to punish me, but the minute you admit that we've been having an affair then it's not going to be you who decides who seduced whom! Think about your position and think about mine. Since I am the secretary here, I have a position of power, and everyone is going to believe that I've been raping you! You can say that you seduced me, but there isn't anyone who's going to listen. Remember, if you really want to help me, you have to refuse to say a word, even if they hold a knife to your throat."

"No problem. If something really does happen to you, I'll wait for you, I'll come and see you wherever you are, and when you get old, I'll look after you."

"It's not going to happen. And if things do go wrong for me, I want you to leave Guojiadian as quickly as you can and go back to the city."

When a woman falls in love with a man obsessively, she is likely to become very stubborn, and that can be difficult for her lover to deal with. Guo Cunxian took hold of Lin Meitang and began to walk her out from under the shadow of the trees: "I'll take you back home."

"No. I can go home by myself. You had better leave a little bit later." Women can be very changeable, and in the blink of an eye, Lin Meitang had gone back to being the thoughtful and sensible person that she was. This was exactly what Guo Cunxian had intended. It was the middle of the night and if, by some mischance, they had bumped into someone on the way home, then he might as well have come right out and confessed everything. But if he refused to escort her home, it would show how cowardly and selfish he really was.

He felt a bit embarrassed. "Won't you be frightened going back on your own?"

"There's only one thing in the world that I'm frightened of right now."

"What's that?"

"I'm afraid that you'll think me a burden, that you'll get bored of me, and that one day you'll just toss me aside. Other than that, there's nothing I'm scared of."

"Meitang!" Guo Cunxian turned round and wrapped her in his arms, pressing her back against the trunk of the tree. His burning lips kissed her lips, her face, her neck, her ears and her hair with sudden passion. "Meitang, I love you. You're so beautiful! Even if they kill me for this, it would all be worth it!" He was overwhelmed with desire, the spark had been lit again, and it carried with it all of his strength and weaknesses.

At dawn, Qian Xishou was jogging around Guojiadian with a smile on his face. All of a sudden, the atmosphere in Guojiadian became markedly more tense, as everyone speculated on what this smile might mean on the face of someone of his position. The more he smiled, the more miserable the people he was investigating ought to be. Since he was smiling in this inscrutable and odd way, might that not mean that Guo Cunxian's future was indeed very uncertain? In these kinds of circumstances, the people of Guojiadian showed their usual skill in thinking the worst. Whether unintentionally or not, they had ignored the fact that a smile can be used to achieve other ends. You can smile to cover up for the fact that you are crying, and a smile can also be a weapon to deceive others. Individual feelings can be very complex and difficult to understand, and there are so many ways in which emotion can be expressed, so many odd and strange ways. There you are feeling embarrassed or depressed, resentful and angry, and yet this can be expressed in a smile, and that smile can be used to calm your emotions and bring back your self-esteem. Anyone looking at the person smiling would find it impossible to imagine that they were being held hostage by someone else, or being controlled by others...

Only Qian Xishou was aware that this might very well be his last visit to Guojiadian.

Qian Xishou had a lot of experience in this matter, because over the years he'd been caught up in all kinds of different political movements and struggles. He was accustomed to the vicissitudes of fate, to the caprices of his superiors, to the fact that he might be forced to retreat even when evidence of wrongdoing was blatant. It was this experience that enabled him to keep running round the village with a smile on his face, keeping his thoughts to himself. From the moment he had failed to get the hoped-for result from the Municipal Committee, and instead received orders to withdraw the investigation team, he had been overwhelmed by a sense of his own failure, for all that he still acted like a victor.

In actual fact, he hadn't failed. Any failure here was to be felt by the higher-ups who had decided to send out the investigation team. He was merely the executive arm. From the perspective of the person on the ground, Qian Xishou didn't feel that he'd been defeated by Guo Cunxian, a mere peasant, but by the fact that he'd underestimated the problems attendant on the complex and difficult relationships between various of his superiors. Divisions had arisen over differences of opinion about what was going on in Guojiadian, and these had only deepened, or perhaps it would be more accurate to say that because there were pre-existing differences of opinion, the problems arising in Guojiadian had exacerbated the situation. He had been caught in the middle but had managed to get out before things got too bad. Who knew whether this might turn out to be a good thing or not?

Since it might turn out to be a good thing, he had to behave as if this were the case. He was going to leave Guojiadian something to think about. He wanted Guo Cunxian to feel the sword of Damocles hanging over his head, threatening to fall at any moment and slay him! He didn't want the peasants here to realise that the Party had misfired on this one, and that they had placed an unbearable burden on the investigation team. Therefore, although he could just have stayed at home and not appeared, sending Feng Hou the necessary documents regarding the final result, he had decided to come back. The investigation had to come to a formal end. He had brought them here in a procession, and now he was going to take them away again the same way. It had been his duty to come here, and now it was his duty to leave.

For other members of the investigation team, leaving Guojiadian ought to have been an unalloyed pleasure, but nobody seemed to be too happy about it. For the investigation to be left hanging, for it to be shelved like that, would mean that they were leaving all sorts of problems unresolved. Leaving with things still unresolved, that was simply letting it slide, and it was very difficult for them to avoid feeling that they'd been messed around, and that finally, the people in Guojiadian had succeeded in getting rid of them. There were very few members of the team who had managed to achieve Qian Xishou's levels of detachment. Because of this feeling that everyone was pulling together, Qian Xishou's orders were carried out with unusual sincerity. Everyone had to write their own mini report, to explain what part they had played in the investigation, what they had achieved and what they hadn't had time to investigate, as well as what they knew about Guo Cunxian. All of the material was taken back to the Municipal Committee where it went into storage. Should the city ever feel the need for any further investigations into Guojiadian, these documents might come in handy.

All that remained was to hold one final meeting before they all went their separate ways. Qian Xishou would then hand over the final report from the investigation that he had personally authored, after which they could pack up and leave. However, as soon as he had finished breakfast, Feng Hou had gone off somewhere outside the village to arrange things for the well diggers, and without him present, they simply could not hold their final meeting.

Feng Hou was just on his way to the eastern fields when he was stopped by Ou Guangming. He was holding up two big fish in one hand, tied together with a nylon line. The two fish were gulping away, and trotting along behind him came a dog. Feng Hou thought this a remarkable scene, so he called out: "Hey! What's the occasion?"

Ou Guangming held the fish even higher, and his eyes glittered: "Mr Feng, I was just on my way to invite you. You've got to come to my house for lunch because my team is going to be setting off this afternoon!"

"Thank you very much. I hope everything goes well for you but I simply cannot make it to lunch, I've got far too much to do."

"That wouldn't be right at all!" Ou Guangming was determined not to let Feng Hou go until he had promised to come. He had his own little scheme up his sleeve, whereby once he got to the city he would be negotiating for contracts on his own, and if he had Feng Hou behind him, wouldn't everything go so much more smoothly? This might all be something Guo Cunyong had put him up to... who knew? Therefore Ou Guangming was making a fuss about it, since he had to make use of this opportunity to build a relationship with Feng Hou on his own account, though he was pretending that Guo Cunxian had asked him to do this, and that he would be furious if the invitation was refused.

Everyone in Guojiadian knew how dictatorial Guo Cunxian could be, and so there was nothing that Feng Hou could do. He was far too easygoing to deal with someone like that. With a bitter smile, he was spun round and dragged back to Guojiadian by Ou Guangming. As it happened, Guo Cunxian had not yet come home when they arrived, and when Zhu Xuezhen saw Ou Guangming holding the two fish and with the dog trotting along behind, she was quite taken aback. She stood there staring at him, and her face went absolutely white. Without saying a word of greeting to Feng Hou (who was, after all, a stranger to her), she shouted at Ou Guangming: "What on earth are you dragging those fish about for?"

Ou Guangming smiled. "To eat them! What do you think?"

"Throw them away!"

"Throw them away?" Ou Guangming thought that she'd gone off her head again. "No!"

"Well, kick the dog away then!"

"Why?"

"It's inauspicious! Someone's going to die!"

She'd gone off her head again. Ou Guangming laughed as he walked away: "You don't need to cook lunch. Come round to my place with Cunxian and eat with Mr Feng."

Having gone a few steps, Feng Hou turned round suddenly. In a low voice, he asked Zhu Xuezhen: "Mrs Guo, why would a dog walking after a fish mean that someone is going to die?"

Zhu Xuezhen was standing stock still, staring after Ou Guangming's retreating back. When she heard the question, she turned to face Feng Hou: "There were two mouths up above a dog, so what Chinese character does that make?" As she spoke she bent down and picked up a stick of charcoal, and wrote it on the ground. It was the character ku (哭), which means 'to cry'.

Feng Hou was shocked. The two fish with their mouths open would be the two mouths in the character, and then dog would be the bottom bit. He was worried that Ou Guangming might notice the character that she had written on the ground, and so he turned round and went to join him. He announced that Guo Cunxian must be out at the eastern fields and that they should head in that direction.

Just as he had expected, Guo Cunxian was there with several other cadres, considering the well-digging programme. Food for the workforce had been arranged without any problem, since that was all the responsibility of the commune, but finding them somewhere to stay was proving more difficult. The investigation team was filling all the empty property. He suggested to Feng Hou that perhaps the answer might be to have the diggers put up in different houses in the village?

Feng Hou said that this wouldn't be necessary, since most of the investigation team would be leaving that afternoon. They could just clean up the rooms and put the diggers in to live where they had been.

Guo Cunxian pricked up his ears: "Did you just say that the investigation team is leaving?"

Feng Hou called him off to one side and told him that the investigation team was leaving, but that Mr Qian had demanded that a couple of people stay a little longer in Guojiadian, with me in command. The Municipal Committee had already agreed to this. However, I can't stay here like I have been, since this is only one small part of my duties. If I have time, I'll come past and have a look at you.

"Qian Xishou is leaving?" This news was so important, and he had come across it so suddenly. For a long time Guo Cunxian had believed that nothing good was going to happen to him ever again, so it was not likely that he would trust anyone bringing him good news. This was going to have to be repeated again and again before he was prepared to take it in.

"Cunxian," Feng Hou said. "It seems to me that the investigation team coming to Guojiadian isn't necessarily a bad thing. At the very least it has rung some alarm bells and got you to tidy up a bit after yourself. When they leave this afternoon, we are all going to have to turn out to see them off and say a few polite words."

Guo Cunxian agreed to that, but a new light was shining in his eyes.

At this time Guo Cunyong was standing off to one side, feeling as if he had just been stabbed in the heart. He had been quite sure that his promotion was within sight, but his dreams were crumbling before his very eyes. Now he had to put all his best efforts into pretending that he was thrilled to see the investigation team go, so that no one would realise his true feelings, particularly not Guo Cunxian.

Realising that he had been, as it were, restored to life, Guo Cunxian seemed to have completely forgotten the promises he had made to Guo Cunyong.

Feng Hou made the necessary arrangements and rushed back to the investigation team. The moment he appeared, Gao Wenping – who was absolutely furious about what had happened but had nowhere to express his irritation – broke in, without waiting for Qian Xishou to formally open the meeting: "Look everybody! Mr Feng here had the right idea about things. He knew from the very beginning that we wouldn't be staying long, so he was thinking about a way out, trying to help out Guojiadian. He was part of the investigation team, but at the same time he's busy making them a well for drinking water. He hits them with one hand and pats them with the other. He's really very clever!"

Feng Hou gave a hearty laugh: "If there is a problem to investigate then that's what I do. But if there's also a difficulty, I think I ought to help out."

"We've been waiting to start until you turned up, just like a dumb woman waiting for her idiot husband."

This was a gauntlet that Feng Hou was not going to pick up. Cui Daben glared at Gao Wenping with a very ugly expression on his face. Everyone else present was hoping that Gao Wenping would not cause any more distractions. They all wanted to hear what Qian Xishou had to say. What reason was he going to give for pulling out a huge investigation team half way through their enquiry?

"Right, everybody is here, we can begin the meeting immediately." Qian Xishou's face, so much like that of an old lady, looked a great deal more conciliatory than on the occasion of previous meetings. It seemed that he was uncomfortable about the anxiety caused to the various members of the investigation team because of all this speculation and waiting around. "I have been to report the progress our investigation team has achieved here in Guojiadian to the Municipal Party Committee. The comrades leading the committee have fully affirmed our work, and they understand that everyone is having a hard time here. Our experienced team has achieved great results, which gives these senior comrades confidence in the way the situation has been handled. They feel that our report will be very valuable for analysing and researching the current situation in rural villages. However, in view of the enormous pressures that some of our colleagues' original work units are under, the situation here cannot continue. We cannot keep such a large investigation team in Guojiadian any longer if it is not absolutely necessary. Therefore the Municipal Party Committee has decided that the majority of our comrades will have to withdraw, leaving behind a three-person team led by Comrade Feng Hou. As to who will leave and who will stay behind, we can sort that out later. Right now I would like to invite Comrade An Jinghui to read aloud the conclusion of our final report, and then we can discuss it and make any final revisions."

Given what he had just said, who had the slightest interest in what this damned final report said? What affirmation of our work? What work unit pressures? This was all finding a way out for oneself, and making it look good with a formal document going to the higher-ups showing what had been 'achieved'. The reader wasn't interested and the listeners weren't concentrating. Everyone was worrying about who was going to be left behind.

Luo Denggao was looking relaxed. He poked Wu Lie, who was sitting next to him, in the ribs and whispered: "You see? What did I say when we first arrived here? These kinds of investigations are quite different from what you are used to in the police. You need to keep something in reserve. If the moment you enter the village you start going at it hammer and tongs, you will make the whole situation impossible. How could you then sort it out amicably?"

"This isn't sorting it out amicably, this is making a pig's ear of things and then waltzing away leaving everything in a mess," Wu Lie said. "This is a joke for Guojiadian, and it's making a complete mockery of our investigation. You're one of the more experienced people on the team. Who do you think is going to be left behind?"

"Well, it won't be me. If they tried to make me stay, I'd refuse."

"What about me?"

"I doubt it."

"Who then?"

Luo Denggao turned his gaze towards Gao Wenping.

Gao Wenping was the most anxious of any of them. The moment An Jinghui had finished reading the conclusion of their report, he could hold himself back no longer. He rushed in to make his objection: "We've been doing really well, so why are we giving up halfway? If we are just going to let it go like this, it shows how useless an investigation team is. What kind of deterrent is that? Everyone is going to be laughing at us."

Cui Daben had decided long ago that he didn't like this show-off would-be Casanova, and since the investigation team was clearly on the way out, it was time for him to be put in his place: "I guess you simply cannot get enough of punishing people, and here at last was a wonderful opportunity for you to get busy. I guess you feel that you haven't had enough of throwing your weight around, and that your itch to punish the wretches that cross your path hasn't been scratched enough?"

At this point Luo Denggao whispered to Wu Lie: "He's the kind of person who uses people, but doesn't understand when they use him back. Leaving two or three people behind is just for show, they don't want to admit that sending the investigation team here in the first place might have been a mistake. So this is 'cutting down the workforce', it isn't abandoning the investigation."

"What are you talking about? Why is everyone trying to get at me?" Gao Wenping was shouting now. "The investigation team hasn't been disbanded yet, but everyone is already going their separate ways!"

An Jinghui was closer to Gao Wenping than any of the others. He liked spending time with her, and on occasion he had bought her snacks or helped her out with this and that. She was the only person who could help him now. "Wenping, this is a real hot potato. There are all sorts of complicated things going on that we aren't in a position to understand. This situation is very unpredictable. You've been complaining so much about missing your wife, and you always say that you can't get anything decent to eat, and where you're staying is really uncomfortable. I don't see why you wouldn't be happy just to go home."

"How do you know that he'll be going home?" Luo Denggao asked. "Someone as interested in this investigation as Comrade Gao Wenping ought to be staying behind, to continue with our mission."

Gao Wenping saw that a way out had been given to him, but he didn't want to take it. "Don't we have to write an 'Internal Reference Document' for our superiors? Do we have a result to report or not? If this investigation team is going to be disbanded now, then that proves we shouldn't have come in the first place. So why does anyone have to stay behind?"

Qian Xishou hurried to explain: "The pertinent Internal Reference Document has already been submitted to the relevant authorities, and by this time it must also have gone to the central government. However, so far, there hasn't been any response from them. The moment there is, everyone will know about it."

"That's just pointless. Maybe there will never be any result, and it's going to be like a stone thrown into the sea!" Wu Lie was now starting to become anxious. "Mr Qian, we don't have any concerns about the conclusion of your report, so how about you announce who is going to leave and who will have to stay behind. The people who are leaving will need to pack, since they will be wanting to get off immediately after lunch."

Everyone was pleased with this suggestion.

Qian Xishou said, in an elegant and unhurried manner: "We've been living here together for more than two months, and everybody has got on really well together. I would like to thank everyone for their support, and I will be providing money to buy a couple of bottles of wine to go with our lunch, so that everybody can enjoy a last meal together before leaving. Let me announce that the senior comrades in charge of our mission here have already agreed that in addition to Comrade Feng Hou, Comrades Cui Daben and Gao Wenping will be staying behind, carrying on the investigation here in Guojiadian."

Everyone burst out laughing, but it was dry laughter and did not last long. Once it had stopped, a dead silence was observed.

In truth, there was nothing to laugh at. Feng Hou was merely a nominal head, and this appointment was to maintain a balance between different factions in the Municipal Party Committee. Cui Daben was in charge of this locale, so he would in effect be staying anyway. To have his name put down as well was a matter of face for the investigation team. For the two of them this was a good move, something that was easily anticipated, and it would allow them to enjoy full honours during their time in the village. Making Gao Wenping stay behind, on the other hand, was a joke that might also be a tragedy. The others would be leaving the member of the team that they most disliked and that they all had the greatest problems in working with. It might be that Qian Xishou had some underlying scheme in mind, that he wanted Gao Wenping to stay so that he could cause trouble for Feng Hou, thereby keeping alive the flame that the investigation team had brought to the village. That would also serve to keep Guo Cunxian on his toes. But it was cruel of Qian Xishou to do this. Ordinarily Gao Wenping was the person who made the most effort to flatter him, who spent time trying to please him. This arrangement was very much to Gao Wenping's detriment; when he was here on his own, the horrible inhabitants of Guojiadian could torment him at their leisure.

"That's great," Wu Lie said in a loud voice. "That's a really good idea on the part of the Municipal Committee, and it's just what Gao Wenping wants."

Gao Wenping didn't want the investigation team to leave, and he didn't want to abandon their work like that, but the idea that out of all of the people who had come from the city, he would be the only one to stay behind, was deeply painful. He couldn't find it in himself to be as respectful as usual to Qian Xishou: "Hey, boss! Don't think you can get away with bullying me like this! Why should I have to stay?"

Qian Xishou glanced at him: "Our superiors thought that you would be the most suitable on a number of counts. First, your work unit doesn't seem to be particularly keen to recall you. And second, we really need to have someone who understands accountancy here."

This put Gao Wenping in an even more awkward position. It seemed as though the people in his work unit didn't particularly like him and would be quite happy to be assured that he'd never be coming back. He felt deeply humiliated: "I'm not staying here, I insist on being allowed to return to my original work unit. They can't just abandon me here, can they?"

"From now on, if you have any problem, you will have to speak to Comrade Feng Hou." Qian Xishou had clearly decided he wanted nothing more to do with this.

Feng Hou sat there looking benevolent. He knew exactly what was going on but he wasn't going to say anything. He kept a smile on his face, with no sign of any irritation or anger.

Cui Daben, on the other hand, was looking scornful. It was quite obvious, nobody could care less about him where he came from, so how could he have the gall to stay behind in Guojiadian and investigate people? Was it likely that the people of Guojiadian would stand for that? The anger everyone had felt about the activities of the investigation team could all be taken out on him. He'd have to pay the price for what they had done, and it was going to be fun to watch.

Gao Wenping had already realised the dangers of his position, and he wanted to cause a massive scene, but he didn't know whether that would get him anywhere. He had to restrain himself.

An Jinghui tried to comfort him: "Don't worry. If you don't want to stay, when I get back I'll think of some way to make your work unit recall you."

Wu Lie was already thinking about going home, and he wanted to have lunch as soon as possible: "Let's go and eat. We can get off as soon as we've had our lunch."

"If we're leaving, we should go as soon as we can," Luo Denggao agreed. "There's no point dragging things out here. If the local peasants find out that we are going, they might well come and cause trouble." Before he could finish speaking, his voice was drowned by the sound of drums and gongs out on the main road, accompanied by enormous numbers of firecrackers being let off, mixed with the sound of shouting and running feet. "What did I say? They want to get rid of us as soon as they can!"

Wu Lie was surprised: "They got the news pretty quick!"

The next person to chime in was An Jinghui, but she didn't seem happy to hear the drums and gongs being played. "From my understanding of village customs, they only have gongs and drums with firecrackers when someone has died, or if they are celebrating the departure of the Plague God."

"Whatever," Luo Denggao said. "The Plague God is still a god!"

It was Feng Hou who explained: "You are all quite wrong. This is to celebrate the digging of the new well!"

Qian Xishou wasn't smiling any more. His face was glacial, and his lips were pressed even more tightly together.

Everybody has something in their hearts that will run wild if not kept under strict control.

If you think about it carefully, sooner or later everyone has a moment where they just want to go berserk. The men hitting the drums and gongs were doing so more and more loudly, faster and faster, as if they were beating a plague out of the village, as if they would have liked to beat a hole in the drums or bashed the gongs so hard that they broke. The people striking the drums were hitting harder, while those listening were getting more excited. The sound of the drums conveyed information faster than any loudspeaker, and everyone understood their message as well as if the village cadres had been going door-to-door. In less time than it takes to eat a meal, the whole village knew that the investigation team was leaving.

The inhabitants of Guojiadian couldn't stay at home, they all wanted to come out to the eastern fields to see what was happening. If there is something going on, who wouldn't want to go and see? The young people who had been lighting firecrackers, with Liu Fugen and Eagle Eye at their head, had also now gone berserk. Sometimes they lit firecrackers which they then threw on the ground; sometimes they put wooden discs on people's heads and lit them there; and sometimes they hung a long string up in the crook of a tree and set light to the fuse. There were double-firing crackers that could be shot off to explode in mid-air, and there were landmine-like crackers that went off under people's feet and enveloped them in a cloud of smoke and confetti.

Light as many as you like, wherever you please. The manager of the food factory, Wang Sun, had already given the word that after they ran out of firecrackers, they could go and find his accountant to get money to pay for more.

If the investigation team was leaving, it was worth spending a bit of money!

It didn't actually matter that much whether the investigation team left, because the people causing all of this racket wouldn't be directly affected either way. It was because they weren't concerned that they wanted to take this opportunity to cause an uproar. They could bang the drums and light firecrackers to their hearts' content. If they felt like it they could shout and scream; if they wanted to harass a woman, they could squeeze into the crowd of girls and young married women and feel them up. Anyone who felt like cursing just cursed, and anyone who felt like laughing just laughed. This was a day of celebration for Guojiadian.

All of a sudden the people out in the western fields found themselves surrounded by drummers and people letting off firecrackers, banging and shouting, yelling at the tops of their voices, with the racket interspersed with explosions. They were just enjoying themselves. Did they really hate the investigation team that much? Was it really a subject for such rejoicing that they were leaving? They were happy for their leader, and the whole village had turned out to celebrate him. They were spending their money in the hope that it would make him happy. Today was a festival for him, and whatever they did, he simply didn't care. How many festivals in the whole of history have been held for a single man?

The Lucky Trees were looking lovely, and underneath them someone had piled up a little mound of soil and stuck three sticks of incense in. A couple of children had climbed up into the trees and were now sitting on branches with their legs hanging down, looking very pleased with themselves. Right up at the very top of the elm, there were a few white 'elm coins' still hanging there, and suspended from the lower branches was a huge banner:

"Warmest Welcome to the Well-Digging Team!

Warmest Congratulations on the Founding of the Guojiadian International Construction Company!

Warmest Congratulations to the Guojiadian Chemical Works on Beginning Production!"

Among those with the most mixed emotions on being at the centre of this excited crowd was Guo Cunyong. He looked at the banner and snorted. These messages were all mere fluff. What Guo Cunxian was actually pleased about was getting rid of the investigation team, so why didn't he just come right out and say so? He was perfectly capable of it!

Ou Guangming and Jin Laixi each had a small baggage roll to hand as they were ticking off the workforce, telling them to put their luggage on the truck that was parked off to one side. The men were all hoping to earn big money by leaving the village to go and work in the city, so they were looking even more excited than the men banging the drums and letting off firecrackers. A large number of other people were now standing around them, and some were even trying to find out how to register to join their ranks.

At the head of this motley group was Wang Shun. He was wandering in and out of the crowd, giving instructions to this one, pointing something out to another, and then every so often he would run over and sit under the great trees to have a cigarette with Guo Cunxian and ask for his advice about something. He saw that trucks were coming out of the chemical works fully laden, and then gestured at the people banging drums and gongs, and the ones lighting firecrackers, that they should all stop. The eastern fields fell silent, but everyone's ears were still ringing. Smoke was still floating in the air, and the Lucky Trees were partially hidden by this haze, so that it seemed as if they were floating. This made the people who still hadn't had enough fun out of the occasion feel for a moment as if they were riding on the clouds.

Trucks were parked by the side of the highway running past the western fields, filled with the products of the Guojiadian chemical works. The works had deliberately chosen a very pretty young woman to keep guard over the trucks. She looked like a flower blossoming among the metal.

Ou Guangming stepped up to the microphone and announced in a loud voice: "I declare this meeting open!"

Since when did he notify us that there was going to be a meeting? "Guo Cunxian is going to say a few words."

Guo Cunxian stood up: "Comrades and fellow villagers, today we in Guojiadian have three, no, four things to celebrate, and in future there may be a further five or six. The first thing we have to celebrate is that Mr Feng has brought a well-digging team here, and very shortly every house will have piped water installed. This shows the care and support that our leaders have for us. The second thing that we have to celebrate is that the entire initial production of the chemical works has already been sold, and there is ever-increasing demand. We can sell everything that we can produce. Who would have imagined that the very first business established in this village would do so well? The third thing that we have to celebrate is the founding of our construction company. We are going to be starting work immediately, and very soon there will be tower blocks all over Tianjin built by people from Guojiadian. The fourth thing to celebrate is that we've had the investigation team here for several months, and in spite of putting us through a fine-tooth comb, for all their digging, they haven't been able to find any evidence of wrongdoing. This is all to the good. It proves that we aren't afraid of being investigated and that we have nothing to worry about. The investigation only shows that we have been vindicated! Today, the majority of the team will be leaving Guojiadian. We need to thank them, we need to give them a good send-off, and we need to show that they will be welcomed if they ever choose to come back. Why do we have these things to celebrate? They are the results of taking risks! If I hadn't risked being severely punished, would we be enjoying these results today? Running a risk doesn't guarantee that you'll get rich, but you definitely can't get rich without taking a chance. You may get punished because you've taken a risk, but being punished is better than being poor. When it comes right down to it, this is all because we don't want to be poor any more. We have to seize the opportunities that we're presented with."

He was cut short by the sound of a shout in the distance: "Guangming, Ou Guangming!"

This strangled noise made everyone start. The people out at the western fields all turned round to look. They saw someone come running up, shouting: "Where is Ou Guangming? Ou Guangming."

Ou Guangming recognised his brother-in-law, Liu Yucheng. He came running as fast as he could towards the crowd.

"Dog's Bollocks has had an accident!"

"What?" Ou Guangming grabbed hold of Liu Yucheng.

"He's been run over!"

"What?" Ou Guangming started running. "Where is he?"

"He's over by the northern highway."

The meeting under the trees was immediately thrown into chaos. Some people were running off towards the north of the village following on behind Ou Guangming. It was exciting for them, and a much more intense thrill than anything that had been going on before, so they had to participate. They had to go and look. They didn't care whether there were three things to celebrate or four; they didn't care whether there was a party or whether they were going to see people off; neither did they care whether this fun had been carefully prepared in advance or whether it was something that came off the top of someone's head. What mattered was that the opportunities here for further uproar were over.

Guo Cunxian stopped Liu Yucheng: "How did Dog's Bollocks get run over?"

"Well, Guangming was leaving, so I thought that it would be a good idea if my sister and nephew came to stay with me for a bit. Dog's Bollocks was late being let out of school, and he was in a hurry to get to the western fields to see the fun, so he just threw his bag at his mum and ran off with a bun in his hand, not even bothering to eat a proper dinner. He ran straight into a truck on the highway."

"Whose truck?"

"The truck just drove off, but the chances are it came from Dahua Steel."

"Is Dog's Bollocks badly injured?"

Liu Yucheng's face was tear-stained: "He's dead."

Guo Cunxian's heart missed a beat. Without saying another word, he turned round and began to head off towards the north.

As he walked away, the village cadres all trotted along in his wake.

Jin Laixi was standing stock still with his hand on the tailgate of the truck. There were various members of his new workforce standing around, trying to get him to express an opinion. "Boss, in the circumstances, Guangming isn't going to be going anywhere, so what do we do?"

"Yeah, it's really inauspicious! We haven't even set off yet and someone's already dead."

"That's what people mean when they say that too much happiness leads to a tragedy, four joys will end in a funeral."

Jin Laixi didn't say a word, no matter what the others said. His head was lowered and his eyes had narrowed to mere slits. He wasn't looking at anybody. As the saying goes, 'women shake their heads and men lower them'. Men like Jin Laixi, who hang their heads and keep their own counsel, are very difficult to deal with.

Guo Cunyong walked over with a serious expression on his face: "Laixi, your partners on this project want you to hurry up. Although Guangming cannot possibly go, you are going to have to take your people off now. When you get to the city, you will have a couple of days to settle in, sort yourselves out and make the necessary preparations. Work is going to begin immediately."

Jin Laixi looked at him, and there was a flash in his tiny eyes, but it was gone in an instant. "Don't we have to wait for the higher-ups to make a decision? If Mr Ou isn't leading the team, who is going to be in charge?"

"Hey, don't try that on me. Ou Guangming was going to be dealing with any political issues, but the work was all going to be down to you. If there's any problem I'm going to come looking for you. This is nothing whatsoever to do with him."

Jin Laixi blinked: "How about you consider coming with us for a bit, to replace Guangming for a few days?"

This was exactly what Guo Cunyong had in mind. If Guo Cunxian wasn't going to lose his job, what was the point in him staying in the village? It was time to play his second card, and try and develop his own independent career. Right now the village had been thrown into confusion, but Guo Cunxian was clearly going to come out on top. There wasn't any point in crawling along behind him hoping for a few crumbs to drop from his table, besides which, he couldn't stand him looking so smug. Guo Cunyong wasn't interested in playing second fiddle to anyone. In future he hoped to find ways to use Guo Cunxian, rather than just being used himself. His current problem was how to get away from Guojiadian as quickly as possible. Ou Guangming, having suffered this tragedy, gave him the perfect excuse. Having realised this, he set off running northwards as quickly as he could.

The excitement that had been taking place in the western fields had now moved to the northern part of the village. There were now several hundred people massed by the side of the highway that led from the city to the Dahua Steel Company works, but nobody was enjoying themselves here. The only sound that could be heard was that of crying. This was real, uncontrollable crying, deep, gut-wrenching sobs. Ou Guangming was cradling the crushed body of his son. He was wailing and banging his head on the ground: "Dog's Bollocks, this is all my fault! I am so sorry! Wait for me, I will get whoever did this to you and then they can shoot me for it. I will be coming to join you."

He was crying hopelessly, a sound filled with regret, shame and overwhelming misery. The people standing around now pressed forward, grabbing hold of his arms. They managed to get Dog's Bollocks' body away from him and put it down on the leaf of a door. Then Ou Guangming's wife, Liu Yumei, came rushing towards them, howling. She was having problems breathing, and then she pitched forward in a dead faint. Fortunately, Lin Meitang and Ou Huaying were right there next to her, so one of them held her up, while the other one brought her round by applying pressure to the acupuncture point on her upper lip. Two of the old men present made sure she was kept warm. If there was one thing the villagers knew about, it was how to look after someone who'd just had something terrible happen to them.

Members of the Ou family and their various relatives by marriage were in floods of tears too, and even those who were just there for the excitement felt a prickling in their noses and their eyes welling up. Lin Meitang should have been trying to get Liu Yumei away, but she simply couldn't say a word and the tears were coursing down her cheeks. She had another reason to be upset: after Dog's Bollocks had been born, she'd persuaded Liu Yumei to undergo sterilisation. It was her fault that this family would now never have another child.

Guo Cunxiao kept a strong grip on Ou Guangming's shoulder as he gave instructions to have Dog's Bollocks carried into the hut. He was laid out there, and a sheet was placed over the body. "Guangming, crying won't help with this. You need to pull yourself together. Someone has to make decisions about the funeral…"

Some of the onlookers added their voices to the chorus but the majority were cursing. They swore, screamed and shouted at the top of their voices. Some of them were swearing that drivers for Dahua Steel were evil bastards, who ran away after killing people. Some of them were swearing that Dahua Steel were monopolising Guojiadian land. Some of them were swearing because their trucks were shaking the houses by the road to bits. And some of them were swearing because over the past few years Dahua Steel's trucks had killed so many chickens, pigs and sheep in Guojiadian. The inhabitants of Guojiadian were standing around, thinking about all the irritations and losses they had suffered. Once their attention had been directed to something, they wanted to fight. Some of them were now grabbing steel shovels and hoes, and in a flash there was a trench dug right across the highway. Dahua Steel's trucks could forget about coming this way in future.

There were also plenty of people to curse Ou Guanghe. They thought he was a complete bastard. If it hadn't been for him forcing his brother and sister-in-law out of the house so they had to live in that little hut right next to the highway, would this tragedy have happened today? Dear little Dog's Bollocks had effectively been murdered by his own uncle.

It looked like Ou Guanghe was feeling bad about what he had done too, because he cried for a bit, and then he cursed for a bit. The more he cried, the redder his eyes became, and the more he cursed, the angrier he felt. In the end he grabbed a steel shovel and headed off in the direction of the Dahua Steel works: "Fuck them! I'm going to get whoever did this!"

"Yeah, we're going to get them!" A group of young men took up the call and they gathered together, some with hoes, some with sickles and some with sticks that they'd just picked up. They were ready to go with Ou Guanghe and make Dahua Steel pay for what they had done.

Guo Cunxian seemed to be joining them in their madness. Shouting at the top of his voice he ran out into the middle of the road to stop Ou Guanghe. "Guanghe, you're a good man. Do you have the guts to go and get whoever did this?"

"Yes!"

"You'll pay the price?"

"I will!"

"Do you know who ran over Dog's Bollocks? Do you know who you are going to go and get?"

"It was a Dahua Steel truck."

"Do you have evidence of that?"

"It's obvious!"

"The fact that it's obvious doesn't mean that you have evidence. Dahua Steel employs more than twenty thousand people. Who are you going to make pay for this? You aren't just going to go in there and start hitting people, are you? You'll be under arrest long before you find the murderer."

Ou Guanghe looked a bit silly and started to calm down.

Guo Cunxian had more than enough stuff in him to keep him in his place: "I promise you that you'll have your opportunity to get them, but right now you have to listen to me. I'm going to appoint some people to keep guard over the scene of the crime, and if any more Dahua Steel trucks come through here they can impound them. However, we're going to wait until the county traffic police turn up before we go any further."

Guo Cunxian turned round and gave instructions to Guo Cunxiao: "Could you go and find Mr Feng as quickly as you can? I want him to phone the county traffic police and ask them to send someone to investigate."

He told Lin Meitang to find a couple of women to look after Liu Yumei, and some men who were standing around doing nothing were told to help Liu Yucheng look after Ou Guangming. "I'll be back as soon as I've sorted out things at the western fields. We can't let this one go. After all, they've killed poor little Dog's Bollocks!"

To have a death in the midst of all these celebrations was very difficult. There would have to be a funeral but the celebrations couldn't stop. The two things should not be allowed to have an impact on each other. Since this had happened, it was an opportunity for Guo Cunxian to show his mettle. He was in charge here and he had to deal with both these situations. First he was going to be cutting the ribbon for the well-digging team, and then he would be sending the construction workers on their way. Who should go instead of Ou Guangming? Qian Xishou and his team were leaving Guojiadian and he couldn't allow them to slip away without any kind of fanfare. He'd promised Feng Hou to give them a good send off and he was happy to do so. He wanted to see them run away with their tails between their legs. However, Dog's Bollocks' death had cast a gloom over all of these celebrations. Nobody was going to be smiling now, not even him.

When Guo Cunxian arrived back at the road running to the western fields, Guo Cunyong caught up with him. "Cunxian, Guangming isn't going to be able to go anywhere anytime soon, but the project in Tianjin can't wait. How about I go with Jin Laixi and the others to the city and start work there, and then when Guangming has sorted out Dog's Bollocks' funeral he can come and join us. You've got enough to do with all the things going on in the village, and you can't afford to have any problems outside. I've been responsible for building up our connections there and I'd feel better if I went myself."

Guo Cunxian didn't raise his head, and he was in no hurry to respond. Guo Cunyong was pretty sharp. The moment the investigation team left, he realised that there would be no future for him in the village, so he had decided it would be better to head off and make some big money elsewhere. However, Guo Cunyong hadn't really crumbled under the pressure brought to bear by the investigation team, the two of them got on pretty well, and he had been very helpful with selling products from the chemical works and getting projects signed up for the construction team. In the situation in which they found themselves, Guo Cunyong had a point; he'd let him go for now. So he said: "With this sudden tragedy I am going to have to let you go and get this project underway. However, once you've got everyone settled I want you to come back immediately, because I have lots of things to discuss with you. I want to pick up where we left off talking the other night. We're going to be setting up various companies and we need to seize the opportunities on offer."

When Dog's Bollocks' mourning tent was put up, it was much larger and lighter than the hut in which he had lived at the end of his short life.

In the middle of the mourning tent there were two long benches. A bed had been erected on top of the benches, and there lay Dog's Bollocks, his body twisted and smashed, covered by a white cotton sheet. The people in charge of the funeral had been told that they shouldn't let anyone lift the sheet to look. Once the police had performed an autopsy on the body, then Dog's Bollocks could be arranged so that he was fit to be seen. The coffin had been prepared with all haste, and it was made with the very finest wood available in the village. It was the same size as would be used for an adult and was made with really thick, solid planks. The kid had never been able to live in a nice house but he wasn't going to suffer more now that he was dead.

The villagers were very upset that poor little Dog's Bollocks had been killed in such a terrible way, and they were very angry with Dahua Steel. Whatever happened, sooner or later there would have to be a reckoning. Ou Guangming was in a dreadful state and couldn't do anything but cry. He felt that he had nothing to live for now. Dog's Bollocks' funeral arrangements were left entirely to a crowd of helpful villagers. Given that this terrible thing had happened, they could not just ignore it;

somebody had to sort things out. This was the custom in the countryside, and it was considered by the villagers to be a fundamental principle governing how to behave.

The more people come to help, the better the family's connections. The best of all is when there is an endless procession of mourners and an endless sound of wailing from the family. The worst thing is when a person dies and there is nobody to cry, when there is a cold silence around the dead. In that kind of situation you have to find ways to make people cry. On the other hand you don't want people to cry too much. If that happens you have to have people step in to talk to the mourners. You don't want the grief to turn dangerous, and you want to give the person crying a way to stop. When holding a funeral you have to understand the rules that govern the realms of the living and the dead; there are various different procedures and you have to complete all kinds of formalities. It is all very complicated and you need experienced people to explain it and then carry it out for you.

Guojiadian did have a little company that organised weddings and funerals. This wasn't something that senior cadres had given orders to establish but a family business handed down from one generation to the next. It had come into existence because it was needed. There are people in every generation who enjoy a good fuss and like to take part in the big events of other people's lives: they weren't afraid of being criticised for interfering, and they were able to gain a sense of self-respect and satisfaction from this kind of work. Every family would ask for their help in the event of a wedding or a funeral, and sometimes they turned up without even being asked. Today, even before Ou Guangming had asked them to come, they all arrived, and it turned out that Guo Cunxian had been in touch. Since factory production could not stop and the managers wouldn't let the people working for them out, he'd summoned various others who were sitting idle in the village. At their head was Zhang Diankui, who everyone called 'Director'. He wasn't tall but he was obviously very strong, and he was both versatile and competent. Zhang Diankui could play the trumpet and banged a good drum, in addition to which he could both sing and strum a fiddle. Just shortly before, he'd been playing first drum out at the eastern fields, and now he'd be taking charge of Dog's Bollocks' funeral. He was making careful note of how much money had been borrowed from the village, how much wood had been bought from which family, not to mention how much matting and steel wire. In future, he would be able to give a good account of the expenditure to whoever was paying. Dog's Bollocks' funeral wasn't going to be like the ordinary kind, for someone who had died of old age or disease. His death had brought out all these officials, so Zhang Diankui needed to be very careful. He sent someone outside the village to keep watch, and instructed them that the moment they spotted the traffic police car, they should immediately come and find Guo Cunxian. He gathered the entire Ou family off to one side to discuss what they were going to ask the police to do.

"You can't just cry," he said to Ou Guangming, "and even if you don't want to live, you have to. You have to look to the future even if you don't feel like it. The most important thing right now is that the people who killed Dog's Bollocks shouldn't get away with it. You will have to take charge of this, because if anyone else lodges a formal complaint then nobody is going to pay the blindest bit of attention."

The traffic police sent out a team of three people. At their head was a very tall man, with dark skin; his tan was even darker than that of the peasants of Guojiadian.

He looked highly authoritative and serious, with a stern and experienced manner. First, he ordered a young policeman to take photographs of the crime scene and then he went to the mourning tent. Accompanied by an older policeman, he lifted the white sheet covering Dog's Bollocks and inspected the injuries, again taking the necessary photographs. This naturally resulted in a wave of howling overtaking the mourners. Liu Yumei had already cried herself hoarse, and now with her mouth flecked with foam, she began to hyperventilate. The people present hurriedly carried her into the hut.

From the way they were crying, the tall, dark policeman had no difficulty in working out who the parents were. He asked Ou Guangming: "Were there any eyewitnesses to the accident?"

Ou Guangming shook his head.

"Who was the first person on the scene afterwards?"

"That would be me and my sister," Liu Yucheng said. "The dead boy was my nephew."

"What did you see?"

"The truck came past and the whole hut was shaking. My sister said that she suddenly felt all funny, and her heart was thumping erratically. She went out of the hut to find Dog's Bollocks, and I went with her saying that I'd help. Then we saw Dog's Bollocks lying in the middle of the highway with blood all over him. The truck had already gone out of sight."

"Was he still alive when you got there?"

Liu Yucheng looked overwhelmed with grief. He shook his head, trying not to cry.

"Did you hear what direction the truck went in?"

"It seemed to be heading towards the Dahua Steel works."

By this time Ou Guanghe had already impounded three Dahua Steel trucks. The tall, dark policemen went over to the truck drivers and started to question them. While he was doing this a Volga car drove out of the village and stopped when it got to the scene of the accident. Then Guo Cunxian, Feng Hou and Cui Daben got out of the car and went into the mourning tent. Dog's Bollocks may have died a horrible death but he'd picked a good time to do it. The most senior cadres of the village and the county all came to pay their respects and see him off. According to local custom, it was considered very disrespectful not to give your condolences if you happened to come across a funeral in progress. Failure to do so would be to brand yourself a pig-ignorant, arrogant bastard. Feng Hou spoke warmly to Ou Guangming as he offered his commiserations, and he also said a few words to the two policemen inspecting the body and taking photographs: "This case is in your hands."

The tall, dark policeman took this opportunity to introduce his two colleagues. "This is Dr Huang, a specialist in forensic medicine, and this is Wang Sheng." Then he gave his own name: "I am Ma Xingjian, captain of the second unit."

"You've been to the scene?" Feng Hou asked.

"Yes, the truck concerned was either headed towards or coming from the Dahua Steel Company. It hit the victim and then drove away. The wheels crushed the child's chest and he died at the scene. There are no eyewitnesses to the truck hitting the victim, so in the absence of further evidence, we cannot be sure that the driver concerned was indeed from Dahua Steel."

"You aren't going to let the driver get away with this!"

"Of course not. When I have finished making my report to you, I will immediately go to the Dahua Steel works."

Feng Hou jerked his head at Ma Xingjian to indicate that they ought to leave the mourning tent. The two men went and stood next to the traffic police jeep: "Do you have any idea who is responsible for this?"

Ma Xingjian nodded. "It is most likely that he was run over by a Dahua Steel truck, and the responsibility lies with the driver. Furthermore, this is an untarmacked road running through a village where there is no pavement and no yellow line marked to indicate that people shouldn't cross it, so the drivers should be particularly alert in case a child suddenly comes darting out from one of the houses, or from one of the piles of firewood."

"Captain Ma, the child died!" Feng Hou was looking and sounding pained not merely because he was upset about the death, but also because he had other worries about what was going on. The relationship between Dahua Steel and the various neighbouring villages had always been tense and difficult because Dahua Steel was illegally occupying land belonging to local farmers, and was causing serious pollution. However, at the same time, some of the peasants were busy stealing electricity and water from Dahua Steel, and they would creep into the works and steal anything they could get their hands on. They were scraping a living and stealing from the company while simultaneously complaining about it. This was the kind of situation that can easily get out of hand.

"Do not worry, Mr Feng, I know exactly what to do." You could see at first glance that Ma Xingjian was a very experienced policeman. He would consider the consequences of his actions, and his words were measured and to the point. This made Feng Hou feel a lot better about the situation. He instructed Guo Cunxian to organise some men to fill in the trench that had been dug across the highway, while getting him to agree that the trucks he had impounded should be allowed to leave.

Guo Cunxian didn't have any reason to refuse. He told Ou Guanghe to fill the trench in immediately. At the same time, he posed a question to Ma Xingjian: "When are you going to find the murderer?"

Guo Cunxian didn't say 'driver concerned', he said 'murderer'.

Ma Xingjian looked slightly more serious than he had before: "If this was done by a driver working for Dahua Steel, we should have the results by the day after tomorrow at the latest. If it's not a Dahua Steel driver, then it's going to take a little more time, but it still shouldn't be too long."

Guo Cunxian glared at him. "This road only goes to the Dahua Steel works, and so if it wasn't a Dahua Steel driver, then it has to be someone connected to the company, bringing things to the works or taking them away. If you get hold of the people there, you are not going to want for clues."

"You have clearly thought about it very carefully. However, there are a number of other villages along this road, just like Guojiadian. They also have cars and trucks coming and going, and we cannot eliminate the possibility that the driver was one of theirs. In order to complete our investigation, in a moment Dr Huang and I will be going to the Dahua Steel works to inspect their trucks, and Wang Sheng will take it one village at a time."

Everyone present was impressed by the care the dark-skinned police captain was taking over the case.

"You are all working so hard," Guo Cunxian said sincerely. "I would like to thank you on behalf of the Village Party Committee and the family of the victim. Once it is all over, if you come back, we would like to show our appreciation."

"No, no, we are only doing our duty."

When 'Director' Zhang Diankui realised that Guo Cunxian had nothing further to say, he chipped in himself: "Captain Ma, once the murderer has been arrested, what can we expect?"

Everyone was interested to know that.

"There are rules about that. The driver in this kind of case can be sentenced to a maximum of seven years in prison."

Immediately people started to shout: "Seven years? Shouldn't he be shot?"

"It was an accident," Ma Xingjian explained. "It wasn't murder. If he had killed someone by running them over and then not run away, he wouldn't be going to prison at all. He would just have to pay blood money."

Zhang Diankui still wanted to find out more about the practical side of things. "So if he goes to prison he doesn't have to pay blood money? What about compensation for the victim's family?"

"There are various different rules governing the payment of compensation to the victim." Ma Xingjian went on to explain them very carefully and in detail. Every criminal case has its own special features, and it would be impossible to establish a one-size-fits-all system to cover every eventuality. The family of the victim could also make demands, and providing that they were reasonable and did not break the law, every effort would be made to see whether they could be met.

Zhang Diankui asked again: "What happens now to the child's body?"

"We've already inspected it and we have our written notes and the photographs. In the absence of any special requests, I think it can be dealt with as the family wishes."

Zhang Diankui immediately gave instructions that people should go and get the white spirit, cotton wool and cotton cloth that he'd prepared earlier and, under Dr Huang's supervision, he started to tidy up Dog's Bollocks' body. The most important thing was to clean the blood off his face, and to bind the wound on his chest, wrapping it with white cotton.

Ma Xingjian checked that the trench had been filled completely flat and then said goodbye to everyone. He told them that he would be in touch as soon as he had news.

Zhang Diankui was absolutely determined that they should not be allowed to leave until they had eaten. He said that he represented the family of the victim, and indeed the cadres in this village, and he heaped flattery upon them. Anybody else would have found it impossible to get away, but Ma Xingjian was an experienced policeman, and he now had an even more stern expression on his dark face as he reminded them that a child had just been killed and he needed to strike while the iron was hot, so he could not possibly stay another minute. The two of them walked together to the car, and they stood side by side talking, like a pair of old friends. Although they had never met before, now that they had been brought together by this funeral, Zhang Diankui was determined that Ma Xingjian should become a friend. He was good at that kind of thing, and in future it might make his job easier. Everyone got to see how in the end Ma Xingjian got out his notebook and wrote out something for Zhang Diankui. Once the captain had got into a Dahua Steel truck with Dr Huang, Wang Sheng drove off in the jeep with the police sign on it. Leaving Guojiadian together, they were quickly lost in the sunset.

Before their eyes the blazing sun turned deep yellow, and then from yellow to red. It seemed bigger and bigger, and the light became more and more feeble. The red clouds in the sky to the west now turned a muddy brown, and as the sun sank further towards the horizon, it was clear that it would soon be dark. Zhang Diankui had organised countless weddings and funerals, but he'd never had an event so complex and difficult before. It was too much responsibility for him; he couldn't possibly manage on his own. He could not make decisions about this. It was impossible that he could be the confident 'director' that he had always been in the past, giving orders about this and sorting out that. He went back to the crowd, where all the most important people in the village were massed. He had to get some guidance from the family about this: "Guangming, it is getting late. Is there anything else that you need me to do for you?"

Ou Guangming stiffened. "Diankui, my mind is a complete blank. If there is anything that needs to be done, you'll have to decide."

"It isn't that I don't want to decide, but I simply cannot do this. Dog's Bollocks' death isn't like an ordinary one, and I can't take responsibility. All I can do is to help you out with some of the donkey work. You ought to ask some of the village cadres to put in an appearance."

With a thud, Ou Guangming went down on his knees and started to kowtow to Zhang Diankui. This was customary; the person asking the 'director' to take charge of a funeral ought to kowtow, wearing the mourning garments of a filial son. However, Dog's Bollocks was a child, and nobody would be able to wear mourning for him. Ou Guangming was too distressed to consider these finer points of etiquette: "Diankui, you don't need to do this for my sake, but because Dog's Bollocks always called you 'Uncle'. Because he was only little when this dreadful thing happened to him, how can you refuse to send him on his way?"

Ou Guangming was completely hoarse, and the tears were now rolling down his face in silence.

Zhang Diankui raised Ou Guangming to his feet. "Don't worry about me, Guangming. But I need you to make a decision. The weather is really hot right now. Dog's Bollocks' body will still be fine tomorrow, but it will start to smell after three days, and there will be decomposition and flies. That would be bad for you and your wife to experience, and I'm sure it's something that nobody in the village wants to see. You can't treat your boy like that. So the pair of you need to make a decision. If you want to do things according to the old ways and we have the funeral on the third day, then you can leave everything to me. You don't have to do a thing, and I promise you that the child will be buried safe and sound. Now, supposing you decide to wait until after the investigation is completed, you will be wanting to make demands, and we don't know if they will agree or not, and if you start arguing, it could all take ages. In that case, what do you want done with the body in the meantime?"

Ou Guangming had already made up his mind. "Supposing that the case isn't closed, or they don't deal with it right. We cannot bury Dog's Bollocks right now!"

"In that case we are going to have to send the child to the cold store at the county funeral parlour," Zhang Diankui said. "But you're going to have to ask Liu Yumei if she is OK with that."

Guo Cunxian asked: "Can we use the parlour's facilities?"

"Just now I asked Captain Ma to write a note for us to that effect. Using the cold store at the funeral parlour will be expensive, so we'll have to work out how much it will cost and then in the end we can ask the defendant to pay." Zhang Diankui had presided over a lot of funerals in his time, knew all about what needed to be done, and he would think more deeply about these things than the family could.

Guo Cunxian took Director Zhang aside and said: "Diankui, Guangming has already kowtowed to you, so you can take charge of the arrangements for Dog's Bollocks' funeral. I have a nasty feeling that this isn't going to go well, so I want you to think about every eventuality, and make sure that you do as much as you can for Guangming and his wife. Right, I've got to go and have a look at what the well-diggers have been up to. If there's any problem, just come and find me."

The cadres were able to leave, so too were the people who were just there for the excitement, but anyone who had come to help with the funeral, whether their role was big or small, had to stay behind. Everyone got a bowl of hot tofu and greens, and there were buns to eat for anyone who was hungry, and hot water in big urns. This was all up to the director to organise. While the family of the dead person might be screaming and shouting in confusion, he has to be thinking about every least little thing and making sure that it is done well. He cannot allow friends and family to assemble from the four points of the compass, together with any helpful villagers, and make a mess of the proceedings. In this case a child had died, and Liu Yumei came from this village, so that made everything much easier. If the dead person were an adult, there might be VIP guests and family from other places, in which case there would have to be four hot dishes and four cold, and he'd have to serve wine. Of course if he had managed to persuade the three policemen to stay, they wouldn't be eating just tofu with greens. The dark little hut that the family had been living in was now set aside for women mourners. Next to the hut a tent had been put up and seats placed inside; that was for male visitors only. A two-burner temporary kitchen had been set up outside this tent, and it was producing a never-ending stream of steamed buns, food and hot water.

The person that Zhang Diankui was most worried about was Liu Yumei. He had been in situations before where a death resulted in a suicide. Fortunately Lin Meitang, who had a very strong sense of responsibility and no other demands on her time, hadn't moved far from her side. The whole afternoon had been spent with her making a shroud for Dog's Bollocks. When it was time to eat then there was a problem, because it didn't matter what he and Lin Meitang said, Liu Yumei was refusing to eat, and she wouldn't say a single word. Ou Guangming now explained to her that he wanted to send Dog's Bollocks to the cold store at the funeral parlour, and that they ought to think of what demands they wanted to make from the guilty party.

After a very long silence, Liu Yumei began to speak. Her voice was rough but they could hear everything she had to say perfectly clearly: "Dog's Bollocks was my baby, and I have to decide what is going to happen at his funeral. If you don't agree with what I have to say, I am going to kill myself right here and now. One, there are two murderers responsible for Dog's Bollocks' death. One is the driver, who will be dealt with according to the law, and the other is a member of the Ou family. I don't want Ou Guangming to be allowed to enter the mourning tent. I don't want him anywhere near my baby. Two, you can make any demands of the driver you want, but you are not allowed to torment my baby any more. He died a horrible death. I don't want him taken away from home and I don't want him to be frozen. You are not going to take him anywhere near the funeral parlour because I want his body buried the day after tomorrow. Three, Dog's Bollocks has to be buried with the rest of the Ou family. I can't bear it that he would otherwise become a lonely ghost. [According to tradition, people who died before they had got married were not allowed to be buried in the family graveyard, they had to be interred outside. It was only in the event of a posthumous 'marriage' that they could be moved inside the cemetery to be reunited with their family.] I want the director to see what he can do about this, and find a girl who has died unmarried, and then we can have a posthumous wedding for Dog's Bollocks. Four, this evening I am going to wash Dog's Bollocks and put him in his shroud, and I don't want anyone with me when I do this. I want to be alone with my baby for a bit. Director Zhang, thank you for taking care of Dog's Bollocks' funeral. Let me kowtow to you on his behalf."

As Liu Yumei finished speaking, her head hit the ground.

Everyone was shocked into silence.

Zhang Diankui rushed forward to stop her. "Yumei, it was the least I could do."

Ou Guangming wanted to say more to his wife about his own ideas, but Liu Yumei wouldn't let him speak: "You can say whatever you like and I'm not going to listen. If you'd had the least sense, you'd have found us somewhere to live in the village, and none of this would have happened. The only thing you ever think about is money. You were going to leave us in that little hut while you went to the city to get rich, and Dog's Bollocks was in such a rush to go and see you off. Would he have run out in front of the truck otherwise? Are you going to agree to the four things that I want or not? My baby is dead. Who cares what you want and whether the guilty party accepts your conditions? If you could bring my baby back to life, I'd agree to anything."

"I didn't say I didn't agree," Ou Guangming said. "We'll do as you say, OK?"

Liu Yumei now directed her gaze towards Zhang Diankui: "What about you?"

Zhang Diankui gave a thumbs-up, though his eyes were full of tears. "Really, Yumei, of course I'll do as you wish. You tell me what you want and that's what I'll do."

"Could you get someone to heat up a basin of water for me?" Liu Yumei opened a box and took out a new towel, and then she walked over to the mourning tent, carrying Dog's Bollocks' shroud. She told Zhang Diankui to keep everyone else outside.

Zhang Diankui had no choice but to obey. He was secretly congratulating himself on having tidied up Dog's Bollocks' injuries already, because otherwise it would have been deeply distressing for Liu Yumei when she dressed him. None of the people who'd come to help dared to stop her, and none of them knew what she was thinking;

normally Liu Yumei wasn't so strong. In all of these years she'd never shown this kind of mettle, she had been gentle and refined, and so everyone had been expecting her just to weep and wail now that her son was dead and, indeed, when the news came that was what she had done. But all of a sudden it seemed as though she had turned into a completely different person. Had she gone mad because her son had been killed? Or had she managed to weep herself into such a state? However, watching her speak carefully and make her own arrangements, she seemed more sensible and stronger than anyone else present. She clearly wasn't off her head in any way. This had the effect of making everyone more frightened and more worried for her than ever.

Zhang Diankui asked a couple of people to stay in attendance outside the mourning tent and keep an ear open, so that if Liu Yumei collapsed, they could carry her away.

Ou Guangming entered the mourning tent behind Liu Yumei. He was carrying a large basin of hot water. Surely she wasn't going to throw him out like the other 'outsiders'? They'd been married for more than a decade, and it seemed as though he had only just got to know her. He felt the situation to be alien and tense.

Zhang Diankui had told him that the bandages round Dog's Bollocks' body shouldn't be moved. It would be unbearable for her if they were touched.

The people on the other side of the matting hung round the mourning tent could hear all that was going on inside, and some of them pulled the matting aside to keep an eye on what Liu Yumei was doing. She pulled aside the white cotton sheet covering her son's body without the slightest cry or moan. She dipped the new towel in hot water and began to wash her son, very gently and carefully, as if Dog's Bollocks were merely sleeping and she was afraid that she might wake him up. Having even cleaned his nostrils, ears, mouth, and eyes, she moved on to his hair and neck.

Her love, her regrets, her pain and her anger were all expressed in washing her son's body. She spoke softly to him, because right now she still had things that she wanted to say. Once he was buried, she might well feel that she never wanted to speak again. Although she was speaking, it probably wasn't anything important. She couldn't say the things that she really wanted to tell him. She felt that she might as well have died with her son.

"I hope this doesn't hurt, baby? You're a good boy, a lovely boy. I've washed you ever since the day you were born for twelve years but this is the best behaved that you've ever been. I'm so sorry, I shouldn't have let you go before you'd had something to eat, I shouldn't have been so careless, I should've gone with you. This is all my fault, all my fault for not wanting to go and join in the fun! If I'd hit you, if I'd held you close, if I'd locked you in the house, then none of this would have happened! I am so sorry. I showed how much I loved you, how much I really cared about you, and now you're dead. I might as well be dead myself! I would be happy to kill myself right now to join you but there are too many people around. They won't let me go. If you miss me then come and see me in my dreams, then I'll come and join you. I must have done something really terrible in a past life, the Ou family must have done something bad, and that's why this horrible thing had to happen to you, which means that the Ou family will die out. Baby, I want you to choose a good family to be born into in your next life. I owe you, because I gave birth to you and then couldn't protect you. I couldn't give you an environment in which you could grow up safe and sound. I don't deserve to be your mother. I might as well never have been born."

Ou Guangming was now in floods of tears but he was afraid of distressing his wife even further, so he forced himself not to make a sound.

He tried to suppress his distress until he couldn't bear it any longer. He hugged his wife against him as he wailed: "Don't say that, Yumei, this is all my fault! Dog's Bollocks has gone, but you can't leave me, whatever happens we have to survive."

The people watching from outside the mourning tent were deeply upset. It was really painful to listen to, and there were only a few that were not in tears. Some of them wanted to go in and speak to her, but they were stopped by Director Zhang. Zhang Diankui realised that Liu Yumei was in a very dangerous state of mind having had something so dreadful happen to her. She needed to be allowed to cry, she needed to say what she had to say, otherwise there might be another tragedy.

Having cried together for a moment, Yumei pushed Guangming away and carried on cleaning her son's hands and feet. Once the whole body had been washed, she put her son into the shroud that she'd just made. When everything had been properly arranged, Liu Yumei sat down by her son's head and said: "You can rest in peace, son. I will be here with you, I will be watching over you. I'm not leaving here until they come and take you for burial!"

Zhang Diankui relaxed. Liu Yumei was a remarkable woman, and once she had made up her mind, she was a great deal tougher than any man. He left a few people to stay overnight, and told the rest to go home.

When it got to about two o'clock in the morning, just at the time when everyone was in their deepest sleep, the people in the hut and on mats in the men's tent were roused by a strangled shout from Liu Yumei, which was followed by Ou Guangming yelling: "Help! Help!"

Zhang Diankui and the other people on night duty came running into the mourning tent. Dog's Bollocks' corpse had disappeared, while Liu Yumei and Ou Guangming were lying in a heap on the ground.

Liu Yumei said that a couple of people had burst into the mourning tent, taking them completely unawares. One of them put a hand over her mouth while the others grabbed Dog's Bollocks and ran off with him. Ou Guangming had been sitting on the matting outside the mourning tent, and hearing the commotion had got up and tried to chase after them, but he'd been violently hurled to the ground by the person guarding the entrance. The man who had hold of Liu Yumei then released her and was the last to run off.

Zhang Diankui and the others ran to the road to have a look, but it was pitch black in every direction. He thought that he heard the sound of a motor heading in the direction of the Dahua Steel works, but when he wanted everyone to listen carefully, there was nothing to be heard. Zhang Diankui had done this kind of work for years, and he had never experienced anything like this. Who on earth would steal a dead body and what for? There only seemed to be one answer: it was the driver from Dahua Steel, who had got together with a few other people to destroy the body to eliminate clues. What other explanation could there possibly be for such a bizarre occurrence?

Zhang Diankui sent two aggressive young men to take a car and chase after them in the direction of Dahua Steel. If they didn't catch up with them, they should go to the works and see what they could find out there, and also go and find Captain Ma and tell him what had happened. He also sent someone to the county police station to report. He wanted to go himself to tell Guo Cunxian what had happened, but Ou Guangming told him to wait until the morning. However, he decided that in the circumstances they couldn't wait.

Zhang Diankui detailed the remainder of his people to keep an eye on Ou Guangming and his wife. He headed off towards the village, moving as quickly as he could in the darkness. Nobody wants trouble at a funeral, and this was going to be a funeral with trouble like no other.

Guojiadian was now on high alert. All the men still at home had been communicated with, and they were assembling north of the village with their weapon of choice.

The young and energetic were already raring to go; people in Guojiadian had never been afraid of fighting. When their fathers and grandfathers were young, it was possible to ride round to one of the other villages for a fight, or to go round to someone else's house and start a punch-up. That was a real fight! Youngsters nowadays might not know that they were born, but they weren't about to allow other people to come to their village, run over a child and then steal the body.

Did they really think that Guojiadian was going to let them get away with it? They were forcing us to fight!

When they heard that Guo Cunxian had taken out his favourite axe, it was clear that the boss was going to show what he was made of. Even the most suspicious and tricky inhabitants now decided that they couldn't be seen to hang back. If another family gets into terrible trouble and you aren't right out there on the front line for them, when you get into trouble yourself, there isn't going to be anyone prepared to help out. Are you going to guarantee that nothing is ever going to go wrong for you? If you'd asked Ou Guangming even two days ago, could he ever have imagined that such a dreadful thing would happen to his family? Everyone is a wolf at heart, and if that wolf is released then other people are killed.

In front of Dog's Bollocks' empty mourning tent, a crowd of several hundred men had formed, and everyone held a piece of farm equipment or a stick which they could use as a weapon. Holding up their hoes and sickles, it looked like a forest of pikes. There was a long line of horse wagons and tractors drawn up by the side of the highway, and the animals seemed to have been affected by their masters, for they snorted and stamped their feet.

People have to pull together, because if they don't join forces in the struggle, they might as well be dead. Their anger having now reached fever pitch, the crowd was about to boil over at any moment. Even the most timorous of mortals realised that they couldn't get out of it now. Zhang Diankui and a few of his men were busy distributing black bands to everyone. They were tied round their arms as a sign of allegiance to this army. Their banner was a length of white cotton. The slogan of this campaign would be written on it and then hoisted up on bamboo poles.

There were a number of worried women present, but they could only stand on the edge of the crowd muttering. They did not dare try to stop their husbands or sons from joining in. The peasant army from Guojiadian was out for revenge. They were waiting for Guo Cunxian to give the word, and then they would march on the Dahua Steel Company.

The majority of them believed that as long as Guo Cunxian stood at their head, there was nothing for them to worry about. Even if the heavens fell, he would hold them up; if something went wrong then Guo Cunxian could deal with it. He was neither a relative nor a friend to Ou Guangming, and he'd been under investigation for the last couple of months, and that wasn't over yet. The higher-ups were clearly still observing him and if anything here went badly wrong, he'd be carted off to prison and maybe even executed. He must have understood that perfectly well and, in spite of that, he wanted to take revenge. That meant they ought to take revenge, and so why should anybody else be afraid of getting into trouble?

Everyone's eyes were fixed on the men's tent. Guo Cunxian was in there with the other village cadres, discussing the plan of action.

Guo Cunxiao came out to give the first round of orders. The people employed in the chemical works, the brick fields, the mill, the chicken and pig farms, together with those helping with the well-digging work were all to go home, since their task was to ensure productivity was maintained. Their job was to stay in the village and keep it secure, and if there was any news, they should get in touch with the main army out on campaign.

Sitting inside the tent, Guo Cunxian looked serious and stern. Once the cadres had finished their discussion, he told someone to find Ou Guanghe and bring him there, because he had something particular to tell him: "Guanghe, I guess you know that the villagers don't have much time for you. You've taken the blame for what happened to Dog's Bollocks, and the fact is that you did wrong in forcing your brother's family to move out."

Ou Guanghe nodded, his eyes fixed on the ground. Ever since Dog's Bollocks had died, everyone had shown open contempt for him, and his sister-in-law had made her hatred of him quite clear. Even if he had been twice the bastard he was, he knew that time was up for him, and he would have to keep his head down and stay on the straight and narrow from here on in. If they went to Dahua Steel now there was guaranteed to be a fight. Without a show of force they wouldn't be able to get what was rightfully theirs. Ou Guanghe ought to be right up front with the shock troops on this mission but, in the circumstances, how could he be? The idea was to make a fuss and cause a scene. Even if they didn't make a fuss, that didn't mean that nothing had happened! This was the reason that Guo Cunxian had decided to light the fuse; he wanted him to get angry, he wanted to fire him up.

"I believe that you're a good man. Right from the day when you went and cursed in front of the investigation team, I was sure that there was something to you. Guojiadian needs men like you. Today you've got to get revenge for what has happened to Dog's Bollocks and you've got to show what you are capable of. You've got to cause a right scene. After all, you're Dog's Bollocks' own uncle, so everyone's going to cut you some slack no matter what you do. However, you are not allowed to hit anyone, and I want you to follow Diankui's directions."

Even though Ou Guanghe was a little confused by what he'd heard, he felt as though an enormous weight had rolled off his body. He was now standing up straight and looking directly at Guo Cunxian, mulling over what he had just said. He had no idea that Guo Cunxian thought so much of him. There were so many people waiting for him outside, he'd been tasked with this mission by the Secretary, and nobody had ever treated him with so much respect.

"Do you understand what I'm saying, Guanghe?" The more tense the situation became, the more patience Guo Cunxian showed.

"I was wrong, I should never have forced my brother and his family to leave. However, I never imagined something like this would happen to Dog's Bollocks. What can I do to make it right?" Ou Guanghe's voice was harsh, and his eyes were shadowed and dazed.

"There is no time right now for regrets about the past. The reason you couldn't find a wife is because you are poor. The reason that other people despise you is because you are poor. You shouldn't blame your brother and sister-in-law, and this is also nothing to do with the house. In olden days, when there were rich landowners, they might have been crippled or blind, they might not have measured up to you in all sorts of different ways, yet there wasn't one of them that didn't get married, and they had their pick of the girls on offer. I'm going to make sure that you get a wife. If an opening appears at the factory I'll get you a job there first, and then wait until you've proved yourself. There'll be lots of girls wanting to meet you. If you really feel that you haven't done right by your brother and his wife, you'd better be prepared to work hard with Dog's Bollocks' funeral, and help them get their revenge. That'll show everyone what you're made of!" Guo Cunxian's encouragement was adding fuel to the fire.

"Just you wait and see!" Ou Guanghe's eyes, which had been red enough already when he arrived, now flashed with an angry light.

"Then you had better be on your way." Guo Cunxian waved his hands, and everyone came out of the tent.

He was the last to leave, and his long thin, knife-like face was full of rage, and his eyes sparkled like lambent flames, with a glare that seemed to see right through to the depths of other people's hearts. In his hand he held a white sailcloth bag, of the kind used by carpenters. The inhabitants of Guojiadian all knew exactly what was in the bag, and so the passions of the crowd were roused to fever pitch, and there was a confused sound of things being struck against each other. The crowd moved agitatedly, seething with anger. Zhang Diankui waved his hands to indicate that everyone should be quiet.

It was customary that, when they went out on campaign, Guo Cunxian had to arrange the order of business. He therefore stepped forward and said: "We all know that a cornered rat will bite a cat. Well, we're cornered people now! A Dahua Steel truck has run over and killed one of our children. That is their first crime. They drove off afterwards, without trying to do anything to save the dying boy. That's another crime on top of the first one. Then today in the middle of the night they stole the body away, to try and hide the evidence of their crime. That's truly evil! This isn't just about Guangming any more. If we let them get away with this, then who knows what is going to happen in future to the Zhang family and the Wangs? They occupy our lands, they shake our houses to bits, they run over our animals, and now clearly they think they can kill us with impunity! If they imagine they can just get away with treating us like shit, then how are we going to survive?"

Guo Cunxian's voice was filled with rage, and the anger grew in the hearts of the listeners: "If they make our lives impossible, then we'll make their lives impossible back! Right here and now, we've got to let them know that we're watching them!"

Guo Cunxian paused for a short while, to allow the peasants to let off steam with their exclamations. Then he laid down the law about what they were trying to achieve: "We're in the right here, and we're not going to go and beat people up, because that would immediately put us in the wrong. We've got three things to do. One, we want Ou Jingfan's body handed back to us. Ou Jingfan is Dog's Bollocks' proper name. Two, we want the murderer to be punished severely. Three, we want compensation. Isn't that right?"

"Yes!"

"Let's go!"

When they set off, the first tractor was hauling Dog's Bollocks' empty coffin and was filled with members of the Ou family. The remainder had packed in according to age. The tractors and wagons at the head of the procession contained the older men, the younger ones came on bicycles, and the ones who didn't have bicycles came on foot. Each of the tractors and wagons had a bamboo pole tied on top, and a white banner fluttered from the pole. Guo Cunxian's three demands were written on them, and they fluttered and snapped in the wind.

This strange semi-mechanised army advanced, rumbling and majestic, on the Dahua Steel Company, with the black coffin and white banners above it, sad and strange. The bright sun rose up above the horizon, the dry wind blew scorching air against them, and yellow dust billowed up and darkened the sky, as they advanced another kilometre in roiling clouds.

In the crowd there were a number of people who'd worked for Dahua Steel at one time or another, and they knew the layout of the place. As they approached the company works, Zhang Diankui had everyone stop and line up. They all got off the wagons and tractors, and then he chose eight strong young men to go in front, carrying Dog's Bollocks' empty coffin. The various members of the Ou family streamed along behind, wailing or cursing as they felt best. The remainder of the company followed in the wake of the Ou family, either carrying tools as weapons, or holding items used in funeral ceremonies. Zhang Diankui walked right at the front with a long whip, while Guo Cunxian was at the very back holding his famous sailcloth bag. Behind him were the wagons and tractors with their white banners fluttering.

Originally, they were heading for the head office of Dahua Steel, but before they got to the works, they passed the school the company had set up for the children of its workforce. Ou Guanghe shouted: "The coffin can't go round corners, so let's take it into the school!"

"That's right!" Eagle Eye, Han Erhu, and the other strong young men shouted their agreement. The people behind them holding hoes, picks, shovels, and backhoes went to work, and pretty quickly the wall round the school had had a hole knocked in it that was a couple of metres wide. A couple of the younger men lit firecrackers in front of them, and paper money was tossed high into the sky. Then came the cold, glossy black lacquer coffin, accompanied by paper horses and oxen, with a guard holding sickle heads and sharp blades, mounted here on a short handle and there on a long pole. There wasn't a single person present who was unarmed. Everyone looked furious, and their eyes showed their rage. Each of them had a black band tied round their left upper arm. Now the tractors and wagons were pulling up in the playground in front of the school, and the children having a physical education lesson there were so scared that they just drew back out of the way, while the pupils in the classrooms ran to the windows to look out.

The coffin was right in the middle of the playground. More firecrackers were now set off, and they started burning the paper horses and oxen, while members of the Ou family wept and keened.

"Jingfan, you died a terrible death. Your father and uncles, and indeed every man in Guojiadian is going to make the person who did this to you pay!"

"Jingfan, you must become a hungry ghost! You must make sure that everyone associated with Dahua Steel dies childless and alone!"

The teachers came running out of the building. The first out was the headmaster or perhaps one of the governors, who asked them crossly: "Who are you? What is this all about?"

Ou Guanghe rushed forward and with his finger pointing just inches from the other man's nose, he said: "Are you blind? Can't you see?"

"Rubbish! Why have you brought the coffin here to the school? How are we supposed to teach under these conditions?"

"You lot have killed a child from our village, and you still want to carry on teaching?" Ou Guanghe raised his fist and shouted a slogan: "Dahua Steel have to pay for this!"

"The murderer must be punished!"

"Blood must be paid for with blood!"

As the peasants raised the hoes and shovels in their hands, the teachers were so scared that they retreated back inside the buildings.

Having caused an uproar in the school, the people of Guojiadian tore down part of the eastern wall and then burst aggressively through the main gate of the Dahua Steel Company, after which they blocked the front entrance with their wagons.

The coffin was placed right in front of the main office building, and the white cotton cloth, like flags or banners, fluttered in the sky overhead. Now paper money was being thrown, paper houses burned, firecrackers let off. Dog's Bollocks' funeral ceremony was well underway.

There were two pillars outside the main office building supporting the heavy roof of the portico. The tractor drivers passed ropes of steel wire round the pillars and then hooked them onto the backs of their tractors. With two tractors pulling at each pillar, the moment Zhang Diankui gave the order, all four would set off at the same time, and pull the two pillars out from underneath the portico roof. Once they were gone, the roof would simply collapse and block the doorway. The peasants were ready to start demolishing the entire works.

The peasants, gloomy and vigilant, occupied the main gate and the courtyard in front of the main building, thus cutting off the main route of communications within the Dahua Steel Company, and surrounding their headquarters. The company was now in trouble, since the people inside couldn't get out and the people outside couldn't get in.

The workers in the workshops and on the factory floor had no idea what had happened. There wasn't anyone to give orders, there wasn't the slightest sign of organisation, and there was no suggestion that they were going to form a united front. They wanted to see what was going on but didn't dare to come too close, and that meant that for the moment the people of Guojiadian were in control.

The heads of the transport and various manufacturing divisions were seated in the main conference room in the headquarters, as the general manager, Zhang Caiqian, presided over the monthly scheduling meeting in his usual elegant and cheerful way. Then there were the most enormous explosions as firecrackers were set off outside, followed by the sound of shouting. It was impossible to carry on with the meeting. Zhang Caiqian went to the window to have a look, and then went quite pale. His office building was already surrounded by a crowd of peasants, and he asked what on earth was going on.

The head of security, Geng Zhijie, explained the outlines of the traffic accident the previous day. Zhang Caiqian was secretly aghast, but he didn't immediately blame his subordinates, since it was already too late to scold them. He asked Geng Zhijie to phone for the police immediately and ask them to send some people as quickly as possible. He also asked the various heads of different divisions trapped with him in the same building, who all looked shocked out of their wits, to each telephone their own work units to make sure that production continued. Nobody was to engage in confrontation or make private contact with the peasants, and even more importantly, they were to avoid any violence, since that would only complicate the situation.

Zhang Caiqian cut short the monthly meeting and returned to his own office, where he personally telephoned senior cadres in the city to report the situation, and to request that the Party Committee send someone suitable as quickly as they could to sort out this impasse.

Geng Zhijie was shouting into the phone from his office, to the point where half the building could hear him loud and clear: "I want you to bring as many people as you can, as many guns as you can, and you'll need lots of bullets. They're all armed. These peasants have organised themselves into a militia, and they have arrived in force to cause trouble at a state-owned enterprise. This is open rebellion! What do you think is going to happen if you don't come and deal with it, and put some of their leaders under arrest? Do we still have any law in this country worthy of the name?"

All of this shouting was just a bluff. He had no idea what to do in this situation, and he was frightened and vacillating. His only thought was to dump the responsibility for this mess on the police and take it out on them a bit. No one in the head office had a clue what do to, and normally none of them gave a shit about what happened to the local peasantry. Why should they?

The people in Dahua Steel suddenly realised that things weren't going to plan here, and they had no idea what to do, since they didn't know the rights and wrongs of the situation.

It wouldn't be right for Zhang Caiqian to appear himself, so he had to send out the president of the union, Hu Yi, and Geng Zhijie, to get a feel for what was going on. Hu Yi was a very conciliatory man, and he wore exactly the same expression on his face as if he'd been paying out funeral expenses or emergency funds for one of his union members. On the other hand, one look at the head of security, Geng Zhijie, was enough to see that he'd spent time in the army. His legs were straight and his back was held stiff, his chest puffed out and his head held high; a picture of military arrogance. The two of them had just walked down the steps when they found their way barred by Ou Guanghe's huge steel spade. "Where do you think you're going?"

Geng Zhijie looked furious: "Hey, I haven't asked you any questions and you're already having a go at me. This is our factory, and I can go wherever I like!"

There were plenty of voices raised in outrage at this: "Oh, so how many people from Guojiadian are you planning to go and kill?"

"Don't do anything stupid! What do you think you're doing? You're all carrying weapons, and you've got together a crowd and burst into a state-owned enterprise!"

"We've come to make you pay."

"If we've broken the law, there are systems to deal with that. In the case of a traffic accident, the traffic police deal with it. Have you thought of the consequences of your behaviour?"

Zhang Diankui picked up the gauntlet: "So what have you done about the person who ran over and killed a child yesterday? And then they stole the child's body last night. Is your law ready to punish that? Or are you allowed to kill people and kidnap the body with impunity, and we aren't allowed to come and complain?"

Hu Yi was shocked. This was now getting more and more appalling. It wasn't just a matter of a simple traffic accident any more. It would be a bad idea to allow Geng Zhijie to make the quarrel worse, so he decided to walk forward and speak up: "You're telling me that you've lost the child's body?"

"What do you think we're here for? And it's not lost, it's your people that came and stole it!"

"How do you know that it's our people who stole it?"

"The people who kidnapped the body came by car, and other than you lot wanting to destroy the body to get rid of evidence, who would want to steal a child's corpse? Besides which, having got hold of the corpse they drove off in the direction of your works." Zhang Diankui spoke with great certainty.

"So what's in the coffin?"

"It's empty. We are waiting until we have Jingfan's body to put back in it. Either that, or you can use it for my body!"

There was a very nasty look in Ou Guanghe's eyes, and behind him the other peasants looked about ready for murder.

Hu Yi thought it best to say something conciliatory: "I am so sorry. The guilty driver was indeed employed at the works here, but yesterday afternoon he ran away. The traffic police have issued a warrant for his arrest."

"He has run off? Even if he has run away, you can't! We want your company to show that justice is going to be done!"

"Please can everyone calm down! I am sure that there is a way to sort this out to everyone's satisfaction."

"Calm down? If it was your child who had been run over and killed, or your father or mother, would you be calm?"

Some of the other peasants were beginning to shout: "Don't bother talking to him. He's just leading you on to waste time."

Zhang Diankui came rushing forward waving his hands. In the circumstances he had to press them on what they were prepared to do: "Can the two of you take responsibility for this? If you can't, can you go and find someone who can? We don't have time to sit here and wait! If you don't produce someone, you are going to have to take the consequences!"

Geng Zhijie had always been a tough guy. His experiences in his past career and his current work had both served to bring out the hardest parts of his character, and he liked to deal with other people in an extremely aggressive fashion, and that included his dealings with the local peasantry. When he caught any of the locals who had come into the works to steal things or to fight with someone, there wasn't much he could do to them, of course, but at the very least he could yell at them at the top of his voice and throw in whatever insults he felt inclined to. Their role in all of this was to try to butter him up, and to smile ingratiatingly. Today he'd had to deal with the peasants of Guojiadian, and he was shocked to find that his usual position with respect to the local people was reversed: it was he who was being cursed and spat at, and he had no idea what to do about it. The peasants were determined to press their cause and they weren't going home without an explanation. Geng Zhijie thought that he'd lost face. This matter should have been handled by him, and it was because he'd failed to deal with it in the first instance that the whole thing had now been blown completely out of proportion. He was now starting to get worried: if he couldn't get rid of these people, how on earth was he going to explain himself to the general manager?

As would always be the case with someone of his temperament, he really wanted to gather the company militia, who outnumbered the people who'd come from Guojiadian, issue them with guns and force these peasants out of Dahua Steel. If that happened, then there would be one of two results. Either the peasants would be scared into running away, or they'd have to fight, in which case the whole situation would become infinitely worse. In a fight between workers and peasants, it would not necessarily be the peasants that found themselves on the losing side. They were united, they were determined to fight at all costs, and they felt they were in the right. He wasn't sure that the workforce here had the same confidence, and they'd be armed only with empty guns, which might well prove not to be as useful as the steel forks and hoes in the hands of the peasants. In that case, would the workers still be prepared to listen to him and obey his orders? The whole company would be thrown into chaos and God alone knows how many people would be injured or killed. The consequences really didn't bear thinking about. Geng Zhijie could only think about these possibilities. With his neck stiff and his eyes bloodshot, without a single soldier under his command or gun in his hand, he was pulled away forcefully by Hu Yi, and dragged back to the main building.

This had already got way past anything that the security office could deal with, and he felt useless and ashamed. All he could do was go with Hu Yi back to the headquarters and report to the general manager Zhang Caiqian quite how serious the situation was. He explained how he'd felt the anger of the peasants at boiling point,

and how shocking and dangerous it had been. Even though you might feel it was
nonsense, clearly there were some reasons for their actions. The fact is that a
company truck had indeed run down and killed one of the village children, and the
driver had run away, and now the body had gone missing.

Zhang Caiqian asked Geng Zhijie what he thought. This really embarrassed Geng
Zhijie: he wanted to come down hard, but he couldn't think of anything to do that
would be sufficiently hard and would solve their problems. His only advice, therefore,
was to wait for the police to arrive. They are an arm of the government, and they
couldn't allow the peasants to just get away with causing trouble like this, could they?
If the police decided to use force… well, that would be another matter, since whatever
trouble then occurred would be nothing to do with Dahua Steel. In actual fact, just at
the moment they were hoping that the police would arrive soon, Feng Hou and Lu
Qing, the deputy chief of police in Kuanhe County, had already arrived at the
entrance to the Dahua Steel Company, together with Captain Ma Xingjian of the
traffic police. Back in Guojiadian, the moment that Feng Hou had heard the news,
he'd phoned Ma Xingjian. When they saw the peasants standing guard aggressively
round the main entrance to the works, they decided not to bother trying to talk to
them. They drove round to enter the works by the back gate. Feng Hou was
determined not to provoke this angry mob in any way. He was here to put the fire out
and had no intention of adding fuel to the flames by getting into a confrontation.
Since their jeep couldn't get near the main office building, they got out some distance
away. Rather than trying to force their way into the building, which would just have
aggravated the peasants, they went first to find Guo Cunxian.

Guo Cunxian was right in the middle of his peasant army. The hordes of men
from Guojiadian stepped aside to let them through. Feng Hou was in front, and he
said hello to people that he recognised as he passed, without any undue haste and
looking very dignified. It didn't matter how much Guo Cunxian liked to throw his
weight around, when he saw Feng Hou he had to be respectful and polite. He was also
a little bit nervous in case Feng Hou blamed him for the situation. He might well
bring up what had happened before and punish him for the two things together. Feng
Hou made the necessary introductions for him and Lu Qing, and Lu Qing, without the
slightest sign of arrogance, measured up Guo Cunxian at a glance and said: "I've
heard so much about you."

"I'm glad that you're here," Feng Hou said to Guo Cunxian. "That means that
we'll be able to keep the situation under control."

His idea was to praise Guo Cunxian in public, and also to give him a way out of
this impasse. He wanted to make his position and responsibilities in this matter quite
clear. He wasn't like an ordinary peasant, and he couldn't just come here and cause
trouble. He was responsible for making sure that the locals kept their noses clean.

Guo Cunxian was on his guard and might not necessarily realise immediately
what Feng Hou was trying to do by saying what he did. However, he understood his
general attitude, and relaxed. He wasn't scared of the Dahua Steel Company, and he
wasn't scared of the police. He was scared of offending Feng Hou, who'd been so
helpful to him, and indeed to the whole of Guojiadian. He became a great deal more
polite to the deputy chief of police. It was clear that Lu Qing would not be easy to
deal with. If he stood on his dignity, and insisted on showing off right there in front of

Feng Hou, what good would come of it? It would be better to listen to what he had to say, besides which, it would look bad if he treated the man rudely after he'd been so polite. He therefore hurriedly replied: "Chief of Police Lu, we local people want to see that justice is done, and we are hoping that the police will see us right!"

"Secretary Guo, I quite understand these people's feelings. You need to listen to Captain Ma when he tells you about what has happened, and then we'll discuss what to do."

"The driver of the car is called Wang Biao," Ma Xingjian said, "and he has been working here for less than a year. He's an unskilled worker. After the accident happened he behaved in an abnormal fashion, and then he asked for sick leave and just ran away. Of course, he is not going to get away from us. We've worked out where he is likely to go, and sent people to investigate his family and friends. We should have him under arrest shortly. I am quite sure that the body-snatching is nothing to do with Wang Biao or his work colleagues. This kind of thing has happened in other villages, and in every case it has been people connected with the local crematorium that have stolen the body."

This Guo Cunxian did not understand: "Why would they want to steal the body?"

"People have gone back to the old custom of being buried, but the crematoriums get fined if they don't reach their target for cremations. Someone who steals a body and takes it to them can get a reward totalling tens of yuan."

"Really?" Ma Xingjian's explanation had startled Guo Cunxian, and the peasants standing around him now felt somewhat less angry.

"All kinds of strange things happen in this world. That is why people in our line of work can't just go jumping to conclusions." Lu Qing's heavy gaze rested on Guo Cunxian.

The peasants standing around them now began to shout: "Trying to make money out of the dead, that's awful!"

"Do the police let them get away with that?"

"Of course not! If we just let them get away with that, we would not be here!" Ma Xingjian explained. "Our people are getting in touch with all the local crematoriums and I'm sure we'll have news soon."

Lu Qing pointed to one of the lengths of white cotton cloth suspended from a bamboo pole. "Are those the three demands that the family is making?" he asked Guo Cunxian.

Guo Cunxian glanced back towards Ou Guangming who was standing beside him. Ou Guangming, his face racked with distress, nodded.

"The first two demands we can do for you, but I imagine that the third one is the most important, is that right?"

"We can talk about that when the time comes," said Ou Guanghe. His voice was hoarse and his words were difficult to make out. It was embarrassing to have to mention money right there in front of everyone. His fellow villagers had come all this way in a great cavalcade to make a scene. Surely this wasn't just about trying to get a bit of money?

Feng Hou gave Guo Cunxian his orders: "In a minute I will go with Chief of Police Lu and Captain Ma to meet with the general manager. I want you to keep an eye on your people, and until you've heard back from me, until you know whether your three demands have been accepted or not, you have to promise me that there isn't going to be any fighting. Feelings are feelings, but the law is the law. If there's any problem, the law will deal with you and by then it will be far too late for regrets."

To have Feng Hou and the deputy chief of police come in person to make peace was just what Guo Cunxian had been hoping would happen. He had already calmed right down. He'd been worried before about how things would turn out, but now Feng Hou had arranged things very nicely for him, so it would be easy for him to climb down. After all, he really didn't want to get into any more trouble. He was perfectly happy to show every respect for Feng Hou as he said: "OK, we'll be waiting."

Feng Hou now knew exactly where he was. Guo Cunxian might run risks, but he wasn't a bastard and he wasn't stupid. He took Lu Qing and Ma Xingjian into the main office building of Dahua Steel. First they went to the security office, where there was a direct-dial telephone that Ma Xingjian could use, because he urgently needed to communicate with his men.

Meanwhile Feng Hou and Lu Qing were taken to see Zhang Caiqian by Geng Zhijie.

According to the system of ranking cadres then in force in China, although Feng Hou held the rank of deputy chief in the county, he was still one grade lower than Geng Zhijie as head of security at Dahua Steel. When officials meet, the first thing that they do is to compare ranks, and then they know what tone to adopt towards each other. The higher-ranking person will speak more arrogantly and will use more colloquial terms. That is certainly what happened with Geng Zhijie. He was determined to put Feng Hou and Lu Qing in their place: "Really, law and order in this place is appalling! First you have peasants stealing the property of a state-owned enterprise and now you have them coming en masse in a violent protest. These incidents are becoming more and more serious. The county police need to use strong methods to establish control. People from shithole places are always out to cause trouble. That saying hits the nail on the head. You have to use force against people like that, it's the only thing they understand. At the very least, the peasants of Guojiadian have to pay compensation for the damage they've caused to our school, and they have to offer a formal apology to the company, to make up for the bad impression they've made."

Feng Hou looked as thoughtful and calm as he usually did. He might have been annoyed, or he might not even have been listening; it was very hard to tell.

Lu Qing was very angry. We come rushing over to Dahua Steel to get you out of this problem and this useless head of security, who is furious because he simply couldn't cope with the peasants coming over here, is now taking it all out on us. He really wanted to say a few things back, or perhaps cause him some other problems and let him take the consequences. That would be perfectly easy for someone in Lu Qing's position. He took a quick look at Feng Hou, who had much better control over his temper and hadn't said a word. If it wasn't for the fact that they'd now arrived at Zhang Caiqian's office, Geng Zhijie would clearly have had more to say.

In stark contrast, Zhang Caiqian was a modest and easygoing man. First he went over the mistakes he'd made that had caused such problems for Feng Hou as county chief, and for the county police, and then he expressed his gratitude that Feng Hou and the police had arrived so promptly to deal with their difficulties. Afterwards he asked about how the case was developing, and inquired minutely about Guo Cunxian and the situation in Guojiadian. Feng Hou told him everything that he knew. Zhang Caiqian listened intently and then asked for his opinion about what they ought to do.

Feng Hou gestured at Lu Qing to speak. Lu Qing glared at Geng Zhijie, and his meaning was very simple: "If your company has got itself into trouble with the local people, you can only deal with this in a conciliatory fashion, you cannot use force. If you can give way then you should, particularly since these folk from Guojiadian have a legitimate grievance. Up to the present time, they haven't actually done anything very wrong, but if you show yourself too intransigent, or you annoy them by adding fuel to the fire in some way, and people do get hurt, I still don't think anyone could blame them, do you?"

Zhang Caiqian nodded, and asked Lu Qing for further advice: "In what way do you think the company should give way? Have the people of Guojiadian made some demand for compensation perhaps?"

Lu Qing explained what the people of Guojiadian had written on their banners, and he put particular emphasis on their third demand: "Normally, when we have been called in to deal with this kind of situation in the past, it all comes down to giving a bit of money to the family of the deceased. However, Guo Cunxian isn't going to let it go at that. He has a position to maintain in the village, and he isn't going to disappoint his followers by being bought off with some small change. As to what demands he is going to make, I really would not like to say. With someone like that you have to show understanding and respect. With Mr Feng present, things will be a lot easier. After all, Mr Feng has been his superior for a long time and has supported him in all of his efforts. Guo Cunxian wouldn't care about anyone else, but he's not going to do anything to upset Mr Feng."

Feng Hou picked up the story: "Yesterday evening, at the funeral, there were people who discussed with the family what demands they were going to make. At the time some suggested sending the child's body to the cold store at the county funeral parlour, and not holding the funeral until you'd agreed to their demands. But most unexpectedly the child's mother said that the law should deal with whoever ran over and killed her son, and she didn't want to use her child's death to make demands about this and that. She wanted her son to be buried on the third day after his death, according to tradition, and if anyone didn't do what she said, she'd kill herself right then and there. She's the kind of person who'd go through with it, too. She has tried to commit suicide more than once since her son died."

Zhang Caiqian looked deeply concerned: "What is the mother called?"

"Liu Yumei. She's a remarkable woman of the kind that you don't often see in villages. Pretty well educated, and she's the kind of person who can see other people's point of view. She doesn't just rush into things. You need to understand that she has already been sterilised, so with this child being killed, the Ou family is going to die out. It is very impressive that she has been able to take the attitude that she has. If it hadn't been for the body going missing, I am sure that none of this would have happened."

Zhang Caiqian brightened up, for it seemed that he had an idea. "Mr Feng, thank you for letting me know what is going on. Our relationship with the inhabitants of the neighbouring villages has always been bad, and responsibility for this situation does not rest entirely with them. I don't want there to be any further confrontations with Guojiadian. Would it be possible for Chief of Police Lu to go down and talk to Secretary Guo, and explain to him that we agree to whatever demands they make, and then ask the family of the deceased to come up here with the relevant village cadres, so that we can discuss the situation in Mr Feng's presence, and work out what is to be done? Do you think that would be OK?"

"No problem." Lu Qing glanced again at Geng Zhijie and walked out.

"Go to the canteen," Zhang Caiqian told Hu Yi, "and have them prepare one thousand lunchboxes, together with two big urns of mung-bean soup. If the main canteen can't do it, then get some of the other workshop canteens to help out. Once you've done that, then have the food sent round to the main gate. Tell them that Mr Feng has organised it."

He turned to look at Feng Hou with a smile: "I do hope you don't mind this being done in your name?"

Feng Hou smiled back. He was very impressed at how sensible and thoughtful Zhang Caiqian's arrangements were.

Zhang Caiqian had Geng Zhijie open the door to the smaller meeting room and prepare tea. Meanwhile he and Feng Hou stood in the doorway waiting for Lu Qing to bring Guo Cunxian, Ou Guangming and Zhang Diankui up, then he went to welcome them. Lu Qing performed the introductions, and then they all sat down in the meeting room. The three people from Guojiadian sat together, looking dishevelled and sunburned, but this served to hide how nervous they were. Each of them was trying to figure out how on earth they were going to proceed. Now Mr Feng was involved, if the other side wasn't actually sincere in trying to resolve the situation, what should they do?

Zhang Caiqian and Feng Hou sat down facing them. The head of this great steel empire had a plump, pale face, and he was wearing a snug-fitting Western-style suit, looking very elegant and graceful. It was easy for anyone in his presence to find themselves feeling awkward, let alone the three peasants seated opposite him today. Zhang Caiqian now solicited Feng Hou's advice: "Mr Feng, how shall we begin?"

Feng Hou didn't want to make a fuss, so he said: "As you wish."

"Let me start then, and if I say something wrong, I want you to break in and criticise. Afterwards Mr Feng can give you his conclusion. He's in charge of Kuanhe County, and that means he's in charge of us all. Whatever he decides, that's what I'll do." Zhang Caiqian was actually a great deal more senior in rank than Feng Hou, but by stressing his seniority, he was setting the tone for the coming discussions and making sure that the three peasants present could not interject.

"I would like to express my deepest condolences about the death of this innocent child. This is a crime committed by the driver of the vehicle, but we too bear some responsibility for what happened. At the very least, we did not provide him with enough instruction, because he really should not have run off leaving the child to die after the accident. The heads of our transport and security divisions did not deal with this matter in a sufficiently timely manner, nor were their actions appropriate in the circumstances. They should have gone to Guojiadian last night to express sympathy to the parents and family of the deceased, and dealt with any problems that arose immediately. It is because they didn't do this that we have this situation today. I would like to express my most sincere apologies for the way in which we have caused unacceptable distress to the local people. I apologise on behalf of the Dahua Steel Company."

Zhang Caiqian had not said a single empty word. His compassion was real, and his analysis of the situation was true. He couldn't help feeling sad himself at some of the things that he had to say. The hearts of the three peasants present might have been moved, but they were quietly telling themselves not to let him get to them, because he hadn't yet said a single thing to the point.

Feng Hou whispered to Lu Qing: "Could you go and hurry Captain Ma up a bit? Do we have any news?"

Lu Qing slipped out, and Zhang Caiqian carried on speaking: "To tell you the truth, in recent years our security team has had to arrest a lot of peasants who've come to our works to cause trouble, but not one of them has come from Guojiadian. I must express my gratitude and respect towards your village. It seems to me that this establishes a basis for us to work together in an amicable fashion. I have heard that Guojiadian has built a number of factories lately in the village, and that Secretary Guo has more things planned, so I was thinking that we might be able to work together and cooperate over building a factory with you. As to exactly what will happen, I will go to Guojiadian in person and explain in detail what I have in mind.

"However, today we are going to be discussing the problem of compensation for the family of the deceased. Of course, that is only money, and can in no way make up for the terrible loss you have suffered and the pain that this has caused. The local people living near our works, including you, have shown great support for the Dahua Steel Company. I have been informed that Comrade Ou Guangming does not have his own home, so our construction arm will build you a new three-room house. Although you are still young, Ou Guangfan was your only child, and with him gone, then there is a problem of who will look after you, his parents, once you are old. If you agree, then you can all come and work here at Dahua Steel, in which case there will be a pension waiting for you. If you don't want to come and work at Dahua Steel, then in addition to the compensation payment that will be agreed according to government guidelines, we will also collect donations from our workforce, which should give you at least another thirty to fifty thousand yuan. This is just something off the top of my head, and if you have any other demands, or you can think of a better way to deal with the situation, there is no need to be polite, please just tell me."

Guo Cunxian looked at Ou Guangming, indicating that in this kind of situation it is important to listen to the parties directly involved.

It was now time to come to the point, but Ou Guangming was stammering: "Mr Feng, this isn't just about money. What about the murderer?"

While Zhang Caiqian had been speaking, Lu Qing had brought Ma Xingjian back into the room. Feng Hou asked him: "Any news about that?"

"The child's body was snatched by your local crematorium," Ma Xingjian said. "We've arrested the four people who stole it, and the body has already been sent back to Guojiadian. Wang Biao's aunt has informed the police that he's hiding at the home of someone he went to school with in the city. We've already sent someone over to arrest him."

Ou Guangming couldn't sit still. Zhang Diankui knew that it was time for him to put his oar in, so he stood up and walked forward: "Mr Feng, General Manager Zhang, since the child's body has been found, we need to get back as quickly as possible to carry on with the funeral. If we delay any longer, the body is going to start going off. As for the financial compensation, I think we should do what General Manager Zhang has suggested, and I thank him on behalf of the family."

Ou Guangming stood up as well, but he simply couldn't find it in himself to say thank you. His son had been killed. How could he thank the work unit who'd run over his son and killed him?

Zhang Caiqian stopped Guo Cunxian: "It is OK if the other comrades hurry back to organise the funeral, but I think it would be best if you, Secretary Guo, left a little bit later. I would like you to go with Mr Feng to have a look at our company, and then we can discuss our future cooperation."

Feng Hou chimed in as well: "You'd better stay, Cunxian."

19

BACHELORS' HALL

It was supposed to be Zhang Caiqian taking Guo Cunxian on a tour of the Dahua Steel Company but, in actual fact, everything that Zhang Caiqian said was directed at Feng Hou, and Guo Cunxian was left trailing along behind, straining his ears to hear what they said. The year that the company went into operation, he'd come to have a look, but he was completely ignorant of developments since then. It was indeed a massive operation, a real industrial empire. When would the works at Guojiadian be on this scale? He was secretly moving the beads on his own abacus, while he waited to see what Zhang Caiqian was prepared to do for him.

Dahua Steel was indeed an empire of metal. The enormous size of the workshops was deeply impressive, with walkways crisscrossing through the space like a huge maze. There were more than twenty factories of different sizes within the company, and they were connected by their own internal network of roads and railway lines which, in turn, connected with the regular rail network outside. This was a company with annual profits in the tens of billions. Guo Cunxian couldn't imagine what that even looked like. They were right here in the same place, and he'd spent decades living in abject poverty, while over here they were rich to the point where you could almost say that the streets were paved with gold. While Zhang Caiqian walked them round, thousands of yuan, or maybe even tens of thousands, had been earned.

No wonder Zhang Caiqian was of so much higher rank that Feng Hou; he had the money. If you can get the initial investment, you can earn money. A small investment brings a small return, a big investment brings a big return. Or to turn it round, if you've got the money, then everything else falls into place. He, Guo Cunxian, had other people interfering all the time in what he was up to and trying to punish him for this or that. Wasn't it all to do with money? If you don't have money then you die in poverty, and if you strive to earn some money, then higher-ups use their power to try and make your life a misery. If you're rich, on the other hand, the rules just don't apply. Look at how polite Chief Feng was being to Zhang Caiqian. Wasn't that all because he was both rich and powerful? Living like Zhang Caiqian must be great fun. He had enough money at his disposal to buy the entire city, if he felt like it, and he had the power to make county officials and the city government sit up and beg.

Zhang Caiqian led them past the open-air pick-up at the steel rolling mill, where there were two great cranes loading steel onto the railroad wagons stationed underneath them with much clanging and noise. Zhang Caiqian stopped there and turned to face Guo Cunxian. "As you probably know," he said, "we have a great gap between supply and demand for steel in China at the moment. There is a shortfall every year of more than thirty million tonnes. As a result, the state has instituted a double-track pricing system. The price of steel that comes within planned production is the same nationwide, and mills are not allowed to set their own higher price for this. But this is in limited supply. At the same time, steel that is produced over and above the planned production quota is priced according to the market, and there is no limit to the supply. That channel iron you're looking at would sell for eight hundred yuan per tonne if it comes within planned production, but if it is extra, then we can sell it for one thousand, two hundred to one thousand, five hundred yuan per tonne."

Guo Cunxian's lips twitched, and he stared at Zhang Caiqian, waiting for him to carry on. Zhang Caiqian turned round and carefully went over the figures with the two people standing behind him, then he picked up the thread of the conversation again: "Every year we have to follow our planned production, because if we don't keep the situation under control, we'd quickly run out of product. In order to have something left over for emergencies, we keep back a good few hundred tons every year so as to have something left over for the third and fourth quarters. So we've decide to give you five hundred thousand tonnes of steel at the set price, which you might want to keep for use in your own industrial developments, or you might want to sell on the open market to give you the financing to purchase other materials or equipment that you need. This five hundred thousand tonnes would have a value of several tens of millions of yuan, which would be enough for your village to do something with."

Whatever he said next, Guo Cunxian was in no condition to listen to. His head was spinning. He felt like a beggar who'd stumbled over a purse of gold in the street. He really couldn't believe that something like this could possibly be true. However, he had to believe it. When the God of Wealth comes looking for you, even if you want to hide, it is impossible to do so. Iron and steel are big business. There was the possibility here to earn a lot of money in a very short time. Money was coming begging. In the past, whatever project he had underway he'd had to go out and get the investment himself, and sometimes it didn't matter what he did, or how hard he worked himself, the money simply wasn't forthcoming. He decided that whatever happened, he would have to make sure that this deal was signed and sealed today, and the documents had better all be witnessed by Mr Feng. He felt like he was in a dream.

Feng Hou saw him standing there in silence with his head lowered, and dug him in the ribs with his elbow. "Didn't you hear what General Manager Zhang said?"

He looked much more calm and collected than would normally have been expected: "Oh, I heard it. When money starts growing on trees everyone pays attention, don't they? I was just wondering whether we in Guojiadian can stand the heat in this particular kitchen? We've already set up a mill, and put in a chemical works and a slaughterhouse, and over that I very nearly came to serious grief. We've all seen how it works. To put it bluntly, to be poor is glorious, to be left-wing is even more glorious, and causing a riot is great. If you're a good actor you can get away with it, and anyone who just goes with the flow ends up in power. Sometimes I really feel that staying within the Communist Party is at the root of all our problems, and I was considering whether we wouldn't be better off going it alone."

Feng Hou laughed: "Really, Cunxian, you don't need to keep on about having had people try to punish you. Anyone would think you've really done something wrong! Everyone knows that now if you get into trouble you're really a hero, besides which, after all their efforts they couldn't actually prove that you'd done anything, could they? In fact, all they've done is make you famous, and once you're famous there are more opportunities for you. Even General Manager Zhang is now supporting you. If you make a success of this, if Guojiadian can pull itself out of poverty, nobody is ever going to try to punish you again. You'll be praised from pillar to post!"

"Thank you for those auspicious words, Mr Feng." Guo Cunxian suddenly bowed deeply to Zhang Caiqian and Feng Hou. "General Manager Zhang, you and Mr Feng here could do great things for Guojiadian, and I hope that the things that you've just been talking about will indeed happen. However, I have another request. I would like to use this money to set up a steel mill. This year we can use the difference in price to deal with the worst poverty, and then next year, we can enrich ourselves with our own production. As I see it, the only way out of poverty for us peasants is industrialisation. If you want to get rich quick, then you have to add commerce into your agricultural production. I'd like you to send people out to help me, because when our iron and steel mill goes into production, if there's something not quite right, I want you to keep an eye on things. I'm going to be relying on you for this, and saying thank you simply isn't enough to express my gratitude. We will have to wait and see what I can do to pay you back. I know that for miles around everyone knows that I've been in trouble recently, but I have my good points too. I'm not the kind of bastard who forgets to pay back!"

"Too kind. Too kind." Zhang Caiqian looked at Feng Hou. "Secretary Guo has indeed lived up to his reputation. I am most impressed. Don't worry about a thing. Our directors of planning and marketing are both here today, and they'll proceed in accordance with your wishes."

The sun was high in the sky, it was already past nine o'clock in the morning, and Bachelors' Hall was being rocked to its foundations by the explosions of firecrackers.

It had been determined that nine o'clock in the morning today was an auspicious hour for earth-moving activities. The demolition team had arrived to tear down Bachelors' Hall, and this had naturally drawn large numbers of villagers who wanted to see the fun. Bachelors' Hall could be said to be the most infamous spot in the whole of Guojiadian, the symbol of their poverty, and the centre of all village gossip, as well as the origin of many an evil rumour. Guojiadian was sorting itself out. Soon there would be factories and hotels, and they were building a new Party Committee office for the village. Were they going to embarrass themselves by leaving Bachelors'

Hall to fester where it was? Let's pull down this horrible building, and that will show that Guojiadian is on the right track.

However, the bachelors weren't stupid. Bachelors' Hall was their home, and if they pulled it down, where were they supposed to hang out? However, the little guy can't fight the big fish: it wasn't going to be possible for them to openly resist the demolition. On the other hand, if they put a few obstacles in the way, what was Guo Cunxian going to do about it? Don't forget that Bachelors' Hall was where so many problems in the community started. Right now the village was busy recreating itself, and everyone was working their socks off, but Bachelors' Hall was still packed with young men idling about all day. This was really annoying Guo Cunxian. Therefore he had cleared his desk of other work for this morning, and was right there standing at the scene to watch over things in person, to see what the bachelors might get up to.

Everyone is happy to push a falling wall, and the villagers had turned out en masse. There was the sound of laughing and joking from them, as the walls of Bachelors' Hall began to give way and then came down with a resounding thud and a huge billowing cloud of dust. Caught up in this musty, foul-smelling cloud, those who'd turned out to see the fun took a hasty step back.

In the midst of this confusion, someone gave an ear-piercing scream: "Snake! There's a snake!"

The onlookers immediately gave the snake plenty of space. It was a black snake about as thick as a spade handle, which came wriggling out of the cloud of dust and headed unhurriedly eastwards. The more nervous villagers ran away, while the braver ones fought to squeeze forward through the crowd so that they could see better. Even the people demolishing the building halted their work and crowded round to see the big snake.

The villagers out in front of Bachelors' Hall were screaming: "Oh my God! That's a huge snake! That's really scary!"

"Maybe it's a snake god! That would make it immortal!"

"If you alarm it then you'll be in for bad luck. Go and get some incense sticks so that we can show it some proper respect."

In this situation, Ou Guanghe and some of the other bachelors were naturally determined to make a thing of it. They danced around holding steel spades, and they picked up lumps of earth with which they were planning to kill the snake. Such a big, fat one would definitely be delicious once it had been roasted!

Guo Cunxian rushed forward shouting at them to stop: "Don't hit it! Nobody is allowed to touch it!"

The black snake wriggled across the road and climbed up the edge of the pit there. By the time everyone had got over there, the snake had completely disappeared.

Everyone stood massed round the head of the pit, unwilling to leave. They all had their own opinion of what they'd just seen: "What on earth is going on? We've never had such a big snake round here before. Clearly Bachelors' Hall must have decent feng shui. Now that such a rare and special creature's been forced out, will that mean good luck or bad?"

"Rubbish! Bachelors' Hall doesn't have any feng shui! If the feng shui there were any good, why would we have so many men that can't get married? I'm guessing that the snake was female, otherwise the bachelors wouldn't be spending all their time in that hall!"

"You don't understand. Out of all living creatures, which has the strongest sexual desire? It's the snake. Snakes will go on having sex for twenty-four hours and they're still not finished. If you don't believe me, have a look the next time you find some snakes mating. They get all coiled up tight together, twisting and turning back and forth, and no matter what you do you can't get them to let go of each other."

"They're enjoying themselves, why should you try to split them up? Snakes are very special creatures, and according to our tradition, if you see one you should pretend that you haven't, and then give them a wide berth."

Guo Cunxian was mulling the whole incident over. He couldn't decide whether the snake leaving Bachelors' Hall when it was demolished was a sign of good luck coming, or bad. Listening to the villagers discuss the matter was making him even more nervous. Then, quite unconsciously, he raised his head and caught sight of Lin Meitang running towards them with her face ashen. When she got close she told him that there had just been an urgent message from the local community office that the following day, the county authorities were going to come out and investigate literacy and family planning projects. If they hadn't met their targets then not only would the whole county be the subject of criticism, there were also going to be fines, and in the worst-case scenario, the village cadres and local Party secretaries would lose their jobs. Damn. The demolition of Bachelors' Hall had been a bad idea, and problems had reared their ugly heads pretty fast!

Everyone immediately quietened down. The villagers were looking at Guo Cunxian. Some of them whispered their own suggestions to him: "You should kill a chicken and a ram as quickly as possible and offer them up here by the pit, to ask the snake for forgiveness."

Guo Cunxian started cursing: "Bastard, ghosts and spirits are afraid of animal sacrifices, not to mention a snake! Now Bachelors' Hall has been demolished, and the snake has gone, which means that misfortune has been expelled and good luck is on its way. Guojiadian isn't going to be poor any more. We're going to do much better in future."

He told Lin Meitang to use the public address system and tell everyone living in Guojiadian that they all had to come immediately to the pit for a meeting. Men and women, old and young, and particularly the heads of the various work units. We are going to hold a sacrifice to the Snake God!

Once they heard Guo Cunxian say that there was going to be a ceremony in honour of the Snake God, the people who were there to watch the fun were even more thrilled. Those who had been intending to just slide away because they didn't want to attend the meeting found that they couldn't leave. They all just stood there watching him. Right now, in his position as the leader of Guojiadian, he had authority, for all that he was as thin as a rake and his face was covered in wrinkles. However, his eyes were exceptionally piercing, and they could shoot glances of great power. Whoever he looked at, they hastily turned their glance aside. The tone in which he spoke now also became more forceful and sharp.

That was exactly the result that Guo Cunxian wanted to see. He stood there by the side of the pit, not saying a word, waiting patiently. He wanted to see what would happen: exactly how long would it take for the people of Guojiadian to assemble? And if there was anyone who dared not listen to his summons, he was going to get them for that. This particular trick was one that he'd played before. He'd often called general meetings on one pretext or another. He liked making speeches, and the more people turned out to listen, the more enjoyable it was. Since he was in charge here, he ought to take every opportunity to have people assemble regularly to listen to what he had to say, since he couldn't rely on his loyal but otherwise quite useless subordinates to keep the inhabitants of the village up to date. They always ended up leaving out the most important bit of his message. Right now it was also crucial for him to call just such a meeting, since he had to get the residents of Guojiadian back into the habit of implicit obedience. He wasn't in the business of doing what other people said or obeying their demands. The people of Guojiadian had been obedient for countless generations and what good had ever come of it? Why shouldn't other people obey us for a change?

Guo Cunxian suddenly felt that his life had taken a turn for the better. The mills of the gods may grind slowly, but at long last, those who've been bullied and kicked around will have the opportunity to be paid back with interest. Just at this moment, the loudspeakers around Guojiadian started to bellow. Lin Meitang was announcing over the public address system that Secretary Guo had an urgent message to transmit. No wonder Guo Cunxian liked and trusted her so much: she could report his words practically verbatim, unlike the people that he normally had to do this kind of work.

It was almost noon, and the villagers had no idea what had happened. People stopped their work, those cooking lunch stopped too, and they all set off in the direction of the pit, hot on each other's heels. Lin Meitang repeated the message quite a few times, and then went in person round the whole of the village, using a recently acquired handheld megaphone to continue to announce the message, hurrying on the latecomers. By the time she arrived at the pit herself, pretty much the entire village had assembled. It was just like when the various important figures in the village came to pay their respects at New Year: you might not be able to remember every single person who turned up, but you would never forget which ones had failed to come. Lin Meitang passed her handheld megaphone to Guo Cunxian: "Why don't you begin, Secretary Guo?"

Ever since the investigation team had left, everyone in the village, and that included Guo Cunxian's friends and supporters, had all stopped calling him Cunxian. Everyone now respectfully addressed him as 'Secretary Guo'. It wasn't that anyone had told them to do this; they had learned it from each other and it had gradually become a habit with them, and this included Lin Meitang. Guo Cunxian lifted the megaphone to his lips. This was the first time he'd ever used one, and he felt a bit silly. It covered quite half his face, so that his subordinates could only see the megaphone. They weren't able to see his expression at all, and this would serve to damage his authority. It would also prevent him from being able to check on their reaction. He put down the megaphone, feeling quite sure that his natural voice would be loud enough and that every villager would be able to hear what he had to say. It would be better to keep the megaphone in his hand as a prop: that would make his gestures even more effective.

"As you can all see, we've knocked down Bachelors' Hall, and one reason for that is that we don't want to have bachelors here any more. In future, men in Guojiadian are going to be getting married, and so I'm here to announce a new policy. From now on, when a bachelor aged over thirty gets married, the village will provide a reward of five hundred yuan."

There was a rustling noise among the crowd. Some people were shouting, some were laughing, some were teasing each other, some were whispering and some were sighing.

Guo Cunxian's heart was thumping. He hadn't discussed this with anyone. In fact, he hadn't even really thought it through seriously himself. He wasn't intending to make any such announcement, but without thinking about it the idea of a reward for bachelors getting married had popped out of his mouth. And since it had popped out, it was now official policy; he wasn't going to go back on his word. Fortunately, he now had the money, and not just a bit of money; he was rich! It was really good to be rich. If you had the money you could live well, you could persuade other people to do what you wanted and you could bend the world to your will.

Now his voice rose again: "What? Right now five hundred yuan would be enough to get you married to a local girl, and it would probably even allow you to buy a wife from the south. Stop muttering! I know exactly what you are saying. You're saying that I've just managed to get my hands on a bit of money and the joy has sent me off my head, the fever to get rich has reduced me to a shadow of my former self. Well, I really hate people who double-cross their benefactors! Other people can see us doing well and they're jealous. Well, people in our own village have taken up their cry: what exactly do you think you're doing? You may think I'm overheating the situation, but heat produces good results. You heat up mud to make bricks, you heat up iron to make steel. Monkey goes into the stove and comes out as Monkey King! You have to go through the furnace to show just what metal you're made of. We here in Guojiadian are going to be showing the peasants all over the country just how to get rich, and if you don't run risks, how are you ever going to get anywhere? If you risk everything and win big, then that shows that you're capable, that you've got some real stuff in you. In this world about five per cent of the population have some real stuff in them and earn big money, and then ninety-five per cent are idiots who stand on the sidelines and complain. Are you going to be the ones earning the big bucks, or are you just going to be the stupid moaners?

"Now I need to turn to the second matter on our agenda. Tomorrow, the county and the local community office is going to send people to our village to investigate how the campaigns to eradicate illiteracy have gone. There have been endless campaigns to eradicate illiteracy here over the past decades, but somehow or other people still think that we can't read. Whatever we do, it seems that they aren't convinced. This situation cannot carry on. From now on we have to have one hundred per cent literacy in Guojiadian. I'm not interested in anything else. This evening, I want illiteracy eradicated once and for all in this village! Stop fussing! Let me explain my idea. Providing you can read a couple of characters, you're not illiterate, are you? If you stay up overnight you can learn a few characters, can't you? If you can't learn to recognise the characters of your own name then change your goddam name! As to what name you pick, well, if you want one word then 'Illiterate' will do, and if you want two, then how about 'Can't Read'!"

The crowd burst out laughing…

Guo Cunxian looked serious: "I'm not doing this for my own amusement, you know. What's the problem with asking you to learn to read? Is it really that difficult? If you can't learn three characters then learn one fewer, and if you can't even manage that, then how about just learning one? One, two, three, four, five, six, seven, eight, nine, ten: even pigs, dogs and monkeys can learn to count that far. Are you content with not even being able to match up to an animal? Remember, this evening Guojiadian has to stop being a village of illiterates, come what may. Everyone over the age of six who can't read has to have learned at least one character by tomorrow morning. If you can memorise more, then you'll get a reward. Ten yuan for every character, so that's one hundred yuan for ten, because when the higher-ups start their investigation tomorrow, if anyone makes a mess of things and stops our village from being fully literate, there's going to be severe punishment. How are you going to be punished? You are going to have to pay the money for everyone else's rewards. That's a heavy enough punishment that you'll regret it for the rest of your life, and if you don't think I mean it, just try and find out tomorrow. Maybe you're thinking it can't possibly apply to you, since you don't have any money and you can't pay that size of fine. Well, it's perfectly true that you may not have that kind of money now, but you'd have to be blind not to see what's going on. In fact, even if you were blind, you'd know, so you'd have to be stupid too. I think everyone has seen the way things are going in Guojiadian. So I'm putting out the word here and now: you don't want to do anything dumb that would mean you get less money at the end of the year, because this year the village is going to be earning ten thousand yuan per household at least. And when the time comes, I don't want anyone to say that they didn't know what would happen."

Ou Guangming's eyes were red, but his face was deadly pale, and he had clearly been drinking. In fact, if it was not for Guo Cunxian's presence, he'd have got himself dead drunk. Guo Cunxian had always used his official position to throw his weight around, and now that he had money too, he'd developed all sorts of tiresome habits, particularly now when he was feeling really good about himself. Recently he had been refusing to see most of his visitors. To tell the truth, this was not something that Ou Guangming particularly minded. In fact, he was happy for Guo Cunxian not to appear. If Guo Cunxian was present, then Ou Guangming would be relegated to the back to listen; he wasn't allowed to say a single word. He also had to be careful about getting too drunk, and it was all really annoying. Once Guo Cunxian had gone, he could come to life. He'd been responsible for looking after all of the visitors they'd had from the steelworks, and then he could say what he pleased, do what he pleased and just be himself. Who would behave any differently in the circumstances? When getting drunk, Ou Guangming had always been difficult and he'd cause terrible scenes while drinking as much as he possibly could. Although he might in theory be encouraging his guests to drink, somehow or other the alcohol ended up in his stomach.

It so happened that among today's visitors was a really tough customer: the head of purchasing at the Tianjin Datong Group, Zhai Faqiang. He wanted 800 tonnes of rebar and 500 tonnes of cold-rolled strip steel, and he was applying pressure to see that the price went as low as possible, making the excuse that the only reason to buy things made in a rural enterprise was because they were cheap and that if it cost the same as a state-owned company then he might as well go to them. He was demanding too big a reduction. Ou Guangming didn't pay the slightest bit of attention to him. After all, if he'd gone to a state-owned company, he couldn't have bought what he needed. The reason that he was here in the first place was because the state-owned companies couldn't fill his needs, so he might as well not bother with all of this showing off. Who did he think he was fooling?

After talking all afternoon they'd failed to reach a deal, and so he'd had no choice but to take him out for dinner to carry on their negotiation. The more Ou Guangming drank, the more he had to say, and the more he had to say, the more he wandered off topic. He forgot all about the reasons for inviting the people out in the first place, and concentrated on drinking as much wine as he could, accompanied by much gross swearing. The various other customers present, who'd come from Handan, Shenyang and Ji'nan, were all perfectly polite. They left it to their host to speak.

Zhai Faqiang's face was liberally coated in pimples, giving him an unpleasant appearance, and he liked to keep up a constant barrage of little insults: "There are rural enterprises like yours springing up all over the place now, but I hope you're going to be leaving something for us state-owned companies. You shouldn't be so keen to put us all out of business."

Ou Guangming found his head ringing and his eyes were protruding. How dare you insult me like that! We are peasants, not beggars!

"Don't be silly. I'm not here to borrow money from you, so you don't need to pretend that you're poor. If you're poor, then I don't know how the rest of us are dragging out our existences! I've seen your house with its nice brick walls and tiled roof, the main living room and the others all properly appointed, and detached too. That's what's called a villa nowadays. Very swanky! And then there's that smart new brick-built hotel that puts the big hotels in the city to shame! I know that your title is merely that of assistant manager of this works, but in actual fact you run it yourself, don't you? Guo Cunxian has the whole village to deal with, and he can't spend all of his time on this. When it comes to the steelworks you're in charge, and you can set the price, can't you?"

The other customers chimed in following Zhai Faqiang's lead. How strange, they said, that Guojiadian had managed to do so well in such a short time. It was almost miraculous. Yes, yes, when you have the money even the gods turn out to help you. Look how lucky they'd been. They needed lots of bricks and wood to build the chemical works and what have you, and then, when they had the bricks and wood for that, they naturally found they needed a whole host of other construction materials. That was how they'd ended up opening their own factory to provide it, and now they had an engineering team out working on further projects. Since they might as well keep the whole thing (and its profits) to themselves, they'd now set up their own construction company.

Ou Guangming was very pleased. What you've seen here in the village is nothing but the local branch. The bulk of our construction company's workforce is out in the city, hard at work.

"You really are qualified to show off about what you've done. You've put Guojiadian on the map in the space of just a couple of years. In order to get your development off the ground, you have had to widen and smooth out that untarmacked road that connects the county seat with Dahua Steel, but the minute the road was sorted out, the whole village started to pick up, and now you're doing really well. You've got all sorts of trucks packed with all kinds of goods, materials and machinery coming and going twenty-four hours a day. There are all kinds of people coming to patronise the businesses you have here in Guojiadian. This place used to be famous for the number of beggars it produced, but now there are banquets held here every day: a little feast for lunch and a massive feast for dinner, every seat filled, packed with your customers day after day."

From what they said, it was clear that they knew a great deal about Guojiadian. However, Zhai Faqiang wasn't actually the least bit interested in praising how well Guojiadian had done, so he was quick to turn the conversation in another direction, and begin working on Ou Guangming again: "I'm guessing that you don't ever eat at home any more, and you just order whatever you feel like." He suddenly shut up once he realised that Lin Meitang was standing right next to him, and the rest of what he had to say ended up being swallowed.

Lin Meitang had been appointed as chief executive of the steel mill by Guo Cunxian, and she was there to exercise authority on his behalf. As a result, whenever a contract was signed with a customer, or they were treated to a meal, she'd be present. Today she was wearing a short snow-white vest and a black silk, semi-transparent jacket. Her hair hung loose about her face, and her eyes were glittering brightly. The men were entranced by her appearance at first glance, and they found her deeply attractive. She picked up the gauntlet that Zhai Faqiang had let drop, and lifted a cup: "Thank you for your kind words about Guojiadian, Mr Zhai. Let me toast you on behalf of Manager Ou."

"Ah, well, if CEO Lin is offering a toast, we have to drink."

Having drunk her toast, Lin Meitang decided to move on to the food: "Do have something to eat. I know the side dishes served this evening don't look like much, but these are the real thing. You simply can't find ingredients of this quality in the city. This is freshly picked sow-thistle, very light and delicious. It's noted for its anti-cancer properties and can lower blood pressure. I know people in the city are always complaining that they can't get good eggs. Well, this is daylily omelette and I guarantee that the flavour is something special."

Without actually saying anything meaningful she monopolised the conversation, since she had so much to say that nobody else could really get a word in edgeways. In this way she was able to control the progress of this banquet. As she was piling food onto other people's plates, she asked them what they would fancy as a final dish? Her meaning was quite clear: no more drinking.

The other guests responded enthusiastically. What was there as a final dish? Lin Meitang said that they were all local specialties. There were delicious wok-cooked rolls with fish, where the flavour of the fish all goes into the rolls. There were also organic leek-stuffed pancakes, or crisp-fried noodles, sorghum noodles, buckwheat noodles, regular noodles, and then for those who'd prefer something lighter, there was yam porridge or millet porridge. Lin Meitang's eyes shone, and they spoke as much as her words did of how attentive she was to every one of her customers. No wonder that people in Guojiadian said that she'd played a crucial role in getting their steel mill off the ground. If she was there to offer a toast to the customers, there was nothing that she couldn't do. If she asked for a loan, she'd get the money. If she wanted to sell a particular product, that's what would be down on the order form. There were all sorts of jokes current in the village and far beyond about how she would drink and offer toasts, and they lost nothing in the telling. In the past, Guo Cunxian had always monopolised any dealings between Guojiadian and the outside world, but now he wasn't willing to go out drinking with their customers. To put it bluntly, this was because he couldn't stand the way they would get drunk and then try and chat up Lin Meitang. They'd tried every trick in the book, and he felt it was rather embarrassing for him to be present. However, right now, he couldn't afford for Lin Meitang not to appear. There were so many things that depended on her, so he just had to say to himself that what the eye doesn't see the heart doesn't grieve about. It appeared that there were various unwritten rules in the business that Guojiadian did with clients from other parts of the country, and one of them was that, if any customer had tried it on with Lin Meitang at the dinner table, when the time came to sign the contract they'd be paying ten per cent over the original price. If they'd tried to grope her or feel her up in any way, then they'd be looking at paying twenty to thirty per cent over the odds.

In the past, the moment Lin Meitang gave the word, Ou Guangming had followed her lead. Even if he'd been twice as drunk, he wasn't about to forget that Lin Meitang was there as Guo Cunxian's representative. Today, things went quite another way. After all, going contrary to what Lin Meitang wanted would show his authority as assistant manager: "Wait a bit, wait a bit. Let's not have the main dish served just yet! We haven't finished drinking, and there are all these dishes on the table that nobody has even touched! Here, this dish of spring onions dressed in shrimp paste is just the snack for when you're out drinking. If you eat this every day, you can keep your erection going for hours! This dish is fried sheep's kidney. It's very nutritious and there are lots of men who eat it right now as a cure for impotence. This one here is something special, stewed donkey penis. Guojiadian is famous far and near for its donkey-penis dishes. Let's have another round of drinks and then we'll have the sheep's kidneys and the donkey penis. Anyone who doesn't drink is a rotten egg!"

Zhai Faqiang now put his oar in: "Great. Mr Ou here is a real man, a real good friend. Since you say we haven't had enough to drink, how about we swap these cups for bowls. I reckon these rice bowls here would be about right. Drink one of these up and we're real friends! When a man becomes friends with another man, he relies on experience. His relationships with women are something else, there he falls in love at first sight." Zhai Faqiang was busy eyeing up Lin Meitang.

Given how much alcohol had already been drunk, he was definitely up to no good in insisting that they swap to larger bowls, or perhaps he had also drunk too much himself. Lin Meitang couldn't care less what Zhai Faqiang did, but she wanted to stop Ou Guangming from going too far. Ou Guangming elbowed her aside, and with his other hand he picked up a bowl of wine and hurled it down his neck. The wine poured all over his chin and down his front, and he didn't even feel the need to wipe it up.

The only thing he cared about was trying to hurry Zhai Faqiang up: "Mr Zhai, your turn now."

Zhai Faqiang set down a bowl of wine, and stared at Lin Meitang: "If CEO Lin is willing to do me the honour of drinking this bowl of wine, then I have the contract here in my briefcase. We don't need to wait until tomorrow morning, we can sign it right now! Either I pay the price that you set, or we can add whatever you want to it."

Lin Meitang was clearly a little nervous. "Ladies don't normally drink wine," she said, "but since Mr Zhai here is making such a point of it, in order to clinch this deal with the Datong Group, you drink first and then I'll follow you."

Zhai Faqiang had definitely misjudged the situation, and now he had to drain his cup to the dregs. Wiping his mouth, he waited for Lin Meitang to proceed. Without a frown or the slightest other change of expression, Lin Meitang downed the bowl of wine in front of them all.

Zhai Faqiang suddenly looked stupid, and the pimples on his face turned bright red. He was staring fixedly at Lin Meitang. Perhaps he was still waiting. A woman who'd drunk so much wine ought to be sodden with it. She ought to collapse, or cry, or beg for mercy, and he could then help her up, cuddle her and give her a good groping. He was there staring at Lin Meitang, while Lin Meitang was staring at the briefcase by his side, and everyone else was watching them, as the situation became more and more embarrassing.

In the end it was Zhai Faqiang who couldn't hold his nerve, but he had no intention of opening his briefcase and bringing out the contract to sign. Instead he turned to Ou Guangming and took his turn: "Mr Ou, today I'm going to tell you that friends come in different kinds. Good friends are like your underpants, and they'll stay with you through everything. Really good friends are like condoms, always there to keep you safe. And your very best friend is like an aphrodisiac, so that when you can't keep it up any more it gives you strength. What kind of friends do you think we are?"

Everyone burst out laughing.

"Well, I think it's time for my turn now," and without waiting for Ou Guangming to respond, Lin Meitang drew everyone's attention to herself. Zhai Faqiang was the first to begin shouting. Great! Great! Let's give the lady a turn. Without the slightest sign of haste, Lin Meitang filled six big bowls with wine right up to the brim, put three of them down in front of Zhai Faqiang, and left the other three for herself. Zhai Faqiang suddenly found himself speechless and the pimples on his face began to turn from red to purple.

"I've heard that men show what they're really like once they're drunk," Lin Meitang said laughingly. "If they go berserk then they're useless. If they start talking rubbish then they're unreliable. But if they stay polite no matter how much they drink, don't forget their promises and do everything they've said they'll do, then that's a good man. Mr Zhai, I'm sure that you're one of the latter, so today I'm determined to toast you three bowls, even if it kills me." Having said this, she drained the first bowl and looked expectantly at him.

There was nothing that Zhai Faqiang could do to get out of it. "Meitang, can I call you that?" Lin Meitang said that he could. "If you toast me, Meitang," Zhai Faqiang said, "then I have to drink. You're doing this to show your respect, and I appreciate that. But I have a condition. It's quite obvious that you're in charge of the steelworks here in Guojiadian. So if I drink down these three bowls then we sign our agreement on my terms. If I can't drink them down, then it'll be on your terms."

Lin Meitang agreed to that, and added that she liked doing business with someone decisive. Zhai Faqiang stretched out his neck and lifted up the bowl of wine, and then began to drink it down with a glugging sound, with the intention of beginning immediately on the next. Having swallowed the first bowlful, his eyes were already fixed on the second, and his hands were reaching for it. However, without knowing quite how it happened, he found himself on his knees in front of Lin Meitang, his hands gripping her ankles and his face pressed against her knees. "You're going to have to let me off this, Meitang, and you can fill in the terms in the contract in my briefcase any way you like."

The people standing around watching how the joke played out now bent down to pick him up. It took a lot of force to get him to let go of Lin Meitang's leg. He was carried out in a heap. Given what had happened, the banquet had to finish now, and Lin Meitang escorted her other customers back to where they were staying. Fortunately, they were all in the same place. On her return she called in at one of the other rooms and dragged out the manager of the chemical works, Chen Erxiong, who happened to be dining there with some staff from the bank. She asked him to help her get Ou Guangming carried back home.

As the two of them hefted Ou Guangming out of the room, one on each side, it so happened that they bumped into Guo Cunyong, who often came swanning in and out. "Where have you been?" Lin Meitang asked crossly. "You know that there was a dinner on this evening, and you also know what Ou Guangming's like. You could have helped to keep an eye on him too."

Guo Cunyong was feeling particularly cheerful. He explained that he'd just come from Cunxian's house, where they'd been discussing building a nightclub. The customers were complaining that after they'd eaten there was nowhere for them to go. The whole place was just dark and dead. You see, there's money just going begging and we aren't picking it up! If the government let us put in a casino too, the money would just come pouring in. He chattered away about nothing as he prepared to take over from Lin Meitang, but Ou Guangming held fast to Lin Meitang's arm and said: "Don't go, Meitang. When we get home I've got something to say to you."

Guo Cunyong moved round to take over from Chen Erxiong. His dinner party hadn't finished yet and he needed to go back to spend more time with his guests. It was true, right now wave after wave of customers were arriving in Guojiadian every day. There were bizarre ones, slippery ones, expansive ones, and then there were those that put on airs, those that shouted at everybody, those who were humble and flattering, and those who were up to something criminal. Some of them brought cheques, some of them had bags of cash, but they all wanted to buy products made in Guojiadian, or join in some project with Guojiadian. Right from the beginning, Guo Cunxian had told his subordinates: I don't care whether you like them or not, you aren't allowed to quarrel with them. Either they are here to make us rich, or they've been invited by us. The only people in this world who spend their whole time smiling at you are beggars, or they want money from you.

The atmosphere around Guojiadian had changed. The village had become like the wilds where mushrooms pop up after the rains. The steel mill stood in a hollow in the salt marshes to the east, and its lights shone through the night in that part of the village, while to the west there were the illuminations from the chemical works. Ou Guangming's feet might be stumbling, but words kept streaming out of his mouth: "Cunyong, you're the smartest person in this whole village after the secretary. It was my idea to start a construction company way back when, but then Dog's Bollocks died and I couldn't leave, you then got the opportunity to go with Jin Laixi in my place and take charge of the workforce. Ever since leaving the village you've done really well for yourself. You've raised the flag high for Guojiadian. In the last two years there have been real opportunities in this village, and you knew how to seize them, didn't you? You came here to recruit people for your workforce, and then you built the steel mill and the hotel with them, and everything was done with the maximum publicity, so that the secretary gets to feel that he really loves you and the way you do things. Well, you've done well for yourselves while I've had all the bad luck, I've lost my family, and everything I do is a failure. Everyone knows for miles around that if it hadn't been for the accident that killed my son, Guojiadian wouldn't be anything like this rich today, but the secretary doesn't trust me. You lot make sure that you're in charge of anything important, and I'm just left to arrange the furniture."

Guo Cunyong stole a glance at Lin Meitang. If she reported what he'd said to Guo Cunxian there'd be serious trouble. He hastily turned the conversation in another direction: "You read too much into things, Guangming. After Dog's Bollocks was killed, the Dahua Steel Company paid you compensation, as indeed they should have done, and the driver concerned went to prison. If you think about it, it is all thanks to the secretary that we were able to get our steel mill off the ground. You have to admit that he's a pretty amazing guy, quick to see an opportunity. At the time, it was him that did all the necessary negotiations with Dahua Steel. Mr Feng was just there to keep an eye on things. The steelworks has been the real source of wealth for our village so, of course, he ought to be in charge there."

"Yes, I know. Do you think I'm stupid? He's the one with real power and access to money. Do you think he'd be willing to hand that over to me? And he was afraid that if I became head of the mill then it would be too obvious that I'd got the job because my son died. By taking that position himself he was able to shut people up." Ou Guangming was swinging his head from side to side and suddenly started to heave. He almost threw up all of the aphrodisiac foods that he'd just been eating. Fortunately, his house was right next to the hotel, the one built by Dahua Steel. At that time, it was the finest private home in the whole village.

When he got to the gate, Ou Guangming fished out his key. Lin Meitang helped him to open first the gate and then the front door. She went in first and switched on the light. The room was filled with brightly coloured things. He had new furniture, new bedding and everything, but the whole place was cold and empty. It didn't look like a house where people actually lived. Guo Cunyong was astonished: "Yumei still hasn't moved back in with you?"

Ou Guangming's head was swaying from side to side again: "I've been round to her brother's house I don't know how many times, and I've talked to her until I'm blue in the face, but she's still refusing. She says she's never going to set foot in the house bought with her son's life. Look at me! I don't have a proper home. I don't have a life. If I'm going to spend the rest of my life alone, what's the point of having this brand new red-brick house?"

"It's too late today," Lin Meitang said, "but tomorrow I'll go and talk to Yumei and see what I can do. I'm sure I can talk some sense into her."

Ou Guangming didn't believe it: "It doesn't matter what you say, it isn't going to make the blindest bit of difference. She has already made up her mind. She's a Buddhist now and spends all her time reading sutras."

"Really?" Guo Cunyong felt quite shocked.

"Cunyong, I know you're really busy, so why don't you go home," Ou Guangming said. "Meitang can stay for a bit longer, because I'd like to talk to her."

Guo Cunyong looked at Lin Meitang because he didn't quite like the idea of leaving her there alone. He tried to get her out of there: "You've had a lot to drink today, Guangming, so how about we both go and leave you alone to get some sleep. Whatever you have to say can wait until tomorrow."

He wasn't expecting Ou Guangming to turn round and glare at him. Go away! he said. I need to talk to Meitang today!

Lin Meitang caught Guo Cunyong's eye: "You'd better go."

The moment Guo Cunyong had gone out of the door, Ou Guangming grabbed hold of Lin Meitang's hands. "Meitang, I'm not drunk. I'm suffering. I need to say something to you that's been on my mind for a long time."

Lin Meitang suggested that he should say whatever was on his mind. At the same time she tried to recover her hands, but Ou Guangming had a grip on them like a pair of pincers. "There are two really unlucky people here in Guojiadian. One of them is me, and the other one is you. You know what people say about us? They say that the money coming into Guojiadian was bought with the life of my son, and with your body."

"Guangming, you're drunk."

"I'm not drunk. I want you to listen to what I have to say. You're a wonderful woman, and what's going to happen to you if you carry on this affair with Guo Cunxian? I've had an idea in my head for quite a while now. How about I don't care about the fact that you've been together with Guo Cunxian all this time, and you don't care that I'm not as rich or powerful as he is. After all, I'm younger than him. We can get married and I guarantee that we'll do OK. If you agree, I'll divorce Yumei right away." As Ou Guangming spoke, he fell to his knees by the side of the bed, in a posture not dissimilar to that of Zhai Faqiang somewhat earlier in the evening.

Now Lin Meitang was really angry. She bounced up from her seat on the bed as if she'd been stung, and did her very best to drag Ou Guangming to his feet. In a furious tone, she said: "What on earth are you talking about?"

"What do you mean? You aren't married to Guo Cunxian, and you aren't some innocent little girl. I have every right to ask you to marry me."

"What about Yumei? Do you have any idea what the people in this village are going to say about this?"

"You don't understand. Yumei has already asked me for a divorce. She was doing that for my sake. She wants me to get married again, so that the Ou family won't die out. After Dog's Bollocks was born, it was you that made her get sterilised, wasn't it?"

Lin Meitang was getting so stressed it made her head ache: "So you want to marry me to get your revenge, is that it, Ou Guangming? I've got to have a kid for you to replace the one that you and Yumei lost?"

"No, stop twisting my words. I love you. I love you as much as anyone could!"

She again tried to force him to his feet. She spoke coaxingly to him: "Get up. We'll talk about it once you've sobered up."

"I'll get up once you've said yes."

As they pushed and pulled at each other, they were too busy to hear the sound of footsteps, and then Guo Cunyong followed by Chen Erxiong burst into the room. Seeing the sight before their eyes they suddenly stopped, frozen with surprise.

Lin Meitang's face had turned bright red, and she looked cross.

Guo Cunyong was the first to recover: "Goodness me, Guangming, what on earth are you doing? Are you teaching her a lesson, or apologising for something?"

Ou Guangming was furious, but he didn't want to admit that he'd made a mistake: "There's nothing wrong in me proposing marriage to Meitang. It's good that you're here, because you can be my witnesses."

Lin Meitang's voice was trembling with rage: "Witnesses to what? Have I agreed to anything? You're drunk!"

Chen Erxiong now chipped in: "Mr Ou, kneeling down to ask for someone's hand in marriage is a Western custom. What you've done is really quite offensive. You shouldn't get drunk and then ask someone to marry you, because that's not showing respect to the woman. Who can say whether you've proposed because you've thought about it and really care, or whether it's just the alcohol talking? You'd better get up." He caught Guo Cunyong's eye and the two of them each grabbed hold of an arm and with a heave they hoisted Ou Guangming up and tossed him onto the bed.

Lin Meitang took advantage of this opportunity to recover her hands, both of which were covered in purple bruises from Ou Guangming's powerful grip.

"Guangming," Guo Cunyong said. "You want to have control over the steel mill, don't you? Erxiong has a good idea about that, and you ought to listen to him."

Chen Erxiong said: "My chemical works is already having problems keeping up with demand, and there have been several big contracts on offer recently that I've had to turn down. I've had a word with Secretary Guo about this. In the past we were only thinking about earning money in a lump sum, we weren't considering cash flow or, indeed, asset accumulation. So I want to turn our chemical works into a corporation, which would mean that we can set up branch works, giving us flexibility in supplying products according to market demand. I've been discussing my idea with the bank, and the loan to make this possible isn't going to be a problem. If Cunyong builds up his business, he can set up a trading company. Jin Laixi has already got his construction company underway, and your steel mill can become a steel company, with you in charge. Then the whole village can establish a group corporation with Secretary Guo as chairman, and we'll be heading our own divisions under his management."

Guo Cunyong poked Ou Guangming with his finger as he said: "You understand? If you start thinking along the right lines, you'll be able to put up a good show, and then the steel works will be yours. Right now you don't need to ask other people to give you authority. You do well enough and the authority's yours. If you don't do well, once the group corporation is set up, even if Guo Cunxian doesn't carry on as head of the steel mill himself, he'll get someone else in to do the job, see?"

Outside there was suddenly the most enormous bang as firecrackers started to go off. The people in the room were all a bit puzzled. Was this a festival or something? Why was someone setting off firecrackers in the middle of the night? Guo Cunyong smiled. Although he didn't spend much time in the village any more, he was still more aware of what people were up to than many who spent their entire lives there. "It must be that the sculptures to expel evil spirits are being put up. Who wants to go with me to see the fun?"

Lin Meitang was desperate to get away from Ou Guangming, so she went out with Chen Erxiong.

To the north of Guojiadian, there were torches and bonfires, not to mention the sound of people shouting. Amid all of this there was the rumbling of a crane and truck motor, with the blaring of horns, as someone directed them to put a three-metre-high sculpture, made from cement on a steel armature, into position on the boundaries between Guojiadian and Mapodian. This sculpture was entitled: 'Cutting the Gordian Knot'. Under the blazing lights of the trucks, a majestic and mighty representation of the God of War, Guan Yu, raised his Green Dragon Crescent Blade in the direction of Mapodian. Clearly he was about to cut all their heads off!

This was exactly what the inhabitants of Mapodian deserved. After all, they'd done their best to make things worse when Secretary Guo got into trouble.

Once the sculpture was erected on the north side of the village, everyone moved, laughing and shouting, to the west. The nearest hamlet to Guojiadian on that side was Wangguantun, and the sculpture to be put there was called 'The Thief Catcher'. It showed a knight with a stern face and a curly beard, his eyes glaring, trampling a turtle beneath one foot.

The explanation for this particular sculpture was a little bit complicated. The name of Wangguantun was derived from an official with the surname Wang, and the same character also appears in the word for 'bastard' and indeed for 'turtle'. That was why this creature was being stamped on. And of course if you're an official it doesn't matter how senior your rank is, you still have to beware of the wrath of heaven. As the saying goes there are things that heaven will not tolerate, and the wrath of heaven follows the enmity of man. Indeed, officials are told that the people represent the will of heaven, meaning that corrupt officials might as well take it easy and just wait to get shot. Here, the knight represented heaven and the will of the people, and that is why it could stamp Wangguantun into the dust, and make sure that they never caused trouble again.

Guojiadian's southern neighbour was Miaojiazhuang, and the sculpture put up there was a great deal easier to understand. It depicted a deer cropping the grass, or 'Miao', and was entitled 'Even the Roots Shall be Grubbed Up'.

To the east stood Hamawo. Their sculpture showed two pythons rearing up and was entitled 'Everything has a Predator'. Snakes like to eat toads, that is 'Hama', and so that should deal with Hamawo.

What on earth was going on!

Chen Erxiong was a young man, and he was speaking in a quiet, unhappy voice: We're supposed to be professionals and we're trying to please our customers. The more friends we have, the better, in fact. Aren't we going to annoy everyone in the nearby villages like this? What happens if they put up something worse? He couldn't stop himself from asking Guo Cunyong: "Whose idea was all of this?"

Guo Cunyong pointed proudly at his own nose.

"So they were made by your cement workers?"

"Hey, you're making it sound as though I've been doing things on the cheap! These were designed by a professor of sculpture at the Dahua Academy of Fine Arts, and he made them working with his students."

Chen Erxiong repressed a squawk of amazement: "A professor from a sculpture department made these?"

Guo Cunyong looked disdainful: "What's so special about being a professor? Why shouldn't he have made this? If you've got the money, you can do anything."

"Does the secretary know?"

Guo Cunyong now raised his voice to an exaggerated pitch: "Are you thick or what? Who would dare do a thing like this without his permission? Cunxian loves this, and he's practically laughed himself sick over the whole thing. It has been years since I last saw him so happy."

Chen Erxiong gulped and didn't say another word.

This was a sign. Guo Cunxian was ready to strike back. Or it might be better to say that Guojiadian was entering the era of Guo Cunxian.

It may be that at the very beginning every myth starts out like that of Guojiadian; it isn't mysterious at all. In fact, everyone is suspicious of it and looks down on all those involved. The people who complained most about Guojiadian were the neighbouring villagers. They all knew exactly what conditions pertained in Guojiadian, and they also knew perfectly well that Guo Cunxian was desperate to get rich. He'd been trying one thing after another for decades, and neighbouring villages had been laughing at him all this time. They'd been quite sure that nothing good would ever happen in Guojiadian even if Guo Cunxian worked everybody to death. They'd just thought Guo Cunxian was a natural-born fighter and that he'd fight for a bit and then he'd be punished. Then after being punished he'd keep on the straight and narrow for a bit, and then after that, he'd start something again, and once that happened it was only a matter of time before he got himself punished all over again.

Once people discovered all of a sudden that this time Guo Cunxian had fought and won big, there were some already at work polishing up the legend, for better or for worse. Those who were polishing the legend for the better made it more and more about luck from the gods. Those polishing it for the worse said that he'd killed people and committed arson, pulling every trick in the book to cheat people out of their money, and that he'd be lucky merely to end in prison, since it was much more reasonable that he be taken out and shot. Previously, when Guo Cunxian had heard this kind of cursing, there'd been nothing that he could do about it. He just had to put up with it. Now he'd decided to put a stop to it, to take a tooth for a tooth and an eye for an eye. If these other villages could join forces to fight Guojiadian, well, let them bring it on!

During the Spring Festival this year, the people of Guojiadian decided to make a show, having made so much money. They began letting off fire crackers on the twenty-third day of the last lunar month, with a constant banging, and they carried on until the evening of the thirtieth of the first lunar month, when they set off fire crackers pretty much constantly throughout the night.

Later on people called this the 'Battle of Guojiadian'.

On the first day of the New Year, everyone went to the temple, and after that there were plenty of people who wanted to go round and see Guo Cunxian at home.

All of a sudden, the people who'd come to wish the Guo family a happy New Year parted like waves to make way for a cavalcade of cars. This was Xiong Wen, secretary of the Provincial Party Committee, who had brought his family to wish Guo Cunxian a happy New Year. With him were his wife, his son and daughter, and three or four grandchildren, as well as his secretary and a journalist: enough people to fill four cars. Just think how impressive that was! The inhabitants of Guojiadian were really pleased. Guo Cunxian had done it again!

The secretary of the Provincial Party Committee was there in ordinary dress, and he looked very friendly. People felt at ease the moment they saw him: "I have often seen news about you on the television or in the papers, so I'm delighted to have the opportunity to meet you here today. In accordance with our old customs, I've come here to wish you a happy New Year. The country attaches great importance to its peasant entrepreneurs, and we're encouraging some people to get rich first. That's how we're going to be supporting the development of rural areas and enriching the peasantry. I am also here to congratulate you on being named as one of our country's top ten outstanding peasant entrepreneurs! This is not just an honour for you, it is an honour for Kuanhe County, for Dahua City, for the entire province! I was originally planning to come out on my own, but everyone was so curious about you, and even my grandchildren wanted to come and see you! I told them that you didn't have three heads or six arms, but that you're a modern-day Nezha [a Chinese Buddhist deity] or Sun Wukong [Monkey King]."

Mr Xiong was very cheerful and he now started laughing at his own joke. Everyone else joined in, adding to the joy of the New Year celebrations at Guojiadian.

When Xiong Wen was sure that everybody had pretty much finished laughing, he carried on speaking: "It's New Year and we ought to go and see our families. It's good to have a few more people about!" He turned round and said to his grandchildren: "Have a good look! This is the famous Guo Cunxian!"

Having the secretary of the Provincial Party Committee come and say such things in front of so many villagers made Guo Cunxian feel even better than the letting off of fire crackers and the visits of so many other people to wish him happy New Year. Guojiadian now had its own six-storey office building, with smart rooms to meet clients in, but the secretary of the Provincial Party Committee had insisted on coming to see him in his home first, to introduce him to his wife and family, and offer his best wishes for the New Year. How could he refuse? Having had a good look at Guo Cunxian's house, Xiong Wen now wanted to inspect the various enterprises in the village, and then he'd hear Guo Cunxian's report.

Guo Cunxian took Xiong Wen and his entourage to the eastern part of the village first. For people who enjoyed seeing other people hard at work, the food factory and the steel mill were the most fun. There was so much to see there that even a whole day would not have been enough. At the food factory there were interesting things to see as well as samples to taste. Attached to it was a 20,000 square metre chicken farm, a 20,000 square metre pig farm, and a ten *mu* (0.67 hectare) dairy herd farm while the steel mill had all the air of being part of a massive enterprise. He quietly gave orders to Wang Shun to stuff the boots of the four cars their guests had arrived in with the very best products from the factory.

Just as he had anticipated, they hadn't seen half of the food factory when it was time for lunch, so he had to ask Wen Xiong to go with him to the canteen, where he could eat while listening to his report. Guo Cunxian made it quite clear that, because it was New Year's Day, it wouldn't be appropriate to talk about work and that if the secretary of the Provincial Party Committee really wanted to know about that kind of thing, he'd come on some other occasion. Instead, he gave a very general introduction: "At present Guojiadian has two industrial zones. The one to the south specialises in electronics and chemicals, with profits of eighty million yuan last year. The one to the east specialises in food and steel, with profits last year of a hundred and forty million yuan. It is estimated that within five years, we will be realising two billion yuan in profits in each zone, and after ten years, we should be looking at ten billion yuan from the eastern zone, and another ten billion from the western one. Guojiadian has an annual output now of two billion yuan."

Xiong Wen had been cheerful on arrival, and he was pleased at what he was being told. He kept saying that this had been a worthwhile trip and he'd learned a lot. He told his secretary to make a note of this place, because they'd be coming back regularly. When they were about to leave, Lin Meitang gave each of the children a red envelope containing 20,000 yuan. This was done behind Xiong Wen's back. Guo Cunxian personally handed Xiong Wen a small memento of his visit. He immediately opened the extremely beautiful mahogany box and took out a gold plaque wrapped in yellow velvet.

"This kind of work can't be done in China," Guo Cunxian explained. "We commissioned this from Shoufeng Gold in Hong Kong. It's made with eight hundred grams of pure gold, and it shows the Lucky Trees that stand at the western approach to our village. The design comes from an original artwork by the famous painter Shen Zhongliang which won an award when it was exhibited in Europe. This represents Guojiadian, and we give it as a memento to those who support us."

Each of the people who'd come with him was given a similar gold plaque, but theirs only weighed eighty grams.

When they'd been seen off, there were some people who were feeling bad about the whole thing. My God! That was so much money, so many things. The secretary of the Provincial Party Committee didn't half do well out of his New Year visit! Our secretary is really throwing his money about...

However, they didn't dare say anything of the kind to Guo Cunxian. It was Wang Shun who realised how they were complaining. He shut them up pretty quick: "Are you all completely stupid? You complain about this little bit of money and you don't think about what it all means. Having the provincial secretary come here to wish Secretary Guo a happy New Year is a massive advertisement for us! If you want to put an ad on TV or in the papers, that costs money too! This money isn't coming out of your pockets, and we've been out arse-licking on your behalf! The way that our secretary has been working is really smooth! I don't care what the rest of you think, the fact is that today I've done my bit to butter them up too. I put a donkey penis stewed in soy sauce into each of the car boots. In the past, we've been beggars, but now high officials are coming here to ask favours from us. Aren't you pleased? I'm not begrudging them a single one of the gifts that we gave!"

PART TWO

20

THE MERRY-GO-ROUND

Another few years passed, and this was Guo Cunxian's own Great Leap Forward. This second Great Leap Forward didn't involve any inflated figures or numbers pulled out of thin air. Real goods were exchanged for the money that poured into Guo Cunxian's bank accounts. Guojiadian's wealth increased exponentially, to the point where it sometimes even terrified him; nobody could have dreamed of such wealth.

Sometimes Guo Cunxian imagined that Guojiadian had become a shop for the entire country, and he was the storekeeper. Senior cadres came in a never-ending stream, like the horses on a merry-go-round, and they clustered around him in a circle. Because they clustered around him, he had the power to do whatever he liked. But when these higher-ups came, he had no choice but to join them. And how could he refuse the power that this gave him? Naturally he ended up as part of the whole merry-go-round, and he circled round them for the power that they could give him. He had been spinning round like that for months and years now – the more he spun, the more famous he was and the richer he became.

New Year's Day visitors will often say some auspicious words like: "May all your wishes come true." In recent years all sorts of things that Guo Cunxian had never wished for had indeed come true. He suddenly found himself a deputy to the National People's Congress – is that the kind of wish that comes true just because you want it to? Every year he had to go to the Great Hall of the People in Beijing to participate in the government of the country and discuss global developments. He couldn't stop himself from thinking about another famous Chinese peasant, Chen Yonggui, a nice old duffer who always wore a hat made from the stomach of a white sheep. He'd started as a deputy to the National People's Congress, and then he'd been promoted to vice premier. He'd also begun life as a peasant. And then there were other things that Guo Cunxian had never even considered, and which made him feel overwhelmed. For example there was this association that wanted him as president, and that organisation that wanted him to be director and was inviting him to attend an event or required him to preside over a ceremony. Even more amazingly, the commune wanted him to become the new mayor...

This had to be some kind of joke. To put it bluntly, he'd rather be head of a rich village such as Guojiadian than mayor of ten communes that were as poor as church mice! Most recently there'd been another rumour that the higher-ups were thinking about having him go to Kuanhe County as deputy mayor. If it had been twenty years ago, for a peasant to make it as mayor of a county, you'd imagine that there'd have to be auspicious omens appearing at the ancestral tombs. But now he really couldn't be bothered. The last couple of years he'd developed a bad new habit: if any senior official arrived at Guojiadian, he'd ask them in a kind of joking voice how much they earned. There were some senior officials who'd laugh when they found out that Guo Cunxian earned more than they did – they seemed very happy that the peasants were getting rich. There were other officials who didn't say a word but who were clearly jealous, and in some cases furious. Right now, Guo Cunxian was earning more than ten times the salary of Gao Jingqi, the party secretary in Dahua – if you want him to go and be deputy mayor of the county and earn so much less than Gao Jingqi, do you expect him to look pleased?

Would he give up Guojiadian for anything, right now? The only thing that would have moved him was a position in Beijing, but the people there didn't seem to have the foresight of Chairman Mao, back in the day. But since news of this kind kept coming, Guo Cunxian increasingly felt that there was nothing he couldn't do. The more confident he became, the more fingers he stuck into different pies. He was circling round power, and power was circling around him, and that brought the banks onto this particular merry-go-round, and once the banks were circling, that meant that money was his for the asking. The banks just kept pressing loans on him. They only talked about loans and never once mentioned repayments – that could be left until later. It seemed as though the banks imagined that, by loaning him money, they were supporting the government's reform programme.

Were they just giving people money? Yes they were, and in particular they were giving it to Guo Cunxian. As the saying goes: 'When opportunity knocks, you answer.'

Since Guo Cunxian had never imagined that so many good things could possibly happen to him, he did indeed feel that all of his dreams had come true. Guojiadian was now rich, lots of people were working there, and they were competent too – it clearly didn't look good that he was merely secretary of a village branch of the Party. He wrote a report for the county committee, suggesting a promotion. The higher-ups immediately agreed and from branch secretary he became Party secretary, which sounded much better. Since he'd begun in life cutting wood for coffins, he liked axes, and from them he'd moved on to liking knives and guns. If there were any qualities that he really appreciated, they were strength, courage and decisiveness. One day he suddenly had a strange thought: what did Guojiadian still lack? It was lacking a police station. But he wasn't going to ask the police to set up a station in Guojiadian – that would be like asking them to come and interfere with what he was up to, and he wasn't about to cause that kind of problem for himself! He wanted his own police station, with him in charge. That would show that Guojiadian was a village in the new style; in effect, it was a little kingdom, with its own legal rights and law enforcement. That would make his people even more courageous and mean that they'd be able to rely less and less on others. However, Guojiadian wasn't a nest of bandits, and he wasn't a bandit chief. There would be no point in establishing his own private police station because it wouldn't have any authority. He had to get permission from the government, and the regular police had to give him a formal letter of appointment as chief; they had to hand out guns and police uniforms. That way his station would have the appropriate authority for a police station.

Once he'd come up with the idea, the excuse was easy. Everyone said that the key to being a good leader was coming up with the ideas in the first place. So Guojiadian reported to the county Party committee and the county police that the village now had more than fifty thousand workers from outside the region, plus a floating population of another two thousand or more coming in and out every day. This had resulted in the creation of a small society drawing in people from the city and the countryside, which comprised both workers and peasants. For their own security, they urgently needed to establish their own police station, and in order to facilitate local law and order management, the Party committee in Guojiadian recommended that Comrade Guo Cunxian act as chief, and that the backbone of the village militia should also take on policing duties, without the need for higher-up police organisations to send out any officers. Having written this report, they needed to find an effective person to bring about the desired result. Guojiadian now had no lack of people who were perfectly well aware of how to bend the rules in today's society, and so permission was given very quickly by the relevant senior officials. After that, guns and bullets were issued, together with a dozen or so police uniforms. Guo Cunxian's letter of appointment as chief was also sent with the rest of the necessary equipment...

Guns make their possessors feel a great deal more confident that nothing nasty is ever going to happen to them, and all of a sudden Guo Cunxian found that he was breathing easy. This gave him a feeling of power of a very special kind. In the past everyone used to say that, as long as you had a seal of office and a gun, there was nothing to fear, you could govern the country as you wished. There were others who said it was the pen and the gun. So he'd set up his own television station and public relations office, to keep control of his image and create favourable public opinion. Everything he said, every event he participated in was recorded and filmed. Every year a huge book was put together from this material to be handed out to the inhabitants of Guojiadian and migrant workers, not to mention being given as a gift to VIPs and reporters.

He now had another thing under his control: moneybags.

It seemed like everything was under his control. If someone had told him there was something he couldn't do, he probably wouldn't have believed it. There had been things in the past that his enterprises, the village or the cadres he controlled couldn't do, but they could be done by his police station. The guns would keep trouble at bay, and if it came in spite of everything, they could deal with it. In the past the village had had a temple to the God of Earth, but few believed in gods any more, so the police station was like a new kind of temple, and it could deal with any evil that transpired. There's an old saying to the effect that every temple is inhabited by the ghosts of dead innocents – if they gather in the temple, then they can't be causing trouble for other people, but once the temple's gone, then they can be out and about bringing the place to rack and ruin.

Now that Guojiadian had its own police station, anyone who was prepared to risk their lives to cause trouble could bring it on!

At this time China still had a planned economy, but Guo Cunxian found himself with a new toy – with guns at his beck and call, why should he worry about anything? The market turned on an axis of his choosing, the city likewise; experts and specialists of every form danced to the tune of his piping; anyone who wanted to get in the way found that they simply couldn't. Guojiadian didn't just have money, it represented opportunity! Guo Cunxian was getting the first bite of every cherry. He was surrounded by reporters from all kinds of media organisations, celebrities of every kind joined him on his merry-go-round. Many women stars were happy to cluster around him because they wanted to appear in adverts, or get him to invest money in something or other, or support their careers. If he was happy with the female star who kissed him or let him grope her, who knew, but maybe he'd be pleased enough to give her a gold plaque weighing a pound or two. As more and more women came clustering around, he began to take aphrodisiacs. Every time Guo Cunyong went to Hong Kong he'd bring back a case full, and yet again he'd have the feeling that there was nothing he couldn't do.

Guojiadian commissioned one load of gold plaques after another, but there were never enough. Originally, the idea had been that these gold plaques would be sent out and he wouldn't have to think about them ever again, but now he was often having to go and ponder on them, trying to work out who should be given one and who could safely be ignored. Money danced around him and he danced around money; women stars chased after him and he chased after them. The whole thing was spinning, spiralling further out of control, and who in such circumstances could guarantee that they would not be overtaken by some kind of *folie de grandeur*?

Guo Cunxian hadn't been overtaken by *folie de grandeur* in just one respect: he now spoke big, thought big, threw his weight around in a big way and felt it incumbent upon himself to have developed a terrible temper. Recently the Party secretary in Dahua City, a man named Gao Jingqi, had come to treat Guojiadian like his own bank, from which he'd make withdrawals a couple of times a year. Guo Cunxian wasn't about to encourage this kind of behaviour. He might treat it as an operational cost, but sometimes he'd just hide and refuse to see the man, while on other occasions, when he was quite visible sitting inside his house, he'd tell his subordinates to say that he was off on a business trip. Obviously he wasn't going to give a gold plaque to Gao Jingqi. He told everyone quite clearly that he didn't have the slightest respect for this man from Dahua. He was also quite sure that Gao Jingqi despised Guojiadian – he'd been trying to cause trouble for them years back when he'd sent in the investigation team. Then the secretary of the provincial Party Committee had come, so it looked bad that he himself never set foot in Guojiadian... Guo Cunxian was quite sure that right now the Party in Dahua City and Gao Jingqi himself needed Guojiadian, but Guojiadian didn't need them. If you're coming here to see me and you're planning to bathe a bit in my reflected glory, then you'd better not think you can look down your nose at me.

He'd never liked it when other people threw their weight about. He now set a new rule: if any cadre of provincial rank or lower came, he wasn't going to see any of them, which happily included all the senior people in Dahua City. There were a few exceptions: on a couple of occasions he'd sent someone to take a letter to Qian Xishou, saying that, if he was willing to admit that he'd made a mistake in coming to Guojiadian, then he'd get one of the gold plaques. Guo Cunxian would also have been happy to see Zhang Caiqian or Feng Hou come to Guojiadian, and he invited them over and over again, and he'd set aside a gold plaque for each of them. Guo Cunxian might be odious in many ways, but he wasn't the kind of person to forget a benefactor. But neither Zhang Caiqian, now mayor of Dahua City, nor Feng Hou, now deputy secretary of the Party Committee there, ever found time to come.

Feng Hou had done particularly well by Guojiadian, but he'd now been called to the city, so of course he must be very busy. However, instead of resting on his laurels or making a fuss over his own seniority, he yet again decided to turn against the tide. At a time when everyone else was joining in the paeans for Guojiadian and Guo Cunxian himself, he wrote a letter to try to cut them down to size. Feng Hou's letter was more than a little acidic. He began by saying that every few days he got to see Guo Cunxian on the television, so it seemed that he had better coverage than any film star. Some nights it seemed like he was on every channel and appeared in front of the cameras more than any national leader, not to mention the overwhelming number of documentaries about him. We are living in a media age, he said, and the media can be holding you up as an example right up to the firing squad: it is best to keep a clear head. He also recommended a couple of articles and suggested that Guo Cunxian might make time to read them.

What were these articles about? The first was entitled '*A Croesus of Antiquity*' and it talked about the incredibly wealthy Shi Chong who lived during the Jin dynasty. His life was one of unimaginable luxury, whereby he dined daily on suckling pig, raised on human milk. His lavatory came equipped with perfumed bags of silk brocade, gharuwood essence and new suits of clothes, not to mention a dozen or more beautiful maidservants in attendance. Anyone who came out of the lavatory was required to change into a new suit of clothing since what they'd worn before might smell foul. He lived to hold regular banquets in his home and invite guests, with yet more beautiful women in attendance, and if one of the guests refused to drink themselves into unconsciousness, then he'd have the beautiful women dragged out and killed. On occasion he might kill quite a few women during a single banquet. Someone like that who enjoys showing off their wealth often gets into competition with other rich men: one person uses malt sugar to clean their pots, so he uses wax candles instead of firewood; another person has a coral tree a couple of metres high, so he has six or seven that are even bigger... just one damn thing after the other until someone forged an imperial edict and went and cut his head off.

Guo Cunxian read the letter while complaining to his subordinates: is he trying to have a go at me? All of these classical citations – he's using the past to criticise the present and bullying us uneducated peasants! When it comes right down to it, he's just jealous. I don't mind if other people are jealous, but he used to be my superior and helped me out a lot, and now he's been promoted to deputy secretary of the Party Committee. How can you be jealous of a peasant you used to praise so much?

The other article that Feng Hou recommended was worse. It was entitled '*A

Conspiracy by Hyenas'. The article said that in the African savannah there lives a kind of hyena that spends all of its time following in the wake of the wild pigs, keeping its eyes fixed on the pigs' hindquarters. The moment a pig has finished excreting, they rush up and lick its anus. The wild pig appreciates this licking and gradually lets down its guard. It will lie down to enjoy this wonderful treatment, and that means it's left behind as the other pigs move on. When that happens, the hyenas suddenly turn on the isolated pig and bite through its anus, pulling out its entrails. It doesn't matter how much the wild pig screams or how angry it gets, the hyenas surround it, pulling out its entrails like a long hempen rope, until the pig falls down dead.

What did that mean? Even an idiot can see that he thinks I'm like the wild pig and the higher-ups and media are the hyenas licking my arsehole! What he says about the media is fair enough, but it's pretty nasty to compare the higher-ups and senior cadres that have supported me to arse-licking hyenas! He's jealous, but why doesn't he come out to Guojiadian? If he came, we'd stuff his car full – he'd get much more than we've given any other senior cadre. He won't come when we invite him, and then he says these horrible things in a backhanded kind of way. What sort of person does that?

Guo Cunxian had spun round his merry-go-round so many times that he no longer had any way to tell a good person from a bad one, or good advice from bad. When someone gets into that kind of state, disaster cannot be far removed...

21

JANGKULEMBI

Jangkulembi is a kind of illness.

The name of this disease, which is derived from the Manchu language, is kind of interesting. It literally means 'to bump into a visitor'. What kind of visitor? An uninvited guest.

This word appears over and over in *The Story of the Stone*: for example in chapter twenty-five Mother Ma says: "If any believer, male or female, will make offerings to the Bodhisattva in a proper spirit of devoutness, he will grant their children and grandchildren his holy peace and protect them from possession by devils, and from the powers of darkness" – that is *jangkulembi*. And when Xue Pan has had too much to drink, he often says: "I had too much to drink last night, and when I was coming back late, I bumped into a visitor on the way" – again, *jangkulembi*.

A Chinese language dictionary published in Taiwan explains: "*Jangkulembi* refers to meeting a ghost or demon. In olden days people believed that any sudden disease could be caused by ghosts or demons."

It is quite possible that this disease is what people nowadays call 'conversion disorder', or 'hysteria'. It refers to an unstable emotional state in which people experience paralysis, they laugh or cry uncontrollably, they talk nonsense, they may experience irrational anger or go into fits.

After Dahua district had been designated as a city, which was entirely thanks to the Dahua Steel Company, the place expanded, and they built a new railway station and a square in the middle of town, as well as widening the roads. But if something really happened, the inhabitants of Dahua could still pull together as one, or they might turn and tear each other apart. On the day in question, the area in front of the train station had turned into an exhibition area for cars. Every model was to be found there, and every colour, all lined up in rows, filling up all available space and blocking the access roads. The lights were flashing, blinking: those drivers queuing up inside wanted to get out, while those waiting outside wanted to get in, and they all leaned on their horns and blared.

Strange to say, all of these expensive cars didn't improve the appearance of the square at all; instead, they made it look like a refugee camp. People were milling around like ants from an ant-heap: gossiping together, bellowing loudly, shouting confusedly, turning around, holding suitcases, carrying bags, pushing and pulling at each other as they threaded their way between the cars.

Those who liked interfering in other people's business were there muttering, trying to work out what was going on. Is there a festival today? Has there been an earthquake, or a fight?

Ha! What do you know about it? The deputies to the National People's Congress in Beijing have returned!

There was more flag waving, blowing of whistles, waving of hands and shouting, as gongs were struck, drums were banged and firecrackers exploded…

The VIP waiting-room in the train station was packed with people, and there were a number of deputies who found that they had to stay out on the platform. Various important figures in the city government were out there too. The most important of them were also deputies themselves, such as Gao Jingqi, the secretary of the Party Committee, and Zhang Caiqian, the CEO of Dahua Steel and mayor of Dahua. The two of them were in a particular hurry to get to the state guesthouse because an international economic forum was about to begin there, and they would be attending the opening ceremony.

This had all been arranged ages earlier; officials are used to it, and this kind of rhythm was just what they needed. The higher-ups seem to have practised rushing from one place to the next, giving the impression that they were massively busy and going from meeting to meeting as if they were actually achieving something. The leadership is there to participate in events, and events are waiting for the leadership to turn up and join in. Otherwise, why should each event be followed hot on the heels by another?

The cars that had come to the station to collect the secretary and the mayor were naturally the biggest and the best – the others just had to squash in where they could, and today many of them found themselves miles away, not even able to get into the square, let alone park near the VIP exit. If the secretary and the mayor had to push themselves out of the regular exit with everyone else who came off the train, what would that look like? I'm afraid that if you want your leaders to be decent, you are going to have to wait patiently.

Luckily the higher-ups present on this occasion had all received excellent training in self-control; at the very least they were able to maintain their usual manner and appearance. They looked just the same as normal and silently contemplated the roiling crowds on the platform with their usual calm. Zhang Caiqian seemed particularly relaxed, though his eyes appeared to flash a slightly mocking smile: who could he be laughing at?

The Party officials who doubled as deputies that were standing around near him had completely lost the refinement and dignity they'd shown at the Congress in

Beijing. Now they were complaining, and some of them were even cursing: what the hell is going on today!

Can't you see that all of the flags outside the station are from Guojiadian? Who other than Guo Cunxian could pull off a stunt like this?

These people were not idle layabouts but had just come back from participating in the government of the country in Beijing – they weren't used to feeling that they were on the losing side. Who was prepared to put up with such a humiliation? The chief of police, a man named Wu Qingyuan, was talking into a mobile phone in one hand as he pushed his way to where Gao Jingqi was standing. He did his best to repress his irritation and unease. A man in his position is used to behaving with great arrogance – how could he cope with such an open indignity? He was trying (and failing) to suppress the rage that he felt, and his chalk-white face showed an expression of cold impatience. He knew that, by giving the senior cadres in the city a big stick with which to beat Guo Cunxian, he'd also get himself off the hook.

"A couple of hundred people and a huge cavalcade of cars have come from Guojiadian to collect Guo Cunxian on his return from the Congress," he said. "They're the ones waving flags and letting off firecrackers. They've occupied the platform and all the best parking places outside in the square, and there are massive traffic jams everywhere. Even police cars can't get through. I'm afraid that you're going to have to wait until he's gone to be able to leave yourselves."

Gao Jingqi kept silent like before. The other deputies simply couldn't stand it any more, and they started to make their complaints to Wu Qingyuan: "The traffic management systems in this city are clearly quite useless. I'm sure I don't know what the traffic police are doing to earn their salaries. You've allowed these cars from Guojiadian to bring the entire city to a standstill.

"Besides which the economic forum is supposed to begin in about fifteen minutes. In addition to various well-known economists and entrepreneurs from our country, there are going to be a couple of dozen foreign scholars and business leaders in attendance, including two winners of the Nobel Prize for Economics. We've invited these people to come, so how can the secretary and mayor possibly be late? If they aren't present for the opening ceremony there's going to be real trouble, I can tell you. It's not going to matter what we say, because they aren't exactly going to have a good impression of Dahua, are they? Is it likely they're going to think that Dahua offers the best possible environment for them to invest?"

Wu Qingyuan always seemed coldly competent. Now his cheekbones showed a deep purple hue, and his jaw was clenched so that the muscles stood out. He spoke even more icily: "What do you want me to do? Guo Cunxian's over there, how about arranging for one of his cars to take the secretary…"

Gao Jingqi stopped him with a wave of his hand. The gaze that had been playing over the middle distance was now collected on his face, and the ambiguous expression in the eyes of the secretary made him feel even more nervous – this was much worse than any public criticism. He'd allowed the Party secretary and the mayor to be openly humiliated in their own city, he'd allowed a peasant upstart to occupy the roads and make a show – what kind of chief of police was he?

Guo Cunxian himself was thrilled by all of this. The moment he got down from the train he was surrounded by people, and when he looked up he saw in the middle of the platform a massive banner bearing the message: 'A Warm Welcome to Our Beloved Leader Comrade Guo Cunxian, Deputy to the National People's Congress, On his Victorious Return from the Meeting in Beijing!'

Oh my God! Anyone reading that banner ended up gulping. All you could say was that at least they'd managed to refrain from adding the word 'Most' in front of the 'Beloved Leader'. Even the VIP waiting room was packed with people from Guojiadian, and they were shouting, barging past and escorting Guo Cunxian as if nobody else were present. Thus they were able to open up a passage for him through the crowds.

With the situation being what it was, you just had to go along with it. Guo Cunxian rubbed his eyes and put a brazen face on it, as the hordes in front and behind swept him in the direction of his own car. He didn't even look in the direction of the senior cadres from the city. He was perfectly well aware that the city cadres were going to be furious that Guojiadian had put on such a big show of welcoming him back – the deputies who'd been sitting with him yesterday at the meeting would now be livid, if not green with jealousy. Even though he couldn't hear what they were saying to each other, he could perfectly well guess: they'll be cursing me for showing off, and they'll be saying that I don't know who I am. The fact is, it doesn't matter what I do, they won't like it. Let them moan. What else can they do? You should know exactly who you are: that is the kind of person who can't even find the train station when they're standing in the square in front of it! You're supposed to be the top people in this city, and if you get all het up and cross over a few cars, that'll really cheer up everyone from Guojiadian! In fact, they've done really well today.

Suddenly, the cars parked in the square all sounded their horns in unison, making a racket and giving everyone in earshot a turn.

The cars of Guojiadian were showing their respect to Guo Cunxian!

Now the people in the square were milling about even more, pushing their way forwards, probably because they wanted to see what Guo Cunxian looked like. The cars behind were still hooting, as the welcome committee from Guojiadian lined up in two neat rows, clearing a path for Guo Cunxian through the square, holding back the crowds as his specially customised Mercedes Royal 600 from Germany rolled majestically away.

After that, the cavalcade of cars from Guojiadian started to move away as well, and the traffic in people and cars around the square began to ease up as the blockage cleared. Anyone who got angry easily could give themselves an ulcer over this – the people packed in front of the station had to cultivate their patience as the Guojiadian cars pulled slowly out of the square like a long, sinuous serpent. Those who wanted to come and join in the fun ran forward like a tidal wave to chase after the line of cars and see what happened next, and they got to see the fleet turn in a magnificent convoy towards the city centre…

In a flash, the square in front of the train station seemed to be completely empty, ringingly empty in fact, and listless.

How impressive was this cavalcade of cars from Guojiadian? Nearly every single one of the more than two hundred luxury cars owned by inhabitants of the village had come. Right up at the front as lead car was an American-made off-road jeep, with the brand name 'Desert Wolf'. Then came Guo Cunxian's own car, and after that were all kinds of other makes – Mercedes Benz, BMW, Lincoln, Buick, Lexus, Nissan. Then right at the back bringing up the rear was another off-road Desert Wolf jeep.

This was indeed something to make a fuss about; it was like a parade. However, in China, parades are very rich in meaning and can be an unexpectedly sensitive subject. Obviously, the inhabitants of Guojiadian were taking advantage of this opportunity to show off a bit. And why shouldn't they? What's wrong with that? They were giving everyone in Guojiadian a bit of face, and making it clear to everyone else that they could fight for what they wanted.

Cars had an almost totemic significance in Guojiadian. The villagers said that when they went to work in the morning and caught sight of Secretary Guo's Mercedes Benz 600 parked outside the main office building, their eyes would brighten and they'd feel happier. They said that the better the car Secretary Guo drove, the better Guojiadian was doing as a whole; the faster his car went, the faster Guojiadian developed. Some people said they felt more safe and secure every day they saw Secretary Guo's huge Mercedes, that they felt like they'd just ingested a tranquilizer. That of course was an inauspicious thing to say – it seemed that even some of the villagers were worried about what was going to happen to Guo Cunxian, that one of these days he just wasn't going to be there any more.

Guo Cunxian had come to be represented by his car. In the eyes of the peasantry, cars meant power, position and wealth. When a peasant gets wealthy, they compete with other people over who has the most expensive car. Some years earlier someone in Guojiadian had read in the papers about a village in the south called Huaxi, where they'd bought a job lot of fifty domestic Jetta cars, and the reporter made a big fuss about how they drove into the village like a red cloud. At the time they'd been deeply envious, but now they were singing to a different tune: shit, who the hell wants a Jetta? And what do you mean by 'red cloud'? We in Guojiadian all drive luxury imported cars: that shows you! If you can't afford it then don't buy it, but if you do buy, you should get the best. Naturally that attracted a huge amount of attention, and the residents of Guojiadian liked to attract attention, particularly when it made other people jealous. That was just tough – particularly if it was city people or senior officials!

Guo Cunxian liked cars, and he liked talking about cars to other people – he'd wasted a lot of time chatting about these cars with other people. There was one time when a reporter came out from Beijing following a senior official on a tour of inspection of Guojiadian, and he asked right out in front of this senior official: What did the peasants living in this village do with all of these luxury cars? Was it just about showing off? What did other people think?

Guo Cunxian was fond of fighting verbal battles, and he immediately came right back with an answer. He said that other people could think what they liked, in fact they could moan to their heart's content and I couldn't care less. If you ask me what I think about it, then I can tell you that these luxury cars have a great economic significance – they represent investment conditions here. We often have foreign clients come to Guojiadian to discuss contracts with us, and we have already established more than thirty joint venture companies. If we all go around riding on donkeys, with bags of dried tobacco swinging from our waists and caps made from white sheep's stomachs on our heads, are foreign investors going to do business with us?

The reporter didn't understand. Why couldn't you talk to a foreign investor if you were riding on a donkey, smoking dry tobacco and wearing a cap made from a sheep's stomach?

Guo Cunxian felt that such a question could only have been posed by a complete ignoramus – it really wasn't worth answering. He gave another example instead: there was a time when a senior cadre asked me what rank I held that I dared use such a fancy car? I shut him up pretty quick: we peasants don't have rank, so you can't compare your rank to mine. There was another time that an old cadre got really upset seeing all of these luxury cars here in Guojiadian. He complained to me, saying that he got where he is today because of the blood he'd shed and the battles he'd fought, and he only got to ride in an ordinary car. You've made a bit of money, Guo Cunxian, it's true, but how dare you have the cheek to go about in such a fancy car? I just laughed and shut him up too: you led poor people into battle against the rich, but I led poor people and made them into rich people: of course I deserve to ride about in a car like this!

The cavalcade from Guojiadian stretched over a kilometre as it set off, and the city folk stared in stupefaction. The pavements on either side of the road were packed with people. For all that cars were the peasants' totem, they were also things that could make city people envious.

The more people who came to line the road to watch, the more the residents of Guojiadian enjoyed themselves, and they decided to show off even more. The Desert Wolf at the front began to hit the horn, and the Desert Wolf at the back chimed in immediately, and then the cars in the middle also started to hoot: woo woo – wooooo. One would rise in pitch as another fell, one would take over when another stopped; the noise was tremendous, an absolutely ear-splitting racket.

God alone knows what had happened to the onlookers: they ran alongside shouting and calling out to each other. This made even more people rush out from various buildings, heading in waves for the main highway through the city.

Just at that moment, everyone seemed to be moving blindly: if someone moved forward, everyone moved forward; if someone stopped, everyone stopped. If people were running away from the crowd, then there were others who forced their way out to run too; if there was someone trying to see what was going on ahead, then others craned their necks too. No one had a clue what was going on, and it was only when they'd pushed their way to the side of the road that they realised it was a bunch of cars. What was so special about a bunch of cars? Cars passed every day on the main highway, so since when did these peasants' cars become a scenic attraction?

It wasn't just pedestrians participating in this spectacle; the cars on other roads also ended up being embroiled in the chaos. There was a truck packed with steel drums, which turned onto Caihong Road from the perfectly peaceful industrial zone: the driver saw the green light up ahead and moved into the intersection without slowing down. Just as he was bearing down on them, he realised that there was a line of cars across the road, and he hit the brake with a blaring of his horn. There was a crashing sound on board his truck as the lids of the drums containing sulphuric acid flew off with the force of the impact. The burning smell of the acid was now assaulting the crowd. All you could hear on both sides was the appalling sound of piercing screaming. People scattered in all directions in panic, pushing and shoving each other, stamping on those who had fallen, a solid mass of humanity.

It was absolute chaos. Dahua City was being brought to a standstill.

Since they hadn't been warned in advance, the police found it impossible to deal with the situation as it transpired. The traffic police stationed at each intersection had no idea what was going on or who might be participating in this convoy. It might have been someone senior in the central government, but then the cars were bigger than they would've used, and they were all foreign – might it not be some foreign head of state? The police walkie-talkies crackled into life; they didn't know whether they should be stopping this cavalcade or letting it through.

By the time they'd discovered where all these cars came from, it was too late to even think about bringing the situation under some kind of control. However the police were not inclined to let the matter go: they'd never felt so messed about with before. Some of them were so furious that they decided they simply didn't care what happened. They began to use their whistles and wave the cars to stop, so that they could give these nouveau riche, thick-as-mince peasants a right ticking-off.

However, in this cavalcade, there was a beginning, a middle and an end, all organised. It would be impossible to stop just one or two cars; if they wanted one to halt, then the entire convoy would have to stop. The moment the procession came to a standstill, it occupied the entire road, in which case anyone hoping to drive through the city was out of luck. Half the city was paralysed. The police weren't willing to just let them go without any interference; that would be allowing them to get away with this show of strength, which wasn't acceptable either.

Besides which the police in Dahua had never felt so humiliated, and they were furious.

Given that the parade was now blocking all the intersections on the main highway, red and green lights no longer had any meaning: when a red light showed you couldn't stop, and when a green light showed you couldn't advance. Each of the crossroads was blocked by a horde of people, and all the neighbouring roads were packed with cars that could neither go forward nor back. Their innocent drivers, now driven to distraction, were leaning on their horns. When they were informed that the cars causing the problem had come from the famous Guojiadian, the shouting and horn honking became even more ear-splitting. Was this a kind of response, or a kind of support, or was it anger and resistance?

It might look like a great city, but that was how useless it was: the sudden appearance of a parade of cars from the countryside could reduce it to chaos.

Guo Cunxian was half-lying across the car seat, his head resting on the soft cushions of the backrest. His eyes were fixed on the back of the driver's head, but in fact he wasn't looking at anything, he was concentrating on the various half-formed ideas that were passing through his mind. It was as though the chaos outside the windows was nothing to do with him. The excitement and pride of his fellow villagers had no power to move him. His excitement had already passed, leaving behind only exhaustion and loneliness.

The beautiful Lin Meitang was pressed up against him, clinging to him. The bright magenta suit that she wore seemed to warm him like a fire; the waves of strong perfume emanating from her stimulated him. He felt the sudden onrush of desire as if it were a physical pain. She was clutching Guo Cunxian's right hand in both of hers, and she was gently pinching and rubbing it. Her eyes, filled with gratification, never left his face for a moment. She murmured: "I'm sure you must be exhausted with the congress going on for so long. We all got to see you on the news!"

"Fuck. It was all over in a flash. Nobody except our own people in Guojiadian would have paid the blindest bit of attention," said Guo Cunxian's adopted son, Liu Fugen, who was sitting up front next to the driver. He couldn't open his mouth without swearing. "Those media reptiles are a bunch of fucking losers. All they know is to run after you arse-licking and demanding cash – not one of them could find their way out of a paper bag. I would've thought they understood that they shouldn't just record your speech, at the very least they should also give you a big write-up. Why can't they see that none of the other deputies can possibly match up to us from Guojiadian? If they cause us any more fucking problems, we'll just buy our own television station!"

Good, he's a good boy, in future he'll do great things! Guo Cunxian opened his eyes and looked at the flash in his adopted son's eyes – the light of someone who is planning to bend other people to his will. This was the first time since he'd got in the car that he smiled, and the woman by his side now smiled too.

Guo Cunxian's own son, Guo Chuanfu, took after his mother and liked to study. Having finished middle school in Kuanhe, he'd managed to get into a university in Beijing, and right now he was preparing to go to the US for graduate school. Guo Cunxian loved his son, and he was very proud of him, but he only got to see him a couple of times a year, so gradually his affection for his son transferred itself to his adopted son, Liu Fugen. Not only did he not complain about his coarseness and vulgarity, he actually thought that he had the right angle on life. His adopted son could always hit the nail on the head when it came to the things that really aggravated him. Guo Cunxian was perfectly well aware that plenty of villagers were privately furious with him for the way he spoiled his adopted son: a brat puffed up with a sense of his own importance who, when it came down to it, was a useless piece of shit.

Ever since he was little, Guo Cunxian had gone regularly to the theatre or listened to a storyteller perform, and there was a tale of a great landowner training up his son that he'd always particularly enjoyed. The great landowner had just the one son, and when he grew up he behaved like a complete brat: he got drunk and went off gambling and whoring. Gradually the great landowner got old, and he gave his son a load of money and allowed him to go to the bad in whatever way he liked. After a year, the son had spent every penny and came back home, and the old landowner asked him what he'd learned, and his son said that women were wonderful, every one of them different, and they were really amazing. The old landowner then gave his son even more money and told him to carry on his studies. Three years later his son came back and told him that all women were just alike, and they were all equally boring. The old landowner was delighted because he knew that his son had graduated, and he could hand over the family property to him. The reason why Shakyamuni was able to achieve Buddhahood was because he'd been a prince, enjoying every kind of wealth and honour. Once he'd become Buddha, then he was able to achieve true peace with respect to his six senses. The reason why Hongyi was able to become such a great

Buddhist master was because he'd been born into a wealthy family – he'd experienced life at that level. Why does an ordinary monk find it so difficult to achieve enlightenment even though he spends all day, every day reading the sutras? It's because he hasn't experienced anything of life. He may be reciting the sutras, but the moment he hears the sound of high-heeled shoes behind him, he can't keep his concentration. He just has to take a peek backwards.

Later on, a professor trying to flatter Guo Cunxian found a real historical example for his theory: Emperor Taizong of the Tang dynasty repeatedly thought about deposing his crown prince, Li Zhi, and Wei Zheng asked him why. Emperor Taizong said that, when he'd been the same age, he'd been a complete hooligan who'd committed every crime in the book. But look at Li Zhi now, so obedient and good. In future he won't be able to govern the empire, or achieve anything of merit, since he'd be the kind of person who'd be easy to topple from power. And later on it turned out just as he said, because Li Zhi was deposed by Wu Zetian.

With imperial sanction, Guo Cunxian thought that he knew where he was, and he allowed his adopted son, Liu Fugen, to get away with more and more.

When it came to this trip to Beijing, he'd had to put in a lot of effort to get himself selected as a deputy to the National People's Congress. However, as far as he was concerned, this was merely the first step on the ladder. In China, if you didn't become a deputy you could forget about becoming a figure of national prominence. Had not that old illiterate peasant from Shanxi, Chen Yonggui, leapfrogged everyone else to be appointed vice premier at the Fourth National People's Congress in 1975? Right, there was a precedent for you: it was natural that Guo Cunxian had the highest hopes of his own participation in the Congress. Although he knew he couldn't quite expect to follow in Chen Yonggui's footsteps any time soon, he thought it quite possible that he could make himself more famous than Chen Yonggui. In fact, now that he thought about it, he was already more famous and more important than Chen Yonggui had ever been...

He understood that the National People's Congress in Beijing is like a bottomless lake; one mistake can see you drowned. Nobody attending the Congress took him particularly seriously. That had been particularly notable in the case of the most senior government figures, many of whom had been to Guojiadian, or whom he'd talked to at a conference. Meeting him this time they carried on as if they'd never set eyes on him before. Ever since Guojiadian had become rich, hordes of people followed Guo Cunxian around wherever he went. The less they knew about him the more curious they were, and they'd come and look at him as if they were making a pilgrimage. He simply wasn't used to people ignoring him.

He didn't want people in Guojiadian to know that he'd gone to the Congress only to be ignored. That was a pain he was happy to keep to himself. But pain had always been his weak point, and in this case he had to keep this secret from everyone in Guojiadian, including the two people in this car, who were the people that he loved and trusted most. Therefore he had no choice but to smooth out the frowning expression on his face, but he remained absent-minded and dazed, as if he'd been enveloped in a cloud so thick that he could no longer breathe.

Lin Meitang turned her eyes away, a gesture that she knew to be deeply seductive. Straightening her body slightly, she took a delicate silver lighter and a packet of

Chunghwa cigarettes from her pocket. She stuck one in her own mouth and lit it, taking a deep puff. Then she took it from between her red lips and placed it in Guo Cunxian's mouth.

The fingers of his left hand cupped round the cigarette as he sucked in the nicotine. Then he fixed his gaze on the beautiful woman by his side like a bird of prey. "What was it that Guo Cunyong was going on about just now at the train station?" he asked slowly. "It was so loud I could barely hear a word. Did something happen to his car?"

Liu Fugen answered from his seat up in front: "His Cadillac was vandalised last night in the car park at the State Guesthouse."

"Really?" Guo Cunxian suddenly pulled himself upright, as if he were on the attack. "Why was his car parked at the State Guesthouse?"

Lin Meitang said lightly: "Our office moved from the Overseas Chinese Building to the State Guesthouse."

Guo Cunxian lay back down again. His eyes had the look of someone who's seen everything. He began to run through his list of questions: "Don't they have security guards at the State Guesthouse? Do we know who did it? Has Guo Cunyong done something to annoy anyone, or is this aimed at Guojiadian? How badly was the car damaged?"

All that Liu Fugen knew was that his brand-new Cadillac had to be scrapped. Guo Cunyong had reported the case to the police, but he didn't know the answer to the other questions. This morning, the main thing for the inhabitants of Guojiadian was to go and welcome back Guo Cunxian. Who had time to think about anything else? Guo Cunxian spat a single command out from between his clenched teeth: do it now!

He told his adopted son to get in touch with Guo Cunyong since he wanted him to come back to the village and report on the vandalism of his car this afternoon. Phone the driver of the Desert Wolf up ahead and tell him to take the cavalcade round past the State Guesthouse. Liu Fugen laughed. He took out his mobile phone and dialled a number.

"I'm guessing that the idiots at the State Guesthouse won't know the first thing about what happened," he said gloatingly. "The last few years the police in this city have been causing endless trouble for us in Guojiadian – they often stop our cars and fine us. It so happens that there's an international economic forum being held at the State Guesthouse, and the opening ceremony is being held this afternoon. There'll be lots of important attendees from at home and abroad. Let's show them the kind of cars that we have at Guojiadian!"

Guo Cunxian suddenly interrupted his adopted son: "Have we been invited to this forum?"

Liu Fugen was listening to the squawking at the other end of the phone, so he just waved a negative. Guo Cunxian did his best to conceal his disappointment. If they were having an economic forum in this city and they didn't invite Guojiadian to participate – and they were right next door – what did that look like? Lin Meitang seemed to have read his thoughts.

"Maybe they knew you were in Beijing for the Congress," she said comfortingly. "I daresay the invitation will arrive any day now!"

Guo Cunxian's mouth curved in an expression of disdain. He gripped Lin Meitang's hand and she obediently pressed her head against his body.

It was nearly noon by the time that the parade of cars reached Guojiadian. Far in the distance, Guo Cunxian caught sight of the Lucky Trees, their branches already green and lush, spreading out across the sky. There were four enormous red balloons hanging in the air above the trees, and suspended below the balloons were huge, colourful banners, which danced in the wind, curved like bright rainbows.

One brightly-coloured banner stated: 'A Warm Welcome to Secretary Guo On his Victorious Return from Attending the National People's Congress in Beijing!'

To one side, there was another brightly-coloured banner: 'Warmest Congratulations to our CEO, Guo Cunxian, on his Successful Participation in Government and National Affairs in Beijing!'

These were the three most important titles that Guo Cunxian held. 'Secretary' referred to his position in the party; 'chairman of the Guojiadian Group' gave his position in the administration of the company; and 'deputy of the National People's Congress' gave his social rank – that is why they'd specially mentioned participating in government and national affairs.

The big archway at the entrance to the village had been freshly painted and was looking most impressive. Once they passed the archway, the whole village was looking really colourful and bright, and in every eye-catching location, huge posters had been affixed bearing the words 'Congratulations on the Successful Completion of the National People's Congress' or 'Welcome, Secretary Guo, on your Return'. This might have given people the impression that Guojiadian was somehow crucial for the proper convening of the National People's Congress; or that Guojiadian had hosted this event: that the success of the Congress had become Guo Cunxian's personal success, and that meant it had been a success for Guojiadian as a whole.

The villagers had become used to this kind of exaggeration, and in turn people found it amusing that they accepted it without query.

Normally, the convoy ought to proceed to the compound in which the main office building was located and stop; the most important people in the village would already have gathered there. They'd want to hear what Guo Cunxian had to say, and he could talk about whatever he liked. Perhaps he might say something about what had happened at the Congress in Beijing, or he might tell them what he'd heard about or seen during his trip, or talk about his own ideas for the future... The whole village knew that Guo Cunxian made a good speech and was never at a loss for the right word. It was a kind of ritual. Since the villagers hadn't seen him for a couple of weeks, they were quite sure that he'd have a lot to say.

This time, however, his subordinates were wrong. Most unusually, Guo Cunxian didn't feel up to going into the village and talking to people, but he was keen to conceal the fact that he was in an unusually depressed mood. Guojiadian needed to maintain its high profile through thick and thin – for him to be obviously depressed would be abnormal, and that would mean something had gone wrong. Therefore the moment he got to the village he told Liu Fugen to pass on the message that it was too late today, the secretary felt that everyone had exhausted themselves by coming to the city to pick him up from the station, so why didn't they go home to eat; they could talk on some other occasion. After that, he instructed his driver to take him straight to his new house in the Talent Park executive residential development.

This area was called 'Guojiadian's Zhongnanhai' by the villagers. There was a magnificent entrance gate, ornamented with lion's heads and guarded day and night by a policeman. This wasn't the kind of security guard that you would see around a gated community in the city, but real armed policemen: they were 'village police'. The main gate at Talent Park was made from stainless steel bars thicker than a fist. Once closed, not even a tank would be able to get through. When all of this was being planned, Guo Cunxian set the standard: in architectural style and decoration, he wanted them to model the building on the Great Hall of the People in Beijing; when it came to quality, he wanted better than any other building in China. Every brick, every tile, every wall, every door, every beam and every column had to be able to withstand an earthquake, a bomb and nuclear attack!

Quite apart from this, the whole area was enclosed by a wall four metres high, and inside that wall were a couple of dozen Western-style villas, two or three storeys tall. The very best location within this community – that is in the place in the main camp where the military strategists of olden times would have put the general's tent – was occupied by a large four-storey red house that dominated the surrounding buildings. The other houses seemed to be playing a supporting role, like the stars surrounding the moon. Of course, this red house was Guo Cunxian's new residence. However, it looked cold and deserted, as if Zhu Xuezhen still hadn't moved in yet to look after it…

While they were talking, the big Mercedes pulled up in front of the red house. Guo Cunxian was lying across the seat and didn't move, since he was waiting for either his driver or the bodyguard to open the door for him. Just as the driver was about to get out, his arm was tugged by Liu Fugen. He was holding his mobile phone and looking a little stunned, murmuring with a dry mouth: "My adoptive mother has got sick again."

Guo Cunxian's heart was pounding. He frowned: "Where is she?"

"In the old house."

He was feeling even more impatient now: "Why hasn't she moved yet?"

Liu Fugen had no idea what had happened, so he could only stammer: "Well, yes, she'd agreed to move this morning…"

Moving house is actually about a person moving. When it comes down to it, a new house isn't a home until your wife has moved in. A home is all about the people who live there, and for a man, the most important aspect is his wife. Once she's moved in, the house becomes a home, it has life to it.

Every item of furniture and all the appliances in this red house were brand new and top of the range. They weren't keeping anything from their old house.

The problem was that Zhu Xuezhen didn't want to move in. She wouldn't tell others why not, but when the house was being built she mentioned something about it to her husband. Guo Cunxian's response had been to shout at her – she always said such unpleasant things. This time she'd said that this part of Guojiadian was haunted, and she kept seeing the house in her nightmares. Surrounded by a high wall, with the only entrance being this terrifying steel gate, guarded day and night by police – she thought it was like a prison. How could anyone possibly live there?

For so many years she'd been tortured by *jangkulembi*, and Guo Cunxian was the only person who knew the true reason for her ill-health. This was why he tried to be considerate toward her, though he never took what she said seriously. Everything was going well for him, so how could he be touched by misfortune? Before he'd gone to Beijing for the Congress, he'd given strict orders that Xuezhen had to move while he was away, and he didn't care whether she wanted to or not. Here he was back again and she still hadn't moved. The only person in the whole village who would dare disobey an order like that was his wife.

There was nothing else for it: he had to tell the chauffeur to turn round and drive to the old house.

When he was still quite a distance away, he could see a number of his more interfering neighbours running in the direction of his old house. You could hear shouting and screaming from both men and women inside, not to mention the sound of things breaking…

Without waiting for the car to come to a proper stop, Liu Fugen jumped out and started running to the house. Lin Meitang glanced at Guo Cunxian's face and then she quickly got out of the car and started running herself. Guo Cunxian was the only one to retain a praiseworthy self-control, in spite of the blood that was pounding in his chest. He remained seated in the car and waited until the chauffeur opened the door for him. Then he walked into his own home with a serious expression on his face, each step across the brick floor resounding with his passage.

A crowd had gathered in the courtyard of his old house, and the whole place was in chaos. Firewood had been kicked about and scattered, and there was a lot of shouting and screaming going on. Everyone knew that someone suffering from *jangkulembi* becomes enormously strong. There were four or five men who'd managed to surround Zhu Xuezhen. One had a grip round her waist, while others were holding onto her arms and legs, and they were trying to lift her into the house.

Zhu Xuezhen seemed to be having some kind of a fit. She had turned into quite a different person, or perhaps a different kind of spirit. She looked really strange, with a hard and cruel glint in her eyes: angry and dangerous. She was screaming and thrashing about, and then with a sudden burst of effort, she was able to throw off the men who had hold of her. Some of them stumbled and fell to the ground, others lost their grip on her, and the remainder were forced into retreat. She now began to shout in an icy but curiously muffled tone of voice, and what she said was quite different from her normal conversation: "Who knows why your mother gave birth to you. Who can know the hour of his own death? In this world, people meet purely by chance, and sooner or later you will have to part. Nobody can stay on top forever, since we are all just repeating the pattern of others. Only the sick are incurable, and you should be grateful for every day that you survive…"

Lin Meitang walked right up to her, speaking in her friendliest voice. In moments like this she always hoped to demonstrate that she was closer to Zhu Xuezhen than anyone else. She didn't really understand what Zhu Xuezhen was trying to say, but she thought there might be something sensible there, and she would have liked her to carry on. At the very least, if she was talking, it was better than having her hit out or in a screaming fit. Just at that moment, everyone advanced, hoping to get Zhu Xuezhen under control again, but she flailed her arms around and forced Lin Meitang and the others back.

Some people busied themselves turning over the woodpile and checking the drains, while others were going through the house poking at the dark corners and heaps of possessions. They believed that the reason Zhu Xuezhen was suffering like this was because the 'Great Immortal Huang' was lurking somewhere, cursing her like the demon he was – otherwise how could she have become so strong, how could she speak or look like she did? The Great Immortal Huang had the weasel as his avatar, so if they could find the weasel and make it go away – or kill it – then Zhu Xuezhen would recover. They turned the whole house upside down, but they didn't find the weasel that was causing all the trouble.

The inhabitants of the village were always shown at their best in situations like this. Some were there to help in a true spirit of sympathy, while others were purely out for sensation, but their motives didn't matter, since once they got in the door they all did their very best. Unfortunately the more people there were, the more Zhu Xuezhen fought...

All of a sudden they froze in the middle of whatever they were doing, because they'd spotted Guo Cunxian standing in the entrance. His expression was as ugly as could be, and the flash of his eyes was arctic – it seemed as though he could see exactly what every single person present was thinking. If you are scared of someone, you are scared of his eyes, and there wasn't a single person in Guojiadian who dared look straight at Guo Cunxian.

All the time he'd been away, he'd been dreaming of stretching out in his comfortable bed at home, eating a bowl of his wife's yam porridge or hot noodle soup with ginger strips, and then snuggling up for a long snooze. But right now, on entering his house, the whole place seemed to have been thrown into chaos – this house was no home, and it was packed with people who didn't belong here. He was furious, even murderous in his rage. His house should be a private place, and it didn't matter what went on there, it should be kept secret. Now he felt as though he'd been the victim of a robbery, or a search-warrant. Anybody could have come through the door whether they were trying to be helpful or just wanting to enjoy the sight of him getting into trouble. He ought to be the most powerful and important person in the village, but now he'd been shown up as a loser, a weakling.

He was resentful, of course, if someone else made fun of him, but sympathy seemed to him an intolerable humiliation. He didn't say a single word, but stood in silence by the door watching them struggle with a most horrifying expression in his eyes. He had to conceal the anguish and fury he was experiencing. He couldn't scream and shout and curse as Zhu Xuezhen was doing, without a care in the world...

The moment the men and women present saw that Guo Cunxian had come home, they immediately calmed down. They stood back to let him pass, and everyone looked most respectful: "The secretary's back...", "Cunxian's come home..."

He didn't answer. He wasn't paying attention.

Some people, entirely of their own accord, started to tidy up the courtyard...

People are most scared of other people, but they also respect other people the most. Although the Great Immortal Huang was supposed to have just tormented Zhu

Xuezhen until she appeared barely human, people didn't show much politeness towards the demon. Guo Cunxian didn't pay any attention towards the complimentary, considerate, questioning, curious or mocking looks that came his way but walked straight up to his wife and grabbed her hard around the shoulders. He had been a carpenter employed to cut the thick planks used in coffins, so his hands were extremely strong. His anger seemed to flow into his hands as well, and you could hear Zhu Xuezhen's screams became quieter, until they gradually died away into moaning. The demon that had possessed her was now losing its grip, and she became more and more feeble, until she seemed barely conscious and unable to stay on her feet.

Guo Cunxian now slowly let go of her, and Liu Fugen and Lin Meitang lifted her onto the *kang*.

The gentle and delicate Lin Meitang now climbed onto the *kang* herself. She arranged a pillow under Zhu Xuezhen's head and made sure she was comfortable. Just now she'd been quite rigid, all her muscles convulsed, so every touch must have been painful. Lin Meitang had been hit and punched on the head and body, so her hair was a bird's nest and several purple bruises marked her face. Now Zhu Xuezhen's body was completely floppy and could be arranged at will. Her face was deathly white and bloodless, but there were beads of sweat on her forehead. Her eyes were closed, and she was breathing deeply. She was worn out from her recent exertions. Lin Meitang grabbed a quilt from one corner of the *kang* and used it to cover Zhu Xuezhen. It all looked so natural and friendly, so thoughtful, as if she really cared about her and wanted to look after her. Everyone was watching her, and she was performing for this audience – for how could it possibly be that she was indeed as friendly towards Zhu Xuezhen as she appeared to be?

Everyone in the entire village knew that it was for Guo Cunxian's sake that she'd never married, even though she was now nearly forty years of age. She ought to hate Zhu Xuezhen, but she had the cheek to come and join in, to help out, to take the burden onto her own shoulders. It was impossible for anyone – even Zhu Xuezhen's own sisters-in-law or Guo Cunzhi's wife – to compete with her. They were reduced to standing around the *kang*. Did this occur because Lin Meitang made it happen that way, or because Guo Cunxian was so powerful that he could force each and every one of them to do his bidding?

Finally Lin Meitang decided there was nothing more that she could do up on the *kang*, and she prepared to get down. The moment she raised her head, a kind of flash went through the eyes of everyone in the room, and her heart gave a sudden thump. Those watching were feeling increasingly awkward; they were trying not to look at each other, and some of them were beginning to make their excuses and edge towards the door. There was no need to have quite so many people just standing around, and the crowds now started to disperse, heading away from the Guo house. A few people on their way out did a bit of tidying up in the courtyard, naturally in order to curry favour. Being able to help out or feel a bit of sympathy for someone like Guo Cunxian, who normally struck awe into his associates, was a great pleasure for the villagers.

Once they'd started to go, the room was soon empty of people, as if the tide had ebbed away. Once sure that there weren't any outsiders present, Lin Meitang asked Huang Suzhen: "Xuezhen was fine this morning – how come she got sick after we left?" This question had been very carefully phrased to make sure that she herself was in the clear: Zhu Xuezhen's turn had nothing to do with her this time.

Huang Suzhen glanced at Guo Cunxian. He was her husband's cousin, but he'd always been particularly close to Cunzhi, so really he was more like a brother. In spite of this she'd always been afraid of him. He hadn't said a word since coming into the room and sitting down on the *kang*. When he heard Lin Meitang questioning Huang Suzhen, he raised his eyes and looked at her. His gaze was icy and dark, and his jaws were tightly clenched. Huang Suzhen was now treading even more carefully. She knew that any question posed by Lin Meitang would be one that Guo Cunxian also wanted to know the answer to, so she began with a sigh. This sigh was like the raising of a stage curtain, and a sign that the play was about to begin.

"This morning she was a bit cross, and she asked me to come over and talk to her. Then it was nearly noon and she reckoned you'd soon be back, so she went out into the courtyard to get some firewood so she could cook. A little bit later I heard her screaming outside. It was quite inhuman and scary, the sound she was making. I rushed out, and she'd already gone kind of blue in the face, and sweat was just pouring off her. She was staring at the bottom of the pile of firewood, and there she was walking slowly backwards, her mouth working. I asked her what had happened. She said that, just when she stretched out her hand to pick up a piece of firewood, she suddenly saw a kind of yellow globular thing, with its head like a corncob, a sharp and pointy chin, and a long and stiff beard. It moved majestically from side to side. Its two eyes were like crystals, and they kept a fixed stare focused on her, as if she'd done something wrong. It was covered in yellow fur, shining like it had been rubbed down with oil, and it had a big old tail streaming out behind it. She was backing out so that she wouldn't be disturbing the Great Immortal Huang any more, and then she went down on her knees and started kowtowing and muttering, saying that the Great Immortal shouldn't blame her for this, I didn't know that the Great Immortal was here, please protect us, please protect my husband, Cunxian..."

Guo Cunxian was no longer listening. With an icy voice he broke into her disquisition: "Who was it that made my wife so angry?"

Huang Suzhen stiffened. Her lips were slightly parted as she stared at Guo Cunxian. The expression in his eyes was explosive, and the situation was clearly becoming dangerous. After a moment's silence she found the right words: "I was afraid you were going to be furious too, so we'd agreed not to say a word to you about it. The fact is that it's nothing too serious. When you were away from home, your wife invited Xiaohui to stay with her. This afternoon the village was completely dead, and Lan Tian – Lan Shouyi's second son – somehow or other managed to inveigle Xiaohui into the nightclub and seems to have sexually assaulted her there. Xiaohui was horrified and ran back home in tears. You know how much your wife loves her niece, but of course making a fuss about it would damage Xiaohui's reputation, so she was feeling more and more upset and miserable, and then all of a sudden she couldn't stand it any more..."

"What a bastard!" Liu Fugen raged. "I'm going to kill him!" He was cursing as he went out the door.

Guo Cunxian's face was thunderous: "Where is Xiaohui now?"

"Once your wife started to get sick, I sent her to my house."

"Did she get raped?"

Huang Suzhen shook her head: "No, she's fine. These things happen when young people get together..."

"Is Cunzhi OK?"

"Oh yes, absolutely. He often asks after you."

22

THE APPEARANCE OF MONEY

The shape of the copper coin reflects the alpha and the omega, the square and the round. People hold it as dear as their closest family members, and they give it the title of Lord Square-Hole. It is respected though it is without virtue; it is held dear though it has no power. It can make its possessor noble and even cause them to enter the palace gates. In a situation of danger it can bring you peace; for those about to die, it can give life; for the noble it can lead to poverty and disgrace; though you live, it can cause your demise. For this reason, when you fight, without money you shall not win; when hidden in obscurity, without money you cannot rise to fame; when you have enemies abroad, without money you shall not be rid of them. The officials in the capital, the provincial nobility, my family and friends, they are nothing without it! Money holds me by the hand and protects me from the beginning of my life until the very end... People today are nothing without money.

A DISCOURSE ON THE GOD OF WEALTH BY LU BAO OF THE
WESTERN JIN DYNASTY (265-316)

Just after midday, six large buses turned off Route 7384 heading for Guojiadian. On board were sitting delegates to the National People's Congress from every corner of the country. That morning they'd been all over Dahua City, and now having eaten lunch they were heading out for a tour of Guojiadian, so clearly they were not afraid of a packed schedule.

Far off in the distance, they could see the Lucky Trees spreading their branches across the sky – those trees were now famous and the symbol of Guojiadian itself. From a distance they looked like one tree, but once you got closer and could see more clearly it was obviously two: one was a pear and the other an ancient elm. Over the course of many years they had intertwined, so that it was difficult to see which was which. It was only by inspecting the bark that you could see that the southern one was the pear and the northern one the elm. Even their crowns had grown together, but to the north there was more elm than pear, and to the south there was more pear than elm. In the middle they were equally matched, crisscrossing, woven together in a dense mass, to the point where it was impossible to distinguish which branch came from which tree.

Anyone who came to Guojiadian had to pass by the Lucky Trees – it was impossible to miss them. Gradually they had become the guardian deities of the village: this was where you had to park your car and get out and walk. Every day, hordes of people parked their cars in the space in front of the Lucky Trees, and the delegates to the National People's Congress were no exception. They were only going to be there for half the day, but according to the rules laid down in Guojiadian, there was a half-day tour and a full-day tour, and if you were staying for two days or longer you got to see a completely different set of sights.

A young woman tour guide provided by the village came out with a megaphone and got all the delegates to assemble in front of the Lucky Trees, whereupon she launched into their story: it wasn't just the residents of Guojiadian but everyone for miles around who thought these trees were auspicious. There wasn't a temple in the village because the two trees were the guardian deities of Guojiadian, so every festival and at New Year, not to mention if there was a wedding or a funeral, or when the superstitious folk of the village wanted to pray for protection from the gods, they'd light incense under the trees and kowtow. From the beginning of spring to the end of autumn, even on ordinary days, the villagers would regularly assemble under the trees just to sit for a while, or they'd stand there, or if they didn't have the time for that, then they'd make sure they walked close by. On summer afternoons the Lucky Trees threw a huge shade, and in the past people from Guojiadian would come out there to take a nap, hold meetings or have a party. If there was nothing going on, you could pass the time sitting under the great trees, while others even went there specially to eat their meals in their shade.

The roots of the huge trees rippled out across the ground, as thick as the trunks of any ordinary trees, polished smooth by the rumps of all the people who'd sat on them over the years. Nobody was sure quite how old these two trees were; even the oldest inhabitants of Guojiadian could only say that the two trees had been enormous when they were children, and when they asked their grandparents, they said that for as long as they could remember the trees had been that big. Their grandparents had asked their grandparents, and they had said exactly the same thing… so they could be anything up to a thousand years old. With trees like this, how could you be sure they didn't have some kind of spiritual power, that they couldn't transform themselves into gods?

Apparently towards the end of the Qing dynasty there'd been a terrible year when the area was hit by lightning, destroying the whole of the pear tree's crown and leaving a charred stump about the height of a man leaning up against the elm. Nobody would have imagined that within a few years it would put out new shoots, and that these new shoots would grow into great branches, right up until the Lucky Trees looked just the same as they always had. This kind of pear – Pyrus xerophila – was used as a rootstock for all kinds of pear cultivars; without it to act as a grafting stock, we wouldn't have pears to eat at all. The elm tree had always been considered a 'money tree' by the Chinese, since from spring onwards its branches were covered in coin-like seeds. It wasn't just that they looked like coins, they were also considered a great delicacy by the local peasantry. In times of famine this elm had provided three crops of seeds per year, and that had prevented a single person in Guojiadian from dying of hunger. When two trees like that grew together, they formed the very best kind of Dragon and Phoenix pairing – later on, the village elders had taken to calling them the Lucky Trees. If they'd been growing in a family garden or clan cemetery, that family would be guaranteed to get rich, or they'd produce great leaders of the nation or famous generals. However, these trees happened to grow by the entrance to Guojiadian, and so the whole village got to enjoy the benefits they conferred.

The delegates to the National People's Congress were struck dumb by all this. Guojiadian was clearly determined to put them through the hoops; they weren't even allowed to enter the village without being forced to listen to a whole heap of superstitious nonsense. How could it be that the famous Guojiadian had got rich merely because it possessed these two big old trees? The delegates, who had just emerged from the palaces of the capital where they had been participating in the government of the country and who each represented their own constituency, had modestly announced that they came to visit and study, but were in fact there to inspect the area. What they were not expecting was that Guojiadian, a place as famous as Dazhai as a model for a new generation, would send out someone to meet them who would proceed to tell them a pack of fairy stories. These strict and serious delegates now found themselves utterly confused. Muttering to themselves, they walked round the Lucky Trees in disbelief. Tied round the trunks of the two trees were auspicious symbols in the form of various lengths of red cloth and yellow paper, and at their feet there were incense burners and piles of fruit as offerings.

Having looked at the huge trees, the delegates were led by their young tour guide to the archway in front of the village. This archway was enormous and featured four columns, three entranceways and five tiers. The guide explained that, added together, this made two times six, and six sixes were of course an auspicious number. The archway was twenty-seven metres tall by fifty-four metres wide, and that made nine times nine: again nine nines is another lucky number. In the past, all of the biggest archways in the world were to be found in China, and the very biggest of all was that in the Yiheyuan Palace in Beijing. However, this archway was even bigger than that, making it the number one archway in all of China. Of course that meant it was also the number one archway in the whole world. Two people together couldn't span one of the vermillion-painted columns, and they soared up majestic and imposing to meet the yellow-tiled roof, the brackets painted in every colour of the rainbow and gilded to boot, in a royal style completely out of harmony with the surrounding landscape. Above the archway there were three hundred and sixty phoenixes sculpted in relief, in openwork and in the round. They were all of different sizes, in different kinds of posture, brightly coloured and lively.

Above the central entrance in the archway was a slogan painted in huge black characters: 'The World in a Nutshell'. The calligraphy was very ugly, but it did not lack force – each stroke looking like a stick of dry firewood, leaning stiff and rigid against the next. It was, moreover, completely inappropriate for the location. The guide informed the onlookers that this had been written by Guo Cunxian himself.

Having gone through the archway they proceeded a short distance only to find their path divided in two. The two parts encircled a flowerbed that was by no means small, but the guide managed to restrain herself from claiming that this was the world's number one flowerbed. However, in the middle of the flowers there was a white metal globe, the diameter of which was fully the size of a two-storey building, with square holes punched all over its surface. The guide explained that this represented a 'divine eye', and yet again it was the world's number one. Of course it couldn't be the world's number one globe because that is the earth itself; none could be bigger than that. This 'divine eye' would be switched on at night, shooting out coloured lights from inside, illuminating the skies above Guojiadian.

The delegates made their way round the 'divine eye' when suddenly they found their way blocked by a magnificent Nine Dragon Wall. This Nine Dragon Wall was built on the same design as that found in Beihai Park in Beijing – the colours were identical, but it was two metres higher and two metres wider, and the dragons were correspondingly bigger and fatter. Naturally, this was the world's number one Nine Dragon Wall.

It was indeed the peasant understanding of the principles of *feng shui* that led to the construction of this wall, which meant that passers-by couldn't actually see the village. The delegates were a varied bunch and some of them were really interested in the way they had done this, and they murmured praise to themselves: Good, good, that's really nice! Guojiadian has really done the trick. It's modern but they haven't done away with their traditional values!

They now had to walk round the Nine Dragon Wall. Clearly it was not at all easy to get into Guojiadian!

The village provided a very lively scene. Stalls lined both sides of the main road, selling everything from items for daily use to grain and fruit and vegetables. There were a great many traders and a great deal of rubbish – it wasn't realistic to expect the road to be spotless under these conditions. With so many different styles of architecture, the village itself gave the same feeling of incoherence as the entrance. There were some brick buildings of the kind you would find in any village in the countryside round there, but then there were also clusters of very elegant buildings. In some places there were heaps of firewood and middens backing onto the road, as well as chickens, ducks, pigs and sheep wandering about looking for food. However, just a step away you might imagine you were in a big city, with one shop next to another, their neon signs flashing. And then beyond that there were the quiet residential areas, with really fine gardens, which looked like gated communities for rich people.

At the heart of the village was the headquarters of the Guojiadian Group. In the empty space in front of the building was an enormous flagpole, and the tour guide informed them that this was the tallest flagpole in the entire world. How on earth did the residents of Guojiadian work that out? Although the flagpole was very tall, there was no flag fluttering from it – who knows what kind of flag they'd hang from it? Several large roads radiated from this spot, heading towards the industrial zones, the science park, the school, the farms… Opposite the headquarters there was a multi-purpose hall, and the delegates from Beijing were now herded in this direction.

A young man was standing in front of the main entrance to the hall. With his broad forehead and an air of authority, his whole body seemed to give off an aura of unrestrained power, combined with the arrogance of a young man who has already achieved great things. A purple jacket was slung over his shoulders, and in one hand he held an electric baton. Two young policemen stood behind him. The tour guide quickly introduced this young man to the assembled group: "This is Mr Liu Fugen, assistant to the general manager of the Guojiadian Group."

Liu Fugen looked suspicious and was entirely lacking in the enthusiasm he ought to show towards these guests. He allowed the guide to marshal the delegates inside the hall, where they all headed straight for the front seats. Once the visitors had settled down, he stood at the front and said a few words of welcome to the delegates to the National People's Congress, but his tone was ironic, and he seemed even a little absent-minded. Afterwards he asked someone to run a film for them.

An enormous head appeared on the screen: a coarse, sharp and cold face, which could even be said to be ugly. Only his eyes were comparatively beautifully set; his temples, forehead and cheeks were covered with pockmarks and lumps, as well as being riven by deep furrows, crisscrossing each other. He had a small, flat head, with bushy eyebrows and thick eyelashes. His eyes were dry and fixed on the distance, with an arrogance that showed a determination to set himself apart from others.

The voice attached to this face was hoarse, and as calmly cold as you might expect: "You have arrived in Guojiadian, and now you are getting to meet me on screen – that is the only way that you can see me. Every day at least three thousand people come to Guojiadian from China's thirty provinces, autonomous regions, special economic zones and Taiwan. These people come in twenty or thirty different groups, and each of those groups wants to meet Guo Cunxian. However, I can meet at most eight groups a day, and even that number would keep me constantly busy with chatting, shaking hands and smiling politely. And any of the groups that I didn't manage to see personally would criticise me and say that I was too proud to have anything to do with them. These last few years I have had four serious problems to deal with: the problem of establishing what direction we need to take when everyone has their own ideas, the problem of economic development in the teeth of endless discussions on the subject, the problem of management style in changing times and the terrible problem of becoming arrogant. There is no choice in this matter: peasants have to sort out their own problems, and without ever taking a penny from the government we have ended up paying hundreds of millions of yuan in taxes every year to the country. It is normal to become proud in such a situation, because we were the ones to pull our fingers out and haul ourselves out of poverty.

"Right now, I am going to begin with a basic outline of the situation in Guojiadian. To put it plainly, Guojiadian is now a national emporium, not just our peasant 'shop'. This village was founded in the time of the Yongle Emperor in the Ming dynasty, and so it has more than five hundred and eighty years of history. The village covers a total area of some six thousand acres, and we have a population of just over five thousand, plus nearly forty thousand workers who come from outside the village. That includes experts, professors and highly skilled technical specialists who we have invited to work here, numbering one thousand six hundred people in total, and more than one thousand managers. There are two hundred and seventy-five businesses based in this village, of which fifty-two are joint venture companies involving a foreign partner. Thirty of these companies have an annual revenue over one hundred million yuan, and they are organised as subsidiaries of six major corporations: our food processing plant, our iron and steel works, Continental Electronics, Global Chemicals, International Construction and Eastern Commerce, as well as an agricultural arm. Last year from farming and industry, our village had a total income of four-and-a-half billion yuan, with after-tax profits standing at six hundred and thirty million yuan. Each villager made one hundred and twenty-five thousand yuan in profit after tax. How does that sound? Twenty years ago Guojiadian was so poor that we had more than seventy bachelors who couldn't find wives, and you can go and see the site where our Bachelors' Hall used to be, but nowadays we're rich!

"People are always so sure that Guojiadian got rich because we were lucky, and even if we'd tried to avoid that outcome, we couldn't have done so. They say we got rich because people gave us money, not because we went out and asked for it. How could that be true? Who could possibly understand how much pressure I was under at that time? Let me make a comparison for you: on one occasion I was sitting in what is currently the largest passenger plane in the world, the Boeing 747, and the air stewardess told me that this kind of plane has to take off at a speed of ten thousand metres per minute, or else it explodes. Some senior cadres simply ignore how much the people of Guojiadian have done for this country. They look at the cars we drive, the money we make, and they go green with envy and say that I'm some kind of peasant emperor. I look at those senior cadres from the city, and see that they are more coarse and vulgar than any peasant could be. If you've got the balls, why don't you try to become a peasant emperor yourself? After all, remove the word peasant and what's left is an emperor!"

This man really was a strong personality, and he had the guts to lay it all right down. When he was speaking, his sharp-featured face jutted forward, and his body kept thrusting forward, as if he were a warhead about to be fired off. You had to admit that Guo Cunxian had an unusual quality to him – he kept saying he didn't have much education, but he could speak well, he could say what he had to and could make a telling comparison or give a neat example, and there was a logic to his conversation. In his own person, he could represent the peasantry and their history, but you could also see that this was no ordinary peasant. He had qualities rare in anyone, and that was the source of his immense charm. This didn't just influence ordinary people, even important figures in the government found themselves affected by it, and it was one of the factors in bringing so many visitors to Guojiadian today.

A number of the delegates present were familiar with the numbers being given, and they knew just how much was behind the figures that Guo Cunxian reported. No wonder Guojiadian was so famous, everything here had been successful in spades, and the whole place lived up to its reputation. Guo Cunxian was a personality, no doubt about it, and he had real money behind him. Without property, he would just have been an ordinary guy, but as it was, with such vast wealth, he had become a major figure in national life.

The mysterious is always tempting. In the film the delegates understood perfectly well that Guo Cunxian was making fun of those who wanted to meet him in person, but this did not prevent them from wanting the same thing for themselves. Actually it made them even more curious and even more determined that they were going to see this remarkable man come what may. The delegates felt quite sure that, whatever Guo Cunxian might say on the film, that was just aimed at ordinary visitors. But they were all delegates to the National People's Congress, and there were so many of them. Their arrival might be termed a visit, but it could also be considered an inspection. Besides which he was a delegate himself, he had to make an appearance! In fact, it was incumbent upon him not merely to make an appearance but also to provide them with what they'd really come for. There were rules about how and when certain people arrived at a certain place, they were to be treated in a particular way…

For the past half century, various different modes of travel had been established by senior members of the Party or cultivated by the more junior on their own initiative. These 'fact-finding missions' offered an opportunity to travel at public expense, and they became a special feature of the cultural landscape in China. During the years of isolation, this was almost the only opportunity for government officials to travel, to broaden their horizons. It was perfectly normal for the delegates to the National People's Congress to take the opportunity to go to Guojiadian now that they'd finished their meetings in Beijing. What they were not expecting was that, having made such a fuss and come all this way, they weren't even going to see the man they'd come to meet, and that he'd sent this young hooligan out to make them go away.

They really hadn't anticipated that Guo Cunxian's assistant, this Liu Fugen, wouldn't play along at all. He told their guide what route she should take and then turned round without even shaking hands, as though he was just going to walk away. The people leading the visiting group simply couldn't stand for this. They dragged him off to a quiet corner and told him that the delegation included cadres heading government departments, not to mention entrepreneurs and intellectuals from a variety of fields. Guo Cunxian simply had to appear.

Liu Fugen didn't move, but he turned his face slightly as he casually announced: "The Master doesn't normally meet any cadre of provincial level or below."

What? Who was the 'Master', and what kind of rule was that?

Liu Fugen smiled, but there was a nasty edge to it. "As for the rules in Guojiadian, didn't you see the video just now? Going back to Dazhai ten years ago, they had only about ten million visitors. Up to the present day, we've had thirteen million come here to Guojiadian. A few years ago, people from the north were all heading south to look at the special autonomous regions, but now southerners come north to see what is going on in Guojiadian. If we don't set some rules about who is going to see what, how would we ever find time to do any work? I know that all of you were delegates to the National People's Congress, so that's why I went with you just now to look at the video. You aren't taking part in government deliberations any more, you are here to observe and study, so you need to sort out your attitudes first. If you think you are going to throw your weight around just because you were delegates, then please go and do this somewhere else."

He then went away, shaking his head.

These remarks were a slap in the face. Those who'd been standing nearby and heard what Liu Fugen had to say were all frozen to the spot.

When the residents of Guojiadian found themselves face to face with Guo Cunxian, they did as they were told, but when meeting some outsider, they liked to throw their weight around too. However the delegates to the National People's Congress had been swanning around Beijing for a couple of weeks now, and they weren't prepared to put up with this kind of treatment. And when you think about it, the whole situation was kind of odd. They'd all been delegates together, and if they'd wanted to meet Guo Cunxian in Beijing during the Congress, it would have been perfectly easy to arrange. If they'd wanted to invite him to a meeting or to participate in some kind of working group to explain the situation in Guojiadian, no doubt he would have been happy to oblige. But who'd given him a second thought at that time? Why was it that the moment the Congress was over, the delegates insisted on visiting Guojiadian? Was it that they wanted to enjoy the prestige of being delegates for a little bit longer, or were they thinking that Guo Cunxian might let them browse at his trough because they'd all been in Beijing together? He was so rich, why would he mind them sticking their snouts in?

Who would have imagined that this 'peasant emperor' behaved like a real emperor once he was back on home turf? Did he really think that he'd removed the 'peasant' from that title? Clearly he didn't like being despised as some kind of hick, and he was determined to step outside his origins. That had become his motive for action and his ultimate goal.

In recent years, what bizarre and strange sights had not appeared at Guojiadian? It is odd, now you mention it, the more you experience, the more bizarre and strange things you get to try. It wasn't like being poor at all, because when you are poor, every day and indeed every year is pretty much the same: all the families in the village lived very much the same kind of life, and if a dog barked it practically qualified as news.

Today, a hot dry day in late spring, many people were milling about. Now all of a sudden an attractive young woman appeared in Guojiadian carrying a baby girl less than a year old. She was stopping people to ask where Guo Cunyong lived, and introduced herself as his wife, just arrived from Hong Kong.

Ha-ha! Well, that was something to enjoy! The more quarrelling there was the more people complained that there wasn't enough going on in Guojiadian – but in the blink of an eye a huge crowd had gathered around, some of them telling the young woman from Hong Kong which way she ought to go, while others were offering to take her straight round to Guo Cunyong's house themselves. Yet more people followed on behind, and as they advanced, they formed a bigger and bigger procession.

Somebody had already rushed off hot-foot to Guo Cunyong's house to report.

Suddenly the village was full of commotion.

Ou Huaying was famous in Guojiadian for her tongue. In the ordinary way of things she'd be right out there giving everyone a piece of her mind. On hearing the news her mind went blank for a moment, and she nearly passed out from sheer rage. However, no matter how angry she might be, no matter how let down she might feel by her husband's deceit, she wasn't the kind of person to make mistakes out of haste. Guo Cunyong would have to pay for what he'd done, but she didn't have time to think about that right now. Right now the most important thing was to prevent this whore from ever setting foot in her house. This was her house – the moment this little cow thought she had her foot in the door, they'd never be able to get rid of her! Guo

Cunyong was an important person in this village, and she herself was now an important person too; she didn't want either of them to become a subject of gossip. This was Guojiadian's Zhongnanhai, so her neighbours were all major figures in the locale. Although her neighbours might not come right out and say it, she knew they'd be perfectly happy to see her come to grief. If there was any open quarrelling here, then she might as well get on the public address system and broadcast it.

The best thing would be to take this whore from Hong Kong off somewhere far away and have it out with her in a place where nobody could stand around with their ears flapping. Ou Huaying was moving quickly now, and her brain was spinning with ideas. By the time she got to the main entrance to her house, she could see a crowd heading towards the gate. She couldn't prevent her heart from thumping erratically. She knew perfectly well what her husband was like, but his turnover of girlfriends was usually pretty quick, so there'd never been problems brought home to her – she'd never had to confront one of his tarts before. Today, even if the skies fell, she'd have to deal with it. One step at a time. The first thing was to get this woman out of here and see what she had to say.

Everyone who'd followed on behind, or had come running from the four points of the compass, stopped the moment they caught sight of Ou Huaying's expression. They stood back, as if clearing a space for the coming drama, assembling in a circle around the main protagonists. The two women were now completely surrounded and would have to perform, whether they wanted to or not.

The woman from Hong Kong had probably guessed who had come out to meet her. They were standing face to face, measuring each other up.

Ou Huaying was furious, and her eyes were like daggers, stabbing at the woman and her baby. This wasn't working: if only she could have stabbed her and had her fall dead at her feet, it would have been wonderful! She seemed to be running a fever, and nobody was surprised. Unfortunately for those who enjoy a good scene, she rarely lost control; she kept telling herself to keep her cool, to think things through, to talk, to deal with one issue at a time and look for her opportunity.

The more Ou Huaying stared at the other woman, the more bitter she felt. Her opponent was so young and seductive, with a dangerous edge to her sexiness. Her long hair was loose about her face, and she kept tossing it back to keep it out of her eyes. A cashmere sweater was draped over her shoulders, and a huge pair of tits were bursting out of her lilac camisole, which was cinched in at the waist with a leather belt. The way her breasts were straining the fabric was really drawing all eyes upon them. To complete this fetching ensemble, she was wearing skin-tight, black, wet-look trousers, tucked in at the bottom to brown high-heeled boots. It was hardly surprising that she'd attracted so much attention on setting foot in the village: the men wouldn't be able to resist, and the women would all be jealous. The moment she caught sight of her, Ou Huaying had been quite clear that if Guo Cunyong had the slightest chance to get a woman like this into bed, he'd have taken it. She knew what he was like.

Ou Huaying had started out in an absolute fury, but now she realised that she was already in trouble. Coming out to meet the Hong Kong woman in this way gave an opportunity for comparison, in which she looked old, countrified, and ugly. If they started fighting, whose side would the onlookers take? The men would naturally all take the tart's side: you just had to look at the way she wiggled her arse from side to side, as if she didn't have a care in the world. She seemed quite oblivious to the dangers and awkwardness of the situation, and she looked at Ou Huaying curiously for a moment, before turning her gaze back to the crowd.

Ou Huaying knew that they couldn't carry on just standing there like that. So she opened her mouth to speak, and even she could hear how the anger had changed her normal tone of voice: "Who are you? What are you doing here?"

The other woman seemed surprised, but she didn't avoid the question. She answered in standard Chinese, but with the slight twang of a southerner: "My name is Guo-Chu Fang, and I come from Hong Kong. I'm looking for my husband, Guo Cunyong. Who are you?"

This was even more infuriating, and Ou Huaying could barely keep her voice steady: "I am Guo Cunyong's wife – we've been married for nearly twenty years. Since when is he your husband?"

This ought to have been a horrible blow for Guo-Chu Fang, but she didn't seem nearly as shocked and surprised as the people standing around had hoped she would be. She just looked innocent and said: "We got married last year in Hong Kong. Does this mean Cunyong is under arrest for bigamy?"

What a silly bitch! She was saying it all right out loud, like she wanted to make sure that everyone knew!

If Ou Huaying hadn't been fully conscious of the fact that the other woman was holding a baby, she'd have begun hitting the whore a while back. "Rubbish! Who the hell do you think you are? It's obvious that you've been fucked and dumped! Who would marry a tart like you? What proof do you have of this so-called wedding?"

"Of course I have proof."

"Well, let's see it then!" She was really hoping that this silly bitch would actually take out her wedding certificate, because then she could tear it into bits. Let's see what she did then!

Guo-Chu Fang looked doubtful. "Here? Are you the police?"

"I may not be police, but I can still deal with a bitch like you! I've seen plenty of your kind, thinking you can cheat me. Right, we're going to the police this instant!"

Ou Huaying rushed forward and grabbed the baby out of Guo-Chu Fang's arms, and then turned round and started running. This was a very neat trick to pull. Guo-Chu Fang shouted and set off in pursuit, and the baby, who'd been terrified by all the yelling, now began to scream, pressed tight as she was against Ou Huaying's chest.

Under ordinary circumstances, a careful and sensible woman like Ou Huaying would have arranged to take Guo-Chu Fang somewhere quiet, like the house of one of her relatives or perhaps a good friend, and then found out what was going on, tried to cajole her or terrorise her a bit (whichever seemed likely to give the best results), and then capped it all off by offering her some money to get this Hong Kong woman to go away. The best would be if she would take the money and leave – then she could just vanish and nobody would be any the wiser. It would have been perfectly easy for her to do, because if there was one thing that Ou Huaying had to hand, it was money. Guo Cunyong was earning over a million yuan a year, together with who knows how much under the table. In her opinion, the best way to keep control of a man was through his finances, so the moment she found out that money had come in, she would rip it out of Guo Cunyong's hands. If he didn't have the cash, there was a limit to how much trouble he could get into. Well, here was the answer. Who would have imagined that a foreign wife would now pop up, complete with a baby? What would he get up to next?

When it comes right down to it, a woman is just a woman. If nothing important is going on, she can be there running her mouth and carrying on like she understands everything much better than anyone else, but the minute something does happen to her, then she does something dumb. Even the people who were there hoping for a scene were surprised. What is Ou Huaying up to? Why did she grab the baby rather than try to explain the situation to the woman? The woman was chasing after them, Ou Huaying was running off, the baby was screaming, the adults were yelling, the onlookers were laughing and cracking jokes, and some of them had even set off running with them.

Of these, some were encouraging Ou Huaying: "Good! You've got the right idea! Don't give the kid back to her! Take it round to the hospital and find out whether Cunyong really is the father."

Others were encouraging Guo-Chu Fang: "Quick! You need to run faster. If you don't have the kid, then Guo Cunyong will just dump you."

The whole of Guojiadian was quivering with sensation. This kind of thing is easy to get excited about: Guo Cunyong's closest friends and family were now out and about, adding their voices to the mix.

When you are quarrelling, the very worst thing is to have other people standing around 'trying to calm things down' because all they do is fan the flames. Even a clever woman like Ou Huaying, with all these other people chiming in with their dumb advice, found the situation slip out of her control. However, whatever happened she wasn't stupid enough to take the baby to the hospital – maybe that had been her intended destination when she grabbed the baby and set off running, but now she had a clear idea of where she was heading: she was going to the village Party committee to find Guo Cunxian. Anyone else in this village might find themselves doing something stupid or not having a clue how to proceed, but her husband's cousin, whatever else you might say about him, was someone that she'd never known to be at a loss for an idea. She'd always liked Guo Cunxian and thought he liked her: he'd be on her side now, he'd take charge, or else he'd tell her exactly what she needed to do.

Of course, she wasn't thinking straight. Although it was perfectly easy to bump into Guo Cunxian when nothing was the matter, the moment you really had a problem he was nowhere to be seen. The guards kept her well away from the front of the office building: wait here, we'll tell him you've arrived, but as to whether he'll see you or not, we just don't know. It's important? Well, various higher-ups have come from the city, do you realise that? And they've got more than forty foreign experts with them, and they're talking to Secretary Guo right this minute in the main VIP meeting-room. How important can your problem be? Would anyone come here if it was just a minor matter? You see over there – there are a whole bunch of reporters from various newspapers big and small, and from China Central Television, not to mention the local station. They're waiting to interview Secretary Guo. They want to know all about us in the 'Number One Village'. Which do you think is more important?

With all of this going on, how could she possibly get into Guo Cunxian's office?

There were all of these important things for him to deal with, he simply couldn't find time for anything else. He must be far too busy to think about other people's problems.

In actual fact, if the guards had just stood back and let everyone who'd come to find Guo Cunxian enter the building, there wasn't one of them who would have been able to locate his office. Although from the outside it seemed as though the building had six storeys, it was actually only five when you got inside: once the stairs reached the fifth floor, that was that. There was a VIP meeting-room on the fifth floor, together with a large conference room, a smaller conference room, a sitting room for guests of honour and then the CEO's own office in the south-eastern corner. This was divided into two large rooms: inner and outer. Sitting in the outer office was the CEO, Lin Meitang. Behind her was a secret door, which in turn led to a little staircase that connected to the sixth floor.

The entire sixth storey was given over to Guo Cunxian. He had his office there, together with a bedroom, a bathroom with attached massage unit, a small dining room, a little room for visitors and so on. All of the furniture was made of sandalwood, and he ate off silver. His taps were gold plated, and the telephone number for his enormous office was 9888 8888, "because eight was a lucky number". Anyone who was lucky enough to be invited into this office was likely to be asked the same question: how does my office compare with Zhongnanhai? Of course, neither the person asking the question nor those answering it had ever even been near Zhongnanhai. The answer to this question wasn't important though; what was important was that Guo Cunxian was determined to make this kind of comparison.

In spite of the fact that he had all of these huge and magnificently appointed rooms at his disposal, Guo Cunxian usually only occupied a very small area. Right at this moment he was trussed up in a Western suit, squatting on top of a large and comfortable leather-covered swivel-chair. That's right. He was squatting and not sitting. He would squat in silence for two or three hours at a time, his posture the same as if he had been out in the fields. He would only sit down if he was tired of squatting or if someone else came in to join him, and then when he had recovered or the other person had gone, he'd be back squatting down. At the same time he'd smoke one cigarette after another, to the point where you could say that he was chain-smoking. He had to have a lit cigarette in one hand, and then whenever he thought about it, he'd drag one mouthful of smoke after another into his lungs. If he forgot about it, the lit cigarette would stay caught between his fingers, the ash falling eventually onto the thick carpet. He had a young woman standing behind him, looking very clean and tidy. It was her job to notice when the cigarette had nearly burned away and then light another one herself, after which she would take the stub of the old one out of Guo Cunxian's hand and replace it with the newly lit cigarette. This would happen again and again, up until the moment that Guo Cunxian left his office.

It sometimes seemed as though Guo Cunxian couldn't think unless he was squatting on his chair smoking. It didn't matter how many people were out there looking for him, how many things needed his attention. Even if the screaming and shouting could be heard throughout the building he would stay squatting on his chair, like an old oil lamp, just breathing, not moving. What he was thinking about as he squatted there, nobody was entirely clear. Maybe he was speculating to himself, or simply dreaming, or maybe not even thinking about anything at all: he just liked being alone and quiet to contemplate his own heart. By himself, as if in a trance, he seemed to be intent upon his own thoughts.

The power that he had he had won for himself: but he never imagined he'd become a legend in his own lifetime. Recently he had come to understand that he simply did not have the necessary experience or intelligence to be able to cope with this, and he was beginning to find it very difficult to deal with other people – he didn't want to discuss anything with them any more. He had to shut himself away in order to be able to maintain the necessary cold ambition. Besides which, if it wasn't easy for the hordes wanting to meet him to clap eyes on him, he would appear even more mysterious. Mystery is necessary for a legend. If you think about people like that, there are many riddles in their behaviour.

Of course, it might be that he was lonely because he was too tough. That loneliness had allowed him to find the toughness that he needed. It gave him independence and freedom. He couldn't engage in pointless small talk any more. He had to wrack his brains for some aphorism or clever slogan in order to deal with the Party leaders, the masses or the media. Whatever he said was either an order or an instruction, and sometimes even an edict. He was endlessly telling his subordinates to make new products that would earn big money, and so his most important job was to think about their production lines and make sure everyone stayed on-message. Just like the spirit of Dazhai all those years ago, he'd come to be trusted by the entire country, and his word was now law among the peasantry.

Guojiadian was now much more famous than Dazhai had been back in the day, but this was nothing to do with its 'spirit', it was because they had a lot of money. It seemed that even fame could be turned to profit nowadays. In this year's Chinese New Year Gala broadcast they'd had three close-ups of him: one full face and two side views. This would have much more impact than three full-length documentaries! Guojiadian had prepared for this for a long time; they had a slot showing the people of Guojiadian light a whole load of firecrackers – that just cost money, ninety thousand yuan in total, thirty thousand yuan for each of his close-ups. He'd originally wanted to buy six close-ups because for New Year's you want something auspicious and six sixes are a lucky number. The TV people had refused, saying there were loads of heroes and model workers, not to mention famous actors who wouldn't necessarily get a close-up in the special gala, and there were various senior cadres who had to have their own shots. If we give you six close-ups, questions will be asked!

Is it true that becoming too famous makes people jealous? Now, even Feng Hou and Zhang Caiqian, the people to whom the village owed all its current prosperity, weren't prepared to come and visit any more. Guo Cunxian really hated them for that, but sometimes he also missed them. Every day now, all he heard was praise and flattery, but he didn't know who his real friends were any more. His true friends, those who'd helped him through the worst of times – Wang Shun, Liu Yucheng, Jin Laixi, Ou Guangming – well, he got to see them barely a couple of times a year. Even if they did manage to meet, they were all respectful and polite. If there was a problem then they'd discuss it, but if nothing much was up, they'd leave right away. The good fellowship of yesteryear seemed impossible to recover...

The sound of footsteps came up the stairs, and his assistant manager, Liu Fugen, pushed the door open and entered. In all of Guojiadian there were only two people who dared to barge right in like that: one was his 'Young Marshal' and the other was Lin Meitang. Liu Fugen moved quickly, with an aggressive manner, and so he brought with him into the room a new atmosphere, and a breath of life.

Guo Cunxian remained squatting in his leather chair. He didn't move but his eyelids flicked up: "Has something happened?"

Liu Fugen began by signing to the woman holding the cigarettes to light him one, and then he began to report to the 'Master' exactly what was going on outside – Guo Cunxian was barely fifty, but the young men of Guojiadian who'd come to power with him liked to call him 'Master' behind his back. This appellation combined a sneer with respect; it showed that the person using this term dared to make fun of the special position occupied by the most important person in the entire village. Liu Fugen was sure to include his own opinion in his report: "We don't have to interfere over this woman from Hong Kong – that's Guo Cunyong's private business and he'll have to wipe his own arse this once. The problem is with the old veterans of the Supervision Committee. They are taking advantage of their position to demand to see you, and they're blocking up the entrance even as we speak. What do you want done about them?"

Guo Cunxian raised his head, his eyes shining. He spoke very sharply: "What is their problem?"

"To cut a long story short, they are objecting to the idea that the Black Forest is going to go into operation today, and so they're demanding the closure of every business on Paris Avenue. They're saying that Paris Avenue is nothing but a line of brothels, and the moment it gets dark you have rich men coming from every corner of the county – even big wheels from the city go there to get their dipsticks stuck in. If the Black Forest goes back into business, then Guojiadian is going to be nothing but a huge red-light district, and the young people here are all going to go to the bad."

"Who's in charge?"

"Who could it be other than Han Jingting? And there's Ou Yutian – he's there because of what happened with his daughter Ou Huaying. In addition to them, you've got Lan Shouyi, trying to get his son off the hook. He's carrying on like it's all Paris Avenue's fault that the little bastard tried to rape Xiaohui..."

Although he never stopped speaking, from start to finish Liu Fugen kept a careful eye out to check for any change in the Master's expression. "We've got to think of a way to deal with those old idiots," he went on. "We cannot allow them to keep on causing trouble for us, imagining that they can make you do whatever they want."

"Where's Guo Cunyong?"

"Maybe he doesn't know a thing about it, or maybe he knows he's really got himself in the shit this time and doesn't dare show his face. I guess he's been hiding, keeping himself occupied with getting the Black Forest ready to open. Once his wife has got rid of this Hong Kong bitch, she'll have a go at him, and he'll be lucky if she doesn't skin him with a blunt knife."

Guo Cunxian was now dragging on his cigarette, one deep breath after another. He stuck his legs out from his chair as he moved to a sitting position. Yes, well, there had been a time when he'd really got into trouble and the old veterans in the village had come out to protect him. You could say that his position as secretary was something that he owed entirely to Han Jingting; to thank the elders in the village he'd set up the 'Supervision Committee of Guojiadian Elders'. He hadn't expected them to become senile in their old age. Here they were assuming an authority that wasn't theirs and trying to use the Supervision Committee to throw their weight around – they really think they can tell me what to do!

All of a sudden Guo Cunxian looked up and questioned his adopted son: "What time is the opening ceremony for the Black Forest?"

"Eight o'clock this evening."

"Go and get the woman from Hong Kong and the baby in here. Inform everyone that we're going to have a Party committee meeting beginning at seven thirty, and those in charge of each company need to attend, particularly Guo Cunyong. I want you to tell him specially, he has to be there."

"What about the old idiots?"

"I don't want to see them."

"And what do we do about the people from the international economic forum?"

Now that was a problem. He felt like closing the door on them and turning a blind eye, after all they hadn't invited him to come from Guojiadian to instruct them. He didn't want to pay any attention to them at all. However, they were important economists, and if he got them on his side, wouldn't that establish his position in the world of economics? If he gave them a sweet to stop their mouths, it would ensure they would praise Guojiadian to the skies. After all, they'd come to Guojiadian to see him! OK, I don't care that they haven't been very polite, they're here and I'm in a good mood today, so they can consider themselves lucky. Guo Cunxian told Liu Fugen to take the experts from the international economic forum to the dining room and wait there – he'd be along as soon as he could.

Guo Cunxian got up and pulled his suit straight. Then he took a turn or two round his office, trying to get the pins and needles out of his feet. He was in many ways the same person he had always been, for all that he now paid ninety thousand yuan for his close-ups, but in the blink of an eye he could turn into a living legend, a sight to be seen and a truly impressive man.

It was very obvious that he liked being presented with problems to solve since they gave him an opportunity to show off his power and his brain. Power is a kind of aphrodisiac, and he felt this particularly when he was solving the problems brought to him by women.

You see, when Liu Fugen went downstairs to announce his instructions, Ou Huaying and her father, Ou Yutian, immediately stopped. He allowed the woman from Hong Kong to enter but kept them outside the entrance – what was that all about? He was clearly trying to make them look bad in front of the entire village. They were very closely connected to Guo Cunxian after all, and even if they weren't, given that they lived in Guojiadian, he shouldn't treat them like that! However, no matter how furious the Ou family were, they wouldn't dare put it into words, and they had to give the baby back to Guo-Chu Fang.

Lin Fugen brought the mother and child up to the fifth floor and handed them over to Lin Meitang, before heading off to carry out his other orders. Lin Meitang went upstairs with Guo-Chu Fang and her baby, gently opening the door of Guo Cunxian's office for them. She told the cigarette girl to leave, and took up the job of lighting and handing over the cigarettes herself.

She began by introducing Guo-Chu Fang to the person in charge here at Guojiadian: Guo Cunxian. When listing his titles he didn't forget to emphasise that he was the head of the police station in Guojiadian. That meant he was in charge of the local forces of law and order.

Guo-Chu Fang made haste to bow and ask how he was.

Guo Cunxian just nodded to her. He was already seated on his leather chair, smoking a cigarette. He weighed up Guo-Chu Fang between narrowed eyelids; he could almost feel his mouth watering. This woman wasn't really very beautiful, but she was certainly eye-catching. Those massive tits, that experienced sexuality, that softness and warmth; she'd be desirable under any circumstances. Guo Cunyong really knew how to pick them!

However, right from the moment that Guojiadian started to get rich, Guo Cunxian hadn't had time for this kind of thing. Although the story behind this woman's appearance had allowed him to put to one side the irritation Feng Hou had caused him, his voice was still ice-cold: "Your surname is Guo?"

"My surname is Chu, but after I married Guo Cunyong I hyphenated it with his surname. I would never have imagined that I'd end up sharing a surname with you." Even Guo-Chu Fang's voice had a sexy, musky undertone. Sitting opposite this bizarre village chief, even though he didn't look anything special, he had a strange kind of dignity about him, which made her feel safe. Her heart was no longer pounding the way it had been.

Guo Cunxian was quite sure that anyone appearing before him would be restrained by his presence, if not outright nervous. Even someone like Lin Meitang, the woman closest to him, always felt the need to keep a close eye on how he was taking what she said; she was cautious and obedient. Guo-Chu Fang was clearly there because she needed his help, in her embarrassing dilemma he was the only person who could help her out, but she was able to remain so relaxed and natural, a slight smile on her face. Really, she was a very attractive woman. Guo Cunxian decided to do his best for her. Although he despised her, he still felt a certain sense of pity.

He carried on the questioning: "Can you prove your marriage to Guo Cunyong?"

"When we got married in Hong Kong we had lots of our friends present – there's the marriage certificate too. Besides which, just look at our daughter! Doesn't she look just like Cunyong? She's the living proof!" The woman held out her baby proudly. Guo Cunxian turned his gaze from the mother's body to the child's face. She was absolutely right: the shape of the head, the wide mouth, the nose and eyes – she was the spitting image of Guo Cunyong.

He turned round to look at Lin Meitang. Her lips curved in a smile.

All of a sudden Guo-Chu Fang's expression changed and her voice took on a sobbing note. Every word she said seemed drenched in tears: "I know that Guo Cunyong loves me, so why did he lie?"

"Love?" Guo Cunxian snorted. "Love always entails an element of deceit. That's just a fact of life. When God gave people the ability to speak, it was to increase their capacity for lying, and whenever someone opens their mouth the chances are that they aren't telling the truth. What is the truth anyway? What is a lie? Are you telling me that you've never lied to anyone yourself?"

He was very calm and collected. Guo-Chu Fang started to get scared: "What am I to do? He's got to pay for this!"

"Why did you come to Guojiadian?"

"After I got pregnant, I lost my job. Guo Cunyong said he'd look after us, but he hasn't been back to Hong Kong for more than six months, and he hasn't been sending me any money."

"That's more like it! Stop trying to tell me it was all a grand romance! I don't care whether you think this is true love and really romantic, because in real life you need power and money to enjoy either. If you don't have food to eat or clothes to wear, it doesn't actually matter how much you love someone. However, you've come a long way, and I won't let you come all this way in vain."

"Really? So you mean you accept that we're legally married?"

"Round here, the law is what I say it is. Guo Cunyong was married long before he met you, so your 'marriage' isn't worth the paper it's written on. However, I can make sure that Guo Cunyong looks after you and the baby, and if he can't Guojiadian will!"

"What do you mean?"

"What job did you use to do?"

"I worked in a beauty salon."

"OK, I'll give you a house here in Guojiadian, and I'll get you the money to open a beauty salon out on Paris Avenue. The conditions are that you have to give up claiming to be Guo Cunyong's wife, and you have to leave him and his family alone. I'm only asking for surface appearance, I don't care about your private feelings in the matter. If you want to carry on your affair in private you can, as long as you don't cause any trouble."

Guo-Chu Fang was confused, she had lost her equilibrium. She didn't know if she ought to agree immediately, but she was certain that she didn't want to refuse the offer.

Lin Meitang looked admiringly at Guo Cunxian. It was a magnificent solution. The two of them had been together for so many years, and the ambiguous nature of their relationship had caused so much gossip, caused so many problems... With Guo-Chu Fang in place, there'd be another target for speculation.

Seeing that she wasn't going to make up her mind right then and there, Guo Cunxian said: "This evening, CEO Lin here is going to arrange a room for you in a hotel, and you can think about what you want to do overnight. If you don't want to stay in Guojiadian, then I want you to go back to Hong Kong tomorrow – I'll pay all your travelling expenses. I'm putting it to you straight, though, this village isn't your private piggybank. Don't think you can come swanning back here causing trouble because you're Guo Cunyong's so-called 'wife'."

Having said this, he waved her away, closing his eyes so that he wouldn't have to look at her again. From his manner, you might imagine that he was quite alone in the room.

Lin Meitang quickly gestured at Guo-Chu Fang to say goodbye. Right up until the moment that they left his office, he didn't move in his chair, and there wasn't the slightest sound from him.

23

VERBAL DIARRHOEA

Right now there is a very common disease. It's called 'verbal diarrhoea'. Real diarrhoea is a condition of the guts, and someone who has it badly can find themselves very sick indeed, and totally emptied out.

Verbal diarrhoea, meanwhile, is when you simply cannot stop talking. The clinical manifestations of this disease are a strong desire to speak, an enjoyment of making reports, a love of performing, the wish to endlessly wag your tongue, to carry on speaking when anyone else would stop, to make comparisons and add details, to talk and talk and talk. True and false, fact and fiction, the dirtiest of stories and the most innocent of jokes, dark and light, useful and pointless, stand-alone or part of a series, verified by someone in the know or made up on the spot, affectionate or frightening, swearing and cursing… it all comes pouring out in a never-ending stream. Sometimes trying to be alarmist, sometimes everything is hearsay, sometimes pretending to be profound, sometimes poking fun, sometimes carrying on an endless monologue until everyone listening longs to sleep, sometimes deliberately dragging skeletons out of cupboards and grubbing up hatchets.

Zhao Rui of the Tang dynasty, writing in the *Classic of Assessing Strengths and Shortcomings*, said: "Someone who gossips, someone who never speaks well of others, who complains day in and day out, slandering others in season and out of season, will find themselves an object of aversion and will be hated by other people." According to research by modern medical experts, verbal diarrhoea is an atypical condition; it is very contagious and many people have been infected. Therefore people nowadays like to get together in large groups, they are happy in crowds, and they really enjoy regular meetings.

Some people in private accused Guo Cunxian of suffering from verbal diarrhoea.

Guo Cunxian arrived at the Alabaster Hall in the Tianbao Hotel in Guojiadian, accompanied by Liu Fugen and Lin Meitang. The guests had been waiting for a while, though they had been given something to drink and trays of nibbles had been circulating. It was kind of rude, not quite right for guests to wait for their host, that senior people should have to wait for their junior, and that a group of high officials should have to hang around for a peasant.

But what could anyone do about it? All kinds of things were happening in Guojiadian that weren't quite right or that shouldn't really be taking place. People there didn't ask for you to come, but you turned up anyway, didn't you? People like to deceive themselves. When everyone tells you that this one person is marvellous, and you insist on going to visit him, you have to be prepared for him to cheat you.

The fixtures and fittings for the Alabaster Hall had cost a fortune. It was all tricked out in gold and silver, really fancy and bright. The most eye-catching feature were the two rows of vast alabaster columns in the main room, six columns in each row. However, the style of the place was neither quite Chinese nor quite Western, and equally, it was neither traditional nor modern. In Guojiadian they knew how to put on the Ritz: decent folk found it impossible in such circumstances to express their unhappiness openly, the most they could do was complain to each other in a whisper.

Once Guo Cunxian arrived, the main room fell silent. When you see such a sight, you have to give it your respect.

He seemed somewhat abstracted, and he didn't really raise his head to look straight at the senior Party cadres and experts from home and abroad who had waited for him so long. However he wasn't stupid, and he took in the scene with a single sweeping glance. He looked disdainful: there were fewer than forty people present, so why did they need to set ten tables? The people who were there to coo and cosset the economists outnumbered them nearly two to one.

He walked straight over to the head table, where the leading cadre and the foreign experts were sitting. This so-called leading cadre was nothing but a secretary; nobody from the real leadership had come. Guo Cunxian had been hoping that Zhang Caiqian would be there. He'd invited him loads of times, and every time he got a positive response, but in the end he somehow didn't show up. If Zhang Caiqian had come with his people today, he wouldn't have been treated like this. The head table was large and could seat seventeen or eighteen people. As Liu Fugen introduced him to the various senior cadres and foreign experts, he shook hands with them as if it were a chore. After that he took his place in front of an empty chair at the head of the main table, without a word of apology for having arrived so late. He also didn't say anything about thanking his visitors for making the journey to Guojiadian – in fact he didn't say even the simplest words of welcome, but launched straight into a speech.

"Banquets are set up to bring people together, so holding a banquet is all about meeting people. To put it even more bluntly, whether it's a banquet or a meeting, it's all about giving people an opportunity to talk. Everybody gets to eat, drink and talk. So right now you are going to eat and drink, and I am going to speak. The main dishes served today will all be specialties of Guojiadian, but for the foreign experts who might not be used to eating that kind of thing, we will also be serving seafood, pork chops and steak. If you are going to have energy to work, you need to eat your fill, and if you get to eat good food, you're going to be happy, you're going to be able to work harder and be able to come up with new ideas. You are all economists, so I'm sure you understand this principle better than I do."

It was a characteristic of Guo Cunxian that no matter how depressed he was, the moment he started to speak he would cheer up. The happier he was, the more he would say; the more he said, the more cheerful he became.

"Personally I like economics, because economics is about earning money. Money can make friends for you, it can bring luck, and it can make sure that every day is filled with excitement and fun. If Guojiadian hadn't become extremely wealthy, you wouldn't have come here and we wouldn't be meeting like this. It is only the poor who are ambivalent about money. They are desperate to get rich, but they spend all their time complaining. They are desperate because they don't have any money, they complain because they'll never get any, and it all comes down to one thing – poverty. It is only rich people who have the right to talk about money. Money is the driving force behind every aspect of modern living. Everything can be attributed to money, and money can be seen as a motive for everything. Money is a symbol of human endeavour, and if you have money, then you have power. People nowadays can only develop their productivity and vitality through the medium of money. Our relationship with money represents our relationship with other people, since this is the basis of our relationship with the rest of society. To put it bluntly, money talks. Take this hall, which I designed myself. Two colours predominate, yellow and white. The yellow is gold, which represents money, the sun, strength, invincible force. The white is silver, and silver also represents money, the moon, softness. OK, if I say any more you will laugh at me. It is now your turn. You've been in Guojiadian for half the day, so if anyone has any questions, or if you want to express an opinion, please feel free."

Having finished what he considered to be his opening remarks, he sat down.

Somehow or other this topsy-turvy, illogical and rambling discourse seemed to please his audience. You had to admit he was an impressive man; they'd had to wait ages for him to turn up but it had definitely been worth it. His eyes were wide open, his voice was hoarse, but he had presence and was obviously strongly independent. One of the foreign scholars, a man with soft and shiny white hair, asked an interpreter to put a question to him: "Guojiadian was just an ordinary Chinese village, so what happened? What was special about this place that you were able to make it like it is today?"

Guo Cunxian stood up again. There was something that he wanted everyone to hear, even though he addressed his remarks to the foreign experts present. "Guojiadian has always been an exceptional place. In the past we were unusually poor and now we are unusually rich. Let me begin by talking about our past poverty. There were families of four or five that only had one bed to sleep in, and there were couples with only one pair of trousers between them, so that when the husband went out to work he had to wear them, which meant that his wife had to spend all her time on the *kang*. Poverty didn't stop couples having children though, and that meant that one generation after another was mired in ignorance and filth. Poverty breeds resentment and anger, poverty results in violence, and there is a popular saying about grinding poverty – the poorer you are, the more you are ground down."

Having brought up this long-standing complaint, Guo Cunxian now found it impossible to stop talking. All the anger that he'd stored up in the years of struggle now came pouring out.

"In those days there were various slogans: 'We will Advance Raising the Red Flag on High'; 'We Swear to Resist Imperialism and Revisionism to the Bitter End'; 'The World is Full of Imperialist and Revisionist Counter-Revolutionaries'; 'When We Sleep We will Keep One Eye Open'. Back then you had your own problems in foreign countries as well, didn't you? Of course, we weren't having too much fun either. We had the old and the new left, the Three Pacifications and the Four Principles. Cadres kept on hammering out the same old tunes, and commune workers simply refused to do anything – if they were forced out into the fields, they just messed around. The rule was that everyone took it in turns, when one person sat down, another would stand up, and then as soon as possible a stop would be called and everyone would go home.

"The way it worked in those days was that people did as little as possible, the commune leaders were hopeless, everyone was just muddling through, and nobody got enough to eat.

"Right, so you may be asking yourselves how come the peasants didn't starve to death during those years. Well, that was all thanks to the vestiges of capitalism – private land. The commune leaders said that private land was a godsend because people could grow a bit of food or keep chickens there. But when it came to dividing up profits, there were always the most massive rows, and the production teams went through the most amazing punch-ups.

"Back then the commune leaders called peasants 'black paws', and that was because they were always digging in the earth and pawing through dung, so their hands were black. Officials and cadres were called 'white paws' because the cadres didn't work so their hands were always clean. Managers in the various departments were called 'leopard paws'. Black paws worked hard, white paws did fuck all and leopard paws just caused trouble.

"It was murder when cadres came down to the village level. The peasants hated the cadres, and the cadres were furious at being sent to the countryside. After the Anti-Rightist campaign they couldn't give orders any more, after the 'Four Cleans' they couldn't extort money, and after the Cultural Revolution they lost power entirely. If only two people were talking together, you would get the truth; if there were three, they'd just be mouthing platitudes; if there were four or more, you'd get nothing but lies out of them."

The audience had now come to life. They were laughing and repeating what he'd said to each other, and some were taking notes. He seemed to have tossed off his remarks about the social problems of those times entirely off the cuff, but they were undoubtedly correct and his audience found them unexpected – he seemed to speak for the people. The most surprising thing was that Guo Cunxian was able to quote all of these slogans from decades before, one after the other, without the slightest hesitation.

That was Guo Cunxian. He hoped every word he spoke would have the whole place rocking with laughter and applause.

This was causing a lot of problems for the interpreters. They were trying to translate and explain his expressions to the foreign experts but it wasn't easy.

However, they were able to give them some sense of the history of this place, and they were becoming more interested in Guo Cunxian and Guojiadian. Without any doubt the foreign scholars found Guo Cunxian as bizarre as the slogans he chanted, but the way he spoke was characteristic of Chinese peasants and charming, and matched with his wrinkled face, marked by the vicissitudes that he'd experienced.

A person who has never taken any risks never comes across like that.

All this time Lin Meitang was sitting by his side with her head down, working away. She was picking crab meat out of the shell one piece at a time. Once that was done, she turned to the fish and pulled the bones out one by one, after which she heaped the safe-to-eat crab meat and the fish on a small plate in front of Guo Cunxian. When chopsticks and a toothpick just weren't enough, she used her fingers to pull apart and prise open the shell with natural and practised movements. She behaved as if nobody else was present, and clearly could not care less what the senior cadres and experts sitting around thought. She looked happy and proud, and every time that Guo Cunxian's speech provoked applause, she laughed with pleasure.

Guo Cunxian sat back down. Under the gaze of his audience, he started to shovel down the crab meat and fish that Lin Meitang had so carefully prepared. This ensured that those watching him felt embarrassed to keep staring at him; some of them turned away, some of them lowered their heads, and the rest felt that they could only watch him out of the corner of their eyes. He took virtually nothing from any of the plates other than the delicacies that Lin Meitang had prepared for him. Maybe he ate these things for her sake, to show that he appreciated her care and attention.

In fact he didn't eat much at all, and this kind of banquet was actually a business meeting for him. Since he was presiding over it as host, he didn't see why he had to eat anything. It was Lin Meitang who'd noticed that, on these occasions, he would just speak and not eat, and she was worried that he was smoking too much as well. Since she was easily satisfied, why not make the woman happy by showing that you appreciated her attentions?

Guo Cunxian could see that he now held the audience in the palm of his hand, and so he stood up again and explained that the circumstances in which Guojiadian had become wealthy were most unusual. This was a great opportunity, and he'd come here exactly because this was an opportunity to talk about himself and Guojiadian. Somehow or other he found himself enjoying these disquisitions more and more, and he was increasingly reckless in what he said. It didn't matter whether it was a plan he'd actually carried out or something that he'd shelved, or maybe even something that someone else had done, or something that had just popped into his head, he would recount these stories as if they were part of his own experience, and he'd make a big show out of it all.

"Just now I was explaining how Guojiadian used to be extremely poor, and now I am going to move on to talk about how we became amazingly rich. As you will have seen, even our pig farm is a kind of United Nations – we have English, Canadian, Belgian, Ukrainian and Chinese breeds, and every year we produce more than twenty thousand head. We've just finished constructing two new three-storey pig-pens, with heating, individual pens and automatic feeders, and the pigs themselves are transported up and down by escalators, with our people keeping an eye on things over the CCTV. You see, here even the pigs have proper houses with electric lights and phones!"

Naturally, there was loud laughter at this point.

"Agriculture is necessary for our national security, but without commerce we cannot survive, without educated people we cannot thrive, without a workforce we cannot get rich. Struggling along in poverty and deprivation is one thing, developing science and technology is another. If we are going to have both the hard workers and the technological know-how, changing our perspective will be crucial. Market forces are not a practice but a system, and they will force great social changes."

The Chinese economics experts, who understood every word he was saying, were now deeply impressed. This man might look like a hayseed, but he was clearly very quick on the uptake, and he was seeing things in everyday life that plenty of officials and scholars in the field hadn't noticed. Once he got going, he went straight to the point and cut right through all the waffle.

"If you are dealing with people who've been poor for many generations, if you want to create wealth, you have to have a proper plan. There are two possible ways to succeed. Either you rely on your own abilities or you rely on other people's mistakes. Their mistakes are your opportunity. I'm going to tell you a story and let all of you great economics experts learn what a peasant can do. In the past, the Soviet Union had sufficient electrical power to be able to keep their iron and steel prices down. After the collapse of the Soviet Union I went into the steel industry in a big way. The Russians were still confused by the changes in their country. Fleets of ships were lying idle, and even their warships didn't have anything to do. I rented some of those ships to transport my steel. Later on the Russians decided that I'd done too well out of the raw materials that I'd purchased, so they slapped on limits. I had my own ideas about how to deal with this change of policy, so I set up joint ventures in Russia and Ukraine. That way they didn't just find that they couldn't interfere in my business, they were thrilled to welcome my investment. Right now we've got the tiger out on the prowl, the monkey up in its tree and the lion on the way out of its den – whoever has the skills and the knowledge gets to make their own success, they are the first to get rich, they are the ones to win big. As to whether China gets rich or not, the key is going to be in organisation. The organisation is responsible for the promotion of cadres, and if the cadres are selected purely for their ability to lick arses, if they nod and agree with every dumb decision of their bosses, if they are only interested in scratching their own backs, if they are endlessly checking which way the wind is blowing, if they only ever carry out other people's orders, if they never query the latest slogan, if they never make up their own minds, if they never say anything wrong, if they never actually do anything, it is going to be impossible for our country ever to get rich! The way I see it, the less interference we get from Party leaders the better. If they don't interfere at all in matters that aren't crucial, that would be best of all, and if they only bother with checking up on what the crucial people are up to, that would be pretty much perfect."

When Guo Cunxian was happily talking away, his wrinkled and ordinary face shone with a sudden light, and his expression became lively yet patient. It was fitting for the kind of things he was saying. His expression bore out his words, and both were persuasive.

Now one of the TV journalists stood up excitedly and issued an invitation right then and there for Guo Cunxian to attend the televised element of the economics forum as a VIP guest. This televised segment was well known and many people watched it – it would be right for him to take part to speak up for the peasantry. What this journalist was not expecting was that Guo Cunxian's face would fall, and he immediately refused: "Just you wait and see. I'm going to make your economics forum a 'Guojiadian forum'. I pay fifteen thousand yuan per documentary that features me!"

The reporter immediately fell silent.

Then another of the foreign experts piped up: "I notice that Guojiadian now has a chamber of commerce, and I am told it used to be your Bachelors' Hall. That is a very interesting memorial of the past. Can I ask you, Mr Guo, if bachelors used to be a common sight in poor villages in China?"

"Put it this way," Guo Cunxian replied. "In the past there were three important events in the lives of each and every peasant – building a house, finding a wife and having a son. Once a son was born, then they'd have to think about building another house and getting another wife for him. One generation after another, this was the cycle of life. Building a house required money, and if you were so poor that you didn't even have a place to live, then it was going to be much harder to get married. When marrying a bride, you have to bring her to your house, so if you don't have one, how are you expecting any woman to put up with that? In the past, emperors owned lots of houses and so they were able to marry lots of wives – they had three palaces and six halls and seventy-two consorts. Are you telling me that this is all about love? And that when a poor man can't even marry a single wife it's because he doesn't want to? I refuse to believe that.

"Everyone is capable of love, but your ability to show it is naturally circumscribed by power, social status, wealth and reputation. There were once more than seventy old bachelors living in Guojiadian, and the oldest of them were fifty or sixty. I issued an order for them to get married, and offered a reward of nine thousand yuan to anyone who could introduce them to a suitable wife. A couple of years later our Bachelors' Hall was empty. And just this afternoon there was an attractive young woman from Hong Kong who was insisting that she wanted to marry a man from Guojiadian. So I have come up with a new policy, which will shortly be announced at a general meeting of the Party Committee. I am offering one hundred young men the opportunity to go abroad to study, and I will encourage them to seek foreign wives, pretty ones too! Whoever brings back a foreign bride to this village will get a big reward. I am going to fight for this, because I want foreign girls to come and marry our Chinese peasant boys. In future, when one hundred of our cleverest young men have married one hundred beautiful foreign brides, they are going to have really great kids. Having kids is a kind of wealth, the most important kind of wealth that any country can have. And this isn't just about having kids, the one hundred foreign brides means that we are going to have one hundred sets of foreign in-laws, and that means one hundred new sets of investors for Guojiadian!"

Ha, that really sounded wonderful! Pretty much everyone was smiling. However, mixed in among those who were genuinely pleased, there were those smiling bitterly or sarcastically.

What did he take these women for? As far as he was concerned they were just like pawns on his chessboard. He clearly hadn't given a moment's thought as to why they would want to marry a man from Guojiadian! And apparently they were supposed to be bringing fat bank accounts with them. He seemed to be setting an interesting condition on the whole venture – he didn't just want beautiful foreign women, they also had to be rich, ideally very rich indeed. That way the young men of Guojiadian would be like piggy-banks for him.

Guo Cunxian couldn't tell that people had other reasons for laughing. Providing that people laughed when he spoke, he was happy and proud. He'd provoked a reaction, his words were having an effect. He also liked to stop when this excitement was at its height, so now he stood up again and banged his chopsticks against his glass as a signal for everyone to quieten down: "I have another announcement to make. You have all come here to Guojiadian and I am not going to let you leave empty-handed. We've got various local specialties including cornmeal, mung beans, sesame oil and so on, all organic and what have you. If you want some, then please raise your hand. If you don't raise your hand you won't get any, because I don't want anyone accusing me of offering bribes."

Everyone thought this was just a joke, so to begin with nobody raised their hand. But Guo Cunxian wasn't smiling, and gradually a somewhat awkward atmosphere began to be felt in the hall. Guo Cunxian looked around the room and then said impatiently: "Since nobody has raised their hand, it means that nobody wants anything. That'll save us some trouble."

Immediately some people raised their hands. First it was some of the workers who had joined the group and reporters, and then some of the experts also raised their hand. If it was on offer they might as well take it, why should they refuse? Guo Cunxian's mouth curved in a slight smile and he raised his voice to say: "That's right! If you are asking a favour, you have to raise your hand." He had the restaurant manager make a note of those who had their hand up and then they were to be given their gift when the banquet was over.

After that Lin Meitang and Liu Fugen both stood up, and he addressed a final few remarks to his audience. "There is a rule here in Guojiadian – when we are at work, we work, and we put our efforts into solving problems. Once work is over, then we have meetings, which are used to discuss issues arising. Members of the Party Committee and managers from various companies are waiting for me, and I will have to leave you now. Please eat your fill, there is no need for you to hurry."

So the host of this evening was leaving and telling his guests to eat up, that there was no need for them to hurry. This guy really was a piece of work. He did his own thing, he paid no attention to anyone else, and he couldn't even manage the most basic politeness.

His visitors could only look on as he stumped out of the Alabaster Hall, his shoulders hunched. He never even turned around.

When one person is really afraid of someone else, what happens? As the saying goes, he wets himself out of sheer terror!

When Guo Cunyong got the message that Guo Cunxian was calling a meeting, his first reaction was a swelling in his bladder and a powerful urge to piss. He had to go to the toilet immediately. He had to go quick, and he had to keep pressing on himself, otherwise he would have peed in his trousers.

It wasn't the first time this had happened. For at least two years, whenever he'd got the message that Guo Cunxian wanted to hold a meeting, he'd had to go and piss first. When he had finished, even though his bladder was empty, he still felt the same intense need to pee, so he went back in, which made him feel a little bit better. When he got to where the meeting was being held, he'd have to go to the toilet again to relieve himself before he could meet with Guo Cunxian.

Guo Cunyong was an important figure in Guojiadian, and he had his own place in village life, but he'd been scared into developing this strange bladder weakness. However, on this occasion he restrained himself and picked up the phone to say in an unconcerned voice: "Why?"

Liu Fugen, that little brat, was now shouting into the phone: "You're asking me? I'm telling you that you need to keep your nose clean right now! Your little piece of fluff from Hong Kong has brought her kid to Guojiadian, and right now she's holed up with the Master in his office discussing the situation. You think your wife is an idiot? She's got a whole bunch of village elders out to complain to the Master, and they've nearly managed to bring down the roof on the village committee. The Master is so furious he is about ready to explode. You're going to have to pay for this, I can tell you."

Guo Cunyong's heart gave a sudden thump, and his brain seemed to have short-circuited – it was completely empty and he felt stunned. Then he started to shake and an icy grip seemed to fasten on the marrow of his bones, chilling him to the very heart. He rushed to the toilet.

The Black Forest was frantically busy with everything that had to be done before opening for business. There were bright colours and flashing lights, the music was thumping away at ear-splitting volume, and everyone was deafened. The staff were all unusually excited, running back and forward screaming and shouting at each other. In actual fact, there was no need for all of this rushing about; some people were there to make a big thing out of it all because they were bored, some had turned up to help but were just in the way, and others were just pretending to be run off their feet. There were also plenty of people simply out to enjoy the fun of the spectacle.

The Black Forest was Guo Cunyong's own project, but now all of a sudden he felt it was nothing to do with him. It was all over, it was time to give up and just close your eyes, this was the end. Right now he didn't want anyone to see him, and he didn't want to see anyone himself; he wanted to find somewhere where he could sit quietly alone. The best thing would be to go back to his own office at Eastern Commerce, where he had his own private bathroom.

Chu Fang, you silly little tart, you've ruined me... Guo Cunyong was now overwhelmed by a sense of regret and fear, much stronger sensations than the love and excitement that he'd felt at the time. Why couldn't his girlfriends be as clever as Ou Huaying? Why were they always as dumb as this Chu Fang? She could have come here at any time, so why now? Though if she came, it wouldn't necessarily be a problem; she should have come to find me first. Why on earth did she go straight to Guo Cunxian? What is she telling him? What is he going to do to her?

Maybe Guo Cunxian wouldn't do anything to her. Perhaps instead of punishing her, he's going to punish me? But how did Chu Fang get into a quarrel with Ou Huaying? Really, you can't keep enemies apart. Once Ou Huaying got wind of what had been going on, there were going to be problems. Chu Fang's brought the baby with her, so clearly she's trying to get money out of me, but is the child really mine? I've always wondered about exactly how she managed to get pregnant like that.

Guo Cunyong could well imagine how much excitement there had been in Guojiadian today. Everyone likes to complain about other people, they enjoy seeing someone else get into a fight, and when a harridan heads out into the main road to curse someone, the louder she shouts and the more foul the insults, the more they enjoy it. This evening he'd be the main topic for discussion in every house in Guojiadian, and they'd find the tale of his bigamy a nice little chaser to go with the food and drink. Fame can be a very frightening mirror. He was now a big man in Guojiadian, and he liked the face he'd acquired and he wanted to keep it. But how?

It was fear for the future rather than any present danger that kept him in its grip.

His house of cards was crashing down. Women really are a source of trouble. When you get to know one, everything is lovely and attractive. But the moment you decide that it's time to back out of the relationship, the problems start. Desires always grow – when it comes to women, men are left helpless. But every pleasure has its cost, and he'd always known that one day he'd have to pay for this.

He couldn't fight his fate!

In recent years he'd gone from dire poverty and endless difficulties to a position of wealth and power. If you can't satisfy your whims and fancies, what's the point of being clever and capable? Without fear and remorse, his pleasures would have lacked that extra spice of the illicit. If it wasn't for the fact that he was endlessly having to balance the two different lives, how would he have found the strength to carry on? But now, none of this meant anything. Guo Cunxian had a girlfriend on the side himself, so what could he do to him? Terror was inextricably linked with hope.

What he was really worried about was that Chu Fang's arrival would bring real disaster down on his head.

He hadn't been sleeping well for days and days. He was busy because he wanted the Black Forest open before Guo Cunxian could find him. With his car having been vandalised in the city, Guo Cunxian wasn't just going to let it go without asking any questions, and once he started his investigations it would quickly become obvious that there was a massive hole in the accounts. He needed the Black Forest to be a success because it would make him a lot of money. That would make him happy, and it might also keep the Master happy for a bit; and the longer that lasted, the more chance he would have to get the money to fill in the hole and get himself out of trouble.

Chu Fang's arrival had probably blown the bottom out of that particular plan.

Would Guo Cunxian not call him in first? Would he just go straight to the Party committee? That would take him down immediately. Guo Cunyong found himself trapped in a maze of sheer terror. He knew Guo Cunxian only too well, and he was the kind of person who could do absolutely anything; but no matter how nasty, he wasn't stupid enough to get caught. The fact is that Guo Cunxian had never been a real peasant, tilling the fields. Right from the beginning he'd worked the axe, getting up to one scheme after another, grasping at power. Now he had the power, and he was going to use it. The reason why he'd been able to become Guojiadian's 'peasant emperor' was because he was as ruthless as any real emperor. In the past, the big families in Guojiadian had taken it in turn to hold power in the village, but whatever their surname, none of them had remained in charge for long. That changed once Guo Cunxian took over, and over the course of several decades, nearly every position of power had been transferred into the hands of the Guo family.

Gradually, Guo Cunxian had stopped just being the head of the village and had become a lifeline for everyone living in Guojiadian. Nobody dared to fight him. To those who flattered and fawned on him, he'd hit hard but then forgive them; if they'd annoyed him or refused to obey orders, he'd strike without mercy, with an impressive venom. Over the past few decades, just look at the people in this village who'd crossed him in some way: which of them had come out of it well? They just dragged out a miserable existence from one year to the next.

If you wanted to get in on the act, then you had to throw in your lot with his, change your allegiance just as he, Guo Cunyong, had done. Back at the end of the Cultural Revolution, he'd helped Guo Cunxian, and then afterwards when he'd been courting Lin Meitang, the two of them had ended up being drawn together. To be absolutely honest, at the time he'd had no idea what was going on with Guo Cunxian – he was a married man with children after all. He hadn't known that he was using his power to force a young girl into bed with him. He'd put a lot of effort into buttering up Guo Cunxian in those years, but at no stage had he realised what was going on.

The fault was his own. He'd been the first person from Guojiadian to finish secondary school, and he'd thought himself pretty much an intellectual. He'd been ambitious and felt that his home town had nothing to offer him. He'd been good-looking too, over one metre eighty tall, with a powerful physique, handsome face and the air of someone who'd be going places. To put it baldly, he was the best-looking young man in the entire village, and everyone who saw him said that he'd got a great future ahead of him. He wasn't going to stay wasting his life in this hell-hole. He'd come back from the county town with a relaxed and free-spirited air, which really drove the girls wild. If he'd wanted, he could have had any girl he liked, but he'd liked the one that he couldn't have: it was Lin Meitang who'd caught his eye.

The two of them were about the same age, and they'd got on very well together, so it had seemed to many that they were an ideal couple. However, it had not worked out the way he'd hoped, and perhaps that wasn't such a bad thing after all. Supposing he'd married Lin Meitang but Guo Cunxian had carried on fucking her – what could he have done about it? He'd have had to put up with being a cuckold with everyone knowing about it. But it had always been a secret agony that he hadn't married Lin Meitang, and the pain had driven him to find other women. After all, the world is a pretty big place, and there weren't that many women in Guojiadian. Once you got away from the village, there were plenty of women far more beautiful than Lin Meitang. When a man marries the woman he really loves, it's easy to get caught up in that relationship; but when a man marries a woman who he doesn't care about, he gets a kind of freedom with it; he's free to fall in love with someone other than his wife. If you want the sex, you'll find plenty of women happy to oblige.

The more women he had, the more dissatisfied he felt. That had always been his problem.

Once he gave up the idea of ever marrying Lin Meitang, he found out that she was always on his side. She passed on information to him, she gave him ideas. He knew that she'd always cared about him. She was a woman, how could she possibly care for a foul old man when she had a handsome guy in love with her? Whenever the two of them met, there was a strange atmosphere, because they both knew how much they loved each other and how deep was the gulf that now separated them. If nobody else was there, they could talk openly, on every subject under the sun. The Viagra and other virility treatments that he was endlessly tasked with buying for Guo Cunxian in Hong Kong would be handed over to Lin Meitang, and she was responsible for giving them to Guo Cunxian when he needed them. This enabled Guo Cunxian to keep face, but it also reminded him of how close Guo Cunyong was to him. He didn't think of himself as a pimp, though that might have struck anyone else. He was giving virility pills to a man he hated, so that he could fuck the woman he truly loved!

Other than Lin Meitang, Guo Cunyong had had relationships with countless women, but none of them had lasted long. They were all short-term relationships and when it didn't work out, they ended up as enemies.

He understood that Guo Cunxian was the kind of person to bear grudges and it had taken a lot of work and a lot of patience over the course of some years to wear away his resentment. You could say that he'd turned himself into a dog. As long as Guo Cunxian kept moving forward, he was right there behind him with the loyal and submissive eyes of a dog. He didn't have a choice. If he wanted to work with the man, he had to show his obedience – and who doesn't bow down before the rising sun?

Guo Cunxian liked to curse Party leaders, he liked to say that they only wanted arse-lickers around them, but he'd turned out to be just the same himself. Guo Cunyong had had to find opportunities to say nice things about Guo Cunxian behind his back, and then make sure that these nice things were repeated to Guo Cunxian. Good God, he'd never spoken so respectfully even to his own parents! Wasn't there some kind of saying about how three things are important for a man? Power, money and women. The only people who ever say bad things about money and power are those who've never been face-to-face with real authority, or up close and personal with real wealth. They are the ones to blame everything on power and money. People make the same basic mistake over and over again – they dare to say the most about things they understand the least. The more incompetent, the happier they are to criticise others.

Three things – money, power, and sex – had all now become integral features in Guo Cunyong's life; the loss of any one of them would make life intolerable. Therefore from the moment he realised that Guo Cunxian was now keeping a close watch on his activities, he was unable to remain unmoved. He was in the grip of icy terror the entire time. Attending on a ruler is like attending on a tiger; partnering a 'peasant emperor' is even worse than spending time with a real emperor. Anyone who didn't understand quite how dangerous he was, anyone who failed to treat Guo Cunxian with the respect that he felt he deserved, was going to find themselves ripped to shreds.

As matters were now drawing towards a crisis, Guo Cunyong found that he had no idea how to proceed, and he'd completely lost any sense of direction in his life. He now weighed more than one hundred kilos, making him pretty big, and he had become used to his comfortable life – how could he cope with the problems now facing him? It is said that cheerful people get fat; being cheerful suggests that you don't get upset about stuff, that you are relaxed and confident, with a sense of humour. Getting fat suggests that you are successful, that you are doing well, it is a healthy kind of fat. He was now fat himself, but not at all cheerful. Normally when you looked at him you saw a pink face, glowing brightly. When he unbuttoned his suit jacket you could see a belt costing two thousand dollars stretched beneath his stomach. He looked successful, he looked like a boss. Who knew how much he suffered, how many things he'd come to regret? Are you really saying that there wasn't somewhere that you could have grabbed a few hundred thousand yuan? If you'd sent that money to Chu Fang earlier, would she have turned up like this to cause you all these problems? The saying 'Lucky in love, unlucky in life' is absolutely right. Given that you knew she was setting a trap, why did you stick your head in the noose? Each night of love was now going to be costing you three million yuan!

As he turned it over in his mind, Guo Cunxian kept thinking that his situation was now desperate. He blamed himself for being seduced by this woman, he blamed himself for his depravity. He realised that, in spite of all the years he'd lived, he was still capable of doing something utterly stupid. In fact all the dumb things he'd ever done seemed to be leading up to this moment. The moment he got himself into real trouble, he discovered what a coward he was. He had absolutely no idea how he was supposed to get out of this mess…

With pain, no matter how bad, there is always a limit. With fear, there are no limits at all.

Thump, thump, thump. Today the music seemed even more hellish than normal, and the sound was even louder and more thunderous, until it seemed to shake the very earth. Guo Cunyong appeared to be pursued by the thumping sounds from the Black Forest. He was breathing hard, he had pains in his chest, and his thin legs were no longer properly supporting the great barrel of his body, so he swayed from side to side as he ran back towards the company office along the most secluded route he could find. Although his mind was far from clear, he didn't forget to avoid pedestrians.

Peasants like to say that the best dog you have will never run faster than a scared dog. Fear adds wings to your feet. Guo Cunyong couldn't remember how many years it had been since he had run so fast, and all of a sudden he realised that his trousers were soaked through.

In disgust, fear and hopelessness he gritted his teeth and ran up the stairs to his third-floor office. When he got there, he was gasping for breath. He was trying to open his mouth wide and drag the air into his lungs, but his body no longer seemed under his own control. In an instant it felt as though countless needles were stabbing at his heart, his heart was rent in pain. The agony forced his fat body into collapse – he could feel himself being twisted by it, deformed by it, as he fell to the ground.

He immediately began to feel an intense, suffocating fear. The pain was becoming worse and worse, and he was feeling more light-headed, as if he was gradually starting to float. At the same time he could smell the dark stench of corruption and death coming from his own body.

A muffled moaning gasp escaped from him... and gradually faded into endless night.

All the most important people in Guojiadian gathered in the small meeting room at headquarters at the appointed time.

When Guo Cunxian called a meeting, no one dared to be late. If anyone turned up after the appointed time, it was him. He reminded everyone constantly that he was a peasant, and that peasants are used to rise with the sun and go to work, and that when the sun goes down they go to bed. That was all they needed to know, so why should they have to worry about the time? Guo Cunxian frequently forgot exactly what time he'd called a meeting for, or when people got together and started chatting with him, he enjoyed himself so much that he forgot that he was supposed to be holding a meeting. He did this because he was having fun.

However this evening he was smoking in silence, and the whole atmosphere was so heavy that everyone else hardly dared to breathe. They seemed to sense already that nothing pleasant was going to be discussed at this meeting.

Lin Meitang was standing beside him. She now reminded him quietly: "Secretary, it's almost eight o'clock."

Guo Cunxian didn't look up. "Is Guo Cunyong here?"

Liu Fugen laughed. "We've been looking for him everywhere but we can't find him. He also won't answer his phone."

"What does he think he is playing at?" Guo Cunxian erupted. "He's caused me a lot of trouble, so does he feel so embarrassed that he's gone off to hide? He can hide today, but what about tomorrow? I didn't say I was going to punish him! I'm afraid that nowadays the only people you can trust are the ones you have pinned down. The moment you let them loose, they're getting up to trouble!"

Ah well, and did the same criticism not apply to him himself? It was only OK for Guo Cunxian to say something like that; nobody else would dare. But those present weren't quite sure if he was saying what he really thought or whether he was just testing their response. Without being sure of what he was up to, they didn't know if they should be furious too, or whether they should keep their calm. However, it didn't seem to be a good sign that he'd gone off like that.

"Well, people have two problems in life – what to do when your desires have been satisfied and what to do when your desires are never going to be satisfied. It's just like how, when you're poor you want to get rich, and when you do get rich you discover that that brings its own problems." Guo Cunxian was muttering darkly to himself, and as he spoke he levered himself up off the sofa. "Let's go. We're moving this meeting to the Black Forest. Today is their opening ceremony and I am supposed to be cutting the ribbon, am I not?"

If Guo Cunxian wanted to go, then they must too. However, going out and getting an airing was better than being stuck in this atmosphere. Everyone looked pleased and got up from their seats, then they followed on behind Guo Cunxian as he walked out of the meeting room.

The evening air was damp, and it was mixed with the green smell of trees and mud, though every so often there was a whiff of nasty chemicals blowing in from the industrial zone. The night-time scene in Guojiadian was as confused and contradictory as its smells. The enormous rotating globe by the entrance to the village was alight, and it was shooting out all the colours of the rainbow in neon lights that went flashing high into the night sky. The industrial zone to the north of the village was dark, but there were regular flashes of light. Every so often a beam of light arced through the sky, flashing and shining, like a series of rolling thunderbolts. By comparison, the western part of the village was quiet, the sky there was dark and the smoke curling up from fireplaces hung in the air.

Paris Avenue was located right in the middle of the village, with shops and nightclubs lining both sides of the road the entire way. They all looked different, with various sign-boards, brightly-coloured and brand new, each announcing what they could offer. Some of these places had bright lights flaring, attracting attention; some looked dark and mysterious; some had loudspeakers out by the door, and the noise was earth-shattering; some had beautiful girls and huge bouncers standing in front, like Beauty and the Beast.

The Black Forest stood in the most desirable location in the busiest part of Paris Avenue. It was a brightly-coloured four-storey building, with a nightclub, recreation centre, sauna and restaurant all under the same roof, together with various other entertainment options. As an eye-catching feature there was a two-metre-tall money tree standing by the entrance, with coins and notes hanging from every golden branch. That had already attracted a crowd. Luckily they'd thought to hire security to marshal the crowds and prevent anyone from touching it. However, some folk simply couldn't resist the temptation of all that money, and the moment the security guards took their eye off them, they stuck out their hands to touch it.

Guo Cunxian cheered up the moment he saw the Money Tree and the dark clouds covering his face vanished in an instant. He couldn't stop himself from praising the idea. *Cunyong may be an idiot, but he does have good ideas sometimes.*

The Black Forest was in a panic. Even though the time for the opening ceremony had passed and all his VIP guests had arrived, Guo Cunyong was nowhere to be seen.

The manager was a thirty-year-old man named Jia Zhenkui, and he looked as newly-scrubbed and nervous as a bridegroom on his wedding day. When he was informed that Guo Cunxian had arrived, he hurled himself down the stairs and nearly fell the last three flights. This was a wonderful opportunity. Having Guo Cunxian over the doorstep was a real coup for the Black Forest. It didn't matter if any one else had failed to turn up, since Secretary Guo's presence was sure to get them off to a good start.

Jia Zhenkui assisted Guo Cunxian up the stairs, explaining what would happen in the opening ceremony for the Black Forest.

Right then the lights were blazing, everything was going hammer and tongs, wine was being poured as if there was no tomorrow – what was he going to say? The people who were talking were shouting their heads off; the people who heard them weren't bothering to listen. Guo Cunxian seemed to remember that the Black Forest had hired nine Russian hookers. He stiffened slightly and then nodded his head in approval.

Although he might not come right out and say so, it was a fact that Guo Cunyong was a pretty smart guy. God knows where he'd managed to lay hands on them, but the moment word got round that there were Russian girls in Guojiadian, everyone for miles around would come rushing to see them – officials, rich men, curious men and all – like flies around a honey-pot. Paris Avenue was going to make him even more of a fortune on the back of this.

But how did Guo Cunyong find out that he wanted to bring foreign brides to Guojiadian? Was he thinking that these Russian girls would be the first round of foreign brides to come to the village? Unfortunately Russia was a bit poor, and these girls would have done their stint as hookers first – if that got out it really wouldn't sound too good. Right now, everyone was envying the people of Guojiadian for being so rich, but if they found out that the foreign brides coming to Guojiadian were all former prostitutes, there were some very nasty connotations to that.

Guo Cunxian was bustled forward into the main room on the third floor.

Jia Zhenkui waved his hands for the musicians to stop, and then he bellowed out his announcement, his neck thrust forward: "Secretary Guo has come in person to attend the opening ceremony for the Black Forest. This is a really great day for all of us here!"

Naturally that caused a round of applause, and once the sound of clapping died away, he moved smoothly on into an invitation for Guo Cunxian to say a few words. The main room fell silent, and Guo Cunxian looked round at the young faces and the girls in their low-cut dresses. His eyes started to shine, and his face took on a gentle and easy-going expression. He cleared his throat and asked: "Right now I should be in a meeting with the Village Party Committee, so do you know why I brought them here?"

He answered this question himself: "Before the Black Forest formally opened, people came to me to complain. They said that Paris Avenue is becoming a red-light district, and that Guojiadian is being ruined. That is the reason I decided I had to come here for myself, to show you my support, to make sure that you carry on! I think that Guojiadian is doing just fine now, and in future we are going to do even better! Others are jealous of our money, so they spend all day cursing us, and they try and find any excuse to criticise us. In spite of all of that, we're doing well, we live in nice houses, we eat wonderful food, everybody owns a car, and we've all got so much money in the bank we couldn't spend it all in two lifetimes. Men have wives, women have husbands, everybody lives in a happy family and we've all got good jobs. How can anyone say that Guojiadian is being ruined? What was so great about going hungry and being unable to get married?

"Just think back to how it was when a woman walked along the road and all the bachelors would have their eyes out on stalks! I haven't seen any 'red-light district'. Round here a red light is just a light, a really pretty and auspicious light. For National Day they hang red lights up all over Tiananmen. I am guessing that, when you go home, you've all got wives to hug, you've all got children to play with. But nowadays in Guojiadian we've got tens of thousands of migrant workers who come here, all unmarried men and women. They are people too, and it's good for them to have somewhere to go and have a bit of fun when they get off work. We can't run Guojiadian like a monastery or nunnery – there is a way that people live when they have money, when they come from a developed place. Whatever they have in the developed countries in the West, we're going to have too. These things are here for a reason. This fact can be compared to the way that weeds grow in fields: if there aren't any weeds, you certainly won't be able to grow crops there either.

"It is because people have great desires that they have great motivation and great satisfaction. Right now people in China know how to work hard, but they don't know how to enjoy themselves. They think that business carries risk, but they don't understand that pleasures can also be risky. Those with money don't understand how to enjoy their opportunities. If you are going to carry on just like before, what's the point of getting rich in the first place? And here I might add that entertainment is a business too, and money in your pocket never stinks.

"I have just been meeting with a couple of dozen foreign economists, and we were talking about how everyone agrees on one common principle at an international level: the main characteristic of money is that you can never have enough. The richer you are, the richer you want to be. Because of this, the more you have the more you want to have, it is never enough, and this has been a major factor in human progress. A dying old man with moneybags stuffed with cash advertises in the papers for a wife, and hordes of twenty- and thirty-year old beautiful women answer. Why is that? Society has changed. Nowadays we mock the poor, not the whores. Today nobody would think of despising a multi-millionaire, and it doesn't matter where his money came from providing there's enough of it. For other people, the ability to achieve great riches is enormously attractive, and the stories everyone wants to hear, the most exciting news, is always connected with money…"

Afterwards he announced the decision of the Village Party Committee (which was of course his decision) to offer financial incentives to encourage one hundred young men from Guojiadian to marry foreign brides. Guo Cunxian's speech was naturally greeted with many acclamations: some in the audience were shouting their approval, some were clapping, some were laughing and some were stamping their feet. Nowadays, men weren't dreaming of getting married any more, they were dreaming of marrying rich, foreign brides.

Two Russian girls with blond hair and blue eyes now walked forward from one side of the room. They were wearing silk brocade cheongsams tied with a gold silk belt, and between them they carried a red silk ribbon. They went to stand right in front of Guo Cunxian. Another pair of girls, both really pretty, came and stood either side of him, and they helped him put on a pair of white silk gloves. Then Jia Zhenkui opened a handsome box and took out a pair of pure gold scissors that he placed in his hand. While everyone watched, he opened the golden scissors and then slowly cut through the silk ribbon, almost as if he were a conductor raising his baton. The music then started blaring and the sound of clapping resounded through the room.

Jia Zhenkui put the golden scissors back in their box, and turning around he handed them to Liu Fugen, who was standing right by his side. Afterwards he came forward and asked Guo Cunxian in a low voice: "Would you like something to eat? Or go to the sauna? Or would you prefer to go to one of the private rooms to sing karaoke?"

Guo Cunxian shook his head at all of these options. After a long silence, he spat out a few words. "I am going to dance."

Dance? That was not something that any of the people present had considered. When did Guo Cunxian learn to dance? Jia Zhenkui smiled and said: "How about you go to a private room to rest for a moment, sir? I'll bring some girls along for you to pick from as soon as I can."

"No, I am going to dance here," said Guo Cunxian, pointing to the other members of the Party Committee. "You'd better find them dance partners too."

Lin Meitang took Jia Zhenkui off to one side and whispered to him: "The secretary is really doing right by you. Think about it, it's going to be huge news that he'd come here to dance, and it'll be a great advertisement for you. Who will complain about the Black Forest in future? You'd better pick out one of the better Russian girls for the secretary as quickly as you can."

How was Jia Zhenkui supposed to know which of the Russian hookers Guo Cunxian would think the best? He let Lin Meitang choose. This was one of the reasons Guo Cunxian had never dumped Lin Meitang – if it happened that he decided he wanted to try something different, that he needed sex with a new woman, he knew that she, Lin Meitang, would find out and so he didn't bother trying to hide it. Lin Meitang would choose someone for him, she would pay the woman off once he was finished with her, and she would never show the slightest sign of jealousy or quarrel with him about it.

In the end, Lin Meitang picked out a girl called Natasha who could speak Chinese. She was slim and long-legged, and wore a lavender halter-dress that showed off her narrow waist and pert breasts. With a bewitching smile fixed on her face, she flitted over towards where Guo Cunxian was standing.

Guo Cunxian was enchanted and found himself immediately excited.

The orchestra had chosen an old song to play for him, which was slow and soothing. Guo Cunxian took the girl stiffly in his arms and began to walk through the steps. The girl's eyes were deep and sultry, an effect highlighted by heavy indigo eyeshadow. She looked straight into Guo Cunxian's eyes and seemed to see right down to the very bottom of his heart.

Guo Cunxian found her fixed gaze a bit uncomfortable, and he wanted to put an end to this awkwardness. However, he needed to give his full attention to his feet and didn't have time for anything else. He also knew that carrying on like this would tighten his screw and when his screw got tight, he'd find it hard to get it going later. He had to say something. He knew that once he got talking he'd be fine. Once he said something, then this foreign whore would no longer have control over the situation.

"You speak Chinese?"

The girl rolled her eyes. "I don't speak well, so I wouldn't say so, but I can speak some."

"Well done! Where did you learn?"

"I studied electrical engineering at university, and after I graduated I spent two years learning Chinese at a language school in Beijing."

Guo Cunxian had obviously never imagined that she was a university graduate, and he was feeling all the more excited and interested: "How come you ended up doing this kind of work?"

"What's wrong with this kind of work?" The girl turned her blue eyes away from him, exaggerating the effect of her question. However, she had no intention of making Guo Cunxian feel awkward, so she told him the real reason very straightforwardly.

"I'm doing this to earn money – it's all about the money. Once I have enough, I'm going to go back home and open my own business."

"Good. There is a lot to know about earning money, and it is a woman's right to get it off a rich man. After all, if your partner is rich and you are pretty, you each have your own advantages. In that sense you are equals. There is no need to complicate things that are in fact perfectly straightforward. Right now we are not in a dog-eat-dog situation. Everyone can live in their own way, and they have the right to succeed on their own terms."

"You really are a great boss!" The hooker had a clear and bell-like laugh. Guo Cunxian felt that her enormous blue eyes seemed to fill her face.

"How right you are, and I am the boss in charge of all of the bosses here. If you want to open your business here, I can help you. This place is open for anyone to do business, and whatever it is that you want to do, we will encourage you and provide you with the necessary investment. What do you think? Think about it, and once you've made up your mind, then come and find me."

The girl looked amazed. Clearly this was no ordinary dance partner. He wanted to talk much more than he wanted to make a move on her, and added to that there was his coarse and brutal appearance. The whole thing was really quite odd. He seemed very out of place.

Guo Cunxian found it impossible to keep his mouth shut in the presence of this woman. He kept trying to find things to say. "How much does the Black Forest pay you per month?"

"I get two thousand and I can keep my own tips."

"In a bit I'll give you two thousand as a tip."

"Wow, thank you!" The girl went up on tiptoe and kissed him quickly on the cheek.

Guo Cunxian was now in full swing, and he squeezed her hand a little bit more tightly, and he could feel the girl's warm breasts brushing against his chest. The music was adding to his excitement and he began to feel a strong sense of desire. The more aroused he felt, the more he carried on talking, partly to hide the fact and partly because he wanted to seduce this girl in a way that he was used to. He now began to show off his 'philosophy of wealth', investing his theory with real emotion: "Money is how rich people show their love and affection. It's a very simple and straightforward way, and throughout history, it's also been the easiest. There's actually no real difference between the people who pursue wealth and the people who pursue women. Rich men and whores are a natural pair. If you know the guy is rich and he's not throwing cash at you, keep well away from him."

The Russian girl looked somewhat confused but she nodded her head. Her eyes glittered seductively. "You're wonderful and I love you!"

"You need to be careful with that kind of thing, sweetheart! When a woman tells a man that she loves him, he's unlikely to take no for an answer afterwards. Whether it is good feeling, or sympathy, or attraction, any of these things can result in a relationship developing. Once you embrace, once you kiss, then you're getting the passport into the other person's private space. Today we've embraced, and just now you kissed me…"

Just as he was enjoying himself in the way that men have since the dawn of time,

Lin Meitang came forward with a horrified expression on her face and told him that Guo Cunyong's family had just found him dead in his office. Guo Cunxian stiffened and then immediately let go of the girl he'd been embracing. Whatever it was that he'd been about to say was cut short, but he didn't forget to mouth a few words at the Russian girl before turning around and walking away.

Lin Meitang came over and looked Natasha up and down. She put her right hand into her handbag and took out a bundle of notes. She had a good feeling for money now, and when she had to pay a bill she didn't need to count, or even to look, she could just use her thumb and index finger to peel off just the right number of notes. She'd been told to pay this woman two thousand and that was what she was going to get, no more and no less. She smiled gently as the Russian girl thanked her, and then walked off quickly to catch up with Guo Cunxian.

24

EVEN IN DEATH, GUO CUNYONG CAN STILL GET YOU

At this point in time, the only person in Guojiadian who dared to express a contrary opinion or make demands of Guo Cunxian was Chen Erxiong, who continued to turn events in the direction he wanted them to take and was prepared to stand up for his own ideas. This was an opportunity for him. Guo Cunyong hadn't been buried yet and there was an awful lot of gossip in the village; in fact there were all kinds of stories making the rounds about how he'd died. Thinking that this was a moment when Guo Cunxian was likely to be too rushed off his feet to resist, Chen Erxiong handed him a report in person, explaining that he wanted to turn his chemical works into the 'Four Seas Chemical Group'.

He knew that this was a sensitive issue and that no matter how carefully he worded his report it was still just a document that Guo Cunxian might well never even bother to look at. The reason why he went in person to hand it over was so that he could explain its importance himself. All he wanted was for Guo Cunxian to give him the nod; he could manage everything else himself. When Chen Erxiong got to meet Guo Cunxian face-to-face, he did indeed carefully explain the drawbacks and limitations of the present management of Guojiadian's chemical works. There were now a number of small companies affiliated to the main one, and these small companies had various small work units attached to them, but they were not properly organised, and some of them were given far too much work to do, while others were left entirely idle. In some instances, the multiplicity of functions they'd been accorded was forming a choke point, some were having problems paying their workforce, some were tasked with things they couldn't do, and some were not being given the big jobs that they were fully qualified to take. In the context of the current situation of the chemical industry at home and abroad, if Guojiadian didn't form its chemical works into a conglomerate, it would hinder further growth in this sector.

By now Guo Cunxian realised that Chen Erxiong had already built up the chemical works into his own little empire. Furthermore, he had no idea that this was even happening. It was a long time since he'd given a thought to industrial development – he spent every day on his endless political schemes. By now every single important position in Guojiadian's chemical empire was held either by someone who'd come up through the business with Chen Erxiong, or who'd been hired in from outside by him. Chen Erxiong had complete control over every aspect of the chemical works in Guojiadian. Whether it was the business side or the technological side, he gave the final word, and most important of all, the contacts with other companies outside all went through him. Developing this company into a group was clearly Chen Erxiong's move, since there could be no other candidate for CEO. And thinking this over, he deserved it, since he built this empire and now he ruled it. The chemical works might have been founded by Guo Cunxian, but it had been built up from pretty much nothing by Chen Erxiong.

But what was now going to happen to Liu Fugen? His official position was that of deputy manager of the chemical company, and the company paid his salary. In the village he also had the title of assistant to Guo Cunxian, but that was just to make it easier for him as he came and went. If the chemical company formed itself into a conglomerate, was Chen Erxiong going to allow Liu Fugen to carry on working there? For many years, Guo Cunxian had noticed that Chen Erxiong made a huge contribution to the village economy, second only to that of the iron and steel works. This did not surprise him at all; when he'd first established the chemical works he knew this was an industry with a great future and would be earning them a lot of money. That was the reason he'd sent his adopted son, Liu Fugen, to work with Chen Erxiong. Officially this was so he could look after him, but what he was actually there to do, Chen Erxiong knew as well as anyone. The problem was that Liu Fugen had realised that Guo Cunxian's own son was too young and so he'd managed to insert himself into the family. However, he'd turned out to be lazy and idle. There were all sorts of good jobs going that he could have taken on, but instead he'd done nothing. In the last ten years or so, the little chemical works had gone on to build up dozens of affiliated businesses, but Liu Fugen had just carried on partying, not even noticing what was going on.

His job at the chemical company seemed to involve showing his face at the office in the breaks between the eating, drinking and enjoying himself. When he'd had enough of partying at home, he'd go off on a holiday abroad. Chen Erxiong would give him however much money he asked for. Sometimes he'd appear if there were visitors from other places, and then he'd get to show off a bit. At the same time, he had another special position – he was Chen Erxiong's personal representative. Whenever Chen Erxiong needed Guo Cunxian to agree to something, he'd always send Liu Fugen to represent him in discussions with his adoptive father. Since this had been the case for such a long time, people had come to feel that Liu Fugen and Chen Erxiong were one and the same person: one was in charge of external matters and one in charge of internal affairs. They seemed to be joined at the hip in this. Liu Fugen did whatever Chen Erxiong wanted him to do; the things Chen Erxiong had, he shared with Liu Fugen. However, once this chemical conglomerate took shape and established itself, Chen Erxiong wouldn't want Liu Fugen to represent him any more; in anything important, he'd want to appear himself.

Guo Cunxian felt threatened and asked Chen Erxiong: if you form this conglomerate then won't it be as big as the village one, in which case who will be giving orders to who? Chen Erxiong said that the village conglomerate ought to be restructured to include the head office of the entire group, which would in turn be solely responsible for the management of both arms – just like a commander-in-chief in the army. Guo Cunxian suspected that Chen Erxiong had already got together with a number of his own subordinates, so he wanted to test him on this matter: is this your own idea or have you already discussed it with others?

Of course, Chen Erxiong immediately realised what was bothering Guo Cunxian, and he claimed he wasn't the kind of person to do something so stupid. He explained that this was entirely his own personal opinion but that he'd been thinking about it for some time, so today he'd finally decided to formally make representations on the subject.

"You're the first person I have talked to about my idea. I reckon that, if I were to announce that I was reorganising the company as a conglomerate, Ou Guangming would immediately follow suit, though I don't know about Wang Shun and Jin Laixi. However Qiu Zhantang's electronics factory still hasn't really found its feet, so at present he won't want to bother with this. The fact is that Jin Laixi has done very well with his building company over the last few years, and he's going to do even better in future. The problem is that he's a right schemer and half the time you have no idea what he's up to. If you were to hold a meeting and explain the current situation, I'm sure everyone would follow you. Where Guojiadian scores is in the capacity we have for production and the economies of scale. If we want to maintain this, we are going to have to develop strong systems and attract management talent who can take us to the very cutting edge. That way Guojiadian will remain competitive. If we don't restructure the management frameworks in Guojiadian, it's going to have a very negative impact, limiting our future development. There are all sorts of work units in other places that have called themselves conglomerates. Anyone who didn't understand the situation here might imagine we're a bunch of clowns without any know-how – that's naturally going to affect their willingness to work with us. If you give the word to allow the companies under your control to reorganise themselves at the same time, it will save a lot of aggravation in future. Everyone will then be admiring how far-sighted you have been."

Chen Erxiong explained it all very carefully, and what he said sounded entirely sensible; in fact, he seemed to be thinking of what was best for Guo Cunxian. But this made Guo Cunxian start wondering all of a sudden whether he was getting old. Was he going to start having problems keeping up with small fry like Chen Erxiong? He now asked: "Once you've reorganised the company, what are you going to do with Fugen?"

This was getting right down to the heart of the matter.

Chen Erxiong had prepared his answer carefully: "If Fugen wanted to, he could certainly stay in the chemical group as a deputy CEO. The problem is that he's never been much interested in that kind of work. He just wanders in and out. It seems a shame not to give him something to do. He's perfectly capable of achieving great things, and if he's going to take over from you one day, then he'd better be appointed to the group headquarters to serve as acting CEO under your command. That way he'll learn how to keep an eye on the bigger picture, and one day he'll be ready to take over control of Guojiadian from you without any major hiccups."

In some ways, this was exactly what Guo Cunxian wanted to hear, but in other ways it stabbed him to the heart. He tried again to find out what Chen Erxiong was really up to: "The fact is that, throughout all these years I've been testing you, your greatest asset is your thoughtfulness and the way in which you always act in a measured and considered way. Everyone knows that you take just thirty minutes to eat your meals, and then you head off to the company while you're still chewing. If I were to hand Guojiadian over to you one day, I'd be happy and I'm sure everyone else would be too. If I were to take you into headquarters, would you do it?"

Chen Erxiong was visibly appalled. He went quite white and then his face flushed red as he vigorously shook his head: "Secretary, you really don't understand me at all. I am not interested in politics in the slightest, and I simply cannot undertake such a terrible responsibility. I am just a businessman. If you insist on bringing me in, I am just going to have to resign my job and go back to being an ordinary person. I'll find some way to build up a company for myself from scratch, set up my own chemical works. In a few years maybe I'll have my own conglomerate anyway, just like the one here in this village."

Guo Cunxian laughed: "I know you! If that were to happen, it wouldn't just be 'like the one here in this village'. It would be twice the size of ours. If you go, then most of the management of our chemical works and all the customers would go with you. Of the ones left behind, who could compete with you? I want you to give up the idea of going it alone, Erxiong, because I am telling you that I will never let that happen. Just think about it for a moment: if you are going to set up your own business, how much is that going to cost? I'll just give you that money. You can have whatever position you want in Guojiadian, and if you want to move to the headquarters then you can. If you don't want that, then stay and build up your own conglomerate. My only concern is that Fugen is used to doing absolutely nothing, and if I promote him people are going to be unhappy about it. Though of course I am not going to let him get away with being idle any more."

"You read too much into things, Secretary. You built up Guojiadian from nothing. If you choose to promote someone, nobody is going to say anything at all, particularly not if it involves Fugen. Haven't you noticed, he's changed a lot recently? In the past, official and noble families often prepared their heirs in this way. Fugen is infinitely better than any of those layabouts from rich families."

"What the hell! Are you comparing me to some local big-wig or nouveau riche pig?"

"What's wrong with being a big-wig? Come to think of it, why should a nouveau riche person be a pig? You've created a huge business here, a model for other people, so how could any of them compare to you?"

"I've already told Fugen to go to Eastern Commerce and take over from Cunyong. With Cunyong dying like that, somebody has to deal with the day-to-day problems, and he needs the experience."

When he heard Guo Cunxian say that, Chen Erxiong silently breathed a sigh of relief. Finally, he'd managed to get rid of that tiresome little sod.

What he said was: "You really do keep the bigger picture in mind, Secretary, and you make your move at just the right moment. It is most impressive the way that you have managed to turn the problems caused by Cunyong's death into another triumph!"

Guo Cunxian was very pleased that he'd managed to find his adopted son such a good position. He went on to agree to Chen Erxiong's proposal and permitted him to restructure his company. However he did not say that other companies could do the same, nor did he mention whether or not the Guojiadian Group was going to be transformed into the office managing each of the conglomerates. He thought that 'Group Head Office' didn't sound as fancy as 'Group'. After all, Group Head Office was just an office but Group was a conglomerate. He thought that ordinary people wouldn't understand which one was the important one and which was not. In addition, he was still interested in seeing what the other people would do. It is exhausting to live in a situation where there is nobody that you can absolutely trust and nobody can trust you. You have to spend all your time arranging safeguards, and when you sleep it is with one eye open. Whatever happened, you had to pay attention to all the possible angles, to avoid falling into a trap. Everyone was out to get you, but they were also all victims of your machinations.

Whatever else you might say about him, Guo Cunyong had been an important figure who'd done a great deal for Guojiadian. That he'd died at the age of just over forty was very sad and unexpected. To show how much Guojiadian appreciated him, Guo Cunxian now made a decision: he wasn't going to be cremated, since burial was the only thing that would be good enough for him, in addition to which it would comfort his family.

Once the secretary said this, his subordinates knew what they had to do. They spent two thousand yuan on buying the body of a beggar, which was then cremated under the name of Guo Cunyong. Of course they also had to spend some money on buying off the staff in the crematorium. Supposedly what went into the coffin was Guo Cunyong's ashes, but in actual fact it was his body, and they made sure that very few people other than family members were present on this occasion.

Items worth several hundred thousand yuan were also stuffed into Guo Cunyong's coffin. He wore a gold necklace as thick as a rope round his neck, a Swiss watch worth more than twenty thousand yuan on his wrist, there were gem-set rings on every finger, and in his pocket there was his regular mobile phone that had set him back more than eight thousand yuan. On one side of his head they placed a tape recorder, while on the other was a camcorder, and a colour television rested beneath his feet. With a full appreciation of Guo Cunyong's needs in the afterlife, they'd put a stack of notes underneath the body, in every denomination from one hundred yuan down to singles. He'd earned so much money in life, he was allowed to take some of it with him in death. He would be buried in luxury with money to pave his way in the underworld, otherwise it just wouldn't have been right.

Guo Cunyong's coffin was naturally also extremely luxurious, being made from three cubic metres of expensive cypress wood and constructed on a grand scale – otherwise how could it have been appropriate to contain all the fine things placed within it? Guo Cunxian had started out in the coffin-making business, but he had never made such a fine one. The whole of Guojiadian could see how much the secretary had valued Guo Cunyong, and sending him on his way in such style showed his appreciation.

Once the coffin lid was nailed down, it was time to bury him.

Early in the morning the day after he was buried, just when it got light, Guo Cunyong's wife was there beating down Guo Cunxian's door. On opening it, he saw Ou Huaying kneeling on the ground, dressed in full mourning and knocking her head against the ground, weeping and wailing and begging that the secretary help her.

Guo Cunxian assisted her into the house, but he had no idea what on earth could have happened. He asked her to tell him, but he was rather annoyed at her because he felt she had a tiresome and difficult personality. No wonder Guo Cunyong had died young! The funeral had been held with such pomp, why should she be dissatisfied? What did she have to be running round here first thing in the morning to complain about?

Ou Huaying screamed: "Secretary, someone's robbed Cunyong's tomb…"

"What!" Guo Cunxian's head was ringing as if he'd just been hit with a baseball bat. However, he immediately pulled himself together and stopped yawning. What a horrible thing to do! There had been stories about people robbing old tombs for the treasures buried within, but why dig up a new one? Was this just about the money, or was it some kind of revenge? According to tradition the recently dead could transform into powerful ghosts, but who could hate Guo Cunyong so much that they were prepared to risk digging him up when he was newly buried? Guo Cunxian really couldn't quite believe it. Maybe it was all because Guo Cunyong had died so suddenly, Ou Huaying couldn't cope and she was having a nervous breakdown that involved seeing things. But when he went with Ou Huaying to the grave site to have a look, he could feel his skin prickling and the hairs rising on the back of his neck.

Guo Cunyong's tomb had indeed been dug up, and the lid of the coffin had been thrown some distance away. His body had been stripped and was now lying naked to one side. Everything that had been buried with him was gone; there was nothing left. Among the villagers of Guojiadian, Guo Cunxian was someone who'd seen something of life, and indeed he'd seen many dead bodies, but he'd never seen anything like this. He was absolutely furious: "Who the hell did this? They're going to have to pay!"

He calmed Ou Huaying down by saying don't worry, we have our own police station right here in Guojiadian now, and they will get whoever did this. Nobody outside the family knows that there were valuables in the coffin with Cunyong, so the culprit must be someone here.

Ou Huaying pointed out that she knew perfectly well who'd done it.

"Who?"

"Lan Xin!"

"This had better not be something that you've just made up. We need real evidence."

"I have evidence that Lan Xin helped some woman dig up Cunyong's grave, and they hired in two people from outside the village to help."

"You mean Guo-Chu Fang?"

"What do you mean Guo-Chu Fang? Her real name is Chu Fang and she's some little whore that Guo Cunyong picked up in Hong Kong who puts a man's name on her own in order to hide the kind of work she does. It's all her fault anyway that Cunyong's dead. She brought terrible bad luck to him and killed him years before his time. I wasn't having a hooker anywhere near us, so I didn't let her see Cunyong one last time, and I wouldn't have her at the funeral. I told her that if she dared to show her face, she'd be taught a lesson she'd never forget. We were all so upset, and I didn't want any trouble when we were burying him. Who could have imagined that the bitch was so vengeful that she'd fuck Lan Xin until he agreed to do this for her?"

"Why do you say that Lan Xin's been seduced by Chu Fang?"

"Don't you know? Lan Xin is famous throughout the village for jumping any woman who holds still. He took advantage of the fact that Chu Fang was here all on her own without anyone to help her. Plus besides which she was the woman of his old enemy Guo Cunyong. He's been humping her for a while, but that was all about taking revenge on Cunyong. This tomb robbery wasn't something Lan Xin was going to be able to think of without her help, and even if he considered the idea, he wouldn't dare actually do anything. But now he's killed two birds with one stone. Chu Fang wanted to see Cunyong one last time – she'd come all the way from Hong Kong and wanted to see him alive or dead. But in addition to that they've stolen everything that was buried with him, which means they've had their revenge. Anyway, having done this, Chu Fang's already gone before the tomb robbery was discovered – even before it got light some people from our village saw her being driven to the train station in Lan Xin's car. Clearly he was getting the bitch out of here. Secretary, you've got to help me, Lan Xin has broken open my husband's tomb. He's caused great distress to a widow!"

"This is appalling. Do not worry, if he's guilty he's not going to get away with it!"

When Guo Cunxian got back to the village he told Liu Fugen to round up a group of young men. Some of them were sent off to put Guo Cunyong back into his coffin and bury him again. Others were sent out under the command of Guo Chuanliang, the new head of security in Guojiadian, to visit all of the Lan family's haunts, arresting Lan Xin and turning up passbooks with a value of several tens of thousands of yuan plus more than four thousand yuan in cash. The passbooks didn't matter, but the cash was a problem – that had quite possibly been stolen from Guo Cunxian's tomb before being divided up among the Lan family.

The world turns, but who could have imagined that things could change so fast or in such profound ways? Industrial development in villages was booming, and these companies were making money hand over fist. Meanwhile, many of the state-owned enterprises in the city could not keep up with market demand, and they began to fail; some of them even went bankrupt or simply had to close down. Even Dahua Steel Corporation found itself in such serious financial trouble that it could not pay its workforce, and so Li Yike, who had previously been head of supply and marketing but was now already deputy CEO, came to Guojiadian to ask Ou Guangming for help.

Outside the main office of Guojiadian's iron and steel works there was now a huge sign that read: 'Sun-Moon Iron and Steel Group'. It was designed to strike the eye and impress anyone who saw it. However Ou Guangming remained very friendly and he took Li Yike's hand in his and simply would not let it go: "I am so pleased that you think so much of Guojiadian that you are prepared to come and ask us for help. Way back when, if it hadn't been for you in Dahua Steel, our Sun-Moon Group could never have come into existence. Tell me, how much do you need?"

Li Yike had now turned bright red, and he was stammering: "Well, in addition to paying the salaries of our workers, we also need to think about how to get back on our feet again. We've been having problems with liquidity, so in total we are going to need over thirty million yuan…"

Ou Guangming took the promissory notes and accounts out of Li Yike's hands and summoned his accountant. He told him: "I want you to transfer enough money into this account immediately to pay off all these loans."

Once the accountant had gone, he said to Li Yike: "You send someone to the bank to tell them that I'll pay this current round of loans off for you. In future if you need more, just let me know. You don't have to come all this way, you can just tell me on the phone."

Although this transaction involved a huge amount of money, Ou Guangming was able to arrange it in the space of moments. Afterwards he insisted on inviting Li Yike to lunch. Li Yike wiped the sweat from his forehead and said that he didn't feel like eating, he had to get back to the company as quickly as possible and report, because this afternoon they needed to be able to pay their workers. We employ a lot of people, so we can't have them going without!

This was a transaction that involved a huge amount of money. Besides which, saving a huge business in a crisis is also a significant event. It would even sound good when put in this way to the upper echelons at Dahua Steel. However, when Guo Cunxian found out what had happened, he nearly kicked over the dining table. Fortunately it was heavy, and he didn't have the strength to overturn it. Thirty million yuan could have bought you the whole of Kuanhe County not that many years ago. Why should Ou Guangming just hand over that kind of sum without the slightest quibble? Where does that leave me? Am I still in charge here? Who is actually in control of Guojiadian?

Guo Cunxian clearly understood that he had become a figurehead; although nominally still in charge, he was becoming more and more sidelined. There were even people who were prepared to say that, with Guo Cunyong dead, it was lucky that Guojiadian still had four good men, the 'Four Bosses' – Ou Gangming, Chen Erxiong, Wang Shun and Jin Laixi. Where did that leave him, Guo Cunxian? Apparently he wasn't a boss any more, he was reduced to the position of a statue in a temple. People show their respect and you just smile in silence.

Guo Cunxian had no intention of just being a figurehead. He had been wondering whether he was right in allowing his subordinates to establish groups. Just as he had expected, the moment Chen Erxiong announced the formation of a group, so did Ou Guangming. It looked perfectly straightforward: if the chemical works could become a conglomerate, so could other work units in Guojiadian. They were proud that their companies were now called a 'Group'. So far Wang Shun and Jin Laixi had not yet dared to follow suit, but some villagers were already calling the companies they were in charge of the such-and-such group: they were the Four Bosses. When people become powerful, their authority, their ambitions, their face and so on grow accordingly. They want to take control for themselves, and they want the same respect shown to them as to anyone at headquarters.

Even though Guo Cunxian was furious, he didn't make a complaint to Ou Guangming directly. Instead he asked Lin Meitang to give Ou Guangming a call and find out what he was really up to. Lin Meitang made the call right in front of Guo Cunxian, and asked him why he hadn't reported to the secretary that he was handing over such a massive sum, totalling more than thirty million yuan? How could he do this on his own authority? What he was not anticipating was that Ou Guangming would show himself to be entirely unrepentant: "What do you mean, a massive sum? I regularly deal with sums in the tens or even hundreds of millions – it's perfectly normal. Do I have to report every single transaction to the secretary? This is my group's money, not anything to do with headquarters, and I can tell you right now that it won't have any impact on how much profit we turn over to the village at the end of the year."

"This is my group's money…" The group was his, and he could do whatever he liked with it, nothing to do with you. Guo Cunxian now began to understand that the rich layer-cake that was Guojiadian had been cut into four pieces: one piece went to each of his old henchmen, but he'd been left with the empty plate. He was furious. In the past Ou Guangming had been one of his closest cronies. If it hadn't been for his help he'd never have been able to get married, and he had started the iron and steel company all by himself, beginning with the agreement with Dahua Steel. He'd built it up from scratch, why should Ou Guangming have it? When he started out he had complete control, but somehow or other he'd become distracted later on, and he'd only managed to keep track of personnel. He'd failed to keep financing in his own hands. Did that mean he'd just handed Ou Guangming everything without a murmur?

How much Guo Cunxian now regretted his past actions! If only he'd played divide and rule among his subordinates, even if there were dozens, even hundreds of work units, they would have been answerable to him, and he would have been necessary to maintain an equal balance between them. Even if there were loads of them and just one of him, it would have been easy to keep them under control. He'd been tricked; he had fallen into Chen Erxiong's trap; he felt as if he'd been persuaded to stick his own head into the noose. Were all of his subordinates now going to turn against him?

Just as Guo Cunxian was worrying about this problem, he heard the sound of shouting outside. He wondered if another woman had turned up, or whether there'd been a second death.

It was Lan Xin's father, Lan Shouyi, who was screaming for justice outside Guo Cunxian's office. Yesterday his house had been searched from top to bottom, and all of his assets had been frozen. Without access to their bank accounts and cash, how was his family supposed to manage? Lan Xin had always been a problem to them, but now he'd been beaten half to death with injuries all over his body, and he might well die if this carried on. Lan Shouyi was now at the end of his tether and seeing no other way out of the situation he'd come to beg Guo Cunxian for mercy. But he hadn't even been allowed into the building, so all he could do was stand outside and shout: "I want to see Secretary Guo! My son is innocent!"

It was not surprising that this had attracted the attention of a horde of curious onlookers. Some were locals from Guojiadian, while others were casual labour from outside. With every moment that passed, the crowd got thicker. The security guard on the gate held Lan Shouyi back. He knew that, without Guo Cunxian giving the word, he would not be allowed into his office, and if he did not speak to him face to face, his problems were not going to be solved. Realising this, he became more and more stressed; and the more anxious he became, the louder he shouted. He was shouting that they were innocent. The louder he shouted, the more likely it was that someone would pay attention.

"Secretary Guo, our whole family has done nothing wrong! I swear on my very life that Lan Xin didn't rob the grave. The day it happened he was visiting his aunt. He came back really early because he was afraid of being late for work. Secretary Guo, please say the word. Otherwise he's going to die."

Guo Cunxian told Lin Meitang to summon the head of security, Guo Chuanliang, to the office. "How is your investigation into the Lan Xin case going?" he asked.

"He's pretty tough," Guo Chuanliang reported. "No matter how hard we hit him, he won't confess."

"Do you have any evidence?"

"If he won't confess, how are we going to get any evidence?" Although Guo Chuanliang was supposed to be in charge of law and order, he seemed to have no idea how to achieve results in this case other than by hitting Lan Xin. The peasant police under his control were only interested in beating people up – that they enjoyed, but they didn't have a clue how to investigate a crime and gather evidence.

Guo Cunxian shook his head. "There was loads of stuff in Guo Cunyong's coffin. There was the television, the camcorder, his mobile phone... if you don't find those things, you are not going to be able to convict Lan Xin. The passbooks and the cash you found in his house doesn't prove anything. If you can't make anything of this, you are going to have to set him free."

"What do you mean, set him free? That's letting him off far too lightly. His father is out there shouting about his innocence, so if we let him go, we'll just look useless. After that, how are we supposed to put the fear of god into people?"

Guo Chuanliang was an idiot, but he was also Guo Cunxian's cousin's son. He might not be a close cousin, but he was still a Guo. Because of this he imagined that he could get away with anything and didn't care who he offended with what he said.

Guo Cunxian was now feeling a curious nostalgia for the days when Ou Guangming had been in charge of security. They had been very hard and difficult days in Guojiadian, but there hadn't been any trouble on his watch. Now he was rich and famous, he had everything he could possibly want, but it was just one damn thing after another...

Just at that moment the shouting from downstairs became even louder. Guo Cunxian stood by the window and looked out. It wasn't just Lan Shouyi who was shouting about how his son was innocent, he'd been joined by a few other elders from the village who were singing the same tune. They were clearly trying to annoy him, and he cursed. "Bastards! When you need them they can never help you out, but it's not enough just to be useless, they also have to pour oil on the flames! Why can't they just do what the Party Committee tells them to? What do they think they are doing? Do they imagine they can get away with this? Do they think they can give me orders?

How am I supposed to maintain order if they are going to carry on like this? They are clearly just trying to annoy me, trying to show off, and I'm not going to let them get away with it."

Guo Chuanliang had been standing in the door, and now he told him: "Lan Shouyi is just looking for trouble. When is he going to give it a rest? If he doesn't find this situation embarrassing, if he's prepared to wash his dirty linen in public, then take him out into the main road and give him a good cursing, teach him a lesson. Your lot are all uniformed police, so you can say you're investigating a criminal case."

Guo Chuanliang was pleased when the secretary gave the word, and he ran downstairs with a few of the lads in uniform. They dragged Lan Shouyi out into the main road and started to 'teach him a lesson'. They began by spitting at him and cursing, but then they decided that this was far from adequate, so they started to punch him and put the boot in. The more they hit him the more they enjoyed it; they were now punching even harder, stamping on him. Although on other occasions these might have seemed perfectly nice and normal young men, if they had the opportunity to hit someone and get away with it, they felt that they might as well take it. Why not? Once the violence began, they became more and more excited, more and more daring, and as they hit the man, they totally forgot what this was all about. They forgot that they weren't supposed to hit him at all.

In the end, the violence became an end in itself. They hit him again and again, their eyes bloodshot and their heads ringing. They hit him with whatever came to hand. Some of them used belts, some of them had sticks, and the worst used hoses tipped with iron, fortified with iron joints. Guo Chuanliang danced around them, screaming like a madman: "Kill him! Kill him and I'll take any blame for it!"

It took just over ten minutes to beat Lan Shouyi, at nearly sixty years of age, to death. Those who hit him hadn't finished enjoying themselves, and so they cursed him furiously: "Old idiot, how come he's so useless?"

This violence brought more than two hundred people to the scene, but not a single one dared to stop them.

Lan Shouyi's daughter hadn't been arrested because she was already married. On hearing the news she rushed to the scene and tried to flag down a passing car to take her father to hospital. There were several hundred cars in Guojiadian, but not a single driver dared to do this for her. Since there was no other choice, she borrowed a pushcart and loaded the old man onto it so she could take him to the village clinic. The doctors in the clinic were not willing to make any effort to save him, so after a few moments they had him moved into the morgue. Maybe this is what people call 'an abuse of power' because we are talking about the power of an individual. This meant that no one in the village was prepared to help someone who had crossed Guo Cunxian; it meant that innocent people became accessories in a murder; it meant that evil men were able to do whatever they liked because a powerful man would protect them. As you will have grasped, Lan Shouyi might have survived, but after a few hours in the cold of the morgue he really was nothing but a corpse.

When Guo Cunxian heard that Lan Shouyi had been beaten to death, he was furious. He shut himself up in his room and ground his teeth with rage. What a bunch of little bastards, not one of them the slightest use to me – all they do is cause trouble!

Did I or did I not tell you just to teach him a lesson? Whatever he did, he didn't deserve to die; and even if he did deserve to die, it shouldn't have been at your hands.

Guo Cunxian was the kind of person who could be cajoled into something, but not forced, and he was not about to herd his subordinates out to take the blame without appearing himself. It was not long before he'd decided how to deal with the matter: a mistake had been made, but it was too late to worry about that now. He had to put pressure on everyone to keep this under control. He would use his authority over Guojiadian to whip up public anger over how the Lan family had robbed Guo Cunyong's tomb, then take stock after Lan Shouyi's funeral. Once things had calmed down, it might be possible to offer the Lan family some kind of financial compensation for what had happened.

That very afternoon a platform was erected on the road in Guojiadian where Lan Shouyi had been beaten to death. Guo Cunxian summoned the entire village to the scene for a struggle session. A number of the guilty men were sitting in a line on the platform, sipping tea without a care in the world. The family of the dead man had been dragged out by peasants in police uniforms and were now standing with their heads bowed at the foot of the platform. Most unusually Guo Cunxian was present, and he personally took charge of this unpleasant situation. He stood up and said: "Lan Shouyi deserved to die. He was guilty of terrible crimes." In order to encourage the villagers in the direction he wanted them to take, he went on: "If you've got the guts, come up here on the platform and expose Lan Shouyi's crimes. If you don't have the guts, stay there and curse."

This was classic Guo Cunxian. He had held innumerable meetings, and he knew how to hold an audience. In fact he was a very fine speaker. Today wasn't about setting forward an argument because he didn't have a leg to stand on, so what was left was appealing to people's baser emotions, while using his authority to prevent anyone from complaining. Once the meeting was over he organised a massive parade through the streets, and since he thought there wouldn't be enough villagers to achieve the kind of thing he had in mind, he tried to call on a number of workers from outside. When it was pointed out to him that most of them were going to be needed at work, he gave orders to close the schools and had the teachers lead the students out onto the streets. He needed to mobilise all his forces against the Lan family; he needed to prevent them lodging any kind of formal complaint. Guojiadian was nothing but a village, and even if it had been twice the size it still wasn't that big. Having a parade of ten thousand men marching around the village was a huge crowd. They really made an amazing amount of noise. As they advanced, they stuck up posters proclaiming: 'The Lan family think they're above the law, they deserve their punishment!' They were also shouting: "Beating Lan Shouyi to death is no crime. He deserved to die!"

Guo Cunxian had completely miscalculated the situation. If you make people feel they have nothing to lose, even a cornered rat will turn and bite you. Have you not noticed how the world works nowadays? Even if you are powerful, even if you have control, it is only in Guojiadian. You don't have power and control in Kuanhe County, let alone in Dahua City. Once the Lan family went to the police, professional policemen arrived in Guojiadian, the murderers were all arrested and every single one of them was convicted.

The whole episode had been a terrible shock to Guo Cunxian. Not only did the police in the county seat and the city pay no attention to him; they showed the tens of thousands of people in and around Guojiadian that the law applied to him and his boys. He was publicly humiliated in his efforts to save them. He shut himself up in his office for nearly a month over this, refusing to see anyone at all and sometimes even refusing to eat. He kept asking himself what he was going to do now. He hated the Lan family, but he also felt sorry for them. When it came to Guo Chuanliang and the lads who'd been convicted, he was angry, but he also felt that he'd let them down. If he hadn't said what he did, none of this would have happened, he'd ruined their lives. Even worse though was the thought that this had made him see how small and useless he really was, that there were things he just couldn't do. A couple of real police had turned up and shown him quite clearly that he was irrelevant, and all his efforts had achieved nothing...

The moment his thoughts turned in that direction he began to boil with anger, and it got worse whenever he caught sight of anyone wearing a police uniform. In fact, he gave orders that the police uniforms he'd been sent should all be burned. He'd originally been so proud of having his own station, but the moment there was a crisis it was revealed to be a fake, completely useless. But are you telling me that the regular police have never beaten anyone to death? Aren't police stations full of ghosts of the innocent dead? But when did you last see a policeman being convicted of his crimes?

After all our efforts, it turns out that people still feel entitled to treat us as second-class citizens. Fine, we'll stay on our own turf in future, where we can do what we like. You may think I don't matter, but right here in Guojiadian, you'd better think again! He gave orders that everyone in the village was to give money to the men who had been sentenced, and assigned a standard to this: every two hundred households in the village were responsible for supporting the family of one of the men in prison.

Because of what had happened, Guo Cunxian concluded that he really loathed the police, but in spite of this feeling, the police decided to come and cause problems for themselves. In fact it was Sun Wenda, a teacher at the Criminal Investigations Department in the Dahua Police Academy, who was the one to suffer his ire. Sun Wenda picked this as the time to bring out a group of police academy students to conduct a social research project in Guojiadian, and he had them wearing police uniforms. The moment they got out of the cars and set to work, the people in Guojiadian could feel the hairs rising on their scalps – what had happened now? Then they found out that it was students from the police academy doing some kind of project, so they gradually calmed down. Naturally they continued to throw spanners in the works whenever they could and acted with open hostility, cursing them in the foulest way, to show how much they hated the police. Guo Cunxian was also furious when he heard about this, and was quite sure that the police were up to something. However, when he went out in person to investigate, he discovered that it was indeed a bunch of children, all dressed up in police uniforms. He asked a few questions but realised he wasn't going to get anything out of it. He then left word that his people could do what they liked and then walked off in a huff. This was to give them an opportunity to take out their anger on these students.

Guo Cunxian's subordinates thought that they ought to be allowed to get away with beating people up. It was one of the perks of the job that they really enjoyed, and they believed it added to the 'authority' of Guojiadian. At the same time, there is an old saying: 'Troubles never come singly'. People have been saying that since ancient times, so there must be a reason. Ever since Guojiadian had seen a couple of its sons convicted and sent to prison, there was a feeling in the village that everyone was waiting for the other shoe to drop.

Liu Fugen had arrived at Eastern Commerce in a perfectly cheerful mood, ready to take over Guo Cunyong's position, but when he started to look into the situation, he discovered that it was just an empty shell: in addition to owing the bank more than two hundred million yuan, there was a hole in the accounts to the tune of more than seventy million yuan. Liu Fugen was furious – he'd originally been under the impression that his adoptive father had found him a cushy number, but now it turned out that everything there was a mess. He wasn't used to the idea of work at the best of times, and he had no idea how to go about sorting out the problems. Instead he pounded round to headquarters to moan about how there was absolutely no money left in Eastern Commerce. Guo Cunxian exploded with rage the moment he heard this. He wasn't just angry about the hole in the accounts, he was furious that everyone at Eastern Commerce had been keeping the dire situation secret from him.

He'd always thought that Guojiadian was under his control, that nothing took place there without him knowing about it, but now he realised that Guo Cunyong had stolen vast sums from under his nose, and nobody had ever even whispered that there might be a problem. This wasn't the first time either. Ou Guangming had lent some outsiders tens of millions of yuan without saying a word to him, and now it turned out that one of the companies owed the bank more than two hundred million yuan, with more than seventy million having been embezzled. Add that to the thirty million... Useless! They were all completely useless!

In his fury, he remembered how other people had once tormented him, and he decided that the time had come for Guojiadian's first investigation team: he himself took the position of team leader, with Liu Fugen as his deputy, and they burst into the offices of Eastern Commerce demanding to see the books. Although Guo Cunxian had always claimed to hate investigations and being investigated, that was just because he'd been a victim. Once the time came for him to do the same to someone else, he started to see the charms of this process.

Yang Zusheng was the chief accountant at Eastern Commerce. This middle-aged man, dressed in a neat suit and with a humble look, now walked into the office of the CEO to bear the brunt of Guo Cunxian's interrogation. Liu Fugen was standing on his left, Lin Meitang was standing on his right, and behind him there were four security personnel in uniform. Guo Cunxian hated the police, but he liked to be surrounded by men in police-like uniforms. It was all very odd.

Yang Zusheng was pushed into position, standing in front of Guo Cunxian. It was Liu Fugen, however, who asked the questions: "Yang Zusheng, you're the chief accountant at Eastern Commerce, so how do you account for such a huge hole in the accounts?"

Yang Zusheng explained the difficulties of his position perfectly calmly: "Although I have the title of chief accountant, I've actually never had any authority. When senior management made decisions about the business, they simply ignored my advice, and even the other accountants in my division felt entitled to ignore me. Whenever the boss wanted to gamble in Macau, I had to give him as much money as he asked for – we had enormous overheads. There were also some extremely peculiar decisions being made about the business, so it's no wonder there's a huge amount of money missing."

"Why didn't you report this to your superiors?"

"I reported it to Guo Cunyong I don't know how many times, but he never paid the slightest attention."

"So why didn't you report it to headquarters?"

"I didn't have the right to appeal over his head. Besides which, if the staff in my own department didn't trust me, nothing good would come of reporting problems to those higher up."

Guo Cunxian suddenly started shouting: "Bastards! You're all completely useless! You're none of you here to work, you're here to ruin Guojiadian!"

Yang Zusheng was shocked, but he very quickly recovered. Having been silent for a few moments, he began to explain: "It's not fair to say that, Secretary Guo. When we were hired by Guojiadian, we were hoping to do great things here, but gradually we found ourselves being sidelined, none of us have any real authority. You don't need me to tell you that there is an unwritten rule here in Guojiadian that unless they marry a local and have kids, people hired in from outside aren't given positions of real responsibility. We're just here to make you look good..."

"Stop blaming other people! I reckon you've been at it yourself. How much have you embezzled?"

"Nothing. I haven't taken a penny. Secretary Guo, I want you to go through the books and when you find that I haven't been stealing from the company, I'm expecting an apology!"

"An apology? You're really expecting me to apologise to you! OK, I'm going to tell you what happens next. As of now you are being stripped of your position as chief accountant, and you are going to have to cooperate with our investigations. When you came here, you were a piece of shit, so now you've gone back to where you started. That's fair, isn't it?"

Yang Zusheng shook his head with a bitter smile. "What kind of language is that? Secretary Guo, you're a respected figure, and you think it is OK to speak to people like that?"

Everyone has aspects of their personality that they would prefer stay hidden, and if one of them should be exposed, they will naturally take this very badly. One of the security guards standing behind him now lunged forward violently, and hit Yang Zusheng two powerful blows across his face. All the while he cursed him: "Who the hell do you think you are! How dare you speak to the secretary like that."

"Good for you," Guo Cunxian said. "I'm rewarding you with five thousand yuan!"

Lin Meitang immediately took a thick stack of one hundred yuan notes out of her bag and handed them to the security guard.

Having taken the money, the security guard went down on his knees in front of Guo Cunxian and started hitting his head against the floor: "Thank you, Secretary, thank you so much!"

Yang Zusheng was stunned at being physically assaulted. However he now pulled himself together and murmured: "Secretary Guo, do you still imagine that you can get away with hitting people?"

When people are reminded of failure, they are almost never going to take it kindly; the usual response is hatred and violence. Guo Cunxian stood up and walked slowly over in front of him. Then he raised his hand and slapped him across the face. "Who's been hitting you?" he giggled. "Has anyone here hit you?"

Yang Zusheng was stunned. He could barely believe what was happening to him.

Guo Cunxian now spoke with a malevolent tone: "You've always got so much to say for yourself, so why don't you speak? Go on, say something!"

Power is a kind of drug, and prolonged exposure to power results in poisoning. It clouds the brain, making the subject imagine that there is nothing he cannot achieve. He looked at Yang Zusheng, an educated man who had come from the city hoping to earn big money here. He had already been beaten to a pulp and was standing there looking stunned. Then Guo Cunxian waved to the four security guards who had escorted Yang Zusheng in: "Take him away and interrogate him thoroughly!"

Liu Fugen had taken over control of a company that turned out to be on the brink of bankruptcy, and his dream of becoming one of the richest men in Guojiadian had been destroyed. There was no way he could go back to the chemical group because his position there had gone in the restructuring, so what was he supposed to do now? He was quietly furious with Chen Erxiong for getting rid of him like that. He'd always thought that Chen Erxiong was his best friend. It was true that at one point he'd been deputy manager in charge of the daily running of the company, but he'd either not bothered to turn up, or he'd made stupid decisions that then had to be rescinded. Liu Fugen had then demanded in a face-to-face meeting with Chen Erxiong that he be given a work unit to practise his management skills on, but he'd just hemmed and hawed and nothing had ever materialised. The fact is that he'd always been trying to keep Liu Fugen at arm's length. That was how Chen Erxiong always behaved, and he'd said time and time again, I don't do deals with people more powerful than me. Of course, Chen Erxiong didn't imagine for a moment that Liu Fugen was more powerful than him, it was Guo Cunxian who he was thinking of. But Liu Fugen was there representing Guo Cunxian.

He'd questioned Yang Zusheng for the rest of the day, but with no joy. The fact of the matter was that nothing good could come of this. The company was bankrupt and there was only one thing left to do: sooner or later it was going to have to close down. Liu Fugen was feeling depressed and had ended up drinking far too much, and then on his way home, he happened to catch sight of Lin Meitang twitching her arse from side to side as she unlocked her front door. His rage and disappointment now seemed unbearable. He rushed forward and dragged Lin Meitang indoors, locking the door behind them, and then he slapped her across the face as hard as he could.

Lin Meitang was shocked at being hit like that: "Fugen, have you gone completely insane?"

Liu Fugen raised his hand and slapped her again: "I am mad. But it is all your fault, you've driven me to it. You deserve to be slapped about for how you've made my adoptive mother suffer all these years."

Lin Meitang was not the kind of person to let him get away with this. She hit him and punched him right back, cursing as she did so: "Who the fuck do you think you are? How dare you do this to me! How dare you hit me! Why don't you take a good look at yourself?"

The two of them ended up wrestling. Liu Fugen then suddenly stopped hitting Lin Meitang and grabbed hold of her, though she carried on punching him. Then he tore off her clothes and pushed her onto the bed, climbing on top of her...

Perhaps even he felt disgusted by what he'd done. After he'd finished raping her, he threw up twice and then put his head down and went to sleep.

When he woke up again, it was almost dawn. He discovered that he was lying naked in Lin Meitang's bed, and so he sat straight up, pulling the covers up across himself. He was then startled to see that Lin Meitang was bending over the ironing-board, ironing his clothes. Hearing his movement, she stood up and smiled at him. "You're awake," she said.

Liu Fugen was looking sheepish and he did not dare catch her eye. If the Master found out about this, there was going to be the most almighty row. After a long, long pause he mumbled: "I am so sorry, I was drunk last night, I hit you. I don't know how I could have done something so awful. I am so sorry, I hope you can forgive me."

Lin Meitang grabbed his clothes and walked over. She was in a generous mood. "I'm very happy to hear you say sorry. For that, it was worth being hit last night. The fact is that people have very complicated relationships and our situation has been awkward for years – sooner or later you were going to take it out on me. If you want to simplify a complicated situation, hitting someone is the easiest way. Now you've hit me, we can all move on. You can stop being angry, you can feel that you've done something for your adoptive mother. Now we can get on better together."

Liu Fugen was feeling guilty and rather frightened. "I feel really bad about what happened. Did I do anything other than hit you?"

Lin Meitang opened her eyes wide and said: "What, you think hitting me wasn't enough? What else did you have in mind? While it's true that I'm not that much older than you, and I don't have any kind of position in your family, the fact remains that I'm your father's second wife. Everybody in the village knows that! Yesterday you threw up all over me, so I've had to be up for hours tidying up. When I finished cleaning you up, I had to wash your clothes. I don't have anything here that a man could wear, so I was worried that you wouldn't have any clothes to put on this morning – you certainly can't spend all day in my bed! So I ended up having to get out my iron and dry them for you that way. Come on! Time to get dressed."

Liu Fugen got dressed and then went down on his knees beside the bed. "From here on in you're going to be treated like my mother, and I won't dare to show you the slightest disrespect." Suddenly he burst into tears and clutched at Lin Meitang's legs: "Nobody's ever spoken to me like that before. Everyone's looked down on me since the day that I was born. In my original village they treated me like dirt.

Everyone said that I was the illegitimate son of a man with a limp, who'd once worked in the commune as a pig-herd. Later on Uncle Guo came along. He saved my life, he really loved me, and so he became my adoptive father. But nobody in Guojiadian takes me seriously. They may not do anything nasty to me but that is just because they respect my adoptive father. The fact is that they despise me, they say I've had it too easy all my life, and there are even some who say I'm Guo Cunxian's illegitimate child, that he humped some woman when he was off making coffins. The only person in Guojiadian who's ever been at all nice to me is my adoptive mother, she's the loveliest person in the world, but I know that she goes off by herself to cry over what's happened. I ought to hate you but I can't. I'd never dare to touch you normally, but then last night I hit you when I was drunk…"

Lin Meitang hugged him. She was feeling deeply depressed. Her tears rained down on Liu Fugen's head. She then made him get up and sit properly on the side of the bed. Putting her hands on his shoulders, she spoke softly to try to comfort him. "I know you've been under a lot of stress lately, but why are you making yourself so miserable? Even if Eastern Commerce goes under there are lots of other companies in Guojiadian. One of them has a place for you. The secretary is going to live for another twenty or thirty years at least, so you've got plenty of time to find your feet."

This made Liu Fugen feel much better about himself. At the same time he was forced to the conclusion that all of these years he'd seriously underestimated Lin Meitang. He'd despised her and that was unfair. She was a most unusual person, and it was no wonder that his adoptive father stuck by her…

25

A FOOL CANNOT DEAL WITH A BASTARD

C onfusion reigned in a huge empty room at Eastern Commerce. There was the sound of shouting, someone begged for mercy, there was screaming and confessing. A string of huge characters had been inscribed in black on the white walls: 'Honesty in business, correctness of thinking'. If this had read: 'Obedience will be rewarded, resistance will be punished', then this place would have been a prison. Another thing was different too – prisons don't have CCTV. But this place was being filmed by Guojiadian TV, who were in a position to record everything that happened during the interrogation. This open access had been decreed some time ago by Guo Cunxian. They were supposed to be recording developments as they occurred in Guojiadian, in order to have documentary evidence of every important event.

The interrogation lasted deep into the night. Liu Fugen kept in mind that he was in charge here until such time as Eastern Commerce actually closed down, so he asked a whole series of searching questions of Yang Zusheng, but no matter how long they went on at him, they still weren't getting anywhere. He was exhausted, and so he headed off to one of the other rooms to grab a bite to eat, then he nodded off. The men who stayed behind completely misunderstood what he wanted them to do – they thought he was deliberately taking himself out of the way so that they could torture Yang Zusheng in peace. Plus, besides which, the previous day they'd seen with their own eyes how the first person to hit Mr Yang had been rewarded with five thousand yuan, so now they were thinking that this was their chance to earn a similar reward for their labours. The result was another appalling bout of violence that saw Yang Zusheng beaten to death.

Sometimes it seems that hitting people is as addictive as any drug, or perhaps violence is infectious? Seven people had just been dragged away from Guojiadian in handcuffs for beating someone to death. The worst offenders had been sentenced to seven years in prison and those who got off lightest to a mere three years. Now those who hadn't been arrested last time carried on in the same old way. Why didn't they realise their mistake? Why did they hit this man even harder?

Lan Shouyi's children, who lived right there in the village, knew enough to get the people who killed their father put in prison. Yang Zusheng came originally from Tianjin, and he'd been invited specially to bring his expertise to Guojiadian – why should anyone imagine that his family would keep silent and just put up with what had happened? The so-called 'Young Master', Liu Fugen, had no idea how to deal with this situation, and he immediately started to panic. He had, however, been to school, and he still remembered learning the saying 'An eye for an eye'. In his terror he rushed off to see Guo Cunxian, to tell him the news that Yang Zusheng had been killed.

The doors and windows in Guo Cunxian's sixth-floor office were all tightly closed, with only a little skylight open a crack for ventilation. He was lying on a huge soft bed, the frame of which was elaborately encrusted in gold, with his two bare feet propped up high and the pillow for his head down low. This was the way that he'd been brought up to sleep since a child, as resting with your head low and your feet high was supposed to slow digestion and stop you from feeling hungry. Now he had more than enough to eat and would never have to worry about hunger again, but when he lay down to sleep, he still arranged himself in this way; it had become a habit. Lin Meitang was lying naked next to him. She was woken up by the sound of running footsteps and a hasty opening of the door, but she knew that there was only one person who had a key and would dare to come in to interrupt them, and that was Liu Fugen. She was therefore in no particular hurry to get up and dress.

The person panicking here was Liu Fugen. This was not because his adoptive father was sleeping with another woman – Lin Meitang wasn't 'another woman' to him any more. The problem was that, the more he thought about how Yang Zusheng had been beaten to death, the more worried he became. This time, he might well be going to prison himself, because the man had died in his office while he was supposed to be questioning him. As a result, his reporting of what had happened was more than confused...

Guo Cunxian sat bolt upright in the huge bed. He was now fully awake and aware of the dangers, but he made sure he appeared completely unconcerned. "Who did it?" he asked.

Liu Fugen stammered out the names. There were four men involved: Guo Chuanzheng, Jin Dabin, Ou Tingyu and Guo Chuanbao. The situation in the village right now isn't great, and I can't deal with this. People are still worried about what happened last time, everyone is afraid. I've already given orders that Eastern Commerce is going to close down and the workforce will be let go. Investigation into what happened has also been temporarily stopped. Once this is over, we'll see what we want to do.

Guo Cunxian shook his head gently. "I want you to remember, Fugen," he said, "in this kind of situation you need to keep a cool head. A fool cannot deal with a bastard! If you want to take charge here, you have to make sure that people are afraid of you. That works much better than trying to be friendly with everyone.

"The problem is that the lads took advantage of my absence just now, and look what they've done! They just rush into things without thinking. They are really hard to control.

"If you can't control them, that's your problem. Right now, we need the lads – they're useful to us. Every dynasty since time immemorial has been founded on the work of lads like them."

Guo Cunxian closed his eyes again and sat in silence on a corner of the bed. He seemed so concentrated. In the face of this problem he appeared amazingly calm and confident. However, in actual fact he was perfectly well aware that things were slipping beyond his control, that the situation in the village was becoming more and more complicated. He understood full well that, as he tried to direct events to his liking, there would be things that he could not do, but he could think of no better way to proceed. There was one thing that he could never forget: in a crisis he needed to demonstrate his authority, and the simplest way was to put pressure on people. He needed his thugs to keep power in Guojiadian. As long as he could protect his power-base, he could deal with whatever problems might be thrown up. As he sat on the bed, he wanted to say a few words, but once he began to speak, he had to stop for a while. He seemed to be trying to give instructions to his adopted son, but he also seemed to be trying to cheer himself up.

"Once you know how society works, you can see that people are born for different destinies. Some are born to take charge, others to have charge taken of them. Whatever your circumstances, you will have to deal with them. What has happened here in Guojiadian shows what you can do when you fight. I've achieved one great thing in my life – I've become rich and famous because of the power I have here. In China, power comes from the land. Ever since ancient times people have fought over cities and farmland. Whoever has land can make himself powerful. But what is land? You always have wilderness right next to fertile farmland, and after the rains come, the weeds grow like nobody's business. In a few days you can see a lushness of growth far greater than that found in your fields. We are seeing that rain now, and we need to be on our guard against the growth of weeds that will come. We need to keep the hoes ready in our hands. The most important task right now is to keep the situation calm, to control the weather, to make sure we don't experience any more storms…"

In spite of all the advice that Guo Cunxian had given him, Liu Fugen was still confused about what he should do. Guo Cunxian therefore had no choice but to explain in detail. "You and the four lads need to go into hiding. We can't handle it like we did last time."

"Where should we go?"

"Go? I told you to hide, and the first thing that comes into your mind is running away! I'm sure the police will be expecting that! Therefore the safest thing to do right now is to go nowhere. You should hide right here in Guojiadian. This is our village and we're in charge here. If the lads don't want to hide in their own houses, then they've got loads of friends and family, right? The village is pretty big, so there's plenty of room to hide a few people, isn't there?"

He now turned his head to give instructions to Lin Meitang: "Give each of the lads some money – it can be a reward for all their hard work. Anyone who can keep them safe will get a further reward in future. We're rich, and spending the money will be easiest for us. In fact, if we can solve this problem by spending some money, then we will. However, you should also make sure that the news gets out that all the people concerned have run away."

Guo Cunxian no longer cared about how rich Guojiadian was; money really didn't mean that much to him. What he really needed was the power to control the situation as it developed.

Once they had got rid of Liu Fugen, Lin Meitang immediately started to put his orders into effect. Guo Cunxian remained sitting up in bed alone, and he smoked one cigarette after another until the room was filled with smoke. After that, he got up. He needed to make a phone call, and there were six gold-plated telephones up on the sixth floor for his personal use – one on the table at the head of the bed, one on his desk, one by the mah-jong table, one next to his massage table and one by the lavatory throne. However, he waited until everyone had started work, and then he went clumping down to Lin Meitang's office on the fifth floor, wearing shoes where he'd stamped down the heels so he could slide his feet in like slippers.

There were some things he wanted to say to his subordinates face to face because he wanted them to understand how much he did for them, and he had no intention of repeating his instructions. He also liked to see his people looking amazed and impressed, and perhaps saying a few words about how much they admired him.

He told Lin Meitang to dial up the number of the incident room at Kuanhe County police station, and then he took the receiver and said: "My name is Guo Cunxian, and I'm the Party secretary at Guojiadian. I have something to report. Last night we had a murder committed here. Just as we were questioning Yang Zusheng about the financial problems at Eastern Commerce here in Guojiadian, a group of people suddenly burst in and beat him to death. Do you think you could come?"

He spoke lightly, almost as if the matter were beneath his notice. Although he'd said he wanted to report a crime, it might be more accurate to say that he was giving them orders. When she heard what he said, Lin Meitang got busy herself, since she needed to tell the people at Eastern Commerce to prepare their testimony in accordance with the secretary's initial phone call.

What the people of Guojiadian were not expecting was that police cars would come out from the city that very afternoon. They went straight to the offices of Eastern Commerce. Soon afterwards the four officers in plain clothes were taken to an empty building where Yang Zusheng had been questioned and then beaten to death. Three police officers went into the building and one remained outside to keep an eye on the surroundings.

Guo Cunxian was immediately informed of their arrival, and he was deeply displeased. He'd reported the crime to the county, so why had police come out from the city? This was very important to him. He had always considered that he'd maintained a good relationship with the county police over the years, and he hadn't been mean when it came to gifts at New Year's and what have you. If they took the case it would be easy to put them on the right track. However, his relationship with the city police had always been much stickier; in fact, you could say that both sides loathed each other without being too far wrong. When the chief of the city police, Wu Qingyuan, had come out to Guojiadian, he'd refused to see the man. In fact, people had suggested giving him one of their gold plaques, but he'd pretended not to hear them. Why should he? The police in Dahua City were endlessly towing away cars belonging to people in Guojiadian, and having been towed, they had to pay enormous fines. And now he was supposed to be giving presents to this man who kept annoying him? Guo Cunxian had never been the kind of person who'd just take it like that. In his own mind, at least, he'd been quarrelling with the city police for years. They were now in charge of this case. How could it go well?

He exploded with rage and bellowed: "I want them stopped!"

Guo Cunxian screamed his instructions into the phone, and with the same speed as if he'd been there in person to order them about, a dozen or so security guards came pouring out of the headquarters of Eastern Commerce, heading straight for the new building. They also made sure that the steel gate was closed behind them. The policeman standing outside, realising that something had gone wrong, made a run for the car. When he saw that more guards were heading out from the main building and running in his direction, he stepped on the accelerator and drove away from the village at top speed.

The person in charge of the city police who'd come out to Guojiadian was Yu Changhe, head of the second bureau within the Criminal Investigation Department. The moment he saw what was happening, he knew exactly where he stood. The security guards who were employed in Guojiadian rushed forward to separate him from his two colleagues. Xing Zhenzhong, a senior guy in the Criminal Investigation Department, had three guards standing next to him. That was probably because he was older and they imagined that three was enough. Meanwhile the clean-cut young forensics expert, Jiang Yuan, had four burly men standing around him. This is what is called 'divide and rule'. Clearly these people had had some training, or else they'd just been given very strict instructions. He looked stern and addressed them formally: "Which one of you is the boss?"

Nobody answered. After a long silence, someone muttered. "We don't have a boss."

"Oh, that's too bad. Well, in that case you're all going to have to take the legal consequences of your actions. Do you understand what it is that you have done? There's a dead body in there, and Secretary Guo Cunxian reported this to the police, and we've received an order to investigate the crime. You're now here causing trouble, which means you've broken at least three laws. One, you are preventing police officers from carrying out their duties. Two, you have illegally restricted the movements of officers of the law. Three, you have deliberately destroyed a crime scene. That could see you all prosecuted as accessories after the fact."

Yu Changhe turned his head slowly to look at each of the guards, as if he were making a note of every detail of their appearance. In the end his gaze came to rest on a security guard who didn't dare look him in the eye: "Go back and report to whoever it is who sent you here. Tell him what I just told you, and tell him my demands – he must immediately remove all the security guards here and restore our freedom of movement, and he has to offer every assistance to our enquiries. If he agrees to my demands, then I may perhaps be willing to let this one go. If not, the consequences will be extremely serious. You really don't want to be involved in this!"

The security guard stood there for a moment, shocked and alarmed, and then he did indeed turn around and walk away.

Yu Changhe now demanded to make a phone call, but the remaining guards just glared at him. They didn't say he could, and they didn't say he could not – they were just making a show of strength. There wasn't a phone in this building, and they weren't going to let him out.

Oh my God, what a bunch of idiots. Actually this was a nasty trick to play. The man in charge never appeared, and he used a bunch of security guards to do the dirty work. If a fight had really broken out, what on earth would that have looked like! Worse still, if there'd really been conflict with the guards, the whole situation would have spun out of control and might well have prevented them from ever being able to solve the case. Of course, that might well be what Guo Cunxian wanted. He reported the incident, but he didn't want anyone to investigate. What was the bastard up to now? If they managed to resolve this confrontation amicably, what did he have in mind to do next?

Xing Zhenzhong was a very experienced officer who was hardly going to let this kind of thing get to him. He put his bag down on the concrete floor and moved to sit with his back against the wall, tilting his baseball cap down so that it shaded his eyes. Then he stretched himself out and said: "You know, it's been a whole week since I've had a decent bit of kip, and I'm extremely tired. Really, these people here in Guojiadian are wonderful with the way they understand my needs, so I'm just going to go right ahead…"

A short time later he was snoring away.

Jiang Yuan took another approach to the situation. He was squatting down next to Yang Zusheng's body in professional mode, inspecting it as if he were looking at some broken antique. He was very carefully touching the corpse here, looking there, and then writing the results up in his notebook. Sometimes he had his eyes fixed on the ground as he walked round the body, and then when he discovered something or other he picked it up with tweezers and put it into a plastic bag. He carried on as if no one else was present, and if one of the security guards got in his way, he pushed them aside.

None of the security guards had ever seen the police carrying out a forensic investigation like this. They liked to hit the living, but they really hated and feared the dead. Because of this they were curious and impressed by Jiang Yuan's activities, and they decided to get out of the way to help him.

That afternoon at three o'clock, Lu Qing, the deputy chief of police in Kuanhe County, rushed out to Guojiadian. He went first to the village Party Committee to see Guo Cunxian. The office of the village Party Committee was closed and the guard on duty by the gate said that Guo Cunxian wasn't there. Then he turned round and rushed to the office of Eastern Commerce, where the security guards also refused to allow him in. No matter who he said he was there to see, they proclaimed that that person wasn't there. Apparently the only people out and about were security guards, but they claimed not to know anything about anything. Clearly he wasn't going to be allowed to enter the crime scene nor rescue his colleagues from the city who were being held, unless he was prepared to use force. However, what kind of 'force' he ought to apply and what the consequences would be, he wasn't entirely sure. All he could do was head back and report what had happened to the city police headquarters and county Party Committee.

In actual fact, Lu Qing's arrival was supposed to give Guo Cunxian an opportunity to climb down gracefully. If he had done so, excuses for his behaviour would have been found, and even if it had proved impossible to paper over all of the cracks, at the very least he would have come out of this situation unharmed. If he had allowed the police to solve the case, he could have carried on being the secretary just as long as he liked. However, he chose this as a moment to be stubborn and refused to take the opportunity given to him to resolve the situation. He felt that Lu Qing had let him down by not coming when he was asked; why should he now rush over when he wasn't wanted? Why didn't Lu Qing realise that he was just a piece of shit allowed here on sufferance? The police in Dahua City were supposed to be really great, weren't they? Anyway, here in Guojiadian we'd put those bastards in their places! If we want to hold them, what are you going to do about it?

He'd spent half his life on the receiving end of other people's attempts to punish him when he stepped out of line, and he'd developed a whole series of prejudices as a result, added to which the police had just arrested one lot of his lads. The mere sight of an official or a policeman irritated him in his current mood. Shortly afterwards, the call from the county Party Committee came through, wanting to speak to Guo Cunxian. It was the secretary of the county Party Committee on the line, speaking personally. To an ordinary village cadre, that was a pretty generous gesture of respect; the man was significantly more senior than Lu Qing, after all. However, Guo Cunxian was no ordinary village cadre, so he turned a cold glance on Lin Meitang: "I won't take the call. Tell him I'm not here. I'm teaching the police in Dahua City where they get off, so this is nothing to do with the county."

That which does not kill us makes us stronger. Guo Cunxian stood up and said cheerfully: "You see? If you stick to your guns, they'll find ways to get you out of trouble. There are always people who want to save their own official positions, so they'll keep on trying to get you off. That's because this is Guojiadian. Every year we pay huge taxes to the government, and I'm a delegate to the National People's Congress – the only one in the whole of Kuanhe County."

Just at that moment, another call came through from the county Party Committee. The person on the other end of the line asked Lin Meitang's name and her role in Guojiadian, then asked her to immediately inform Guo Cunxian of the orders that had been given by the Party Committee: "Another person has now been beaten to death in Guojiadian, and the police are investigating in accordance with the law. No work unit or individual has the right to interfere with or obstruct their work for any reason. You must immediately release the police who are being held in Guojiadian, and you must guarantee their personal safety and their ability to perform their duties. This must be done right now, without delay."

Guo Cunxian closed his eyes and thought for a moment, and then he gave his orders. That evening at eleven o'clock he would send a fax through to the county Party Committee, but whether they received it or not would be up to them. If all of those old idiots had eaten dinner by then and gone back home to bed, whereby they didn't get my fax, then I'm afraid it's just tough for those three policemen – they're going to have to spend the night with a corpse. We'll let them go tomorrow morning.

The fax should read: "Today at midday four plain-clothes officers came from Dahua City and entered the offices of Eastern Commerce where they started bullying the staff, only to be held by the security guards. I have only just arrived back, and the moment I received the message from the Party Committee I realised this was a mistake, so I have immediately given orders to treat the police with proper respect and to give them every facility to allow them to investigate this case."

Guo Cunxian thought he'd played a really neat trick this time: he'd taught both the county and the city police where they got off, while obstructing and delaying their investigation of the crime. At the same time, he was creating a breathing space for the lads who'd beaten Yang Zusheng to death; he was giving them time to hide and allowing the witnesses to sort out their testimony. Now was the moment for him to start thinking about backing down gracefully.

People like to imagine they are going to get away with things, particularly when they've achieved great success in their lives. Guo Cunxian was going to find, when he tried to back down, that it was now all too late. This time there would be nobody to dig him out of the mess he'd got himself into.

Just before dawn, the security guards who'd been watching the three policemen slipped away. A short time later someone else appeared, to represent Eastern Commerce and to explain to Yu Changhe that it had all been a terrible mistake. He said that he would invite him to breakfast, to give him a good meal before sending him off.

He was not expecting Yu Changhe to refuse. "We aren't going anywhere, so why are you seeing us off? Also we don't need breakfast. We seldom eat until we've solved our case. What we need is for you to help us out here. We need to question the men who beat Yang Zusheng, so that we can find out exactly who killed him."

In his fax to the county Party Committee, Guo Cunxian had promised to give the police every facility in investigating the crime – he couldn't go back on his word. The problem was that, if these three bastards were refusing to leave in spite of the fact they'd been kept hungry for twenty-four hours, it meant that they must have discovered something. If they were questioned, the killers would be sure to make a mistake. If the lads didn't appear, or if they were said to have run away already, then it would be as good as a confession. It would be perfectly obvious to the police who they ought to be arresting for the murder...

Guo Cunxian still hadn't made up his mind about how he was going to deal with the situation when he heard the sound of police sirens coming ever closer, blaring with an ear-splitting noise. In the blink of an eye, four police vehicles arrived, moving through the early morning rush-hour as commuters came into the village for work: three cars and a mini-bus. Everyone quickly made way for them, gathering curiously by the side of the road, watching as they headed for Guo Cunxian's office building.

The villagers were nervous, and they were moving restlessly. The police cars formed an impressive parade, and they looked like they meant business as they pulled up in front of the main building. Seven or eight men in uniform got out of the three cars. They were clearly under orders that they fully intended to carry out. Ten men from the armed response squad got out of the mini-bus, of whom two stayed with the cars, while the rest followed the others into the building.

As this scene unfolded, everyone could see that Guojiadian was now in real trouble.

The security guards from the village who were responsible for keeping an eye on the main gate might look impressive under everyday circumstances, but the minute they came across some real police making a show of force, they were useless. They were in no position to make the slightest protest. If they had tried to stop them, they'd have been put under arrest immediately. And it was true that they hadn't received orders not to let the police into the building, so they didn't dare say a word. The police paid no attention to them whatsoever but headed straight for the main door and went up to the fifth floor, which was supposed to be the location of Guo Cunxian's office.

The room was full of smoke. In addition to Guo Cunxian and Lin Meitang, a handful of other people were present, and they were struck dumb at the interruption. Nobody seemed to have a clue what to do next. In the end it was Guo Cunxian who pulled himself together first and came forward to bring the situation under control: "I don't know what you think you're all doing here, we've only had the one person killed after all!"

Lu Qing indicated Wu Lie and began to introduce him: "Comrade Guo Cunxian, this is the head of Dahua City Criminal Investigation Department..."

Wu Lie raised his hand to stop him: "We know each other."

The moment he came through the door, Wu Lie had started to weigh up Guo Cunxian: he was after all both rich and famous, as well as getting on in years. Wealth had not resulted in him becoming fat; quite the contrary, the man looked positively skeletal, like an opium addict from olden times. The biggest difference was that in the past the wrinkles on his face had been laugh-lines, but now they were set in patterns of arrogance and distain.

Wu Lie pulled a document out of his pocket and began to read it aloud to Guo Cunxian: "I am here to inform you of the following orders issued by the Public Security Bureau at Dahua City. First, you are to immediately release Comrades Yu Changhe, Xing Zhenzhong and Jiang Yuan, who arrived in Guojiadian yesterday to investigate a crime. They are to be brought here straight away."

Lin Meitang glanced at Guo Cunxian and realised from his expression that he had no intention of refusing the instruction, so without waiting for him to say anything, she told a young man standing next to her to make sure that this was done. Wu Lie then announced the second order. "The local station here in Guojiadian is disbanded with immediate effect. Therefore I will be removing the ten automatic rifles with which you have been issued, together with the one thousand five hundred rounds of ammunition, also five Type Sixty-Four handguns, with five hundred rounds of ammunition."

The office was dead silent. Wu Lie glared at Guo Cunxian and pressed the point. "Where are your guns and ammunition? You need to hand them over right now."

Guo Cunxian would never have imagined that the city was going to go after him in this way – so that's why Wu Lie had come! He had no time for the police, but he'd clean forgot that his own local station was actually under the control of the Public Security Bureau. This was a real blow below the belt, and he was totally unprepared for it. He immediately started to complain: "I don't understand why you've been ordered to do this. If you take away our local station, how can you be protecting the development and reform taking place here in Guojiadian? This will have a very negative impact on production, on morale – the consequences could be most serious! How are we supposed to carry on working here…?"

Wu Lie shouted at him to shut up: "First you have to obey orders. Where are your guns and ammunition? Take my men there to collect them!"

At this moment, Guo Cunxian realised that, for all his cleverness, there was nothing he could do. If he dared to refuse to obey orders, the police might well pull out their guns. Wu Lie had turned up with so many police, it was clear that he'd made preparations for every eventuality. In this situation, if it came to any kind of fight, he was going to lose. Helplessly, he gestured to Lin Meitang.

Lin Meitang knew exactly what he meant. In a low voice she said to Wu Lie: "The guns are here, but we don't have all of the ammunition. There's been some target practice carried out, which has used up about one hundred rounds. The rest is all kept in the duty room at Zhongnanhai… ah, that's the gated community we live in. Two of the rifles are kept there, with ten rounds of ammunition. The duty rooms at the head offices of our four main groups each have an empty gun, and all the other weapons and ammunition are right here on the sixth floor."

Oh, right, so Guo Cunxian had kept the guns and ammunition for his own personal use, where he could paw them over any day… what a joker!

Lu Qing took six of the police officers up to the sixth floor, following in the wake of Lin Meitang. Another of Wu Lie's men took some of the other police officers downstairs to visit the other sites where guns and ammunition were kept; they were to be shown where to go by a young man. That left just Guo Cunxian and Wu Lie in the office together, and they sat face to face looking at each other, though neither was prepared to break the silence by actually speaking. The atmosphere in the room was very unpleasant, to the point where it was almost impossible to breathe.

Fortunately it was not long before Yu Changhe and the others arrived. They didn't bother to say much to Guo Cunxian, but Jiang Yuan took this opportunity to make his report to Wu Lie: "I counted more than four hundred separate injuries inflicted on the dead man – in fact you could say he was beaten almost to a pulp. Not only was he punched and kicked, there were also clear signs of trauma inflicted by a blunt weapon. When I carried out my investigation, I found that there were twelve places where severe subcutaneous bleeding had occurred. He also suffered compound fractures to eight ribs, there was an internal haemorrhage in the right side of his chest cavity containing about four hundred millilitres of blood, and his liver and spleen were ruptured in three places. Judging by the state of his injuries and the blood loss, he died of shock. There were footprints from five different individuals at the scene of the crime, as well as various other traces. The guards on duty on the gate that night have given evidence that nobody else entered the interrogation room, so we can be pretty sure that the killers are those five men."

Guo Cunxian could feel the chills going up and down his spine. The police had been stopped almost as soon as they arrived in the village, but apparently on the basis of a night spent with the corpse, they'd effectively worked out how the man died! "Have you talked to the suspects yet?" Wu Lie asked.

"We haven't had the opportunity," Yu Changhe said, "but we've identified our targets."

"Good," Wu Lie nodded. "You've done well, the three of you. There's food in my car, and some hot water. Go and have something to eat now, and in a while when we've collected the guns and ammunition, we can both get to work a bit more on our assignment."

The hidden door communicating with the sixth floor slid open, and Lu Qing and the four policemen came out, carrying the guns and ammunition. Lin Meitang followed behind them with the documentation. Lu Qing remained behind to report to Wu Lie what had happened when the guns and ammunition had been sorted out, while Yu Changhe and his companions went downstairs with the other police officers to stow the weaponry away in the car.

Having got the guns and ammunition back, Wu Lie felt much more cheerful. He turned his head to speak to Guo Cunxian: "There are another couple of things that we are going to need your help with. First, we need to arrest these suspects as quickly as possible. If they aren't arrested today, we'll have to talk to their families, and we'll be wanting to search their houses and any other place that they might be hiding. Tomorrow we're going to be sending out a team to the village with the necessary search warrants."

The young man who'd gone off with the police to collect the guns now came back as well, and he looked very tense. He came up to Guo Cunxian as if he wanted to speak to him, but Wu Lie was quick on the uptake and got in ahead of him with his question: "Was there a problem with collecting the guns?"

The young man was startled into replying: "Not at all. The four guns and ten rounds of ammunition have already been put in your cars."

Seeing that Wu Lie had no further questions, the young man put his mouth close by Guo Cunxian's ear and whispered: "They're saying that our village has been completely surrounded by the police..." He was now gabbling, and his voice was getting lower and lower, to the point where the other people in the room simply could not hear what he said.

The anger that Guo Cunxian had been keeping pent up the whole morning now exploded, and he jumped up from his chair as if he'd been stabbed with an awl. He shouted at Wu Lie: "What do you think you are doing? I'm telling you, if there's any trouble over this, you're going to pay for it! We peasants don't understand the law, I don't understand the law myself. If it comes to a fight, are you going to take responsibility? If you're here to arrest me then go right ahead, but you don't need to bring so many people. I'm not the kind of person who you can subdue with a show of force."

"Calm down!" Wu Lie said. "It is perfectly true that there are four hundred police waiting three kilometres outside Guojiadian. They have been deployed there by the Public Security Bureau. Yesterday you placed police officers who were carrying out their duties under illegal restraint – if you dared to do that, what else can we expect from you? Given that you had guns and ammunition, and since there are many people here in Guojiadian who have come from god knows where, we had to make some arrangements, we had to be prepared for the worst. I hope you can understand and cooperate with our enquiries..."

"I'm supposed to cooperate with you? Why aren't you required to cooperate with me? I am definitely resigning from here on in!"

He threw open the door and rushed out, heading in a frenzied run for the broadcasting room, which also happened to be located on the fifth floor of the same building. A few moments later, the loudspeakers that were located at strategic points throughout Guojiadian were transmitting his irate voice: "Fellow villagers, fellow colleagues, we are now facing an extremely serious crisis. The city has sent a large number of armed police to lie in wait outside Guojiadian. They have cannons, tear-gas, attack dogs and guns, and they want to come into the village to search the place. I believe that they are not here to investigate a crime. It is their intention to destroy the economic foundations of Guojiadian. We must be prepared for our development to suffer, for production to drop and for our incomes to go down. However, we are not afraid! We will never turn back! Never! I am now declaring that every company in the village must stop work, every factory must cease production for one month, and the schools will also be closed. However, you will receive your salaries as normal, and if any employer cannot afford this, I am prepared to use my personal reserves. If they think they can bully us, we can show them they've bitten off more than they can chew!

"I want everyone to assemble as soon as they can, we need to mobilise the entire village. Get whatever weapons you have to hand and prepare to defend your homes. I want you to close all the roads, to prevent evil men from entering the village and causing trouble. We need to protect Guojiadian! We need to defend the Guojiadian Group! Everyone dies sooner or later. You can live for twenty years or you can live for sixty years, either way it ends in death. I refuse to live in chains! I would rather die..."

Everyone in the office got to their feet. Lu Qing shouted: "The man's gone stark staring mad!"

Wu Lie used his walkie-talkie to give orders to his subordinates outside. "Tell our men to get in the car and not to get into any kind of fight with the villagers. You are to wait for further orders." Afterwards he turned to Lin Meitang, and his tone was now very harsh. "Where is your broadcasting room? Take me there immediately!"

Lin Meitang was about to go with him, when they were stopped by Lu Qing: "Mr Wu, there are loads of guns and ammunition in those cars. If the locals really start attacking our people, there could be serious trouble..."

Wu Lie knew that Lu Qing's concerns were entirely justified, but if he left right now, gossip would say that they'd been thrown out of Guojiadian, and that would give Guo Cunxian the upper hand. However, in this situation, they really should pull out because it would be a bad idea to get into any kind of conflict with the villagers. In the circumstances, he had to give his message to Lin Meitang.

"As you can see, Guo Cunxian is trying to whip up public anger, and that is very dangerous. You must keep calm, and I hope you can encourage him to keep his temper and not do anything stupid. Let me repeat, we'll be back tomorrow to arrest our suspects, and we'll have the necessary warrants to summon people for questioning and to search property. In order to avoid trouble, we will be leaving now."

Lin Meitang nodded her agreement. She was young and far from stupid. She could see perfectly well which way the wind was blowing. She escorted Wu Lie and the other men out of the building herself; if anyone had tried to stop them, nothing would have happened as long as she was present. She also rather suspected that if she hadn't offered to escort them, they might well have taken her hostage, to be released once they had safely left the village.

Guojiadian was now in turmoil, although at least on the surface everyone seemed to be enjoying the situation. People were running out of their houses and gathering together in the streets. Some had absolutely no idea what on earth was going on, but they ran along with the others shouting and screaming, enjoying the excitement. The so-called 'Number One Village in the World' was quickly reduced to utter chaos.

Some people had genuinely gone to arm themselves; they were carrying brooms, cudgels, picks and shovels. It was perhaps the case that the villagers in Guojiadian had been under too much pressure, too much control lately. They had been through decades of political movements and investigations, and once the political movements and investigations were over, then the village had produced a man who demanded constant respect and admiration. As a result, hitting people, even beating them to death, offered a kind of release from this pressure, an excitement similar to a festival. Today presented an opportunity for them to let their most vicious instincts run wild, they could reach a climax. This time they were going to be beating the police, and every single person in the village was going to join in.

Lin Meitang watched Wu Lie and the others get into the police cars, and then standing out in the road, she ordered the peasants to stand back and make way for them. She watched the four police cars as they drove off, sirens blaring. The villagers who saw these events simply didn't understand what she was doing. Weren't they supposed to be beating the police up? Why did Lin Meitang, who always turned out to represent Guo Cunxian, allow the police to leave?

Seeing all of these people rushing about excitedly like blue-arsed flies, first shouting about this, then screaming about that, Liu Fugen felt a certain sense of surprise that he wasn't at all interested himself. He had hidden himself away, but then he decided to come out again for some reason. The fact is that he didn't have any family in Guojiadian and had been lying low in Lin Meitang's house, but then he decided it wasn't safe. If the police started searching, they weren't going to leave her house off the list. Even more importantly, he felt that he'd caused all of these problems, and he decided that it wouldn't look too good if, at a moment like this, he stayed hidden away and his adoptive father had to deal with all the fall-out. When the last man had been beaten to death, the Four Bosses and all the other senior figures in the village had gone into hiding, including Guo Cunxian's own brother-in-law, Qiu Zhantang, who claimed to be away from home the entire time. That gave him an excuse for not receiving any messages, but he hadn't said anything to Guo Cunxian in advance about being away. Right now Liu Fugen and Lin Meitang were the only ones who could be relied on. So if he went into hiding too, wouldn't that put his adoptive father in a very difficult position? Liu Fugen's concerns resulted in him becoming increasingly anxious. He found the confused situation in the village comical, but then immediately felt that finding any humour in this was an act of disloyalty to his adoptive father. He was furious with himself for feeling that his boundless confidence in Guo Cunxian had been shaken at this crucial moment.

Liu Fugen admired Guo Cunxian enormously. He'd always thought he was a wonderful man, and a great man for all that he was a peasant. He understood how many hopes his adoptive father had invested in him; his own son had no interest in Guojiadian and would soon be leaving to study in the United States. It was him who'd be looking after his adoptive father in old age, and so it was him who would be handed the baton of power over Guojiadian. Guo Cunxian's only worry was that he couldn't pick it up. That was the nub of the problem: when the Master was gone, he couldn't possibly keep control. Even if others obeyed him, the Four Bosses wouldn't. He understood perfectly well that the reason the Master was making such a fuss was to try to use the fact that a man had been beaten to death to scare people, because this was an opportunity to establish his authority. The problem was that he couldn't imagine it would work. Liu Fugen was young but he had a good feeling for what was going on. Right now his feelings were telling him that people weren't scared, and that his adoptive father was running serious risks for nothing...

The loudspeakers now came to life again, but this time it was Lin Meitang's voice that they heard. She was reporting an order from Party Secretary Guo that the four groups were each to be responsible for guarding an entrance to the village: north, south, east and west. Trucks were to be used to block the roads, and they were to organise a militia to patrol the area. The remaining peasants and workers should assemble in the square in front of the main office building. The village had to mobilise a militia of twenty thousand men, and at the key moment in time, they would be under the command of the village Party Committee. However, they were to be gathered in the main square in one hour's time in order to be passed under review by Secretary Guo. The Public Security Bureau had taken away our local station, so we were going to have to form a militia to protect our reforms! They had taken away our guns and ammunition, but we had other weapons!

The people gathered in the roads, at the doors of their houses, in parks and in factories. Then, having heard their instructions being broadcast, they poured into the square in front of the headquarters. Men and women, old and young, with their improvised weapons in their hands, they looked like temporary labourers touting for work, or perhaps like workers going out to build a canal. Trucks and forklifts from every local company thronged the main roads through Guojiadian, blocking every exit. The loudspeakers were now playing stirring music: first it was *The March of Athletes*, and then it was *The March of the Volunteers*. More and more people were crowding into the square, shouting at each other, their weapons held high. The peasants had already been through 'Combatting Local Tyrants and Redistributing Land', they'd been through collectivisation, not to mention the militarisation programme of 1958 and the Cultural Revolution, so this was all very familiar. Provided you went about it the right way, everyone would come when you called.

The music stopped and the square gradually began to quieten down. A short time later, Guo Cunxian came downstairs accompanied by his bodyguards. This provoked a susurration from the crowd. When he looked around, all the anger and depression that he'd just felt was swept from his mind, to be replaced with excitement and pleasure. He was so delighted that he completely forgot about getting into his own

Mercedes-Benz, but climbed instead into one of the trucks. He grabbed a megaphone and shouted to the crowd: "You've worked so hard!"

The peasants in the square ought to have shouted back: "You too, Secretary Guo!" or perhaps: "We are Serving the People!", but they didn't know that. There was nobody to organise them or give them instructions, so the whole thing began to seem rather awkward. Suddenly a young child realised what was required and started shouting out slogans: "We Don't Interfere if Nobody Interferes With Us!" and followed that up with: "If Someone Interferes With Us, We Will Fight Back!"

This made everyone laugh. However, mobilising civilians is much, much more difficult than mobilising soldiers.

Now Guo Cunxian asked: "Are you scared?"

This time a few people bellowed back: "No!"

"Those who lose are scared. Winners are never scared!"

"Great!" Guo Cunxian was now beginning to whip up his troops. "As long as we stay united, we can protect the fruits of our labours. We can carry on enjoying the good life. We've always been right on the front line, haven't we? From the beginning, we have been showing the whole country the way, otherwise we wouldn't have these bastards trying to get at us! Just now they were still trying to put pressure on me to shut up, ordering me to stay calm. They tell me that, no matter how high the river gets, it can't drown the bridge. Who says so? If the river really rises high enough, it can drown the bridge no problem. It can even cover huge buildings and entire villages! In ancient times, didn't the waters once cover Jinshan? From now on, the young men of our village are going to be organised according to work unit to patrol the village and keep watch, while old people and small children will stay on the alert at home. If you hear the order, then I want the whole village to attack! I refuse to accept what they're trying to do. They're trying to bully us, trying to turn us peasants out of our own homes! We suffered enough when we were poor, and now that we're rich they still despise us! Today we're going to stand up to them and show them what we peasants can do! Right?"

This time there were shouts from around the square: "Right! Right!"

His words sounded fine, and his enthusiasm was infectious. When his speech was over he decided to go on a tour of inspection of the four roads leading into the village, so he told his driver to take him to the west where the traffic was heaviest; the chemical group was responsible for blocking the road there. As the truck passed the Lucky Trees, he discovered they were covered in dead branches and desiccated leaves. The great green canopy seemed to have been stripped bare. This was a shocking sight to meet his eyes.

What on earth had happened to the Lucky Trees? He realised that it was a very long time now since he'd last come out to look at the trees, because otherwise he would have noticed they were sick... or perhaps they'd suffered insect attack? Or could the cause be chemical pollution? Why had nobody told him? If there was something wrong with the Lucky Trees, that was a serious problem for him, and he started to feel frightened.

He didn't have time to think about it right now since he needed to inspect the arrangement of his forces.

He stood up on top of the truck and could see huge lorries, heavily laden, pulling into the village along the highway without even having to slacken their speed. He was puzzled; he really couldn't believe that there was anyone in Guojiadian who would dare to openly disobey his orders. When his truck got a bit closer he could see what was going on. It looked as though there were four huge lorries parked across the road and blocking it, but each of the drivers sitting in the cabs was allowing cars in and out. When they heard the sound of a horn, they would go into reverse and pull out of the way to the side of the highway. When Guo Cunxian's truck approached, the same thing happened. They didn't wait for him to get to the entrance of the village before the four lorries that were supposed to be blocking the road had pulled back to let him pass.

Guo Cunxian was furious. He stopped his truck and summoned the four drivers. "Who told you to do this?" he shouted. "Aren't you supposed to be blocking the road?" The drivers were petrified, and to begin with they didn't dare say a word. However, they knew that sooner or later they'd have to tell him something. Guo Cunxian shouted again: "Cat got your tongue?"

In the end, one of the braver men muttered something about how this was what his superiors had instructed. Anything that wasn't a police car they were told to let through, because otherwise it would have a terrible effect on traffic through the village and cause problems in production. This sounded perfectly reasonable; they wouldn't have dared to act this way if they hadn't had direct orders from the boss. They couldn't tell him exactly who the boss was. They didn't want to take the blame for this, but they also didn't want to betray the company they worked for, nor did they have any intention of being punished for passing on information to the secretary.

Guo Cunxian suddenly realised that, for all that he'd spent the day looking over his forces, the only people he could actually rely on were Lin Meitang, Liu Fugen and his own bodyguards. He was very pleased to see that his adopted son had come of his own accord to be by his side in this crisis, and he thought he'd picked well. After all, the Four Bosses had once been his very closest friends, but not one of them had come. It wasn't just that they'd let him down; were they likely to act independently from now on? His good mood over 'reviewing his troops' had now disappeared. Without going to the other three roads into the village, he knew exactly what he would find there.

"Let's go back to the office," he said crossly to Lin Meitang. "Tell the bosses of the four groups that I want to see them immediately. I don't care how busy they are, they are to come now!"

Once he was really angry, nobody dared to disobey orders. Within a very short space of time the Four Bosses were standing in front of him. Guo Cunxian pointed to Chen Erxiong: "I told you to block the roads. What on earth do you think you are doing?"

Chen Erxiong already knew exactly what had happened, so he now tried to speak up for himself: "You can't really mean to block the roads, can you? It won't stop the police and it will just cause us problems. We take over two hundred deliveries a day, and that's just my group of companies. You cannot seriously mean to inflict such a loss on us, can you?"

How dare the little bastard speak back! Guo Cunxian was so enraged that he started to shout: "Of course I do! Stop just thinking about money! Just look at the crisis we are in. We've got the people and now is the time to use them! You've got enough money to last three lifetimes, so why can't you stand up for the people at this critical moment?"

Chen Erxiong was now so frightened he didn't dare say another word. He hung his head and didn't look at Guo Cunxian directly. Looking into his eyes would have been like staring into the muzzle of a gun; it was far too dangerous.

Ou Guangming was nearly fifty years of age now, and he had an unassailable position in Guojiadian, so he tried to speak up for Chen Erxiong. "Secretary," he murmured, "I've sent people out to have a look all round our village and the police have gone. We shouldn't be working ourselves up like this over nothing. Besides which, just think about it. If they really want to come in, we've just got a few trucks and a couple of hundred, maybe a thousand men in all. How are we going to stop them?"

"Even if we can't stop them, we ought to try. We ought to try! A hard man will still be afraid of a violent man, and a violent man will still be afraid of a man who's decided he doesn't care whether he lives or dies. Besides which, I don't think they'd dare massacre us or anything like that. Jin Laixi, come on! You say something!"

Jin Laixi was no longer the smarmy and cowardly individual of a couple of decades ago. He was about the same age as Guo Cunxian, and he was one of the men who'd made Guojiadian rich; in fact he was now one of the Four Bosses. More importantly, nobody would ever now dare criticise his family background. It was his turn to speak, he could say anything he liked. However, in addressing Guo Cunxian he still used a low voice and humble demeanour, but this should not have fooled anyone. This was the iron hand in the velvet glove.

"Secretary, I think the two of them have a serious point. We've worked hard for decades to get to where we are today, and it's been tough. We don't want to ruin it all just because someone's been beaten to death here. There's still a great future for Guojiadian if we don't mess it up. We peasants can't fight the government. How are our people supposed to fight against the Public Security Bureau and the government at city and county level? The way I see it is that we've had our fun, we've managed to run the police out of here, so you've been able to show them that you don't want to be messed about. Tomorrow, when they come back to investigate the case, we let them come, they do whatever is necessary, and we draw a line under this and move on. We have lots to do right now, and we don't want to be wasting our time on this."

"He's right, Secretary. We've all worked so hard to get to where we are today. I'm begging you, please think of the bigger picture. Don't ruin us for nothing, I'm begging you!" Wang Shun didn't wait for Guo Cunxian to start questioning him, but went down on his knees with a thud.

It wouldn't have mattered if he was the only one to go down on his knees, but the others now followed suit. "Secretary, we are begging you, stop this now! If this carries on any longer we are heading for disaster!"

Up until this point Liu Fugen hadn't dared to say a word. He had no idea what else to do but join the others in kneeling down. Guo Cunxian was now furious, and raising his foot he kicked his adopted son to the ground, screaming with rage: "Traitor! Villain! You think you don't need me any more, but we'll see. You're all right, I'm always in the wrong. Piss off! I want all of you to go to hell!"

The others now shamefacedly struggled to their feet, but Wang Shun remained kneeling. "If you don't give the villagers the orders to go home, I'm not getting up and I don't care what you do to me. We can't let them run such terrible risks. Please!"

In actual fact, in spite of having decided to strike fear into others, Guo Cunxian was now himself deeply disturbed. Day and night, the moment he closed his eyes he seemed to see a black hole within his mind, a bottomless pit, and he felt as though an irresistible force was pulling him into it, into the darkness and terror, and he would come out in a cold sweat. This black hole was getting bigger and bigger, to the point where he was no longer brave enough to face up to this hallucination, and he had no idea how to stop it other than by never shutting his eyes and never switching off the light. He now bent down and pulled Wang Shun to his feet: "It's been many years since you've spoken so honestly to me."

"I couldn't speak like that in front of other people, they might say I wasn't being respectful enough towards you..."

"You're one of the Four Bosses now, so how come your food business is the only one that hasn't changed its name to a group?"

"It's just a name, isn't it? I was a butcher, but now I sell a bit more than I used to. As far as I'm concerned it's the same thing. However, if you want me to do this, I will."

"You're the only one who's still on my side..." Guo Cunxian suddenly felt cold all over, as a sense of terrible confusion crept over him. He had managed to get himself into this impasse and now had no idea what it was that he'd been hoping to achieve. He'd always been in charge of things before, it was his role to come up with ideas for what everyone else should be doing and his brain had been ever fertile. As soon as one idea passed, another popped into his head, sometimes pausing to put out new shoots and leaves. It was something that surprised everyone who had to deal with him, and it had always garnered him a lot of respect. However, it also had the result of making him underestimate those around him, and to rely only on himself for the big decisions. Today, though, he finally came to realise that there were some circumstances in which he didn't understand himself at all. He had no idea why he'd done what he'd done, and it had been impossible to control himself.

A couple of days later, Wu Lie, the head of the Criminal Investigation Department, was summoned into the office of Wu Qing, the chief of police. The chief of police was clearly in a very good mood, smiling and looking cheerful, and he waved his hand to indicate that he should sit down opposite him. However, he was more than a little nervous because under ordinary circumstances he would only be called in like this for a serious talk if there was a difficult mission ahead. But no matter how he wracked his brains, he couldn't think of anything of that kind being on the cards, and nobody had hinted anything in advance, so why would the chief of police want to talk to him?

Wu Qingyuan saw how nervous his subordinate was looking and gestured at him to indicate that he should sit down. Afterwards, he asked in a slow voice, with just a hint of teasing: "Has Guojiadian's peasant militia been disbanded?"

Wu Lie nodded. "Yes."

"Have you arrested the murderers?"

"Yes, we got all of them."

"Good!" Wu Qingyuan now moved in for the kill. "Now you've got to go back and arrest Guo Cunxian!"

As if stung by a bee, Wu Lie jumped from his chair: "Arrest Guo Cunxian?" He stared at the chief of police, wondering whether he'd misheard.

Wu Qingyuan was now smiling. He waved a hand to gesture that he ought to sit down: "Make yourself comfortable. I'm just telling you to go and arrest a peasant, why should you be so surprised?"

"But he's a famous peasant entrepreneur and a delegate to the National People's Congress!"

Wu Qingyuan looked serious, and his voice was stern: "Right now, Guo Cunxian is nothing but a criminal. He's done terrible things, and he's never going to be representing the people again. I can list for you a number of the crimes that he's committed just off the top of my head – accessory before and after the fact, attempting to pervert the course of justice… In fact he's even tried to interfere with police officers trying to carry out their duties. Any one of these offences is enough to see him arrested and brought to justice, don't you think?"

Perhaps it was because he was so surprised that Wu Lie asked an even more stupid question: "Is this the decision of the city's Party Committee?"

"Don't ask." Wu Qingyuan ticked him off for impertinence. "However, I can tell you that this arrest has been approved at a provincial level. They agreed with my recommendation, and all we have to do is to report our actions to the Party Committee here in the city. Your job is to actually perform the arrest."

"Great!" Wu Lie leapt to his feet. He looked in an immense hurry to get going. "That bastard should have been dealt with years ago! I'll grab a couple of my men, and then we'll go and get him."

"There's no need to get too het up about this." Yet again Wu Qingyuan waved him back into his seat. "We want this done without anyone even noticing, and certainly without violence. Let me tell you exactly what I want you to do…"

26

UNDER ARREST

Guojiadian calmed down again. Even though the barricades that had been constructed on all four sides of the village were still there, it was no longer like a powder keg. A couple of thousand villagers who'd picked up iron bars or picks and shovels to serve as weapons, together with more than ten thousand young men from outside, now either went back home or returned to work. Nobody was on patrol day and night around the village any more. The criminals who'd caused all the trouble had been arrested, and Yang Zusheng's family had come to take the body away. All that remained was for the trial to be held, convictions to be handed down and compensation paid to the family of the victim. However, this was not something that the ordinary folk of Guojiadian felt a strong sense of involvement in.

When everyone thought that the worst was over, Guo Cunxian got a call from the Party Committee in Dahua City. The secretary, Gao Jingqi, wanted to invite him to a meeting at the International Hotel to discuss the situation over a meal. He was perfectly aware that he might never come back from this meeting, and indeed those around him encouraged him not to go. In the past, he could have ignored the city Party secretary: if you want to see me, you'll have to come out to my village, otherwise you're shit out of luck. But now he no longer dared to behave like that. With one person after another having been beaten to death, he now found himself entirely out of his depth, and for the first time in his life he felt that his own destiny and that of the village had slipped from his grasp.

Besides which the person who gave him the message over the phone had been really polite, suggesting that he not read too much into things. With all that had happened lately it wasn't appropriate for Party leaders to be visiting the village, and the International Hotel was perfectly comfortable, so that was the location picked for the meeting. After all, it wasn't just the city Party secretary, a whole load of other senior people in the city government would also like to meet him, and this would be a great opportunity to build up a strong working relationship with them.

Whoever it was on the phone sounded entirely sensible. Guo Cunxian agreed straight away because he had no reason not to, and once he'd agreed then he had to go. They are treating me with such respect, I have to show some appreciation. As a peasant you have to admit that you obey orders from your superiors in the county and city administration, and right now you really need to find out what they are up to.

The fact is that, if his superiors were really out to get him, there was no need to go to all this trouble. When they arrested the lads, they could easily have got him too. The police were armed, and he was far from sure that his guards – for all that they were happy enough to beat other people to death – would have risked their lives when it came to that kind of pinch. In the circumstances it was best to pull his horns in a little, make others think he was frightened and that he had learned his lesson. However, he was not about to let his guard down. He took four huge bodyguards with him, and they set off in a three-car convoy. Guo Cunxian was riding in the middle car with one to lead the way and one to bring up the rear. They would be able to deal with pretty much any kind of trouble.

No matter how serious the situation is, you always hope that somehow or other things will turn out well in the end. The International Hotel was only used as a venue for meetings with important guests, so Guo Cunxian thought that if the city government really wanted to punish him, they wouldn't pick a place like that to do it, would they? He walked into the entrance hall surrounded by his bodyguards and was greeted by two smiling young women desk clerks, who informed him that the comrades from the city administration were waiting for him in the small salon, and could Secretary Guo please come this way, though his people would have to stay in the entrance hall.

It really was a most impressive building. The entrance hall to the International Hotel was magnificently appointed, very grand and very quiet. Without a second thought, Guo Cunxian agreed to the young women's request. Even if he had thought about it, he would have had to respect the rules. Nobody is allowed to take their bodyguards into a discussion with senior officials.

He gestured at his bodyguards that they should stand off to one side, and he followed the clerk down the corridor and through another door. The room was empty: Gao Jingqi and the other senior officials in Dahua City were nowhere to be seen. Instead he was confronted with a number of armed police officers, and even before Wu Lie gave his orders he understood that he'd fallen into their trap. There wasn't even time for regrets, and there was no point even asking whether his bodyguards were now under arrest too.

Here, Guo Cunxian was being arrested, there the Dahua City Party Committee was holding a standing committee meeting in one of its smaller seminar rooms.

Secretary Gao Jingqi had a broad forehead and a well-preserved complexion. He now proceeded to give everyone the shocking news in a completely calm manner: "Today's meeting is to inform everyone that, in the wake of a series of murders in Guojiadian, Comrade Wu Qingyuan communicated with the provincial authorities, and with the agreement of the General Office of the Party, a few moments ago the former Party Committee secretary of Guojiadian, Guo Cunxian, was arrested at the International Hotel."

With the exception of Wu Qingyuan himself, everyone was struck dumb.

Gao Jingqi had fully mastered the art of judging a situation, and his eyes now swept round the members of the standing committee. He continued speaking with a regular tempo: "I am sure that some of those present will be feeling surprised, or perhaps you may feel that this has all been too dramatic, but this is the inevitable result of what has happened. Over the years, when it comes to the development of Guojiadian, there has always been conflict within society, with one group offering staunch support and the other showing a suspicious or even negative attitude. Those who supported the people of Guojiadian observed the way in which the village got rich so quickly and admired their success, making them legendary money-makers. Those with a negative perspective thought they had taken the wrong path and believed that the methods Guojiadian was using needed to be looked at carefully. Sometimes they even suspected that these methods were underhand and hence not something that should be promoted or that other people should be encouraged to learn from. They considered that, if other undeveloped regions took the same route, the result would be agricultural stagnation.

"In the past, Chairman Mao encouraged cadres over and over again to read books, particularly historical works. So in order to understand what has been happening in Guojiadian, I've been reading *The Spring and Autumn Annals of Lü Buwei*. In one chapter it says: 'Of the methods used by the sage-kings of antiquity to guide their people, the first in importance was devotion to farming. When the people farm, they remain simple, and being simple are easy to use. When people abandon this fundamental occupation to pursue a secondary task, they become fond of using their wits, and because they are fond of using their wits, their scheming increases. When scheming increases, the people try to outsmart law and order by making right into wrong and wrong into right.' *The Discourses on Salt and Iron* also says: 'Merchants are practised liars, artisans are skilled at deceit. They are ever ambitious and they lack any sense of shame. This means that the niggardly are cheated by them, and even the liberal become niggardly.'

"Guo Cunxian's life has borne out the criticisms of these ancient writers with uncanny accuracy. Here you have a very intelligent and capable peasant who has managed to get increasingly rich, until he was bedazzled by the shine of his gold, which overwhelmed his simple and honest peasant nature. Thus his original sincerity and ideas about how to escape poverty and get rich were perverted, and he took one step after another on the wrong path. This is sad, but it is also wrong. Now I would like to ask for your opinion."

The members of the standing committee had no idea what they ought to say. Gao Jingqi had kicked off by saying that he had information for everyone, that he was telling them something they needed to know, but then he'd asked them to discuss and come up with an opinion. If, once it is all over, you ask people for their opinion and you end up not agreeing, then what? Having gone over the heads of the standing committee and then asking them to express an opinion, what do you expect them to say? All they can do is agree and offer their support. In this extremely oppressive and uncomfortable silence, Zhang Caiqian, mayor and deputy secretary of the municipal

Party Committee, spoke. He had always been honest and straightforward, with a sound and balanced personality. However, at this moment his expression was ugly in the extreme. When he stood up, he announced that this was a very odd meeting of the standing committee since it seemed to contravene standard practice, not to mention Party principles.

The members of the standing committee had great interest in what he had to say, and the room was entirely silent. Zhang Caiqian had helped build Dahua from nothing, and he was a power in the city government, and in the Party. It was he who'd created the Dahua Steel Company, and that came even before the city was ever founded. Dahua was built because of Dahua Steel; without Dahua Steel there would have been no Dahua City. Everyone waited quietly to hear what their mayor had to say.

Zhang Caiqian looked stern, but he was clearly not angered. His voice was unhurried and he gave full weight to every sentence that he spoke: "Just now Comrade Jingqi has given everyone some news. Regardless of whether the standing committee agrees or not, it is already too late because you've gone ahead and done it. This puts the standing committee in an impossible situation, and it contravenes Party policy. Something so important should have been discussed by the standing committee in advance and then we could have made a report to the provincial authorities. Comrade Wu Qingyuan, what have you been up to? Is the idea to take the standing committee by surprise? Right now I don't want to talk about Guo Cunxian's crimes, I want to talk about the fact that many people played a role in the situation we have before us now. We helped Guojiadian get where it is today, we made Guo Cunxian a model. The situation changes every day, so how can he not change with it – don't we bear some responsibility? Does arresting him put us in the right? Is there anyone here who hasn't been to look at what happened in Guojiadian? Is there anyone here who didn't support what Guo Cunxian was doing? If he's committed crimes, then we've pushed him into doing them! We discovered him, we helped him, we supported him, and we let him get away with things. We promoted him to the point where he became famous in ways that he'd never anticipated or asked for, and now we've had enough, so we're going to go after him for it. What do you think that looks like? What do you mean by this? What do you want us to tell people? Are we supposed to say that government policy has changed? That attitudes are different?

"And another thing. Have you thought at all about Guojiadian? There are more than one hundred companies in Guojiadian, including some famous businesses, and our national banks have billions of yuan of loans tied up there – we're not talking about Guo Cunxian's personal wealth here. So now you've arrested Guo Cunxian, but have you considered how big an impact that's going to have? What is going to happen to Guojiadian? What's going to happen to the more than one hundred companies based there? What about those bank loans? We could have dealt with Guo Cunxian in a much better way. We could have gone through the Party to remove him from his position, or maybe even stripped him of Party membership, lessening his influence on Guojiadian and on the companies based there. We could then have punished Guo Cunxian for his mistakes – his crimes – as a matter for the individual concerned, while protecting the residents of Guojiadian and maintaining their productivity. Wouldn't that have been so much easier? Why should the Party Committee of Dahua

City deal with such an important matter in such an overblown and emotional way? Have you thought about what impact this is going to have on the country? At the same time, have you considered doing right by Guojiadian, or even by Guo Cunxian himself?

"Today I really regret my past actions, and I feel that I've let him down. In a way I am to blame for everything that has happened. When all of this started I had great respect for Guo Cunxian, I supported him and worked with him. However, in recent years I've been disappointed in some of the things that he's done, so I didn't see him any more. If I'd had any sense, I would have gone to Guojiadian a couple of times and talked to him. Guo Cunxian was never a fool, perhaps I could have turned him in a different direction and things would never have gone this wrong. Have any of you tried to talk to him? The Party tells us that we cadres ought to be ready to do that kind of work, right? When we could have gone and talked to him, we didn't. And now we're cross with him and we've caught him out in a mistake, so we're going to use that as an opportunity to get rid of him. You have been frivolous and irresponsible. Have you even thought about the consequences of all this? Right now, Guojiadian is earning a fortune for us here in Dahua City, and that money isn't going into Guo Cunxian's pocket. In punishing him like this, you may well throw the whole of Guojiadian into a tailspin from which it'll take them a decade or two to recover. You've totally ignored the bigger picture here, but you still have the cheek to say that you've been enforcing the law, you've been doing right by the Party and right by the people! So let me conclude by giving my opinion. First, I do not agree with your course of action. Second, I want you to report my words to the provincial authorities."

Zhang Caiqian kept saying "you" and everyone knew that this meant Gao Jingqi, since without his say-so Wu Qingyuan could never have got in touch with the provincial authorities off his own bat. However Gao Jingqi remained as self-possessed as ever, and as always when he encountered a difficult problem, he showed a mature attitude in the face of criticism – though some people would say that this was pure hypocrisy. However, his abilities in this direction made him the embodiment of his era. Therefore no matter how pointed Zhang Caiqian's words might be, Gao Jingqi would continue to remain in charge of the proceedings. This allowed him to follow up Zhang Caiqian's words: "Your opinion is very important to me, Mayor, but the situation is what it is, and we now need to think about how to reduce any negative impact and preserve the economic development of Guojiadian. Comrade Qingyuan, the trial and sentencing going forward must strictly abide by legal procedures, and you must guarantee Guo Cunxian's personal safety. I imagine that many will try to speak up for him, but you must handle the case impartially and investigate thoroughly. If you find a problem, you know what to do. If you realise people are innocent, then you need to release them. We must take responsibility for Guojiadian, for Guo Cunxian and for the whole city. Does anybody else have anything fresh to say?"

He was clearly getting up to go because he wanted this meeting to draw to a close. If they carried on their discussion, nobody was going to say anything positive.

"I have something to say," said Deputy Secretary Feng Hou, who wasn't going to let Gao Jingqi get away with bringing the meeting to a close like that. "I absolutely agree with what Comrade Caiqian has just said. Arresting Guo Cunxian like that is at the very least too hasty, and the consequences have not been properly considered. This isn't just a legal problem, it is a governmental problem. Whether you like it or not, Guo Cunxian and Guojiadian have a symbolic significance. What happens to him is not just a problem for Dahua City. Just now Comrade Jingqi discussed two different opinions concerning the development of Guojiadian, and these show a theoretical problem – or perhaps a cognitive problem – but not a legal one, and certainly present no reason to place Guo Cunxian under arrest. *The Spring and Autumn Annals of Lü Buwei* and *The Discourses of Salt and Iron* were blown to pieces by Western gunboats at the end of the Qing dynasty. Classic concepts of industry and business in the West are derived from the theories of Montesquieu. He said that commercial activities spread civilisation and noble ideals among the barbarians of northern Europe. Wherever trade flourishes, virtue will prevail…"

The villagers had been worried enough already when Guo Cunxian headed off for the city, but when they saw that his car had come back along with his bodyguards, but he himself was nowhere to be seen, they surrounded his car in an instant. When the bodyguards emerged with their heads hung low, they reported that the secretary was under arrest.

Guojiadian was thrown into turmoil at this news. Some of the people present vented their anger on the bodyguards themselves, spitting at them and cursing: You're all completely useless! The master spent so much money on you, and normally you're right there harassing anyone you don't like the look of, but the moment you're really needed, you're nowhere to be seen! With the secretary being arrested like that, how do you have the face to come crawling back here?

But with the higher-ups having decided that they wanted to take down Guo Cunxian, how could a couple of bodyguards prevent it?

Those villagers who really cared about what happened to Guo Cunxian now began to look for anyone who could help and discussed how to rescue him. Even ordinary peasants stopped what they had been doing and went around asking each other questions, in and out, muttering their heads off, rushing from place to place like blue-arsed flies. This made the atmosphere in the village very tense, as if disaster might overtake them all at any moment. Yet at the same time it was very quiet – nobody dared to say anything in a loud voice, and many people just glanced at each other as they passed in the streets. Some refused to leave their houses in this crisis; they locked the doors and tried to work out what would happen to Guojiadian with Guo Cunxian gone. What were they going to do themselves?

Lin Meitang was panicking herself. Forgetting to grab a car, she started running like a madwoman in the direction of the chemical group headquarters, which stood some way outside the village. She was hoping to find Chen Erxiong and ask him what to do. Out of all of the Four Bosses he was the cleverest. However, as she ran she began to slow down, and eventually she came to a stop. In her opinion, the four main groups of companies in Guojiadian would collapse pretty quickly with Guo Cunxian gone, but the question was, would Chen Erxiong agree with that assessment? He might take the opposite view. Guojiadian now had many important people but it didn't have a leader; nobody in the village could give orders to everyone. Why should

Chen Erxiong listen to her? Would he tell her what he really thought about the situation? From now on, the person in Guojiadian in the most awkward and difficult position would be herself. She ought to understand that and think about how to protect herself. Out of the Four Bosses, the only ones who might be prepared to show her a bit of consideration were Ou Guangming and Wang Shun, so she now changed her mind and headed for the iron and steel works. However, yet again, she halted before she got even close. If she went to see them now, what could she do other than complain about what had happened? Right now the most important thing was to find out what was actually going on, and best of all would be if she could think of a way to proceed and then go and discuss it with them.

All of a sudden she called to mind An Jinghui. She was a very competent woman, and in this crisis she might know what to do. Fortunately, they'd remained in touch through the intervening years. When the fleet of cars set off for the big city at New Year's and other festivals to hand out presents, Lin Meitang always made sure that her name appeared on the list. Now she might have a good idea about what to do next, and at the very least she'd be in a position to provide reliable information... At this point Lin Meitang turned round and headed for home, since she was now in a hurry to get An Jinghui on the phone. An Jinghui was deeply shocked to hear the news that Guo Cunxian had been arrested. She was very concerned, and there was not the slightest evasion or hesitation in what she said. Clearly this had piqued her journalistic interest. She immediately promised Lin Meitang that she'd find someone to ask what was going on, and once she had any news she'd ring back.

After putting down the phone, Lin Meitang didn't dare leave the house. She stayed sitting by the phone, but she did also switch on the television. The arrest of someone like Guo Cunxian should be the top news story, but she was hoping that he wouldn't appear at all. As long as there were no reports in the media, there would still be room for manoeuvre. They could apply pressure at various points, and things might yet turn in a better direction. Once this made the TV news then everyone would know about it, people would be watching them and discussing what happened, so both the people wanting to punish him and the person being punished would find themselves boxed into a corner. In that case, Guo Cunxian was done for.

Lin Meitang was really suffering, and time seemed to drag on endlessly. An Jinghui didn't ring back until after dark. She was an amazing person, capable of reporting the deliberations of the standing committee in Dahua City as if she'd been there in person. All the key points of their discussion were now reported back to Lin Meitang. She begged her: "There's nobody else I can ask, you have to help me, Jinghui. Save Guo Cunxian! I don't care how much it costs. I'll bring you the money tomorrow."

An Jinghui didn't respond to these overtures one way or the other, but her tone was cold: "Meitang, this isn't going to be something you can fix with money. The background to this arrest is very complicated, and the situation is now out of your hands. I am afraid that the people who want to punish him won't be bought off. Try not to worry too much. I am going to do my best for you. If I need money, I'll tell you."

Lin Meitang was deeply moved. To tell the truth, she'd never been that fond of An Jinghui, but now in this crisis she'd had to ask her for help and she'd clearly done her very best. She didn't make the slightest attempt at putting her off; it was almost as if the more difficult the situation, the more effort she was prepared to put in. Lin Meitang thought a lot of An Jinghui's advice. She needed to report this immediately to Guo Cunxian's family and the Four Bosses, and then they could discuss how to get him off. Just at that moment, the TV news came on. She decided to watch it and then head out of the door. First the national news was played, and Lin Meitang breathed a sigh of relief. Then the announcer's voice changed as they gave one last item in the time slot remaining: following a series of murders in Guojiadian, the famous entrepreneur and former secretary of Guojiadian, Guo Cunxian, had been arrested today…

She could feel her mind was almost stunned by this blow, and her chest felt as if constricted, her breathing difficult, but one thought conquered all: this is the end! Guo Cunxian would never be coming back. Now everyone knows that he's been arrested. If An Jinghui was right, those behind the arrest couldn't care less that the members of the standing committee were opposed to it, so that is why they had decided to go public like this. They wanted to put the thing to bed, and that meant Guo Cunxian might well be facing the death penalty. She suddenly felt prickles of fear up and down her spine, and she hesitated as to whether she ought to inform the Guo family about what had occurred.

Everyone would have been watching the news just now, so if she turned up with further bad news, wouldn't she just be adding to the general pain and causing needless aggravation? Having vacillated for a long time, in the end she decided to go, but this was not because she expected other people to ask her what was going on, but because she needed to ask others what they thought and what they intended to do about it. She was utterly confused, she had no idea what was going on, but if she stayed at home she'd either sink into depression or go mad. As Lin Meitang walked out of her house, in the distance she could hear firecrackers going off. Sometimes it was huge firecrackers with a sound like thunder, sometimes it was little firecrackers that sounded more like popcorn on the stove. Then there was the sound of running feet.

Clearly people had come to the village from neighbouring communities and were now setting off firecrackers, and it sounded as if Guojiadian were under attack from all sides. She was puzzled: was this some kind of festival? Why were they setting off firecrackers like this? Were they trying to make a thing of the fact that Guo Cunxian was in trouble? She crossed the main road to the west, and she could hear shouting at the entrance to the village, when suddenly one voice rang out louder than all the rest.

"Fuck off you bastards from Wangguantun and Miaojiazhuang! You think people here are going to let you get away with this? I'll fuck eight generations of your ancestors first!"

It was Ou Guanghe's voice.

In the darkness came another angry voice: "How about we set off some firecrackers of our own? I've got a bag of huge crackers from Xiaodingzhuang. That'll show them!"

Someone else stopped him: "Bastard! Do you want it to look like we're celebrating the secretary's arrest too?"

Lin Meitang's heart was thumping. If neighbouring villages were being invited to set off firecrackers, they must be celebrating Guo Cunxian's arrest!

They must all have seen the TV news just now. But why did they hate us so much? Were they jealous of the money coming into Guojiadian, or were they still angry about those unfortunate statues? Why were they so angry? Of course, as everyone knows, it might all be the result of malicious gossip. The general public don't understand what is going on, they don't see what is happening behind the scenes, and sometimes without you even noticing, someone does become famous overnight. Or the other way around, someone can find their life ruined because the people or the government has turned against them for no reason at all.

Be that as it may, it had been a terrible mistake for Guojiadian to do nothing to improve relations with neighbouring villages after they got rich. It wasn't just a problem with neighbouring villages either. If they'd maintained good relations with the county and the city, would this have happened today? However, it was now too late for regrets.

She didn't have time to stay and listen to people shouting at each other by the entrance to the village. She now hurried in the direction of Guo Cunxian's home. From the gate to the house, upstairs and down, it was full of people. The sitting-room was packed: Guo Cunzhi and his wife were there, and so were Guo Cunzhu and her husband, Qiu Zhantang, not to mention Liu Yucheng and his sister. They were all sitting with Zhu Xuezhen, while Ou Guangming and Wang Shun were standing off to one side. Other villagers were standing or sitting anywhere there was space. Unable to say much useful, they contented themselves with sighing, or making an angry comment now and again, interspersed with a few curses. The most important thing was that they'd come round to see the Guo family, they were looking after Zhu Xuezhen. Whether they actually said anything didn't matter.

When Ou Guangming caught sight of Lin Meitang making her way in, he broke the silence immediately: "Have you heard any news?"

Lin Meitang said to Zhu Xuezhen: "This morning I spoke to An Jinghui and she just phoned me back to say that it was the Public Security Bureau in Dahua that secretly arrested Secretary Guo. This was done without any prior warning, and immediately after the arrest there was a meeting of the standing committee at which Mayor Zhang and the former county chief Feng Hou both quarrelled with Secretary Gao. They are really opposed to this arrest. However, the city leaders are hand-in-glove with the police over this, and they got permission from the provincial authorities. I've asked An Jinghui to help us get Secretary Guo out of this mess, whatever it costs. Tomorrow I'm going to the city to give her the necessary money."

"Whatever it costs, I'll pay," Qiu Zhantang said. "In a sec, I'll get someone to give you the cash."

Lin Meitang waved him away. "Don't worry, I have the money. An Jinghui said on the phone that she didn't want me to bring cash, but even if she doesn't agree I'm still going to do this. Right now we need to find out who has a say in this matter, and we go and visit all of them. After all, we can't know exactly who will be able to put in a good word at the right moment. If I understand An Jinghui correctly, the only people now who can save Secretary Guo would be the provincial governor or someone from the Central Committee."

"OK," Ou Guangming said, "tomorrow I'll go and talk to the provincial secretary."

"I'll go to Beijing for a look-see," Wang Shun said. "In recent years I've got to know a few people there, and they might have an idea. Somehow or other we've got to get Guo Cunxian off. If I can't even manage that, how could I have the gall to stay in Guojiadian with my family?"

The atmosphere in the sitting-room immediately started to improve. People stopped feeling so helpless and depressed, they were going to find a way to get him off, there were still things that they could do.

Zhu Xuezhen was sitting on the sofa, and from start to finish she didn't say a word, she didn't even move. Her expression never changed. Although she didn't appear to be panicking, she also didn't seem to be moved at all by the friendliness and helpfulness of those in the room. She didn't even say a word of thanks, and it seemed as though she held out no hope for her husband's future. Lin Meitang had originally intended to go over to try to cheer her up, but when she saw Zhu Xuezhen's face, she didn't dare say a word.

Although Guo Cunxian was now under arrest, he found it hard to believe that such a thing could be happening to him. Even when he'd been pushed into the police car, he was still arguing with himself, and still questioning: Can this be true? Have they really dared to arrest me? Am I going to be held for just a couple of days until all of the fuss about the man dying has had a chance to calm down, or is this a real arrest? Whose idea was it, anyway? It cannot possibly be the Public Security Bureau on its own. Even though Wu Lie never liked me and I reckon he's a nasty piece of work, he doesn't have the authority to touch me! So who in the city is behind all of this? It wouldn't be the mayor, Zhang Caiqian, he's always helped me and would never agree to my arrest. How about Secretary Gao Jingqi? That's not very likely. Although I don't like him much, he's done a lot of grazing at Guojiadian's trough over the years. He's not going to want to see his road to riches threatened. The person who's most likely to want to cause trouble for me is that bastard Qian Xishou, but surely he doesn't have the authority? Do the higher-ups know that I've been arrested?

Guo Cunxian's mind was spinning in confusion. It would be a lie to say he wasn't frightened, or that he wasn't panicking, but things weren't desperate yet. He seemed to be trying to make his way through an endless maze, in which his questions had no answers. This was worrying him because, if he couldn't think, he couldn't deal with what other people were likely to throw at him. After all, he'd been in charge of Guojiadian and that made him important, there was no doubt at all about that. If they now arrested him, did that mean they'd already made up their minds that the case was over? Was there going to be some new big political movement? He'd got himself into this mess, now he'd have to find his own way out.

What is going to happen now that I've been arrested? Will they send me to prison? If so, for how many years? What are they going to be accusing me of? You should know that right now we peasants are in the ascendant. Are you so afraid of not being able to control us that you are prepared to kill the goose that lays the golden eggs? Guo Cunxian was overcome by a sense of terrible fear. His heart had never been good, and he might well die before he even found out who was behind all of this.

Fame is a very fragile, very feeble thing, and the fates that can overtake the famous can really surprise you. However, there are circumstances in which it can protect you from danger, as well as cause you trouble – one of the key aspects of fame is the way in which you handle it. If you are always throwing your weight about, you can really find yourself in a dangerous position.

He was having a very bumpy ride in the police car. They turned first this way and then that, all the time lurching over a road apparently composed entirely of boulders. Gradually he felt that his heart had started to beat properly, and he was no longer feeling suffocated – he was now sure he was going to be OK. But maybe he was now going to be heading down from heaven into hell. It was surprising to him that his heart, which normally played up at the least little thing, now seemed to have decided that, in this genuine crisis, it needed to be beating regularly. It seemed as though, in his present troubles, he'd have to rely entirely on himself. Once you make up your mind to deal with it, life is just one damn thing after another. You just have to take it one step at a time. As officials often say, you have to cross the river by feeling the stones. But if you fall in, there's no point in complaining that your clothes are all wet.

Finally the police car turned in through a huge, heavily guarded gateway. The courtyard was almost empty, yet there was a feeling that many people were watching. Once Guo Cunxian got out of the car, the police took him into a small room. Out of sheer curiosity and nerves, and in order to be prepared for whatever was coming next, he looked around carefully. There was a large table in the middle of the room, and behind it were three armchairs, while in front there was a stool. That was obviously there for him to sit on.

Once he was seated on that little stool, he'd be staring straight across at the huge red words on the opposite wall: 'Speak the truth and you will be treated well. Resistance will be punished!' These eye-catching words seemed to stab him to the very heart. He couldn't stop shaking.

It was somewhat odd to see a small, beat-up sofa up against one wall. This did not fit at all with the rest of the appointments in the room. He laughed to himself. This is going to be my seat. Wherever I go, I am still Guo Cunxian, and even when I'm under arrest I still get special treatment. Oh well, since it's here I may as well make use of it. He threw himself full-length on the sofa.

He was going to be keeping control of the situation, showing everyone who was boss. That would tell whoever showed their face who was in charge here!

He still hadn't decided how he was going to deal with whatever happened next; he was just going to have to wait until someone came in. Oh, not him again! Even though they'd never really spoken to each other, Guo Cunxian hadn't forgotten his face. This was the man who had brought the investigation team to Guojiadian way back when, and then a little while ago it was him who'd come to Guojiadian to take away their guns and arrest people. Now it was him who'd brought him here, when he'd be quite happy never to see the man ever again. When you see a familiar face under such circumstances it is best to pretend not to recognise them; it is an even better idea if the person is an enemy! However, the expression in this man's eyes was so alien that he even wondered whether he'd made a mistake. Right now every time he saw a policeman he felt like this was someone he'd already seen but that might well just be the effect of the uniforms. The very obvious fact that this is a professional policeman obscures his other personal features. In Guo Cunxian's eyes, all the police that he'd met today looked pretty much the same. They were stern-faced and held themselves rigidly, looking confident but abstracted, without the slightest sign of individuality. If you'd been asked to describe them, you would have been hard put to do so. Of course, this might also be because he himself was confused. When you have just been arrested it is hard to remain calm, so prisoners probably always have difficulty in telling individual police officers apart.

After coming in, the man walked straight over to the table and sat down in the chair in the middle. He then put down the file that he'd been holding in a place where he could consult it easily. From his unconcerned air, you might think that Guo Cunxian wasn't in the room at all. When he turned to look at him, Guo Cunxian felt his heart give a sudden thump. He tried to calm himself. You couldn't have said that he was frightened by this man, but he thought him strange, or perhaps his reaction was the result of anger. For years now he'd been looking at people, and they fell generally into a handful of basic categories: there were those cosying up to him, those trying to flatter and fawn on him, those who were frightened of him, those who were admiring and envious, those who were jealous and those who were curious. Even very senior government officials, when they met him, would show friendliness and curiosity in their eyes. But this man's expression was so calm: he was serious without it being a deliberate pose, and without being in the least tense, his face was entirely expressionless. What was going on here? Doesn't he know how important I am? Whatever crimes I might have committed I'm still in charge of Guojiadian – isn't he even slightly curious about me? Is he just pretending not to have noticed that I'm sitting here?

No. If he was pretending, this man would be really difficult to deal with.

He wanted to hide how nervous all this was making him, so he deliberately leaned back, putting his legs up, draping his arms over the sofa armrests. The other man's face was still as cold as ever, but now he spoke: "Guo Cunxian! Come and sit on this stool in front of me."

Of course he wasn't going to move. He waved a hand carelessly. "Whatever. Why can't we speak here?" Ha! He was carrying on like it was his own office. OK, so that's how it's going to be. Who the hell do you think you are?

The new arrival looked at him blackly, and he spoke with even greater severity: "No. You are going to be questioned now, so you have to come and sit over here."

"So who's this sofa for?"

"The sofa isn't there for you to sit on, that's for sure. It's there for when an interrogation goes on for a very long time, or when people collapse because of stress. Get yourself over here, or do you imagine that you're still going to get special treatment even in this place?"

How dare he have a go at me like that! For more years than he could remember, it had always been Guo Cunxian who attacked other people – nobody treated him like that! The man sitting on his chair looked pretty nasty, and his tone of voice and the expression in his eyes all said that he wasn't the kind of person to let anyone get away with disrespecting him. Clearly if he didn't accept his fate, the man would call in the police officers standing by the door to help him... Oh well, there's nothing one can do about it, this isn't Guojiadian, and the fact is that, ever since ancient times, people have always had to climb down over this kind of thing. As the saying goes, when you're under someone else's roof you have to bow your head. It is the mark of a real man that he knows how to give way gracefully. So he got up and moved to sit on the little stool in front of the table, and that immediately made him feel uncomfortable. What a horrible thing to do to anyone. There was no support for the back, which soon made it exhausting to hold yourself up, and so you'd end up having to hunch forward. Once you started hunching forward, your legs are going to have to be curled up to support your body, and your arms will hang down – you'll be pushed into a defensive posture. How can you then stop yourself from feeling guilty of something? Now that he looked like a criminal, the man immediately started his interrogation.

"Name?"

"What! Are you telling me you arrested me without knowing who I am?"

"Stop fussing, we haven't arrested the wrong man. We need you to tell us your name. That's the rule here."

"Guo Cunxian."

"Date of birth?"

"First of January, nineteen thirty-eight." Listen up, someone with such a lucky date of birth isn't supposed to end up sitting here like this! Everyone who's ever told my fortune has said the same thing, with a birthday like that you are going to end up rich and famous!

"Family background and education?"

Suddenly he felt that he couldn't stand this any longer. This interrogator wasn't asking about anything important, he was just asking questions to which he obviously already knew the answers. Was he trying to grind him down, or was he pretending to be stupid in order to annoy him? He snapped back: "What has my family background got to do with me ending up sitting here? If you cared about my background and education, would you have arrested me like that? I have nothing to say on this subject. My memory is terrible, so I simply don't remember any more. There's no point in asking me."

"This is part of the legal process and you have to answer my questions. If you don't have a good memory, then you can tell me about yourself one year at a time, starting from birth."

The man was staring deep into his eyes and was clearly weighing him up. Of course Guo Cunxian stared straight back, trying to work out what kind of person he was dealing with. Right now it is one-on-one, and only the smart deserve to survive. Could he keep clear of the traps the other man was setting? Maybe he's deliberately trying to look as if he has all the time in the world, because he thinks that'll get me to talk. This is a test. He must know that I am not going to let him get anything out of me so easily.

However, the situation right now required calmness; it would be dangerous to get upset. The moment he became anxious, the person in control of events would be in a position to go on the offensive. After all, he was in control of the situation, and not you. Although his position was not dissimilar from that of the lamb in the lion's den, he did not despair of winning the battle of wits. Who knew how many hours that would take? But if the man sitting opposite was really smart, there was no need to be wasting all this time on petty details. Guo Cunxian then rattled off a few dates and events, pretending to be impatient. The interrogator didn't hear all of them clearly and asked him to repeat. This allowed him to strike back: "I've said what you asked me to. If you can't be bothered to listen, what am I supposed to do about it?"

The man sitting opposite started, and then sketched a grin. He didn't insist on him answering the questions properly, but looked down and took out a piece of paper from the folder in front of him. In an even harder voice he started to read aloud from it: "According to the laws of the People's Republic of China [and here he cited the relevant statute], you are now placed under arrest. Sign here, please."

Guo Cunxian felt as if he'd been hit over the head. This was actually for real! At least he was in some way prepared. He knew that once he got into the clutches of the police it would not be so easy to extract himself again, but to hear such an announcement in such a place – his heart was thumping erratically. Did that mean the Public Security Bureau had the requisite permission? They would have had to go pretty high up the food chain for that, so who had they found to approve this?

People may seem tough, but it is hard to maintain this attitude when you are in the grip of the law. The law is like the mills of the gods, which grind exceedingly small. However, he was still trying to look tough and show how little he cared about these proceedings: "You insisted on arresting me, so what am I supposed to do about it? If I didn't agree, then what? However, I am not going to sign this."

The interrogator now stopped looking quite so cheerful and started glowering at him again. "I am telling you that signing this document is a standard legal procedure. Once an arrest warrant is issued then it goes into effect immediately. If you imagine you can leave today, you are quite wrong."

"Why am I under arrest? What is your evidence?"

"Don't worry, we have plenty. Otherwise, how could we arrest someone like you?"

"You've asked me all of these questions, so can I now ask you something? Can I at least know who's responsible for having me arrested, and who's going to be questioning me?"

"My name is Wu Lie, and I've been to Guojiadian a good few times, so you ought to know me. Just now I was in charge of the team arresting you at the International Hotel, but I guess you were so confused you didn't notice me. Maybe you should have been arrested more than a decade ago, but the time simply wasn't ripe then. Now the moment has come and I've got you bang to rights. I've been put in charge of investigating your case all over again. It seems that destiny keeps bringing us together. However, there is no need for you to worry too much. I work to the facts and the evidence."

Sooner or later, enemies always meet in a narrow lane. Now he'd fallen into the clutches of someone who was really out to get him. With a bastard like this in charge of the case, how on earth was he going to get off? He hid his fright and worry and refused to pick up the gauntlet that Wu Lie had so casually tossed down. He decided not to focus on the past, but to ask another even more important question: "In a while, am I going to be in a cell on my own, or will I be sharing with other prisoners?"

"We're putting you in with some others."

"I want my own room. If it's a question of money, then I can tell people to come from Guojiadian with the necessary. You name the price, I'll pay it."

"This isn't anything to do with money. This is the rule. We have to take responsibility for your safety."

"Responsibility for my safety? You don't imagine that I'm going to commit suicide, do you? I'm not the kind of person to kill himself."

"Of course, of course, someone like you isn't going to do something stupid like that! But if you're so full of confidence, why are you worried about being in with other people?"

"I've always had problems sleeping, particularly in any new place. Even at home, in my own room, with a doctor to provide massage before I got to bed, I still often cannot sleep at all. If you put me in a cell with lots of other people, it may well kill me. If you drive me insane with lack of sleep, I'm sure you're not going to get anything out of questioning me."

"I am afraid this is not your home, this is a jail and we don't make exceptions. Whether you like it or not, you are just going to have to put up with it. If we were going to let you stay in a grand room all by yourself with a personal masseur, why would we have bothered to arrest you in the first place? The most important thing for you right now is to think about what you've done and what you're currently doing, and think carefully. If there's one thing you have now, it's time to think."

Wu Lie was finally showing irritation. He waved his hand at the two police officers by the door, and they came in and took Guo Cunxian away. It was obvious that he was now going to be put in a cell somewhere.

He was starting to worry. Just now, was I too argumentative with this Wu Lie? Maybe I should have just signed the paper the way that Wu Lie said. It doesn't seem to make any difference whether I sign or not. He was mulling over this first round of questioning: where had he scored, where had he made a mistake? Having turned first this way and then that, he was taken by the two police officers down yet another corridor. Just before they got to the end, they unlocked the iron door to one of the cells. They escorted him in and then closed the door with a thud and locked it.

The first thing he saw in the cell was a row of bunk beds, but at the same time he realised that the room was full of other people. Their eyes were questioning, sarcastic, unpleasant, enjoying his downfall and filled with evil intentions of all kinds. Glances were shot at him from every corner of the room, from men lying in bed and from men standing beside their beds. He could almost feel himself being flayed by their gaze.

He was nervous and couldn't prevent himself from shaking. He could smell the stench of blood coming from somewhere. This was like being locked in a cage with wild animals and the best you could say was that they hadn't attacked him yet. Guo Cunxian didn't utter a word but balled up his fists where they couldn't be seen. He was preparing to fight for his life. Just as the saying goes, when the tiger loses its claws even a dog will bully it. Way back when, I fought in battle. I may be old now, but I've nothing to fear from you horrible lot! After a while he calmed down, and he could see that nobody was occupying the bed by the door. In fact both the upper and lower bunk beds were empty. Perhaps that was the reason he'd been placed in this cell, it was simply because there were empty beds here. He went over and sat down on the lower bed.

By his reckoning, the other bastards in this cell should have had a good look at him by now and have some idea of what they were dealing with, so now it was his turn to measure them up. He stared at them one at a time. Most of them were between the ages of twenty or thirty, with unpleasant expressions and nasty-looking eyes, and attitudes suggesting that they were men of violence. Really, they might as well have been provided by central casting. They couldn't have looked more savage if they tried. Perhaps they'd appeared different before they got put in here, but now no matter how handsome and charming they might have been, they'd turned into brutes. This thought having crossed his mind, a cold shiver suddenly ran down his spine. Wasn't he now one of these brutes himself?

He suddenly came to notice two hunched-up old men in the furthest corner of the room. From the looks of things they were a good bit older than he was. Without entirely understanding why, he found himself feeling a strange sense of disgust, but also relief, as if at the very least there were people in this cell who were in a worse position than him. Nobody said anything and the atmosphere was extremely tense, as if the place was going to explode any moment. He didn't know whether this was normal, or whether it was because he'd just arrived that people were behaving in a strange way. Just as he was puzzling over this, the door opened with a thud and the police thrust another prisoner in.

The new arrival was a very good-looking man, but whether from anger or fear, his handsome face was distorted. His gritted teeth made his jaw stand out, revealing his conceit and determination. The police officers who'd brought him there under guard now stood by the door and stared into the cell for a moment. Then they shut the door and walked off. Six or seven of the men in the cell now stood up, and they looked at the new arrival. What on earth was going on? There hadn't been a welcome like that when he'd been put in the cell just now. Maybe they'd all been involved in the same case, and the person who'd just come in was their boss. Guo Cunxian was speculating to himself when he saw the others violently attack the new arrival, and before he could really see what they were up to, they'd put a hand over the man's mouth to keep him quiet while they punched his head, and they grabbed hold of his arms to leave themselves free to kick him. One of the men then opened the lavatory behind the main door. The pan was already full of piss and shit, and the cell immediately filled up with a foul stench. This had obviously been prepared in advance. Before the new arrival had time to even scream, his head was thrust down into the pan. A bastard with a really nasty face slammed the lid down on his neck and then applied pressure with his foot.

The wretched new arrival fought back as hard as he could, and twisted his whole body this way and that, but how could he possibly get away? Now his movements were getting weaker, he was gradually losing strength, and in the end his body went slack and stopped moving entirely. The ferocious man with the appallingly scarred face now gestured to the door and someone immediately ran over and started thumping on it, yelling at the top of his voice: "He's killed himself! Someone's drowned themselves in the lavatory!"

The sound of running footsteps came down the corridor and the iron door was quickly thrown open. The police who came in immediately covered their mouths and noses with their hands. By this time all the prisoners were back on their own beds, leaving the man who'd choked on the piss and shit squatting next to the lavatory. From the shoulders on up was just a horrible mess.

The moment the police looked at this scene they ought to have understood what had happened; nobody could possibly kill themselves like that. Even if you did choose to stick your head into the lavatory, would you be able to commit suicide that way? The police were disgusted but didn't seem to want to ask any questions, as if they had no interest whether this man had killed himself or not. One of them gestured at a couple of the others and told them to take the dead man out into the courtyard and run him under a tap, as if once he'd been cleaned up, that would be enough.

Once the police had left, Scarface ordered some of the other younger criminals to open the windows of the cell, and to wash out the lavatory area. Clearly he was in charge of this cell. At some point in the past someone must have stabbed him in the face deliberately; the scars crisscrossed his face evenly, making a horrifying spectacle. But it was remarkable when you looked into his eyes what a spirit you saw there. It should immediately put you on high alert. Could it be that everyone who comes into this cell has to undergo this kind of baptism? So why had he been spared? Was this because he was special, because he had connections, that they didn't dare kill him? Or was it because the other man was special, meriting a treatment that would not be meted out to anyone else? Good God, he'd have to be sharing a room with these animals! He wasn't going to be able to sleep, because even if he dared to close his eyes in their company, he couldn't actually rest. Even if he dared to try to sleep, would he be able to do so?

Just now, Wu Lie had put a lot of emphasis on one sentence: he said I should have been arrested more than a decade ago. Now what did he mean by that?

27

DEATH IN LIFE

When someone is knocked loose from their foundations, they find themselves spinning without any sense of gravity, lost in a dark and unpredictable realm. The very night is filled with lights, and that is even more frightening than the pitch blackness. In every direction there were spots of darkness, soft and viscous, and powerfully attractive. They made his floating body spin faster and faster, and he fell at an ever-increasing speed. He was scared witless and felt as though his head were about to explode. Even as he jerked awake, Guo Cunxian found that he was soaked in sweat.

He knew that he wasn't going to be able to get back to sleep tonight, whatever else happened. Sleep comes when your mind is at rest. Having got to this age and being in jail for the first time, and on the first night, how could he possibly relax? But even though he was not at rest, how could he endure the whole night without closing his eyes? The moment he tried to close his eyes and calm down, he found himself feeling very uncomfortable, his mind wandered, unable to fix itself upon anything. He could feel evil spirits and ghosts pressing in upon him, and this was terrifying.

When he opened his eyes, he found he was lying just like before on a hard wooden bed, with bright lights shining. A searchlight out in the courtyard lit up everything in the cell as bright as day. Although he hadn't been injured at all, his whole body was suffering, there wasn't a single place that didn't hurt. No matter how he tossed and turned the pain was still there, and he felt as though any moment now his skeleton would be falling apart. Was this a sign of old age? Maybe he was now really old. But he was just over fifty, and he should be in the prime of life. It was all the fault of those bastards out in the village – just a year or so ago they'd started calling him the Master. Since this was supposed to be a sign of respect, he'd enjoyed hearing them do so, but it was now making him feel old. It was only here in the cell that he was able to admit this to himself, because he had to. He couldn't take any more, his bones were suffering. It had to be because he was getting old.

Night ought to be black, it ought to be dark, with blackness and darkness hiding everything, to assist with concealment and evasion. When you can see nothing you are willing to shut your eyes, and then your mind begins to clear. Light, on the other hand, is the source of all reality. The reason why prisons are equipped with so many searchlights is so as to allow the incarcerated no opportunity for evasion; so that even on the darkest night there is no way to conceal anything, and that includes what they have done. If you are forced to confront reality at every moment, then you have to endlessly face up to the disgusting facts that are drawn to your attention.

Clearly he was going to have to learn how to sleep with his eyes open.

Everyone has experienced a sleepless night that they actually enjoyed, a night spent pondering past triumphs. If you have a good life it is easy to sleep, and when you do, you have sweet dreams. The night belongs to women, it belongs to couples. When you hug a woman against you, even though you cannot sleep, it can still be a truly wonderful experience. But in custody, all you can think of are terrible things, and whichever way your mind turns, it moves inexorably towards the most depressing outcomes. He could not keep thinking about what Wu Lie had said because that would mean the direction of his thoughts was being determined by the man. That way, he would have fallen into his trap. He was trying to stop him from sleeping. But if you can dream sweet dreams in this kind of situation, doesn't it suggest that you are truly heartless? Either you are inhuman or you are a great hero, the kind of person who doesn't blink an eye when the heavens come crashing down on his head. Well, you could describe Guo Cunxian as that kind of hero, couldn't you?

In wartime, heroes who had fought in battle were admired. Everyone knew their names and people talked all the time of the great things they'd done. Heroes direct social trends, they purify the national spirit, and they elevate the character of the people and society as a whole. After the Liberation, model workers were lauded, they were heroes on the frontline of national reconstruction. However, during the Cultural Revolution, people began to despise heroes and they came under constant attack. This was the age of anti-heroism. Now, economic heroes were in charge, so if you could earn big bucks then you are a hero, anyone who gets rich is a hero. Didn't everyone say: "Anyone who turns a deficit into a profit is a hero"? The marketplace is like a battlefield, and successful entrepreneurs are the heroes of a market economy. Money can make you practically divine, and society always praises the rich to the skies. If you're the richest man in the world, then you're a hero to men and women, old and young, all over the world. Right now all sorts of beauty queens, the lovely young women who are TV stars, models or singers, are all in mad pursuit of businessmen and want to marry men who are the bosses of their own companies. That is the modern world for you, just like in the past girls all wanted to marry heroes or model workers. That is how it has always been: amazing people do amazing things, amazing things result in amazing achievements. Guo Cunxian thought he'd done amazing things, an amazing person with amazing achievements. So what if he had to be imprisoned for a while, he ought to look on this as yet another strange episode in his remarkable existence. You still have to eat and sleep, and when you sleep you should dream sweet dreams. That is the way to hold out under pressure, and that is how to live long.

He spent ages trying to cheer himself up like this, but he still could not get to sleep. The fact is, the more he told himself he was special, the more miserable he felt about his present situation. Being unable to accept what had happened to him, he could not sleep. If you give up, then you can sleep soundly, after all sleep is a kind of death. Don't people often say 'sleeping like the dead'? If sleep is like death, then waking up is a kind of return to life. Guo Cunxian had lost all sense of time, and he kept tossing and turning, wishing that he could just stop breathing and that he could really just die. Then his pain would be over, it would be a good death, and it would be better than his present suffering. Once he died it would all be over, it would be quick, and very soon his body would have rotted away. If he didn't die, there'd still be a lot of suffering to endure. If he died tonight, then what? The night belongs to death. People often die in the night of old age or disease. It is only those who die by violence who don't pick the time. There is a terrible curse in Chinese: 'May you suffer a bad death!'

Once you are put in prison, any hopes for a good death are probably over. It may yet happen of course, supposing that you are not sentenced to death, you can still hope. Maybe you can yet achieve a good death all by yourself. Many great people in this world have achieved fame in prison. After all, the great hero Yue Fei, invincible in battle, was killed in prison, but later generations built temples to his memory and prayed to him as a god. If the Monkey King Sun Wukong had not spent five hundred years under a mountain, how could he ever have become the Great Sage?

The fact is that he couldn't yet be sure whether being arrested and held in custody was going to be a good or a bad thing. He must have done great things in his past life, not to mention this one, to allow Guojiadian to flourish like this under his leadership. He'd become nationally famous as a result. The remarkable development that had taken place in Guojiadian was big news, and this wasn't just a source of pride for him or the village; it was important for China. So now he'd been arrested and put in prison. Who would dare to judge him? What were they going to accuse him of? He refused to believe that nobody would come forward and speak up on his behalf.

If he wasn't in prison himself, he could never have imagined how packed the cells were. From a very early stage in human development, mankind started to build prisons, and in the last couple of thousand years, all kinds of things have disappeared from the world, but prisons are definitely still with us, and more and more are built every year. How is it that prisons have become something human society cannot manage without? Some people say that 0.1 per cent of the entire global population is in prison at any one time. There are some Western countries where prisons are so full that it is a serious problem. The richer the country, the worse the prisons. Now was the moment for someone sensible to start building new prisons. You could earn a lot of money doing that... What are you thinking? If it wasn't for the money, would you be locked up now? Here you are lying in your cell bed too miserable to sleep, and you are thinking about building prisons to earn more money! Really, how stupid can you get?

The young man sleeping in the bunk above Guo Cunxian's head kept tossing and turning. You could imagine how upset he must be. To have your head thrust into a pile of shit and piss – it's disgusting just to think about. How do you ever recover from being exposed to such filth? Clearly the police were very experienced, or perhaps they have to deal with this kind of thing all the time, because this afternoon the minute they realised he'd choked on it, they dragged him out to be hosed down. And then having been hosed down, it turned out that he wasn't dead after all. He'd managed to survive having his head plunged into the lavatory like that.

But what a thing to live through! How can you ever feel clean again?

When he was sent back to the cell, he didn't immediately lie down on his own bunk and rest, but he stood in the entrance weighing up all the other people in the room, as if he were remembering and checking up on exactly who had been involved in assaulting him that afternoon. He didn't seem angry, or indeed scared. He was perfectly calm and even polite about it. This terrified the others. The cell went cold and was filled with fear. The inmates just glanced at each other, since they knew what they were in for. Each of those who'd hurt him turned their heads away, avoiding his gaze, and nobody dared to strike up a conversation with him.

Let's just wait and see. Those who'd injured him would now be in serious trouble.

For some people, humiliation is worse than death. They'd done such disgusting and filthy things to him, really it would have been better if they'd just killed him. When someone like that comes back, they don't come back as a human being; they've been transformed into a vengeful ghost, into a wild beast. He seemed to be so calm because he was bitterly angry. He'd already decided exactly how he would take his revenge, and he was sure that he was going to be successful. Whether you liked it or not, this little bastard had skills.

The most admirable demonstration of bravery is composure in the face of danger. Composure when you find yourself in a difficult situation is a remarkable characteristic, and as always, if you can keep your composure there is always hope. If I ever get out of here, I'm going to pay whatever it takes to get this man to come to Guojiadian to help me keep an eye on things.

The bed swayed gently. He thought that the young man in the upper bunk was getting down to pee. Such a young man to be having bladder problems! Or was this the result of what had happened to him this afternoon, did he still need to purge himself of the foulness in his guts? He was waiting to hear the sound of piss hitting the lavatory pan. During this unendurably long night, listening to someone else pee was something to mark the slow turn of the hours. However, for the longest time, there wasn't the slightest movement. Perhaps he simply couldn't hear what was going on.

Suddenly Guo Cunxian's mind went on high alert, though he realised that any attack would not be made on him. At night in the cells, the quieter it was the more frightening it became. He could feel his skin prickling with fear. All around him was the sound of grinding teeth, of whimpers and moans, of people talking in their sleep as if they were caught up in some nightmare. Was the young man walking in his sleep? Or was this the moment that he would strike?

Although sleep has certain similarities to death, once you die your soul leaves the body forever. Modern medicine has already confirmed the existence of the soul and the weight of the spirit, as well as how the soul leaves the body. When doctors treat epilepsy, they use electrodes to stimulate the patient's gyrus. The patient then feels 'light and bodiless', able to sense their soul floating out of their body, looking down at themselves lying on the bed, looking at their own feet and legs.

So scientists continued to experiment and put some people who were about to die on a set of high-precision scales. When the patient died, the balance shifted, and somewhere between ten and forty grams of weight suddenly disappeared. This lost weight should be the weight of the soul. Individuals are different, so the weight of their soul varies. In order to prove this, scientists performed the same experiment with dying dogs. Dogs at the moment of death didn't lose any weight. This shows that dogs do not have souls.

If you despise someone, you might say that he is a 'lightweight'. You aren't talking about how much he actually weighs, but about his spirit instead. You are saying that he doesn't have weight in that sense. Since people have spirits of different values, then of course they have very different qualities. If the spirits of the prisoners locked in this cell were allowed out, what good could possibly come of it? You would have evil, wickedness, trickery, violence, nastiness, greed, lecherousness... each of these qualities would appear in all their loathsomeness, showing their claws and fangs. This is a prison, after all. All sorts of horrible people have been imprisoned here, and plenty of them have died here too. This is a place with male and female ghosts, old ghosts and young ghosts, powerful ghosts and murderous ghosts, not to mention the ghosts of the innocent and suffering dead. This cell is a kind of hell.

This is why prisoners hate to be alone. The moment you are put in solitary confinement, you realise the importance of light. Prisoners are all afraid of the dark, and they are all afraid of closing their eyes. With your eyes open, nothing is a problem. But once darkness falls and you close your eyes, you hear all kinds of noises, sharp sounds and sudden cries, sobs and moans. Sometimes you may even hear men and women talking and laughing together, the sound of their cries, the clack of high heels walking along the road. Otherwise, why would prisons need such high walls? It is to prevent ghosts from coming in and harming people.

Suddenly there was a strangled gasp and a strange movement in the cell.

A breath of cold air whistled past Guo Cunxian's ear and the bed shook. It seemed as though the young man from the upper bunk was climbing back in.

In the circumstances, it wasn't just officials who were keeping well away from Guojiadian, even ordinary people were doing so, lest they get into some kind of trouble. Those staying furthest away were the cadres from Dahua City. Nearly all of them had been to Guojiadian in the past, and they'd all come back with something. This might turn out to be important, or it might not – just like when a toad jumps on your foot, it may not bite you, but it's still going to be disgusting. Senior cadres from Dahua City were now wishing there was no such place as Guojiadian, and that they'd never even met Guo Cunxian. After all, who knew where his interrogation might lead – who he might turn on to try to draw attention away from himself?

It was at this point that the deputy secretary of the municipality, Feng Hou, made time in his busy schedule to go out to Guojiadian. He was worried, and he wanted to find out whether his concerns were justified. He had had a bad feeling about things when Guo Cunxian had been in trouble before, and now that he'd been arrested, how could he not feel an even greater concern? When he got to the village, he realised that his worries were entirely justified. In fact, the situation was much worse than he'd imagined. In the past thousands of visitors arrived in Guojiadian every day, but now the whole place was dead and nobody was out and about on the streets, and there was no traffic. A foot-thick layer of straw, wheat-straw and dried bean pods was scattered on top of the road, all drying in the sun. Since Feng Hou's car wouldn't be able to get past, he told his chauffeur not to try to enter the village but to drive round and have a look at the two industrial zones on the outskirts of Guojiadian. There was a tarmacked road heading out to the industrial zones, but it was completely empty. No workers could be seen, nor any cars. There was also not the slightest sound of anyone doing any work because all the factories were closed.

Now he knew where he was, he had to find people and talk some sense into them. He had his car stop at the western entrance to the village, and then he went in on foot, climbing over a thick layer of wheat-straw. He was shocked as he walked past the Lucky Trees. These two ancient trees no longer flourished as they had in the past, and they were covered with dead branches and dried leaves. Even the parts that weren't dead were diseased and decayed. The branches were spindly and sick-looking, and the leaves wizened. Fortunately someone was sitting under the trees, and given that this was the person he'd been searching for since the moment of his arrival in Guojiadian, he turned his steps that way.

It was almost noon and the air was warm. The man was sitting with his back to the tree, snoozing with his head in his hands. He looked just like Second Uncle, back in the day. However, he didn't have the wild hair, nor was he bearded. Feng Hou came close and joked: "Oh my God! Second Uncle's come back to life!"

The man suddenly opened his eyes: "How do you know that Second Uncle's dead?"

"Oh well..." Feng Hou fell silent. He looked carefully at the man. He was about fifty years old, looking a bit like Guo Cunxian, and then he asked: "Are you Guo Cunzhi?"

Guo Cunzhi said: "I recognise you, you're Feng Hou. Way back when you did a lot to help my older brother out, so how come he's now been arrested?"

Feng Hou sighed gently: "Well there are reasons for that, but it's a long story and this isn't the place to talk about it."

Guo Cunzhi got up from his place by the tree and said: "You've got to save him!"

"Right now nobody can guarantee saving him, but I have some ideas about how to help your village. Who can I discuss this with? Who's in charge round here?"

"Nobody. Guojiadian is finished. Even the Four Bosses have given up."

"Is your sister-in-law OK?"

"With all that's happened, how can she be?"

"I've heard that Cunxian's son is doing well?"

"Oh yes, he's gone to the United States to study, the first from Kuanhe County since the Liberation. He just cannot believe that his father would fall from grace like that."

"And do you have children?"

"Two girls. Mr Feng, when uncle was dying he told me to help my brother. At that time I didn't understand, and I thought that either I'd misheard or that he'd said something wrong. My older brother was always about a million times more competent than me. Right from when we were little it was always him who helped me, so how am I able to help him? But ever since he got into trouble I've been sitting under the trees trying to puzzle it out, and I'm thinking that what he said was something that I ought to ask you to do. After all, you've done so much for my brother already. You can save him, can't you? If you weren't going to, you wouldn't be here now, would you?"

"Cunzhi, before we go into all of that, can you help me with something?"

"What?"

"Can you go and get the Four Bosses and your sister's husband Qiu Zhantang... and anyone else you can think of who has a position in your village. Tell them I want to see them. I'll be waiting in the office of the village Party Committee."

"OK, I'll find some people to deliver the message for you." Guo Cunzhi set off at a jog.

Feng Hou followed on behind and went into the village, looking closely at everything there was to be seen. Very few people were out and about in the village, but there were plenty of pigs and chickens rooting about here and there, and the streets were filthy. He headed straight for the building housing the village Party Committee. The square out front was absolutely empty, and there wasn't a sign of any of the security guards. The door was secured with an ordinary bicycle lock. The fact that he couldn't see anybody didn't mean that nobody was looking at him. In fact he'd been under observation by the people of Guojiadian since the moment he arrived in the village.

After Guo Cunxian was arrested, very few cars came to Guojiadian, and of course the villagers knew perfectly well that no senior officials would be turning up. However, this meant that the presence of Feng Hou was more concerning and suspicious. But if he was here to arrest more people, why weren't there police and police cars with him? The villagers naturally knew that he'd played an important part in making Guojiadian successful, but the fact that he hadn't visited at all in recent years showed that he had a problem with what Guo Cunxian was doing. Even if he hadn't given orders to arrest him, at the very least it meant that he was onto something. So was he here today to prove that he'd been correct all along? Was he laughing at Guojiadian? Or was there going to be trouble? If anything happened in Guojiadian now, it would just about put the tin hat on things. When he was walking around the square in front of the main building, the villagers started to assemble, just a few at first, but then more and more were standing around him. Nobody said a word. The villagers in Guojiadian had been traumatised by all that they'd been through. You could see the worries and alarm in their eyes.

Feng Hou looked around and couldn't find a single familiar face, but he wasn't prepared to let them carry on staring at him like that, so he said in a loud voice: "I guess you'd be happy to pull me limb from limb after what has happened! However, you'd better not forget that everything you have today, you owe to my help in the first instance. As the saying goes, when you drink fresh water, don't forget the guy who dug the well. It seems to me you need to be reminded of that. Besides which, don't you want to know why I'm here today?"

The crowd looked at each other. Nobody said a word, but they seemed to surround him less tightly, and some of them even started to wander away. Feng Hou now felt much more relaxed, but the atmosphere was still a little awkward. Luckily Ou Guangming came running up at this moment, shouting: "Mr Feng, Mr Feng..." He was gulping for air as he shouted at everyone to move back: "What do you think you are doing? Piss off! Go away! Guojiadian owes a great deal to Mr Feng here, do you really think that he was behind Cunxian's arrest? Do you think anyone involved in Cunxian's troubles would be here in Guojiadian right now? They'll all be off hiding somewhere."

Feng Hou noticed that Ou Guangming wasn't calling Guo Cunxian 'Secretary' any more; he'd gone back to his old form of address. This had the effect of making him seem more friendly and concerned. He pushed his way through the crowd to grab hold of Feng Hou's hand. "Thank God you're here! We've been like a bunch of headless chickens. Nobody knows what to do and we can't get any reliable information. Everyone we try to talk to just runs away and hides."

As Ou Guangming spoke, his eyes filled with tears. He wasn't the silly young man that he had once been. He was now starting to go bald and get a pot-belly, but he had kept the same straightforward and open character.

Feng Hou shook his hand and asked: "How've you been? And how is Yumei?"

"We're both fine," Ou Guangming replied. "We get along OK, thanks for asking. I know I didn't do right by Yumei, and the fact is that we couldn't have more kids, but growing old just the two of us together is fine by me."

"Tell Yumei that I asked after her. And your younger brother is married?"

"Oh yes, he married a girl from Anhui who came here to find work. They've got a boy."

Feng Hou congratulated him again. Good! Good!

Ou Guangming suddenly reacted to their surroundings: "Don't let's just stand here, we should go inside." The problem was that the door was locked and when he asked, nobody seemed to know who had the key. He told someone to go and call Lin Meitang, perhaps she had it. However, he seemed unwilling to wait, and walking to the back of the building he found a grappling hook. This might have been a weapon at one point or had maybe even been used for beating people. He hooked it into the lock and pulled it open. There was a nose-prickling smell of dust and mould coming from inside the closed building. He called on the villagers assembled in the square for help, and they all went up to the second floor to open the windows of the meeting room.

Feng Hou went up to the second floor with everyone else, to find the tables, chairs and sofas all covered in a thick layer of dust. The villagers helped to sort things out: some of them were giving items a shake, others were wiping them down. Within a very short time he saw the people he needed to talk to come in one after another, and he came forward to say hello. Unlike the other bosses and peasant entrepreneurs, Liu Yucheng was still dressed exactly like the other villagers, and he couldn't stop himself from asking curiously: "How's the agricultural team doing, Mr Liu?"

Liu Yucheng looked as cheerful as ever, and he still had the same serious manner: "Mr Feng, I know people say that we don't take agricultural production seriously around here, but that's really not fair. We've got half as much again of land under cultivation, but we're getting three-and-a-half times as much grain. We're paying the largest amount of grain to the government of any team in the commune, and we're in the top ten in this county, plus we have the best quality year after year. I don't want to put myself in the wrong, so I always send our very best grain up to the government. Don't forget that our agricultural team comprises only fifty labourers, and we're cultivating land for the whole village, which has more than four thousand inhabitants."

Here, Ou Guangming broke in: "When the Indian minister of agriculture came to our village to have a look, he really couldn't stop admiring all that Yucheng had achieved here. He was going to invite him and his wife to visit India. However, with Cunxian's problems, I'm afraid it's not going to happen…"

"Oh, but it must," Feng Hou said. "Give me the letter of invitation from the Indian government and I'll make sure it happens." As he was speaking he raised his eyes and saw Lin Meitang come in, and he gave a little start: "Ah, Comrade Lin Meitang is here. Great! I thought you were still in Beijing."

Lin Meitang smiled coldly, but it very quickly turned into a miserable grin. "I couldn't stay there in the circumstances. Why should I let everyone gossip and laugh at us, making snide remarks behind our backs? With the problems we have, we're going to be poor, we're going to have people cursing us, but we might as well experience this all in the comfort of our own homes right here in Guojiadian."

Feng Hou suddenly found himself feeling a lot more respect for this woman. "Don't worry about gossip. That'll soon pass."

The last of the Four Bosses to arrive was Wang Shun. He came in red-faced and reeking of alcohol, and even with his wife, Hong Fang, there to help him, he was swaying from side to side. The moment he caught sight of Feng Hou, he pushed his wife aside and then stood to attention, bowed and announced: "Mr Feng, we know you're a great man, and you shouldn't let these little things get to you. No matter how annoyed you may have been in the past with Guo Cunxian, the fact remains that you helped him a lot. So I'm begging you to save him. I'm going to kowtow to you right here and now!"

As he spoke, he did indeed go down on his knees.

Feng Hou rushed forward to stop him, but he now squatted down on the ground and started to cry, his arms wrapped round his head. Hong Fang squatted down next to him, one arm round her husband to comfort him, while she tried to explain the situation to Feng Hou. "You mustn't mind him. Ever since Secretary Guo got into trouble, he's been so upset. He's been rushing around from pillar to post with money and presents, trying to find someone to intercede. He's been in business for so many years and he's met all kinds of people, some of them really senior too, but the moment you need them, they've either been refusing to see him or they've been putting him off politely. Some people have been worse, of course, they've taken the money and then done nothing at all. He's been begging all of these people for help, it's cost us an absolute fortune, but nothing seems to have worked. Then since yesterday he's been refusing to carry on like this, he's been drinking from the moment he opens his eyes in the morning, then he gets drunk and goes to sleep, and when he wakes up he starts drinking again…"

"You really are a good man, Mr Wang," Feng Hou sighed. "Guo Cunxian is lucky to have a friend like you. I've heard that, when you were trying to stop him making any more mistakes, all four of you went down on your knees in front of him! In your position, that must have been hard to do. Unfortunately he didn't appreciate your efforts, and that resulted in the terrible situation he's facing now."

As he spoke he assisted Wang Shun to get up and made sure he was comfortably ensconced in a chair, and then he continued his conversation: "The mayor, Zhang Caiqian, and I were informed at a meeting that Guo Cunxian had come to grief. We weren't told anything about it until after he'd already been arrested. We both really regret not coming out to Guojiadian at all in the last two years. If we'd come more regularly and kept an eye on things, we could have joined you in warning him of the dangers he was running and perhaps none of this would have happened. My visit to Guojiadian today is a private one. I haven't been sent by the city government or the municipal Party Committee, but I wanted to come and see you all. What I've seen has confirmed all my worst fears. Leaving agricultural work to one side, given that this is not the busiest time of year anyway, how can the four big industrial groups close their doors? You've got great businesses there and you've already established your brands. Are you really going to throw all that away and let Guojiadian go back to the way that things used to be?"

"If the country doesn't care," Wang Shun shouted, "why should we? If we start up again, won't we be letting Cunxian down? We need to show them that, without Guo Cunxian, Guojiadian wouldn't exist!"

"I don't care," Ou Guangming snorted. "I don't have any kids, so who am I going to leave all this money to anyway?"

"I know you're angry," Feng Hou shook his head. Then he turned to Chen Erxiong: "What do you think?"

Chen Erxiong looked deeply depressed. "Right now everyone is really worked up about the whole situation. You mustn't think that it was easy having Secretary Guo around because he made everyone so tense. Today he'd be suspicious of one person and then next day he'd be doubting whether someone else was telling him the truth. It created an environment in which everyone was terrified of him and they had to spend lots of time covering their own backs. That meant nobody dared to say what they really thought, and sometimes you had to lie to him because otherwise he'd turn on you. But because he was arrested like that, we all feel bad. We remember his good points, and there are more and more families that actually worship him…"

Feng Hou was shocked. "Worship him? You mean people are treating him like a god or something?"

"Oh yes," said Chen Erxiong. "It was already happening a few years back, when Guojiadian first got rich. For New Year's, everyone wanted to have a God of Wealth and I don't know quite how it started, but people were saying that Guo Cunxian was Guojiadian's God of Wealth. The one that they'd all been praying to for hundreds of generations was no damn use, but once Guo Cunxian was born, Guojiadian had its own real live God of Wealth. They kept their old statues of the god, but pasted a photograph of Guo Cunxian over the face…"

When Feng Hou heard this his heart was thumping as if he'd heard some very bad news: what on earth would happen here if Guo Cunxian never came back? There are plenty of failed heroes in Chinese history, and many of them became deified. The fact that they died in appalling circumstances seems to have aroused people's sympathy. Feeling sympathy then creates a feeling of closeness, that closeness results in legends, and legends can so easily be turned into myth…

Chen Erxiong saw that Feng Hou's expression had changed and that he appeared upset, so he stopped talking and looked at him. Feng Hou asked instead: "What has

Guo Cunxian becoming a God of Wealth got to do with the fact that you've ceased production? If you all go out of business, won't that mean Guo Cunxian has failed as a God of Wealth?"

"We had to stop," Chen Erxiong said. "We had some big jobs in hand at my place, and we're losing money hand over fist as it is. But if I didn't close down then the villagers would be cursing me, and if the worst came to the worst they might well sabotage my machines. They wouldn't dare turn on the police, but they'd take out their rage on me, make no mistake about that!"

Feng Hou was always a restrained and polite man, but at this he jumped up with some sign of agitation. He looked at these people who held the fate of Guojiadian in their hands, and he spoke in serious tones: "Don't you understand? What you are doing is very dangerous for Guo Cunxian, you are showing everyone that it was right to arrest him. He's really nothing but a nouveau riche peasant when you come right down to it, and Guojiadian's wealth was built on loans from state-owned banks, so the minute the banks cut your credit lines the four groups here were bankrupt. This is nothing about how much you produce, and Guo Cunxian's biggest achievement isn't the fact that he made Guojiadian rich. What he did was to provide an example of a really poor agricultural area getting rich at exactly the right time. That kind of example is the only thing that anyone can hand down to later generations. There have been tens of thousands, hundreds of thousands of super rich people in history. Which one of them was able to hand their wealth on to posterity? With him being arrested, you are supposed to pick up the baton and carry on his idea. This world doesn't belong to the powerful, and it certainly doesn't belong to the rich, it belongs to those who have ideals. As long as Guojiadian flourishes, Guo Cunxian will flourish too. It doesn't matter where he is, nobody will ever forget him. If Guojiadian fails, then it doesn't matter whether Guo Cunxian is in prison or not, because nobody will care one way or the other."

The conference room was dead silent. For the last few days, Guojiadian had been completely cut off from the outside world, but now the corridor outside the conference room and the stairs was packed with people, because they all wanted to hear what Feng Hou had to say. The fact is that many of them wouldn't be able to hear clearly, and even if they heard every word wouldn't necessarily understand, but the Four Bosses of Guojiadian needed Feng Hou to help them find their way out of this impasse. They were furious about what had happened, they were deeply upset, but they still weren't necessarily prepared to see the companies they'd built up from nothing go to the wall. Once Feng Hou's words were reported around Guojiadian, they could all go back to work.

Feng Hou now suddenly asked: "Are you blaming Guo Cunxian for getting Guojiadian into trouble? Of course I don't mean that he did it on purpose, he'd never want to do anything to hurt Guojiadian, but what he's done has resulted in all sorts of problems for this village, hasn't it? It would be great if he hadn't been arrested because then everything could carry on like normal. Isn't that what you think?"

Nobody said a word, either in the room or outside, so he carried on: "If you don't say anything, then I'm assuming you agree with my assessment. At the very least you must agree that what he's done hasn't been good for Guojiadian, right?"

This time some people nodded, while others murmured their agreement.

He waved his hands. "You're wrong. If you take the long view, you might even say that he's saved Guojiadian!"

The room fell so silent that you might have imagined even the air had congealed.

"What has happened this time here in Guojiadian is something that was going to happen sooner or later," Feng Hou continued. "With the way that you were all carrying on, if it didn't happen to Guo Cunxian himself, it might have happened instead to one of the Four Bosses or maybe some other senior management person. Guo Cunxian is a test. He's providing you with a lesson, he's telling you that things have to change. Don't you understand that? For example, he's telling you how to deal with government officials – you cannot pin all your hopes on any one higher-up, nor even a group of leaders, and you cannot imagine that your money and power will get you out of every kind of trouble. He's telling you how to deal with the government – do not get into open conflict over showing off your wealth. If a peasant enterprise does well, it's because the circumstances allow this. You cannot take all the credit yourself. No matter how successful you are, you do not operate in isolation. You always need help from the situation in which you find yourself. He's also telling you how to deal with the media. The moment you think you've bought them and that they'll be saying nice things about you from now on, all you've done is leave evidence of corruption in their hands. What Guo Cunxian has told you here are the facts of life. He wants you to understand that the principles that govern the way the world works are rigid, but the way that you must proceed is flexible. It is only by approaching the situation in a flexible way that you can understand how rigid the rules are. I am sure that in future Guojiadian will not go back to being the way it was in the past, but you also have to move on from the way that it used to be when Guo Cunxian was in charge here. That is the lesson to draw from Guo Cunxian's arrest, and you must not let this have happened in vain."

Everyone understood exactly what Feng Hou meant by this, particularly the Four Bosses, all of whom were listening intently. They almost felt a sense of enlightenment. He now lowered his head and whispered to Wang Shun by his side: "Have you sobered up now?"

Wang Shun nodded. "I'm sober and I feel as if I've woken up from a dream. I feel I've learned more in the last few minutes than I did in ten years of school!"

"How about you invite me to lunch then?" Feng Hou said.

"It would be a pleasure."

"Great! Find someone to go to the western entrance to the village and call my chauffeur here. Tell him not to forget that I've got a good bottle of wine in the car, I brought it especially as a present for you..."

"Aaaahhh...!" A strange scream, sharp and terrifying. It didn't seem to be a human noise, and everyone in the cell was jerked upright.

Scarface, who'd yesterday pushed the man sleeping in the bunk above Guo Cunxian's head into the lavatory pan, had now been found hanging.

He was hanging from a fine noose attached to the uppermost rung on his own bunk bed, and his feet were just inches from the ground. The person who started screaming first was the man who slept on the uppermost bunk. The whole cell was in chaos, but in the midst of all the confusion he managed to pull himself together and say: "Quick, get him down! From the looks of things he may not be quite dead yet. When people die by hanging, don't they have bug-eyes and protruding tongues? Look, his eyes are shut! Maybe he's doing it on purpose to scare us..."

Everyone leapt forward to assist, some undid the noose, while others took hold of his legs and torso. They were all unusually excited, and with lots of shouts and yells they managed to put Scarface back on his own bed. Afterwards they tugged at him, thumped him, slapped his face and pummelled his chest. But in spite of all their efforts, Scarface was dead.

Right from the beginning Guo Cunxian had been quite sure that Scarface wasn't going to be coming round. It was likely that he'd been garrotted long before he was strung up like that. Although he wasn't surprised to discover that Scarface was dead, he nevertheless sat up bolt upright in alarm when the screaming started. Of all the people in the cell, the man in the bunk above him was the only one who carried on just lying there, not moving, not looking, not saying anything and certainly not participating in all the fuss, as if it were not in the slightest bit interesting that someone was found hanging right opposite his bed. This little bastard was pretty damn calm and collected, whatever else you might say about him.

Nobody had a clue what to do, so the cell began to quieten down a bit.

Just at that moment the man in the bunk above Guo Cunxian suddenly said: "Shithead, there's only one thing to do if you want him to recover."

From the moment he entered the cell the previous day, this was the first time he'd spoken. His voice was gentle and refined, but it was also decisive. The person he called Shithead was the one in the bunk above Scarface's head, and he looked a complete thug. He now quickly asked: "What?"

"Get some water and spray it on his face."

"But we're all locked in. Where do I get water?"

"You've got pee in your bladder, haven't you? That's water!"

Immediately other people started to chime in: "Yeah! When someone's in a faint you spray them with water and then they wake up." The criminal types locked up in this cell were all the sort who'd go looking for trouble and who'd be up for anything. First they are up to one thing and then they are up to something else.

The man in the bunk above Guo Cunxian was lying down on his own bed staring at the ceiling. He didn't look at anyone, but he spoke with even greater determination: "Listen up, Shithead! If you don't pee on Scarface and get him to wake up, you're going to be dragged off God knows where later today."

Shithead was really nervous: "What do you mean? Aren't you just trying to get back at Scarface by getting me to pee on him? If you want him peed on, then come down and do it yourself..."

"There is a limit to my patience, bastard, and pretty soon I'm not going to be giving you any more good advice. Right now, we've got Scarface dead, and he was hanging right next to your head. Are you saying that you didn't hear a thing? Once you discovered him hanging there, you deliberately destroyed the crime scene – and your fingerprints are now all over the noose round Scarface's head, and on his bed. If he doesn't come round, you're going to be the first to be suspected of the crime."

"Yeah, you're right!" The little brutes who'd been making such a racket screaming and shouting were now speaking up for the guy on the upper bunk, and doing their best to scare Shithead.

Shithead was now really angry, and he came over to Guo Cunxian's bunk, shouting: "You're the one..." But the next word was choked in his throat. Guo Cunxian didn't see clearly the moment that the man got down from the bunk above him, but he grabbed hold of Shithead's right wrist and threw him onto the bed, and then in a single move he lifted him back up again, with his right hand holding tight to Shithead's throat, his fingers digging deep into the flesh. Scarface, who was supposed to have hanged himself, didn't have his eyes protruding, but Shithead's eyes were nearly starting from their sockets. His ugly and filthy face turned dark purple. He didn't say anything, but he went up on tiptoe to try to kick out at his attacker, but he wasn't able to get him to let go.

He was strangling him to death right in front of their eyes! Everyone in the cell was so terrified they hardly dared even to breathe.

The man from the upper bunk gave his orders: "Either I dunk your ugly head in the lavatory pan, or you pee into Scarface's mouth for me. Your choice!"

Shithead didn't say anything, he just nodded his head. At the same time as the man let go of him, he pushed him forward, so Shithead fell into the empty area in front of the door to the cell. When he sat up, he felt his throat with his hands. There were deep marks on his neck from the fingers. If he'd applied a bit more pressure, the man's fingers would have ended up embedded in his flesh.

Guo Cunxian decided that anyone who'd taken part in yesterday's attack must now be truly terrified.

Shithead crawled to his feet. He didn't dare look again at the man in the upper bunk. He went over to where Scarface was lying, his head hung low, and then he peed into his mouth just as he'd been ordered to.

The man in the bunk above Guo Cunxian's head now spoke again: "Right, listen the fuck up you bastards. You know exactly who did what to me yesterday, and I know too. I realise that you were just there to help beat me up, Scarface wouldn't dare try it alone. But you see, I damn near died, but now I'm back again. Do you know what that means? It means I'm back to kill whoever did this to me. If you're scared of what you've done to me, then you'd better be bloody careful in future. My name is Shang Yi. Just remember that I don't let any little bastards get past me."

Just at this moment there was a sound from outside the cell, the huge iron door to the jail was being opened, and then came the sound of running feet inside the building. The cell door was thrown open with a crash and a policeman was standing in the door frowning at them and rubbing his nose. The policeman's eyes swept round the cell: "What's up?"

For the longest time there wasn't the slightest sound. The policeman fastened his gaze on Guo Cunxian and the question was obviously directed at him. It was at that moment that he realised he was the only person in the entire cell who was sitting up in bed; everyone else was lying down with their eyes shut, pretending to be asleep. He could almost have burst out laughing. Who did they think they were kidding? Just now there'd been all this racket and now they were pretending to be fast asleep. Did they imagine the police would believe that! However, he'd only just arrived and he didn't know the rules operating in the cell, so although he knew he shouldn't say anything, he felt the need to speak: "Someone's hanged themselves."

"A suicide? Who?"

He gestured to Scarface's bed.

The policeman walked over and carefully looked Scarface up and down from head to foot, using his nightstick to poke and prod. After that he checked the noose that Scarface had been strung up in; it was made from a strip of cloth torn from the sheet. The sheet on Scarface's bed had indeed had a strip torn off it. Finally the policeman straightened up and bellowed: "Everyone down and standing to attention!"

The prisoners seemed to have been waiting for this command. They came tumbling down from their beds and lined up in the empty space by the door to the cell. They were clearly used to this exercise.

Guo Cunxian was still unaccustomed to thinking of himself as a prisoner, and he wasn't used to having people speak to him with the attitude and tone that the policeman had just used, but what could he do about it? Very unwillingly he crawled out of bed and stood at the back of the line.

Only the dead Scarface lay on his bed in a puddle. The fact that he wasn't obeying the policeman's orders was the final proof that he was dead. The policeman stood in front of everyone and his eyes flicked from one face to another: "Who found the body?"

Shithead raised his hands: "I wanted to get down to pee, but when I turned over, I got a massive shock."

"So you were so scared you weed on his bed?"

"I've heard it said that you can bring someone round from a dead faint by sprinkling water on their face. Anyway, there wasn't any water in the cell, so I had to pee on him..."

The policeman nodded. The whistling sound of breath being expelled from between his teeth was chilling: "Well, why not – if he'd still been alive at that point you could have drowned him in your pee! That was a pretty nasty thing to do. Anyone else join in on peeing all over Scarface?"

Shithead made haste to explain: "It was just me. The others didn't have time before you came in..."

"Oh, so if you'd had the time, you would all have peed over the man, would you?" The policeman moved a step closer to Shithead and his gaze was fixed on him, not allowing him to turn his eyes away. "So was it just you that cut Scarface down?"

"That was all of us..."

"Who is all of us?"

Shithead had to point out the guys who'd taken part.

"Why didn't you tell us what had happened? We have lots of experience with this kind of thing, or were you in a hurry to destroy the scene of the crime?"

"No, no, no. Oh my god, what are you talking about..." Shithead was now terrified and regretful, he was waving his hands about, as if praying. "To tell you the truth, none of us imagined that he was actually dead, we were trying to save him. And then, before we'd thought about telling anyone, you came rushing on in."

"What happened to your neck?"

"Oh, I scratched it. I don't know what it was that bit me, but it really itches."

"Did you scratch it, or did someone else grab you?" The policeman shone his torch on Shithead's neck and turned him round, looking for any other injuries anywhere on him.

"Surely you know me better than that, sir! It's because I've always been a coward and unable to stand up for my own point of view that I've ended up in here. Look at me, I'm tiny! Even if I had twice the courage, I couldn't possibly attack anyone."

Shithead was perfectly capable of handling this kind of situation. He made a big show of being terrified but whatever the policeman asked him he had his answer ready. You could see that the police had never managed to really get to him. Just now, was he genuinely frightened of Shang Yi, or was he just pretending?

Guo Cunxian was still thinking about Shithead when the policeman turned his attention to the man in the overhead bunk. "Shang Yi, what were you doing when all of this happened?"

Shang Yi looked straight into the policeman's eyes. Just like before he used a straightforward manner to answer: "I was asleep."

"You were able to sleep?"

"I had my head rubbed in human waste, and even now I feel all faint at the thought. When I breathe in, all I can smell is shit and piss."

"Did you hear anything during the night?"

Shang Yi didn't say a word, he simply shook his head.

The policeman turned back to the others: "Did anyone hear anything last night?"

They all shook their heads, as if they had been stirred by the wind. It is best to keep out of things, just don't get involved. In this tiny room, in which a dozen or so men were crammed together, all terrified to the point where none of them could sleep easily, it was true that they could hear all kinds of mumbling and moaning, people farting and grinding their teeth. So how could you fail to hear the sounds of someone dying? Although it had happened and everyone said they hadn't heard it, who would believe them?

Of course the policeman didn't believe a word of this. It didn't matter whether Scarface killed himself or was murdered, sounds must have been made, and if sounds were made then people must have heard them. He kept his gaze moving from one man to another, and in the end he fixed his attention on Guo Cunxian: "I've heard that when you are at home, Guo Cunxian, you suffer from insomnia even with a trained doctor to provide special massage. Last night must have been the first night you ever passed in a cell, so I'm guessing you weren't fast asleep and unable to hear anything?"

The criminals all turned their faces towards him, and the cell became very quiet.

After a long pause he said: "No, I was awake pretty much the entire night."

"Did you hear anything?"

"Oh, there was noise almost the whole night through."

"Oh really? What kind of noise?"

"Grinding teeth, mumbling, moaning, people talking in their sleep, tossing and turning…"

Some of them were giggling to themselves now, and the tense atmosphere in the cell seemed to have lifted.

The police officer didn't give up: "Was there any sound of fighting or violence?"

"No. Not at all. If you started fighting in here, you'd wake everyone up immediately. Just before dawn there was a kind of muttering noise, but I thought it was someone talking in his sleep, and after a while there was silence again."

"You are quite sure you didn't sleep at all last night?"

"If I couldn't even tell if I was awake or not last night, I'm sure you wouldn't have bothered to arrest me and incarcerate me here. Do you know how hard it is being an insomniac?"

"You would be prepared to bear witness?"

"Hey, what is all of this? I'm telling you the truth. I hope you don't imagine that you can make me take the blame for this guy dying!"

The policeman stiffened. It was somewhat unexpected that he'd failed to pick up this gauntlet. Probably there wasn't anyone else in the place who'd dare speak to him in that tone of voice. Just at that moment a bell started to ring and everyone jumped. They could practically feel their hair standing on end.

In point of fact, this was the bell that sounded to get the prisoners out of bed. In here, everything was done extra loud. If you spoke to someone you shouted, if you looked at someone you glared, and if you were angry then you started a fight. In the evening, there was an ear-splitting bell to inform prisoners that it was bedtime. Even those who were so tired they were already asleep at this point were jerked awake, and some more nervous types found themselves with heart complaints as a result of long-term imprisonment.

The bell to get everyone out of bed interrupted the policeman in his questioning of Guo Cunxian, and afterwards he decided not to continue with it. He gestured to two of the criminals and told them to carry Scarface's body out. The policeman bent over and heaped up everything Scarface owned, together with the noose and the bedding, and carried it away. Just as he was about to go out of the door, he didn't forget to order the people in the cell to open the window and clean up the lavatory.

The sun had now come up and there was the sound of movement in every cell. The jail had come back to life. However, Guo Cunxian wasn't sure which would be worse, day or night. When the policeman instructed them to "clean up the lavatory" that meant they could use the facilities in turn and remove the filth that had accumulated overnight. There was a tap next to the lavatory, and once the bell for getting everyone up had sounded, the water would be switched on, so the prisoners could clean their teeth and wash their faces. There were more than a dozen people in this cell desperate for the lavatory and wanting their turn at the tap. Their bladders and guts were full, but who would go first? Was this going to be a free-for-all? No wonder everyone wanted to pee on Scarface, because that would mean they didn't have to wait their turn!

The night before, Shithead had already explained to Guo Cunxian that there were rules that applied in any cell, and that you had to take things in turns. You were not allowed to move out of your place. If it wasn't your turn, even if you were so desperate that you peed in your pants or messed yourself, you shouldn't try to occupy the lavatory. The order was determined by the head guy. He'd be first on the lavatory, first to the tap and he – Shithead – was currently in last place. If there was any new arrival, in this case Guo Cunxian and Shang Yi, they'd be after him. It might be that a new arrival launched a successful coup, in which case they would then have the right to reorder the men in the cell, putting a stop to some of the old rules and setting up their own. This wasn't something that Shithead said, but it was what Guo Cunxian worked out for himself. This is how a pecking order works.

The head in this cell had been Scarface but he'd now been carried out feet first. Now his second-in-command ought to be taking first place at the lavatory and tap. He didn't dare assume these privileges, and he kept looking at Shang Yi.

Shang Yi took over smoothly and immediately announced the new rules: "I don't care what kind of crime you've committed on the outside, once you're in here then you're all the same. Nobody is better than anyone else and nobody is worse. Starting today we are going to take it in age order – oldest first and the young ones after them. There are going to be two people who don't go in age order. I am going to be in second place and Shithead is going to be last, and he's also going to be responsible for keeping the lavatory scrubbed nice and clean. Any objections? If anyone's unhappy, they can go after Shithead!"

This guy was hot stuff, and he clearly knew how to control people. However, what he said was also pretty fair, so who was going to disagree? The only person who was obviously unhappy was Shithead, and he didn't dare show it. Guo Cunxian was the third oldest; ahead of him were one man of seventy-two and one of sixty-nine. They got busy one after the other, it was quite a spectacle.

There was a strict time schedule. Once everyone had washed, breakfast arrived. They each got a bun, a plate of pickled vegetables and a bowl of porridge. Really, this is another kind of torture. For decades prisoners had been fed exactly the same bun-veg-porridge breakfast every day. It is like trying to deal with little kids; if they feed you well then you won't want to leave, but if they feed you badly you're going to tell them everything that you've done wrong, so that you can get out of here a little bit quicker. Is that how they imagine that this works?

Haven't they considered that it may provoke prisoners into a confrontational and angry state of mind, which is definitely a bad thing if you want to get any kind of confession out of them? Guo Cunxian hadn't had anything to eat for lunch or dinner the previous day, so he was feeling more than a little hollow. But now when he caught sight of his bun-veg-porridge meal, he felt no desire to eat and was even a little nauseous. As he sat looking at his own breakfast he was trying not to throw up. But the trays of everyone else in the cell had now been cleaned, and greedy eyes were glancing at his tray, some of them looking straight, some of them glancing, some of them covetous, some of them desperate to steal his food, but none of them daring to be the first to stretch out their hand.

Shang Yi whispered to him: "We've only just got here, Old Guo, and the first few days are going to be really difficult. Don't look at it but just eat it, because you're going to need something in your stomach."

"I'll give it a go, but aren't people nowadays promoting starvation cures? I've heard it can be really good for you."

"You really aren't going to eat it?"

He pushed his tray into Shang Yi's hands. Shang Yi began by wolfing down the porridge in huge gulps, and then he handed the bun over to Shithead: "You've had a horrible morning, so this is a present from Old Guo."

Just as he spoke, a policeman came in and took Shang Yi away. The others in the cell looked at each other, and nobody dared to make a sound. They didn't know whether he was being taken away because of Scarface's death, or whether it was all to do with the original case against him.

Shortly afterwards the police called back again for Guo Cunxian. The policeman took him back into the same interrogation room as yesterday. Apparently this room had been set aside for his personal use. Two other policemen were sitting there, and Wu Lie was sandwiched between them. His attitude seemed much nastier and more serious than the previous day.

Guo Cunxian had prepared himself carefully for this moment, and he calmly sat down on the little stool in front of him. When the enemy arrives, the general goes into action. You ask the questions, I'll give my answers. Right now, I still reckon I have a chance to come out on top.

Wu Lie was pretending to be concerned about him: "Did you sleep well last night?"

Fuck off! You know perfectly well already whether I slept well or not! Who do you think you are fooling with this faked show of concern? If I say I didn't sleep well are you going to let me go, or put me in a cell by myself? So today I need to show a bit more metal: "Oh, I didn't sleep at all, but other than that everything is fine."

"Guo Cunxian, you were clearly awake all night, so you must know about the death of Liu Shuang, the one they called Scarface."

"He died by hanging."

"Did Shang Yi, the guy in the bed above you, get up in the night?"

"I don't know."

"Guo Cunxian, trying to pervert the course of justice is a crime!"

Whatever's bothering you, why don't you just spit it out? Why keep calling my name? Plus besides which I am much older than you, so why should you endlessly insult me by using my personal name? Giving my name in full every time is disrespectful, it's humiliating, as if he endlessly feels the need to remind me that I am his prisoner. "What do you want me to say? Did anyone tell me that I had to stay awake all night and watch whether Shang Yi got out of bed or not?" He closed his eyes and paid no further attention.

"Guo Cunxian, look at me. You're under interrogation now, and I want you to show a proper attitude."

He opened his eyes. What is it this time?

"Do you admit your guilt?"

This is a trap. If I admit that I've done something wrong then he'll insist that I explain exactly what happened and what crimes I've committed, and the more I speak, the more I put myself in the wrong. Guo Cunxian shook his head. "No. I have done nothing wrong. I've done right!"

"If you've done nothing wrong, then why are you sitting here?"

"Ask yourself that!"

"OK, I can tell you exactly what you've done wrong. The thing is that it's quite different if I say it or if you admit it yourself, and it will have a big impact on what happens next. Raise your head and look at what it says on that wall."

He was not happy about what it said in red characters on the wall, and the more he stared at it, the more unhappy he became. He was quite sure that you could take the most law-abiding and decent person and make him sit for a few hours looking at that slogan, and he'd come up with a whole long list of crimes that he'd committed. Then either he'd have a nervous breakdown or he'd go mad. If Wu Lie would like to stop trying to force him to answer questions, he'd be prepared to give this a go. If you want to avoid being crushed by the slogan, then you have to change it and give it a new meaning. It was likely that every criminal hated and feared that slogan, so he started to play around with the wording and added a different ending: 'You'll Spend Your Life in Prison!' And: 'You'll be Home for New Year!' Then it became: 'Speak the Truth and You'll Spend Your Life in Prison! Resistance will mean You'll be Home for New Year!' That shows how they were trying to trick you and catch you off-guard.

He looked at the slogan painted on the wall as if he found it truly fascinating, his eyes narrowed down to little slits, and his head swayed from side to side. Let's just see who cracks first. Before long, Wu Lie started shifting restlessly in his seat. It seemed as though he wanted to strike while the iron was hot, he wanted to carry on the interrogation one question after another. If the prisoner doesn't speak, then the interrogator has failed. So he started speaking again, taking the tone of someone offering helpful advice: "Guo Cunxian, clearly you need me to explain some basics of the law. Luckily I have the time, and it is my job to do this. Right, listen up, the longer this all takes, the worse it is for you. What you need to do right now is to take this opportunity to confess what you've been up to. The law is based on facts, and the fact is that you are going to be convicted whether you speak or not. The law is based on principle, this is how the law works, so if you don't say anything it amounts to a confession of guilt."

The more he tried to provoke him into speech, the more determined he was to keep his mouth shut. Today his plan was to say nothing.

Why do jails make so much of the interrogations that go on there? Without an interrogation you cannot get a conviction. So for a criminal, the interrogation is like passing through the Gates of Death, what in olden times used to be called 'passing through the courts'. You get through and maybe you find yourself in heaven, or maybe you're in hell. What's the big difference between being sent to prison in this world and being sent to hell in the next? That is why the first principle in any interrogation is stick to your guns, whatever happens.

Once you are dead, you don't make mistakes, because the dead don't know the difference between right and wrong. If you die, then you can leave. Hadn't Scarface been able to go? He got his freedom this way. But Guo Cunxian didn't want to die, so he played dead and that is another interrogation technique.

If you are going to play dead, you have to be able to keep your mouth closed. When you have no idea what to do for the best, just shut up. Why do people say that silence is golden? When a lump of gold is put into water, you can immediately see the difference in weight. Speaking makes you weak. It is the gold that is hard, and that is worth real money. Guo Cunxian had always enjoyed the benefits of cleverness and eloquence. Maybe he was in all of this trouble because when he was happy he told everyone about it, and when he was unhappy he also told everyone all about it. Now the situation was quite different: he was a prisoner, and the qualities he'd been so proud of before were now his weaknesses. Why do houses have front doors, back doors, bedroom doors and bathroom doors? Why do you need all these different kinds of doors? It is because the doors are there for safety. Once closed, those outside cannot see in. When you are a criminal, you need to keep your own doors closed: the doors of right and wrong, the doors of life. This is not the moment to think about showing off. Your lips are a magical gateway, so if you keep them closed, your thoughts can find expression in silence. In silence you can think, you can run away, you can attack. Keeping silent is a way to summon your guardian deities. Silence is in and of itself a powerful protection. Since Wu Lie wanted to strike while the iron was hot, you have to be even more determined to keep silent, because in that way you will be stronger than him. If you can keep silent, he can say what he needs to, you can think what you will, but you don't allow your thoughts to be directed as he wishes. If you let him control your thoughts, then you are walking into his trap. Think about this and that, turn your mind from one thing to another, but make sure you don't leave any room for him to get at you.

"The law does have coercive power. Law without that power is like a fire that does not burn, or a light that doesn't shine. So if you keep silent, in the end the only person who will be hurt by this is yourself. When the time comes for you to be convicted, it will only make the penalties worse. There will be no reason for us to seek clemency. To put it to you in a clearer way, the law is given to us by God. It encourages you to be honest and prevents you from behaving badly. Don't you like making comparisons with Western cultures? Right, let me tell you a story from the Bible. When God discovered that Adam was ashamed of his own nakedness, and so did not dare to come out to see him, he asked him whether he'd eaten the forbidden fruit. Adam said that Eve gave it to him. God then asked Eve, and she said that the serpent had tempted her. You could say that this is the first interrogation of the first criminal in human history!"

This gave Guo Cunxian a clue: "So you are saying that the ancestors of the human race are criminals? That crimes were committed from the moment that humankind first appeared? How do you know that by arresting me you haven't committed a crime yourselves? At the very least you've destroyed a model for peasant development."

If his opponent left himself open for attack, then he couldn't stop himself from speaking. But the moment he opened his mouth, he was in danger. He saw that Wu Lie wasn't angry at all, in fact he was laughing. He quickly came to his senses; how difficult it is to make someone who likes to talk shut up for a change! Intelligence and cleverness all comes out through speech. A clever and intelligent person can find himself speaking without meaning to. If he was going to be able to keep silent, he would need to stop himself from giving way to his thoughts. That way he wouldn't make any mistakes during the interrogation. If he considered every thought, every word and every action from all possible angles first, then he could keep himself safe.

Wu Lie gave an unexpected laugh. "I know what you are thinking. You have got yourself into this situation and you can't face up to the fact, you don't dare admit to yourself that you are already a criminal. Just like an ostrich you are burying your head in the sand, imagining you can get through this if you hide from reality. Just think about it. We've arrested you to keep you out of trouble. If your circumstances in the past had been able to protect you, you wouldn't be here now. Let me tell you, nobody is above the law. If the law applies to the greatest in the land, how can it not apply to a peasant like you? Right, tell me what happened, starting with the first man to be beaten to death in Guojiadian…"

"Chairman Mao said: 'Though death befalls all men alike, it may be weightier than Mount Tai or lighter than a feather…' But I can't remember anything specific."

"This was a murder case and it wasn't that long ago. How can you dare say you don't remember? I'm sure you think about it every day."

"I didn't eat well and I didn't sleep last night, I am feeling all confused and I have a splitting headache. What is it that you want me to remember? I can tell you for free, this is what happens when you get old. You know the eight problems when you get old? You don't sleep at night but nap during the day, you can remember things that happened ages ago but not what happened last week, you can see things far away but not what's right in front of your nose…"

Wu Lie now had no idea how to proceed. He couldn't just sit there while Guo Cunxian laughed at him, but it would also be a mistake to get angry. Ah, a successful counter-attack. Who would have imagined that turning the subject would be so effective? Silence is a form of concealment. Talking about something else and annoying him with irrelevancies is also a form of concealment – it is called silent speech. Using silence to counter interrogation makes any kind of questioning useless.

Everyone has secrets that other people would like to know. Guo Cunxian wanted to know what they had in mind for him. Wu Lie's interrogation was aimed at provoking Guo Cunxian and tricking him into telling him what he wanted to know. Guo Cunxian was clever enough to understand that he had to prevent his opponent from getting at his deepest secrets. Either he had to divert him, or he had to keep silent, but keeping completely silent when you are being interrogated is much easier said than done. Maybe it would be best to just cut your tongue out and have done with it.

In the past, Guo Cunxian had always disliked silence, and he only experienced isolation and loneliness if he had absolutely no choice in the matter. Silence is by its very nature full of surprises and dangers. Now that everything else had been taken away from him, the only thing he had left was silence, and it was only in silence that he found any self-respect, any sense of self. True silence is the foundation of all life. In silence the soul can control itself without interference from outside. For someone undergoing an interrogation, silence is the very loudest of declarations. Once even silence is taken from you, you have no further cards to play.

When you are under interrogation day in and day out, you have to learn to accept it.

Interrogation is a two-character play; if the person being questioned doesn't open his mouth then the interrogator has more to say, and clearly Wu Lie prepared carefully before each day's performance, really going to a great deal of trouble over the whole thing.

So today, he started off as follows: "Guo Cunxian, clearly you still think you are enjoying the same glory as you did in the past and don't want to come out of the clouds. However, I don't have a problem with talking about the past. It can be useful for revealing how your life has gone and explaining how you ended up in your present position. But if you only care about the past and try to avoid facing up to your current circumstances, that would be a terrible mistake. That really would be a tragedy. Whatever happened in the past cannot protect you today, and indeed it is because of your past that you are in this situation now. There is a well-known expression about how, if you are in a hole, you should stop digging, but I have never heard of any suggestion that you can get yourself into that hole all of a sudden. If you are so caught up in the past that you can't extricate yourself from its grasp, then I can listen to you, I can hear you out. I have the patience for that, and it's my job. But I will tell you here and now that time is not on your side, it is not going to wait for you. Furthermore, we need to see your attitude, and that will determine what happens next.

"The fact is you've based your entire career on just one concept – causing trouble! When you didn't get enough to eat you went out and caused trouble, when you had enough to eat you were still out there causing trouble. If it was important you fought tooth and claw, if it was not important then you made sure that nobody had a moment's peace until you got whatever the hell it was that you'd decided you wanted. Sometimes you were there raising hell among your subordinates, sometimes you were raising hell among your superiors, and then you took up beating one person to death after another in your village. You seem to only be happy if you are causing trouble to someone else! You've always claimed that you became famous because of the way you were punished, but the moment you got to punish other people yourself, you set about it hammer and tongs. There seems to be only one thing that matters to you and that is causing trouble! To begin with other people caused trouble for you, later on they couldn't do that any more so you started causing trouble to other people, be they your subordinates, your superiors or just anybody that you didn't happen to like, and now, having caused trouble left, right and centre, you've ended up here. There are only two kinds of people, those who like causing trouble and those who suffer the results. Those who like causing trouble will do so to their graves, while those who don't are always at a disadvantage. However, those who like causing trouble will in the end cause trouble for themselves. It's a kind of disease, a contagious, modern disease, and you only escape it when you die."

"It's a nice conclusion," Guo Cunxian said, "but you've got it the wrong way round. It's always been you lot causing trouble for me. It is superiors causing problems for inferiors. Right now, aren't you causing trouble for me and not the other way round?"

Interrogation isn't just a test of your intelligence, it also tests your will, your experience and your wit. It is a kind of cross-talk, in which I cap your line and you cap mine, with one trap following on from another, and if you aren't paying attention and fall in, then your whole story may collapse. So Guo Cunxian was extremely alert. During the day Wu Lie interrogated him, and at night he interrogated himself back in his cell, trying to work out what he'd said that was right and what was wrong. Tomorrow, what would Wu Lie use as his entry point, what would he get his teeth into? As a result, he couldn't always decide if the next interrogation actually happened or was just something he'd played out in his own mind.

"Guo Cunxian, are you going to admit that you really don't care about the people who died or not? It seems to me that you are inured to seeing people die in all kinds of different ways, and you've always used the deaths of others to your own advantage. So for example, when you were younger you survived by making coffins. You'd have been happy to see people die providing you got to make money from the dead. When you'd just become head of the brigade, the son of a distant cousin was the cashier and he took three hundred yuan from the brigade in order to be able to get married. Then you screamed and cursed at him until the wretched young man went off and killed himself. I've heard that was just after the wedding too."

"Oh, are you talking about Guo Chuangui? That was absolutely nothing to do with me. It was Han Jingting who was secretary at the time. I wasn't the one who discovered the problem and I didn't talk to him either. Some people thought they could punish me because of this, and Chuangui got really depressed and killed himself in the hope of covering up his mistake. I had no idea that, after so many years, you were going to grub that up and try to blame me for it. It actually doesn't matter whether he was my nephew or not, or how much money he took, the fact is he was always greedy. In those days three hundred yuan was a lot of money for a village, and you can't say that I just let it go. I did criticise him strongly over it, and I told him he had to give the money back. I can't be blamed for the fact that he got depressed over it all. He decided to kill himself to atone for his crimes and use this as a way to wipe out his shame at his own actions. That's what a real man would do, and I'm proud that the Guo family can produce someone so right-thinking. I buried him properly after he died, and I've always looked after his wife right up until she found a really good new man and married him. Tell me what it is that I'm supposed to have done wrong? You're sitting today in the interrogator's seat. So are you telling me that the village shouldn't have investigated him and that we should just have let him get away with stealing the money?"

"Stop trying to twist my words. You know that's not what I meant. What happened wasn't your fault, and you could say that what you did was right, you put the general good above family loyalty. I mentioned it because I want you to recognise the ruthless streak in your own character and how you are accustomed to using other people's deaths to your own advantage. Do you remember the fire at the Frog Marshes more than twenty years ago? We still haven't solved the case. And the really strange thing is that a couple of days after the fire, Lan Shoukun, who was responsible for arresting the arsonist, had his son disappear too, never to be seen again. Later on Lan Shoukun and his wife both left Guojiadian, and that's another mystery. It was that tragedy which meant you were lucky enough to be able to become secretary of the village branch of the Party."

"What do you mean by that? Are you accusing me of being an accessory or are you trying to scare me? Oh well, I'm at your mercy, so are you planning to make me take the blame for all the cases that the police cannot solve?"

"We don't need to make you take the blame for any other cases. We've got enough on you for the crimes that you've committed. I am talking about a phenomenon, and that explains a principle. It tracks your biography, or perhaps you could say it tracks the trajectory of your crimes. Like with the death of Dog's Bollocks. You seem to have been waiting for that death for a long time, because the moment it occurred your life completely changed direction. You were able to get rid of the investigation team, you were able to take up with Dahua Steel, and then you could use poor little Dog's Bollocks' life as a tool to allow Guojiadian to get rich overnight. Factories mushroomed out of the ground, and money accumulated faster than you could count it. The way that Guojiadian got rich seems like a conjuring trick."

"Surely that's not right? All it shows you is that death is an end, but it is also a beginning. Death is the start of new life, and it is a part of life, perhaps even the most important part. The life that you create out of death is incomparably powerful, it is extremely strong. I think you have misunderstood what life and death are really about, and in the process you have exposed your own hypocrisy. In your own career you must be much more used to seeing death than I am, and you use death for your own purposes. You use the law as a tool for making the deaths of others seem rightful punishment, so you are really the person here who has benefited from the demise of other people. Why is it that this is OK for you, and you won't accept that I came to understand the value of life through my own experiences of death?"

"What, so you are saying that you used other people's deaths to make sure that you could survive, and used other people's deaths to make your own life more valuable? So are you telling me that being here today is also part of making your own life more valuable? The fact is you were trying to use Guo Cunyong's death to destroy your enemies. You were hoping this was an opportunity for you, so you ended up killing people and behaving with complete disregard of human life, thinking you could do whatever you liked. This is what is called being blinded by wealth. Do you really think that you got rid of the investigation team way back when? The fact is, after the investigation team left Guojiadian, people never stopped checking up on you, and we've been collecting paperwork on your activities all the while. Now the time is ripe so we've brought you here, because that will make the next stage of our investigations easier."

28

MIRACLES DO HAPPEN

Another day had passed, but every day now seemed to drag on endlessly. It was very difficult to get through. It was evening by the time Guo Cunxian had made his way back to the cell, and he felt quite at the end of his tether. He wolfed down his evening meal of two buns, a small dish of pickled vegetables and a bowl of soup. The really scary thing was not knowing how long this was going to last, how many more days like this were waiting for him. For an insomniac, the nights are hard. For a prisoner being interrogated, the days are even worse than the nights.

What does it mean to lose your freedom? Prisoners are treated like dogs, like they are no longer entirely human. You aren't allowed to sit down or stand where you like any more; you aren't allowed to go where you wish. Every part of your body is no longer under your own control. And then you have a really hair-raising situation that occurs when the supervisor appears; you must go immediately wherever he demands. In the evening, when you go back to your cell, at the very least you have the right to sit or lie down as you please.

During a police inspection, the prisoners in the cell all adopted the same pose and sat in a line in front of their beds, their backs straight, their hands on their knees, their eyes looking straight ahead. Each one of them looked like a monk in meditation. That is how it is: at the same time as you lose your freedom, there are other things that you gain, and circumstances will force you to think about many things that you have previously tried to ignore. Even with freedom itself, there are great differences and significant variables. Sometimes the greater the degree of freedom, the fewer options for independence you have, and vice versa. In Wang Shun's chicken farm, if you want them to lay eggs, you have to shut them up; likewise in the pig farm, if you want to fatten them, then you put the animals into a pen. If you can make use of imprisonment and lack of personal freedom to meditate, this may give your mind the opportunity to release itself from its shackles, and your imagination can roam free, in which case you are sure to benefit greatly. Otherwise how could the prisoners in this cell live so happily, eating and sleeping peacefully, without a care in the world? It is because they have a technique for dealing with their lack of personal freedom. This is a skill, but it is also something that needs to be practised. The reason Guo Cunxian could not achieve such detachment is because he considered himself to be different from the others locked up in there. He refused to believe that the higher-ups, the important people who he'd had dealings with, would simply leave him there without concerning themselves over his fate. And the reporters from China and abroad, when they heard that he'd got into trouble, wouldn't they be making a massive fuss and putting his superiors under pressure to deal with the situation? Without him, Guojiadian would pretty quickly collapse, so were those who'd ordered his arrest really prepared to take responsibility for that?

Shang Yi's meal was still sitting on a little table next to the head of Guo Cunxian's bed, and it was the focus of much attention. If this food had been left for anyone else, it would have been stolen and eaten by the other inmates long before this. But nobody dared to touch Shang Yi's food. Some thought he wouldn't be able to come back to the cell this evening. That was certainly Shithead's opinion and he expressed it with a great deal of fervour: "He'll have been beaten to a pulp during the course of the day. Do you think the police are easy to hoodwink, and they'll just believe everything you say? If they've managed to keep him alive, they'll be questioning him round the clock, so there's no way he's going to be allowed to come back here to sleep."

"Suppose he can't stand it and splits on us," another asked, "won't he be coming back?"

"If he splits," Shithead said, "it will be bad for all of us. I hope they put him in solitary with handcuffs and manacles. He's too dangerous, that one. Who knows who'll be the next to die if he's on the loose overnight?"

"Oh, that's obvious, it's going to be you!"

Shithead glared: "He wouldn't dare!"

"Yeah, right! When the wildcat loses its claws, anyone can kill it!"

"Yeah, when he's not here, you like to sound off, but I notice you're not touching his food for all that you've been staring at it…"

"I don't feel like eating today. I even had to force down my own food."

"Hey, you could have told us that earlier. We would've helped you clean your plate!"

"Shithead, is it right that you're going to be sentenced pretty soon? How about telling us about what you've done before you have to leave us?"

"You know all about me, so how about we let Old Perve speak. He's nearly eighty and he still goes out and rapes a girl. He must be pretty hot stuff!"

"Bastard! I'm old enough to be your grandfather and you still think you can make fun of me? It looks great, doesn't it, when you bully an old man like me."

"Bastard yourself! If it wasn't for Scarface looking out for you, why the hell should you be allowed to pee ahead of me? You do these disgusting things and then throw your weight around because you're older than the rest of us. Well fuck that!"

"Oh well, we can't expect too much of a piece of shit like you!"

"What do you mean, a piece of shit? Fuck you! So what if I've committed a few crimes, so have you or you wouldn't be here. Stop going around arse-licking and trying to look innocent. All you're good for is getting up to really foul things."

"How about you give it a rest?"

"Give it a rest yourself. Hey, Old Bai, how about you divine a character for me? Today the guy interrogating me was behaving kind of weirdly and I'm worried that things are going against me. They might even be looking for an exemplary punishment."

"You pick a character, and I'll do the divination for you."

"I want *lai*, the *lai* that means 'to come'."

"The character *lai*, in full-form, is written 來 with three 'men' and a cross... that which has come, that which is coming, that which will come, it encompasses everything and everyone. Do nothing, and light will come. You have nothing to worry about. I guarantee they won't seek an exemplary punishment for you."

"Hey, Old Bai! You're being very mysterious. Does this actually work?"

"What do you mean, does it work? You shouldn't have to ask. Of course it bloody works! Have you heard about how, way back when, Zhang Zuoling, the one they called King of the Northeast, died? He was living in Chessboard Alley in Beijing, and he was commander-in-chief. His house was located between two train stations. On the one side was Yongding Gate station and the other was Beijing Main train station. That site was picked out for him by a geomancer, who said that, as long as he stayed there, he'd be happy as a clam. If he was living right there in Beijing, no one could touch him. But he decided to move back to Manchuria, and the old commander-in-chief got himself ambushed on the railway by the Japanese devils, who blew him to kingdom come!"

One of the other prisoners now piped up: "Can you do a divination for me too?"

"What character do you want?"

"The *mao* (毛) that means 'hairy'."

"Well, look at you! You must be feeling brave!"

"It's a test for you, to see how you divine the character."

"Don't bother with setting me tests, it doesn't work. The character for hairy is the same as hand but it is bent the opposite way around, so people with the surname Mao are particularly good at striking out backhanded, the whole of their lives are spent doing things in reverse. The four encirclement campaigns during the civil war laid the foundations, and then we had the land reform and its attacks on local powers, the anti Chiang Kai-shek campaign, the anti-American imperialism campaign, Anti-Revisionism, the Three Antis and the Five Antis, and then the Anti-Capitalist campaign. Pretty impressive, don't you think, to always be able to get what he wants, for all that he sets about it in reverse? Who the hell do you think you are? How dare you pick a character like that! I know it was just a joke, but it's still a sign of Heaven's will! If you take my advice, you'll be very careful in future."

"Fuck you, what does it matter whether I'm careful or not? So what if they shoot me. The sooner I die, the sooner I can reincarnate in a better form."

"Oh, ho, ho. You must think a lot of yourself! With what you've done, how can you be so sure you're going to reincarnate in a better form?"

"What's so special about being reincarnated, surely everyone is? I bet you when you were born your face was all wrinkled like a little old man, and that's because you

were reborn from being a wrinkled big old man. Right now there's no damn point in
being reincarnated as a person because, after all, if you get reborn as an animal then
you get looked after. Just look at pandas, or lions and tigers! Hell, even if you get
reborn as a donkey you are worth the same amount of money as a brand-new car.
Whereas even if a whole bunch of people die down a coal mine, their families just get
eighteen thousand yuan as compensation. I reckon that the best thing is not to be
reborn as a human being."

"Hey, hey, hey! How about you all give it a rest? I'm already fed up with having
been questioned all day, and now I'm back in cells I want to relax. I don't want to
have to listen to your lectures, OK? Come here and I'll tell you a story. That'll cheer
everyone up."

Listening to the prisoners bickering, you cannot help but be amazed at how
difficult and painful it must be to stop yourself from speaking freely. Everyone in the
cell had been holding their tongues for an entire day, and if they did talk at all they
twisted and turned what they said to make it difficult for anyone to get at the truth.
This pent-up feeling was really uncomfortable, so the moment they came back to the
cell, they took the opportunity to take the bridles off their tongues and say whatever
they felt like, no matter how silly or stupid, because for them the most important thing
was the fun of being able to say what they wanted. The ability to speak is a wonderful
thing, you can go on talking forever, and it is a crucial part of daily life. Who knows
how much you will say in the course of your life, or how many words you will use?

The human mind is a wonderful repository. It can preserve all of the conversations
you hear in the course of a lifetime and will never forget the important things that you
yourself have said. Words can sometimes bring about miracles, and they can
constitute powerful weapons. Before a prisoner falls to a bullet or is sentenced to
many years in jail, he has already been subjugated by words during his interrogation.
Just as all of the prisoners were laughing and joking back and forth, a young man
came over and sat down on Guo Cunxian's bed. He said that he'd never imagined that
he'd meet someone like him in a place like this. His name was Fu Xinhui, and he was
twenty-seven years old. Originally he'd been a bank employee, and in the four years
he'd worked in a bank after graduation from the University of Finance and
Economics he'd managed to steal more than ten million yuan from them. He'd been
driving to and from work in his own BMW and if anyone asked him about it, he'd
either say that he'd borrowed the car from a friend or that he'd won it by gambling. In
this day and age, what kind of friend gives you a brand new BMW to drive around in,
and what must you have had to give them in exchange? There was this one time he
suddenly decided that he wanted to eat grapes, so he hired a plane to fly him to
Xinjiang for the weekend. There he was, staying in the best hotel in Urumqi, eating
grapes from Turfan, and then he flew back on the Sunday evening.

He really knew how to live it up! But he'd been too young, with too much money,
and because it had been so easy to get his hands on it, he'd failed to realise quite how
much trouble he was in. He'd been showing off all over the place and so of course
he'd attracted attention. His original idea had been to carry on for another half year,
put together twenty million yuan and then get out of the country, but he had not
expected that when he went back again to stick his hand in the till the same way as
before, he would end up getting caught. The fact is that they'd set a trap for him, so of

course they got him. There were clearly some impressive people in this cell for all that they were criminals, and Guo Cunxian couldn't help but feel sorry for Fu Xinhui. He felt a strange kind of sympathy for his predicament and couldn't stop himself from saying that he thought he must be a pretty clever guy. Anyone who can conjure a huge amount of money out of thin air like that is a genius of a kind, and nowadays nobody thought any the less of someone who got rich by illegal means. And as for his ultimate failure, well, that was just fate, wasn't it?

"You know what happens to geniuses?" Fu Xinhui said. "Either they live a wonderful life, or they end up in prison. That's true of you too, isn't it? You were a peasant genius, and at one time you were there being promoted by our leaders, and now you're in here with thieves and murderers."

With Fu Xinhui's help, Guo Cunxian started to get a handle on the other people in there with him.

Shithead's real name was Shen Fumin, and he was a burglar. He specialised in going round the Second Ring Road stealing things because he was quite sure that the local residents were far too casual about their doors and windows. The Second Ring Road is busy and lit up twenty-four hours a day, so who would have the guts to go there and commit a crime with the whole place as bright as day? Well, he had the guts! Before his arrest this time, he'd managed to go all round the Second Ring Road stealing things, and walked away with more than three hundred and seventy thousand in cash in the space of one month, not to mention all kinds of other valuable items.

The one known as Old Perve was really called Liu Quan, and he was the oldest man in the cell. He had a few dry wisps of grey hair stuck to his pate, and his face was deeply wrinkled. He was under arrest for the sexual assault of an under-aged girl. There were four of them in it together, and they'd ganged up to sexually assault the mentally handicapped daughter of one of their neighbours. The oldest of them was eighty-four, the youngest sixty-seven; the other three were being held in different cells in the jail.

The guy doing the divinations was Bai Liang, who was the second oldest man in the cell. He looked pretty clean-cut and spoke well, but his crime was nevertheless an unpleasant one: he was in the habit of spying on his daughter-in-law when she took a shower, and then one day when his son wasn't at home, he raped her. It is such a horrible thing, but the fact is that nowadays adverts for Viagra and other virility pills are everywhere, as if there isn't a single man who doesn't have problems in this line. How is it that the old men in this jail not only don't have the slightest difficulty in getting it up, they end up being over-sexed in some way and that gets them put under arrest? It really is a topsy-turvy world.

Driiing... an ear-splitting bell sounded. The prisoners who'd been chatting immediately shut up. Nobody dared to make a noise at a time like this, because if the warders heard you, you'd be in serious trouble. Just as the bell was sounding, Shang Yi walked back into the cell. The prisoners who were already in bed either turned their faces or raised their heads to look at him, and everyone had the same question in mind: what had happened to him, was he still intact, because judging by what normally happened in these kinds of circumstances, he must have suffered appallingly all day. They were curious. Shang Yi seemed to want everyone to have the opportunity to inspect him, since when he came in through the cell door he paused and looked at everyone in turn. He seemed relaxed and self-confident, and his clothing was perfectly neat and tidy, so obviously they hadn't been beating him up. In fact, he looked even better than when he'd left the cell first thing in the morning. Some of his cellmates glared at him, and then they quickly turned their heads away and pretended to fall asleep. He saw that there was a tray sitting on a little stool, so he bent down and picked up a bun without even asking if it had been left for him, and he bit it in half.

Guo Cunxian wriggled over to one side of the bed and then patted the other side, to indicate that he should sit down and eat in comfort. Shang Yi then dragged the stool with the tray of food over towards him, and sat down next to Guo Cunxian's head. He asked gently: "How did it go? Are you OK?"

One of the police suddenly shouted from the doorway: "Shang Yi, what's all this racket? Didn't you hear the bell?"

Shang Yi didn't move a muscle. He was still chewing on his bun. "Can't you see I've only just got back? How about you let me eat something? Otherwise, why bother with providing any food?"

"Hey, what is this? You don't say a word all day and now you start talking the moment you have something to eat!" The police officer clearly wasn't willing to waste any more time, so he muttered a few complaints and then walked away.

"Did you really not say anything all day?" Guo Cunxian asked him.

"Whatever happens it's the death penalty for me, so I really don't care. All that will come from opening my trap is that I die a bit quicker and look like a coward."

"I guess they tried everything to make you talk, so how did you stand it?"

"Look, if someone's tried to choke you to death in a pile of shit, you learn how to stand things. If someone's thinking about killing you to make sure you stay silent, then opening your mouth means certain death. There was this guy in France back in olden days called Voltaire who said that the two most difficult things in life are keeping a secret for someone else and knowing how to spend your leisure time. Seems to me that he was giving good advice to us prisoners."

Shang Yi ate by just shovelling the food into his mouth; you couldn't really spot him ever chewing. In the blink of an eye everything had been gulped down, and he wiped his mouth before he put his head right down next to Guo Cunxian's. They weren't chatting any more, but whispering.

"Do you remember Liu Jianmei from a few years back, the guy who made a fortune in overseas trade? Every year he was paying fifty million dollars to the city, but he was arrested because there was less than thirty thousand yuan that couldn't be accounted for when his books were inspected. His people went straight to the mayor, and pretty much immediately they were put in touch with the right people, and then off they went to the prison to collect him with the paperwork from the higher-ups, only to discover that he'd already admitted taking bribes to the tune of more than one million yuan. With him singing like a canary, even the gods couldn't get him out of here. It doesn't matter who you are, it doesn't matter what kind of connections you have on the outside, you can't get a self-confessed criminal out of this place. If you want to leave here, there's only one way to do it – insist you are innocent and stick to it, come what may. That gives those who want to save you an opportunity. Plus besides which this really isn't the kind of place where you can justify what you did, so keeping your trap shut is the best defence. Even if they kick your teeth in, you have to stay silent."

He had a point. If you want to survive, you have to have a strong will. But will is not the same as destiny; your life is the outcome of the struggle between the two. With Shang Yi being so nice to him, was that because of his position, or was it because he hadn't told the police about him getting up in the middle of the night?

Quite soon it was a month since the time of Guo Cunxian's arrest, which meant that the time they were allowed to question him was up. Either they had to formally press charges, or they had to let him go. It was for this reason that, for the last couple of days, his interrogation had been particularly intense, covering all kinds of different topics past and present. Wu Lie seemed to imagine that, by hitting him hard with an endless battery of questions, he'd be able to get at him. It was a horrible experience and even Guo Cunxian could feel that he was almost starting to fail. It might appear that he was holding out well. He was staying as quiet as possible, and if he spoke, he said as little as he could get away with. Furthermore they hadn't got a lot of useful information out of him, so he reckoned they wouldn't be able to press charges on the basis of what they had so far. But even supposing that they didn't press formal charges, would they let him walk free? According to what Shang Yi had told him, if a high-status personage was arrested, on the first day there'd be a whole load of people speaking up in his defence, but they would then ebb away like the tide. After a week, there would be an awful lot fewer who'd turn out to try to help, because some of them would now be frightened they'd get into trouble themselves, or they'd discovered it wasn't so simple and so they gave up. It was the couple of days at the end of the first month that were crucial. If they couldn't get the person out then, you could forget about it. After one month, there would be nobody to speak up for you.

Guo Cunxian asked the other prisoners who'd been in for the longest whether they'd ever come across someone spending more than a month under arrest and then in the end being released without charge. His cell-mates said that they'd heard of such a thing, but they'd never come across it themselves. To enter in chains and to leave as a free man... that would be practically a miracle, and miracles don't happen every day.

It so happened that one afternoon he wasn't summoned for questioning by Wu Lie, and that increased Guo Cunxian's hopes. Maybe they were discussing his release? They would need a good excuse to do so, of course, because if they let him go, they would have to do so in such a way that they didn't have to admit they were wrong to arrest him in the first place. They didn't want to give him any opportunity to sue them for wrongful arrest. As far as he was concerned, all they had to do was to let him go, and everything else would be fine. He would guarantee never to undertake any kind of legal action against Wu Lie and whoever it was who put him up to this.

That afternoon the miracle happened. Nobody in the entire cell could believe it, but Shang Yi was released.

It should be explained that he, more than anyone else in the same cell, had really been through the mill, and for nearly a month he'd hardly had a moment to himself. For a long time he'd been under constant interrogation, and then without a break they'd spring yet another round of questioning on him. Right up to the moment when his release was announced, they'd still been at it hammer and tongs, shouting and screaming at him for hours at a time. They'd been trying to convince him that he was never going to get out of there alive. The problem was that he thought he was going to be sentenced to death whether he spoke or not, so he'd decided to die properly, hence all his anger and suffering was suppressed. He was determined to maintain his self-respect to the last.

Who would have imagined that, after this final awful few minutes of silence, the interrogator would change his tune and tell him he was allowed to leave. It came so suddenly that he couldn't quite understand it, he couldn't grasp what "you can go" must mean. Where could he go other than straight back to the cell? The prison guard shouted at him impatiently: "Saying you can go means that you are going to be released. Haven't you spent long enough in here? Do you want to spend a few days more?"

It was because he hadn't said anything that the police couldn't get enough evidence to prosecute, in addition to which a massive effort had been made by his friends outside to get him out of there. When the time came, they had to let him go. Guo Cunxian now understood why people talked about this as a miracle. It is a miracle because what you are looking at is like a dead person coming back to life. You have to be dead to stay silent. Shang Yi had been able to keep his mouth shut, and he'd obviously made up his mind to expect the death penalty. This was how he was able to survive. If you make it absolutely obvious that you consider yourself to be dead meat, then you become incredibly strong. Once you have achieved that kind of strength, you may yet have the opportunity to get out in one piece.

Sometimes things in this world are difficult to predict, and travelling the roundabout route may bring you closer to your destination than taking the direct path. Suddenly he felt a strange excitement. Shang Yi's unexpected release reminded him of something. Perhaps the fact that he hadn't been called for interrogation all day – a most unusual circumstance – might mean something. Clearly this place was not as impenetrable as it seemed, and all the stories about how once you were arrested you never saw the light of day again were exaggerated. What actually happens is that you are arrested all of a sudden, and then you are released all of a sudden. You weren't expecting to be dragged off to jail, and you get let out again when you don't expect it. Guo Cunxian might well find this applied to him.

He was on tenterhooks and so overwrought that he could neither sit nor stand. His ears were pricked up to catch any sound from the corridor outside the cell, and he was full of hope. The miracle was going to happen! Moreover, having lived this long it is not as though I haven't experienced a miracle or two in my time. The biggest miracle of all was being able to set up the iron and steel works. With the price rises that year in building materials, I was able to earn more than one hundred million yuan annually. Even if Lin Meitang spent all day every day counting the money we were earning, she couldn't have counted it all. That was a miracle, and it took me right to the top, so I guess I can't expect another one to happen.

Just as he was dreaming about miracles, Wu Lie came in unexpectedly and announced that he'd come to see him. He didn't say that they were formally pressing charges, but neither did he say that he was being released. What was the bastard up to? Was he deliberately trying to provoke him by tormenting him in this way? Was he trying to mislead him by not mentioning that he was under interrogation to begin with, so as to encourage him to hope, and then destroy all of his illusions at a stroke?

He might enjoy this kind of game, but Guo Cunxian didn't. He decided to cut right to the chase: "You've had me here for a month now, so surely I should be released today?"

Wu Lie said lightly: "We've already received special permission from our superiors that we can question you for another month."

Guo Cunxian was furious. "Does the law still apply to you lot or not?"

Wu Lie chuckled. "Oh, there's a law that covers this. In special circumstances you can use special measures."

Guo Cunxian had been keeping up his confidence all along, because he was quite sure that he had as many if not more people outside working towards his release compared with Shang Yi, and they were much more powerful. The reason why he wasn't being released was probably all to do with his attitude. His attitude had always been quite the opposite of Shang Yi's, because even after he'd been arrested and thrown in a cell, he'd been unwilling to face up to the fact, and he'd kept trying to argue with Wu Lie about it. He was so desperate to get out that he couldn't keep his mouth closed, and so his attitude simply wasn't tough enough.

If you have hope then you make demands, and if you make demands then you show your weakest points. In such circumstances it is very easy to be deceived. For the past several decades he'd been in charge of so many people, he'd taken charge of so many things, he'd managed so much money, so why was he now having such problems keeping guard of his own tongue? Once imprisoned in this kind of place, your tongue was the only thing left for you to guard, other people were in charge of everything else. Guo Cunxian, you need to remember how to sham dead! In the past, you were punished time and time again, and you got through it because you were tough. In an age when people were punished for the smallest thing, he had relied on his courage and daring to build up his self-confidence and prestige. That was how a carpenter had become the leader of a production team, and the leader of a production team had become a secretary. It was not fear of being punished that brought about subsequent success. In the past, a miracle would always occur sooner or later, so what is wrong this time?

Success is the source of all failure; are you already unprepared to challenge yourself? If so, that's the reason you aren't going to be given another opportunity. Or is it because you are getting old? The fact that the police have been given an extension to question you means that either no efforts have been made by the people outside to save you, or that those with the power to get you out have no interest in coming to the rescue. He was so frightened and suspicious that he had to ask Wu Lie for some sleeping pills.

Wu Lie said no. He asked why not. You must know that someone who doesn't sleep night after night can't survive for long. Is the idea to drive me into an early grave so that you don't have to bother with assembling a case against me? Aren't you afraid that I'll leave some final words accusing you of driving me to my death?

No way, said Wu Lie. You may be unable to sleep but that's not something that drugs can solve. Your crimes have caught up with you and you are fighting with yourself. If you choose to work with me, then you can get it all off your chest. Once that has happened, you'll sleep like a baby.

He pointed out that there was nothing at all that he wanted to get off his chest, and that if he couldn't sleep, it was because of rage.

Wu Lie asked if he was angry about the extension they'd been granted. You need to wake the fuck up, you can no longer expect other people to come forward to speak on your behalf. Stop dreaming that you have a future outside of here.

He said that nearly everyone thinks about their own future, but the vast majority of them are wrong. I never think about the future, because I know exactly what is coming. So what if I've been arrested? So what if I am sentenced to death? Everyone is sentenced to death from the moment they are born, and that includes you. All that can happen is that the time of execution for some is closer than for others. However, all that happens then is that you live for a few years, or a few decades, as opposed to seventy or eighty years. What's so bad about dying a little early? What's so great about living a few years more?

Wu Lie said that this was all too negative, that's not your style at all. So according to you, life's a bitch and then you die. In which case, how do you make your life worthwhile? If you really felt like that, why did you work so hard to see Guojiadian get rich in the first place? What would be the point? People need to make their lives valuable. It is hard to live a worthwhile life, and it is even more difficult to die a worthwhile death. This is because dying pointlessly can devalue everything that you have achieved before. You seem a bit confused to me. How about I bring a doctor in to have a look at you?

A short time after he had left, he returned with a young doctor in tow. The doctor subjected Guo Cunxian to an endless examination. He took his pulse, listened to his heart, tested his reflexes and he had him open his mouth so that he could look deep into his throat. And then afterwards it was one question after another. Was this some kind of interrogation? He became furious. You know what happens to people here! Why do you need to ask all of these questions? What kind of doctor are you, anyway?

The doctor wasn't cross at all. He patiently explained that there are four techniques used in treating the sick, based on sight, smell, hearing and knowledge of the pulse. You can't be a good doctor without mastering these four skills. If you can't do these things, then you have to be the God of Medicine to be able to save people.

"OK, so you've done your bit. What's wrong with me?"

The medic explained that he had all sorts of health problems. His liver and spleen, heart and kidneys all showed signs of trouble, but the issues with his stomach and lungs were much more serious. It seemed as though there weren't too many of his internal organs that could be said to be doing their jobs properly, and the fact that he was feeling a bit depressed was quite frankly the least of his problems... but right now there was no sign that anything was about to go seriously wrong.

Guo Cunxian suddenly understood. Wu Lie couldn't care less about his insomnia. He wanted the final confirmation that his organs weren't about to fail. And that meant that, since he was unlikely to die of any of his health problems, he would be afraid of accidents.

Before leaving, Wu Lie told him that he would be given a packet of sleeping pills by the guard before lights out. Guo Cunxian crossly refused. He felt that his mood today was particularly bad, because Shang Yi's release had made him angry with himself, and he was also angry about what Wu Lie had just said. He had made up his mind to guard his tongue, to keep his mouth shut come what may, and see how Wu Lie dealt with that. However, his plan had gone badly wrong. Why had he asked him for the sleeping pills? If he was determined to die, then what did it matter whether he slept or not? How could it be that he showed less determination than Shang Yi, a young guy in his thirties? Where did the courage, bravery and wisdom of the past disappear to?

Early one morning, as Wu Qingyuan's car pulled up at the gate to the Public Security Bureau, the guards there saluted and let him through. Just at that moment a fashionably dressed young woman leapt out from one side to block his route. As the car came to a halt she got in, and just as the chauffeur was about to make a fuss, he recognised her as the famous reporter from the *Dahua Daily News*, An Jinghui. Wu Qingyuan smiled helplessly: "I should have known that there was only one person in the whole of Dahua City who'd do a thing like that, and that is you. OK, what's up?"

An Jinghui allowed a bewitching smile to play across her face: "I'd like to be allowed to attend your meeting this afternoon."

Wu Qingyuan looked angry: "You really are on the ball, aren't you? You know exactly what cases are coming up for discussion and when! We must have a spy in our midst…"

An Jinghui continued to use a conciliatory tone, in the hope of wearing him down: "Guo Cunxian's arrest is big news, and there are many things that haven't come out yet. This could be a real scoop for me. My editor has told me to keep right on top of the case, and he wants me to get the evidence first hand. He wants the story of one man's rise and fall. You've got to help me out here, given that you're the chief of police."

"There are strict rules about this kind of thing. We don't allow reporters to attend meetings where we are discussing progress on individual cases."

That might be what Wu Qingyuan said, but he looked so relaxed and cheerful that it almost seemed he was encouraging An Jinghui to continue. Right now he was in a wonderfully good mood, you could even say that he felt as if all his dreams had come true. Arresting Guo Cunxian had been his happiest moment since joining the police. Or perhaps it would be more accurate to say it was the most important moment in his official career. First he had to establish the basic facts and then put pressure on from all sides, pushing again and again, and now the outlines of his case were settled. If Guo Cunxian was convicted, then Guojiadian itself was finished. That would also put an end to the careers of those who'd supported Guojiadian, and that would make it impossible for them to remain in control of what happened in Dahua City – and then his own plans would succeed. Since he was so confident, he took extra care to keep An Jinghui onside. Besides which, it might be useful to see her publish certain information in the paper.

"I have a great deal of sympathy for your position, and I do see that Guo Cunxian would be a great subject for you in future. However, it's impossible for you to attend the meeting this afternoon, and it's unnecessary anyway, because today we aren't going to be discussing the details of the case but the underlying principles of government policy. That isn't going to be useful for you. How about we drive you round to the Propaganda Department and you can wait there for me. The moment the meeting is over I'll come right over, and I can bring along the head of the department, and we can have a good chat."

That was very polite of him, and An Jinghui knew that she had to accept his offer. She remained seated in the car and the chief of police got out. He waited until the car had turned round and driven away before he went in to the main building of the Public Security Bureau headquarters and made his way upstairs to the meeting room. The other members of the special investigative unit had all arrived already, so the moment he took his seat he opened the meeting.

"The arrest of Guo Cunxian has caused a huge shock throughout the entire country, so the reporters who used to go out to Guojiadian have now all taken up residence in the Propaganda Department of the metropolitan Party Committee. The secretary of the metropolitan Party Committee, Gao Jingqi, has been having to explain progress on the case on a pretty much day-to-day basis, and we understand that everyone has been under enormous pressure. This has created a huge workload for everyone as you have to deal with a mountain of evidence. However, we now have approval from the Procuratorate so we can formally press charges against Guo Cunxian. From today, the prosecutions involving Guojiadian will go through normal procedures, and our special investigative team can be disbanded. However, before the team is disbanded we need to hear their final report, in which all necessary information will be passed on, and then we can see if there are any remaining questions we need to draw to the attention of the people taking over the case. Alternatively, you may have some special requests or wishes concerning how the case is handled. They can also be discussed. Then this afternoon I will report back to the municipal Party Committee."

As Wu Qingyuan's words died away someone raised their hand. "OK, let's have Comrade Qian up first, and we can hear what the People's Congress has to say."

Comrade Qian was none other than Qian Xishou. After his retirement he'd become a member of the standing committee of the Municipal People's Congress. The problem with that was that he had nothing to do, and he didn't have any kind of home life either. Since he really needed something to keep him busy, he became a director of the People's Congress Law Committee. That gave him a desk in its office, and if he wanted, he could find plenty to occupy his time. Qian Xishou now cheered up significantly, and his wrinkles seemed to have smoothed themselves out a little, but he was still far too thin. Sitting in his big chair he seemed to be just the outline of a full human being. His mouth had sunk inwards and his cheekbones jutted out, making him look even more like a toothless old crone than ever. However, the moment he opened his mouth, his voice was as shrill as usual: "The standing committee of the Municipal People's Congress has received more than a hundred complaints and several hundred letters concerning the case from the masses, and the vast majority demand that Guo Cunxian should be tried in public so that the case can be prosecuted in the most fair and open manner possible. We need to know who was helping him behind the scenes, who was connected to him, and each one of them should be dealt with so that we can offer the public an account of our actions, and provide a lesson for the masses."

As he spoke, he opened a folder in front of him and took out a heap of documents to show that he was telling the truth. "Everyone has the same question," he said. "How could someone like Guo Cunxian appear in our Dahua City? How could he have got to where he is today without the support of some very senior people? And given the situation today, shouldn't they be taking some of the responsibility? I have explained to everyone over and over again how more than a decade ago I took a team to investigate him, only to see him protected by those higher-up, so that the investigation was abandoned half-way through. As we can all now see, the people who thought they were protecting him back then were actually harming him. We investigators were actually helping him. If we'd been allowed to carry on back then, yes, he would have lost his position as secretary, but he would have been able to carry on being a peasant, and he wouldn't be under arrest now for being caught up in a murder case. The standing committee of the People's Congress has the right to know about progress on this case, so we hope the Public Security Bureau will remain in regular contact with us."

Clearly he was on the attack, but who was he out to get? Was it Zhang Caiqian or Feng Hou? But Gao Jingqi had been many times to Guojiadian himself, hadn't he? It seemed that making trips to Guojiadian wasn't considered the same thing as 'supporting' Guojiadian, and maybe never going near the place was going to see you brought down for 'protecting' Guo Cunxian. How very complicated! Qian Xishou's bombshell stunned everyone in the room, and Wu Qingyuan wasn't pleased that he'd thrown it like that. Who exactly do you think you are scaring in this way? There are some things that you just can't say right out, or at least that you don't want to put too plainly. No wonder people don't like him. However, Wu Qingyuan didn't allow his expression to change. He moved his pieces out of checkmate with a light laugh.

"It is easy to see that Comrade Qian Xishou has a background in ideological theory. He has posed us a very interesting question, and the situation with Guo Cunxian is not only worthy of careful study, but I am also afraid that his example is going to prove only too typical across the entire country, which is another topic that we need to consider carefully. That means we need to think about this from another angle too. Investigating him and criticising him is actually the best way to support him. After all, last time he was investigated, it made him famous. It brought him interest and sympathy. Later on it was his fame that helped to bring in a lot of investment. As Guo Cunxian himself would put it, punishment made him famous and then it made him rich. However, we shouldn't confuse things. Senior cadres have been supporting the reforms and opening up of the peasants in Guojiadian, and they are happy to see them climb out of poverty, but that does not mean they have supported Guo Cunxian's criminal activities, and you should also not confound Guojiadian's economic success with Guo Cunxian's crimes. Today we are discussing developments in the case, and issues of ideology will have to wait for another time. Next let us hear Comrade Wu Lie's report on the development of the case."

Wu Lie merely gave the bare bones of the case since he really didn't trust this special team set up by the municipal Party Committee, and he was afraid that any leak from it would have a serious impact on the case. Nevertheless, Wu Qingyuan listened carefully to what he had to say. He sat up very straight, making him half a head as tall again as any of the others sitting round the table. He wore a pair of fine, white-rimmed glasses, and the skin on his face was extremely pale, but his gaze was cold, secretive and arrogant. The impression he gave was more than a little uncomfortable. When Wu Lie had finished his report, he immediately expressed his own opinion on the topic since he was clearly unwilling to allow this routine meeting to run on indefinitely.

His recommendation was also absolutely straightforward: "I've looked at the records of every interrogation Guo Cunxian has undergone over the course of the last month, and he's told us almost nothing of any value. The psychological gap is just too great. He does not dare face the facts, and he is desperately trying to preserve his fantasies. He still imagines that we won't be able to prosecute him. Because of this he takes every opportunity to show off and to proclaim how wonderful he is. From what's happened in the last couple of days, I don't think it's a good idea to keep Wu Lie in charge of questioning him. Guo Cunxian resents him, and Wu Lie has consistently been trying to provoke him or confuse him, rather than attempting other kinds of interrogation strategies. Of course that is good too because it allows us to keep Guo Cunxian's murderous energies under control. However, Chen Kang, the deputy head of our Interrogation Division, has just wrapped up the other case he was involved in, so in future he will be responsible for questioning Guo Cunxian. Chen Kang, tell us what you think."

Chen Kang was short and fat, and bald to boot, and he looked very cheerful. "I've been familiarising myself with the paperwork but right at the moment I don't have anything much to say. I would be much more interested in hearing my colleagues' opinions."

Wu Qingyuan also put in a word of encouragement: "OK. Our finest interrogator is asking for help, so if anyone here has something to say, please feel free to give us your advice."

The meeting room was now filled with hubbub. Clearly everyone had their own ideas about how to question others, and it was particularly exciting to imagine this happening to someone like Guo Cunxian, who'd once been so powerful and had now fallen so low. Some wanted a hardline approach, others thought that Guo Cunxian wouldn't be bothered by interrogators screaming at him, so it was best to go soft, and then alternate between the two.

After letting this continue for a while Wu Qingyuan decided that, since time was nearly up, he should draw the proceedings to a close: "OK. Everybody has given us some really valuable opinions, now how about we let Chen Kang get on with it?"

He turned to face Chen Kang and spoke to him in a serious tone: "Remember, you will never have interrogated anyone like Guo Cunxian before. He was at no point in his career an official, but he was quite convinced that he could well have become a senior figure in the government. He's not a hardened criminal, but he has been punished over and over again, so he has experience of being questioned. I'm going to give you two pieces of advice. One, don't be condescending. You need to be accurate in observing and assessing your opponent's mental state, and you both have to consider the questions that arise from the same level. Once you are absolutely on the same wavelength as Guo Cunxian, you can get him. Two, the real art of an interrogator lies in being able to anticipate exactly what factors his opponents will rely on in resistance and then finding ways to make use of this knowledge to convince them that resistance is useless. All of Guo Cunxian's illusions stem from his belief that he built Guojiadian from scratch. You need to wear away at this, to use his faith in this myth to destroy it. After that, the rest will be easy…"

Guo Cunxian was convinced that there was a ghost in the cell. He'd seen it appear day after day, so how could he possibly be wrong?

This wasn't the kind of poltergeist-type ghost from ancient stories; this ghost didn't cause the slightest trouble. It would float in during the silent watches of the night, sometimes looking like a white fluffy bobble and at other times like a black shadowy blob. On some occasions it would be resting quietly by the door; on others it would come close and plunk itself down next to his pillow. It would pause there until he moved to try to catch it, and then it would suddenly disappear. You might have thought it would be terrifying to have a ghost constantly appearing to you, but the fact is that it didn't bother him in the slightest. Why wasn't he frightened of the ghost? Possibly it was because he felt his position to be pretty much the same. If you are going to be scared, it is people who are terrifying! What is so bad about ghosts? His insomnia was bothering him night after night, and the hours just dragged on endlessly, so he was kind of pleased to have a ghostly friend to keep him company, to chat with about this and that. Besides which he was curious to know about what went on in the other world. And this wasn't some kind of nasty ghost, it didn't look as if it were there to take revenge by killing people. In fact it didn't seem to have any interest in hurting anyone. It also wasn't pestering him in any way. If it really wanted to get him, it could have done so by now.

It seemed quite possible to him that this was an insomniac ghost that found it impossible to sleep, and so, being lonely and cold, it had decided to make its way into the cell to enjoy a little bit of human warmth. Maybe this ghost had come specially to meet him, and if it was a benevolent ghost, maybe it wanted to tell him something important. Therefore he really ought to keep it a secret, a wonderful secret all of his own.

His cellmates were all experienced prisoners. During the day, the only thing on their minds was getting enough to eat, and then at night they fell asleep as soon as their heads hit the pillow, and then they slept like the dead. As long as the ghost didn't climb on top of them and try to wring their necks, they weren't going to notice it. But if any of them did find out that Guo Cunxian was in nightly communication with a ghost, it was guaranteed that they would kick up an unbelievable fuss, which would in turn make the warders suspicious and cause God-knows-what other kinds of trouble. He was not anticipating that one day Fu Xinhui would suddenly announce he'd seen a ghost, after which everyone started screaming and shouting. It was at this point that Guo Cunxian discovered lots of people in the cell had seen ghosts. Shithead boasted that he'd once had a female ghost to keep him company all night, and he'd had the time of his life riding her. In order to calm the terrified Fu Xinhui, the diviner, Bai Liang, used his own spit to write a ghost-repelling talisman in each corner of the room, and then he muttered an exorcistic chant:

"I call upon Sun Wukong from the east,
I call upon the White Tiger Star from the west,
I call upon Guanyin from the south,
I call upon the Great Lord Jiang from the north!
I call upon the gods and spirits from every corner of the earth,
And I call upon the Great Helmsman Mao Zedong!
Let ghosts and demons, abominations and plagues make haste to surrender.
Let each and every one of them accept their bonds..."

That night, having finally drifted off into an uneasy doze, Guo Cunxian found himself being violently jerked awake by something. Instantly on the alert, he saw someone standing over by the door. He thought he might have been woken up by his call, and he could vaguely make out his appearance. He was dressed like a villager, with a cap on his head made from the stomach of a white sheep. His face was furrowed, and his expression was calm and serious, with eyes deeply-set like two caves. He gave off an air of remote arrogance that served to keep everyone else at a distance.

Guo Cunxian recognised him: "Oh, it's you! What are you doing here?" He couldn't help wondering if this cell ghost was some innocent soul who'd died in here, because how could a ghost come in from outside?

"Who says I'm a ghost?" When his interlocutor spoke, his voice was tired and hoarse, but it went straight into his ears. "If you die you're going to become a ghost for sure, but what makes you think the two of us are the same? Haven't you always been secretly trying to out-compete me? Now you find yourself in this situation, shouldn't I come and take a look?"

Guo Cunxian was furious: "You're enjoying my misfortunes, aren't you? You want to see me brought low. Let me tell you that, in spite of all that's happened, I'm still better than you! Guojiadian has already become a symbol of the very greatest peasant enrichment. Our brands are worth at least ten billion yuan. How many hovels like yours could you buy for that kind of money? You are really a model impoverished peasant, struggling through from one day to the next, and poor generation after generation. I, on the other hand, am a classic example of a nouveau riche. I thought big and took risks, and that made me famous. What you represent is nothing but humiliation and stupidity, while I stand for self-respect and intelligence. Leaving everything else on one side, just take a look at my glasses. They are gold-rimmed, bought in Hong Kong, and they set me back nine thousand, nine hundred and ninety-eight yuan. My annual salary was one million, eight hundred and eighty thousand yuan. I never wore the same garments twice. I smoked the same top-quality cigarettes as those made especially for Zhongnanhai. Just look at what you are wearing! A white cotton handkerchief round your head, coarse cloth on your body. That was what you had in life and it's also what you have in death. By what right do you criticise me?"

"Yeah, of course you're the greatest, that's why you're here! You get all these mass murderers and serious villains who come into prison saying how they don't care, but somehow or other they find it impossible to sleep. If they close their eyes they have nightmares, and even with their eyes open they find they are surrounded by ghosts – ghosts of the living and ghosts of the dead. Do you know why that is? You are half-way to becoming a ghost yourself by now…"

"If I do become a ghost, I'll be a better one than you! At the very least I'll be a rich ghost, one that fought to survive. That's got to be better than being the ghost of someone who starved to death or who died in the wilderness with no home to go to."

"Don't you find it exhausting spending all day, every day boasting and showing off? Do you really not get bored of it? This edifice you've built up is going to crumble any moment now, so you might as well go back to being yourself again. I'll tell you the truth – seeing as how we both used to be peasants, I might well be prepared to help you out. If I can't, I can put you in touch with even higher powers. I know you keep trying to show your contempt and distain for me but as far as I can see, deep down you envy me, you are eaten up with jealousy, and even in your dreams the wish to be like me rears its head. This is because, the moment a peasant is successful, they want to stop being a peasant. Those who despise peasants the most are peasants themselves. You are one of them. I'm not fooled by the way you make such a fuss of being a peasant yourself and then put yourself out to complain about officials, taking every opportunity to make fun of them or curse them. You are desperate to be an official yourself, and a senior one at that. It's the only thing you've thought about for years! If you could buy the position that I used to hold, you'd have done it ages ago! Pride, envy and greed – these three ropes delivered you here bound hands and feet. It may annoy you, but it's a fact. Today, you cannot possibly consider yourself to be better than me in any way. Though you may despise me, the fact remains that I've moved on into another world. I have my place in heaven but your place in this world is one that you probably won't hold much longer. You've committed terrible crimes, otherwise you wouldn't be in this kind of place, and the sort of people who die in here mostly go straight to hell. I don't believe you aren't frightened, that you don't regret the past, and I'm sure you want me to help you."

This old ghost might look nothing special but he had a nasty turn of phrase, and what he'd just said was like a kick in the guts for Guo Cunxian. As far as he could see, the real disaster was that Chairman Mao died too soon to be of any use to him. Otherwise he could have invited Chairman Mao to come to Guojiadian. If he'd set foot in Guojiadian just the once, whatever disasters overtook Guo Cunxian after that, he'd have been guaranteed to come out on top. He could have become a second Chen Yonggui, or maybe even surpassed him. Of course since it was a ghost he was dealing with, even though this was just something that Guo Cunxian thought, he did not need to put it into words for the other to know.

"I find it all very odd," he said. "It was economic liberalisation that allowed you to get rich. So why now you've been imprisoned do you care so much about Chairman Mao, who was after all an opponent of liberalisation?"

"Aren't you the same? You must miss him more than I do. If it weren't for Chairman Mao you'd still be a ditch-digger in a hell-hole somewhere or other! You were bloody lucky to be invited to his birthday banquet in Zhongnanhai. That's like being summoned to the palace by the emperor to be given a goblet of wine in olden days, you went right to the top! Then what Chairman Mao said about you was reported across the country: 'Yonggui is a good man, a really good man' or something like that. Is that supposed to be an order from the Party leadership too? And then he said something about impressive people coming from poor backgrounds. The fact is that Chairman Mao was in a good mood at the time, so he said a few polite words, and that resulted in a kind of mass movement because of the contemporary political situation. When it comes right down to it, Chairman Mao really trusted us peasants. We sang *The East is Red* and called him the Helmsman for a reason..."

"What is this? You seem to know all about it."

"I'll tell you the truth, then. The last few years I've been studying your history in every spare moment. You were bloody lucky, you know that? Your fiftieth birthday was celebrated in the Great Hall of the People, wasn't it? You must have been so proud. More than ten thousand senior cadres, including plenty from the central government, all gathered together in the Great Hall of the People to look at you respectfully and listen to you speak for a couple of hours with bated breath. You looked then just as you do today, a cap made from white sheepskin and clothes of coarse cloth. When you walked up to the rostrum you had a cigarette in your hand, and after taking your seat, you spoke while chain-smoking, your left hand gesturing as you made your points. You carried on smoking for the next couple of hours, and the ashtrays filled up one after the other with ash, but there was never a stub to be seen. Your audience was stunned. They'd never seen such a thing. When one cigarette had been smoked down to the stub, you'd fish out another one with your right hand, and then without even looking and carrying on speaking the whole time, you'd apply the end of the old butt in your left hand to the tip of the new cigarette, then you'd put it in your mouth and carry on smoking. Take a long hard look at yourself – virtually uneducated, no skills to speak of other than as an agricultural labourer, and yet you end up as vice premier, that's like prime minister in imperial times. That's never happened before in China or anywhere else in the world! A billion people or so suffered for decades, all so that you could get right to the top!"

"Look at you, just look at you, so jealous you must nearly be choking on your own bile! As a human being you can't simply go with the flow, drifting about hither and thither. When the time comes to stand up and be counted, then you have to stand up. When you have to hold out under pressure, then you should. The crucial thing is what you are made of. If you're pure gold, even if they break you into pieces, you still have value. If you were worthless before, break you and you're still worthless. What do you mean by saying that there's never been a peasant prime minister or a peasant chancellor anywhere in the world? How much do you know about world history? There have been plenty of peasant prime ministers in Chinese history, not to mention peasant emperors! This has been an agricultural country for thousands of years, and so many feudal emperors started out as peasants. Aren't you a peasant yourself? And you say I'm uneducated!

"Do you know what culture is? It comes from civilisation and from military might. A civilisation needs military strength in order to build its own culture. There are two kinds of culture. In the first kind you totally ignore what everyone else is doing and devote yourself to study. In the second you make history, make experience, you make culture itself! I created a legend, I made history. Are you telling me I didn't make culture at the same time? You've been making fun of a peasant prime minister, but once a peasant becomes prime minister he's not a peasant any more. You keep moaning about my clothes, but these are my trademark, just like Chairman Mao's suit or Zhou Enlai's twisted arm. I never behaved as you have. The moment you got rich you tried to hide the fact that you started out as a peasant, but it doesn't matter how expensive your glasses are or how splendid your clothing, the moment people look at you they can tell that you're a peasant, and that you've been warped and twisted by trying to pretend you're not! You're just like a monkey – dress it in human clothes and it still looks like a monkey and not a person. The way you have behaved shows your lack of self-confidence and that deep down you don't think much of yourself at all. I, on the other hand, have always kept on looking the same, that's my style.

"Let me tell you, the greatest reward of success is success itself. All a man needs is self-confidence, intelligence and ability. It doesn't matter what kind of clothes he wears or what brand of watch he sports. I am a peasant, but I'm also more than just a peasant. That's what ordinary people responded to and something that even senior Party members admired. It can happen that you get into a situation where you seem to be the only person who matters, even the sun seems to revolve around you, and if you're in the right, then the world around you is right too. Look at what's happened to you now. You're in prison, everything you've worked so hard to achieve may well be ruined, and you refuse to even consider your own role in all of this..."

"It's true enough that when it comes to power and position, you got to the highest level possible for a peasant, but you really don't seem to know anything about wealth. It may be that, from that perspective, I reached the highest possible level for a peasant. So how do we decide which of us did better? Who is on top now? Maybe you did do well, but you never made yourself rich. You weren't interested in money, so money forgot all about you. Do you have any idea what it feels like to be rich? Money brings in more money, riches attract wealth. It comes looking for you and you simply can't turn it away. It comes rolling in, wave after wave, ceaselessly. It's the most wonderful experience in the world. Money is something that you can never have enough of. Pursuing wealth, accumulating wealth, that's what life is all about! I may never have reached the high rank that you did, but I ate and drank my fill, I had my fun, I built up an enormous empire of gold, and with that gold I lived better than you can possibly imagine. Money is the only thing that can improve the quality of your life, that's how you really experience what wealth means. There are two things that happen when you get rich – you earn shockingly huge amounts of money and you live the kind of life others can never even dream of. Even though you achieved such high office that other people had to show some respect, the people whose requests you turned down would still have cursed you as a vulgar upstart behind your back. You may not know this, but it doesn't matter whether you are a peasant or not, the moment you have money in your hand you become wonderful, you become mysterious and powerful, there is nobody who dares despise you and nothing that you cannot do. You end up feeling that you are almost another species. Who in the past ever took peasants seriously? But now nobody would dare to look down on some nouveau riche peasant, they queue up to flatter and fawn on us! Why shouldn't we show off a bit? Why shouldn't we be proud? So what if I've ended up here today, it's been worth it. I have no regrets."

"Whatever. Look at where you are today and stop trying to fool yourself. You may not choose to admit it to yourself but you are eaten up with regrets. Do you imagine that I don't know exactly how you became so rich and famous? You got rich because of other people's mistakes. A loophole in government policy meant people like you got showered with money. You kept it, but some people in your position didn't. You've been busy transferring the money from state-owned banks to your own village for years now, it's a kind of theft. People who get rich often don't understand how to appreciate this. They use their money to buy things they don't need, and their desires are never satisfied. You have material possessions but you are eaten up with a desire for further acquisition. Yet once acquired, you immediately lose interest. It's a kind of disease. So what if you are rich? You don't need to use other people's poverty in order to show off your wealth! In your eyes everyone else is dirt poor, bastards scrabbling around begging for crumbs from your table. Why should anyone put up with this! You've never had any other plan except self-aggrandisement. You boast about yourself and you pay other people to puff you. How can you not get into trouble like this?"

"If I didn't have guts I wouldn't be alive today. That's the only thing that can keep you going when you suffer misfortune. Other people are out to get you. If you are a coward, you are your own worst enemy. If you are brave, you can become your own biggest supporter. Understand? Running risks is the price you pay for the chance to be successful. And if it comes to boasting, haven't you been doing enough? You don't even care about the wishes of heaven where you are, and you're out and about causing trouble all the time. Ghosts kill people and then people are angry. But you make your reputation out of that. The more people you kill, the more they suffer, the more famous you become. How great and glorious can you be in such circumstances?"

"And aren't you just the same? Tricky and treacherous, sadistic in inflicting pain on others, and even more famous now you've been thrown into prison. But history is not going to keep giving you opportunities to put yourself right. You still don't seem to understand the situation. It is only when something is already rotten that the maggots start to appear. I've now got beyond all of that, I understand more than you possibly could, I've seen through the hollow nature of human passions, and I don't care any more who is rich and powerful and who is poor…"

29

CHEN KANG PAINTS A PICTURE

W u Lie came with a fat little policeman in tow to tell Guo Cunxian that he'd now been formally charged. Guo Cunxian wasn't surprised by this development, and he also didn't seem particularly upset or angry. He just made one request: "Since you're now formally charging me, can I have a lawyer?"

Wu Lie was surprised: "Wow! You certainly know your rights!"

"You could lock up a cretin in any jail and they'd pretty soon turn out to be an expert on the law. It's just the same for the police. The reason why you'll never be any good at your job is because the only thing you ever think about is locking other people up. You've never been in prison yourself."

Wu Lie looked at him sarcastically: "People need the law to clarify the evil nature of criminal acts."

"Don't give me that! Law depends on courts and lawyers. It doesn't matter what it says in the legal code, if you don't have lawyers you might as well leave the pages blank. If you don't let me see a lawyer, I'm going to kill myself. If you don't believe it, then just wait and see. You know perfectly well that if I go berserk, I can kill myself as easy as winking."

"Have I said that we're not going to let you see a lawyer? Do you have one in mind or do you want us to find one for you?"

"I have my own," Guo Cunxian said firmly, "and I'd like to be able to see my lawyer tomorrow."

"Who?"

"Zhu Xuezhen. She teaches at the primary school in Guojiadian."

Wu Lie was amazed: "Your wife?"

"That's right. Zhu Xuezhen is an educated woman and very law-abiding. She's the perfect person to act as my lawyer."

"No way. The law says that family members involved in the case can't act for you. You'd better ask for a proper lawyer, or else we'll find one for you."

"You know perfectly well that Zhu Xuezhen has nothing to do with this case. Plus besides which, I don't want anyone else."

Wu Lie thrust out his lower lip. "What is this? Are you missing your wife?"

Guo Cunxian came right back at him: "What, is that against the law too?"

"No, no, it is perfectly normal, I quite understand. Anyone else you miss other than your wife?"

"Right now there are two people I miss. The first one is my wife, of course. I'd like to be able to tell her that marrying her was the best thing that ever happened to me."

"And the other one is your son, right?"

"Of course I miss my own son! However, I don't really have time to think about him right now, because the other person I miss most is Second Uncle. For the last couple of days every time I close my eyes I see my Second Uncle standing in front of my bed, but he doesn't say a word to me. Do you think you could find Second Uncle for me? Could you tell me whether he's alive or dead? In that case I'll confess whatever you like."

Wu Lie looked at the fat police officer standing next to him, but he didn't say yes or no. For many days after this encounter, Guo Cunxian wasn't summoned for questioning, though of course Xuezhen didn't come to see him either. He was trying to puzzle out whether they were genuinely making an effort to find Second Uncle. Or did they really believe that he wanted Xuezhen to act as his lawyer and were reporting to their superiors to this effect? He tried to consider every possibility and thought the whole thing through, but in the end he couldn't decide what to do next.

If there really are tricks and traps for the soul in this world, then you can see them in action in jails, and they are set by the police and not by the prisoners. If the police refuse to give up, even if they can't get anything out of you by interrogation, then whatever you do and whatever you say, they can grind you down. Even if that doesn't work, they can just wait it out. All kinds of brutal criminals, thieves and murderers, right nasty bastards, not to mention professional confidence tricksters, come into jail and they are all chewed to a pulp. For the last couple of days Guo Cunxian calculated that he'd barely slept a couple of hours each night and he'd eaten virtually nothing. He was feeling confused all day with a splitting headache. He kept thinking about dashing his head against the nearest wall and putting an end to this misery. He was now genuinely suicidal because anyone shut up in this kind of place does end up thinking a lot about death, but he'd come to feel that the only way to preserve his self-respect was to die decently.

How can you die decently locked up in a cell? The fact is that he hadn't made up his mind to do it, and the situation wasn't yet desperate. There might yet be a way out, and if that was the case he wasn't going to die before he found it. In the very worst-case scenario he might be sent to prison, but how long could that possibly be for? He hadn't actually killed anyone himself, so he might get away with a couple of years. After he served his time he'd be released on probation and that would be for a maximum of seven years. Sooner or later he'd be able to go back to Guojiadian, and then he'd really show everyone what he was made of. So right now he had to survive. Even if he didn't want to eat the kind of food served in jail, he had to force himself to swallow it. He would gulp down a mouthful or two and then wash it down with water. That never killed anybody.

He was hoping to be summoned for questioning because then he'd get news and could let off some steam.

As he sat in his cell, he decided that sooner or later they'd have to interrogate him some more. Finally one of the police officers called his name. As he came to the door of the interrogation room, it so happened that he bumped into the fat police officer he'd seen the other day. The officer smiled at him and called him "Mr Guo", and then he said something about how "I hope you've had a good rest…" But the remainder of his polite enquiry was swallowed. Whatever it was that he'd wanted to say, there was no need; Guo Cunxian's face had already answered him. His skin was dull and yellowing, his eyes puffy, his hair like a bird's nest, and his greying beard resembled a tuft of dead grass. Asking someone who looked like that whether they've had a good rest is worse than pointless.

It wasn't just that. Since Guo Cunxian had been arrested, this was the first time he'd seen a smiling face and the first time anyone had spoken to him and not called him by name. That meant he was being polite. Unfortunately he'd already stopped smiling, so he couldn't respond. In fact there was no need for him to do anything of the kind, since this sort of cheerful-looking hatchet-man is very hard to deal with. Wu Lie might seem tough to the nth degree, but Guo Cunxian had never been frightened of him. The fat man introduced himself as Chen Kang and explained that he was taking over the case from Wu Lie.

Guo Cunxian thought to himself that this fat little man must be a lot harder than Wu Lie or they would never have let him take over. But under his left arm there was a notebook and several sheets of cartridge paper, while in his left hand he clutched a fistful of brushes, and his right hand was grasping a small box. He seemed entirely occupied with the task, and was clearly finding that he didn't have enough hands. He seemed to have brought an awful lot of rubbish with him.

After they took their seats, Chen Kang didn't stare at him aggressively the way that Wu Lie always had, trying to terrify him into a submissive frame of mind. Instead he was busy opening his little box, from which he removed a packet of cigarettes and a lighter. As he pushed them over towards Guo Cunxian, he explained: "I know you normally only smoke top-quality Chunghwa cigarettes, but I couldn't get any, so I bought you ordinary ones. I paid the proper price too, but I don't know if they are counterfeit or not. I've also brought a box of walnut brittle. If you feel hungry, please help yourself. However, I have to explain something first – these aren't a present from me, I can't afford to do that. All of these things are going to go down on your account, and eventually you'll have to pay for them. Right now you are still not allowed family visits, so they can't send you things. I've already told my superiors that you want to see your wife. The moment I hear back, I'll let you know."

As he said this he pushed over a little notebook and a pen. "Can you check if this is right? If the price and the items are satisfactory, then sign your name. In future if you want anything, just let me know. If it's not on the forbidden list, I'll get it for you."

Guo Cunxian smoked half a cigarette with just one intake of breath. Then he ate two squares of walnut brittle. It seemed as if he'd never smoked such a good cigarette in his entire life, nor eaten anything quite so delicious. The officer in charge of recording their session poured him a glass of water, and as he smoked and ate, Chen Kang painted something on the paper with a fat brush.

"What are you painting?" Guo Cunxian asked suspiciously.

"Your portrait."

Guo Cunxian took alarm at this, after being treated so unusually well: "What do you mean? Is this some kind of final picture before they take me out and shoot me?" He tried to make his comment humorous, but his voice was hoarse and there was a quaver in it.

Chen Kang looked at him, but the brush in his hand never faltered. "What are you talking about? I started out studying to be a painter but what with one thing and another I ended up in the police. The other day when we met I noticed that you had a most remarkable face, and I just couldn't help myself, I really wanted to paint you. I do hope you don't mind. I'd like to do a portrait that you'll be happy with."

What on earth was he up to? Why was he painting a portrait during an interrogation session?

Chen Kang seemed to have noticed his suspicious attitude: "Today is the day that I officially take over your case, but I don't want to dive straight into a discussion of your problems. Apart from anything else, they are blindingly obvious. There's no need for any investigation here, the facts are perfectly clear and literally thousands of people are aware of the situation and can testify to what has gone wrong. It is my responsibility to make you face up to these facts, so I want to talk to you first about how sick you are."

"My sickness? What's wrong with me and how do you know about it?"

"Not a regular kind of sickness," Chen Kang said.

"Oh, I get it, everything that happens to me is serious. My heart is giving out and I could suffer a heart attack at any moment. My knees hurt so I can't walk any distance. And then there's my terrible insomnia. That can really drive you mad if it goes on…"

"Those aren't the worst problems that you have. There are other things that are much more serious. If you don't believe me, then just think back to when you were an itinerant coffin-maker. Think how happy and content you were. You were highly thought of in your village, you had a beautiful and kind wife, you were living a good life. But then you began your official career and were promoted higher and higher, you held the power of life and death over others, and then you really did start to want to kill other people. Aren't you horrified yourself by the change that came over you? You have more money than you could spend in two lifetimes, but as the saying goes it's shirtsleeves to shirtsleeves in four generations. However, at the very least your children and grandchildren could live well. But then you ruined everything, isn't that perverse? Your road to riches wasn't an easy one, there were problems every step of the way, and there were many times that you ran terrible risks, you were investigated time and time again, but in the end you survived it all. This year your output is valued at six billion yuan, and it is predicted to be over ten billion next year. So what happened? You've apparently never asked about this, but don't you find it strange? Don't you sometimes have difficulty in retaining self-control, and haven't you wondered whether you might not be sick in some way?"

Guo Cunxian was confused. Was this a trap or was there hope for him yet? Does he want me to admit psychological problems? Because if I really do suffer from mental ill-health, then whatever illegal acts I've committed I can't be held responsible for my actions.

Chen Kang spoke in a thoughtful tone of voice, and as he did so, from time to time he carefully drew a few lines on the paper in front of him. He would glance at Guo Cunxian and then turn his attention back to his sketch, raising his head and then lowering it again, raising it and lowering it. He was clearly fully occupied.

"Right, I'm going to put it to you straight. As far as I can see you are pretty sick. And what is wrong with you? 'Money mania' would be one way of putting it. Or perhaps 'insane greed'. Getting rich is important, of course. As the saying goes, men risk their lives for money the way that birds and beasts risk their lives for food. How much money you have can have a really major impact on your personality, but it also changes the way other people think about you and how they behave around you. Suddenly becoming enormously wealthy is a complicated thing. You not only become famous and admired, but it can also provoke great jealousy and betrayal. Many people are quite schizophrenic in their attitude towards wealth. On the one hand they want to be rich themselves, but on the other they are endlessly suspicious that the rich have obtained their money by illegal means. This doesn't mean that money is the source of all evil and that people should give up their wealth. Of course, that would be impossible. Just like the air we all breathe, the food we all eat, or the way that some people get sick and others don't, money is innocent. It is human beings who are the problem. The classic symptoms of 'insane greed' are suspicion and social isolation, narrow-minded jealousy or envy, a strong belief in the importance of revenge, being easily angered or enraged, rushing into ill-considered judgments, a strong sense of self-righteousness, an overweening self-confidence, selfishness and so on. Let me read you this medical history..."

He took a clipping out of his notebook and read it out loud: "In the beginning I couldn't sleep, and then I stopped being able to eat. Things that used to make me happy seemed disastrous, I felt deeply depressed, and it was impossible for me to control my feelings any more. I had lost faith in everything, I might as well have been mad. I didn't understand, and couldn't understand, why lavatory manufacturers didn't fit their products with explosives so that you could just blow yourself up when you flushed. I didn't understand, and couldn't understand, why my wife when cooking noodles didn't boil the annoying phone at the same time. I didn't understand, and couldn't understand, why the arrogant bus driver didn't simply smash through the plate glass shop windows and grab some of the great items on display. Then, in the end, I was in my car one day and out on a crowded street when I suddenly felt as if I was driving my own tank. I aimed it at the people in front of me, at any obstacle in my path, crushing them to death like ants. It was wonderful!"

Guo Cunxian really couldn't stand it any longer, he felt deeply humiliated. Shouting in protest he said: "What is all of this nonsense? Just spit it out! If you want to insult me, you don't have to do it in this roundabout fashion."

Far from being annoyed, Chen Kang laughed. "You think I'm insulting you in a roundabout way? There you have it! A normal person, if they get sick, will make an effort to find a doctor, and in order to make sure that the medic takes their problem seriously, they may go so far as to somewhat exaggerate their symptoms. The quicker you are to deny the possibility, and the stronger your reaction is, the more you prove that you are sick, and seriously sick at that! That's because people with this kind of problem treasure their disease. They imagine it's something that makes them unique, that it is special, that sets them apart from others."

Guo Cunxian lit another cigarette.

"Why don't you say something, Mr Guo?" Chen Kang remarked. "Think about it. When you gave orders to beat someone up, wasn't that an enormous psychological burden?"

"I've never given that kind of order. It was the rage of the masses spontaneously erupting."

"Oh really? Well, let us analyse exactly how the Guojiadian masses under your rule found their rage erupting spontaneously. We don't need to go back too far in time. Let's begin with the death of Guo Cunyong..."

"Haven't you said enough? Surely it's my turn to be allowed to say something?" Guo Cunxian was determined to counter-attack. Having eaten and drunk his fill, he now felt an even more intense desire to speak. And having bottled up this feeling for days, he might well get sick if he couldn't say his piece. At the same time he wanted to make Chen Kang stay, he wanted to stay as long as possible in the interrogation room. There was food and drink on offer here, and cigarettes, so it was much better than being in the cell.

At this point, the interrogation started to become interesting. If the person being questioned demands to be allowed to speak, what was there for Chen Kang to worry about? His mind cleared and any clouds dissipated. Guo Cunxian was getting into his stride: "How can you say it's just me who is sick? Why don't you talk about how other people are sick, or how our leaders are sick, or how society is sick, or indeed how the whole world is sick? You wanted to know when I first started to suffer from this 'insane greed', didn't you? Well, every single person of any importance from the city, and then the province, and then the country, came one after the other to Guojiadian. The disease is endemic! Do you know how I got past the door the very first time I went to see a Party secretary? I took two *jin* of sesame oil and a watermelon and went to the front door to ask to be let in, and the guard on the door took me straight in.

"There are two ways to get to the very top of the tree here in China. Either you go abroad or you're the sort of person who appears in photos with our leadership. People often imagine that important people have everything they could possibly want in their homes, so it isn't easy to give them presents because they won't want anything. Actually, that's quite wrong. They love everything they get given. That is the way peasants work, and their methods are effective, because our higher-ups are all peasants too. If you don't believe me, just try it. Take ten *jin* of sesame oil and a truckload of watermelons, and you'll maybe find it's not that easy to get in so see the Party secretary. Why not? People won't trust you, but they'll trust a peasant, and they'll trust a rich peasant like me easiest of all. If someone rich comes to their house, the greedy find themselves thinking about money so much more, they start wondering what lovely things I might not be bringing them. That piques the curiosity of these senior cadres and makes them even more acquisitive. So I get the green light, and you in the Public Security Bureau just get annoyed..."

Well, that's where you went wrong, Chen Kang thought to himself. You could have given these people nothing at all, you could have held back from trying to play senior leaders, from getting into mind games with them, because all that's happened is that you've lost.

"And then there were all sorts of experts and scholars, as well as professors from the Academy of Sciences trying to get my favour. Again and again they praised what I had done, making sure that other people heard good things about me, or straightforwardly flattering me to my face. Whatever I did, they would make it sound good. What is more, they would find good reasons for it. They designed my mansion, the ornamental gates to the village, the Nine Dragon Wall, the 'Divine Eye'... They pulled every trick they could think of to find out what I wanted, to make sure it happened, to see my delight. Take the four sculptures that were supposed to keep down neighbouring villages. You say that's nothing but feudal superstition, but do you really believe that a peasant like me could come up with something like that? They were made by experts, who told me about how feng shui worked and how I could use it to curse people. I might think that it would be pretty to have a sculpture of a beautiful nude, but then higher-ups would give me grief over it, so I'd put a tail on her and say she was a mermaid. But Guojiadian isn't anywhere near the sea, so why do we have a mermaid?

"What I am trying to say is that peasants like to hide anything that's potentially embarrassing, so they'll put a tail on or add trousers. If this is how high officials and experts behave, what can you expect of anyone else? When Guojiadian was at the height of its prosperity, you had to squeeze sideways down the street at rush-hour. There were visitors all over the village, as well as those hoping our streets were paved with gold. Many people simply couldn't find a place to lay their heads and ended up sleeping by the side of the road. We were also visited by senior officials, journalists and tourists from more than one hundred different countries, and all of them were astonished. They found Guojiadian an amazing place, and it left a deep impression on their minds. There they were giving us the thumbs-up, telling us that everything was wonderful. Are you telling me this is a symptom of my disease? Was this brought about by what you are calling 'insane greed'? When you come right down to it, everyone wants money. The poor want to get rich, and the rich want to get richer! Money gives you control over what happens, and it allows you to control other people. Tell me the truth. If you suddenly became as rich and powerful as me, wouldn't you change too?"

Chen Kang said that would just be pointless speculation. I can never become like you, and you could never turn into someone like me. There are lots of rich people in this world, but how many of them are like you?

"What's wrong with being like me? If you want to understand what has happened in China, once you start talking about reform in agricultural villages in any historical era, will it be possible to avoid discussing me? My experiences, the things I've done, have become legendary among Chinese peasants. Anyone who wants to deal with Chinese agricultural reform or the fate of our peasants has to deal with me and Guojiadian. Arresting me, and bringing me here, may just be the capstone to the legend of Guo Cunxian! Without me, Guojiadian will collapse. Guojiadian's collapse will show just how important I was.

"How people in future will judge this is very hard to say. I'm sure you've heard a lot of gossip about me, many will have been wanting to criticise and complain, but the fact remains that I've managed to survive in an atmosphere of constant carping, and that's also a sign of my success. If you don't have some quality, even if you want other people to complain about you, are they going to have noticed your existence? I'm absolutely sure my name will be found in history books. I'm going to be a historical personage. History won't pass me by in silence because I've done my bit, I've helped history move on. Let me tell you something – it doesn't matter how you treat me now, whether you convict me or not, or how many years you send me to prison for, sooner or later I'm going to become a god. Don't look at me like that, I'm not joking. Last year for the New Year's celebrations every single family in Guojiadian worshiped me as the God of Wealth. There were some families that had a table with a statue of the God of Wealth on it, holding a sword in his hand and with a long beard. The face, though, was mine. This wasn't ordered by anyone in the village, it was the peasants themselves who did it, it was their idea. The fact of the matter is that I've brought them wealth, they've become rich because of me – me, and not the old God of Wealth, Guan Yunchang. I imagine that, among the tens of thousands of people who've come to Guojiadian to work, there may well be others who worship me as the God of Wealth..."

Chen Kang stopped painting and opened up the bag by his side. He took out a New Year's print from Guojiadian with a picture of Guo Cunxian on it as the God of Wealth. Suddenly a phrase popped into his head about how even the gods have ugly faces, and he found himself laughing.

Guo Cunxian would never have imagined that Chen Kang would collect and keep this kind of delightful memento, and it was enormously encouraging for him. He said happily: "You may not be aware of it, but for the last couple of years the women of Guojiadian have been accustomed when they get pregnant to come to my office and let me stroke their bellies. That's regardless of whether it was a baby within the family planning rules that they were going to keep, or whether they were going to have to have an abortion..."

Chen Kang could not help himself laughing. He pointed at Guo Cunxian: "Are you saying that all the women in Guojiadian have let you grope them?"

"Hey, what kind of second-rate policeman are you anyway to be reading things into this?"

"I'm not reading anything into it. You said it."

"It's a fact. The women whose bellies I stroked went off to have their abortions safe and sound, with no problems afterwards. The ones who got to keep their babies all had lovely healthy children."

"Oh, so I guess the women in Guojiadian whose bellies you stroked all had boys! Well in future Guojiadian is going to look like a monastery. Are you planning to rebuild Bachelors' Hall, or are you going to try to find wives for them from other villages?"

"Not other villages, from abroad! Our lads in Guojiadian aren't going to be landed with just any girl. We've been so successful, we can do things our own way. Now you have to admit that, even though I've ended up in here, I'm still more important than the others. Don't talk to me about how it hurts a lot when you get sick, it's really serious. It's only when the wound goes deep that it's painful, and it's weight that makes it serious. Seriousness testifies to weight, and it's another way of assessing value."

Chen Kang didn't really seem to be listening, but the brush in his hand was never still. He was on his third sketch of Guo Cunxian's head and was painting away when he remarked completely out of the blue: "Your hair is too long and your beard too coarse. I'll bring a barber along tomorrow to give you a cut and shave."

Guo Cunxian had been enjoying himself but was now brought up short. This took away all his pleasure in their conversation, and he couldn't stop himself feeling a bit cross: "Haven't you been listening to anything I've been saying? Is this an interrogation or a portrait sitting?"

From his tone, he didn't just object to Chen Kang painting his portrait, it was arousing latent hostility and fear in him. It seemed as though he was happy to be questioned, but not to be painted. Chen Kang paused his brush and looked at him, his expression calm and his eyes serious. He said in a very friendly manner: "Don't worry about it. In my profession we are trained to use our eyes, ears and brain all at the same time. I've been paying attention to everything that you've said. If there's anything I've missed, then our session is being recorded. Just now you were enjoying giving that disquisition, showing just how much value you attach to your life before and after death, so that anyone might imagine that you are looking forward to it. You are quite wrong. People can only become gods after they die. So if you want to become a god, you're going to have to be dead first. The fact that a clever man like you has embarked on a criminal career speaks a great deal about your way of life, and that is a more accurate reflection of your personality than any wish for posthumous regard. But you have forgotten the limitations that experiences impose upon you that are almost impossible to set aside. You may imagine you have reached a high point, but in fact you are at your lowest ebb. Beyond the sky there is outer space. The wind races ahead of the wind that buffets you now. Beyond the road you walk, there are other roads.

"Just now you were talking about history, which is more patient than any human being. Without making a sound it watches you, waiting for you to walk step by step towards the trap it has laid for you. For example, you say you've become a god in Guojiadian. Do you know what a god is? A god is something beyond the mundane world, it exists high above us, it is independent. Over and over again you have either condoned or ordered people's deaths. Ultimately, is this not the result of internal conflicts? To put it more bluntly, you have felt that you are losing control of the situation, the Four Bosses are now acting independently, and you have not kept power over the cashflow in your own hands – the Four Bosses have control over that. Again and again you have tried to provoke incidents so as to grab back some power, which in future will go to that adopted son of yours…"

Guo Cunxian felt like a pig lying on the butchering block as Chen Kang used his knife to peel back his skin, hack at his bones and cut out his heart. He might look perfectly ordinary, but he was clearly extremely intelligent. He could explain what he'd done with much more clarity than he could himself. If he had originally thought about things with this degree of insight, perhaps he could have fixed his problems in a less controversial fashion, and then none of this would have happened. As it was he'd been thrown into jail and his adopted son was in terrible trouble.

At present the Four Bosses seemed to be safe and sound, which meant that there was yet a chance to turn this situation around. But if they carried on working and the companies continued to function as normal, then that would prove that Guojiadian could get along just fine without him, or maybe do even better. That would put him in a very difficult position. How could he come back from that? It would be even worse than being condemned to death. From the very beginning of his imprisonment, he'd been hoping that his four old friends would take his side, that from the day of his arrest they would have ceased production, or at the very least slackened off as much as possible, so that their groups collapsed and went bankrupt, destroying Guojiadian. That was the only way to show how important he was; Guojiadian couldn't survive without him, and arresting him meant ruining Guojiadian. But would they do it? Some of them might. On the other hand others might be secretly pleased to get rid of the 'emperor' and stand on their own two feet, establishing their own power and authority.

On the second day, Chen Kang did indeed bring a barber with him, and before the interrogation began, he cut Guo Cunxian's hair and gave him a shave.

Chen Kang liked to conduct his interrogations with plenty of spontaneity. He used this unexpectedness to probe the personality of his opponent, with all its strengths and weaknesses. He gave the impression of someone who never got angry. But in fact he was simply picking his moment. Sometimes the meat needs to simmer for a while, and you don't want to take it too fast or too slow. But when the time came to bring things to the boil, the person he was interrogating would be in a much worse state than him. After the cut and shave, Guo Cunxian was clearly feeling a lot better.

"I must say you look a lot younger now you've had your hair cut," said Chen Kang, mixing his colours. "I feel a lot more confident in you. If you face up to the past and get lenient treatment on the back of it, there'll be many years for you to enjoy once you get out of here."

These words were enormously encouraging to Guo Cunxian, but he didn't make a sound.

Chen Kang started painting Guo Cunxian's portrait as quickly as he could, and as he did so he said: "You really do look completely different. I'm going to take this opportunity to do several sketches. Sit down and we'll continue our conversation from yesterday, but today we're going to get down to details. Straight after seven of your lads were convicted over beating a man to death, you had a teacher and students from the police academy beaten up. What was that all about? You don't have to explain because I know exactly why you did it, but I'd like to hear you come up with an account for your actions."

Unlike the previous day, Guo Cunxian now had no interest in building up his morale by boasting of this and that, so he dealt with this question by saying that it was nothing to do with him, or with his lads either. The students from the police academy had brought it on themselves by their arrogant behaviour. What's so special about being in the police? What gives them the right to behave like that? They treat everyone like they are criminals, they went round the shops throwing their weight around, breaking things and cursing the counter staff. Weren't they just asking for trouble?

"That can't be right. I am sure that's not what happened. They were students from the Dahua City Police Academy studying criminal investigations and they came out to Guojiadian with their instructor, Sun Wenda, to carry out a sociological study. They had your permission for this. In the course of their investigations some villagers reported that you'd collected more than four hundred thousand yuan in 'voluntary' donations for the men who'd been convicted. Some people were wondering what you were up to collecting all of this money. Was it really to fund the murderers or was it intended for some other use? Of course there were also other points of conflict. One of the students, Cheng Wei, used up all his tapes making recordings and went to a shop in the village to buy more. What he did not know was that the shops had all received your orders not to serve them – or perhaps this was merely something ordered by your subordinates. The shop had the tapes he needed but refused to sell them, and when he insisted, they produced some old ones. What was that all about anyway? The students naturally asked what was going on, not anticipating that the manager would immediately shout for security, and they beat the students up. They had their faces masked, so we don't know who they were. But they then dragged off the students who'd just been thumped to your office to let you decide what should happen to them. So you are entirely responsible for what happened after that."

"What's all of this stuff about responsibility? There's no such thing, and stuff happens for no particular reason, either. Some people are born to suffer, others are born to lord it over them. Why don't you ask them why they suffer? Why don't they get to lord it over others?" Guo Cunxian was showing his impatience and started to try to turn the subject.

Every time this happened, Chen Kang would just laugh, without the slightest sign of irritation. He picked up a large brush in his right hand and, without taking his eyes off him, made full note of the change in Guo Cunxian's mood. He also continued speaking: "Don't move, don't move, look at me... That's right. Well, the fact is that it happened, and there's a reason for it. You can forget about making a few excuses. That's not going to get you off."

"There are always plenty of rules in this world, and if you've got the power, you set the rules. In every situation, you can make your own laws. And the opposite is also true – if you don't have power, it doesn't matter what the rules say, they're worthless. Right now you have power in your hands, what you say goes. If you want to summon me for questioning you can, and if you don't feel like it then I just sit in my cell and wait."

"Oh, so what you're trying to tell me is that in those days you were the most powerful so you didn't need to obey the law, you could just do whatever you liked. So in actual fact it was arranged right from the beginning. The security guards in the shop were told to beat up the students and then take them to you. That was to give you an excuse to question them, right?"

"When I saw that bunch of very suspicious young men being dragged in, of course I wanted to question them."

"What did you want to ask, and how did you question them?"

"Oh, I had a lot of questions. Why were they interfering in our business here in Guojiadian and why had they smashed the glass counter in one of our shops? Were they here to study or were they just out to cause trouble? Why had they picked Guojiadian for their investigations? Were they up to something here? Who were they investigating and what had they discovered? Had they found any black-market goods? I really don't remember any more."

"So what did you find out?"

"Nothing much. Shortly afterwards the teacher called Sun something-or-other turned up with the other students. I had no idea that these student bastards would have an instructor who was just as much of a pain in the arse! He wasn't there to deal with the situation, he wanted to throw his weight around because he was in the police, and he was doing this to me in my own village! I wasn't going to pay any attention to him, so I went out to make a call, to see if I could find out who he was…"

"Wait a moment, don't move." Chen Kang stretched out his arm and made a gesture with his brush to indicate that Guo Cunxian should stay put exactly as before. "Just before you left Lin Meitang's office on the fifth floor, you said one thing that turned out to be really important, really crucial for the case. Surely you remember?"

"I say a lot of things. What is it that you are thinking of?"

"'If you don't tell me now, you'll find yourselves in real trouble after I leave.'"

"Yeah, I did say that. So what?"

"Since you know perfectly well, I don't understand why you're bothering to pretend. What happened next occurred precisely because you said that. When you said that about 'real trouble' it might have been thought to be a threat aimed at the students, but in fact you were giving orders to your thugs. Afterwards you saw the results of 'real trouble' for the police academy students and their instructor, but you didn't see the process of how this was inflicted, so now I'm going to tell you exactly what happened there. It began with one of your security guards going up and slapping Mr Sun across the face. It seems that this was a signal because then, all the other Guojiadian thugs piled in, punching and shouting: 'Who the hell do you police think you are? This is Guojiadian, and we can hit you any time we like!'"

Chen Kang's brush sped across the paper, and his words now came even more quickly: "The really shocking thing was that even women took part, like Lin Meitang. Ordinarily she really doesn't look like the kind of person who'd beat someone up, but there she was grabbing a student by the hair so she could kick and punch him, and cursing all the while: 'You bastards! You deserve a good thumping!' It really was quite horrible. They were beating up people because they thought they could get away with it, and because they might as well. Your people seemed to find it really exciting to be able to behave like this, it was like a festival for them and they obviously enjoyed it. Everyone took part and when it was over they let them go. For the victims, of course, it was quite a different matter. Mr Sun lost teeth and the hearing in one ear, and he suffered a haemorrhage in his left eye. There were twenty-one students beaten on the same occasion, of whom five were so severely injured they ended up in hospital. Of course they weren't allowed into your village hospital. They were held here for seven hours, and it was only when they got back to the city that they received the necessary medical attention. You're very lucky none of them died. But then before we'd even finished dealing with the fallout from that, just two weeks later you beat the chief accountant of Eastern Commerce to death. You beat up outsiders, you beat up your own employees, and step by step the numbers increased. First you had a couple of thugs, then a dozen, then a few dozen, until you ended up with several thousand men in military uniforms in open resistance to the lawful activities of the police."

Chen Kang got up from his seat and walked round Guo Cunxian, his painting in his hands, measuring him up. "What on earth did you think you were doing? I've never heard of anything like this. It sounds like a modern version of a tale from *The Thousand and One Nights*. So I've been wondering all this time, did this kind of sadism become addictive? Did your thugs get used to behaving like this, so that if anything didn't go just right, their first reaction was to lash out physically, to ball up their fists and start punching? I know that crime can be addictive. Some criminals find committing crimes so intensely pleasurable that they carry on, trying to recover that emotion. Even if they want to stop they are unable to do so. Terrorists are like that, and serial killers, sometimes burglars too. They commit crimes in a way that they enjoy, and every time there are certain things that they do, like leaving a signature to their activities. This is what criminal psychologists call 'repeat offending'. Now tell me, do you agree with my reading of the situation?"

Having received an order to this effect from the chief of police, Chen Kang was waiting in his office for a visit from An Jinghui. This was quite contrary to usual practice. From the fact that this had never happened before, you could see how remarkable this woman journalist was. What was even more remarkable was that, even though half an hour had passed from the time set for their meeting, An Jinghui still had not turned up. Given that she was asking a favour from Chen Kang and not the other way around, she still had the crust to behave like that.

Well, she was a woman and a famous woman at that. Chen Kang was trying to imagine what the most famous woman in the city would be like when he finally heard the tapping of high heels out in the corridor. Someone opened the door to his office and informed him that the reporter was here. Immediately afterwards a billow of delicious perfume enveloped him. Chen Kang raised his head and was amazed: good heavens, this famous reporter looked like the woman in that film about the assassination attempt on Lenin – hunched shoulders, pulled-in neck, lips blue with cold... or maybe she'd deliberately painted her lips that colour.

For all that she looked frozen to death, An Jinghui never lost her sex appeal. She was wearing a dark silk skirt and a camel-hair coat, a small bag slung over her shoulder and her arms crossed over her chest. She walked up to Chen Kang with a smile on her face, but she did not say a word.

Chen Kang got up to say hello and then let her take a seat: "Please do sit down. You must be the famous journalist An Jinghui, whom I've heard so much about."

An Jinghui didn't sit. "You can cut the big build-up," she said. "Call me Jinghui."

She weighed him up with eyes that were not at all unfriendly, and the smile curved in an even more confiding way: "You're the famous one here. An expert interrogator of legendary ability..." She was stamping her feet and rubbing her hands, complaining about how cold the weather was, and how icy his office. Why are we having a cold snap at this time of year? Suddenly she called him by his name, just as if they were old friends: Chen Kang, do you think you could continue the glorious tradition of the police showing their care and concern for the people by rubbing my hands to warm them up a bit?

Chen Kang was most embarrassed. He would actually have quite liked taking her hands in his to warm them, but he simply didn't dare. Moreover, given that this was the first time they'd met, her request was outrageous! However, he didn't really dislike her for it. In fact quite the opposite, it made him more relaxed and more interested in her. He took off his jacket and walked round behind her to drape it over her shoulders.

"Thanks. You're a real gentleman." An Jinghui's smile was becoming more and more ambiguous. She teased him, saying: "Actually, I'm trying to test the Public Security Bureau's attitude…"

"The office of the chief of police have already been in touch. I understand you want to look at the footage from Guojiadian?"

"Yes. But your office is freezing. Would it be possible for me to borrow the footage so I can watch it in comfort?"

Chen Kang was now quite nervous. "Impossible."

"Then how about I bring in a blank tape and make my own copy to take away?"

"That's also impossible."

An Jinghui didn't seem put out at all, and as before she turned laughing eyes on him in the hope of tempting him into an indiscretion: "Well, if this is impossible and that is impossible, what am I allowed to do?"

Chen Kang smiled bitterly: "I'm very sorry but those are the rules. I'm only obeying orders. If it wasn't for special permission from the chief of police, you wouldn't even be able to watch the footage here. But only you are going to be allowed to see it, you aren't allowed to make any kind of recording, and you aren't allowed to write anything or tell anyone about what you have seen. Do you agree?"

"I agree," An Jinghui said formally. "So let's get on with it."

The moment she started work, she seemed very professional and stopped trying to provoke him. She also stopped complaining about the cold. There was an awful lot of film and plenty of it was really boring, but she kept her eyes glued to the screen from start to finish, occasionally scribbling a word or two on her pad. Chen Kang did nothing to stop her.

The scenes playing on the screen were extremely confusing. There was footage from various different rooms in which people were being interrogated or beaten up. There was screaming, pleading, the sound of crying and the voices of people trying to make excuses for themselves. From outside you could hear the blaring sound of loudspeakers broadcasting Guo Cunxian's voice…

Chen Kang sat next to An Jinghui explaining what was going on, and she reached into her bag and fished out a packet of cigarettes and a lighter. "Can I smoke?" she asked.

Chen Kang nodded. "Of course." An Jinghui put the packet down in front of him but he waved it away. "I don't smoke, but please go ahead."

A couple of thuggish-looking police officers appeared on the screen, dragging a well-dressed and refined-looking middle-aged man in a suit off into an office. An

Jinghui couldn't stop herself from asking: "Why were there so many police at Guojiadian? The whole place seems to have been nothing but officers and security guards."

"They had their own dress-up police, to try to put the fear of God into people. It's a place where they admire brute force, so they thought they could give themselves more authority by wearing police uniforms, and then they could go out and throw their weight around. In fact all that happened is they revealed their guilty conscience. Everyone will unconsciously try to protect their psychological weak points, and if you don't feel secure you'll try to defend yourself in some way. Guo Cunxian hates the police so he liked to have all of these people dressed up like policemen to follow him around, because that made him feel safe."

After she had finished watching the footage, An Jinghui spoke as if she were talking to herself: "What a strange man Guo Cunxian is. Sometimes he seems very macho, but he's clearly quite nervy, and never, ever forgets an enemy. But at other times he can be unbelievably generous…"

She suddenly turned to face Chen Kang and asked him: "Who took this footage?"

"Of course it was Guo Cunxian himself who ordered the filming. They had top quality equipment out at Guojiadian, and their own TV station. "

"Was he off his head? He was giving you all the evidence you need."

Chen Kang laughed: "You're absolutely right, he has gone off his head. However, when he gave orders for this film to be made, he wanted to show off his success and flaunt his authority. He wanted it to look as if everything was right and proper and he had nothing to fear. In addition to that, he has a strong sense of history, so he was hoping that by recording all of this footage he'd make his way into the history books. Normally he had a team of cameramen and sound technicians recording everything he said and did, and afterwards this material would be edited and turned into documents to give to the villagers, or kept until the end of the year when it would be compiled into a book. Eventually, no doubt, he was hoping to see a *Selected Works* and a *Complete Works*. I'm sure he never imagined that this film would end up as evidence of his criminal activities."

A few days later, the *Dahua Daily News* published An Jinghui's article, entitled 'The Fall of a Billionaire'.

Recently a peasant has made the news, shocking the entire country. Of course, he is no ordinary peasant, but the famous 'Keeper' of the Guo Family Shop at Guojiadian and member of the National People's Congress: Guo Cunxian. That's right, Guo Cunxian is in trouble, serious trouble, and people have been killed. So he is under arrest.

As we all know, the Cultural Revolution came to an end in 1976. The following year was spent in hope, in waiting and in thinking. And then in 1978, the peasantry couldn't stand it any longer, and they launched themselves into action in another way. In a village called Xiaogangcun in Fengyang County, Anhui Province, peasants from eighteen households smeared their lips with blood and swore an oath to divide land equitably among themselves and then work it to their own private profit.

It was at this time that peasants with a bit more guts and ability from across the country started to set up factories, go into haulage and deal with logistics. This was because peasants were sick and tired of poverty. They'd had enough, they weren't prepared to put up with it any more, and they weren't scared to fight for what they wanted. They did anything to earn a bit of cash, even if it was just a couple of dozen yuan, and once they'd got a few hundred yuan together they were ready to take on something bigger. If you were clever, if you were prepared to work hard, you could make some real money very quickly.

At that time there was a discussion in our country about what was the biggest problem facing China. Our peasants were the biggest problem, and if you don't understand peasants, you don't understand China. Peasants form the bulk of Chinese society, so if they don't live well, society as a whole has a serious problem. Therefore, reform had to begin with the peasantry, and throughout the period of agricultural reform in the Eighties, most important leaders of this movement came from provinces with big agricultural production.

Hot on the heels of this movement, township enterprises came to the fore with peasants at the helm. They took the lead in shaping the social trends of this period. Guo Cunxian himself played a key role in all of this, and he was one of the most important figures in this era. He demonstrated the wisdom, diligence and courage of our peasantry to the full. He had his own philosophy, his own mysterious way of doing things, and he lacked neither self-deprecation nor a sense of humour. In a time of great social change, when old and new rules were endlessly in conflict, he grabbed every opportunity to push things on at high speed. He kept moving forward, trampling on anything that got in his way, going through one red light after another, and somehow or other he got away with it. In the space of just over a decade, Guojiadian became what was indubitably the richest agricultural village in the country, and so it was natural that Guo Cunxian should become a hero of this economic advancement, the living embodiment of a new era in peasant development.

To use an old expression, he was a 'model', a model of peasant enrichment. From land reform to collectivisation, from the 'Four Cleans' to the Cultural Revolution, each and every one of these movements produced their own peasant models, but none of them lasted long. The individuals concerned may be different, but the underlying principles and the way they rose and fell were very much the same. So what conclusions can we draw? Can model peasants never hope to escape this kind of fate? Everyone has been watching Guo Cunxian, they had high hopes of him. Therefore, we need to think seriously about what happened to him after he became a rich model peasant. Now he is under arrest, does this predict the destiny of other peasant tycoons?

The media is currently engaged in endless analysis of these peasant tycoons. In 1999 the state commended five hundred peasant entrepreneurs, but within two years more than a quarter of them had withdrawn from the scene for one reason or another. It is as if their riches existed only in a dream. Once they woke up, they found themselves back at square one, as poor as they had ever been. Some didn't make it even that far; they ended up in prison or dead.

The media in Beijing report that we have been through three stages of peasant entrepreneurship.

Stage One lasted from 1978 to 1984. The individuals concerned mostly had just primary school education, and the majority were village secretaries, team leaders or in possession of a skill. They managed their businesses in a highly paternalistic manner, and they completed the transformation from an agricultural economy to a basic market economy.

Stage Two lasted from 1985 to 1990, and the people concerned at this stage had attended junior high and high school, and a few had even been to university. They introduced an institutionalised style of management, and their greatest historical contribution was in moving small-scale production into mass marketing.

Stage Three was from 1990 to 1994, and these people came armed with a high school diploma, a degree and sometimes even a post-graduate qualification. In management, they started to bring in cutting-edge techniques from overseas, and they deliberately led their enterprises into high-tech fields or modern industrialisation.

From this you can see that Guo Cunxian clearly belongs to the first generation of peasant entrepreneurs. But a new crop appeared every few years, and they kept popping up like mushrooms.

According to their calculations, the average life expectancy of a rural enterprise in China is seven years, and many who got rich in Stage One found themselves stripped of their wealth later. These included the reckless, those who ended up overextended, those who relied on connections with the powerful, those who tried to get their own people into top positions, those who placed all their eggs in one basket, the over-aggressive, the corrupt and those who risked too much on the stockmarket. Now, to which of these categories does Guo Cunxian belong?

Why is it that, once a peasant gets rich, he wants to make others feel his wrath, and this violence becomes deeply enjoyable to him? It is terrible to have to admit it, but Guo Cunxian was no exception. Let me give you various examples of this kind of sadism that have recently been exposed by the media:

In Baijiaocun, a wealthy seaside village in Zhangzhou County in Fujian Province, the deputy secretary of the local branch of the Party, Lin Lizhi, hired an assassin to murder the director of the village Party Committee, Wang Yijie.

In Taoyingxiang, under the administration of Dengzhou City in Henan Province, a number of village cadres, including Zhang Zexin and Liu Changzhi, were ordered by the village head, Duan Zhanqing, to beat a peasant named Chen Zhongshen to death after he reported to the authorities various problems in the administration of the village and illegal sales of land.

In Shuangmiaozhen, a village in Woyang County, Anhui Province, nearly ten cadres, including Guan Erhui and Wang Bujiu, used 'carrying out family planning policy' as an excuse to force their way into the houses of local people – sometimes even breaking down doors – whereupon they would attack any women they found inside and gang-rape them.

In Longquancun, a village in Yongnian County in Hebei Province, a young peasant Zhang Yanqiao got into an argument with the director of the village Party Committee. He was then arrested by local cadres and beaten to death.

Such examples were not confined to the newly rich in the countryside. When the first generation of wealthy men in Guangzhou, Wuhan, Shanghai and Shenyang came under investigation, it was exactly the same. Some of them were guilty of corruption and embezzlement, and then there were those who'd been gambling and whoring, and now found themselves addicted to drugs. Others had business empires built on fraudulent schemes, and then there were those who'd turned violent and launched themselves on a life of crime.

Violence spreads like the plague. It has destroyed many rich men, and many of those who wanted to get rich too.

Goodness breeds further good deeds. But where there is evil and misfortune, it all goes to nurture hatred. Guo Cunxian suffered greatly in the past, and so he stored up a powerful desire for revenge. Such things can be concealed when you are poor, but once you get rich, particularly if you get very rich, when you have fame, power and a position in the world, then the anger you have stored up in your heart over the course of decades will burst its bonds like a demon.

Guo Cunxian liked to compare his position to that of high officials, but in actual fact he hated them for holding appointments more important than his own. He beat to death his chief accountant Yang Zusheng because he despised intellectuals and believed they always looked down on peasants like him. He would often talk about how he was doing things to make life better for peasants, whatever he did was supposed to be for their benefit, but then he would pick one of their number and beat them to death. The fact of the matter is that he really couldn't stand peasants! In the past, peasants were denied many freedoms because they didn't have money. Under Guo Cunxian's leadership they may have had money, but they still lacked many freedoms because they had to obey his orders in all things.

Right from the beginning there were people who complained about Guo Cunxian, saying that he was undermining socialism, that he was destroying state-owned enterprises and that his aims were entirely capitalistic. He responded by pointing out that Guojiadian represented capitalism without the -ism. He was quite right, this was about capital and he didn't understand capitalism in the slightest. If anything, he was reverting to feudalism. He was the saviour of Guojiadian, their very own God of Wealth, and the entire village showed boundless admiration and trust in this economic strongman. In planning, management and execution his word was law, there was absolutely no control imposed on him, and so it should not surprise anyone that Guo Cunxian has ended up where he is today.

Guo Cunxian is the secret behind Guojiadian's rags-to-riches story.

No wonder that some experts have said: "The phenomenon of Guo Cunxian is a purely Chinese one. Looking at all walks of life, at agricultural, urban and industrial areas, what success, what successful work unit, does not have someone like Guo Cunxian behind it? Is there any strongman whose political operations don't far outweigh his economic manipulations?"

Is Guo Cunxian a strongman? Only superficially.

Lack of faith breeds crime, violence shows weakness. Guo Cunxian had people beaten up, even beaten to death, in order to cover up his weaknesses and shortcomings. At the very moment that he imagined he was so powerful that he could condemn others to death, he showed that he was a weakling and a failure.

After Guo Cunxian got into trouble, a strange riddle was posted on the big entrance gate out at Guojiadian:

'Cunxian – Secretary – Master – Guo Cunxian!

Old man – Sick Man – Lunatic – Common Criminal!'

I will try to explain my answer to this riddle. From the way that the people in Guojiadian addressed Guo Cunxian, you can see the way his fate unravelled. To begin with everyone in the village, old and young, liked to call him 'Cunxian' – that was friendly and kind. You could say this was the happiest time in his life. Later on he became an official and so they had to be respectful and call him 'Secretary'. Otherwise he would get angry. Later on as he got older, people called him 'Master', which gave the impression he was a clan head, or perhaps the boss of a Triad gang. This was appropriate for a peasant emperor. Now he was a criminal, and his position was lower than that of any ordinary peasant, nobody needed to be frightened of him or show their respect, so everyone now called him 'Guo Cunxian'!

He started out as a peasant, and it was his ambition to get rich. After he achieved this ambition he was old. As his wealth grew it seemed to trap him in unhealthy attitudes. The things he did were more and more abnormal. Later on he became even more sick, in fact you could say he went mad, kidnapping police officers and trying to mobilise Guojiadian to fight the authorities. The result of his lunatic behaviour was that he was thrown into prison as a common criminal.

Such was the life of Guo Cunxian.

30

JUDGMENT DAY

The interrogation that afternoon did not proceed as normal. The police did not take Guo Cunxian to the room where he was usually questioned, but instead directed him to an empty room off the main courtyard. He was utterly unprepared for the fact that Zhu Xuezhen was there waiting nervously for him, holding a huge bag of stuff. He froze in the doorway, his heart wrenched with pain. In less than six months, Zhu Xuezhen had aged more than ten years. Soon she'd be an old woman.

It was dreadful to think that such a lovely person had suffered so much because of him.

He had forgotten how much he had changed too; to begin with Zhu Xuezhen didn't even recognise him. It wasn't just that he looked so much older, but he seemed to have changed physical form. He was now so thin he looked skeletal, nothing but a bag of bones. Zhu Xuezhen didn't dare cry, but she also couldn't open her mouth to speak. The door was open and flanked by two armed guards, their guns loaded with live ammunition. Now she began to cry, with ever greater intensity.

For a long time now she'd been eating very little, and then yesterday on receiving the news that she'd be allowed to visit, she hadn't slept at all. Now, suddenly seeing that her husband had become an old man, she was horrified. She could feel her legs trembling, and her hand lost its grip so her bag fell to the ground. Any moment now she was going to collapse in a heap... Guo Cunxian stepped forward and caught her. Afterwards he sat down on the stool and pressed the ball of his thumb hard against her upper lip to bring her round from her faint. After a long while, the blood started to come back into Zhu Xuezhen's chalk-white face, and her blue lips became warm again. When she opened her eyes she struggled out of Guo Cunxian's embrace and sat down weakly on a little stool to one side. She pointed to the bag on the ground, gesturing at him to open it.

Guo Cunxian was desperate to open the bag and look inside, but he was afraid that once he saw the contents he'd want to start eating. He was constantly hungry now, but he was afraid the sight of him ravening would make Zhu Xuezhen even more worried about him, so he forced himself to put the bag of food to one side. He kept his eyes fixed on his wife's face as he said in a humble voice: "I demanded to be allowed to see you, and threatened to kill myself if they refused because I wanted to apologise to you face-to-face. If there is anyone in this world who I've genuinely hurt, it is you. I am so sorry for the way I've treated you. If I ever get out of here, the first thing I'm going to do is to visit Xiayangpo with you. I want to kowtow to your parents' grave and apologise to them because I haven't been able to keep the promises I made when we first got wed."

Zhu Xuezhen started to cry again, but she waved her hand to show that he shouldn't say any more: "I've never blamed you..."

She didn't want her husband to talk about such things in front of the police, so she took a letter out of her coat pocket and was just about to hand it over to Guo Cunxian when suddenly one of the police officers yelled at her. She wasn't allowed to show Guo Cunxian anything with writing on it. She put it straight back and said: "A letter came from Chuanfu in America..."

Guo Cunxian leapt up off the stool with a thud. "He's gone then?"

"It was entirely by coincidence. He left the day after your arrest."

"I've been so worried, thinking that I might have ruined his future... That's good, he's been able to get away. God has been good to me."

"Chuanfu's doing really well in America. He's got a fully funded PhD place, and his supervisor found him a job as a teaching assistant, so he's got more than enough to pay all of his expenses over there. He's now busy doing the paperwork so I can go and join him."

"That's wonderful." Guo Cunxian kept muttering the word 'wonderful'. "Xuezhen, the best thing I've ever done was getting married to you. It was because of having such a wonderful wife that I could have a good son like Chuanfu. He takes after you, after all you come from an educated family. We Guos have never produced a scholar before, and thank God my son doesn't take after me! Does he know what's happened?"

"Of course he knows! It's been big news on TV and in the papers."

"What does he say? Does he hate his old man?"

"It doesn't matter whether he's a scholar or not, he's still your son. How could he possibly hate you? In his letter he said to tell you that you've got to get through this, whatever happens. He said this is a watershed moment in your life. If you don't get through it then you'll always be nothing but a peasant entrepreneur, but if you do make it through, you'll be considered a peasant philosopher."

"Did he really say that?"

"Would I say it if he hadn't told me? I did bring the letter in my pocket, but the police won't let you see it..."

Guo Cunxian leaned forward and took hold of his wife's hand. Zhu Xuezhen looked at the police officers by the door and tried to pull her hand back, but he held it in a grip like a vice and she couldn't get free. Guo Cunxian's face was now right in front of hers and his eyes were opened wide.

"Xuezhen, you've got to promise me – in fact I'm begging you – when Chuanfu's done the paperwork, you should immediately go to the US to join him. You can look after our son, and you must let him look after you. Let the boy pay back all that I owe you. Then I know you'll be safe and sound, and whatever happens here there'll be nothing to be afraid of."

Zhu Xuezhen said lightly: "I've already written to our boy to say we'll go together once you get out."

Guo Cunxian was now anxious, and he shook off Zhu Xuezhen's hand. "Are you completely stupid? Even if I do get out of here, they aren't going to let me leave the country. Right now the person I worry most about is you. If you're out of here I can relax, everything will be easier... Second Uncle came to see me yesterday."

Zhu Xuezhen was amazed, and she stared at him. "What are you talking about? Don't scare me like that!" she said.

Guo Cunxian shook his head: "I'm not trying to scare you and it wasn't a dream. Second Uncle came to my cell and he had Blackie with him... it's the size of a small ox nowadays! The last few days Second Uncle has been in and out a few times, but he never says anything to me. I know he must be very disappointed in me, so he's not paying me any attention. Second Uncle was always much more fond of Cunzhi. But yesterday we sat up half the night chatting."

Zhu Xuezhen could feel the hairs on the back of her neck prickling: "What did Second Uncle say?"

"He said I saved Guojiadian and that in future it's going to do even better than when I was in charge. In the past I often used to claim that I was blasting through the barriers to rural reform, but now I've been blown up myself, I really can't complain. Power is like a wild beast – the greater your power, the wilder the beast. It won't let someone ride quietly on its back. Whoever you are, when the wild beast goes berserk, it will toss you onto the ground. He said I'm going to have to pay for my brutality and arrogance and that I should feel profound regret over the way I've become emblematic of someone with an overinflated estimation of their own abilities. He said that I've been pushed into a corner by the concerted efforts of those who love me and those who hate me, and that I have now reached the end of the road. He said I shouldn't ignore this final fulfilment of my destiny. Isn't that pretty much what Chuanfu wrote in his letter?"

"Did Second Uncle say what you should do?"

"Yeah, I asked him about that. Here I am surrounded by all these disgusting and filthy criminals, does this not mean I'm going to end up dead? Second Uncle said that manure is disgusting, and filthy too, but how come when you spread it on the fields you can grow good crops? And those crops are clean, they keep us alive. Doesn't it all depend on whether you've got decent land to work? Or whether you use your brain or not? On a decent piece of land, manure doesn't stink, and things that smell horrible can turn out to be the most nutritious. If you've got the brains, you can achieve great things as a result of suffering."

Zhu Xuezhen laughed. "You're just making that up! Second Uncle would never say anything of the kind."

"Without Second Uncle's advice, I couldn't have said it either." Guo Cunxian took a wooden block one inch by three out of his pocket and handed it to Zhu Xuezhen. "Do you remember this?"

Zhu Xuezhen took a closer look. The little wooden block was completely smooth, with a depression carved in the middle. A hole had been drilled in the centre of this depression and a moveable bolt inserted. This mysterious object had been beautifully worked, but she didn't understand what her husband meant by this, so she raised her eyes and looked at Guo Cunxian.

"This was the lock on the door of our house," Guo Cunxian explained. "I made it myself. You can't have forgotten, it changed our lives. I didn't have it with me the day I was arrested, besides which when the police searched me on arrival in jail, they'd have found it and taken it away. Second Uncle gave it to me last night. Look at the back. There are two lines newly carved on it. I didn't write them. It's not the kind of thing that would ever occur to me..."

Zhu Xuezhen turned it over. As he had said there was a couplet carved on either side of the depression in tiny characters:

When you have seen through worldly illusions, it is terrifying.
When you have understood human emotions, it is chilling.

One evening a few days later, the police came to call Guo Cunxian just before lights-out. He guessed that this would be the last time Chen Kang would be questioning him. The odd thing was that he didn't feel even slightly relaxed, but nervous and helpless instead. The next thing that would happen would be the court case, and he had no idea how that would go. If he was sentenced to a short period of imprisonment that would be OK, but recently he'd sensed that things were not trending that way. If the higher-ups were making such a fuss about his case, it really didn't seem likely that he would only be lightly punished. If he only got sent down for a few years, wouldn't that mean the leadership was blatantly letting him get away with it? How were they going to explain that to the country, to society as a whole, to the public? If he was going to be severely punished, he would rather carry on answering Chen Kang's endless questions.

Even he could sense how much he'd changed. When he'd just been arrested he wanted to see his family, or indeed anyone from Guojiadian or anyone at all for that matter, so as to encourage them to curse and scream, to declare his innocence, to plead for him with the higher-ups. Now the only person he wanted to see was his wife. He also felt very fond of Chen Kang, though he didn't know when this had started, and now the interrogation was coming to an end.

Chen Kang was clearly very relaxed. He was smiling so much that he seemed quite globular. His head was round, his face was round, and his shoulders were round – even his body seemed round. When he saw Guo Cunxian he was so pleased his eyes went quite round too, and he rushed forward to open the portfolio he was holding: "I simply couldn't make time to see you until now, so I had to bring you here this late."

Chen Kang then revealed his portrait of Guo Cunxian. With his eyes fixed on him he asked: "What do you think? Are you satisfied?"

Guo Cunxian's eyes flashed and he stared at the painting. Chen Kang had produced a wonderful likeness, a real living likeness, but at the same time there was an unusual quality to it. Some aspects of the painting exercised a strange fascination on him. He loved the self that appeared in this portrait, that short hair, the long eyebrows, the straight nose, that square chin. He was completely familiar with every aspect of his own appearance. But Chen Kang had put all of these features together in a face that was fresher and more cheerful than his own. He bore a thoughtful expression, his eyes were calm, he seemed kindly and serious. It revealed a gentler personality than he expected, with less sharpness coming through.

He wanted to thank Chen Kang. It was worth being interrogated for months to get this kind of portrait painted. Another idea also came into his head – this painting ought to go to Guojiadian, and then for the New Year's prints they could use it as the model for the God of Wealth. That would be much nicer, and this face was one that people would feel more friendly towards.

A portrait is different from a photograph, particularly in the context of a jail. When an interrogator paints a portrait of the person he is questioning, that has a very special meaning, and more than that, it is a matter of good fortune, a kind of glory. After all, it is not everyone in jail who can experience this kind of good fortune and glory. Chen Kang asked him again if he liked the picture.

Do you need to ask? It was obvious he liked it, but he said in hesitating tones that it was a good portrait, although he felt it somewhat alien.

Chen Kang stopped laughing: "That's right! People's feelings change all the time and your expression will change too in response to that. I did dozens of sketches of you the last few months. The two of us were communicating all the while, not just verbally, but at the level of our minds and spirits. The painting is finished, so questioning you is also over. Until the interrogation was concluded, I couldn't complete my portrait. I know you weren't happy about the sketches I did of you before, but that's because they revealed you in a state of change. In the circumstances your face couldn't be reflective of who you really are. The reason why you like this painting is that it reflects your emotional journey. You've done with lunatic fantasies and are prepared to reveal a softer side hidden deep inside you. That's given you an opportunity to rediscover your soul. That's why you can now look so calm, that's why there is hope in your eyes. This is who you really are."

As Chen Kang said this, Guo Cunxian was struck by the realisation that there was a lot less that he wanted now. Most of the time his mind was completely free from desires of any kind. He couldn't even be bothered to waste time speculating on whether he would get out alive or not. His life had become very simple; all that was left was life itself, nothing else. He'd originally thought this was a sign of weakness, of surrender, but being thrown into prison had stripped him of much useless baggage. Losing his freedom had paradoxically allowed him to see clearly what his life had been all about. He'd thought a lot about the past, and he could now analyse things in a much truer light.

Chen Kang asked him: Do you know who your greatest enemy has always been? It has always been yourself. You've been constantly fighting yourself. Now you've stopped that, and you're not going to start again. Power and wealth are external things. It doesn't matter that you keep on talking about the rough patches you've been through or the glory that you've enjoyed. These are things that it has been easy for you to accomplish. But your soul is something internal, something that is very hard to capture. You should know that better than anyone else. In the past you used violence and fear to force other people to do your bidding, but at the same time you frightened yourself. We are connected as human beings in so many different ways. The lessons that strike hardest and are most unforgettable come through setbacks and blows. There is nothing that can beat the education you receive from adversity. A while back you were discussing history with me, and analysing the place you will enjoy in history books. Well, going to prison will correct some of your analysis, but as far as history is concerned, this is just an afterthought.

"You know about Czechoslovakia and how the current president is Václav Havel. He spent time in prison too, and when he came out he wrote a book called *The Power of the Powerless*. In this book he talks about how going to prison is a kind of invisible power, it allows you to send a message. Everyone has their own history, even the most insignificant of individuals, and they participate in history. In this way we each obtain the right to be respected. I'm saying this because I want to tell you that keeping a soft spot in your heart, giving your emotions free rein, isn't a sign of weakness or pessimism. Quite the opposite in fact. Wisdom is a form of strength, and right now the only source of strength that you have left is your intelligence. Dignity and respect are very powerful words. In the past you were respected, but then that respect became tinged with other emotions. When you go before the judge, if you can deal with whatever comes the way you did in the past, if you understand what it is that you've done wrong, you can regain your sense of self-respect."

"Am I going to be sentenced soon?" Guo Cunxian asked.

"Yes, probably in the next couple of days. You need to be prepared."

Originally Guo Cunxian had intended to ask how long he was likely to be sent to prison. But as the words trembled on his tongue, instead he asked: "There are lots of other people involved in my case, but there hasn't been any suggestion that they've been questioned too. How can they convict me of anything?"

Chen Kang laughed. "Well, your interrogation is over, and this evening is probably the last time we can have a long chat, so I'm going to tell you a story. During the reign of the Tongzhi Emperor during the Qing dynasty, the manager of a pawnshop received a set of elephant-chess pieces made of the finest emerald-green jade, exquisitely carved and beautifully designed. The engraving was done by famous artists, too. And so he wrote a ticket for five hundred taels of silver, with a limit of ten days. When the pawnshop owner came back he was furious, since he thought the manager had been cheated and that he should have realised the chess pieces were rubbish. The manager felt deeply humiliated after the boss cursed him like that, and he said that he'd pay back the five hundred tael loss, but that he was also going to resign and go home. As he said that, he picked up the chess set and threw it into the canal by the pawnshop. On the ninth day the original owner came back wanting to redeem his chess pieces with a thousand taels of silver. The boss was overcome with amazement. The owner told him that the chess pieces were priceless; they'd been bestowed upon his grandfather by the emperor, and that since the time wasn't yet up, if the pawnshop didn't hand over the goods, he'd pay with his head. The boss was terrified and rushed off to find some swimmers prepared to trawl the bottom of the canal, but the current was fast and there was a build-up of silt, so they simply couldn't find the little chess pieces. The boss was at the end of his tether and had no idea what to do next, so he had to bring his manager back to help him find the set, cost what it may.

"The manager said that he didn't want money. You screamed and shouted at me in front of many people the other day, so I want you to bring everyone back and apologise to me in front of them. You have to take back all of those hurtful things you said, and then I'll think of a way to get those chess pieces back for you. The boss told his staff to gather everyone sitting around near the canal, and when they heard what was happening a crowd quickly assembled. Anyway, the manager took out two pieces from this elephant-chess set from his pocket – when he tipped the others into the canal he kept back the 'Red Commander-in-Chief' and the 'Black General'. He then tied a silk string onto the Commander and the General which in turn was attached to a rope, and sent people out in a boat to fish where the pieces had been thrown in. They moved the rope back and forward many times. When they lifted it up, there was a whole chess set clinging to the end of the rope. All the missing pieces were there. The onlookers were stunned, and news soon resounded through the entire city. The manager explained that right from the beginning he'd known that these were very special objects, and the stone from which they were made had magnetic properties. As long as he had the General and the Commander-in-Chief pieces under his control, getting the others back would be as easy as winking."

"You said that if you got me, it would be easy to deal with others in Guojiadian..." Guo Cunxian muttered. "Thanks for saying something so nice about me. You are an amazing interrogator, Mr Chen, and if I'd met you way back when I'd never have ended up in this mess. If one day, and I'm saying 'if', I get to go back to Guojiadian, I'd like you to act as my legal advisor. Would you be interested?"

Chen Kang was perfectly amicable in response: "Well, we can talk about it later. Even after I've handed all the paperwork about this case over to the authorities, you can still come and find me if there's any kind of problem. Just let the guards know, and I'll come to see you."

"I have a request to make," Guo Cunxian said.

"Go ahead."

"Tomorrow morning. could you buy me two *youtiao* fritters?"

"Fine, tomorrow morning I'll invite you to breakfast right here in this room. You've already ordered *youtiao*, but would you like soft beancurd with that, or soy milk, or maybe wonton soup? And would you prefer sesame flatbreads, plain buns or rolls?"

Lin Meitang was surprised to get a call from An Jinghui: "I've been trying to get hold of you for ages, Meitang. At least this time you're in. Let me cut a long story short, I really need to see you, so tell me, do you want me to go to Guojiadian or will you come to the city?"

Lin Meitang was startled. "It surely won't be convenient for you to come here, so how about I come to you?"

"Great! We can meet at the Rose Garden for dinner. I'll see you there."

Lin Meitang was now completely free. She could go wherever she wanted without having to explain to anyone what she was up to. She began by sitting down in front of the mirror to do her make-up. Ever since Guo Cunxian got into trouble, people had been keeping a really close eye on her, as if they could read things in her face: Lin Meitang's looking terribly old all of a sudden, all of those wrinkles! Her hair has gone quite white, and she's trying to avoid anyone seeing her... She wore heavy make-up whenever she went out, though she didn't care in the slightest how she looked. Whatever happens will happen, whether she liked it or not. Let them say what they like.

Once she'd made up her mind to appear in public, the rest was easy. She chose an old rose velvet jacket that she'd bought a while back but never worn, which she paired with black cashmere trousers, light but warm and very comfortable to wear. Once everything was ready she picked up her bag, locked the door and took a moment to breathe deeply on the steps before she set out. She could have asked for any of the company cars to take her, or phoned up any private car owner, and she was sure they would have been happy to drive her into the city, but she didn't want to ask any favours.

She walked out of Guojiadian's Zhongnanhai all on her own, with back straight and head held high. She headed out of the village in the hope of finding a taxi by the entrance. A taxi driver who'd brought a fare out and didn't want to go back empty might wait for a bit to see if they could find someone going to the city. And even if she couldn't get a taxi, there was a bus every half hour, and in a little over one hour she'd be in the city. Lin Meitang steeled herself to accept what it was like to live as an ordinary person in some out-of-the-way village. You may never get to live the good life, but there is no limit to the suffering you can experience. Guo Cunxian was a classic example of this. Women are supposed to be good at putting up with things; well, that was her plan.

Guojiadian was carrying on. Without saying a word, the four big conglomerations had gone back to work and they were doing fine. The Four Bosses had got away with it. They had all learned their lesson, and they weren't going to cause a fuss like Guo Cunxian. However, it seemed as though it wasn't quite business as usual. The conglomerates' customers went straight to their offices, bypassing the village entirely, leaving the community out in the cold. A Guojiadian without Guo Cunxian gave the impression of missing something. Missing what? It had lost its spirit, there was no human warmth here, its time had passed. Well, you had only to look at the Lucky Trees and it was perfectly obvious, they were dying too. It was all very odd. Second Uncle was gone, Guo Cunxian had been arrested, and it seemed as if the Lucky Trees weren't going to survive much longer either. Who were they continuing to live for? Lin Meitang couldn't bear to look at the huge trees that she'd always thought so beautiful.

There were traces of Guo Cunxian all over Guojiadian, lots of signs that he'd written still hanging on buildings round the village, but the locals seemed to have already forgotten him. Life carries on, never stopping for a second, and if someone has fallen by the wayside, well, that's just too bad. The fact is, nobody is indispensable. The residents of Guojiadian had their own lives to live, and they'd clearly already moved on from Guo Cunxian's chapter. On realising this, Lin Meitang felt a sudden stab of terrible pain in her heart. Guo Cunxian had spent more than half his life in this place, but was it really worth it?

It was very quiet by the entrance to the village – no taxis, of course, and even the buses had changed their schedules. She waited for nearly an hour and then was lucky enough to catch a passing bus. People can change really quickly. This was true of her as well. You have to change as circumstances develop, you have no choice. At every important juncture, you need to adjust to the changing situation around you – you must constantly change the way you do things. The first thing she changed was to stop being irritable. Her time was now worth nothing at all, and never again would there be important things, urgent things, needing her attention. She wasn't ever going to have to be in a hurry again. She didn't worry any more about things being slow, she wasn't afraid of having to wait, she had plenty of time. She was bored of sitting at home doing nothing, so at least standing at the entrance to the village waiting for a bus was something to do. She had a goal, she was going into the city to see someone.

Luckily there were seats available on the bus, and as she sat down the bus rattled on its way. Sooner or later it would arrive at its destination. She didn't want to see anyone, and she didn't want anyone to see her, so the moment she was in her seat she closed her eyes. Recently, the moment she closed her eyes, she'd found herself mulling over all the things that had happened. But right at this moment, to pretend to be napping while turning things over in her mind, was perhaps the best way to occupy the time that she was going to have to spend on this bus.

Earlier on she'd been sorting out some old photographs at home, and her attention had been drawn to an old newspaper that she found in with her pictures. The lead article was kind of interesting. Supposedly Mao Zedong had posed a question to Zhou Enlai and Liu Shaoqi: how can you make a cat eat chili peppers? Zhou Enlai and Liu Shaoqi racked their brains for an age and thought of a variety of possible answers, but all of them were wrong. She hadn't read to the point where Mao Zedong gave the right answer when she received the call from An Jinghui. Having been distracted like that she completely forgot about how to make cats eat chili peppers. But now all of a sudden she remembered the story and she really wanted to know the answer. How do you get a cat to swallow a chili pepper?

Maybe she should get a pet. She liked dogs and had been thinking for ages that she ought to get an Alsatian, but then she'd thought about how Guo Cunxian would come to join her in bed without any warning. A loyal dog that thought it ought to protect her might be tiresome. The mistress of a married man can't keep a dog. On the other hand it would be fine now. She'd like to have a sensitive and clever animal to live with. There was also now no concern that it might be problematic; she could have whatever pet she liked. If she wanted someone to cuddle she could have that too, or find someone to look after her. For a woman in her position, there'd be no problem in financing a toy boy, and if she wanted an older man to take care of her, that would be perfectly straightforward too. In the last few weeks there had been plenty of bastards imagining they could take her over, and there had also been an awful lot of gossip and rumours about her. That was all because she'd been Guo Cunxian's mistress. All of these men wanted to try being in his shoes.

So had she been Guo Cunxian's pet all this time? In the years that she'd been sleeping with him, he never gave her a penny; there was just one occasion after he got rich that he did give her some money. That was towards the end of the year when the iron and steel works was set up. One afternoon when they were alone together he handed her a big bag with one million yuan of cash inside, telling her to look after it. Previously there had been all this talk about millionaires as if this is something special, but a million is nothing! This money is to guarantee your future, and you should try to save as much as you can from your salary. Right now if we need to spend money on anything it should come out of the village's pocket. We've earned whatever money there is in this village, so we ought to be allowed to spend as much as we like. That day he laid down a rule for her that any time she went out, even if she was just leaving the office for a moment, she had to have at least fifty thousand yuan in cash in her pocket. In the past they'd been terribly poor, and now they had money, so they were going to have to make sure that there was money available at all times, in case there was a sudden need for cash and they couldn't lay their hands on any, which would just let other people despise them. So from the perspective of outsiders, it was always her who'd spent money on whatever it was he wanted. It looked as if she were taking care of him.

So could you say that Guo Cunxian had been her pet? Other people might not see it that way, but that was always how she'd thought about it and how she behaved. He might seem a very strong and determined character, and indeed to begin with this was what had really seduced her. She liked men to be clever and powerful and stronger than herself. Even today she could clearly remember how it had been the first time she gave him her body. As he crushed her beneath him she felt like the whole house had fallen down on top of her. His love was destructive. At that time her separate consciousness and will left her, but his conquest of her was also creative. From that day on, she felt renewed, as if everything had changed. Even if nobody else in the world could understand her, she was quite clear about it herself. This sudden and violent explosion of emotion was love, and she should cherish it. If it doesn't come suddenly you can't really call it love. By the same token a man's qualities have to be discovered by women, they are created by women. He was so thin he looked like a monkey, with deep wrinkles running across his face, the spitting image of an opium addict in old pictures, but she discovered his qualities. She was deeply troubled by his wild ambitions. This was no ordinary peasant. When he looked at people you could see an inexplicable and mysterious authority in his eyes.

However, in all of Guojiadian, she was the only person who could make Guo Cunxian back down. He had such a terrible temper, everyone was afraid of him and had been cursed by him. But who had ever seen him get angry with Lin Meitang? And not only that, even his power was implemented through her. In Guojiadian everyone was replaceable, with the sole exception of her. What happened later only served to reinforce this point. He left her because he was thrown in prison, and now everything had gone wrong. She had thought about what would happen to her in future many times, but her fate was inextricably linked with that of Guo Cunxian, and she could never have imagined that things would turn out like this. All of his ambitions and ideals have led to this stupid and destructive denouement.

How could she make sure that he obeyed her over the course of the decades? It is only when a man respects and trusts a woman – and truly can't do without her – that he will never get angry with her. Other people might think that he ruined her life. Crucially, even Guo Cunxian might think so, and so she had every right to criticise him, to blame him, but in fact she'd never spoken a single angry word to him. You can't discuss the rights and wrongs of the situation with a man; men only want women who don't complain. The less she criticised and blamed him, the more important she became, and the more he owed her. But if she'd ever said one word of criticism, if she'd ever said one word of blame, he would have written all of that off. There were times when she could have destroyed him, but she protected him instead – she was determined that he should never feel her to be a burden. Since she owed everything to him, why would she make the stupid mistake of complaining? Since she'd always done what he wanted, since she'd always been happy and never caused him the slightest problem, why shouldn't he trust her? Absolutely every aspect of his life was arranged by her. She even sorted out his sexual encounters, since she looked after the aphrodisiacs Guo Cunyong bought for him in Hong Kong. Besides which, in recent years Guo Cunxian had ruined his health. He might look impressive enough on the surface but he was just the shell of his former self. He couldn't do anything without her help. In the end she was the only person with whom he could keep his self-respect going. She knew how to prevent him from overtaxing himself, and she made it easy for him to feel good about it. She was now the only woman with whom he could enjoy such successful encounters.

The night before he was arrested, he didn't go home at all. He stayed with her in the bedroom on the sixth floor. He seemed to have a sixth sense warning him of impending disaster. He must have known on some level that it was likely that tomorrow he would leave and never come back. But he had to go, after all he'd told the Public Security Bureau that if they wanted to arrest him all they had to do was say so and he'd turn himself in. It was the secretary of the metropolitan Party Committee who had invited him to go. That was a nice gesture and he had to show his appreciation. Even knowing it was a trick, he had to go. But, having prepared for the worst, he decided that his last night as a free man would be spent with her. It was some kind of compensation and recompense. Sometimes he'd even gone so far as to tell her that she was just his daytime wife. The daytime wife was someone to show off to other people, someone who could sparkle in front of other men. Since she was young and beautiful, it was best to make her the daytime wife. In fact he called her his daytime wife to set limits on their relationship, even though love is omnipresent. To make love to one another in broad daylight brought a piquancy to their affair. Sometimes in the evening he would have sex with her and then head back home to his night-time wife. There were occasions when she really wished he could stay overnight with her, but she'd never said so. Every time she watched him get dressed in silence and then let him go without a word. That night, which might well have been the last night of his life, was given to her. It was a heartwarming moment for her, a deeply satisfying occasion. Before they'd even begun to have sex she was already lost in his strange, dark gaze. She was so confused she gave him a double dose of Viagra, thinking that it wouldn't matter if it killed him. They were only too familiar with each other, so desire struck them like a wave, ebbing and cresting, one wave after another, completely naturally. Your body is there to bring you pleasure, not to be hidden away. As he thrust again and again he began to curse and swear – who knows what whore taught him that kind of language! And then, most unusually, she suddenly lost all desire. She didn't want him to find out, so she faked a series of orgasms. Somehow or other faking it reignited her passion, her need for sexual release became stronger and stronger, and in the end she had no idea whether she was still faking or whether it was real.

After sex, he hugged her against him and said that if he never came back after tomorrow there was one wish that was still unfulfilled. She asked what wish; even if it killed her, she'd see it fulfilled. He laughed – for the one and only time that whole day – and said you can't help. I started out making coffins, and I've made more coffins than I can count, of every kind. I've seen all sorts of different manners of death, and in the end it was me who helped to tuck them in safe and sound in their shrouds. I guess that counts as a good deed. My wish would be to make a good coffin for me when I get old, and not just one either, but it will be a matter of luck whether you get to use yours. If I die first, that's just your bad luck. You'd better find a new man and get married, get away from here. If Xuezhen dies first, then I'll marry you right away, it doesn't matter how old I am. That way when you die you can be buried in the Guo family graveyard without anybody complaining, and in the next world just like in this one I'll have you on one side and Xuezhen on the other to keep me company...

She scrambled on top of him, wailing . She'd never cried like that in front of him before. He didn't shed so much as a single tear, and if anything, he cheered up at her reaction. He told her that he'd had a good life, and having someone to cry like that was a fine way to send him on his way.

After he said that she did her very best to hold back her tears. Even so, they didn't sleep at all that night.

It was dark by the time the bus arrived in Dahua City. As the bus made its way through the busy streets, Lin Meitang indicated that she wanted to get off. She then found a taxi to take her to the Rose Garden. An Jinghui was waiting for her by the main entrance, wearing a pair of snow-white loose trousers, which really stood out under the multi-coloured rainbow lights. The waist of the trousers was cinched in with a wide, soft-textured elastic band, giving a very sexy feeling. Anyone seeing it would be tempted to reach out and give it a tug. She was wearing a tiny denim jacket as well, which made her look young and energetic. In fact the whole impression given by her outfit was of a lively personality. Lin Meitang felt a spasm of envy. Look at her, she's never been pretty, but somehow or other in all these years she doesn't seem to have aged at all. She got out of the taxi, and the two women embraced.

With that embrace both of them could feel the other's sincerity and affection, and in that moment these two very different women became friends. As friends, there was no need for formality. To carry on standing by the door saying polite nothings was obviously an empty gesture; it would destroy the harmony and fellow-feeling between them at a stroke. Without saying a word, An Jinghui grabbed hold of Lin Meitang and started walking.

She was obviously a regular customer, as comfortable here as in her own home. She turned first this way and then that through the maze-like passages of the Rose Garden, making her way to a private dining room on the second floor. There was a beautiful little powder compact sitting on the table, making it look as if An Jinghui had already been in there. From this private dining room you could look out on the dance-floor in the main dining room at the Rose Garden. Floor shows were held there every evening from eight o'clock, then at eleven it was turned over to any customers who fancied the exertion, and they could carry on dancing right through to the early hours when the place closed at two o'clock. Once the door was closed, however, they could be private. Inside there was a dining table and sofas to sit on. In the middle of the room there was a marble paved area, just for the people using this private dining room, where they could get up to whatever they liked.

After taking the measure of her surroundings, An Jinghui didn't take her eyes off Lin Meitang's face. Lin Meitang, on the other hand, seemed unable to concentrate and unwilling to meet her gaze. An Jinghui broke the awkward silence: "You seem to be keeping your spirits up. You're looking better than I expected, but... what on earth have you done to your face? That was what I was afraid of. Now that everything's gone so wrong, you've stopped caring. Come, let's get that clown makeup washed off. I'm simply not going to be able to face eating anything this evening until we've fixed your face."

She picked up her compact off the table and led Lin Meitang by the hand to the bathroom attached to their private dining room. Once inside, Lin Meitang lost all control. She slumped against An Jinghui's breast and burst into tears. Even though she was crying with great intensity, she did not dare to completely let herself go. The feeling that even now she had to hold back, keep the noise down was unendurable. She cried so hard that her back was shaking and her whole body trembled. Then, afraid that her tears would be spotting An Jinghui's clothes, she used both hands to wipe her face.

An Jinghui hugged her tightly and patted her gently on the back. "Just have your cry, you'll feel better afterwards. There's no point trying to put a good face on things. The fact is that good things happen at the right moment, but bad things always happen at absolutely the wrong time." Most unexpectedly, as she said this, her own tears started to drip down Lin Meitang's neck.

After a while, the tensions that had been building up in Lin Meitang's mind were released, and the storm of tears began to ebb, so she now haltingly explained: "This is the first time I've cried since Guo Cunxian was arrested. You know, I haven't had anyone to talk to about it. Besides which, even if I felt like crying, it wasn't the right time or place."

As she said this she burst into tears again. An Jinghui rushed forward to try to soothe her, helping her to take off her coat: "That's fine, there's nothing to worry about, it's all my fault anyway, I should have come to see you before. If we'd met sooner we could have had a good chat and you could have got it all off your chest. Now wash your face, your makeup is all over the place." She turned on the tap and made sure it was the right temperature.

Lin Meitang lowered her head and washed her face. The tears vanished in the flowing waters, and she gradually started to calm down.

An Jinghui opened up her make-up case: "This is Estée Lauder from France – I got it specially for you. Women change their make-up in order to change their mood. If your make-up is good, you're naturally going to feel so much better about things. With the situation being what it is, you really should think about yourself for a change. After being through such a terrible time, you need to be even stronger, even tougher than before."

The two women started to work on Lin Meitang's face. Here a darker shade, there a lighter one, rubbing a bit here, putting in a line of colour there. With all of this powdering and painting, Lin Meitang did really begin to feel better. The two of them started to talk and smile, even giggling a bit.

When An Jinghui had finished working on Lin Meitang's face, she inspected her critically, adding a few final touches. All the while she was humming snatches from a pop-song:

The common belief that we can be happy,
That vulgar faith in happiness
In a world where everything has lost its meaning
Survives, yet without respect...

They spent more than half an hour in the bathroom before they finally emerged. Lin Meitang was already looking a great deal better.

When they sat back down at the dinner table their mood was completely different, and they were obviously much more cheerful. An Jinghui started to order a real spread – she didn't even look at the menu but discussed what she wanted with the waiter: "It's really hard to order for just two people. You want quality but not huge portions, so let us have a crab each, female 'round navel' ones. And fried shrimp, pig's trotters in a soy-glazed sauce – that's so good for the skin – and for our vegetable dish let's have asparagus soup. With a couple of cold dishes that should be about right. Today we don't want to have hard liquor. It's bad to drink when you're already upset. Since we're having seafood I think we should order white wine, so please bring us two bottles of a dry white from France..."

While they were waiting for the food and wine to be served, An Jinghui was so desperate for information that she started to ask questions: "What is going on in Guojiadian right now?" She had come with many questions to ask. She was planning a series of articles about Guo Cunxian, and if it worked out she might even write a book about him. This evening she was hoping to get a real reaction from Lin Meitang, so she was preserving an unconcerned air, as if the questions she was asking were just a matter of natural concern.

In fact Lin Meitang didn't have any objection. There was a lot that she wanted to get off her chest: "What you'd expect. If you don't know about what's been happening you might imagine that everyone's moved on. The whole place is dead quiet. It's like a line has been drawn through Guo Cunxian's name. But if you think about it in another way, Guojiadian has turned over a new leaf. Guo Cunxian has saved it for a second time! He's really helped some people an awful lot."

An Jinghui raised her eyebrows – this was interesting! "What do you mean?"

"All these years Guo Cunxian has been training up a group of cadres in his image at Guojiadian. When he was around, they were all as quiet as mice. But then in the blink of an eye they all turned into mini-Guo Cunxians, up to one damn thing after another, constantly in-fighting. Even if nothing happened this time, there'd be disaster sooner or later. If it wasn't Guo Cunxian who got into trouble, one of the others would have. Well, as it turned out, it was Guo Cunxian for the chop. After he was arrested, Feng Hou came out to Guojiadian to read the riot act and everyone came to their senses right away, particularly the Four Bosses. They're now doing even better for themselves than when Guo Cunxian was in situ. They've silently gone off to set up foreign companies and opened offices abroad to engage in joint ventures. First they transfer the money out of the country and then their families leave. Wang Shun's wife and children have emigrated to Canada. Chen Erxiong is spending a lot of time in Australia nowadays and I hear he's got dual nationality. Jin Laixi has handed management of the company over to his son, and he and his wife are on a world tour. They wouldn't dare behave like that if Guo Cunxian was still around. They aren't going to be like Guo Cunxian, stupidly thrashing around and just waiting for someone to come and get him! They may say that they have the utmost respect and admiration for Guo Cunxian, but they are afraid that he might come back – it would be best if he rots and dies in prison. That way everyone is happy, and I guess that when the day comes they'll hold a huge funeral for him in Guojiadian."

An Jinghui was stunned. She was not expecting such a thorough and incisive analysis of the situation from Lin Meitang. It seems that there are some things where thinking deeply isn't enough, you have to experience them personally. She sighed: "So they've hollowed out Guojiadian? There's an awful lot of government money – banks' money – invested there."

"Exactly! But all of that money was borrowed in Guo Cunxian's name. They ought to have thought about that when they arrested him. Now he's in prison, you think anybody is ever going to see any of that money back?"

"So the country is going to have to take a big loss because Guo Cunxian was arrested? In the past nobody ever cared about the economy when ordering arrests, it was always all about politics, but now I wonder whether they don't still think the same way. They really should have considered the problem before he was arrested. Besides which he was always presented as a model of business success, not as some kind of moral exemplar. Politics is very odd. Sometimes political mistakes are what is really needed."

The waiters brought in the food and wine, so An Jinghui stopped talking. Once everything had been served, she said laughingly: "We're going to be talking about private matters so we don't want to be disturbed. I'll call you if we need anything."

She poured a glass of wine for Lin Meitang and then raised her own glass: "This first toast is to you, Meitang, you can now start your life afresh. Cheers!"

"Thanks." The two women drained their glasses and then Lin Meitang grabbed the bottle and poured them both a top-up. "To tell you the truth, I do sometimes feel as if I've set down an enormous burden. It is true that Guo Cunxian offered me great support, he was the one and only man in my life, but we weren't ever married – I never had a properly defined position. Nobody has a clue what that's been like year in and year out. I never tried to force him into anything. In fact, I was always a little frightened of him. I always had to think about how to please him in everything I did, and at the same time consider how it would affect his position. It was so exhausting. Now I don't have to be afraid of anyone, and the worst has happened. In future, nothing and nobody can scare me."

"That's women for you. It's in our nature to be devoted, and that expresses itself in many ways. You've been living on a knife-edge, trying to keep your balance – no wonder you've been so badly hurt. There's a theory that people compensate for whatever it is that they lack, so blind people have super hearing, the deaf are extra sensitive and so on, so in a way imperfection is the key to perfection. There are many people whose success is built on covering up their problems. If Guo Cunxian hadn't got into trouble, wouldn't things just have carried on like before? And he was the kind of person who is never satisfied. I've heard his wife was absolutely beautiful when she was young, but he still goes out and has affairs with other women, not just you. The most desirable women were the ones who said no. He really was insatiable in his greed. He was just creating problems for himself. Even when he seemed to be living perfectly happily, he was quietly sabotaging himself. There was a restless quality about him, and it was mysterious and powerful. As a man he was both self-confident and sensitive, but he could be extraordinarily narrow-minded and self-obsessed. Sometimes he seemed intensely lonely. At the same time he liked puzzles, playing tit for tat, strategising – he was an idealist and a player of power politics.

"But above all else he admired success, he wanted Guojiadian to fulfil his utopian vision. It's not surprising that so many people turned against him in the end, not just one or two. It was the entire system that had supported him, and the leaders who'd once been on his side who moved against him. How could he not end up where he is today? He may have been a great man, but he was a terrible husband. There seem to be lots of good men out there, but not so many that you'd actually want to marry... Oh well, it's all over now. How about I introduce you to some suitable men here in the city? That way you can get out of Guojiadian and lead a happy life somewhere else."

Lin Meitang quickly waved her away. "That's impossible. A nice man wouldn't want someone like me, and if he's not nice, why would I want him?"

An Jinghui gazed at her, mockingly: "Who knows? There are loads of gorgeous studs out there and right now it's really fashionable to have a younger man in tow. If you've got the money, you might find yourself a great lover..."

"The woman in the film, *The Bridges of Madison County*, said something that made a deep impression on me. She said that that man gave her an entire life, a complete universe. Well, Jinghui, you've got a good position yourself, but haven't you stayed single too?"

An Jinghui laughed: "It's because I have a good position that I can stay single. Right now it's a sign of high status to not be married."

"Well, so what are you going to do now?"

"Live well, enjoy as many good things as I can, write some surprising things. There is plenty I want to achieve. I've never lacked for new ambitions. But I've never taken them too seriously." She took out a cigarette but gave one to Lin Meitang first. Lin Meitang used the lighter to light first her companion's cigarette and then her own. The two women took their first puff at the same time, looking at each other with a smile.

An Jinghui suddenly changed the subject. "What kind of person is Guo Cunxian's wife? I really regret that when I was back in Guojiadian all those years ago I didn't go to her house to meet her and have a good talk."

Lin Meitang dragged on her cigarette. She then said thoughtfully: "Supposing the whole of Guojiadian was completely rotten and there was only one good person left. That would be her. Everyone in the village speaks well of her. Even those who absolutely loathe Guo Cunxian wouldn't say anything bad about Zhu Xuezhen. She's always been quite the opposite of Guo Cunxian's aggressive and powerful personality. She's really weak. I don't just mean that she's always had terrible health, but she always gives you the impression of being quite feeble. I'm afraid that some of

Guo Cunxian's people bullied her behind his back. But no matter what other people do to her, she's a really lovely person. It's not that she's trying to please anyone else, but that her sweet personality just naturally shines through. She's always been the same, she's really nice to everyone, even to me, and she never, ever says anything unkind. But although you might say she's weak, there are times when she can be as tough as anything. When Guo Cunxian got into such terrible trouble to begin with it felt like the sky had fallen in on Guojiadian. People rushed round to the house to look after her because they were afraid she might give way. They were worried she might be suicidal. But Zhu Xuezhen was pretty much the same as ever. She wasn't angry, or even particularly worried or upset. She was carrying on as normal. She really isn't like the other peasants at all, and other people don't understand her in the slightest for all that they appreciate how good a person she is. Nobody has a clue what she thinks about all of this. Guo Cunzhi told me that, many years ago, she'd already predicted that Guo Cunxian would end up in prison…"

"Really?" An Jinghui lit another cigarette excitedly. "She sounds a most remarkable person. So she definitely wouldn't have been involved in her husband's activities?"

"Of course not! The other village women sometimes jokingly call her a visitor from another planet."

"But now she's been caught up in her husband's problems…"

"If she's got nothing better to do, she likes playing cards. The four of us widows often play together now."

"Four widows?"

"Guo Cunyong's wife, Ou Huaying, she's a real widow. The rest of us are grass widows – that's Ou Guangming's wife, Liu Yumei, Xuezhen and myself."

The sound of laughter burst in on them from outside, and the serving staff were tittering and giggling. The gales of amusement disturbed the two women in their elegant room. Having got up to close the door, An Jinghui suddenly cut short what she was saying: "Meitang, is it true that all the villagers feel that Guo Cunxian's sentence was too harsh?"

"Of course! Twenty years is far too harsh. The thugs who carried out those beatings got five years or seven years. In the worst case it was eleven. The higher-ups clearly don't want him to come out of prison alive. He's already over fifty, so how on earth is he going to survive two decades in prison? It's obvious that Guo Cunxian will die behind bars."

An Jinghui was startled. "And what do you say?"

"It's perfectly clear that he's been sentenced so harshly because those higher up want him dead. Other people now also think that way. If he were just sentenced to a few years and then came back to Guojiadian, there'd be no place for him in the village any more – everybody is doing well all by themselves. They wouldn't want him to take power again, and the whole situation would be really awkward. I imagine that he doesn't want to survive. He knows what everyone else is hoping to see happen, and he'll understand that whatever happens he's going to be surplus to requirements. After the sentencing, he made the decision that he doesn't want to see anyone other than his wife. He's even refused to see his brother and sister, so you'll understand that he doesn't want to see me or any of the Four Bosses. The only reason he sees his wife is because he's forcing her to go to the US to be with their son. It's all arranged, and she should be off next month at the latest. Once she's gone, I imagine things will start to happen. If he doesn't manage to kill himself, he might be released early for medical treatment or on compassionate grounds, and in that case I'll look after him. We can be together until the end, and things could be a lot worse..." Lin Meitang's face was covered in tears as she raised her head with a jerk and gulped down the remaining wine in her glass.

An Jinghui stood up and hugged her, and then went out to ask that a particular piece of music be played for them. Shortly afterwards, a cold high-pitched voice singing an operatic aria began to play over the loudspeakers:

Though I travel with my pack,
Human existence is but an illusion.
I have been on an endless journey:
Through trackless forests,
Over countless mountain peaks,
To where the Yangtze river rolls.
I have struggled through icy clouds and clammy mists;
I have suffered through bitter rain and chilling winds.
The passes stand strong:
Our rivers and mountains are yet safe.
Nobody recognises me:
When dressed in rags, I arrive in Xiangyang...

Without quite noticing it, they'd managed to drink two bottles of white wine. An Jinghui went out to ask a waiter to bring them another bottle.

"Meitang, do you think you could get me in to see Guo Cunxian? From what you've been telling me, I'd be really interested to know what kind of state he's in, and how he's changed..." This was what An Jinghui really wanted to ask this evening, and it was the real reason that she came to see Lin Meitang.

Lin Meitang shook her head, a bitter expression on her face: "No, or at least, not yet. I've been told that, now he's been sentenced, he can receive visits from family and friends, but only if he agrees. If he doesn't agree, nobody can see him. Nearly one hundred people went from the village with Zhu Xuezhen on her first visit, but in the end she was the only one he would agree to see. It didn't matter how much the others begged and pleaded. You've helped so much in this case that I'll do my very best for you. If he agrees to see me, I'll take you in with me. I refuse to believe that he's going to be hard-hearted enough to never see me again."

An Jinghui slapped the table: "What on earth is that all about?"

Lin Meitang heaved a deep sigh. "I think he's really angry because, with the exception of his adopted son, everyone at Guojiadian has betrayed him. When they had the open session in court, Liu Fugen was the one to stand up to them the most strongly, but of course he had the right. He took full responsibility himself. He said that those who beat Yang Zusheng to death were employed by his company, that he gave orders for the beating, and it was nothing to do with his father. The judge told him to call the prisoner by name, and so he said 'my adoptive father, Guo Cunxian' or 'the party secretary in Guojiadian, Guo Cunxian'. He may not be Guo Cunxian's own flesh and blood, but he certainly takes after him. But everyone else referred to him as 'Guo Cunxian'. I know him very well, and he really hates people using his name to address him. He considers it an insult, and so for the people from Guojiadian who came to give evidence, including the men who actually carried out the murders, to do this meant that they were openly showing hatred and contempt. They betrayed him. He took responsibility for everything, so he must have imagined that got his people off the hook…"

"Oh dear, oh dear, after all that's happened, he still doesn't understand. What is all of this about loyalty and betrayal when you can't have one without the other? It's easy to be loyal before everything comes out in the open. Once all is revealed, there's going to be betrayal. But you've always been on his side. Why doesn't he want to see you? Surely he must miss you."

"I can't explain it either. Maybe that open session in court just destroyed his faith in human nature. When I was called into court all I could do was speak the truth. I never had the kind of position that Liu Fugen did, so I couldn't possibly claim responsibility for what happened on his behalf. But to tell the truth in that kind of situation is also a betrayal. To begin with I called him Secretary Guo, but the judge said that he was now a prisoner, so I ought to refer to him by name. I did then call him Guo Cunxian. More than anyone else there I had the right to call him by his name. I wanted to scream and shout and curse him: You bastard, Guo Cunxian, what the hell do you think you've been doing? I've wasted my life on you! Look at what you've done! Fine, you've kicked over the hornet's nest and can now rest quietly in prison, but what's going to happen to me?"

Lin Meitang was now drunk and her voice rose higher and higher, her face was puffy and red, and she kept bursting into tears. Really, she was crying almost all the time today. An Jinghui came hurrying over and patted her, drying her tears.

But Lin Meitang still wasn't finished. Like a runaway car she ploughed on, her voice breaking with sobs: "Afterwards they summoned other witnesses involved in what had happened at Guojiadian, and they kept calling him Guo Cunxian. Some of them managed to work his name into everything they said. They were doing it on purpose. In the past none of them would have dared call him by his name. Now they had the chance, they wanted to scratch that itch – they wanted to take it out on him by calling his name, they wanted him to take the blame for absolutely everything. Think about it: how could Guo Cunxian cope with being openly humiliated like that? I imagine it was worse than being sentenced to twenty years in prison…"

The music outside was getting louder, so simply keeping the door shut was no longer working. An Jinghui rested her half-smoked cigarette against the lip of the ashtray and dragged Lin Meitang to her feet. The two of them stood face to face, holding hands, and then they started to sway their bodies in time to the beat of the music. An Jinghui was a good dancer, moving seductively in time to the music, her mind relaxed and her eyes far away. Lin Meitang was much stiffer, and her feet were having difficulty in keeping up. After dancing for a little while she wanted to sit down again, but An Jinghui kept hold of her. Gradually the two of them started to slow down.

An Jinghui jokingly patted Lin Meitang's bottom. "You've got great hips and that arse is almost like an African woman's – very sexy and strong. Men love that kind of arse."

Lin Meitang sighed. "I started out with a good body, and then what with not getting married and not having kids, I kept it for a long time. But now I've noticed that my arse is spreading and my waist is getting thicker."

"A woman's body needs a man's touch to feel good." An Jinghui whispered in Lin Meitang's ear: "Have you thought about getting a boyfriend?"

Lin Meitang shook her head.

"So are you spending all your time at home guarding an empty house and a sack of cash? What's the point of that?"

"I go out every day, either to the county town or to the city. I go shopping, or to the cinema, and then have a meal and a glass of wine, and when I get back home I fall asleep as soon as my head hits the pillow. If you are physically exhausted, you don't think too much about things."

The two women clung to each other and carried on slowly dancing a few steps. An Jinghui was inspired to recite a few lines that had just come into her head. Her voice was lovely and so melodious that she almost seemed to be singing:

All alone, unhappy and distressed,
It is hard to decide what to do:
And I am still caught up in the intensity of my feelings...
After gazing deep into each other's eyes,
Drifting off into a confused sleep,
Dreams are shattered by illusory fears.
Look into the distance at the mountains and rivers:
People come and go,
It is hard to make out their features, they are so far away.
From this point on
There is but suffering and bitterness,
Just like tonight.

She seemed to be in a very sentimental mood, but then she sprang a question on Lin Meitang that came out of the blue: "Are reporters still pestering you out at Guojiadian?"

"No. Reporters are only interested in the latest thing. Guojiadian is old news by now, so what would a reporter be doing there?"

"I'd like to come and see you, stay for a couple of days, maybe talk to a few people. Would that be OK?"

"Sure, I'd like to have you to stay. You want to come now?"

"I can't, there are a few things that I still need to sort out here. Why don't you come and stay with me for a couple of days, and then we can go back together when I've got these things off my hands?"

"No, I'm not comfortable doing that, particularly at a time like this when it might get you into trouble. I'll go back to the village now and wait for you." Lin Meitang suddenly thought about the time. Looking at her watch it was nearly midnight.

An Jinghui grabbed the bill and paid. Walking out of the Rose Garden they could see a number of taxis waiting by the entrance. They hugged each other again and said goodbye, with assurances that they would meet again in a few days' time, yes, absolutely. Then Lin Meitang climbed into one of the taxis.

The driver asked her where she wanted to go, but she didn't say anything, she just stuck out her chin. The driver put the car in gear and started to move off, and as he did so, she took a mirror out of her bag, hesitating as to whether or not she was going to inspect her face. Then she took out a cigarette and lit it. The driver saw that she was now finished getting herself comfortable and so asked again: "Where would you like to go, madam?"

"Guojiadian." As she said this, the taxi driver suddenly slammed on the brake.

"What's wrong?" she asked.

The driver was trying to think of an excuse to get her out of his cab. "Guojiadian's too far away, and it's really late, but even if it was broad daylight I wouldn't be guaranteed a return fare, so coming back my taxi's going to be empty. I can't afford that kind of loss. You won't pay me for there and back, will you? So you'd better find another taxi."

Bastard. The minute he's told to go to Guojiadian it isn't "madam" any more, its "you". She breathed out a mouthful of smoke and asked slowly: "How much for there and back?"

"At least two hundred."

Lin Meitang reached two fingers into her bag and took out two one hundred yuan notes. She handed them over with a single word: "Go!"

With the money in his pocket the driver cheered up. The crucial thing was that his fare was a woman, so he wasn't in any danger himself. Once they were out of the city, he wanted to talk and so he began by asking: "So you live in Guojiadian, lady?"

Oh, so now I'm a lady. Lin Meitang didn't pay any attention to him.

The driver realised that she wasn't going to answer, and he guessed she might be feeling nervous, which he found a pleasing idea. "Hey, lady, aren't you frightened going all this way late at night?"

Lin Meitang was looking out of the window. It was pitch black out there. Now she slowly asked: "Why should I be frightened? What is there to be scared of? Should I be scared of you?"

"Yeah, I am a man after all. Aren't you scared I might grope you or something?"

"What, you think you might be able to grope me?" Lin Meitang seemed amused. "Just drive your goddam car! If there's anyone here who should be scared, it's you!"

Now it was the driver's turn to laugh. "Me? What kind of man is frightened of a woman?"

"But you're alive and I'm already dead. Just think about it. Who should be afraid of who?"

All of a sudden the taxi driver could feel his hair rising as cold chills ran up and down his spine. He didn't dare look back at her, and even his voice had changed: "Stop trying to frighten me, lady!"

Lin Meitang suddenly burst out laughing, but there was a hysterical edge to her voice, and then as she laughed she suddenly burst into tears.

The driver was now even more terrified. Either she was a ghost, or else he had a lunatic in the back of his car.

ENDNOTES

3. Food Substitutes

1. In Chinese folklore, Yang Silang is the fourth son of Yang Ye, a reputed general adept at martial arts and famed for his valiant defence of the Song dynasty 960-1279CE, especially in its wars against the Liao (Khitan) aggressors. Yang Ye had eight sons in total and all served the Song militarily. Various, mostly fictionalised stories have been told about the Yang family's bravery and loyalty to the Song Emperor. In the Peking Opera *Silang Visits His Mother* (*Silang tan mu* 四郎探母), we hear the tale of how the Song Emperor was invited for peace talks with the Liao. Believing it to be a trap, however, the eldest son of the Yang family is sent disguised as the Emperor, with his brothers serving as his royal retinue. They are, of course, ambushed. Three sons perish, four escape and Silang is captured. Not knowing his true identity, the Liao are soon won over by Silang's handsomeness and his skills in combat, never suspecting he is the son of a mortal enemy. Eventually, he is freed from bondage and allowed to serve the Liao Emperor. He does this for nearly 15 years, winning the favour of the Liao Empress, and ultimately wedding her daughter. All the while, his true identity remains concealed, until finally, on the eve of yet another battle with the Song forces, Silang learns that his brothers, and even his mother, are in the Song camp. Nearly overcome with longing to see his family, he confesses his identity to his wife and tells her he must see them. Shocked, but understanding, she aids him in sneaking past the Liao frontlines to rendezvous with his long estranged mother and brothers. Overjoyed to learn that her son is alive, Silang nevertheless tells them that he has promised to return to his wife, to his son and to the enemy Liao. As he returns, however, he is caught and soon the Liao Empress discovers his real identity. Enraged by the betrayal, she orders his execution. The blade doesn't fall, however, as the Empress' daughter, Silang's wife, begs for mercy. Finally relenting as she doesn't wish to see her favoured grandson without a father, Silang is freed once more and lives the remainder of his days with the Liao.

7. Earth And Soil

1. There are many versions of the story of Lady Meng Jiang. Considered one of China's 'Four Great Folktales', it underscores the devotion a wife has (to have) towards her husband. While earlier snippets of the story can be found in the classical historical narrative *Commentary of Zuo* (*Zuozhuan* 左傳), the most developed version is set during the Qin dynasty (221-206BCE). In the tale, Lady Meng Jiang's husband is conscripted by the First Emperor to help build the Great Wall. Hearing nothing from him after his forced departure, Lady Meng Jiang, in a show of great loyalty, bundles up clothes and food and sets off for where her husband has been toiling away. She arrives to tragedy, however, as upon her arrival she learns he has died from exhaustion, his bones buried under the section of the Wall she now stands in front of. Overcome with grief, Lady Meng Jiang breaks into tears, wailing so loudly, according to the story, that the Wall under which her husband lays collapses and reveals his bones. She is thus able to bury him properly, after which, in a true expression of her devotion, she laments she is alone in the world with no father, no husband and no son, with nothing left for her to do but die. The story is ultimately included in the Han dynasty (206BCE-220CE) *Biographies of Exemplary Women* (*Lienüzhuan* 列女傳), wherein the commentary remarks on how Lady Meng Jiang serves as a most pure example of wifely commitment to her husband.

13. Women's Fate

1. Cao Cao (c.155-220CE) was a prominent general during the final years of the Han dynasty (206BCE-220CE). He was posthumously credited with being the first Emperor of Wu (220-266CE), a kingdom that vied for control of China in the aftermath of the Han dynasty's collapse. Yang Xiu (175-219CE) was an official and adviser under Cao Cao. The reference above to chicken soup alludes to a story in *The Romance of the Three Kingdoms* (*Sanguo Yanyi* 三國演義), a 14th century historical epic attributed to Luo Guanzhong 羅貫中 (c. 1330–1400CE or c. 1280–1360CE). In the story, Yang Xiu is

variously described as an able and talented official, but Cao Cao believes he is a little too boastful and full of himself. He was eventually executed by Cao Cao for a presumptuous command given to the warlord's troops. Evidently, after bringing Cao Cao some chicken-rib soup and hearing his commander mutter about the bones, Yang Xiu mistakenly believed Cao Cao was using the complaint directed at the soup to indicate his army should retreat. This was the order Yang Xiu delivered, after which, enraged by his meddlesomeness, he was executed for insubordination, as well as cowardice since Cao Cao, after all, would never have retreated.

ABOUT THE AUTHOR

Jiang Zilong was born in 1941 in Hebei Province, northeast China, and spent his formative years in the countryside before moving to the city of Tianjin at the age of fourteen. He served an apprenticeship at a machine tool factory and then joined the navy in 1962. From 1965 to 1982, he worked at a factory in Tianjin, rising to the ranks of senior management and publishing his first written works on the side. He has been a full-time author since leaving the factory and became known as the founder of 'Reform literature', which deals with the policy of reform and opening up that was initiated by Deng Xiaoping following the death of Mao Zedong. Many of Jiang's stories are set in the industrial world and examine the impact that the seismic socio-economic changes have had on the lives of ordinary Chinese citizens. His works have won national literary awards many times and been translated into multiple languages including English, French, German, Russian, Japanese and Spanish.

Lightning Source UK Ltd.
Milton Keynes UK
UKHW041140280119
336125UK00006B/27/P